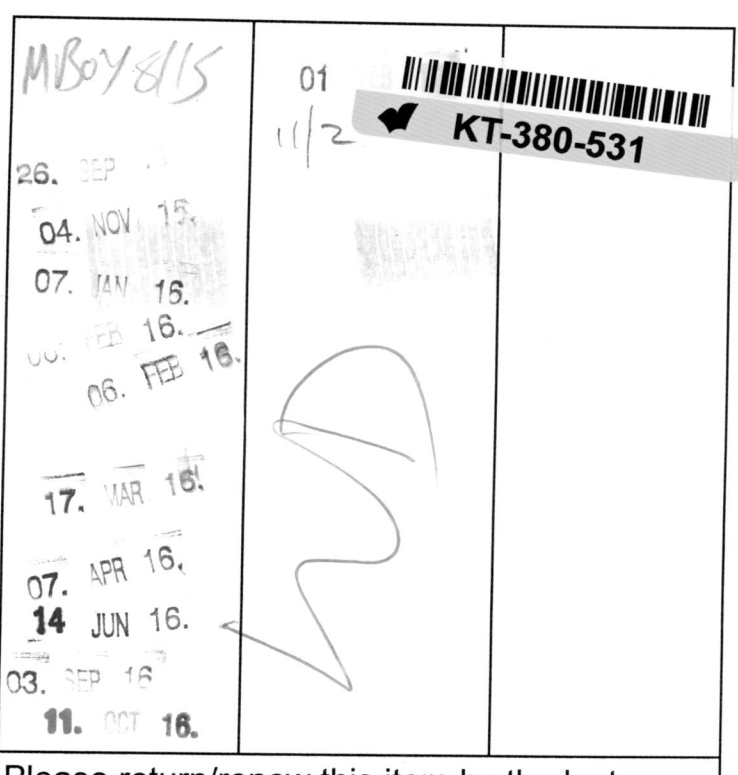

MBoY 8/15

01
11/2

KT-380-531

26. SEP
04. NOV 15.
07. JAN 16.
06. FEB 16.
06. FEB 16.
17. MAR 16.
07. APR 16.
14 JUN 16.
03. SEP 16
11. OCT 16.

Please return/renew this item by the last date shown. Books may also be renewed by phone or Internet.

 www.rbwm.gov.uk/web/libraries.htm

☎ 01628 796969 (library hours)

☎ 0303 123 0035 (24 hours)

The Royal Borough

Windsor & Maidenhead

Windsor and Maidenhead

38060000000020

The Special Dead

The Special Dead

LIN ANDERSON

MACMILLAN

First published 2015 by Macmillan
an imprint of Pan Macmillan
20 New Wharf Road, London N1 9RR
Associated companies throughout the world
www.panmacmillan.com

ISBN 978-1-4472-9831-1

Copyright © Lin Anderson 2015

The right of Lin Anderson to be identified as the
author of this work has been asserted by her in accordance
with the Copyright, Designs and Patents Act 1988.

All rights reserved. No part of this publication may be reproduced,
stored in a retrieval system, or transmitted, in any form, or by any means
(electronic, mechanical, photocopying, recording or otherwise)
without the prior written permission of the publisher.

This book is a work of fiction. Names, characters, places, organizations
and incidents are either products of the author's imagination or used fictitiously.
Any resemblance to actual events, places, organizations or persons,
living or dead, is entirely coincidental.

Pan Macmillan does not have any control over, or any responsibility for,
any author or third party websites referred to in or on this book.

1 3 5 7 9 8 6 4 2

A CIP catalogue record for this book is available from the British Library.

Typeset by Palimpsest Book Production Ltd, Falkirk, Stirlingshire
Printed and bound by CPI Group (UK) Ltd, Croydon, CR0 4YY

This book is sold subject to the condition that it shall not, by way
of trade or otherwise, be lent, hired out, or otherwise circulated without
the publisher's prior consent in any form of binding or cover other than
that in which it is published and without a similar condition including
this condition being imposed on the subsequent purchaser.

Visit **www.panmacmillan.com** to read more about all our books
and to buy them. You will also find features, author interviews and
news of any author events, and you can sign up for e-newsletters
so that you're always first to hear about our new releases.

For Detective Inspector Bill Mitchell

If you are reading this then I am dead.

To know a person's name is to conjure with it.

1

The green eyes were regarding him candidly. Mark suspected she was weighing him up and wasn't sure she liked what she saw. Jeff, on the other hand, was having an easier time with the girl's friend. *Trust Jeff to strike it lucky, the bastard*.

Mark took another slug of his pint. If the girls came as a pair, then the fact that green eyes didn't fancy him might mean Jeff got the brush-off too, which would bring Mark no end of grief. As though reading his mind, Jeff threw him a look that urged him to try harder.

When Jeff had suggested he come through to Glasgow for a Friday night on the town together, Mark had jumped at the chance. True, he'd had to cover his tracks a bit with Emilie and make out he was playing five-a-side football with Jeff and his mates. She'd been a bit suspicious about that, until Mark had suggested she could come with him and watch if she liked. That had done the trick. Plus he'd promised to be back to take her out for lunch in Edinburgh on Saturday. A promise he meant to keep.

They'd been in four pubs before this one and Mark had lost count of the variety of drinks he'd consumed. None of the previous pubs had produced the possibilities of this one and he owed it to Jeff to play it out. Mark marshalled himself for one more go, but he didn't get the chance.

'So,' she said suddenly. 'Want to come back to my place?'

To say he nearly fell off the chair was putting it mildly. He shut his mouth, realizing it had dropped open, and tried to look nonchalant.

'Sure thing.'

She immediately stood up. Mark expected the pal to get up too, but she didn't. The two girls exchanged some unspoken message and the pal laughed. Jeff, equally surprised by the way things were going, looked askance and not a little jealously at Mark, who grinned in triumph, then followed green eyes to the door.

Outside, he offered to wave down a taxi.

'No need. It's just round the corner.'

Mark felt himself stir in anticipation. It looked as though Jeff wasn't the lucky one after all.

She ushered him inside and shut the door firmly behind him. A black cat appeared from nowhere to rub itself against her ankle. When she lifted it, the purring grew louder. The cat fastened its eyes on Mark and he was struck by their similarity to the girl's eyes. Through the alcoholic haze, sharpened by the coke he'd snorted in the last pub toilet, the scene took on a bright hallucinatory hue.

The long hallway was dimly lit and painted blood red. He identified a series of doors that shifted and merged until he closed one eye.

'In here,' she said, throwing open a door on his right. She gave him a slight push and he stumbled inside what was definitely a bedroom. The cat, discarded from her arms, mewed in annoyance and darted off, tail stiffly upright.

'Take off your clothes,' she ordered. 'And lie down on the bed.'

Mark had experienced a variety of sexual encounters

under the influence of alcohol and coke before, but he'd never been bossed about. He found he rather liked the experience.

'Are you for real?' he grinned.

'Just do it.'

Her expression suggested if he didn't do what was asked, he would be out the door. Something he definitely didn't want.

Mark pulled off his shirt, then his jeans and stood in his boxers.

'What's your name?' he said, suddenly feeling he should know what to call the girl he was about to have sex with.

'You're not here to ask questions.' She ran the green eyes over him from top to toe. 'Now the boxers.'

In a show of bravado, Mark exposed himself.

She studied him intently, then licked her lips. The result of which was a shot of an aphrodisiac he didn't require.

'Okay. Now lie down.'

Relieved that he had passed muster, Mark did as ordered.

The few clothes she wore were removed in seconds, then she stood before him in all her glory. Mark drank in the smooth white skin, the pink pointed nipples, the neat brush of auburn hair highlighted between the long smooth legs.

Who was the lucky one now?

When the cat suddenly jumped on the bed to spoil his view, Mark tried to sweep it aside.

'Leave it,' she said sharply.

Before he could protest, the cat had settled on his face, its silky warm body acting like a suffocating blindfold. The purring rose to a crescendo as its open claws kneaded his shoulder. Mark's surprised cry was smothered in hot fur.

He could no longer see the girl, but he felt her climb

aboard and firmly straddle him. As she lowered herself, pain and pleasure met and exploded in his head.

His stomach heaved, bringing him back to consciousness. Mark rolled onto his side and vomited a pool of warm stale beer on the carpet.

Where the hell was he?

He shivered suddenly in his nakedness. Flashes of memory began bombarding his brain. The girl staring down at him. The smothering action of the cat. The crazy coupling. He turned to check the other side of the bed but there was no one there. The luminous dial on his watch told him it was five o'clock in the morning.

Sitting up, he swung his feet out of bed, trying to avoid the wet patch caused by his vomit, but not entirely succeeding. He contemplated his next move, which should be to get dressed and leave as quickly as possible. Rising a little shakily, he located the pile that was his clothes. As he dressed, a pair of green eyes appeared suddenly in the semi-darkness.

He recalled the cat settling on his face and the girl ordering him to leave it there. The memory brought a rush of pleasure. For a moment he was back there, wanting more of the same, then the whiff of his vomit reminded him it was wiser to leave. Now.

Dressed, he checked the corridor, found it empty and stepped out of the room to be presented with four doors leading off the hall, all of them closed. Mark stood for a moment, trying to recall last night and which door might be the exit point. Finally accepting that he had no idea, he chose one and attempted to open it as quietly as possible.

Immediately the cat tried to squeeze past his ankles,

mewing loudly. Mark swore under his breath, attempted to stop it with his foot and tripped over it instead. The cat sprang into the room, tail bristling, with Mark stumbling headlong into the darkness in its wake.

He eventually righted himself and stood very still, praying the room, whatever its purpose, was unoccupied. Moments later, he decided it was, although something had definitely spooked the cat. Its mewing had changed into a high-pitched keening sound that reverberated through his brain and would eventually rouse anyone else who might be in the flat.

Which meant he should get out of here, and quickly.

Mark swung round, desperate now to make his exit, and immediately walked into a small hanging object. As spooked as the keening cat, he tried to sweep it aside only to have it swing back at him, and poke him in the eye.

Swearing under his breath, he caught the offending item in his hand.

In the faint light from the hall, he now saw it was a doll.

Naked, long-legged, with pert breasts and flowing silver blonde hair, it hung from the ceiling via a length of cord wound tightly round its neck.

Jesus. Last night had been weird, but this was even weirder.

Mark released the doll in distaste and it swung away from him, only to immediately collide with something else, setting off a series of eerie clicks and clacks accompanied by the creak of moving objects.

What the hell was that?

Mark stood stock-still, knowing he shouldn't turn, but aware he would anyway.

When he did, he found that the doll wasn't alone.

There were at least twenty of them, swinging in the light

filtering through from the hall. Blondes, brunettes, redheads, naked, eyes glinting. All were suspended from the ceiling by a string tied round their necks, all set in perpetual motion by his action.

The swaying scene was grotesque, but not as terrible as what Mark now discerned beyond the hanging dolls, and the true reason for the cat's distress.

2

Rhona stared up at the ceiling. Beside her, the soft sounds of Sean's breathing only emphasized how awake she was herself.

This is one of the reasons I prefer sleeping alone.

She threw back the covers, knowing leaving the bed wouldn't wake Sean from his slumbers. Grabbing a dressing gown against the night air, she went through to the kitchen. The wall clock said 3.25 a.m., which meant she'd had about three hours sleep. Not enough to face a day's work, but judging by her busy brain, she was unlikely to get any more.

She spooned some coffee into the filter and filled the water reservoir. If she was determined to be awake, there was no point in avoiding caffeine. She took up her favourite stance at the window as the coffee machine hummed into action. Three storeys down, and bathed in a soft spotlight, the statue of the Virgin Mary stood resolute against the surrounding darkness. Soon the lights of its neighbouring convent would spring on, heralding the nuns' early start to the day.

In that respect, at least, I would make a good nun, Rhona mused as she poured herself a mug of coffee. She carried the coffee through the hall to the living room, pausing for a moment to glance in at the sleeping Sean. He had moved onto his back, losing the duvet in the process. Naked, his body seemed to gleam like marble in the moonlight that shone in through the open curtains.

If she chose to go back in there now and stroke him into wakefulness, they would carry on where they'd left off. Rhona contemplated the prospect, albeit briefly, before entering the sitting room and closing the door behind her.

Settling herself at the desk, she opened her laptop and logged on. As though on cue, Tom arrived to take up his place on her lap. She was never sure if the cat sought company or her warmth, or simply liked the comforting electronic hum to accompany his own soft purring.

Beyond the window, dawn was beginning to break over the great sleeping mammoth that was Glasgow. Unlike New York or London, Glasgow did at least appear to slumber, usually between three and five in the morning. Or it seemed that way from her vantage point, high above the green expanse of Kelvingrove Park.

Dispensing with this thought, Rhona turned her attention to the screen.

The case she was in the process of writing up hadn't proved forensically challenging. A middle-aged man had visited a gay bar where he'd picked up a teenage foreign national and taken him home, only to be stabbed to death.

The perpetrator had dumped the knife in a nearby bin along with his backpack. Later, apprehended by the police, he'd confessed to the killing, stating that his victim had launched an attack on him during sex, and that he had retaliated.

As far as Rhona was concerned, the crime-scene forensics matched the perpetrator's story. Deposits of both men's semen and blood had been identified at the scene. The victim's fingerprints had been retrieved from the perpetrator's neck, suggesting he'd been throttled, perhaps during the sex act.

The knife cuts on the perpetrator's scrotum had definitely been inflicted by a left-handed person, i.e. the victim. Furthermore, the stab wounds in the victim's chest had been made by the same knife, wielded by a right-handed person, which the perpetrator was. The toxicology report suggested both men had been high on crystal meth at the time. The sexual game, perhaps begun by mutual consent, had ended in death.

Tragic, horrifying and almost inevitable, if the sad saga of abuse that had been the perpetrator's life was true. It seemed that the victim had been seen by the young man who'd killed him as just one more abuser, against whom he had finally retaliated.

One life lost, another ruined, the path that had led to murder seemingly unavoidable. The darkest corner of her mind believed that, yet the 'if only' aspect still prevailed. What if the victim had treated the young man differently? What if he hadn't tried to control him? Abuse and threaten him? What if they had shown respect for one another?

Both might be alive, and no one a murderer.

But that 'what if' was of no use now. The deed was done, recorded forensically to be shown in court.

Two hours later, her report complete, Rhona shut the laptop, just as a still-naked Sean appeared in the doorway.

'Was I snoring?' He looked apologetic.

'No, I had a report to write.'

'And you've finished?'

'Yes.'

'I'll make us some breakfast.'

9

'No, thanks. I've had coffee already.'

He regarded her with a smile. 'So you still don't eat breakfast?'

Rhona gave him a pointed look in return. 'And you still make coffee looking like that?'

Sean glanced down, as though only just registering his nudity. 'I'll go and get dressed.'

Rhona rose, picking up her laptop. 'Don't bother. I'm on my way out, anyway.'

Sean looked a little nonplussed by that. 'Will you be at the jazz club later?'

'Not sure,' Rhona said, determinedly non-committal.

A small smile played at the corner of Sean's mouth. 'Fine,' he said and was gone.

Rhona heard the tap running, then the spurting sound of the coffee machine, accompanied by Sean's distinctive whistling of a well-known Irish tune.

He hasn't changed and neither have I. If it didn't work the first time, why should it work now?

She and Sean Maguire had history. Lots of it. The Irish musician had walked into her life at the fiftieth birthday party of DI Bill Wilson, her friend and mentor, held in the jazz club which Sean part-owned. Sean's dark hair and blue eyes, coupled with his Irish charm and musical skill on the saxophone, had been difficult to resist. In fact, Rhona hadn't really tried. Sean had approached her with a bottle of wine when he came off stage and asked if he might be allowed to join her. She'd said yes. When he'd walked her home, Rhona had asked him up without hesitation.

Last night I did the exact same thing. Talk about history repeating itself.

As Rhona set about packing up her laptop, her mobile

rang. A glance at the screen indicated it was not a caller she particularly wanted to speak to. Nevertheless . . .

'DS McNab?' she said.

'Dr MacLeod. Top of the morning to you.'

The jibe, aimed no doubt at the reappearance of her Irish lover, only served to irritate Rhona, which is what McNab intended.

'What do you want?' Rhona said, keeping her voice even.

'I'd like you to take a look at a suspicious death.'

'Why me?'

'DI Wilson suggested it should be you.'

Rhona bit off a further retort. If Bill wanted her there, then she would go. Of course McNab knew that, which is why he said it. Whether it was true or not was another matter.

'I'll send a car for you,' he said before she could ask for further details.

'Tell them to buzz when they get here.'

Rhona rang off before McNab could indulge in any more comments on her love life.

She quickly showered, then dressed in the bathroom, keen to avoid encountering Sean again, naked or otherwise. Maybe he had the same plan, because he didn't reappear, although she heard the notes of his saxophone from the spare room.

The familiarity of that sound in the flat disturbed her, but she reminded herself that the instrument was only there because they'd come straight from Sean's gig at the jazz club the previous night. Its presence in no way signified that Sean had become a permanent fixture.

She contemplated asking when he was leaving, but the buzzer sounded before she could bring herself to, so she made a swift exit with a shout of goodbye. Hopefully when she returned, Sean would no longer be there. Rhona was pretty sure he had got that message, although Sean had a habit of interpreting her responses in a way more suited to himself.

Now, outside the main door, Rhona realized the car McNab had 'sent' was in fact his own. It was a neat trick. He was well aware that had he indicated he would be the driver, she would have definitely declined. As it was, she now had little choice.

Rhona slid into the passenger seat without comment.

'Chrissy's on her way,' McNab offered by way of an olive branch.

'Good.'

He headed for town.

Travelling with McNab was never uneventful. He always drove as though he had a blue light flashing even when he didn't. The one-way system didn't serve as any deterrent. Glasgow city centre was as busy on a Saturday as during the weekday rush hour, which made the experience even more hair-raising than usual. Rhona was aware he was trying to provoke her into remonstrating with him, so she chose not to. In a show of determination, she didn't even grip the seat.

He finally took a sharp right into a back lane, just off Hope Street, where a police van was already parked.

'Okay?' he said.

'Never better.'

Short looks and few words were all they exchanged these days. The secret that they both shared lay uneasily between them. McNab had offered her the chance to 'spill the beans' to Detective Inspector Bill Wilson. Rhona hadn't as yet, knowing that it might end McNab's already shaky career. She'd told herself that was the reason, but was unsure if it was, and the longer she kept quiet, the more difficult it had become.

McNab gestured to an open door. 'First floor.'

Rhona got out and began kitting up. The lack of conversation in the car meant she had no idea what she was about to walk in on, which could be an advantage. Forensically, the first image of a crime scene was a powerful and informative one. From her experience, the questions that immediately sprang to mind were often the most important ones. There was, of course, a routine to be followed, a structure to every investigation, to ensure nothing was forgotten in the emotional impact of the moment, but first impressions mattered. A lot.

The steps of the stairwell were well worn, the walls patterned with glazed green tiles. When she reached the first landing, she found the single door there standing open, an officer on duty.

Recognizing her, he stood aside to allow Rhona entry.

She tucked her hair under the hood and pulled up her mask, then stepped over the threshold onto one of the metal treads already laid out on the floor to avoid contamination, indicating that McNab was treating this suspicious death seriously.

The hall was painted red and poorly lit. There were four inner doors, three of which stood open. A swift look established that one led to a bedroom, another a kitchen, and the third a toilet and shower room. A crime-scene photographer was already busy in the bedroom. When he spotted her, he indicated the closed door was the one she sought. Rhona nodded her thanks and approached it. Then she heard a terrible sound, which made the hairs on the back of her neck stand up. High pitched, almost a scream, she recognized it as a cat in distress.

'It's in there with the body,' the photographer told her. 'We haven't been able to catch it yet. They've contacted the SSPCA.'

As Rhona cautiously opened the door, the suffocating scent of death escaped, her mask barely weakening it. She stepped inside and quickly shut the door.

The image that presented itself in the blazing light from two arc lamps shocked even her. Rhona had prepared herself for a body, and a mourning cat, but not for the curtain of naked Barbie-type dolls that hung from the ceiling.

The draught generated by her entry had set them in motion, the noise of their hard plastic limbs clicking off one another as disquieting as the sight of them. What was even more disturbing was what she glimpsed beyond the curtain of dolls.

The young woman was naked, her body suspended from a large hook in the back wall via a red cord wound round her neck. Her green eyes were wide open and staring, the tongue protruding between swollen lips. At her feet stood a large black cat, hair bristling, tail upright, the tip swishing back and forth in a warning.

Rhona met its green glare and knew that it meant business, and with the cat there, she had no chance of examining its owner. She didn't even attempt the *Here kitty* routine. Her best chance, she decided, was to let it come at her, which it surely would, then do her best to catch it.

As she got closer to the body, the cat arched its back and hissed. Rhona braced herself, conscious that the flying claws might pierce her forensic suit. But it had given her too much warning and she was ready for it. With a practised hand she grabbed it by the scruff of the neck and held it away from her body, the paws and tail thrashing thin air.

Rhona made for the bathroom. The shower cubicle seemed the ideal place to corral it. She dropped it in and swiftly shut the door. The cat, further infuriated by its enclosure, clawed and spat at her through the glass.

Retreating, Rhona shut the door behind her, before warning the photographer of the menacing presence in the bathroom.

'I've never seen a cat so mad before,' he said.

'Neither have I,' Rhona agreed. 'Let me know when the SSPCA arrive.'

Free of the enraged feline, Rhona re-entered the room and was struck again by the image of the dolls and the body.

Hanging was a fairly common method of suicide. Accidental hangings were less common, and homicidal hangings rare. True, murderers sometimes tried to cover strangulation by stringing up their victim afterwards, not realizing that the signs of each method of death were easily distinguished.

Most suicides, if determined to succeed, stepped off a raised object, such as a chair or a ladder. No such object existed in the room. In fact, the room was bare apart from the victim and the spooky dolls.

The body hung four inches above the floor. On closer inspection, the cord proved to be a knotted plait of a red silky material. Looped round what resembled a large meat hook, it was finally tied together at the right-hand side of the neck to fashion the noose.

The body appeared unmarked apart from two tattoos, consisting of a small Celtic cross in the middle of the forehead and a pentagram about two inches in diameter in the region of the heart. The hair was dark auburn, cut short, the body slight, the breasts small. There were no piercings apart from the earlobes, where the small silver earrings were the same design as the forehead tattoo.

The face was very pale; the green eyes had dilated pupils, their whites marbled red by tiny burst blood vessels. The protruding tongue was cyanosed – coloured blue by deoxygenated blood. All features of hanging.

In cases of suicide, the ligature mark generally followed the line of the lower jaw, before going upwards behind the ear, depending on whether a fixed or running noose was used.

The mark from the plaited cord was incomplete and above that normally seen in strangulation by ligature. The forearms, hands, legs below the knees, and feet showed evidence of lividity, which suggested the body had been suspended for at least three to four hours after death.

It had all the hallmarks of a suicide, but the question remained. How had the victim got herself onto the hook?

The door opened and Rhona turned to find Chrissy, her forensic assistant, eyes wide above her mask as she registered the dolls.

'I used to have one of those,' she said. 'Two if you count Ken.'

Chrissy began zigzagging her way through the curtain of dolls, sending them into a paroxysm of stilted movements, their outstretched arms and legs glancing off one another like maracas. Finally she emerged to confront Rhona and the body on the back wall.

Chrissy ran a practised eye over the victim.

'If it had been a man I would have taken a guess at

auto-erotic strangulation, especially with the field of naked female dolls on view.'

A thought already contemplated by Rhona.

'So what do you think?' Chrissy said.

'I think it's a suspicious death.' That's all Rhona would commit herself to.

Chrissy looked about, obviously checking for the missing step.

'There wasn't one,' Rhona said.

'So she managed to hang herself without her feet touching the ground? *Very* suspicious, I would say.' Chrissy wasn't one to mince her words.

Rhona set Chrissy to work on the surrounding area while she concentrated on the body.

A little over an hour later, Chrissy had completed her forensic search of the room and Rhona had almost completed her sampling of the front portion of the body. A presumptive test for semen had indicated the likelihood that the victim had had sex prior to her death. Rhona had swabbed all orifices and taped the skin, locating two white fibres from the roof of the mouth.

The fingernails had also proved fruitful. This time the fibres were fine and red and may have come from the ligature, something she would check in the laboratory under the microscope. A presumptive test for blood under the nails had proved negative, so it didn't look as though she had fended off an attacker. Neither did Rhona find evidence of obvious bruising anywhere on the body.

Although women were less likely than men to indulge in erotic asphyxiation, there was an outside chance this could be the reason for the hanging. If so, the victim would have needed help to suspend herself and someone on hand to rescue her after climax had been achieved.

If that had been the case, the sexual partner may have panicked and left when things went wrong, thinking it better to make it look like suicide than be blamed for her death.

Rhona set about recording the scene for herself. She wouldn't remove the cord prior to the post-mortem, for fear of damaging evidence. Only when it was taken off could they be sure that there were no other marks on the neck indicating injury before the hanging.

By now the heat and the smell in the room were becoming overpowering, and Rhona could feel the trickle of perspiration constantly running down her body inside the suit. Thinking about a shower reminded her of the cat and she wondered if it had been removed by the SSPCA yet. She hoped not.

Emerging into the hall, she was rewarded by a cool draught from the open front door and the sight of an SSPCA officer heading into the bathroom. Rhona followed him.

The cat stood in the cubicle, hair bristling, defying anyone to approach.

'Sorry, we're a bit overstretched,' he said, explaining the time lapse since they'd been contacted. He eyed the cat's angry glare. 'Well done in isolating it.'

'It was standing guard over its mistress's body.'

'Unusual for a cat.'

'Are you going to sedate it?'

'It might be necessary. It's pretty distressed.'

Rhona explained her thoughts on how the animal might provide evidence, if she could take some samples.

'Okay, give me five minutes and ignore any screams from me or the cat in the interim.'

18

Rhona moved into the hall and shut the door, silently wishing him good luck.

Laid out now on the bathroom mat, the cat bore little resemblance to the furious creature she'd first encountered. Rhona focused on the front claws, where a presumptive test indicated the presence of blood. Under a magnifying glass, she also located skin particles. She had managed to avoid its claws, but it seemed it had succeeded in attacking someone, and recently.

Once the cat was safely on its way, Rhona checked with the photographer, who told her the cat had been in the room when he'd arrived.

'Do you know who discovered the body?'

'DS McNab said it was the postman. He found the front door lying open, heard the squealing cat, knew something was wrong and called the police.'

'Did the postman or McNab enter the room?'

He didn't know for certain. 'You'll have to ask the DS.'

Rhona had only glimpsed the bedroom in passing. Now she studied it in all its glory. Painted a midnight blue, the drawn curtains were similar in colour, patterned by silver stars and crescent moons. The room was dotted with candles and night lights, particularly round a mirror shaped like a five-pointed star. To add to the reflective possibilities, the wall behind the bed was occupied by a large ornate mirror, as was the ceiling above it and the opposite wall. The room smelt of vomit and sex, barely masked by the scented wax of the candles.

'The bed's covered in cat hairs,' Chrissy informed her. 'There's evidence of blood in small quantities on the pillow and semen on the undersheet. And, of course, the watery

LIN ANDERSON

vomit on the carpet next to the bed. Beer, I would say, but thankfully no diced carrots. Plenty of fingerprints. I retrieved a decent man-size bare footprint from the carpet, probably from inadvertently standing in the vomit.'

'So more than just the victim in the room recently?'

'I would say so.'

Rhona nodded, pleased at Chrissy's thoroughness.

The body, released from the hook, now lay on the floor, the crooked stiffness of its limbs mirroring those of the surrounding dolls.

As the photographer captured this on camera, Rhona checked the victim's back to find no obvious signs of cuts or bruising. She counted nine knots tied in the cord, including one at each end, probably to prevent fraying. The remaining seven were distributed evenly along its length. She would need to wait until the cord was cut free of the neck to study the noose knot in detail.

Whatever had taken place here, the red silk cord looked significant to the proceedings. If it was a suicide, then the victim had knotted the cord round her own neck. Easy enough to do that, then step off a ladder or a chair, but . . .

'You nearly done?' McNab's voice came from the doorway. He was kitted up to match Rhona, only the blue eyes showing above the mask. 'The mortuary van's here.'

Rhona nodded. 'I've left the rope in place until the PM.'

'So you don't think it's a straightforward suicide?'

'Do you?'

McNab looked up at the hook. 'How the hell did she get herself up there? That's what I'd like to know.'

'Me too.' They could agree on this at least.

'Fancy a coffee when you've finished? I'd like to discuss

this further,' he added, as though to make things perfectly clear.

Rhona still brushed him off. 'Let's wait for the post-mortem, then we might have something to discuss.'

McNab's eyes flashed back at her. He looked as though he might argue, then wisely chose not to.

'I'll leave you to it,' he said curtly, then turned on his heel.

Rhona heard further murmured words and laughter and realized he'd moved on to Chrissy. Her forensic assistant held McNab in high regard and had reason to. He had saved her unborn son by taking a bullet in his own back. McNab was a hero in Chrissy's eyes.

The memory of that night and McNab's near-death experience didn't make Rhona any more comfortable with the situation that currently lay between them.

Damn blast the man, for putting her in this position.

Taking down the dolls for transport to the laboratory was more time-consuming than moving the body. There were twenty-seven of them and, on closer inspection, they proved to have patterns drawn on them similar to the victim's tattoos. Each one was attached to the roof with a large tack, via a length of standard household string wound round the doll's neck.

They had worked out a method of getting them down which consisted of Rhona standing on a chair taken from the kitchen and Chrissy bagging each doll as she took possession of it.

'My brothers used to pinch my Barbie and torture it,' Chrissy informed Rhona as they worked.

This latest revelation about the male members of Chrissy's

family came as no surprise to Rhona. Chrissy had three brothers, only one of whom, Patrick, Chrissy had any time for. The other two were carbon copies of her father. Mean, spiteful, drunken, brutish pigs.

'It used to reappear with a leg missing or an eye put out,' she elaborated. 'But I always got my own back.'

Rhona had to ask how.

'Various ways. Mostly involving their prize possessions.'

'Which were?'

'Their pricks, of course.' Chrissy grinned up at her. 'Remember itching powder?'

She took a flame-haired doll from Rhona and slipped it into an evidence bag. 'I always wondered why it was okay to give the female doll tits, but the male equivalent, Ken, had no dick.'

Rhona decided there was no answer to that.

Once the room was bare of body and dolls, Rhona settled down to write up her notes while everything was fresh in her mind. Now that the smell of death had been removed, other scents resurfaced, the predominant one being damp.

There was only one window in the room. Grimy with the dirt of the inner city, it looked out over the back lane in which she'd been deposited abruptly by McNab some hours before. Looking out, she suddenly registered exactly where she was. The block directly in front of her was the north side of the Lion Chambers, an art nouveau building, eight storeys tall, listed, but in critical need of repair. Originally designed and built as artists' studios, it was an early example of reinforced concrete construction, waiting, she suspected, to be knocked down. Yet its countenance was still regal, even though the lion carvings were encased in wire netting.

Looking down into the lane, she noted that there was only one car there now, Chrissy having hitched a ride back to the lab with the dolls via the forensic van. The car, she suspected, was McNab's. She pictured him sitting there, waiting for her to emerge, with an offer of a lift back, either to the lab or home.

Rhona exited the flat and the officer on duty closed the door behind her. She stepped out of the forensic suit, conscious of the stink of perspiration, chemicals and death about her person. Catching the tube or a taxi smelling like this was out of the question. She would accept a lift from McNab, regardless.

He was sitting in the driver's seat, deep in thought. Rhona stood for a moment in the doorway, watching him, before he sensed her presence and turned. For a moment he smiled, that dazzling smile that had melted a few hearts before her own. Then the dark clouds were back.

Settled into the passenger seat, Rhona responded to his questioning look.

'Home,' she said quietly, then added, 'please.'

The *please* slackened McNab's taut jawline. He visibly relaxed and the return journey was considerably less fraught. He even slowed on approaching traffic lights as though hoping they would change before he got there. Still they didn't speak until Rhona finally asked if he or the postman had fought off the cat.

'The postman claims he didn't go into the flat. The open door and the noise from the cat was enough to make him call us. He said the girl, Leila Hardy, treated the cat like a person.

'I took a look in the room,' he went on. 'It was obvious

23

she was dead, so I backed out to avoid the cat. No point contaminating the locus. Then I called you.'

'You said you spoke to Bill first,' Rhona said accusingly.

'I knew you would agree if you thought the boss wanted it.'

When Rhona didn't respond to his honesty, he said, 'Why did you ask about the cat?'

'I retrieved blood and skin from under its claws.'

McNab waved his unmarked hands briefly in the air. 'Not guilty.'

The words *not guilty* escaped his mouth to hang between them like a bad smell.

McNab, sensing this, covered his dismay by suddenly upping speed, only to have to brake suddenly as a bus pulled out in front of them.

Rhona almost felt sorry for him in that moment.

Perhaps sensing this, McNab turned and said, 'So, when do we go to the boss and tell him what happened that night in the stone circle?'

It was the question Rhona didn't want to answer.

3

McNab watched the door swing shut behind Rhona. He'd broached the subject for the third time and still received no answer. She'd just observed him with those eyes, examining what churchgoers might call his soul. McNab thought of it more as his Mr Hyde, although he wasn't at all sure that his outer persona had ever reached the standards of Hyde's better half, Dr Jekyll.

They had to eventually talk this through. He knew that. She knew that. The unspoken secret just kept getting bigger.

One option would be for him to go to DI Wilson alone and confess. After all, it was his actions that had created the problem. But, he acknowledged, Rhona's inaction in not immediately revealing what had happened put her in the frame too. Which was, of course, his fault. He had gone against her wishes that terrible night barely two months ago in the stone circle. He'd let a killer die while she'd been trying to keep him alive. *Let him die or made him die?* Had he been Hyde that night or Dr Jekyll?

The circular nature of these thoughts frustrated him further and brought to mind a saying of his late mother. *When in doubt, do nothing.*

It had been her way of encouraging him to think before he acted. Acting on the spur of the moment had proved his downfall on a number of occasions. She had been well aware of that and had often sought to persuade him to go more cautiously.

Well, he'd definitely been cautious on this occasion, and it had only made matters worse.

McNab turned the car round and headed back to the police station.

Shannon Jones was twenty-four years old, petite, blonde and very frightened. She'd arrived at the dead girl's flat late Saturday afternoon, worried by the fact that her friend wasn't answering her mobile. When she'd discovered the police presence, she'd had a nervous breakdown on the doorstep, which only got worse on hearing that her friend was dead.

McNab had asked DS Janice Clark to talk to her before he did. He couldn't order Janice to do anything, since he was no longer her superior officer. In fact, this was the first time he'd had to engage with Janice since his demotion.

When he was first a DS, she was a DC. When he was promoted to DI, she was promoted to DS. In that particular game of snakes and ladders, he'd found himself quickly sliding down the snake, and was now on the same level as his former right-hand woman.

It wasn't a comfortable place to be, but Janice, as always, strove to make it so. McNab hadn't encountered any animosity or glee at his demotion from that quarter, although there were others, particularly Superintendent Sutherland, who obviously relished it. He continually wore the *I told you so* expression. Sutherland didn't like officers who wouldn't play the game as dictated by him, even if they got results. The search for Stonewarrior had been a case in point. McNab going AWOL had got a result. Two results in fact. They had caught the perpetrator and McNab had lost his promotion.

McNab thought that a fair exchange. Sutherland regarded it as a personal triumph. Fortunately, their paths rarely crossed now that McNab was lower down the ranks again, which suited both of them very well.

Shannon brought the cup of coffee shakily to her lips. The movement reminded McNab of when he'd been drinking heavily and his hand had trembled just like that.

Not any more.

'Tell me about Leila,' he said gently.

They were seated in a side room which housed a coffee machine, a few easy chairs and a table. Used to give bad tidings, it wore the scent of absorbed despair.

'She was funny and clever.' Shannon wobbled a little on the past tense, a common reaction when the idea of someone being dead hadn't quite registered. 'She liked a laugh.'

'And you were out having a laugh last night?' McNab said.

'We went out for something to eat and a drink after work.'

'Where did Leila work?'

'With me, at Glasgow University library.'

'Tell me about last night.'

She cleared her throat as though about to make a speech. It sounded guilty but probably wasn't. She was blinking a lot, but contrary to popular opinion that didn't mean she was about to lie, just that she was stressed. Then again, people get stressed when they're lying.

'We ate pizza in the Italian in Sauchiehall Street near the Buchanan Galleries, then went for a drink at The Pot Still in Hope Street.'

McNab knew the place, mainly because of its extensive

collection of malt whiskies. Many of which he'd enjoyed, probably too much. He nodded at her to continue.

'Two guys started chatting us up. At first Leila didn't look interested, but I knew she was playing him along, making him worry. Then she suddenly stood up, gave me a knowing look and off they went together back to her place.' She halted, fear crossing her face. 'He looked okay. He'd had a drink, but he wasn't really drunk.' She rushed on. 'If I'd thought he would hurt Leila . . .'

McNab interrupted her. 'We don't know that he did.'

Shannon looked from McNab to Janice and back again.

'I don't understand. You said Leila was dead. How did she die if he didn't kill her?'

'She was found hanged.'

The shock of his words hit her face like a punch, draining it of blood. 'Hanged?' she repeated in disbelief.

'We have yet to establish whether it was suicide.'

'No way.' She shook her head vehemently. 'Leila would *never* commit suicide.'

If McNab had a tenner for every time he'd heard the friends and family of suicide victims say exactly that . . . He waited a few moments before continuing. 'We won't know for certain until after the post-mortem.'

The girl wasn't really listening to him. 'Leila took him home for sex,' she said firmly. 'That's what she wanted last night. That's what she did. For fun. No strings attached. That's the way she liked it.'

McNab sat back in the chair and contemplated the young woman before him. He believed her when she said that's what Leila did, but he wasn't sure that was the whole story.

'And what about you? Was that your intention too?'

Blood flooded back into her face, reddening her cheeks in embarrassment. 'Maybe, but it didn't work out like that.'

'Why?'

'After they left, the other guy went to the toilet and never came back.'

McNab looked at the girl before him, pretty and probably willing with a little wooing, and wondered why her suitor had given up so easily.

'Why do you think your one bailed?'

It was a harsh question, indicated by Janice's frown, but you couldn't always be nice in this job.

Shannon said outright, 'I wondered that myself. We were getting on well, better than Leila and his mate. He looked really pissed off when they left.' She paused. 'I think they had a bet on who would score first. And when it wasn't him, he lost interest.'

'Do you remember their names?'

'It was noisy in the pub. I think mine said George.'

'And the other one?'

She shook her head. 'No idea.'

'And you didn't exchange numbers?'

'We hadn't got that far.'

'Is there any chance he followed Leila and his mate?'

She looked startled by the suggestion, then took a moment to think about it.

'Time-wise it's a possibility. But why would he do that?'

McNab could think of a number of reasons. None of them pleasant. If there had been two of them, getting the victim onto the hook would have been easy. His imagination working overtime, he did a rerun of the previous night's events. Leila taking guy number one back to her flat. Guy number two joining them there.

29

'She definitely didn't hang herself,' Shannon said again. 'Leila wasn't suicidal. She had . . . beliefs.'

McNab's ears pricked up. 'What sort of beliefs?'

Shannon shifted a little in her seat. 'New Age stuff. That life is precious. That we're one with the universe. That sort of thing.'

'What about bondage and sadomasochism?' McNab said.

'What?' Her eyes widened.

'Could Leila have hanged herself during sex?'

The face paled again. 'No way.'

'What about the room with the hanging dolls?'

There was a moment's silence while she digested his words and tried to make sense of them. 'I don't know what you're talking about.'

'There were nearly thirty Barbie-type dolls hanging from the roof in the room where we found her.'

Shannon was definitely freaked by that. 'No way. I never saw that room.'

McNab changed the subject. 'Have you given Detective Sergeant Clark a description of the two men?'

Shannon looked a bit worried by this. 'I did, but I was pissed to be honest, and it's a bit of a blur.'

'We need to contact Leila's family. Do you have a phone number or address?'

'She has a brother who lives in Glasgow. His name's Daniel. He's a musician. Plays in a band called the Spikes. They're on Facebook if you want to contact him. I don't have an address.' She looked grief-stricken at the thought of him being told about his sister.

McNab gave her a moment to collect herself, then thanked her and told her she could go.

'When will you know what happened to Leila?'

'In a couple of days,' he said, hoping it was true.

Janice was the one to show Shannon out, while McNab took advantage of the coffee machine. Strong coffee had replaced whisky as his stimulant of choice. The buzz wasn't as good, but then again there was no hangover. He chose a double espresso, drank it in one go, then pressed the button for another.

When Janice came back he asked if she wanted one. She asked for a latte and he did the honours. He realized he felt easier in Janice's company since his demotion. In fact, he felt better because they were now equals. He couldn't boss her and she couldn't boss him.

'Well,' he said. 'What do you think?'

'That she's telling the truth. They had a drink and met two guys. Leila took hers home. What happened next, I don't know. When's the post-mortem?'

'Scheduled for Monday morning, first thing. D'you want to come along?'

She nodded.

They sat in easy silence for a moment. McNab pondered this strange turn of events. That he and DS Clark should be comfortable in one another's company. He stole a sideways look at her as she sipped her latte. Her expression said she was also pondering something. There was a small crease in her forehead and a faraway look in her eyes. She wore no make-up. She wasn't pretty, but she was certainly arresting to look at. He thought of a younger Annie Lennox or Tilda Swinton.

When they'd first met he'd hit on her. She'd turned him down, which had irked at the time. So he'd put it about that she must be gay. DI Wilson had ordered him into his office and torn strips off him. McNab still flinched at the memory.

He'd retreated after that. Janice hadn't held a grudge. In fact, if it hadn't been for her support in the last case, he might have lost his life, rather than just his promotion. He contemplated whether he should offer to buy her a drink as a belated thanks, then remembered he was on the wagon.

'What's the plan, then?' Janice said.

'How do you feel about contacting the brother?'

It was by far the hardest of the jobs and she knew it.

'Okay,' she said.

'I'll speak to The Pot Still contingent.'

Janice raised an eyebrow, which suggested that word had got out about him being off the booze.

'We can swop if you like,' McNab offered.

'No need.'

What she was really saying was that she trusted him, although in view of the *Stonewarrior* case, she had little reason to.

McNab felt a surge of respect for Detective Sergeant Janice Clark. When Janice climbed the ladder to detective inspector, she wouldn't slide back down the snake, as he had done.

4

The delicious smell of cooking met Rhona as she approached her front door. Her plan had been to order in food, for despite being in the presence of death most of the day, she was starving. But the aroma suggested that Sean, rather than leave, had stayed to cook for her.

She paused before putting the key in the lock, trying to decide how to deal with this. If she appeared welcoming, that might suggest she was glad Sean had stayed on. If she was annoyed, that might give the impression she didn't want him there at all.

Neither way was how she felt.

On entry, the cat came bounding towards her. Tom was no longer the small furry ball Sean had bought after her first cat, Chance, had been killed, murdered by a psychopath as a warning to her. She'd been annoyed with Sean for making the decision about a new cat without consulting her, but had gradually warmed to Tom's presence. Yet the cat, appearing now, simply reminded her of the psychological games her former live-in lover was wont to play.

Rather than seeking Sean out, Rhona dropped her forensic bag, removed her jacket and headed straight for the shower. Fifteen minutes later, smelling a good deal better, she entered the kitchen to find it empty.

The table was set for one, with a note on the waiting plate.

Food in the slow cooker. Should be ready by six, but won't spoil. White wine in the fridge. Enjoy. Sean x

The wrath Rhona had nursed under the heat of the shower dissipated and she felt foolish, and then a little annoyed.

Why? Because he'd done what she'd wanted and left?

Rhona retrieved the wine and poured herself a glass. The slow cooker, bought by Sean when they'd lived together and which she'd buried in a cupboard when she'd told him to leave, was back in pride of place on the work surface and emitting the delicious aroma she'd encountered on the stairs.

Rhona decided not to ponder Sean's motives or how she should interpret them, but rather just eat the food he'd prepared for her. The contents of the cooker turned out to be chicken casserole. That and the wine were definitely up to Sean's usual standards and, she had to admit, better than the meals she generally phoned out for.

Hunger assuaged, she took her wine through to the sitting room and settled on the couch with her laptop. There was a message from Chrissy to say she'd logged the samples taken from the flat, including the creepy dolls, then gone home. As Rhona read this, another email pinged in, this time from McNab.

Rhona regarded it for a moment. The title 'Monday morning' immediately made her think he'd decided to confess to Bill Wilson. She hesitated, then opened it, and found it was simply alerting her to the post-mortem on the possible suicide.

Her relief at this irritated her. She wasn't usually prone to indecision, but this case wasn't usual. If McNab would just lay off the subject, she would make up her own mind what to do. Even as she thought this, she was aware that this line of reasoning was just a way of blaming McNab for her indecision.

Well, he'd put her in this position.

To take her mind off McNab, she fired up the photographs from the crime scene. Scrolling through them, she decided the images of the dolls were almost as disturbing as those of the victim.

Now, observing the dolls en masse, Rhona realized they were arranged in three rows of nine, and that each row was divided into three, by hair colour, making nine blondes, nine brunettes and nine redheads in total. Since the cord used in the hanging was also knotted nine times, it did seem that the number nine was significant in some way or other to the victim.

She decided to do a little online numerology research.

When she entered 'the significance of nine' into the search box, Wikipedia popped up first. The detailed and substantial entry provided a great deal of information on the place of nine in mathematics, including the simple fact that when you multiply any number by nine, then add the resulting digits and reduce them to a single digit, it always becomes a nine. Intrigued by this, Rhona tried a few herself just to make sure. It seemed, said the entry, 'that from a numerological perspective, the 9 simply takes over, like the infamous body snatchers'.

There was also a mention of nine in Chinese lore and in Tolkien's *Lord of the Rings*, with the nine companions of the ring and the nine Ringwraiths, matching good and evil. She learned quite a bit from her study of the number nine, but none of it offered an insight into the pattern of nine in the hanging dolls or the use of nine knots in the plaited cord.

Of course, should the post-mortem conclusion be that it wasn't suicide, then the cord might have been the property of the perpetrator, rather than the victim. Which led Rhona to wonder if the presence of the dolls could also be the work of the perpetrator.

Her first thought when she heard the door buzzer was that it might be Sean returning, but she dismissed that as unlikely. At ten o'clock he would just be starting his set at the jazz club.

When she answered the intercom, there was a moment's silence as though her visitor might have rung the wrong flat. Rhona was about to put the receiver down when McNab finally spoke.

'Can I come up?'

'No.'

'Please? We need to talk.'

Rhona wanted to tell him to go away, but found herself unable to. Maybe he was right. Maybe they did need to clear the air.

Rhona released the door and let him in.

Michael Joseph McNab looked better than he had done for some time. Gone were the shadowed eyes. He'd shaved, and he definitely hadn't been drinking. When she'd offered him a whisky, he'd turned it down and asked for coffee instead.

'Make it strong,' he requested.

Rhona did as asked then poured herself another glass of wine.

McNab sniffed the air. 'Been cooking?'

'I don't cook. You know that.'

He smiled. 'Smells good whoever made it.'

Rhona sipped her wine in silence. McNab swallowed the coffee and held the cup out to be replenished.

Eventually he spoke. 'I'm in a better place now. Off the booze, for a start.' When Rhona didn't respond, he went on. 'That night at the stone circle, I'd had God knows how many drugs pumped into me. I was high and mad and when I saw that bastard on top of you, I . . .' He halted.

His words had conjured for Rhona a memory as vivid as when it had happened. Suddenly she could smell him again, feel his weight bearing down on her. She stood up and walked to the window and looked down on the tranquil scene below, trying to dispel that other image.

'I've written it all down,' McNab said. 'Everything I can remember. You can read it if you want, before I hand it to the boss.'

Rhona didn't turn from the window.

'We were both debriefed. Neither of us told the full truth then,' she said.

'I'm going to tell it now,' McNab said.

'If you do, then I'll be the liar. By omission.'

'Not the way I've told it.'

'Then it's not the truth,' Rhona said.

She turned and their eyes met and held for the first time since that fateful night in the dark, in the middle of the stone circle.

'I have to fix this,' he pleaded.

Rhona slowly shook her head. 'It's unfixable.'

McNab was trying to read her expression. 'You want to let it go?' he said, surprised.

In that moment, Rhona made her decision. 'Yes.'

A flurry of emotions crossed his face, relief and hope among them. Rhona felt a little of both herself. McNab had offered on numerous occasions to reveal the last moments of the serial killer they had come to know as Stonewarrior, yet she had refused to discuss it with him.

Now that she had made a decision, it was as though the weight of the killer's body had been lifted from her.

'Can we change the subject now?' she said.

'Gladly.'

'I've been studying the photographs from the suspicious death,' Rhona said.

'And?'

'Did you notice the presence of the number nine?'

'Not particularly,' he said cautiously. 'Unless you mean that twenty-seven dolls constitutes three times nine.'

Rhona beckoned him to follow her through to the sitting room and fired up the laptop again. She showed him the photographs she'd taken of the dolls. McNab's recoil at that image reflected her own.

'There are nine of each hair colour,' she said. 'Each row is made up of nine dolls, divided into threes.' Rhona pulled up an image of the red cord still encircling the victim's neck. 'You'll have to take my word for it until the PM, but there are nine evenly spaced knots in the ligature used to hang her.'

'So what's special about nine?'

'Lots of things.'

She brought up the Wikipedia page and watched as McNab's eyes glazed over.

'For fuck's sake. Don't make it maths or we'll have to bring in the nutty professor again,' he said, alluding to Professor

Magnus Pirie, criminal psychologist and McNab's very own bête noire.

Rhona ignored the dig at Magnus. 'I don't think it's anything to do with the maths properties, but it's significant in some way.'

'Her pal said Leila was a New Age believer, if that helps,' McNab offered.

'It might.'

Rhona tried a search on 'nine' and 'New Age'. What appeared was anything but enlightening, unless you believed that the Masonic Lodge was behind the Twin Towers attack and that both the Bible and the devil used the number nine in their scriptures.

Rhona closed the laptop.

'I didn't think you would give up so easily,' McNab said.

'I haven't.' She looked pointedly at her watch.

McNab took the hint. 'Okay. I'd better head for the pub, before it's closing time.'

'What?' Rhona said.

He smiled at her reaction. 'To talk to the barman on duty last night when Leila met her man.'

She didn't return the smile, irritated at him for setting her up, but then again, that was the real McNab. She walked him to the door.

Rhona didn't want him to bring up their earlier discussion and was keen for him to leave. Sensing this perhaps, he exited, but as she made to close the door behind him, he stopped her.

'We *are* okay, Dr MacLeod?' he said.

Rhona wasn't willing to go quite that far.

'Let's wait and see,' was all she could manage.

He appeared to accept this, because he nodded, then headed downstairs.

Rhona stood for a moment, listening to his echoing footsteps, hearing the main door slam shut behind him.

What the hell had she done? Whatever way you looked at it, she had bound herself to McNab by keeping the secret.

And secrets, she knew, had a habit of coming back to bite you.

5

Mark checked his watch for the umpteenth time.

They must have found her by now.

He felt his heart quicken at the thought. Funny how he'd never noticed the speed of his heart before, not even when he was playing football. Now he heard every beat resounding in his head.

What the hell had he done?

The trouble was he had no idea. He remembered fucking her, the weird cat digging its claws into his shoulder, then nothing until he was sick. *What happened in between? How had she got in that room and onto that hook? And the dolls. Those freaking dolls.*

He suddenly registered Emilie calling to him from the bedroom.

'Coming,' he shouted back.

He observed himself in the mirror, then splashed his face with cold water. He needed to stay calm and focused. Emilie didn't suspect a thing. He'd turned up at her flat as promised to take her to lunch. She hadn't seemed interested in knowing about the football, but had regaled him with her own story of a meal out with friends.

After lunch they had come back to her place.

Emilie had been up for sex and he'd obliged, but only after he'd snorted a line to blot out last night's lingering

41

image. She'd spotted the cat's claw marks on his shoulder, but appeared to buy the story of a fall during the football game.

Re-entering the bedroom, he gave an audible groan and even managed to limp a bit. Emilie was sitting up in bed, arms stretched above her head, her breasts eyeing him in the hope of a second round.

Something Mark didn't think he could manage.

He groaned again.

'What's up?' Emilie said.

'My shoulder where I fell. Think it's stiffening up.'

She eyed his penis, which definitely wasn't.

He gave her a plaintive look. 'Would you mind if I went home for a kip?'

This time suspicion did lurk in those baby-blue eyes.

Mark leaned over and kissed her. 'I could come back later?'

Somewhat mollified, she stroked his hair. For some reason, that got a response where the pointed breasts had not. Noting this, she slid her hand downwards to massage his growing erection.

Mark blanked all thoughts of last night and got on with it.

He left Emilie at nine o'clock. After round two, she'd phoned out for pizza. Mark had eaten his quickly, after which he'd indicated just how tired he was by a series of yawns, and had eventually been permitted to leave.

Outside now, he took a deep breath of cool night air, then pulled out his mobile, which he'd kept switched off all day. There were three messages from Jeff, all brief, asking in a variety of ways how he'd got on last night. The final one had come in around eight o'clock.

Mark decided to look at that positively. Jeff obviously hadn't heard about the body of a female being discovered in a flat near the pub, or he would surely have mentioned it.

He knew he should text back. Jeff would expect that. But what to say?

I had sex with her, then found her hanging in the next room.

The half-digested pizza flipped in his stomach, making him feel nauseous.

Let's face it, I'm fucked whatever I do.

He set off towards the Grassmarket, deciding a pint would help him think.

The night was fine and pleasantly warm. Being Saturday, the tables outside the string of pubs that called the Grassmarket home were full.

Mark gave up on an outside seat and, choosing the bar emitting the least noise, went inside. It took him a good five minutes to order a drink, but he did manage to find a small corner table next to the toilets, where he could sit in relative peace.

Free now of Emilie and her keen observance, he ran over last night's proceedings. At least, what he could remember of them. He could recall how everything had been sharpened by the coke. Colours, sounds, touch, all enhanced by that snap pack of white powder. He had a sudden memory of laughing when she'd ordered him to strip. God, that had been a turn-on. He realized with a start that had she wanted to whip him, he would have readily agreed to that as well.

Which stirred a sudden memory. *The knotted cord.*

After she'd ordered the cat off his face, she'd made him

sit up and, his penis still inside her, had bound them together round the waist with a red knotted cord, pulling it tighter as he'd reached climax.

Mark's heart was racing now, as though he'd taken another line of coke. He brushed away a drop of perspiration that ran down the side of his face, realizing if she hadn't been dead, he would have gone back for more.

A thought struck him.

What if she wasn't dead? What if he'd been hallucinating with the mix of coke and alcohol? What if it had all been a bad dream?

Then he remembered the smell.

When he'd opened the door and the cat had pushed its way in, there had been a bad smell. Like piss or shit. Then the cat had wailed and he'd seen her, the red cord round her neck, those eyes staring at him.

That's what he'd smelt in that room. Death.

His hand trembling a little, Mark drank down the remainder of his pint and ordered another, then set about scouring the news on his mobile, looking for some mention of a dead girl found last night in Glasgow.

Twenty minutes later, he had nothing, which either meant she hadn't been found or that the police hadn't released details yet. But she would be found eventually and, he decided, probably by the friend.

The friend who had watched him leave with her, which would make him a suspect. And he'd watched enough cop dramas to know he was all over her, the bedroom *and* the red cord. Still, DNA was no use without a suspect to match it to, and he didn't have a record.

So, he persuaded himself, he was safe. Unless they picked him up.

Mark suddenly realized how important it was to talk to

Jeff. If Jeff had broken the golden rule and given out his real name and mobile number, the police would be able to trace him via Jeff.

He pulled up Jeff's number. It rang out four times, then Jeff picked up.

'Hey, mate, at last. Where are you?'

'Back in Edinburgh.'

'How was she?'

While Mark figured out what his answer should be, Jeff came back. 'The bitch ditched you before you got a taste?'

Mark couldn't help himself. 'Oh no. I made it into the garden all right,' he heard himself boasting. 'How about you?'

'Same.' Jeff gave an appreciative whistle.

'Seeing her again?' Mark said.

'No way. A one-off as agreed, to spice up the regular love life.' He paused. 'I take it Emilie bought the five-a-side routine?'

'No problem. Did you tell her your real name?' Mark checked.

'Treated myself to a new one. George. How about you?'

'Never got round to names, too busy doing other things,' Mark said.

'Excellent. See you next month for more of the same?'

'You bet. And, Jeff? Whatever happens, we were never in that pub. Agreed?'

'Agreed.'

Mark felt better when he rang off. Maybe he could survive this. He had tomorrow to get his head straight before work on Monday. He would avoid Emilie until next weekend. Plead too much work. Play it safe. Play it low.

The phone call had calmed him a little.

Now that he had thought it through, he was pretty sure that the sex games they'd played had never reached that room with the dolls. So, if he didn't have a hand in her death, then how did it happen?

He'd been trashed by drink, drugs and sex. Not so much asleep as unconscious. And while he was comatose, had someone else come into the flat? He'd toyed with the idea that she'd committed suicide, but it didn't fit with the way she'd acted. Why invite him there for sex then top herself?

He'd blotted out the image of her on the hook, but he forced himself to recall it now. She had been off the ground and there was no upturned chair.

So how the hell had she got up there?

Someone must have entered the flat while he was asleep. It was the only explanation. And that someone must have killed her. Did the killer realize he was in the bedroom? If so, why wasn't he killed too?

It only took him seconds to work out why.

He was the mug that would take the blame. The last one seen with her alive and the one whose DNA was all over her and the murder weapon.

Let's face it, he was totally fucked.

6

Saturday night and the pub was busy, both with regulars and, McNab could hear from the voices, tourists, come to taste the wide variety of whiskies on offer. He made his way through the throng to the bar and, showing his ID, asked to speak to Barry Fraser.

The young woman disappeared round the back and, minutes later, a tall, blond man emerged, looking worried.

McNab flashed his ID again. 'Barry Fraser?'

When the guy nodded, McNab asked, 'Anywhere we can talk in private, Barry?'

He looked unsure. 'The cellar's about the only quiet place tonight.'

'That'll do.'

Barry looked nonplussed at this, but realizing McNab was for real, lifted the counter and ushered him inside. As they passed the shelves lined with malt whiskies, McNab kept his eyes firmly on Barry's back.

A narrow corridor led to a door that opened on a set of stairs. Barry headed down them and McNab followed. The cellar was tidy and well stocked with a row of barrels attached to pipes leading upwards. There were shelves with whisky bottles all arranged by distillery. It was something a connoisseur would notice and McNab did. How the hell anyone worked here and didn't imbibe, he had no idea. Barry took up a stance in front of a barrel and waited with worried eyes for his interrogation to begin.

'I wanted to ask you about someone who was in here last night.'

Barry gave him a disbelieving look. 'Have you any idea just how many folk were in here last night?'

McNab nodded. 'This one you would have noticed.'

'Okay. Try me.'

'A young woman. Auburn hair. Green eyes. About five five. A real looker. She was with a pal. Pretty, petite, blonde. They were in here about ten o'clock?'

The barman eyed him warily. McNab guessed he had seen Leila. She would have been hard to miss and he thought Barry Fraser would be well practised at bird spotting in his bar.

Barry was considering his reply and wondering what it might lead to. Curiosity tinged with a little concern eventually decided him.

'It sounds like Leila Hardy. Why, what's happened to her?'

McNab ignored the question. 'You definitely saw them?'

He nodded. 'Sure. They were over in the corner with two lads.'

'Can you describe these lads?'

He shook his head. 'I notice the lassies, the lads don't interest me.'

It was a fair comment. Had McNab been asked to describe one of the crowd of blokes propping up the bar tonight, he would have been hard pressed to do so.

'Did you see Leila leave?'

In that split second, McNab knew his barman was about

to tell a lie. Call it police intuition or psychology in action, but he just knew.

'No.'

'What about the blonde one?'

'Leila, I noticed. The pal not so much.'

'How well do you know Leila?'

McNab already suspected the answer to that, but he was pretty sure Barry wouldn't reveal it. Not until he sussed out why the policeman was interested.

McNab decided to go for the jugular.

'Leila Hardy was found dead this morning.'

Barry's eyes widened. The shock appeared real enough for him to seek a seat on the edge of a nearby barrel.

'Jesus,' he whispered under his breath. He looked up, his face now suffused with anger. 'You bastard, you never said anything about that on the phone.'

McNab decided not to warn him about swearing at a police officer, but waited as Barry tried to pull himself together. Eventually he did and rose to his feet again. 'What happened to her?' he said, genuine concern in his voice.

'That's what we're trying to establish.'

Barry searched McNab's expression. 'You mean she was murdered?'

'She was found hanged in her flat.'

Barry looked as if he was trying to compute and couldn't. 'Leila committed suicide?'

When McNab didn't respond, Barry came back. 'No way. Leila had everything going for her. She really enjoyed life.'

'So,' said McNab, drawing the conversation back to where he wanted it to be. 'When did she leave the pub and who was she with?'

This time Barry thought. Hard. 'I came down here to

change a barrel sometime after ten. When I went back up she had gone and the blonde was on her own.'

'You were keeping an eye on Leila?' McNab suggested.

'I wasn't stalking her if that's what you mean,' Barry declared.

'Just taking a keen interest?' McNab smiled. 'I take it you two were once an item?'

Judging by Barry's expression, he was contemplating another lie, then thought the better of it. 'No, but we did get together on occasion.'

'You had sex with Leila *on occasion*?' McNab said.

'Sometimes she asked me back to her place,' Barry said defensively.

Lucky you, McNab thought. 'But not last night?'

'No. Not last night.'

'The guy she did take home with her. What did he look like?'

Now that Barry knew that Leila was dead, he was more forthcoming about his rival. 'Tall, maybe six foot. Late twenties, early thirties. Blond. Worked out by the shape of him. Was wearing a blue striped shirt with short sleeves and jeans. By the clothes, the Gucci watch and the wallet, I'd say he wasn't short of cash,' he added.

The description, McNab noted, was a close match to Shannon's, although she hadn't mentioned that he'd looked affluent.

'What about the mate?'

'Dark hair, not as tall, dressed the same, but he never came near the bar. They moved in on Leila and the blonde quite quickly after that.'

'You don't know Shannon?'

He shook his head. 'Leila came in a lot, living round the corner.'

'What about security cameras?' McNab said.

'One on the front door, one on the side.'

So they might have footage of Leila and the guy leaving, if they weren't obscured by a crowd of smokers. McNab thanked him.

'Someone will be round for the security tapes.' He handed Barry a card. 'If you remember anything else, give me a ring.'

McNab fought a desire to reward himself with a dram and headed outside. As he suspected, the entrance was en-circled by smokers all within sight of the security camera. He took a look in the back lane and discovered the fire exit standing wide open. Just inside was the Gents, so the mate could have exited here when he'd deserted Shannon on the pretext that he was going to the toilet. If so, there was a chance that the back camera had caught him.

McNab left the lane and took the short walk between the pub and Leila's flat. There were plenty of revellers about the city centre at this time on a Saturday night. No doubt there were folk about last night too, who might have spotted the auburn-haired Leila and her tall blond companion walking the short distance home.

Once the post-mortem was over, they could get down to the business of looking for witnesses, unless the pathologist decided McNab's intuition was suspect and that Leila Hardy had simply taken her own life. That was a possibility, of course. Suicides were extremely adept at carrying out their wishes, often against the odds. If their aim was a cry for help, that was usually evidenced by the method they chose and the circumstances in which they made the attempt, which often had a 'way out'. A bit like driving down the wrong side of the road until you met an approaching car, then swerving to avoid it. Alternatively, courting death could be used to make life more exciting or maybe just bearable.

A condition McNab had been known to suffer from himself.

Tonight, the real and present danger presented itself in the form of numerous bars, from which music, chatter and female laughter escaped to surround him in a warm embrace.

McNab walked with a determined step, eyes forward, fighting the desire to say 'Fuck it!' and head into the next one he passed. He hadn't drunk alcohol in the last three weeks and planned a month at least, just to show that he could. Relieved to find that he could function without it, he'd convinced himself that although he'd been drinking heavily, he was not, yet, dependent on it.

Back at his own flat, he contemplated how to pass the midnight hour, alone and sober, knowing that tomorrow, Sunday, wouldn't be any easier. He phoned out for a pizza and put the recently purchased coffee machine on. While the coffee was brewing, he stripped to his boxers and did fifty press-ups. Anything to keep his mind off the open bottle of whisky in the cupboard near the sink. Kept there undrunk, it had become a symbol of his success.

Sex would have helped, but staying away from pubs had meant the only females he met were the ones he worked with. He'd long ago made his way through the fanciable ones, apart from Janice, and was pretty sure none of them would welcome a return visit however fit and sober he was now.

Janice had suggested, as they parted company, that now he was no longer a DI, he might like to come out for a drink with the team again. McNab was secretly pleased by her suggestion, but didn't trust himself to do that, yet.

Then there was his Rhona obsession.

He may have kidded himself in the past that they might get back together *on occasion* but he knew that wasn't going to happen. Ever. He was like the barman, with one eye on the object of his affection and a constant hope that she might just, in a weak moment, ask him back to her place.

Sad bastards, the pair of them.

McNab slipped on a T-shirt and answered the buzzer for his pizza delivery.

Sitting on the couch now, feet on the coffee table, a double espresso already drunk, he was reminded of another night, when Rhona had sat opposite him, sharing a pizza. They'd exchanged words over the girl he'd been bedding at the time, young enough to be his daughter.

Rhona had been less than impressed, and she'd been right.

But the memory of those sexual encounters with Iona were as difficult to forget as the bottle of whisky. McNab abandoned the remains of the pizza and headed for the shower.

Ten minutes later, reddened by the force of the hot, then cold shower, the bullet scar on his back glowing, he poured another coffee and carried it through to the bedroom. The room was stuffy and warm, so he opened the window a little, then lay down naked on top of the bed and listened to the siren sound of his fellow officers dealing with the fallout from too much alcohol on a Saturday night.

Staring at the ceiling, McNab set his caffeine-buzzed brain to figuring out what had happened to Leila Hardy after she left the pub and headed home for sex with the unknown blond guy.

In all the possible scenarios he came up with, not one, but two men figured.

One thing his gut told him.

Leila Hardy hadn't died by her own hand.

7

It wasn't a requirement for the investigating officer to attend a victim's post-mortem and many simply chose not to. Seasoned officers, well acquainted with the variety of terrible ways that humans dispensed with one another, often found viewing the systematic surgical dissection of a body too difficult to deal with.

Familiarity with the aftermath of murder, however messy and horrific that might be, was not the same as actually being present when a knife sliced its way through flesh, and an electric saw cut its way through bone. The variety of noises alone were often hard to bear, although earplugs could be employed, and often were.

When Rhona arrived in the changing room, DS Clark was already there.

They'd exchanged pleasantries as they'd donned the overalls, both managing to avoid mentioning McNab's recent demotion. Rhona gained the impression that Janice was more relaxed about working with McNab as an equal, which suggested that he was definitely making an effort.

This pleased her.

When the object of her thoughts arrived, he wasn't hungover, which had often been the case in the past. Glancing from one woman to the other, you could see what he was thinking, so Rhona put him straight.

'We weren't talking about you.'

McNab's feigned expression of indifference made Janice smile.

'So what were you talking about?' he asked airily.

Rhona ignored the question and posed one of her own.

'How did you get on with the barman?'

McNab located a forensic suit and began to pull it on.

'He saw Leila leave with a man fitting Shannon's description. He admitted that he had the hots for Leila himself and that he and she were an *occasional* item.' He threw Rhona a swift glance which she ignored.

'What about the suicide angle?'

'He was as adamant as Shannon that Leila wouldn't kill herself.'

'Well, let's see what the pathologist has to say,' Rhona said, pulling up her hood and raising her mask.

Dr Sissons didn't glance up on their entry. His usual behaviour was to simply ignore the presence of others at the post-mortems he conducted. He and Rhona had an unspoken understanding that they did not cross the boundaries between their specializations unless absolutely necessary. Sissons did not like his judgement questioned. Like a surgeon in an operating theatre, he gave out orders and did not take them. To break into his train of thought would probably result in being told to leave.

All three of them were aware of this, and stood in absolute silence as he recorded the bodily measurements and condition of the body, then the signs of rapid anoxial death.

Anoxia, the scientific term for a lack of oxygen, could develop over a long period of time, due to a variety of illnesses, where the lungs and the heart weren't working properly. Rapid anoxial death was an entirely different matter. If the flow of oxygen from the atmosphere to the tissues was interrupted suddenly, then rapid anoxial death occurred. Classification of such deaths included suffocation, choking, strangulation, compression of the chest, cyanide poisoning, drowning and hanging. Some of these methods were swifter than others. In very rapid deaths, the oxygen supply to the body and brain was cut off and the victim immediately became quiet and pale, and passed swiftly into unconsciousness then death.

Such a quick death usually caused little disturbance at a scene. In more slowly progressing rapid anoxial death, the situation was quite different. Once anoxia had started, the victim fought for breath, often lashing out at an attacker. The result was the obvious signs of a death struggle, evidenced by bruising on both victim and attacker, and DNA exchange often through scratches and blood transfer.

When Sissons stated that he was about to remove the cord from round the victim's neck, Rhona asked permission to record this and Sissons gave a curt nod. From observation, she had deduced that the main knot was a slip knot or simple noose. Watching it being unravelled would confirm this.

Now that the neck was free of the cord, it was clear that there were no pressure fingermarks or bruises associated with strangulation. As was common in hanging, the mark of the ligature was incomplete, evident only at the front. The mark was depressed, pale and parchment-like, the pattern of the plaited cord evident.

Dr Sissons recorded this evidence in his usual dry tone. As he did so, McNab's eyes met Rhona's above the mask.

'I found some fibres in her mouth,' Rhona said.

Sissons acknowledged this with a nod and went in for a

look himself, extracting a further fibre from deeper in the throat, suggesting, as Rhona had surmised, that a cloth of some sort might have been put in the victim's mouth or even pushed into her throat to cut off the air supply.

Gagging was common in homicidal suffocation, along with plastic or wet material covering the nose and mouth, and in some instances shoved down the throat.

Rhona could feel McNab's growing impatience; Sissons wasn't known for speed in post-mortems, even when the cause of death appeared obvious to everyone round the table.

But Sissons got there eventually.

In the pathologist's estimation, the victim had something wedged in her mouth, causing her to pass out. This had then been removed and the cord tied round her neck while she was unconscious. She had then been hung on the hook.

He finished this by stating, 'There is, of course, the chance that all of this was done as part of auto-erotic hanging, which she may have consented to.'

Now back in the changing room, all three stripped off their suits and dumped them in the basket.

'So she was gagged,' McNab said. 'What with?'

'The fibres I extracted were a cotton synthetic mix. I sent Chrissy back to the flat to check for anything that might match.'

'I don't buy the auto-erotic bit,' Janice said. 'If she was into all that, we would have found other stuff in the flat. Plastic gags, blindfolds.'

'There's something else to consider,' McNab said.

'What?'

'I believe the other guy left the pub immediately after Leila and her man. I have a feeling he followed them.'

If that were true, it could change everything.

'We're checking the security cameras.' McNab turned to Janice. 'Any luck with the next of kin?'

'The brother's band, the Spikes, are on tour in Germany. I've emailed the manager but he hasn't come back to me yet.'

'Did you ask Shannon about the dolls?' Rhona said.

'She says she was never in that room,' McNab said. 'You still think the dolls are significant?'

'Who hangs twenty-seven dolls from their ceiling unless it means something?'

'Put that way,' McNab agreed. 'I take it you never discovered the secret of nine?'

'What's this about the number nine?' Janice came in.

Rhona explained about the nine knots in the cord and the pattern of dolls. 'Any ideas?'

Janice shook her head. 'But it's intriguing.'

'I thought I might run it past Magnus. He's back in Glasgow.' Rhona had been planning to drop that suggestion into her conversation with McNab the previous night, but had decided not to, in view of the circumstances.

'Good idea,' chimed Janice.

McNab had opened his mouth, no doubt to protest, but changed his mind and shut it again.

'I'll give him a call,' Rhona said. 'And let you know what he has to say.'

Back now at the lab, Rhona logged the arrival of the cord, then surveyed the sea of dolls laid out in rows on the table.

She had filled her Sunday with work, preferring to spend time at the lab to wondering if Sean would get in touch. It seemed, however, that he'd got the message. There had been no phone calls, no texts, and when she'd returned home early Sunday evening, she'd found no evidence he'd been back in the flat, despite still having a key. Rhona had found herself mildly irritated that he had taken her at her word and a little sorry not to encounter the scent of a cooked meal waiting for her.

Nevertheless, Sunday had been fruitful. A deserted and peaceful lab had resulted in a considerable amount of work being done. She'd established from the swabs that the victim had had sex before she'd died. There had been no bruising in the genital area, which Dr Sissons had confirmed at the PM, so the sex appeared to have been consensual.

More interestingly, fine fibres plucked from Leila's navel matched those of the red silk cord, suggesting it had also been round her waist. From sweat on the cord, she'd extracted samples of two different strands of DNA. One from the victim and the other matching that taken from the semen.

So her sexual partner that night had also been in contact with the cord.

Examining the red cord in more detail, Rhona found that the nine knots were identical and, from the chirality of each, she deduced they'd been tied by the same person, since the direction of movement was consistent.

Now she replayed the short movie she'd taken as Dr Sissons slowly untied the knot that had fixed the cord round Leila's neck. Rhona had suspected a slip knot or simple noose and this was proved to be right. After replaying a couple of times, she retied it herself to make sure.

It wasn't possible to definitely determine whether the person who tied a knot was left- or right-handed, but it became apparent that replicating the chirality of the slip knot felt awkward, and since she was left-handed, she suspected whoever had tied the slip knot wasn't. As for the nine knots, they were too simple to be certain. The postmortem hadn't established whether Leila was left- or right-handed. That was something McNab would have to find out from Leila's pal, Shannon.

Rhona was tackling the knots in the dolls' cords when Chrissy appeared and waved through the glass, indicating it was time to eat.

Abandoning the dolls, she joined Chrissy in the office where the warm scent of baking emanated from a paper bag, reminding Rhona how hungry she was.

Chrissy busied herself spooning coffee into the filter and unpacking what turned out to be four large sausage rolls.

'Help yourself.'

Rhona did as commanded.

Coffee machine on, Chrissy plonked herself down next to Rhona with a bottle of ketchup and proceeded to dollop some on her sausage roll before attacking it with gusto. It was clear there was to be no conversation until her forensic assistant had satisfied her hunger. Rhona had to wait until Chrissy had demolished two sausage rolls and half of Rhona's second one.

Settled back at the desk with her coffee, Chrissy finally said, 'I've brought a few items back that might match your fibres. How did the PM go?'

Rhona relayed what Sissons had said.

'Okay, but I don't think she was a gasper. I double-checked all her belongings. There's no evidence she was into erotic asphyxiation unless it's on the laptop the Tech guys took along with her mobile.'

'Except for the hanging dolls,' Rhona reminded her.

Chrissy made a face. 'I used to love my Barbie. Wasn't so fond of Ken though. He always seemed a bit of a wimp.'

'I'm going to give Magnus a ring. See if he has any ideas about the pattern of nine and the dolls.'

Chrissy considered this. 'McNab won't like that.'

'He agreed,' Rhona assured her. 'Or at least Detective Sergeant Clark thought it was a good idea.'

'And McNab didn't bite her head off?'

'No.'

Chrissy looked impressed. 'Changed days, eh?'

But for how long? Rhona wondered.

8

Professor Magnus Pirie was a typical Orcadian, if such a thing existed. He had grown up surrounded by the sea, spent a great deal of time battling against the wind that stripped the islands bare of trees, made his own home-brewed beer (a dying art). He spoke with an Orcadian accent when at home in Houton Bay and had mixed ancestry with the Inuits of Northern Canada via the Hudson Bay Company. Apart from these typical characteristics shared by many of those who inhabited the windy northern isles, he also had a powerful sense of smell which, at its best, was a blessing. At its worst, a curse.

Today it was a curse.

The train back from Edinburgh, packed as it was with teatime commuters, had developed a fault which prevented it from regulating the temperature in the carriage. The resultant heat was accentuating every aftershave, perfume and not-so-pleasant bodily odours that radiated from his fellow travellers.

He'd survived the journey so far by focusing on the book he'd brought to read en route. A prescribed text for his students of forensic psychology, they were currently studying the chapter on 'Police Psychology', in particular the section entitled 'Canteen/Cop Culture'. The term 'canteen culture' had been coined to differentiate it from the more general police culture, since rank-and-file officers' cultural norms rarely matched those of their management.

Magnus's own experience of police work had brought him into contact with many of the features of 'cop culture' discussed. Cynicism, conservatism and suspicion being just three of them. Most working officers didn't take kindly to a forensic psychologist being foisted on an investigation, his arrival being seen as an indication that senior management didn't trust the judgement of its detectives.

Rank-and-file officers regarded forensic psychology as nothing more than unproven mumbo jumbo. Forensic science had been accepted over time, particularly if it helped convict 'the bastards'. Psychology, on the other hand, was not regarded as a science and had no basis in reality, as far as most cops were concerned.

It was often bracketed with social work, and social workers were known to try and get people off by relating some sob story about a perpetrator, just as psychologists strove to understand and explain the criminal mind.

As far as the majority of front-line officers were concerned, bad people did bad things and must be stopped. End of story. At times, Magnus found himself in complete agreement with them.

He closed the book and slipped it in his bag as the train approached Queen Street Station. He always enjoyed his trips to Edinburgh. Much as he loved the vitality and 'in-your-face' nature of Glasgow, a trip to its sister city, so different in manner and architecture, reminded him of the eternal dichotomy of the Scottish psyche.

Built on seven hills, always breezy and rather fond of its own importance, Edinburgh's outward appearance was of douce respectability. Industrial Glasgow, on the other hand, having known real hardship, preferred to lace life with irony and dark humour.

The trip east had involved a visit to Edinburgh University to give a guest lecture on his criminal profiling work. The lecture theatre had been packed with eager students, who, in the main, were there to ask about his involvement in the high-profile *Stonewarrior* case, which had set their social media sites alight, involving as it did an alternative reality game, which, it appeared, the whole student world had been eager to play.

The case having never reached court, because of the death of the perpetrator, Magnus had been free to give some indication of the role he'd played in apprehending the killer, although he deemed it to be a small one.

He'd also been perplexed and not a little perturbed to discover from one student that a well-known gaming company was already putting the finishing touches to a new game entitled *Stonewarrior Unleashed*.

Thus the fiction of the original *Stonewarrior*, which the perpetrator had played out as fact, was to become the new fiction. Something, Magnus suspected, the perpetrator would have relished from his prison cell, a desire for notoriety being a psychological feature of his personality.

Emerging from the station into the noise of traffic circling George Square, Magnus caught the vibration of his mobile in his jacket pocket. Retrieving it, he found Rhona's name on the screen and immediately answered.

'Rhona. How are you?'

'Good. And you?'

'Fine. Back from Orkney and in downtown Glasgow as you can tell by the noise.'

'I wanted to run something past you, but now doesn't sound like a good idea.'

Magnus immediately came back. 'I'll be at my flat in twenty minutes, if that helps?'

Rhona was silent for a moment, then said, 'Might I come round? I'd like you to take a look at some photographs.'

'Of course,' Magnus said, trying to keep delight from his voice.

When Rhona rang off, Magnus upped his pace. If he was quick he could pick up some food on the way home and perhaps persuade Rhona to stay and eat with him after their discussion. They'd had no contact since the *Stonewarrior* case and he hadn't been called on to do any further police work. Initially this had suited him, and he'd immersed himself in his university tasks, but now he was ready for another challenge, especially one brought to him by Dr Rhona MacLeod.

Half an hour later, having welcomed Rhona into his riverside flat, Magnus found himself regarding a photograph on her laptop that deeply disturbed him. The image was of a room, bare of furniture, but festooned with naked Barbie-type dolls, attached to the ceiling via cords round their necks.

The grotesque image reminded him of another case he and Rhona had been involved in that had also featured dolls. Then, the baby dolls had been much more realistic. Termed *Reborns*, they'd been beautifully fashioned replicas of real babies, who had died shortly after birth. The man who had created them had been a psychopath.

The dolls before him now were hard plastic imitations of an impossibly shaped female body. Skinny catwalk models with pert breasts, bright eyes and avid smiles. Not to mention too much hair.

Rhona's voice interrupted his thoughts. 'There are twenty-seven of them, arranged in three rows of nine,' she said.

Magnus drew his eyes from the grotesque nature of the image and checked what she'd said.

'So there are,' he noted with interest. 'And arranged in threes by hair colour,' he added.

Rhona changed the image on the screen. 'This was behind the curtain of dolls.'

A young woman, naked, hanging on a hook, her eyes staring, her mouth and tongue swollen. If the dolls were bad, this was much worse. Magnus couldn't prevent himself recoiling in horror from such a death scene.

Rhona immediately apologized. 'I'm sorry, Magnus, I should have warned you.'

Composing himself, Magnus brushed her concerns away. 'I take it she was murdered?'

'We believe so.'

Rhona gave Magnus time to absorb the scene and recover from its impact, before continuing. 'The pattern of nine and three is continued in the cord used to hang her. It consisted of three strips of red silk, plaited, and had nine knots tied in it, evenly spaced out along its length.'

A series of facts Magnus found intriguing.

'And this pattern of nine is what you wanted to ask me about?'

'That and the possible significance of the dolls.'

Magnus reviewed the images as he considered Rhona's question. 'Nine is significant in mathematics, for lots of reasons. It also features in most religions.' He caught Rhona's eye. 'But you know all that, I take it?'

'I did spend some time researching online,' she said with a smile.

'But nothing you read seemed to fit?'

She nodded. 'There's forensic evidence to place the cord round the victim's waist, as well as her neck. And she had sex before she died. The DNA from the semen also matches a sample taken from the cord, which suggests her sexual partner also handled it.'

Magnus gave her a keen look. 'Are you saying that the death may have occurred during a sexual encounter?'

'Or shortly after.'

A flood of thoughts raced through Magnus's mind. He attempted to slow and order them.

'What do we know about the victim?'

'The night she died, she was drinking in a pub with a friend where they picked up two men. The victim left with one of them, according to her friend. She says the intention was to go back to the flat for sex.'

'Did the friend know about the dolls?'

'She says not. However, she did tell McNab that the victim was into New Age stuff.'

It appeared Rhona had sparked an idea. She watched as Magnus went over to the bookshelves and began a search. Some minutes later, he pounced on a book on the top shelf. Withdrew it and brought it across to her.

'Medieval Orkney had a fearful reputation as a haven for Witches and warlocks,' he said. 'I did some research on this a few years ago.' He leafed through the large blue book, which was entitled *Complete Book of Witchcraft*, eventually stopping at a chapter headed 'Magick'.

'How long was the cord?' Magnus said.

'Approximately nine feet. Is that important?'

'It could be a cingulum.' Magnus began reading out loud. *'Three times three makes nine, the perennial magick number. It should be red, the colour of blood, the life force, and nine feet in length,'* he looked to Rhona, *'made with three lengths of red silk if possible.'*

'What about the knots?' Rhona said.

Magnus read on in silence for a moment, then said, 'It seems the nine knots are storage cells for the magical energy required to make a spell.' He turned to the next page. 'And here we have the sexual aspect.'

The illustration he indicated featured a couple having sex and bound together by a cingulum tied round their waists.

'Looks like your victim may have been dabbling in Witchcraft.'

'And the dolls?'

'At a guess, something to do with the importance of the Goddess in the Wiccan religion.'

He surrendered the book to Rhona.

'Take a look while I make us something to eat, unless you have other plans?'

'Food would be good,' she said.

'Sex magick is one of the most potent forms of magick, for we are dealing here very much with the life forces.' The more Rhona read of the chapter, the more it seemed that Magnus might be right and that the coupling before Leila's death, using the red cord or cingulum, might have been, for her at least, a *magick* ritual.

Magnus's voice calling Rhona to table broke into her thoughts.

'It's just pasta, I'm afraid, but it is fresh and the sauce is my own.'

'I was planning a takeaway, so this is an improvement.'

The last time she'd eaten with Magnus had been at his house on Orkney, overlooking Scapa Flow. Back then, he'd cooked her fresh scallops and served home-brewed beer. The memory of that meal came swiftly back to her. She'd been unsure about accepting his offer of a room for the night. A deluge of midsummer tourists, combined with a stream of police personnel come to investigate a murder at the famous Ring of Brodgar neolithic site, had filled all available accommodation, so she'd had little option but to stay with Magnus, despite her misgivings.

Initially things had been awkward, on her part at least. She and Magnus had history, not so much romantic as tragic. Thrown together on a case that had changed their lives, the memory at that time had still been raw.

'How much do you know about the Wiccan religion?' Rhona asked when they'd reached the coffee stage.

'Not much,' Magnus admitted. 'The research on Witchcraft was more about the past than the present, but I found that book fascinating and informative. It's difficult to find covens and speak to members about their beliefs and practices. They tend to keep very low key. There's still a great deal of prejudice and misunderstanding about Wiccans – and Pagans, for that matter.'

'The Wiccan Rede doesn't sound very murderous,' Rhona said.

'"An' it harm none, do what thou wilt,"' Magnus quoted. 'Present-day practitioners deny any cavorting with the devil. It's more New Age tree hugging and eco-friendly, but then again, maybe it always was. I think burning Witches was more about gaining sadistic sexual gratification from torturing women than a desire to rid the world of evil. There were psychopaths back then too.'

A thought struck Rhona.

'Maybe that's why she died,' she said. 'Maybe she was killed because she was a Witch.'

'Well, after burning, hanging was the most popular method of dispensing with a Witch. Followed by drowning.'

'Is that true?' Rhona said, surprised.

'It is. So maybe your theory has some validity.'

'Or maybe she made the mistake of taking a sadistic psychopath home with her.'

'An equally valid theory.'

Rhona glanced at her watch, sensing it was time to go.

'There's a strategy meeting tomorrow about this. I take it you would be willing to attend, if asked?'

'I look forward to hearing what Detective Sergeant McNab makes of the Witchcraft angle.' Magnus gave a wry smile.

'I'll run it past DI Wilson first.'

'A wise move.' Magnus walked her to the door. 'Well, good luck with the investigation. And if there's anything else I can help with, feel free to call me.'

The subway was quiet and her journey to Byres Road swift and uneventful. The short walk that followed brought her to the jazz club by nine. As she descended the steps to the cellar she heard the sound of Sam on piano.

Sam, an Ibo from Nigeria, was close to completing his medical degree at Glasgow University. He and Chrissy had been an item long enough to produce a son who had inherited, as was often the case in a mixed relationship, the

71

most attractive qualities of both parents, which made him perfectly beautiful as well as good-natured.

Chrissy had proved herself to be a rather good mum, without losing her essential 'Chrissyness'. Her relationship with Sam had brought an end to her own parents' marriage, because her father found he didn't like the idea of a 'black' grandchild. Her mother had disagreed. The resultant split had been no bad thing, according to Chrissy. In fact, she'd declared that she'd wished it had happened years earlier. Chrissy's mother, finally free from having to deal with a domineering and often drunken husband, was thoroughly enjoying being a 'hands-on' granny.

So, there were people like Chrissy who could form lasting relationships in the most difficult of circumstances, thought Rhona.

Just not me.

Rhona made for the bar and ordered a glass of white wine. She'd half-expected to find Chrissy there. She often came in on the nights that Sam was playing. That way she got to see him, their paths rarely crossing during the day. But there was no sign of Chrissy tonight. Mildly disappointed by this – she had hoped to get Chrissy's take on Magnus's revelations – Rhona made a swift decision. Lifting her glass of wine, she headed through the back to Sean's office to find the door closed and the low sound of voices inside.

Once upon a time Rhona would have walked straight in and expected a welcome. Now, things being different, she hesitated before knocking on the door.

The voices inside fell silent, then the door was flung open.

Sean's surprise was evident, but he quickly masked it with a smile.

'Rhona, to what do I owe this pleasure?'

Rhona wasn't often stumped for an answer, but she was now. When she didn't immediately reply, Sean waved her inside.

The woman in the room was in her twenties, pretty and a little put out by Rhona's appearance. The feeling, Rhona decided, was mutual.

Sean, seemingly unperturbed, made the introductions.

'Rhona, Merle. Merle, Rhona.'

The two women eyed one another. By Sean's expression, he was rather enjoying the moment.

'Merle is our new singer. Rhona is . . .' he hesitated, then opted for, 'an old friend.'

Rhona didn't relish that description of herself.

But what could he say? *Rhona and I are old news, resurrected now and again when sex is required.*

'Hi, good to meet you.'

'And you.' Merle's voice was melodious and husky, as a jazz singer should sound. She glanced at Sean. 'I'd better go through. I'm due on shortly.'

Rhona smiled a goodbye as Sean ushered Merle to the door with words of encouragement. Rhona felt like following her out, but couldn't.

Sean shut the door.

He regarded her for a moment, then approaching, removed the glass from her hand and set it down on the desk.

'So, why *are* you here?'

Rhona didn't have an answer, at least not one she was willing to give.

When nothing was forthcoming, Sean brushed her cheek, his eyes meeting hers. It was a gentle gesture that led to nothing more. He dropped his hand.

'Are you planning on staying?'

Every ounce of sense she possessed screamed *no*. Yet she almost nodded her agreement, before a sense of reality regained the upper hand.

'I have to prepare for a strategy meeting in the morning.'

'That's a pity.'

They stood in silence for a moment, before Sean said, 'I'd better go in and catch Merle's spot.'

'Of course.'

If only he had tried just a little harder.

Rhona followed Sean to the door.

9

Shannon tensed as she heard the main door open below, and waited as the voices and footsteps passed by on their way upstairs. Normally, she liked hearing the comings and goings of her neighbours. It made her feel safe to be surrounded by people, but since Leila's death, she'd jumped every time the buzzer had sounded and viewed all approaching footsteps as a possible threat.

Tonight, she'd turned on the news at ten only to discover Leila's face staring out at her. Unnerved before, she'd crumpled in shock. Despite being adamant when speaking to the policeman that Leila would never have committed suicide, Shannon had secretly wished that might be the explanation, however unlikely, because the alternative was so much worse.

Plus I lied to the policeman when he asked about the dolls.

It had been the preservation instinct that had provoked her reaction. The first rule was to tell no one what they really were. So she'd blurted out that Leila was a New Age believer.

How stupid was that?

The news item had given details of the man Leila had left the pub with, which was of course the description Shannon had given to the police. So, she reasoned, the man

75

who had killed Leila would know that she, Shannon, was able to identify him.

Which puts me in danger too.

That fearful thought had driven her through to the bedroom.

Unrolling the circular mat, she spread it out on the floor at the foot of the bed.

Having cast a circle around her and lit the four candles, setting them at north, south, east and west as required, Shannon felt a little better, but not safe enough. Leila had always been the strong one, the sure one. The one who had faith in all the rituals.

I was only a follower.

The insistent ringing of her mobile eventually forced her to break the circle. The number was withheld but she knew who it would be.

'You didn't tell them, did you?'

'No.'

'If you do, I'll know.'

'I won't, I promise,' she insisted, but the caller had already gone.

Shannon dropped the mobile and crawled back inside the circle, chanting the words to help reseal it. Hugging her knees, she watched as the dark shadows cast by the candle flames danced about her.

10

Mornings minus a hangover were beginning to become a habit.

McNab swung his feet out of bed, relishing the non-pounding of his head, a mouth that didn't taste like a cat had pissed in it and eyes that could face daylight without splintering pain.

Likewise, his morning shower felt less like an attempt to wake the dead, and a look in the mirror didn't involve squinting and images of bloodshot eyes. All in all, he decided, being sober had its plus points. The negatives, however, also had to be faced.

His bed had been empty of female company since the alcohol had dried up, so no good memories of wild coupling the previous night and no repeat performance in the morning to set him up for the day. In fact, craving sex had now taken over from craving drink. If he didn't get laid soon, McNab feared he would seek religion, if only to satisfy his desire to have something to get ecstatic about.

Then there were the nightmares.

Whisky had aided sleep to the level of unconsciousness. If he'd experienced bad dreams, he rarely remembered them. Now, however, his sleep was often like a night at the movies, of the horror genre. The latest serial dream replayed the finale of his last case in glorious Technicolor, accompanied by smell, the overpowering nature of which made him even sympathetic to Professor Pirie. Something he would admit to no one, even himself.

So apart from bad dreams and no sex, he was doing okay.

Dressed, coffee machine on, McNab contemplated visiting Shannon Jones, who wasn't answering her mobile. He'd tried three times the previous night, only to be diverted to the messaging service.

They'd not yet succeeded in contacting Leila's brother Daniel in Germany. Shannon wasn't a relative, but McNab would rather have let her know they were treating her friend's death as murder before she heard it on the news, though it was probably too late for that now.

He swallowed down the remainder of his coffee and headed out, having decided to call in at Glasgow University library on his way to the meeting. He owed Shannon that, at least.

In general, McNab preferred to avoid the university precinct. True, the female talent on show there was good, but definitely too young. He'd learned his lesson on that score. As for the guys, they were way too clever and confident for his liking.

Needless to say, McNab's route to his present position had not been via a university degree. His mother would have liked it to be, but money was tight and McNab decided not to make it any tighter. He'd briefly contemplated the army, but didn't fancy returning in a body bag, so he'd joined the police instead.

In the end he *had* seen the inside of a body bag and had lived to tell the tale, evidenced by the bullet scar on his back, not to mention the damage done to his internal organs.

It had turned out, for him at least, that fighting crime was every bit as dangerous as combat duty in some foreign land.

The only college he'd attended had been police college, where, it seemed, most of his fellow recruits had come via university, after studying forensic and criminal psychology and, of course, sociology. A fact that had irked McNab and which probably accounted for his distrust of such subjects, and those who taught them, like Professor Magnus Pirie.

Irritated with himself for thinking about Pirie again, McNab flashed his ID at the reception desk and asked to speak to Assistant Librarian Shannon Jones.

The man peered at him over his spectacles.

'I'm not sure Shannon's in yet. Let me check.'

He abandoned McNab and headed for a desk phone. Moments later he was back.

'Shannon's not in, I'm afraid. She wasn't in yesterday, either.' He gave McNab a searching look. 'Is this to do with Leila's death? I saw it on the news last night. A terrible business.'

McNab ignored the question. 'Did Shannon call to say she wasn't coming in?'

'I have no idea, I'm sorry. She doesn't work in this part of the building.'

'Where does she work?'

'Archives.'

'Can I speak to someone in Archives?'

The man looked nonplussed. 'I can't leave the desk, but I'll get someone to take you there, if you'll wait a moment.'

The student queue forming behind McNab was growing restless. McNab turned and gave them the police eye, which shut them up long enough for his guide to appear. At a guess, she was in her mid twenties, with long brown hair, and very presentable.

'Detective Sergeant McNab.' He presented his ID, hoping she might give him her name in return. She didn't.

'If you'll follow me,' she said.

It took five minutes to get to their destination. During the journey in lifts and corridors, McNab asked if she knew either Leila or Shannon, and was rewarded with, 'Not really.'

'So you didn't socialize?'

She shook her head.

'Or drink in the same pubs?'

'Everyone drinks in Ashton Lane at some time or another.' She gave him a scrutinizing look. 'Maybe that's where I've seen *you* before?'

'Could be,' McNab said casually, hoping he hadn't been inebriated at the time.

She opened a door and stood back to allow him entry.

'Grant!' she called to what looked like an empty room apart from multiple rows of stacked shelves.

A man McNab guessed to be in his fifties appeared, a frown on his face at being disturbed at whatever one did in Archives.

'This is Detective Sergeant McNab,' his guide announced. 'He wants to talk to you about Shannon.'

'She isn't here,' Grant said, the frown lines deepening.

'I know,' McNab said patiently.

'Get Grant to call reception when you're finished and I'll come back for you,' his guide offered.

McNab thanked her.

After she'd gone, he asked Grant for the young woman's name.

'Freya Devine. A post-graduate student in medieval history.'

Perfect name McNab thought, and definitely too brainy for him.

Sensing this wasn't going to be over quickly, Grant asked McNab to follow him between the shelves into a small office. There were two desks, one of which he indicated was Shannon's.

'I can offer you a coffee?'

'Great. As strong as possible, please,' McNab said.

Grant indicated that McNab should take Shannon's seat, before spooning three scoops of instant coffee into a mug and adding hot water from a thermos.

'Milk, sugar?'

'Just as it is, thanks.'

Grant handed it over and, retrieving his own mug, sat down opposite McNab.

'Shannon phoned in yesterday. She said she was ill. It sounded as though she'd been crying. Then I saw the news last night and realized what was wrong.'

'You knew Leila Hardy?'

'Only really by sight. She works elsewhere in the building, but I knew that she and Shannon were friends.'

'I'm having difficulty getting in touch with Shannon. She's not answering at the number she gave me,' McNab said.

'Really? Maybe she's too upset.'

Or she doesn't want to talk to the police again.

'Could you try her for me?' McNab said.

'Of course.' Grant checked a pad next to the phone for her number and dialled. McNab heard it ring out, but no one answered. Eventually Grant hung up. 'Should we be worried?'

McNab showed Grant his notebook. 'Is that her current address?'

'Yes. You're going to check she's all right?'

McNab assured him he would. He gulped down the remainder of his coffee and asked if his guide could be called, to direct him back to the entrance.

'Of course. It is a bit of a warren.'

Freya appeared a few minutes later. McNab was aware that he had only five minutes to make her acquaintance properly, before she ushered him out the front door. He wondered if it was worth the effort since she was, he feared, out of his league.

'Could we have met in the jazz club in Ashton Lane?' he offered as they wound their way towards the lift.

'You're a jazz fan?' She sounded surprised.

'Sometimes,' he hedged his bets.

'Me too,' she offered.

'The piano player, Sam Haruna. Have you heard him play?'

'No, I haven't. Is he good?'

'Very.' McNab decided to go for it. 'He's on tonight.'

'Really?'

'Maybe I'll see you there,' McNab tried.

'Maybe.'

Well, at least it wasn't a no.

When they reached reception he handed her his card. 'If you think of anything that might help me, however small, give me a call,' he said.

Her face clouded over at that and McNab thought he might have overstepped the mark.

She left him at reception, but with a farewell smile. McNab had the feeling those intelligent eyes could see right through him and they weren't sure they liked what they saw. Still, he had tried.

Once outside the building, he called DS Clark.

'Where are you? The strategy meeting's in fifteen minutes,' she said.

'At the university library looking for Shannon.'

'Well, I suggest you get here, and fast.'

11

Detective Inspector Bill Wilson swivelled the chair round to face the window just to hear it girn – a Scottish term for which he could find no English equivalent, but which described the sound perfectly, while endowing the seat with character.

How many cases had he attempted to solve while sitting in this seat? He didn't dare count. And had he made the world a safer place?

That he could answer. No.

His spell at home with his wife Margaret, during her second bout of cancer treatment, had brought out the philosopher in Bill. Or, put more simply, he'd spent too much time thinking dark thoughts and questioning what the point of his years in the force had been. Whether the time wouldn't have been better spent with his family. So he had hung around at home, trying to make himself useful, until Margaret, ever the pragmatist, had told him to please go back to work, so she could have her old Bill back. And so he had obliged.

And what of his protégé?

Bill had come to the decision that we each have a place in which we do the most good. DS McNab had tried a different place, and it hadn't worked out for him. Yet, in Bill's opinion, Michael Joseph McNab was a bigger and better man than those above him in rank could ever imagine, let alone achieve.

During the debriefing after the *Stonewarrior* case, Bill had been aware that something was being left unsaid. That something had driven a wedge between McNab and Rhona. They had history already, spiky at times, tragic at others, but this was something else, and it bothered and fretted Bill like a sore that would not heal. Secrets, he knew from his job and his personal life, had a cancerous habit of growing bigger.

This morning's strategy meeting, he decided, was likely to be more enlightening regarding the investigative team than the murder they were seeking to solve. An early-morning visit by Rhona had persuaded Bill to add one more player to the game. Professor Magnus Pirie. Solid, reliable, knowledgeable, yet esoteric, he brought a questioning to an investigation that most officers felt uncomfortable with.

In this job, it was always more reassuring to regard life and the humans that inhabited it as purely black and white, with no grey areas. Thus Magnus was, in the words of Gandhi, first ignored, then mocked, then fought against by the front-line troops, before occasionally winning. McNab wouldn't like it, of course, although DS Clark would be relaxed, and Rhona, from her forensic analysis of the crime scene, deemed it necessary, which was good enough for Bill.

He turned from his view of the city and checked his watch.

It was time for the fray.

The room was packed. A murder investigation involved far more people than could be imagined by the general public. They saw only a limited number, the focus on a few faces representing the full team. The superior officer who fronted the investigation on media broadcasts was the one the public grew to recognize, although it wasn't he, or she, who did the groundwork.

Before him were those who would perform the irritatingly tedious jobs, such as watching endless hours of security camera footage, and interviewing the public, with all their prejudices, lack of observation and self-obsession. Attention to detail was everything, however long and mind-numbingly slow that might be. Success was achieved because each police officer on the case did their job properly.

The whole was only as good as its individual parts.

Then there was the digital world that now ran parallel to their own, recording and illuminating it in a way that couldn't have been imagined even five years ago. The information gathered was vast, and complex. All of it had to be sifted through and examined, registered as important or discarded. Added to this was the insatiable demand of the mainstream media, forever hungry and keen to refashion the facts to suit its own agenda.

Surveying the sea of faces, Bill noted the presence of Rhona, Magnus and DS Clark, but as yet no DS McNab. The questioning look he sent Janice brought the response, 'On his way, sir.'

Bill called the assembled company to order and directed their attention to the screen and its collection of photographs. In truth, the images had perturbed Bill in a way he found hard to explain. He had been at many murder scenes. All of them horrific. All had affected him to a greater or lesser degree. Why then was this one particularly disturbing?

He had come to the conclusion it was because Barbie dolls normally evoked a memory of his teenage daughter's innocent childhood, yet here they appeared to symbolize something else entirely – the female of the species, stripped, abused and hanged. And behind that curtain, a real female, treated in the same manner.

What did that say? What did it mean?

If Bill had learned anything from his time on the force it was that to every kill there is meaning. Not one the majority of the human race would recognize as valid, but valid to the perpetrator nonetheless. And the staged nature of the death scene screamed *meaning* at him.

At this point he would have asked McNab to come to the front, since he had been first on the scene, but as McNab hadn't yet put in an appearance, Bill asked Rhona to give her version of events.

She gave a brief résumé of the results of her forensic examination so far, together with the post-mortem findings. She then asked them to study the photographs again and raise any points they thought might be significant.

'The way in which the dolls are arranged?' DS Clark offered. 'The different hair colours together in groups of three?'

Someone else piped up. 'There are three rows of nine dolls.'

'There are,' Rhona confirmed, 'and yes, the arrangement seems precise.'

Bill had spent a great deal of time on the photographs, but he hadn't noticed the pattern of nine, or of three. Once mentioned though, it seemed obvious, as evidenced by the sounds of first surprise, then affirmation from the assembled company.

Bill watched intently as Rhona brought up an enhanced image of the cord used to hang the victim.

'The noose is plaited silk, that is, made up of three

individual strands. If you count you will see that there are nine knots in it, evenly spaced out. What I can also tell you is that the overall length of the cord is nine feet.'

This piece of information brought a gasp from her listeners and then the question that Bill too wanted to ask.

'So what's significant about the number nine to the perpetrator?'

Rhona took a moment to answer. 'I'm not sure it is significant to the perpetrator, but it may be of significance to the victim.' She went on to explain about the forensic evidence found on the cord and the probable role it had played in the sexual act prior to the victim's death. 'Professor Pirie identified the cord as a possible cingulum, which is a ritual cord used in British traditional Wicca, or what is more commonly termed Witchcraft.'

Magnus approached the front in an outbreak of excited chatter.

Now this was news as far as Bill was concerned. He wondered if McNab was party to this development.

Magnus was prone to nervousness at strategy meetings. Bill didn't blame him for that. Front-line officers in general didn't rate criminal profilers. Magnus had had some success in his work with them, but he'd also screwed up, which tended to be what was gossiped about, and remembered.

Bill indicated he wanted silence while Magnus composed himself before speaking.

'I was involved in an extensive study of Witchcraft for an Orkney project some years back and when Dr MacLeod showed me images of the cord, it triggered a memory of a cingulum. The cingulum is used in a variety of rituals and should be nine feet in length with nine knots in it. It should also be red to represent the life blood. When sexual magick is performed, the two participants are bound together round the waist by the cingulum. However, contrary to popular belief, reinforced by the Christian Church, Wicca is not satanistic. The Wiccan Rede in its briefest form says "An' Ye Harm None, Do What Ye Will."'

He continued, 'The Wiccan religion has dual deities in the God and Goddess, often represented by small statues. Unlike in Christianity, in Wicca the male and female are regarded as equals – in fact, the Goddess is often seen as the more powerful and influential of the two.'

Bill intervened at this point. 'In your opinion, did the victim's death have anything to do with Wicca?'

'There are ways it may have,' Magnus said.

'Such as?'

'Three possible scenarios suggest themselves. One, that the sexual partner reacted badly to the idea that he was being used in a spell and killed the victim for that reason. Two, they were both participants in a sexual game which went too far. However, I'm unaware of a ritual using sexual magick where auto-erotic practice is involved. And thirdly, the cingulum may have been used simply because it was available to the perpetrator, and had no significance for him whatso- ever.' Magnus ground to a halt, his expression suggesting he was clear on nothing, and had therefore not been much help.

Bill thanked Magnus anyway, and moved on to dealing out jobs, which the team looked relieved about. Working out *who* had killed Leila Hardy was, in their eyes, a better proposition than *why* it had been done.

Once he'd set everyone to work, Bill asked DS Clark to get DS McNab on the phone and find out why the hell he hadn't come to the meeting.

12

McNab tried the doorbell one more time and listened to it echo in what sounded like an empty flat. It seemed that Shannon Jones was neither at work, nor at home.

Why didn't he believe that?

McNab held open the letter box and peered inside. The poor view this afforded was of a small shadowy hallway with three doors leading off, only one of which was closed.

'Shannon,' he called, trying to keep his voice friendly. 'Shannon, it's DS McNab.'

His attempt was greeted by silence.

'Shannon, please open the door. I'd like to speak to you.'

When there was no response to his second plea, McNab tried a different tack.

'I have news on how Leila died.'

Shannon had been very keen to know what had happened to her friend. If she was in there, surely that would bring her to the door, ill or not?

It didn't.

McNab checked his watch. He was now late for the strategy meeting, and he didn't have the decent excuse of a chat with Shannon Jones about her dead pal. He stood for a moment contemplating his choices, which, he decided, were limited. Either he forced entry or he walked away and faced the music back at the station. McNab examined his reason for coming here one more time and found it still valid. He was uneasy about the well-being of Shannon Jones. If he walked now, he would be none the wiser.

McNab pushed the letter box open again, and then he spotted it. A pool of water seeping from under the only shut door in the hallway.

Jesus, what has she done?

McNab put his shoulder to the door. The force he exerted rattled the door in its frame, but that was all.

Fuck's sake.

Pulling out his wallet, he fished out his Costa Coffee card. The tried and trusted method of springing a snib on a door, but only if she hadn't turned a mortice lock as well.

It took no more than a second to slip the card between the door and its frame. Another to find the right combination of angle and force, then the snib clicked free and McNab stepped into the hall. He didn't bother checking the rooms that lay open but made immediately for the third, squelching across a sodden carpet, while praying she hadn't locked herself in.

She hadn't. The door swung back to reveal the real reason Shannon Jones hadn't answered his calls.

This time, there *was* an upturned chair in the room. Tilted against a filled bath, its rear two legs were off the ground. Sitting on it was a naked Shannon, her head and shoulders submerged, tendrils of blonde hair floating in strands on the surface of the water.

Christ, girl. What happened?

McNab reached in and gently lifted her head, already knowing that Shannon Jones was long gone. The pretty face was white and puckered, the lips a mottled blue. The cold eyes that stared up at him seemed to say *Why didn't you come sooner?*

McNab checked the remainder of the flat. The main room, which also housed a small kitchen area, looked undisturbed. Entering the bedroom, he immediately caught a strong scented smell. On the floor at the foot of the bed was a circular green mat. Around its perimeter were four candles, one still fluttering, emitting the fragrance he'd caught on entry.

As McNab watched, the final candle spluttered and went out.

He had no idea what the circle and the candles meant, but instinct told him that Shannon had constructed it as an imagined place of safety. A forlorn hope as evidenced by the scene in the bathroom. McNab felt something akin to despair wash over him. Shannon had been shocked and terrified by her friend's death. That much had been plain at her interview. She'd also been adamant that Leila hadn't taken her own life.

McNab had assumed that Shannon, like him, considered the man Leila had taken home as being instrumental in her death. She'd even blamed herself for not spotting the danger.

But had that been the whole truth?

Shannon had denied all knowledge of the dolls' room, which McNab found hard to believe if they were such good mates. Then she'd blurted out that Leila had been into New Age things, as though that was nothing to do with her.

Looking at the circle and the candles suggested McNab's instinct had been right. Whatever Leila had been involved in, so too had Shannon.

With a heavy heart, McNab pulled out his mobile and dialled the station.

Janice answered almost immediately.

'Where the hell are you?' she began.

McNab interrupted her. 'Can you get a forensic team and pathologist to come to . . .' He gave her the address.

'Who—?' she began.

'Shannon Jones. I found her drowned in the bath.'

'My God.' The shock in her voice was palpable.

'Can you organize a team?' McNab said. 'I'll stay here and wait for them.'

Janice had collected herself. 'Of course. Do you want Dr MacLeod to come?'

McNab didn't answer immediately. Rhona didn't have to do the forensic but then again if it wasn't suicide, and there was a link to Leila's death, Rhona's expertise would be the best option.

'Try her first,' he said.

'Will do.'

McNab rang off. For the first time since he'd been off the drink, he had an almost unbearable craving for it. Had a half-bottle been in his pocket, he wouldn't have hesitated. If he were at home now, the bottle in the kitchen cupboard would have been out and open.

He checked his hands and found they were trembling. What he needed was the buzz of strong coffee to dull the craving, but there was little chance of that until the team arrived. He checked his pockets for any sign of a packet of cigarettes, his other habit, which he'd beaten before but which occasionally raised itself from the grave, trying to steer him into one.

Thankfully there were no remnants of his smoking days

lurking anywhere in his jacket. So McNab chose to do the only compulsive action left to him. He strode up and down in an agitated fashion.

The first cop car arrived twenty minutes later. After Janice brought him briefly up to date on the strategy meeting, McNab handed over the preservation of the crime scene to her, then took himself outside, ostensibly for some fresh air, but really to await the arrival of Dr MacLeod, which occurred ten minutes later.

'What happened?' she said as soon as she stepped out of the van.

'Shannon didn't go in to work the last two days and I couldn't reach her by phone. So I decided to come and find her. That's why I wasn't at the meeting.'

Rhona's expression told him that she could read him like a book. His thoughts, his distress, his horror at what he'd found and what she must now face herself.

'You did the right thing,' she said.

McNab didn't reply.

Rhona pulled on her forensic suit. 'Bill will be here shortly. He says to stay put, he wants to talk to you.'

'There's a coffee shop on the corner. Tell him I'll be there,' McNab said.

As he set off, he prayed that there wouldn't be a pub in the vicinity of the coffee shop, and definitely not one en route. His prayers were thankfully answered.

He stepped into the cafe and quickly ordered two double espressos. Carrying both to an unoccupied table, McNab drank one down and waited for the craving to subside.

When the caffeine hit home, he pushed the empty cup to one side and drew the full one in front of him. He then tried to order his thoughts in advance of DI Wilson's appearance.

It wasn't just the coffee that had driven him here. McNab really didn't want to face the boss while Rhona was in the vicinity. However much they may have appeared to patch things up, there was still an awkwardness between them, and he was pretty sure the boss had spotted it.

Therefore the less he saw of them together, the better.

When DI Wilson arrived minutes later, McNab was struck by how thin and tired he looked. His stint at home should have seen the boss rested, but McNab had gathered from Janice that watching his wife deal with the return of her cancer had eaten away at Bill, so much so that Margaret had ordered him back to work.

The depth of commitment between the boss and his wife was something McNab admired. At times, he thought he wanted something similar for himself, but couldn't see it ever happening. His personal relationships seemed to be motivated, for the most part, by lust. Self-sacrifice just didn't figure anywhere in them.

But if he met the right woman?

I have met the right woman. It's just that the feeling isn't mutual.

Bill acknowledged his sergeant's presence and the two espresso cups in front of him.

'Another?'

'I still have one to drink, sir.'

Bill ordered a filter coffee with cold milk and carried it over to the table.

'Has anyone filled you in on what happened at the strategy meeting?'

'I heard from DS Clark that Professor Pirie knows a lot about Witchcraft,' McNab said drily.

Bill ignored the barbed nature of the reply and continued,

'He had some interesting theories involving the Wiccan religion, which appeared to fit with what Rhona found at the crime scene.'

'There's a suggestion of something similar at Shannon's place,' McNab admitted, describing the mat and candles.

Bill looked thoughtful at that. 'Have you had any luck tracing the man Leila took home with her?'

'We have a decent description and I'm waiting for results from the security cameras.'

'And now another death. Did Shannon Jones say anything to you that suggested she was afraid for her life or that she might be suicidal?'

'She was very shocked and upset about Leila, but was adamant that Leila wouldn't have hanged herself.'

'Which we now believe to be true.' Bill paused. 'We have to pick up the main suspect and soon.'

'We will,' McNab said.

'What about the other guy?'

'The description of him isn't so good. I'm hoping he'll appear on the camera in the back lane. We think he may have left that way.'

'Could they be working as a pair?'

'It's something I've considered.'

'I want to know if Leila was a practising Witch, and if so, who she was practising with. Check with the Tech department. See what they have from the mobile and laptop.' A thought struck him. 'What about a mobile or laptop in Shannon's flat?'

McNab said no. It had been the first thing he'd checked for. 'Maybe the search team will have more luck.'

Bill observed his sergeant.

'Why did you force the door?'

McNab hesitated as though he wasn't sure how to answer that. 'A gut feeling, sir.'

That was good enough for Bill. 'I want you to liaise with Professor Pirie on the Witchcraft angle. He has the knowledge.'

McNab's expression suggested that was the last thing he wanted to do, but he didn't argue, which Bill realized was probably a first.

13

The pathologist had come and gone, required only to certify death.

The dribbling tap had been turned off, but the water still lapped around her feet, transferring any movement Rhona made into tiny waves of energy that crossed the floor tiles to break against the pile of the hall carpet.

The bathroom was small. *Not much bigger than a coffin.*

Rhona had heard about Leila's friend, who had been with her the night she'd died, but hadn't viewed an image of her. The hair floating in tendrils in the water reminded Rhona of a painting of Ophelia. Contrary to popular opinion, drowning wasn't an easy death, unless the victim was comatose to begin with.

The notion that you could enter water, deny your lungs air and not experience pain and terror, was a cruel fallacy. Which was why waterboarding as a means of torture was so widely used and successful.

She had already taken her 'before' photographs, as had the Return To Scene team. Now, they would require taking again, without the water. As the last liquid was pumped out of the bath into a container to be transported to the lab, Rhona took close-ups of the exposed face and upper body, then stepped outside and gave the Return To Scene personnel access. Their 360-degree recordings of before and after would be invaluable.

McNab had departed, due, Rhona surmised, to her presence or a desire for Bill not to engage with them together. A wise move on McNab's part. Rhona was well aware that the tension between them was tangible, despite their mutual agreement to 'let things lie'. Secrets had a habit of revealing themselves, eventually.

And Bill, she knew, was a natural detective.

Still, she reminded herself, *I made the right decision*.

Waiting for R2S to complete their recording, Rhona checked out the other rooms in the flat. A forensic team was already at work, eyes above the masks acknowledging Rhona's presence. The flat was tidy and pretty in an understated way. No room of hanging dolls, no evidence of anything but normality, except in the bedroom.

A circular mat had been laid out at the foot of the bed. Around it, at four locations, stood candles. Rhona's first thought was that Shannon had been meditating recently, soft music and candlelight being a common method of relaxation. Then again, the circular mat might have something to do with the Witchcraft angle.

With that in mind, she gave Magnus a call.

'Describe the bedroom scene to me,' he said.

Rhona did so, including the candles.

'Are they set at the points of the compass?'

Rhona tried to work out where north was via her knowledge of Glasgow landmarks.

'Probably,' she said. 'Any chance you could come and take a look?'

'I have a lecture shortly, so it will have to be after that,' Magnus said.

'Not a problem, I'm likely to be here for some time.'

Rhona rang off and headed back to the bathroom.

Roy Hunter and his colleagues at R2S had worked along-side Rhona on many jobs, including the most recent *Stonewarrior* case. Vastly experienced, particularly in some of the more forensically challenging crime scenes, Rhona always valued Roy's opinion.

'What do you think?'

'Suicide drownings usually involve slit wrists and a warm bath. So I don't buy the chair and submersion,' Roy said. 'Who would hold their own head under water long enough to drown? But, then again, she may have been under the influence of drugs or drink at the time.'

Roy's thoughts mirrored her own. If Shannon had taken her own life, then it was a difficult way to do it. McNab had reported her as very distressed and frightened by her friend's death, so there was no doubt she was in a vulnerable state. The scene in the bedroom only served to emphasize this.

Perhaps Shannon had run a bath to help her relax? The chair she sat on, painted white and made of light wood, looked as though it belonged in the bathroom. Shannon's clothes were in a pile close by on the floor. The bath water, Rhona suspected, had had lavender oil added to it, a bottle of which stood nearby.

All of which suggested Shannon was trying to calm herself.

There had been no evidence of alcohol being consumed and no evidence of drugs on the premises. They would have to wait for toxicology tests to discover if Shannon had ingested any drugs prior to her death, legal or otherwise.

Had Shannon been intent on killing herself, the easiest

way, as Roy suggested, was to ease the passing with drink and drugs and simply allow herself to sink under the water. In this case Shannon was sitting on the chair, which had been turned to face the bath and her head submerged. Either by accident or by force. Shannon wasn't tied to the chair, although she might have been at the time. Rhona checked the wrists first.

The hands were small and slim, the fingers free of jewellery. On initial inspection, there was no obvious bruising on the narrow wrists. Rhona examined the chair for evidence of anything having been tied to the legs or main body and found nothing. Using the magnifying glass, she took a closer look.

The fingernails were bleached white from the water, but there was something caught beneath them. Rhona extracted a fibre and bagged it, then swept below the nails on both hands.

She then examined the neck, finding no evidence of bruising.

The scalp was more of a problem, covered as it was by thick wet hair.

Rhona visualized a hand forcing Shannon's head underwater and where the fingers of that hand might have gripped, and was rewarded by a surface cut on the crown which could have been inflicted by a fingernail.

After sampling the head and all its orifices, Rhona called for some help to tip the chair back. Slim and undoubtedly light in life, Shannon had become heavy and waterlogged in death.

With Roy's help, Rhona set the chair upright and Shannon with it. From this vantage point, it was clear that her knees had been pressing against the side of the bath, perhaps as her head had been held under the water.

Having freed her from her watery grave, Rhona stepped outside to allow Roy to record the scene again. Once that was done, she set about cataloguing the body forensically, every square inch covered, every nook and cranny sampled. If Shannon Jones had been manhandled, evidence of her attacker was on her. It was up to Rhona to find that evidence.

Magnus arrived a couple of hours after she'd called him. He appeared suddenly in the bathroom doorway, immediately recognizable despite the forensic suit, mainly because of his height. His eyes above the mask registered his dismay.

Rhona took a moment to describe the original scene, before they'd emptied the bath and uprighted Shannon.

'Her head and shoulders were underwater while still on the chair?' Magnus said.

'The chair was tipped forward as you can see by the pressure marks on her knees, although it's not certain whether the bruising occurred before or after death.'

'So she drowned?' Magnus said.

'That's what it looks like, although we'll have to wait for the post-mortem to be certain.'

'Forced?'

'Perhaps,' Rhona conceded. 'Again, it's too early to say.'

Magnus nodded. 'Can you show me the circle?'

Rhona led him through to the bedroom.

Magnus studied the mat, bending down to sniff at the candles before asking Rhona whether a cingulum or any other Wiccan artefacts had been found in the flat.

'Only the mat and candles so far,' she told him.

'The mat is a type used to create a magic circle. The

candles are normally placed at the four points of the compass. If your victim was frightened for some reason, it would be natural for her to make a circle and stay inside it until she felt better.' He paused. 'I picked up the scent of lavender in the bathroom. I assume she'd added it to the bath water?' Magnus asked.

'I think so.'

He nodded. 'There was another scent in the bathroom, one I'm not so sure of. It's not present in here. Can we go back?'

Magnus stopped outside the third room. 'What's in there?'

'The sitting room and kitchen.'

Rhona followed Magnus in. The room was small, with the kitchen tucked into a corner. There was a single window overlooking a back court, an L-shaped settee, a coffee table, a small gas fire and a flat-screen TV. There was also a forensic officer dusting for prints. Nothing looked unusual or out of place.

Magnus exited, without speaking, and went back to the bathroom, where he sniffed the soap at the sink, then shook his head.

'Maybe it's the smell of the chemicals I'm using,' Rhona suggested.

Magnus shook his head again. 'No. I can identify them, having met them all before at various times.' He stood for a moment, eyes closed, deep in concentration, breathing in slowly through his nose.

'It could be a man's cologne, it smells astringent. Citrus, spicy.' He shrugged his shoulders in defeat, then hunkered down to look more closely at the victim.

'Was she tied to the chair?'

'Not when she was found.'

'But maybe?'

'There were fibres under her nails, but no obvious pressure marks on her wrists.'

'Finding her like that reminds me of a ducking stool,' Magnus said.

'What?'

'In medieval times Witches were primarily disposed of in three ways, as I said before. They were either burned at the stake, hanged or they were drowned by tying to a ducking stool.'

14

The front security camera had a good view of Leila but a rather poorer showing of her male companion. Just as he emerged, a group of smokers had gathered, obscuring the camera's sight of him. From what McNab could make out, Barry's description held. The guy was blond and tall, and looked fit. He was wearing a shirt as described, and jeans. There was even a brief sighting of his watch worn on the left wrist. His face, however, wasn't visible.

McNab asked the officer to rerun the sequence one more time, peering at the screen in his frustration. It was no good, he could be any one of hundreds of fit young males in shirt and jeans on a night out in Glasgow. The best they could do was show it on a news bulletin together with the description, and hope it rang a bell with someone.

The back-door camera proved equally useless. The only thing it picked up was a couple having a shag against a wall, oblivious to the fact they were being recorded. Then again, maybe that's why they'd chosen to do it there. If the second male had definitely left the pub shortly after Leila and his pal, the angle of the camera hadn't recorded him.

Running through the front-door footage again proved just as fruitless. In the time sequence following Leila's departure, dozens of people exited the pub, some to smoke, but plenty heading off elsewhere.

Frustrated, McNab abandoned the video and called the pub again.

His enquiry after Barry brought the response, 'I'll get him for you,' then the sound of the phone being carried elsewhere. Eventually Barry came on the line.

'Yes?'

'It's DS McNab here. We spoke before about Leila Hardy. On the night she died,' McNab added for emphasis.

'Yes?' Barry said, sounding nervous.

'You said the blond guy with Leila looked affluent by his clothes, the Gucci watch and wallet.'

'Yeah, he did.'

'How did he pay for the drinks?'

Silence.

'Did he use cash or a card?'

Pause. 'I can't remember. I served loads of people that night.'

'Try.'

'I honestly can't remember.'

'But you remembered he had an expensive wallet and a fancy watch,' McNab reminded him.

'Because he flashed them at me.'

'Did he also flash a card?'

McNab could almost hear Barry thinking out loud. What should he say? Cash or card? And what would that mean for him?

Eventually, Barry came back with his decision. 'No, I remember now. Cash. He paid cash for the drinks. His wallet was full of it.'

Bastard.

'You're sure of that?'

'Yes.'

'Okay. We'll need a list of all your card transactions that night anyway,' McNab told him.

There was a gasp at the other end of the line, which McNab ignored. 'Someone will pick them up tomorrow.'

McNab rang off, irritated that he hadn't checked the card angle when he'd first spoken to Barry. In his experience people paid by card when out on the town. Carrying wads of cash was becoming a thing of the past. Still, if you didn't want anyone to know what you were up to, cash was the better option. That way you didn't leave a trace of your transactions and their location on your debit or credit card. If Barry had told the truth, then their suspect's card details wouldn't be on that list, but they would have to go through them all anyway.

He headed for the coffee machine in the corridor and topped up his caffeine levels. What he really needed was food, but that would have to wait. Mid afternoon now, he planned to check out the contents of Leila's mobile and laptop before he finally went for something to eat.

McNab didn't like the Tech department, mainly because it made him feel inadequate, and those who did the job seemed very young, thus highlighting both his lack of digital skills and the fact that he was getting old.

The *Stonewarrior* investigation had introduced him to the digital world in some detail, wherein he had met Ollie, who looked as though he should be in the second year of secondary school. Overcoming such prejudices on McNab's part had proved difficult but he had managed it, after a fashion. And he had to admit that Ollie's skills in forensic computing had been extensive and had helped McNab to crack the case.

Entering the digital domain again, McNab sincerely hoped Ollie was still around and that he wouldn't need to forge new allegiances. In that he was lucky.

Ollie greeted him with a grin, his eyes wide behind the round glasses.

'DI McNab, good to see you again.'

'It's detective sergeant now,' McNab reminded him.

Ollie's face fell, his expression moving from pleasure at encountering McNab again, to outright anger.

'You fucking solved the *Stonewarrior* case.'

'You helped,' McNab said.

'So why the fuck did they demote you?'

McNab listed a few of the many actions that had brought him down. 'If I'd been a soldier they would have shot me at dawn.' McNab smiled. 'I put you in the shit too, as I recall.'

'It was well worth it,' Ollie said with relish.

They acknowledged the righteousness of their joint indignation.

'So,' said Ollie, 'how can I help?'

'The laptop and mobile belonging to Leila Hardy. I want to know what's on them.'

'Come this way.'

Ollie led McNab across the room between the various desks, each one a hive of digital activity, then gestured at him to take a seat alongside.

Back in front of a series of screens, McNab screwed up his eyes. How the hell these guys did this for a living he had no idea.

'Just tell me what you found,' he said.

Ollie looked sympathetic. 'Okay, your victim was unusual in that she has *no* social media presence. No Twitter account, no Facebook page. Her email account is the one for the university library and its entries are all to do with work. Basically, she's offline.'

'No personal email?' McNab was stunned. He thought he was the only one in the world not tuned in to the digital revolution. 'What about her mobile?'

Ollie handed McNab a list of contacts. It was short. A dozen at the most, at least half of them relating to university departments.

'That's it?'

Ollie nodded.

'I don't believe it. Even I have more mobile contacts than this.'

'Maybe she had another mobile. Possibly a pay-as-you-go?'

'Well, it wasn't in the flat.'

Ollie shrugged his shoulders. 'Sorry.'

'Her Internet history?'

'Limited, although she did order some stuff recently from Amazon.'

'Such as?'

Ollie pulled up a list on the screen for McNab to look through. The orders were all from the same site.

'It sells New Age stuff mostly,' Ollie said. 'Amulets, crystals, books, etc.'

McNab had to ask. 'Is there anything there related to the Wiccan religion?'

'Probably. Why?' Ollie looked intrigued.

'There's evidence to suggest the victim may have been a practising Witch,' McNab said cautiously.

Ollie looked interested. 'I knew a guy at Edinburgh University who practised Wicca,' he said.

'In Edinburgh?' Witchcraft in Scotland's douce capital city. McNab could hardly believe it.

Ollie seemed unfazed by McNab's reaction as he continued. 'Joe was really into it. Had the altar and all the stuff in his room at the halls of residence. Even performed spells to help us pass our exams and get girls,' Ollie said.

'Did they work?' McNab said sarcastically.

'Passing exams got me here.' Ollie shrugged. 'The love potions weren't so successful.'

'Join the club,' McNab said with feeling.

'Anyway, Joe's coven had a rented room in the Vaults just off the Royal Mile.'

'Are you still in contact with this guy?' McNab said. 'If so, I'd like to talk to him.'

'I can probably locate him.'

'Do that,' McNab said. 'So, how do we find out if our victim was a member of a coven?'

'Mmm. Tricky. Covens don't normally advertise in case they attract nutcases.'

McNab was about to laugh, then realized Ollie was serious.

'You get to join by recommendation. Sometimes the shops that sell the tools and gear you need know the local covens. There's bound to be at least a couple in Glasgow and Edinburgh. I could check for you.'

'Do that.'

Departing the Tech department, McNab made for the incident room, the printouts Ollie had given him clutched in his hand. Someone could make a start on contacting what few email and phone contacts Ollie had retrieved. McNab glanced at his watch. The public appeal to identify the suspect was due to be broadcast shortly, using the description and the security camera footage.

When McNab arrived, all eyes were turned to the TV screen on which DI Wilson was giving a brief résumé of events surrounding the discovery of Leila's body at her flat. An image of the pub appeared, then the CCTV footage of the couple as they exited. Leila was in clear view, her companion not so much. The identikit image of the main suspect followed, based on Shannon's written description in her testimony to DS Clark. It was a reasonable match for Barry's version, although McNab thought the suspect's height, build and general good looks were more likely to provide evidence of sightings, rather than the constructed facial image.

Then followed a request for the two men who had met Leila and her friend to come forward to allow them to be eliminated from the enquiry. No mention was made of Shannon's death, although they wouldn't be able to keep that under wraps for long. The appeal ended with the repeated image of the man they wanted to interview – tall, good-looking, blond, and sporting a Gucci watch with a black leather strap.

Where the hell was that guy?

15

Mark opened the snap pack and gently shook out a line along the black granite kitchen surface.

When he'd bought the flat six months before, the estate agent had waxed lyrical about the excellent kitchen and its incredible view over the park to the distant crags of Arthur's Seat. Mark had never cooked in the kitchen, but the granite surface had been well used, and he'd enjoyed the view on numerous occasions, including tonight, until the latest news bulletin had hit the giant TV screen and spoiled it all for him.

The bottle of cold beer, which he'd also been enjoying, had met its end on the tiled floor as the grainy video of himself exiting the pub with *that girl* had filled the screen. Jumping up, he'd listened open-mouthed to the description of himself and a request for Jeff and him to come forward and help the police with their enquiries.

Like fuck he would.

Then the killer ending with the photo-fit picture, and the mention of his bloody Gucci watch. That had brought the beer climbing back up swifter than it had gone down. He'd made the sink just in time, spewing it out like poison. After that, alcohol just didn't offer what he required for his sanity, hence the hit.

Mark gripped the edge of the sink and waited for the

panic to be replaced by something more pleasurable. Gradually, it was. With a sigh of relief tinged with excitement, he loosened his hold and turned on the cold tap, rinsing away the evidence of his fear. Then he studied the now famous Gucci watch.

The other girl, the blonde, must have noticed it.

Mark removed the offending item and laid it on the surface.

How many people know I have a watch like this? Jeff. Emilie. And all my co-workers at the bank. After all, I've flashed it often enough.

But then again, he reminded himself, the watch wasn't unique. You could buy it at House of Fraser if you were willing to spend a grand and more. So he wouldn't be the only male in Edinburgh wearing one. Or in Glasgow either.

But he had been in that pub on Friday night wearing it. And he had left with that girl, whose name he now knew was Leila Hardy.

The memory of him asking her name came surging back. *You're not here to ask questions*, had been her reply.

Fuck, that had been a turn-on. That and her ordering him to strip.

Snorting the coke, he realized, had made him high and aroused. He thought back to the mad coupling, the crazy cat smothering him, the mix of pain and ecstasy.

One thing's for certain. I didn't kill her.

He was sure of that. Or was he? The flashbacks had become more frequent and more varied. Once or twice, he thought he recalled another man in the room with them, taking part in the action. Doing other things that involved the red cord round her neck.

Could that be true?

Mark pushed the offending watch off the kitchen surface to the floor. Resilient, it bounced a little then lay unhurt, staring back up at him accusingly. He lifted his foot and stamped on it, grinding his heel into its face, hearing the glass shatter, putting all his energy, frustration and fear into its destruction.

If anyone asked, he would say it had been stolen.

He poured himself a large whisky and settled on the couch. He needed to think. Destroying the watch wouldn't be enough to cover his tracks. Emilie knew he'd been in Glasgow on Friday evening. If she saw the CCTV footage, would she recognize him from those images? The thought horrified him.

And what about Jeff? What would he do when he saw the police appeal?

They'd agreed to say nothing about that night, whatever happened. But would Jeff keep his word once he heard the girl was dead? Jeff had more to lose than a girlfriend if it got out that he'd been there that night.

They both had more to lose than a girlfriend.

16

McNab glanced at his mobile, expecting the station, only to find a number he didn't recognize. He let it ring a few more times before finally answering.

'Detective Sergeant McNab,' he offered.

There was a short silence, as though the caller thought they'd dialled a wrong number.

'Hello,' he tried again.

'Sorry, this is Freya Devine from the university library.'

'Hello, Freya. What can I do for you?' McNab tried not to sound too jubilant about the call.

A hesitation. 'I was just wondering if you'd managed to contact Shannon Jones yet.'

Now it was McNab who was hesitating. This was a tricky one.

'Why?' he ventured.

'Grant still hasn't managed to reach her on the phone. I said I could go round and check if she's okay.'

'No, don't do that,' McNab said quickly.

'Why?' Her voice had risen in fear.

McNab made his voice calm. 'I need to speak to you first.'

'Is something wrong?' she said quietly.

McNab ignored the question and asked one of his own. 'Where are you exactly?'

'Outside the library.'

'Walk down to Ashton Lane. I'll meet you there.' McNab rang off before she could question him further.

He knew he was taking a risk. Freya Devine might well decide to go round to Shannon's place anyway and spot the police activity. They wouldn't tell her anything and nor should he, but the fear in her voice had decided him. Freya had said she didn't know Shannon very well, but McNab wasn't so sure that was true.

This way he might find out.

She was standing outside the jazz club, waiting for him.

'What's wrong with Shannon?' she demanded as soon as McNab drew near.

McNab led her to an outside table and motioned her to sit down. She looked as though she might argue, then didn't.

'Do you want something to drink?' he said.

She shook her head.

The waitress appeared and McNab ordered two espressos.

When they were alone again, he said, 'I went to Shannon's flat directly after I left the library. She didn't answer the door, so I forced an entry. I'm sorry to have to tell you that Shannon is dead.'

The shock of what McNab was saying hit her and she swayed a little in the seat. McNab grabbed her arm to steady her.

'I'm sorry. There was no easy way to tell you that.'

She looked at him in horror. 'How?'

He shook his head, indicating he couldn't say.

'Did somebody kill her?' she demanded.

McNab didn't answer.

'My God, somebody killed her,' she said, shaking her head in disbelief.

McNab intervened. 'We won't know exactly how she died until the post-mortem.'

She examined his expression, those intelligent eyes missing nothing.

'Leila, now Shannon. Who's doing this?'

'Why do you think the deaths are connected?' McNab said swiftly.

'Don't you?' she challenged him.

'Why *would* they be connected?' he tried again.

He watched as she collected herself, then carefully chose her words.

'It's all over the news about the man Leila picked up in the bar. Shannon could identify him. Isn't that reason enough?'

It was a possibility, although McNab wasn't sure he bought it. Shannon wasn't the only person who could identify the chief suspect. He changed tack a little.

'It's important that you don't discuss what I've told you with anyone until it's official.'

'When will that be?'

'In the next twenty-four hours.'

At that moment the coffees arrived. McNab immediately drank his down, then eyed hers.

'Have it,' she offered. 'I don't like espresso.'

'Can I buy you a drink instead then?' he said, certain of a rebuff.

She surprised him by considering his offer, then asking if he'd eaten yet.

'No. If you're hungry we could order something here?' he suggested cautiously.

She glanced about at what was now a busy after-work crowd. 'I'd rather go somewhere quieter.'

'I know just the place,' McNab said.

*

Twenty minutes later, they were settled in a quiet corner of a small Italian restaurant he occasionally frequented on Byres Road, their order taken and a bottle of very nice red Italian wine uncorked on the table in front of them.

McNab poured her a glass.

'Aren't you having some?' Freya said.

'Tell me if you like it first,' he said, stalling for time.

She sipped a little and pronounced it very good. McNab, familiar with the vintage, knew it would be. He was just questioning whether he could stop at wine.

Well, it was time to find out.

He poured himself a small amount, then filled their water glasses, internally reminding himself *one glass of wine, one glass of water*.

'Grant said you were a post-grad student in medieval history,' McNab began on what he thought was safe ground.

It wasn't.

'You asked Grant about me?' she said, perturbed.

'A police habit,' he quickly apologized. 'So why medieval history and why Glasgow?'

'You noticed I don't come from here,' she said with a small smile.

'Newcastle?' he guessed.

'Correct.'

'Honorary Scot,' he assured her.

'Everyone says that.' She relaxed a little and took a sip of wine. 'I chose Glasgow because it's home to the Centre for Scottish and Celtic Studies and I have access to the Baillie collection, which is a prize collection of printed medieval and modern sources in Scottish, Irish and English history.'

'That all sounds good,' McNab said, as though he understood the significance of Glasgow University's medieval attributes.

She seemed amused by his expression. 'I chose medieval research because it's like being a detective, although all the cases are cold. Very cold.'

McNab smiled back. 'Now, I understand.'

As the food arrived, McNab allowed himself a mouthful of wine instead of water. After weeks of abstinence, it tasted pretty bloody good. He admonished himself silently and weakened its impact with more water.

They lapsed into silence as they each tackled their plates of spaghetti. McNab felt strangely at ease in Freya's presence, something he wasn't used to experiencing with attractive and desirable women. Wearing a plain blue dress, sporting no make-up or jewellery – he'd noted the lack of a ring in particular – she was, he decided, quite lovely.

And out of my league.

The spaghetti eaten, he offered to refill her glass.

'If you have more, too,' she said. 'Or maybe you're still on duty?'

'No,' he said and poured some for himself.

McNab was feeling better after the food and the wine, and her company, but he still had a job to do.

'May I ask you a question?' he said.

She studied him intently. 'If it will help find the person who did this to Shannon and Leila.'

'It will,' he said. 'Are you a practising Witch?'

The glass, halfway to her mouth, halted abruptly. 'What?' she said in mock amazement.

'Do you practise Wicca?'

'Why do you ask me that?'

'Do you?' he insisted.

She contemplated lying, but by her expression, lying wasn't something she was comfortable doing.

119

Finally she said, 'Yes,' and met his eye. 'Why?'

'Because both Leila and Shannon also practised Wicca, as I expect you already know.'

She shifted a little in her seat and he waited as she considered another lie. 'I was aware of that, yes.'

'And you didn't think it important to tell me?'

'No. If they were practising Catholics or Buddhists or agnostic, I wouldn't have mentioned that either,' she said defensively. 'Has the fact they practised Wicca something to do with their deaths?'

'There was a room of naked Barbie-type dolls in Leila's flat. Twenty-seven of them hanging from the ceiling.'

Her face, already porcelain in colour, became transparent. McNab watched the blood beat rapidly at her temple, dark blue against the white. He'd surprised and frightened her and he felt sorry for that, but he couldn't give up now.

He told her what had not, as yet, been reported in the media, although it was bound to come out soon.

'Leila was found hanged in that room, just like the dolls, with a red plaited silk cingulum round her neck.'

Her hand flew to her mouth and McNab wondered for a moment whether she might throw up. So did the waiter, who was glancing over at them anxiously.

She stood up.

Realizing she was planning on leaving, McNab said, 'I'm sorry. Please sit down and I'll explain.'

She was fighting herself. McNab also suspected that the possible link between the deaths and Wicca had just hit home, and that connection had spooked her.

'If you think there may be a link between their beliefs and their deaths, I have to know, *if* I'm going to find who killed them,' he emphasized quietly.

Her frightened eyes met his and she sank into the seat again. McNab gave her a few moments to compose herself.

'I won't spring anything else on you,' he promised.

The waiter, sensing the furore had come to an end, approached and offered them dessert. Freya declined, as did McNab, but he did order an espresso.

'Talk to me,' he said when some of the colour had re-appeared in her cheeks.

She gathered herself before she spoke. 'My research involves the practice of Wicca and the occult in medieval times. The university has a substantial collection on the occult called the Ferguson collection. Shannon looked after it. That's how I knew about her involvement with Wicca, although we never discussed it in detail. Leila was more obvious. One staff night out in Ashton Lane, she revealed that she believed in sexual magick.' She glanced at McNab to check if he knew what that was. When he shook his head, she said, 'Spells cast during sexual inter-course are believed to be more potent, because of the energy released during climax. Leila was adamant that this was true.'

'Which is why she made a habit of picking up men for sex?' McNab said.

'Possibly.'

'And the significance of the dolls?'

'That I don't know, although the Goddess is an important deity in Wicca.'

McNab tipped the rest of the wine into their glasses and drank his down, before hitting the coffee.

'I'd like to go home now,' she said.

'Of course.' He waved at the waiter for the bill. 'I'm sorry I frightened you.'

'No, you're not,' she said sharply.

McNab decided there was no point in arguing. He had done his job and by doing it had blown his chances.

Outside, they stood awkwardly for a minute, before McNab said, 'Please call me at any time, if you want to talk about this, or if anything frightens you about it.'

She nodded in an unconvincing manner, then turned and walked away.

With a stab of regret, McNab registered that Freya Devine was unlikely ever to seek him out again.

He retraced his steps to Ashton Lane, entered the first pub he came to, ordered a double whisky and carried it outside.

17

Laid out in three rows of nine, matched by hair colour, they were in the same formation as when she'd first seen them hanging from the ceiling in the murder room.

Except the last one was missing, because Chrissy held it in her left hand and in her right hand was a scalpel.

'Okay?' She looked to Rhona.

Rhona nodded.

Chrissy inserted the tip of the blade between the breasts, then cut a clean line between there and the navel, making an L-shape at top and bottom, a classic incision used in many post-mortems. Laying down the scalpel, Chrissy used forceps to pull back the plastic and reveal the inside.

'There it is,' she said, her eyes glinting in excitement.

Chrissy had spent the afternoon examining the dolls. Dusting for prints, and combing the hair for trace evidence. During the procedure she'd spotted that some of the dolls had an incision between their legs, and suspected this had been done to insert something into the body.

Now she was proved right.

Picking up a pair of tweezers, Chrissy carefully extracted what appeared to be a rolled-up piece of paper from the body of the doll.

The triumphant grin behind the mask was obvious.

With gloved hands, Chrissy carefully unrolled the paper

and laid it flat on the table to reveal an outline sketch of what appeared to be a male figure, including the genitals with the penis dominant and erect. Below the drawing was a set of symbols.

'Well, we know what the drawing represents, but what's that below?' Chrissy said.

Rhona reached for a magnifying glass and took a closer look. 'They look like runes of some sort.' She handed the glass to Chrissy. 'How many dolls have been cut in this way?'

'Nine, including this one.'

'Okay,' Rhona said, 'we'll each take four and check if there's anything inside.'

Twenty minutes later the other eight dolls had had their own post-mortems and their contents removed. All had contained a similar drawing of a man in a state of arousal, but the body shape and height of each male was different. Some had distinguishing marks on them, such as a symbol that might be there to represent a scar. The size of the genitals differed too. All of them had a different set of runes below.

'Are these replicas of the men she had sex with?' Chrissy said.

Rhona was thinking that too. 'It looks like it.'

'Maybe the sex was rubbish so she cast a spell on them,' Chrissy suggested with a laugh.

'Or maybe she had sex with them in order to cast a spell,' Rhona suggested, remembering what Magnus had said about sex magick. Rhona glanced at her watch. 'You head off. It's been a long day.'

'My mum's got wee Michael for the night. Fancy a drink?'

'What about Sam?'

'He's playing tonight, so I'm headed to the club.'

Rhona contemplated what visiting the jazz club might mean in terms of facing Sean and decided to delay her decision.

'I want to photograph the drawings and email them to Magnus first. Can I catch you up?'

Chrissy threw her a suspicious look. 'How long will you be exactly?'

'Half an hour,' Rhona promised.

Once Chrissy had gone, Rhona set about photographing the nine sketches and transferring the images to her laptop. They had made some progress since the morning strategy meeting. While Chrissy had concentrated on the dolls, Rhona had examined the cingulum in more detail. Unplaited and spread out on a lab table, shaking the silk had resulted in two hairs from the strands. A light brushing had brought forth flakes of skin. If, as it appeared, the cingulum had been used in a number of sexual encounters, then other partners may have left trace evidence of themselves behind, depending how often it had been washed.

The attempt at making the drawings particular to different shapes and sizes of men did seem to indicate they were replicas of real people. Would Leila's final partner feature among them?

She prepared an email for Bill, copy to Magnus, describing what Chrissy had found, then attached the images. Just before she sent it, she considered adding McNab's name to the recipients, then decided she would leave that up to Bill.

The more distance she kept between herself and McNab, the better.

As she logged her results and tidied up, Rhona contemplated heading for home. Chrissy would no doubt call when she didn't appear at the jazz club, but she would have her excuse ready. The post-mortem on Shannon Jones was scheduled for tomorrow morning, and it had been a long day. Whatever the excuse, Chrissy was smart enough to know the real reason for Rhona's non-appearance.

Not for the first time did Rhona regret inviting Sean back into her bed. Not because she hadn't enjoyed the experience, but because she'd enjoyed it too much. It would be easy to slide back into that relationship, but only if she forgot how it had played out the last time. Still, she should be able to go for a drink with Chrissy without agonizing over it. With that thought in mind, she turned her steps towards the jazz club.

The night was fine with a clear late-summer sky. The inhabitants of the West End were out in force, taking advantage of the pleasant weather. The outside tables in Ashton Lane were packed, the doors and windows of the various eateries and pubs standing wide open.

As Rhona made her way through the throng she spotted a figure she recognized. He sat alone, apparently deep in thought. In front of him was a glass of amber liquid that she suspected was whisky. Rhona watched as he raised the glass to his lips, then lowered it again untasted.

As she tried to make up her mind what to do, if anything, McNab glanced up and spotted her. Their eyes met for a moment, before he nodded briefly and turned away. There was something in his manner that troubled Rhona enough to make her approach.

McNab acknowledged her arrival with an enquiring look.

'Dr MacLeod. What can I do for you?'

'You can buy me a drink,' Rhona said. 'A white wine, please.'

A ghost of a smile passed his lips. 'My pleasure.'

When he'd disappeared inside, Rhona checked out what was in his glass and found it was whisky, although she suspected he'd drunk none of it, yet.

McNab appeared minutes later with a bowl of peanuts and a glass of white wine.

'I thought you might not have eaten yet.'

'I haven't,' Rhona said gratefully.

He watched as she sampled both the wine and the nuts, but made no attempt to take a drink himself. Rhona wondered how long he had been sitting there and whether this was his first drink. She realized she had little idea how to deal with this version of McNab. Their relationship before *Stonewarrior* had consisted of flashes of insight, barbed comments and occasional sexual congress. This silent, non-confrontational McNab bothered her. When he made no attempt to engage her in conversation, Rhona decided to open the proceedings.

'When Chrissy examined the dolls, we found nine of them had small sketches hidden inside.'

That caught his attention. 'Sketches of what?'

Rhona described the drawings. 'I sent image files to Bill and Magnus.'

'And me?'

She hesitated. 'I thought Bill would pass them on.'

That didn't please him and she saw a flash of the old McNab in the look he gave her.

'Fuck you, Dr MacLeod,' he said quietly.

She didn't react, because she probably deserved his anger. 'I sent them to Magnus because I thought he might be able to interpret the runes.' Which was true, but sounded like an excuse.

'And I wouldn't?' McNab gave a little snort of derision.

'I'm sorry,' she said.

'So am I.' McNab lifted the glass and drained it dry.

Rhona watched him walk away, hoping it wasn't her lack of faith in him that had broken his resolve.

McNab had done exactly what he'd vowed not to do, and it had felt good, which was why he'd left immediately after. Had he hung around he would have had another, and another. Rhona had done him a favour dissing him like that, although his anger at her failure to include him in the latest discovery had been real enough.

Christ, she could really get under his skin.

Emerging on Byres Road again, he stopped to make a call.

Magnus answered on the third ring.

'McNab here. Are you at home?'

'Yes,' Magnus said, sounding guarded.

'I'd like to come over, if that's okay? I need to talk to you about Witchcraft.'

18

The feeling of nausea that had hit in the restaurant swept over her again. Freya stopped for a moment and, leaning against a nearby garden wall, fought to quell the fear that was causing it. Focusing on the stone, still warm from the day's sunshine, she watched as a spider extended its web from an overhanging clematis, instantly trapping one of the tiny insects that occupied the evening air.

She grabbed the plant, tearing the cobweb, its sticky tendrils now clinging to her hand instead of the foliage, but the fly was already dead.

Just like Shannon.

Breathing deeply, she contemplated turning back. Seeking out the detective again. Revealing her innermost thoughts.

But did they make any sense?

Or was she just in shock at the death of a friend? Even though neither Shannon nor Leila were really friends. They had just shared an interest in Wicca.

And he thinks that's why they were killed.

Collecting herself, she walked on, heading back towards the university. The library would still be open, but that wasn't where she was going. On the crown of the hill, she turned right, entering the main gates.

The last time she and Shannon had spoken, Shannon had mentioned she had access to the room that had originally housed the famous Ferguson collection. Shannon seemed excited by this, but hadn't said exactly why.

One of the reasons Freya had chosen Glasgow for her PhD had been the Ferguson collection, something she'd mentioned to the policeman. John Ferguson, former Regis Professor of Chemistry at the university, had amassed 7,500 volumes, including 670 books on the history of Witchcraft, the subject of her own thesis. Now housed in the main library, its original home had been in the main Gothic building.

Once inside the deserted quadrangle, Freya made for the staircase to the tower and climbed to the second level. She'd been up here only once before, as a pilgrimage more than anything. Her initial interest in both this area of study and the collection had been sparked by a lecture she'd attended by Emeritus Professor of Astronomy Archie Roy.

He hadn't visited Newcastle University to talk about celestial bodies, but to discuss his other interest – psychical research. Both funny and entertaining, he'd told the sceptical audience of science students how, as a young lecturer in physics at Glasgow, he'd inadvertently visited this part of the old building only to discover a library he never knew existed. Curious, he'd entered and found numerous tomes on the occult, and realized he recognized some of the authors as eminent scientists. He reasoned that if these men wrote books on the subject, then it must be worth investigating. Freya had immediately felt the same way.

She stood for a moment on the landing, getting her bearings, then made for the double doors midway along. There was no sign on the wall or the doors to tell her she was in the right place, but memory told her she was.

The outer room was being refurbished, which was why Shannon had been called to check it out before workmen stripped out the original bookcases. Piles of old shelves sat in the centre of the room and dust danced in the late sunlight that streamed through the Gothic-shaped windows.

The door in the back wall was the one she sought. Crossing to it, Freya tried the handle, establishing it was locked. She felt in her pocket for the set of keys she'd taken earlier from Shannon's desk, and slipped the larger of the two into the lock.

With a satisfying clunk it turned. Freya pushed open the door and stepped inside.

19

Rhona took a breath, then let her body sink. Relaxing her muscles sent her arms floating of their own accord, her breasts swaying gently with the water. She thought of her pregnancy, almost two decades before. How she'd loved lying in a warm bath, the mound that was her unborn son a small island in the water. Almost twenty years ago.

I was a child, who bore a child and gave it away, to be raised by strangers.

As her brain repeated the mantra she periodically rebuked herself with, her muscles began tensing again. Rhona breathed in and this time dipped her head below the water. Despite her efforts, small bubbles of air immediately escaped through her mouth and nose.

How long before I breathe in water? Not long and even less if I panic.

She was counting now. Counting down the seconds before she would have to give up and rise to the surface. The water enveloped her and she had the sensation of being pulled deeper, reminding her of an incident when she was a child. Paddling at the edge of a loch, her feet had gone from under her and she'd dropped like a stone into the freezing water. The shock had made her gasp and she'd breathed in water. It might have been over in seconds had her father not pulled her out unceremoniously by the hair.

'Rhona?' The voice floated towards her from what seemed like an immense distance.

She opened her eyes just as a hand reached in and yanked her to the surface.

'Christ, Rhona, what the hell are you doing?'

She finally opened her mouth and sucked in air, with all the desperation of a smoker taking a nicotine hit.

Sean's expression was so furious, Rhona almost laughed.

'A scientific experiment,' she said.

'Like fuck it was.'

He hauled her upright.

'Here.' He thrust a towel at her. 'You're freezing. How long have you been in there?'

Rhona ignored the proffered towel, stepped out of the bath and took her robe from behind the door. 'A while. I was thinking about drowning.'

'What?'

'About the science of drowning. Anyway, how did you get in?'

'I still have keys, remember?' He flourished them at her.

Rhona tied her robe, suddenly conscious of her nakedness beneath, and headed for the kitchen, Sean following.

'Chrissy said you were coming to the jazz club.'

'I decided on a bath and an early night.'

'So you weren't avoiding me?'

'No,' she lied.

He didn't look convinced. 'Have you eaten?'

'Not yet.'

He opened the fridge door and took a look inside. 'I could make us an omelette?'

'I'm having a takeaway.'

'What did you order? Chinese or pizza?'

By the sceptical look on his face, it was time for the truth. 'I haven't ordered, yet.'

Sean extracted the eggs and some Edam cheese she'd bought days ago and started breaking the eggs into a bowl.

'I brought chilled white wine. A nice Italian. Two bottles.'

'I'll get dressed,' Rhona said.

'Don't bother. Relax. Pour the wine.' He gestured to a bag. 'There's olives and bread.'

She poured them both a glass, put the olives in a bowl and cut up the bread. Already the barriers were breaking down. This is what they did well. Eating, drinking and talking, although the talking usually led to sex.

'How's McNab doing?' Sean said as he whisked the eggs.

'Okay,' Rhona conceded.

'He's a one-off. Like you. A free spirit. That's why he's good at what he does.'

Rhona struggled to respond to that. 'He was demoted,' she reminded Sean.

'Who the fuck cares? McNab will never fit the mould, but he understands how people tick. Good or bad.'

It was a fair assessment. 'I thought you didn't like him?' she said.

'You don't know men, although you think you do.' Sean flipped an omelette onto a plate and handed it to her. 'I like him.'

They ate together in silence. It always amazed Rhona that Sean could conjure a meal from nothing and make it taste good. It was a skill she didn't possess. She also killed plants despite strenuous attempts to keep them alive. Why was that? Did she possess a life force that destroyed? Both plants and food, and men?

Sean, on the other hand, was a creator. Of both music

and food. She merely grazed on the fallout of life. The good and the bad. But mostly the bad. Analysing and reporting it. Not a pretty thought.

Christ, she even studied drowning while in the bath.

'Music?' he suggested when she'd cleared her plate.

'How's the new singer?' she countered, suddenly remembering the woman in his office who had looked less than impressed by her arrival.

'Good, although she's only here for a month,' Sean said as he stacked the dishes in the dishwasher.

'Why's that?'

'Her boyfriend's a musician. When he tours, she goes with him.'

Sean's mention of touring made her think of Leila's brother.

'Have you heard of a band called the Spikes?'

Sean looked surprised at the question. 'Yes, why?'

'The police are trying to get in touch with a band member, Daniel Hardy. He's the dead girl's brother. They think he's touring in Germany.'

Sean shook his head. 'No. He's in Glasgow. I saw him a couple of days ago.'

'Are you sure?' Rhona said, surprised.

'Pretty sure.'

'If he's here, he must know about his sister. It's been all over the news. Why didn't he contact the police?'

Sean looked thoughtful. 'Maybe he has and McNab hasn't mentioned it yet.'

It was possible, but unlikely. 'I think I should tell him.' Rhona rose and went in search of her mobile. Contacting McNab was an ideal way of terminating the cosy wine-drinking session in the sitting room before it progressed to other things. McNab's phone rang out a couple of times then went to voicemail. Rhona left a message relating Sean's sighting of Daniel Hardy, then rang off.

As she made her way back to the sitting room, she met Sean in the hall.

'I'm heading back to the club, if that's okay?'

She covered her surprise. 'Of course. Thanks for the meal.'

'My pleasure.'

In that moment, Rhona wished he wasn't going. This was always the way of it. If she felt Sean was manipulating her, she rejected him. If he appeared to reject her, she wanted him.

Sean dropped his set of keys on the hall table.

'You don't have to . . .' she began.

'Yes, I do.' He smiled. 'Call me.'

Rhona stood at the open door, listening to Sean's footsteps descend the stairs. Well, she'd got what she wanted. So why didn't it feel good?

20

On his arrival, Magnus had welcomed him in with no sign of animosity. That in itself had irritated McNab because Magnus's magnanimity had always been a sore point. Then, of course, Magnus had offered him a whisky, a rather good Highland Park. The taste of the earlier whisky still in his mouth, McNab had had to strive hard to turn down the offer. He was aware that his curt refusal had appeared to be more like bad grace than abstinence, but again Magnus had seemed unperturbed as he set up the coffee machine to produce McNab's requested caffeine hit.

They were now seated at the table by the open French windows, with a view of the flowing river below and the compelling Glasgow skyline above. Magnus was nursing a whisky, McNab a mug of strong coffee. Before them the big book on Witchcraft lay open, wherein McNab had read the selected passages with a mixture of interest and outright disbelief. Now they were looking through the photographs on the laptop screen. The ones Rhona had sent Magnus and omitted to send to McNab.

From the moment he had set eyes on them, McNab had loathed those dolls.

A psycho who hangs a woman from a hook, probably for sexual pleasure, was something he understood and could deal with. He didn't want the dolls to play a role in the story of her death. But it seemed they might.

He marshalled himself to ask the necessary question. 'Why would the victim place drawings inside the dolls?'

'I don't know for certain,' Magnus said. 'I'm assuming it was something to do with casting a spell.'

McNab didn't like the word 'spell' either, but he couldn't ignore it.

'A *spell* to do what?'

Magnus shrugged. 'Again, I have no idea.'

Fuck this, McNab thought, but didn't say out loud. Instead, he tried a different angle. 'What are spells used for in general?'

'Anything you desire. The Wicca code suggests you can do what you like, provided it harms no one.'

God, he would like a whisky, and that would harm no one, except of course himself. McNab held out his mug. 'More coffee?'

As Magnus went to get a refill, McNab eyed the whisky bottle.

If he added some to his coffee, did that count as drinking?

When the mug reappeared, McNab drew his eyes from the whisky and focused on the drawings on the screen.

'Okay. We know whether these guys were short or tall, well hung or not. What we need are names.'

Magnus surprised him by saying, 'I think we may have them, or at least a first name.' He indicated the symbols below the first drawing. 'These look like runes from the Seax-Wica alphabet, which is popular in occult writing.' He flipped through the Witchcraft book. 'Here are the runes and their alphabet equivalent.'

'If we exchange each rune below the first drawing with its alphabet equivalent, this is what we get.' He passed McNab

a sheet of printed paper with the symbols above and the letters he recognized below.

'Are these their real names?' McNab said.

'There's no way of knowing. True Wiccan names are chosen personally by each member of the circle. They usually relate to plants, the elements, like wind, rain or fire, animals such as raven or wolf, Gods or Goddesses like Freya, or special gifts that someone might have. This list doesn't contain any names like that.'

'They could also have fed her a false name,' McNab said.

'True, but I think Leila Hardy was intelligent enough to discover their real names if that was the case.'

McNab studied the list.

One name jumped out at him and that was Barry. Could it be the barman, Barry Fraser? If so he had a scar which, by its position, might be the result of an appendectomy. According to the sketch, the barman also had a package big enough to incite male envy.

If Barry Fraser was the one named, what were the chances that the last man seen with Leila before she died was also there? McNab studied the drawings again. There were three tall figures which could match the suggested build of their suspect, but there was no indication as to their age or hair colour, so not enough to pinpoint the tall blond man that Leila had left the pub with.

McNab cautiously reviewed his earlier anger. Rhona had been right to send the drawings to Magnus. He allowed himself a brief grudging acceptance of the man observing him from across the table.

'Thanks, this has been helpful and informative,' McNab managed.

Magnus appeared momentarily discomfited by the unexpected approbation, then added, 'There's one thing more I should mention, although I'm not sure if it's significant.'

'What's that?'

Magnus drew the book forward and indicated the passage that followed the table of runes. *'To know a person's name is to have a hold over them. For to know the name is to be able to conjure with it,'* he quoted.

A shiver ran up McNab's spine, something that didn't happen often and which he didn't like.

'You think that's why the drawings are named? Leila conjured up something *with* these men?'

'Or *against* them,' Magnus said.

'You're suggesting she made sexual magick with them in order to curse them?'

McNab had been cursed by a variety of women, most, if not all of them – including Rhona – with justification. But there was a difference between being cursed at and being cursed. Even he could appreciate that.

'A revenge killing?' he offered.

'It's a possibility.'

There were too many possibilities and now too many possible suspects.

Identifying the nine men of the apocalypse would be difficult, if not impossible, especially with the death of Shannon Jones. McNab's thoughts moved to Freya. Might she recognize any of the descriptions contained in the dolls? Or maybe their best bet was the brother, the elusive Daniel Hardy.

'I should get going,' McNab said. 'Thanks for your help.'

'I'll write a report on the drawings and send you and DI Wilson a copy.'

'And Rhona.'

'And Rhona.' Magnus seemed pleased at being reminded.

Once back at street level, McNab checked his mobile messages and found one from Rhona regarding Daniel Hardy, which made him immediately call the incident room. He was surprised to find Janice still on duty.

'DS Clark, have you no home to go to?'

'I could say the same about you.'

'Okay, we're both sad bastards. I got a call from Rhona. She says Daniel Hardy's been seen in Glasgow. Has he contacted the station?'

'Not that I'm aware of.'

'Have we got an address for him?'

'Yes. Give me a minute and I'll get it.'

Janice came back on the line and quoted an address.

'Want me to come with you?' She sounded almost keen.

'No need. Go and have a drink with the team. I'll see you in the morning.'

McNab rang off and checked his watch. It was after ten now. If Daniel Hardy was set on avoiding the police, he was unlikely to hang around at home waiting for them to call. But then again, he wouldn't be expecting an unwelcome visitor at this time.

The address for Daniel Hardy was a flat in the East End, on the High Street, not far from the location of the first investigation Professor Magnus Pirie had been involved in. The East End had seen a makeover since then, the Great Eastern men's hostel refurbished, the nearby wasteland where they'd searched for bodies transformed by the erection of brightly coloured blocks of flats. Somewhere below ground the Molendinar burn still ran through its brick-built caverns, taking Glasgow's fresh water run-off from Hogganfield Loch down to the River Clyde. Thinking about what had happened in those caverns didn't bring back good memories for McNab, of Magnus, Rhona or himself.

He parked the car near the cathedral precinct and walked down the hill. The refurbishment hadn't quite reached this section of the High Street, although one or two coffee shops had opened since last he'd been here. McNab was never sure if he welcomed the infiltration of old Glasgow by the latte brigade, yet the place did look better for their arrival and suggested that at least some of the locals now had money to spend on fancy coffees.

None of the coffee shops were open at this late hour. Neither did he encounter a pub, which was a blessing in his current state of mind. He might have missed the shop, intent as he was in following the street numbers to his chosen destination. Ollie had said he would check for covens via local magick shops. McNab realized he should have recalled this one, which had been here on the High Street as far back as he could remember, although he'd always assumed it was simply selling New Age rubbish, left over from the hippy era.

Now he saw it was much more than just joss sticks and hookah pipes. The poster in the window advertised a visit by a well-known Wiccan warlock and a promise of all things required for magick inside. The proximity of the shop to the brother's flat seemed noteworthy.

One puzzling aspect of Leila's flat, apart from the dolls and the cingulum, was the singular lack of evidence that Leila had worshipped there. According to Magnus there should have been an altar complete with candles, an incense burner, various dishes and a goblet, together with figures to represent the female and male deities.

McNab noted that the window display offered a selection of such items, the Goddess being available as a picture or a statue, both of which were nakedly beautiful, with long flowing hair and voluptuous bodies.

McNab crossed the road and a couple of blocks further down found the number he was looking for. There were no names on the various entry-phone buttons, just flat numbers, which hadn't been included with the address. McNab chose a button at random and pressed it. When there was no answer, he tried another. This time he was lucky and a male voice answered.

'Daniel Hardy?' he tried.

'Wrong flat, mate.'

'Can you let me in, then?'

'Why should I?'

'Because I'm the police,' McNab said sharply.

The lock clicked free. On the way up the stairs, McNab met his interrogator at an open door. It was a man in his sixties. McNab flashed his ID at him. 'Which door?'

'Top landing on the left.'

McNab continued up the stairs, aware of the guy's eyes following him. Reaching the door in question, he registered that the nameplate wasn't Hardy but Carter. McNab rapped on the door. It took two more raps for someone to finally answer.

The door was pulled open only to the length of a thick metal chain, thus obscuring McNab's view of a frightened female face. McNab showed his ID.

'Detective Sergeant McNab. Is Daniel Hardy at home?'

By her expression she would rather he'd declared himself a mad axe murderer than a policeman.

'No,' she finally said.

'May I speak to you then?'

'What about?'

'His sister.'

Through the crack in the door he watched the pale face grow paler.

'I don't know anything about his sister.'

'I'd still like to talk to you,' McNab said, making it sound more like an order than a request.

He was rewarded by the chain being removed and the door opened. His gatekeeper was a little over five feet, with cropped bright pink hair, black rimmed eyes and a nose ring. She wore a T-shirt with the word 'Spikes' on it, which suggested she was a fan, if not a girlfriend.

McNab softened his look. 'May I come in?' he said, aware he sounded a little like a vampire requesting entry.

When she eventually nodded, McNab stepped over the threshold into a small hall with a washing line strung along one wall, on which hung a variety of garments including boxer shorts.

'Is there somewhere we can talk?'

Her eyes flitted about, unsure. She glanced at a couple of doors, dismissing them, while McNab tried to establish if there was anyone else in the flat with her. A block which housed three flats on each landing wouldn't be spacious. He decided two bedrooms at the most, or maybe only one, with the sitting room made into another. That would leave the kitchen as the only communal room.

Eventually she led him to a door, beyond which was the kitchen. In here was a table and two chairs, with a window that looked out on a small concreted back court. It was tidier than his own place, despite his increased attempts at house-keeping. She took a seat at the table and McNab joined her there.

'When will Danny be back?'

'I don't know.'

'Is he playing somewhere tonight?'

'I don't know,' she repeated.

'Yet you're a fan?' McNab gestured to the T-shirt.

She immediately folded her arms over the offending advertisement.

'What's your name?'

She'd been preparing for another question about Danny and was openly disarmed by this one.

'Maggie Carter.'

'May I ask if you and Danny are an item?'

'We just flat-share.'

McNab wasn't sure he believed her, but let it go anyway.

'We've been trying to contact Danny because of the death of his sister, which has been widely reported on the news. It's important we speak to him.'

His words seemed to shatter her defences.

'He doesn't want to. I told him to, but he won't.' She sounded and looked really upset by this.

'When did Danny get back from Germany?'

She studied the table. 'He didn't go on the tour.'

'Danny's been here in Glasgow all the time?'

She nodded.

McNab said a silent curse at the public in general, and Danny Hardy in particular, for pissing the police about. He pushed his card across the table.

'Tell Danny if he isn't in touch within the next twenty-four hours, I'll issue a warrant for his arrest.'

The alarm that caused suggested she would do her best, which is all he could ask.

Outside now, McNab contemplated his next port of call, which should be a further chat with Barry Fraser. If he was swift, he might just catch him before the pub shut. Then again, he would be visiting a pub, with a wide range of excellent whiskies on offer – a tempting thought.

21

The night was still young, Mark decided, as he stood glassy-eyed in front of the mirror. Robotically checking his watch, he found an empty wrist.

Fuck. He would have to stop doing that.

But, then again, it was a natural reaction in someone who'd recently had an expensive watch stolen. Emilie had been sympathetic and urged him to report it and make an insurance claim. He'd said he would, but hadn't, obviously. The last thing he wanted was to make his presence in Glasgow on that night known to the police with the added extra that he'd been wearing a Gucci watch with a black leather strap.

Mark wiped his nose of any excess coke and rubbed his finger along his gums.

Three days now and no one had linked him to those images on CCTV. No one at work or Emilie or even Jeff had mentioned the footage. The silence from Jeff's end had surprised Mark. He'd contemplated calling him, but had decided against it. If Jeff had viewed the police appeal, it seemed he'd decided to keep well clear of involvement. A wise move on both their parts.

Especially since it involved murder.

Thinking the word immediately replayed the image of that room and the curtain of clicking swaying dolls. Mark tried desperately to halt the rerun before it reached the view of what lay beyond those dolls, and failed. There she was. The naked body with its pink-tipped breasts, the auburn mound between the long slim legs. As his eyes rose to the cord round her neck, he felt himself harden.

Why did that happen? Was it because I killed her?

His stomach churned as the numerous vodka shots he'd swallowed threatened to resurface. No way could he do that to a woman. But if he had been out of his head? He'd watched plenty of porn, some of it rough, but that wasn't unusual among his circle of mates, including Jeff. It didn't mean he actually wanted to hurt anyone. And, Mark reminded himself, she had been the one to order him about, not the other way round. She had been the one to tie them together. Recalling that aspect of the encounter did nothing to soften his prick. In fact, it made it harder.

Fuck it. He would have to leave the Gents soon or his absence would be noted.

Mark set about imagining his father's face if he ever found out. The coke would be bad enough. HIGH COURT JUDGE'S SON CAUGHT SNORTING COKE would make a great headline. But hey, HIGH COURT JUDGE'S SON AS MURDER SUSPECT was so much better. Imagining the second headline had the required effect on his erection.

Mark washed his hands, dried them and headed out.

As he climbed the stairs to the main bar, the coke began to lighten his mood. It would be okay, he assured himself. He was sorry about the girl, but it had had nothing to do with him, and if it emerged that he'd been with her that night, a lot of people would be hurt. No, devastated. Emilie for one. His father, for obvious reasons. His mother, who he definitely didn't want upset, not in her present condition.

He had no choice, really.

As Mark weaved his way through the crowd towards his colleagues, a figure suddenly stepped out in front of him.

'What the fuck are you doing here, mate?' Mark said, his stomach dropping to his feet.

'Don't fucking *mate* me, you bastard,' Jeff blazed back at him.

'Keep it down,' Mark hissed as a couple of heads turned in their direction.

'Whatever happens, we were never in that pub?' Jeff sneered. 'Whatever happens?'

'Let's go outside,' Mark said. 'And talk.'

Jeff lifted the shot in front of him on the bar and downed it. Mark wondered how many had gone the same way. Jeff could drink him under the table, and he looked pissed as well as mad. A volatile combination. Jeff was known for his bad temper, when provoked. Mark had rescued him from a number of angry Glasgow encounters where Jeff had taken offence for some throwaway comment. But tonight he was the target of Jeff's anger.

He led Jeff past the tables out to the centre of the paved Grassmarket, where they served lunches under the trees. A cool wind from the Forth was rattling the leaves, reminding them that autumn was on its way. Mark shivered as he tried to marshal his thoughts. How much was he planning to tell Jeff? How much was it safe to tell him? Maybe a lie would be better? Whatever he said must convince Jeff to keep quiet. If neither of them came forward, the police had nothing more than that crappy video, and that would take them nowhere.

Jeff was glaring at him, his fists clenched by his side. 'What the fuck have you done?' he said.

'Nothing,' Mark said. 'Nothing,' he repeated.

'That girl's dead.'

'I know.'

'*You* were the last one to see her alive.'

'No, I wasn't.'

'You went back with her. You're on CCTV.'

'I didn't go back to the flat. She blew me off.'

'What?' Jeff looked incredulous.

'She said it was a joke to see if I'd fall for it.' Rising to the lie, Mark rushed on. 'You saw the look she gave her mate. I think they had a bet on, like we do sometimes.'

'You didn't fuck her?' Jeff said.

'No way. She blew me off,' he repeated.

Mark watched as the lie took root.

'Why didn't you come back then?' Jeff said suspiciously.

'Cos you looked as if you might make it. You were getting on much better than me. Remember?'

Jeff did remember.

'And you did get it, didn't you?' Mark reminded him.

Jeff nodded.

Mark clapped him on the back. 'I didn't want to fuck up your fun.'

Jeff eyed him. 'So what do we do now?'

'Keep schtum, as agreed.' Mark warmed to his argument. 'Someone will have seen her after she left me and tell the police. They have no way of finding us. The video's crap.'

'What about the other girl?' Jeff said.

Fear leapt in Mark's chest. 'You're not in contact with her?'

'No way.'

'Good. So, we lie low. And say nothing. Agreed?'

Jeff slowly nodded.

'Let's go back to my place. Have a drink together. The booze here is way overpriced,' he added, knowing that Edinburgh prices were a favourite gripe of Jeff's.

He watched Jeff agree, and was relieved. He would get him to stay over. Make sure everything was still okay in the morning. Besides, it was better if they weren't seen together by his colleagues. Just in case. He would make an excuse tomorrow about his disappearance. Tell them Emilie called, keen for sex.

Mark congratulated himself as he led a now docile Jeff in the direction of his flat. He'd been fucking brilliant back there. Defused the situation and convinced Jeff that he'd never been in the dead girl's flat.

It would all blow over. They would find the guy that did it, because it definitely hadn't been him.

22

As he approached his front door, a figure stepped out of the shadows. McNab, immediately on alert, felt instinctively for a gun he didn't possess, a result of undercover work he'd rather forget.

'It's only me,' Freya said apologetically as she entered the light.

To say he was surprised to see her there was an understatement. He'd given her his card with a mobile number and the station number. He had definitely not mentioned where he lived.

'How did you find out my address?'

She gave him a disarming smile. 'My job is to find out things about people who lived centuries ago. Finding you was less difficult. Besides, you mentioned where you ordered your pizza from.' She pointed across the street. 'After that it was easy.'

McNab was impressed. 'You haven't any relatives in the Italian Mafia?' he said.

'I'm from Newcastle, remember?'

He met her smile. 'Only a little less scary.'

'Can I talk to you in private?' she said quietly.

'Want to come inside?'

'Please.'

Opening the door, McNab said a silent thank you for the

fact that the place didn't smell of stale food and whisky – a definite upside to his new-found sobriety.

Freya glanced about. 'You live alone?'

'Always,' McNab said firmly, then regretted it.

When she came back with, 'Me too,' and an understanding look, something shifted inside him.

God, he was on dangerous ground.

'Fancy some coffee?'

'That would be great. Black, please.'

'Take a seat,' he said as he spooned fresh coffee into the filter.

McNab heard her settle behind him and imagined her there on his sofa, wishing the circumstances were different. Memories of Iona, his last attempt at a relationship, resurfaced. Admittedly, Iona had been about sex. Only sex. Most of their sex had been fuelled by whisky and in her case coke. Something he'd chosen not to notice at the time, preferring to believe the big pupils were all about her excitement at being screwed by him.

As the boiling water filtered through the coffee grains, McNab fetched two mugs from the cupboard, keeping his eyes averted from the whisky bottle that stood alongside. He hadn't avoided The Pot Still and Barry Fraser tonight to come home and repeat his earlier mistake.

'I wouldn't mind a tot of whisky in mine,' she said from behind him.

'Sure thing,' McNab said and lifted the bottle out.

Everything went into slow motion after that. He poured a decent measure in her coffee, then the bottle headed towards his own mug. His fumbled attempt to prevent this resulted in a spill on the kitchen surface. When the sharp scent of the spilt whisky met his nostrils, McNab fought a desire to scoop it up with his finger and lick it.

He turned away swiftly and carried both mugs over, setting hers down on the coffee table in front of her.

'Hope it's not too strong,' he said.

'My father used to make me a hot toddy when I had a cold. He swore by them. I didn't like the taste of whisky then, but I like it now.'

'A hot toddy in Newcastle?'

'My dad came from Inverness.'

McNab swallowed a mouthful of coffee. For some reason, the caffeine didn't provide its usual kick. He must be getting used to it. Just as you did with whisky, which was why one was never enough.

'What did you want to speak to me about?'

She had moved on to whisky with water. He'd finished the coffee and made another pot, stronger this time. There was a scent in the air. At least there was for him. It was the mingled aroma of a woman and whisky. Freya was, he thought, a little drunk. She was also frightened.

The tale she'd told him had been an odd one and he wasn't sure he recognized the significance she placed on it. But it meant something to her. It seemed Shannon had hinted that she'd found something in the old library in the main building which had originally housed the Ferguson collection of manuscripts on the occult.

'And?' McNab had said.

'We were interrupted at this point and I never found out any more. Then she didn't come into work and . . .' Freya's voice had tailed off in distress.

'You think Shannon found something important?'

'The Ferguson collection is world renowned,' she'd explained, then gone on to mention a selection of famous pieces it contained.

McNab had made suitable noises, at the same time thinking that writings about casting spells and turning metal into gold were about as believable as parables about turning water into wine and feeding the world on a few loaves and fishes. Eventually he came to understand that whatever Shannon had thought she'd found, it was no longer there.

'And you think this possible discovery could have something to do with Shannon's death?'

Freya had thrown him a look of exasperation at this point.

'Such documents are priceless. Someone might kill for them.'

Now those two statements did make sense to McNab.

'So Shannon mentioned finding something to you. You took the key to the room from her desk and went looking for whatever it was, after I told you about her death?'

She nodded. 'And there was nothing there.'

'Could she have been the one to move it?'

Freya shrugged. 'I don't know.'

'What about Grant?'

'I asked him. He said Shannon had never mentioned anything to him, but he'd check it out.' Freya asked McNab for another drink.

McNab took the glass from her and went to fetch a refill. There had been half a bottle's worth and there wasn't a lot left. Perhaps it was safe now for him to have one. He couldn't go out and buy another bottle at this late hour. McNab made a decision and shared the remainder. His neat, hers diluted.

155

When he arrived back with the two glasses, she looked pleased.

'I thought you were still on duty,' she said.

'Time to knock off for the day.'

'Good.'

She shifted along the couch towards him. That surprised McNab, but not as much as what happened next. He was used to being the one to make the first move. Often he overstepped the mark and was rebuffed. Iona had made a play for him in the pub on the night of his promotion. He'd succumbed only after Rhona had turned him down. Iona, he liked to think, had caught him on the rebound.

The lips that met his were moist and whisky-laden. The tongue that sought his even more so. She tasted good, and smelt even better. As she arched her back he felt the press of her breasts against him.

It had been a long time since McNab had experienced sober sex. The eagerness was there, but the desperate fumbling, forgotten in the morning, didn't have to be, he told himself. McNab stood up and offered Freya his hand. When she took it, he led her through to the bedroom.

He woke as dawn filled the room to find Freya no longer beside him. For a split second, McNab thought she had been no more than an erotic dream, then he spotted something on the pillow next to his. It was a figurine, a small replica of the Goddess statue he'd seen in the magick shop window. On its base was the name Freya.

Under the shower, McNab relived their encounter. With a clear head, he recalled everything in detail. He had become the perfect witness. The one the police longed for. The one who could describe a suspect in detail, down to the exact location of a freckle or a mole.

McNab could recollect the timbre of Freya's voice, the sound of her sigh, every curve and plane of her body, the taste and smell of her. If he'd walked into a crowded room, he suspected he would know immediately if she was there.

It was something he'd experienced only once before.

As he dried and dressed, McNab moved from thoughts of Freya to what she had further revealed after they'd made love. It was that moment when closeness made you say things you might come to regret.

'I rarely saw Leila or Shannon at work. Most of my time in the library is spent on research. I didn't know they were practising Wicca until I met them at a coven meeting.'

McNab had sprung to attention at that point. 'Where was this?'

'In Edinburgh. There's a meeting place in the Vaults under the Bridges. It's not a secret. Tourists who visit the Vaults during the day can look through a grille at the room. But,' she said, 'the members don't advertise their identities.'

McNab recalled Ollie mentioning his friend Joe using the Vaults for a coven meeting.

'And you three are members?' he said.

'Just visitors. Shannon and Leila were as surprised to see me as I was to see them.'

'Were they members of any Glasgow coven?'

'No. And neither am I. It's perfectly possible to practise Wicca alone or in a group of two or three.' She hesitated. 'Leila and Shannon worked together, but Leila was the leader. And I think she was using her skills as a Witch in other ways.'

'How exactly?'

'Selling sexual magick.'

'You mean casting spells during sex?' he'd said with a dismissive laugh.

Freya had pulled away from him at that point. 'You shouldn't mock something you don't understand,' she'd warned.

'Or you'll put a spell on me?'

Her hurt expression had cut McNab to the core. 'I'm sorry. That was way out of order,' he'd said, keen to make amends. When Freya had eventually nodded an okay to his apology, McNab had felt his stomach flip in relief.

Don't fuck this up, a small voice had warned him.

'What made you think Leila had been selling sexual spells?' he'd said, having finally registered the true significance of her statement.

'Because of something she said once.'

'And what was that, exactly?'

'That men were willing to pay for sex, and pay even more for sex magick.'

23

Rhona disrobed and deposited her suit in the bin. This morning's post-mortem on Shannon Jones had proved to be straightforward. In the pathologist's opinion, Shannon had in fact died of suffocation, after which her head and shoulders had been immersed in the bath water. Opening up the body, he'd discovered evidence of congestion in the lungs and the heart muscle, consistent with undue pressure.

How she was smothered was less obvious. A plastic bag over her head was a possibility. Or a pillow from the bed next to the circle which she'd hoped would keep her safe.

The small incision on her crown had been noted, together with pressure marks on the skull, suggesting her face may have been held against a pillow. Alternatively, it may have happened when her dead head was being forced beneath the water.

A heavy impact caused blood vessels to rupture even after death, particularly areas engorged with post-mortem hypostasis. Oozed blood in the tissues produced a visual effect similar to ante-mortem bruising. The most reliable way of determining whether bruising had occurred before or after death was to examine whether a large number of white blood cells had been dispatched to the area to deal with an injury. Dr Sissons's conclusion had been that the contusions on Shannon's knees had happened post-mortem.

Undressed now, Rhona stepped under the shower.

The piping hot water felt good after the chill of the mortuary. McNab hadn't shown up for the post-mortem and she'd heard nothing back from him regarding her message about Daniel Hardy. Her first thought was that he'd fallen off the wagon after their brief meeting in Ashton Lane, and, she decided, that might be her fault.

But, then again, McNab needed very little to persuade him to do what he wanted to do anyway. If he wanted to drink, he would. Yet his attempt at abstinence had appeared to be going well, although the substantial increase in caffeine had created its own edginess.

She turned her face to the spray, rinsing out her mouth, dispensing with the taste of death and chemicals. DI Bill Wilson hadn't been present at the PM either, nor DS Clark, which suggested that Bill had assumed McNab *would* be there. Yet he wasn't, and Rhona wondered why.

She turned off the water and stepped out, grabbing a towel.

In truth, she was as annoyed with herself as she was with McNab, because she was letting him get under her skin, despite her efforts not to.

Just as I'm doing with Sean. Another uncomfortable thought.

Once dried and dressed, she checked her mobile and discovered a message from Bill asking her to drop round after the PM. It could be that McNab's absence had been noted or, more hopefully, Bill wanted to discuss the drawings found in the nine dolls.

The day was overcast, the air distinctly cooler. It had been an exceptional summer in Scotland and it seemed her residents, by their apparel, were determined to pretend it would continue that way, despite the obvious change in temperature. But Glasgow was no Los Angeles, even though this summer the tans had been more real than fake. Autumn was coming. The trees knew it, even if the residents pretended not to.

She contemplated the result of the PM on Shannon Jones as she drove. As Magnus never failed to remind them, a perpetrator always had a rational reason for a kill, although it may never appear rational to a normal person. They also had a reason for the manner in which they killed, the location they chose and, assuming they weren't disturbed, the state in which they left the crime scene.

Which led to a number of questions.

Where had Shannon been suffocated? If it was in the bedroom, why transport her to the bathroom and half immerse her in the bath, if not to try and give the impression she'd drowned? Most people had no idea how drowning was actually determined, and that despite few outward signs of suffocation, a post-mortem could reveal them.

Then there was Magnus's revelation about the favoured manner in which Witches were disposed of. Hanging, drowning or burning. Could the attempt at portraying Shannon's death as being caused by drowning have anything to do with the fact that she was a practising Witch? As she parked and made her way to Bill's office, Rhona decided she was none the wiser, but hoped Bill was.

She hesitated before knocking, aware that this had been McNab's office too in the short time he'd served as DI. It couldn't have been easy for McNab to take up residence here. McNab worshipped the boss, that much was plain. Had DI Wilson been around to support him in his new position, maybe things would have gone differently.

Then again, maybe not. McNab's *don't give a fuck about authority* mode was hardly going to bode well for him in any position of seniority. Although, she reminded herself, Bill hadn't risen through the ranks despite his obvious ability, probably because he didn't care for prestige and position either.

Maybe the two men weren't that different.

You look too thin, she thought, as Bill turned from the window to welcome her. Rhona's forensic eye quickly estimated the loss of a couple of stone from a body that had been trim in the first place. She suspected he'd lost it in tandem with Margaret, as she'd entered her second bout of cancer treatment. Worry killed the appetite as much as chemotherapy.

But maybe now he was back at work?

Rhona had already spied the mug of tea on the desk, left to go cold just the way Bill liked it, alongside a plate piled high with chocolate biscuits.

'Rhona.' Bill's face broke into a smile. 'It's good to see you.'

'You too,' she said. 'How are the troops treating you?'

He indicated the biscuits. 'Feeding me up. Or trying to. You haven't brought more, I hope?'

'No, but I'm happy to help you demolish those,' Rhona said, suddenly feeling hungry.

When she accepted his offer of coffee, Bill stuck his head out the door and placed the order, his voice, unlike his body, anything but frail.

'So,' he said, indicating that she should take a seat. 'The dolls have provided a clue to their existence.'

'Chrissy's eagle eye,' Rhona said.

'Have you read Magnus's take on it?' Bill said.

'No, I was at the PM on Shannon . . .'

When she halted, Bill said, 'And?'

'Suffocation, followed by immersion.'

'So not drowned, voluntary or otherwise?'

'Apparently not.'

'You and McNab discuss it?' Bill said as the coffee arrived. There was no avoiding an answer.

'So he didn't turn up?' Bill's expression indicated that McNab should have. 'Is he drinking?'

'A great deal of coffee,' Rhona said, honestly. 'And he's definitely on the case. Both cases.'

Bill nodded. 'He went to see Magnus last night. Apparently they discussed the drawings and Magnus came up with some interesting information regarding the symbols.' Bill pulled up an image on his screen. 'Take a look.'

Below the first photograph, Magnus had added a graphic which took each of the symbols and translated them into a letter of the alphabet.

'In his detailed email he says the symbols are those of the Seax-Wica alphabet, which is popular in occult writings.'

'Magnus thinks the runes represent the first names of possible sexual partners?'

Bill nodded. 'It's something, although with Shannon dead, we have no way of identifying these men, aside from a possible first name and rough description.'

'You've had no luck with the CCTV footage?'

'Lots of calls. None leading to a suspect.'

Rhona decided it was time to tell Bill the latest news. 'We may have more than a name and a description.'

Bill waited for her to continue.

'I found traces of semen on each of the nine drawings,'

Rhona said. 'It looks like Leila may have left a DNA marker, as well as a description and a name.'

It made sense in terms of sexual magick as described by Magnus. The power of the spell was in the seed. So the seed must be retained for the magic to continue. They could create a DNA profile for each of the nine men who had indulged in sexual magick with Leila, but if they weren't recorded on the database already, even that wouldn't be enough to find them.

Rhona encountered the elusive McNab as she exited Bill's office. He was in an animated conversation with DS Clark, a totally different man from the one she'd encountered last night in Ashton Lane.

Her first thought was that he and Janice had become an item, an idea that rather pleased her. She liked Janice, but was well aware that McNab had hit on her in a spectacular fashion when she'd first arrived. Then, when rejected, had behaved like a misogynist idiot and been duly chastised for it by the boss. Rhona had already noted a different relationship between them now they were both the same rank, but a romance she hadn't anticipated.

A closer look convinced her that McNab had definitely hit it lucky somewhere, but not necessarily with DS Clark.

'Dr MacLeod. Good to see you.'

McNab gave her his signature grin while Janice shot her a look, one that matched Rhona's reading of the situation. Detective Sergeant McNab was the tomcat who had got the cream but that cream wasn't Janice.

'You missed the PM,' Rhona said to burst his bubble.

'Let me guess. She was suffocated, then dumped in the bath?'

'You spoke to Sissons?' she said suspiciously.

164

'No, but I'd like to speak to you. Fancy a coffee?'

Rhona was about to suggest he would be better seeing the boss first, but a persuasive look from Janice made her agree instead.

They made their way to the room that housed the drinks machine. Luckily, the room was unoccupied. McNab immediately selected a double espresso then asked what she fancied. Rhona settled for a black coffee.

As soon as the espresso arrived, McNab knocked it back and pressed for another.

'That's a lot of caffeine,' Rhona ventured.

'Better than too much whisky.'

'How's that going?'

'Good,' he said. 'Better than good.' The smile that passed his lips wasn't meant for her, but for some thought he was having.

The question had to be asked.

'Who is she?'

'What do you mean?' McNab feigned puzzlement.

'I've seen your post-sex expression. Remember?'

The grin he bestowed on her was infectious. 'Oh, I remember all right, Dr MacLeod.'

'That's why you weren't at the PM?'

'No. I was in fact in the Tech department discussing Witches' covens with my friend Ollie. I've arranged to visit one and wondered if you'd like to accompany me?'

'What?' Rhona said, taken aback at this turn of events.

'Apparently there's an *esbat* tonight. That's the name of a regular meeting, to the uninitiated.'

He was definitely trying to annoy her with his newly acquired insider knowledge. Rhona decided not to rise to the bait.

'Where is this meeting?'

'In the Edinburgh Vaults.'

Rhona was tempted. 'Why me? Why not DS Clark?'

'If you don't fancy it . . .'

'Have you spoken to Magnus about this?'

'No, but I plan to.' McNab threw the empty cup in the bin. 'I'll pick you up at eight.' And with that McNab and his Cheshire grin was gone.

Rhona pondered McNab inviting Magnus to participate, coupled with his upbeat attitude. She should be glad of it, yet . . . McNab with a hangover was tricky to manage, but at least she had some experience of that. McNab in love would take some getting used to.

And who the hell was the female involved?

The person to ask was obviously Chrissy. Nothing got past her forensic assistant's network of informers. If Chrissy didn't know who McNab had got lucky with, no one would.

'No way,' Chrissy said later, when presented with the circumstantial evidence. 'Are you sure?'

'I know that look,' Rhona said.

Chrissy was already checking her mobile for any messages regarding McNab's love life which she may have missed. There apparently were none.

'He's not even been to the pub.' Chrissy's brow creased in thought. 'So where the hell did he meet her?'

'No point looking at me,' Rhona said. 'You're always the first to know. You must be slipping.' It felt rather good to be one step ahead of Chrissy for a change, even though the step was a small one.

Chrissy was immediately on the case. 'It must be someone

he met during the investigation. After all, he's been working twenty-four-seven, according to Janice. I'll give her a call.'

'You do that.'

Having off-loaded the detective work on to Chrissy, Rhona headed into the lab.

24

The Pot Still was a different beast at ten o'clock in the morning. No crowds wearing the whisky glow and talking the talk; it was empty apart from a young guy who wasn't Barry, bottling up.

When McNab asked for Barry, he was informed that he was due in shortly. McNab decided to wait. In the meantime he would take advantage of their breakfast menu. He ordered the biggest plate on offer, together with a pot of coffee, and, retreating to a corner table, reflected on how Glasgow had changed when you could have something other than a liquid breakfast in a pub of a morning.

He was well through the offering of square sausage, bacon, black pudding and egg when Barry arrived. McNab watched as he was cornered by his colleague and a whispered conversation ensued. Then Barry turned his gaze on the corner, where McNab had just popped the final bit of sausage in his mouth. To say that Barry wasn't pleased to see him would be an understatement.

In contrast, McNab gave him a welcoming smile. 'Barry. Come and join me.'

Barry made a weak effort not to comply. 'I have to start work.'

McNab glanced at the guy behind the bar. 'I'm sure your

colleague can manage without you for just a little longer. Take a seat.'

Barry did so grudgingly.

'The details of the card payments?' McNab said.

Barry looked a little flustered. 'I'll get them for you.'

'Later,' McNab said, pushing the cleared plate to one side and easing back in his seat. 'I have a couple of questions to ask you.'

'I've told you everything I know,' Barry protested.

'Not everything.' McNab gave Barry time to worry about what was coming next, before asking, 'Have you had an appendectomy?'

Puzzlement flooded Barry's face. 'What?'

'Have you had your appendix taken out?'

'What's my appendix got to do with anything?'

McNab pushed his mobile across the table. On the screen was the image of the drawing of the man that just might be Barry, with a stitched scar on his abdomen.

Barry stared down at the sketch in disbelief.

'What is this?'

'The rune below says it's someone called Barry. So I'd hazard a guess and say it's you, assuming the size of the genitals are exaggerated.'

Barry pushed the mobile away from him, but said nothing.

'These sexual encounters with Leila. Did they involve tying you together with a red cingulum and casting a spell when you climaxed?'

Barry's face was now a tumult of emotions. If asked to translate them into a well-known phrase or saying, McNab would have settled for *I'm fucked*.

Barry gave up. 'Okay. Okay. That's what she was into, and I didn't see any harm in it.'

'We'll require you to give a DNA sample.'

'But I was here the night she died. I have witnesses.'

McNab was about to ask Barry where he'd been on the night Shannon had died, when the door opened and a tall, slim, auburn-haired guy walked in.

Barry sprung to his feet. 'We're not open yet, mate.'

The guy turned and, seeing Barry's warning expression, immediately backed towards the door, but McNab was there before him.

'Of course they're open. I've just had breakfast,' McNab said with a smile. 'Take a seat and Barry here will serve you. Won't you, Barry?'

The newcomer hesitated, trying to weigh up the situation. There was no doubt in McNab's mind that these two men knew one another. He also suspected that the man standing nervously in front of him was Leila Hardy's brother.

'So, Danny, we meet at last.'

The impasse had endured until McNab introduced himself as Detective Sergeant McNab, investigating officer in the Leila Hardy murder enquiry. The stark announcement appeared to have the desired effect. Danny no longer resembled a colt about to bolt, although he definitely still wanted to.

McNab gestured him to take a seat and promptly ordered a worried Barry to bring more coffee.

When Barry took himself off, albeit reluctantly, McNab observed the troubled young man before him.

'I'm very sorry about your sister—'

Danny broke into McNab's attempt at sympathy. 'Have you found the bastard who did it?'

'Not yet,' McNab admitted.

'Why not? He was seen leaving the pub with her.'

'So you've been following the investigation. Yet you didn't get in touch with us?'

'I didn't need you to tell me Leila was dead.' His voice broke a little on her name.

'But we need you to identify her body.'

Danny looked shocked at the prospect. 'Shannon Jones, her mate, can do that. She saw her more often than me.'

'You and your sister weren't on speaking terms?' McNab said.

'We got on okay. We just didn't hang out together.'

'That doesn't explain why you avoided contacting us, especially under the circumstances.'

Danny turned on him at that. 'You should be looking for the bastard who killed my sister. Not trying to find me.'

Nothing is right about this interchange.

The young man before him was obviously shocked and angry about his sister's death, yet had deliberately not come forward to speak to the police. Why?

'Did you know your sister was a Witch?' McNab said.

'A Wiccan. She was a Wiccan,' Danny spat back. 'And, yes, I knew. There's no crime in that.'

'No. But she may have died because of it.'

Danny should have reacted to that announcement, but didn't. No shock. No demand to know why McNab had said such a thing. Just a closed-down expression that suggested to McNab that Danny Hardy already suspected that to be the case.

Just then, Barry arrived back with the coffee.

'Join us,' McNab ordered.

It seemed that Barry might protest, but then thought the better of it.

171

McNab waited until he was seated then looked pointedly from one to the other, before stating, 'Shannon Jones is dead. She was found murdered in her flat yesterday.'

Both men's shocked reaction to this announcement was instantaneous and apparently genuine, leading McNab to surmise that Barry had known Shannon better than he'd admitted up to now.

Danny, suddenly suspicious, eyed McNab. 'You fucking bastard. You're lying.'

'It's not a lie,' McNab said. 'I was the one who found her.'

Danny muttered some obscenity under his breath and stood up.

'If you're not arresting me, I'd like to leave.'

McNab realized that despite his announcement, or because of it, the discussion was at an end. He contemplated ordering Danny to stick around a while longer, but decided he would keep him until later.

'You are both required to report to the police station within twenty-four hours to give a statement and provide a DNA sample.' He turned specifically to Danny. 'You will also formally identify your sister.'

25

DI Bill Wilson and Detective Superintendent Sutherland went back a long way. The road they'd travelled together had often been a rocky one, with bad blood on occasion. Something which Bill chose not to dwell on, although Sutherland liked to allude to it now and again. The rocky and bloody patches usually featured DS Michael Joseph McNab. As it did again today.

Sutherland was a man Bill thought he understood. They were similar in age, both married, with teenage children, although their careers had not followed similar paths. Bill had always sought to stay close to front-line policing. Sutherland, on the other hand, had striven to get away from it as swiftly as possible. At times, Bill thought the super had forgotten what it really meant to be a detective. What had to be done, sometimes outside the rule book, to get results.

The image before him now confirmed this – the carefully groomed hair, the smart uniform, even the neatness of the desk, suggested someone who had forgotten that life and death was as disordered as those involved in it.

Apparently there had been some *disquiet* regarding McNab's participation in the current murder case. Bill had interrupted the doublespeak at this point, to remind Sutherland that it had been DS McNab who'd had the sense to check on Shannon Jones.

'And forced entry in the process,' Sutherland said.

'And that's what the *disquiet* is about?'

'McNab does not maintain the discipline of a police officer. He acts like a wild card with no respect for the law, which has been, I must remind you, a big contributor in his downfall.'

'He caught Stonewarrior, sir,' Bill reminded him, 'when the combined might of the UK police forces couldn't.'

'You exaggerate, Inspector.'

Bill bit back a retort. Annoying Sutherland further wouldn't help McNab's case.

'So there isn't an official complaint, just some *disquiet?*' Bill tried to nail down the reason for his summons.

'I thought it apt to remind you that DS McNab is your responsibility.'

'I am aware of that, sir.'

Sutherland shot him the look of a superior making a point of his superiority.

Bill ignored it. 'Is that all, sir?'

On Sutherland's curt nod, Bill exited.

So there was *disquiet* about the investigation. He would have put it more forcibly than that. And it had nothing to do with McNab's part in it. Bill's *disquiet* came from the fact that they had not yet picked up their main suspect, despite numerous showings of the CCTV footage. And now they were about to release details of the Shannon Jones murder.

In his opinion it was no unlucky coincidence that Shannon Jones had met her death so swiftly after that of her friend. Neither death, he thought, was random. Both had been planned, but the reason for them escaped him. True, it might be that the second killing had occurred because the perpetrator viewed Shannon as a threat to his continued freedom. But Shannon Jones hadn't been the only one to see the suspect that night in the pub. The barman McNab had interviewed had given a good description, even added to it with details of the expensive watch and wallet. If Shannon had been in danger because she'd had a close-up of their suspect, so too was the barman.

And what about the suspect's mate, who was even more elusive? If he was innocent of any wrongdoing, why hadn't he come forward? Then again, maybe the deaths were the work of two men rather than one.

Bill re-entered his office and took up residence in his swivel chair, turning it to face the window with its view over his city. He registered that he was grateful to be back here with more to think about than Margaret's illness and was then flooded with guilt that he had stopped thinking about it, even for a moment.

But dwelling on Margaret's cancer hadn't stopped it returning and wouldn't make it go away. That's what she'd said when confronting him with her demand that he go back to work. Thinking about an investigation, on the other hand, could help solve it.

His wife was a wise and courageous woman, both attributes Bill acknowledged she had in greater abundance than her husband.

On Margaret's orders, Bill now turned his thinking skills back to the task in hand.

Rhona's recent revelation regarding possible DNA identification of the nine men whose sketches were in the dolls could be a game changer, but only if they were already on the database, and that was only a possibility if they'd already been found guilty of a crime.

*

There were a number of presumptive tests used in the detection of semen which weren't dependent on the presence of sperm cells. One was the acid phosphatase (ACP) test, used both in the search for seminal stains and in their presumptive identification. ACP was an enzyme secreted by the prostate gland and found in very high concentrations in seminal fluid compared to other bodily fluids. If a stain was seminal fluid, exposure to the ACP test would result in a purple colour in less than half a minute. However, the colour also developed when other bodily fluids were present, such as vaginal fluid, although the reaction time was much longer.

The definitive test, the one Rhona had chosen to use, was the p30, which detected the presence of a protein of the same name produced by the prostate gland. Among bodily fluids, p30 was found almost exclusively in seminal liquid. Its other advantage was that the identification of semen was unaffected by the absence of spermatozoa. So if the owner of the seminal fluid had had a vasectomy, or was affected by a condition known as azoospermia, it didn't matter.

Once the existence of seminal fluid on the nine pieces of paper stored in the dolls had been established, the next step was to produce a DNA profile for each of them and run them through the database. Besides DNA profiles, they'd already amassed a sizable collection of trace evidence – hair, fibres, skin flakes, urine traces from the toilet, vomit, fingerprints and even a naked footprint. All useful in building up a picture of who had been in Leila's flat. Even the chirality of the knots used in the noose made from the cingulum provided another piece of the jigsaw.

Rhona checked the time on the wall clock. If she was going to Edinburgh with McNab, she would have to get a move on. Go home, eat, change and be ready for his arrival. Chrissy had departed already, having not yet solved the mystery of McNab's love life. Before leaving she'd instructed Rhona in the art of interrogation. Not for the first time Rhona had thought Chrissy would make a good detective.

'Why don't you just call him?' Rhona had suggested. 'After all, you two are bosom buddies.'

It seemed Chrissy had already considered doing that. 'He would see it as failure on my part that I had to ask,' Rhona had been told, with an exaggerated sigh.

Rhona had found the only way to put an end to the conversation was to go into the lab and firmly shut the door.

She eventually left at seven. On the way home she stopped at the deli and bought some cold cuts and potato salad. One thing Sean had done by intermittently reappearing in her life had been to highlight the paucity of her culinary horizons – namely, pepperoni pizza and no. 12 on the Chinese menu. Both fell short of Sean's freshly cooked food. The cold cuts and potato salad weren't freshly cooked either, but at least they offered some variety.

Showered, Rhona contemplated what should be worn to the meeting of a Witches' coven. Obviously if one had a gown, what was worn beneath, if anything, didn't matter. Eventually, having dressed as normal, she settled down to her deli meal.

The buzzer sounded dead on eight o'clock. Approaching McNab's car, Rhona found Magnus already in the passenger seat and registered that the two men looked relatively comfortable in one another's company, which was as surprising as McNab's new loved-up persona.

McNab drove in his usual fashion, reminding Rhona why she preferred to travel in the back when he was at the wheel. Judging by the stiff set of Magnus's shoulders, he was bracing himself rather than openly gripping the seat.

Once on the motorway, things improved a little. The traffic was relatively thin, the road straight. McNab cruised along at just over seventy, slowing for speed cameras where necessary. Magnus relaxed a little and Rhona decided it was time to bring both of them up to date on the sketches and the probability of DNA profiles from the deposits of semen.

'I showed Barry Fraser the sketch with his name under it,' McNab said. 'By his reaction, I would say he thought it might be him. He also admitted to the cingulum playing a role in his encounters with Leila.'

'Did he have any idea who the others were?' Magnus asked.

'I didn't reveal there were nine. I'll keep that for when he comes in for his DNA test.' McNab paused. 'I also ran into Danny Hardy, who seems to be mates with Barry.'

'Did Danny know what his sister was involved with?' Rhona asked after McNab had described their encounter.

'He knew she was a Wiccan. Said there was no law against it, and he's right.' McNab looked about to add something, then didn't.

Magnus had remained silent during McNab's story, but Rhona could tell by his expression that he was deep in thought. Her rendition of his name had no effect, so Rhona tried again.

'Magnus?'

This time he did respond. 'I wonder if the nine men involved are a defined group.'

'You mean like a coven?' Rhona said.

McNab again looked as if he would say something, then stopped.

'That's twice you've done that,' Rhona accused him. 'What is it?'

There was a moment's silence, then he said, 'A workmate of Leila's thought she was selling sex magick.'

'Someone from the library?'

McNab nodded. 'Her name's Freya Devine. She's a PhD student in medieval history and also a Wiccan.'

'So there were actually three of them?' Rhona said.

'Freya didn't know about the other two until they met at the Edinburgh coven. Like her, they weren't members, just visitors.'

'Are you sure she was telling you the truth?' Magnus joined in with Rhona's concern.

Now McNab's *yes* sounded slightly hesitant. 'They weren't close friends, not like Shannon and Leila.'

'So she couldn't be linked to them other than through the library?' Magnus said.

'No,' McNab said in a manner which indicated he no longer wished to discuss the woman in question, which immediately raised suspicions in Rhona's mind.

Was this the female Chrissy had been seeking?

'I'd like to talk to Freya Devine,' Magnus said. 'Is that possible?'

By the set of McNab's jaw, he was now regretting ever mentioning her name.

'Maybe.'

Magnus looked as though he might pursue this, but catching Rhona's warning glance, wisely decided not to.

26

Rhona had never visited the Vaults before, although she knew about them.

The series of chambers, up to 120, had been formed by the building of the nineteen arches of the South Bridge during the 1700s. Originally used to house taverns and tradesmen and as stores for illicit goods, they'd eventually become home to the poor of Edinburgh.

After they too had moved out in the 1800s, the caverns had been filled with the detritus of those who lived or worked above ground.

Now, they were a popular location for ghost tours and in this case a coven meeting.

The owner of this section of the Vaults warned them as he threw open the gates that the ground was uneven.

'Some of the caverns have power but the passage is unlit, so watch your step.'

McNab had had the sense to bring a torch, as had Rhona, but even then the going was tricky, the stone floor rising and falling intermittently.

The owner gave them a running commentary as they walked, which included a complaint about a band that had taken to practising in one of the caverns without paying for the privilege.

'The coven, on the other hand, are excellent tenants,

although they haven't met for a while due to the warlock being in hospital with gallstones.'

There was a pregnant silence before McNab ventured, 'I take it there are no spells to prevent gallstones.'

'It seems not.'

They made one stop before their destination, orchestrated by Magnus who asked why an empty cavern had a ring of large stones set out on the floor.

'The coven say the room had an evil presence which they're trying to contain within the stones,' the owner told them. 'They advise that no one steps within the circle.'

Rhona heard a muttered 'Fuck's sake' from McNab, thankfully at low level.

A few yards further on, they stopped outside a metal grille with a gate, through which they could see a room. Candlelit, with an altar, the floor had a painting of a five-pointed star and was surrounded by nine low stools with red cushions.

At first it seemed there was no one in there, until a figure in a long black embroidered robe stepped into view.

'Derek,' said the owner, 'I've brought your visitors.'

The man who came towards them was middle-aged, stout and balding. He unlocked the gate and, swinging it wide, invited them to enter. His voice was deep and melodious, reminding Rhona of a Church of Scotland minister.

McNab showed his ID and introduced Rhona as Dr MacLeod and Magnus as Professor Pirie. Derek gave his surname as White and welcomed them.

'The others should arrive shortly. Would you prefer we wait?'

'We can start without them,' McNab said.

'Of course.'

Magnus had already wandered away, apparently intent on examining the room and its artefacts. Rhona stayed close to McNab, interested in how the interchange would develop.

'I understand you had three visitors at your last meeting?' McNab began.

'Yes. As I said on the phone. Three young women.'

'Were they together?'

'Two were. The other came alone. She was a post-grad student at Glasgow who got in touch with me about her thesis on Witchcraft.'

'And the other two?'

'They were on a night out in Edinburgh and asked to drop by.'

'Were they known to anyone in your circle?'

'Not that I am aware of.'

'Then how did they get in touch?'

'There's a shop in Glasgow on the High Street. They contacted me through the owners.'

By now people were filtering in, glancing with interest at the visitors as they donned gowns and made ready for whatever was in store. They all looked perfectly normal. Most were middle-aged, although there was a younger man among their ranks who came over as soon as he spotted McNab.

'DS McNab? I'm Joe, Ollie's mate from uni.'

They shook hands.

'Great job on the *Stonewarrior* case. Ollie told me all about it, or at least what he was permitted to tell,' he added cautiously.

'We'll have to start the ceremony soon,' Derek interrupted. 'So, if you'd like to talk to the others?'

Being surrounded by a group of people dressed in star

and moon embroidered gowns wasn't in McNab's comfort zone, but he did the job admirably, giving out just enough information and getting a good response. Many hadn't picked up on the death of Leila Hardy, or hadn't linked any mention of the murder to their recent visitors. At the news of the second death, a babble of noise erupted.

McNab held up his hand for silence.

'The murder of Shannon so soon after Leila suggests that their deaths may be linked. Of course, that link may not be because of their involvement with Wicca, but the nature of both crime scenes suggests that it might.'

McNab then gave brief details of the room of dolls and of the cingulum, which caused a lot of consternation. Rhona had been studying the reactions of the group while McNab talked. All were distressed, but one man, in particular, had looked increasingly uneasy. By the sheen on his skin he was sweating, although the vaults were cool, verging on cold. On one occasion he had darted a look towards Rhona and swiftly away again when he realized she was watching him. After that he'd made a point of not catching her eye.

When McNab began talking about the men they believed Leila had performed sex magick with, the man had swiftly made an exit. Rhona followed to find him in the passageway leaning against the wall.

'Are you okay?'

'I'm a little claustrophobic,' he explained. 'The room is small and with the extra people . . .' He tailed off.

'It wasn't a pleasant story to listen to,' Rhona said.

'No. It wasn't.'

'Did you meet the women when they visited?'

He nodded. 'They were young and enthusiastic.'

'And now they're dead.'

He looked sick at that.

'Is there anything you know that might help find who killed them?'

He was struggling with himself. Rhona wasn't sure if his story of claustrophobia was true, or whether he, like most people, merely struggled with the horror of murder. She, McNab and even Magnus forgot that the world they inhabited was something unimaginable to people living ordinary lives, even if, like the man before her, they practised Witchcraft.

'I'm sorry, I didn't mean to upset you.'

'I am upset, but more because I may have been a party to what happened to those young women.'

When they'd emerged from underground Edinburgh, McNab had quickly located the nearest pub, where they were now seated in a quiet corner. The man, whose name was Maurice, had a large brandy in front of him, half of which he'd already consumed. Minus his robe, he looked more like a bank manager than a warlock. A frightened one.

'When she asked my advice, I reminded her of the creed,' he said.

'*An' it harm none, do what thou wilt,*' Magnus quoted.

Maurice looked swiftly at him. 'Yes. There was no harm intended, she assured me of that.'

'Then what was intended?' McNab said sharply.

'The men wanted something important to their future prosperity, she said.'

'They all wanted the same thing?'

Maurice shook his head as if trying to remember. 'They were in it in some way together, so it was binding on them, I think.'

'So you advised her to keep a record?'

'Yes.'

'To blackmail them?'

He looked shocked by that. 'No. Sexual magick is made powerful by the life force. Men's seed is that force. More powerful than a name.'

'To know a person's name is to have a hold over them. For to know the name is to be able to conjure with it,' McNab said, with a glance at Magnus. 'Did she say how many men were involved?'

'No, she didn't.'

'Did *you* suggest she sketch them?' Rhona asked.

'I suggested a drawing would serve in place of a clay model.' He drank the remainder of his brandy, his hand shaking as he raised the glass to his mouth.

'Who was party to this discussion?' McNab said.

'Only Leila. She asked to speak with me alone after the ceremony.'

'The other two weren't involved?'

'The one called Freya left first. The other two stayed until the end. That's when Leila spoke to me.'

'Why you?' McNab said.

'She'd read a pamphlet I'd written about sexual magick.'

Rhona suspected he was telling the truth. Magnus's expression suggested he did too. McNab, ever the detective, worked on the assumption that everyone was lying until proved otherwise.

'Would you be willing to give a DNA sample?' Rhona said. 'To prove you weren't one of the group?'

Maurice looked surprised by the request, then relieved.

'Of course. Can I give it now?'

'If Detective Sergeant McNab is okay with that, we can do it now.'

McNab nodded and stood up, masking the general view while Rhona swiftly donned gloves, took a mouth swab, slipped it in a container and put it in her bag.

Now that he had seemingly proved his innocence, Maurice relaxed, going so far as to offer to buy them a drink. McNab said thanks, but no thanks. They had to get back to Glasgow.

They left him there at the bar buying himself another. Confession and forensic science had seemingly restored him to his former innocent self.

The journey home was memorable mostly for its silence. What had happened had given them all food for thought. Rhona was glad she'd come with the two men, but wasn't sure her presence had achieved much, apart from one DNA sample.

Magnus, whatever his thoughts, had chosen not to share them. McNab was keyed up. Rhona could tell that by the nerve that beat in his cheek, but he too remained silent.

On entering Glasgow, McNab headed for Rhona's place first. She'd hoped to talk to him in private about Freya Devine, but that wasn't to be.

As the car drove off, Rhona had the distinct impression that McNab was determined on a private conversation, but not with her.

27

McNab waited until he'd dropped Magnus before calling Freya. Almost midnight, he decided to only let it ring three times. If she didn't answer, he would assume she was asleep and wait until the morning to get in touch with her.

Freya answered on the second ring.

'You're still up?' he said.

'I'm a Witch, remember? I'm contemplating the full moon.'

She sounded pleased to hear from him, at least McNab let himself think so.

'Where are you?' she said.

'In the car, heading home.'

'Come here instead.'

When he didn't immediately answer, she said, 'It's late, I know.'

'I don't care about the time.'

'Then you'll come?'

'Yes.'

She told him the address.

'I'll be there in ten minutes.'

McNab did a great deal of thinking in those ten minutes. Mainly around the question: *What the hell am I doing?* Regardless of how he might try and persuade himself otherwise, Freya was part of the investigation and he was pursuing a relationship with her. Not professional and not wise. But what worried him more was the concerned reaction of Rhona and Magnus to Freya's existence. True, Maurice had confirmed that the three women hadn't come together to the coven, which meant Freya had told McNab the truth about that. *But*. And this was the big but. The three women were connected by Wicca, and whatever he might think of that, it might place Freya in danger.

Which is why I need to watch over her.

It was a good line to feed himself, he thought, as he pressed her buzzer. She answered immediately and freed the door. She was waiting for him on the first landing. There was a moment's hesitation as neither of them knew quite how to greet one another.

Freya settled for a smile and ushered him inside.

McNab followed her through to an open-plan room with a sitting area and kitchen combined. A large bay window gave a distant view of the university towers.

'Coffee?' she said.

McNab answered in the affirmative, although he would have preferred alcohol.

She was dressed in tracksuit bottoms and a T-shirt and he thought she looked beautiful. While they waited for the coffee, he told her he'd been at the coven meeting in the Vaults.

She registered this with surprise. 'Tonight?'

He nodded. 'That's where I was coming from when I called you.'

Her open look suggested she wasn't worried about what he'd discovered there, because she'd told him the truth about her visit. McNab was so used to people lying to him, or at the very least avoiding the truth, he found her honesty disconcerting.

'Was it helpful?' she finally said.

'It was.' McNab took a mouthful of coffee. 'Do you know anything about a pamphlet on sexual magick?'

She thought for a moment. 'I've seen incunables on sexual magick.'

'What's an incunable?'

She smiled at his confusion. 'A book or pamphlet printed in Europe, before the year 1501.'

'This pamphlet is more recent. Written by a man called Maurice Wade. A member of the Edinburgh coven.'

She shook her head. 'I haven't seen it. Is it important?'

'That's why Leila was there, to speak to him about it.'

She looked thoughtful at that. 'So what I said was true? She was performing sex magick?'

'According to Maurice, yes, she was.'

'And you think that's why she died?'

McNab was suddenly weary of it all. He didn't want to talk about violent death with this woman. He wanted to be here for a different reason.

As though reading his mind, Freya said, 'Shall we go to bed?'

McNab hadn't been invited into a woman's bedroom for what felt like forever. His sexual encounters, even with Rhona, had not been at her place. Iona had turned up at his unkempt, unpleasant-smelling flat and seemingly hadn't cared. But then, if you're high on drugs and drink, who does?

McNab was stone cold sober now, and he cared.

This time *she* led him through to the bedroom.

The scent of her was here in abundance, encompassing

him, heightening his senses. He had the buzz, but it wasn't from drink.

She chose to undress him first. Her gentle moves excited him more than any mad tearing off of clothes. Standing before her was a revelation. He had never felt so naked before, physically or emotionally. The feeling both frightened him and flooded him with pleasure.

Undressing Freya, he was seized by an overwhelming need to protect her.

No one will frighten or hurt you while I'm here.

McNab imagined he only thought the words, but realized by her reaction that he must have said them out loud.

She touched his cheek and it felt like fire.

When he woke she was beside him. That in itself filled McNab with wonder. If he was honest, most of his couplings involved himself or the woman leaving in the middle of the night. In truth, he often preferred it that way. No awkward morning silences. No uncomfortable goodbyes. No lies about calling them.

Freya was still asleep, her expression content, her breathing quietly even.

He took time to study her in detail, feeling wonder that someone so lovely would invite him into her bed. Perhaps sensing his attention, she opened her eyes.

'Good morning,' he said.

She smiled and drew him to her.

He stayed to breakfast, which was another first. Minus a hangover, loved up and verging on happy, McNab felt like a stranger to himself. The more cynical side of him muttered an occasional internal *It won't last*, which he did his best to ignore.

Freya pottered about, brewing fresh coffee, toasting bagels and spreading them with honey. Watching her eat one, her tongue licking the honey from her lips, was an erotic experience. McNab realized if he didn't leave soon, he was unlikely to leave at all.

He stood up.

'You have to go to work,' she said, sounding sorry.

'Don't you?'

She nodded. 'I have a thesis to research and write.'

'On Witchcraft.'

She smiled. 'Does that worry you?'

'I spend my days chasing killers. Does that worry you?'

A shadow crossed her face, making him want to take back the words. They had said nothing of the case from the moment she'd led him to her bed. He wanted to keep it that way.

'Can I phone you later?' McNab said.

'Yes, Michael.'

McNab was unused to being called by his first name, but found he liked it. When Freya said it, he forgot for a moment that he was Detective Sergeant McNab. The feeling didn't last long. He was barely out of the building when his phone rang.

'Dr MacLeod. This is an early call.'

'Can you come by the lab?'

'Not if you intend interrogating me,' he said, keeping his voice light.

'There's something you should know.'

'Okay,' McNab said, noting her serious tone. 'I'm on my way.'

His first instinct was that the secret he shared with Rhona was no longer a secret. That would account for her obvious concern. Also, she wouldn't want to reveal this in a phone call, hence the request for his lab visit. McNab's joie de vivre evaporated and he was back in the real world.

She was in her office when he arrived. Security had buzzed him in, commenting on his early visit, to which McNab had feigned a jocular reply. A mood he was no longer in. Dread had descended again. The dread he used to experience when he first opened his gritty eyes and knew he had another day to face, half of which would involve a hangover. The light mood with Freya had gone so quickly, McNab questioned whether it had really happened or whether it could ever happen again.

Seeing Rhona only served to heighten this feeling.

Her studied look reminded him that Dr Rhona MacLeod was the only woman who had ever come close to *knowing* him, and not just in the biblical sense.

'It's Freya Devine,' he said, seeing no point in hiding the fact from Rhona.

She smiled and he thought it was from pleasure on his behalf. 'I thought so.'

'I went to see her last night.' His confession rolled on like a Catholic who'd just found a long-sought-for priest.

She nodded, although he detected her thoughts were elsewhere.

'So why am I here?' he ventured.

She caught his look. 'It isn't about your love life or about . . . the other matter.'

McNab registered relief.

'What is it then?'

28

Her intuition had been right.

The results were in for the first samples she'd dispatched last night before heading for Edinburgh. Of the five she'd sent, four had registered against the Scottish Database as a no show, which meant the men involved had not been convicted of a crime north of the border. The fifth result was rather unexpected.

Rhona handed McNab the printout. 'This one found a match, but the details have been withheld. From me, at least.'

McNab scrutinized the paper. 'Has this ever happened to a search you've done before?'

'No, but I did have forensic evidence removed from the lab fridge once. A dismembered foot found on a beach in Skye. The Ministry of Defence decided they preferred to deal with it themselves.'

'The MOD interfered with your investigation?'

'They took it over in the interests of national security.'

It was a long and sorry tale, which had happened before she and McNab had met, but the memory of the mishandling of the case and its aftermath still rankled.

McNab was studying her. 'You think this is something similar?' he said.

'I think that someone in a position of authority doesn't

want this particular person to be *openly* identified as part of the investigation.'

She watched as McNab processed what that might mean, something Rhona had done already. Just because your details were currently on the database didn't mean you were guilty of a crime. You may have given a DNA sample voluntarily in an investigation for the purposes of elimination, just as Maurice had done last night.

It might be that the case you were attached to hadn't yet reached a conclusion. Under Scots law, your details would be removed from the Scottish Database once the case was decided, or you were not charged with an offence. They only remained there if you were found guilty. There was one exception to this, which involved sexual offences, where a suspect, not convicted, would have their details retained for three years.

English law was different. Once on the database you stayed there, even if innocent of any crime. All profiles on the Scottish DNA Database (except volunteers for intelligence-led screenings) were exported to the National DNA Database, which gave all police forces throughout the UK the ability to search for profile and crime-scene matches. But once you were removed from the Scottish Database, you then had to be removed from NDNA.

McNab was well aware of all of this, so Rhona didn't remind him. The true consequence for the investigation of being denied access to the details of the match, he got immediately.

'If Magnus is right and we do have a group of nine, then having a lead on one of them could take us to the other eight,' McNab said.

'My thoughts exactly.'

'We can't let this go unchallenged.'

'I agree.'

'So?'

Rhona took a moment to savour the fact that McNab was asking for her advice. Her first instinct when she'd viewed the printout had been not to show it to McNab. The old McNab would have acted first and thought about the consequences later, but this wasn't the old McNab.

'I think you should take this to the boss,' Rhona said.

All leads should be followed and all possibilities eliminated – that was the rule of an investigation. Bill had said exactly that when he'd sought an interview with Superintendent Sutherland to ask why details of the search match had been denied to the submitting forensic scientist, Dr MacLeod.

Now that he had been granted leave to state his case, Bill continued, 'DS McNab's work with Professor Pirie leads us to believe the nine men may form a group. Identify one and we may be able to identify them all.'

Sutherland interrupted before Bill could continue.

'The person you refer to is not a suspect, and their connection with the case will be dealt with at a higher level.'

Bill felt his anger rising. 'Who is this special case?'

'You don't need to know,' Sutherland said curtly.

'If you want me to explain why this is necessary to my team, *I* need to know who we're shielding and why.'

Sutherland considered this, then appeared to come to a decision.

'The owner of one of the DNA samples presented himself to a senior officer as soon as the case hit the news. He met the victim briefly, some months ago. I repeat, he is not a suspect.'

'That's for me to decide,' Bill retorted.

'On the contrary, Inspector, it is for me to decide.' Sutherland's tone had turned icy.

So the identity of someone currently on the database had to be kept secret. Those who worked in crime enforcement and were therefore likely to visit crime scenes had their DNA recorded for elimination purposes. In fact, so did anyone visiting a crime scene in an official capacity. His was on there, as was McNab's and Rhona's.

Bill took a calculated guess. 'He's one of ours.'

When Sutherland didn't respond, Bill tried a few possibilities. 'A serving police officer? Someone working undercover? Or just someone very important?'

The only evidence that he might have hit home was a blink at the final suggestion on his list. Hardly evidence that would hold up in court, but intriguing nonetheless.

Sutherland suddenly gave full attention to some papers on his desk. 'Thank you, Detective Inspector, that will be all.'

Summarily dismissed, Bill took his leave, accepting he'd met a dead end. Besides, he had other ways of discovering the truth. He didn't command a room full of eager detectives for nothing.

The thought briefly occurred that Sutherland's earlier concern about McNab's role in the investigation had been occasioned by this development. McNab had a reputation for ferreting out information which many of those in positions of power would prefer to keep out of the public eye.

Politics and policing – a shit sandwich, but one that was served up all too frequently in his opinion.

Bill glanced at his watch. It was time to talk to the troops.

29

The nightmare had been sudden, vivid and frighteningly realistic.

The green-eyed girl's intonations as she tightened the cord that bound them together. His determined thrusts and the resulting ecstasy which became the sole reason for his being.

Then the hand stuffed something into her mouth, silencing her words.

But whose hand?

Then she was choking, the green eyes bulging with fear, as he fell into the sweet abyss of climax, where nothing and no one mattered more than his own release.

Mark had woken at that point, launching himself upright, bathed in sweat, gasping for air, his heart banging painfully against his ribs.

Jesus.

He'd taken a deep breath and willed his heart to slow. When it hadn't, he'd risen and gone through to the kitchen. Throwing open the freezer door, he'd upended an open bag of ice on the kitchen surface, sending cubes slithering to the floor.

Grabbing some, he'd shoved them in his mouth. The instant and shattering cold had stunned him, but he'd known it would work. Apparently there was a nerve in the roof of your mouth. If you froze it, your heart slowed. He'd learned the trick from his mother, although her galloping and erratic heartbeat was a symptom of her illness and owed nothing to over-indulgence in coke and alcohol.

Or to guilt-ridden nightmares.

As his heart had finally begun to slow, the tight pain in his chest had loosened its grip. Mark had turned and spat the remains of the ice in the sink.

I'm doing too much coke. That's the reason.

He'd opened the balcony doors and stepped outside. In the distance, the imposing shadow of Arthur's Seat had been a blot on a midnight horizon. Up in the penthouse flat, he'd always considered himself on a par with the rock, with the scattered lights of Edinburgh spread out below him.

Which was why he'd bought the flat.

Thinking of buying the flat had immediately brought his father to mind, because a large chunk of the deposit had come from him, and Mark hadn't wanted to think about that.

He'd turned from the view then, and gone back inside. As he'd closed the patio doors he'd tried to relive his earlier success with Jeff. Jeff had definitely been contained for the moment. If Mark went to the police, Jeff's presence that night would also be revealed. And no upwardly mobile young lawyer would want to be associated with a suspect in a murder enquiry.

At that point Mark had congratulated himself. He'd been so convincing with Jeff, he'd almost believed it himself. Until an internal voice had reminded him yet again . . .

You did have sex with the girl and she died while you were in that flat.

On re-entering, he'd picked up his mobile from the coffee table and had noted an unread text from Emilie and, worse, a voicemail from his father.

The text he'd left unopened. The voicemail was another matter.

His heart speeding up again, Mark had listened to voice-mail service.

The call had come in at eleven, shortly after he'd passed out on the bed.

'I want to speak to you, Mark,' the cultured Edinburgh voice said. 'Come to my club at eight, tomorrow night.'

Mark had dropped the mobile at this point as though it was red hot.

Shit! Why did his father want to see him? What had he done wrong now?

Then a terrible thought had struck. Had his father seen the CCTV footage? Had he recognized his only son?

Jesus fuck.

He'd immediately started thinking of a list of possible excuses not to go. None of which, he knew, would be accepted. What his father wanted, his father got.

He will know something's wrong. He will know I'm lying.

A High Court judge for twenty years, his father could spot a liar with ease.

The rest of the night had brought little sleep, but he had made it into work at the bank this morning, although there wasn't much actual work being done.

Mark tried to take his mind off the meeting with his father and concentrate on the task in hand. The presentation was due to be given tomorrow and he'd prepared less than a third of it.

Who the fuck cares?

I'll care when I have to stand up in a room full of people and talk about it.

When his attempt to focus didn't work, Mark considered a trip to the Gents for a line of coke. Maybe half a line would be enough to get his enthusiasm going. If he finished the presentation by the end of the day, he could meet his father with a feeling of success.

The truth was, the *only* way he could face his father tonight was via a line of coke coupled with a very stiff drink, and if he did indulge his father would know. He'd seen too many drugged-up individuals in the dock. Sent many of them down. Including murderers.

I'm not a murderer. I had sex with a girl I met in a bar. It was consensual. In fact, she was the one in charge. I woke to find she wasn't in the bed. I vomited and, embarrassed by this, I went home.

He'd spent the hours awake last night rehearsing his confession. Always missing out the trip through to that room and the image of the girl hanging on the hook behind the swaying dolls.

Mark froze at the memory. Jesus, he couldn't go on like this. It was screwing with his brain.

Maybe I should go to the police? Tell them I was the guy on CCTV. Explain what happened. After all, my father is a High Court judge. That has to count for something?

His mobile pinged, bringing his mind back from that terrifying scenario.

Mark checked the screen to find a photo message from a number he didn't recognize. His first thought was to delete it, but curiosity won instead.

When it opened he stared at the screen for a moment, unsure what he was looking at. It was like one of those puzzle pictures taken at a strange angle to confuse you. Then he made out the plaited red cord. Just as he realized what it was, the image began to move, revealing it as a video clip.

200

It only lasted seconds, but Mark knew the male in the clip was him and the female most definitely the dead girl, bound together in a heart-stopping embrace until . . .

A hand – his hand? – stuffed a cloth in her mouth.

Mark made a dash for the Gents, causing consternation among his colleagues. Entering a cubicle, he immediately rid his stomach of a part-digested lunch of chicken and salad wrap.

A cold sweat swiftly followed. He pulled himself to his feet and flushed the toilet with an unsteady hand. His night-mare was fast becoming a reality. Someone else had been in that flat, in that room, while he was with the girl. They'd even filmed him fucking her. Had filmed him stuffing some-thing into her mouth.

So it *was* true. He *had* made her choke.

Mark couldn't face that thought, or the one that followed on from it. Not without help. He felt in his pocket for the coke and shook out a line on the cistern.

He would say he was feeling ill. A stomach bug. Go home. Try and think this through. He stood, hands gripping the cistern, waiting for the coke to take effect. Then he heard someone enter and Campbell, the guy on the next desk to him, shouted, 'You okay in there, Mark?'

'Not so good, mate. A stomach bug, I think.'

'Go home. I'll tell the boss what happened.'

Mark thanked him. He would leave work, but he wasn't sure if he would go home. If the third person that night knew his mobile number, chances were they knew his address too.

Ten minutes ago, he'd thought he was in deep shit.

Now, Mark acknowledged, it was much worse than that.

30

The two young men waiting in Room 1 stopped their argument immediately she entered, unaware that she'd been listening to it through the door.

The one with dark auburn hair she knew to be Leila's brother without an introduction. The similarity in eye and hair colour was striking. Leila had been beautiful, her brother equally handsome. According to McNab, there was only ten months between them, Leila being the elder. An only child herself, Rhona had no experience of the closeness of siblings, but imagined that with less than a year between them, the brother and sister must have felt like twins. Yet according to McNab, Danny had claimed that he and his sister weren't close.

The argument raging as she'd approached the room had suggested the two men were at odds over Leila's death. How exactly, Rhona wasn't able to make out, except for the fact that they both blamed each other.

As Rhona introduced herself, she was acutely aware of Danny's appraising glance. Barry kept his eyes averted.

'So you're a doctor?' Danny said with a smile.

'Of science,' Rhona replied.

'Still, a bit too important to be taking swabs?'

Rhona let that one go and asked him to open his mouth. From the corner of her eye she noted that Barry looked decidedly worried about what she was doing. Danny on the other hand was gallusness personified. He even gave her a wink as she circled the inside of his mouth with the swab.

When it came to Barry, she saw fear in his eyes, but then again McNab had run a drawing past him which suggested his DNA might have already been found at the scene of crime. If this sample was a match to the semen found inside the doll, then Barry was one of the nine.

'So,' said Danny as she prepared to leave, 'will I see you again, Dr MacLeod?'

Rhona met his challenging look with one of her own.

'Unlikely, unless it's in court.'

Danny didn't like that answer. A cloud suddenly covered those handsome green eyes.

He immediately came back at her with, 'Why would I be in court?'

'To see your sister's killer brought to justice.'

'If you lot ever fucking find him.'

Rhona wanted to say, 'We'll find him, all right,' but chose not to, which she decided irked him even more.

DS Clark and McNab were waiting outside for her.

'Well?' McNab said.

'Barry's worried about the swab, Danny not so much,' she told him.

'Looked like Danny was chatting you up.'

'He *is* very handsome,' Rhona said, with a glance at Janice.

'And knows it,' Janice agreed.

McNab intervened. 'If you have the hots for Danny, I'd better do his interview.'

'Barry's not bad either. He definitely works out,' Janice said.

McNab looked from one woman to the other.

'You're shitting me.'

'Took you a while to work that one out, Detective,' Rhona said as she departed.

Back at the lab she found Chrissy eager to tell her the news regarding McNab's love life. Rhona decided not to burst her bubble by revealing that she knew already. Her plan failed, as she suspected it might. Chrissy McInsh had an eye for a lie.

'You know,' she said accusingly.

'McNab told me himself, first thing this morning.'

'He did?' Chrissy looked taken aback. 'Why would he do that?'

'Confession's good for the soul?' Rhona tried.

Chrissy, the Catholic, didn't go for that. 'He wanted to make you jealous.'

'Why would he want to make me jealous?'

'Were you?'

'No.'

Chrissy eyed her speculatively. 'Is it the real thing?'

'I believe he likes her. Very much,' Rhona said truthfully.

Chrissy seemed at a loss for words at this, but only briefly.

'Well, good on him. He deserves it.'

Rhona couldn't have agreed more.

Danny had been in Glasgow when his sister had died. His excuse for not going on tour was that he'd been ill.

'Ill with what?' McNab said.

'Flu.'

'You went to the doctor?'

'No. I sweated it out and got better.'

'When did you last see your sister?'

Danny threw him an evil look. 'In a drawer in the mortuary twenty minutes ago.'

McNab didn't rise to the bait. 'Before that?'

'I don't keep a diary. Maybe three weeks ago.'

'What did you talk about?'

'She talks. I don't listen.'

'What was the room of dolls in her flat about?'

'Never saw it. Don't go there.'

'Where do you meet then?'

'We have coffee some place.'

And so the conversation had progressed mainly into dead ends. The most important question was where Danny had been on the night his sister died and that was one that demanded an answer.

'I told you. I was ill. So I was in bed.'

'Anyone vouch for that?'

Danny nodded, and McNab could swear he was very pleased with his reply.

'Maggie Carter.'

So the plan was for Maggie to give him an alibi.

'Funny she didn't mention that when I spoke to her.'

'You didn't ask,' Danny said with a smirk.

'Been conducting your own interview?' McNab said.

'A policeman comes to the door, I want to know why.'

McNab had left it there, for the moment. Danny was cocky and confident. Maggie not so much. He had a feeling she had a greater respect for the truth than her flatmate, or lover. Did he think Danny might have killed his sister? Most murders were committed by someone known to the victim. Few were carried out by a stranger.

McNab had a strong feeling that Danny and his sister's

lives were far more intertwined than he had been willing to admit. He also thought Danny had a plan. To do what, he didn't know. He would love to put a tail on Danny if he could convince the boss that it would be worth the man hours and the money. And McNab didn't have anything other than a feeling, yet.

Once he'd finished with Danny, he checked on DS Clark. The room she'd occupied with Barry was empty, so he went to top up his caffeine levels at the machine before seeking her out. This was the time in an investigation when you were bombarded with spurious bits of information, possible witnesses and false leads. It could sometimes feel like you were wading through treacle.

And still no pointers to the man Leila had left the pub with.

McNab was beginning to believe the guy wasn't local. Both Shannon and Barry had maintained he was Scottish, but that didn't mean he lived in Glasgow, or even Scotland. If one or both of the men had been up in Glasgow for the weekend, and departed swiftly afterwards, they had little chance of locating either of them.

If McNab had been a praying man, he would have prayed for some luck.

As he downed the double espresso, a call came in from Ollie.

'Hey, Ollie.'

'I have some good news for you. We found Shannon's mobile.'

'Where?

'Tossed in a litter bin not far from her flat.'

Somebody had just made a big mistake. McNab said a silent thank you to the God he hadn't prayed to.

'It's been damaged, but not badly enough. Want to come and see?'

McNab very much wanted to come and see.

31

As she headed home through Kelvingrove Park, the rain came on. The dark clouds amassing on the horizon as she left the lab should have been enough to warn Rhona of the impending deluge. The first drops were large, although infrequent. They sent the summer-clothed Glaswegians scurrying onwards along the path, or heading for the nearest tree to take shelter.

A flash of lightning split the sky above the Gothic grandeur of the university main building. Seconds later, they were treated to an exaggerated roll of thunder that might have heralded the entry of that master of horror, Boris Karloff.

Then the rain began in earnest.

The force of it on her head and shoulders drove Rhona, like the others, to seek any kind of shelter. Advice about not standing under a tree during a thunderstorm was heeded by no one. Getting soaked was a certainty, being hit by lightning less so.

The panic changed to screams of laughter as the group under the tree squeezed together in an effort to give house room to those who still needed to get under cover. Beside her, a pram, with hood up, provided the best refuge of all, the baby inside gazing out with saucer eyes at the antics of the grown-ups.

The deluge lasted a full fifteen minutes. Tropical rain rather than that usually experienced in Glasgow. Even the term 'pelting' didn't do it justice. Eventually her fellow shelterers grew bold and stepped out into it. Glasgow folk were used to rain, after all, and at least the stuff coming out of the sky today was warm.

Rhona added herself to the departing throng.

Strangely, getting soaked had put a spring in her step. By now the rain had lessened to a warm shower, pleasant and invigorating. The grass steamed and the park turned into a scene from *Avatar* minus the wild beasts and gangly blue inhabitants.

Her mobile rang as she exited the park gates. She hesitated when she saw the name on the screen, but answered nonetheless.

'Where are you?' Sean said.

'Coming out of the park.'

'You're wet?'

'Very.'

A distant roll of thunder emphasized what had just happened.

'I called to ask you out to dinner.'

That foxed her. Rhona played for time. 'When?'

'Tonight.'

'Where?' Rhona suspected it would be his place. Sean considered himself a better cook than most chefs. In that he was probably right.

'You choose,' he said, surprising her even further.

Rhona named a popular restaurant in Ashton Lane.

'We might not get a table, but I'll try,' Sean said. 'I'll text you the time.'

Ringing off, Rhona found herself rather pleased by the

call, and the invitation. Not to mention the prospect of a proper meal, and some male company, unconnected with the investigation.

On entering the flat, she was immediately besieged by Tom, desirous for food and affection. She dealt with both demands, then took herself off for a proper shower, which also involved soap and shampoo.

Dressed and ready, she awaited the promised text. When it finally arrived, she had ten minutes left until the allotted time. According to Sean, he'd waited in her desired restaurant foyer for a full hour in the hope of a no-show or a cancellation, and had finally struck it lucky.

Rhona immediately called herself a taxi. As she headed for the door, she spotted something on the floor. Tom had a habit of bringing in dead things from the roof, where he spent a lot of his time. Her first thought was that it was the remains of a bird.

She considered ignoring it and dealing with it on her return, but that would give Tom time to dissect the carcass, leaving bits scattered throughout the flat for her to step on. Rhona bent for a closer look and discovered it wasn't a dead bird, but a small stick figure made of twigs. It was lying close to the wall under the coat rack, next to a pool of water from her dripping jacket.

How did that get there?

Her first thought was that it had to have been brought in by Tom, but he only had access to the roof. How could such a thing have got on the roof? Rhona glanced at the letter box. Had it arrived that way? Had it been there when she'd first come in?

Her mobile rang a warning that the taxi had arrived.

She could either leave it where it lay and trust Tom not

to dismember it, or take it with her. She opted for the latter, creating a makeshift evidence bag using a couple of clean paper hankies.

The taxi driver, having had no response from the mobile call, was now ringing her buzzer.

Rhona slipped the stick figure into her bag, already aware that her planned evening of no thought of work wasn't to be. A figure made of sticks in her hall she might have contrived to find an explanation for. One with what looked like human hair glued to its head and a red thread wound tightly round its neck would be more difficult.

Double-locking the door, Rhona headed downstairs to the waiting taxi.

The rain having cleared, the people of Glasgow were back out in force to enjoy the evening. During the journey to Ashton Lane, Rhona pondered whether it would have been better to have cancelled the outing in the wake of her find. If she'd done that, Sean would have rightly asked for an explanation and what could she have said?

The deaths of Leila and Shannon had hit the news now big time, especially the Wicca aspects. Although nothing about the Witchcraft angle had been officially released by the police, the tabloids had managed to ferret out that aspect to the story. Passing a newsagent on their way up Byres Road gave evidence of that, the latest headline in the evening paper declaring SECOND GLASGOW WITCH FOUND DEAD.

They were on the third course when Sean finally asked her what was wrong.

Arriving at the restaurant, she'd resolved to put the stick figure out of her mind for this evening at least. There would be time enough tomorrow to consider its implications.

Meeting Sean like this for a meal was bizarre enough, so she'd concentrated in dealing with that, and then found herself enjoying both the food and the company. When Sean was in the mood to entertain the ladies, he couldn't be faulted. The only thing missing in what was obviously a courtship meal, was a serenade on his saxophone. Maybe he had plans to do that later.

But despite Sean's best efforts, he'd found himself with a non-attentive companion.

'This was a bad idea?' he suggested quietly.

In a sudden rush of emotion, Rhona remembered all the reasons why she'd been with Sean. His kindness, the fact he was non-judgemental, and his support when she'd chosen to search for her son, Liam. And when they'd finally met, Liam had taken to Sean in a big way.

'No,' Rhona said. 'It wasn't a bad idea. I just have something on my mind.'

Sean accepted that and didn't ask what the something was. He knew her well enough not to.

Just at that moment the coffee arrived, along with two Irish whiskeys.

When the waitress departed, Sean reached over and took Rhona's hand. That small gesture ruined her resolve. She reached into her bag and placed the parcel on the table, opening it up to expose her find. Against the white of the tablecloth, the twig figure, with its wisps of hair and holes where eyes should be, was a disturbing image.

Whatever Sean had been expecting, it hadn't been this. Rhona watched as he tried to assess what he was looking at.

'May I pick it up?'

'Better not touch it,' Rhona said.

'Where did you find it?'

'In my hall, near the front door, as I was about to leave.'

Sean absorbed her answer and read its implication. 'Has it something to do with the Witchcraft case?'

'I don't know.'

'It's female?'

'I'd say so.'

'And the string round the neck . . .' Sean said.

'Leila Hardy was found with a cingulum round her neck.'

'Cingulum?'

Rhona explained the meaning of the term and what a cingulum was used for.

'So this is a representation of her death?'

'Maybe,' Rhona said.

She placed the stick figure inside a clean napkin and put it back in her bag.

Sean started asking the questions she'd been asking herself.

'Was the lower door open when you got home?'

'No, but by using the common buzzer anyone might be let into the close.'

'How would the person who delivered it know where you lived?'

Rhona shrugged. If someone was determined to find out an address, they probably could.

'Were you followed through the park, maybe?'

Rhona cast her mind back to the torrential rain and standing in close proximity with dozens of others under that tree. It had been like the subway at peak time. Someone could have slipped it in her pocket in the crush, and it could have fallen out when she'd hung up her jacket. She said as much to Sean.

'I think the more important question is why was it delivered?' Sean finally said the words Rhona had been avoiding.

Rhona lifted her whiskey. Having spoken of the figure, she now wanted to forget it, how it had got into her hall and definitely why.

Sean read her expression and interpreted it correctly.

'I'll come back with you.'

32

The New Town Club didn't open its doors to just anyone. Mark Howitt Senior was a member. His son was not. He could be signed in as a guest, but was only allowed access to certain public rooms, such as the one he was in now.

Having already consumed a couple of good measures of high-strength Russian vodka in a pub on the Royal Mile, Mark had also ordered a vodka tonic from the waiter, while awaiting his father's arrival.

Seated in a high-backed leather chair, with the drink on a polished table next to him, he contemplated the thick-carpeted, wood-panelled room, which hadn't changed since the first time he'd been allowed entry to the hallowed halls. It struck him that this stuffy room resembled his father. Both, in Mark's eyes, had always been old.

His father had consistently looked, and acted, the same throughout Mark's childhood, adolescence and early adult-hood. A formidable figure, he had always seemed remote, even when at home in the large town house in central Edinburgh which the family had shared.

Mark had never seen his parents kiss or even embrace in public, or at home, except for a peck on the cheek. As an adolescent, he'd spent a lot of time wondering if they ever had sex. They'd definitely had it once because he was here, but there was a phase when he thought he might have been adopted, because he felt sure he was in no way genetically connected to his father.

On the other hand, Mark loved his mother, quite fiercely at times. He couldn't have said why, but she generated an affection in him which he found worrying, because it was seldom repeated in his other personal female relationships. His mother was kind, loving, thoughtful and wished her son well. She didn't cling to him, but almost pushed him away, so that he might 'find his own feet'.

Mark sometimes thought it was because she wanted him away from his father. But why? His father wasn't a cruel or bad man. He was supportive of his son. Interested in his future. He supplied Mark with money when necessary, but Mark knew the difference between his parents. His mother loved him unconditionally. His father, on the other hand, was disappointed in his only son.

And disappointment was harder to deal with than dislike.

At this thought, Mark attacked the vodka tonic, swallowing down half of it. He considered heading to the Gents, then remembered he'd left the line of cocaine at the flat as a precaution, having decided vodka would be his only prop.

The waiter was hovering nearby, so Mark emptied the glass and indicated he would like another. Should his father enter now, it would look like his first drink.

As it was, his order and his father appeared at the same time.

A big man, both in girth and height, Sir Mark Howitt Senior QC was a striking figure. Mark had seen him in action in court and been impressed, despite himself. His own inability to be certain about anything seemed entirely at odds with his father's view of the world and those in it.

His father glanced about and, spotting Mark, immediately headed in his direction.

Mark stood to attention like a soldier in front of a commanding officer.

'Mark.'

The handclasp his father offered was cool and firm, the opposite of Mark's warm, nervous, damp one. Mark withdrew his offering as quickly as possible.

'Good. I see you've ordered,' his father said as the vodka tonic was placed on the side table. 'I'll have my usual,' he told the waiter.

The usual was, as Mark knew, a double measure of his favourite single malt, served with a small jug of water. That, too, hadn't changed over the years.

His father sat down opposite him, his figure dwarfing even the voluminous high-backed leather chair.

'How are you, Mark?'

'Fine,' Mark said. 'Work's going well.'

'Good.' His father looked down for a moment as if squaring up to reveal the real reason why Mark was there, which definitely wasn't to enquire about Mark's job.

There was a pause in the proceedings when the waiter arrived with the pale malt in the crystal glass and the jug of water. His father thanked him, then waited until they were alone again, before speaking.

His father had always been forthright, a feature Mark had not inherited. Whatever his reason for bringing Mark here, it would be said clearly and unequivocally. Mark waited in silence for his nightmare to begin.

'I asked you here to tell you that your mother is dying. She has at best two months, but I don't believe it will be that long.'

The words Mark heard and attempted to process were not the ones he'd expected. Tensed and ready to spill lies as necessary, he was suddenly faced with the clear words of a truth too terrible to contemplate.

'What?' Mark said stupidly.

'She didn't want me to tell you, but I felt you should know.'

When rehearsing his confession, Mark had consistently heard his mother's voice, telling him he was right to go to the police and she was proud of him for doing so. It had been his 'get out' clause. His safety net. Whatever he did, his mother would still love him.

'I haven't been to see her,' Mark said, suddenly aware of how long it had been since his last visit.

'But you've spoken on the phone,' his father reminded him.

Mark realized his father was simply repeating his mother's words, and her excuses for his infrequent visits.

'I'll come home with you now.'

'No,' his father said swiftly. 'The nurse is with her and she'll be asleep, anyway.'

A tidal wave of emotion threatened to drown Mark. 'When, then?'

'I'll have to break it to her that I've told you. Then I'll call and let you know when to come.' His father lifted his glass and swallowed the whisky down. In that moment he looked vulnerable and bereft. Something Mark couldn't bear to behold.

'Why didn't she want me told?' Mark said.

His father contemplated him for a moment.

'Your mother has been courted by death for most of your life. She didn't want you to be courted by it too.'

The job done, his father rose. 'If you'll excuse me, I have another matter I must deal with before I go home.'

Mark followed his father's glance. A man had just entered the room. With a jolt Mark realized he recognized the man's face, but from where? Not sure his legs would support him, Mark stayed seated as his father approached the man, greeted him, then ushered him into a side room.

Mark lifted his drink with a shaking hand as the memory of where he'd seen the man came flooding back. It had been on television at a press conference about the Glasgow Witch murders. The man meeting with his father was the detective in charge of the investigation.

33

The rest of the Tech team had gone home, the main lights had dimmed, yet the machinery still hummed and blinked, giving the impression of a spacecraft automatically piloting itself through the outer darkness.

McNab didn't like this room, and felt inadequate when in it. What value had instinct, intuition and years of experience when faced with the vastness of the digital mind, the ability to process at a rate approaching the speed of light, cross-referencing and calculating?

Ollie, on the other hand, resembled a child with a toy, playing a complicated game. No fear. No trepidation. No lack of confidence in his abilities to master the digital world. That made Ollie a proper scientist.

What does that make me?

McNab suddenly recalled the term 'urban warrior' had been used by his superiors and definitely not in a complimentary way.

'Shannon received a single short phone call that evening, from this number,' Ollie said, bringing McNab back to the task in hand.

'Who was it?' McNab demanded.

A name appeared on the screen.

Jesus fuck. No wonder the bastard had looked so frightened

when he'd been told about Shannon's death. Or maybe he'd known
already? Maybe he'd been the one to kill her?

'Barry Fraser,' he said softly.

'You know him?' Ollie said.

'I know him, all right.'

Ollie moved on to the list of contacts and the more recent
texts he'd retrieved. The university library number was
among them, as too was Freya's mobile number. Seeing
Freya's name on the list gave McNab a jolt.

'How many calls or texts from, or to, that number?' He
pointed to Freya's name.

Ollie did a quick check. 'Eleven in total. There's a call
from it the day you found the body, which wasn't answered.'

McNab experienced a sense of relief that Freya's version
of events and the level of her friendship with Shannon
appeared to be true, at the same time admonishing himself
for ever doubting her.

Daniel Hardy was also on the list, as often as Barry. When
McNab had first interviewed the barman, Barry had been
quick to deny he'd even noticed Shannon in the pub, only
admitting to knowing Leila. For someone he didn't know
he was on the phone to her a lot, including speaking to her
the night she'd died.

It was time to talk to Barry Fraser again.

The earlier rain clouds had disappeared, leaving a clear sky
and a rosy sunset. McNab toyed with the idea of saving
Barry for the morning and calling Freya instead. The police
had revealed to the press that Shannon's mobile was missing,
but hadn't updated them with the news that it had now
been found. So assuming Barry was following the investigation, he wouldn't be currently concerned about his call being

discovered. Barry Fraser, McNab decided, wasn't going anywhere.

He contemplated going by The Pot Still just to check on the guy, but if he was seen it might alert Barry to what was to follow. No, McNab decided. Let the bastard do his shift and go home. They would bring him in tomorrow, and he would take great delight in tearing Barry's story to shreds.

McNab pulled out his mobile and called Freya's number.

This time he let it ring longer than just three times, but still she didn't answer. McNab was a little taken aback by the degree of his disappointment. He checked his watch, only now taking note of the time. He should have called earlier, before he met up with Ollie.

Maybe she'd given up on him and was out somewhere she couldn't hear her mobile? Alternatively, she'd spotted the name of the caller and decided not to answer. A thought that didn't go down well.

Eventually Freya's voice asked him to leave a message. McNab said, 'Hi, moon lady. Sorry it's so late. Call me, please.'

What to do now? In past times, he might have headed for the jazz club. Had a drink there and talked to colleagues. Maybe he would catch up with Sam, if Chrissy wasn't about. It was a tempting thought, but a dangerous one.

He would go home. Pick up a pizza on the way and watch some TV. He hadn't replaced the half-bottle of whisky he and Freya had shared. Hadn't even thought of doing so, until now.

A hole had opened up in his evening. A place he'd assumed would be filled by Freya, but now a bottle of whisky was vying for second place. In that moment his self-belief went, his conviction and determination with it. He knew he would buy a bottle of whisky on his way home. The off-licence was next to the takeaway. It was too easy.

McNab tried to persuade himself that that particular scenario wouldn't necessarily happen. That he'd made a commitment and would stick to it. Then he thought of Freya and his resolve evaporated. He tried to raise it again by checking his phone. But there was no answering message. No request that he come by.

I cannot depend on this woman to stop me from drinking.

But if not her, then who?

The answer came in the form of a phone call. McNab almost missed it, so intent was he in his approach to the pizza place and, of course, the off-licence. He didn't even glance at the screen, so hopeful was he that it was Freya calling back.

The voice that answered wasn't Freya, but it was the voice of a lost love.

'Dr MacLeod,' he said.

'Why don't you call me Rhona?'

'Because you told me we could never be friends again,' he said, knowing he sounded pathetic.

'What's wrong?'

'Nothing,' he lied.

'Have you been drinking?'

'Not a drop,' McNab said with honesty.

'Come over,' she said. 'Please.'

McNab had waited a long time to hear those words spoken by this woman.

'Why?'

There was a moment's silence. 'Because I'm asking you to.'

Her voice sounded worried and sad and evasive all at the same time. McNab knew he would agree because he'd never been able to say no to Rhona MacLeod, except that one night, in the stone circle.

'I'm on my way.'

Their history was as complex as the numerous investigations they'd worked on together. When he was being honest with himself, McNab knew exactly what Rhona thought of him. The term 'infuriating' came immediately to mind. She'd called him many things in the time they'd known one another; most of the terms used or implied had been less than complimentary. He also knew that she cared about him. Deeply and loyally. McNab would trust Rhona MacLeod with his life, as she could trust hers to him.

When he arrived, the flat was a blaze of light, every window facing the street lit up. When he buzzed, Rhona didn't free the door until she'd heard his voice. As McNab climbed the stairs, the thought occurred that something had spooked Rhona. This in itself spooked McNab, because one thing he knew about Rhona was, she didn't frighten easily.

When she opened the door to him, he was surprised to find her dressed as though for a date. He gave her an appraising look, which was quickly quashed by an unspoken warning from her.

The words, 'You didn't have to get dressed up for me,' died on McNab's lips.

She led him into the kitchen. No subdued lighting here either, every corner free of shadow. The window which normally stood open to allow the cat access to the roof was firmly closed and, McNab suspected, locked.

'What's going on?' he said.

She gestured to the table. On it lay a clear evidence bag with something inside. McNab picked the bag up and checked out its contents. The bundle of sticks it contained took shape and became a woman with long hair, wearing a red thread round her neck. There was no mistaking the image the figure conjured up.

'Where did you get this?' he said.

'I found it in the hall when I got back from work—'

He interrupted. 'Why didn't you call me?'

'I just did.' She sounded exasperated.

'Four hours later.'

'I had a date. I decided to keep it.'

McNab wondered who with, but didn't ask.

'Can I look at it out of the bag?'

She brought him gloves and a pair of tweezers.

'Who's touched it?' he said.

'Only me, and maybe the cat.'

She handed him a magnifying glass. 'There's something scratched on the body.'

At first McNab didn't see what she was talking about, so faint were the marks.

'What are they?'

'Runes,' she said.

'Fucking runes.' McNab felt his exasperation mount.

Rhona pushed a piece of paper towards him. On it was the alphabet table he'd seen in Magnus's book on Witchcraft. McNab expected her to translate for him. The fact that she didn't, worried him.

'What does it say?' he demanded.

Rhona hesitated for a moment. 'I think it says Freya.'

At the utterance of the name, McNab's stomach dropped like a stone.

Rhona immediately added a proviso. 'Freya is the name given to the Goddess in Wicca, so it's not unusual to see it on replicas.'

McNab remembered the little statue the real Freya had left on her pillow. He'd carried it with him since that morning. He produced it now and showed it to Rhona.

She studied the little green figure, noting the name on the base.

'Freya gave you this?' she said.

McNab nodded. 'That's a true depiction of the Goddess and there isn't a cingulum round her neck.'

'Have you spoken to Freya recently?' Rhona said.

McNab had his mobile out and already on fast dial. 'I tried calling her earlier. She didn't pick up.' He felt his throat tighten as his call rang out unanswered. Eventually Freya's voice came on asking him to leave a message.

'I'm on my way round to your place,' McNab said, trying to keep his voice even.

He pocketed his mobile.

'I'm not convinced this has anything to do with your Freya,' Rhona said. 'I called you as a precaution.'

He understood that. 'Thanks.'

'If she's stayed late at the library, her mobile may be switched off,' Rhona offered.

'I'll check there too.'

Rhona went with him to the door.

'You'll let me know?'

'Yes.' McNab suddenly remembered. 'We have Shannon's mobile. Barry Fraser called her the night she died.'

As he descended the stairs, he heard Rhona shut and double-lock the door behind him.

*

Rhona turned as the sitting-room door opened and Sean emerged.

'How did it go?' he said, concerned.

'He's going round to check on Freya.'

'You did the right thing.'

Rhona wasn't sure she had. She'd interpreted the runes as reading 'Freya', but even with the magnifying glass it wasn't clear that they did. She hadn't announced the name at first because she'd wanted McNab to attempt his own translation, to reinforce her own reading of the runes. Tomorrow, under a proper microscope, she could be more certain. But she hadn't wanted to wait until tomorrow.

'The doll might not be a threat,' Sean said.

'What could it be, then?' Rhona said sharply.

'A plea to find Leila's killer?'

Rhona halted the retort in her throat. Sean was right. She'd had pleas before, some by letter, some via email. When people realized she was forensically involved and the crime was personal to them, they sent her messages, either castigating her efforts or encouraging her to do more. The general population had great faith in the power and truth of forensics, mainly because of watching TV crime shows. It was both humbling and worrying.

'Freya is an established name for the Goddess,' Sean reminded her. 'And McNab's Freya wasn't a friend of the dead women. Just an acquaintance, like all their other colleagues in the library.'

'They weren't Wiccan,' Rhona said.

'How do you know?' Sean smiled. 'If I suddenly revealed that I practised Wicca, what would you say?'

He had her there. 'You *are* joking?' she said.

'I was brought up an Irish Catholic, worshipping a man

who died a couple of thousand years ago. According to my teacher and the local priest, women were temptresses, destined to bring a man down. I find I'm rather drawn to the Wiccans, with their female Goddess.'

'There's a male God too,' Rhona reminded him.

'Equality between the sexes. Who would have thought?'

He had lightened the moment, which of course had been Sean's intention.

'Freya has a champion in McNab,' he reminded her. 'She can trust him with her life.' Sean smiled. 'Now will you come to bed with me?'

34

The library building was in darkness as he drove past on his way to Freya's flat. If Freya had been working late, as Rhona had suggested, she wasn't there now. Approaching the traffic lights at the foot of University Avenue, McNab ignored the red signal and drove straight through, taking a swift left up into the grid of streets behind the university union.

The arrival of the stick figure had initially annoyed rather than worried him. The papers had hyped up the Witch aspect of the killing of the two women. Black magic and sex sold newspapers and the tabloids were making the most of it. That sort of coverage attracted nutters, who liked to get involved. There had also been outrage from so-called Wiccans, defending their beliefs, accusing the police of a witch-hunt. Delivering a token like the stick figure to a member of the investigating team was on a par with all of that.

He'd been singled out on numerous occasions by angry members of the public who thought he wasn't doing his job properly, as had Rhona. McNab suspected the real reason she'd waited four hours before calling was because she hadn't initially spotted the faint runes or translated them. Once she had, she'd felt compelled to tell him, especially in view of the blurted confession in the lab about his love life.

Turning the car into Freya's street, McNab saw a figure

exit the main door to her set of flats and walk swiftly away. It was a young man, tall, slim, his back towards McNab, hood up, his face unseen, yet there was something recognizable about him. McNab was momentarily tempted to follow the guy, just to check him out, then he spotted a light on in Freya's place.

To say his heart lifted would have been an understatement.

With no empty spaces on the narrow street, McNab parked alongside a wheelie bin, despite the police warning notice that he would be towed away if he committed that particular crime. As he turned off the engine, his mobile rang and the name he'd longed for lit up the screen.

'Freya.'

'I just got your messages. When you didn't call earlier, I went to the library to work and forgot my mobile.'

McNab said a thousand silent thank yous. 'I'm sorry, I got held up at work.'

'Are you home now?' she said.

'No. I'm standing outside your flat.'

There was a moment of surprised silence. 'How long have you been there?'

'I just arrived.'

Another short silence. 'Are you planning on coming up, or staying on sentry duty outside?'

'I'll come up,' he said.

The door buzzed open.

She met him in the hall, already naked. The fear he'd striven hard not to acknowledge drove McNab now, and he swept her into his arms, lifting her high in delight. Freya responded by encircling him with her legs. McNab carried her through to the bedroom, their laughter and desire colliding.

Laying her carefully on the bed, McNab undressed.

Before he could lie down, she moved to the edge of the bed and took him in her mouth. The action was unexpected and explosive. But McNab didn't want this. He gently caught her head in his hands and drew her up. He wanted to cradle the face that was coming to mean so much to him. He wanted to kiss her. To make every nerve in her body sing. Freya was alive. She was safe. McNab hadn't known until this moment just how much that meant to him.

He lay and watched her sleep. McNab had rarely done that with a woman before, except perhaps Rhona MacLeod. The opportunities to do so with Rhona had been rare, and precious, to him at least. For her, he knew, not so much. There had been genuine affection in her responses, even passion at times, like the day he'd reappeared from the dead. That was the encounter he liked to remember most.

Would this relationship be any different?

McNab removed a wisp of hair from Freya's cheek, so that his view of her face was unimpeded. She was younger than him, by ten years at least. Was that a problem? He was a detective sergeant destined to go no further than that. Her career, on the other hand, was only just beginning. If they were together, could she cope with his strange existence, his brushes with drink and his obsession with work?

The boss had a wife and a family, McNab reminded himself. Bill and Margaret had been together almost as long as the woman before him had been alive. Now that was a sobering thought.

But he wasn't Bill Wilson. If McNab had been asked to

liken himself to anyone, it would have been Rhona, although her obsessions were better controlled than his. Neither of them had truly committed to one partner. McNab had accepted long ago that there was only one man who stood a real chance with Rhona MacLeod, and it certainly wasn't him.

But maybe his chance of happiness lay facing him?

What future did this woman, Freya, Wiccan goddess, and he, Detective Sergeant Michael Joseph McNab, recently demoted, have together?

As he contemplated this, Freya turned in her sleep and McNab was met with her back. In view of his current thoughts, it was an uncomfortable image. Women had a habit of turning their backs on him.

McNab lay down behind her, craving again the warmth and touch of her skin. She moved a little to meet him. The closeness of her sprung him into action again. McNab retreated, not wanting to impose himself on her when she was so obviously asleep.

Just then his hand touched something protruding from under her pillow. He found it and took hold, sliding it free from its hiding place. McNab knew what it was, even before he saw it. He could feel the shape of the plaited silk and judge its long length as it uncurled. Had she intended using the cingulum tonight? Had she planned to wrap it round them, tightening it as they reached climax?

The idea both disturbed and excited him.

Freya had made no secret of the fact that she was Wiccan, he reminded himself. She had been, McNab believed, completely honest with him up to now. If she'd wanted him to take part in sexual magick, she would have asked. His answer, McNab wasn't so sure of.

At that moment Freya stirred into wakefulness, moving close to press herself against him. It was the signal McNab had been waiting for.

35

He stood in the darkened room, the cold damp smell of disuse enveloping him. Gone was the warm scent of incense, the glint of candlelight and the soft music of her chanting.

In vain he searched the shadows for any sense of her presence, and found none.

Then it hit him. If Leila's spirit was absent from this place, then she *had* truly gone.

The finality of this struck with a terrible intensity that stopped both his breath and his heart. Seeing her lying in the mortuary, white and cold, the shining hair already dull, the green eyes closed, he hadn't recognized that lifeless mannequin as his sister. He'd been angry to have been forced to look at it. To pronounce it as his sister.

At that point hate had taken possession of him and he'd directed that hate at the detective, because Danny couldn't face the truth – that Leila was probably dead because of him.

In this place, surrounded by her altar and candlesticks, her robe and wall hangings, her God and Goddess statues, he knew it was true.

His beautiful, wonderful sister had gone from him.
Where are you?

He shouted his thoughts and his voice hit the concrete walls and echoed back at him unanswered.

What use is your magick now?

Danny sat down on the circular mat, with his back against her altar, put his arms about his knees and wept.

Sometime later, he stood up and lit all the candles and the incense burner, then topped up the dishes, one of salt and one for water. Finally, he filled the goblet with wine.

Her book of spells he placed at the back between the statues of the God and Goddess. Danny thought of the red cingulum, which should have been here, but was being kept by the police as forensic evidence.

I don't need forensic evidence to find out who killed my sister.

He lifted the green Goddess and turned her upside down. Made of china, the figure had a small hole in the base. Below the hole, the name Freya was etched. He lifted it to the candlelight and tried to see inside.

If the other Freya was right, this was where he might find it.

Danny stepped back a little and, swinging the hand that held the statue, struck it hard against the surface. It shattered, sending sharp shards to litter the altar. One sliced the palm of his hand, breaking the skin, sending a trickle of blood to fall on the salt dish, quickly colouring its contents red.

There was nothing hidden in there.

Freya had been wrong. There was no contact list. Nothing to help him track down Leila's killer or killers. All he had were three video clips and without being able to identify the men in them, he had failed.

In Wicca there was no retribution after death. No hell and damnation awaiting the wicked. Witches believed you got your rewards and punishments during your life, according to how you lived it. Do good and you will get good back. But do evil and evil will return.

What had Leila done to deserve such evil?

'Give of yourself – your love; your life – and you will be thrice rewarded. But send forth harm and that too will return thrice over,' Danny intoned.

That part of the Wiccan Rede, he did agree with.

Danny lifted the sacrificial knife and the Book of Shadows from the altar and blew out the candles.

36

When his father had disappeared into the side room with the policeman, Mark had waved the waiter back over and ordered another double vodka, then pulled out his mobile and called Jeff, despite the disapproving look from an elderly man sitting two chairs away.

Jeff had answered after three rings. 'I thought we agreed—'

Mark had cut him off. 'Listen. It's important.'

The tenor of Mark's voice had had the desired effect on Jeff. 'Okay?' he'd said cautiously.

'I'm coming through to yours. Now.'

'Why the fuck would you do that?' Jeff had sounded genuinely perplexed.

'I've had a video message on my mobile. It's of me . . . and the girl.' Mark hadn't been able to bring himself to say the name because that would have made her real.

'Where was it taken? In the bar?'

At that point, Mark had suddenly remembered he'd told Jeff he'd never had sex with her. *Jesus fuck.* The lies just kept mounting up.

'In the street, near her place, just before she told me to fuck off,' he'd lied again.

'Can you see your face in it?'

'A bit.' Another lie because in the video you couldn't see his face, just most of his naked body.

'Who the hell sent it?'

'I don't know, do I?' Mark had said, thinking what a stupid bastard Jeff could be at times. Christ, if he got a lawyer like Jeff on his case, he'd be done for.

'Maybe the killer?' Jeff had said in a frightened voice.

'That's why I want to lie low for a bit at your place. In case he knows where I live, as well as my number.'

'How could he know your number? You didn't give it to the girl, did you?'

'No.' Mark had asked himself the same question and didn't like the answer he'd come up with. He'd been out of his head on coke and drink that night. He didn't remember anything after fucking the girl. Didn't remember passing out. Didn't even remember if he'd smothered her. But somebody had seen all of it and no doubt when Mark *had* passed out, had taken his mobile number for future reference. But to do what?

'Maybe they're planning on blackmailing you. If they find out your father's a judge—'

Mark had interrupted him at that point and told Jeff he was catching the next train. 'Meet me in the Central Hotel bar.' He'd rung off then, not keen to get involved in any further discussion, especially one involving his father and blackmail.

Now at Waverley Station, his mobile rang again. Checking the screen, he saw Emilie's name. Mark ignored it. He would text her once he was on the train. He could tell her he'd been sent home ill, but then she might come round to see him. No, he decided, he'd make some excuse about being away on a course for a couple of days. She might buy that.

The train to Queen Street was busy. Mark found himself sharing a table with three young women, all dressed up for a night out clubbing in Glasgow. No drink was allowed on the trains after nine o'clock, but that hadn't thwarted them.

Mark soon discovered that the Costa Coffee cups they'd carried on didn't contain coffee, but a pink alcoholic concoction. Their subterfuge worked well, probably because, although chatty, they didn't appear drunk and behaved impeccably when the inspector arrived to check their tickets. When he left the carriage, the girls offered to 'share' their lethal cocktail with Mark and he accepted readily. Even better than the booze and chat, the one opposite, a dark-haired brown-eyed beauty, removed her shoe and used her foot to massage his crotch under the table, which helped Mark forget the mess he was in, for the length of the journey, at least.

Hanging back as the train drew into Queen Street, he let the giggling girls get off. His crotch nuzzler delayed long enough to pass him her mobile number. Mark gave her a grateful smile in return.

He watched the three of them clip clop their way up the platform, either the ridiculous heels or the cocktails they'd consumed contributing to their unsteady gait. As they exited through the barrier, his admirer turned back and gave him a wave which Mark returned, wishing with all his heart that it had been her he'd met on that fateful night out.

The hour of pleasure over, reality came back with a vengeance. Not only that, his bladder seemed suddenly keen to get rid of the vodka tonics he'd downed in his father's club, augmented by the cocktail potion. His mobile buzzed as he jumped the turnstile into the Gents. Mark expected to discover Emilie's name on the screen again, having totally forgotten to contact her on the train. However, the text wasn't from Emilie, but from the unknown number.

Mark's first instinct was to stamp on the mobile and throw it in the nearest bin. Then the bastard couldn't contact him, ever again.

But that might prompt his tormentor to contact the police instead.

Mark made for a cubicle, went in and shut the door. Feeling unsteady, either through drink or fear, Mark lowered the lid and sat down.

Then he opened the text.

The buzz of drink and cocaine was wearing off and stark terrifying reality settling back in. He was still high as evidenced by the enhanced colours and sharp vibrant sounds, but the fall was coming and fast. He'd planned to be high when he met his tormentor, but had timed it wrong.

Anger split through the sudden despair and he shouted a litany of silent abuse at the girl who had so fucked up his life. Why had the bitch taken *him* home? Why not Jeff or any other stupid fucker in that bar? A rush of nausea swept over him and he thought that he would throw up, there on the street.

He stopped and waited, cold sweat popping his forehead.

Gradually the inner swell subsided, but it had brought a flashback of that morning when he'd stood in his own vomit in the dead girl's bedroom. God, would he never rid himself of these images?

Go to the police and tell them what happened.

The cool, calm voice that appeared in his head was that of his mother. It was so real, so clear, that Mark could have sworn she was standing there beside him.

He straightened up and came to a decision. He would meet his tormentor as planned, but he would tell him that he was going to the police. If he had choked that girl, then it had been an accident. And he definitely hadn't hung her on that hook.

Buoyed by his new-found flicker of courage, Mark upped his pace.

The rain came on as he approached the meeting place. He stood at the entrance and looked down the narrow, dark, rain-splattered lane. The last time he'd come here, *she* had been leading the way. All he could think about as he'd walked behind her was the sex that was to follow. Now, he had no idea what awaited him here.

37

Despite heading out early, McNab found the council had been true to their word and had removed his car. He called the appropriate number, but his excuse that he'd abandoned the car to chase the perpetrator of a crime didn't wash with the man on the other end. In fact, he sounded delighted to have shafted a police officer.

'You'll have to pick it up from the pound, like everyone else, *Detective Sergeant*. But maybe you can claim the fee on expenses and make the good citizens of Glasgow pay for it,' he added for good measure.

Normally McNab would have given him a mouthful in return, but not this morning. He headed back upstairs to say a proper goodbye to Freya.

'You can stay for coffee, then?' she said in response to his announcement.

McNab didn't see why not, and besides, he'd decided to broach the subject of the stick figure. He didn't want to frighten Freya, just encourage her to be vigilant and to report any unexpected visitors or deliveries.

When he'd finished his brief description, Freya immediately asked if the figure had been given a name. That threw McNab a little and he contemplated saying no, then decided against it. If Freya was being honest with him, he had to be honest with her.

'There were runes scratched on it. When translated, we think they said Freya.'

'So that's why you came by last night? Because the runes said Freya? You were worried for my safety?'

'That, and to see you again.'

She looked touched by this, then glanced down and studied her coffee for a moment.

'I did have a visitor last night, just before you arrived,' she said.

Now McNab was the surprised one. 'Can I ask who?' he said cautiously.

'Leila's brother, Danny.'

It was the last name McNab had expected to hear. 'Danny Hardy?'

In flashback, McNab remembered turning into the street and glimpsing the man emerging confidently from her main door, then the sensation that he recognized something about the guy, despite not seeing his face. He now knew what it had been – the bloody swagger of the man.

'Why was Danny here?' he said, striving to keep his voice calm.

In an instant McNab suspected Freya was about to lie to him, and he desperately didn't want her to. As she avoided eye contact, a terrible series of thoughts hit McNab. She'd asked him on the phone how long he'd been outside, because she wanted to know if he'd seen Danny. When she'd met him in the hall, she was already naked. And the worst thought of all – the red cingulum below her pillow hadn't been there for him, but for Danny.

McNab recalled the way Danny had looked at him in the interview room, as though he was revelling in some secret

McNab didn't know about. Maybe the secret was that he was shafting him?

Jealousy and suspicion bloomed, then grew exponentially. The detective in McNab took over and with it the belief that everyone is a liar until proved otherwise. Including Freya.

'You're sleeping with him.' The words were out before he could stop them.

She flinched as they hit home. McNab found himself interpreting her non-answer as guilt and convinced himself he was right. When she didn't respond to his accusation he tried again.

'Are you sleeping with Danny Hardy?'

'I'm sleeping with you,' she said quietly.

McNab ignored her response because the thoughts were coming too rapidly, and all of them were bad. 'You were telling the truth when you said you didn't know Leila that well, but what you didn't say was that you knew her brother. Intimately.'

'Michael,' she tried.

His look as she uttered his name silenced her.

'I'll have to ask you to come down to the station and give a statement regarding the deaths of Leila Hardy and Shannon Jones, and your relationship with the deceased's brother Daniel Hardy.'

The face he'd watched in sleep last night, drained of colour. Freya looked as though she might protest, or try and explain, then chose not to.

Now McNab saw sadness in Freya's eyes, rather than guilt, and knew that whether he was right or wrong, what had happened in the last few moments was irreparable.

'I am not having sex with Daniel Hardy. He came here last night to talk to me about Leila. What he told me, I want to tell you.'

Seconds had elapsed since McNab's outburst, but it felt like hours. He'd messed up. Big time. He hadn't given her a chance to speak. He'd failed to trust her, because he didn't trust himself.

They sat on either side of the kitchen table, the warm coffee pot between them. McNab could still smell its aroma and with it his feelings about having breakfast with her. But the man who'd shared her bed and looked so tenderly on her sleeping face was no more. He knew it and she knew it. Whatever she said now wouldn't change that. He'd screwed up whatever had been possible between them, just as he'd feared he would.

She waited for him to acknowledge what she'd said before she continued. McNab took refuge in his detective demeanour. It was a shabby thing to do, but once he thought of her as a suspect or a liar, he found himself incapable of moving away from that premise. This, he decided, is why I cannot sustain a relationship in this job.

'Leila was performing sex magick, according to her brother, almost exclusively for a group of men who occupy positions of power,' Freya said. 'She had been sworn to secrecy about this. One night when high or drunk she told Danny. He was worried, so he decided to film what was happening, to safeguard his sister.' She paused to let the words sink in. 'Barry knew about it.'

Her words drifted over McNab, not really registering, because he couldn't draw his emotions away from what had just happened between them. Eventually his brain engaged and analysed what she'd been saying. 'There's footage of her meetings with the Nine?' he said.

'According to Danny, there's some footage, but not of all the men in the group.'

'Why did he tell you?' McNab said.

'Danny wants to find his sister's killer. He thinks you . . . the police aren't doing enough. He asked what I knew about the covens and Leila's place in them. And did I know anything about the Nine.'

'And do you?' McNab said.

'No. What I told you is true. Leila, Shannon and I were work colleagues who shared a similar interest. That's all. It was a coincidence that we were all at the Edinburgh coven that night.'

McNab wished she hadn't used that word. One thing the boss had taught him was not to believe in coincidence.

'Why didn't Danny tell me about the video footage in his interview?'

'He said you didn't like or trust him, and you didn't want to listen.'

Both could be said to be true, but McNab didn't buy it. Danny Hardy had a mission and McNab wasn't convinced it was the one he'd assigned to Freya.

'What's he planning?'

'I don't know. He had a call, probably around the time you arrived downstairs. He said he had to go. That's when I called you.'

McNab recalled Danny's swift exit from the building, plus the fact that he'd avoided looking in the direction of the arriving car. McNab's detective heart told him that Danny had been warned of his imminent arrival, and not by an external call. That heart shattered as he formed the words, but he said them anyway.

'I don't believe you were at the library. I don't think you forgot your mobile. I think you didn't answer because you and Danny were fucking. When you got the second message, you knew I was on my way, so Danny had to leave, and fast. That's why you were naked when you opened the door to me.'

Freya stood up, that lovely face white, sad and furious.

'I want you to go. Now,' she said.

McNab deliberately drank down the remains of his coffee before standing up.

'Be at the station sometime this morning. Detective Sergeant Clark will take down your statement.'

He waited a moment on the landing after she'd shut the door on him, listening to the sound of her weeping, knowing if he was wrong, then he'd just fucked up the best thing that had ever happened to him.

38

So he didn't need whisky to press the self-destruct button. He could do that when stone-cold sober.

As he walked towards town, McNab relived every word he'd said, and saw his expression as he'd said them. It wasn't a pretty sight or sound. He'd conducted the conversation like an interview with a known criminal – with sarcasm, innuendo, accusation and cruelty.

McNab felt his chest tighten and his throat close. He had been a bastard to her. Then he remembered Danny's expression in the interview room when he'd been coming on to Rhona. His manner while McNab was interviewing him. The arrogance. The sense that Danny had something on McNab and was very pleased about it.

Then, to crown it, an image of Danny and a naked Freya came into his head.

Had there been an object he could punch at that point, McNab would have done it.

He forced himself to think about what Freya had told him. The Nine were important men and Danny had footage of some of them with Leila. McNab's first instinct said it wasn't true and she'd said it to deflect him from his rant about Danny's visit. Why would Freya tell him something like that? Did Danny tell her to?

None of it made any sense.

If only he'd stayed calm and not let suspicion take over, he might have learned more. But, he reminded himself, suspicion was at the heart of being a detective.

Everyone was a liar until proved innocent.

For once the mantra didn't work. He'd conducted himself badly. He should have asked more questions, instead of throwing accusations. Janice would make a better job of it – that is, if Freya turned up at the station as ordered.

He would call and warn Janice that Freya was on her way. Bring DS Clark up to date on what he'd been told about Danny. He would also ask for a warrant for the arrest of Daniel Hardy. Barry Fraser, he would keep for himself.

A brisk walk and a phone call later, he was outside The Pot Still.

Last time he'd been here, Barry had turned up ten minutes from now, just as McNab had finished his breakfast. The thought of anything other than a liquid breakfast didn't appeal at the moment. McNab stood for a moment, composing himself, rehearsing the word 'coffee' rather than 'whisky' before heading inside.

The same guy was bottling behind the counter. His expression when he spotted McNab's entry was anything but welcoming.

'He's not in,' he said before McNab could ask after Barry. 'Didn't turn up last night either. I had to come in and cover for him.' He didn't include *bastard* in the complaint, but McNab got the flavour of it.

'You have his number?' McNab said.

'I've tried it twice already this morning. He's not answering.'

McNab gave his order and went back to his table in the corner. As he waited for the coffee to arrive, his mobile rang and DI Wilson's name lit up the screen. McNab hesitated before answering, aware he'd been off the radar for a while, and would have to explain his reasons.

'Boss?'

'Where are you?'

Another hesitation. Should he tell him he was in the pub?

McNab came clean. 'The Pot Still, looking for Barry Fraser.'

'Get round to Bath Street Lane. Now.'

McNab rose to his feet, just as the pot of coffee was plonked on his table.

'What's up, sir?'

'A council worker just called in to report the body of a male, behind the Lion Chambers.'

He lay curled in a corner, his face and knees close to the wall, a thick pool of congealed blood seeming to cushion his head against the cracked concrete. From the back, McNab estimated him as around six feet tall. Dressed in shirt and jeans, his broad muscled shoulders stretched the cotton. Blond, twenties to thirties, worked out – a description of plenty of the blokes who may have frequented the Hope Street area last night.

McNab would have given anything to have checked out the face, but knew that wasn't possible. With the forensic team not here yet, he couldn't step any closer to the crime scene without contaminating it.

The tape was already up cordoning off entry to the lane, two uniformed officers on sentry duty. The bloke who had found the body had been told to stay put until someone interviewed him. His anxious face sought McNab over the barrier, seemingly keen to tell all.

McNab departed the body and went to talk to him.

Up close, the man had a pinched look, the voluminous yellow jacket dwarfing his thin frame. His face was pale and sickly, not surprising when he'd come to clear up rubbish and found a body instead.

McNab introduced himself and showed his ID. 'What's your name?'

The man looked surprised to be asked. 'Tattie McAllister.'

'Your real name?'

He looked taken aback by the question. 'That is ma real name.'

'Well, Mr McAllister –' McNab couldn't bring himself to say 'Tattie' – 'tell me how you found the body.'

'I came in to pull out the wheelie bin for emptying and he was lying there.' He gestured at the corner, but averted his eyes.

'Did you touch the body?'

He shook his head. 'No way. I knew he was dead, so I kept away.'

'What time was this?'

Tattie checked his watch. 'Half an hour ago.'

'Any sign of a weapon?'

'Naw, but it might be in the bin,' he suggested helpfully.

McNab hoped so. Just then he saw the team arrive, including the forensic van. He thanked Tattie and said he could go, but to leave his contact details with one of the uniformed officers at the cordon.

'I haven't emptied the bin,' the man said, looking worried.

'We'll do that,' McNab assured him.

251

McNab recognized Rhona's figure despite the shapeless forensic suit. McNab joined her and began kitting up himself.

'Any ID?' Rhona said as she taped her gloves and pulled on a second pair.

McNab explained about the position of the body. 'I haven't got close enough to check.'

Back inside the cordon, Rhona followed McNab along the cobbled lane, round the Lion Chambers building and into the rear concreted area behind a wheelie bin, passing the door into Leila's flat en route. Rhona stopped six feet back and studied the scene. The body lay close in to the corner, where the back of the Lion Chambers building met a neighbouring block of flats. The cramped location would make securing a tent a problem. Something she didn't have to tell McNab, who'd been crime-scene manager on a number of incidents.

Rhona approached with caution, trying to assimilate and question as she did so.

The smell was of warmth and rotting refuse near the bin, but as she got closer to the body she also picked up a faint scent of male cologne.

The position had struck her as odd from six feet away. Now nearer, it seemed even odder. Why was he so close to the wall, almost hugging it? Had his assassin pulled him into the corner to hide him from view of the few windows that did look down on the lane? Or was it to make it difficult to see his face? The pool of blood didn't look disturbed and there was no evidence of him being dragged into the corner.

Rhona hunkered down and began to check the accessible pockets of the jeans. All of them were empty. If he'd had a wallet or a mobile phone, they appeared to have been taken.

At this angle, she couldn't see his face without moving his head. Remaining crouched, she took some shots to indicate the exact angle of his head, then handing her camera to McNab, she gently turned the head enough to expose the face.

Any hope of instant recognition was immediately quashed, although the method of death became apparent. The eye sockets had been pierced and gouged out by a sharp implement. Both cheeks and the forehead had been cut in the shape of a cross, in what looked like an attempt to make the victim unrecognizable.

McNab crouched beside her. 'Jesus, God.'

'You know him?' she said.

McNab shook his head. 'I thought it might be the barman, Barry Fraser, but there's no telling from that face.'

'Why Barry?'

'He and Danny were apparently filming some of Leila's encounters with the Nine, supposedly as a safeguard for Leila. Then again, maybe it was for blackmail. The Nine are apparently pillars of our society.'

'Who told you all this?' Rhona said.

McNab gave a little shake of his head, indicating he wasn't willing to divulge his source. 'I'm not saying it's true, but if it is . . .' McNab reached over to double-check the pockets, then said, 'There's no watch.'

'Maybe he didn't wear one,' Rhona suggested.

McNab stood up as though he'd just realized something. 'I think the bastard took his watch,' he said, amazed.

'Who, the killer?'

'No, the guy who found him. He swore he didn't go near the body, but he looked shifty about it.'

'What about the wallet and mobile?'

253

'Maybe he got the whole lot before we arrived.' McNab cursed himself. 'I'd better locate Tattie McAllister before he gets rid of his plunder.'

'Before you go, what happened about Freya?' Rhona felt she had to ask.

'She was fine,' McNab said curtly.

The difference in his demeanour from that of last night suggested Freya might be fine, but McNab definitely wasn't, and neither was their relationship.

Rhona wanted to say, 'What happened?', but settled for, 'That's good,' instead. When McNab's expression closed down, it was better not to probe too deeply.

In the end, with rain threatening, Rhona had made the decision to move the body away from the wall in order to raise a forensic tent. Once enclosed, with the heavy patter of rain on the roof, she'd continued with her forensic examination in situ.

A police pathologist had come and gone. Expecting a knife crime but not in the manner it was presented, he'd been a little taken aback at the gouged eye sockets and slashed face, and had stayed just long enough to pronounce death.

Judging by the knees of the victim's jeans, it appeared he'd been kneeling prior to his death. The walls that met on that corner were green with slime from a leaking drainpipe which ran down the back of the Lion Chambers building. The corner also housed some rather artistic graffiti, perhaps as a tribute to the Chambers' former use as a set of artists' studios.

There were deposits of green fungus on the victim's palms and under the fingernails. Rhona imagined him on his knees facing the wall, his hands on the stone. Whoever had killed him had made him a supplicant first. If that had been his position, then why not slit his throat? Easy to do and less chance of blood on your clothes. Why bother with the messy business of stabbing out the eyes, unless it had some meaning for the perpetrator?

The state and temperature of the body suggested he'd been killed the previous night, which matched McNab's story of the missing Barry. Having been with him for such a short period of time to take a mouth swab, her one abiding memory of Barry Fraser was the fear in his eyes. And now those eyes were gone.

When her mobile rang, she'd already finished work on the body and was in the process of writing up her notes. Outside, she could hear the movements and calls of the forensic team scouring the lane. Chrissy had worked the area inside the tent and had now joined her colleagues who were decanting the contents of the wheelie bin, looking for a possible murder weapon.

Rhona fished inside her forensic bag for her mobile, assuming it would be McNab to give her news on the missing items, but the call came from an unknown number.

'Dr Rhona MacLeod?' a voice said hesitantly.

'Yes. And you are?'

'Freya Devine. I'm a research student at Glasgow University.'

McNab's Freya.

'How did you get this number?' Rhona said.

There was a moment's embarrassed silence. 'From Detective Sergeant McNab's mobile.'

By the tone and manner of her reply, it seemed clear to

255

Rhona that McNab knew nothing of this acquisition. She waited for an explanation for the call and it eventually came.

'There's something I need to speak to you about. Will you meet with me?'

'If it's to do with the current case, then you should contact the police directly,' Rhona told her.

'It's about Michael.'

Hearing McNab's first name spoken in that concerned manner, coupled with McNab's earlier demeanour, decided Rhona.

'Okay, let's meet.'

39

The video clip had arrived on his mobile shortly after McNab had left Rhona at the crime scene. He'd barely had time to contact the council and get details for Tattie McAllister, who it appeared had knocked off work early because of his shock at finding a body in Bath Street Lane.

McNab thought it more likely that Tattie was disposing of his loot and with it the identity of the corpse. Of course, he could be wrong. Tattie could be an upright citizen who, after a bad experience, needed a lie-down. Experience and intuition suggested otherwise.

The message that heralded the video clip immediately caught his attention.

It said, 'This is the man you're looking for,' followed by a mobile number.

McNab launched the video.

There was a moment when he could make out nothing but flickering candlelight and dancing shadows. Then he saw them. They were seated upright on the bed, Leila straddling the man. Around their waists was fastened the red cingulum. There was no sense from their actions that they were aware of a camera recording them, but then again, maybe they were acting for the camera. Leila's face was in clear view. The male's face was barely visible and only briefly.

The shoulders were broad, the upper body toned. The chest hair suggested he might be blond.

On the top right-hand corner of the recording was a date and a time. If they were correct, this had happened the night Leila had died. There was no sound on the recording, but it was clear that they were approaching climax as Leila reached down and began tightening the cingulum.

McNab realized that the *thump thump* was the sound of his own heart in his ears. He had a sudden and overwhelming desire to shout *Stop*, then the video jumped as though it had halted on his command then started again.

Now he saw only Leila's face, her eyes wide with excitement or maybe the beginnings of fear, as a male hand appeared to push a cloth into her mouth.

Without sound, the image of panic in her bulging eyes was even more horrific.

McNab waited for her hands to appear to pull the cloth free, but they never did.

The screen went black. It was over.

Around McNab life continued. Pedestrians stopped and checked out the yellow tape and were moved on. A bus trundled past, those on this side craning their necks to see why so many police were about. A young woman appeared with a pram. She and McNab exchanged glances as she realized something bad had happened behind that tape.

'I'm sorry,' she said as she walked past, as though she could do anything about it.

McNab didn't answer, intent as he was on what he had just viewed.

Freya had said that Danny had footage of some of Leila's encounters.

If that were true, was this one of them?

258

He dismissed that as a probability. If Danny had shot this video, then surely he would have prevented his sister's death?

So if Danny hadn't taken it, who had? And who was the guy in the video?

McNab rang Ollie and warned him he was forwarding him the clip and message.

'I want to know who sent it and who owns the mobile number in the message. The guy in the video could be our prime suspect. See if you can match him with the CCTV footage. I'll call in after I've spoken to the boss.'

'Will do.'

McNab checked the time. The boss was expecting a report in person, and he certainly had plenty to tell him.

The rain that had given them problems earlier had eased in the interim, although judging by the thick mass of dark clouds, they could look forward to another downpour soon enough.

McNab headed off on foot, aware he should have done something about his car. That something was to turn up at the pound and pay the fine. For that he needed to borrow a vehicle and a driver to transport him. All of which took time. Something he didn't have.

The incident room was working full out – on the wall board photographs of Leila and Shannon, alive and dead, plus a myriad of other material. Despite everything being recorded on Return To Scene software and accessible by all, there was still a demand to see it up there – to watch the placing of each piece in what seemed like a giant jigsaw puzzle. If the recent victim was Barry Fraser, then they had yet another death to add to the puzzle.

At least now he could walk into the boss's office and tell him that they might have a lead on the perpetrator.

DI Wilson was in his seat facing the window. When he heard the door open he swivelled round to face McNab. The face was still too thin, but there was a light in his eye and a firm set to his mouth. A look that McNab knew only too well. That look was usually present when he or some other member of the team had screwed up and let the boss down. McNab had met that look often and deserved it.

Surprisingly, when DI Wilson realized that it was McNab, the look changed.

This time McNab was waved to a seat.

'I'm sorry, boss, about being out of touch,' McNab began.

DI Wilson shook his head, dismissing McNab's opening line of apology.

'Tell me about the Bath Lane body.'

McNab described the scene, and the possibility that the victim might be Barry Fraser.

'Has his home address been checked?'

'Someone's gone round. I'm still waiting for the officer to get back to me,' McNab said.

'Why do you think it might be Barry despite the injuries to his face?'

McNab decided it was time to reveal what Freya had told him. Even as he outlined what she'd said about Danny and Barry being involved in taking footage of Leila's sexual encounters with the nine pillars of the establishment, he could hear all the things he should have asked her resound in his head. The boss was looking at him with a questioning air, no doubt wondering the same thing.

'I told her to come in this morning and give a full statement, sir,' he finished.

There were a few moments of silence, then the question: 'Were you aware that Freya Devine was in contact with Daniel Hardy?'

'No, sir. Not initially,' McNab added.

The eyes were boring into him now.

'And when did you become aware of this, Sergeant?'

McNab's throat closed and he covered it with a cough. This was turning into an interrogation with him on the receiving end, and the boss was ace at scenting a lie.

'Daniel Hardy was at her place, just prior to my arrival, sir.'

'And you were there, why?'

Now he was on tricky ground. He could come clean and admit he was sleeping with a possible witness, or lie. He never got the chance to do either.

'Since when, Sergeant?' DI Wilson said, a hard glint in his eye.

'I met her at the university library. She turned up one night at the flat, frightened about the death of two of her colleagues. That's when she told me about their visit to the Edinburgh coven.'

The boss had risen as McNab talked, and walked back to his spot by the window, so that McNab was addressing his back.

'Did you learn nothing from the *Stonewarrior* case, Sergeant?' the voice said.

'I learned to curb my drinking, sir.'

The boss turned to face him. 'But not yet to vet your sexual partners before bedding them?'

'She's a post-grad student from Newcastle working part-time at the library. She's not a criminal,' McNab said defensively.

261

'But she *is* a possible witness.'

McNab couldn't refute that. Freya hadn't appeared to be when they'd first met, but that excuse wouldn't wash with the boss.

'I severed my relationship with Freya Devine as soon as I realized that might be the case, sir.'

If the boss did the maths, he would know the timeline didn't quite match his pronouncement. McNab didn't wait for that to happen. He took out the mobile and laid it on the desk.

'I received a video recording a short while ago accompanied by a message stating that this is the man we're looking for for Leila's murder, together with a mobile number.'

McNab set the video in action.

DI Wilson had sat back down and was now staring at the mobile screen. When the video ended, he played it again.

'I've already given it to the Tech department,' McNab said. 'They should be able to trace who sent it.'

DI Wilson nodded. 'We need to pick up Daniel Hardy. If he took this video, he was there when his sister died. If it wasn't him, I want to know who it was.'

'Yes, sir.'

McNab made to rise.

As he did so, DI Wilson surprised him by saying, 'I called in a favour on the missing DNA report.'

McNab waited in anticipation.

'My source confirmed that one of the Nine is a serving officer.'

40

'You should be telling this to a police officer,' Rhona said.

'I don't want to get Michael into trouble.'

McNab was already in trouble, Rhona thought, but didn't say so. The young woman looked worried enough.

She'd arranged to meet Freya Devine in The Pot Still, which seemed appropriate, considering its role in the investigation and its proximity to the crime scene. When Rhona arrived, Freya had been sitting in a corner alone, a pot of tea in front of her.

Rhona had approached and introduced herself.

'I'm very grateful that you agreed to see me,' had been the reply.

Rhona had ordered a coffee and taken a seat across the table from her. Freya was young, but definitely not as young as McNab's previous disaster of a relationship that had nearly cost him his career. She also looked and sounded intelligent, another improvement on the previous one.

Rhona had waited for her coffee to be delivered before she'd encouraged Freya to tell her why she'd asked to speak to her. Then it had all come tumbling out. Freya's original meeting with McNab at the university. Her shock at Leila's death. Her conversation with Leila about sexual magick. Then Shannon's non-appearance at work.

'I wanted to go round and check on her, but Michael

stopped me. He already knew by then that Shannon was dead.' A shadow crossed her face, then she pulled herself together and went on. 'He was very kind to me.' She looked as though she might say more on that, but didn't. 'He came to check on me after you received the stick figure. Told me to be careful of visitors or deliveries, and to inform him if anything odd happened. So I told him about Danny Hardy's visit.'

Rhona waited for her to continue. When she didn't, Rhona said, 'And that didn't go down very well with McNab?'

'He thought that Danny and I were –' she paused and looked directly at Rhona – 'which we aren't. Danny told me he didn't trust the police to find Leila's killer, and he knew that Leila had kept a list of the men she was performing sexual magick with, but he didn't know where it was. He thought I might know.'

'And did you?'

'No, but I suggested a possibility and he said he would look there.'

'Where?'

'On her altar in her Goddess statue.'

'Where is her altar?' Rhona said.

Freya looked surprised. 'I thought she worshipped at home.'

'There was no altar in her flat.'

'That's strange. I got the impression Danny knew where it was.'

'He didn't mention a location?'

Freya shook her head. 'Shannon would have known . . .' She stumbled to a halt.

Which was probably why Shannon was dead, was left unsaid by either of them.

'If Leila didn't worship at home, then where might she choose?' Rhona persisted.

Freya inclined her head a little as though in deep thought. 'My mother had a little hut in our garden. I use a box room in my flat.' She thought again. 'Somewhere quiet where she was unlikely to be disturbed. A basement maybe, easily accessible.'

'The university somewhere?' Rhona tried.

'I thought Shannon might have been using one of the rooms that originally housed the Ferguson collection.'

'On the occult,' Rhona added.

Freya seemed surprised she should have heard of it.

'Professor Pirie, who works with us as a profiler, spoke about it,' Rhona explained.

'I found a set of keys in Shannon's desk.' Freya produced a simple ring with two keys on it, one large, the other much smaller. 'The bigger one opens a small back room there. Shannon had let slip something. I thought . . .' Freya hesitated.

'Thought what?' Rhona urged.

'Shannon said something about a Wiccan secret.'

Rhona waited for her to continue.

'I thought she might have unearthed a manuscript left behind when the collection moved to the main library. Or maybe she'd been using the room to worship in. But there was nothing there.'

'Shannon's bedroom had a circular mat but she didn't have an altar either,' Rhona told her.

Freya looked at her, wide-eyed. 'So maybe she and Leila were worshipping together?'

Rhona suspected so. 'But where?' she said.

Freya shook her head. 'I have no idea.'

'I suggest you go down to the station and give a full statement. Tell them everything you've told me,' Rhona said.

Worry crossed Freya's face. 'It was me who came on to Michael. I don't want him to get into trouble because of it.'

'Just tell them the whole story. That's the best thing.'

Freya didn't look convinced but eventually nodded. 'You're right. That's what I'll do.'

'Why did you contact me in particular?' Rhona had to know.

'Michael gave the impression . . .' Freya seemed to want to choose her words carefully, 'you were someone he trusted.'

Who can I trust?

In answer to the internal question, two names immediately sprang to mind – Bill and Chrissy. At one time she would have also said McNab, but since the *Stonewarrior* case, she wasn't so sure. Sean's name hadn't occurred, and she questioned why.

Perhaps it wasn't possible to truly trust a lover? Then she thought of her adoptive parents, who'd been both friends and lovers until death had finally parted them. Bill and his wife Margaret were the same.

As to Chrissy and Sam, Rhona wasn't so sure. The cracks in that relationship were already showing. Sam, Chrissy believed, would go back to Nigeria when his training as a doctor was complete. Chrissy had already declared that she wouldn't go with him. She was also determined that their child, named after McNab, would stay in Scotland with her. Circumstances had drawn her and Sam together, and it appeared that circumstances would break them apart.

As for McNab and Freya . . .

Rhona recalled how upbeat McNab had been since he'd met Freya. Seeing McNab joyous had been a revelation. One that hadn't lasted long. He'd always said, in his job, everyone was a liar until proved otherwise. It seemed McNab had decided that was also the case with Freya.

But maybe he was wrong?

Freya hadn't asked Rhona to plead her case with McNab, but Rhona decided she just might, given the opportunity.

Had she registered the padlock in passing, even subconsciously? *No.* Her focus had been on the body and its immediate vicinity. Searching the surrounding area had been the prerogative of the crime-scene manager.

She hadn't considered the padlocked door at all, not until Freya had shown her the key ring she'd found in Shannon's desk and stated how the larger key opened a door in the previous Ferguson library in the old building, but what the smaller key was for, she had no idea.

At that point Rhona had asked if she could have the smaller of the keys to study and Freya had handed it over without argument.

Rhona retrieved the said key from her pocket and approached the door on the lane side of the Lion Chambers, yards from where the latest body had been discovered. This entire section of the building reeked of damp, its crumbling concrete sprouting glossy green growth, fed by a broken drainpipe further up the narrow eight-storey property.

All the metal on the door and the security-grilled windows was corroded, including the thick chain, but strangely not the padlock itself, where the area around the keyhole gleamed clean with use.

Rhona eyed the small key.

If Freya was right and Shannon and Leila had worshipped together, might it not have been near Leila's flat?

It just could be.

Rhona whispered a silent *please*.

As though in answer, the key turned swiftly to the right. The padlock clicked and fell open.

According to the two officers sent to check out Barry Fraser's flat, there had been no sighting of him in the last two days. Apparently he lived alone but entertained frequently, often after the pub shut.

'No music, no noise, no nothing, according to his downstairs neighbour, who sounded pretty relieved about that,' the uniforms had told McNab.

They hadn't forced entry, unlike McNab with Shannon's flat. Mainly because McNab was of the opinion that the body currently on the mortuary slab was Barry Fraser. He was just awaiting DNA comparison with the mouth swab taken in the interview to prove it. McNab anticipated that the same swab would prove that the barman, although an occasional sexual partner of Leila's, wasn't one of the nine 'important' men featured in the dolls.

The method used to kill him, a sharp implement shoved into his eyes, had a ritual feel to it. Knives were often the weapon of choice in Glasgow, but the eyes weren't the usual entry point. McNab couldn't help but feel that stabbing someone's eyes out indicated that the killer hadn't liked what Barry had viewed with them. If what Freya had said was true – McNab could hardly say her name even to himself without feeling pain – then Barry and Danny had truly pissed off Leila's important customers.

En route to the Tech department, McNab stopped at the coffee machine for a double espresso. He drank it down and pressed the button for another, aware that coffee had been his only sustenance apart from anger since he'd risen from

Freya's bed that morning. He'd assumed he'd have to go hungry for a while longer, but cheered up as he approached Ollie's cubicle and spied what awaited him on the desk.

Ollie grinned round at him.

'I took the liberty of ordering a double helping, seeing as you ate most of mine the last time.'

McNab eyed the giant filled roll with delight.

'Sausage, bacon, egg and tattie scone special,' Ollie informed him. 'And strong black coffee. Is that okay?'

McNab's mouth watered in anticipation. 'Better than okay.'

Ollie waved him to a seat and pushed the plate and cup towards him. McNab set about the roll with vigour, while Ollie retrieved the display he'd obviously had planned for McNab's visit.

A name appeared on the screen alongside the number sent to McNab's mobile phone.

'The number belongs to a Mark Howitt. I did some research on him. He's on LinkedIn, has a Facebook page and tweets now and again.'

Ollie pulled up a photograph.

'He works for RBS in Edinburgh, a trader of some sort. Aged twenty-seven. Has a penthouse flat built in the grounds of the former Royal Edinburgh Infirmary overlooking the Meadows, so not short of money. Went to Edinburgh Academy, which is a fee-paying school, followed by Edinburgh University, where he studied law.' Ollie paused here, while McNab polished off the remains of the roll and had a slug of coffee.

'Now the really interesting part.' Ollie paused for effect. 'It appears that Mark Howitt has an illustrious father. Sir Mark Howitt Senior QC.'

'Jesus,' McNab said as he registered the name. 'His old man's a High Court judge?'

'Assuming the lead you were sent is true.'

Now came the crunch. 'Is he the guy in the video with Leila?' McNab said.

'Probably,' Ollie said.

'What do you mean probably?'

'According to the software there's a sixty per cent probability that the partial view of the face in the video is a match for Mark Howitt,' Ollie said. 'However . . . the video jumps just after the climax scene and before we see the hand approach the victim's mouth.'

He ran it again for McNab, stopping it at the spot mentioned.

'When it starts again, only the female's face is visible. I'm not sure where her hands are.'

McNab remembered waiting for Leila to pull the cloth from her mouth.

'The two slices of video are taken at different times?'

'I believe so. Unfortunately, we don't have a good shot of the man's hands during sex, so we can't compare them to the hand at the end. I've been trying to find clear images of Mark Howitt's hands but no luck so far.'

'So we bring him in,' McNab said.

'That would be good.'

'And if we have the ID wrong . . .' McNab imagined the fallout if that were the case.

He took a mouthful of coffee. His heart was already beating rapidly and he didn't need the caffeine, but the coffee felt the equivalent of a celebratory drink.

'What about the judge?' Ollie said.

McNab acknowledged they would have to tread carefully. He could approach the boss and give him the news. Let DI Wilson decide. Alternatively . . .

'Can we forget you discovered Mark Howitt's *possible* illustrious connections for the moment?' McNab paused. 'Just long enough for me to check out the suspect.'

Ollie gave him a long, slow smile. 'Sounds like a good plan to me.'

Back in the incident room, McNab looked for DS Clark only to be told she was taking a statement from a friend of the two female victims. The elation he'd experienced in the Tech department fell away and was replaced by a dull anger, whether at himself or Freya he wasn't sure.

He checked which room they were in, then went to take a look.

From the observation point next door, he studied the two women sitting across the table from one another. Janice looked calm and assured, Freya nervous and distressed. McNab's stomach flipped as she inclined her head to the right, a gesture he realized he'd come to love about her. It was something she did when thinking deeply.

In that moment, McNab wished the previous twelve hours had never happened. That he'd arrived ten minutes later at Freya's flat and, as a result, had never seen Danny Hardy leave.

Would that have made a difference to his reaction when Freya told him of Danny's visit?

Yes, because he wouldn't have immediately linked her nakedness to Danny's exit.

McNab wanted to listen in, but found himself incapable of doing so. He'd lost all confidence in his ability to analyse, accept or reject anything Freya said. He would have to leave that up to Janice. McNab left the viewing room and shut the door firmly behind him.

It was time to do something he *was* capable of.

41

Rhona stood for a moment considering her next move. Already kitted up, she could enter alone or wait and locate McNab. There were still a couple of SOCOs further down the lane, but Chrissy, she knew, had accompanied the evidence retrieved from the body back to the lab.

Rhona pulled at the chain and it rattled through the double handles and fell free.

As she pushed the door inwards, the scent of incense wafted out, faint but recognizable. Water dripped somewhere, each plop echoing back at her from the concrete walls.

A sudden mad fluttering saw a trapped pigeon avoid the glare of her torch and escape upwards through a hole in the ceiling, seeking the windowed and brighter upper level. In return, daylight drifted down, exposing the emptiness and dereliction of the room, with its covering of concrete dust and bird shit.

Yet she could still smell incense – of that she was certain.

According to Magnus, the area required to perform the rituals and work magick could be a whole building, a room or just part of a room. A place kept solely for rituals, in perhaps an attic or basement, like the vaults they'd visited in Edinburgh, would be ideal.

The room had to be clean and would have been scrubbed out with salt before the temple was constructed. Rhona checked the floor again. If there was a room, then there should be a noticeable pathway through the dust that led to it. She switched off her torch and stood for a moment, accustoming herself to the grey light.

Then she spotted it.

Rather than head across the room, the path snaked left. The room had been a shop at one time, as evidenced by the long counter and shelved back wall. Rhona followed the path behind the counter to an abrupt end at an old-fashioned wooden stool that stood between the counter and the shelves.

Rhona moved the stool back to expose a small brass handle embedded in the floor, signalling the existence of a trapdoor. She slipped her finger through the ring and pulled upwards. With a sigh the wooden door released itself and rose.

Immediately the scent, she recognized now as sandalwood, escaped.

Glancing down, she saw a steep ladder of perhaps a dozen or more steps.

Minutes later, Rhona was standing in the temple.

Entering at the north-west corner of the basement room, she faced the altar, which stood in the middle of the circle. To the east was the opening on the circle. The walls were painted the magickal symbolic colours: the north wall painted green, the east yellow, the south red and the west blue. On the south wall, which faced her, stood a couch draped in red. Above, black writing on the red wall read:

Here do I direct my power
Through the agencies of the
God and Goddess.

Directionally opposite, smoke still drifted from the censer that stood on the altar. According to Magnus, a special charcoal briquette was lit and sprinkled with incense, then placed in the censer, allowing it to burn slowly. Hence the lingering scent. Around the circle and in all four corners of the room stood a burnt-out candle. Only one remained alive, fluttering its way to extinction. The candles and censer suggested someone had been in here recently, maybe only hours before.

As Rhona approached the altar, she spotted the broken pieces of what looked like the Goddess statue scattered among the other ritual items, which included the statue of the God.

Freya had said she'd told Danny to check Leila's Goddess statue and it looked like either he or someone else had done just that. Rhona studied the altar and came to the conclusion that it wasn't only the Goddess that was missing. Salt and water dishes were there, as was a beautifully inscribed horn for wine. Two goblets for the God and Goddess stood on either of the altar. On the floor before it stood two further goblets for participants, confirming that two Witches used this temple for worship.

Magnus had said that every Witch has a personal knife, called an *athame*, or in the Scottish tradition, a *yag-dirk*. Usually made of steel, it was a double-edged blade. A ceremonial sword lay on the altar, normally used for marking the circle, but there was no knife, although there was clearly a place for it.

Rhona recalled the body outside with its gouged eyes. A double-edged knife would have been a perfect implement to achieve such a result.

If Danny had come here to search for the list, had he taken the knife?

Freya had told McNab that Danny and Barry had both been involved in taking videos of Leila and her sexual partners. If the victim in the lane was Barry, was it possible Danny had killed him? If so, why?

Rhona retreated upstairs. Back in the lane, she called McNab.

'Dr MacLeod?'

'I've located Leila's temple,' Rhona told him.

'Where?'

'In the Lion Chambers building.'

'That's been checked.'

'They missed a basement in the downstairs shop on the lane side.'

'You're fucking kidding me, right?'

She didn't answer the rhetorical question but asked one of her own. 'Can you come down?'

'I have something I have to do first. Are there SOCOs still about?'

'Chrissy's gone but I can bring her back,' Rhona offered. 'And I could ask Magnus to take a look?'

'Do that.'

His swift agreement surprised Rhona.

'Are you okay?' she said.

'Fine. Why shouldn't I be?'

Rhona could think of at least one reason. She decided to come clean.

'I found the temple because of Freya.'

She broke the loaded silence that followed. 'She showed me the keys she found in Shannon's desk. One looked like a padlock . . .'

McNab cut in, his voice a splinter of ice. 'You had no business interviewing Freya Devine.'

'I didn't interview her,' Rhona said. 'She called and asked to speak to me about Shannon.' That wasn't exactly true but . . .

'How did she get your number?' McNab asked sharply.

'I'm not sure,' Rhona lied. 'But I think what Freya told me was the truth.'

'Really?'

Rhona ignored the sarcasm. 'I'll let you know if we find anything.'

'You do that, Dr MacLeod.'

He rang off before Rhona could tell him about the missing knife.

Stupid, argumentative, stubborn bastard. No wonder he made a piss poor DI.

But, a small voice reminded her, *that stubborn bastard never gives up, no matter what it might cost him.*

And in this case, it looked as though it might have cost him Freya.

McNab threw the mobile on the passenger seat and tried to concentrate on the road. Having commandeered a vehicle, he was now on the M8 heading east. The afternoon traffic was steady which meant he wasn't going anywhere fast. McNab thought about putting on the blue light and hitting the accelerator. He would relish a burst of speed and some serious driving right now. On the other hand he was so angry, he was probably a danger to the public as well as himself.

He forced himself to stay in the left-hand lane at a steady sixty and tried to think things through. He'd done it again. Cut Rhona off with sarcasm, instead of questioning her about her find. And it was a find, one that he or his team had failed to achieve. The main search had made use of the front entrance to the Lion Chambers. All rooms had been checked but no one had spotted the basement entrance. Congratulations should have been in order and instead he'd given Rhona grief.

Was he a worse bastard sober than when he'd been drinking? Or was he just a bastard?

And what had Freya told Rhona that she believed? He hadn't even asked. So much for being a detective.

When he pulled in at Harthill services for petrol and a coffee fix, he found a text message from Ollie. It seemed the mobile used to send the video was a pay-as-you-go, which had since gone quiet. No surprise there. The next bit of news was more interesting. Mark Howitt had made a call in the last hour *to* Edinburgh *from* the Glasgow area. If true, then McNab was heading in the wrong direction if he wanted to speak personally to his suspect.

'Where in Glasgow?' McNab asked when he rang Ollie back.

'City centre area.'

'Who did he call?'

'An Emilie Cochrane.'

'Do we know anything about her?'

'Quite a lot.'

'Tell me.'

McNab listened to the details of Emilie's life, including her place of work, which was a high-end fashion store on George Street.

'Okay, keep a trace on Mark. I'll get back to you.' McNab rang off and finished up his coffee. If Emilie was the girlfriend then chances were she knew exactly where Mark was.

LIN ANDERSON

McNab began to wish he'd taken the train as he entered the city centre. Glasgow traffic was bad enough with its one-way system, which inevitably meant you went round the block while trying to get to your destination. Edinburgh had its own unique problems, including the addition of the trams on Princes Street and the rule on buses only. Running in parallel, George Street was wide with two-way traffic but getting a parking place was no easy matter. He finally located one at Charlotte Square and, paying his dues via the meter, began his walk, fetching up outside a rather smart clothes shop that had no prices in the window.

McNab headed inside.

The scent in here was not of incense or candles but of money. It was funny how money had a smell. A very pleasant one. McNab enjoyed the aroma for a moment before taking a look around for a possible Emilie.

Mark Howitt was by all accounts a tasty and well-heeled bloke, even if he might be a killer. McNab imagined a girlfriend would be his equal. He spotted who he thought might be Emilie moments later. She emerged through plush blue curtains and came walking towards him, although walking was an inadequate word to describe the movement she made.

She was tallish, blonde and very classy. McNab gave her a silent ten out of ten.

'Can I help you?' she said with a coquettish smile.

McNab killed that smile when he produced his ID and introduced himself. She observed him in a puzzled, defensive manner. Dealing with the police would be like dealing with riff-raff, is how McNab read it.

She collected herself and assumed a caring, bewildered look.

278

One McNab had met many times before, usually among those who thought themselves above and beyond the law.

'I'm investigating the murder of a young woman in Glasgow last Friday night.' He paused to allow that to sink in. 'And I'd like to speak to a Mark Howitt who I believe is a friend of yours.'

Whatever she'd expected, maybe a parking offence or a burglary in the vicinity, it hadn't been death, or a mention of Mark.

McNab barged straight ahead. 'We know he was in Glasgow at that time. We have him on CCTV leaving the pub with the female in question. We'd like to know where he is now.'

The lovely face became a turbulent mass of emotions, including outright shock, but McNab could see the calculations behind them. How much to say? How much to get involved?

'Can we go somewhere and have a quiet coffee?' McNab suggested with a reassuring smile. 'No one need know why I'm here.'

She saw and immediately clung to that smile and its reassurance. Image was everything here. If she was linked to a murderer, he suspected the job and quite a few other relationships might be over.

'I'll just tell them I'm popping out.'

McNab told her he'd wait for her outside.

She appeared moments later having donned a jacket to match her outfit. In the interim she'd collected herself and her look was now one of steely determination. McNab suspected she was about to shaft Mark Howitt, whatever their relationship had been.

She suggested a nearby cafe and chose to sit inside in

the darkest corner she could find. McNab went along with her desire for anonymity. Edinburgh was a small place, and he presumed George Street and its environs were even smaller.

When the waiter, decked out in long black apron, approached, McNab ordered his usual double espresso. Emilie asked for chamomile tea, to settle the nerves, no doubt. Left alone while they waited for their order to arrive, McNab asked Emilie what her relationship with the suspect was.

'We go out together – now and again,' she added, making it immediately impermanent.

McNab accepted that to put her at ease.

'Were you aware he was in Glasgow on Friday night?'

By her expression, this was a tricky one for her. If she revealed the truth, it might be construed that she knew Mark better than she wanted to admit.

Eventually, she said, 'He told me he was playing five-a-side football with Jeff in Glasgow.'

'Jeff?'

'Jeff Barclay. They went to university together. I've only met him once when he came through to Edinburgh. He and Mark get together once a month—' She came to a sudden halt, aware she was giving the impression that her relation-ship with Mark was long-standing.

McNab smiled again to further reassure her.

'Do you have Jeff's phone number?'

'No, but he's a lawyer for a big Glasgow firm.'

'Where is Mark now?'

'He said he's on a course for the next few days, in Glasgow.'

'When did he tell you this?'

She hesitated. 'He called this morning.'

'When did you last see him?'

Another hesitation. 'Saturday. He took me out to lunch.'

'How did he seem?'

She didn't like this, that was plain to see, as every answer indicated that she knew Mark better than she wanted to admit.

'Hungover, and –' she went in for the kill – 'he had a bad scratch on his right shoulder. He said he got it at the football.'

McNab thanked her and handed her his card.

'If Mark gets in touch again, you'll let me know?'

She stared at the card. 'I don't want to talk to him,' she said, shaking her head.

'Just let me know if he calls, or tries to see you.'

She didn't relish the thought of either possibility.

'Am I safe?' she said.

'We don't know that Mark's guilty of anything yet,' McNab said. 'That's why we need to talk to him.'

She wasn't sold on that. Mark was plainly guilty of lying to her and picking up other women. Her expression said as much.

'The sooner we contact him the better,' McNab said. 'So anything you can do to help would be much appreciated.'

Mollified by this, she slipped the card into her jacket pocket.

'I'd better get back,' she said.

McNab offered his hand and thanked her again for all her help.

When she'd gone he called the waiter over and ordered another espresso, this time to go. Emilie's chamomile tea was left untouched.

McNab picked up the car and headed up the Mound, intent now on checking out Mark's pad. He didn't have a search warrant, but that didn't necessarily mean he couldn't glean some information from a visit. Leading to the Royal Mile, this was the part of town most tourists flocked to. Crossing the Mile, he spotted the university in the distance and, to the west, the old Royal Infirmary.

Just inside the main gate was a reception area for those interested in purchasing a property on this prime site. According to Ollie, Mark's penthouse wasn't in the older building, but part of the new block which overlooked the extensive parkland known as the Meadows.

Parking in one of the many residents' bays, McNab headed for the block in question. The view even from ground level was pretty spectacular and the location was only a fifteen-minute walk from Princes Street. McNab thought of his much more modest backstreet flat as he gazed upwards at the structure that rose in turrets of glass. If the view was ace down here, what must it be like in the penthouse?

He turned in at reception where he was pleased to find a concierge on duty. McNab introduced himself once again and flashed his badge, which caused some interest.

'Aye, how can I help you, officer?'

'Mr Mark Howitt. The penthouse flat? Is he home?'

The man lifted a phone and pressed a number, which turned out to perform much like the buzzer in McNab's own less palatial residence.

'He's not in.' The concierge waited on the next development.

'Have you seen him recently?' McNab said.

'No. Why? Is something wrong?'

McNab assumed a serious expression. 'We're concerned for Mr Howitt's welfare. Is there any way we can check the flat just in case he *is* in there?'

'Well,' the man mulled this over, 'if you think something might be wrong with the bloke, I could use the pass key.'

'Thanks.'

Mission accomplished, they proceeded to the glass lift which sped them swiftly skywards. The door opened with a swish and McNab was presented with a bird's-eye view of the volcanic crag that was Arthur's Seat. The view alone must have added a hundred grand to the asking price.

As the concierge unlocked the door and pushed it open, McNab took his arm.

'If you could wait here, sir. Just in case.'

The concierge looked as though he might argue, so McNab added, 'We were alerted to the fact that Mr Howitt was suicidal. Better that you should stay out here.'

The 'suicide' word did the trick.

'I'm not supposed to leave my desk, officer. I'll head back down. I hope the bloke's all right.'

McNab waited until the lift sped downwards, then entered and shut the penthouse door behind him.

The smell of money was in here too, just like in the fancy clothes shop.

He stood for a moment admiring the wide open space that stretched from the glossy kitchen area to the floor-to-ceiling windows, which occupied three sides of the room. The furnishings were all black leather, the flat wall-mounted TV as big as a small cinema. Mark Howitt had *the pad*, all right.

McNab noted the whisky bottle and the glass on the granite kitchen surface. Next to which was undoubtedly a film of white powder. McNab rubbed his finger in it and tested it on his tongue.

So last time Mark was here, he'd indulged in some coke washed down with whisky.

Next stop, the bedroom.

Colours here were the same. Black bedding, leather head-board, white rug on the polished floor. Above the bed was a mirror, another on the ceiling, just like in Leila's apartment. The doors stood wide on the wardrobe, a couple of the drawers disturbed, suggesting Mark had maybe packed for a journey.

McNab checked Ollie's information for Mark's work number and gave it a ring. There was only one way to determine if Mark was actually on a course and that was to ask.

It took a few minutes to get through to his department where the call was fielded by someone called Cameron. This time McNab didn't mention police but just asked to speak to Mark Howitt.

'He's off sick, I'm afraid. May I help?'

McNab said he preferred to deal with Mr Howitt. 'Any idea when he'll be back?'

'I'm afraid not.'

McNab thanked him and rang off.

So Mark Howitt Junior had definitely flown the coop and McNab suspected his hideout to be pal Jeff's place. Jeff hadn't come forward as a witness despite the nationwide appeals featuring the CCTV images, suggesting he and Mark had decided to keep quiet together.

McNab took a last look round, then exited and shut the door. Emerging from the lift, he bestowed a reassuring look on the concierge.

'He's okay?'

'He's been located in Glasgow,' McNab said. 'Thanks for your help in this. Much appreciated.'

'You're very welcome.'

Once back at the car, McNab retrieved the whisky glass with the nice clear fingerprint on it and popped it in an evidence bag, then he called Ollie and asked him to seek out one Jeff Barclay who worked for a big firm of Glasgow lawyers.

'His home and work address,' he said, then added 'please' as an afterthought, to keep the troops happy.

'I take it this is about the Mark bloke?' Ollie said.

'He's hiding out in Glasgow. You did a good job tracking down the girlfriend. Now I need you to track down the mate.'

42

The temple was laid bare, the mystical nature of it dispersed by the harsh entry of the arc lights. Rhona shivered a little, and wished she'd put another layer on under the boiler suit. The cellar wasn't damp, not like the upper floors, but there was a definite chill down here which crept into your bones.

She'd called both Chrissy and Magnus, both of whom would appear shortly. In the interim she would take her own set of stills and a video recording, before embarking on a forensic examination of the room.

From the layout of the altar and the couch, this may have been the most likely place for the sex magick to occur. If that were the case then Leila's encounter with the man in the bar seemed random and perhaps nothing to do with the Nine.

Rhona recalled McNab's assertion that Danny had been filming some of the encounters in secret. If that was true, then here would be a better place to do it than Leila's bedroom, but where exactly in this room might a camera or a person with a camera or camera phone be hidden?

It took her thirty minutes to work out what she believed was the best possible location. Once decided it seemed obvious. The altar under its long white tablecloth consisted of a circular stone tabletop balanced on a wooden frame. It stood tall enough for someone to crouch beneath.

When Chrissy and Magnus arrived, Rhona ran her theory past them. Chrissy's response was that they should try it out.

'If Danny or Barry took the video they would have to fit under there. Both of them are tall, maybe not as tall as Magnus . . .' Chrissy eyed Magnus speculatively.

Under Chrissy's intense scrutinizing gaze, Rhona could swear he winced.

Chrissy snatched Rhona's mobile from her hand and gave it to a reluctant Magnus.

'Okay, you get under the altar.'

Magnus, seeing he had little choice other than to agree, dropped to his knees and did as commanded. It was a tight squeeze for a man of his height and build, but he managed it.

'Right, boss, now's your chance with me on the couch,' Chrissy said with glee.

After much laughter and many sexual innuendoes, the deed was accomplished.

Rhona played back the video. It was clear that the location under the table was a good vantage point should someone want to capture anyone using the bed for sexual magick.

With the fun over, Chrissy set to work on the room while Rhona and Magnus discussed the altar. Rhona explained her thoughts on the missing knife and the wounds on the most recent victim found in the lane.

'There should be a *yag-dirk* here,' Magnus agreed. 'And it would be capable of inflicting damage like that, but there's something else missing too.'

'What?' Rhona said.

'Leila's Book of Shadows. There's a chance she might

287

have brought it with her each time she came to the temple, but if that was the case, I assume you would have found it in her flat.'

'What would it look like?'

'It's the Wiccan equivalent of a Bible. Witches will create their own. They're often bound and very ornamental.'

'There was nothing like that in her flat.'

'Assuming Leila and Shannon were worshipping together here, the Book of Shadows would contain the rituals they practised and the spells they performed.'

'Including the ones cast with the Nine?' Rhona said.

Magnus nodded. 'It might give you a clue as to what the Nine were involved in, and what their desires were.'

'Which makes you wonder who removed it, and the knife?' Rhona said.

'From a profiler's viewpoint, nothing feels right,' Magnus said. 'Leila met the main suspect for the first time the night she died. She took him home and they had sex. In her flat, *not* here. If he did kill her, the act would appear to have been random, perhaps fuelled by drink or drugs, or as a reaction to the idea that she was putting a spell on him via the cingulum. So why hang her on a hook in that room? Why not just get out of there and fast?' He shook his head in consternation. 'This isn't the profile of a random killer. It does, however, fit the profile of a serial offender or,' he paused here, 'someone who is intent on wiping out everyone who might identify him.'

'One of the Nine?' Rhona said.

'Or all of them. Killing as a group makes it far more difficult to pin the blame on anyone.'

'If Leila threatened to expose them,' Rhona began, 'or Danny tried to blackmail them with the videos he'd taken, and your theory is correct, then maybe McNab is right, and the latest victim is Barry Fraser.'

'Which means Daniel Hardy is the only one left alive who's able to testify to any of this.'

An uncomfortable thought reared up in Rhona's mind. 'Danny made contact with Freya Devine recently. It was Freya who suggested he look in the Goddess statue for the list.'

From Magnus's expression he didn't like that piece of information one bit. 'I believe anyone who may have a link to this case will be considered a threat to the perpetrator *or* perpetrators,' he said. 'Can you ask McNab to keep a watch over Freya?'

43

'He's not here.'

'I'd like to take a look inside to confirm that, sir,' McNab said.

Jeff Barclay appeared about to refuse, then caught McNab's eye and decided to back off. As a lawyer, he must have been aware how things would go if he obstructed a police officer in a murder hunt.

McNab was permitted to enter and the door shut behind him. No doubt Jeff didn't fancy his neighbours knowing his business. He waved his arms in a dismissive manner. 'Go right ahead, Sergeant. Search the place. He's not here, as you'll see.'

McNab soon did see. The place, though not as expensive a pad as Mark's, was definitely upmarket. Situated in the Merchant City area of the city centre, McNab suspected this had been the place Mark had made his last call from. At the top of a renovated building, it had a view of Glasgow Concert Hall. With a similar layout to the penthouse, minus the floor-to-ceiling windows, it didn't have many places to hide.

McNab checked them all and found nothing.

Returning to the kitchen, he spied a bottle of Russian vodka and two shot glasses standing next to the sink, one of which had traces of vodka in it. McNab pointed and asked who Jeff had been entertaining.

The response was swift. 'My girlfriend, Carla.'

'And where is Carla now?'

'She left before you arrived.'

'How soon before I arrived?'

'Ten minutes.'

'She didn't finish her shot.'

'She's not a big drinker.'

It seemed to McNab that Jeff was growing more confident with every passing second, which suggested he felt safer now than when McNab had entered. McNab wondered why.

Then he saw the swift glance he wasn't supposed to see, and knew.

McNab lifted the bottle and checked it out as though he recognized good Russian vodka when he saw it. Meanwhile he calculated how he planned to play this out.

The long window on the street side sported what appeared to be a narrow ironwork balcony only big enough to house a couple of pot plants. Then again, maybe not.

McNab set the bottle down, strode swiftly across the room and opened the window. Behind him, he could swear he heard an intake of breath, but no warning shout. So maybe he was wrong.

The glass door now open, the noise of the Merchant City swept in. McNab stepped out and took a look round. The railing was four feet high. Beside it was a drainpipe that ran up to a flat roof which was surrounded by a low stone facade. A fit guy could make his way up there, no problem.

McNab re-entered to find Jeff looking even happier.

'I told you he wasn't here.' He could hardly keep the delight from his voice.

'We have witnesses who saw you and Mark Howitt at The Pot Still the night Leila Hardy died. I don't need to remind you that it appears you have been withholding information in a murder enquiry.'

Jeff's smirk dissolved and he produced a concerned and earnest expression to replace it.

'I *was* with Mark that night in the pub, but he left with a girl. I don't watch TV and had no idea what happened to her until now. If I had, I would of course have gone to the police.'

McNab listened as the man before him slithered like a snake round the truth. Lawyers in his opinion could be very good at bare-faced lies, or telling the truth as their clients perceived it. McNab chose to nurse his anger. He would fan the flames when he was ready.

'I want you down at the station to give a statement and a DNA sample. If Mark Howitt gets in touch, I want to know.'

Jeff gave a small smile of success. 'Of course, Detective Sergeant. Now that I'm aware of the circumstances, I'd be delighted to help.'

McNab could have cheerfully spat in his eye, but he'd already decided to save Mr Smoothie for later. An hour in an interview room with Jeff Barclay was a prospect he would relish.

On exiting the flat, McNab fired his next shot.

'I'd like to take a look on the roof.'

The satisfied smile slid from Jeff's face.

'That's not possible,' he said swiftly. 'There's no access.'

McNab pointed at the trapdoor in the ceiling above the top landing. 'If we pull that down, there will be steps. You should have a pole with a hook on the end to do that.'

Jeff quickly shook his head.

'I don't have anything like that,' he insisted.

'Then bring a chair.'

Jeff took so long to comply with the request, McNab suspected the bastard was texting his mate, so he went for a look. It turned out Jeff had taken refuge in the toilet, obviously stalling for time.

McNab took a chair from the dining table.

As he suspected, the freed trapdoor revealed a set of pull-down steps.

In minutes he was on the roof. From this vantage point it was obvious that anyone emerging here could make their way along the building and choose to exit via one of the other stairways in the L-shaped block of flats. If Mark Howitt had come up here, he was long gone. McNab chose to walk the roof anyway, checking behind the redundant chimney stacks, just in case.

Ten minutes later he was back in the flat. Jeff had emerged from his sojourn in the toilet and awaited him, the self-satisfied look he'd worn earlier back in place.

McNab stood for a moment in ominous silence, then said, 'Did you know that if someone drinks from a glass of water, by the time they've drunk two thirds of it, the remainder is pretty well all DNA from their saliva?'

Jeff blanched, having an inkling of where this might be going.

'You made a statement to a police officer, captured on my mobile, that you had been entertaining your girlfriend Carla. Let's see if that was true.'

McNab produced a pair of forensic gloves, two plastic evidence bags and a mouth swab. He donned the gloves, sampled the vodka with a mouth swab and, lifting each glass, placed them in a separate bag.

Jeff suddenly remembered he was a lawyer and began protesting.

'Also,' McNab interrupted him, 'if you made a call to the suspect while in the toilet, our Tech team will have logged it.'

This wasn't strictly true, but it was worth it to see the effect his announcement had.

McNab made that his parting shot, before he headed down the stairs.

44

Freya had been nervous and jumpy all day. Having spoken to Dr MacLeod and given the police her statement, she should have felt better by now, but didn't. From her high vantage point by the window in the library, she watched as dusk fell over the university grounds and a grey mist crept in to envelop the towers of the main building.

Never did this ancient seat of learning look more like Dracula's castle than it did at this moment.

Tucked in a corner, encircled by shelves of manuscripts and ancient tomes, her laptop open on the desk before her, Freya had written nothing. How could she think about anything other than the deaths of Shannon and Leila and what had happened between herself and Michael?

It had stung her that Michael believed she'd lied to him, but it stung even more that he had been right. When Grant had asked her to fetch the detective from reception, little did she know that the chance meeting would have such a profound effect on her life. At first glance, she'd been intrigued by the tall, auburn-haired man with the bright blue eyes. It appeared to her that the interest had been mutual and she'd found herself flattered by that. He was both intriguing and scary, an exciting combination.

In the aftermath of Leila's death, Detective Sergeant Michael McNab had also made her feel safe. So, when

Shannon hadn't turned up again for work, Freya's first instinct had been to call him. Listening to the tone of his voice when he'd asked her not to go round to Shannon's flat, she'd known something terrible had happened.

That's when everything changed.

That's when she'd forged the lie that had come between them.

She and Danny had never been an item, but she had met him before the previous night when McNab had seen him leave her flat. He and Leila shared many characteristics, to the extent that they might have been twins. Both extremely attractive, charismatic and openly sexual, it wouldn't have been difficult to fall for Danny's advances.

But she hadn't, so in that McNab had been wrong. She should, of course, have told him the truth, but the hurt and suspicion that had radiated from him had stopped the words in her throat, so she'd chickened out and insisted she'd never met Danny in person before that night.

And once a lie had been told, it immediately multiplied.

McNab, good detective that he was, would discover that she'd met Danny before, because he would eventually meet up with Danny and he would simply ask him.

She recalled Dr Rhona Macleod's quiet expression this morning as she'd listened to Freya's tale. She hadn't told the entire truth then either, although she'd hoped by explaining to someone McNab obviously trusted that she'd helped in some way.

And what of the key Rhona had taken?

'Freya?' A quiet voice brought her back from her tumultuous thoughts.

She looked up and found Grant standing there. 'Sorry. I was miles away.'

'How's the thesis progressing?' He eyed the pile of books beside the laptop, all of which were unopened.

'Not so well,' she admitted. 'Can't seem to concentrate.'

He smiled an understanding. 'Could you spare a few minutes then for a visitor?'

'Who?' For a moment she hoped it might be Michael, however improbable that might be.

'A benefactor of the library, who's interested in the Ferguson collection and your work on it.'

Freya's heart sank, but how could she refuse?

'Sure, Grant. I'd be happy to speak to them.'

'He's waiting for you over at the old building where the collection was previously housed.'

She looked at him, puzzled. 'What about the workmen?'

'They've gone until Monday. It'll be nice and quiet there to chat. Use the back room. You'll find a key for it in Shannon's desk.'

Freya opened her mouth to say she already had the key, then shut it again.

'Okay. Who am I looking for exactly?'

'Dr Peter Charles,' Grant said. 'Don't worry about the books. I'll put them back for you.'

'Thanks, Grant.' Freya slipped her laptop into her bag and lifted her coat from the back of the chair. 'I'll see you tomorrow, then?'

'See you tomorrow.'

Freya took the lift down to the ground floor and said a goodnight to the guard on the door. Buttoning her coat against the evening chill, she set off across the road and through the main gates. Anything happening in the main building would already be over, but there were still a few students wandering the echoing cloisters on their way to the exit.

Freya headed for the tower that had housed the old library.

As she did so, a text arrived. She stopped to read it, hoping it might be from Michael, but it was Danny's name on the screen. Did she really want to make contact with Danny again? Maybe if she ignored his calls and texts, she could extract herself from this entire mess? Good sense told her that, but she still didn't heed it.

The text was brief.

Barry's dead. Be careful.

'Barry's dead,' she repeated, stunned.

She had never met Barry, but she was aware he was somehow involved in all of this. And now he was dead? Like Shannon and Leila? And why did she have to be careful?

With trembling hand Freya pressed the call button. It rang out, shrill and insistent.

'Why don't you answer?' she pleaded.

At that point a figure appeared from the shadows. Tall, distinguished, suited, with grey hair and a kind face, he quickly approached her.

'Freya Devine?' He held out his hand. 'Peter Charles. Thank you for agreeing to meet with me.'

Freya slipped the mobile in her pocket and grasped his proffered hand.

'Grant said there's somewhere we can chat about your thesis on Witchcraft?'

Freya pulled herself together. 'He suggested the old library where the Ferguson collection used to be housed.'

'Excellent idea,' he said with a smile.

As she led her visitor up the winding stone staircase, Freya made up her mind to contact Rhona immediately after Dr Charles left. Her first thought had, of course, been Michael, but that was no longer possible.

As she opened the door to the inner room, she recalled Michael's promise that night in her bed: 'No one will frighten or hurt you while I'm here.'

But you're not here, Michael. Not any more.

She turned and invited Dr Charles to follow her inside.

45

The question, 'Is she a danger to us?' hung in the air, awaiting its answer.

Dinner had been served and enjoyed and the brandy and whisky glasses recently filled. The waiter, having completed his duties, had exited, closing the double doors on the private dining room behind him. No one else would enter until called.

The meal had been eaten by candlelight as it always was, no man's face exposed to the glare of electric light. The faces flickered in the shadow, indistinguishable, but the voices they could recognize.

Over the years, they'd indulged in a variety of entertainments since the group had been formed. None of which had quite grabbed their attention as much as that which had been put before them the last time they had met.

No one believed in magic, but one of their group had a great deal of knowledge of its practice in both medieval and modern times. At this point in the proceedings he'd handed round a number of images of sexual magick being performed. Some came from ancient tomes he and they were trading in, some were present day.

The images had provoked what could only have been described as a frisson of excitement, even more powerful than making money had. They'd questioned him avidly, particularly about the photograph featuring the red-headed Witch, Leila Hardy.

'She would be my choice,' the promoter of sexual magick had said, satisfied at their response. 'It would of course be up to each of you to decide which spell you would demand of her.'

'And she's willing?' The voice came from the far end of the table.

He'd confirmed she was. 'On condition that the spells you choose fit the Wiccan Rede.

'Which is?' a rich baritone had asked.

'"An' Ye Harm None, Do What Ye Will."'

An explosion of laughter had followed the quotation.

And so the fun had begun and the spells cast.

Back then it had been exciting; now it had become problematic. It was time to deal with the fallout from their forage into magick.

He looked round the circle of faces. These men were not friends, but they were bound together and, provided they kept faith, they would both survive this and continue to prosper.

'Gentlemen,' he began. 'It is time to put our affairs in order.'

46

As she approached the steps to her front door, Danny Hardy appeared from the shadows and smiled at her. The smile held a promise of something . . . but what exactly? Rhona had encountered that smile in the interview room, when she'd taken the swabs from him and Barry. During the interchange, Daniel Hardy had indicated that they would meet again, somewhere at sometime.

It seemed that time and place was here and now outside her flat.

'Can we talk?' he said, then added a 'please'.

Daniel Hardy was effectively on the run, with a warrant out now for his arrest. She suspected he'd probably been the last person to visit Leila's temple. The one who had broken the Goddess statue and maybe removed the Book of Shadows and the knife. He was also a man in mourning for his sister, with possible revenge on his mind. For his sake, and McNab's, she should accept his offer. She should also endeavour to keep him talking until the police might be called.

If she could persuade him to go to a cafe nearby, the encounter would be in full view of the clientele, thus guaranteeing her safety. There might also be the opportunity to visit the toilet and, once out of sight, contact McNab.

'Where?' Rhona said, realizing if she was too firm about the location of their discussion, he might anticipate why.

Danny hesitated, her immediate agreement having surprised him.

'Your place?' He looked up at her window, indicating that he knew exactly where she lived.

Rhona suddenly realized something. 'It was you,' she said. 'You posted that stick figure through my letter box.'

Danny looked as though he might dispute the accusation, then nodded.

'Why?' Rhona prompted.

'You lot needed to get your act together,' he said angrily. 'If you had, Barry wouldn't be dead.'

'You think the body in the lane is Barry?'

'You don't fucking know?'

'There was no ID on the body and his face had been mutilated. We're awaiting the DNA results.'

It was obvious from his shocked expression that Danny knew none of the gory details but had simply assumed it had been Barry.

He shook his head. 'If it isn't Barry, where the fuck is he?' he demanded.

Rhona ignored the rhetorical question. 'Come on. There's a coffee shop round the corner.'

At close quarters, Danny's eyes suggested sleep had evaded him for some time, and access to washing and shaving had been minimal. Rhona was aware McNab had put a watch on Danny's flat and wondered where he'd been sleeping, then remembered the couch in Leila's temple.

If that had been his place of refuge, it was no longer available.

Danny quickly drank half the contents of the large cup of strong black coffee he'd ordered, making Rhona think she should have offered to buy him food as well. While standing at the counter, waiting for them to make her latte, she'd considered trying to text, but the table Danny had chosen had been picked for a reason. That reason being its clear view of the queue at the counter.

Rhona sipped her coffee and waited. Eventually Danny spoke.

'Have they got the guy who went home with Leila?' His voice broke a little on his sister's name.

Rhona shook her head. 'Not yet.'

'I don't think he killed her,' Danny said.

'Then who did?'

'One of the Nine.'

'You have proof of that?'

'Maybe.'

It was what she wanted to hear. 'Then give it to the police.'

'No way. They won't touch the bastards.'

'Why do you say that?'

Danny gave her a withering look. 'All are establishment figures. One's something to do with the law. They killed my sister to cover their tracks. Just like they killed Shannon and Barry. No doubt I'm next.'

'Then hand yourself in. Give the police everything you have on them.'

'And watch it disappear?'

Rhona thought back to the DNA sample to which access had been denied. There was no way Danny could have known about that.

'Then what do you propose to do?' she said.

The look he gave her was penetrating. 'Can I trust you?'

'You must have thought so, otherwise I wouldn't be here.'

He shook his head. 'No, it's Freya who trusts you.'

Rhona felt compelled to ask. 'How long have you known Freya?'

'A while. Why?'

'Were you ever an item?' If she was going to divulge any of this to McNab, she would have to be sure.

Danny was weighing up her question before responding. 'The detective saw me that night at her flat and got pissed off?'

'You could say that,' Rhona said.

'We never fucked. That night or any other. Will that do?'

It would.

McNab stood undecided. *What next?* Mark Howitt was proving as elusive as the truth. He checked his watch and realized he hadn't eaten since early morning. The thought of heading home to an empty flat didn't appeal, although entering the off-licence en route did.

He decided instead to seek out one of the many eateries Glasgow city centre had to offer. The Merchant City dwellers had already finished work and were duly at play. He didn't feel like staying in this quarter. He'd had enough of mixing with Glasgow's wealthier citizens.

So he headed west, then up towards Sauchiehall Street and the Italian restaurant Shannon had identified as the location of her last meal with Leila. This wasn't his first visit to the restaurant and he was duly noted in the queue that was beginning to form in the doorway and waved inside. One of the perks of being a police officer.

Guiliano ushered him to a tiny cubicle next to the kitchen door.

'You look like a policeman,' he told McNab. 'I don't want to put off my diners' appetites.'

McNab took this in good spirits. He was happy to be incognito and out of sight.

He ordered a pizza, a small carafe of red wine and a jug of water. Guiliano brought him the wine, water and some bread and olives.

'On the house,' he said. 'You look hungry.'

He was right. McNab fell on the bread and olives with gusto. By the time the pizza came, he'd ordered a refill on the wine and was beginning to feel mellow. Something he hadn't experienced for some time.

Before eating, he'd set his mobile on the table beside him. Halfway through the three-cheese pizza, it came to life. McNab checked the name on the screen before abandoning his knife and fork and answering.

'Dr MacLeod?'

'Where are you?' she said, the note of suspicion in her voice suggesting she thought the noisy location might be a pub.

McNab told her.

'I'll come to you,' she said, and rang off.

McNab returned to his pizza. Rhona was either coming here to lecture him about Freya or to tell him something she didn't want to say over the phone. When she hadn't arrived by the time he ordered coffee, McNab toyed with the idea of having a single malt to go with the espresso. He would have to down it and get rid of the glass before Rhona appeared, to avoid that look of hers.

He realized, with a pang, how furtive that would be. He told himself that he was in control of his drinking and should he want a whisky, he saw no reason not to have one. Waving

Guiliano over, he ordered a double out of defiance, then purposefully left it there untouched for Rhona to see.

From his location, his line of sight to the main entrance was constantly interrupted by the opening of the kitchen saloon doors as the waiters exited with piled-high plates. The buzz of the place and the lively chatter was the first semblance of normal life McNab had experienced since he'd sat across the kitchen table from Freya in what seemed a lifetime ago, but was actually only that morning.

He was eyeing the whisky glass, eager to taste its contents, but still testing his resolution, when Rhona appeared and slipped into the seat opposite.

'Daniel Hardy did not have sex with Freya, either last night or previously,' she immediately told him. 'They were never an item.'

'He told you that?'

'He did.'

'And you believed him?'

'Yes.'

McNab eased himself back in the chair and met her look head on, then lifted his whisky glass. 'I'll drink to that,' he said.

When the spirit hit the back of his throat, it tasted even better than he remembered.

'And that's what you came here to tell me?' His voice, he knew, dripped with cynicism, yet inside his head a small flame of hope had been ignited.

'In part.' She paused. 'Danny says Leila let slip that one of the Nine is something to do with the law, and that he – Danny – has short video clips which feature three of them.'

McNab took that in. 'The boss said he believed the denied DNA match was a serving officer.'

He watched as the implications of that hit home.

A small smile played at the corner of Rhona's mouth. McNab had seen that smile before and welcomed it at that moment.

'If that's true, then whoever it is must be on the database because they're involved in a current case. Once the case comes to court, their details will be removed.'

McNab nodded. 'So we identify and locate everyone currently in that situation. That's a tall order.'

'But not impossible,' Rhona said.

'I believe the boss would be up for that, but we can't broadcast what we're doing or Sutherland will be on to it like a shot. Would Danny be willing to surrender the video clips?'

'He doesn't trust the police to expose one of their own.'

'With good reason.' McNab thought about an alternative. 'Could you tell him what we plan to do and get him to meet with Ollie in the Tech department? A fair exchange, wouldn't you say?'

'He didn't give me a way of contacting him and won't hand himself in anyway,' Rhona stressed.

'We could meet at Ollie's place.'

'That might work if we can figure out a way of getting a message to Danny,' Rhona said.

McNab felt the flame of hope leap a little higher. 'Would you be able to check for any officer who's been entered on the DNA database recently because of a current case?'

When Rhona indicated she would, McNab could have hugged her.

He took out his mobile and showed Rhona the video he'd received. Her response after watching it a couple more times was, 'The hand at the end looks different.'

'Ollie agrees. The person who sent it gave us what he claims was the first guy's mobile number. His name is Mark Howitt. His girlfriend confirms he was in Glasgow on the night Leila died.' McNab told her about his meeting with Emilie Cochrane.

'What is it?' he said, reading Rhona's expression.

'You said Mark Howitt?'

'Yes.'

'Could he be related to Mark Howitt QC?'

'His son,' McNab admitted.

'Jesus, McNab, does the boss know?'

'Not yet.'

'And when were you planning to tell him?'

'When I bring Howitt in.' Seeing Rhona's doubtful look, McNab rushed on. 'If Sutherland finds out you know, what will happen?'

'Your career or what's left of it will be dead in the water,' Rhona said.

'But if I bring him in and charge him, it can't be hushed up.'

Rhona looked troubled. 'That video isn't proof he killed Leila. Danny doesn't think he did. He maintains it was one of the Nine. And he blames himself for his sister's death, because of the videos.' Then she told him Danny's suspicions about the identity of the body in the lane, something McNab didn't need to be convinced of.

'Is that everything?' McNab said, sincerely hoping it was.

By the look in Rhona's eye, it wasn't. Then she told him about Danny's fears for Freya's safety.

47

'Michael?' Freya said in disbelief.

When his name had appeared on her mobile screen she'd thought she was imagining it. Then she'd hesitated, worried he might still be angry with her, still unforgiving. The words that followed convinced her that neither was true.

'Are you okay?' His voice, although not as warm as it had been prior to their argument, gave her hope.

'I am,' she said, feeling that she now was, because of his phone call.

'Rhona spoke to Danny,' he began.

Freya interrupted him. 'He texted me to be careful. He said that Barry was dead.' Fear suddenly swept over her again, all consuming.

'We don't know for certain the body in the lane is Barry.'

Freya knew by Michael's tone that he was trying to reassure her.

'But it probably is,' she said.

'There's a strong chance.'

'Then Danny was right. He and I are the only ones left directly connected with Leila and Shannon.'

'You weren't involved with the Nine?' He hesitated, as though he wanted to check that was true.

Freya came in swiftly. 'I knew nothing about the Nine.'

He went quiet for a moment before saying, 'I believe you.'

Those three words opened a floodgate in Freya.

'I should have said that I'd met Danny before with Leila, but you were so angry, I couldn't. But I never slept with him, and we were never an item.'

'It doesn't matter if you were. I'm the one with the problem. In my line of work everyone is guilty until proved innocent.'

They were both silent as each absorbed the other's confessions.

'I want you to take Danny's advice,' he said. 'Lock up well and be careful.'

'I will.'

There was a moment when she thought the conversation was over, then he came back with, 'I could come round, if it makes you feel safer.'

'Please,' she said, her voice breaking.

His voice was bright when he answered. 'I'll text you when I'm on my way, but it might be late.'

'It's a full moon tonight and I'm a moon lady, remember?'

She rang off, her heart soaring. Michael would solve this. Once it was over they could start again. She found herself imagining Michael meeting her at the library. The two of them going out to dinner together. His presence in her flat. In her bed.

There were two things she knew she must do now, for Leila and Shannon and for herself.

Up to this point she had not been able to say goodbye to her fellow Witches. Now was the time. She headed to the small box room she'd transformed into her temple. Donning her moon lady gown, she filled the various dishes and lit the incense, then used the sword to draw her circle. Stepping within, she experienced an immediate sense of safety. She sounded the horn. The low warm note filled the room and resonated within her own body. Her skin prickled with energy, warm blood bringing a flush to her face.

She took up her stance before the altar and spoke, her voice no longer her own but that of the Wiccan priestess she had become.

'I, moon lady, sound the horn for Leila, known by her magick name of Star, and for Shannon, known by her magick name of Rowan. They are no longer in this Circle, which saddens me. I send forth my good wishes to bear them both across the Bridge of Death. May they return at any time should they wish to be with me again.'

She pointed her *athame* at a spot behind the altar and imagined Leila and Shannon standing there. The power of suggestion was strong enough to visualize them as they had been at the Edinburgh coven, Leila wearing her bright star robe, Shannon's patterned by rowans rich with red berries.

'I wish you all love and happiness. Let you both be at peace.'

Satisfied that she'd done what was required to celebrate those who had passed, Freya now turned her attention to the future. On this occasion she would choose the priapic wand. Twenty-one inches long, the final nine inches were carved in the shape of a phallus to symbolize the continuation of life. A life she hoped to share with Michael, for as long as he chose to share it with her.

She pulled her robe over her head and dropped it at her feet. Now naked, her skin glistened in the candlelight. Where her voice had spoken of loss in the first instance, this time it would speak of joy and affirmation.

Pointing the priapic wand towards the statues of the God and Goddess, she visualized a naked Michael standing before her, just as he had been that night in her room. She smiled, drinking in the memory of him and what had followed. It was as though he were there with her, his fingers burning her skin.

She took a deep breath and spoke the words:

'Thus runs the Wiccan Rede.
Remember it well. Whatever you desire;
Whatever you would ask of the Gods;
Whatever you would do;
Be assured that it will harm no one – not even yourself
And remember that as you give
So shall it return thricefold.'

McNab rose from the table.

'I'm going to head round to Freya's.'

Rhona smiled. 'So I heard. This time if Freya tries to tell you something, please listen to her.'

'You're giving me relationship advice?' He grinned. 'Well, here's mine to you. Give Sean Maguire a call.'

He left her there in the booth. Glancing back as he exited, he noted that Rhona was studying the menu, and didn't appear to be following his advice.

Waving down a taxi, he took great pleasure in instructing the driver to take him to Freya's flat. In his mind's eye he saw her, naked, waiting for him in the hall. He imagined how he would gather her in his arms. The mental picture almost stopped his breath. When his mobile rang, he answered without checking the caller's name, believing it to be Freya.

In the next moment, his dream for tonight evaporated.

'There's a man at the station who wants to talk to you,' Janice said.

'For fuck's sake,' McNab exploded in exasperation. 'It's after ten.'

'He says his name's Mark Howitt and that *you* would know why he's here?'

The news stunned McNab into silence for a moment, then he said, 'Keep him there, I'm on my way.'

He rang off and knocked on the intervening glass.

'Change of plan.' He told the surprised driver to take him to the police station.

He would have to text Freya rather than call her, because he couldn't bear to hear the disappointment in her voice.

'I take it you're a cop?' the taxi driver said knowingly.

'Always,' McNab announced.

He's very like Barry Fraser. In height, build, even the bloody hairstyle. Is there a fucking mould they use to fashion these guys? Like a plastic male mannequin. Or is it all down to gym membership?

Despite the smart clothes and handsome face, Mark Howitt looked like shit. Guilt and fear oozed from all his pores. Across the table from him, McNab was getting wafts of it. For a moment his sense of smell seemed the equal of Magnus Pirie.

Howitt's face was pale, the sheen on his skin suggesting acute stress, or perhaps he was coming down from a high. In that respect McNab had some sympathy with the man before him. Like cocaine, the highs of whisky were good, the downtime hellish.

McNab considered how he should conduct this meeting to get what he wanted. He didn't have a degree in psychology, but had enough experience to recognize a soul ravaged by guilt and despair. He'd been there himself, too often to recall.

'You were at Jeff Barclay's flat when I visited. You went up on the roof to avoid me.'

'Yes.' The voice was low, almost eager.

McNab had the sense he was the priest in the confessional. If he played this right, he would get everything. Maybe even the truth of that night. McNab sat back in the seat, creating more space between them. Give the man air. Give the man support. Let him talk. Let him release his soul.

The story poured out like liquid gold. How he and Jeff had gone on a drinking spree, looking for sex. How they both had partners, but wanted the excitement of something different. Even as he spoke, McNab could feel the thrill that had fed that night. Something out of the ordinary. They'd had no luck until The Pot Still and the two women. One auburn-haired, sexy, exciting. The other blonde, more accessible and pretty.

'Jeff went for the blonde. He always does. She seemed to like him as much as I can remember. Me, I had to persuade the other one.' He halted as though recalling.

'I didn't think I had a chance,' he went on. 'She was so beautiful, but I didn't think she fancied me. Jeff was playing a better game. He looked a cert. Then she suddenly invited me home with her.'

He stopped there, exhibiting his amazement at what had happened.

'A set-up?' McNab asked.

He thought about that. 'Maybe,' he said reluctantly.

'And?' McNab encouraged him.

'She lived nearby. We were there in minutes. She practically pushed me into the bedroom. Then she ordered me to

315

strip.' He wiped a drip of sweat that threatened his eyes. 'I thought she was going to tell me to fuck off because I wasn't good enough. I was high and drunk. It was the most exciting thing ever.'

McNab understood his pleasure. Recognized the intense desire spurred on by drink and drugs. He'd been there himself.

'She ordered me to lie on the bed, then that bloody cat sat on my face and clawed at my shoulder. I tried to push it off but she stopped me. After that . . .'

'What?' McNab said.

'We had sex and she tied a red cord round our waists.' He paused, remembering. 'I must have passed out. When I came to, she wasn't there. Then I was sick. I got out of bed, my head still swimming, and stood in the vomit. I just wanted out of there. The weird sex, the cat—' He stopped in full flow and shuddered.

'Go on,' McNab said.

'I went into the hall, but there were all these fucking doors . . . I opened one and the cat tripped me up and started screaming. Those dolls clicking and clacking. Hitting my face.' He blanched at the memory. 'Then I saw her.'

He shook his head as though to dispel the terrible image of what had hung beyond the dolls. An image McNab could share with him.

He produced a mobile and pushed it towards McNab.

'Someone sent me this.'

McNab knew what he was about to watch, but viewed it anyway.

The same snippet of video. The two figures tied together by the cingulum. Then the climax and the terrible finale.

'Is that me?' Mark said when it finished, his face as white as a sheet.

It was something McNab wanted to know as much as Mark.

'Put your hands on the table,' McNab ordered.

'Why?'

'Just do it.'

Ollie's program would compare those hands with the one in the video, but McNab didn't need a program to tell him what was plain to the naked eye.

'That's not your hand,' McNab said.

Mark looked from his own hands to the one now frozen on the screen.

'It isn't my hand,' Mark repeated, relief flooding his face.

'But that doesn't mean you weren't there when it happened,' McNab said, wiping that look of relief away. 'The person who sent you this. Have they been in contact again?'

Mark shifted uneasily in his seat. Whether he was contemplating a lie or uneasy at the thought that what McNab had said might be true, McNab wasn't sure.

Eventually Mark came to a decision. 'Yes.'

McNab scanned the texts he was shown.

'You met him?'

'I went into the building as directed, but no one appeared.' Mark looked relieved at this.

'Has there been any mention of blackmail?'

'No.'

'Then why send the video?'

'To frighten me?'

'Or to use against your father?' McNab suggested.

That obviously hadn't occurred to Mark.

'They never mentioned my father. Not once.'

'But that doesn't mean they don't know who he is.'

Mark tried to raise the coffee McNab had supplied him with to his mouth, but his hand was trembling too much, so he set it down again.

McNab stood up. 'You did the right thing coming in and giving a statement. We will of course require your mobile to trace whoever sent the video.' He signalled to the duty lawyer that the interview was over.

'I suggest you make contact with your father. I'm sure he'll want to hire a defence lawyer for you.'

Mark shook his head. 'I don't want to speak to my father.'

'Considering your father's a respected QC, my superior officer will want to inform him as soon as possible.'

Mark shrugged. 'I'm dead to him now.'

48

The door of the cell shut with a clang. Mark stood for a moment in the silence that eventually followed, realizing this was the first time he'd stopped running since that terrible night.

He took a seat on the bed, his knees drawn up, back against the wall. The only light now was the emergency one above the door. He was finally alone.

Or was he?

One thing he hadn't told the detective. Something he could hardly admit to himself. But now here in the dark silence of his cell, he would have to.

The girl Leila had died, but she hadn't gone from him.

Her presence had grown stronger with time. The more and further he ran, the stronger it had become. No amount of coke or alcohol had silenced her voice in his head. From whispers in his subconscious, her voice had become a torrent.

He had no memory of her saying the words when they were together, so why did he hear and recognize them now?

Give of yourself – your love; your life – and you will be thrice rewarded. But send forth harm and that too will return thrice over.

Like a chant it never stopped, the phrases overlapping one another so that at times it became a cacophony.

He was stressed, he knew that, but having now confessed to his role in the night she'd died, he had hoped, even prayed, that Leila's voice would be gone.

But now, here in the absolute silence, he realized that it hadn't and perhaps never would.

In that moment he made his decision. He would do what was required of him and bring this thing to an end.

Mark retrieved the paper and pen he'd asked for and, taking a seat at the small table, began to write by the emergency light.

His confession to the detective had been heartfelt, but it hadn't been complete. He hadn't killed Leila Hardy, but he was responsible for what followed, because he hadn't gone to the police. Had he done so, Shannon and the barman would still be alive.

That's what the man had said. The man he hadn't told the detective about. The man in the Lion Chambers.

And something much worse: the fact that his father was somehow involved with the group of men Leila had been partnering in sexual magick. Something that would become common knowledge if the Nine were exposed. Mark had refused to believe this at first. His father visiting Leila for sex? But the man had seemed so certain and knew so much about his father.

'Your mother, I understand, has only weeks to live. Wouldn't you rather she spent them with your father?' the man had said.

That was the question that had troubled him the most. The question that had decided him. He didn't want his father exposed, even if he had done what was claimed.

I've hurt my parents enough.

'No one else will die?' Mark had asked.

'No one,' the voice had reassured him.

Mark picked up the pen.

320

49

Rhona stared into the darkness, much-needed sleep eluding her. In her self-imposed solitude she hoped that McNab and Freya were together. In a way she felt Freya held the key to all of this, because she was the only one who truly understood the two worlds they were dealing with.

On the other hand, there was nothing magical about death. She'd met it often enough to know that. If Danny was right, his sister had died because she'd become a threat to men with the power to remove her. But had they done it themselves or paid for it to be done? Had Mark Howitt been chosen as a scapegoat? The man who would be blamed for Leila's murder? But they'd taken things too far, linking the manner of Leila's death with her activities as a Witch. So Shannon had become a threat too and had to be disposed of. Danny had claimed both girls' deaths as his fault, believing he had spooked the Nine by taking the videos.

If he was right, ironically, trying to protect Leila may have resulted in her death.

Giving up on sleep, Rhona rose and went through to the kitchen where the wall clock informed her it was half past midnight. She wished now she'd taken McNab's advice for once and called Sean. Too late now. Or was it?

She settled for a text. If he was on stage or the club was

busy, he wouldn't hear it anyway. If he responded, she could always change her mind.

In the meantime she made herself a coffee and, bringing through her laptop, logged on to check on possible updates on the R2S software file.

It seemed that the remainder of the DNA samples from the dolls had come back without a match. With Barry having been eliminated as one of the possible nine samples, that meant only one of the Nine was on record, but they weren't permitted to know who that was, which made Rhona all the more determined to find out.

The DNA from the body in the lane had found a match with the swab she'd taken from Barry Fraser. McNab had been right all along on that one, as had Danny. Which meant – as Danny had pointed out – that he, and to a lesser extent Freya, were the only ones left alive who could be linked to Leila and her practice of Witchcraft.

That thought discomfited Rhona, but she reassured herself that McNab had taken the warning on Freya's safety seriously, and was with her now.

At that point her mobile screen lit up with Sean's name.

She let it ring three times before she made up her mind to answer.

'Have you eaten?' were Sean's first words.

Rhona laughed. 'You always ask me that.'

'I always have to. Well?'

'I thought about Italian but instead stopped at the chippie on the way home.'

'What about company?'

'I'd welcome some,' Rhona said honestly.

'Will I do?'

'Yes.'

'I'll bring my supper with me. I'm always hungry when I've been playing, as well you know.'

'I remember.'

'Okay. I'll see you in fifteen minutes.'

The relief she felt at the prospect of company that didn't involve work, surprised her. Or maybe McNab's happy expression as he'd departed the Italian restaurant had inspired her to forsake the lonely menu, however tasty, and head for home.

Hunger pangs had made her stop at the local chippie. There she'd chosen Chrissy's favourite, a smoked sausage supper. She'd managed the sausage but not the chips. The resultant feeling of hunger unsatisfied made her wonder what Sean would bring with him in the way of food and wine.

Rhona discovered soon enough.

Sean arrived with a covered dish and asked her to put it in the oven for fifteen minutes at 180 degrees.

'I could microwave quicker,' she offered.

The look he gave her silenced any other suggestions on that front.

'A white for you. A red for me.' He plonked the two bottles on the table. 'It's chilled,' he added, also producing a French stick that smelt hot and very fresh. 'The new bakery close to my flat. They try and catch the late-night brigade.'

'Like us,' she offered.

He set the table, moving about the kitchen as though it were his own. Rhona had no wish to argue. Sean had come when she called, which put them on an even footing as far as she was concerned. He could use her kitchen as he wished.

'Should be ready now.' Sean swept the dish from the oven and placed it on the table. Peeling back the foil, he revealed three giant stuffed mushrooms oozing scents that Magnus would have loved.

'Two for me. One for you. Or if you're not hungry, three for me.' Checking her expression, Sean scooped one onto her plate, then offered her bread to dip in the sauce.

They ate in comfortable silence. At moments like this, Rhona wondered why she'd asked Sean to leave, but the truth was, she needed her own place free from emotional involvement and, she suspected, Sean needed the same.

As he served them coffee, Rhona tackled one of the reasons she'd invited him here.

'Danny Hardy was outside the flat when I came home earlier.'

Sean looked concerned. 'And?'

'He told me things about the case, which I've duly told McNab,' Rhona said. 'However, I need to get a message to Danny from McNab.'

'This isn't a police trap to take Danny into custody?'

'No. Quite the opposite,' Rhona said.

Sean raised a quizzical eyebrow. 'McNab's playing off the park again?'

'You could say that.'

Sean considered her request.

'Give me the message and I'll do my best.'

'Thank you.'

'Is that all?'

'Not quite.'

Something had changed between them. The sands on which their relationship had been built had shifted. Imperceptibly perhaps, but Rhona had experienced a sense of it on the previous two occasions Sean had been here.

And she felt it even more strongly now as she lay in his arms.

She thought back to the beginning, when she'd been searching for her son. How Sean had gone to Paris, asking her to go with him, but she'd refused.

She had eventually joined Sean there, when she had found her son, or when he had found her. Stepping off that train in Paris, her joy at seeing Sean had matched the intensity of her emotions at finding Liam. It had been a moment to savour and hold in her heart.

Maybe this was how it could be?

Rhona allowed herself a moment of happiness before she closed her eyes and drifted off to sleep.

50

The interview over and report written, McNab made for the coffee machine. Already one o'clock, he wondered if he should really visit Freya. Exhaustion had taken over from his earlier elation and his mind seethed with the story Mark Howitt had just told him.

He checked his mobile but there was no response to his earlier message.

He drank the espresso and pressed the button for another. When it failed to appear, McNab punched the machine in frustration.

At that moment a uniform appeared at the door of the waiting room. McNab shot him a warning look, assuming his arrival had been occasioned by his argument with the coffee machine.

It hadn't.

'Sir . . . can you come down to the cells?'

McNab read his shocked expression. 'Why?'

'It's Mark Howitt, sir. He's dead.'

I, Mark Howitt, confess to the killing of Leila Hardy, Shannon Jones and the barman Barry Fraser. I killed Shannon Jones and Barry Fraser because they could identify me as the man who left the pub with Leila that night. No one else will die now.

McNab threw the confession down on DI Wilson's desk.

'This is shite, boss. Mark Howitt had sex with Leila Hardy, then ran away when he found her dead in that room. He didn't kill her and he didn't kill the others.'

'You're sure about that?'

McNab hesitated. He was sure, but it would take more than his word to prove it. 'Forensic results should show he wasn't in Shannon's flat or anywhere near the body of Barry Fraser.'

'What if that's not the case?'

A wave of anger broke over McNab. He'd chased Mark Howitt but had never caught him. Mark had given himself up in the end and last night had told his story. A story that had rung true to McNab.

'The hand in the video wasn't his,' he said.

'That doesn't mean he wasn't there,' Bill countered, just as McNab had done earlier with Mark. 'Way back when we discussed this, we contemplated that there might be two perpetrators involved. What about the friend?'

'I ordered him to come in and give a DNA sample and a statement.'

'Has he done it?'

McNab ran his hand through his hair. 'I don't know, sir.'

DI Wilson gave him a sympathetic look. 'You've been here all night. Go home, Sergeant. Get some sleep.'

McNab laughed. 'Like that's going to happen, sir.'

'A death in custody is a serious matter, especially the death of the son of a prominent QC.'

McNab grimaced. 'Mark's last words to me when I mentioned contacting his father were, "I'm dead to him now".'

The duty doctor examined the prisoner Mark Howitt and found him to be in good physical condition, although low in mood.
He had not been put on suicide watch, although a police officer had checked him at half-hourly intervals. He had surrendered his valuables and had been deemed as having nothing on his person which might be used to harm himself or others.

He had requested paper and a pen to write to his parents, which had been duly supplied. He had been seen shortly after this, writing at the desk. At the next check he was on his bed apparently asleep with his face turned to the wall.

The next time he was checked, he lay in the same position but there was a smell from the cell which suggested that he may have soiled himself. On entering the cell the officer found that the prisoner had taken off his socks and wedged them deep into his throat. The doctor then called tried to resuscitate the prisoner but failed. He was pronounced dead at 12.55.

Bill had phoned Mark Howitt Senior in person that morning to tell him the news of his son's suicide in custody. Bill chose not to elaborate on the circumstances until he met him in person. He owed him that much at least.

He and Mark Howitt Senior were friends from way back, when Bill had been at the police college and Mark a defence lawyer. They'd kept in touch over the years, although sporadically. As QC and detective inspector they did not move in the same social circles, but that didn't mean they didn't appreciate the role each of them played in upholding the law. Bill was aware that, though unsaid, Mark Howitt Senior had little time for Superintendent Sutherland, although they were often required to be seen together. In that, as in other things, they shared a common bond.

Despite his exalted position and wealth, Bill regarded

Mark Howitt as a man he could deal with. A man he could trust. A man who deserved to be told the whole truth about his son, as far as Bill was aware of it.

The formalities of the identification of his son over, Bill suggested they go somewhere quiet to talk.

'I'd prefer outside the station,' said the man who'd appeared to age ten years in the last half an hour. 'I don't want to be away from Sarah for long. I've chosen not to tell her. I hope I may not have to.'

Bill had no words to say what he felt at this moment.

'Can we talk somewhere in the open? A park perhaps?'

Bill had led him to the nearby square and they were seated there now. The morning sun played on the trees that were already showing signs of autumn.

Bill spoke slowly and quietly, aware that what he was about to say would be difficult to take in, even for someone of the intelligence and discernment of the man before him. He explained how Mark had come into the station and confessed to being the man who'd left The Pot Still with Leila Hardy on the night she died.

'He admitted he was high on drugs and drink and had sex with Leila, but insisted he didn't kill her. My detective sergeant believed him and there is some video evidence sent to Mark's mobile which suggests he was being pressured into believing he had suffocated the girl. This has been proved false, although he could have been present when it happened.'

The face before him had become etched in stone, each line deepened like scores on granite.

'I suspected something was wrong when we met to discuss his mother. The news of her impending death was a shock to him. He wanted to come and see her but I forbade it. That was a mistake.'

'Mark left a statement admitting to all three murders. He insisted that he killed Shannon Jones and the barman who served them that night, because they could identify him.'

'Is that possible?'

'It could be if we have forensic evidence to put him at those crime scenes.'

Mark Howitt Senior stared straight ahead.

'I don't believe we should discuss this any more. I thank you for giving me the details of Mark's death and the circumstances that led up to it.'

He rose and held out his hand to Bill. The handshake was as firm as ever.

'Let me know when I can have the body of my son.'

Bill watched him walk away, a broken man who had lost his son and, it seemed, would soon lose his wife. But Bill had read something else on that granite face. His old friend had wanted to tell Bill something, but found he couldn't. Or not yet, anyway.

He brought out his mobile and called home. Margaret answered almost immediately.

'Bill, what is it?' she said, sounding worried.

'Nothing,' he lied, 'I just wanted to hear your voice.'

51

McNab stepped into the shower and turned it to the power setting. The impact on his skull felt like a pneumatic drill pounding his brain. He stood like that for all of five minutes, then moved the impact to his neck and shoulders.

After this he would eat, he promised himself, even if his stomach wasn't asking for food.

He stepped out after fifteen minutes, finishing with a blast of cold water. If he'd been asleep on his feet before, he was awake now.

Dried and dressed, he went through to the kitchen and put on the coffee machine, doubling the required number of spoonfuls of fresh coffee for the amount of water he poured in.

He'd purchased enough ingredients for breakfast in the local corner shop on his way home. He could have stopped at a cafe en route but feared that he would fall asleep, his face in whatever they served him.

He fired up the gas and, adding oil to the pan, set about frying the big breakfast pack of sausage, bacon, black and white pudding. Once cooked, he slipped the slices into the oven to keep warm and fried himself two eggs to go with it.

Once he began the process of eating, hunger took over and he demolished the food in record time. Wiping the plate clean with bread, he poured himself another coffee. Feeling human again, he said a silent thank you that he was not facing a hangover. He'd survived last night probably because he hadn't taken to whisky.

Opening the window wide, he stood in the draught of cool air and took a deep breath of Glasgow oxygen.

Now he would go and see Freya. She had to be told what had happened last night that had stopped him going round there, and it was better he did that in person. Trying her number, he heard it ring out unanswered. Well past nine o'clock now, he told himself she would be at the university library, and that's where he should head first. He left a message on voicemail to that effect, apologizing for not coming over due to an emergency at work, which he would explain when he saw her.

McNab then put his dishes in the sink, ran some water on them, fetched his jacket and set off.

The food and the shower had brought a clarity to his thinking that had escaped him in the long hours of the night. His gut feeling told him that Mark had lied. Not about the night he spent with Leila, but about his contact with the person who'd sent him the video clip.

That someone had in some manner persuaded Mark to kill himself. 'No one else will die.' That phrase had jumped out at McNab. His own initial response to it had been positive, because he wanted to believe that now Freya would be safe. But who had said, 'No one else will die'?

McNab didn't think those words had come from Mark, but from someone who'd persuaded Mark that if he confessed, that would be the case.

Mark had sacrificed himself, but for whom and for what?

The image of the Nine reared again in his head. Power, money, influence. That's what the men Leila had performed sexual magick with all had.

'Fuck them,' McNab said out loud. 'I'm going to fuck them, if it's the last thing I do.'

Rhona had risen to the drill of her mobile.

Sean, on the other hand, slept on. This time Rhona didn't resent his peaceful sleep but merely acknowledged it. She thought about placing a kiss on his forehead, but decided against it. He might stir and envelop her in his arms and she would succumb. She must save dessert for a later date.

The caller was Chrissy, her voice high with excitement or shock.

'Mark Howitt handed himself in and confessed to the three murders then suffocated himself in his cell.'

A stunned Rhona asked Chrissy to repeat this more slowly.

'A mate called me. When she went on duty this morning, the station was alive with the news. Mark Howitt, the QC's son, gave himself up last night. Confessed to McNab that he was the man who'd taken Leila Hardy home. Then wrote a further confession in his cell. He claimed that he also killed Shannon and Barry Fraser to cover his tracks.'

Rhona called a halt at this point.

'We have no forensic tests to prove that the man with Leila that night was also present at the other crime scenes.'

'Well, we'd better prove it or not, soon,' Chrissy said in her usual forthright manner. 'My bet's on a false confession.'

Rhona was inclined on instinct to agree.

'Why would he do that?'

'He said that no more killings would happen,' Chrissy told her.

'Has this hit the news?'

'Not so far. Want to take a bet how long it takes? Witch

333

killer and son of QC confesses all, then commits suicide. He promises in his confession that no one else will die.'

'You should be a reporter,' Rhona said.

'I'd write a damn good headline,' Chrissy retorted. 'But seriously, you need to get down to the mortuary.'

There are some places in life that are necessary. There are places necessary for the dead too. A room full of drawers of dead people sounded like something from a horror film, yet here they were. As necessary as air was, to those who lived.

The scent of death was masked in here by the presence of cold. Deep, penetrating cold that halted, or at least suspended, the organic disintegration of the human body that was both inevitable and essential.

Dust to dust, ashes to ashes, or rather decomposition, which didn't sound so philosophical, but did sound less messy. In her time, Rhona had had her hands in gloop consisting of human remains, mud and blood, so looking on cold marbled bodies could be thought of as easy in comparison.

Except it wasn't.

The young man before her was a perfect specimen of a male human body. Sculptured. Bone and sinew in complete harmony. Handsome even in death. The enormity of the loss of possibility was there to view.

Mark Howitt had gone out for a night of fun. The penis that lay there cold and flaccid had driven him to pastures new. Excitement heightened by cocaine and alcohol. But at the end of the day he was driven by a male's need to have sex. Primeval, maybe, but nevertheless the reason why humans continued to exist. Without that drive, there would be no future. No future generation.

It seemed that Leila had responded to this need, matching

it with her own desire. There had been no coercion, except perhaps on her part.

Neither of those two young people had wished evil, but nevertheless it had been visited on them.

An' it harm none, do what thou wilt.

How did following such a creed end in such evil?

There would be a post-mortem, but the result was already known. Mark Howitt had died by his own hand. So determined had he been to end his life that he had stuffed his socks so far down his throat that it would have been impossible to stop his own suffocation.

He had died as he thought Leila had died. A fitting retribution.

Or was it?

Rhona indicated that she'd seen enough and the mortuary assistant shut the drawer.

Bill was seated in his usual place at the window, the mug of cold coffee or tea on the desk beside him. Rhona waited while he turned, the resultant girn sounding like an old friend reappearing in difficult circumstances.

'You saw him?' he said.

'Yes.'

'I broke the news to his father. We know one another from way back.' He halted for a moment. 'It was Mark Howitt QC who I consulted about the denied access.'

'My God,' Rhona said.

'Strange how circular life is.'

'And now his son is implicated.'

'Do you believe his confession?' Bill said.

'The DNA sample I took from his body will indicate whether he was with Leila the night she died,' Rhona told him.

'What about the other crime scenes?'

'We should know in forty-eight hours.'

'How would you feel if your son was a murderer?' Bill said to the air, but also to Rhona. 'Would it be your fault?'

'There must be a time when a child becomes an adult and makes their own choices.'

'That sounds like Magnus talking,' Bill said. 'Do we not make the child that becomes the adult?'

'You and I both know that no matter how good and loving a childhood might be, psychopaths still exist.'

'Was Mark Howitt a psychopathic killer or a daft boy who found himself caught up in something terrible?' Bill said.

'That's what we have to find out.'

Forensics were a way of mapping out what happened in intricate detail. There was no emotion involved, only science. The science of who, where and when.

There was a cleanness in that. A certainty. Yet nothing was certain. In the past, the present or the future. It was how you viewed it that mattered.

Imagine a fence post above a ravine where a body lies. Whose DNA was on it? Those who had placed their hand there as they climbed over the fence to take a closer look at what lay below? The man who had cut the post? The man who had hammered it into the ground? All had imprinted their person on it. Only one DNA sample belonged to the person who'd held on to that post as he'd tossed his victim into the ravine.

DNA wasn't enough, but in Mark's case, it might be sufficient to make the authorities believe the man who made the confession was in fact guilty of all three murders.

On the other hand, DNA could also be purposefully placed

at a crime scene to implicate the innocent. In Rhona's opinion, Mark Howitt's confession hadn't cleared up the mystery, but only added to it.

Rhona told Bill what she thought.

'I'll request Magnus watch McNab's interview with Mark,' Bill said, 'and also examine his written confession. Maybe he can give us some insight into the thought processes that led to his suicide.'

As she made to leave, Bill added, 'You and McNab sort out your differences over the *Stonewarrior* case?'

The sudden question had caught her unawares, but Rhona answered as honestly as she could. 'McNab and I will always have differences of opinion. But we're okay, I think.'

'Good.'

The text came in as she pulled up in her parking space at the lab. Seeing it was from Danny, she said a silent thank you to Sean. The answer to her message about meeting with Ollie was short and sweet.

I'll be there.

The second task McNab had allotted her, of helping identify a list of police officers currently on the DNA database, would take a lot longer. In that, she had DI Wilson's help. Bill had surprised her by bringing up the subject himself just prior to her departure from his office. His message had been suitably oblique, but she knew Bill well enough to believe that he too was on the case.

52

Freya had chosen to sleep within the magick circle. After receiving McNab's text, she'd resigned herself to the fact that he wasn't coming, tonight at least. She'd fetched a pillow and duvet and, wrapping herself in it, had lain down before the altar. The smell of incense and flickering candles comforted her and had eventually lulled her to sleep. That and the sense that both Leila and Shannon were there with her.

The box room had no window and therefore no daylight penetrated the space. Eventually the distant sound of cars outside roused her and she'd woken to the lingering fragrant smell, but a thick darkness, as the candles had all burned themselves out.

She rose, groaning a little at the stiffness of limbs that had spent the night on a hard floor. Every morning since Leila's death, she'd woken with a tight knot of fear in her stomach. This morning it had lessened, although hadn't disappeared altogether.

She showered and put on the coffee machine.

Checking her mobile, Freya listened again to McNab's voicemail just to hear his warm tone of concern for her, but wishing too that there was a further message from him.

He's a police officer, she told herself. That's his life. If I want to be with him, I'll have to get used to it.

She left the flat just after nine and began her walk to the university library, determined to make proper use of her day. The deadline she'd set herself on her thesis wouldn't be met if she didn't start applying herself again. Grant had been kind to her over the whole business, checking up on how the thesis was going, encouraging her to talk to him about the investigation and her place in it. He'd even allowed her to skip a few of her shifts in Archives to allow her more time with her research.

She'd discovered in their talks just how well informed Grant was on the Ferguson collection and on the occult in particular. It was easier to ask him a question sometimes than to go searching the catalogue for the answer. He could often point her to the exact pamphlet or volume to refer to. Considering there were 670 books in the collection on the history of Witchcraft, Grant's recall was considerable.

Freya knew Grant was aware of her Wiccan beliefs and respected them. She found their talks on the subject reassuring and often enlightening. He'd apparently had similar discussions with Leila and Shannon.

Dr Peter Charles had been equally interested in her work. They'd spent an hour in the old library together. He'd revealed he'd been a chemistry student at the university and since the Ferguson collection had originally been under the auspices of the chemistry department, he'd seen the old library in its original form. He'd voiced his disappointment that the precious collection was now housed 'in that soulless glass tower block'.

'But it's safer there,' Freya had remonstrated.

His smile at that point had been thoughtful and not a little sad. Afterwards, they'd walked together through the cloisters, but rather than head for the exit he'd urged her to accompany him to what she'd always considered the front of the building, the Gothic face that overlooked Kelvingrove Park and the art gallery below.

He'd walked her round, describing the meaning and purpose of the elaborate carvings and statues.

When they'd eventually reached the gates again, he'd held her hand in his and thanked her kindly for taking the time to talk to an old man much obsessed with 'what we don't yet understand'.

Her reply – 'Is that not what a place of learning should be obsessing about?' – had brought a grateful smile.

When he'd departed down University Avenue, Freya had crossed to the Wellington Church, whose doors stood open. It wasn't a place for her religion, yet from the moment she'd come here to Glasgow and the university precinct, she'd admired its splendour. With its neoclassical portico, complete with a full colonnade of Corinthian columns, it stood in direct contrast to the Gothic splendour of the university across the way.

Standing there in the entrance had reminded Freya that Wiccans needed no stone palace in which to worship, but only the magick that came from acknowledging their place in the eternal cycle of being. Freya had had the feeling that Dr Peter Charles would agree.

This morning as she approached the library entrance, she spotted a figure she knew was waiting for her. Had the auburn-haired man been Michael, she would have run towards him and thrown herself into his arms. When she realized it was Danny, Freya stopped, her desire to turn away and hope he hadn't seen her uppermost in her mind.

But he had seen her and there was to be no escape. From

Danny or from the stomach-churning fear his reappearance had brought her.

'I need to talk to you.'

Freya registered the sunken eyes and ashen skin.

'You look terrible,' she said.

Danny brushed her concerns away and indicated the rucksack he had over his shoulder. 'There wasn't a list in the Goddess statue, but I have Leila's Book of Shadows.' Before Freya could respond, he rushed on. 'Leila recorded all the spells she cast with the Nine. I think we can work out who they are.'

'Then you have to give the book to the police,' Freya said.

He read her determined expression. 'I will, after we figure it out.'

Freya wasn't convinced.

'If I hand it over now, what will they do? These people don't understand what's in there. And they don't believe in magick. Leila did, Shannon did and you do.' Danny looked imploringly at her. When she didn't respond, he added, 'Chances are they'll come to you anyway.'

In that he might be right.

'Okay,' Freya said. 'I'll take a look, but that's all.'

Relief flooded Danny's face. 'Thank you.'

'Let's go inside. I can find a quiet corner for us in Archives. Then if Leila made reference to anything in the collection, we can check it out.'

Freya knew she should ask permission from Grant to bring Danny into the library, but was pretty sure he wouldn't object, not if he thought it might help. She signed Danny in as a visitor and led him to the lift. Minutes later they were ensconced in her usual corner at the desk near the window.

'We're not allowed coffee in here,' she apologized, 'although you look as though you could do with one.'

'I'm okay,' Danny said. He pulled up a chair and sat down, shielding the contents of the desk from anyone who might suddenly appear from beyond the shelves that enclosed them. Once he seemed certain there was no one in the vicinity, he withdrew the Book of Shadows from his rucksack and placed it on the table.

It is quite beautiful, Freya thought, *like Leila*.

Fashioned from green leather, the surface etched with a pentagram held in the hands of the Goddess, it was fastened by two beautifully fashioned brass clasps.

Traditionally, a personal Book of Shadows should be destroyed on the owner's death. Seeing it here before her made Freya feel that Leila was still alive.

Danny unclipped it and, as he began carefully turning the pages, Freya glimpsed elegant and intricate writing and drawings, all in Leila's hand.

'What's in here will mean more to you than it does to me,' Danny said, 'although I can sense my sister when I touch it.'

He leafed through, eventually finding the section he was looking for, entitled 'The Nine'. 'There's a page for each of them,' he said, his voice bristling with anger.

Freya ran her eyes over the first entry, which consisted of a full-body sketch of a man and a date, which looked like a date of birth. Alongside this was what she guessed was a reduced version of the date of birth resulting in a single digit – the owner's birth number.

Below were two paragraphs of dense script written in what looked like the Seax-Wica runic alphabet, the first of which was in couplets.

'What does it say?' Danny said eagerly.

'I think the first part may be the spell, but it'll take time to decipher both sections,' Freya explained.

'How much time?'

'I'll have to get a copy of the runic alphabet and see what I can match up.'

Danny looked exasperated.

'I thought you would know.'

'I'm sorry. I will try, but I'll need to concentrate.'

Danny seemed to accept that. He glanced at his watch. 'I have to be somewhere. Can I call you later? See how you got on?'

Freya was relieved at the suggestion. She certainly couldn't focus with an impatient Danny there beside her. As he rose to leave, a figure popped his head round the shelves.

'Freya?' Grant said in surprise. 'I didn't know you were in.'

Freya, flustered, stood up. 'I'm sorry. I was planning on coming to talk to you but got a little waylaid.'

Grant's glance had fallen on the book, despite Danny's attempt to shield it.

'What have you got there?'

Freya didn't see any reason to lie, but still she hesitated to tell the entire truth.

'It's a Book of Shadows, my friend found. He thought I might be interested in taking a look at it.'

Grant was scrutinizing Danny, and Freya realized with a jolt that of course anyone who'd known Leila would recognize the likeness between them.

Danny took the initiative and held out his hand. 'I'm Danny, Leila's brother.'

Sympathy flooded Grant's face as he took Danny's hand.

'I'm so sorry about your sister. She was such a lovely young woman.'

Danny nodded his appreciation.

'Is that Leila's Book of Shadows?' Grant said.

'It is.'

'I understood that it was normal practice for a Witch's book to be burned on her passing?'

'There's nothing normal in the way my sister died.'

Grant looked aghast at having upset Danny. 'I apologize. That was an inappropriate thing to say.' He turned to Freya. 'If you need any help deciphering the contents – I assume that's what you're doing – then I put myself at your disposal.'

'Grant knows a lot about the various Wiccan alphabets,' Freya said.

'I'd rather it was kept between Freya and me,' Danny said. 'It's all I have left of my sister.'

Grant nodded. 'Of course. I understand. I'll leave you to it.'

When Grant disappeared, Danny looked at Freya.

'Can he be trusted?'

'Leila trusted him. Shannon too. He knew they were Witches. He knows I'm one.'

'I don't want him looking at the book.'

'Okay,' Freya said. 'If you like I'll take it home to study.'

Danny looked relieved when she didn't argue. 'I'd rather you did.'

'I'll need to check out a couple of reference books to help.'

Danny nodded. 'I'll call you later.' He turned back as he remembered something else. 'I've spoken to the forensic woman. I think she's on our side.'

His words were unexpected, but nevertheless made Freya's heart lift.

'I hope so.'

53

Danny's decision to come to Ollie's flat had forced McNab to change plans, so he never made the library and still hadn't met up with Freya.

Instead he was now seated beside the man who, after Mark Howitt, he'd sought the most. Danny Hardy looked even more like his sister than McNab had previously registered, but then he'd never seen Leila alive, only some photographs. He had no wish to recall the terrible image of her corpse hanging in that room.

McNab was glad Danny had never witnessed that, although seeing his sister laid out in the mortuary was bad enough.

Danny Hardy was clearly a man in mourning, who also had revenge on his mind. McNab could empathize with that. He'd made his own vow to expose the Nine. Mark Howitt's death had only strengthened his resolve on that front. So he and Danny shared a common goal. McNab just had to make sure they played their cards as close to the law as was necessary, to avoid any of them paying a heavy price for actions such as the one they were involved in now.

'Okay.' Ollie peered at them through his trademark specs. 'I've uploaded the three video clips and enhanced the quality. I can do more work on them, frame by frame, but that will take time.'

'Who took these?' McNab asked Danny.

'I set it up beforehand and Leila agreed to start the recording, secretly of course.'

'Which goes some way to explain the quality, and why the camera isn't always focused on the right spot,' Ollie said as he set the film running.

Initially there was more sound than image, but eventually two figures appeared in the camera's line of sight. McNab felt the tension in Danny's body as the lens found Leila's naked back. In this instance, Leila's body shielded the man's face, but they did have a partial view of the left hand.

'Stop,' McNab ordered. 'Can you zoom in there?'

Ollie selected the area and did as asked.

'That's a pinkie ring. Is there a crest of some sort on it?'

Ollie eased in further. 'A horse or maybe a unicorn?' he suggested.

'Any views of his face?'

The male had his back against the raised end of the sofa, Leila astride him, continuing to block their view.

'Did she do that on purpose?' McNab said, exasperated.

'I had a hard time persuading her to let me film it at all. From Leila's point of view I was messing with the spell,' Danny explained.

It was clear when they reached the end of the clip that their only means of identifying the first male was by the ring.

The man in the next video was just as hidden, although there was a good shot of his right ear.

'Ears are pretty unique and identifiable, provided we come up with a suspect,' Ollie assured them.

Number three was the best of the bunch. This man was tall and broad, so that even though Leila was astride him, she wasn't totally blocking his face. Ollie paused the video at the appropriate moment and zoomed in.

The hairline was grey, the dark eyebrows distinctive, as were the brown eyes.

'That's better.' Ollie voiced what McNab had been thinking. 'Particularly having access to the eyes.'

Danny regarded McNab. 'What happens now?'

McNab didn't want to promise something he couldn't deliver.

'It's a start, but it's not enough. Not until we have suspects to compare them with.'

'What if one of the men in the video clips is a police officer?'

'Did Leila say he was?'

'She hinted it,' Danny said.

'If that's true, that would help.' McNab explained why the DNA of serving officers was stored during a live investigation.

'So you have access to details on this group, even images of them we could compare to?' Danny said excitedly.

'In theory, yes, although they'll probably be in the hundreds and they'll cover all of Scotland.'

'If I run their photos through the comparison software . . .' Ollie began. 'We might get lucky.'

A glimpse of a hand, a bit of an ear – McNab only wished he had Ollie's faith it would be enough. The Nine had been scrupulous about keeping their identities secret up till now. He believed they had killed to keep it that way. And all he had were three video clips that showed almost nothing and the vague hope of outing a policeman, against the express orders of their superiors.

'What spooked them enough to kill your sister?' McNab said.

Danny didn't like the question, that much was plain from his face.

347

'Well?' McNab insisted.

'I think they found out about the recordings.'

'So they know they exist?'

'I'm not sure. Leila may have given the game away.'

'You didn't try some blackmail?'

Danny shook his head vehemently. 'No.'

'What about Barry?'

'He was keeping an eye on Leila for me. Who she met in the pub, that sort of thing.'

So Barry had been watching out for Leila at her brother's request. McNab eyed Danny. 'You've definitely told me everything?'

'Yes.'

Danny's expression was set on stubborn, so McNab let it go, for the moment. His gut feeling was telling him there was something else, maybe just a thought Danny had had, but he wasn't willing to divulge it at the moment.

'Both Ollie and I are going out on a limb on this,' McNab told him firmly. 'By rights I should be interviewing you under caution, asking where you were on the night Barry Fraser died, maybe even charging you with withholding evidence.'

'You know I had nothing to do with Barry's death. And maybe I should be in custody. I'd feel fucking safer.'

Danny was right up to a point. He had brought the video recordings as requested.

'We're evens,' McNab said, 'for the moment, but as soon as we have something on these guys, I want you at the station giving a full statement.'

'When will you have a result?' Danny said.

'Forty-eight hours,' McNab said. 'Keep out of sight until then.'

54

Freya nestled the backpack against her shoulder, feeling the weight and significance of its contents. Grant had been right. A Witch's Book of Shadows should be burned on her passing.

She imagined how they might do that, she and Danny, when this was all over, then suddenly realized it would never truly be over for Danny and that Leila's precious book would become a piece of evidence handled by scores of people.

Such a thought brought her deep disquiet.

Leila's spells were hers alone, their potency dependent on her power as a Witch. Their exposure, the secret of her thoughts and wishes, might mean she would enjoy no peace in the afterlife.

For that reason, the Book of Shadows should be burned.

Taking the Book of Shadows home now seemed wrong. Leila's place of worship felt the lesser violation but, as far as she was aware, the police were still in there.

Then a thought struck.

If she couldn't gain access to Leila's place of worship, perhaps access to Leila's flat might be possible? There she would be close to Leila, maybe even gain her spirit guidance in what she was about to attempt. Wiccans believed in reincarnation, but there was also 'the time between', the length of time spent between lives, when those who had passed became spirit guides or guardian angels for those left behind. That comforting thought grew in Freya's mind until it was the only one.

Rhona was in the midst of checking all the forensic results received. It was as yet a sporadic picture and she had no clear indication that Mark Howitt's confession had any forensic basis in the truth.

One thing was certain, however. She believed the person who'd tied the knots in the cingulum used to hang Leila was right-handed and she now knew that Leila and Mark Howitt, the chief suspect and the man she'd taken home that fateful night, were not.

Neither Leila nor Mark had tied the slip knot that had been used to hang her.

Added to that, the video McNab had shown her of the hand inserting the material into Leila's mouth had been of a right-handed man.

People didn't lead by the right if they were left-handed.

She was also running a search on the DNA database, identifying police officers currently involved in a case. It was a valid search on her part and hadn't as yet caused any disquiet. How she would deal with the list this achieved was something Rhona wasn't yet sure of.

Her mobile rang around eleven and Rhona was pleased to see Freya's name on the screen.

'Freya?'

'I'm sorry to call on a Saturday.'

'No worries. I'm at home, but working.'

The voice on the other end hesitated.

'What is it?' Rhona said encouragingly.

'I have Leila's Book of Shadows.'

It was obvious by her manner that Freya thought Rhona would know what she was referring to. Thanks to Magnus, Rhona did.

'May I ask how you have it?'

'Danny brought it to me this morning.'

So it had been Danny who'd removed the book from the altar. Rhona waited, giving Freya time to continue.

'It may contain references which might be useful to your investigation,' Freya said.

'How can I help?' Rhona immediately offered.

'This may sound strange,' Freya rushed on, 'but I think it would be easier to interpret the writings if I felt closer to Leila.'

'How?'

'Could you and I gain access to the place she died?'

'Her flat?'

'Yes.'

As Chief Forensic Scientist, Rhona could request to revisit the crime scene, but should she take Freya with her?

'What do you want to do there?'

'Decipher what Leila wrote about the Nine.'

A sense of death still lingered here. The smell of it had dissipated, replaced by chemicals used in the forensic examination, plus dust and disuse. Rhona imagined she could hear the steady beat of her heart in the depth of the silence and could see from the rapid pulse in Freya's neck that her heart was racing.

'Which room would be best?' Rhona said.

'Where did Leila die?' Freya was struggling to hold her voice steady.

'Probably the room with the dolls.'

Freya was looking at her, puzzled. 'What dolls?' she said.

Rhona pointed at the closed door, her memory of the last time she'd opened it as powerful as ever.

'There were twenty-seven Barbie-type dolls hanging in there, in rows of nine and split by hair colour, red, blonde and brunette. We found Leila's body behind them.'

After hesitating about whether she should reveal this fact at all, Freya's reaction was the last thing Rhona expected.

Freya gave a little laugh.

'The pattern of three and nine is very powerful in Wicca,' she explained, 'and the dolls I believe represented the Goddess Freya. This was Leila's way of making the room powerful. They shouldn't have killed her in there.'

'I don't understand,' Rhona said.

'Wiccans believe if you give of yourself – your love; your life –you will be thrice rewarded,' Freya said. 'But send forth harm and that too will return thrice over.'

55

'I would suggest you get the advice of a handwriting expert,' Magnus said. 'But in my opinion this is a false confession.'

'Why?' Bill said.

'I've watched the taped interview with McNab. The suspect wants to confess to what he remembers happened and by his mannerisms, his voice, the words he chooses, I would say he's telling the truth. He feels enormous guilt, which of course might also be present if he had killed Leila, but the honest detail he gives convinces me that he didn't. The relief too, when McNab points out that the hand in the video isn't his.'

'So what changed between that interview and the written confession in the cell?' Bill said.

Magnus indicated the copy before him.

I, Mark Howitt, confess to the killing of Leila Hardy, Shannon Jones and the barman Barry Fraser. I killed Shannon Jones and Barry Fraser because they could identify me as the man who left the pub with Leila that night. No one else will die now.

'Compared to the examples you have of the suspect's normal handwriting, this script suggests he's doing this under duress, like a confession looks when given under torture. And the last sentence: *No one else will die now*. Who's saying that? I don't believe it's the suspect. It sounds to me like a repeat of something he's been told.'

Bill nodded his agreement. 'DS McNab believes Mark met with the man who sent the video, although as you saw he denied this in the interview.'

'Something was done or said to cause Mark to both confess, then commit suicide.'

'Mark's father is a well-respected QC with a terminally ill wife, who isn't expected to live much longer.'

Magnus contemplated this. 'So, the psychological pressure on the suspect was even greater than I was aware.' He paused. 'Were Mark and his mother close?'

'Apparently so, although she'd kept the extent of her illness a secret from him. When his father revealed it, Mark wanted to go and see his mother, but his father refused to allow that.'

'Can I ask why?'

'Apparently the mother had forbidden her husband to tell Mark how close the end was.'

'Yet he did?' Magnus said. 'May I ask what you plan to do about this?'

'Make sure that Mark Howitt's confession and his suicide do not close down this enquiry.'

It was a meeting that had to be faced, yet Bill wasn't sure it was quite the time to do it. If he revealed he'd been conducting his own private enquiry into the identity of the police officer who'd had sex with Leila Hardy, that search was unlikely to be permitted to progress any further.

Superintendent Sutherland might be persuaded into giving his reasons for keeping the name of the officer under wraps, but Bill didn't hold out much hope that he would. There could be many reasons for doing so, one of which stood uppermost in Bill's mind, namely that by making the officer's identity common knowledge, it might endanger his life.

Having made his decision, Bill knocked on the door and awaited permission to enter.

When that didn't happen, Bill chose to walk in anyway. He found Sutherland on the phone. When he was shot a warning glance, Bill chose to stand his ground, which essentially meant the phone call had to come to an end.

'Sorry, sir, I thought I heard a "come in".'

'You didn't, Detective Inspector.'

'Then would you prefer me to come back later, sir?'

'No.'

Sutherland didn't wave him to a seat, so Bill continued standing. He preferred it that way because he got to look down on his superior officer rather than meet him eye to eye.

'Go on, Inspector. What did you wish to say?'

'We believe the confession from the suspect Mark Howitt is a false one, made under duress.'

Sutherland was immediately on to that. 'What duress?'

'We believe he met with the person blackmailing him about his involvement with the victim and was persuaded to help end the killing by taking responsibility for it.'

'Why would he do such a thing?'

Bill said what he had expressly come to say. 'I believe either his father or his mother were threatened, sir, and that tipped him over the edge.' As he spoke, Bill studied Sutherland's expression. Always closed, never giving anything away, except perhaps irritation, Bill detected a flicker of surprise in his eyes. Sutherland, he decided, had not seen that one coming.

'And your evidence for this?'

'His interview with DS McNab was viewed by criminal psychologist Professor Magnus Pirie. He suggested that when Mark used the words "No one else will die" in his confession, he was repeating the words of his blackmailer.'

Sutherland swung his chair round at this point, blocking Bill's view of his expression. It was a tactic Bill used himself and he understood the reason for it. He waited quietly for Sutherland to turn to him again.

'I believe you and Mark Howitt QC are old friends, and that you spoke to him personally about the death of his son,' Sutherland said.

'I did, sir.'

'Did you run this theory past him?'

'No, sir. I hadn't formulated it by then.'

'Did he give any indication that he thought he might be under threat?'

'No, sir, he did not.'

'Clearly this will be a distressing time for him. I would like him shielded from the press as much as possible, particularly since his wife's death seems imminent.'

'I agree, sir.'

'And where are we in identifying the Nine?'

It was a question Bill didn't expect to be asked, so wasn't sure how to answer. Eventually he went for the truth. 'No further forward except for the serving officer.'

Sutherland looked slightly taken aback at this. 'You have identified him, Inspector?'

'I have a list of possibilities,' Bill said honestly.

'Then we should discuss them.'

56

She'd helped Freya carry a small writing table and chair from the bedroom through to the dolls' room. There Freya had reverently laid the green leather Book of Shadows and the volumes on runic script, the ones she'd checked out of the library.

Rhona was keen to view the contents of Leila's book, but got the impression that Freya didn't want her to. Yet.

'A Witch's Book of Shadows is very personal. It shouldn't be handled by others. I promised Danny to keep it safe,' Freya said. 'Once I do what he asked, then he says he'll hand it over to Detective Sergeant McNab.'

It was a reasonable request and, Rhona decided, one she could comply with. So she took herself into the kitchen and set up her laptop there. From what Freya had said, McNab wasn't yet aware of the book's existence and that Freya now had it.

Rhona contemplated warning him of this, then decided not to.

She had a feeling he would find out soon enough.

The quiet in the flat continued unbroken. Had she been asked to describe it, Rhona would have said it was the silence of the dead. Wandering through to the bedroom, she had a sense of what the flat must have been like when Leila lived there. One thing was obvious: Leila had loved bright colours

357

and pretty things. She had been a vibrant, intelligent woman who should have had a long life ahead of her. A life someone had stolen.

Two hours passed before Freya called out to her.

On entering the room, Rhona discovered the table and chair had been moved to the place Leila had been found hanging. The hook itself was now stored with the other forensic evidence taken from the flat, and Rhona hadn't mentioned the spot's significance.

'This is where she died, isn't it?' Freya said.

'Yes, it is.'

'Where are the dolls now?'

'Stored with the other forensic evidence.'

'Did the dolls tell you anything?'

'Nine of them had a sketch inside, together with semen samples.'

'There's a sketch of each of the men in here too.' She gestured Rhona over. 'But I haven't been able to translate the runes. They don't match what's in the books I brought.' Worry and exhaustion etched Freya's face. 'I'm sorry.'

Freya pushed the open book across for Rhona to view.

This time the drawings were more detailed, making the others hidden in the dolls mere pointers to their entry here.

'Is that a date of birth?' Rhona said.

'I think so. The following number is their birth number derived from it. Then I think it's the spell she cast, and a paragraph maybe about the outcome of the spell, or further details of the subject associated with the spell.'

'Which would be very useful,' Rhona said.

'I know.' Freya looked dejected.

Dusk had fallen outside and the room was filled with long shadows. The view across the lane was of the curved windows of the upper floors of the Lion Chambers, and the empty rooms beyond.

'Shall we call it a day?' Rhona said. 'Get something to eat and try again tomorrow?'

Freya thought about that.

'Can you fetch something in and some coffee? I'd like to stay a little longer.'

'You'll be all right here on your own?' Rhona asked.

'I'm not alone,' Freya assured her.

When Rhona departed, Freya took out her mobile. Keen not to be disturbed, she'd switched it off on her way here. Two texts pinged in. One from Michael suggesting they meet up. The other from Danny asking what was happening with the Book of Shadows.

Freya dialled a different number.

'Grant, I need some help with the runic alphabet in Leila's Book of Shadows.'

57

Danny pressed the buzzer again, keeping his finger on it longer this time.

Freya had said she was taking the Book of Shadows home, therefore she must be here.

Eventually someone from a different flat let him in just to stop the noise.

Danny took the stairs two at a time. When he'd got no response from Freya's mobile, he'd assumed she was concentrating and didn't want to be disturbed.

Now he wasn't so sure that was the reason.

I shouldn't have left her.

I should have taken her home. I should have made sure she was okay.

When he reached her door, Danny stood for a moment, determined to calm himself, not wanting Freya to see his fear.

He rapped and waited.

When there was no response, he tried again, louder this time.

The third time he banged and shouted through the letter box: 'Freya, it's Danny!'

At that point a door opened on the upper landing and a guy's head appeared above him.

'For fuck's sake, mate, give it a break. She's either not in or she doesn't want to speak to you.'

Danny quashed his desire to shout abuse back.

'Have you seen Freya this morning?'

'No. And she's not in now.'

As Danny had one more go at the door, the guy started down the stairs. Tall and muscled like a rugby player, Danny got the impression he intended tipping him over the banisters if he didn't leave of his own free will.

Danny stepped back from the door.

'Okay. Okay. I'm going.'

Muscleman stood three steps up and waited, a determined look on his face.

Danny had no alternative but to leave.

Back out on the street, he considered his options. Having tried once again to call Freya, with no response, he decided to head back to the library. Maybe Freya had remained there after all. Maybe the books she needed to decipher the runes couldn't be signed out.

Calmed by this thought, Danny set a course for the university.

Why don't you answer?

McNab flung the mobile on the table. He'd thought Freya had forgiven him, but it seemed he'd screwed up again. He should have been round to her place by now. Or should at least have spoken to her.

But that wasn't going to happen. Not for some time yet.

He lifted the espresso cup and drained the contents.

He and the boss were about to interview Jeff Barclay, who'd just presented himself at the front desk. But before that he needed some time alone with the boss. There was the little matter of the video clips to discuss.

McNab headed to the Gents first. The shower and decent

breakfast had perked him up earlier, and he wanted to keep that wide awake feeling. Hence the double espresso. He made use of the urinal first, the result no doubt of too much caffeine, then spent a few minutes splashing his face with cold water. Examining himself in the mirror above the sink, he acknowledged the bloodshot eyes and the rather too bristled chin, something he should have taken account of earlier.

It was always better to look smart and awake when about to go into the confessional.

The confessional had been a big feature of his Catholic upbringing. That and the implicit belief that as a Catholic he had a guardian angel. Something McNab was pretty sure wasn't available to Protestants. But back then, let's face it, there was a lot of pish talked. Most of which he'd now discarded, except the guardian angel, who'd saved his life more than once. McNab hoped he was still on side.

Refreshed, McNab approached the boss's office and knocked.

The voice that told him to come in sounded upbeat, which heartened McNab.

On entry, things continued to look good as he was told to take a seat.

McNab did so.

Now they were face to face across the desk, DI Wilson appeared to be waiting for McNab to begin the proceedings. Not sure how this meeting would pan out, McNab was keener that he not serve first. So he waited.

Eventually DI Wilson said, 'I believe you've been withholding information, Detective Sergeant.'

Rather taken aback by this announcement, McNab came in quickly with his denial. 'Not exactly, sir. I asked to see you so that I might *present* information.'

The boss sat back in his chair.

'Present away.'

McNab began with a brief résumé of how Mark Howitt had appeared on his radar and how he'd asked Tech to check the mobile number.

He was interrupted at this point, 'When were you aware that Mark Howitt was the son of a High Court judge?'

'Not *immediately*, sir.' McNab crossed his fingers. 'I contacted the girlfriend and she told me about Mark and Jeff's night out in Glasgow. She also mentioned the scratches on his shoulder.'

'So you thought you had your man?'

'Not right away, sir,' McNab said. 'I then checked Mark's home address and was granted access by his concierge.'

The boss's left eyebrow was raised at this point which flustered McNab a little. He raced on to counteract this. 'It looked as though he'd left in a hurry, taking some clothes with him. His work said he'd been signed off sick, so I thought I'd check the mate's place in Glasgow.'

The boss was listening intently now, so McNab carried on.

'Jeff Barclay denied Mark was there, but when he let me enter there were two glasses on the kitchen surface with a bottle of vodka nearby.' McNab explained about his search of the roof and how he'd taken the two shot glasses for fingerprint and DNA analysis.

'And that led to Jeff Barclay presenting himself here?'

'Yes, sir.' McNab relaxed a little.

Maybe things were going okay after all.

'What about the tapes you've been viewing?'

How the fuck did he know about that?

'I was just about to mention them, sir. Danny Hardy

brought the tapes and they were viewed by myself, Danny and someone from Tech,' he said, trying to keep Ollie's name out of it.

'And?'

'There are only partial views of three men. A set of hands. A right ear. And the upper part of a face to include the hairline, eyebrows and eyes.'

'So not distinguishable without comparisons?'

'No, sir.'

McNab thought he was through the worst, until the next question arrived.

'I take it Daniel Hardy is now in custody?'

The boss would be fully aware he wasn't in custody, so it was crunch time.

'I asked him to get back in touch in twenty-four hours and he agreed at that point to hand himself in,' McNab was swift to answer.

'And you believed him?'

McNab decided to come out fighting this time. 'Danny didn't kill his sister or Shannon or Barry Fraser, sir. In fact, he's probably the one most in danger now.'

'Which is all the more reason why he should be in custody, Sergeant.'

McNab had no good answer to that.

58

'He looks worse than me,' McNab thought, not without some pleasure.

Jeff Barclay was definitely outside his comfort zone. That much was obvious. Where McNab had been the intruder in Jeff's upmarket Merchant City apartment, now he was on McNab's home turf. One, McNab surmised, Jeff had not visited before. He suspected the man in front of him was about to see a slice of life he wasn't familiar with, and wouldn't enjoy very much.

As DI Wilson went through the usual routine of setting up the recording and advising Jeff of his rights, McNab kept a beady eye on his opponent, who kept a close eye on the tabletop.

'When was the last time you saw Mark Howitt?' Bill said.

'He stayed at my place on Thursday night.'

'What about yesterday?' McNab intervened. 'When I arrived.'

'I told you he wasn't there and he wasn't.'

'You called his mobile while you were in the toilet.'

Jeff looked as though he might deny this then thought the better of it.

'Okay, I did call Mark, but it was to tell him to hand himself in to the police.'

'Which he did,' Bill said.

Jeff looked taken aback at this. 'Mark's here? I didn't know that.'

'So you haven't been in touch?'

'No. He never answered his phone.' Jeff was observing their faces. 'He's handed himself in. That's good, isn't it?'

Bill answered swiftly. 'I'm sorry to have to inform you that Mark Howitt took his own life last night.'

'What?' Jeff shook his head. 'No. No way. Mark would never do that.' As he rose from his seat, Bill commanded him to sit down.

A brief silence fell as Jeff took to examining his hands as though they might explain what he had just been told.

Eventually Bill spoke, his voice low but firm.

'Mr Barclay. You have already admitted lying to a policeman in pursuit of a suspect. As a lawyer, you must be aware how serious that is?'

Jeff nodded. 'I'm sorry.'

'Let's get back to the night in question. The night Leila Hardy died.'

It took an hour to extract the whole story.

According to Jeff, he had departed the pub after Mark and the girl, using the excuse that he was going to the toilet. When questioned as to why, his reason had been that he'd felt sick through too much drink and decided to go home.

'I left by the fire exit.'

'When was that exactly?' McNab said.

He shrugged his shoulders. 'I have no idea. I was very drunk by then.'

'You must have crawled out, because you're nowhere to be seen on CCTV in the back lane and, believe me, I've watched it all,' McNab said. He looked to the boss, who nodded.

'Please put both your hands palms down on the table,' McNab said.

'Why?'

'Just do what Detective Sergeant McNab says,' Bill urged.

When Jeff laid his hands as requested, McNab took a photograph of them.

'Hey, what's that for?' Jeff protested.

'To eliminate you from our enquiries. We will also require a mouth swab.'

59

'Where are you?'

'At Leila's flat,' she admitted. 'I thought it might help to be in the place she died.'

'Oh, Freya. I'm so sorry.'

There was a moment's silence during which she thought Grant might let her down, but he wasn't about to.

'I can't help you decipher over the phone. You'll have to come back to the library.'

When Freya didn't respond, Grant continued. 'I think I know the volume you need. Leila expressed an interest in it a while back. It contains a variety of the less common runic scripts. Maybe that's the one she used.'

Grant was right. She would have to go back.

'Okay,' Freya conceded. 'I'll be half an hour.'

'I'll look it out and have it ready,' Grant said.

Freya repacked her bag, taking particular care of the Book of Shadows. She'd been so certain if she came here, the place where Leila died, that she would be able to decipher what was written there. She'd been wrong.

Rhona hadn't arrived back with the coffee yet.

Rather than wait, Freya decided to leave a note instead. *Rhona can't help me with this anyway.*

Freya stood for a moment in the ever-darkening room, wishing she could hear Leila's voice again. Watch her bright figure in the library. Hear her laugh with Shannon, the blonde and auburn heads close together.

She recalled the intensity of Leila's expression as she'd spoken of sexual magick and the power of the spells it generated. She'd been intoxicated by it. Had she in casting those spells forgotten the Wiccan Rede? Had she been courting the darker side of magic?

As she moved to close the window, opened earlier to aid her concentration, Freya heard a movement behind her and turned to discover a pair of green eyes observing her from the doorway.

The big black cat held her in its gaze for a moment, before opening its mouth and emitting a high keening sound that cut Freya like a knife. In that moment she was back in the room Rhona had so vividly described with the twenty-seven dolls clicking and clacking against one another in the draught from the open window, all eyes focused on her as they swayed like the pendulum of a clock. Telling Freya that time was running out and that she must hurry.

60

'You left her in that flat on her own?' McNab couldn't believe what he was hearing.

'I went out to buy us coffee and something to eat,' Rhona said. 'She was having difficulty translating the runes, she thought being there would help.'

'That wee bastard Danny said he wasn't withholding any more evidence. Now I find both you and Freya were keeping this book a secret too.'

'Keeping secrets is something we're both good at. Remember?' Her retort was below the belt, but Rhona still enjoyed saying it.

The silence on the other end was deafening.

'This Book of Shadows will be full of pish, Dr MacLeod. Wiccan pish. What the hell were you thinking, exposing Freya to it?'

'In case you've forgotten, Freya believes in the pish, as you call it. And maybe if you'd treated her better, she would have asked you for help instead of me.'

'For fuck's sake, as if you always do things right. You fuck me in extremity, you fuck Sean Maguire when you fancy a decent dinner. Who are you to give relationship advice?'

The stand-off between them came to an end when McNab said, 'Where is Freya now?'

'She said she was going back to the library.'

*

Returning to Leila's flat with coffee and sandwiches only to find Freya's note had frankly worried Rhona. Freya was fragile and frightened, yet determined, something Rhona admired. She didn't believe in 'the pish' either, as McNab had called it, but locations created strong emotions. She was well aware of that. For her, standing in this room again conjured up all the images she'd encountered the first time she'd been here.

Not just images, but smells: incense and death and the sound of the cat wailing for the dead. Even now, standing in this room devoid of swaying dolls, Rhona could hear that cry.

After their spat on the phone, McNab had indicated he was at the station, having just completed an interview with Jeff Barclay.

'I don't trust the bastard,' had been his interpretation. 'He said he left the pub by the fire exit, but we have no evidence to confirm this.'

'You have a DNA sample from him?'

'Yes, and a photo of his hands.'

At that point McNab had explained about the videos.

'We're getting closer,' Rhona had said.

'Too close,' McNab retorted.

'What do you mean?'

'That serving policeman on the list? Turns out he's not as low level as we thought. In fact, *much higher*.'

'Do we have a name?' Rhona said.

'No. *We* don't, but I suspect the boss does.'

'So what happens now?'

'We find out which of the Nine did the three murders and the remaining establishment figures will be protected.'

'That's the plan?'

'You've been here before, Dr MacLeod. You know how the world works.'

Rhona took a last look round before locking up. She'd left the table and chair in the dolls' room. There seemed little point in moving them back. She had no idea what would happen to Leila's flat once the enquiry was completed. She didn't know whether Leila owned it or whether it was rented. Either way, eventually Danny might remove some of his sister's things and let it go.

Re-entering the hallway, she was struck by a sudden and strong smell of cat urine.

Rhona stood for a moment, perplexed. The smell hadn't been there when she'd entered the first time with Freya. Had a stray cat found this place and taken up residence here?

She recalled Leila's cat and its determination to protect the body of its mistress. But it had been taken away by the SSPCA. No doubt it was still with them, if it hadn't already found a home elsewhere.

An image of the cat's angry spitting face returned, making Rhona wonder if it could ever find a new home. If it had been deemed unmanageable, then the only recourse the charity had was to put it down, simply a more oblique way of saying 'kill it'. Not an outcome Rhona liked to consider.

She decided to go back through the flat and check the windows, just in case a stray had found its way inside.

The window in the dolls' room was the only one left open a little. Rhona was about to shut it, then changed her mind.

At least you can get out again, she thought as she locked the front door.

61

Freya caught the subway at Buchanan Street. She'd felt bad at not waiting for Rhona's return, but the vision of the dolls and the cat had persuaded her not to hang around any longer.

Seated next to the door, Freya hugged the backpack close to her. Even now in the crowded carriage, she could hear the terrible sound of the cat crying. Her upset that Leila hadn't visited her in the flat had dissipated. Leila *had* been with her, was *still* with her. Freya was convinced of that now. The Book of Shadows was the answer to all of this. And she would decipher it, because Leila wanted her to.

Exiting Hillhead station onto Byres Road, she cut up through Ashton Lane. Passing the jazz club where she'd met with Michael, she had an urge to call him, but quashed it. She should talk to no one, not Michael, not Danny, until she'd accomplished her task. She didn't want to have to explain her actions or her reasons. No matter what they said, neither men understood what it meant to be a Wiccan. Michael had joked about it. Danny had tolerated his sister's beliefs, but they didn't understand how deeply and profoundly they were held.

On the final stretch to the library a text arrived. Glancing at the screen, Freya saw that it was from Grant, so she opened it.

Have taken the book to the old Ferguson room for privacy – not strictly off campus! You'll have peace there to work on it. Grant.

'Thank you,' Freya said quietly.

Entering by the main entrance to the old university, Freya registered what sat astride the gates. A unicorn on the left, a lion on the right. She recalled what Dr Charles had told her when they'd walked the surroundings together and viewed the magnificent stone figures on the ancient staircase next to the memorial chapel on the west side of the old building.

'The unicorn symbolizes Scotland, the Lion England. This staircase comes from the old College building on the High Street. It was transported to Gilmorehill in 1870 when the University of Glasgow moved to its new West End site.'

The image of the unicorn seemed portentous to Freya, and positive.

Freya was pleased to be back amid the empty cloisters. Glad of her thoughts as she moved through them.

Every sound seemed magnified as she climbed the stone steps to the old Ferguson library. She was approaching the place where it had all begun. Her interest in Wicca had been sparked by the lecture by Professor Roy at Newcastle University. His own interest as a young physics lecturer had been awakened by finding this place.

Freya emerged on the landing. Ahead of her was the set of double doors that led into the Ferguson room.

She pushed open the right-hand door and entered.

*

'She doesn't answer my calls.'

'She's okay,' McNab said. 'Dr MacLeod is in touch with her. She went back to the library to consult another book.'

Danny's reaction to this wasn't what McNab expected.

'I don't fucking trust that guy.'

'What guy?' McNab said.

'He creeps about, popping up when we're examining the Book of Shadows. Definitely wants a look. He was like a man smelling a sexed-up pussy. Believe me, Freya should not trust that guy.'

The image was ripe, but one McNab appreciated and understood.

'Okay. I take your point, but they're at the library. Freya's safe enough there. I've been inside. It's like a police station in its security.'

'People die in police stations,' Danny reminded him.

'Where are you?' McNab said.

'Headed to the library.'

'I'll be with you shortly.'

Life sometimes moved in slow motion. It had happened to McNab on numerous occasions, usually when things got tough. Maybe it was life's way of reminding you what was important. What was memorable.

Danny's call had unnerved him.

He had met Grant, the library guy. Nothing about him had made McNab wary. But he had been wrong before. And he would no doubt be wrong again. People hid themselves, often in the trappings of their professions. Jeff had tried that, on occasion quoting them lawyer speak, but his actions had belied his weasel words.

What about Grant?

McNab realized he didn't even know the librarian's second name. His fault. He should have asked. He should have interviewed him. After all, he had known both deceased women. Had known about their Wiccan beliefs.

He should have asked.

He should have asked the entire fucking world.

McNab wanted a drink now more than he had wanted anything in his life before.

He was in Ashton Lane again. Location of his initial meeting with Freya and, he reminded himself, his subsequent meeting with Rhona. Neither had gone that well and both relationships, if he was honest with himself, were on the rocks.

Sooner or later, I always rub people up the wrong way.

McNab did a quick left turn on that thought and entered the jazz club. Heading downstairs, he found himself in a busy space. Early Saturday evening jazz was proving popular in the West End of Glasgow. McNab almost turned away and headed back up the steps. Would have done had a voice not called his name.

McNab turned, knowing the voice and welcoming it.

They had been rivals more often than friends, but Sean Maguire had proved his worth on more than one occasion. McNab hated the Irishman at times, as much for his knack of enticing Dr Rhona MacLeod into his bed as his ability to play sexy music on his saxophone.

'What's up?' Sean said, his tone suggesting his concern.

McNab didn't answer.

'Fancy a drink?' Sean asked. 'We could use my office.'

McNab had used that office as a bedroom once. That room and a camp bed had provided him with a place of safety and sanity.

When McNab nodded, Sean led him through the crowd, who were listening to a female singer McNab had never heard before. She was tidy too, oozing sex from the way she handled the microphone as much as through her voice and the words she sang.

'She's only here another week,' Sean said when McNab expressed his opinion. 'Heading to Europe after that.'

'More's the pity,' McNab ventured.

'Rhona doesn't think so.'

'Jealous?' McNab ventured.

'Distrust. Rhona thinks I'm liable to stick it in any woman who looks and sounds like that.'

'Is she right?'

'She's not totally wrong,' Sean admitted.

There was a bottle of Irish whiskey on the desk and a couple of glasses. McNab almost salivated when he saw it.

'You don't have to,' Sean said. 'I can give you something soft.'

McNab laughed. 'When people say that, I always imagine a soft prick. Which is strange since mine's never been harder since I eased up on the booze.'

Sean poured a couple of shots. 'Like everything in life. Whiskey should be enjoyed in moderation. Are you able to do that?'

McNab eyed the glass as Sean handed it over. 'Let's hope so.' He examined the golden liquid. 'I was very rude to Rhona on the phone. Told her not to give me advice on relationships. Said some rough things.'

Sean gave him a wry smile. 'You screw up. I screw up. Rhona screws up. The important thing is we care enough to face up to that.'

'The wise old man of Ireland talking.'

'We Irish can talk the talk right enough.'

McNab set the untouched whiskey firmly on the table. 'Thanks for the chat. And good luck with Rhona.'

'I fear I need more than luck.'

McNab finally crested the hill and made his way up to the library. His sojourn with Sean had made him even more resolute about progressing things with Freya. He had no idea what Leila's book of spells might reveal. Based on what had happened up to now, he didn't think it would be much, but if Freya believed in it, he would try his best to support her on that.

In McNab's opinion, they needed to expose the Nine and what the boss was doing was perhaps more likely to achieve that than studying spells.

At the front desk, he showed his badge and asked to speak to Freya. A couple of phone calls ensued, before he was informed that she wasn't in the building. A subsequent enquiry after Grant revealed his surname as Buchanan and that he wasn't in the building either.

'Do you know where they are?' McNab demanded.

'It's Saturday evening. I assume they're at home,' the woman said, as though she too wished to be there.

'But I understood that Freya was coming here.'

The woman behind the desk shrugged. 'She checked in first thing, then left. Grant was in earlier too, but checked out about an hour ago.'

McNab emerged to find Danny approaching.

'Well?' he demanded.

'Freya isn't here,' McNab told him.

'What the fuck?'

McNab's sentiments exactly.

'And the Grant guy?'

'He's not here either.'

'I don't like this,' Danny said.

McNab could not have agreed more.

'You're the detective. What do we do now?' Danny demanded.

62

Freya set the Book of Shadows out on the table beside the book of runic alphabets Grant had signed out of the library for her. He'd also supplied coffee and biscuits, just as he used to do for Leila and Shannon.

'Thank you. I really appreciate this.'

Grant nodded. 'What else do you want me to do?'

Freya observed his worried face and decided to come clean.

'Danny thinks Leila's Book of Shadows contains information about the nine men she was performing sexual magick with. He wanted me to try and identify them.'

'Has he shown the book to the police?' Grant asked.

'Not yet, but he will once I've deciphered it. Danny believes one or more of these men may have been responsible for Leila's death, and Shannon's, and even the death of the barman who served them that night.'

Grant looked perturbed. 'But I heard the guy Leila left the pub with has confessed to all three murders.'

Freya was taken aback. 'When did you hear that?'

Grant shook his head. 'I'm not sure. I think it was on the rolling news this morning.'

'So they've got the guy?' Freya said, relieved.

'Looks like it.'

'Oh, Grant, that's wonderful, if it's true.'

'So maybe you don't need to translate after all. Maybe Leila's Book of Shadows can be laid to rest.'

Freya thought about that. 'I'm not so sure. When I was in her flat something happened.'

'What?'

'Her cat was there crying to me and I saw an image of the hanging dolls in the room where they found Leila.'

Grant looked askance at this.

'I know you're not a believer, Grant, but it was very real. It seemed Leila was asking me to do this.'

Grant nodded. 'Okay. Let's find out the truth.'

It was as Grant had suggested. The writing Leila had used was obscure, mainly because it was a mixture of alphabets, each symbol intricately drawn as though Leila had intended that anyone striving to interpret it shouldn't find it easy.

But before she tackled the translation, Freya spent some time on the drawings. There was one in particular she kept returning to, because there was something familiar about the figure of the man. He was naked but with no obvious discerning features on his trunk. Slimly built, he appeared tall in comparison to some of the others. He also had hair which Leila had shaded in as grey. The eyes were blue.

None of his features struck a chord with Freya, except perhaps the hands – on the left one of which was a pinkie ring. Using the magnifying glass Grant had brought her from the library, Freya examined the ring more closely and eventually decided that the engraving on the gold was of a tiny unicorn.

The last time she'd seen a ring like that, it had been worn by the man who'd visited her here. Dr Peter Charles. Freya thought back to his kindly face, his interest in her work, his fascination with the unicorn statue in the west quadrangle of the university.

Grant had indicated Dr Charles was a benefactor of the university library, in particular the Ferguson collection, which was why he'd been keen to talk to her, and was probably the reason for the signet ring.

Freya moved to look more closely at the details beside the drawn figure.

What she'd assumed to be the date of birth was given as 7/7/1949, which made his sign Cancer, his birth colour green, indicating finance, fertility and luck. His birth number involved adding all the digits together to reduce them to a single digit, in this case coming eventually to 1. A single runic word followed this, which might be his magic name, usually chosen to match the birth number.

There were numerous alphabets used in writings on Witchcraft. Seax-Wica alone had many variations in the runes used – Germanic, Danish, Swedish-Norse, Anglo-Saxon. Added to that there was the Theban script, popular among Gardnerian Witches, referred to incorrectly as the Witches' Runes, as it wasn't runic at all.

Some covens used Egyptian hieroglyphics, others the Passing the River alphabet. Then there was the Angelic alphabet and the Malachim, the language of the Magi. The PectiWita, in the Scottish tradition, had two interesting forms of magickal writing. One was a variation on runes, the other based on the old and very decorative Pictish script.

In the past Magicians often worked alone and jealously guarded their methods of operation, not from the Christian Church, but from other Magicians. Contemporary Witches continued this practice for the same reason of secrecy, but also for another motive.

One way to put power into an object is to write appropriate words on it whilst directing your energies into the writing.

Writing in everyday English didn't require the same amount of intense concentration. Creating runic script directed your energies, your power, into what you were working on.

Freya understood this, because it demanded the same energy, concentration and power to decipher the words Leila had written. It appeared that she'd chosen to mix alphabets, dropping from Anglo-runes to Angelic script with a sprinkling of Pictish thrown in. As solitary Witches, Leila, Shannon and herself could manage their faith as they chose. There were no rules, no requirement to ascend through the rankings of an Order or coven. They were as free as the first Witch. Leila had chosen to be as varied and free in her writings, choosing what suited her best.

She'd also divided her Book of Shadows into three sections, the final one being the pages concerning the Nine. The preceding page to this section consisted of a sketch of the Goddess in the form of a Warrior Queen with a shield and spear. Unlike the version on the leather cover, this Goddess bore a strong resemblance to Leila herself, the hair being short and auburn, the face bearing the same small tattoo as Leila had worn.

As Freya began the laborious task of identifying each symbol and transposing them, a strange thing happened.

Grant had gone to fetch fresh coffee, promising to be back soon.

He had shut the door behind him, but at this moment it chose to blow open. The swirling draught that entered caught Freya by surprise, almost whipping the paper she was writing on from under her pen. She rose and, fighting the sucking draught blown up from the windy cloisters below, she reshut the door.

When she returned to her seat to resume her task, she discovered that the pages of the Book of Shadows had flipped back, returning to the page featuring the Goddess.

Now Freya noted a continuous line of runic text running round the circular shield of the Warrior Queen. Intrigued, she wrote down the symbols and began to translate them.

This time the pattern came easily, each rune swiftly finding its English equivalent.

I've finally cracked the code, Freya thought.

She regarded the long string of letters, beginning at the top of the circle and moving to the right. It took only moments for her brain to break up the string into nine words that brought a chill to Freya's heart.

If you are reading this then I am dead.

63

McNab and Danny had adjourned to the nearby student cafeteria.

McNab's impression that Danny, in his quest to nail his sister's killers, hadn't been able to work and therefore had no money for food, was proved right. When McNab came back with two coffees plus two of the largest burgers on offer, Danny attacked his with a vengeance.

McNab was hungry too, but for inspiration rather than food.

He was more studied in his eating while he tried to work out what to do next. The most obvious move was to inform the boss about this latest development, although that in itself would not produce a lead on where to look for Freya. He could ask DI Wilson to send a uniform round to her flat and to force entry if necessary.

Something ice cold attacked the pit of his stomach at this thought. He quashed it, because he already knew she hadn't been there when Danny visited as she'd been with Rhona in Leila's flat.

His next and better move would be to eat humble pie and contact Rhona. She'd been the last person to see Freya and would know her state of mind. She might also have an idea where Freya would go if not to the library.

Both moves were required. One would be easier than the other.

McNab chose the easy one first.

The boss listened quietly, then agreed to have someone sent round to Freya's flat.

'You believe this book Leila left is important?'

'Who knows? It's Wiccan stuff, but Danny says it holds information on the men involved with Leila. I'll have to take his word for that because I haven't seen it.' McNab wanted to make sure the boss knew he hadn't been withholding information this time round.

The boss rang off then, with strict instructions to McNab that he was to be kept informed on the search for Freya.

McNab couldn't stomach the rest of his burger. When Danny realized this he asked if he could have it.

'Go ahead. Take the chips too.' McNab pushed the plate across. 'I'm going outside to make a call.' The last thing he wanted was for Danny to be party to his next conversation.

She had come here as though it were a place of refuge. Maybe it was. Her reason for coming was more complicated than a way to spend leisure time or even a love of jazz, which she didn't possess.

She fully understood McNab's anger and vexation, and why he'd voiced it, some would say truthfully, over the phone. She too was concerned about Freya's well-being, which was why she'd agreed to take her to Leila's flat.

It hadn't worked, but it had been worth a try.

Now, Rhona decided, she would await news and have a drink.

She ordered white wine and took a seat at the bar. Sam was doing a stint serving, having played earlier. Chrissy, he informed Rhona, was staying over at her mother's with young Michael. He sounded sorry about that and Rhona sensed an end in sight for that relationship, despite their mutual love for McNab's namesake.

At that moment the end of any relationship seemed almost inevitable.

She hadn't sought Sean but he found her anyway, news of her arrival having travelled swiftly to the boss of the establishment.

'It's quieter in the office,' he offered.

Rhona wasn't in the mood for a get-together, a dark impenetrable cloud having descended on her thoughts, but rather than argue, she followed him through. Sean ushered her inside, closed the door behind them and turned the key.

'We need to talk,' was his explanation for that.

Rhona spied the two glasses and bottle of whiskey on the desk, and interpreted Sean's remark and the evidence of a drinking buddy in the same scenario.

'McNab's been here?' she said.

'Briefly.'

'How brief?'

'One drink's worth,' Sean said. 'He told me you fell out.'

'That's an understatement.'

'He said some bad things?'

'Bad, but truthful. As did I,' Rhona admitted.

'He seemed very worried about Freya.'

'She was with me earlier at Leila's flat, which he didn't like. I went out to get us some coffee. When I got back, she'd disappeared. The message said she'd gone back to the library.'

'Where he was heading when I saw him.'

'If he was in a hurry, why stop for a drink?' Rhona said.

'You're worried, and you came here for one.'

'Piss off.'

'If you want me to.'

There was no point taking her frustration out on Sean. It wasn't his fault. She said so.

'It *is* possible to have a personal life outside work,' Sean declared firmly.

'Do you really believe that?' she said, her cynicism obvious.

'I do, although I know you and McNab don't.'

'The Irish have a fine way with words,' Rhona countered.

'Exactly what McNab said. You're more alike than you're prepared to admit.'

Rhona was grateful when her mobile rang. Despite Sean's look suggesting she ignore it, she answered, even though it was McNab's name on the screen.

'She's not at the library and neither is Grant Buchanan, the guy in charge of the Ferguson collection. Apparently he checked out a book earlier on runic scripts in Witchcraft.'

Rhona could taste McNab's concern. What he really wanted to ask her was where the hell they had gone to study it. A question she might be able to answer.

'Freya has a key to the old Ferguson collection library. She took it from Shannon's desk. There were two keys. One for Leila's altar in the Lion Chambers. The other to the old library.'

'You think she's there?' McNab said eagerly.

'It's a possibility,' Rhona said.

'Where is it?'

'Somewhere in the main building. That's all I know.'

388

64

If you are reading this then I am dead.

There was no doubt what the message on the shield said, and no doubt in Freya's mind that Leila had hoped, or even intended, that someone should find this message in the event of her death.

The fact that it was placed here on the drawing of herself as the Goddess and in the foreword to her section on the Nine seemed also significant.

Freya checked the Warrior Queen again in case she'd missed anything else, then flipped over the page and began on the spell cast for the first of the Nine.

So deep in concentration was she that she didn't hear Grant's entry.

'Coffee's here.'

Freya caught the aroma at the same time as she heard the words.

The door opening had brought another blast of wind from the spiral staircase that led from the cloister to the tower. It flapped at the pages of the Book of Shadows, sending them scurrying towards the end.

Grant forced the door shut.

'Have you got the key? We may have to lock it to prevent it blowing open again.'

Freya pointed to her rucksack. 'It's in the front pouch with my mobile.'

The door secured, Grant handed over her coffee.

'How's the translation going?'

'Quite well,' she told him. 'I've figured out the mix of scripts Leila used and, since she's been pretty consistent about the pattern of usage, I'm getting a little faster in translation now.'

'Good,' Grant said, offering her a biscuit. 'How long will this take? I'll have to head home soon.'

'You've been great, Grant. Go home. This may take some time. When I finish, I'll call DS McNab and hand the book and the translation to the police as you suggested.'

Grant nodded. 'You could leave the other book in here and I'll pick it up in the morning.'

'One thing,' Freya said.

'Yes?'

'I think Leila believed herself to be in danger.'

'What makes you say that?'

Freya explained about the shield. 'The translated message said, "If you are reading this then I am dead."'

Grant's face paled. 'That's not good. Maybe she had a premonition.'

'Maybe. One other thing?'

'Yes?' Grant was staring out of the window, where the rising wind was tearing at the trees.

'One of the nine figures Leila drew is wearing a signet ring engraved with a crest featuring a unicorn. I wondered about its significance.'

Grant turned. 'Was it the unicorn alone or the unicorn and the lion?'

'Only the unicorn.'

'When they're together, Scottish Unicorn on the right, English Lion on the left, they symbolize the union of the crowns of Scotland and England on the marriage of James VI of Scotland to Margaret Tudor. Dr Charles wears one like that. Maybe he's related to royalty.' He smiled. 'If the unicorn is on its own, it's probably merely decorative.'

'Okay,' she said. 'Thanks.'

'I'd better get going. Will you be all right here alone?'

'I'll be fine,' Freya assured him.

'I'll see you on Monday, then. And good luck.'

The main gates were shut and locked, but the right-hand side gate still stood open. With no sign of anyone they could ask to direct them, they had no choice but to head into the main building and trust to luck that they would meet someone who knew their way around. McNab had visited Rhona's lab on a number of occasions, but that wasn't in the old building and he had no idea of the geography of the place.

They eventually found their way into the cloisters, fighting the wind that seemed to be coming from all directions, but every door into the main building they met was firmly locked.

McNab came to a grinding halt and pulled out his mobile.

He'd tried Freya's number three times since leaving the cafeteria. Surely eventually she had to pick up? He let it ring until it went to voicemail, then simply begged her to tell him where she was.

He made a second call, this one to the station to check the outcome of the watch on Freya's flat, and found she hadn't been there. This time when he rang off, he turned his wrath on Danny.

'If you hadn't given her that fucking book, this would never have happened.'

Danny didn't have an answer to that. 'So what do we do now?' he said.

'We find whoever looks after this place at night and get them to let us in.'

Rhona had night access to her own block at the foot of the hill, but had no access to the main university building after hours.

Eventually, after a few calls, she was passed to one of the caretakers, who arranged to meet her at the gate, provided she could produce her ID.

When they finally met up, the man was pretty flustered by being called out at this late hour, and even more perplexed at being asked to direct her to a place he didn't know existed.

'The old library where the Ferguson collection was held before it was moved to the main library,' Rhona tried again.

He shook his head. 'Never heard of the Ferguson collection.'

'I think it was in one of the towers.'

'We can check the towers, but it'll be pretty dark by now. No one's supposed to be in the building.'

'My colleague, Detective Sergeant McNab, is somewhere around here,' Rhona said.

'Not to my knowledge.' The caretaker looked affronted.

Rhona rang McNab's number again, grateful when he answered.

'I'm here and I have a caretaker with me,' she said. 'Where are you exactly?'

'In the west quad,' came the reply.

'Stay there.'

*

Freya wasn't aware of the surrounding darkness or the circling wind that buffeted the thick stone walls and lattice windows of the tower room. She had just completed a translation of what she thought might be the final spell, and had discovered it was more of a declaration.

I am the Warrior Queen!
Defender of my people
With strong arms do I bend the bow
And wield the Moon-axe

I am sister to the stars
And mother to the Moon
Within my womb lies the destiny of my people
For I am the Creatrix

I am also she whom all must face
at the appointed hour
Yet am not to be feared
For I am sister, lover, daughter
Death is but the beginning of life
And I am the one who turns the key.

Should I die, I ask the first reader
To burn my Book of Shadows
For its death will avenge my own.

Freya sat back, and rubbed her eyes. Outside the window, all was dark. In here she had only a desk light to work by. But she'd translated enough to know what Leila had been doing. And to know that she'd taken risks with her worship that might well have threatened her life.

Grant's revelation that the chief suspect had confessed, Freya hoped was true. Otherwise, she believed, one or all of the Nine were implicated in Leila's death.

She was ready now to talk to Michael about this. To show him the translated notes and to give him at least the magic names Leila had allotted to the members of the group, their birthdates and therefore their age. That and the spells they'd requested Leila to conjure up.

All of which may have gone against the Wiccan Rede.

Now she understood why Leila was asking her to burn the book. It was traditional that the Book of Shadows be burned on the owner's death, but that wasn't why Leila wanted it to happen. Her desire was for vengeance on those who had taken her life and Shannon's.

Whether there was a possibility of that happening, Freya didn't know.

She rose from the table and went in search of her mobile. She would arrange to meet Michael at the jazz club and hand the Book of Shadows over. She had promised Danny she would tell him the result of her translation first, but she now feared what he might do with her findings.

It was better for everyone if she handed the book directly to Michael.

As she searched in vain for her mobile in the front pocket of the backpack, then in the main pouch, she caught the faint scent of smoke. Setting the bag down, she saw the first trail of it coming under the door.

Then she heard a crackling sound from the outer room, like kindling sticks sparking and catching alight. The room, she knew, was still filled with the debris of old, dry, varnished shelves, stripped from the walls.

A veritable tinderbox.

Freya grabbed at the door, remembering that Grant had left and she hadn't locked it behind him. When it wouldn't open she was seized by confusion.

Had she locked it after all?

The curls of smoke were increasing, rising to the ceiling of the small room, catching the back of her throat.

She must have locked the door against the wind. What had she done with the key? Now the light was no longer enough, illuminating as it did only a portion of the desk.

Frantic now, Freya dropped to her knees and began feeling the floor around the desk. When that didn't produce the key, she up-ended the backpack and shook it, to no avail.

By now she was coughing, the acrid taste of smoke deep in her throat.

She had to get out of here.

Freya tried the door again, using all of her remaining strength. When that didn't work, she took off her jacket and laid it along the foot of the door to try and slow the flow of smoke. A solution that would prove only temporary.

Coughing and spluttering, her eyes on fire, she moved the chair close to the window and stood up on it. If she could open the window, then maybe she could breathe again.

The catch was stiff but manageable.

Freya flung open the window and the wind surged in, scattering her papers from the desk, flapping the pages of the Book of Shadows. As the oxygen surged into the room, helping Freya to take a breath, it also rattled the door, forcing its way round the edge and beneath, giving sustenance to the flames in the room next door.

Freya heard a roar as the fire beyond the door gained momentum, and a crash as a window exploded.

As she slumped in the furthest corner from the door, she

saw the first sparks arrive, whipped in on the wind, landing on the flapping pages of the Book of Shadows.

Freya knew she should try to save it, shelter it between her body and the wall. Make it survive, even if she didn't. But another voice told her to *let it burn*. That way those responsible would pay the price.

Freya began her own chant, echoing Leila's words because all three Witches, she, Leila and Shannon, would soon be reunited.

> *'I, moon lady*
> *Salute my sisters*
> *Of the stars and the trees.*
>
> *We are She whom all men must face*
> *At the appointed hour*
> *Yet I am not afraid*
> *Death is but the beginning of life*
> *And I am the one who holds the key.'*

They were crossing the west quad when McNab picked up the scent, faint but immediately recognizable. In moments they saw flames coming from the nearest tower.

The caretaker began babbling about dialling 999. McNab grabbed him by the scruff of the neck and told him to open the lower door first and let him in.

The man thrust a set of keys into his hand. 'It's the one marked "tower2",' he said, then pulled out his mobile and began his emergency call.

McNab thumbed his way through the keys, cursing the lack of light and his own ineptitude. Eventually he thrust a key into the lock and tried to turn it, outwardly praying it was the right one. There was a moment's hesitation as the lock resisted. In that moment McNab found himself praying to any god that was willing to listen that it would work.

'Thank you!' he shouted as the key turned and his prayer was answered.

McNab pushed the door open and smoke billowed out, engulfing them. As he headed inside, Rhona's hand caught his arm. 'The old library is on the second floor.'

McNab sensed Danny behind him as he darted upwards through the swirling smoke. By the first-floor landing he could hear the crackle and spit of the fire. Running up the staircase had taken its toll and McNab instinctively took in air, regretting it immediately as his lungs and throat objected, sending him into a paroxysm of coughing.

'Cover your mouth and nose,' Danny shouted at him.

McNab copied Danny as he took off his jacket and held it to his face.

Now Danny darted ahead, disappearing up the spiral staircase that led to the next level. McNab raced after him through the thickening smoke and the increasing noise from above. He found himself mouthing, 'Please don't let her be up there. Please God she's in a different tower. Please let her be alive.' And all the time he could picture Freya, already comatose, her smoke-filled lungs no longer taking in oxygen to pump her precious heart.

McNab threw himself onto the second level, to find no sign of Danny.

Ahead a set of double doors flapped madly in the gusts that whined up the stairwell from the open door below and blasted in through the shattered windows of the old library. Beyond the doors, as seen through the missing glass, the fire raged like a mad red beast intent on devouring every-thing in its path.

Freya can't be alive in that.

Horror engulfed McNab as he tried to breathe through the jacket, his eyes streaming. Pushing open the door, he could see that the fire had taken hold among the discarded timber of old shelves. Like a fifth of November bonfire, it blazed in the centre of the room but hadn't yet engulfed the high ceiling, although it was already licking the right-hand wall.

This couldn't be the room Freya had been working in, but he had to be sure. Entering, he heard Danny screaming Freya's name. McNab lowered his jacket and joined in, desperately trying to raise his voice above the roar of the fire.

Then he saw her or thought he did. A female figure through the flames looking directly at him as though chal-lenging him to come to her.

'Freya!' McNab shouted, fearing his voice had been snatched and devoured by the din.

'In there,' he heard Danny shout in return, pointing to a door in the right-hand wall.

As they both moved towards the door, McNab from the right, Danny from the left, another window suddenly burst in the heat, shooting shards of glass like confetti in Danny's direction. McNab saw Danny try to cover his face with his arms but not speedily enough. He crumpled and fell, his face a mess of blood.

'Danny!'

Danny urged McNab onwards to the door as he tried to right himself. 'Get Freya.'

McNab hesitated, but only for a moment, then darted round the bonfire which licked at his legs and feet. He stumbled at its touch and, reaching out a hand to steady himself, met the blistering heat of the right-hand wall. The burning pain of the connection seemed to belong to someone else as McNab grabbed the door handle and tried to turn it. For a split second it appeared to give, before a sudden halt.

'Fucking bastard!' McNab screamed.

This time he put his shoulder to the door. He'd done this before. Many times. Forced a door with his shoulder. He could do it again now. The flames were licking from behind as he retreated to harness more power. He felt the burst of heat on the bullet wound in his back, and he remembered with sudden clarity what it meant to die.

That couldn't happen to Freya. Not Freya.

His first attempt shook the door on its hinges. His second attempt, he knew, had torn the lock. Once more and he would blast the fucking door from its frame. McNab retreated one more time, backing further into the heat and flames. This time he had to do it.

He launched himself at the door. As he slammed against it, he felt his right arm exit his shoulder with a sickening pop, but not before the door had sprung open.

McNab fell into the room, his right arm now hanging uselessly from its socket.

'Freya? Are you in here?'

He strove to focus in the darkness, his eyes blurred by the biting smoke. The fire, having eaten its way through the intervening wall, was now licking its way across the ceiling.

'Freya! Where are you?'

A series of sparks as the flames met the varnish of the bookshelves suddenly lit up the room like fireworks and for a moment McNab caught a glimpse of the layout. Shelves, a desk and chair, and nothing else.

She's not here. She's not in here.

As McNab stood, sensing defeat, but not yet willing to accept it, there was an explosion behind him, its force propelling him further into the room. Then he saw it laid open on the desk, the pages already curling in the heat. The Book of Shadows.

If it's here, so is Freya.

At that moment, the book flared like a paper taper and began to burn before his eyes. In its cold green light he saw her tucked under the desk, her arms about her legs, her head resting on them.

McNab dropped to his knees beside her.

'Freya.' This time his voice was as soft as a caress, as desperate as a wish he dared come true.

'I'm here, Freya. I've got you now.' As he took her arm, it dropped free and limp and she fell towards him, her body as heavy as death.

'No!' McNab shouted, tugging at her with his left arm, his right one useless. 'Please, Freya, come to me.'

When there was no response and unable to move her, McNab sat down and drew Freya to him, cradling her head against his chest, shielding her from the smoke and heat with his body.

Accepting that there was nothing he could do except stay here with her, McNab planted a kiss on Freya's head and told her he loved her and that he was sorry. It seemed to him that she stirred at his words, shifting a little against him. McNab closed his eyes, blotting out fire, replacing the image with one of his own. Freya laughing, naked, as he'd swept her off her feet and carried her into the bedroom.

Before, when he'd faced death, he had done so alone. Not now. Not ever again.

The cocoon they shared rocked as something fell across

it, tossing the burning Book of Shadows to the floor in front of him. McNab gazed on it, hatred foremost in his mind.

You fucking did this to her, Leila. You and your fucking book of spells.

His exploding anger rolled him out of their hiding place.

He wasn't giving up. He would get Freya out of here somehow or die trying. McNab got onto his knees and, dragging Freya up with only his left arm, succeeded in pulling her over his shoulder.

Now all I have to do is stand up.

He extracted his right knee. Unbalanced now, he leaned against the desk and, steadying himself with his left hand, tried to get up. Painfully slowly, every sinew striving to raise himself and the precious cargo he carried.

Then he was upright, or as upright as he would ever be. His right arm flapping uselessly beside him, he stumbled with Freya over his shoulder towards the doorway and out into the inferno.

McNab had no idea how far he walked through the hell that was the Ferguson room before he heard and felt the force of cold water as a fire hose reached the shattered window of the room, hissing and spluttering as it met the flames and turned them into steam.

Then the figure of a firefighter loomed before him, and in moments Freya was plucked from his shoulders and carried away before him down the stairs and into the night air.

Relieved, McNab turned, searching now for Danny in what was left of the room.

65

Rhona turned to face Sean's back and curled herself against him. He slept the sleep of the angels, undisturbed by her sudden warm presence. She imagined that was what he was, in waking or sleeping . . . undisturbed by her presence.

She rose, leaving him there in his slumber.

Her own sleep had been short. After they'd made love, brought on by the instinct for survival, Rhona had dozed fitfully. Sean, on the other hand, had rejoiced in Freya's survival, and celebrated it through sex then deep sleep.

Rhona envied him his ability to do that.

Now in the kitchen, she set the coffee machine up and switched it on. Tom didn't even open an eye at her early arrival in his domain.

Would you stand and howl at my grave like Leila's cat did? I think not.

Rhona walked to the window. Not yet dawn, the light on the statue of the Virgin was still distinguishable in its rosy glow. Warm, but not the flash of red fire.

The terrible memory of what had happened only hours before suddenly engulfed her. A blur of noise and soaring flames, McNab like a man possessed, diving up that stairwell. Being pulled away herself by a burly firefighter and ordered to stand as far away as possible and let them do their job.

She'd shouted at him that three people were in there,

not knowing if she'd been heard through the frantic bustle and noise. Then the terrible wait, the seconds as long as hours until the firefighter had finally reappeared with Freya in his arms. Her joy when she saw them, and then the swift despair when no one else followed him out of that door.

'He's dead,' she'd heard herself say, knowing she'd been in this place before, when McNab had died in front of her.

She'd spotted Danny first, the glow of the fire setting his own auburn head ablaze, his face a mass of blood. Then she realized that he was supported by a stumbling McNab.

Rhona had stood back as all three were loaded into an ambulance and the screaming siren had taken them from her and the burning tower.

Freya had survived, but it seemed the Book of Shadows had not, although no one – forensic expert or otherwise – was to be allowed inside the tower room to check that was the case until it was deemed safe.

All three survivors were currently in hospital, smoke inhalation being the main reason, although Danny had also been badly cut about the face and McNab had had to endure the agony of having his right shoulder put back in. Despite his obvious discomfort, McNab had opted to sit with Freya, his blistered hands forgotten in his desire to be with her when she opened her eyes.

Rhona hoped she would open them soon.

66

'He wore a signet ring with a unicorn on it. Grant said it was a unicorn and a lion but it wasn't.'

Freya had gripped his blistered hand, but McNab refused to react to the pain, so happy was he to see her awake and alive.

'Who?' he said, trying to make sense of what appeared to be ramblings.

'The man who wanted to talk about my thesis. Dr Peter Charles. We met in that room.'

'Last night?' McNab said, confused by the timeline.

She shook her head. 'No, on Friday. Then I saw the drawing.' She looked wildly at him. 'I think it was him in the drawing.'

'You met a man on Friday in the old library and you think he was in the Book—'

She interrupted him: 'The Book of Shadows. What happened to it?'

'The room was gutted. It can't have survived.'

McNab expected Freya to be upset by this, but instead she said, 'Good.'

He wondered if it was the drugs talking. 'I don't understand,' he said.

'Leila wanted that to happen.'

When she'd fallen into what appeared to be a peaceful sleep, McNab had disengaged his hand gently from Freya's and gone to check on Danny. His final memory of last night had been pulling Danny upright and helping him down the stairs.

'Hey,' McNab said, 'you're awake.'

'How's Freya?' was Danny's immediate response.

'She's going to be okay.'

Relief swept Danny's face. 'What happened? How did she get locked in there?'

'She thinks she locked the door after Grant left to prevent it blowing open in the wind, then couldn't find the key.' McNab explained the rambling story about the signet ring in the drawing and the man she'd met last week, Dr Peter Charles. 'He's a benefactor of the Special Collections in the university library. He was supposedly interested in her thesis on Witchcraft.'

Danny halted him. 'Freya never saw the video. The guy with the signet ring?' he reminded McNab.

Jesus. How could he have forgotten?

'Grant wanted to find out what Freya knew,' McNab said, suddenly understanding.

Danny nodded. 'I would say so.'

'If I go and check this out, will you keep an eye on Freya for me?'

'Sure thing.'

On McNab's departure Danny dressed and, as requested, went to check on Freya.

He stood for a moment in the doorway, observing her. She was, he decided, still in that place between sleep and wakefulness. He hesitated to disturb her by entering the room, but perhaps sensing his presence, Freya opened her eyes.

Her smile reminded him of Leila.

'McNab sent me to look after you. He had to report for duty.'

'I guess it's always going to be like that.'

Danny pulled up a chair. 'He told me about the drawing and the ring. What you didn't know was that a ring like you described appears on one of the three video clips Barry and I took.'

Freya pulled herself up in the bed. 'So he may have been one of the men who visited Leila?'

'How did he get in touch?'

'Through Grant. He arranged for us to meet at the old library to discuss my thesis.'

Danny's heart missed a beat.

'Grant introduced you?'

'Not exactly. He set up the meeting and I went along. Dr Charles was completely charming and very knowledgeable.'

Danny's conjectures were fast falling over one another.

'Did Grant suggest the old library last night too?'

'I called him from Leila's flat and asked him for help. He said he would take the book I needed there for me.'

'So he *did* suggest the old library?'

'He said it was quiet there and we wouldn't be interrupted.' She halted, her expression suggesting she didn't believe where this was leading. 'You can't think Grant has anything to do with all of this?'

'He was ultra-keen to take a look at Leila's Book of Shadows,' Danny reminded her.

'Of course he was. Anyone with his interest in the occult would be.' Freya stopped, remembering something. 'Grant told me the man Leila met that night had confessed to all three murders. Is that true?'

'It is, but he couldn't have known that. Not last night.'

'He said it was on the news.'

Danny shook his head. 'It wasn't. I only know because McNab told me.'

'Maybe Grant was mistaken,' Freya said hesitantly.

'Maybe,' Danny said carefully, although he was thinking the opposite. He swiftly changed the subject. 'How much can you remember of the translation?'

A shadow crossed her face. 'A fair bit. One thing in particular.'

Danny listened as Freya told him of a circular message on the shield that seemed to predict his sister's death. Then the final words Leila had written:

> Should I die, I ask the first reader
> To burn my Book of Shadows
> For its death will avenge my own.

Danny didn't believe in Witchcraft, in spells, rituals, chants or incense. He didn't believe in Gods and Goddesses or any of the other artefacts that had adorned Leila's altar. But he did believe in revenge, and he wasn't willing to leave its enactment to a spell cast by his dead sister.

67

'Mark Howitt Senior was found dead beside his wife this morning. It's not confirmed, but from initial reports it appears he decided his life would end when hers did,' Sutherland said.

Bill sank down on the nearest chair, his legs no longer able to hold him up.

Sutherland waited, giving Bill time to compose himself.

'I believe you and he were old friends?'

'We were,' Bill acknowledged.

'Then maybe that's why he left a letter addressed to you at the scene.' Sutherland slid a white embossed envelope towards Bill.

Bill hesitated before picking it up, unsure how to react to this. Sutherland, he could tell, was keen to know the letter's contents. Bill, on the other hand, had no wish to either open the letter in his presence, nor share what was inside unless he had to.

He rose, letter in hand. 'If you'll excuse me, sir?'

Sutherland gave a reluctant nod, before adding, 'Obviously, if the contents have any bearing on his son's case . . .'

Bill didn't bother answering as he exited the room.

Seated now in his chair, the letter still sealed lying on the desk in front of him, Bill pondered what he should do. The last time he'd met with his old friend had been at the city mortuary where he'd come to identify the body of his son. It was a task no parent should ever have to do. After that Bill had had to explain that his son had been implicated in the deaths of three people. Had in fact confessed to all three murders.

For an ordinary man, that would have been tragic. For a High Court judge, who'd spent most of his life presiding over such cases, it must have been catastrophic.

All his own life in the police force, Bill had had one overriding fear. That a close family member might become a victim of a serious crime, or even a perpetrator. The idea that only evil people were driven to do bad things was, of course, a fallacy.

We are all capable of murder given the right circumstances.

Bill recalled their conversation in the park and the sense that his friend had wanted to reveal something, yet could not, at that time.

It seemed the time had now come.

Bill slit open the envelope, extracted the letter and began to read.

There is a catharsis in telling the truth. You and I both know that. We have seen it in interviews and in court. When we met I wanted to tell you this, but wasn't brave enough to do so. Funny how we, you and I, have spent our lives urging others to confess, yet when it came to it, I was unable to do so. At least face to face.

I became aware of Leila Hardy when seeking alternative treatments for Sarah. We had been through every available medical procedure possible. As you know, none of them worked. She was dying and I was desperate. Suffice to say that Leila Hardy was my last resort. She was kind to me. Kind and persuasive. She offered me her strongest magic and I'm ashamed to say I took it. Perhaps as much for myself as for what it promised for Sarah.

Like all other routes, it led nowhere except death.

I was the undisclosed DNA sample found in her flat. I had recently visited a crime scene with a jury and had been recorded. Immediately I heard of Leila's death, I contacted Superintendent Sutherland and explained about my indiscretion. He advised me to wait. Again I took the coward's way out and did so, convincing myself that such a revelation might destroy Sarah's remaining time alive.

My biggest failure I think was not to have faith in my son. Sarah always did. Mark sensed my disappointment, when he should have sensed my love.

For what it's worth, I knew nothing of the group you term the Nine, although I suspect they had found out from Leila about me. When you said you thought Mark might have been blackmailed into confessing, my first thought was that I might have been the tool they used to manipulate him.

If that was the case, then I think he died to protect Sarah, and perhaps even me.

I sensed when we talked that you believed Mark to be innocent, as do I. I hope you can clear his name, but even more I hope you can apprehend the person, or persons, who killed Leila Hardy and her friends.

McNab looked up from the letter, his expression sombre.

'We'll get Buchanan,' he said. 'But not the Nine,' he added bitterly.

'The wheels of the Lord grind slowly, but they grind exceedingly fine,' Bill quoted a favourite saying of his late mother's.

'You believe that?' McNab challenged him.

'In a religious sense, no. But we've made a start, and the case can't be closed until we find the other members of the group.' Bill examined McNab's demeanour. He looked like a man still on the wagon, with maybe even some joy in his life, despite the frustration of the Nine.

'How's Freya?' Bill asked.

A small smile played McNab's mouth, something not often seen, Bill thought.

'She's okay, thank you, sir.'

McNab indicated the letter.

'Do you intend making this public knowledge, sir?'

'The super already knows. I'd like you to inform Rhona. I believe that's enough for the time being.'

'Thank you for telling me, sir.'

68

After the preceding forty-eight hours, the quiet of the lab felt like heaven. Having done her best to bring Chrissy up to date, Rhona had chosen to be alone, the quiet study of science a welcome relief after the psychological turmoil of recent events.

Freya was alive; the book they'd pinned their hopes on had gone.

But there was copious forensic material, which when assembled, might give them an insight into what had happened up to this point.

Traces of the suspect's DNA had now been identified at all three crime scenes. In the first, it had already been established that he'd had sex with the victim, and that the cingulum had had contact with his skin.

The evidence at the other two sites was less conclusive. A swab taken of Shannon's mouth had traces of Mark's DNA on it. But there was something else as well. A microscopic fibre of the same type to that found in Leila's throat. The cloth may well have carried DNA from one scene to another, by accident or on purpose.

Other things didn't add up.

The hand that had pushed Shannon's head underwater, nicking her skin and leaving DNA in the cut, didn't belong to Mark. The shape and dimensions of the fingerprint bruising didn't match him either. Like the original crime scene, he may have been present, but in Rhona's considered opinion, Mark hadn't done the deed.

The third scene was the most puzzling of all and posed for Rhona the maximum number of questions. Mark could not have inflicted those wounds, unless he had done so with his least-used hand.

Once your brain decided whether it was left- or right-handed, humans used the chosen hand. Some were lucky enough to be able to use both, but as far as she was aware, Mark Howitt was not ambidextrous. To exert a force like throwing a ball, a punch, stabbing, you used your strongest arm.

The arm that had forced the knife into Barry Fraser's eyes was not the arm that Mark led with. On that alone, Rhona found it difficult to believe that he'd inflicted the fatal wounds. Yet his DNA was on the face and neck of the victim.

If the cloth that suffocated Leila had been used again . . .

She updated the R2S software with her findings.

At the end of the day, should it ever come to court, the jury would decide.

But who could be brought to court to face the charges?

Not Mark Howitt.

Writing reports eased the mind. Rhona always made them as detailed and explicit as possible. That often meant she wasn't required to appear in court to support them. Science was clean, but couldn't stand aside from the inevitable.

Why did people do what they did?

She realized she longed to talk to Freya about what had happened that fatal night in the tower room. She wanted to examine the residue and establish what had caused the fire. But most of all, she needed to know what had happened to the Book of Shadows. Without realizing it, the book had become uppermost in her mind.

It wasn't scientific. It had, for Rhona, no basis in reality, yet it held, she suspected, a window on the truth.

And all forensic scientists wanted to look through that window.

She was surprised by McNab's arrival in the lab, but not exactly put out by it. She was in truth glad to see him out of hospital, despite the bandaged arm and shoulder.

'Coffee?' she offered, to break the tension between them.

He nodded enthusiastically and she set about filling the machine, usually Chrissy's job, and spooning in the coffee.

'Make it strong,' he urged.

As she did so he told her about a letter to Bill from a deceased Mark Howitt Senior, explaining how he had become involved with Leila Hardy. Rhona dropped the scoop and the final spoonful of coffee sprayed along the surface.

'He chose to die with his wife,' McNab went on. 'He left the sealed letter for the boss at the scene.'

'So Mark's father was the owner of the denied DNA?' Rhona said.

'Yes, although not one of the Nine.'

'And the theory that Mark died to protect him . . .'

'Probably true,' McNab said.

Rhona set the coffee machine on. Listening to it humming seemed the only normal thing about this moment. They remained silent until she handed the coffee to McNab.

'We're not going to find them, are we?' she said.

'The boss won't give up, and neither, I suspect, will we.'

69

There are three ways to traditionally kill a Witch. Hang her, drown her or burn her.

The fire in the tower had raged all night. He recalled another fire that had happened before he'd come here, in the 100-year-old Bower Building just off University Avenue. The building had been completely destroyed, including a great deal of research material.

Maybe that had been his inspiration?

But like then, as apparently now, there had been no fatalities reported, so the chances were the Witch hadn't died.

His anger rose to burn in his throat.

He was in the section on the occult and had asked not to be disturbed. In truth, he was amending the catalogue to take account of the missing items, including the book on runic alphabets he'd taken to the old library on Saturday evening.

He couldn't imagine it had survived.

He had his story straight for whoever came to speak to him. And someone would come. He had nothing to hide. He had helped a colleague out by supplying a book she required. A little against the rules as the book in question should never have left this building, but then the main building was still on campus as he'd said jokingly in his conversation with Freya.

There was the small concern regarding the signet ring and the likelihood that he would be questioned about Dr Charles. He could only answer in good faith. The man had presented himself as a benefactor of the Special Collection and asked to speak to their current PhD student whose thesis was on Witchcraft, a strong interest of his.

That much was true. The fact that he and Dr Charles also shared a worldwide interest in the trade in ancient tomes and pamphlets on the occult need not be revealed.

At this point in the thought process, a small niggling doubt arose. Should he land in trouble over this, he doubted whether he would have the back-up of Dr Charles or anyone else in the group. As such, he had material hidden away that he knew they would be interested in, to trade with. It was all a matter of planning and organization.

He withdrew a book to gaze again on the illustrations which featured the many and varied methods used to torture and dispose of Witches. The colours were still as bright as when they'd been painted. The terror and cruelty as vivid on the page as in the minds of those who had devised them.

People imagined that Witchcraft was no more and that the enlightened mind had taken its place. He knew differently. Witchcraft was as powerful and established as it had always been. Its ancient artefacts and writings were eagerly sought by those in power, throughout the world. Like fine wine, it only rose in value.

He would have preferred to have retained Leila's Book of Shadows as a reminder of all that had happened, but because of what it was suspected to contain, it had needed to be destroyed.

He was a little sorry about that.

Hearing the sound of the door opening, he returned the

book to its allotted place and went to see who had disturbed him.

As he passed the main gates, McNab registered that the smoke and the acrid smell of the fire had gone, yet he could still taste it on his lips and feel its effect in his lungs. He stopped before attempting the hill to the main library and tried to take a deep breath, which only resulted in a fit of coughing. He checked his mobile for any message from Danny. When there wasn't one, he decided to assume all was well with him and Freya.

There were questions he required answering and Grant Buchanan, he believed, was the only man who could do so.

When he asked for Mr Buchanan at the front desk, he was informed that he was working and had asked not to be disturbed. McNab showed them his badge and insisted.

The man behind the desk made a call which wasn't answered.

'I'm sorry, he's not picking up.'

'Then someone can deliver me to him.'

'We're a bit short-staffed at the moment.'

'Tell me where to go and I'll find him myself.'

Grant waited for his visitor to appear, ready with an admonishment for disturbing him after strict instructions not to.

At that moment something strange happened. He thought he saw Leila's auburn head pass by on the other side of the bookshelves. It was both familiar, yet disquieting. Then the face appeared, her face and yet not her face. He stared, slightly unnerved, as his brain finally reminded him that this was Leila's younger brother who stood looking at him.

His first instinct was to be angry, both for having been

417

frightened by the similarity and by his sudden appearance, but instinct warned him that this was not the reaction required. He must remain solicitous, just as he had been before when he'd found Danny and Freya here with the Book of Shadows.

'Danny. I'm so pleased you're here. I've been calling the hospital and the police trying to find out if Freya was still in the building when the fire—'

'Freya's in hospital. She's fine. The Book of Shadows was destroyed in the fire.'

Grant adopted a suitably sad expression. 'That's unfortunate.'

'But then, as you reminded me, a Witch's Book of Shadows should be burned on their passing.'

'That was a throwaway remark. I apologize for it. As long as Freya's all right.'

How like his sister, he looks, Grant thought. Those green eyes, the hair, even the shape of the face and the flashing anger when challenged.

'How did you know the suspect had confessed to my sister's murder?'

A cloud appeared on his horizon, a dark cloud that suggested a storm was brewing.

'I didn't,' was all he could muster.

'Are you calling Freya a liar?'

Leila's male equivalent had moved towards him with, he thought, the stealth and quietness of a cat about to spring.

He took a step backwards and met the desk where he'd been viewing the images of tortured Witches.

'Do you know what Leila's instructions were about her book?' Danny spat at him.

He shook his head, no longer trusting his voice.

'That by burning it, her death would be avenged.'

He composed himself. Things were not as acute as they had at first seemed. The brother knew nothing. He was merely angry and upset. Before he could find a suitable retort however . . .

'I don't believe that Wiccan stuff. I prefer my own version of revenge.'

The *yag-dirk* now in Danny's hand was undoubtedly Leila's, taken like the Book of Shadows from her altar. He accepted in the seconds that followed that he should have cleared her temple when he'd had the chance. The night he'd met with the suspect in that building, he had chosen not to, because it would have aroused suspicion.

He was paying the price now for that error of judgement.

He contemplated shouting, but the basement was soundproof, as was most of the library, the idea being that you shouldn't be disturbed. He might wrestle with the young man but he would surely lose. Then again, if the young man harmed him, he became the criminal.

He therefore chose to say what he really thought about Leila Hardy. 'Your sister overstepped the mark. She thought herself more important than she was. She actually believed the stuff she peddled, but she wasn't selling magick, she was selling sex.'

The remark hit home as he knew it would. Danny made a lunge at him, which he'd prepared himself for. What he hadn't anticipated was an addition to the fray. The policeman appeared from nowhere, like an avenging angel, grabbing the blade in his bandaged hand.

There was a brief struggle as the two men fought for supremacy, but there was no doubt in his mind who would win. Eventually order was restored.

'As you saw, this mad man attacked me—' he began.

The look the detective threw him stopped him mid-sentence.

'I'd like you to come with me to the station, Mr Buchanan. We have some questions to put to you regarding the deaths of Leila Hardy, Shannon Jones and Barry Fraser.'

70

It was a strange group that gathered one week after the fire, in so much as two of those present weren't police officers or forensics or those normally associated with the investigation of a crime or crimes.

Danny and Freya looked out of place, and definitely not of this world, Rhona thought.

Danny was clean shaven, his hair now cut as short as his sister's. Freya, tall and striking in a quieter way, looked both resolute and a little apprehensive.

And who could blame her?

Addressing a room full of detectives was a daunting prospect.

Magnus too was there, standing at the back, his part in the investigation acknowledged.

Bill asked Freya to begin by telling her story as she recalled it. All of it from the beginning. Rhona felt McNab's tension, and his affection, as Freya mustered herself to speak to the assembled officers.

Once begun, she spoke well and with authority. It was obvious that she'd chosen to ignore any preconceived ideas the company might have against Wicca and Witches in general. In a short space of time her honesty and forthrightness had won most of them over, not as believers, but at least as willing to try and understand.

She spoke of the importance of the Ferguson collection, and its value worldwide.

'Think of the tablets from Mount Sinai,' she explained, 'or the original writings of Jesus or Mohammed. Witchcraft is practised everywhere in the world in many various forms, like Christianity or Islam. Whatever has been written about it is precious and very valuable to both believers and un-believers.'

She spoke of Leila and Shannon and what she'd discovered in the Book of Shadows. Her recall was explicit, not of all the details of the Nine entries, but of Leila's translated wish that the book should be burned, because by doing that, her death would be avenged.

Finishing on that particular statement, Freya took her seat.

Rhona took to the floor immediately afterwards, silencing the ripple of discussion that had followed Freya's pronouncement. Scientific findings rather than Wiccan predictions proved a more comfortable place for the team.

Leaving aside how the fire had been started, Rhona concentrated on the debris they'd sifted from the back room.

'There was no key anywhere in the inner room. The only way the door could have been locked was from the main room, and that's where we found the key. Which means that Freya had been locked in and, according to the fire department, the fire started deliberately.'

Even if they couldn't get Grant Buchanan on the other killings, they could certainly charge him with the attempted murder of Freya Devine.

In the excited babble that followed, McNab took centre stage and introduced Danny, who then spoke about his concern for his sister and the video clips he'd taken. The

00

clips were shown and the link between Freya's story of the signet ring highlighted. The mock-up of the man who'd called himself Dr Peter Charles now appeared on the screen.

'We believe this man may already have left the country. Freya recalled some data she translated on him including, importantly, his date of birth. The name Peter, which was recorded in the Book of Shadows, she believes was his chosen magick name. His real first name she suggests will have the same name number. The letters will add up and subsequently reduce to 1, as does his date of birth.'

Bill indicated the image now on the screen:

1	2	3	4	5	6	7	8	9
A	B	C	D	E	F	G	H	I
J	K	L	M	N	O	P	Q	R
S	T	U	V	W	X	Y	Z	

P+E+T+E+R = 7+5+2+5+9= 28=10=1

'We'll maybe get the Tech team to deal with all the possibilities conjured up by that,' Bill said as a ripple of amused consternation went through the group.

The atmosphere in the room is upbeat, Rhona thought. *We have Buchanan and we have the possibility of his accomplice. It wasn't everything, but it might prove enough.*

Freya asked to speak to Rhona when the meeting was over and Bill offered them his office. McNab didn't accompany them, although Rhona could tell by his body language that he really wanted to.

Rhona was aware he was still concerned about Freya, but he hadn't revealed why, even though she and McNab were on better terms now, the *Stonewarrior* secret they shared diminished by more recent events.

Once they were alone, Freya said, 'I wanted to thank you for your help. You were right to let me visit Leila's flat. I shouldn't have left there without speaking to you first. If I had, things may have turned out differently.' She paused. 'But what I really wanted to ask was this: Do you have the forensic evidence to prove Grant killed Leila and Shannon?'

Her full report was taking form, but despite the extent and depth of the forensic analysis, Rhona doubted whether it would be enough to guarantee a conviction. In particular, the hand on the video had not been a match for Grant Buchanan and his DNA had not been included in the dolls. She saw little point in raising Freya's hopes.

'We have evidence, but it isn't conclusive. What I can say with conviction is that Mark Howitt wasn't responsible for their deaths, or the death of Barry Fraser. We *are* clear that Grant Buchanan attempted to murder you.'

Freya nodded. 'Then their deaths may go unavenged?'

'The law isn't about revenge, Freya,' Rhona said.

Freya gave her a small smile. 'No, you're right. It isn't.'

Rhona thought back to Freya's words later as she stood at the kitchen window, watching the sun set over the convent garden.

She'd wanted to add that the law was about seeking justice for the victims of crime, but had stumbled at that point for two reasons. One was the look on Freya's face, the other, Rhona's own sense that she had somehow failed the victims.

A pair of arms surrounded her.

'What are you thinking about?'

'A cat,' Rhona said.

'Tom? He's in the sitting room on the sofa.'

'No, Leila's cat. I called the SSPCA. Apparently they re-homed it, but it didn't stay at the new owner's for very long. I think it may be hanging around Leila's, hoping she'll come back.'

'Are you planning to rescue it?' Sean said.

In truth, Rhona hadn't considered it, but now that Sean had mentioned it, maybe she should?

'A Witch's cat should really live with a Witch,' Sean said. 'What about Freya?'

Rhona smiled, imagining McNab's reaction to the big black cat making Freya's flat its home.

'I'm not sure the cat would stay, even if Freya agreed to take it.'

'Some cats are better left alone,' Sean stated.

He turned her round and kissed her.

'You ready to eat now?'

'Yes,' Rhona said, 'I am.'

71

When McNab woke in the early hours of the morning Freya was no longer beside him, the place she'd lain cold to the touch. He rose and went looking for her, knowing where she would be.

The door to her temple was closed, but he detected the scent of incense and saw the flickering candlelight below the door.

McNab knew he couldn't disturb whatever ritual was being played out beyond that door. Her trust in Wicca was important to Freya. She'd told him she'd looked on death that night in the old library, and hadn't been afraid, because of her beliefs.

But the time Freya spent in there seemed to be getting longer.

When he'd questioned her about it, she'd mentioned something about scrying, which apparently enabled a Witch to see into the past or the future. She'd shown him a mirror, one whose face had been painted with black enamel, its gilt frame painted with symbols.

'Wiccans believe if we focus our thoughts on the black mirror, we can look into the past and sometimes the future.'

McNab could tell by her expression that Freya was trying to be honest with him, and reminded himself that his mother had been a firm believer that Jesus had died on the cross for his sins, of which there were many. He'd loved his mother, but hadn't believed a word of it. The same went for Freya.

'Okay,' he'd said. 'What does the black mirror tell you?'

'What happened the night Leila died.'

What had surprised McNab most was that Freya's inter-pretation of events matched his own so closely, to the extent that the team were already working that line of enquiry.

Grant Buchanan, he believed, *had* been watching Leila and *had* been in The Pot Still or its environs that night. He'd followed Leila and Mark home to the flat and contacted the man they knew as Peter. The plan had been to dispose of Leila and pin the blame on the man she'd picked up. The hand in the video seen stuffing the cloth into Leila's mouth had not been Grant's, however. And they had no way of proving it belonged to Peter Charles, unless they found him, although they were fairly certain he was the signet ring wearer on Danny's clip. The other two men in the clips hadn't been identified.

Both Buchanan and the elusive Peter had been involved in stealing artefacts from the Ferguson collection. Shannon had suggested to Freya that she'd found something out about the collection via the old library. That in itself probably put Shannon in danger.

As for Barry Fraser, he'd been set the task of keeping an eye on Leila by Danny and he'd been involved in making the videos, but McNab also thought there was a chance Barry had spotted Buchanan at The Pot Still that night, but hadn't known who he was until later. A good enough reason for his death.

Danny had done the right thing in lying low. It was prob-ably the only reason he was still alive. Buchanan had been vociferous in his claims that Danny Hardy had attacked him with a knife in the university basement and that only McNab's intervention had saved his life, something McNab had flatly contradicted. He'd given a different version of the story, omitting the knife, which fortunately the boss had believed. Leila's knife now lay on Freya's altar alongside her own.

Freya had watched him carefully as she'd told her black mirror story, noting the moments of recognition on his face.

'That's what *you* think happened, isn't it?' she'd said.

'Close to it,' had been all McNab was prepared to admit.

Jeff Barclay hadn't figured anywhere in Freya's deliberations, which fitted as well. Jeff's DNA hadn't found a match with the samples taken from Leila's flat. How and when he'd left the pub was still uncertain, but he had been charged with obstructing police enquiries.

All in all, Freya's contemplation of the black mirror had produced as good an understanding of the crime as he and his team had. As for the Nine, as they'd called them, Barry's DNA hadn't been a match for his namesake in the doll, and although Mark Howitt Senior had been identified as one of Leila's nine, he'd claimed not to know such a group existed. If so, then maybe Leila had placed him with the others because he'd bought sex magick from her as they had, or simply because of the significance of the number nine in Wicca. The Book of Shadows was gone with all its fine detail of the men she'd encountered, but, McNab reminded himself, they still had the DNA samples, Leila's simple drawings and what might be their first names. Not enough to go on at the moment, but maybe in the future?

The chanting from within had stopped.

McNab, keen that Freya wouldn't find him lurking there, went back through to bed.

When she climbed in beside him minutes later, he drew her into his arms.

'You okay?' he asked.

'I am now,' she said with a satisfied smile.

72

The book on the varieties of runic scripts used in Witchcraft would have brought an excellent price. He was sorry that it had gone, but its destruction had served a greater purpose.

The man whose name had been given as Dr Peter Charles congratulated himself on the outcome. The old library had been destroyed and with it the Witch's Book of Shadows. Anything the Witch had written about the group of men she'd serviced was gone.

He was aware of the confession and the subsequent suicide of the suspect, Mark Howitt. Had they known that night that the man Leila would take home was the son of a judge who had connections to the Witch, the plan would have been changed. However, the connection had proved to be beneficial in the long run.

Had the brother not interfered, it would have gone no further than the first Witch. On his head lay the blame for the subsequent deaths. Still, sufficient forensic evidence had been planted on the other two to give credence to Mark Howitt's confession.

True, one Witch remained alive, although her connection had been more with the Book of Shadows and, according to the report he'd received, she hadn't shown it to the police before it had been destroyed.

She might recall their meeting, of course, but he had

departed the country by the time of the fire and there was little chance of tracing him. There was one other loose end, his contact in the Ferguson collection, who had since been apprehended with regard to the fire, but he was confident that nothing the man might say could lead directly to him.

The group were now dispersed and would no longer be in contact with one another, at least for a while. Should they wish to reconvene, another European city would be chosen. Lucerne would be his choice.

The Ferguson collection had drawn them to Glasgow and he'd succeeded in making some of the rarer items available to the members of the group. Some of them were copies, but still valuable in the worldwide trade of precious and significant writings on the occult.

The man fingered his ring, as he was wont to do when thinking. His instinct told him that all would be well, and he trusted his instinct. His flight would be boarding soon, but there was still time for another drink. He waved the waiter over and ordered a double gin and tonic.

Ten minutes later he noted from the departure board that it was time to make his way to the gate, and decided to visit the Gents first. Toilets on aircraft were narrow and cramped, and the first-class lounge offered a better alternative.

The lounge had been quiet, the toilet was empty.

He chose a cubicle and entered, securing the door behind him.

As he unzipped his fly a strange thing happened. He heard what sounded like a cat hissing and was immediately reminded of the Witch's cat. The night he'd visited her in the altar room, it had been sitting there, its green eyes focused on them as she had brought him to climax. She had pushed him backwards at that point to lie on the sofa, her

431

knees gripping his waist. Then to his surprise she'd shouted an order and the cat had sprung up to settle on his face, its claws kneading his shoulder, the suffocating feel of it on his face heightening the intensity of his pleasure.

As he allowed the memory to wash over him, his prick hardened, preventing him from urinating.

He gripped himself, encouraging the memory now, playing it live here in the cubicle. He felt the cat on his face, his open mouth full of its fur. He heard the loud purring, the chants of the spell she'd chosen. He experienced the tightening of the cingulum, the desperate need for air, all driving him towards ecstasy.

Then suddenly the imagined grip of the cingulum became like a metal band constricting and compressing his chest. He let go of his penis as the pain grew in intensity, spreading over his shoulder to descend his left arm like a red-hot poker.

I need to breathe.

He tried madly to push the imagined cat from his face, knowing all the time he wasn't choking on its fur, but having a heart attack.

As he dropped into unconsciousness, he was back in the Witch's temple, the suffocating body of the cat on his face, its claws tearing at his shoulder. As he felt the Witch move against him, there was no mounting ecstasy, only pain, each of her thrusts, he knew, propelling his heart swiftly towards its final beat.

73

When he opened his eyes, the doll was there on the pillow, green eyes staring into his, red hair wild. Of course he'd been dreaming, because when he woke up properly, the doll had gone.

Some nights later when they'd put out the lights, he heard the sound of their hard plastic bodies clicking and clacking together. The noise had invaded his cell, keeping him awake.

He knew a great deal about magick, although he didn't believe in it. Therefore he ascribed his symptoms to stress at the upcoming trial. He asked to see a doctor, but chose not to describe what kept him awake at night, saying only that he couldn't sleep.

Shortly after that, the visitations became more frequent and were now a combination of vision and sound. They consisted of a curtain of swaying dolls, their colliding limbs like the cackle of Witch laughter as they swung from the ceiling on their red cords, their shiny bead eyes fastened on him.

It was at this point that he considered his options.

Death being one, the other, confession.

Time and his state of mind would tell which one he chose.

74

The cat dropped from the roof onto the ledge and eased its way in through the open window, springing silently to the floor.

No longer sleek and well-fed, its green eyes wore a hungry look.

Hearing a sound in the hallway, it headed in that direction.

A snap of the letter box saw three circulars thrust through. The cat stood for a moment, anticipating something else, its tail upright, the tip swishing.

A draught from the open window heralded a series of clicks and clacks from the room it had entered by.

The cat made a beeline back there to stand and stare up at the swaying dolls. It turned, sensing a presence, and sprang towards it, rubbing its body against the slim legs, weaving between them, its purr as loud as the clicking curtain of colliding limbs.

Notes and Acknowledgements

My lecturer in astronomy at Glasgow University was Professor Archie Roy. He really was ambidextrous and could draw two circles and fill them in with diagrams at the same time.

I met him again many years later when he had become the foremost authority on the paranormal in Scotland, while also Emeritus Professor of Astronomy, with an asteroid named after him: (5806) Archieroy. I called him up one day to discuss a speculative piece for television that I was writing and we met in the university common room where he told me many tales about his work with the Scottish Society for Psychical Research.

Later I attended a series of lectures run by the SSPR at the university in which he told the story of the old library and what it contained and how this had sparked his interest in investigating the paranormal. So that much is true. I merely substituted Freya at Newcastle University for my own experience at Glasgow.

The Ferguson collection does exist and details about it can be found on the university library's website, some of which I used. As far as I am aware, it is still intact, and is still as valuable in terms of its contribution to our understanding of such matters. When I tried to locate the exact position of the old library as described by Professor Roy, I was unsuccessful, so I chose my own location in the tower, mainly because I used to have lectures in moral philosophy in one of the tower lecture theatres. I particularly remember the cooing sound of the pigeons directly above us as we tackled Plato's *Republic*.

As to Wicca, I found during my research much to commend it as a way of worship, including the Wiccan Rede, oft quoted in the text. Witchcraft is not merely legendary; it was, and is, still real. Some would say its doctrine is far more relevant to the times than the majority of established church texts, insofar as it acknowledges a holistic universe, equal rights, feminism, ecology, attunement, brotherly and sisterly love, planetary care – all part and parcel of Witchcraft, the old, yet new, religion.

However, misconceptions still abound and my knowledge is not great enough to prove them all wrong. Suffice to say that every religion has its dark and bright side. And every force for good can be changed into one for evil. You only have to recall the Inquisition to know that.

Torturing and killing women by naming them as Witches was a job perfectly designed for those who delighted in the sexual torture of the female of the species. As Magnus says in the book, there were psychopaths back then too.

I couldn't help but think as I did my research that Rhona's knowledge of forensics and the science of DNA would have been seen as a type of Witchcraft not so long ago. In fact in some parts of the world, Rhona, the forensic scientist, would be regarded as a Witch at this very moment.

Lin Anderson

KU-211-026

The Modern Law
of Evidence

The Modern Law of Evidence

Eighth Edition

ADRIAN KEANE LL.B
of the Inner Temple, Barrister,
Professor of Law and Director of Professional
Programmes, the City Law School,
City University, London

James Griffiths B.Soc.Sci.
of the Middle Temple, Barrister,
and Senior Lecturer, the City Law School,
City University, London

Paul McKeown LL.B, LL.M
of Lincoln's Inn, Barrister
and Senior Lecturer, the City Law School,
City University, London

OXFORD
UNIVERSITY PRESS

OXFORD

UNIVERSITY PRESS

Great Clarendon Street, Oxford OX2 6DP

Oxford University Press is a department of the University of Oxford.
It furthers the University's objective of excellence in research, scholarship,
and education by publishing worldwide in

Oxford New York

Auckland Cape Town Dar es Salaam Hong Kong Karachi
Kuala Lumpur Madrid Melbourne Mexico City Nairobi
New Delhi Shanghai Taipei Toronto

With offices in

Argentina Austria Brazil Chile Czech Republic France Greece
Guatemala Hungary Italy Japan Poland Portugal Singapore
South Korea Switzerland Thailand Turkey Ukraine Vietnam

Oxford is a registered trade mark of Oxford University Press
in the UK and in certain other countries

Published in the United States
by Oxford University Press Inc., New York

© Oxford University Press 2010

The moral rights of the authors have been asserted
Database right Oxford University Press (maker)

This edition 2010

All rights reserved. No part of this publication maybe reproduced,
stored in a retrieval system, or transmitted, in any form or by any means,
without the prior permission in writing of Oxford University Press,
or as expressly permitted by law, or under terms agreed with the appropriate
reprographics rights or ganization. Enquiries concerning reproduction
outside the scope of the above should be sent to the Rights Department,
Oxford University Press, at the address above

You must not circulate this book in any other binding or cover
and you must impose the same condition on any acquirer

British Library Cataloguing in Publication Data
Data available

Library of Congress Cataloging in Publication Data
Data available

Typeset by MPS Limited, A Macmillan Company
Printed in Great Britain
on acid-free paper by
Antony Rowe Ltd, Chippenham, Wiltshire

ISBN 978–0–19–955834–6

10 9 8 7 6 5 4 3 2 1

PREFACE TO THE EIGHTH EDITION

The twin aims of this work remain unaltered. The first aim is to explore the theory of the law of evidence and its practical application, bearing in mind the varied needs of its readers: judges, practitioners, and students studying law at both the undergraduate and the vocational stage. The second aim is to seek to state the law in a way which is not only accurate, but also readable, with the focus, wherever possible, on modern aspects of the subject.

Although the aims of this work remain constant, this new edition reflects three types of significant change. The most important change is to its authorship. It is a quarter of a century since the first edition of this book was published, and this seems a good time for me to share the pleasures and challenges of preparing new editions. I am delighted that my colleagues James Griffiths and Paul McKeown have agreed to become co-authors. I have no doubts about their expertise, enthusiasm, and thoughtful input. Together, we hope that feedback from readers will remain complimentary and positive.

A second set of changes relate to presentation, a new feature, and a new accompanying resource. The presentation of the book has changed with a view to improved 'navigation' and readability. The new feature is a 'key issues' section at the start of each chapter, designed to provoke readers, especially those coming to the subject for the first time, to think about the issues, in particular the policy issues, before looking at the laws themselves and their given rationale. The accompanying resource takes the form of an Online Resource Centre (www.oxfordtextbooks.co.uk/orc/keane8e/), which will contain regular updates to the text of the published work and a list of weblinks to other relevant sites.

The third change is the one to be expected, the incorporation of the changes in the law since the seventh edition. There have been a number of important developments. They include the Criminal Evidence (Witness Anonymity) Act 2008 and the detailed guidance on its meaning provided by the Court of Appeal in *R v Mayers;* the Law Commission's Consultation Paper on the Admissibility of Expert Evidence in Criminal Proceedings in England and Wales; the decision of the European Court of Human Rights in *Al-Khawaja and Tahery v United Kingdom*, and the subsequent decision of the Court of Appeal in *R v Horncastle,* on the right of an accused to examine or have examined witnesses against him; the decision of the House of Lords in *C plc v P* on the scope of the privilege against self-incrimination; and the many important case law developments in relation to bad character, hearsay, and 'without prejudice' privilege.

The authors are grateful to OUP, for their ongoing support, and to readers, for their helpful feedback. My thanks go, as ever, to my wife Rosemary, whose understanding and encouragement remain quite boundless. James' thanks go to his wife, Kate, for her love and patience. Paul dedicates his work on this edition to his father, Michael Joseph McKeown.

The responsibility for errors and other imperfections rests with the authors, who have attempted to state the law as at 7 September 2009.

Adrian Keane
Thurston End, Suffolk
September 2009

OUTLINE CONTENTS

DETAILED CONTENTS

TABLE OF STATUTES

Page references in bold indicate that the text is reproduced in full

TABLE OF STATUTORY INSTRUMENTS

Page references in bold indicate that the text is reproduced in full

Page references in bold indicate that the text is reproduced in full

TABLE OF CASES

Introduction

Key Issues

- What is 'evidence' and 'the law of evidence'?

- Typically, the parties to litigation dispute the facts. What are the factors that operate to prevent the court from looking at *all* the evidence that could assist in discovering where the truth lies?

- What human factors can operate to prevent the court from discovering where the truth lies?

- Are there any good reasons to restrict the evidence taken into account *more* when the tribunal of fact is a jury or lay justices than when it is a professional judge?

- Should the law of evidence be codified or allowed to continue to evolve by way of common law development and piecemeal statutory reform?

Evidence is information by which facts tend to be proved, and the law of evidence is that body of law and discretion regulating the means by which facts may be proved in both courts of law and tribunals and arbitrations in which the strict rules of evidence apply.[1] It is adjectival rather than substantive law and overlaps with procedural law.

At the risk of oversimplification, the broad governing principle underlying the English law of evidence can be stated in no more than nine words: all relevant evidence is admissible, subject to the exceptions.

Truth and the fact-finding process

In most litigation the parties will dispute the facts. In an ideal world, perhaps, the court inquiring into those facts would take account of all evidence which is relevant to the dispute, that is all evidence that logically goes to prove or disprove the existence of those facts and would thereby get to the truth of the matter.[2] In the real world, however, a variety of factors operate to restrict the evidence taken into account. First, there are practical constraints inherent in the fact-finding process and common to all legal systems: considerations of time and cost and the need for finality to litigation.[3] Secondly, under the English adversarial system of trial, whatever its undoubted merits, the court itself cannot undertake a search for relevant evidence but must reach its decision solely on the basis of such evidence as is presented by the parties. Thirdly, there is the law of evidence itself, much of which comprises rules which exclude relevant evidence for a variety of different reasons. For example, evidence may be insufficiently relevant or of only minimal probative force; it may give rise to a multiplicity of essentially subsidiary issues, which could distract the court from the main issue; it may be insufficiently reliable or too unreliable; its potential for prejudice to the party against whom it is introduced may be out of all proportion to its probative value on behalf of the party introducing it; its disclosure may be injurious to the national interest; and so on. Thus the court may aspire to the ascertainment of the truth, but at the end of the day it must come to a decision and settle the dispute even if the evidence introduced is inadequate or inconclusive.

The risk that the court will not get to the truth of the matter is heightened by virtue of the fact that litigation is, of course, a human endeavour and therefore will, in one way or another, provide scope for differences of opinion, error, deceit, and lies. Thus judges, who are called upon to decide what evidence is relevant and to be taken into account, may take different views about whether one fact is relevant to prove or disprove another. As to the parties to litigation, they are hardly impartial and may well be more concerned with winning their case than in assisting to establish the truth. As to the fact-finders, they are most likely to use inferential reasoning to supplement the evidence in the case and fill the gaps in it, which may involve the creation of non-existent facts.[4] Finally, there are the witnesses who, if not telling the truth, will either be lying or mistaken. As to

---

[1] The strict rules of evidence do not apply, for example, to civil claims which have been allocated to the small claims track (see CPR r 27.8) or at hearings before employment tribunals (see r 14(2), Employment Tribunals Rules of Procedure, Employment Tribunals (Constitution and Rules of Procedure) Regulations 2004, SI 2004/1861, Sch 1).

[2] In support of the view that trials should be a search for the truth, see the Government's White Paper, *Justice for All*, Cm 563 (2002) at 32 and Lord Justice Auld's *Review of the Criminal Courts of England and Wales*, HMSO, 2001, para 154, ch 10.

[3] See Morgan, *Introduction to the American Law Institute Model Code of Evidence* (1942) 3–4.

[4] See generally Pennington and Hastie, 'The story model for juror decision making' in R Hastie (ed), *Inside the Juror* (Cambridge, 1993).

mistakes, there is obvious scope for error, not only in their observation of events, but also in their memory of it and in their recounting of those events in court. There is also the risk that witnesses may give truthful but unreliable evidence of facts which have been created by parties involved in the legal process, a classic example being evidence of a false confession produced during the interrogation of a suspect.[5]

The development of the law

The largely exclusionary ethos of the modern law of evidence reflects its common law history. Many of the rules evolved at a time when the tribunal of fact comprised either jurors or lay justices to whom the judges adopted a paternalistic and protective attitude, excluding relevant evidence such as hearsay evidence, evidence of character, and the opinion evidence of non-experts on the basis that lay persons might overvalue its weight and importance, or even treat it as conclusive. A typical example is evidence of the accused's previous convictions or of his disposition towards wrongdoing which, to an extent, remains inadmissible because of fears that it might influence jurors disproportionately against the accused and distract their attention from other evidence tending to prove his guilt or innocence. Distrust of the jury probably had little to do with the origin of the rule against hearsay evidence, but much to do with the delay in the growth of exceptions to that rule. Historically, the judges also suffered from an ingrained fear of the deliberate concoction or manufacture of evidence by the parties to litigation and their witnesses. This accounted for the general ban on statements made out of court by a witness and consistent with his present testimony (the rule against previous consistent or self-serving statements). In large measure, it also explained why an out-of-court statement, even if it could be shown to be of virtually indisputable reliability, was generally excluded as evidence of the truth of its contents under the rule against hearsay. The dread of manufactured evidence went much further than the exclusion of specific kinds of evidence: it also meant that whole classes of persons were treated as incompetent to give evidence at all. For example, the incompetence of persons with a pecuniary or proprietary interest in the outcome of the proceedings, including the parties themselves in civil cases, was not fully abolished until the mid-nineteenth century, and it was not until the Criminal Evidence Act 1898 that the accused and his spouse were entitled, in all criminal cases, to give evidence on oath. Another factor which contributed to the largely exclusionary nature of the law of evidence in criminal proceedings stemmed from an understandable desire, at a time when the dice were unfairly loaded against the accused, to offer some judicial protection against injustice. Trials were often conducted with indecent haste, accused persons enjoyed far less legal representation, and convictions could be questioned only on narrow legal grounds.[6]

In civil cases, nowadays, trial is usually by a judge sitting alone who is perfectly capable, by virtue of her training, qualifications, and experience, of attaching no more weight to an item of evidence than the circumstances properly allow. In criminal cases, the scales can no longer be said to be unfairly loaded against the accused, especially since the coming into force of the Human Rights Act 1998. No doubt, it remains necessary to prevent some material being placed before juries on the grounds of irretrievable prejudice against the accused, but the quality of juries and lay magistrates has greatly improved and it is questionable whether they

---

[5] See M McConville, A Sanders, and R Leng, *The Case for the Prosecution* (London, 1991).

[6] See Criminal Law Revision Committee, 11th Report, *Evidence (General)*, Cmnd 4991, paras 21 et seq.

are incapable, given clear and proper judicial direction, of properly evaluating the weight and reliability of some relevant evidence which continues to be excluded, such as evidence of the previous consistent statements of witnesses.

Over the years, there has been much statutory reform, sometimes significant, including in particular the enactments designed to bring domestic law into line with the European Convention on Human Rights. Statutory reform has done much to reduce the number of restrictions on the admissibility of relevant evidence, to rationalize and clarify the law, to enhance the discretionary powers of the judge, and to remove some of the more anomalous and unnecessary discrepancies between the rules in civil and criminal cases. Reform, however, has been piecemeal, sporadic, slow, and usually limited to one specific area of the law, with little or no consideration of the impact of change on other related areas of the subject. The current law of evidence, therefore, may be likened to a machine which has been constructed on common law principles by judicial engineers, but which is subject to periodic alteration by parliamentary mechanics, who variously remove or redesign parts or bolt on new parts. The judges oil and maintain the machine, and continually seek to refine, modify, and develop it to meet the continually changing needs it is designed to serve. But there are constraints and limitations. Developments can only occur in relation to the specific issues brought before the judges by litigants, some of which are slow to surface.[7] Moreover, in relation to the issues that do surface, the basic framework of the law may be so unprincipled or out of line with con-temporary needs or moral and social values that the judges, bound by *stare decisis* or saddled with antiquated legislation, can only act on a 'make do and mend' basis and put out a call for parliamentary assistance.[8] Whether the call is answered, however, is something of a lottery, with the odds improving if the proposals are based on, or supported by, the recommendations of a law reform agency. Some proposals, however, are simply unacceptable to the government of the day or too dull to win votes, being technical or relating to the quality rather than the content of the law.

Speaking generally, statutory reform has done much to improve the civil rules across a range of subjects. Additionally, and as a result of Lord Woolf's review of the procedural rules in the civil courts,[9] the Civil Procedure Act 1997 provided for the creation of the Civil Procedure Rules (and supplementary Practice Directions). The rules, which replaced the former Rules of the Supreme Court and County Court Rules, and which may modify the rules of evidence,[10] constituted the most radical reform of the ethos and procedure of civil litigation since the Supreme Court of Judicature Act 1875. The jury is still out on whether they render the civil justice system as a whole more accessible, fair, and efficient,[11] but concerning the law of evidence, they have done much to simplify and rationalize the relevant procedural rules.

Parliament has also rationalized and improved many of the criminal rules. The most recent of the major reforms, the Criminal Justice Act 2003, has brought about radical change in relation to hearsay evidence and evidence of bad character. The provisions are premised on

[7] For example, it was only in the early 1990s that the courts were first asked to give detailed consideration to the applicability, in criminal proceedings, of the general doctrine of public interest immunity.

[8] For example, there have been repeated judicial requests for reform of the privilege against self-incrimination. See also the comments in *C v DPP* [1995] 2 All ER 43, HL, concerning the presumption of *doli incapax*, subsequently abolished by statute.

[9] Access to Justice, Final Report (HMSO, 1996).

[10] See Sch 1, para 4 to the Act.

[11] See s 1(3) of the Act.

a welcome new confidence that fact-finders can be trusted to evaluate evidence correctly, reflecting the view in Lord Justice Auld's *Review of the Criminal Courts of England and Wales* that 'the English law of criminal evidence should, in general, move away from technical rules of inadmissibility to trusting judicial and lay fact finders to give relevant evidence the weight it deserves'.[12] As to the procedural rules, the Criminal Procedure Rules 2005[13] represented the first steps towards the creation of a new consolidated and comprehensive criminal procedure code of the kind recommended by Lord Justice Auld in his *Review of the Criminal Courts of England and Wales*. Although, initially, the rules merely consolidated and adopted all the pre-existing rules of court, rule 1.1 sets out a new overriding objective of the code that criminal cases be dealt with justly. Under rule 3.2, the court must further the overriding objective by actively managing the case, which includes ensuring that evidence, whether disputed or not, is presented in the shortest and clearest way; and under rule 3.3, each party must (a) actively assist the court in fulfilling its duty under rule 3.2, without, or if necessary with, a direction; and (b) apply for a direction if needed to further the overriding objective.

'It would be unfortunate', it has been said, 'if the law of evidence was allowed to develop in a way which was not in accordance with the common sense of ordinary folk',[14] not least, one might add, because it has to be used and understood not only by professional judges, but also by part-time judges, lay magistrates, jurors and, increasingly, the police. Recent developments give some cause for cautious optimism. Looking at the law of evidence overall, however, there are strong grounds for believing that fairness, coherence, clarity, and accessibility will only come, not from common law development coupled with piecemeal statutory intervention, but from codification.

ADDITIONAL READING

McConville et al, *The Case for the Prosecution* (London, 1991).

Pennington and Hastie, 'The story model for juror decision making' in Hastie (ed), *Inside the Juror* (Cambridge, 1993).

Research Board of the British Psychological Society, *The Guidelines on Memory and the Law* (2008).

Twining, *Rethinking Evidence* (Oxford, 1990).

[12] Para 78.
[13] SI 2005/384.
[14] Per Lawton LJ in *R v Chandler* [1976] 1 WLR 585 at 590, CA.

Preliminaries

Key Issues

- What are the only facts that should be open to proof (or disproof) in any given trial?

- What forms can evidence take in a trial?

- What is 'circumstantial evidence'?

- Should adverse inferences be drawn if a party to a trial (a) fails to give evidence or call witnesses; or (b) can be shown to have told lies about the facts in dispute?

- What is meant by evidence 'relevant' to the facts in dispute?

- When and why should evidence be excluded notwithstanding that it is relevant to the facts in dispute?

- What is meant by the 'weight' of an item of evidence?

- In a jury trial, which evidential issues should be for the judge and which for the jury?

- When and why should a question about the admissibility of an item of evidence be decided in the absence of the jury?

- Should the admissibility of evidence be governed entirely by rules of law or should the judge have discretionary power (a) to admit evidence inadmissible in law; and/or (b) to exclude evidence admissible in law?

Facts open to proof or disproof

The facts which are open to proof or disproof in English courts of law are facts in issue, relevant facts, and collateral facts.

Facts in issue

A fact in issue is sometimes referred to as a 'principal fact' or *'factum probandum'*. The facts in issue in any given case are those facts which the claimant (or the prosecutor) must prove in order to succeed in his claim (prosecution) together with those facts which the defendant (or the accused) must prove in order to succeed in his defence. The nature and number of facts in issue in a case is determined not by the law of evidence, but partly by reference to the substantive law and partly by reference to what the parties allege, admit, and deny. For example, in an action for damages for breach of contract in which the defendant simply denies the facts on which the claimant relies for his claim, the facts in issue will be those facts which, if proved, will establish the formation of a binding contract between the parties, breach of contract by the defendant, and consequential loss and damage suffered by the claimant. However, if the defendant, in his defence, pleads discharge by agreement, admitting that the contract was made but denying the breach and loss alleged by the claimant, then the facts in issue will then be those which, if proved, will establish breach by the defendant and consequential loss and damage suffered by the claimant together with those facts which, if proved, will establish that the parties discharged the contract by agreement. Another possibility is that the defendant admits the contract and its breach and makes no counterclaim. The only facts in issue will then be those which, if proved, will establish consequential loss and damage and the amount of damages to which the claimant claims he is entitled. There are many other possibilities. In civil proceedings, the facts in issue are usually identifiable by reference to the statement of case, its very purpose being to set out the factual (and legal) issues on which the parties agree and disagree so that they and the court know in advance exactly what matters are left in dispute and what facts, therefore, have to be proved or disproved at the trial.[1] Under CPR rule 16.4(1):

> Particulars of claim must include—
> (a) a concise statement of the facts on which the claimant relies; . . .

Under rule 16.5(1):

> In his defence, the defendant must state—
> (a) which of the allegations in the particulars of claim he denies;
> (b) which allegations he is unable to admit or deny, but which he requires the claimant to prove; and
> (c) which allegations he admits.
> As a general rule, a defendant who fails to deal with an allegation shall be taken to admit it.[2]

---

[1] See *Esso Petroleum Co Ltd v Southport Corpn* [1956] AC 218 at 241, HL; *Farrell v Secretary of State for Defence* [1980] 1 WLR 172, HL.

[2] CPR r 16.5(5). Under r 16.5(3), a defendant who fails to deal with an allegation but sets out in his defence the nature of his case in relation to the issue to which that allegation is relevant, shall be taken to require that allegation to be proved. Under r 16.5(4), where the claim includes a money claim, a defendant shall be taken to require that any allegation relating to the amount of money claimed to be proved unless he expressly admits the allegation.

In criminal cases in which the accused pleads not guilty, the facts in issue are all those facts which the prosecution must prove in order to succeed, including the identity of the accused, the commission by him of the *actus reus*, and the existence of any necessary knowledge or intent on his part,[3] together with any further facts that the accused must prove in order to establish any defence other than a simple denial of the prosecution case. However, under section 10 of the Criminal Justice Act 1967, any fact of which oral evidence may be given in any criminal proceedings may be admitted for the purpose of those proceedings by or on behalf of either the prosecution or defence and an admission made by any party of any such fact shall be 'conclusive' evidence of the fact admitted. In other words, a fact which is formally admitted under the section is not open to contradictory proof and in effect ceases to be a fact in issue: the court must find the fact to have been proved.[4]

Relevant facts

A relevant fact, sometimes called a 'fact relevant to the issue', an 'evidentiary fact' or '*factum probans*', is a fact from which the existence or non-existence of a fact in issue may be inferred. If the only facts which were open to proof or disproof were facts in issue, many claims and defences would fail. If, for example, the fact in issue is whether a man shot his wife, obviously an eye-witness to the incident may be called to give evidence that he saw the shooting. However, in many cases a statement by a witness that he perceived a fact in issue with one of his senses, which is described as 'direct evidence', is quite simply unavailable. Very often the only available evidence is that which can establish some other fact or facts relevant to the fact in issue, for example the evidence of a gunsmith that on the day before the shooting the man bought a gun from him, the evidence of a policeman that after the shooting he found that gun buried in the garden of the man's house, and the evidence of a forensic expert that the gun bore the man's fingerprints. Evidence of relevant facts is described as 'circumstantial evidence', some further examples of which are given later in this chapter. Where a party to proceedings seeks to establish a relevant fact the existence of which is denied by his opponent, the relevant fact may also be said to be a 'fact in issue'.

Collateral facts

Collateral facts, sometimes referred to as 'subordinate facts', are of three kinds: (i) facts affecting the competence of a witness; (ii) facts affecting the credibility of a witness; and (iii) facts, sometimes called 'preliminary facts', which must be proved as a condition precedent to the admissibility of certain items of evidence tendered to prove a fact in issue or a relevant fact. As to the first, an example would be that a potential witness suffers from a mental handicap rendering him incompetent to testify. An example of a collateral fact of the second kind would be that a witness, who testifies to the effect that he saw a certain event at a distance of 50 yards, suffers from an eye complaint which prevents him from seeing anything at a distance greater than 20 yards. Such a witness may be cross-examined about his eye complaint and, if he denies its existence, evidence in rebuttal may be given by an oculist.[5] Similarly, a witness may be cross-examined about his bias or partiality towards one of the parties to the proceedings and again, if

---

[3] Per Lord Goddard CJ in *R v Sims* [1946] KB 531 at 539.
[4] See further under Ch 22, 673 under **Formal admissions**.
[5] See per Lord Pearce in *Toohey v Metropolitan Police Comr* [1965] AC 595 at 608, HL (see Ch 7).

he denies it, evidence may be called to contradict his denial.[6] A collateral fact of the third kind may be illustrated by reference to an exception to the rule against hearsay: in criminal proceedings a statement made by a participant in or observer of an event is admissible as evidence of the truth of its contents, by way of exception to the rule against hearsay, *on proof that* it was made by a person so emotionally overpowered by the event that the possibility of concoction or distortion can be disregarded.[7] Another illustration is an exception to the general rule that a party seeking to rely upon the contents of a document must adduce the original: a copy is admissible as evidence of the contents *on proof that* the original has been destroyed or cannot be found after due search.[8]

Where a party to proceedings seeks to establish a collateral fact the existence of which is denied by his opponent, the collateral fact may also be said to be a 'fact in issue'. The existence or non-existence of a preliminary fact in issue is, as we shall see, decided by the judge, not the jury, as part of his general function to rule on all questions concerning the admissibility of evidence.

The varieties of evidence

The evidence by which facts may be proved or disproved in court is known as 'judicial evidence'. Judicial evidence takes only three *forms*, namely oral evidence, documentary evidence, and things. Judicial evidence, however, is open to classification not only in terms of the form in which it may be presented in court but also in terms of its substantive content, the purpose for which it is presented and the rules by which its admissibility is determined. Thus, any given item of judicial evidence may attract more than one of the labels by which the varieties of evidence have been classified. The principal labels are 'testimony', 'hearsay evidence', 'documentary evidence', 'real evidence', 'circumstantial evidence', and 'conclusive evidence'.

Testimony

Testimony is the oral statement of a witness made on oath in open court[9] and offered as evidence of the truth of that which is asserted. 'Direct testimony' is a term used to describe a witness's statement that he perceived a fact in issue with one of his five senses. In other words, it is testimony relating to facts of which the witness has or claims to have personal or first-hand knowledge.[10] Direct testimony, or 'direct evidence' as it is sometimes called, is a term commonly used in contrast with 'hearsay evidence'. The term is also used in contrast with 'circumstantial evidence'.

---

[6] See per Geoffrey Lane LJ in *R v Mendy* (1976) 64 Cr App R 4, CA at 6 (see Ch 7).

[7] See Ch 10 and s 118(1) of the Criminal Justice Act 2003.

[8] *Brewster v Sewell* (1820) 3 B&Ald 296 (see Ch 9).

[9] In criminal proceedings, some witnesses may give their evidence by live television link and video recordings of interviews of some witnesses may be admitted as their evidence-in-chief: see Ch 5. In civil proceedings, the court may allow a witness to give evidence through a video link or by other means (eg by telephone): see CPR r 32.3.

[10] An appropriately qualified expert may give oral evidence of opinion, as opposed to fact, on a matter calling for the expertise which he possesses and may do so even though substantial contributions to the formation of his opinion have been made by matters of which he has no personal or first-hand knowledge: see per Megarry J in *English Exporters (London) Ltd v Eldonwall Ltd* [1973] Ch 415 at 423. A statement of opinion may also be made by a non-expert witness, but only as a way of conveying *facts* personally perceived: see generally Ch 18.

Hearsay evidence

In common parlance, hearsay is used to describe statements, often gossip, that one hears but does not know to be true. In the law of evidence, the word is used in a broader technical sense. The common law concept of hearsay may be defined as any statement, other than one made by a witness in the course of giving his evidence in the proceedings in question, by any person, whether it was made on oath or unsworn and whether it was made orally, in writing, or by signs and gestures, which is offered as evidence of the truth of its contents. If the statement is tendered for any purpose other than that of proving the truth of its contents, for example to prove simply that the statement was made or to prove the state of mind of the maker of the statement, it is not hearsay but 'original evidence'. Provided that it is relevant to a fact in issue, original evidence is admissible. At common law, hearsay could only be received in evidence exceptionally. Under the modern law, in civil cases the rule has been abrogated; in criminal cases there are a variety of statutory exceptions; and in both civil and criminal cases a number of common law exceptions have been preserved and given statutory force.

The meaning of 'hearsay' and 'original evidence' and the distinction between them is perhaps best understood by way of examples. Suppose a fact in issue in criminal proceedings is whether a man, H, shot his wife, W. X was an eye-witness to the shooting and later said to Y: 'H shot W'. Y repeated X's statement to Z. If X is called as a witness to the proceedings he may, of course, give direct testimony of the shooting. It is something of which he has personal or first-hand knowledge, something he perceived with his own eyes. However, X may not narrate to the court the statement that he made to Y in order to prove that H shot W unless his statement comes within one of the exceptions to the rule against hearsay. The statement was made other than in the course of giving evidence in the proceedings in question and would be tendered in order to prove that H shot W (the truth of its contents). For the same reasons neither Y nor Z, if called, could recount X's out-of-court statement unless, again, it comes within one of the exceptions to the rule against hearsay. Now suppose a fact in issue in criminal proceedings is whether D is physically capable of speech. D is charged with obtaining property by deception. The prosecution allege that he dishonestly obtained money from a charity by pretending that he was incapable of speech. D, leaving the offices of the charity, held a conversation with E. E, if called as a witness for the prosecution, may give evidence of what D said, not to prove the truth of anything that D said, but simply to prove that D's statements were made, that D could speak. D's out-of-court statements are received as original evidence.

These are simple examples of difficult concepts. The meaning of hearsay evidence and the distinction between hearsay and original evidence give rise to difficult legal problems which are explored fully in Chapter 10. The numerous common law and statutory exceptions to the rule against hearsay comprise the largest topic in this work. They are considered in Chapters 10–13.

Documentary evidence

Documentary evidence usually consists of a document or a copy of a document, produced for inspection by the court. However, in some cases the evidence may be presented electronically, by a simultaneous display to all parties via courtroom monitors, thereby ensuring that all involved are looking at the same item of evidence at the same time. Presentation of evidence in this way is encouraged in fraud and other complex criminal cases because of its potential for saving time.[11]

---

[11] See the Protocol for the control and management of heavy fraud and other complex criminal cases [2005] 2 All ER 429, para 6(vi).

THE VARIETIES OF EVIDENCE

A document, for the purposes of the law of evidence, has no single definition. The meaning of the word varies according to the nature of the proceedings and the particular context in question. Suffice it to say, for present purposes, that in certain circumstances the word is defined to include not only documents in writing, but also maps, plans, graphs, drawings, photographs, discs, tapes, videotapes, films, and negatives.[12] Documents may be produced to show their contents, their existence, or their physical appearance. The contents of a document may be received as evidence of their truth, by way of exception to the hearsay rule, or for some other purpose, for example to identify the document or to show what its author thought or believed. It is convenient to regard the contents of documents as a separate category of judicial evidence because although, like oral statements, they are subject to the general rules of evidence on admissibility, their reception in evidence is also subject to two additional requirements. One of these relates to the proof of their contents.[13] The matter is explored fully in Chapter 9. It is mentioned here merely in order to explain the distinction, mainly of importance in connection with documents, between 'primary evidence', which may be regarded as the best available evidence, and 'secondary evidence', that is evidence which by its nature suggests that better evidence may be available. As a general rule, a party seeking to rely on the contents of a document must adduce primary evidence of those contents, which is usually the original of the document in question, as opposed to secondary evidence of those contents, for example a copy of the document, a copy of a copy of the document, or oral evidence of the contents.[14] Where a document is produced to show the bare fact of its existence or its physical appearance, for example the substance of which it is made or the condition which it is in, it constitutes a variety of 'real evidence'.

Real evidence

Real evidence usually takes the form of some material object produced for inspection in order that the court may draw an inference from its own observation as to the existence, condition or value of the object in question. Although real evidence may be extremely valuable as a means of proof, little if any weight attaches to such evidence in the absence of some accompanying testimony identifying the object in question and explaining its connection with, or significance in relation to, the facts in issue or relevant to the issue. In addition to material objects, including documents, examples of real evidence also include the physical appearance of persons and animals, the demeanour of witnesses, the intonation of voices on a tape recording, views, that is inspections out of court of the *locus in quo* or of some object which it is impossible or highly inconvenient to bring to court, and, possibly, out-of-court demonstrations or re-enactments of acts or events into which the court is enquiring. Real evidence is considered in greater detail in Chapter 9.

Circumstantial evidence

General

Circumstantial evidence has already been defined as evidence of relevant facts (facts from which the existence or non-existence of a fact in issue may be inferred) and contrasted with 'direct evidence', a term which is used to mean testimony relating to facts in issue of which a witness

---

[12] See further Ch 9.

[13] The other concerns proof of the fact that the document was properly executed.

[14] The distinction between primary and secondary evidence is also of importance in relation to the proof of facts contained in a document to which a privilege attaches: see Ch 20.

has or claims to have personal or first-hand knowledge. Circumstantial evidence may take the form of oral or documentary evidence (including admissible hearsay) or real evidence.

'It is no derogation of evidence to say that it is circumstantial.'[15] Its importance lies in its potential for proving a variety of different relevant facts all of which point to the same conclusion, as when it is sought to establish that an accused committed murder by evidence of his preparation, motive, and opportunity for its commission, together with evidence of the discovery of a weapon, capable of having caused the injuries sustained by the victim, buried in the accused's back garden and bearing his fingerprints. Circumstantial evidence, it has been said, 'works by cumulatively, in geometrical progression, eliminating other possibilities'[16] and has been likened to a rope comprised of several cords:

> One strand of the cord might be insufficient to sustain the weight, but three stranded together may be quite of sufficient strength. Thus it may be in circumstantial evidence—there may be a combination of circumstances, no one of which would raise a reasonable conviction or more than a mere suspicion; but the three taken together may create a conclusion of guilt with as much certainty as human affairs can require or admit of.[17]

In criminal proceedings in which the Crown's case is based on circumstantial evidence, there is no rule of law requiring the judge to direct the jury to acquit unless they are sure that the facts proved are not only consistent with guilt but also inconsistent with any other reasonable conclusion.[18] However, as Lord Normand observed in *Teper v R*:[19]

> Circumstantial evidence may sometimes be conclusive, but it must always be narrowly examined, if only because evidence of this kind may be fabricated to cast suspicion on another. Joseph commanded the steward of his house, 'put my cup, the silver cup in the sack's mouth of the youngest', and when the cup was found there Benjamin's brethren too hastily assumed that he must have stolen it.[20] It is also necessary before drawing the inference of the accused's guilt from circumstantial evidence to be sure that there are no other co-existing circumstances which would weaken or destroy the inference . . .

Examples

The circumstances in which a fact may be said to be relevant to a fact in issue, in the sense that the existence of the former gives rise to an inference as to the existence or non-existence of the latter, are many and various. Certain types of circumstantial evidence arise so frequently that they have been referred to as 'presumptions of fact' or 'provisional presumptions' such as the presumptions of intention, guilty knowledge, continuance of life, and seaworthiness, all of which are more conveniently considered in Chapter 22. Another type of circumstantial evidence is evidence of facts which are so closely associated in time, place, and circumstances with some transaction which is in issue that they can be said to form a part of that transaction. Such facts, referred to as facts forming part of the *res gestae*, are more conveniently explored in Chapter 12: the *res gestae* doctrine is mainly concerned with the admissibility of statements of fact as evidence of the truth of their contents by way of

---

[15] *R v Taylor, Weaver and Donovan* (1928) 21 Cr App R 20, CA.
[16] Per Lord Simon in *DPP v Kilbourne* [1973] AC 729 at 758, HL.
[17] Per Pollock CB in *R v Exall* (1866) 4 F&F 922 at 929.
[18] *McGreevy v DPP* [1973] 1 WLR 276, HL.
[19] [1952] AC 480 at 489, PC.
[20] See Genesis, 44: 2.

common law exception to the hearsay rule and has been described, not unfairly, in terms of a 'collection of fact situations . . . so confusing in its scope as almost to demand that a reader cease thinking before he go mad'![21] The following examples of circumstantial evidence are more typical and pose less danger to mental health.

Motive. Evidence of facts which supply a motive for a particular person to do a particular act is often received to show that it is more probable that he performed that act. Such evidence is admissible notwithstanding that the motive is irrational.[22]

> Surely in an ordinary prosecution for murder you can prove previous acts or words of the accused to show that he entertained feelings of enmity towards the deceased, and this is evidence not merely of the malicious mind with which he killed the deceased, but of the fact that he killed him . . . it is more probable that men are killed by those that have some motive for killing them than by those who have not.[23]

Conversely, evidence of absence of motive may be relevant to show the relative unlikelihood of a particular person having performed a particular act.[24]

Plans and preparatory acts. Facts which tend to suggest that a person made plans or other preparations for the performance of a particular act are relevant to the question of whether she subsequently performed that act. Thus evidence may be given of the purchase by an alleged murderer of poison, or as the case may be, of a gun or dagger. On the question of whether a person's declaration of intention to do a certain act is relevant to prove its performance by him, the authorities conflict.[25]

Capacity. Evidence of a person's mental or physical capacity or incapacity to do a particular act has an obvious relevance to the question of whether he in fact performed it.

Opportunity. Circumstantial evidence of opportunity is evidence of the fact that a person was present at the time and place of some act allegedly performed by him, for example evidence, to establish adultery in divorce proceedings, that a couple occupied the same hotel bedroom for two nights.[26] Conversely, evidence of lack of opportunity is evidence of the fact that a person was absent, which, in a criminal case, may assist the accused, for example alibi evidence, or the prosecution, for example evidence that after his arrest the accused had no opportunity to commit further offences (coupled with evidence that no further offences similar to those with which he is charged were committed in the same area).[27]

Identity. Circumstantial evidence of identity often takes the form of expert testimony that the fingerprints of the accused[28] or samples taken from his body match those discovered on or taken from

---

[21] Wright, 20 Can B R 714 at 716.

[22] *R v Phillips* [2003] 2 Cr App R 528, CA at [30], disapproving *R v Berry* (1986) 83 Cr App R 7, insofar as it suggests otherwise.

[23] Per Lord Atkinson in *R v Ball* [1911] AC 47, HL at 68; affirmed in *R v Williams* (1986) 84 Cr App Rep 299, CA. Any doubt that may have been cast upon this classic statement in *R v Berry*, ibid, should be disregarded: *R v Phillips* [2003] 2 Cr App R 528, CA at [26].

[24] See *R v Grant* (1865) 4 F&F 322.

[25] See *R v Buckley* (1873) 13 Cox CC 293, *R v Wainwright* (1875) 13 Cox CC 171 etc (see Ch 12).

[26] *Woolf v Woolf* [1931] P 134, CA.

[27] *R v Wilson* [2009] Crim LR 193, CA.

[28] *R v Castleton* (1909) 3 Cr App Rep 74; cf *R v Court* (1960) 44 Cr App R 242, CCA.

some material object at the scene of the crime or the victim of the offence in question.[29] It can also take the form of evidence that a tracking dog tracked the accused by scent from the scene of the crime.[30] Identity may also be established by evidence that both the accused and the criminal share the same name, the same physical idiosyncrasy, for example left-handedness, the same style of handwriting, or the same particular manner of expression in speech or writing.[31] In civil proceedings, evidence as to the paternity of a person may be given by expert medical evidence of blood tests showing that a man is or is not excluded from being the father of that person.[32]

Continuance.   The fact that a certain act or event was taking place at one point in time may justify the inference that it was also taking place at some prior or subsequent point in time. Thus evidence of the speed at which someone was driving at a particular point in time may be given to show the speed at which he was likely to have been driving a few moments earlier[33] or later.[34]

Failure to give evidence or call witnesses.   In civil cases, one party's failure to give evidence or call witnesses may justify the court in drawing all reasonable inferences from the evidence which has been given by his opponent as to what the facts are which the first party chose to withhold.[35] Thus adverse inferences have been drawn from the unexplained absence of witnesses who were apparently available and whose evidence was crucial to the case.[36] In *Wisniewski v Central Manchester Health Authority*[37] Brooke LJ derived the following principles from the authorities on the point.

1. In certain circumstances a court may be entitled to draw adverse inferences from the absence or silence of a witness who might be expected to have material evidence to give on an issue in the action.

2. If a court is willing to draw such inferences they may go to strengthen the evidence adduced on that issue by the other party or to weaken the evidence, if any, adduced by the party who might reasonably have been expected to call the witness.

---

[29] It is for the prosecution to prove formally that the *sample* fingerprints were taken from the accused and evidence, by him, that he cannot explain, or does not know, how 'his' fingerprints were found on the material object does not amount to an admission that the fingerprints were his: *Chappell v DPP* (1988) 89 Cr App R 82. The police have the power to take fingerprints, including palm prints, of a person without his consent. The circumstances in which this may be done include (i) where he is detained at a police station, if he is detained in consequence of his arrest for a recordable offence or he has been charged with, or informed that he will be reported for, such an offence; and (ii) where he has been convicted of a recordable offence, given a caution in respect of a recordable offence which he has admitted or has been warned or reprimanded for a recordable offence: ss 61, 65, and 118 of the Police and Criminal Evidence Act 1984.

[30] See *R v Haas* (1962) 35 DLR (2d) 172 (Court of Appeal of British Columbia). Evidence of tracking by a dog is admissible provided that (i) there is detailed evidence establishing the reliability of the dog by reason of its training and experience; and (ii) the jury are directed to consider the evidence carefully and with circumspection: *R v Pieterson* [1995] 2 Cr App R 11, CA. See also *R v Sykes* [1997] Crim LR 752, CA.

[31] See, eg, *R v Voisin* [1918] 1 KB 531: 'Bloody Belgian' written as 'Bladie Belgiam'.

[32] In any civil proceedings in which the paternity of any person falls to be determined, the court may direct the taking of blood samples from that person, the mother of that person and any party alleged to be the father of that person: s 20 of the Family Law Reform Act 1969. Section 20 also makes provision for the taking of 'bodily samples', defined as samples of bodily fluid or tissue taken for the purpose of scientific tests (which could include eg DNA genetic fingerprint tests).

[33] *R v Dalloz* (1908) 1 Cr App R 258.

[34] *Beresford v St Albans Justices* (1905) 22 TLR 1. See also the presumption of continuance of life, Ch 22.

[35] See per Lord Diplock in *British Railways Board v Herrington* [1972] AC 877 at 930.

[36] *Karis v Lewis* [2005] EWCA Civ 1637. See also *Baigent v Random House Group Ltd* [2006] EWHC 719, Ch D at [213]–[215] and *Raja v Hoogstraten* [2005] EWHC 2890, Ch D.

[37] [1992] Lloyd's Rep Med 223.

3. There must, however, have been some evidence, however weak, adduced by the former on the matter in question before the court is entitled to draw the desired inference: in other words, there must be a case to answer on that issue.

4. If the reason for the witness's absence or silence satisfies the court then no such adverse inference may be drawn. If, on the other hand, there is some credible explanation given, even if it is not wholly satisfactory, the potentially detrimental effect of his/her absence or silence may be reduced or nullified.

The inferences that may be drawn, in criminal cases, from the accused's election not to give evidence, call for a more detailed analysis. The subject is covered in Chapter 14. Concerning the accused's failure to call a witness (other than his or her spouse), in appropriate cases the judge may comment adversely on the fact that the witness was not called, but should exercise the same degree of care as when commenting on the failure of the accused himself to give evidence and in particular should avoid the suggestion that the failure is something of importance when there may be a valid reason for not calling the witness.[38] Whether a comment is justified and, if so, the terms in which it should be cast, are matters dependent upon the facts of the particular case. In *R v Khan*[39] the Court of Appeal gave the following guidance. (1) A universal requirement to direct the jury not to speculate would be unfair. On the other hand, to give no direction could invite speculation and work injustice; and to comment adversely might work injustice, since there might be a good reason but one which it would be unfair to disclose to the jury. Moreover, there might be an issue between the prosecution and defence as to whether a witness was available. There was no simple answer and much depended upon the judge's sense of fairness. (2) The dangers of making adverse comments, and failing to warn the jury not to speculate, are the paramount considerations. (3) On the other hand, now that a defendant's failure to disclose his case in advance can be the subject of comment, the case for permitting comment on an absent witness may be stronger. (4) If the judge comments on a failure to call a witness, a reference to the burden of proof may be appropriate. (5) A judge who is proposing to make a comment should first invite submissions from counsel in the absence of the jury.

Concerning the failure of the spouse of an accused to testify, comment by the *prosecution* was prohibited by proviso (b) to section 1 of the Criminal Evidence Act 1898. The Criminal Law Revision Committee proposed the lifting of this prohibition,[40] a proposal rejected by Parliament. Re-enacting the relevant parts of the proviso, section 80A of the Police and Criminal Evidence Act 1984 (the 1984 Act) provides that:

> The failure of the wife or husband of a person charged in any proceedings to give evidence in the proceedings shall not be made the subject of any comment by the prosecution.

Under proviso (b), it was held that where counsel for the prosecution does make an adverse comment on the failure of the accused to call his spouse to give evidence on his behalf, it is the duty of the trial judge, depending upon the circumstances of each case, to remedy that breach in his summing-up, especially when the accused is a man of good character and this is

---

[38] Per Megaw LJ in *R v Gallagher* [1974] 1 WLR 1204, CA. See also *R v Wilmot* (1988) 89 Cr App R 341 at 352, CA and *R v Couzens* [1992] Crim LR 822, CA; and cf *R v Weller* [1994] Crim LR 856.

[39] [2001] Crim LR 673, CA.

[40] Para 154 (Cmnd 4991) (1972).

central to his defence.[41] It may be assumed that a breach of section 80A should be remedied in the same way.

Section 80A applies only to the prosecution. In appropriate circumstances, therefore, the *judge* may comment on the failure of the spouse of the accused to testify. However, if the judge, in the exercise of his discretion, does decide to make a comment, he must, save in exceptional circumstances, do so with a great deal of circumspection.[42] The same degree of circumspection would also seem to be required in the case of comment on failure to call cohabitees, who are not covered by section 80A.[43]

A breach of section 80A is unlikely to result in a successful appeal if the judge, in summing-up, makes appropriate and suitable comments on the failure of the spouse to testify: the error made by counsel is subsumed in the summing-up.[44]

Failure to provide evidence.   Under section 23(1) of the Family Law Reform Act 1969, if, in any civil proceedings in which the paternity of any person falls to be determined, the court directs a party to undergo a blood test and that party fails to obey the direction, the court may draw such inferences as appear proper in the circumstances.[45] Similarly, section 62(10) of the Police and Criminal Evidence Act 1984 provides that where an accused has refused without good cause the taking from him of an intimate body sample the court, in determining whether there is a case to answer, and the court or jury, in determining whether he is guilty of the offence charged, 'may draw such inferences from the refusal as appear proper'. Section 62 is considered further in Chapter 14, together with the inferences that may be drawn, pursuant to statute, from an accused's silence or conduct.

Lies.   Lies told by an accused, on their own, do not prove that a person is guilty of any crime.[46] However, such lies may indicate a consciousness of guilt and in appropriate circumstances may be relied upon by the prosecution as evidence supportive of guilt, as in *R v Goodway*[47] in which the accused's lies to the police as to his whereabouts at the time of the offence were used in support of the identification evidence adduced by the prosecution. It was held that whenever a lie told by an accused is relied on by the Crown, or may be used by the jury to support evidence of guilt, as opposed merely to reflecting on his credibility (and not only when it is relied on as corroboration or as support for identification evidence), a direction should be given to the jury that: (1) the lie must be deliberate and must relate to a material issue; (2) they must be satisfied that there was no innocent motive for the lie, reminding them that people sometimes lie, for example, in an attempt to bolster up a just cause, or out of shame or a wish to conceal disgraceful behaviour; and in cases where the lie is relied upon as corroboration,[48] (3) the lie must be established by evidence other than that of the witness

[41] *R v Naudeer* [1984] 3 All ER 1036, CA. See also *R v Dickman* (1910) 5 Cr App R 135 and *R v Hunter* [1969] Crim LR 262, CA.

[42] Per Purchas LJ in *R v Naudeer* [1984] 3 All ER 1036 at 1039, CA.

[43] See *R v Weller* [1994] Crim LR 856, CA.

[44] See *R v Whitton* [1998] Crim LR 492, CA.

[45] See *McVeigh v Beattie* [1988] 2 All ER 500.

[46] *R v Strudwick* (1993) 99 Cr App R 326, CA at 331.

[47] [1993] 4 All ER 894, CA.

[48] See Ch 8.

THE VARIETIES OF EVIDENCE

who is to be corroborated.[49] It was also said, however, that such a direction need not be given where it is otiose, as indicated in *R v Dehar*,[50] ie where the rejection of the explanation by the accused almost necessarily leaves the jury with no choice but to convict as a matter of logic. An example is *R v Barsoum*,[51] where the lie related to the presence of another person, M, at the scene of the crime and if M was present, B was entitled to be acquitted, but if M was an invention it automatically followed that B must be guilty.[52] Where a direction is given, it should also make the point that the lie must be admitted or proved beyond reasonable doubt.[53]

The topic has spawned much case law and in *R v Middleton*[54] it was held, *per curiam*, that when the question arises whether a direction should be given, it will usually be more useful to analyse the question in the context of the individual case by examining the principles to be derived from the authorities rather than by trawling through hosts of cases. The court emphasized that the point of the direction is to avoid the risk of the forbidden reasoning that lies necessarily demonstrate guilt: where there is no risk that the jury may follow this prohibited line of reasoning, a direction is unnecessary. It was also said that, generally, a direction is unlikely to be appropriate in relation to lies told by an accused in evidence because that situation is covered by the general directions on burden and standard of proof. Furthermore, even where a specific direction could be given about a lie told in evidence, it is not required if it will do more harm than good.[55]

In *R v Burge*[56] it was held that a *Goodway* direction, which is often referred to as a *Lucas* direction,[57] is usually required in only four situations, which may overlap:

1. Where the defence relies on an alibi.

2. Where the judge suggests that the jury should look for support or corroboration of one piece of evidence from other evidence in the case, and amongst that other evidence draws attention to lies told or allegedly told by the accused.

3. Where the prosecution seek to show that something said in or out of court in relation to a separate and distinct issue was a lie and to rely on that lie as evidence of guilt, ie to use it, in effect, as an implied admission of guilt.

4. Where, although the prosecution have not adopted the approach described in (3), the judge reasonably envisages that there is a real danger that the jury may do so.[58]

---

[49] Applied in *R v Taylor* [1994] Crim LR 680, CA. See also *R v Taylor* [1998] Crim LR 822, CA. If a lie is relied on merely to attack credibility, a direction may be appropriate in exceptional circumstances, as when the lie figures largely in the case and the jury may think that the accused must be guilty because he lied: *R v Tucker* [1994] Crim LR 683, CA.

[50] [1969] NZLR 763, NZCA.

[51] [1994] Crim LR 194, CA.

[52] Cf *R v Wood* [1995] Crim LR, CA, where the accused may have been influenced by panic or confusion and therefore guilt was not the only possible explanation for the lies he told. But see also *R v Saunders* [1996] 1 Cr App R 463, CA at 518–19, where it was held that a direction was not required, the accused having explained his lies on the basis that he was confused and under pressure, and the judge having dealt with that explanation fairly in his summing-up.

[53] *R v Burge* [1996] 1 Cr App R 163, CA.

[54] [2001] Crim LR 251.

[55] *R v Nyanteh* [2005] Crim LR 651, CA.

[56] Ibid.

[57] See *R v Lucas* [1981] QB 720, CA.

[58] However, the Court of Appeal is unlikely to be persuaded that there was such a danger if defence counsel did not ask the trial judge to consider giving an appropriate direction: *R v Burge* [1996] 1 Cr App R 163 at 174. The failure of defence counsel to raise the matter at trial may also be taken into account in cases in which both the third and the

The Court of Appeal stressed that the direction is not required in run-of-the-mill cases in which the defence case is contradicted by the evidence of the prosecution witnesses in such a way as to make it necessary for the prosecution to say that the accused's account is untrue. Similarly, in *R v Hill*[59] it was said that a direction is not required simply because the jury reject the evidence of an accused about a central issue in the case, since that situation is covered by the general direction that the judge will give on burden and standard of proof. *R v Landon*[60] is to similar effect. In that case Hobhouse LJ emphasized that a direction should be given where lies told by the accused are relied upon by the Crown, or may be relied upon by the jury, as *additional* evidence of guilt, and not where there is no distinction between the issue of guilt and the issue of lies.[61]

Concerning the first situation identified in *R v Burge*, the Judicial Studies Board specimen direction relating to evidence called in support of an alibi concludes with the warning:

> even if you conclude that the alibi is false, that does not itself entitle you to convict the defendant. The prosecution must still make you sure of his guilt. An alibi is sometimes invented to bolster a genuine defence.

In *R v Lesley*[62] it was held that this version of the *Goodway* direction should be given routinely, although whether a failure to do so renders a conviction unsafe depends on the facts of the case and the strength of the evidence. The accused in that case had served an alibi notice but did not call the person named in it and did not give evidence himself. The prosecution infer-entially invited the jury to conclude that the alibi was false and therefore evidence of guilt. Having regard to some weaknesses in the evidence given by the chief prosecution witness, it was held that failure to give the standard direction rendered the verdict unsafe.[63] *R v Lesley* was distinguished in *R v Harron*,[64] in which it was held that the judge had not erred in failing to give the standard direction because the central issue in the case was whether the prosecution witnesses were lying (rather than mistaken) or the accused was; it would only have confused the jury to have directed them that, if they accepted the evidence of the prosecution witnesses as to the presence of the accused, and therefore rejected the accused's evidence to the con-trary, his evidence might have been falsified to bolster a genuine defence.[65]

R v Genus[66] furnishes an example of the third situation identified in *R v Burge*. The accused claimed to have been acting under duress. The prosecution case was that the accused had told lies to the police, and in their evidence, on collateral issues, ie issues not directly relevant to the question of duress, by reason of which the jury should disbelieve their evidence of duress. It was held that the case cried out for a *Goodway* direction. In *R v Robinson*[67] the accused was charged

---

fourth situations arise, and may lead the Court of Appeal to conclude that the absence of a direction did not make the conviction unsafe: *R v McGuinness* [1999] Crim LR 318, CA.

[59] [1996] Crim LR 419, CA. See also *R v Harron* [1996] 2 Cr App R 457, CA, below.

[60] [1995] Crim LR 338, CA.

[61] Nor is a direction likely to be required in the numerous cases of handling in which the accused denies knowledge or belief that the goods were stolen, including those in which the accused has given different and inconsistent ver-sions as to how he came by the goods and the prosecution assert that the evidence is a lie: *R v Barnett* [2002] Crim App R 168, CA.

[62] [1996] 1 Cr App R(S) 39, CA.

[63] Cf *R v Drake* [1996] Crim LR 109, CA, and see also *R v Peacock* [1998] Crim LR 681, CA.

[64] [1996] 2 Cr App R 457, CA.

[65] See also *R v Gultutan* [2006] EWCA Crim 207.

[66] [1996] Crim LR 502, CA.

[67] [1996] Crim LR 417, CA.

with possession of drugs with intent to supply. In his summing-up the judge gave considerable prominence to the issue whether the accused, in his evidence, had lied about when he had first complained to the police that they had planted the drugs on him. It was held that the issue whether the allegation of planting was a late invention was a separate issue, not a central one, and fell clearly within the fourth situation identified in *R v Burge*. The jury should have been directed on the possibility that the accused had lied to bolster a potentially weak defence.

Standards of comparison. In cases where it is necessary to decide whether a person's conduct meets some objective standard of behaviour, evidence of what other persons would do in the same circumstances is admissible as a standard of comparison. Thus, in *Chapman v Walton*,[68] where it was alleged that a broker was negligent in failing to vary the terms upon which certain goods were insured on receiving ambiguous information concerning their destination, evidence from other brokers as to what they would have done in such circumstances was admitted for the purpose of deciding whether the broker had exercised a reasonable degree of care, skill, and judgment in the performance of his duties. Similarly, where the issue concerns the existence of a practice in a trade carried out in a particular location, evidence may be admissible of the existence or non-existence of that practice in a similar trade located elsewhere. In *Noble v Kennoway*,[69] for example, the issue being whether underwriters were entitled to repudiate liability on an insurance of a ship's cargo on the grounds that its discharge in Labrador had been unreasonably delayed, it was held that evidence of a practice of delaying the discharge of cargo in the Newfoundland trade was admissible to show the likely existence of a similar practice in the Labrador trade.

Conclusive evidence

Conclusive evidence operates to prove a matter and to bar any evidence that might go to disprove it. An example is section 21(a) of the State Immunity Act 1978, whereby a certificate issued by the Secretary of State for the Foreign and Commonwealth Office is conclusive evidence as to whether any country is a State for the purposes of Part 1 of that Act.[70]

Relevance and admissibility

Such evidence as a court will receive for the purpose of determining the existence or non-existence of facts in issue is referred to as admissible evidence. The admissibility of evidence is a matter of law for the judge. The most important feature of the English law of evidence is that all evidence which is sufficiently relevant to prove or disprove a fact in issue and which is not excluded by the judge, either by reason of an exclusionary rule of evidence or in the exercise of her discretion, is admissible.[71] In *R v Terry*[72] it was held that evidence will be admissible if it

---

[68] (1833) 10 Bing 57.

[69] (1780) 2 Doug KB 510. See also *Fleet v Murton* (1871) LR 7 QB 126.

[70] See also Civil Evidence Act 1968, s 13, Ch 21.

[71] However, there is no principle that a judge cannot read or hear material that is actually or potentially inadmissible, especially if he is judge of both law and fact: see *Barings plc v Coopers and Lybrand* [2001] EWCA Civ 1163, [2001] CPLR 451, where it was held that to read background documentation in preparation for a long and complex case involved no danger of the judge being so influenced by the material that he would not decide the case on the basis of the admissible evidence.

[72] [2005] 2 Cr App R 118, CA at [34].

is relevant *and* such that a jury, properly warned about any defects it might have, could place some weight on it. This is probably best understood not as the introduction of some new two-limb test for admissibility, but as a recognition that a judge's determination as to whether evidence is sufficiently relevant to be admissible will depend, to some extent, on his or her assessment of its weight.[73]

It will be convenient (i) to consider the meaning of relevance; and (ii) to examine, in outline, some of the exclusionary rules of evidence to which the bulk of the remainder of this book is devoted. Reference will then be made to the principles of multiple and conditional admissibility and an evidentiary ghost of marginal contemporary significance known as 'the best evidence rule'.

Relevance

The classic definition of relevance is contained in Article 1 of Stephen's *Digest of the Law of Evidence*,[74] according to which the word means that—

> any two facts to which it is applied are so related to each other that according to the common course of events one either taken by itself or in connection with other facts proves or renders probable the past, present or future existence or non-existence of the other.

Stephen also suggests that relevance may be tested by the use of a syllogism,[75] a form of reasoning in which a conclusion is drawn from two given or assumed propositions, a major premise, a generalization, and a minor premise, which in the context under discussion is a proposition of fact the relevance of which is being tested. For example, to test the relevance of motive on a charge of murder, the major premise is the generalization that those who had a motive to kill a person are more likely to have done so than those who had no such motive; the minor premise is that the accused had a motive to kill the person; and the conclusion is that the accused is more likely to have killed the person than those without a motive for killing him. As Cross and Tapper point out, care may have to be taken in selecting the appropriate major premise.[76] Indeed, the validity of this form of reasoning depends entirely upon the validity of the major premise, which has to be formulated having regard to common sense and general experience. This accords with the requirement in Stephen's definition of relevance that it be determined 'according to the common course of events'.

As Stephen's definition also makes clear, a fact may be relevant to the past, present or future existence of another fact. *R v Nethercott*[77] provides an example of relevance to the past existence of a fact. N's defence was that he had acted under duress as a result of threats by his co-accused G and gave evidence that he feared for his own safety having regard to the way in which G had acted on previous occasions. It was held that evidence of the fact that three months later G had stabbed N with a knife was also relevant because it made it more likely that N, at the time of the offence, had genuinely feared for his safety.

As one commentator has pointed out,[78] Stephen's definition of relevance appears to set the standard too high in that it requires a relevant fact to 'prove or render probable' the fact

---

[73] See further under **Weight**, at 29 below.
[74] 12th edn.
[75] *General View of the Criminal Law* (1st edn) 236.
[76] *Cross and Tapper on Evidence* (9th edn, Butterworths, London, 1999) 56.
[77] [2002] 2 Cr App R 117, CA.
[78] IH Dennis, *The Law of Evidence* (2nd edn, Sweet & Maxwell, London, 2002) 54–5.

requiring proof. In contrast, under the simpler working definition of Lord Simon of Glaisdale in *DPP v Kilbourne*,[79] the relevant fact need only make the matter requiring proof more (or less) probable:

> Evidence is relevant if it is logically probative or disprobative of some matter which requires proof. I do not pause to analyse what is involved in 'logical probativeness' except to note that the term does not of itself express the element of experience which is so significant of its operation in law, and possibly elsewhere. It is sufficient to say, even at the risk of etymological tautology, that relevant (i.e. logically probative or disprobative) evidence is evidence which makes the matter which requires proof more or less probable.[80]

In *R v Randall*[81] Lord Steyn cited and applied the statement appearing in the fifth edition of this book that 'relevance is a question of degree determined, for the most part, by common sense and experience'. R and G were tried together on a charge of murder. Each raised a cut-throat defence, each blaming the other for the infliction of the fatal injuries. Both therefore lost the protection of section 1 of the Criminal Evidence Act 1898[82] and were asked questions about their previous convictions and bad character. R had relatively minor convictions for driving offences and disorderly behaviour. G had a bad record, including convictions for burglary, the most recent being for burglary committed by a gang in which G had been armed with a screwdriver. G also admitted in cross-examination that at the date of the killing he was on the run from the police, having been involved in a robbery committed by a gang, all the robbers having been armed with knives. The House of Lords held that the evidence of G's propensity to use and threaten violence was relevant not only in relation to the truthfulness of his evidence, but also because the imbalance between that history and the antecedent history of R tended to show that the version of events put forward by R was more probable than that put forward by G.

Other examples of evidence sufficiently relevant to prove or disprove a fact in issue have already been given under the rubric of circumstantial evidence which, it will be recalled, is a term used to refer to evidence of *relevant* facts. Consideration may now be given to some examples of evidence which has been excluded on the grounds of irrelevance or insufficient relevance. *Holcombe v Hewson*[83] concerned an alleged breach of covenant by the defendant, a publican, to buy his beer from the plaintiff, a brewer. The plaintiff, in order to rebut the defence that he had previously supplied bad beer, intended to call publicans to give evidence that he had supplied them with good beer. Excluding this evidence, Lord Ellenborough said:

> We cannot here enquire into the quality of different beer furnished to different persons. The plaintiff might deal well with one, and not with the others. Let him call some of those who frequented the defendant's house, and there drank the beer which he sent in . . .

In *Hollingham v Head*[84] the defendant, in order to defeat an action for the price of goods sold and delivered, sought to establish that the contract was made on certain special terms by evidence that the plaintiff had entered into contracts with other customers on similar terms.

---

[79] [1973] AC 729 at 756, HL.

[80] Concerning the role of probability theory in legal proceedings, see Sir R Eggleston, *Evidence, Proof and Probability* (2nd edn, 1983).

[81] [2004] 1 All ER 467 at 474.

[82] See now s 101 of the Criminal Justice Act 2003.

[83] (1810) 2 Camp 391, KB.

[84] (1858) 27 LJCP 241.

The evidence was held to be inadmissible on the grounds that it would have afforded no reasonable inference as to the terms of the contract in dispute.[85] On a charge of manslaughter against a doctor, expert evidence may be adduced as to the doctor's skill as shown by his treatment of the case under investigation, but evidence of his skilful treatment of other patients on other occasions must be excluded.[86] Evidence that after an accident the defendants to a negligence action altered and improved their practice has no relevance to the question whether the accident was caused by their negligence: 'Because the world gets wiser as it gets older, it was not therefore foolish before.'[87]

Where two criminal trials arise out of the same transaction, evidence of the outcome of the first will generally be inadmissible, because irrelevant, at the second; some exceptional feature is needed before it is considered relevant.[88] This is the position, *a fortiori*, where the earlier trial related to a different event.[89] It has been said that the rationale for the 'rule' is that the evidence amounts to nothing more than evidence of the opinion of the first jury,[90] but taken alone that would be a reason for never admitting evidence of a previous verdict. The true rationale, in the case of an earlier acquittal, is that in most cases it is not possible to be certain why a jury acquitted.[91] The 'exception' to the rule is where there is a clear inference from the verdict that the jury rejected a witness's evidence, on the basis that they did not believe him, as opposed to thinking that he was mistaken, and the witness's credibility is directly in issue in the second trial.[92] An example is where an officer who has given evidence of an admission in a trial resulting in an acquittal by virtue of which his evidence can be shown to have been disbelieved, faces an allegation, in a subsequent trial, that he has fabricated an admission.[93] Another example is where the prosecution allege that as part of a joint enterprise, A and B, one after the other, raped C; A and B are tried separately; the prosecution case against each man depends almost entirely on the evidence of C and therefore the jury have to decide which side is lying; and A is tried first and acquitted.[94]

In *R v Sandhu*[95] it was held that, insofar as an offence of strict liability involves no proof of *mens rea*, evidence of motive, intention, or knowledge on the part of the accused is inadmissible because irrelevant to the issue of his guilt and merely prejudicial to him.[96]

---

[85] Evidence of 'similar facts' is not invariably excluded, however: see, eg, *Hales v Kerr* [1908] 2 KB 601, DC; *Joy v Phillips, Mills & Co Ltd* [1916] 1 KB 849, CA; and *Sattin v National Union Bank* (1978) 122 Sol Jo 367, CA, all considered in Ch 15.

[86] *R v Whitehead* (1848) 3 Car&Kir 202.

[87] Per Bramwell B in *Hart v Lancashire & Yorkshire Rly Co* (1869) 21 LT 261.

[88] *Hui Chi-ming v R* [1991] 3 All ER 897, PC. See also, concerning the admissibility, at a retrial, of the first jury's acquittal on some counts and failure to agree on others, *R v H* (1989) 90 Cr App R 440, CA; *R v Greer* [1994] Crim LR 745, CA; *R v Scott* [1994] Crim LR 947, CA; and, generally, A L-T Choo 'The Notion of Relevance' [1993] *Crim LR* 114.

[89] *R v Terry* [2005] 2 Cr App R 118, CA at [34].

[90] *Hui Chi-ming v R* [1991] 3 All ER 897, PC.

[91] *R v Deboussi* [2007] EWCA Crim 684. The rule also seems to apply in the case of an acquittal based on a judge's ruling that there is insufficient evidence for the case to go to the jury: *R v Hudson* [1994] Crim LR 920, CA. As to the relevance and admissibility of previous convictions as evidence of the facts on which they were based, see Ch 21.

[92] *R v Deboussi*, ibid.

[93] *R v Edwards* [1991] 2 All ER 266, CA. See also *R v Hay* (1983) 77 Cr App R 70, CA and *R v Cooke* (1986) 84 Cr App R 286, CA.

[94] *R v Deboussi*, ibid.

[95] [1997] Crim LR 288, CA.

[96] See also, applying *R v Sandhu*, *R v Byrne* [2002] 2 Cr App R 311.

Another, but controversial, example of irrelevance is to be found in the decision of the House of Lords in *R v Blastland*.[97] The appellant B was charged with the buggery and murder of a boy. At the trial B admitted that he had met the boy and engaged in homosexual activity with him but said that when he saw another man nearby, who might have witnessed what he had done, he panicked and ran away. B gave a description of the other man which corresponded closely to M and alleged that M must have committed the offences charged. At the trial there were formal admissions[98] by the prosecution. Some related to M's movements on the evening in question and others showed that M had been investigated by the police after the murder and had been known to engage in homosexual activities in the past with adults but not children. The defence sought leave to call a number of witnesses to elicit from them that, before the victim's body had been found, M had made statements to them that a boy had been murdered. The trial judge held this evidence to be inadmissible. B was convicted on both counts. Before the House of Lords the appellant submitted that, although the statements made by M were inadmissible hearsay if tendered for the truth of any fact stated, they were admissible, as original evidence, if tendered to prove the state of mind of their maker, ie to show M's knowledge of the murder before the body had been found.[99] Lord Bridge, giving the judgment of the House, held that original evidence of this kind is only admissible if the state of mind in question 'is either itself directly in issue at the trial or is of direct and immediate relevance to an issue which arises at the trial'. The issue at the trial was whether B had committed the crimes and what was relevant to that issue was not the fact of M's knowledge but how he had come by it; since he might have done so in a number of different ways, there was no rational basis on which the jury could be invited to draw an inference as to the source of that knowledge or conclude that he rather than B was the offender. The evidence, therefore, had been properly rejected. The flaw in this reasoning, it is submitted, is the unwarranted introduction of the requirement that the evidence be 'of direct and immediate' relevance. The evidence was no less relevant than the evidence relating to M's movements which was thought to have been properly admitted, albeit neither item, by itself, could show that M, rather than B, was the offender.[100]

It is submitted that an unnecessarily strict approach to relevance was also taken in *R v T (AB)*[101] The complainant alleged that A, the appellant, B and C had each sexually abused her. There was no suggestion that they had acted in concert or that any one of them was aware of the abuse of either of the others. B admitted the allegations against him, but died before his trial, and C pleaded guilty to counts of indecent assault. It was held that evidence of B's admission and of C's guilty plea was inadmissible because irrelevant to the issues of whether A had abused the complainant and that while it was 'tempting' to say that it was relevant to the issue

[97] [1986] AC 41, HL, applied in *R v Williams* [1998] Crim LR 494, CA. See also *R v Kearley* [1992] 2 AC 228, HL, Ch 10; and *R v Akram* [1995] Crim LR 50, CA.

[98] See under **Facts open to proof or disproof, Facts in issue** at 7 above. There were also a number of *informal* admissions, M having successively made and withdrawn admissions of his own guilt of the offences in question, but these were properly rejected by the trial judge as inadmissible hearsay: see *R v Turner* (1975) 61 Cr App R 67, CA.

[99] See under **The varieties of evidence, Hearsay evidence** at 10 above.

[100] Contrast the approach taken in *Wildman v R* [1984] 2 SCR 311 (Supreme Court of Canada) and *R v Szach* (1980) 23 SASR 504 (Supreme Court of S Australia). See also *R v Gadsby* [2006] Crim LR 631, CA, where it was held, obiter, that evidence may be relevant if capable of increasing (or diminishing) the probability of facts indicating that some other person committed the crime, eg evidence that a person with the opportunity of committing the crime had a propensity to do so; and *R v Greenwood* [2005] Crim LR 59, CA, where it was held that an accused charged with murder is entitled to seek to establish that a third party had a motive to murder the victim.

[101] [2007] 1 Cr App R 43, CA.

of her credibility, evidence is inadmissible simply to bolster credibility because this would be a form of 'oath helping' which has never been a permissible ground for admitting evidence.

Evidence of demeanour may be relevant, depending on the circumstances. For example, in the case of an accused charged with murder, the evidence of an experienced physician that the accused was calm and uninterested when the baby was found to be dead may be relevant, but not evidence of the fact that the accused did not appear emotional at the funeral, because 'outward appearances at a funeral home offer no reliable barometer of one's grief'.[102] The demeanour of the victim of a crime immediately after its commission may be relevant and admissible to support his or her account, by analogy with the principle of *res gestae*.[103] However, it is submitted that the *res gestae* conditions[104] do not have to be met: the evidence is not hearsay. Similarly, the condition in *R v Keast*[105] seems unduly restrictive. In that case, it was held that unless there is some concrete basis for regarding long-term demeanour and state of mind of an alleged victim of sexual abuse as confirming or disproving the occurrence of such abuse, it cannot assist a jury bringing their common sense to bear on who is telling the truth.[106]

On a charge of causing death by dangerous driving, evidence that the accused took cocaine shortly before the accident is relevant, even without evidence as to the amount taken,[107] but evidence that the accused took drink will not be relevant without evidence to show that the amount taken would adversely affect a driver.[108] The reasoning for the distinction appears to be based on the dubious generalization that a modest dose of cocaine has a greater capacity to impair driving ability than a modest intake of alcohol.[109] Much, it is submitted, should turn on both the timing and the amounts.

There are occasions when the effect of evidence, albeit technically admissible, is likely to be so slight that it is wiser not to adduce it, particularly if, in a criminal trial, there is any danger that its admission will have an adverse effect on the fairness of the proceedings.[110] Evidence of marginal relevance may also be excluded on the grounds that it would lead to a multiplicity of subsidiary issues which, in addition to distracting the court from the main issue,[111] might involve the court in a protracted investigation[112] or a difficult and doubtful controversy of precisely the same kind as that which the court has to determine.[113] In *Agassiz v London Tramway Co*[114] the plaintiff, a passenger in an omnibus, claimed damages for serious personal injuries arising out of a collision allegedly

[102] *R v MT* [2004] OJ No 4366 (Ont. CA).

[103] *R v Townsend* [2003] EWCA Crim 3173.

[104] See Ch 12.

[105] [1998] Crim LR 748, CA.

[106] See also, applying *R v Keast*, *R v Venn* [2003] All ER (D) 207 (Feb), [2003] EWCA Crim 236; and cf *R v Townsend* (2003) LTL 23 Oct.

[107] *R v Pleydell* [2006] 1 Cr App R 212, CA.

[108] *R v McBride* (1961) 45 Cr App R 262, followed in *R v Thorpe* [1972] 1 WLR 342.

[109] See *R v Pleydell* [2006] 1 Cr App R 212, CA at [27] and [28].

[110] Per Lord Lane CJ in *R v Robertson; R v Golder* [1987] 3 All ER 231 at 237, CA in relation to the admissibility of evidence under s 74 of the Police and Criminal Evidence Act 1984. See also *R v Williams* [1990] Crim LR 409, CA.

[111] See per Byrne J in *R v Patel* [1951] 2 All ER 29 at 30.

[112] See per Rolfe B in *A-G v Hitchcock* (1847) 1 Exch 91 at 105 and per Willes J in *Hollingham v Head* (1858) 27 LJCP 241 at 242: 'litigants are mortal . . . '

[113] Per Lord Watson in *Metropolitan Asylum District Managers v Hill* (1882) 47 LT 29, HL, where a majority of the House was of the opinion, without deciding the point, that in considering the effect of a smallpox hospital on the health of local residents, evidence of the effect of similar hospitals in other localities on their residents would be admissible. See also *Folkes v Chadd* (1782) 3 Doug KB 157.

[114] (1872) 21 WR 199.

caused by the driver's negligence. The action was dismissed for want of evidence as to how the accident had happened. After the accident, the conductor, in reply to the suggestion of another passenger that the driver's conduct should be reported, said: 'Sir, he has been reported, for he has been off the points five or six times today; he is a new driver.' Kelly CB held that this evidence was properly excluded, since it neither related to the conduct of the driver at the relevant time nor explained the actual cause of the collision, but merely gave rise to a multiplicity of side issues.

On charges of possession of drugs with intent to supply, there is a difficult distinction to be drawn between evidence which is relevant to the intention to supply the drug found, and evidence which, although of some relevance to that issue, is unduly prejudicial because it relates to past dealing or dealing generally.[115] In *R v Batt*,[116] a charge of possession of cannabis resin with intent to supply, the Court of Appeal did not question the admissibility in evidence of B's possession of weights and scales (on which there were traces of cannabis resin), but held that evidence of the discovery of £150 in an ornamental kettle in her house was inadmissible because it had nothing to do with intent to supply in future the drugs found, but had a highly prejudicial effect as 'a hallmark of a propensity to supply generally, or a hallmark of the fact that there had been a past supply, or that the money will be used in future to obtain cannabis for future supply'.

However, it seems that *Batt* has not laid down any general principle that evidence of possession of money is never admissible on a charge of possession with intent to supply, and on one view the decision in that case turned upon the fact that the trial judge had failed to direct the jury as to how they could properly use the evidence of the possession of money.[117] In *R v Wright*[118] it was held that drug traders needed to keep by them large sums of cash and therefore evidence of the discovery of £16,000 could have given rise to an inference of dealing and tended to prove that the drugs found were for supply. This approach was followed in *R v Gordon*,[119] where it was held that although evidence as to past deposits in, and withdrawals from, savings accounts was irrelevant, because it could only found an inference of past drug dealing, evidence of the discovery of £4,200 in G's home was admissible ('cash for the acquisition of stock for present active drug dealing must be relevant to a count of possession with intent to supply'), subject to an appropriate direction on any possible innocent explanations for the presence of the cash.[120] The jury should be directed that they should regard the finding of the money as relevant only if they reject any innocent explanation for it put forward by the accused, but that if they conclude that the money indicates not merely past dealing, but an ongoing dealing in drugs, they may take into account the finding of it, together with the drugs,

---

[115] The principles to be derived from the cases in the ensuing text are unaffected, it is submitted, by s 101 of the Criminal Justice Act 2003: see generally Ch 17.

[116] [1994] Crim LR 592, CA.

[117] See *R v Morris* [1995] 2 Cr App R 69, CA, and *R v Nicholas* [1995] Crim LR 942, CA. Alternatively, it should be regarded as a case confined to its own facts, remembering that £150 was too small, and its hiding place too unremarkable, to be the hallmark of present and active drug dealing: *R v Okusanya* [1995] Crim LR 941, CA.

[118] [1994] Crim LR 55, CA.

[119] [1995] 2 Cr App R 61, CA. See also *R v Morris* [1995] 2 Cr App R 69, CA.

[120] Concerning the accounts, cf *R v Okusanya* [1995] Crim LR 941, CA: evidence of money in three accounts was admissible to rebut O's explanation for having £8,800 in his possession (that, as a Nigerian, it was not his custom to put money in banks). But see also *R v Smith (Ivor)* [1995] Crim LR 940, CA: evidence that £9,000 had been deposited in S's account in recent months, of which £2,100 was unexplained by various legitimate transactions, was admissible (subject to an appropriate direction).

in considering whether intent to supply has been proved.[121] The jury should also be directed not to treat such evidence as evidence of propensity, ie not to pursue the line of reasoning that, by reason of past dealing, the accused is likely to be guilty of the offence charged.[122]

At one stage it was thought that where possession of drugs is in issue, evidence of possession of money or drugs paraphernalia can never be relevant to that issue.[123] However, in *R v Guney*[124] the Court of Appeal, declining to follow the earlier authorities, held that although evidence of possession of a large sum of cash or enjoyment of a wealthy lifestyle does not, on its own, prove possession, there are numerous sets of circumstances in which it may be relevant to that issue, not least to the issue of knowledge as an ingredient of possession. The issue in that case was whether the accused was knowingly in possession of some 5 kilos of heroin or whether it had been 'planted', and the defence conceded that if possession were to be proved, then it would be open to the jury to infer intent to supply. It was held that, in all the circumstances, evidence of the finding of nearly £25,000 in cash in the wardrobe of the accused's bedroom, in close proximity to the drugs, was relevant to the issue of possession.[125]

The exclusionary rules

Evidence must be sufficiently relevant to be admissible, but sufficiently relevant evidence is only admissible insofar as it is not excluded by any rule of the law of evidence or by the exercise of judicial discretion. The consequence, of course, is that some relevant evidence is excluded. Thus although statutes make provision for the admissibility of various categories of hearsay, not *all* relevant hearsay is admissible.[126] Relevant evidence, including highly relevant evidence, may also be withheld as a matter of public policy on the grounds that its production and disclosure would jeopardize national security or would be injurious to some other national interest.[127] The opinion evidence of a non-expert is generally regarded as being insufficiently relevant to a subject not calling for any particular expertise but, whatever its degree of relevance, is generally excluded on the basis that the tribunal of fact might be tempted simply to accept the opinion proffered rather than draw its own inferences from the facts of the case.[128] These and other exclusionary rules make up much of the law of evidence and are considered throughout this book.

Multiple admissibility

Where evidence is admissible for one purpose, but inadmissible for another, it remains admissible in law for the first purpose (although it may be excluded by the exercise of judicial discretion). For example, an out-of-court statement may be inadmissible for the purpose of proving the truth of its contents, being inadmissible hearsay, but admissible, as original evidence, for the purpose of proving that the statement was made. The principle has been described,

---

[121] *R v Grant* [1996] 1 Cr App Rep 73, CA; cf *R v Antill* [2002] All ER (D) 176 (Sep), [2002] EWCA Crim 2114. However, the judge is not tied to this or any other particular form of words: *R v Malik* [2000] Crim LR 197, CA.

[122] See *R v Simms* [1995] Crim LR 304, CA, and *R v Lucas* [1995] Crim LR 400, CA.

[123] See *R v Halpin* [1996] Crim LR 112, CA and *R v Richards* [1997] Crim LR 499, CA.

[124] [1998] 2 Cr App R 242.

[125] Applied in *R v Griffiths* [1998] Crim LR 567, CA. See also *R v Edwards* [1998] Crim LR 207, CA and *R v Scott* [1996] Crim LR 652, CA.

[126] See generally Chs 10–13.

[127] See Ch 19.

[128] See Ch 18.

somewhat misleadingly, as one of 'multiple admissibility'.[129] Where it applies, the judge is often required to warn the jury of the limited purpose for which the evidence has been admitted.[130] The risk that the jury may misunderstand or ignore such a warning is felt to be more than outweighed by the greater mischief that would be occasioned if the evidence were to be excluded altogether.[131]

Conditional admissibility

An item of evidence, viewed in isolation, may appear to be irrelevant and therefore inadmissible. Taken together with, or seen in the light of, some other item of evidence, its relevance may become apparent. Evidence, however, can only be given at a trial in piecemeal fashion, by degrees, and it may be difficult to adduce the second item of evidence before the first. In order to overcome this difficulty, the first item of evidence may be admitted conditionally or *de bene esse*. If, viewed in the light of evidence subsequently adduced, it becomes relevant, it may be taken into account. If, notwithstanding the evidence subsequently adduced, it remains irrelevant, it must be disregarded. The operation of the principle may be illustrated by reference to the admissibility of accusations made in the presence of the accused, the relevance of which may depend on evidence, subsequently adduced, of the accused's reaction to them. An accusation made in the presence of the accused upon an occasion on which he might reasonably be expected to make some observation, explanation, or denial is, in certain circumstances, admissible in evidence against him, provided that a foundation for its admission is laid by proof of facts from which, in the opinion of the judge, a jury might reasonably draw the inference that the accused, by his answer, whether given by word, conduct, or silence, acknowledged the truth of the accusation made. The accusation may be admitted in evidence, however, even where the evidential foundation has not been laid, provided that, if evidence is *not* subsequently adduced from which it can be inferred that the accused did acknowledge the truth of the accusation made, the judge directs the jury to disregard the accusation altogether.[132]

The best evidence rule

The so-called best evidence rule, at one time thought to be a fundamental principle of the law of evidence, is now applied so rarely as to be virtually extinct. The eighteenth-century case of *Omychund v Barker*,[133] suggests that it was an inclusionary rule, allowing for the admissibility of the best evidence available that a party to litigation could produce. The rule, however, was rarely used in this way, and as an inclusionary doctrine of general application certainly finds no

---

[129] Wigmore *A Treatise on the Anglo-American System of Evidence* (3rd edn, 1940) I, para 13.

[130] For example, where a confession, admissible as evidence of the truth of its contents by way of exception to the hearsay rule, implicates both its maker and a co-accused, the trial judge is duty bound to impress upon the jury that it can be used only against its maker and not against the co-accused: *R v Gunewardene* [1951] 2 KB 600, CCA (see Ch 13). Cf *R v Randall* [2004] 1 All ER 467, HL at p 478, Ch 17. Similarly, where a statement containing an admissible confession also contains inadmissible material which cannot be edited out without prejudice to the sense of the confession, the jury should be directed to ignore the inadmissible material: *R v Flicker* [1995] Crim LR 493, CA, where the court appears to doubt, wrongly it is submitted, the existence of a discretionary power to exclude the whole statement. See also *R v Norman* [2006] EWCA Crim 1622.

[131] See per Tindall CJ in *Willis v Bernard* (1832) 8 Bing 376 at 383.

[132] Per Lords Atkinson and Reading in *R v Christie* [1914] AC 545, HL at 554 and 565 respectively. For another example, see *R v Donat* (1985) 82 Cr App R 173, CA.

[133] (1745) 1 Atk 21 at 49.

place in the modern law of evidence. The authorities show that the rule was normally treated as being of an exclusionary nature, preventing the admissibility of evidence where better was available.[134] As an exclusionary principle, however, the rule is now virtually defunct. The rule that a party seeking to rely upon the contents of a document must adduce primary evidence of the contents, secondary evidence being admissible only exceptionally,[135] is sometimes said to be the only remaining instance of the best evidence rule,[136] notwithstanding that it pre-dates the best evidence rule, but in *Springsteen v Flute International Ltd*[137] it was held, in this context, that it could be said with confidence that the best evidence rule, long on its deathbed, had finally expired. Prior to that decision, the rule did make a rare appearance in *R v Quinn and R v Bloom*.[138] The accused, two club proprietors, were charged with keeping a disorderly house. The charge arose out of certain allegedly indecent striptease acts performed at their clubs. One of the accused sought to put in evidence a film made three months after the events complained of and showing what the performers actually did, together with evidence that the performances shown in the film were identical with those in question. The Court of Criminal Appeal held that this evidence had been properly excluded. Ashworth J, giving the judgment of the court, said:

> it was admitted that some of the movements in the film (for instance, that of a snake used in one scene) could not be said with any certainty to be the same movements as were made at the material time . . . this objection goes not only to weight, as was argued, but to admissibility: it is not the best evidence.[139]

Although out-of-court demonstrations and re-enactments are admissible as a variety of real evidence,[140] the court held that a reconstruction made privately for the purpose of constituting evidence at a trial is inadmissible.[141]

The best evidence rule is of no more than marginal contemporary significance, but where a party fails to make use of the best evidence available and relies upon inferior evidence, the absence of the best evidence or the party's failure to account for its absence may always be the subject of adverse judicial comment. The inferior evidence may be slighted or ignored on the grounds that it lacks weight.[142] For example, in *Post Office Counters Ltd v Mahida*,[143] a

---

[134] See, eg, *Chenie v Watson* (1797) Peake Add Cas 123, where oral evidence relating to the condition of a material object was excluded on the grounds that the object itself ought to have been produced for inspection by the court; and *Williams v East India Co* (1802) 3 East 192, where circumstantial evidence was excluded because direct evidence was available. Both cases have, on the point in question, been reversed: as to the former, see now *R v Francis* (1874) LR 2 CCR 128 and *Hocking v Ahlquist Bros Ltd* [1944] KB 120 (which are considered in Ch 9); as to the latter, see now *Dowling v Dowling* (1860) 10 ICLR 236.

[135] See Ch 9.

[136] See, eg, per Lord Denning MR in *Garton v Hunter* [1969] 2 QB 37 at 44, CA and per Ackner LJ in *Kajala v Noble* (1982) 75 Cr App R 149, CA at 152.

[137] [2001] EMLR 654, CA.

[138] [1962] 2 QB 245.

[139] Cf *R v Thomas* [1986] Crim LR 682, a case of reckless driving in which a video recording of the route taken by the accused was admitted to remove the need for maps and still photographs and to convey a more accurate picture of the roads in question.

[140] See, eg, *Buckingham v Daily News Ltd* [1956] 2 QB 534, CA: a demonstration of the way in which a worker cleaned the blades of a rotary press in a printing house.

[141] Cf *Li Shu-ling v R* [1988] 3 All ER 138, PC: a video recording of a re-enactment of the crime by the accused may be admitted in evidence as a confession (see Ch 13).

[142] See per Lord Coleridge CJ in *R v Francis* (1874) LR 2 CCR 128.

[143] [2003] EWCA Civ 1583, (2003) The Times, 31 Oct.

debt action, it was held that the claimant company, which relied upon secondary evidence of documents submitted to it by the defendant, having itself destroyed the originals, had failed to prove the debts in question.

Weight

The weight of evidence is its cogency or probative worth in relation to the facts in issue. The assessment of the weight of evidence is in large measure a matter of common sense and experience, dependent upon a wide variety of factors such as: (i) the extent to which it is supported or contradicted by other evidence adduced; (ii) in the case of direct testimony, the demeanour, plausibility, and credibility of the witness and all the circumstances in which she claims to have perceived a fact in issue; and (iii) in the case of hearsay, all the circumstances from which any inference can reasonably be drawn as to the accuracy or otherwise of the out-of-court statement including, for example, whether the statement was made contemporaneously with the occurrence or existence of the facts stated and whether its maker had any incentive to conceal or misrepresent the facts.[144] Weight, like relevance, is a question of degree: at one extreme, an item of evidence may be of minimal probative value in relation to the facts in issue; at the other extreme, it may be virtually conclusive of them. Where the evidence adduced by a party in relation to a fact in issue is, even if uncontradicted, so weak that it could not reasonably justify a finding in his favour, it is described as 'insufficient evidence'. Where the evidence adduced by a party is so weighty that it could reasonably justify a finding in his favour, it is described as 'prima facie evidence'. Somewhat confusingly, however, this term is also used to describe evidence adduced by a party which is, in the absence of contradictory evidence, so weighty that it does justify a finding in his favour. 'Conclusive evidence' might be thought to denote the weightiest possible evidence. In fact, the term refers to evidence which, irrespective of its weight, concludes the fact in issue: the fact ceases to be in issue and is not even open to contradictory proof because the court must find the fact to have been proved.[145]

The issue of the weight to be attached to an item of evidence is related to, but distinct from, the issue of its admissibility. The weight of evidence is a question of fact, its admissibility a question of law. Thus, in a jury trial, the judge decides whether an item of evidence is relevant and admissible and, if the evidence is admitted, the jury decides what weight, if any, to attach to it. It does not follow from this, however, that the weight of evidence is solely the concern of the tribunal of fact. For a variety of different purposes, the judge must also form a view as to the weight of evidence. In determining admissibility, he must consider whether evidence is sufficiently relevant and this will depend, to some extent, on his assessment of its weight. In examining the evidence adduced to establish preliminary facts, which, it will be recalled, must be proved as a condition precedent to the admissibility of certain items of evidence, the weight of the evidence should be taken into account. As we shall see, a judge should withdraw an issue from the tribunal of fact where a party has adduced 'insufficient evidence' in support of that issue. As we shall also see, the judge has a discretion to exclude certain items of evidence and for these purposes also may have regard to, inter alia, the weight of the evidence in question. Last, and by no means least, in his summing-up the judge is entitled to comment upon the

---

[144] See s 4 of the Civil Evidence Act 1995 (Ch 11).

[145] See, eg, s 10(1) of the Criminal Justice Act 1967 (Ch 22) and s 13(1) of the Civil Evidence Act 1968 (see Ch 21).

cogency of the evidence admitted, provided that he does not usurp the jury's function as the tribunal of fact.[146]

The functions of the judge and jury

The division of functions between judge and jury, which dates from a time when jury trial was the norm in both civil and criminal proceedings, has left a deep impression on the modern law of evidence, even as it now applies in cases tried without a jury. It will be convenient to explore the division and the extent to which the judge controls the jury under the headings of: (i) questions of law and fact; (ii) the *voir dire* (or trial within a trial); (iii) the sufficiency of evidence; and (iv) the summing-up.

Questions of law and fact

The resolution of disputes in courts of law gives rise to questions of fact, or questions of law, and often both. In jury trials, the general rule is that questions of law are decided by the judge and questions of fact by the jury. This is not as straightforward a division as it may appear at first blush, because some questions of 'fact' for the jury, for example the issue of dishonesty in theft and related offences, may be considered to be as much questions of law as of fact, and some questions of 'law' for the judge, for example the existence or non-existence of preliminary facts, are essentially questions of fact.[147]

Questions of law for the judge include those relating to the substantive law, the competence of a person to give evidence as a witness, the admissibility of evidence, the withdrawal of an issue from the jury, and the way in which he should direct the jury on both the substantive law and the evidence adduced. Questions of fact for the jury include those relating to the credibility of the witnesses called, the weight to be attached to the evidence adduced and ultimately, of course, the existence or non-existence of the facts in issue. In trials on indictment without a jury, ie complex fraud cases and trials where there is a real danger of jury tampering, the judge decides all questions of both law and fact and, if the accused is convicted, must give a judgment which states the reasons for the conviction.[148] In the case of a trial by lay justices, the bench decides all questions of both law and fact, but on questions of law, including the law of evidence, questions of mixed law and fact, and matters of practice and procedure, should give heed to the advice of its clerk or legal adviser.[149] Theoretically in the same position, district judges (magistrates' courts) tend to decide questions of law as well as fact. In civil cases tried by a judge sitting alone, the judge decides all questions of both law and fact.

Although questions of fact are generally decided by the jury, the judicial function includes the investigation of preliminary facts (for the purpose of determining the admissibility of evidence), the assessment of the sufficiency of evidence (for the purpose of deciding whether to withdraw an issue from the jury), and the evaluation of evidence adduced (for the purpose of commenting upon the matter to the jury in summing-up). Each of these matters is considered

---

[146] *R v O'Donnell* (1917) 12 Cr App R 219; *R v Canny* (1945) 30 Cr App R 143.

[147] See generally Glanville Williams, 'Law and Fact' [1976] *Crim LR* 472 and Allen and Pardo, 'Facts in Law and Facts of Law' (2003) 7 *E&P* 153.

[148] Section 48(3) and (5) of the Criminal Justice Act 2003.

[149] For the duties of the clerk or legal adviser, see para 55, *Practice Direction (Criminal Proceedings: Consolidation)* [2002] 1 WLR 2870.

separately below. Additionally, there is a variety of special cases in which questions of fact are also capable of being questions of law or are treated as being questions of law or for some other reason fall to be decided, wholly or in part, by the judge. They include the following.

The construction of ordinary words

The modern authorities are in a state of disarray on the important question whether, in criminal cases, the construction of ordinary statutory words is a question for the tribunal of fact. The leading authority on the point, *Brutus v Cozens*,[150] expressly supports an affirmative answer. The appellant, during the annual tennis tournament at Wimbledon, had gone on to No 2 Court while a match was in progress, blown a whistle, and thrown leaflets around. He was charged with using insulting behaviour whereby a breach of the peace was likely to be occasioned under section 5 of the Public Order Act 1986. The magistrates dismissed the information on the grounds that the appellant's behaviour was not insulting. On a case stated, the question was whether, on the facts found, the decision was correct in law. This assumed that the meaning of the word 'insulting' in section 5 was a matter of law. Allowing the appellant's appeal against the decision of the Divisional Court, the House of Lords rejected this assumption. Lord Reid said:[151]

> The meaning of an ordinary word of the English language is not a question of law. The proper construction of a statute is a question of law.[152] If the context shows that a word is used in an unusual sense the court will determine in other words what that unusual sense is. But here there is in my opinion no question of the word 'insulting' being used in any unusual sense. It appears to me . . . to be intended to have its ordinary meaning. It is for the tribunal which decides the case to consider, not as law but as fact, whether in the whole circumstances the words of the statute do or do not as a matter of ordinary usage of the English language cover or apply to the facts which have been proved. If it is alleged that the tribunal has reached a wrong decision then there can be a question of law but only of a limited character. The question would normally be whether their decision was unreasonable in the sense that no tribunal acquainted with the ordinary use of language could reasonably reach that decision.

Applying this dictum in *R v Feely*,[153] an appeal from a trial by judge and jury, Lawton LJ held that whereas the word 'fraudulently' which was used in section 1(1) of the Larceny Act 1916 had acquired a special meaning as a result of case law, the word 'dishonestly' as used in section 1(1) of the Theft Act 1968 was an ordinary word in common use. Accordingly, it was a question of fact for the jury and required no direction by the judge as to its meaning.[154]

---

[150] [1973] AC 854.

[151] [1973] AC 854 at 861.

[152] See also *R v Spens* [1991] 4 All ER 421, CA: it is for the judge to construe binding agreements between parties, and all forms of parliamentary and local government legislation, including codes which sufficiently resemble legislation as to require such construction, eg the City Code on Takeovers and Mergers; and cf *R v Adams* [1993] Crim LR 525, CA, and *R v Morris* [1994] Crim LR 596, CA.

[153] [1973] QB 530, CA.

[154] See also *R v Harris* (1986) 84 Cr App R 75, CA: the words 'knowledge or belief' are words of ordinary usage and therefore, in most cases of handling stolen goods contrary to s 22(1) of the Theft Act 1968, all that need be said to a jury is to ask whether the prosecution has established receipt, knowing or believing that the goods were stolen; *R v Jones* [1987] 2 All ER 692, CA: whether a person is 'armed' while being concerned in the illegal importation of cannabis contrary to s 86 of the Customs and Excise Management Act 1979; *Chambers v DPP* [1995] Crim LR 896, DC: 'disorderly behaviour' contrary to s 5 of the Public Order Act 1986; and *R v Kirk* [2006] Crim LR 850, CA: 'indecent or obscene' under the Postal Services Act 2000, s 85(4).

In *DPP v Stonehouse*[155] the question whether acts are sufficiently proximate to the intended complete offence to rank as an attempt, was treated as a question of fact. This was justified by Lord Diplock on the grounds that the concept of proximity is a question of degree on which the opinion of reasonable men may differ and as to which the legal training and experience of a judge does not make his opinion more likely to be correct than that of a non-lawyer.[156]

Lord Reid's dictum, however, although never expressly disowned, has largely been ignored. As one commentator has observed, the number of cases when *Cozens v Brutus* ought to have been cited but was not 'are as the sands of the sea'.[157] This disregard extends to the House of Lords itself. In *Metropolitan Police Comr v Caldwell*,[158] for example, 'recklessly' was held to be an ordinary word, but given a legal definition. A similar approach has been taken in relation to the word 'supply' in section 5(3) of the Misuse of Drugs Act 1971[159] and the word 'discharge' in section 5(1)(b) of the Firearms Act 1968.[160] The need for such legal definition of ordinary words stems from the potential diversity of interpretation by jurors, and indeed judges, and the concomitant risk of inconsistent verdicts, and for these reasons, it is submitted, Lord Reid's dictum should continue to be ignored until it is expressly repudiated.

In civil cases tried with a jury, there is old authority to support the view that the meaning of ordinary words is a question of construction for the judge.[161]

Defamation

As a result of Fox's Libel Act 1792—which provides that, in criminal prosecutions for libel, it is for the jury, having been directed by the judge on the law, to give a general verdict of guilty or not guilty upon the whole matter put in issue—there has developed a rule whereby the judge decides whether the writing in question is capable of the defamatory meaning alleged by the prosecution and, if satisfied that this is the case, the jury, construing the writing, then decides whether it does, in fact, constitute a criminal libel. This division of functions between judge and jury also applies in civil proceedings for libel.[162]

Corroboration

In the now rare cases in which a conviction cannot be based on uncorroborated evidence, it is for the judge to direct the jury as to what evidence is capable, in law, of amounting to corroboration and for the jury to decide whether that evidence does, in fact, constitute corroboration.[163]

---

[155] [1978] AC 55, HL.
[156] [1978] AC 55 at 69. See now s 4(3) of the Criminal Attempts Act 1981.
[157] D W Elliott, 'Brutus v Cozens; Decline & Fall' [1989] *Crim LR* 323 at 324.
[158] [1982] AC 341, HL.
[159] *R v Maginnis* [1987] AC 303, HL.
[160] *Flack v Baldry* [1988] 1 All ER 673, HL.
[161] Per Parke B in *Neilson v Harford* (1841) 8 M&W 806 at 823.
[162] *Nevill v Fine Arts & General Insurance Co Ltd* [1897] AC 68, HL. Where a defendant claims qualified privilege for a report as a fair and accurate report of the proceedings of an inquiry within the Schedule to the Defamation Act 1952, the issues of fairness and accuracy are questions of fact for the jury, as are questions of public concern and public benefit under s 7(3) of the Act: *Kingshott v Associated Kent Newspapers Ltd* [1991] 2 All ER 99, CA.
[163] *R v Tragen* [1956] Crim LR 332; *R v Charles* (1976) 68 Cr App R 334n, HL; *R v Reeves* (1979) 68 Cr App R 331, CA. See generally Ch 8.

Foreign law

In the courts of England and Wales, questions of foreign law, that is questions relating to the law of any jurisdiction other than England and Wales, are issues of fact to be decided, on the evidence adduced, by the judge. Section 15 of the Administration of Justice Act 1920 provides that:

> Where for the purposes of disposing of any action or other matter which is being tried by a judge with a jury in any court in England or Wales it is necessary to ascertain the law of any other country which is applicable to the facts of the case, any question as to the effect of the evidence given with respect to that law shall, instead of being submitted to the jury, be decided by the judge alone.

This provision applies to criminal proceedings only,[164] but has been re-enacted, in relation to High Court proceedings and County Court proceedings, by section 69(5) of the Supreme Court Act 1981 and section 68 of the County Courts Act 1984 respectively. Foreign law is usually proved by the evidence of an appropriately qualified expert, who may refer to foreign statutes and decisions, or by the production of a report of a previous decision by an English court of superior status on the point of foreign law in question.[165] Where necessary, the judge must determine the point by deciding between the conflicting opinion evidence of the expert witnesses.[166]

Questions of reasonableness

What is reasonable is a question of fact and therefore normally decided by the jury. In some civil cases, however, it must be decided by the judge on the basis of facts which, if not agreed, have been ascertained by the jury. In an action for malicious prosecution, for example, it is the function of the jury to ascertain the facts, if disputed, which operated on the mind of the prosecutor, and the function of the judge, on the basis of the facts thus ascertained, to decide whether the prosecutor did or did not have reasonable and probable cause for commencing the prosecution in question.[167]

Perjury

The offence of perjury is committed where a person lawfully sworn as a witness or interpreter in a judicial proceeding wilfully makes a statement *material* in that proceeding which he knows to be false or does not believe to be true.[168] Section 1(6) of the Perjury Act 1911 provides that 'the question whether a statement on which perjury is assigned was material is a question of law to be determined by the court of trial'.

Autrefois acquit and convict

An accused charged with an offence which is the same as an offence in respect of which he has previously been acquitted or convicted or an offence in respect of which he could on some previous indictment have been lawfully convicted, may tender a special plea in bar of *autrefois acquit* or *convict* in order to quash the indictment. Where such a plea is tendered, it is for the judge to decide the issue, without empanelling a jury.[169]

---

[164] *R v Hammer* [1923] 2 KB 786, CCA.

[165] See Ch 18. For the circumstances in which judicial notice may be taken of points of foreign law, see Ch 22.

[166] See, eg, *Re Duke of Wellington, Glentanar v Wellington* [1947] Ch 506.

[167] *Herniman v Smith* [1938] AC 305, HL, applied, in relation to the tort of procuring the grant of a search warrant falsely, maliciously, and *without reasonable and probable cause*, in *Reynolds v Metropolitan Police Comr* (1984) 80 Cr App R 125, CA.

[168] Perjury Act 1911, s 1(1).

[169] Criminal Justice Act 1988, s 122.

The *voir dire*, or trial within a trial

Preliminary facts, as we have seen, must be proved as a condition precedent to the admissibility of certain items of evidence. For example, where the prosecution propose to adduce evidence of a confession made by the accused and the defence object to its admissibility on the grounds that it was or may have been obtained by oppression of the accused or in consequence of something said or done which was likely, in the circumstances, to render unreliable any confession which might be made by him in consequence thereof, the court shall not allow the confession to be admitted except in so far as the prosecution prove to the court that the confession was not obtained by such means.[170] Proof of due search for the original of a lost document, on the contents of which a party seeks to rely, is a condition precedent to the admissibility of a copy of that document.[171] Similarly, it may become necessary to show that a person is competent to give evidence as a witness or that a witness is privileged from answering a particular question. Questions of this kind are matters of law for the judge. The preliminary facts may be agreed or assumed, but where they are in dispute it is for the judge to hear evidence and adjudicate upon them.[172] The witnesses give their evidence on a special form of oath known as a *voir dire*. The hearing before the judge is called a hearing on the *voir dire* or a 'trial within a trial'.

In general, disputes about the admissibility of evidence in civil proceedings are best resolved by the judge at trial rather than at a separate preliminary hearing, because at such a hearing the judge will usually be less well informed and such a hearing can cause unnecessary costs and delays.[173]

In the Crown Court, questions of admissibility, including those involving the hearing of evidence on the *voir dire*, are usually determined in the absence of the jury because of the impossibility of deciding such questions without some reference either to the disputed evidence, which in the event may be ruled inadmissible, or to other material prejudicial to the accused. Thus where the prosecution propose to adduce a certain item of evidence and counsel for the defence intends to make a submission that it is inadmissible, that intention will be conveyed to the prosecution either at the Plea and Case Management Hearing or immediately before the trial commences so that the evidence is not referred to in the presence of the jury, whether in the prosecution opening speech or otherwise. The prosecution will adduce their evidence in the normal way but at that point in time when the evidence would otherwise be admitted, counsel will intimate to the judge that a point of law has arisen which falls to be decided in the absence of the jury and the jury will be told to retire.[174] Whether or not the jury, on returning to court, hear the disputed evidence depends, of course, on the judge's

---

[170] Police and Criminal Evidence Act 1984, s 76(2) (see Ch 13).

[171] *Brewster v Sewell* (1820) 3 B&Ald 296 (see Ch 8).

[172] However, where the preliminary facts are identical with the facts in issue, the condition precedent is held to be established if the judge is satisfied that there is *sufficient evidence* of it to go before the jury. For example, if a party seeks to adduce a tape-recording in evidence, the question of whether it is genuine and original being ultimately for the determination of the jury, the judge need satisfy himself by no more than prima facie evidence that the tape is genuine and original and therefore competent to be considered by the jury: *R v Robson, R v Harris* [1972] 1 WLR 651; cf *R v Stevenson* [1971] 1 WLR (see Ch 4). See also *Stowe v Querner* (1870) LR 5 Exch 155 and per Lord Penzance in *Hitchins v Eardley* (1871) LR 2 P&D 248. However, it has also been said that the judge must reach a definite decision on the preliminary fact in question: see per Lord Denman CJ in *Doe d Jenkins v Davies* (1847) 10 QB 314.

[173] *Stroude v Beazer Homes Ltd* [2005] EWCA Civ 265.

[174] Occasionally it is necessary to determine admissibility immediately after the jury has been empanelled, eg, where the evidence of a confession is so crucial to the prosecution case that, without reference to it, their case cannot even be opened: see *R v Hammond* [1941] 3 All ER 318.

ruling on its admissibility. In *R v Reynolds*[175] Lord Goddard CJ was of the opinion that the determination of preliminary facts in the absence of the jury is confined to exceptional cases, such as those relating to the admissibility of a confession, where it is almost impossible to prevent some reference to the terms of the confession.[176] However, the modern practice is to ask the jury to retire whenever there is a risk of them being exposed to material which might be ruled inadmissible or which, in any event, would be likely to prejudice the accused.[177] The modern position, therefore, is probably accurately reflected in rule 104(c) of the United States Federal Rules, which provides that hearings on the admissibility of confessions shall always be conducted in the absence of the jury and that hearings on other matters shall be so conducted when the interests of justice require.

In *F (an infant) v Chief Constable of Kent*[178] Lord Lane CJ observed that since the function of the *voir dire* is to allow the arbiter of law to decide a legal point in the absence of the arbiter of fact, in proceedings before magistrates, where the justices are judges of both fact and law, there can be no question of a trial within a trial. In that case, it was held that once the question of the admissibility of a confession has been decided as a separate issue, the magistrates having heard evidence on the preliminary facts and having ruled in favour of admissibility, it is unnecessary for the evidence about the confession to be repeated later in the trial proper. Lord Lane CJ also held that it was impossible to lay down any general rule as to when a question of admissibility should be taken in a summary trial or as to when the magistrates should announce their decision on it, every case being different. This flexible approach was reiterated in *R v Epping and Ongar Justices, ex p Manby*,[179] where the accused contested the admissibility of certain documentary evidence tendered by the prosecution and sought leave to have the question resolved as a preliminary issue. The magistrates refused and admitted the evidence as providing a prima facie case for the accused to deal with later, if he saw fit. The Divisional Court held that the justices had not erred: within statutory constraints, they should determine their own procedure.

Section 78 of the 1984 Act, whereby a criminal court has a discretion to exclude evidence on which the prosecution propose to rely on the grounds that it would have an adverse effect on the fairness of the proceedings,[180] is not a statutory constraint for these purposes and accordingly does not entitle an accused to have an issue of admissibility settled as a preliminary issue in a trial within a trial.[181]

In *Halawa v Federation Against Copyright Theft*[182] it was held that the duty of a magistrate, on an application under section 78, is either to deal with it when it arises or to leave the decision until the end of the hearing, the objective being to secure that the trial is fair and just to both sides. Thus, in some cases there will be a trial within a trial in which the accused is given the opportunity to exclude the evidence before he is required to give evidence on the main issues (because, if denied that opportunity, his right to remain silent on the main issues is impaired); but in most cases the better course will be for the whole of the prosecution case to be heard,

[175] [1950] 1 KB 606.
[176] See further Ch 13, 390 under **The *voir dire***.
[177] See *R v Deakin* [1994] 4 All ER 769, CA.
[178] [1982] Crim LR 682, DC.
[179] [1986] Crim LR 555, DC.
[180] See further below.
[181] *Vel v Owen* [1987] Crim LR 496, DC.
[182] [1995] 1 Cr App R 21, DC.

including the disputed evidence, before any trial within a trial is held. In order to decide, the court may ask the accused the extent of the issues to be addressed by his evidence in the trial within a trial—a trial within a trial might be appropriate if the issues are limited, but not if it is likely to be protracted, raising issues which will have to be re-examined in the trial proper.

Where justices resolve to exclude under section 78, evidence of statements made by an accused, they should consider, after seeking the views of the parties, whether the substantive hearing—if there still is one—should be conducted by a differently constituted bench.[183]

Section 76(2) of the 1984 Act[184] is a statutory constraint and an exception to the generally flexible approach. In *R v Liverpool Juvenile Court, ex p R*[185] the Divisional Court held that if, in a summary trial, the accused, before the close of the prosecution case, represents to the court that a confession was or may have been obtained by the methods set out in section 76(2), the magistrates are required to hold a trial within a trial, in which the accused is entitled to give evidence relating to the issue of admissibility, and are also required to make their ruling on admissibility before or at the end of the prosecution case.[186] In such a case, an alternative contention based on section 78 would also be examined at the same trial within a trial, at the same time.[187]

Somewhat surprisingly, given the importance of the matter, there is little authority on the question whether the tribunal of law, whether judge or magistrates, in deciding what evidence is admissible for the purpose of proving or disproving disputed preliminary facts, is bound by the rules of evidence which apply at the trial proper,[188] including those relating to oaths and affirmations.[189] Under the United States Federal Rules,[190] the judge is only bound by those rules of evidence which concern privilege.

The sufficiency of evidence

The obligation on a party to adduce sufficient evidence on a fact in issue to justify a finding on that fact in his favour, is referred to as 'the evidential burden'.[191] A party discharges an evidential burden borne by him by adducing sufficient evidence for the issue in question to be submitted to the jury (tribunal of fact). Whether there is sufficient evidence is a question of law for the judge. If the party has adduced enough evidence to justify, *as a possibility*, a favourable finding by the jury, the judge leaves it to them to decide whether or not the issue has been

---

[183]   *DPP v Lawrence* [2008] 1 Cr App R 147, CA, *per curiam* at 153–4.

[184]   See above.

[185]   [1987] 2 All ER 668, DC.

[186]   A trial within a trial will only take place before the close of the prosecution case if a representation is made pursuant to s 76(2). If no such representation is made, the accused may raise the question of the admissibility or weight of the confession at any subsequent stage of the trial. However, at this later stage in the proceedings, although the court retains an inherent jurisdiction to exclude the confession, as well as the power to exclude by virtue of s 78, it is not required to embark on a trial within a trial: see per Russell LJ at 672–3.

[187]   *Halawa v Federation Against Copyright Theft* [1995] 1 Cr App R 21, per Ralph Gibson LJ at 33.

[188]   In the case of statutory exceptions to the hearsay rule, it has been held that preliminary facts call for proof by admissible evidence: see per Lord Mustill, obiter, in *Neill v North Antrim Magistrates' Court* [1992] 4 All ER 846, HL, at 854, applied in *R v Belmarsh Magistrates' Court, ex p Gilligan* [1998] 1 Cr App R 14, DC and *R v Wood and Fitzsimmons* [1998] Crim LR 213, CA. But cf *R v Foxley* [1995] 2 Cr App R 523, CA. See also *Edwards v Brookes (Milk) Ltd* [1963] 1 WLR 795, QBD.

[189]   See *R v Greer* [1998] Crim LR 572, CA, and contrast *R v Jennings* [1995] Crim LR 810, CA.

[190]   Rule 104(a).

[191]   The meaning of this term is considered fully in Ch 4.

proved; if the evidence is insufficient, the judge withdraws the issue from the jury, whatever their view of the matter, directing them either to return a finding on that issue in favour of the other party or, in appropriate circumstances, to return a verdict on the whole case in favour of the other party. For example, in criminal proceedings, the evidential burden in relation to most common law defences is borne by the accused. If the accused, on a charge of murder, fails to adduce sufficient evidence of, say, provocation, the judge will withdraw that issue from the jury, directing them that it must be taken as proved against the accused.[192] The prosecution normally bear the evidential burden in relation to all those facts essential to the Crown case. If the prosecution fail to adduce sufficient evidence in relation to an essential element of the offence, they not only fail on that issue, but also in the whole case and the judge will direct the jury to acquit.

In criminal cases tried with a jury, the defence, after the prosecution have adduced all their evidence and closed their case, may make a submission of no case to answer.[193] If there is no evidence that the alleged crime has been committed by the accused, no evidence of an essential ingredient of that offence, or no corroborative evidence where corroboration is required as a matter of law, the submission will be upheld. Likewise, if the judge comes to the conclusion that the Crown's evidence, taken at its highest, is such that a jury properly directed could not properly convict on it, it is his duty to stop the case.[194] However, where the Crown's evidence is such that its strength or weakness depends on the view to be taken of a witness's reliability, or other matters which are, generally speaking, within the jury's province, and where on one view of the facts there is evidence on which a jury could properly conclude that the accused is guilty, the submission will fail; the judge should give brief reasons to enable the defence to understand why the submission has failed,[195] then the accused should call his evidence in the usual way and the case should go before the jury.[196] Cases in which the evidence is purely circumstantial are not in a special category; the judge should not withdraw the case from the jury simply because the proved facts do not exclude every reasonable inference besides that

[192] *Mancini v DPP* [1942] AC 1, HL. But see also *Bullard v R* [1957] AC 635, PC (see Ch 4).

[193] The submission should be made in the absence of the jury and, if the trial proceeds thereafter, should not be referred to by the judge in his summing-up: see *R v Smith and Doe* (1986) 85 Cr App R 197, CA, and, in the case of visual identification evidence, *R v Akaidere* [1990] Crim LR 808, CA (see Ch 8). See also *Crosdale v R* [1995] 2 All ER 500, PC: if the judge rejects the submission, the jury need know nothing about the decision—no explanation is required; and if the judge rules in favour of the submission on some charges but not on others, all the jury need be told is that the decision was taken for legal reasons—any further explanation will risk potential prejudice.

[194] See, eg, *R v Bland* (1987) 151 JP 857, CA, where the only evidence that the accused had assisted a man in the commission of an offence was that she was living with him at a time when he possessed and dealt in drugs. It was held that knowledge could be inferred from the circumstances, but assistance, though passive, required more than knowledge; there should have been some evidence to prove the further element of encouragement or control. Cf *R v Suurmeijer* [1991] Crim LR 773, CA; *R v McNamara* [1998] Crim LR 278, CA; and *R v Berry* [1998] Crim LR 487, CA.

[195] *R v Powell* [2006] All ER (D) 146 (Jan).

[196] See generally per Lord Lane CJ in *R v Galbraith* [1981] 1 WLR 1039, CA; cf *R v Beckwith* [1981] Crim LR 646. The Royal Commission on Criminal Justice recommended replacement of the rule in *R v Galbraith* by a new power for the judge to withdraw from the jury an issue or the whole case if he considers the evidence too weak or demonstrably unsafe or unsatisfactory: see para 42, ch 4, *Report of the Royal Commission on Criminal Justice*, Cm 2263 (1993). For the correct approach in cases where the issue is mistaken identity, see *R v Turnbull* [1977] QB 224, CA and *Daley v R* [1993] 4 All ER 86, PC (Ch 8). Where a judge improperly rejects a defence submission of no case to answer, a conviction may be set aside on appeal on the grounds that he made a wrong decision on a question of law. As to the position on appeal in cases where, subsequent to the improper rejection of the submission, evidence was given entitling the jury to convict, see *R v Power* [1919] 1 KB 572; and contrast *R v Abbott* [1955] 2 QB 497 and *R v Juett* [1981] Crim LR 113, CA.

of guilt,[197] but should ask the simple question, looking at all the evidence with appropriate care: is there a case on which a jury properly directed could convict.[198]

The judge also has a power to withdraw a case from the jury at any time after the close of the prosecution case, even as late as the end of the defence case, and whether or not a submission of no case to answer has been made at the end of the prosecution case. This is a power to be very sparingly exercised and only if the judge is satisfied that no jury properly directed could safely convict.[199] However, it is not open to a judge to entertain a submission of no case before the close of the prosecution case, because it is only at that stage that it is known what the evidence actually is and until then the most that can be known is what it is expected to be.[200] A ruling may be made at an earlier stage, where it is admitted or agreed what the outstanding prosecution evidence will be, but any direction to return a not guilty verdict should normally await the end of the prosecution case unless, of course, the Crown bows to the ruling and offers no further evidence. Similarly, before the calling of any evidence, the parties may agree that it would be helpful for the judge to rule on the question whether, on agreed, admitted, or assumed facts, the offence charged will be made out, with a view either to the Crown offering no evidence or to the accused considering whether to plead guilty.[201]

In criminal cases tried by magistrates, the position is not entirely clear. The test, contained in a *Practice Direction*, used to be that a submission of no case may be properly made and upheld (1) when there has been no evidence to prove an essential ingredient of the offence alleged;[202] or (2) when the evidence adduced by the prosecution has been so discredited as a result of cross-examination or is so manifestly unreliable that no reasonable tribunal could safely convict on it.[203] This *Practice Direction* was revoked[204] but not replaced. There can be no doubt that the first limb of the *Practice Direction* remains good law. As to the second limb, it is submitted that it should continue to apply, on the basis that the magistrates are the tribunal of fact as well as law. Thus although it has been said that questions of credibility, except in the clearest of cases, should not normally be taken into account by justices on a submission of no case,[205] if magistrates conclude that the prosecution evidence has been so discredited or is so manifestly unreliable that they cannot safely convict on it in any event, there can be no point in allowing the case to continue.

In civil cases tried by a judge sitting alone, a defendant can submit that there is no case to answer at the close of the claimant's case, but in most cases the judge will only rule on the submission if the defendant elects not to call evidence.[206] In *Benham Ltd v Kythira Investments Ltd*[207]

---

[197] *R v Morgan* [1993] Crim LR 870, CA; *R v P* [2008] 2 Cr App R 68, CA.

[198] *R v P*, ibid.

[199] *R v Brown* [2002] 1 Cr App R 46, CA.

[200] *R v N Ltd* [2009] 1 Cr App R 56, CA. Nor does the judge have power to prevent the prosecution from calling evidence and to direct an acquittal on the basis that he thinks that a conviction is unlikely: *Attorney General's Reference (No 2 of 2000)* [2001] 1 Cr App R 503.

[201] See *R v N Ltd*, ibid at 66.

[202] See, eg, *Chief Constable of Avon and Somerset Constabulary v Jest* [1986] RTR 372, DC.

[203] *Practice Direction (Submission of No Case)* [1962] 1 WLR 227.

[204] *Practice Direction (Criminal Proceedings: Consolidation)* [2002] 1 WLR 2870.

[205] *R v Barking and Dagenham Justices, ex p DPP* (1995) 159 JP 373, DC, in which it was held that the prosecutor should be given the opportunity to reply to the submission or, where the magistrates are minded to dismiss the case of their own motion, to address the court.

[206] *Alexander v Rayson* [1936] 1 KB 169 at 178, CA.

[207] [2003] EWCA Civ 1794, followed in *Graham v Chorley Borough Council* [2006] EWCA Civ 92.

the Court of Appeal, after reviewing the authorities, held that there were two disadvantages of entertaining a submission of no case to answer without putting the defendant to his or her election. First, it interrupted the trial and required the judge to make up his mind as to the facts on the basis of one side's evidence only, applying the lower test of a prima facie case, with the result that, if he rejected the submission, he had to make up his mind afresh in the light of further evidence and on the application of a different test. Secondly, if the judge acceded to a submission of no case, his judgment might be reversed on appeal, with all the expense and inconvenience of resuming or retrying the action. The court concluded that rarely, if ever, should a judge trying a civil action without a jury entertain a submission of no case, although it conceded that 'conceivably', as Mance LJ had suggested in *Miller v Margaret Cawley*,[208] there may be some flaw of fact or law of such a nature as to make it entirely obvious that the claimant's case must fail, and the determination at that stage may save significant costs. The decision, it is submitted, is unnecessarily inflexible, especially in the light of the wide powers of case management under the Civil Procedure Rules, which should enable a court to consider a submission with or without putting the defendant to his election. In some cases, albeit rare, there will be grounds for contending that the claimant has no reasonable prospect of success whether or not the defendant gives evidence, as when the judge forms the view that the claimant is not a reliable witness of fact and that the position will not change even if the defendant calls evidence.[209]

In civil cases tried with a jury, the judge has a discretion whether to rule on a submission of no case to answer without requiring the defendant to elect to call no evidence[210] and a submission may also be made, after all the evidence has been adduced, that there is insufficient evidence to go before the jury.[211] The test would appear to be the same test as is used in criminal jury trials,[212] namely whether the evidence, taken at its highest, is such that a jury properly directed could not properly reach a necessary factual conclusion.[213]

The summing-up

At a trial on indictment, after the conclusion of all the evidence and closing speeches by counsel, the judge must sum up the case to the jury. In addition to directing them on the substantive law and reminding them of the evidence that has been given, the judge must also explain a number of evidential points.[214] Many directions will reflect or be based upon the specimen directions of the Judicial Studies Board.[215] The judge should begin with a direction as to which party bears the obligation to prove what facts and the standard of proof

---

[208] [2002] All ER (D) 452.

[209] See *Mullan v Birmingham City Council* (1999) The Times, 29 July, QBD.

[210] *Young v Rank* [1950] 2 KB 510.

[211] *Grinsted v Hadrill* [1953] 1 WLR 696, CA. In civil cases, with or without a jury, if the judge rejects a submission of no case to answer, albeit improperly, and the defendant subsequently adduces evidence and is found liable, the Court of Appeal may consider all of the evidence adduced, including that of the defendant: *Payne v Harrison* [1961] 2 QB 403, CA.

[212] See *R v Galbraith* [1981] 1 WLR 1039, CA, above.

[213] See *Alexander v Arts Council of Wales* [2001] 4 All ER 205, CA per May LJ at [37].

[214] It would be helpful if prosecuting counsel made a check list of the directions on the law which they considered the trial judge ought to give and drew the attention of the judge to any failure on his part to give an essential direction before the jury retired: per Watkins LJ in *R v Donoghue* (1987) 86 Cr App R 267, CA.

[215] See <http://www.jsboard.co.uk>.

required to be met before they are entitled to conclude that those facts have been proved.[216] He should remind the jury of the evidence adduced by the prosecution and defence[217] and refer to any defence which that evidence discloses,[218] even if it has not been relied upon by defence counsel.[219] He should also explain, where necessary, that the onus of disproving certain defences, such as provocation and self-defence, rests on the prosecution. Depending on the nature of the case and the evidence called, it may be necessary: (i) to give a warning on or to explain the requirement for corroboration, indicating the meaning of that word and pointing out the evidence capable in law of amounting to corroboration; (ii) to direct on any relevant presumptions of law, making it clear, where necessary, that if the jury are satisfied that certain matters are proved, they *must* find that other matters are proved; (iii) to warn of the special need for caution, where the case against the accused depends wholly or substantially on the correctness of one or more identifications, before convicting in reliance on the correctness of the identification or identifications; and (iv) to explain that certain items of evidence can only be used for certain restricted purposes, for example that a confession made by an accused implicating both himself and a co-accused is evidence only against the accused and not the co-accused. On all these and other such matters the judge is duty bound to direct the jury.

The judge is entitled to comment on the plausibility and credibility of the witnesses and the weight of the evidence. He may do so in strong or emphatic terms provided that he also makes it clear that, apart from whatever he says about the law, the jury are in no way bound by any view of his own about the evidence which he may have appeared to express.[220] The specimen direction of the Judicial Studies Board concerning comments by the judge on the evidence includes the following passage: 'If I mention or emphasize evidence that you regard as unimportant, disregard that evidence. If I do not mention evidence that you regard as important,

---

[216] See *R v McVey* [1988] Crim LR 127. See also, as to burden of proof, *R v Donoghue* (1987) 86 Cr App R 267, and as to standard of proof, *R v Edwards* (1983) 77 Cr App R 5 and *R v Bentley (Deceased)* [2001] 1 Cr App R 307, CA. Where the prosecution case depends solely on the identification of a single witness, it is particularly important to give a general clear and simple direction on burden and standard: *R v Lang-Hall* (1989) The Times, 24 Mar, CA. In cases involving injuries to a very small child, any temptation on the part of the jury to succumb to emotion should be countered by a very clear direction on the burden of proof: *R v Bowditch* [1991] Crim LR 831, CA.

[217] *R v Tillman* [1962] Crim LR 261. See also *R v Gregory* [1993] Crim LR 623, CA, and cf *R v Sargent* [1993] Crim LR 713, CA. It may be that, in a straightforward case, failure to sum up on the facts is not necessarily a fatal defect (*R v Attfield* (1961) 45 Cr App R 309), but in the majority of cases it is clearly desirable that the judge should do so: *R v Brower* [1995] Crim LR 746, CA.

[218] *R v Badjan* (1966) 50 Cr App R 141. The judge is under no duty to build up a defence for an accused who has elected not to testify, but need only remind the jury of any relevant matter contained in pre-trial statements and interviews with the police and the assistance, if any, provided by the Crown's witnesses: *R v Hillier* (1992) 97 Cr App R 349, CA. See also *R v Curtin* [1996] Crim LR 831, CA. If the accused has said nothing in police interviews and adduces no evidence to refute, qualify, or explain the case against him, the judge is under no duty to remind the jury of the defence case: *R v Briley* [1991] Crim LR 444, CA.

[219] *R v Porritt* (1961) 45 Cr App R 348. See also *R v Bennett* [1995] Crim LR 877, CA and *R v Williams* (1994) 99 Cr App R 163, CA. The duty only arises, however, if there is a reasonable possibility of the jury finding in favour of the defence, and not where the matter is merely fanciful and speculative: *R v Johnson* [1994] Crim LR 376, CA.

[220] It is undesirable for judges to make comments which place police witnesses in any special category or which may lead a jury to think that there will be adverse consequences for police officers if a verdict of not guilty is returned: *R v Harris* [1986] Crim LR 123, CA. Nor should the prosecution suggest that an acquittal will ruin a prosecution witness: *R v Gale* [1994] Crim LR 208, CA. If the witness refers in his evidence to the consequences of his evidence being disbelieved, the judge should direct the jury that their verdict should not be influenced by such a consideration: *R v Gale*. See also *Mears v R* (1993) 97 Cr App R 239, PC, where the comments were unduly weighted against the accused.

follow your own view and take that evidence into account.' Such a direction is best given at the start of the summing-up, especially if the judge is minded to express strong views on the evidence.[221]

The judge should never give an express indication of his own disbelief in relation to the evidence of a witness, especially the evidence of an accused, even in a case in which the evidence warrants incredulity;[222] and on certain matters, such as the accused's failure to call a particular witness,[223] the judge is restricted in the comments that he may properly make. Although it is clear that if a judge is satisfied that there is no evidence before the jury which could justify them in convicting the accused and that it would be perverse for them to do so, it is his duty to direct them to acquit, there is no converse rule. If he is satisfied on the evidence that the jury would not be justified in acquitting the accused and that it would be perverse of them to do so, he has no power to direct them to convict, because the jury alone have the right to decide that the accused is guilty. In *DPP v Stonehouse*,[224] from which this principle derives, the trial judge had directed the jury that if they were satisfied that the accused had falsely staged his death by drowning, dishonestly intending that claims should be made and money obtained by his wife under policies on his life with insurance companies, that would constitute the offence of attempting to obtain property by deception. This amounted to a withdrawal from the jury of the question of fact of whether the accused's conduct was sufficiently proximate to the complete offence. A majority of the House of Lords held that this was a misdirection, being of the opinion that even where a reasonable jury properly directed on the law must on the facts reach a guilty verdict, the trial judge should still leave issues of fact to the jury. However, since no reasonable jury could have had the slightest doubt that the facts proved did establish the attempt charged, it was further held that no miscarriage of justice could have resulted from the direction. The proviso to section 2(1) of the Criminal Appeal Act 1968 was applied and the conviction affirmed.[225] In *R v Wang*[226] the House of Lords has confirmed that there are no circumstances in which a judge is entitled to direct a jury to convict and that no distinction is to be drawn between cases in which a burden lies on the defence and those in which the burden lies solely on the Crown, because that distinction is inconsistent with the rationale of the majority in *DPP v Stonehouse*, which is that no matter how inescapable a judge may consider a conclusion to be, in the sense that any other conclusion would be perverse, it remains his duty to leave the decision to the jury and not to dictate what the verdict should be. The jury therefore retain the power to return a perverse verdict, a power which has been memorably exercised from time to time.[227] This is viewed by some as a blatant affront to the legal process,[228] but by others as a means of controlling oppressive state prosecutions and ensuring that the law conforms to the layman's idea of justice.[229]

---

[221] See *R v Everett* [1995] Crim LR 76, CA.

[222] *R v Iroegbu* (1988) The Times, 2 Aug, CA. See also *R v Winn-Pope* [1996] Crim LR 521, CA and *R v Farr* [1999] Crim LR 506, CA.

[223] *R v Gallagher* [1974] 1 WLR 1204, CA.

[224] [1978] AC 55, HL.

[225] See also per Lloyd LJ in *R v Gent* [1990] 1 All ER 364, CA at 367 and cf per May LJ in *R v Thompson* [1984] 3 All ER 565, CA at 571, approved in *R v Gordon* (1987) 92 Cr App R 50n, CA.

[226] [2005] 1 All ER 782, HL.

[227] See, eg, *R v Ponting* [1985] Crim LR 318.

[228] See Auld LJ's *Review of the Criminal Courts of England and Wales: Report* (2001), paras 99–108.

[229] See Lord Devlin 'The Conscience of the Jury' (1991) 107 *LQR* 398.

Where there has been a direction to convict and the decision as to guilt was not in reality made by the jury at all, a conviction will be quashed, but an appeal may be dismissed, notwithstanding a direction to convict, if the jury were left to make a decision and retired to do so and the evidence of guilt was overwhelming.[230]

Many of the rules governing the way in which a judge should sum up rest on largely uninvestigated assumptions about the way in which jurors analyse and evaluate evidence. Section 8 of the Contempt of Court Act 1981 operates to prevent research involving real juries and therefore research within the jurisdiction has been confined to simulated and shadow juries, who obviously do not meet real parties and are not responsible for making real decisions. However, the research, together with research projects undertaken elsewhere with real jurors, has shed much light on the extent to which jurors understand, recall, and apply directions on such matters as the standard of proof and the use to which character evidence may be put. It also indicates the need for clearer guidance for juries at the start of the trial, for the use of simpler language, and for greater use of written material in what remains a predominantly oral process.[231]

Judicial discretion

If all evidence was either legally admissible or legally inadmissible, the law of evidence would be more certain. The price of such increased certainty, however, would be a rigidity that would do nothing to promote the integrity of the judicial process because it would sometimes occasion injustice by the exclusion of highly relevant evidence or the admission of evidence that would be unduly prejudicial or unfair to one of the parties. This can be avoided if the judge, over and above his general duty to rule on the admissibility of evidence as a matter of law, has a discretionary power to admit legally inadmissible evidence and to exclude legally admissible evidence. The former, inclusionary discretion, is virtually non-existent in English law. The latter, exclusionary discretion may be exercised in civil cases in favour of either party and in criminal cases in favour of the accused. It will be convenient to consider each separately.

Inclusionary discretion

Despite the absence of express authority on the point, it seems clear that at common law, in both civil and criminal cases, a judge has no discretionary power to admit legally inadmissible evidence. In *Sparks v R*[232] the accused, a white man aged 27, was convicted of indecently assaulting a girl. At the trial, the judge held that evidence by the girl's mother to the effect that shortly after the assault her daughter had said 'it was a coloured boy' was inadmissible. The child gave no evidence at the trial. The Privy Council held that the evidence had been properly excluded as hearsay evidence which came within no recognized exception to the rule against hearsay in criminal cases.[233] It seems clear that Lord Morris, who delivered the opinion of the Privy Council, was operating on the assumption that where evidence is inadmissible as a matter of law, there is no inclusionary discretion.[234]

---

[230] See *R v Kelleher* [2003] EWCA Crim 3525, approved in *R v Caley-Knowles* [2007] 1 Cr App R 197, CA.

[231] See W Young, 'Summing-up to Juries in Criminal Cases—What Jury Research says about Current Rules and Practice' [2003] *Crim LR* 665, which refers to much of the relevant literature.

[232] [1964] AC 964, PC.

[233] The appeal was allowed on different grounds.

[234] [1964] AC 964 at 978. See also per Lord Reid in *Myers v DPP* [1965] AC 1001 at 1024.

Exclusionary discretion

Civil cases

Prior to the introduction of the Civil Procedure Rules, a judge in a civil case had no discretionary power to exclude evidence that would otherwise be admissible as a matter of law. There was an exception, arguably, in the case of information given and received under the seal of confidence. On one view, the judge had a wide discretion to permit a witness, whether or not a party to the proceedings, to refuse to disclose information where disclosure would be a breach of some ethical or social value and non-disclosure would be unlikely to result in serious injustice in the case in which it was claimed.[235] In *D v National Society for the Prevention of Cruelty to Children*[236] Lords Hailsham and Kilbrandon were of the opinion that such a discretionary power did exist, but Lords Simon and Edmund-Davies disagreed. Lord Simon was of the view that although the judge could exercise a considerable 'moral authority' on the course of a trial, by which he could either seek to persuade counsel not to ask the question or gently guide the witness to overcome his reluctance to answer it, when 'it comes to the forensic crunch . . . it must be law not discretion which is in command'.[237]

CPR rule 32.1(2) has introduced a general exclusionary discretion in civil cases.[238] Rule 32.1 provides as follows:

(1) The court may control the evidence by giving directions as to—
    (a) the issues on which it requires evidence;
    (b) the nature of the evidence which it requires to decide those issues; and
    (c) the way in which the evidence is to be placed before the court.
(2) The court may use its power under this rule to exclude evidence that would otherwise be admissible.
(3) The court may limit cross-examination.

When the court decides to exercise its power to exclude evidence under rule 32.1(2), as when exercising any other power given to it by the rules, it must seek to give effect to the 'overriding objective',[239] which is to enable the court 'to deal with cases justly'.[240] Rule 1.1(2) provides as follows:

(2) Dealing with a case justly includes, so far as is practicable—
    (a) ensuring that the parties are on an equal footing;
    (b) saving expense;
    (c) dealing with the case in ways which are proportionate—
        (i)   to the amount of money involved;
        (ii) to the importance of the case;
        (iii) to the complexity of the issues; and
        (iv) to the financial position of each party;
    (d) ensuring that it is dealt with expeditiously and fairly; and
    (e) allotting to it an appropriate share of the court's resources, while taking into account the need to allot resources to other cases.

[235] 16th Report of the Law Reform Committee, *Privilege in Civil Proceedings* (Cmnd 3472) (1967), para 1.
[236] [1978] AC 171.
[237] [1978] AC 171 at 239.
[238] Including claims allocated to the small claims track: CPR r 27.2(1).
[239] CPR r 1.2.
[240] CPR r 1.1(1).

Rule 32.1(1) invests the court with extraordinarily wide powers, whereby it can override the views of the parties as to which issues call for evidence, the nature of the evidence appropriate to decide the issues, and the way in which the evidence should be given, eg in documentary form rather than orally.

Rule 32.1(2) also confers extremely wide powers: subject to rule 1.1, there are no express limitations as to the extent of the power or the manner of its exercise.[241] As we have seen, civil courts already have the common law power to exclude evidence of marginal relevance.[242] In theory rule 32.1(2) allows the court to exclude evidence even if plainly relevant, but it has been said that the more relevant the evidence is, the more reluctant the court is likely to be to exercise its discretion to exclude and that the power to exclude under rule 32.1(2) should be exercised with great circumspection.[243] However, rule 32.1(2) can be used to exclude peripheral material which is not essential to the just determination of the real issues between the parties[244] and, in appropriate circumstances, evidence that has been obtained illegally or improperly.[245] It can also be used, it is submitted, to restrict the number of witnesses and exclude superfluous evidence.

At common law the judge has a discretion to prevent any questions in cross-examination which in his opinion are unnecessary, improper or oppressive. Cross-examination, it has been held, should be conducted with restraint and a measure of courtesy and consideration to the witness.[246] Rule 32.1(3) supplements the common law powers of the judge and may be used to impose limits on the time permitted for cross-examination.[247] It may also be used to limit cross-examination about a witness's previous convictions. Thus although a witness may be asked about his convictions even where the offence is not one of dishonesty, in order to attack his credit,[248] rule 32.1(3) gives the judge a discretion as to which previous convictions can be put. However, where sitting with a jury, he should be more hesitant to exercise the discretion because it is for the jury to decide what weight to give to such matters in relation to a witness's credibility.[249]

Because circumstances vary infinitely, it is submitted that it would be undesirable for the courts to go beyond the wording of rule 1.1(2) with a view to providing additional guidance as to the way in which the discretion under rule 32.1(2) and (3) should be exercised. It is further submitted that exercise of the discretionary powers should only be impugned on appeal if perverse in the *Wednesbury* sense,[250] ie where the court makes a decision which no reasonable tribunal could have reached.

Criminal cases

That a judge in a criminal trial has a discretion to exclude legally admissible evidence tendered by the prosecution has been accepted for some time[251] and was confirmed by the House

---

[241] *Grobbelaar v Sun Newspapers Ltd* (1999) The Times, 12 Aug, CA.

[242] See 19 above, under **Relevance and admissibility**.

[243] *Great Future International Ltd v Sealand Housing Corporation* (2002) LTL 25 July.

[244] See *McPhilemy v Times Newspapers Ltd* [1999] 3 All ER 775, CA.

[245] See Ch 3, 54 under **Discretion, Civil cases**.

[246] See *Mechanical and General Inventions Co Ltd v Austin* [1935] AC 346 at 360 and generally Ch 7, 192 under **The permitted form of questioning in cross-examination**.

[247] *Rall v Hume* [2001] 3 All ER 248.

[248] See Ch 7, 192 under **The permitted form of questioning in cross-examination**.

[249] *Watson v Chief Constable of Cleveland Police* [2001] All ER (D) 193 (Oct), [2001] EWCA Civ 1547.

[250] *Associated Provincial Picture Houses Ltd v Wednesbury Corpn* [1948] 1 KB 223, CA.

[251] See, eg, *R v Christie* [1914] AC 545, HL.

of Lords in *R v Sang*.[252] The House was of the unanimous albeit obiter view[253] that the judge, as a part of his inherent power and overriding duty in every case to ensure that the accused receives a fair trial, always has a discretion to refuse to admit legally admissible evidence if, in his opinion, its prejudicial effect on the minds of the jury outweighs its true probative value.[254] Exercise of the discretion is a subjective matter,[255] each case turning on its own facts and circumstances.[256] The judge must balance on the one hand the prejudicial effect of the evidence against the accused on the minds of the jury and on the other its weight and value having regard to the purpose for which it is adduced. Where the former is out of all proportion to the latter, the judge should exclude it. In one sense, of course, all relevant evidence adduced by the prosecution is prejudicial to the accused and the greater its probative value, the greater its prejudicial effect. In some cases, however, there will be a serious risk that the jury will attach undue weight to an item of evidence which is, in reality, of dubious reliability or of no more than trifling or minimal probative value, and in these circumstances the judge should exclude. In the words of Roskill J in *R v List*:[257]

> A trial judge always has an overriding duty in every case to secure a fair trial, and if in any particular case he comes to the conclusion that, even though certain evidence is strictly admissible, yet its prejudicial effect once admitted is such as to make it virtually impossible for a dispassionate view of the crucial facts of the case to be thereafter taken by the jury, then the trial judge, in my judgment, should exclude that evidence.

The case law on the basis of which the House of Lords in *R v Sang* came to its conclusion shows the discretion operating in a number of different sets of circumstances in relation to particular kinds of evidence. Their Lordships, however, were of the firm view that the cases were no more than examples of the exercise of a single discretion of general application and not of several specific or limited discretions.[258] Moreover, it was recognized that the existing cases were not the only ones in which the discretion could be exercised. Lord Salmon said:[259]

> I recognize that there may have been no categories of cases, other than those to which I have referred, in which technically admissible evidence proffered by the Crown has been rejected by the court on the ground that it would make the trial unfair. I cannot, however, accept that a judge's undoubted duty to ensure that the accused has a fair trial is confined to such cases. In my opinion the category of such cases is not and never can be closed except by statute.

There has been much scope for exercise of the discretion in relation to otherwise admissible evidence of the accused's bad character. For example, where the accused became liable to cross-

---

[252] [1980] AC 402.

[253] A view affirmed by Lord Roskill in *Morris v Beardmore* [1981] AC 446, HL at 469.

[254] This 'fair trial' discretion may be exercised not only in the case of evidence the prejudicial effect of which outweighs its probative value, but also in the case of evidence obtained from the accused, after the commission of the offence charged, by improper or unfair means: see per Lords Diplock, Fraser, and Scarman at 436, 450, and 456 respectively. See Ch 3.

[255] Per Lord Fraser at 450.

[256] Per Lord Scarman at 456. See also per Lord Guest in *Selvey v DPP* [1970] AC 304 at 352: 'If it is suggested that the exercise of this discretion may be whimsical and depend on the individual idiosyncrasies of the judge, this is inevitable where it is a question of discretion.'

[257] [1966] 1 WLR 9 at 12.

[258] Per Lords Scarman and Fraser at 452 and 447 respectively.

[259] At 445. See also per Lord Dilhorne at 438.

examination about his previous convictions and bad character under section 1(3)(ii) of the Criminal Evidence Act 1898, ie where the nature or conduct of the defence was such as to involve imputations on the character of the prosecutor or witnesses for the prosecution (see now section 101(1)(g) of the Criminal Justice Act 2003), the judge could exercise his discretion to disallow it.

> He may feel that even though the position is established in law, still the putting of such questions as to the character of the accused person may be fraught with results which immeasurably outweigh the result of questions put by the defence and which make a fair trial of the accused person almost impossible.[260]

There is also scope for exercise of the discretion in relation to hearsay. In *Grant v The State*[261] it was said to be clear that the judge in a criminal trial has an overriding discretion to exclude evidence judged to be unfair to the accused in the sense that it will put him at an unfair disadvantage or deprive him unfairly of the ability to defend himself, and that conscientiously exercised it affords the accused an important safeguard where statute permits the admission of hearsay.

A judge can also exercise his discretion to exclude evidence otherwise admissible under section 27(3) of the Theft Act 1968. Under that subsection, where a person is charged with handling stolen goods and evidence is given of his possession of the goods, evidence that he has within the five years preceding the date of the offence charged been convicted of theft or handling stolen goods is admissible to prove that he knew or believed the goods to be stolen. The trial judge has a discretion to disallow the admission of such evidence, albeit strictly admissible, if, on the facts of the particular case, there is a risk of injustice. This may occur, for example, where possession is in issue in the case and it will be difficult, therefore, for the jury to appreciate that the evidence is relevant not to that issue but only to the issue of guilty knowledge.[262]

The discretion can also be used to exclude an out-of-court accusation directed at the accused which is admissible in evidence against him because by his conduct or demeanour it is possible to infer that he accepted, in whole or in part, the truth of the accusation made. Again, in these circumstances, the judge may exercise his discretion to exclude where the prejudicial effect of the evidence in the minds of the jury is out of all proportion to its true evidential value.[263]

Having considered some specific examples, it remains to note two matters of general importance relating to the exercise of the discretion now under discussion. First, the discretion may only be exercised to exclude evidence on which the prosecution, as opposed to any co-accused, proposes to rely. There is no discretion to exclude, at the request of one co-accused, evidence tendered by another. This principle, and the description of it appearing in the third edition of this work, were approved by the Privy Council in *Lobban v R*.[264] In that case L and R were charged with three murders. R, under caution, made a 'mixed' statement, ie a statement which contained admissions as well as an exculpatory explanation. An integral part of the exculpatory explanation implicated L by name. The prosecution tendered R's statement for the truth of its contents against R—it was no evidence against L. Counsel for L submitted that the trial

---

[260] Per Singleton J in *R v Jenkins* (1945) 31 Cr App Rep 1 at 15, approved in *Selvey v DPP* [1970] AC 304, HL.

[261] [2006] 2 WLR 835, PC.

[262] *R v List* [1966] 1 WLR 9, Assizes, a decision under s 43(1) of the Larceny Act 1916, which was repealed by the Theft Act 1968 but re-enacted, with some modification, in s 27(3). The decision was approved in *R v Herron* [1967] 1 QB 107, CCA. See further Ch 17.

[263] See per Lord Moulton in *R v Christie* [1914] AC 545, HL at 559.

[264] [1995] 2 All ER 602, PC.

judge should have exercised his discretion to edit R's statement so as to exclude the parts which implicated L on the basis that the prejudice to L by allowing the whole statement to be admitted outweighed the relevance of the disputed material to the defence of R. The Privy Council held that no such discretion existed—counsel's submission, if accepted, would result in a serious derogation of an accused's liberty to defend himself by such legitimate means as he thinks it wise to employ. It was held that the discretionary power applies only to evidence on which the prosecution propose to rely. Although R's statement was *tendered* by the prosecution, the disputed material supported R's defence and the prosecution were not entitled to rely on it as evidence against L. Thus, although a trial judge has a discretion to exclude or edit evidence tendered by the prosecution which is wholly inculpatory and probative of the case against one co-accused on the ground that it is unduly prejudicial against another co-accused, there is no discretion to exclude the exculpatory part of a 'mixed' statement on which one co-accused wishes to rely on the grounds that it implicates another. One remedy to the latter situation is to order separate trials, but if that is not done then the interests of the implicated co-accused must be protected by the most explicit direction by the judge to the effect that the statement of the one co-accused is not evidence against the other.[265]

The second matter to note is that because exercise of the discretion is, as we have seen, a subjective matter, each case turning on its own peculiar facts, it is difficult to appeal successfully against a judge's decision not to exclude. Thus although an appellate court will interfere with exercise of the discretion if there is no material on which the trial judge could properly have arrived at his decision, or where he has erred in principle,[266] it is not enough that the appellate court thinks that it would have exercised the discretion differently. However, the appellate courts have from time to time set out guidelines for exercise of the discretion in relation to various types of evidence.[267] This assists judges. It also assists defence counsel in advising and deciding tactics, to predict whether the discretion will be exercised.

The discretionary common law power to exclude evidence on the basis that its prejudicial effect outweighs its probative value has now been supplemented by section 78(1) of the 1984 Act, which provides that:

> the court may refuse to allow evidence on which the prosecution propose to rely to be given if it appears to the court that, having regard to all the circumstances, including the circumstances in which the evidence was obtained, the admission of the evidence would have such an adverse effect on the fairness of the proceedings that the court ought not to admit it.

Section 78(1) is of general application. Other statutory provisions empower a criminal court to exclude, in the exercise of its discretion, specific varieties of otherwise admissible evidence.[268]

[265] But see also *R v Thompson* [1995] 2 Cr App R 589, CA: without a discretion to exclude evidence which is relevant and therefore admissible in relation to an accused but inadmissible and prejudicial in relation to a co-accused, the only safeguard is the cumbersome device of separate trials. The court observed that this seemed undesirable and that it might be preferable to allow a discretion where the prejudice is substantial and the evidence is of only limited benefit to the accused.

[266] See per Viscount Dilhorne in *Selvey v DPP* [1970] AC 304, HL at 342 and per Lord Lane CJ in *R v Powell* [1986] 1 All ER 193, CA at 197.

[267] See, eg, per Lawton LJ in *R v Britzman; R v Hall* [1983] 1 All ER 369, CA at 373–4.

[268] See, in the case of hearsay, s 126 of the Criminal Justice Act 2003 (Ch 10), which expressly preserves the general power to exclude under s 78; and in the case of evidence of the bad character of the accused, s 101(3) of the Criminal Justice Act 2003 (Ch 17), which also, it seems, provides protection additional to s 78(1): see *R v Highton* [2005] 1 WLR 3472.

Although section 78(1) is formally cast in the form of a discretion ('the court may'), the objective criterion whether 'admission . . . would have such an adverse effect on the fairness of the proceedings' in truth imports a judgment whether, in the light of the criterion of fairness, the court ought to admit the evidence.[269]

A simple example of the application of section 78(1) is *R v O'Connor*[270] B and C were jointly charged in one count with having conspired to obtain property by deception. B pleaded guilty and C not guilty. The evidence of B's conviction was then admitted at the trial of C under section 74 of the 1984 Act to prove that B had committed the offence charged.[271] The Court of Appeal held that the conviction should have been excluded under section 78 because evidence of B's admission of the offence charged might have led the jury to infer that C in his turn must have conspired with B.[272]

Section 78(1) operates without prejudice to the discretionary common law power to exclude. Section 82(3) of the 1984 Act provides that 'Nothing in this Part of this Act shall prejudice any power of a court to exclude evidence (whether from preventing questions from being put or otherwise) at its discretion'. The terms of section 78(1) are clearly wide enough to apply to items of prosecution evidence already subject to the common law discretion[273]—and the weighing of probative value against prejudicial effect can be an important factor in exercising the discretion under section 78(1)[274]—but section 78(1) is not confined to such cases.

Section 78(1) directs the court, when considering exercise of the discretion, to have regard to all the circumstances, 'including the circumstances in which the evidence was obtained'. Thus, although it is clear that section 78(1) can be applied by a court in the absence of any illegality or impropriety,[275] the chief importance of the subsection lies in its potential for the exclusion of evidence illegally or improperly obtained. That topic is considered in Chapter 3.

Applications to exclude evidence in reliance on section 78(1) should be made before the evidence is adduced: the section applies to evidence on which the prosecution 'propose' to rely.[276]

Proof of birth, death, age, convictions, and acquittals

Birth and death

The normal and easiest way of proving a person's birth or death is by (a) producing to the court a certified copy of an entry in the register of births (deaths),[277] which is admissible under an exception to the hearsay rule[278] and admissible, therefore, as evidence of the truth of its contents; *and* (b) adducing some evidence to identify the person whose birth

---

[269] Per Lord Steyn in *R v Hasan* [2005] 2 AC 467, HL at [53]. See also per Auld LJ in *R v Chalkley and Jeffries* [1998] 2 All ER 155, CA at 178.

[270] (1986) 85 Cr App R 298, CA. See also *R v Curry* [1988] Crim LR 527, CA; *R v Kempster* (1989) 90 Cr App R 14, CA; and *R v Mattison* [1990] Crim LR 117, CA (see Ch 21).

[271] See Ch 21.

[272] Cf *R v Lunnon* [1988] Crim LR 456, CA, and see also *R v Robertson; R v Golder* [1987] 3 All ER 231, CA (see Ch 21).

[273] See *Matto v Crown Court at Wolverhampton* [1987] RTR 337, DC, per Woolf LJ at 346: '[s 78] certainly does not reduce the discretion of the court to exclude unfair evidence which existed at common law. Indeed, in my view in any case where the evidence could properly be excluded at common law, it can certainly be excluded under s 78.'

[274] Per Lord Lane CJ in *R v Quinn* [1990] Crim LR 581, CA.

[275] *R v Samuel* [1988] QB 615, CA; *R v O'Leary* (1988) 87 Cr App R 387, CA at 391; *R v Brine* [1992] Crim LR 122, CA.

[276] *R v Sat-Bhambra* (1988) 88 Cr App Rep 55, CA.

[277] See s 34 of the Births and Deaths Registration Act 1953.

[278] See generally Chs 10–12.

(death) is in question with the person named in the birth (death) certificate.[279] Proof of birth or death may also be effected by the testimony of someone present at the time of birth (death), by hearsay statements admissible under either the Civil Evidence Act 1995 or the Criminal Justice Act 2003[280] or, in proceedings in which a question of pedigree is directly in issue, by a declaration as to pedigree made by a deceased blood relation or spouse of a blood relation.[281] A person's death may also be proved in reliance on the presumption of death, which is considered in Chapter 22, or by the testimony of someone who saw the corpse and was capable of identifying it as that of the person whose death is in question.

Age

The date of a person's birth being contained in his or her birth certificate, the normal way of proving a person's age is by (a) producing to the court a certified copy of an entry in the register of births, which, as we have seen, is admissible as evidence of the truth of its contents; *and* (b) adducing some evidence identifying the person whose age is in question with the person named in the birth certificate. A person's age may also be proved by the testimony of someone present at the time of his or her birth, by inference from his or her appearance,[282] by hearsay statements admissible by statute, and by declarations as to pedigree.

Convictions and acquittals

Section 73 of the 1984 Act, which superseded a variety of outdated statutory provisions, is a modernized provision for the proof of convictions and acquittals by means of a certificate signed by an appropriate court officer together with evidence identifying the person whose conviction (acquittal) is in question with the person named in the certificate. It provides as follows:

(1) Where in any proceedings[283] the fact that a person has in the United Kingdom been convicted or acquitted of an offence otherwise than by a Service court is admissible in evidence, it may be proved by producing a certificate of conviction or, as the case may be, of acquittal relating to that offence, and proving that the person named in the certificate as having been convicted or acquitted of the offence is the person whose conviction or acquittal of the offence is to be proved.

(2) For the purposes of this section a certificate of conviction or of acquittal—

    (a) shall, as regards a conviction or acquittal on indictment, consist of a certificate, signed by the proper officer of the court where the conviction or acquittal took place, giving the substance and effect (omitting the formal parts) of the indictment and of the conviction or acquittal; and

---

[279] See also s 1 of the Evidence (Foreign, Dominion and Colonial Documents) Act 1933 whereby an Order in Council may be made providing for the proof by authorized copy of extracts from properly kept public registers kept under the authority of the law of the country in question and recognized by the courts of that country as authentic records. Concerning births (deaths) on board ship, see the Merchant Shipping (Returns of Births and Deaths) Regulations 1979, made under s 75 of the Merchant Shipping Act 1970.

[280] See Chs 10 and 11.

[281] See Ch 12.

[282] See, eg, s 99 of the Children and Young Persons Act 1933 and s 80(3) of the Criminal Justice Act 1948.

[283] 'Proceedings' means criminal proceedings including proceedings before a court-martial or Courts-Martial Appeal Court.

(b) shall, as regards a conviction or acquittal on a summary trial, consist of a copy of the conviction or of the dismissal of the information, signed by the proper officer of the court where the conviction or acquittal took place or by the proper officer of the court, if any, to which a memorandum of the conviction or acquittal was sent;

and a document purporting to be a duly signed certificate of conviction or acquittal under this section shall be taken to be such a certificate unless the contrary is proved.

(3) In subsection (2) above 'proper officer' means—

(a) in relation to a magistrates' court in England and Wales, the designated officer for the court; and

(b) in relation to any other court, the clerk of the court, his deputy or any other person having custody of the court record.

The section contains a saving for 'any other authorised manner of proving a conviction or acquittal'.[284] The issue of identity in section 73(1) is a question of fact for the jury.[285] In *Pattison v DPP*[286] the following general principles were said to apply when section 73(1) is relied on by the prosecution to prove the conviction of an accused.

(a) Identity must be proved to the criminal standard.

(b) This may be effected by a formal or informal admission,[287] by evidence of fingerprints, or by the evidence of someone present in court at the time.

(c) There is no prescribed means of proof: identity can be proved by any admissible evidence, for example a match between the personal details of the accused and those on the certificate.

(d) Even if the personal details, such as the name, are not uncommon, a match will be sufficient for a prima facie case.

(e) The failure of the accused to give any contradictory evidence can be taken into account and may give rise to an adverse inference under section 35(2) of the Criminal Justice and Public Order Act 1994.

ADDITIONAL READING

Aitken and Taroni, 'Fundamentals of Statistical Evidence—a Primer for Legal Professionals' (2008) 12 E&P 181.

Anderson and Twining, *Analysis of Evidence* (London and Boston, 1991).

Choo, 'The Notion of Relevance' [1993] *Crim LR* 114.

Eggleston, *Evidence, Proof and Probability* (2nd edn, London, 1983).

Elliott, '*Brutus v Cozens*; Decline and Fall' [1989] *Crim LR* 323.

Grove, *The Juryman's Tale* (London, 1998).

Heaton-Armstrong et al (eds), *Analysing Witness Testimony* (London, 1999).

Wigmore, *The Principles of Judicial Proof* (2nd edn, Boston, 1931) 17–31.

Young, 'Summing-up to Juries in Criminal cases—What Jury Research says about Current Rules and Practice' [2003] *Crim LR* 665.

---

[284] Section 73(4).

[285] *R v Burns* [2006] 1 WLR 1273, CA and *R v Lewendon* [2006] 2 Cr App R 294, CA.

[286] [2006] 2 All ER 317, QBD.

[287] As to the former, see Criminal Justice Act 1967, s 10, Ch 22; as to the latter, see Ch 13.

Evidence obtained by illegal or unfair means

3

Key Issues

- When and why should relevant evidence obtained illegally, improperly, or unfairly be admitted at trial?

- When and why should relevant evidence obtained illegally, improperly, or unfairly be excluded at trial?

- Should the law of evidence admit or exclude relevant evidence obtained by (a) torture; (b) inhuman or degrading treatment; (c) entrapment; and (d) undercover operations?

- Should decisions on the foregoing issues be governed by rules of law or the exercise of judicial discretion?

- When and why should the law of evidence, in dealing with the foregoing issues, differentiate between criminal and civil cases?

This chapter concerns the circumstances in which relevant evidence can be excluded, as a matter of law or discretion, on the grounds that it was obtained illegally, improperly, or unfairly. It also considers a related matter, the circumstances in which criminal proceedings should be stayed as an abuse of the court's process on the grounds of entrapment.

Evidence may be obtained illegally, for example by a crime, tort, or breach of contract, or in contravention of statutory or other provisions governing the powers and duties of the police or others involved in investigating crime. Evidence may also be obtained improperly or unfairly, for example by trickery, deception, bribes, threats, or inducements. At one extreme, the view could be taken that evidence which is relevant and otherwise admissible should not be excluded because of the means by which it was obtained, whether illegal, improper, or unfair; to exclude it would, in some cases, result in injustice including the acquittal of the guilty. On this view, all evidence which is necessary to enable justice to be done would be admitted; and those responsible for the illegality or impropriety could be variously prosecuted (in the case of crime), sued (in the case of actionable wrongs), or disciplined (in the case of conduct amounting to breach of some statutory, professional, or other code of conduct). The view at the other extreme would be that illegally or improperly obtained evidence should always be excluded; to admit it might encourage the obtaining of evidence by such means or at any rate bring the administration of justice into disrepute. On this view, all such evidence would be excluded, even if this would sometimes result in injustice, including the guilty going free, in order that those responsible for the illegality or impropriety are in future compelled to respect, and deterred from invading, the civil liberties of the citizen.

The modern law of evidence in this country represents a compromise between these two extreme views. Thus although, generally speaking, it reflects the first view in relation to admissibility *as a matter of law*, it also empowers the trial judge to exclude *as a matter of discretion*. In civil cases, the discretion to exclude was introduced under the Civil Procedure Rules (CPR) and has generated little case law. In criminal cases, there is discretion to exclude prosecution evidence both at common law and under section 78(1) of the Police and Criminal Evidence Act 1984 (the 1984 Act). As to the former, the discretion is clearly established in relation to admissions and confessions, but in relation to other types of evidence is of unclear scope and appears to operate only in relation to material which may be regarded as analogous to, or the physical equivalent of, an admission or confession. Under section 78(1), prosecution evidence obtained by illegal or unfair means may be excluded where it would have such an adverse effect on the fairness of the proceedings that the court ought not to admit it. The court will consider the nature of the illegality or unfairness and may also have regard to the general and specific rights set out in Article 6 of the European Convention on Human Rights. However, almost all of the voluminous case law to which section 78(1) has given rise indicates that the discretionary power should only be exercised where the illegality or unfairness has affected the reliability of the evidence in question and, thereby, the fairness of the proceedings. Thus although it has been said that the fact that the police acted *mala fide* can be taken into account, which suggests that at least part of the rationale for exclusion is promotion of the integrity of the criminal process, it has also been held that the discretion should not be used to discipline the police. Furthermore, where the illegality or unfairness has *not* affected the reliability of the evidence, the courts have not been prepared, either at common law or under section 78(1), to consider the exercise of its powers by balancing the reliability or cogency of the evidence together with the desirability of convicting a criminal against other important public policy objectives such as the desirability of adhering to provisions designed to protect the rights of a suspect and of promoting the integrity of the criminal justice system as a whole by preventing it from being brought into disrepute.[1] However, where the conduct of the police has been so seriously improper as to bring the administration of justice into disrepute, or a prosecution would affront the public conscience, as when police conduct brings about state-created crime, then rather than hold a trial and exclude prosecution evidence, the criminal proceedings will be stayed.[2]

Law

Subject to exceptions, the rules of English *law* make no provision for the exclusion of relevant evidence on the grounds that it was obtained illegally or improperly. One exception concerns privileged documents. Although there is a general rule allowing secondary evidence of privileged documents to be adduced, even though obtained illegally or improperly,[3] a party to litigation who obtains by a trick documents belonging to the other party and brought into court by him will not be permitted to adduce copies of those documents, because the public interest in the ascertainment of truth in litigation is outweighed by the public interest that litigants should be able to bring their documents into court without fear that they may be filched by their opponents.[4] A second exception relates to a confession made by an accused that was or may have been obtained by oppression or in consequence of anything said or done which was likely, in the circumstances, to render unreliable any confession which might be made by him in consequence thereof.[5] Oppression, for these purposes, is defined to include torture,[6] in respect of which there is a broader common law exclusionary principle. In *A v Secretary of State for the Home Department (No 2)*[7] it was held that as a matter of constitutional principle evidence obtained by torture may not lawfully be admitted against a party to proceedings in a British court, irrespective of where, or by whom, or on whose authority the torture was inflicted. Such evidence falls to be excluded both at common law and in accordance with the European Convention on Human Rights, which takes account of the United Nations Convention Against Torture and Other Cruel, Inhuman or Degrading Treatment or Punishment 1987.[8] Evidence obtained by inhuman or degrading treatment contrary to the Convention, and in breach of the privilege against self-incrimination, may also fall to be

---

[1] Cf the position in Australia and other Commonwealth jurisdictions: see Choo and Nash, 'Improperly obtained evidence in the Commonwealth: lessons for England and Wales?' (2007) 11 *E&P* 75. For an interesting analysis of the question whether to admit illegally obtained evidence and the shortcomings of the exclusionary principle, see AAS Zuckerman, *The Principles of Criminal Evidence* (Oxford, 1989) Ch 16. See also P Mirfield, *Silence, Confessions and Improperly Obtained Evidence* (Oxford, 1997).

[2] *R v Looseley; Attorney General's Reference (No 3 of 2000)* [2001] 1 WLR 2060, HL.

[3] See per Parke B in *Lloyd v Mostyn* (1842) 10 M&W 478, applied by Lindley MR in *Calcraft v Guest* [1898] 1 QB 759 at 764, CA. See Ch 20.

[4] *ITC Film Distributors v Video Exchange Ltd* [1982] Ch 431. Cf *R v Tompkins* (1977) 67 Cr App R 181, CA. See Ch 20.

[5] Police and Criminal Evidence Act 1984, s 76(2). See Ch 13. See also s 17 of the Regulation of Investigatory Powers Act 2000, which renders inadmissible evidence which tends to suggest the commission of an offence of intentional interception, at any place in the United Kingdom, of any communication in the course of its transmission by means of a public postal service or by means of a public telecommunication system.

[6] Police and Criminal Evidence Act 1984, s 76(8).

[7] [2005] 3 WLR 1249, HL.

[8] See per Lord Bingham at [51] and [52]. The definition of torture for these purposes appears to be that adopted in s 134 of the Criminal Justice Act 1988, namely the infliction of severe pain or suffering by a public official in the performance or purported performance of his official duties: see per Lord Hoffmann at [97].

excluded.[9] Incriminating real evidence recovered as a direct result of torture should always be excluded, but evidence secured as an indirect result of statements obtained by inhuman treatment may be admitted if it is only accessory in securing a conviction and its admission does not compromise defence rights.[10]

Subject to the exceptions, the law is accurately represented by the following words of Crompton J in *R v Leatham*:[11] 'It matters not how you get it; if you steal it even, it would be admissible in evidence.' Thus evidence remains admissible in law if obtained by the use of *agent provocateurs*,[12] or by invasion of privacy,[13] or by the unlawful search of persons or premises.

In *Jones v Owens*[14] a constable, in unlawfully searching the accused, found a number of young salmon. The evidence was admitted on a subsequent charge of unlawful fishing on the grounds that to exclude evidence obtained by illegal means 'would be a dangerous obstacle to the administration of justice'. In *Kuruma, Son of Kaniu v R*[15] the accused was charged with the unlawful possession of ammunition which had been found in his pocket by officers who were of insufficiently senior rank to have carried out the search. Evidence of the search was admitted and the accused was convicted. His appeal to the Privy Council was dismissed. Lord Goddard CJ was of the opinion that where evidence is relevant and admissible the court is not concerned with how it was obtained. The same proposition was readily accepted by the Divisional Court in *Jeffrey v Black*.[16] The accused, who was charged with unlawful possession of cannabis, was originally arrested for stealing a sandwich. Police officers, without the accused's consent and without a search warrant, then searched his home and found the cannabis which formed the subject matter of the charge. The magistrates excluded evidence of the finding of the cannabis on the grounds that it had been obtained as a result of an illegal search and dismissed the charge. An appeal by way of case stated was allowed.

Discretion

Civil cases

Prior to the introduction of the Civil Procedure Rules, such authority as there was suggested that in civil proceedings there was no discretion to exclude evidence obtained illegally or improperly.[17]

Under CPR rule 32.1(2) the court may now exclude evidence that would otherwise be admissible, and in deciding whether to do so must seek to give effect to the overriding objective of enabling the court to deal with cases justly.[18] It is submitted that, in appropriate circumstances, therefore, the court may exercise the discretionary power to exclude evidence which,

---

[9] *Jalloh v Germany* [2007] Crim LR 717, ECHR.

[10] *Gäfgen v Germany*, Application No 22978/05, 30 June 2008.

[11] (1861) 8 Cox CC 498 at 501.

[12] *R v Sang* [1980] AC 402, HL.

[13] *R v Khan (Sultan)* [1997] AC 558, HL.

[14] (1870) 34 JP 759.

[15] [1955] AC 197, PC.

[16] [1978] QB 490.

[17] See per Lord Denning MR in *Helliwell v Piggott-Sims* [1980] FSR 582.

[18] See Ch 2, 43 under **Exclusionary discretion.**

although relevant, has been obtained illegally or improperly. In *Jones v University of Warwick*,[19] a claim for damages for personal injuries, the defendant was allowed to introduce a video of the claimant obtained by trespass and in breach of Article 8 of the European Convention on Human Rights (the right of respect for private and family life). Inquiry agents acting for the defendant's insurers had gained access to the claimant's home by deception and had filmed her without her knowledge. It was held that the court should consider two conflicting public interests, on the one hand the achieving of justice in the particular case and on the other, considering the effect of its decision upon litigation generally, the risk that if the improper conduct goes uncensored, improper practices of the type in question will be encouraged. The weight to be attached to each public interest will vary according to the circumstances. The significance of the evidence will differ as will the gravity of the breach of Article 8, and the decision will depend on all the circumstances. In the case before it, the Court of Appeal held that the conduct of the insurers was not so outrageous that the defence should be struck out and that it would be artificial and undesirable to exclude the evidence, which would involve the instruction of fresh medical experts from whom relevant evidence would have to be concealed. However, it was also held that the conduct of the insurers was improper and unjustified and that the trial judge should take it into account when deciding the appropriate order for costs.[20]

Criminal cases

The background

That a judge, in criminal proceedings, has a discretionary power to exclude otherwise admissible evidence on the grounds that it was obtained improperly or unfairly was, until *R v Sang*,[21] only clearly established in relation to evidence of admissions and confessions. The power to exclude, as a matter of discretion, an otherwise admissible admission or confession is a large and complex topic which is considered separately in Chapter 13. Admissions and confessions apart, there was also an unbroken series of dicta from a variety of impressive sources to suggest that in criminal proceedings the trial judge also has a general discretion to exclude evidence tendered by the prosecution which has been obtained oppressively, improperly, or unfairly[22] or as a result of the activities of an *agent provocateur*.[23] However, despite these weighty dicta, this discretion was rarely exercised. A very rare reported example is *R v Payne*[24] where the accused, charged with drunken driving, agreed to a medical examination to see if he was suffering from any illness or disability on the understanding that the doctor would

---

[19] [2003] 3 All ER 760, CA.

[20] See also *Niemietz v Germany* (1992) 16 EHRR 97 and *Halford v UK* (1997) 24 EHRR 523.

[21] [1980] AC 402, HL.

[22] See per Lord Goddard CJ in *Kuruma, Son of Kaniu v R* [1955] AC 197, PC at 203–4 (evidence obtained 'by a trick'); per Lord Parker CJ in *Callis v Gunn* [1964] 1 QB 495, DC at 505 (evidence obtained 'oppressively, by false representations, by a trick, by threats, by bribes, anything of that sort'); and per Lord Widgery CJ in *Jeffrey v Black* [1978] QB 490, DC at 497–8 (exceptional cases where 'not only have the police officers entered without authority, but they have been guilty of trickery, or they have misled someone, or they have been oppressive, or they have been unfair, or in other respects they have behaved in a manner which is morally reprehensible'). See also per Lord Hodson in *King v R* [1969] 1 AC 304, PC at 319.

[23] See per Lord McDermott CJ in *R v Murphy* [1965] NI 138, C-MAC, a case decided before the rejection of entrapment as a defence. See also *R v Foulder, Foulkes and Johns* [1973] Crim LR 45; *R v Burnett and Lee* [1973] Crim LR 748; and *R v Ameer and Lucas* [1977] Crim LR 104, CA.

[24] [1963] 1 WLR 637.

not examine him to assess his fitness to drive. At the trial the doctor gave evidence of the accused's unfitness to drive and the Court of Criminal Appeal quashed the conviction on the grounds that the trial judge should have exercised his discretion to exclude the doctor's evidence. In *R v Sang*[25] Lords Diplock, Fraser, and Scarman regarded the decision as based on the maxim *nemo tenetur se ipsum prodere* ('no man is to be compelled to incriminate himself') and analogous, therefore, to cases in which an accused is unfairly induced to confess to, or make a damaging admission in respect of, an offence.[26]

In *R v Sang* the House of Lords held that the judicial discretion to exclude admissible evidence does not extend to excluding evidence of a crime on the grounds that it was instigated by an *agent provocateur*, because if it did it would amount to a procedural device whereby the judge could avoid the substantive law under which it is clearly established that there is no defence of entrapment.[27] The primary importance of *R v Sang*, however, is the obiter answer given to the certified point of law of general importance, namely 'Does a trial judge have a discretion to refuse to allow evidence, being evidence other than evidence of an admission, to be given in any circumstances in which such evidence is relevant and of more than minimal probative value?' On that wider issue, the House was of the unanimous opinion that: (i) a trial judge always has a discretion to exclude prosecution evidence where its prejudicial effect outweighs its probative value;[28] but (ii) since the court is not concerned with how evidence sought to be adduced by the prosecution has been obtained, but with how it is used by the prosecution at the trial, a judge has no discretion to refuse to admit admissible evidence on the grounds that it was obtained by improper or unfair means except in the case of admissions, confessions, and evidence obtained from the accused after the commission of the offence. Although the judgment in this respect was obiter, Lord Roskill declared later that it would be a retrograde step to enlarge the narrow limits of, or to engraft an exception on, the discretion to exclude as defined in *R v Sang*.[29] Unfortunately, however, the scope of the discretion defined, despite their Lordships' apparent unanimity, is far from clear, particularly insofar as it extends to 'evidence obtained from the accused after the commission of the offence'. For Lord Diplock, that phrase seems to refer to evidence tantamount to a self-incriminating admission obtained from the accused by means which would justify a judge in excluding an actual confession which had the like self-incriminating effect[30] and there is no discretion to exclude evidence discovered as the result of an illegal search.[31] For Lord Salmon, the decision whether to exclude being dependent upon the 'infinitely variable' facts and circumstances of each particular case, the category of cases in which evidence could be rejected on the grounds that it would make a trial unfair was not closed and never could be closed except by statute.[32] Lord Fraser appears to

---

[25] [1980] AC 402.

[26] At 435, 449 and 455 respectively. Cf *R v McDonald* [1991] Crim LR 122, CA, a decision under s 78 of the Police and Criminal Evidence Act 1984: it is not unfair for a psychiatrist to give evidence of an admission made by the accused on a non-medical issue in the course of a psychiatric examination. *R v McDonald* was followed in *R v Gayle* [1994] Crim LR 679, CA and, in the case of confessions to probation officers, *R v Elleray* [2003] 2 Cr App R 165, CA.

[27] See *R v McEvilly*; *R v Lee* (1973) 60 Cr App R 150, CA; *R v Mealey*; *R v Sheridan* (1974) 60 Cr App Rep 59, CA. As to the discretion to exclude, however, see now *R v Looseley* [2001] 1 WLR 2060, considered under s 78 of the Police and Criminal Evidence Act 1984, below.

[28] See Ch 2, 42 under **Judicial discretion**.

[29] *Morris v Beardmore* [1981] AC 446, HL at 469.

[30] See also *R v Payne* [1963] 1 WLR 637, CCA, above.

[31] [1980] AC 402 at 436. See also *R v Adams* [1980] QB 575, CA, below.

[32] [1980] AC 402 at 445. See also per Lord Fraser at 450.

have understood the phrase as referring to evidence and documents obtained from an accused or from premises occupied by him, but also said that their Lordships' decision would leave judges with a discretion to be exercised in accordance with their individual views of what is unfair, oppressive, or morally reprehensible.[33] For Lord Scarman, it referred exclusively to the obtaining of evidence from the *accused*.[34]

The subsequent case law has done little to clarify the meaning of the phrase 'evidence obtained from the accused after the commission of the offence' but has put a major gloss on *R v Sang* to the effect that the discretion should not be exercised if those who obtained such evidence unlawfully did so on the basis of a bona fide mistake as to their powers. In *R v Trump*[35] the Court of Appeal, while acknowledging that the phrase was not fully considered by the House, treated it as referring to cases analogous to improperly obtained admissions. The accused was convicted of driving while unfit through drink. Following an unlawful arrest, a specimen of blood was obtained without the accused's consent within the meaning of section 7 of the Road Traffic Act 1972. It was held that although the giving of blood by the accused was very close to an oral admission by him that he had drunk to excess, and was therefore subject to the discretion, the judge would have erred if he had excluded the evidence because, although the sample was given as a result of a threat, the police officer in question was acting in good faith and the evidence could not undermine the fairness of the trial. On a similar charge in *Fox v Chief Constable of Gwent*[36] the House of Lords held that evidence of a breath specimen obtained by officers acting in good faith and in accordance with the statutory procedure was not inadmissible merely because the accused had been unlawfully arrested. Lord Fraser said:[37]

> Of course, if the appellant had been lured to the police station by some trick or deception, or if the police officers had behaved oppressively towards the appellant, the justices' jurisdiction to exclude otherwise admissible evidence recognized in *R v Sang* might have come into play. But there is nothing of that sort suggested here. The police officers did no more than make a bona fide mistake as to their powers.[38]

In *R v Khan (Sultan)*[39] it was held that evidence of an incriminating conversation obtained by means of a secret electronic surveillance device did not fall within the category of admissions, confessions, and other evidence obtained from the accused after the commission of the offence, on the basis that the accused had not been 'induced' to make the recorded admissions.

In *R v Apicella*[40] the accused was convicted on three counts of rape. Each of the victims had contracted an unusual strain of gonorrhoea. The accused, whilst held on remand, was suspected by the prison doctor to be suffering from gonorrhoea. The doctor, for solely therapeutic reasons, called in a consultant who took a sample of body fluid in order to enable diagnosis. The consultant assumed that the accused was consenting. In fact, he submitted because he had been told by a prison officer that he had no choice. The sample showed that the accused

[33] [1980] AC 402 at 450.
[34] ibid at 456.
[35] (1979) 70 Cr App R 300, CA at 302.
[36] [1985] 3 All ER 392, HL.
[37] Ibid at 397.
[38] Applied in *Gull v Scarborough* [1987] RTR 261n. See also *DPP v Wilson* [1991] RTR 284.
[39] [1997] AC 558, HL.
[40] (1985) 82 Cr App R 295, CA.

was suffering from the same strain of gonorrhoea as the victims, and the prosecution called evidence to that effect. The Court of Appeal flatly rejected a submission that the evidence was the physical equivalent of an oral confession.[41] It was held that use of the evidence was not unfair and the judge correct in the exercise of his discretion not to exclude it.[42]

Section 78 of the Police and Criminal Evidence Act 1984
Section 78 of the 1984 Act provides as follows:

(1) In any proceedings the court may refuse to allow evidence on which the prosecution proposes to rely to be given if it appears to the court that, having regard to all the circumstances, including the circumstances in which the evidence was obtained, the admission of the evidence would have such an adverse effect on the fairness of the proceedings that the court ought not to admit it.

(2) Nothing in this section shall prejudice any rule of law requiring a court to exclude evidence.

The effect of section 78(2) is that if an item of evidence is inadmissible by virtue of any of the exclusionary rules of evidence, it *must* be excluded. As to the discretionary power to exclude under section 78(1), the question of exclusion may be raised by any accused against whom the evidence is to be used. Section 78(1) confers a power in terms wide enough for its exercise on the court's own motion.[43] However, if the accused is represented by an apparently competent advocate, who does not raise the issue, perhaps for tactical reasons, the judge is under no duty to exercise the discretion of his own motion, even in the case of a flagrant abuse of police power, although he may make a pertinent enquiry of the advocate in the jury's absence.[44] Section 78(1) refers to evidence on which the prosecution *proposes* to rely. Thus, in *R v Harwood*[45] it was doubted whether section 78(1) empowers a judge to exclude evidence, after it has been adduced, in the absence of any submission to exclude before it was adduced. At trials on indictment, if there is a dispute as to the circumstances in which the evidence was obtained, it would seem to be necessary to hold a trial within a trial.[46] Thus if the accused disputes that he was cautioned, it is the duty of the judge to hold a *voir dire* and make a finding on the issue.[47] However, concerning the admissibility of identification evidence, it has been held that although there may be rare occasions when it will be desirable to hold a *voir dire*, in general the judge should decide on the basis of the depositions, statements, and submissions of counsel.[48] It is not clear under section 78(1) where the burden of proof lies.[49] If there is a dispute as to the circumstances in which the evidence was obtained, in principle, it

---

[41] No reference was made to *R v Trump* (1979) 70 Cr App R 300, above.

[42] See also *R v Adams* [1980] QB 575, CA, where it was held that a judge should not exercise the discretion to exclude as evidence articles obtained by means of an unlawful entry, search, and seizure: 'There is no material suggesting that the error of the police as to the continuing validity of the warrant . . . was oppressive in the sense that the adjective is used in *R v Sang*.' According to Lord Diplock in *R v Sang*, evidence discovered as the result of an illegal search is not even subject to the discretion to exclude.

[43] *Re Saifi* [2001] 4 All ER 168, DC at [52].

[44] *R v Raphaie* [1996] Crim LR 812, CA.

[45] [1989] Crim LR 285, CA.

[46] Concerning proceedings before magistrates, see Ch 2, 30 under **The functions of the judge and jury**.

[47] *R v Manji* [1990] Crim LR 512, CA.

[48] *R v Beveridge* [1987] Crim LR 401, CA (identification parade evidence); and *R v Martin and Nicholls* [1994] Crim LR 218, CA (evidence of informal identification). Cf *R v Flemming* (1987) 86 Cr App R 32, CA. Concerning confessions, see also *R v Keenan* [1990] 2 QB 54, CA (Ch 13).

[49] Acknowledged, *per curiam*, in *R v Anderson* [1993] Crim LR 447, CA.

is submitted, there should be an evidential burden on the accused, on the discharge of which there should be a legal burden on the prosecution to disprove those facts beyond reasonable doubt.[50] However, it was said in *Re Saifi*,[51] in the context of extradition proceedings, that the words of section 78 provide no support for such a contention, and that the absence from section 78 of words suggesting that facts are to be established or proved to any particular standard is deliberate, leaving the matter open and untrammelled by rigid evidential considerations.

Concerning the scope of section 78(1), it applies to *any* evidence on which the prosecution proposes to rely, whether tendered by the prosecution or (presumably) a co-accused. Thus it may be used to attempt to exclude, inter alia, the following types of otherwise admissible evidence: hearsay evidence, including depositions and documentary records[52] and admissions and confessions;[53] evidence of opinion, including identification evidence;[54] and evidence of an intoximeter reading.[55] Insofar as the subsection may be used to exclude evidence obtained by improper or unfair means, it is *not* confined, as is the common law power described in *R v Sang*, to admissions, confessions, and evidence obtained from the accused after the commission of the offence—it extends to any evidence on which the prosecution proposes to rely, whenever it was obtained and whether it was obtained from the accused, his premises or any other source.[56]

In deciding whether or not to exercise the discretion, section 78(1) directs the court to have regard to all the circumstances, including those in which the evidence was obtained. In particular, the court may be invited to take into account any illegality, impropriety, or unfairness by means of which the evidence was obtained, including conduct in breach of the European Convention on Human Rights, or any abuse by the police of their powers under the 1984 Act, and the Codes of Practice issued pursuant to that Act, including those relating to stop and search (Code A), the search of premises and the seizure of property (Code B), detention, treatment and, questioning (Code C), identification (Code D), and audio recording of interviews (Code E).[57] When considering breaches of an earlier Code, the provisions of the current version may well be relevant to the question of unfairness under section 78, because they reflect current thinking as to what is fair.[58] The discretion can only be exercised, however,

---

[50] See generally Ch 4.

[51] [2001] 4 All ER 168, DC at [50]–[61].

[52] *R v O'Loughlin* [1988] 3 All ER 431, CCC.

[53] *R v Mason* [1987] 3 All ER 481, CA.

[54] *R v Nagah* (1990) 92 Cr App R 344, CA. See also *R v Deenik* [1992] Crim LR 578, CA (voice identification).

[55] *McGrath v Field* [1987] RTR 349, DC.

[56] Contrast, *sed quaere*, the dictum of Watkins LJ in *R v Mason* [1987] 3 All ER 481 at 484: 's 78 . . . does no more than restate the power which judges had at common law before the 1984 Act was passed.'

[57] Even where the evidence in question was obtained by someone other than a police officer (or a person charged with the duty of investigating offences or charging offenders—see s 67(9) of the 1984 Act, Ch 13), the principles underlying Code C may be of assistance in considering the discretion to exclude under s 78(1): *R v Smith* (1994) 99 Cr App R 233, CA. The Cleveland guidelines, contained in the report of Butler-Sloss LJ on the Inquiry into Child Abuse in Cleveland, set out what is considered to be the best practice, when children are interviewed in connection with sexual abuse, in seeking to ensure that a child's evidence is reliable. If they are not observed, there are grounds for a judge or jury to consider with particular care whether the child is reliable. Much the same, it is submitted, can be said of *Achieving Best Evidence in Criminal Proceedings: Guidance for Vulnerable or Intimidated Witnesses, Including Children ('The Memorandum')*, published by the Home Office: see *R v Dunphy* (1993) 98 Cr App R 393, CA, a decision on the precursor to the current Memorandum. See also C Keenan et al, 'Interviewing Allegedly Abused Children' [1999] *Crim LR* 863.

[58] *R v Ward* (1993) 98 Cr App R 337, CA at 340.

if in all the circumstances admission of the evidence would have an adverse effect on the fairness of the 'proceedings'. The first use of the word 'proceedings' in section 78(1) suggests that it means 'court proceedings' rather than both the investigative and trial process. Section 78(3), since repealed, which referred to 'proceedings *before* a magistrates' court' supports such an interpretation.

Trial judges, as we have seen, already have a duty to ensure that the accused receives a fair trial, in the exercise of which they may exclude any evidence the prejudicial effect of which outweighs its probative value. Section 78(1), however, goes beyond this. Thus although the fact that evidence was obtained improperly or unfairly will not by itself automatically have such an adverse effect on the fairness of the proceedings that the court should not admit it, it is implicit in the wording of the subsection that the circumstances in which the evidence was obtained *may* have such an adverse effect.[59]

In *R v Quinn*[60] Lord Lane CJ said:

> The function of the judge is therefore *to protect the fairness of the proceedings*, and normally proceedings are fair if a jury hears *all* relevant evidence which either side wishes to place before it, but proceedings may become unfair if, for example, one side is allowed to adduce relevant evidence which, for one reason or another, the other side cannot properly challenge or meet, or where there has been an abuse of process, eg because evidence has been obtained in deliberate breach of procedures laid down in an official code of practice.

It is, of course, impossible to catalogue, precisely or at all, the kinds of impropriety which will be treated as having an adverse effect on the fairness of the proceedings. A breach of the 1984 Act or of the Codes does not mean that any statement made by an accused after such breach will necessarily be excluded—every case has to be determined on its own particular facts.[61] Equally, the fact that evidence has been obtained by conduct which may be typified as 'oppressive' will not automatically result in exclusion, because oppressive conduct, depending on its degree and actual or possible effect, may or may not affect the fairness of admitting particular evidence.[62]

A judge's exercise of her discretion under the subsection can be impugned if it is perverse according to *Wednesbury* principles,[63] ie a decision to which no reasonable trial judge could have come, in which case the Court of Appeal will exercise its own discretion.[64] The Court of Appeal will also interfere if the trial judge exercised his discretion on a wrong basis, eg by adverting to an out-of-date version of a relevant Code of Practice.[65] Circumstances vary infinitely, and for this reason it has been said that it is undesirable to attempt any general guidance on the way in which the discretion should be exercised,[66] but some such guidance is available from the reported decisions. They show, with a reasonable degree of clarity, that

---

[59] Per Woolf LJ in *Matto v Crown Court at Wolverhampton* [1987] RTR 337.

[60] [1990] Crim LR 581, CA.

[61] Per Lord Lane CJ in *R v Parris* (1988) 89 Cr App R 68, CA at 72. See also per Hodgson J in *R v Keenan* [1990] 2 QB 54 at 69.

[62] *R v Chalkley and Jeffries* [1998] 2 All ER 155, CA at 177–8.

[63] *Associated Provincial Picture Houses Ltd v Wednesbury Corpn* [1948] 1 KB 223.

[64] *R v O'Leary* (1988) 87 Cr App R 387 at 391, CA; *R v Christou* [1992] QB 979, CA; *R v Dures* [1997] 2 Cr App R 247, CA; and *R v Khan* [1997] Crim LR 508, CA. See also Tucker J, *per curiam*, in *R v Grannell* (1989) 90 Cr App R 149, CA: the citation of decisions of judges or recorders of the Crown Court, not being High Court judges, is of no assistance to the Court of Appeal in deciding whether a judge has exercised his discretion properly.

[65] See *R v Miller* [1998] Crim LR 209, CA.

[66] Per Hodgson J in *R v Samuel* [1988] QB 615, CA.

the purpose of section 78(1) is not disciplinary, but protective, and that although deliberate or wilful misconduct on the part of the police may render exclusion more likely, the determinative factor is the extent to which the suspect has been denied the right of a fair trial by reason of breaches of the provisions governing procedural fairness from the time of being stopped or questioned through to the time of trial.

The disciplinary principle

The *effect* of excluding relevant evidence which has been obtained improperly or unfairly may be to discourage the police from obtaining evidence in such a way, but a decision to exclude under section 78(1) should not be taken *in order to* discipline or punish the police.[67] The Court of Appeal may well deplore police ignorance of the provisions of the Codes[68] and lament deliberate, cynical, and flagrant breaches of such provisions,[69] but as Lord Lane CJ said in *R v Delaney*:[70] 'It is no part of the duty of the court to rule a statement inadmissible simply in order to punish the police for failure to observe the Codes of Practice.' Similarly, in *R v Chalkley and Jeffries*,[71] in which it was held that a determination under section 78 is distinct from the exercise of discretion in determining to stay criminal proceedings as an abuse of process (which, according to the circumstances, may involve balancing the countervailing interests of prosecuting a criminal and discouraging abuse of power), Auld LJ stressed that the critical test under section 78 is whether any impropriety affects the fairness of the proceedings: the court cannot exclude evidence under section 78 simply as a mark of its disapproval of the way in which it was obtained.[72] This view, it is submitted, clearly accords with the wording of section 78. Nonetheless in some of the authorities great stress has been placed on whether the police acted *mala fide*, *deliberately* flouting the law or *wilfully* abusing their powers, and evidence of such conduct has been allowed to tip the scales in favour of the accused. In some cases, the impropriety does *not* affect the reliability of the evidence but does involve the breach of important rights. An example is *Matto v Crown Court at Wolverhampton*.[73] In that case the accused was convicted of driving with excess alcohol. Police officers, when requesting a specimen of breath on the accused's property, had realized that they were acting illegally. The specimen was positive. The accused was arrested and later provided another positive specimen of breath at the police station. Allowing the appeal, it was held that the officers, having acted *mala fide* and oppressively, the circumstances were such that if the Crown Court had directed itself properly it could have exercised its discretion to exclude the evidence under section 78. In other cases, deliberate misconduct has rendered the evidence unreliable. For example, in *R v Mason*[74] where a confession had been made after the police had practised a deceit on the accused and his solicitor by alleging that they had fingerprint evidence which they did not in fact have, it was held that the trial judge should have excluded the confession under section 78.[75]

---

[67] See per Watkins LJ in *R v Mason* [1987] 3 All ER 481 at 484, CA.

[68] See per Hodgson J in *R v Keenan* [1989] 3 All ER 598 at 601, CA.

[69] See per Lord Lane CJ in *R v Canale* [1990] 2 All ER 187, CA at 190 and 192.

[70] (1988) 88 Cr App R 338 at 341, CA.

[71] [1998] 2 All ER 155, CA.

[72] [1998] 2 All ER 155 at 178–80.

[73] [1987] RTR 337.

[74] [1987] 3 All ER 481, CA (see Ch 13).

[75] See also *R v Alladice* (1988) 87 Cr App R 380, CA, and *R v Canale* [1990] Crim LR 329, CA, below; and cf *R v Christou* [1992] QB 979, CA.

The protective principle

General.   The governing principle is protective, ie to protect the suspect from breaches of important provisions set out in the 1984 Act, the Codes, and elsewhere, governing proce-dural fairness on arrest, search, detention, etc that will have a sufficiently adverse effect on the fairness of the proceedings. It is clear that the discretion may be exercised on this basis whether the breaches in question were wilful or merely ignorant. Thus in *R v Alladice*,[76] a case of improper denial of the right of access to a solicitor under section 58 of the 1984 Act, it was held that if the police had acted in bad faith, the court would have had little difficulty in ruling any confession inadmissible, but that if they had acted in good faith, it was still necessary to decide whether admission of the evidence would adversely affect the fairness of the proceedings to such an extent that the confession should be excluded. Similarly, in *R v Walsh*[77] Saville J, referring to breaches of section 58 or the provisions of the Code, said:

> although bad faith may make substantial or significant that which might not otherwise be so, the contrary does not follow. Breaches which are themselves significant and substantial are not rendered otherwise by the good faith of the officers concerned.

This does not mean, however, that in every case of a significant or substantial breach the evidence in question will be excluded—the task of the court is not merely to consider whether there will be an adverse effect on the fairness of the proceedings, but such an adverse effect that justice requires the evidence to be excluded.[78] This is the most likely explanation for the *obiter dicta* in *R v Cooke*,[79] a rape case, that where a sample of hair is not taken in accordance with the relevant statutory provisions but obtained by an assault, and is then used to prepare a DNA profile implicating the accused, the evidence will be admitted on the basis that the means used to obtain the evidence have done nothing to cast doubt on its reliability and strength. This approach has been buttressed by the obiter comments of Lord Hutton in *Attorney General's Reference (No 3 of 1999)*,[80] another rape case in which there was no question as to the reliability of the DNA evidence the admissibility of which was in dispute. Lord Hutton was of the view that in a case of the kind in question, involving the commission of a very grave crime, in exercise of the section 78 discretion the interests of the victim and the public must be considered, as well as the interests of the accused.

The reasoning in *R v Cooke* and *Attorney General's Reference (No 3 of 1999)*, it is submitted, is preferable to the approach taken in *R v Nathaniel*.[81] In that case a DNA profile taken from the appellant's blood in relation to charges of raping A and B, of which he was acquitted, was not destroyed in accordance with section 64 of the 1984 Act, but formed the main pros-ecution evidence on a charge of raping C. It was held that the evidence should have been excluded. The accused was misled, in consenting to give the blood sample, by statements and promises which were not honoured. He was told that it was required for the purposes

---

[76] (1988) 87 Cr App R 380, CA.

[77] (1989) 91 Cr App R 161 at 163, CA. See also *R v Quinn* [1990] Crim LR 581, CA, below, *DPP v McGladrigan* [1991] Crim LR 851, DC, *R v Samms* [1991] Crim LR 197, and *R v Brine* [1992] Crim LR 122, CA.

[78] *R v Walsh* (1989) 91 Cr App R 161 at 163, CA and *R v Ryan* [1992] Crim LR 187, CA.

[79] [1995] 1 Cr App R 318, CA.

[80] [2001] 1 All ER 577, HL at 590.

[81] [1995] 2 Cr App R 565, CA.

of the case involving A and B; that it would be destroyed if he was prosecuted in relation to A and B and acquitted; and that if he refused without good cause to give the sample, the jury, in any proceedings against him for the rape of A and B, could draw inferences from his refusal.[82]

The reasoning in *R v Cooke* also serves to explain the admission in evidence of the fruits of an improper search, as in *R v Stewart*,[83] where, following an entry involving a number of breaches of Code B, the accused was found in possession of apparatus to divert the gas and electricity supplies so as to bypass the meters. The outcome was the same in *R v Sanghera*[84] where, a search having been conducted in breach of the Code without written consent, there was no issue as to the reliability of the evidence as to what had been discovered. However, it should be otherwise if the means used to obtain the evidence could have affected its quality, for example a case in which the accused, following a search of his premises during which he was improperly kept out of the way, claims that the property found was 'planted'.[85] Equally, although officers are entitled to delay taking a suspect to a police station in order that a search may be conducted with his assistance, if they abuse that entitlement to ask questions, beyond those necessary to the search, on matters which properly ought to be asked under the rules of Code C applying at a police station, the answers may be excluded on the grounds of unfairness.[86]

It is clear that the outcome depends upon the precise facts. In *R v Pall*[87] it was said that the absence of a caution was bound to be significant in most circumstances, and in *R v Nelson and Rose*[88] it was held that a failure to caution should have led to the exclusion of the whole of an interview. However, in *R v Hoyte*[89] a confession was admitted, despite a failure to caution, on the basis that the police had acted in good faith and in the particular circumstances there could have been no unfairness.[90] Similarly in *R v Gill*[91] it was held that lies told during an Inland Revenue investigation of tax fraud were admissible, despite a failure to caution. Clarke LJ said that the principal purpose of the caution was to ensure, so far as possible, that interviewees do not make admissions unless they wish to do so and are aware of the consequences, and not to prevent interviewees from telling lies. Although lies may be excluded where there has been a failure to caution, each case depends on its own facts. On the facts, the Revenue had not acted in bad faith and the appellants were aware that criminal proceedings were in prospect and

---

[82] See now s 64(3B) of the 1984 Act.

[83] [1995] Crim LR 500, CA. See also *R v McCarthy* [1996] Crim LR 818, CA.

[84] [2001] 1 Cr App R 299, CA.

[85] But see *R v Wright* [1994] Crim LR 55, CA, where evidence of a search was admitted notwithstanding that a record of it had not been made in W's custody record (contrary to s 18(8) of the 1984 Act) and there were said to have been breaches of Code B in that no communication was made with W, he was not present at the search, and no proper list had been made of the property. Noting that there had been no deliberate breach of the Code, it was held that the judge had taken into account the breach of s 18(8) and the other matters could not have placed W at any disadvantage. See also *R v Khan* [1997] Crim LR 508, CA.

[86] *R v Khan* [1993] Crim LR 54, CA, applied in *R v Raphaie* [1996] Crim LR 812, CA.

[87] (1991) 156 JP 424, CA.

[88] [1998] 2 Cr App R 399, CA.

[89] [1994] Crim LR 215, CA.

[90] See also *R v Ibrahim* [2008] 2 Cr App R 311, concerning the application of s 78 to 'safety interviews' under Sch 8 of the Terrorism Act 2008, where it was said that much will turn on the nature of the warning or caution given, if any.

[91] [2004] 1 WLR 49, CA.

must have known that they were not obliged to answer the questions.[92] In *R v Aspinal*[93] the accused, a schizophrenic, was interviewed, about 13 hours after his arrest, without an 'appropriate adult', in breach of what is now paragraph 11.15 of Code C, and without a solicitor. It was held that an accused of this kind may not be able to judge for himself what is in his best interests, which may put him at a considerable disadvantage, not least because the record of the interview may not seem unreliable to a jury. However, in appropriate circumstances the confession of a mentally disordered accused may be properly admitted notwithstanding that it was made in breach of paragraph 11.15.[94]

Another good example, in this regard, relates to the right to legal advice in section 58 of the 1984 Act, which has been judicially described as 'one of the most important and fundamental rights of a citizen'.[95] It has been held that significant and substantial breaches of that section (or the provisions of Code C) will, prima facie, have an adverse effect on the fairness of the proceedings.[96] Breach of the section, however, is no guarantee of the exclusion of any statement made thereafter. In *R v Alladice*, for example, it was held that if the trial judge had considered section 78, he would not have been obliged to exclude the confession, because the circumstances showed that the accused was well able to cope with the interviews, understood the cautions that he had been given, at times exercising his right to silence, and was aware of his rights, so that, had the solicitor been present, his advice would have added nothing to the knowledge of his rights which the accused already had.[97] In *R v Parris*,[98] on the other hand, another case involving breach of section 58, it was held that evidence of a confession should have been excluded because, had a solicitor been present, the accused would probably have accepted his advice to remain silent. Furthermore, the solicitor could have given evidence on whether the police had fabricated the confession; alternatively, his presence would have discouraged any such fabrication.[99]

In *R v Konscol*[100] the trial judge admitted evidence of an interview with K, containing lies, conducted by a Belgian customs officer. There was no dispute that K had said what was recorded, and that the interview was conducted fairly according to Belgian law, but K was neither cautioned nor advised that he could have a lawyer present. The Court of Appeal

---

[92] See also *R v Senior* [2004] 3 All ER 9, CA, applied in *R v Rehman* [2007] Crim LR 101, CA (questioning by customs officers to establish ownership of a suspicious baggage, prior to administering a caution) and *R v Devani* [2008] 1 Cr App R 65 (the questioning of a suspect, who was a solicitor, without a caution, but in the presence of her principal).

[93] [1999] Crim LR 741, CA.

[94] See *R v Law-Thompson* [1997] Crim LR 674, CA

[95] Per Hodgson J in *R v Samuel* [1988] 2 All ER 135, CA. See also *Brennan v UK* [2002] Crim LR 217, ECHR: the right to consult with a lawyer *in private* is part of the basic requirements of a fair trial and follows from Art 6(3)(c) of the European Convention on Human Rights.

[96] Per Saville J in *R v Walsh* (1989) 91 Cr App R 161 at 163, CA. However, in the case of drink-driving offences the public interest requires that the obtaining of specimens should not be delayed to any significant extent to enable a suspect to take legal advice: *Kennedy v DPP* [2003] Crim LR 120, DC. See also *Campbell v DPP* [2003] Crim LR 118, DC, *Kirkup v DPP* [2004] Crim LR 230, DC, and *Whitley v DPP* [2003] All ER (D) 212, [2003] EWHC 2512 (Admin). Similarly, in the case of juveniles, there is no reason to delay the obtaining of specimens in order for an 'appropriate adult' to be present: *DPP v Evans* [2003] Crim LR 338, DC.

[97] See also, to similar effect, *R v Dunford* (1990) 91 Cr App R 150, CA.

[98] (1988) 89 Cr App R 68, CA. See also *R v Walsh* (1989) 91 Cr App R 161.

[99] This argument could have been, but was not, employed in *R v Alladice* (1988) 87 Cr App R 380, CA, where fabrication was also alleged.

[100] [1993] Crim LR 950.

dismissed the appeal and declined to lay down guidelines as to when a court should admit a statement made overseas according to rules which did not coincide with the provisions of the 1984 Act.[101]

In *R v Keenan*[102] records of an interview with the accused were compiled in plain breach of Code C: the record was not made during the course of the interview; the reason for not completing it at that time was not recorded in the officer's pocket book; and the accused was not given the opportunity to read it and to sign it as correct or to indicate the respects in which he considered it inaccurate. The accused's defence, unknown to the trial judge at the time when the submission on admissibility was made, was that the interview had been fabricated. The judge, ruling that any unfairness to the accused could be cured by the accused going into the witness box and giving his version of the interview, admitted the evidence. On appeal, it was held that the relevant provisions of Code C are designed to make it difficult for detained persons to make unfounded allegations against the police which might otherwise appear credible and to provide safeguards against the police inaccurately recording or inventing the words used in questioning a detained person. Where there have been significant and substantial breaches of the 'verballing' provisions, evidence so obtained should be excluded, because if the other evidence in the case is strong, then it may make no difference to the eventual result if the evidence in question is excluded, and if the other evidence is weak or non-existent, that is just the situation where the protection of the rules is most needed. It was wrong to assume that any unfairness could be cured by the accused going into the witness box: if he intended not to testify if the evidence was excluded, then its admission unfairly robbed him of his right to remain silent; if the defence case was to be (as it turned out to be) that the evidence was concocted, then its admission forced the accused to give evidence and also, by attacking the police, to put his character in issue; and if the defence was to be that the interview was inaccurately recorded, it placed the accused at a substantial disadvantage because he had been given no contemporaneous opportunity to correct any inaccuracies. For these reasons, the conviction was quashed.

In *R v Canale*[103] the way in which records of two interviews with the accused were obtained involved breaches very similar to those which occurred in *R v Keenan*. In this case, however, at two subsequent and contemporaneously recorded interviews, the accused repeated admissions allegedly made in the first two interviews. On the *voir dire* and in evidence the accused admitted that he had made the admissions but said that they were untrue and that the police had induced him to make them by a trick. The Court of Appeal held that by reason of the flagrant and cynical breaches of the Code, the judge was deprived of the very evidence which would have enabled him to reach a more certain conclusion on the question of admissibility and, had he ruled in favour of admission, the jury would have been deprived of the evidence necessary to decide the truth of the accused's denial of the offence. The initial breaches affected the whole series of alleged admissions, all of which should have been excluded.[104]

---

[101] See also *R v Quinn* [1990] Crim LR 581, CA and *R v McNab* [2002] Crim LR 129, CA.

[102] [1990] 2 QB 54, CA.

[103] [1990] 2 All ER 187, CA.

[104] See also *R v Absolam* (1988) 88 Cr App R 332, CA, and *R v Sparks* [1991] Crim LR 128, CA; and cf *R v Langiert* [1991] Crim LR 777, CA (failure to record the reason for not making a contemporaneous record), and *R v Rajakuruna* [1991] Crim LR 458, CA (failure to inform a person not under arrest that he is not obliged to remain with the officer).

Many of the reported decisions have involved breaches of Code D (identification). Under paragraph 3.12 of Code D, whenever (i) a witness has identified or purported to identify a suspect; or (ii) there is a witness available who expresses an ability to identify the suspect, or there is a reasonable chance of the witness being able to do so, and the suspect disputes the identification, an identification procedure shall be held, ie a video identification, an identification parade, or a group identification. The exception is where an identification procedure is not practicable or it would serve no useful purpose, for example when it is not disputed that the suspect is already well known to the witness.[105] Breach of paragraph 3.12 will not necessarily result in the exclusion of the other evidence of identification, of which there may be an abundance.[106] The critical issue is the impact of the breach on the fairness of the trial.[107] Thus in *R v Samms*,[108] where it was not shown that it was impracticable to hold a parade (or group identification),[109] it was held that it would be unfair to admit the evidence of identification of the suspect by confrontation because the confrontation that occurred partook of the dangers sought to be prevented by a parade (or group identification).[110] It will also be unfair to make use of identification evidence obtained by a video identification procedure which uses images of persons bearing an insufficient resemblance to the accused.[111] On the other hand, in *R v Grannell*[112] it was held that no unfairness arose from the failure, in breach of what is now paragraph 3.17 of the Code, to explain to the suspect prior to an identification procedure, such matters as the purpose of the identification and the procedures for holding it; and in *R v Ryan*[113] it was held that a clear breach of what is now paragraph 3.11 of the Code—an officer involved with the investigation of the case took part in the identification procedures—had caused no prejudice to the accused.[114]

Where a breach of Code D has been established but the judge has rejected an application to exclude the evidence in question, he should explain to the jury that there has been a breach

[105] For the issues that arise where a suspect admits his presence at the scene of the offence, but denies committing the offence, see Andy Roberts 'Questions of "Who was there?" and "Who did what?": The Application of Code D in Cases of Dispute as to Participation but not Presence' [2003] *Crim LR* 709.

[106] See *R v McEvoy* [1997] Crim LR 887, CA, a decision under an earlier version of para 3.12.

[107] This remains the case where the identification is not strictly governed by Code D at all (see *R v Hickin* [1996] Crim LR 584, CA) or where the evidence of identification has come into existence abroad as a result of arrangements made by a foreign police force (see *R v Quinn* [1990] Crim LR 581, CA).

[108] [1991] Crim LR 197, CC.

[109] See also *R v Johnson* [1996] Crim LR 504, CA (confrontation by video).

[110] See now para 3.23, Code D. See also *R v Martin and Nicholls* [1994] Crim LR 218, CA (evidence of informal identification by young witnesses a very long time after the offence and in unsatisfactory conditions outside the court while the accused and witnesses were awaiting allocation of the case to a court). Cf *R v Tiplady* [1995] Crim LR 651, CA (a group identification in the foyer of a magistrates' court where T had been bailed to attend). It was held that the venue was not inappropriate and *Martin and Nicholls* was distinguished on the basis that whereas in that case there were striking limitations on the choice open to the identifying witnesses (the accused wore 'funky dreads') in *Tiplady* at any one time between 20 and 30 people had been present, most of them in T's age group. Cf also *R v Quinn* [1990] Crim LR 581, CA: evidence of an informal identification as a result of a chance meeting would be admissible. See also *R v Oscar* [1991] Crim LR 778, CA, and *R v Rogers* [1993] Crim LR 386, CA.

[111] See *R v Marcus* [2005] Crim LR 384, CA.

[112] (1989) 90 Cr App R 149, CA.

[113] [1992] Crim LR 187, CA. See also *R v Jones (Terence)* [1992] Crim LR 365, CA, and *R v Khan* [1997] Crim LR 584, CA; and cf *R v Gall* (1989) 90 Cr App R 64, CA, and *R v Finley* [1993] Crim LR 50, CA.

[114] See also, *sed quaere, Marsh v DPP* [2007] Crim LR 163 (failure, in breach of para 3.1(b), to make a record of a witness's description of a suspect *before* participation in any identification procedure).

and how it has arisen and invite them to consider the possible effects of the breach. For example, in the case of an improper failure to hold an identification parade, the jury should ordinarily be told that a parade enables a suspect to put the reliability of the identification to the test, that he has lost the benefit of that safeguard, and that they should take account of that fact in their assessment of the whole case, giving it such weight as they think fair. However failure to direct the jury about a breach of Code D will not necessarily infringe an accused's right to a fair trial or render a conviction unsafe.[115]

Entrapment and undercover operations. *R v Looseley* and *Attorney General's Reference (No 3 of 2000)*[116] are the leading authorities on the circumstances in which criminal proceedings should be stayed, or evidence excluded, on the grounds of entrapment.[117] Hearing both appeals together, the House of Lords held as follows:

1. Entrapment is not a substantive defence, but where an accused can show entrapment the court may stay the proceedings as an abuse of the court's process or it may exclude evidence under section 78.

2. As a matter of principle, a stay of the proceedings rather than exclusion of evidence should normally be regarded as the appropriate response. A prosecution founded on entrapment would be an abuse of the court's process. Police conduct which brings about state-created crime is unacceptable and improper and to prosecute in such circumstances would be an affront to the public conscience.[118]

3. In deciding whether conduct amounts to state-created crime, the existence or absence of a predisposition on the part of the accused to commit the crime is not the criterion by which the acceptability of police conduct is to be decided, because it does not make acceptable what would otherwise be unacceptable conduct on the part of the police or negative misuse of state power.[119]

4. A useful guide is to consider whether the police did no more than present the accused with an unexceptional opportunity to commit a crime. The yardstick for these purposes is, in general, whether the police conduct preceding the commission of the offence was no more than might have been expected from others in the circumstances. 'The State can justify the use of entrapment techniques to induce the commission of an offence only when the inducement is consistent with the ordinary temptations and stratagems that are likely to be encountered in the course of criminal activity . . . But once the State goes beyond the ordinary, it is likely to increase the incidence of crime by artificial means.'[120] Of its nature, the technique of providing an opportunity to commit a crime is intrusive. The greater the degree of intrusiveness, the closer will the courts scrutinize the reason for using it.

---

[115] See *R v Forbes* [2001] 2 WLR 1, HL.

[116] [2001] 1 WLR 2060, HL.

[117] See A Ashworth, 'Redrawing the Boundaries of Entrapment' [2002] *Crim LR* 161.

[118] The possibility of a stay on the basis of entrapment by non-state agents, eg journalists, seems to be remote: see *Re Saluja* [2007] 2 All ER 905, QBD at [81].

[119] Cf *R v Moon* [2004] All ER (D) 167 (Nov), CA, where the absence of predisposition on the part of M to deal with or supply heroin was regarded as a critical factor in concluding that a test purchase by an undercover officer, who claimed that she was suffering from heroin withdrawal symptoms, was an abuse of process.

[120] Per McHugh J in *Ridgeway v The Queen* (1995) 184 CLR 19 at 92.

5. Usually, a most important factor, but not necessarily decisive, will be whether an officer can be said to have caused the commission of the offence, rather than merely providing an opportunity for the accused to commit it with an officer rather than in secrecy with someone else. A good example of the latter situation is furnished by *Nottingham City Council v Amin*[121] where a taxi driver who was not licensed to ply for hire in a particular district, and was flagged down by plain clothes officers in that district, took them to their stated destination. Lord Bingham CJ said:[122]

    > it has been regarded as unobjectionable if a law enforcement officer gives a defendant an opportunity to break the law, of which the defendant freely takes advantage, in circumstances where it appears that the defendant would have behaved in the same way if the opportunity had been offered by anyone else,

    by which he meant, in that case, that the officers behaved like ordinary members of the public in flagging the taxi down. They did not, for example, wave £50 notes or pretend to be in distress. The test of whether a police officer acted like an ordinary member of the public works well and is likely to be decisive in many cases of regulatory offences committed with ordinary members of the public, such as selling liquor without a licence, but ordinary members of the public do not become involved in large-scale drug dealing, conspiracy to rob, or hiring assassins. The appropriate standards of behaviour in such cases are more problematic; and even in the case of offences committed with ordinary members of the public, other factors may require a purely causal test to be modified.

6. The causal question cannot be answered by a mechanical application of a distinction between 'active' and 'passive' conduct on the part of the undercover policeman. For example, drug dealers can be expected to show some wariness about dealing with a stranger and therefore some protective colour in dress or manner as well as a certain degree of persistence may be necessary. Equally, undercover officers who infiltrate conspiracies to murder, rob, or commit terrorist offences could hardly remain concealed unless they showed some enthusiasm for the enterprise. A good deal of active behaviour may therefore be acceptable without crossing the boundary between causing the offence to be committed and providing an opportunity for the accused to commit it.

7. Ultimately the overall consideration is always whether the conduct of the police was so seriously improper as to bring the administration of justice into disrepute. Other formulations substantially to the same effect are: a prosecution which would affront the public conscience[123] or conviction and punishment which would be deeply offensive to ordinary notions of fairness.[124] In applying these formulations, the court has regard to all the circumstances of the case. One cannot isolate any single factor or devise any formula that will always produce the correct answer. There are a cluster of relevant factors but their relevant weight and importance depends on the particular facts of the case. The following are of particular relevance.

---

[121] [2000] 1 WLR 1071, DC.

[122] At 1076–7.

[123] Per Lord Steyn in *R v Latif* [1996] 1 WLR 104, HL at 112.

[124] Per Lord Bingham in *Nottingham City Council v Amin* [2000] 1 WLR 1071, DC at 1076.

(a) The nature of the offence. The use of proactive techniques is more appropriate in the case of some offences, for example dealing in unlawful substances, offences with no immediate victim, such as bribery, offences which victims are reluctant to report, and conspiracies. The secrecy and difficulty of detection, and the manner in which the criminal activity is carried on, are relevant considerations. However, the fact that the offence is a serious one is not in itself a sufficient ground for the police to ignore the provisions of the Undercover Operations Code of Practice (issued jointly by all UK police authorities and HM Customs and Excise in response to the Human Rights Act 1998) or for the courts to condone their actions by allowing the prosecution to proceed.

(b) The reason for the particular police operation and supervision. As to the former, the police must act in good faith. Having reasonable grounds for suspicion is one way good faith may be established. It is not normally considered a legitimate use of police power to provide people not suspected of any criminal activity with the opportunity to commit crimes.[125] However, having grounds for suspicion of a particular individual is not always essential. The police may, in the course of a bona fide investigation into suspected criminality, provide an opportunity for the commission of an offence which is taken by someone to whom no suspicion previously attached, as in *Williams v DPP*.[126] This can happen when a human or inanimate decoy is used in the course of the detection of crime which has been prevalent in a particular place. Sometimes, random testing may be the only way of policing a particular trading activity. As to supervision, to allow officers or controlled informers to undertake entrapment activities unsupervised carries great danger, not only that they will try to improve their performances in court, but of oppression, extortion, and corruption. The need for reasonable suspicion and proper supervision are both stressed in the Undercover Operations Code of Practice.

(c) The nature and extent of police participation in the crime. The greater the inducement held out by the police, and the more forceful or persistent their overtures, the more readily may a court conclude that they overstepped the boundary. In assessing the weight to be attached to the police inducement, regard is to be had to the accused's circumstances, including his vulnerability. It will not normally be regarded as objectionable for the police to behave as would an ordinary customer of a trade, whether lawful or unlawful, being carried on by the accused.

(d) The accused's criminal record. This is unlikely to be relevant unless it can be linked to other factors grounding reasonable suspicion that he is engaged in criminal activity.

8. A decision on whether to stay the proceedings is distinct from a decision on the fairness of admitting evidence.[127] Different tests are applicable to these two decisions. If an application under section 78 is in substance a belated application for a stay, it should be treated as such and decided according to the principles appropriate to the grant of a stay. If the court is not satisfied that a stay should be granted, the question under section 78

---

[125] See, eg, *Ramanauskas v Lithuania* [2008] Crim LR 639, where an officer acted on mere rumours about a prosecutor's openness to bribery.

[126] [1993] 3 All ER 365. See below.

[127] Citing *R v Chalkley* [1998] 2 Cr App R 79, CA at 105.

is not whether the proceedings should have been brought but, as Potter LJ held in *R v Shannon*:[128]

> It is whether the fairness of the proceedings will be adversely affected by admitting the evidence of the agent provocateur or evidence which is available as the result of his action or activities. So, for instance, if there is good reason to question the credibility of evidence given by an agent provocateur, or which casts doubt on the reliability of other evidence procured by or resulting from his actions, and that question is not susceptible of being properly or fairly resolved in the course of the proceedings from available, admissible and 'untainted' evidence, then the judge may readily conclude that such evidence should be excluded.

9. Neither section 78 nor the power to stay proceedings has been modified by Article 6 of the European Convention on Human Rights and the jurisprudence of the European Court of Human Rights. There is no appreciable difference between the requirements of Article 6, or the Strasbourg jurisprudence on Article 6, and the English law. Nor is there anything in *Teixeira de Castro v Portugal*[129] which suggests any difference from the current English approach to entrapment.

In *R v Smurthwaite and Gill*[130] the Court of Appeal considered the application of section 78(1) to evidence obtained as a result of police undercover operations. It was held that the relevant factors include:

1. whether the undercover officer was acting as an *agent provocateur*, ie enticing the accused to commit an offence he would not otherwise have committed;

2. the nature of any entrapment;

3. whether the evidence consists of admissions to a completed offence or relates to the actual commission of an offence;

4. how active or passive the officer's role was in obtaining the evidence;

5. whether there is an unassailable record of what occurred or whether it is strongly corroborated; and

6. whether the officer abused his role to ask questions which ought properly to have been asked as a police officer and in accordance with the Codes.[131]

Both *Smurthwaite* and *Gill* were trials for soliciting to murder. In each case the person solicited was an undercover police officer posing as a contract killer and the prosecution case depended upon secret tape recordings of meetings held between the undercover officer and the accused. In S's case, the Court of Appeal was not persuaded that the officer was an *agent provocateur*. There was an element of entrapment and a trick. However, the tapes recorded not admissions about some previous offence but the actual offence being committed; they showed that S made the running and that the officer had taken a minimal role in the planning and had

---

[128] [2001] 1 WLR 51, CA at 68.

[129] (1998) 28 EHRR 101. See further below.

[130] [1994] 1 All ER 898.

[131] The same factors also apply in the case of evidence obtained by undercover journalists acting on their own initiative and not on police instructions: *R v Shannon* [2001] 1 WLR 51, CA and *Shannon v UK* [2005] Crim LR 133, ECHR. See also Hofmeyr, 'The Problem of Private Entrapment' [2006] *Crim LR* 319. As to the sixth factor, see also *R v Christou* [1992] QB 979, CA, and *R v Bryce* [1992] 4 All ER 567, CA, both below.

used no persuasion towards S; they were an accurate and unchallenged record; and the officer had not abused his role to ask questions which ought properly to have been asked as a police officer. In these circumstances, the judge's decision not to exclude the evidence was upheld. The outcome was the same in G's case: the facts were very similar and although the first meeting between G and the officer was not recorded and there was a stark conflict of evidence as to what was said at that meeting, the existence of a total record was only one factor, and both the contents of the subsequent taped conversations and statements made by G in her formal police interviews supported the officer's account of the first meeting.[132]

R v Governor of Pentonville Prison, ex p Chinoy[133] concerned the setting up of a bank account to facilitate the laundering of money alleged to be the proceeds of drug trafficking. The Divisional Court held that the fact of entrapment was one of the circumstances which should be taken into account when carrying out the balancing exercise under section 78(1), but concluded that the circumstances did not require the exclusion of the evidence. It was held that the detection and proof of certain types of criminal activity may necessitate the employment of underhand and even unlawful means. On the facts, although the evidence was obtained by means which were criminal in France and, according to French law, in breach of the European Convention on Human Rights, there was no breach of English law and the means employed by the undercover agents were appropriate to the situation they were investigating and did not require the exclusion of the evidence they obtained. In *R v Latif*[134] S was convicted of being knowingly concerned in the importation of drugs which had been brought into the country by an undercover customs officer. Although S had been lured into England by the deceit of an informer, and both he and the undercover officer had possibly committed the offence of possessing heroin in Pakistan, the House of Lords upheld the judge's refusal to either stay the proceedings or exclude the informer's evidence under section 78.[135]

An application under section 78 will not succeed where a police officer gives an accused an opportunity to break the law, of which the accused freely takes advantage, in circumstances in which the accused would have behaved in the same way if the opportunity had been offered by anyone else. An example is *DPP v Marshall*,[136] where, on a charge of selling alcohol without a licence, evidence was received of purchases made by plain clothes officers. The same approach was adopted in *Ealing London Borough v Woolworths plc*,[137] in which it was held that, on a charge under section 11(1) of the Video Recordings Act 1984, justices were in error in excluding evidence that a boy aged 11, acting under instructions of officers of the Trading Standards Department, had entered the store and purchased an 18-category video film. In *Williams v DPP*,[138] the trick, based on the expectation that someone might act dishonestly, was to leave in a busy street an insecure van containing an apparently valuable load, a stratagem which, it was held, left the accused free whether to succumb or not.

It seems that the police cannot circumvent section 78(1) by using, as *agents provocateurs*, informants who will not be called as witnesses. Thus if an informant, C, acting on police instructions rather than on his own initiative, incites or entraps an accused, D, into committing

---

[132] Cf *Re Proulx* [2001] 1 All ER 57, DC.

[133] [1992] 1 All ER 317.

[134] [1996] 1 WLR 104.

[135] See also *R v Pattemore* [1994] Crim LR 836, CA, and *R v Morley* [1994] Crim LR 919, CA.

[136] [1988] 3 All ER 683, DC.

[137] [1995] Crim LR 58, DC.

[138] [1993] 3 All ER 365, DC.

an offence (the supply of drugs, say) and D is then approached by E, an undercover police officer, in whose presence the offence is committed (D supplies E with drugs), this may form the basis of a submission to exclude E's evidence under section 78(1) notwithstanding that E, by reference to the relevant factors as set out in *Smurthwaite and Gill*, behaved throughout with perfect propriety.[139]

Undercover operations after commission of an offence. Whether section 78(1) operates to exclude evidence obtained by undercover operations or other forms of trickery *after* commission of the offence, usually turns, as in the case of other types of evidence, on the reliability or otherwise of the evidence to be adduced, and not just on the extent to which the accused has been deprived of his important procedural rights, each case turning on its own facts.

Many of the cases have involved covert recording or filming. In *R v Bailey*[140] two co-accused, having exercised their right to silence when interviewed, were charged and placed in the same bugged cell by officers who, in order to lull them into a false sense of security, pretended that they had been forced to put them in the same cell by an uncooperative custody officer. Evidence of incriminating conversations obtained by this subterfuge was held to be admissible. In *R v Khan (Sultan)*[141] the House of Lords held that the fact that evidence has been obtained in circumstances which amount to a breach of Article 8 of the European Convention on Human Rights (the right to respect for private life, home, and correspondence) may be relevant to exercise of the section 78 power, but the significance of the breach turns on its effect on the fairness of the proceedings. In that case the police had made a recording of an incriminating conversation relating to the importation of heroin, by means of an electronic surveillance device attached to a house without the knowledge or consent of the owner or occupier. It was held that the judge had been entitled to conclude that the circumstances in which the evidence had been obtained, even if they constituted a breach of Article 8, were not such as to require exclusion of the evidence. The European Court of Human Rights subsequently held that although the recording was obtained in breach of Article 8, its use at the trial did not conflict with the right to a fair hearing under Article 6, because there was no risk of the recording being unreliable, the accused had the opportunity to challenge its admissibility, and if its admission would have given rise to substantive unfairness, the domestic court could have excluded it under section 78.[142] The European Court has reached similar conclusions in relation to evidence obtained in breach of Article 8 by the unlawful installation of a listening device in the accused's home[143] and, in *PG and JH v United Kingdom*,[144] by the unlawful use of covert listening devices in police cells.[145] In *PG and JH v United Kingdom*, where the recordings did not contain any incriminating statements, but were used at trial as a control to identify the voices of the accused on other tapes, it was held that they could be regarded as akin to blood, hair, or other physical or objective specimens used in forensic analysis and to

---

[139] See *R v Smith (Brian)* [1995] Crim LR 658, CA, and cf *R v Mann* [1995] Crim LR 647, CA.

[140] [1993] 3 All ER 513, CA.

[141] [1997] AC 558.

[142] *Khan v United Kingdom* (2001) 31 EHRR 1016.

[143] *Chalkley v United Kingdom* [2003] Crim LR 51.

[144] [2002] Crim LR 308.

[145] See also *R v Mason* [2002] 2 Cr App R 628, CA; and *R v Button* [2005] Crim LR 571, where the 'startling proposition' that the court is bound to exclude any evidence obtained in breach of Art 8 because otherwise it would be acting unlawfully was rejected on the basis that any breach of Art 8 is subsumed by the Art 6 duty to ensure a fair trial.

which the privilege against self-incrimination does not apply. In that case the European Court also reiterated that:

> Whilst Article 6 guarantees the right to a fair hearing, it does not lay down any rules on the admissibility of evidence as such, which is therefore primarily a matter for regulation under national law . . . . It is not the role of the court to determine, as a matter of principle whether particular types of evidence, for example unlawfully obtained evidence—may be admissible or, indeed, whether the applicant was guilty or not. The question which must be answered is whether the proceedings as a whole, including the way in which the evidence was obtained, were fair.[146]

The European Court has followed the same approach in relation to covert filming. In *Perry v United Kingdom*,[147] the applicant having failed to attend identification parades, the police, infringing official guidelines, filmed him covertly for the purposes of a video identification of which neither he nor his solicitor were aware. It was held that the application was manifestly ill-founded on the grounds that the use of evidence obtained without a proper legal basis or through unlawful means will not generally contravene Article 6(1) so long as proper procedural safeguards are in place and the source of the material is not tainted.[148]

In *R v P*[149] it was argued that although telephone intercept evidence was properly obtained in accordance with the Convention and the law of a country overseas, its use in an English trial was contrary to Article 6 and the policy of the English law. Rejecting this argument, the House of Lords held that the fair use of intercept evidence at a trial is not a breach of Article 6, that even if it was unlawfully obtained, the criterion of fairness in Article 6 is the criterion to be applied by the judge under section 78, and that there is no principle of exclusion of intercept evidence independently of the statutory provisions.[150] The House has also held that where intercept evidence is inadmissible pursuant to statutory provisions, there is no rule prohibiting the use of the intercepts at police interviews and, subject to section 78, such use will not render the interview evidence inadmissible, although the interview transcript will need to be edited to remove any direct or indirect references to the intercept.[151]

In *R v Christou*[152] the police set up a shop staffed by two undercover police officers who purported to be willing to buy stolen jewellery. Transactions in the shop were recorded, the object being to recover stolen property and obtain evidence against thieves or receivers. The accused, charged as a result of the operation, unsuccessfully sought to exclude all the evidence obtained thereby. It was argued that the evidence was obtained by a trick designed to deprive visitors to the shop of their privilege against self-incrimination and that a caution should have been administered.

---

[146] For a fuller examination of approaches to exclusion of evidence obtained in breach of Art 8, see D Ormerod, 'ECHR and the Exclusion of Evidence: Trial Remedies for Article 8 Breaches' [2003] *Crim LR* 61. See also R Mahoney, 'Abolition of New Zealand's Prima Facie Exclusionary Rule' [2003] *Crim LR* 607.

[147] [2003] Crim LR 281.

[148] See also *R v Loveridge* [2001] 2 Cr App R 591, CA, where the accused were covertly filmed in court, which was both unlawful and in breach of Art 8, to enable comparison with pictures of the crime as recorded on a CCTV film; *R v Marriner* [2002] All ER (D) 120 (Dec), [2002] EWCA Crim 2855, where the accused were covertly recorded on video and tape by undercover journalists; and *R v Rosenberg* [2006] Crim LR 540, CA, where the accused and the police were aware of surveillance by the accused's neighbour that had been neither initiated nor encouraged by the police.

[149] [2002] 1 AC 46.

[150] See now the Regulation of Investigatory Powers Act 2000.

[151] *R v Sargent* [2003] 1 AC 347, HL.

[152] [1992] QB 979, CA.

The Court of Appeal, distinguishing *R v Payne* and *R v Mason*,[153] held that the accused had voluntarily applied themselves to the trick (in the sense that what they did in the shop was exactly what they intended to do) and this had resulted in no unfairness.[154] Concerning the alleged breach of Code C, the court acknowledged that the officers had grounds to suspect the accused of an offence, but held that the Code was not intended to apply in the present context. The Code was intended to protect suspects who are vulnerable to abuse or pressure from officers or who may believe themselves to be so. Where a suspect, even if not in detention, is being questioned by an officer, acting as such, for the purpose of obtaining evidence, the officer and the suspect are not on equal terms: the officer is perceived to be in a position of authority and the suspect may be intimidated or undermined. On the facts, however, the accused were not questioned by officers acting as such, conversation was on equal terms, and there was no question of pressure or intimidation.

In *Christou* the court held that it *would* be wrong for the police to adopt an undercover pose or disguise to enable them to ask questions about an offence uninhibited by the Code and with the effect of circumventing it, and it would then be open to a judge to exclude under section 78. On the facts, however, the questions and comments of the officers were, for the most part, simply those necessary to conduct the bartering and to maintain their cover, and not questions about the offence. Thus, although officers had asked questions about the origin of the goods, they had formed a part of their undercover pose as receivers: receivers need such information to prevent them from re-selling goods in the area from which they were stolen.[155] In *R v Bryce*,[156] on the other hand, in which an undercover officer, posing as a potential buyer of a car, asked B how recently the car had been stolen, it was held that evidence of the answers should have been excluded. The questions were not necessary to the maintenance of the undercover pose. They went directly to the issue of guilty knowledge, they were hotly disputed, and there had been no caution and no contemporary record.

In a number of cases the trickery, or subterfuge, has involved the use of an accomplice. In *R v Cadette*[157] B, arrested as a suspected drugs courier, was asked by customs officers to telephone C, in accordance with an arrangement previously made between B and C, but to pretend that she had not been arrested and to try to persuade C to come to the airport. Evidence of their conversation, which was recorded, was held to have been properly admitted. The court observed that, in practical terms, there comes a point when officers move from following up available lines of inquiry to obtain evidence against others involved to a stage where they seek in effect to deprive a suspect of the protection afforded by the 1984 Act and the Codes, but held that the officers had not crossed the line. The provisions of the 1984 Act did not apply; there was a reliable record of the conversation; and the ruse, of itself, did not give rise to unfairness for the purposes of section 78.[158]

---

[153] [1963] 1 All ER 848 and [1987] 3 All ER 481.

[154] Similar reasoning was applied in *R v Maclean* [1993] Crim LR 687, CA, and *R v Cadette* [1995] Crim LR 229, CA, both below. See also *R v Deenik* [1992] Crim LR 578, CA (police evidence of voice identification, D not having been warned that an officer was listening).

[155] See also *R v Lin* [1995] Crim LR 817, CA.

[156] [1992] 4 All ER 567, CA.

[157] [1995] Crim LR 229, CA.

[158] See also *R v Jelen; R v Katz* (1989) 90 Cr App R 456, CA and *R v Edwards* [1997] Crim LR 348, CA.

The line was crossed, however, in *Allan v United Kingdom*[159] A, suspected of murder, was interviewed by officers on several occasions but, acting on legal advice, consistently refused to answer questions. H, an experienced informer, who had undergone coaching by police informers, was fitted with recording devices and placed in A's cell for the specific purpose of questioning him to obtain information about the murder. At the trial H gave evidence, which proved to be decisive, that A had admitted his presence at the scene of the murder, but this conversation had not been recorded on tape. A was convicted. The European Court of Human Rights was satisfied that using statements obtained in a manner which effectively undermines a suspect's right to make a meaningful choice whether to speak to the authorities or to remain silent infringes procedural rights inherent in Article 6. The court acknowledged that whether the right to silence is undermined to such an extent as to invoke Article 6 will depend upon the circumstances of the case, but, distinguishing *Khan v United Kingdom*, was satisfied that evidence of the conversation had been obtained without sufficient regard to fair trial guarantees:

> the admissions allegedly made by the applicant to H . . . were not spontaneous and unprompted statements volunteered by the applicant, but were induced by the persistent questioning of H who, at the instance of the police, channeled their conversations into discussions of the murder in circumstances which can be regarded as the functional equivalent of interrogation, without any of the safeguards which would attach to a formal police interview, including the attendance of a solicitor and the issuing of the usual caution.[160]

The conviction was subsequently quashed by the Court of Appeal[161] on the basis that H was a 'police stooge' carrying out the equivalent of interrogation after A had exercised a right of silence, impinging on that right and the privilege against self-incrimination.

ADDITIONAL READING

Ashworth, 'Redrawing the Boundaries of Entrapment' [2002] *Crim LR* 161.

Choo and Nash, 'Improperly obtained evidence in the Commonwealth: lessons for England and Wales?' (2007) 11 *E&P* 75.

Home Office, *Achieving Best Evidence in Criminal Proceedings: Guidance for Vulnerable or Intimidated Witnesses, Including Children ('The Memorandum')* <www.homeoffice.gov.uk>.

Keenan et al, 'Interviewing Allegedly Abused Children' [1999] *Crim LR* 863.

Mahoney, 'Abolition of New Zealand's Prima Facie Exclusionary Rule' [2003] *Crim LR* 607.

Mirfield, *Silence, Confessions and Improperly Obtained Evidence* (Oxford, 1997) Chs 2, 6, and 12.

Ormerod, 'ECHR and the Exclusion of Evidence: Trial Remedies for Article 8 Breaches' [2003] *Crim LR* 61.

Roberts, 'Questions of "Who was there?" and "Who did what?": The Application of Code D in Cases of Dispute as to Participation but not Presence' [2003] *Crim LR* 709.

Zuckerman, *The Principles of Criminal Evidence* (Oxford, 1989) Ch 16.

---

[159] (2002) 36 EHRR 143.
[160] At para 52.
[161] *R v Allan* [2005] Crim LR 716, CA.

The burden and standard of proof

4

Key Issues

- Where facts are in issue in either a civil or criminal trial, which party should have an obligation to prove those facts, and why?

- Where a party in a criminal trial has an obligation to prove facts, why should a judge, before allowing the party to attempt to prove the facts to a jury, first require the party to adduce sufficient evidence to make out a prima facie case?

- How persuasive must the evidence of facts adduced by a party be before those facts can be regarded as having been legally proved (a) where the party is prosecuting; (b) where the party is the accused and is relying on those facts in his defence; and (c) where the party is a party in a civil trial?

- Should an accused have an obligation to prove facts in his defence?

The burden of proof

Standing alone, the expression 'burden of proof' is self-explanatory: it is the obligation to prove. There are two principal kinds of burden, the legal burden and the evidential burden. The legal burden is a burden of proof. However, as we shall see, it is confusing and misleading to speak of the evidential burden as a burden of proof, first because when borne by a defendant it may be discharged by evidence other than the evidence adduced by the defence and therefore may not in substance be a burden at all,[1] and secondly because it can be discharged by the production of evidence that falls short of proof.[2]

The content of the first half of this chapter is largely concerned with the rules governing which party bears the legal and evidential burdens on which facts in issue. The practical importance of these rules is fourfold. They can, of course, determine the eventual outcome of the proceedings. Additionally they determine which party has the right to begin adducing evidence in court; in what circumstances a defendant, at the end of the case for the prosecution, or claimant, may make a successful submission of no case to answer; and how the trial judge should direct the jury. However, easy as it is to outline the nature and importance of this subject, detailed analysis is made difficult by problems of classification and terminology. It will be convenient, then, to begin by defining and distinguishing the legal, evidential, and other burdens before considering in detail which burden is borne by each of the parties on the various facts in issue in any given case.

The legal burden

This burden has been referred to as 'the burden of proof' or 'probative burden'[3] and as 'the ultimate burden'. Another label, 'the burden of proof on the pleadings',[4] is used to show that this burden is sometimes indicated by the pleadings. Two further phrases, 'the risk of non-persuasion'[5] and 'the persuasive burden', are used to show that a party bearing the burden on a particular fact in issue will lose on that issue if he fails to discharge the burden. Most of these labels are, to some extent, misleading, and in the ensuing text this burden will be referred to simply as 'the legal burden'.

The legal burden may be defined as the obligation imposed on a party by a rule of law to prove a fact in issue. Whether a party has discharged this burden and proved a fact in issue is decided only once, by the tribunal of fact, at the end of the case when both parties have called all their evidence. The standard of proof required to discharge the legal burden depends upon whether the proceedings are criminal or civil. In the former the standard required of the prosecution is proof 'beyond reasonable doubt', in the latter the standard required is proof 'on the balance of probabilities'. A party who fails to discharge a legal burden borne by him to the required standard of proof will lose on the issue in question.

The legal burden relates to particular facts in issue.[6] Most cases, of course, involve more than one issue and the legal burden of proof in relation to these issues may be distributed

---

[1] See *Bullard v R* [1957] AC 635, PC, below, and per Pill LJ in *L v DPP* [2003] QB 137, DC at [23].

[2] Per Lord Devlin in *Jayasena v R* [1970] AC 618, PC at 624.

[3] See *DPP v Morgan* [1976] AC 182, HL.

[4] Phipson, *Law of Evidence* (16th edn, London, 2005) ch 6 para 6-02.

[5] Wigmore, *A Treatise on the Anglo-American System of Evidence* (3rd edn, Boston, 1940) ch IX, paras 248–9.

[6] A question of construction is a question of *law* in respect of which no burden lies on either side; but if a party relies on surrounding circumstances as an aid to construction, then the onus is on him to prove them: see per Nourse LJ, construing a conveyance in *Scott v Martin* [1987] 2 All ER 813, CA at 817.

between the parties to the action. We shall see, for example, that in a criminal case where insanity is raised by way of defence, the legal burden in relation to that issue is borne by the defendant, whereas the prosecution may well bear the legal burden on all the other facts in issue. In civil proceedings, an example would be a negligence action in which the defendant alleges contributory negligence: the claimant bears the legal burden on the issue of negligence, the defendant on contributory negligence. The obligation on a party to prove a fact in issue may oblige that party to negative or disprove a particular fact. In criminal proceedings, for example, the prosecution bear the legal burden of proving lack of consent on a charge of rape.[7]

In civil cases, a judge may find it impossible to make a finding one way or the other on a fact in issue, so that it will then fall to be decided by reference to which party bears the legal burden on the issue. The principles governing this situation were summarized in *Stephens v Cannon*:[8] the situation has to be exceptional but can arise in relation to any issue; and the court is only entitled to have such resort to the legal burden if it cannot reasonably make a finding, in which case it should tell the parties that it has striven to make a finding and explain why it cannot do so, except in those few cases where such matters can readily be inferred from the circumstances.

Which party bears the legal burden of proof in relation to any given fact in issue is determined by the rules of substantive law discussed below. Judges sometimes refer to the 'shifting' of a burden of proof from one party to his opponent. The phrase is apt to mislead. The only sense in which the legal burden may be said to shift is on the operation of a rebuttable presumption of law. Rebuttable presumptions of law are considered in detail in Chapter 22, but it is convenient, at this stage, briefly to consider their operation. Where such a presumption applies, once a primary fact is proved or admitted, in the absence of further evidence another fact must be presumed. The quantity and quality of evidence required to rebut the presumed fact is determined by the substantive law in relation to the presumption in question. The party relying on the presumption bears the burden of proving the primary fact. Once he has adduced sufficient evidence on that fact, in the case of a 'persuasive' presumption his adversary will bear the legal burden of disproving the presumed fact. The burden may be said to have shifted. However, when judges refer to a shifting of the burden in circumstances other than on the operation of rebuttable presumptions of law, they mean that the burden may, at any given moment in the course of the trial, *appear* to have been satisfied by the party on whom it lies by virtue of the evidence adduced by that party. Insofar as this places a burden on that party's opponent, the opponent bears a 'tactical' burden. The legal burden has not shifted because, as noted above, whether the legal burden has been discharged by a party is only determined once and that is at the end of the trial when *all* the evidence has been adduced.[9] The tactical burden is discussed more fully in contrast with the evidential burden.

---

[7] The operation of the legal burden in rape cases has been affected by the creation of presumptions of lack of consent under the Sexual Offences Act 2003 where certain circumstances or acts are proved by the prosecution. The presumptions are mostly 'evidential' presumptions, but in rare cases a 'conclusive' presumption may arise. Presumptions are touched on shortly in this chapter and dealt with more fully in Ch 22.

[8] [2005] EWCA Civ 222.

[9] See per Sir Christopher Staughton in *Re W* [2001] 4 All ER 88, CA at 93–4. See also per Mustill LJ in *Brady (Inspector of Taxes) v Group Lotus Car Companies plc* [1987] 3 All ER 1050, CA at 1059.

The evidential burden

This burden is also referred to as 'the burden of adducing evidence' and 'the duty of passing the judge'. It may be defined as the obligation on a party to adduce sufficient evidence of a fact to justify a finding on that fact in favour of the party so obliged. In other words, it obliges a party to adduce sufficient evidence for the issue to go before the tribunal of fact. It is confusing and misleading, therefore, to call the evidential burden a burden of *proof*: it can be discharged by the production of evidence that falls short of proof.[10] Whether a party has discharged the burden is decided only once in the course of a trial, and by the judge as opposed to the tribunal of fact. The burden is discharged when there is sufficient evidence to justify, as a possibility, a favourable finding by the tribunal of fact. Thus in a criminal trial in which the prosecution bear the evidential burden on a particular issue, they must adduce sufficient evidence to prevent the judge from withdrawing that issue from the jury. If the prosecution discharge the evidential burden, it does not necessarily mean that they will succeed on the issue in question. The accused will not necessarily lose on that issue, even if he adduces no evidence in rebuttal, although if he takes that course that is a clear risk he runs. If the prosecution also bear the legal burden on the same issue, and fail to discharge the evidential burden, they necessarily fail on that issue since the judge refuses to let the issue go before the jury. However, it does not follow that a discharge of the evidential burden necessarily results in a discharge of the legal burden; the issue in question goes before the jury, who may or may not find in favour of the prosecution on that issue.

Like the legal burden, the evidential burden relates to particular facts in issue. The evidential burden in relation to the various issues in a given case may be distributed between the parties to the action. Normally, a party bearing the legal burden in relation to a particular fact at the commencement of the proceedings also bears an evidential burden in relation to the same fact. However, this is not invariably so. Thus although, as we shall see, the prosecution bear the legal burden of negativing most common law and certain statutory defences (including the defences of provocation, self-defence, duress, and non-insane automatism), such a defence will not be put before the jury unless the accused has discharged the evidential burden in that regard. Equally, and to complicate matters further, the evidential burden borne by the accused in these circumstances may be discharged by *any* evidence in the case, whether given by the accused, a co-accused, or the prosecution, and in this sense the so-called evidential burden is not a burden on the accused at all.[11] If the evidential burden is discharged, whether by defence or prosecution evidence, the prosecution will then bear the legal burden of disproving the defence in question, but if there is no evidence to support the defence, then the judge is entitled to withdraw it from the jury.[12]

As in the case of the legal burden, judges sometimes refer to the 'shifting' of the evidential burden. The evidential burden may sensibly be said to shift on the operation of a rebuttable presumption of law of the 'evidential' variety.[13] However, the phrase has also been employed in

[10] Per Lord Devlin in *Jayasena v R* [1970] AC 618 PC at 624.

[11] Per Pill LJ in *L v DPP* [2003] QB 137, DC at [23].

[12] *R v Pommell* [1995] 2 Cr App R 607, CA, where it was also held that although normally a judge will not have to decide whether to leave a particular defence to the jury until the conclusion of the evidence, in rare cases where the nature of the evidence to be called is clear, it may be appropriate, in order to save time and costs, for the judge to indicate at an early stage what his ruling is likely to be.

[13] Where a party relying on an 'evidential' presumption has adduced sufficient evidence on the primary or basic fact, his adversary will bear an evidential burden to adduce some evidence to rebut the presumed fact. See further Ch 22.

other circumstances. Where a party discharges an evidential burden borne by him in relation to a particular fact, his adversary will be under an obligation, referred to as the provisional or tactical burden, to adduce counter-evidence in order to convince the tribunal of fact in his favour. If he chooses not to adduce such counter-evidence, he runs the risk of a finding on that issue in favour of the other party. It is in these circumstances, also, that judges refer to a shifting of the evidential burden.[14] This conjures up a vision of the trial as a ball-game, with the evidential burden as the ball, which is continuously bounced to and fro between the contenders. This is misleading because although examination followed by cross-examination of witnesses often results in swings of fortune for and then against a party, normally in a trial, whether civil or criminal, one party first adduces all of his evidence before his adversary then adduces his. But there is a more important sense in which the phrase misleads. The evidential burden only needs to be considered by the court on two occasions, first at the beginning of a trial, to determine which party starts, and secondly when, during the trial, the judge determines whether sufficient evidence has been adduced to leave an issue before the tribunal of fact. If the judge decides at the latter stage that insufficient evidence has been adduced, the issue will be withdrawn from the tribunal of fact and further consideration of the evidential burden is irrelevant. But further consideration of the evidential burden is equally irrelevant when the judge allows the issue to go before the tribunal of fact. It is certainly possible to say, at this stage, that the evidential burden has shifted to the opponent and that he, by adducing counter-evidence, may cause the evidential burden to shift back to the first party, and so on, but such observations are of no legal significance. So far as the court is concerned, the evidential burden requires no further consideration; the only burden remaining at this stage is the legal burden.[15]

The incidence of the legal burden

Which party bears the legal burden is determined by the rules of substantive law set out in the precedents and statutes. Speaking generally, the determination of where the legal burden falls is a matter of common sense. If certain facts are essential to the claim of, for example, the claimant in civil proceedings or the prosecution in criminal proceedings, that party must prove them. A useful starting-point—although, as we shall see, a far from reliable guide—is the maxim 'he who asserts must prove' (*ei incumbit probatio qui dicit, non qui negat*). In *Wakelin v London and South Western Rly Co*[16] a widow brought an action in negligence under the Fatal Accidents Act 1846. The only available evidence was that her husband had been found dead near a level crossing at the side of a railway line. Lord Halsbury LC held that the widow bore the burden of proving that her husband's death had been caused by the defendants' negligence; if she could not discharge that burden, she failed. Even assuming that the husband had been knocked down by a train while on the crossing, the evidence adduced was as capable of leading to the conclusion that the husband had been negligent as it was of showing the defendants' negligence and, accordingly, the defendants' negligence was not proved.[17]

A detailed examination of the incidence of the legal burden of proof requires that criminal and civil cases be considered separately.

---

[14] See, eg, per Lord Goddard CJ in *R v Matheson* [1958] 1 WLR 474, CCA at 478. See also *Rickards and Rickards v Kerrier District Council* (1987) 151 JP 625, DC.

[15] See *Sutton v Sadler* (1857) 3 CBNS 87 (see Ch 22).

[16] (1886) 12 App Cas 41, HL.

[17] Cf *Jones v Great Western Rly Co* (1930) 144 LT 194, HL.

Criminal cases

Speaking generally, the legal burden of proving any fact essential to the prosecution case rests upon the prosecution and remains with the prosecution throughout the trial. Negative as well as positive allegations may be essential to the case for the prosecution. Thus the prosecution bear the legal burden of proving absence of consent on a charge of rape or assault.[18] Generally, therefore, the accused bears no legal burden in respect of the essential ingredients of an offence, whether they be positive or negative and whether or not he denies any or all of them. In *Woolmington v DPP*[19] the accused, charged with the murder of his wife, gave evidence that he had shot her accidentally. The trial judge directed the jury that once it was proved that the accused had shot his wife, he bore the burden of disproving malice aforethought. The House of Lords held this to be a misdirection and Lord Sankey LC said, in a now famous passage:[20]

> Throughout the web of the English criminal law one golden thread is always to be seen, that it is the duty of the prosecution to prove the prisoner's guilt subject to what I have already said as to the defence of insanity and subject also to any statutory exception . . . No matter what the charge or where the trial, the principle that the prosecution must prove the guilt of the prisoner is part of the common law of England and no attempt to whittle it down can be entertained . . . It is not the law of England to say, as was said in the summing up in the present case: 'if the Crown satisfy you that this woman died at the prisoner's hands then he has to show that there are circumstances to be found in the evidence which has been given from the witness-box in this case which alleviate the crime so that it is only manslaughter or which excuse the homicide altogether by showing it was a pure accident . . .

The rule enunciated by Lord Sankey is subject to three categories of exception: where the accused raises the defence of insanity, where a statute expressly places the legal burden on the defence, and where a statute impliedly places the legal burden on the defence. The statutory exceptions are often referred to as reverse onus provisions. Since the coming into force of the Human Rights Act 1998, any such provision is open to challenge on the basis of its incompatibility with the presumption of innocence guaranteed by Article 6(2) of the European Convention on Human Rights. This aspect of the topic receives separate treatment, below.

Insanity. Where an accused raises insanity as a defence, he bears the legal burden of proving it.[21] The justification is based on the difficulty of disproving false claims of insanity, given that the accused may not cooperate with an investigation of his state of mind.[22] Where an accused is charged with murder and raises the issue of *either* insanity *or* diminished responsibility, the prosecution, pursuant to section 6 of the Criminal Procedure (Insanity) Act 1964, is allowed to adduce evidence to prove the other of those issues. In this event, the prosecution bear the legal burden of proving the other issue on which they have adduced evidence.[23] If an accused is alleged to be under a disability rendering him unfit to plead and stand trial, the issue may be raised, under section 4 of the 1964 Act, by either the prosecution or defence. If the issue is

---

[18] *R v Horn* (1912) 7 Cr App R 200; *R v Donovan* [1934] 2 KB 498. But see also ss 75 and 76 of the Sexual Offences Act 2003.

[19] [1935] AC 462, HL.

[20] [1935] AC 462 at 481–2.

[21] *M'Naghten's Case* (1843) 10 Cl&Fin 200, HL.

[22] For a critique of the justification, see Ashworth, 'Four threats to the presumption of innocence' (2006) 10 *E&P* 241 at 263–5.

[23] The standard to be met by the prosecution in these circumstances is proof beyond reasonable doubt: *R v Grant* [1960] Crim LR 424.

raised by the prosecution, they must prove it and satisfy the jury beyond reasonable doubt;[24] if the issue is raised by the defence, they must prove it, but only on a balance of probabilities, the lower standard of proof.[25]

Express statutory exceptions. A number of statutes expressly place on the accused the legal burden of proving specified issues. The legal burden of proof in relation to all issues other than those so specified remains on the prosecution. For example, section 2(2) of the Homicide Act 1957 places upon the accused the legal burden of establishing the statutory defence of diminished responsibility on a charge of murder.[26] Section 2(2) does not contravene Article 6 of the European Convention on Human Rights.[27] Other examples are considered at 86 below under the heading of **Reverse onus provisions and the Human Rights Act 1998**.

Implied statutory exceptions. Section 101 of the Magistrates' Courts Act 1980 (the 1980 Act), formerly section 81 of the Magistrates' Courts Act 1952 (the 1952 Act), provides as follows:

> Where the defendant to an information or complaint relies for his defence on any exception, exemption, proviso, excuse or qualification, whether or not it accompanies the description of the offence or matter of complaint in the enactment creating the offence or on which the complaint is founded, the burden of proving the exception, exemption, proviso, excuse or qualification shall be on him; and this notwithstanding that the information or complaint contains an allegation negativing the exception, exemption, proviso, excuse or qualification.

This section applies to summary trials but at common law similar principles applied to trials on indictment and it was held by the Court of Appeal in *R v Edwards*,[28] and confirmed by the House of Lords in *R v Hunt*,[29] that the section sets out the common law rule in statutory form. If this were not so, then in the case of an offence triable either way, the incidence of the burden of proof could vary—but for no good reason—according to whether the accused is tried summarily or on indictment.

Implied statutory exceptions within section 101 of the 1980 Act are capable of derogating from Article 6 of the European Convention;[30] and the cases, in the ensuing text, in which, by virtue of section 101 or the common law principles on which it is based, particular statutory provisions have been construed to impose a legal burden on the accused, must now be read subject to the Human Rights Act 1998 and the cases in which reverse onus provisions have been challenged on the basis of incompatibility with Article 6.[31]

Section 101 applies to statutory provisions which define a criminal offence and use words such as 'unless', 'provided that', 'except', or 'other than', to set out an exception, proviso, etc

---

[24] *R v Robertson* [1968] 1 WLR 1767, CA.

[25] *R v Podola* [1960] 1 QB 325, CCA.

[26] Section 2(2) not only dictates which party shoulders the burden of proof once the issue is raised, but also leaves it to the defence to decide whether the issue should be raised at all; if, therefore, the defence does not raise the issue but there is evidence of diminished responsibility, the trial judge is not bound to direct the jury to consider the matter but, at most, should in the absence of the jury draw the matter to the attention of the defence so that they may decide whether they wish the issue to be considered by the jury: per Lord Lane CJ, obiter, in *R v Campbell* (1986) 84 Cr App R 255, CA.

[27] See *R v Lambert; R v Ali; and R v Jordan* [2001] 2 WLR 211, CA.

[28] [1975] QB 27.

[29] [1987] AC 352. HL.

[30] See per Clarke LJ in *R (Grundy & Co Excavations Ltd) v Halton Division Magistrates' Court* (2003) 167 JP 387, DC at [61].

[31] See below.

which amounts to a defence. The definition of an offence, and the exception or proviso to it, are not always readily distinguishable. However, before considering the kind of statute capable of giving rise to difficulty, two reasonably straightforward examples of the kind of provision to which section 101 applies may be given: (i) section 87(1) of the Road Traffic Act 1988, which provides that it is an offence for a person to drive a vehicle on a road otherwise than in accordance with a licence;[32] and (ii) section 161(1) of the Highways Act 1980, which provides that if a person, without lawful authority or excuse, deposits anything whatsoever on a highway in consequence of which a user of the highway is injured or endangered, that person shall be guilty of an offence. In *Gatland v Metropolitan Police Comr*[33] Lord Parker CJ held that although it was for the prosecution to prove that a thing had been deposited on the highway and that in consequence thereof a user of the highway had been injured or endangered, it was for the accused to raise and prove lawful authority or excuse pursuant to section 81 of the 1952 Act.[34] In *Westminster City Council v Croyalgrange Ltd*,[35] by contrast, no reliance could be placed on what is now section 101 of the 1980 Act. A company which had let premises to a person who used them as a sex establishment without a licence was charged under Schedule 3, paragraph 20(1)(a), of the Local Government (Miscellaneous Provisions) Act 1982, whereby a person who knowingly causes or permits the use of premises contrary to Schedule 3, paragraph 6, commits an offence. Paragraph 6 provides that no persons shall use any premises as a sex establishment except under and in accordance with a licence. The House of Lords held that section 101 was inapplicable because the exception in question qualified the prohibition created by paragraph 6 and not the offence created by paragraph 20(1)(a). The prosecution bore the burden of proving, inter alia, that the directors of the company knew that no licence had been obtained by the tenant.[36]

Nimmo v Alexander Cowan & Sons Ltd[37] was another case giving rise to some difficulty. This was a Scottish case brought by an injured workman under section 29(1) of the Factories Act 1961, which provides that 'every place at which any person has at any time to work . . . shall, so far as is reasonably practicable, be made and kept safe for any person working therein'. The workman alleged that his place of work was not kept safe but did not aver that it was reasonably practicable to make it safe. Section 155(1) of the 1961 Act makes a breach of section 29(1) a summary offence and although the case in question was a civil one, the House of Lords referred to the Scottish equivalent of section 81 of the 1952 Act and Lord Pearson made it clear that the incidence of the burden of proof would be the same whether the proceedings were civil or criminal.[38] The House held, Lords Reid and Wilberforce dissenting, that there was

---

[32] On being charged with this offence, it is for an accused to prove that he satisfies the proviso of holding a current driving licence. See *John v Humphreys* [1955] 1 WLR 325, DC. See also *Leeds City Council v Azam* (1988) 153 JP 157, DC: it is for the accused to prove that he is *exempted* from the need for a licence for the operation of a private hire vehicle under s 75 of the Local Government (Miscellaneous Provisions) Act 1976.

[33] [1968] 2 QB 279, a decision under s 140(1) of the Highways Act 1959, re-enacted in s 161(1) of the 1980 Act.

[34] Cf Offences Against the Person Act 1861, s 16: a person who without lawful excuse makes to another a threat, intending that the other would fear it would be carried out, to kill that other or a third person shall be guilty of an offence. In *R v Cousins* [1982] QB 526, CA, it was held that on a charge under s 16, the onus is on the prosecution to prove absence of lawful excuse for making the threat.

[35] (1986) 83 Cr App R 155, HL.

[36] See also, construing s 33(1)(a) of the Environmental Protection Act 1990, *Environment Agency v ME Foley Contractors Ltd* [2002] 1 WLR 1754, DC.

[37] [1968] AC 107.

[38] [1968] AC 107, HL at 134. Although Lord Reid dissented, his opinion on this point, at [115], was the same.

no burden on the plaintiff employee to prove that it was reasonably practicable to keep the premises safe; the defendant employers bore the burden of proving that it was *not* reasonably practicable to keep the premises safe. In reaching this decision, the majority was of the opinion that where, on the face of the statute, it is unclear on whom the burden should lie, a court, in order to determine Parliament's intention, may go beyond the mere form of the enactment and look to other, policy, considerations such as the mischief at which the Act was aimed and the ease or difficulty that the respective parties would encounter in discharging the burden. Given that the defendant was better able to discharge the legal burden than the plaintiff, the construction of the majority, it is submitted, best achieved the object of the enactment in question, namely to provide a safe place of work.

On its wording, section 101 applies to summary trials. Concerning trials on indictment, the leading authorities are *R v Edwards*[39] and *R v Hunt*.[40] In *R v Edwards* the accused was convicted on indictment of selling intoxicating liquor without holding a justices' licence authorizing such sale contrary to section 160(1)(a) of the Licensing Act 1964. Edwards appealed, one of his grounds being that the prosecution had not called any evidence to prove that he did not hold a licence. It was submitted, on his behalf, that at common law the burden of proving an exception, exemption, proviso, excuse, or qualification fell on the defence only when the facts constituting it were peculiarly within the defendant's own knowledge[41] and that in the instant case they were not. The clerk to the licensing justices for any district is statutorily bound to keep a register of local licences and accordingly the police had access to a public source of knowledge. The Court of Appeal held that the legal burden of proving that the accused was the holder of a justices' licence rested on the defence and not the prosecution. After an extensive review of the authorities, Lawton LJ continued:[42]

> In our judgment this line of authority establishes that over the centuries the common law, as a result of experience and the need to ensure that justice is done both to the community and to the defendants, has evolved an exception to the fundamental rule of our common law that the prosecution must prove every element of the offence charged. This exception . . . is limited to offences arising under enactments which prohibit the doing of an act save in specified circumstances or by persons of specified classes or with specified qualifications or with the licence or permission of specified authorities. Whenever the prosecution seeks to rely on this exception, the court must construe the enactment under which the charge is laid. If the true construction is that the enactment prohibits the doing of acts, subject to provisos, exemptions and the like, then the prosecution can rely upon the exception.
>
> In our judgment its application does not depend upon either the fact, or the presumption, that the defendant has peculiar knowledge enabling him to prove the positive of any negative averment.

In *R v Hunt*[43] the accused was charged with the unlawful possession of morphine contrary to section 5 of the Misuse of Drugs Act 1971 (the 1971 Act). Under the Misuse of Drugs Regulations 1973 (the 1973 Regulations), it is provided that section 5 shall not have effect in relation to, inter alia, any preparation of morphine containing not more than 0.2 per cent

---

[39] [1975] QB 27, CA.

[40] [1987] AC 352, HL.

[41] See *R v Turner* (1816) 5 M&S 206 at 211, followed in *R v Oliver* [1944] KB 68 (dealing in sugar without a licence) and *John v Humphreys* [1955] 1 WLR 325, DC (driving without a licence). See also *R v Ewens* [1967] 1 QB 322, CCA (possessing drugs without a prescription).

[42] [1975] QB 27 at 39–40.

[43] [1987] AC 352, HL.

of morphine. At the trial the defence submitted that there was no case to answer because the prosecution had adduced no evidence as to the proportion of morphine in the powder which had been found in Hunt's possession. The judge ruled against the submission. Hunt changed his plea to guilty. The appeal to the Court of Appeal was dismissed. In support of his further appeal to the House of Lords the accused raised two arguments: (i) *R v Edwards* was wrongly decided; and (ii) on the true construction of the provisions in question, the prosecution bore the burden of proving that the facts fell outside the 'exception' contained in the 1973 Regulations. The prosecution submitted that *R v Edwards* did apply and that the burden was on the accused to show that the facts fell within the 'exception'.

The House of Lords allowed the appeal. The reasoning was as follows:

1. When, in *Woolmington v DPP*,[44] Lord Sankey used the phrase 'any statutory exception', he was not referring *only* to statutory exceptions in which Parliament has placed the burden of proof on the accused expressly. A statute can place the legal burden of proof on an accused either expressly or by implication, ie on its true construction.[45]

2. Where a statute places the legal burden on the accused by implication, that burden is on the accused whether the case be tried summarily or on indictment; section 101 of the 1980 Act reflects and applies to summary trials the rule relating to the incidence of the burden of proof evolved by judges on trials on indictment.

3. *R v Edwards* was decided correctly subject to one qualification: on occasions, albeit rarely, a statute will be construed as imposing the legal burden on the accused although it is outside the ambit of the formula given by Lawton LJ. The present case did not come within the formula, which was 'limited to offences arising under enactments which prohibit the doing of an act save in specified circumstances or by persons of specified classes or with specified qualifications or with the licence or permission of specified authorities'. The formula, although 'a helpful approach'[46] and 'an excellent guide to construction',[47] was not intended to be and is not exclusive in its effect.

4. In the final analysis, each case must turn on the construction of the particular legislation. If the linguistic construction of a statute does not clearly indicate on whom the burden should lie, the court, in construing it, is not confined to the form of wording of the provision but, as in *Nimmo v Alexander Cowan & Sons Ltd*,[48] may have regard to matters of policy including practical considerations and in particular the ease or otherwise that the respective parties would encounter if required to discharge the burden.[49] Parliament, however, can never lightly be taken to have imposed the duty on an accused to prove his innocence in a criminal case and the courts should be very slow to draw any such inference from the language of a statute.[50]

[44] [1935] AC 462, HL.
[45] See per Lords Griffiths and Ackner [1987] AC 352 at [6]–[7] and [15] respectively.
[46] Per Lord Ackner at [19].
[47] Per Lord Griffiths at [11].
[48] [1968] AC 107.
[49] On this basis it is possible to explain cases formerly difficult to reconcile with *R v Edwards* such as *R v Putland and Sorrell* [1946] 1 All ER 85, CCA, *R v Cousins* [1982] QB 526, CA, above, *R v Curgerwen* (1865) LR 1 CCR 1, and *R v Audley* [1907] 1 KB 383.
[50] Per Lord Griffiths [1987] 1 All ER 1 at 11.

5. Policy, in the present case, pointed to the legal burden being on the prosecution. This would not be an undue burden because in most cases the substance in question would have been analysed before a prosecution was brought and therefore there would be no difficulty in producing evidence to show that it did contain a certain percentage of morphine. If the burden was on the accused, however, he would have real practical difficulties because the substance is usually seized by the police and he has no statutory entitlement to a proportion of it. Moreover, the substance may already have been analysed by the police and destroyed in the process.

6. The question of construction being one of obviously real difficulty and offences involving the misuse of hard drugs being among the most serious of offences, any ambiguity should be resolved in favour of the accused. For these reasons, therefore, the appeal was allowed.

In its 11th report, the Criminal Law Revision Committee was strongly of the opinion that both on principle and for the sake of clarity and convenience in practice, burdens on the defence should be evidential only.[51] In *R v Hunt*, Lord Griffiths thought that such a fundamental change was a matter for Parliament and not a decision for the House of Lords.[52]

Reverse onus provisions and the Human Rights Act 1998. Since the coming into force of the Human Rights Act 1998 (the 1998 Act), any reverse onus provision is open to challenge on the basis of its incompatibility with Article 6(2) of the European Convention on Human Rights, under which 'Everyone charged with a criminal offence shall be presumed innocent until proved guilty according to law.' Clearly, a reverse onus provision will not inevitably give rise to a finding of incompatibility,[53] but if a provision does unjustifiably infringe Article 6(2), the further issue will arise whether it should be read down, in accordance with the obligation under section 3 of the 1998 Act, so as to impose an evidential and not a legal burden on the accused.

The underlying rationale of the presumption of innocence in both domestic law and in the Convention, is that it is repugnant to ordinary notions of fairness for a prosecutor to accuse an accused of a crime and for the accused then to be required to disprove the accusation on pain of conviction and punishment if he fails to do so.[54] Under domestic law, as will be apparent from the foregoing text, Parliament does not regard the presumption as an absolute or unqualified right. Equally, the Article 6(2) right is neither absolute nor unqualified. In reaching a decision on the question of incompatibility, the test is whether the modification or limitation of the Article 6(2) right pursues a legitimate aim and whether it satisfies the principle of proportionality: a balance has to be struck between the general interest of the community and the protection of the fundamental rights of the individual.[55] In *Attorney General's Reference (No 4 of 2002)*[56] Lord Bingham considered the scope of the presumption under the Convention. After an extensive review of the jurisprudence of the European Court, including the leading authority of *Salabiaku v France*,[57] his Lordship summarized the relevant principles to be derived from the Strasbourg case law:

[51] Subject to two minor exceptions: see Cmnd 4991, paras 140–1.
[52] [1987] 1 All ER 1 at 12.
[53] Per Lord Hope in *R v Lambert* [2002] 2 AC 545, HL, at [87].
[54] Per Lord Bingham in *Attorney General's Reference (No 4 of 2002)* [2005] 1 AC 264, HL, at [9].
[55] Per Lord Hope in *R v Lambert* [2002] 2 AC 545, HL, at [88].
[56] [2005] 1 AC 264, HL, at [21].
[57] (1988) 13 EHRR 379, ECHR.

The overriding concern is that a trial should be fair, and the presumption of innocence is a fundamental right directed to that end. The Convention does not outlaw presumptions of fact or law[58] but requires that these should be kept within reasonable limits and should not be arbitrary. It is open to states to define the constituent elements of a criminal offence, excluding the requirement of *mens rea*. But the substance and effect of any presumption adverse to a defendant must be examined, and must be reasonable. Relevant to any judgment on reasonableness or proportionality will be the opportunity given to the defendant to rebut the presumption, maintenance of the rights of the defence, flexibility in application of the presumption, retention by the court of a power to assess the evidence, the importance of what is at stake and the difficulty which a prosecutor may face in the absence of a presumption. Security concerns do not absolve member states from their duty to observe basic standards of fairness. The justifiability of any infringement of the presumption of innocence cannot be resolved by any rule of thumb, but on examination of all the facts and circumstances of the particular provision as applied in the particular case.

In *R v Lambert*,[59] L, found in possession of a duffle bag containing two kilograms of cocaine, was charged with, and convicted of, possession of cocaine with intent to supply, contrary to section 5(3) of the 1971 Act. L had relied upon section 28 of the 1971 Act, asserting that he did not believe or suspect or have reason to suspect that the bag contained cocaine or any controlled drug. The trial judge had directed the jury that in order to establish possession of a controlled drug, the Crown merely had to prove that L had the bag in his possession and that in fact it contained a controlled drug, and that thereafter the burden was on L to bring himself within section 28 and 'to prove', on a balance of probabilities, that he did not know that the bag contained a controlled drug. The House of Lords held, by majority, that since the trial had taken place before the coming into force of the 1998 Act, L was not entitled to rely on an alleged breach of his rights under the European Convention. However, the House was of the view (Lord Hutton dissenting) that section 28 is not compatible with Article 6(2) and, under section 3 of the 1988 Act, may be read as imposing no more than an evidential burden on the accused.

Lord Steyn approached the question of compatibility by applying a three-stage test: (i) whether there has been a legislative interference with the presumption in Article 6(2); (ii) if so, whether there is an objective justification for such interference; and (iii) if so, whether the interference is proportionate, ie no greater than is necessary. As to the first stage, it was held that, taking account of the fact that under section 28 an accused will be denying moral blameworthiness and that the maximum penalty for the offence is life imprisonment, knowledge of the existence and control of the contents of the container is the gravamen of the offence, and therefore section 28 derogates from the presumption of innocence. Lord Steyn also reached this conclusion on broader grounds. His Lordship noted that the distinction between constituent elements of the crime and defensive issues will sometimes be unprincipled and arbitrary: a true constituent element may not be within the definition of the crime but cast as a defensive issue and conversely a definition of the crime may be so formulated as to include all possible defences within it. It is necessary, therefore, to concentrate not on technicalities and niceties of language, but on matters of substance. A defence may be so closely linked with *mens rea* and moral blameworthiness that it will derogate from the presumption of innocence to place the burden of proving that

[58] See Ch 22.
[59] [2002] 2 AC 545, HL.

defence on the accused. In the case before the House, the issues under section 28, even if regarded as a pure defence, bore directly on the moral blameworthiness of the accused and therefore derogated from the presumption of innocence.

As to the second stage, Lord Steyn was satisfied that there is an objective justification for the legislative interference with the presumption of innocence, namely that sophisticated drug smugglers, dealers, and couriers typically secrete drugs in some container, thereby enabling the person in possession of the container to say that he was unaware of the contents. Such a defence is commonplace and poses real difficulties for the police and prosecuting authorities.

As to the third stage, it was held that the burden is on the state to show that the legislative means adopted were no greater than necessary. The principle of proportionality required the House to consider whether there was a pressing necessity to impose a legal rather than an evidential burden. The burden of showing that only a reverse legal burden can overcome the difficulties of the prosecution in drugs cases is a heavy one. In a case of possession of controlled drugs with intent to supply, although the prosecution must establish that controlled drugs were in the possession of the accused and that he knew that the package contained something, under section 28 the accused must prove on a balance of probabilities that he did not know that the package contained controlled drugs. If the jury is not satisfied of this on a balance of probabilities, or considers that the accused's version is as likely to be true as not, they must convict him. Thus a guilty verdict may be returned in respect of an offence punishable by life imprisonment even though the jury may consider that it is reasonably possible that the accused has been duped. It was held that section 28 was a disproportionate reaction to perceived difficulties facing the prosecution in drugs cases. A new realism had significantly reduced the scope of the problems faced by the prosecution. First, possession of the container presumptively suggests, in the absence of exculpatory evidence, that the possessor knew of its contents. Secondly, section 34 of the Criminal Justice and Public Order Act 1994, enabling a judge to comment on an accused's failure to mention facts when questioned or charged, has strengthened the position of the prosecution.[60] Thirdly, where a 'mixed statement', ie an out-of-court statement made by the accused which is partly inculpatory and partly exculpatory, is introduced in evidence, and the accused elects not to testify, the judge may point out to the jury that the incriminating parts are likely to be true whereas the excuses do not have the same weight, and may also comment on the election of the accused not to testify.[61] For these reasons, Lord Steyn concluded that section 28 was incompatible with Article 6(2). However, it was further held that under section 3 of the 1998 Act, where section 28(2) and (3) require the accused to 'prove' the matters specified, the word can be read to mean 'give sufficient evidence', thereby placing only an evidential burden on the accused.

R v Lambert was distinguished in *L v DPP*,[62] which involved a charge of being in possession of a lock-knife in a public place contrary to section 139 of the Criminal Justice Act 1988, in relation to section 139(4), which provides that it shall be a defence for an accused to prove that he had good reason or lawful authority for having the knife with him in a public place. It was held that, striking a fair balance, section 139(4) does not conflict with Article 6 of the Convention.[63] Six reasons were given. (1) Unlike section 28 of the 1971 Act,

[60] See Ch 14.

[61] See *R v Duncan* (1981) 73 Cr App R 359, Ch 6.

[62] [2003] QB 137, DC.

[63] See also *R v Mathews* [2004] QB 690, CA: the court, agreeing with and adopting the reasoning in *L v DPP*, held that neither s 139(4) nor s 139(5) of the 1988 Act was incompatible with Art 6.

under section 139 it is for the prosecution to prove that the accused knowingly had the offending article in his possession. (2) There is a strong public interest in bladed articles not being carried in public without good reason. Parliament is entitled, without infringing the Convention, to deter the carrying of bladed or sharply pointed articles in public to the extent of placing the burden of proving a good reason on the carrier. (3) The accused is proving something within his own knowledge. (4) The accused is entitled under Article 6 to expect the court to scrutinize the evidence with a view to deciding if a good reason exists, whether he gives evidence or not. (5) Although there will be cases in which the tribunal of fact may attach significance to where the burden of proof rests, in the great majority of cases it needs to make a value judgment as to whether, upon all the evidence, the reason is a good one, without the decision depending on whether it has to be proved that there is a good reason. (6) In striking the balance, some, albeit limited, weight should be given to the much more restricted power of sentence for an offence under section 139 than for an offence under section 5 of the 1971 Act.

R v Lambert was also distinguished in *R v Drummond*[64] in relation to the so-called 'hip flask' defence in section 15 of the Road Traffic Offenders Act 1988, under which it is for the accused to prove that he consumed alcohol after the offence but before providing a specimen. It was held that driving while over the limit and causing death by driving while over the limit are both social evils which Parliament sought to minimize by the legislation and that the legislative interference with the presumption of innocence was not only justified, but no greater than was necessary. Four reasons were given. (1) Conviction follows after a scientific test which is intended to be as exact as possible. (2) In most cases the test is exact or, to the extent that it is less than exact, the inexactness works in favour of the accused. (3) It is the accused himself who, by drinking after the event, defeats the aim of the legislature by doing something which makes the scientific test potentially unreliable. In many, perhaps most cases, the accused will have taken the alcohol after the event for the precise purpose of defeating the scientific test. (4) The relevant scientific evidence to set against the result ascertained from the specimen of breath or blood, including the amount which the accused drank after the offence, is all within the knowledge or means of access of the accused.

In *R v S*[65] the Court of Appeal considered section 92(5) of the Trade Marks Act 1994, which provides that it is a defence for a person charged with the unauthorized use of a registered trade mark to show that he believed on reasonable grounds that the use of the sign was not an infringement of the registered trade mark. It was held that section 92(5) imposed a legal burden on the accused and was compatible with Article 6(2). The same issue arose, but did not call for decision, in *R v Johnstone*,[66] in which the House of Lords, approving *R v S*, was of the same, albeit obiter, view. Lord Nicholls, in a speech endorsed by Lords Hope, Hutton, and Rodger, said:[67]

> for a reverse burden of proof to be acceptable there must be a compelling reason why it is fair and reasonable to deny the accused person the protection normally guaranteed to everyone by the presumption of innocence . . . A sound starting point is to remember that if an accused is required to prove a fact on the balance of probability to avoid conviction, this permits a conviction in spite of the fact-finding tribunal having a reasonable doubt as to the guilt of the accused . . . This

[64] [2002] 2 Cr App R 352, CA.
[65] [2003] 1 Cr App R 602, CA.
[66] [2003] 1 WLR 1736, HL.
[67] At [49]–[51].

consequence of a reverse burden of proof should colour one's approach when evaluating the reasons why it is said that, in the absence of a persuasive burden on the accused, the public interest will be prejudiced to an extent which justifies placing a persuasive burden on the accused. The more serious the punishment which may flow from conviction, the more compelling must be the reasons. The extent and nature of the factual matters required to be proved by the accused, and their importance relative to the matters required to be proved by the prosecution, have to be taken into account. So also does the extent to which the burden on the accused relates to facts which, if they exist, are readily provable by him as matters within his own knowledge or to which he already has access. In evaluating these factors the court's role is one of review. Parliament, not the court, is charged with the primary responsibility for deciding, as a matter of policy, what should be the constituent elements of a criminal offence . . . The court will reach a different conclusion from the legislature only when it is apparent the legislature has attached insufficient importance to the fundamental right of an individual to be presumed innocent until proved guilty.

As to section 92(5), Lord Nicholls had regard to the fact that counterfeiting is a serious contemporary problem with adverse economic effects on genuine trade and adverse effects on consumers in terms of quality of goods and, sometimes, on the health or safety of consumers. His Lordship also noted that the section 92(5) defence relates to facts within the accused's own knowledge. Two other factors were said to constitute compelling reasons why section 92(5) should place a legal burden on the accused. First, those who trade in brand products are aware of the need to be on guard against counterfeit goods. Secondly, by and large it is to be expected that those who supply traders with counterfeit goods, if traceable at all by outside investigators, are unlikely to be cooperative, so if the prosecution are required to prove that traders acted dishonestly, fewer investigations will be undertaken and there will be fewer prosecutions.

The concept of facts within the accused's own knowledge is separate from the concept of ease of proof, but in some cases both will point in the same direction. *DPP v Barker*[68] concerned section 37(3) of the Road Traffic Act 1988, whereby a disqualified driver may hold a provisional licence and drive in accordance with its conditions. In support of the conclusion that it was proportionate for the accused to bear the burden under the subsection, it was said that, as to being the holder of a provisional licence, the burden could easily be discharged by producing the licence and, as to the conditions of the licence, in some cases, in the absence of any information from the accused as to the identity of a passenger, it would be impossible for the prosecution to establish his identity and that he was the holder of a licence and therefore qualified to be supervising the accused.[69]

By contrast, in *DPP v Wright*[70] it was held that it was disproportionate to impose a legal burden on an accused who sought to rely on an exemption under section 1 of the Hunting Act 2004. The

---

[68] [2006] Crim LR 140, DC.

[69] See also *R v Makuwa* [2006] Crim LR 911: the prosecution will find it difficult, if not impossible, to prove, for the purposes of the defence set out in s 31(1) of the Immigration and Asylum Act 1999, that the accused's life or freedom was *not* threatened overseas and that he had *not* presented himself to the UK authorities without delay, matters on which the accused is likely to be as well, if not better, informed than the prosecution. Note also, *R v Clarke* [2008] EWCA Crim 893, CA, where the accused, charged with providing immigration services without being qualified to do so contrary to s 91 of the Immigration and Asylum Act 1999, bore a legal burden. The burden was held not to be onerous since the accused had ready access to evidence to prove his qualification, whereas if he bore an evidential burden and had only to raise the possibility that he was qualified, it would be exceedingly complex for the prosecution to disprove.

[70] [2009] 3 All ER 726, DC.

section makes it an offence for a person to hunt a wild mammal with a dog unless his hunting is exempt under section 2, being within a category of hunting specified in Schedule 1 of the Act. The court noted the 'diverse and massive potential content' of the categories in Schedule 1 and considered that if the burden was a legal one, an accused would have to prove the substantial (and difficult) issues in the case once the prosecution had proved the prima facie (and easy) fact that he had been in pursuit of a mammal with a dog. Accordingly, the exemption was read down to impose an evidential burden only. Imposition of a legal burden would have been '...an oppressive, disproportionate, unfair and, in particular, an unnecessary intrusion upon the presumption of innocence in article 6'.[71]

In *Attorney General's Reference (No 1 of 2004)*[72] a five-judge Court of Appeal heard five conjoined appeals. The first two appeals concerned sections 352, 353(1), and 357(1) of the Bankruptcy Act 1986. Under section 353(1), a bankrupt is guilty of an offence if he does not inform the official receiver of a disposal of a property comprised in his estate. Under section 357(1), a bankrupt is guilty of an offence if he makes, or in the five years before the start of the bankruptcy made, any gift or transfer of, or any charge on, his property. Under section 352, a person is not guilty of an offence under either section 353(1) or 357(1) if he proves that, at the time of the conduct constituting the offence, he had no intent to defraud or to conceal the state of his affairs. It was held that section 352, as it applies to section 353(1), does not breach Article 6. The reasons given to justify this reverse burden included the fact that concealment or disposal of assets to the disadvantage of creditors can be done alone and in private and whether there has been fraud will often be known only to the individuals in question.[73] It was also held, however, that section 352, as it applies to section 357(1), does breach Article 6 and should be read down so as to impose only an evidential burden. The reason given for this conclusion was the very wide ambit of section 357. For example, it can apply to disposals made long before the commencement of bankruptcy and possibly at a time when there was no indication of insolvency and the prosecution does not have to prove that the bankrupt was aware of the possibility of his insolvency and does not have to establish anything unusual or irregular in relation to the gift or disposition.

The third appeal related to section 1(2) of the Protection from Eviction Act 1977, whereby a person is guilty of an offence if he unlawfully deprives the residential occupier of any premises of his occupation or the premises 'unless he proves that he believed, and had reasonable cause to believe, that the residential occupier had ceased to reside in the premises'. Three reasons were given to justify this reverse burden: that the essence of the offence is unlawful deprivation of occupation, the defence only being available to the accused who can bring himself within a

---

[71] At [85]. See also *R v Charles* [2009] EWCA Crim 1570: where an accused is charged with breaching an anti-social behaviour order the burden of proving a reasonable excuse under s 1(10) of the Crime and Disorder Act 1998 is evidential only. The legal burden of proving lack of reasonable excuse lies with the prosecution. See also, to similar effect, in respect of breach of a restraining order under the Protection from Harassment Act 1997, *R v Evans* [2005] 1 WLR 1435.

[72] [2004] 1 WLR 2111, CA.

[73] The court was of the view that the decision in *R v Carass* [2002] 1 WLR 1714, should be treated as impliedly overruled by *R v Johnstone*, a view endorsed by the House of Lords in *Attorney General's Reference (No 4 of 2002)* [2005] 1 AC 264 at [32]. See also *R (Griffin) v Richmond Magistrates' Court* [2008] BPIR 468, concerning the failure to deliver up books in a 'winding up': the defence under s 208(4)(a) of the Insolvency Act 1986, that there was no intent to defraud, imposes a legal burden on the accused.

narrow exception; the circumstances relied upon by the accused are peculiarly within his own knowledge; the public interest in deterring landlords from ejecting tenants unlawfully.

The fourth appeal concerned section 4 of the Homicide Act 1957. Under section 4(1), it is manslaughter and not murder for a person acting in pursuance of a suicide pact between himself and another to kill the other. Under section 4(2), 'Where it is shown that a person charged with the murder of another killed the other, it shall be for the defence to prove that the person charged was acting in pursuance of a suicide pact between him and the other.' This reverse burden was justified on the basis that it provides protection for society from murder disguised as a suicide pact killing and that the defence only arises once the prosecution have proved murder and the facts necessary to establish the defence lie within the accused's knowledge.

The fifth appeal concerned section 51 of the Criminal Justice and Public Order Act 1994. Under section 51(1):

A person commits an offence if

(a) he does an act which intimidates, or is intended to intimidate another person;
(b) he does the act knowing or believing that the victim is assisting in the investigation of an offence or is a witness or potential witness or a juror or a potential juror in proceedings for an offence; and
(c) he does it intending thereby to cause the investigation or the course of justice to be obstructed, perverted or interfered with.

Under section 51(7), if the matters in section 51(1)(a) and (b) are proved, the accused shall be presumed to have done the act with the intention required by section 51(1)(c) unless the contrary is proved. This reverse burden was justified on the basis that although it related to an ingredient of the offence rather than a special defence, witness and jury intimidation, which continues to increase, is a very serious threat to the proper administration of criminal justice, and in balancing the potential detriment to the accused against the mischief which Parliament is seeking to eradicate, the balance comes down firmly in favour of the prosecution.

In *Attorney General's Reference (No 1 of 2004)*, Lord Woolf CJ, giving the judgment of the court, noted the significant difference in emphasis between the approaches of Lord Steyn in *R v Lambert* and Lord Nicholls in *R v Johnstone*, and noted in particular the likelihood that 'few provisions will be left as imposing a legal burden on Lord Steyn's approach'.[74] It was held that until clarification of a further decision of the House of Lords, lower courts, if in doubt as to the outcome of a challenge to a reverse burden, should follow the approach of Lord Nicholls. With a view to further assisting the lower courts, Lord Woolf also set out 'General Guidance' in the form of 10 general principles. However, in *Attorney General's Reference (No 4 of 2002)*,[75] the House of Lords held that both *R v Lambert* and *R v Johnstone*, unless or until revised or supplemented, should be regarded as the primary domestic authorities on reverse burdens; that nothing said in *R v Johnstone* suggested an intention to depart from or modify *R v Lambert*, which should not be treated as superseded or implicitly overruled; and that the differences in emphasis were explicable by the difference in the subject matter of the two cases. The House also expressly declined to endorse Lord Woolf's 'General Guidance', save to the extent that

---

[74] At [38].
[75] [2003] 3 WLR 1153, HL.

it was in accordance with the opinions of the House in *R v Lambert* and *R v Johnstone*.[76] Lord Bingham said that the task of the court is never to decide whether a reverse burden should be imposed on a defendant, but always to assess whether a burden enacted by Parliament unjustifiably infringes the presumption of innocence, and questioned Lord Woolf's assumption that Parliament would not have made an exception without good reason. Such an assumption, it was held, may lead the court to give too much weight to the enactment under review and too little to the presumption of innocence and the obligation imposed on it by section 3.

In *Attorney General's Reference (No 4 of 2002)*, the House heard two conjoined appeals. The first concerned section 5(2) of the Road Traffic Act 1988, whereby it is a defence for a person charged with an offence of being in charge of a motor vehicle on a road or other public place after consuming excess alcohol, to prove that at the time he is alleged to have committed the offence, the circumstances were such that there was no likelihood of his driving the vehicle whilst the proportion of alcohol in his breath, blood, or urine remained likely to exceed the prescribed limit. It was held that even on the assumption that section 5(2) infringes the presumption of innocence, it was directed to the legitimate object of preventing death, injury, and damage caused by unfit drivers and met the tests of acceptability identified in the Strasbourg jurisprudence. It was not objectionable to criminalize conduct in these circumstances without requiring the prosecutor to prove criminal intent. The accused has a full opportunity to show that there was no likelihood of his driving, a matter so closely conditioned by his own knowledge at the time as to make it much more appropriate for him to prove the absence of a likelihood of his driving on the balance of probabilities than for the prosecutor to prove such a likelihood beyond reasonable doubt. The imposition of a legal burden did not go beyond what was necessary.

The second appeal concerned section 11(1) and (2) of the Terrorism Act 2000, which are in the following terms.

(1) A person commits an offence if he belongs or professes to belong to a proscribed organisation.

(2) It is a defence for a person charged with an offence under subsection (1) to prove—
   (a) that the organisation was not proscribed on the last (or only) occasion on which he became a member or began to profess to be a member, and
   (b) that he has not taken part in the activities of the organisation at any time while it was proscribed.

The House of Lords was of the unanimous opinion that the ingredients of the offence are set out fully in section 11(1) and that section 11(2) adds no further ingredient to section 11(1). The House also held, by majority, that section 11(2) was incompatible with Article 6 and should be read and given effect as imposing on the accused an evidential burden only. Six reasons were given for the conclusion of incompatibility with Article 6. (1) The extraordinary breadth of section 11(1) and the uncertain scope of the word 'profess' are such that some of those liable to be convicted and punished under section 11(1) may be guilty of no conduct which could reasonably be regarded as blameworthy or such as should properly attract

---

[76] See per Lord Bingham at [30] and [32]. Lords Steyn and Phillips agreed with the speech of Lord Bingham and Lords Rodger and Carswell appear to endorse these parts of Lord Bingham's speech.

criminal sanctions. As to the breadth of section 11(1), for example, it covers a person who joined an organization when it was not a terrorist organization or when, if it was, he did not know that it was. It also covers a person who joined an organization when it was not proscribed or, if it was, did not know that it was. There would be a clear breach of the presumption of innocence and a real risk of unfair conviction if such persons could exonerate themselves only by establishing the defence provided and it is the clear duty of the courts to protect defendants against such a risk. (2) As to section 11(2)(b), it may be all but impossible for an accused to show that he had not taken part in the activities of the organization. Terrorist organizations do not generate minutes or records on which he could rely and although he could assert his non-participation, his evidence might well be discounted as unreliable. (3) If section 11(2) imposes a legal burden and the accused fails to prove the matters specified, there is no room for the exercise of discretion—the court must convict him. (4) The penalty for the offence, imprisonment for up to ten years, is severe. (5) Security considerations carry weight, but they do not absolve member states from their duty to ensure that basic standards of fairness are observed. (6) Little significance can be attached to the requirement in section 117 that the Director of Public Prosecutions gives his consent to a prosecution because Article 6 is concerned with the procedure relating to the trial of a criminal case and not the decision to prosecute. As to the reading down of section 11(2), there could be no doubt that Parliament intended section 11(2) to impose a legal burden on the accused because section 118 of the Act lists a number of sections which are to be understood as imposing an evidential burden only and section 11(2) is not among those listed. For the majority, however, section 11(2) should be treated as if section 118 applied to it on the basis that although that was not the intention of Parliament when enacting the 2000 Act, it was the intention of Parliament when enacting section 3 of the Human Rights Act 1998.[77]

According to the authorities, the imposition of a legal burden on the accused is likely to be more acceptable in the case of offences which are concerned to regulate the conduct of particular conduct in the public interest and which are not regarded as 'truly criminal'. In *R v Lambert*,[78] Lord Clyde said:

> The requirement to have a licence in order to carry on certain types of activity is an obvious example. The promotion of health and safety and the avoidance of pollution are among the purposes to be served by such controls. These kinds of cases may properly be seen as not truly criminal. Many may be relatively trivial and only involve a monetary penalty. Many may carry with them no real social disgrace or infamy.[79]

R v Davies[80] concerned section 40 of the Health and Safety at Work Act 1974, which requires the accused to prove that 'it was not reasonably practicable to do more than was in fact done' to satisfy his health and safety duties. It was held that section 40 is not incompatible with the Convention, but justified, necessary and proportionate.[81] In reaching this conclusion,

[77] As one commentator has observed, the reasoning is ingenious but unconvincing given that when the 2000 Act was passed Parliament must be taken to have had full knowledge of s 3 of the 1998 Act: see Dennis, 'Reverse Onuses and the Presumption of Innocence: In Search of Principle' [2005] *Crim LR* 901 at 916.
[78] [2002] 2 AC 545, HL at [154].
[79] See *R v S* [2003] 1 Cr App R 602, CA at [48], where this dictum was applied.
[80] [2003] ICR 586, CA.
[81] See also *R v Chargot Ltd (trading as Contract Services) and others* [2009] 1 WLR 1, HL, where the reverse burden under s 40 was not rendered *disproportionate* by the fact that penalties had been increased under s 1(1) and (2) and Sch 1 of the Health and Safety (Offences) Act 2008.

the court relied upon the regulatory nature of the 1974 Act and the 'convincing and extremely helpful' analysis of Cory J in the Canadian Supreme Court in *R v Wholesale Travel Group*.[82] Cory J expressed the rationale for the distinction between truly criminal and regulatory offences as follows:

> Regulatory legislation involves the shift of emphasis from the protection of individual interests and the deterrence and punishment of acts involving moral fault to the protection of public and societal interests. While criminal offences are usually designed to condemn and punish past, inherently wrongful conduct, regulatory measures are generally directed to the prevention of future harm through the enforcement of minimum standards of conduct and care.
>
> It follows that regulatory offences and crimes embody different concepts of fault. Since regulatory offences are directed primarily not to conduct itself but to the consequences of conduct, conviction of a regulatory offence may be thought to import a significantly lesser degree of culpability than conviction of a true crime. The concept of fault in regulatory offences is based upon a reasonable care standard and, as such, does not imply moral blameworthiness in the same manner as criminal fault. Conviction for breach of a regulatory offence suggests nothing more than that the defendant has failed to meet a prescribed standard of care.

Justifying the distinction by what he called the licensing argument and the vulnerability justification, he continued:

> while in the criminal context the essential question to be determined is whether the accused has made the choice to act in the manner alleged in the indictment, the regulated defendant is by virtue of the licensing argument, assumed to have made the choice to engage in the regulated activity. Those who choose to participate in regulated activities have in doing so placed themselves in a responsible relationship to the public generally and must accept the consequences of that responsibility . . . Regulatory legislation . . . plays a legitimate and vital role in protecting those who are most vulnerable and least able to protect themselves.

In *R (Grundy & Co Excavations Ltd) v Halton Division Magistrates' Court*,[83] it was held that the offence of tree felling without a licence contrary to section 17 of the Forestry Act 1967 was a case of the kind which Lord Clyde had in mind in *R v Lambert* and which Cory J had in mind in *R v Wholesale Travel Group*: it was a classic regulatory offence, designed to protect the nation's trees, involving only a monetary penalty and carrying no real social disgrace or infamy and no real moral stigma or obloquy.

To some, including the authors of this work, it remains repugnant in principle, especially in the case of imprisonable offences, that jurors or magistrates should be under a legal duty to convict if left in doubt as to whether the accused has established his defence, or are of the view that his version of events is as likely to be true as not. In some cases, as we have seen, the courts will rule that the reverse onus provision in question is incompatible with Article 6 and can be read down so as to impose only an evidential burden. However, Parliament has decided not to legislate that all burdens borne by the accused should be evidential only. In previous editions of this work, reference has been made to the views of one distinguished commentator who pointed out that if Parliament did not intervene and therefore the question of compatibility fell to be determined in respect of each reverse onus provision, there would be a long period of uncertainty and much expensive and wasteful litigation, with inconsistent

---

[82] (1991) 3 SCR 154.
[83] (2003) 167 JP 387.

results, because courts would have differing views.[84] That prediction is proving to be all too accurate, and the scale of the problem remains vast because some 40 per cent of the offences triable in the Crown Court impose a legal burden on the accused to prove at least one element of the offence or statutory defence.[85]

For a number of reasons, the various criteria that have been developed to determine compatibility compound the problems of uncertainty and inconsistency. Some courts are clearly adopting a 'pick 'n' mix' approach to the criteria; there is no guidance as to the weight to be attached to such important and potentially competing criteria as the seriousness of the potential punishment, the ease of proof, and whether a matter is within the knowledge of the accused; the criterion of deference, albeit limited, to the considered opinion of Parliament is of dubious validity given the very nature of the obligation under section 3 of the 1998 Act; and the distinction between 'truly criminal' and regulatory offences is inherently tenuous, not least because views are bound to differ as to which particular regulatory offences involve moral fault. In these circumstances, in many cases it will be as easy to draw a rational conclusion of compatibility as incompatibility.[86] As another commentator has put it, in the absence of broader principles for applying the relevant factors, decisions will continue to resemble a 'forensic lottery'.[87]

Civil cases

The general rule, in civil cases, is that he who asserts must prove. Certain issues are 'essential' to the case of a party to civil proceedings in the sense that they must be proved by him if he is to succeed in the action. The legal burden of proof will generally lie on the party asserting the affirmative of such an issue. For example, in an action for negligence, the claimant bears the legal burden of proving duty of care, breach of such duty, and loss suffered in consequence. The legal burden of proving a defence which goes beyond a simple denial of the claimant's assertions, such as *volenti non fit injuria* or contributory negligence, lies on the defendant. The burden of proving a failure to mitigate is also borne by the defendant.[88] Similarly, the legal burden of proving a contract, its breach, and consequential loss lies on the claimant; and the legal burden of proving a defence which goes beyond a simple denial of the claimant's assertions, such as discharge by agreement or by frustration, lies on the defendant.

In *BHP Billiton Petroleum Ltd v Dalmine SpA*[89] it was held that, although in most civil proceedings the statements of case are likely to be a good guide to the incidence of the legal burden of proof, they cannot be definitive, because a party cannot, by poor pleading, take

---

[84] See Professor Sir John Smith's commentary on *R v DPP, ex p Kebilene* [1999] Crim LR 994.

[85] See Andrew Ashworth and Meredith Blake 'The Presumption of Innocence in English Criminal Law' [1996] *Crim LR* 306. There is also a legal burden on the defendant in confiscation proceedings in the Crown Court; see *Grayson v United Kingdom* (2009) 48 EHRR 30.

[86] For a good example, see *R v Keogh* [2007] 2 Cr App R 112, where the Court of Appeal, 'read down' ss 2(3) and 3(4) of the Official Secrets Act 1989 on the basis that the reverse burden was not a necessary element in the operation of ss 2 and 3, it being 'practicable' to require the prosecution to prove that the accused knew, or had reasonable cause to believe, that the information disclosed related to such matters as 'defence' and that its disclosure would be damaging.

[87] Dennis, 'Reverse Onuses and the Presumption of Innocence: In Search of Principle' [2005] *Crim LR* 901 at 927. See also Ashworth, 'Four threats to the presumption of innocence' (2006) 10 *E&P* 241.

[88] *Geest plc v Lansiquot* [2002] 1 WLR 3111, PC, disapproving *Selvanayagam v University of the West Indies* [1983] 1 WLR 585, PC.

[89] [2003] BLR 271, CA at [28].

upon himself a burden which the law does not impose on him, or free himself from a burden which the law does impose on him. Thus a party cannot escape a legal burden borne by him on a particular issue essential to his case by drafting his claim or defence, in relation to the issue, by way of a negative allegation. In *Soward v Leggatt*[90] the plaintiff, a landlord, alleged that his tenant 'did not repair' a certain house. The defendant replied that he 'did well and sufficiently repair' the house. Lord Abinger CB, observing that the plaintiff might have pleaded that the defendant 'let the house become dilapidated', held that it was not the form of the issue which required consideration, but its substance and effect. Accordingly, it was for the plaintiff to prove the defendant's breach of covenant.[91]

The incidence of the legal burden of proof in civil cases can often be discovered from the precedents concerned with the issue of substantive law in question. In the absence of such a precedent, however, the courts are prepared to decide not on the basis of any general principles but more as a matter of policy given the particular rule of substantive law in question.[92] In *Joseph Constantine Steamship Line Ltd v Imperial Smelting Corpn Ltd*[93] a ship on charter was destroyed by an explosion the cause of which was unclear. The charterers claimed damages from the owners for failure to load. The owners' defence was frustration. The charterers argued that the owners could not rely upon frustration unless they proved that the explosion was not caused by fault on their part. The owners replied that they could rely upon the defence of frustration unless the charterers showed that the explosion was caused by their fault, that is fault on the part of the owners. The House of Lords held that in order to defeat the defence of frustration, the burden of proof was upon the charterers to prove fault on the part of the owners. Accordingly, the cause of the explosion being unclear, the appeal of the owners was allowed. It is possible to justify this outcome on the basis that it is more difficult to prove absence of fault than it is to prove fault. This justification, however, should not be regarded as an inflexible *rule*: in bailment cases, for example, the bailor having proved bailment, the bailee has the onus of proving that the goods were lost or damaged without fault on his part.[94] Similarly, in an action for conversion, the burden is on the bailee to prove that he dealt with the goods in good faith and without notice.[95] Thus the cases have been decided as a matter of policy on their own merits.[96]

In civil, as in criminal cases, the incidence of the legal burden of proof may be determined by statute. For example, whereas it is for the former employee claiming unfair dismissal to prove that he was dismissed, it is for the employer to show the reason for the dismissal and that it

---

[90] (1836) 7 C&P 613.

[91] See also *Arbrath v North Eastern Rly Co* (1883) 11 QBD 440, CA, concerning an action for malicious prosecution in which the plaintiff bore the burden of proving both that the defendant had instituted proceedings and had done so without reasonable and probable cause This was because, according to Bowen LJ, the assertion of a 'negative' was an essential part of the plaintiff's case. The case was affirmed on appeal ((1886) 11 App Cas 247, HL) and applied in *Reynolds v Metropolitan Police Comr* (1984) 80 Cr App R 125, CA (procuring the grant of a search warrant falsely, maliciously, and *without reasonable and probable cause*).

[92] See Stone (1944) 60 LQR 262.

[93] [1942] AC 154, HL.

[94] *Coldman v Hill* [1919] 1 KB 443, CA; cf *Levison v Patent Steam Carpet Cleaning Ltd* [1978] QB 69, CA.

[95] *Marcq v Christie Manson and Woods Ltd* [2002] 4 All ER 1005, QBD.

[96] In some civil cases exposition of the law is rendered difficult by a judicial failure to make clear which burden, legal or evidential, is in contemplation. One example is where rape is pleaded as a defence to adultery. It is unclear whether the legal burden is on the petitioner to prove that the intercourse was consensual or on the defendant to prove that it was non-consensual. In *Redpath v Redpath and Milligan* [1950] 1 All ER 600, CA the judgment of Bucknill LJ suggests the former, that of Vaisey J the latter, although neither distinguished between the legal and evidential burden.

constitutes one of the grounds set out in the statute on which a dismissal is capable of being fair. If the employer fails to show such a reason, the dismissal is automatically unfair.[97] Equally, the parties themselves may expressly agree upon the incidence of the burden of proof.[98] The parties may do this, for example, in the case of written contracts, but in the absence of express agreement the matter becomes one of construction for the court. In *Munro, Brice & Co v War Risks Association*[99] an insurance policy covered a ship subject to an exemption in respect of loss by capture or in consequence of hostilities. The ship in question had disappeared for reasons unknown and a claim was made. The question for the court was whether the plaintiffs had to prove that the ship was not lost by reason of enemy action. The court found for the plaintiff on the basis that the defendants bore the burden of proving that the facts fell within the exception and this they had clearly failed to do.[100] However, where a claimant in these circumstances relies upon a proviso to an exemption clause, the burden of proving that the facts fall within the proviso may well be on him. In *The Glendarroch*[101] the plaintiffs brought an action in negligence for non-delivery of goods, the goods in question having been lost when the boat carrying them sank. Under the bill of lading, there was a clause exempting the defendants in respect of loss or damage caused by perils of the sea provided that the defendants were not negligent. It was held that the plaintiffs bore the burden of proving the contract and non-delivery; that if the defendants relied upon the exemption clause, it was for them to prove that the facts fell within it, ie that loss was caused by a peril of the sea; but that if the plaintiffs then relied upon the proviso to the exemption clause, it was for them to prove that the facts fell within the proviso, ie that loss was caused by the negligence of the defendants.

The incidence of the evidential burden

As a general rule in both civil and criminal proceedings, a party bearing the legal burden on a particular issue will also bear the evidential burden on that issue. This rule has given rise to little difficulty or case law in civil proceedings. As in criminal cases, the incidence of the evidential burden in civil cases may be affected by the operation of a presumption, a matter considered in detail in Chapter 22.[102] In criminal cases, where, as we have seen, the prosecution generally bear the legal burden of proving those facts essential to the Crown case, the prosecution normally also bear the evidential burden in relation to those facts. Similarly, where the defence bear the legal burden of proving insanity (as required at common law) or

---

[97] See Employment Rights Act 1996, s 98. A further example is the Consumer Credit Act 1974, s 171(7): if a debtor alleges that a credit bargain is extortionate (within the meaning of ss 137 and 138), it is for the creditor to prove to the contrary. See also s 63A of the Sex Discrimination Act 1975 and s 54A of the Race Relations Act 1976. However, the burden is, 'counter-intuitively', on the employee to prove victimization under the 1976 Act. See *Oyacre v Cheshire County Council* [2008] 4 All ER 907, CA.

[98] See, eg, *Levy v Assicurazioni Generali* [1940] AC 791, PC and *Fred Chappell Ltd v National Car Parks Ltd* (1987) The Times, 22 May, QBD.

[99] [1918] 2 KB 78.

[100] Cf *Hurst v Evans* [1917] 1 KB 352.

[101] [1894] P 226, CA.

[102] See, eg, s 30(2) of the Bills of Exchange Act 1882: 'Every holder of a bill is prima facie deemed to be a holder in due course; but if in an action on a bill it is admitted or proved that the acceptance, issue, or subsequent negotiation of the bill is affected with fraud, duress, or force and fear, or illegality, the burden of proof is shifted, unless and until the holder proves that subsequent to the alleged fraud or illegality, value has in good faith been given for the bill.' The effect of this provision is that if a party sues on a bill of exchange he only bears the evidential burden on the issue whether he gave value for the bill in good faith if the defendant has adduced prima facie evidence that the acceptance, issue, etc of the bill is affected with fraud, duress, etc. See *Talbot v Von Boris* [1911] 1 KB 854 at 866, CA.

some other issue (pursuant to an express or implied statutory exception), the defence also bear the evidential burden on such issues.

In the case of all common law defences except insanity, the evidential burden is on the defence and, once discharged, the legal burden of disproving the defence is then on the prosecution.[103] However, the evidential burden may be discharged by *any* evidence in the case, whether adduced or elicited by the defence, a co-accused, or the prosecution;[104] and where there is sufficiently cogent evidence of such a defence, then the judge must leave it to the jury, even if it has not been mentioned by the defence[105] or has been expressly disclaimed by them[106] (or they have conveyed to the judge their opinion that he should not leave it to the jury)[107] and notwithstanding that it may be inconsistent with the accused's defence.[108] The above principles apply to the common law defences of provocation,[109] self-defence,[110] duress,[111] non-insane automatism,[112] and drunkenness.[113]

In relation to the defence of provocation, it has been held that the judge is required to leave the defence to the jury only if there is some evidence, from whatever source, suggestive of the reasonable possibility that the accused might have lost his self-control due to provoking words or conduct. If there is no such evidence, but merely the speculative possibility of an act of provocation, the issue does not arise and suggestions in cross-examination cannot by themselves raise the issue.[114] Equally, a judge is under no duty to put before the jury strained and implausible inferences to create a defence of provocation for which there is no true basis.[115] In *R v Cox*[116] it was held that where there is evidence of provocation and the defence

---

[103] This is also the case in relation to a variety of statutory defences. See, eg, s 3(1) of the Criminal Law Act 1967 (reasonable force in the prevention of crime etc) and *R v Cameron* [1973] Crim LR 520, CA and *R v Khan* [1995] Crim LR 78, CA. See also s 75 of the Sexual Offences Act 2003 and s 118(2) of the Terrorism Act 2000.

[104] *Bullard v R* [1957] AC 635, PC.

[105] *Palmer v R* [1971] AC 814, PC at 823. See also *R v Hopper* [1915] 2 KB 431; *R v Cascoe* [1970] 2 All ER 833, CA; *R v Bonnick* (1977) 66 Cr App R 266, CA; *R v Johnson* [1989] 2 All ER 839, CA; and *DPP (Jamaica) v Bailey* [1995] 1 Cr App R 257, PC.

[106] *R v Kachikwu* (1968) 52 Cr App R 538, CA at 543.

[107] *R v Burgess and McLean* [1995] Crim LR 425, CA and *R v Dhillon* [1997] 2 Cr App R 104, CA. But see also *R v Groark* [1999] Crim LR 669, CA, below.

[108] See *R v Newell* [1989] Crim LR 906 and generally Sean Doran, 'Alternative Defences: the "invisible burden" on the trial judge' [1991] *Crim LR* 878.

[109] *Mancini v DPP* [1942] AC 1, HL and *R v Cascoe* [1970] 2 All ER 83, CA. See also *R v Rossiter* [1994] 2 All ER 752, CA and *R v Cambridge* [1994] 2 All ER 760, CA.

[110] *R v Lobell* [1957] 1 QB 547, CCA. See also *Chan Kau v R* [1955] AC 206, PC.

[111] *R v Gill* [1963] 1 WLR 841, CCA. See also *R v Bone* [1968] 1 WLR 983, CA.

[112] *Bratty v A-G for Northern Ireland* [1963] AC 386, HL. See also *R v Stripp* (1978) 69 Cr App R 318, CA at 321 and *R v Pullen* [1991] Crim LR 457, CA. The situation is different in the case of insanity, because that defence places a burden of proof on the accused, although in rare and exceptional cases the judge may of his own volition raise the issue and leave it to the jury: see *R v Thomas (Sharon)* [1995] Crim LR 314, CA.

[113] See *Kennedy v HM Advocate* 1944 JC 171 and *R v Foote* [1964] Crim LR 405. However, in *R v Groark* [1999] Crim LR 669, CA, it was held that if, in a case of wounding with intent, there is evidence of drunkenness which might give rise to the issue whether the accused had the specific intent, but the defence is that the accused knew what was happening and acted in self-defence, if the defence object to a direction on drunkenness in relation to intent, such a direction need not be given.

[114] *R v Acott* [1977] 1 WLR 306, HL. See also *R v Kromer* [2002] All ER (D) 420 (May), CA, *R v Miao* (2003) The Times, 26 Nov, CA and *R v Serrano* [2007] Crim LR 569, CA.

[115] *R v Walch* [1993] Crim LR 714, CA. See also *R v Wellington* [1993] Crim LR 616, CA.

[116] [1995] 2 Cr App R 513, CA.

do not rely upon it at trial, it is most unsatisfactory that the judge's failure to direct the jury on it can then found an appeal against conviction, and therefore if it appears to counsel for either side that there is evidence of provocation, it is their duty to point it out to the judge before he sums up.[117] It is submitted that this duty should not be confined to cases of provocation, but should be extended to the other common law and statutory defences in respect of which the accused bears the evidential but not the legal burden.

Where the defence of non-insane automatism is raised by an accused, the judge must decide two questions before it can be left to the jury: whether there is a proper evidential foundation for it and whether the evidence shows the case to be one of insane or non-insane automatism. If the judge rules it to be a case of insanity, the jury must then decide whether the accused is guilty or not guilty by reason of insanity.[118] It was held by the Court of Appeal in *R v Burns*[119] that where the issues of both insanity and non-insane automatism arise in the same case, the judge should direct the jury that while the accused bears the legal burden of proving insanity, he bears only the evidential burden in relation to non-insane automatism.

The law relating to the above defences is reasonably well settled and clear. It is less clear, however, whether the defence bears the evidential burden in relation to a defence which amounts to nothing more than a denial of the prosecution case and therefore raises no new issue. On one view, an accused should not bear an evidential burden in relation to a defence of, say, alibi or accident, because the onus is already on the prosecution to prove, in the one case, that the accused was present at the scene of the crime and, in the other, that he had the requisite *mens rea*.[120] There are obiter dicta, however, to the effect that the evidential burden, in the case of both of these defences, is on the accused.[121] Moreover, in *R v Bennett*[122] it was held that the accused bore the evidential burden in relation to impossibility on a charge of conspiracy to contravene the provisions of the Misuse of Drugs Act 1971[123] and in *Bratty v A-G for Northern Ireland*, as we have seen, the accused was held to bear the evidential burden on non-insane automatism.

Where the evidential burden alone, in relation to a particular defence, is borne by the accused, the judge, if he decides that insufficient evidence has been adduced on the matter, will direct the jury that the issue must be taken as proved against the accused. If the defence has adduced sufficient evidence, the judge will direct the jury that the prosecution bears the legal burden of negativing the defence in question and must satisfy them beyond reasonable doubt on the

[117] Where there is sufficient evidence of provocation but the judge fails to leave the issue before the jury, the Court of Appeal may nonetheless conclude that the conviction is safe: see *R v Van Dongen* [2005] 2 Cr App R 632, CA.

[118] *R v Burgess* (1991) 93 Cr App R 41, CA.

[119] (1973) 58 Cr App R 364; cf *Bratty v A-G for Northern Ireland* [1963] AC 386 at 402–3.

[120] See Professor Glanville Williams (1977) 127 *NLJ* at 157–8 and generally per Lord Hailsham LC in *R v Howe* [1987] 1 All ER 771, HL at 781 et seq.

[121] *R v Johnson* [1961] 3 All ER 969, CCA (alibi); *Bratty v A-G for Northern Ireland* [1963] AC 386, HL per Lord Kilmuir LC at 405 (accident). There is no dispute, however, that if the defence do adduce evidence in support of an alibi, the prosecution bear the legal burden of disproof (*R v Helliwell* [1995] Crim LR 79, CA and *R v Fergus* (1993) 98 Cr App R 313, CA) and ideally the judge should give a specific direction on the burden of proof in relation to the alibi (*R v Anderson* [1991] Crim LR 361, CA and *R v Johnson* [1995] Crim LR 242, CA). See also *R v Mussell* [1995] Crim LR 887, CA: a specific direction is needed if the nature of the alibi is that the accused was at a specific place elsewhere, raising the question why he did not call witnesses in support, but not if the evidence amounts to little more than a denial that he committed the crime.

[122] (1978) 68 Cr App R 168, CA.

[123] However, it was further held that if the prosecution have in their possession evidence which might show that at the time when the agreement was made the carrying out of the agreement would have been impossible, it is the duty of the prosecution either to call the evidence or to make it available to the defence.

matter. However, where the legal burden is borne by the accused, the jury should be directed that it is for the defence to satisfy them on a balance of probabilities and that if they are not so satisfied the issue must be taken as proved against the accused.[124] Accordingly, the judge may direct the jury that if they cannot decide on the evidence whether the defence case is more probable than not, they should find against the accused.

The right to begin

The right to begin adducing evidence is determined by the incidence of the evidential burden. As a general rule, the claimant has the right to begin adducing evidence in civil proceedings and the prosecution in criminal proceedings. In civil cases, the claimant has the right to adduce his evidence first unless the defendant bears the evidential burden on every issue.[125] In *Mercer v Whall*[126] an attorney's clerk brought an action for unliquidated damages for wrongful dismissal. The defendant admitted the dismissal but pleaded justification on the basis of the plaintiff's misconduct. It was held that the plaintiff was entitled to begin because he bore the evidential burden in relation to damages. The defendant would have had the right to begin if the claim had been for a liquidated sum because the only fact in issue would then have been the question of misconduct on which the defendant bore the evidential burden. In criminal cases where there is a plea of not guilty, the prosecution will normally have the right to adduce their evidence first. The reason appears to be that they will almost always bear an evidential burden on at least one issue. However, this may not be the case where the accused has made formal admissions pursuant to section 10 of the Criminal Justice Act 1967 or agreed to a statement of facts admitted in evidence pursuant to section 9 of the same Act. Where the accused pleads *autrefois acquit* or *convict* and there is a dispute of fact requiring evidence, the accused has the right to begin.

The standard of proof

The legal burden

Whether a party to civil or criminal proceedings has discharged a legal burden borne by him in relation to a particular issue is, as we have seen, decided by the tribunal of fact at the end of the case. To discharge the burden and succeed on that issue the evidence adduced by that party must, in the opinion of the tribunal of fact, be more cogent or convincing than that adduced by his opponent. How much more cogent or convincing the evidence is required to be is determined by rules of law relating to the standard of proof. If the evidence adduced by a party is sufficiently cogent or convincing to meet the appropriate standard of proof, the legal burden will be discharged and facts in issue will be legally proved and taken to have happened. In *Re B (Children) (Sexual Abuse)*,[127] Lord Hoffmann explained this process in the following way:[128]

> If a legal rule requires a fact to be proved (a 'fact in issue'), a judge or jury must decide whether or not it happened. There is no room for a finding that it might have happened. The law operates a binary system in which the only values are 0 and 1. The fact either happened or it did not. If the tribunal is left in doubt, the doubt is resolved by a rule that one party or the other carries

---

[124] See *R v Evans-Jones, R v Jenkins* (1923) 87 JP 115, and *R v Carr-Briant* [1943] KB 607.
[125] See *Pontifex v Jolly* (1839) 9 C & P 202 and *Re Parry's Estate, Parry v Fraser* [1977] 1 All ER 309.
[126] (1845) 14 LJ QB 267.
[127] [2009] 1 AC 11.
[128] At [2].

the burden of proof. If the party who bears the burden of proof fails to discharge it, a value of 0 is returned and the fact is treated as not having happened. If he does discharge it, a value of 1 is returned and the fact is treated as having happened.

The standard of proof required to discharge a legal burden depends upon whether the proceedings are criminal or civil, the standard being higher in the former than in the latter. In criminal proceedings, the standard required of the prosecution before the jury can find the accused guilty is proof beyond reasonable doubt.[129] In civil proceedings, the standard of proof required to be met by either party seeking to discharge a legal burden is proof on a balance of probabilities.

The notion of a third and intermediate standard of proof lying between the standards required in criminal and civil cases has not found favour in the courts.[130]

Criminal cases

The rules prescribing the standard of proof are a matter of law for the judge. Whether the evidence adduced meets the standard is a question for the jury as tribunal of fact. In criminal trials, therefore, the judge must direct the jury on the standard of proof that the prosecution is required to meet.[131] In *Miller v Minister of Pensions*[132] Denning J described the standard of proof required to be met in a criminal case, before an accused person may be found guilty, in the following terms:

> It need not reach certainty, but it must carry a high degree of probability. Proof beyond a reasonable doubt does not mean proof beyond the shadow of a doubt. The law would fail to protect the community if it admitted fanciful possibilities to deflect the course of justice. If the evidence is so strong against a man as to leave only a remote possibility in his favour, which can be dismissed with the sentence 'of course it is possible but not in the least probable' the case is proved beyond reasonable doubt, but nothing short of that will suffice.

Given the enormous difficulty of defining degrees of probability clearly as well as precisely, Denning J's dictum might fairly be regarded as a model. However, as we shall see, definitions and explanations are generally to be avoided and there is no requirement to use any formula or particular form of words.

Definitions and explanations. In *R v Yap Chuan Ching*[133] the judge in his summing-up had directed the jury that it was for the prosecution to prove the charges so that they were sure that they had been made out, or to prove them beyond a reasonable doubt. The judge

---

[129] The same standard has to be met: (i) by a judge determining the facts for the purpose of sentence, the accused having pleaded guilty and having put forward a version of the facts which differs significantly from the prosecution's version (*R v McGrath and Casey* (1983) 5 Cr App R (S) 460 and *R v Ahmed* (1984) 6 Cr App R (S) 391); (ii) by a jury in a coroner's court considering a verdict of unlawful killing (including cases where an issue of insanity is raised) or suicide (*R v West London Coroner, ex p Gray* [1987] 2 All ER 129, DC, *R v Wolverhampton Coroner, ex p McCurbin* [1990] 2 All ER 759, CA, and *R v HM Coroner for District of Avon ex p O'Connor* [2009] EWHC 854, DC); and (iii) by a Solicitors' Disciplinary Tribunal investigating what is tantamount to a criminal offence: *Re a Solicitor* [1991] NLJR 1447, DC. See also reg 10 of the Disciplinary Tribunals Regulations 1993, Annexe N, Code of Conduct of the Bar of England and Wales and *Campbell v Hamlet* [2005] 3 All ER 1116, PC.

[130] See, eg, per Lord Tucker in *Dingwall v J Wharton (Shipping) Ltd* [1961] 2 Lloyd's Rep 213 at 216, HL.

[131] See Ch 2, 39 under **The summing-up**.

[132] [1947] 2 All ER 372 at 373–4.

[133] (1976) 63 Cr App R 7, CA.

explained that these were two different ways of saying the same thing. After retirement the jury came back into court and the judge understood the foreman to ask for a further direction on the standard of proof. The judge repeated the test of proof beyond a reasonable doubt and continued:

> A reasonable doubt . . . is a doubt to which you can give a reason as opposed to a mere fanciful sort of speculation such as 'Well, nothing in this world is certain, nothing in this world can be proved' . . . It is sometimes said the sort of matter which might influence you if you were to consider some business matter. A matter, for example, of a mortgage concerning your house, or something of that nature.

Four minutes later the jury returned to court and found the defendant guilty on one count by a majority of eleven to one. The Court of Appeal thought that the judge's direction on the standard of proof in his summing-up could not have been clearer or more accurate. However, taking judicial notice of the fact that one of the popular forms of television entertainment is reconstructed trials which have a striking degree of realism, and observing that most jurors currently know something about burden and standard before they even get into the jury box, the Court of Appeal concluded that in most cases judges should not attempt any gloss upon the meaning of 'sure' or 'reasonable doubt'. The court held that judicial comments of that kind usually create difficulties and are more likely to confuse than help. 'We point out and emphasize . . . that if judges stopped trying to define that which is almost impossible to define there would be fewer appeals.'[134] However, it was acknowledged that in exceptional cases the jury does require help. The case in question was such a case and, so far as his additional direction was concerned, the judge was right in what he did. The appeal was accordingly dismissed.[135]

In fact, as we shall see, judges often define and explain the burden to the jury.[136]

Formulae. On the basis that definitions and explanations are generally regarded as undesirable, it would not be unreasonable to expect a requirement that judges use a particular form of words when referring to the standard of proof. In fact, the authorities have been consistently opposed to such a course. 'It has been said a good many times that it is not a matter of some precise formula or particular form of words being used.'[137] However, in *Ferguson v R*[138] Lord Scarman observed that 'though the law requires no particular formula, judges are wise, as a general rule, to adopt one'. The particular formulae that judges are wise to adopt are, as we shall see, 'sure of the defendant's guilt' and 'satisfied beyond reasonable doubt'. This is, of course, tantamount to a requirement of that which is being proscribed, a certain form of words. The point is well illustrated by *R v Kritz*,[139] where the trial judge had directed the jury that they must be 'reasonably satisfied' and did not use the words 'satisfied beyond reasonable doubt'. On appeal, Lord Goddard CJ held that the accuracy of a summing-up did not depend on the use of a particular form of words and continued:[140]

---

[134] (1976) 63 Cr App R 7 at 11.
[135] See also per Goddard CJ in *R v Hepworth and Fearnley* [1955] 2 QB 600, CCA at 603.
[136] See *Walters v R* [1969] 2 AC 26, PC
[137] Per Fenton Atkinson LJ in *R v Allan* [1969] 1 All ER 91, CCA at 92.
[138] [1979] 1 WLR 94, PC.
[139] [1950] 1 KB 82, CCA.
[140] [1950] 1 KB 82 at 89–90.

It is not the particular formula that matters: it is the effect of the summing up. If the jury are made to understand that they have to be satisfied and must not return a verdict against a defendant unless they feel sure, and that the onus is all the time on the prosecution and not the defence, then whether the judge uses one form of language or another is neither here nor there . . .[141]

Proper and improper directions. The most reliable guidance as to how a judge should properly direct a jury is discovered by contrasting those directions which, on appeal, have been approved and disapproved. 'The time honoured formula is that the jury must be satisfied beyond reasonable doubt.'[142] Although in *R v Summers*[143] Lord Goddard objected to the use of this phrase, three years later in *R v Hepworth and Fearnley*[144] he approved of it, explaining that his earlier objection was based on the difficulties of explaining to a jury what a reasonable doubt is. To explain to a jury that it is not a fanciful doubt offers no real guidance and to tell them that it is such a doubt as to cause them to hesitate in their own affairs does not convey any particular standard; one jury member might say he would hesitate over something whereas another might say that that would not cause him to hesitate at all.[145] In *R v Stafford, R v Luvaglio*[146] Edmund Davies LJ said:

We do not . . . agree with the trial judge when, directing the jury upon the standard of proof he told them to 'Remember that a reasonable doubt is one for which you could give reasons if you were asked', and we dislike such a description or definition.[147]

In *R v Gray*[148] the trial judge defined a reasonable doubt as 'a doubt based upon good reason and not a fanciful doubt' and as 'the sort of doubt which might affect you in the conduct of your everyday affairs'. The Court of Appeal held that if the judge had referred to the sort of doubt which may affect the mind of a person in the conduct of important affairs, there could have been no criticism, but a reference to 'everyday affairs' might have suggested to the jury too low a standard of proof. In *Walters v R*[149] the Privy Council upheld the direction of the trial judge that 'a reasonable doubt is that quality and kind of doubt which, when you are dealing with matters of importance in your own affairs, you allow to influence you one way or the other'.[150] In *R v Hodge*,[151] a murder case where the prosecution evidence was entirely circumstantial, the jurors were directed by Alderson B that before returning

[141] Cited with approval by the Privy Council in *Walters v R* [1969] 2 AC 26.
[142] Per Lord Scarman in *Ferguson v R* [1979] 1 WLR 94, PC. The phrase has been approved by the House of Lords in *Woolmington v DPP* [1935] AC 462 and *Mancini v DPP* [1942] AC 1.
[143] (1952) 36 Cr App R 14 at 15.
[144] [1955] 2 QB 600, CCA.
[145] [1955] 2 QB 600 at 603. Cf Lord Diplock in *Walters v R* [1969] 2 AC 26, PC: it is otiose to describe 'doubt' as subjective; it is the duty of each individual juror to make up his mind and inevitably, because of differences of temperament or experience, some jurors will take more convincing than others.
[146] (1968) 53 Cr App R 1 at 2, CA.
[147] Cf per Barwick CJ in *Green v R* (1971) 126 CLR 28 at 32–3: 'Jurymen themselves set the standard of what is reasonable in the circumstances . . . A reasonable doubt which a jury may entertain is not to be confined to a "rational doubt" or a "doubt founded on reason".'
[148] (1973) 58 Cr App R 177.
[149] [1969] 2 AC 26, PC.
[150] Cf *R v Wanhalla* [2006] NZCA 229 per Hammond J at [166]: 'The gravity of the criminal context (where the liberty of the subject is at stake) should not be watered down by the quite different context of a domestic setting'.
[151] (1838) 2 Lew CC 227.

a verdict of guilty they should be satisfied that the evidence was consistent with the guilt of the accused and inconsistent with any other rational conclusion than the defendant's guilt. However, the House of Lords in *McGreevy v DPP*[152] held that there is no rule requiring a special or additional direction where the evidence against the defendant is wholly or partially circumstantial; it suffices to direct the jury that the prosecution has the burden of proving the defendant's guilt beyond reasonable doubt.

Another classic formulation of the criminal standard of proof is to direct the jury that in order to return a guilty verdict they must 'be sure' or 'satisfied so that they feel sure'.[153] In *R v Hepworth and Fearnley*[154] Lord Goddard CJ held that it is a proper direction to say, 'You, the jury, must be completely satisfied', or better still, 'You must feel sure of the prisoner's guilt.' In that case the appeal was allowed because the judge had merely directed the jury that they must be 'satisfied'. To direct the jury to be 'satisfied' without any indication of the degree of satisfaction required is an inadequate direction.[155] However, it is sufficient to direct the jury to be satisfied so that they are sure of guilt, and it is not helpful to seek to draw a distinction between being sure of guilt and being certain of guilt.[156] In *Ferguson v R*[157] the two classic formulations were combined and Lord Scarman held that: 'It is generally sufficient and safe to direct a jury that they must be satisfied beyond reasonable doubt so that they feel sure of the defendant's guilt.' However, the current 'specimen direction' on the standard of proof confines itself to the formulation of 'making the jury sure':

> How does the prosecution succeed in proving the defendant's guilt? The answer is- by making you sure of it. Nothing less than that will do. If after considering all the evidence you are sure that the defendant is guilty, you must return a verdict of 'Guilty'. If you are not sure, your verdict must be 'Not Guilty'.[158]

Where the accused bears the legal burden. In criminal cases, the legal burden is, as we have seen, generally borne by the prosecution. Where the legal burden on a particular issue is borne by the accused, it is discharged by the defence satisfying the jury on a balance of probabilities.[159] So, where the defence bear the legal burden of proving insanity[160] or diminished responsibility,[161] the burden is discharged by satisfying the jury on a balance of probabilities.[162]

---

[152] [1973] 1 WLR 276, HL.

[153] See per Lord Goddard CJ in *R v Kritz* [1950] 1 KB 82, CCA at 89–90 (approved by the Privy Council in *Walters v R* [1969] 2 AC 26 and in *R v Summers* (1952) 36 Cr App R 14, CCA at 15).

[154] [1955] 2 QB 600 at 603, CCA.

[155] See also per Fenton Atkinson LJ in *R v Allan* [1969] 1 All ER 91, CCA.

[156] *R v Stephens* (2002) The Times, 27 June, CA.

[157] [1979] 1 WLR 94 at 99, PC.

[158] Specimen Direction 2B, available at <http://www.jsboard.co.uk/criminal_law/cbb/index.htm>. Where the jury are told in clear terms that they should return a verdict of guilty only if they are sure, failure to tell them that they should return a *not guilty* verdict if they are *not* sure will not necessarily render a conviction unsafe: *R v Blackford* LTL 22 July 2009.

[159] See *R v Carr-Briant* [1943] KB 607, CCA, In particular see ibid 612.

[160] *Sodeman v R* [1936] 2 All ER 1138 at 1140, PC.

[161] *R v Dunbar* [1958] 1 QB 1.

[162] See Specimen Direction 2C for the model direction proposed where the defence bear a legal burden, available at <http://www.jsboard.co.uk/criminal_law/cbb/index.htm>.

Civil cases

In civil trials, the standard of proof required to be met by either party seeking to discharge the legal burden of proof is on a balance of probabilities.[163] The same standard should also be used in reaching a decision on a submission of no case to answer when the defendant has elected not to adduce any evidence.[164] In *Miller v Minister of Pensions*[165] Denning J described as well settled the degree of cogency required to discharge the legal burden in a civil case. He continued:[166]

> It must carry a reasonable degree of probability, but not so high as is required in a criminal case. If the evidence is such that the tribunal can say: 'we think it more probable than not', the burden is discharged, but if the probabilities are equal it is not.

To the general rule on the standard of proof in civil proceedings are a number of clearly defined exceptions. First, the appropriate standard in committal proceedings for civil contempt of court is the criminal standard, proof beyond reasonable doubt.[167] Second, the criminal standard may also be required in civil proceedings pursuant to statute.[168] Third, it has been held that an exacting civil standard of proof, which for all practical purposes is indistinguishable from the criminal standard of proof, applies to the following civil proceedings: applications for sex offender orders (in relation to the condition, set out in section 2(1)(a) of the Crime and Disorder Act 1998, that the person against whom the order is sought is a 'sex offender');[169] applications for football banning orders under section 14B of the Football Spectators Act 1989;[170] and applications for anti-social behaviour orders (in relation to the condition, set out in section 1(1)(a) of the Crime and Disorder Act 1998, that the person against whom the order is sought has acted 'in an anti-social manner').[171] As to the last case, it has been held that magistrates, to make their task more straightforward, should always apply the *criminal* standard.[172]

There are only two standards of proof, the civil and the criminal standard. There is no intermediate standard. Nor is the civil standard to be broken down into sub-categories designed to produce one or more intermediate standards.

However, although there is a single civil standard, it is flexible in its *application*. In particular, the more serious the allegation or the more serious the consequences if the allegation is proved, the stronger must be the evidence before a court will find the allegation proved on

---

[163] The same standard is not necessarily appropriate for interim applications. For example, an application for summary judgment is decided not by application of the normal standard of proof but by application of the test whether the respondent has a case with a real prospect of success: *Royal Brompton Hospital NHS Trust v Hammond* [2001] BLR 297, CA.

[164] *Miller v Cawley* (2002) The Times, 6 Sept, CA.

[165] [1947] 2 All ER 372.

[166] [1947] 2 All ER 372 at 374.

[167] *Re Bramblevale Ltd* [1970] Ch 128, CA; *Dean v Dean* [1987] 1 FLR 517, CA; see also *Re A (A Child) (Abduction: Contempt)* [2009] 1 FLR 1, CA. Proceedings to bind over for breach of the peace are probably criminal proceedings, but even if properly classified as civil proceedings, call for proof to the criminal standard, because failure to comply with an order to enter into a recognisance may result in imprisonment: *Percy v DPP* [1995] 3 All ER 124, DC.

[168] See *Judd v Minister of Pensions and National Insurance* [1966] 2 QB 580.

[169] *B v Chief Constable of Avon and Somerset Constabulary* [2001] 1 WLR 340, DC.

[170] *Gough v Chief Constable of the Derbyshire Constabulary* [2002] QB 1213, CA.

[171] *R (McCann) v Crown Court at Manchester* [2003] 1 AC 787, HL.

[172] Ibid.

the balance of probabilities.[173] Thus although there are indications in some of the authorities that the flexibility of the standard lies in an adjustment of the degree of probability required for an allegation to be proved,[174] the flexibility does not lie in any such adjustment but in the strength or quality of the evidence required for the allegation to be proved on the balance of probabilities.[175] 'The more serious the allegation the more cogent is the evidence required to overcome the unlikelihood of what is alleged and thus to prove it.'[176] As Morris LJ remarked in *Hornal v Neuberger Products Ltd*, 'the very elements of gravity become a part of the whole range of circumstances which have to be weighed in the scale when deciding as to the balance of probabilities'.[177]

Some authorities clearly focus on the seriousness of the allegation rather than the seriousness of the consequences if the allegation is proved, on the reasoning that the more serious the allegation the less likely it is that the event occurred, and that the inherent probability or improbability of an event is itself a matter to be taken into account.[178] However, this rationalization will take due account of the seriousness of the consequences if an allegation is proved, because in general the seriousness of an allegation is a function of the seriousness of its consequences. Nonetheless, there will be cases where proof of an allegation may have serious consequences even though it cannot be said that the matter alleged is inherently improbable, and in such cases the more serious the consequences, the stronger the evidence required to prove the matter on the balance of probabilities.[179]

Issues calling for flexibility in the application of the civil standard defy comprehensive classification, but will be explored by reference to (i) allegations of crime in civil proceedings; (ii) matrimonial causes; and (iii) a miscellany of different cases.

Allegations of crime in civil proceedings.   Prior to the decision of the Court of Appeal in *Hornal v Neuberger Products Ltd*,[180] it was unclear, on the authorities, what standard of proof was appropriate in civil cases in which a party made an allegation of criminal conduct. One line of authorities supported the view that the standard was as high as that required of the prosecution in a criminal case.[181] Other authorities took the view that the appropriate standard was the normal civil standard on a balance of probabilities.[182] In *Hornal v Neuberger Products Ltd*

[173] See *R (D) v Life Sentence Review Commissioners* (Northern Ireland) [2008] UKHL 33, where it was held that although the civil standard of proof was unvarying, it was flexible in its application. For a conceptual framework for understanding the civil standard of proof, see Mike Redmayne 'Standards of Proof in Civil Litigation' (1999) *MLR* vol 62, 167.

[174] See, eg, per Denning LJ in *Bater v Bater* [1951] P 35 at p 37 and in *Hornal v Neuberger Products Ltd* [1957] 1 QB 247.

[175] Per Richards LJ, after an extensive review of the authorities, in *R (on the application of N) v Mental Health Review Tribunal* [2006] QB 468, CA, at [60]–[62].

[176] Per Ungoed-Thomas J in *Re Dellow's Will Trusts* [1964] 1 WLR 451, Ch D.

[177] [1957] 1 QB 247, CA at 266. These words of Morris LJ were approved and adopted by the House of Lords in *Khawaja v Secretary of State for the Home Department* [1983] 1 All ER 765 in relation to the detention pending deportation of persons alleged to be illegal immigrants: see per Lord Scarman at 783–4.

[178] See *Re H (Minors) (Sexual Abuse: Standard of Proof)* [1996] AC 563, followed in *Secretary of State for the Home Department v Rehman* [2003] 1 AC 153.

[179] Per Richards LJ in *R (on the application of N) v Mental Health Review Tribunal* [2006] QB 468, CA at [64].

[180] [1957] 1 QB 247.

[181] See, eg, *Issais v Marine Insurance Co Ltd* (1923) 15 Ll L Rep 186, CA (allegations of arson on the part of the assured in an action on an insurance policy).

[182] See, eg, *Hurst v Evans* [1917] 1 KB 352, KBD (an allegation of theft on the part of the servant of the assured in an action on an insurance policy).

the plaintiff claimed damages for breach of warranty or alternatively for fraud. The defendant company had sold a lathe to the plaintiff. The plaintiff alleged that one of the company directors had represented that the lathe had been 'Soag reconditioned'. If the director did so represent, there was clearly a fraudulent misrepresentation because he knew that the machine had not been reconditioned. The question became whether the representation had been made or not. Dismissing the claim for damages for breach of warranty on the grounds that the parties did not intend the director's statement to have contractual effect, the trial judge said that he was satisfied on a balance of probabilities, but not beyond reasonable doubt, that the statement was made and accordingly awarded damages for fraud. On appeal, the Court of Appeal held that on an allegation of a crime in civil proceedings the standard of proof is on a balance of probabilities.

One of the reasons for the decision was put clearly by Denning LJ:[183] 'I think it would bring the law into contempt if a judge were to say on the issue of warranty he finds the statement was made, and that on the issue of fraud he finds it was not made.' In support of his conclusion that the civil standard applied, his Lordship referred to the views which he had expressed in *Bater v Bater*[184] where he said that civil cases must be proved by a preponderance of probability, but there may be degrees of probability within that standard. However, as we have seen, it is now recognized that the flexibility of the civil standard does not lie in an adjustment of the degree of probability but in the strength of the evidence required for serious allegations to be proved.

Against the background of conflicting authorities preceding it, *Hornal v Neuberger Products Ltd* would appear to have settled this area of the law in favour of the normal civil standard. It was applied in *Re Dellow's Will Trusts*,[185] civil proceedings in which the issue was whether a wife feloniously killed her husband. As Ungoed-Thomas J pertinently observed: 'There can hardly be a graver issue than that.' It was also applied in *Post Office v Estuary Radio Ltd*,[186] where an allegation of a criminal offence under the Wireless Telegraphy Act 1949 was made on an application for an injunction under the same Act.[187] Similarly, in *Re B (Children) (Care Proceedings: Standard of Proof)*,[188] the House of Lords held that the normal civil standard applied where allegations of sexual crimes against children were made in care proceedings, notwithstanding that such allegations were grave.[189]

Matrimonial causes. The authorities remain in conflict as to the standard of proof appropriate to matrimonial causes, earlier decisions requiring the criminal standard of beyond reasonable doubt, more recent cases favouring the ordinary civil standard on a balance of probabilities.

[183] [1957] 1 QB 247 at 258.
[184] [1951] P 35 at 37, CA.
[185] [1964] 1 WLR 451, Ch D.
[186] [1967] 1 WLR 1396, CA.
[187] See also *Piermay Shipping Co SA and Brandt's Ltd v Chester, The Michael* [1979] 1 Lloyd's Rep 55 (an allegation of deliberately scuttling a ship); *Khawaja v Secretary of State for the Home Department* [1983] 1 All ER 765, HL (detention pending deportation of persons alleged to be illegal immigrants), distinguished in *Ali v Secretary of State for the Home Department* [1988] Imm AR 274, CA; and *Parks v Clout* [2003] EWCA Civ 1030 (an allegation of obtaining letters of administration by fraud).
[188] [2009] 1 AC 11, HL.
[189] Followed in *Re D (Children)* [2009] EWCA Civ 472. See also *Smithkline Beecham Plc v Avery* [2009] EWHC 1448 QB which, drawing on *Re B*, at [59]–[61], determined that a single civil standard applied in a claim for an injunction to restrain harassment under s 1(1)(A) of the Protection From Harassment Act 1994.

THE STANDARD OF PROOF

In *Ginesi v Ginesi*,[190] where it was held that adultery must be proved to the criminal standard, the Court of Appeal relied upon the fact that adultery was regarded by the ecclesiastical courts as a quasi-criminal offence.[191] In *Preston-Jones v Preston-Jones*.[192] A husband petitioned for divorce on the ground of adultery and proved that his wife had given birth to a normal child 360 days after the last opportunity he could have had for intercourse with her. The House of Lords held that adultery had been proved beyond reasonable doubt, Lord MacDermott stressing the gravity and public importance of the issues involved: 'The jurisdiction in divorce involves the status of the parties and the public interest requires that the marriage bond shall not be set aside lightly or without strict inquiry.'[193] Because the result of a finding of adultery would have been in effect to render the child illegitimate, this decision may be regarded as little more than an application of the law, as it then stood,[194] that the presumption of legitimacy could only be rebutted by proof beyond reasonable doubt.[195]

When the question of the appropriate standard in matrimonial causes next fell to be considered by the House of Lords, in *Blyth v Blyth*,[196] the tide had begun to turn. A husband petitioning for divorce on the ground of adultery sought to negative the presumption of condonation which arose from his sexual intercourse with his wife on a date subsequent to the adultery. The question arose as to the standard of proof required to negative condonation. The majority of the House, comprising Lords Pearson, Denning, and Pearce held that proof was required on a balance of probabilities. Lord Pearson was of the view that the requirement of proof beyond reasonable doubt was confined to the grounds of divorce and did not extend to the bars to divorce. Lord Denning, however, held that both the grounds for and the bars to divorce may be proved on a preponderance of probability. His Lordship disapproved *Ginesi v Ginesi*, preferring *Wright v Wright*,[197] a decision of the High Court of Australia in the same year, and relied upon his own dicta in *Bater v Bater* and the decision in *Hornal v Neuberger Products Ltd*. Lord Pearce also drew the distinction made by Lord Pearson between the grounds for and the bars to divorce, but expressed his agreement with Lord Denning's views on *Ginesi v Ginesi*[198] and *Wright v Wright*, and, in this connection, did not find *Preston-Jones v Preston-Jones* in conflict.[199]

In the light of the various dicta in *Preston-Jones v Preston-Jones* and *Blyth v Blyth*, it was not surprising to find the Court of Appeal in the ensuing case of *Bastable v Bastable and Sanders*[200] openly expressing the difficulties of determining what standard of proof should be applied in relation to proof of adultery.[201] Wilmer LJ adopted the dicta of Lord Denning in *Bater v Bater*,

---

[190] [1948] P 179, CA.

[191] See also *Bater v Bater* [1951] P 35, CA. However, contrast *Briginshaw v Briginshaw* (1938) 60 CLR 336, a decision of the High Court of Australia favouring proof to the civil standard.

[192] [1951] AC 391.

[193] See also *Galler v Galler* [1954] P 252.

[194] See now Family Law Reform Act 1969, s 26, but see also *Serio v Serio* (1983) 13 Fam Law 255, CA, below.

[195] See particularly the speech of Lord Simonds. See also *F v F* [1968] P 506.

[196] [1966] AC 643.

[197] (1948) 77 CLR 191.

[198] [1948] P 179, CA

[199] [1966] AC 643 at 673. His Lordship said at 673, 'The real question in *Preston-Jones* was whether, on the assumption that proof beyond reasonable doubt was needed to establish adultery, such proof had been forthcoming on the evidence under review'.

[200] [1968] 1 WLR 1684.

[201] See per Willmer LJ [1968] WLR 1684 at 1685.

which were approved in *Hornal v Neuberger Products Ltd*, that the court requires a degree of probablilty proportionate to the subject matter. Accordingly, he was satisfied that the commission of adultery is a serious matrimonial offence and held that a high standard of proof is required.

Bastable v Bastable, it is submitted, is a decision which accords with the spirit of the then un-enacted Divorce Reform Act 1969,[202] which abolished the old grounds for divorce, largely based on the concept of the matrimonial offence, replacing them with one ground, that the marriage has irretrievably broken down. The fact that the ecclesiastical courts regarded adultery as a quasi-criminal offence is, under the present philosophy of divorce law, not a convincing reason for the application of the criminal standard of proof, especially now that the civil standard of proof is held to be appropriate in civil cases in which allegations of crime are made. The matter may be one of statutory construction; under the current legislation irretrievable breakdown may be established if the petitioner 'satisfies' the court of one of five facts. The same word 'satisfied' was used in the legislation prior to the Divorce Reform Act 1969 under which the decisions set out above were decided. However, it seems most unlikely that the criminal standard will even be re-imposed by way of statutory construction or because of the importance of divorce to the parties and to the state.

Miscellaneous.   On various different issues arising in civil cases it has been suggested either (a) that the appropriate standard is higher than the ordinary civil standard (sometimes as high as the criminal standard) or, in any event, (b) that the more improbable the event being alleged, the stronger the evidence required to prove it (on a balance of probabilities). The following examples may be given.

1. A party desiring to prove an intention to change domicile must do so 'clearly and unequivocally'.[203]

2. There is a strong common law presumption that a marriage ceremony celebrated between persons who intended it to constitute a valid marriage is formally valid. Evidence in rebuttal is required to be 'strong, distinct, and satisfactory'[204] or 'evidence which satisfied beyond reasonable doubt that there was no valid marriage'.[205]

3. A party claiming rectification is required to prove his case by 'strong irrefragable evidence'.[206]

4. In cases involving the care of children, the standard is the ordinary civil standard but it had been held that the more serious or improbable an allegation of abuse, the stronger the evidence required to prove both the abuse[207] and the identity of the

---

[202] See now the Matrimonial Causes Act 1973.

[203] *Moorhouse v Lord* (1863) 10 HL Cas 272 at 236. See also *Fuld's Estate (No 3)* [1968] P 675 at 685.

[204] *Piers v Piers* (1849) 2 HL Cas 331 at 389.

[205] *Mahadervan v Mahadervan* [1964] P 233 at 246.

[206] *Countess of Shelburne v Earl of Inchiquin* (1784) 1 Bro CC 338 at 341. See also *Earl v Hector Whaling Ltd* [1961] 1 Lloyd's Rep 459, CA.

[207] See *Re H (minors) (sexual abuse: standard of proof)* [1996] AC 563, HL and *In re U (a Child) (Serious Injury: Standard of Proof)* [2005] Fam 134, CA. See also V Smith 'Sexual Abuse: Standard of Proof' [1994] *Fam Law* 626 and J Spencer 'Evidence in child abuse cases—too high a price for too high a standard?' (1994) 6 JCL 160.

abuser.[208] This approach must now be considered in the light of *Re B (Children) (Sexual Abuse: Standard of Proof)*[209] which emphasized that the standard is the simple balance of probabilities and that the seriousness and probability of an allegation are simply factors to be taken into account when determining where the truth lies.[210] In *Re B*, Baroness Hale observed that there is no 'logical or necessary connection' between the seriousness of an allegation and the probability that what is alleged occurred, as a serious allegation can be more or less probable according to other evidence.[211] Her Ladyship noted that:[212]

> It may be unlikely that any person looking after a baby would take him by the wrist and swing him against a wall, causing multiple fractures and other injuries. But once the evidence is clear that that is indeed what has happened to the child, it ceases to be improbable. Some-one looking after the child at the relevant time must have done it. The inherent improbability of the event has no relevance to deciding who that was. The simple balance of probabilities test should be applied.

5. The standard required to make a finding of paternity is a heavy one, commensurate with the gravity of the issue, and although not as heavy as in criminal proceedings, more than the ordinary civil standard of balance of probabilities.[213]

6. For a court to approve medical treatment for an incompetent mentally ill patient without infringing Article 3 of the European Convention on Human Rights, it must be 'convincingly shown' that the proposed treatment is medically necessary, a standard that may be met notwithstanding that there is a responsible body of opinion against the proposed treatment.[214]

7. Cogent evidence is in practice required to satisfy a mental health review tribunal, on the balance of probabilities, that the conditions for continuing detention under sections 72 and 73 of the Mental Health Act 1983 have been met.[215]

8. The gravity of civil recovery proceedings under Part V of the Proceeds of Crime Act 2002 is 'very great indeed' and evidence that the property sought to be recovered is or represents property obtained through unlawful conduct must satisfy the court to a standard that is commensurate with the gravity of the case.[216]

---

[208] *Re G (A Child) (Non-accidental Injury: Standard of Proof)* [2001] 1 FCR 97, CA. See also *Re M (Children)* [2008] EWCA Civ 1216.

[209] [2009] 1 AC 61, HL.

[210] Per Lord Hoffmann at [70]–[73]. There is no necessary connection between seriousness and probability, as a serious allegation can be more or less probable according to other evidence. It could be rare for a person to harm a child he is looking after, but it ceases to be improbable if other evidence shows that the child sustained injuries at a time when being looked after.

[211] Ibid [72].

[212] At [73].

[213] *W v K* [1988] Fam Law 64. See also *Serio v Serio* (1983) 13 Fam Law 255, divorce proceedings in which the paternity of the wife's son was in dispute. The Court of Appeal held that notwithstanding s 26 of the Family Law Reform Act 1969, the standard on an issue of paternity is slightly higher than the balance of probabilities.

[214] *R (N) v Dr M* [2003] 1 WLR 562, CA.

[215] *R (on the application of N) v Mental Health Review Tribunal* [2006] QB 468, CA.

[216] Per Tugendhat J in *The Assets Recovery Agency v Virtuso* [2008] EWHC 149. (QB) at [18].

The evidential burden

Whether a party to civil or criminal proceedings has discharged an evidential burden borne by him in relation to a particular issue is, as we have seen, decided by the judge as opposed to the tribunal of fact. This may account for the dearth of authority on the standard required to discharge the evidential burden. In criminal cases, the standard required to discharge the evidential burden depends upon whether it is borne by the prosecution or defence. We have seen that in criminal trials either party bearing an evidential burden must adduce sufficient evidence to prevent the judge from withdrawing the issue in question from the jury, and this is done when there is sufficient evidence to justify as a possibility a favourable finding by the tribunal of fact. Where the evidential burden is borne by the prosecution, it is discharged by the adduction of 'such evidence as, if believed and if left uncontradicted and unexplained, could be accepted by the jury as proof'.[217] This means that the prosecution must adduce sufficient evidence to justify as a possibility a finding by the tribunal of fact that the legal burden on the same issue has been discharged, discharge of the legal burden, of course, requiring proof beyond reasonable doubt. However, where the evidential burden is borne by the accused, it is discharged by the adduction of such evidence as 'might leave a jury in reasonable doubt'.[218] This standard applies only where the defence bear the evidential but not the legal burden on a particular issue, as when the defence is one of provocation, self-defence, or duress. Where the defence bear both the legal and evidential burden in relation to an issue, as when the defence is one of insanity or diminished responsibility, the evidential burden is discharged by the adduction of such evidence as *might* satisfy the jury of the probability of that which the accused is called upon to establish.[219] In civil cases, whichever party bears the evidential burden on a particular issue, it is discharged by the adduction of sufficient evidence to justify as a possibility a finding by the tribunal of fact that the legal burden on the same issue has been discharged, discharge of the legal burden, of course, requiring proof on a balance of probabilities.

The burden and standard of proof in a trial within a trial

Preliminary facts are those facts which must be proved as a condition precedent to the admissibility of certain items of evidence. It is for the judge alone, if necessary in a trial within a trial, to determine whether preliminary facts have been proved. The burden of proving such facts is borne by the party who alleges their existence and who seeks to admit the evidence in question.[220] On the question whether a witness is competent to give evidence in criminal proceedings, it is for the party calling the witness to satisfy the court on a balance of probabilities that the witness is competent.[221] Where the prosecution bears the burden of proving preliminary facts, the standard of proof required to discharge the burden is proof beyond

---

[217] Per Lord Devlin in *Jayasena v R* [1970] AC 618 at 624.

[218] Per Lord Morris in *Bratty v A-G for Northern Ireland* [1963] AC 386 at 419, HL.

[219] See per Humphreys J in *R v Carr-Briant* [1943] KB 607 at 612.

[220] See, at common law, *R v Jenkins* (1869) LR 1 CCR 187 (a dying declaration) and *R v Thompson* [1893] 2 QB 12 (a confession). As to the former, see now s 116 of the Criminal Justice Act 2003. As to the latter, see now s 76(2) of the Police and Criminal Evidence Act 1984. See generally, Pattenden, 'Authenticating 'Things' in English Law: Principles for Adducing Tangible Evidence in Common Law Jury Trials' (2008) 12 *E&P* 273, especially at 281.

[221] Youth Justice and Criminal Evidence Act 1999, s 54(2).

reasonable doubt.[222] It would seem to follow that where the burden under discussion is borne by the defendant in criminal proceedings, or by either party to civil proceedings, the appropriate standard is proof on a balance of probabilities.[223] In *R v Ewing*[224] the Court of Appeal considered what standard of proof was appropriate to the question whether samples of handwriting, allegedly written by the accused, were 'genuine' for the purposes of section 8 of the Criminal Procedure Act 1865. That section provides as follows:

> Comparison of a disputed writing with any writing proved to the satisfaction of the judge to be genuine shall be permitted to be made by witnesses; and such writings, and the evidence of witnesses respecting the same, may be submitted to the court and jury as evidence of the genuineness or otherwise of the writing in dispute.

In the earlier decision of *R v Angeli*,[225] the Court of Appeal, on the basis that the 1865 Act applied to the criminal courts a provision which had already been in operation in the civil courts, held that the standard of proof under the section, whether applied in criminal or civil proceedings, was the civil one, on the balance of probabilities. In *R v Ewing* the Court of Appeal, unable to agree with this reasoning, and of the view that *R v Angeli* was decided *per incuriam*, held that, since section 8 did not deal with the standard of proof required to satisfy the judge, the matter was governed by common law. O'Connor LJ said:[226] 'It follows that when the section is applied in civil cases, the civil standard of proof is used, and when it is applied in criminal cases, the criminal standard should be used.'

There are cases similar to, but quite distinct from, those discussed above in which the judge, before allowing particular issues to go before the jury, must be satisfied of certain matters by prima facie evidence. For example, if the prosecution seeks to admit a confession allegedly made by the accused, the defence case being that the confession never was made, the judge must be satisfied by prima facie evidence that the accused did make the confession.[227] Likewise, if the prosecution seeks to adduce a tape recording in evidence, the judge must be satisfied that the prosecution has made out a prima facie case of originality and genuineness by evidence which defines and describes the provenance and history of the recording up to the moment of its production in court.[228]

---

[222] See *R v Sartori* [1961] Crim LR 397 in relation to confessions, *R v Jenkins* (1869) LR 1 CCR 187 in relation to dying declarations, and generally *R v Ewing* [1983] 2 All ER 645. By contrast, in Australia, New Zealand and Canada, the civil standard has been held to apply: see *Wendo v R* (1963) 109 CLR 559; *R v Donohoe* [1963] SRNSW 38; *Police v Anderson* [1972] NZLR 233; and *R v Lee* (1953) 104 CCC 400.

[223] See, in the case of a defence application under s 23 of the Criminal Justice Act 1988, *R v Mattey and Queeley* [1995] 2 Cr App R 409, CA.

[224] [1983] 2 All ER 645.

[225] [1978] 3 All ER 950.

[226] [1983] 2 All ER 645 at 1047.

[227] See further, *Ajodha v The State* [1981] 2 All ER 193, PC (see Ch 13).

[228] In *R v Rampling* [1987] Crim LR 823, CA the Court of Appeal gave the following general guidance upon the use in trials of tape recordings and transcripts of police interviews: (i) the tape can be produced and proved by the interviewing officer or any other officer present when it was taken; (ii) the officer should have listened to the tape before the trial so that he can, if required, deal with any objections to its authenticity or accuracy; (iii) as to authenticity, he can, if required, prove who spoke the recorded words; (iv) as to accuracy, he can deal with any challenge, eg that the recording has been falsified by addition or omission; (v) the transcript of the recording can be produced by the officer who, before the trial, should have checked it against the recording for accuracy; the tape recording is the evidence in the case and can be made an exhibit; the transcript, not in itself evidence, may be used as a convenience to the jury; (vi) use of the transcript is an administrative matter to be decided in his discretion by the trial judge; in many cases the accused will agree to its use and will not require the tape to be played at all, in which case

In *R v Robson, R v Harris*[229] it was held that in these circumstances the judge is required to be satisfied to the civil standard, on a balance of probabilities, because application of the higher standard of proof, beyond reasonable doubt, would amount to a usurpation by the judge of the function of the jury. If the judge satisfies himself that the evidence is competent to be considered by the jury and should not be withdrawn from them, the very same issues of originality and genuineness may then fall to be considered by them. The standard of proof is then proof beyond reasonable doubt. It has been convincingly argued, however, that a better approach, also involving no usurpation of the function of the jury, would be for the judge to decide the issue in exactly the same way as he is required to decide whether an evidential burden has been discharged.[230] In other words, the judge should not be required to be satisfied on a balance of probabilities; the test should be whether the party seeking to put the evidence before the jury has adduced sufficient evidence on the facts in issue to justify, as a possibility, a finding by the jury on those facts in that party's favour.

ADDITIONAL READING

Ashworth, 'Four threats to the presumption of innocence' (2006) 10 *E&P* 241.

Ashworth and Blake, 'The Presumption of Innocence in English Criminal Law' [1996] *Crim LR* 306.

Dennis, 'Reverse Onuses and the Presumption of Innocence: In Search of Principle' [2005] *Crim LR* 901.

Harmer, 'The Presumption of Innocence and Reverse Burdens: A Balancing Act' (2007) 66(1) *CLJ* 142.

Ho,'Re-imagining the Criminal Standard of Proof: Lessons From the 'Ethics of Belief'' (2009) 13 *E&P* 198.

Roberts and Zuckerman, *Criminal Evidence* (Oxford, 2004) Ch 8.

---

the transcript will be read out by the officer who produced it; however, the accused is entitled, if he so wishes, to have any part of the tape played to the jury; (vii) if any part of the tape is played, it is for the judge to decide whether the jury should have the transcript, in order to follow the tape, and have it with them when they retire; the use of the transcript is within the judge's discretion and not dependent on the consent of the parties; a transcript is usually of very considerable value to the jury but each case has to be decided on its own facts. See also *R v Emmerson* (1990) 92 Cr App R 284, CA; *R v Riaz* (1991) 94 Cr App R 339, CA; and *R v Tonge* [1993] Crim LR 876, CA (all in Ch 5); the Code of Practice on Tape Recording of Interviews with Suspects, Code E; para 43 of *Practice Direction (Criminal Proceedings: Consolidation)* [2002] 1 WLR 2870; and John Baldwin and Julie Bedward 'Summarising Tape Recordings of Police Interviews' [1991] *Crim LR* 671.

[229] [1972] 1 WLR 651; cf *R v Stevenson* [1971] 1 WLR 1.

[230] *Cross & Tapper on Evidence* (9th edn, London, 1999) at 170.

Witnesses

5

Key Issues

- Which types of witness should be eligible to give evidence and which ineligible?

- Which types of witness, if eligible to give evidence, should the court have the power to compel to give evidence?

- When and why should witnesses be allowed to give evidence through a live television link?

- When and why should parties to litigation be allowed to call additional evidence after the close of their case?

- In civil proceedings, what are the advantages of (a) exchanging witness statements prior to trial; and (b) allowing a statement to stand as a witness's evidence-in-chief?

- When and why should witnesses in criminal proceedings be allowed to give their evidence-in-chief by video-recording?

- What measures can be taken to minimize the ordeal and trauma experienced by children and other vulnerable or intimidated witnesses when giving evidence in criminal cases?

- When and why should witnesses be allowed to preserve their anonymity?

- Why is witness training or coaching prohibited?

Competence and compellability

A witness is said to be competent if he may be called to give evidence and compellable if, being competent, he may be compelled by the court to do so.[1] A compellable witness who chooses to ignore a witness summons is in contempt of court and faces the penalty of imprisonment.[2] The same applies in the case of a compellable witness who attends court but refuses to testify, although such a witness may be entitled, on grounds of public policy or privilege, to refuse to answer some or all of the questions put to him.[3]

No party has any property in the evidence of a witness. Even if there is a contract between a party and a witness under which the latter binds himself not to give evidence to the court on a matter on which the judge can compel him to give evidence, it is contrary to public policy and unenforceable. Thus an expert witness is compellable if, having inadvertently advised both parties, he is loath to appear on behalf of one of them.[4] However, once a witness in criminal proceedings has given evidence for the prosecution, he cannot be called to give evidence for the defence;[5] and an expert witness may not be called by one party if his opinion is based on privileged information, such as communications with the other party, and cannot be divorced from it.[6]

The general rule

At common law, the law of competence and compellability is governed by a general rule with two limbs. The first limb is that anyone is a competent witness in any proceedings. This part of the general rule has now been put on a statutory footing in criminal cases. Section 53(1) of the Youth Justice and Criminal Evidence Act 1999 provides that: 'At every stage in criminal proceedings all persons are (whatever their age) competent to give evidence.' The second limb of the general rule is that all competent witnesses are compellable.

There used to be many categories of exception to the first limb of the general rule, but these were whittled down, over the centuries, by piecemeal judicial and statutory reform: see, in the case of non-Christians and atheists, *Omychund v Barker*[7] and the Evidence Further Amendment Act 1869; in the case of those with criminal convictions or with a personal pecuniary or proprietary interest in the outcome of the proceedings, the Civil Rights of Convicts Act 1828 and the Evidence Act 1843; in the case of the parties to civil proceedings and their spouses, the Evidence Act 1851, the Evidence Amendment Act 1853 and the Evidence Further Amendment Act 1869;[8] in the case of the accused as a witness for the defence, section 1 of the Criminal

---

[1] In civil cases a witness summons may be issued by the court: see CPR r 34.2–34.6. In trials on indictment, the attendance of witnesses may also be secured by means of a witness summons: see Criminal Procedure (Attendance of Witnesses) Act 1965. For the position in magistrates' courts, see s 97 of the Magistrates' Courts Act 1980.

[2] See *R v Yusuf* [2003] 2 Cr App R 488, CA.

[3] See Chs 19 and 20.

[4] *Harmony Shipping Co SA v Saudi Europe Line Ltd* [1979] 1 WLR 1380, CA.

[5] *R v Kelly* (1985) The Times, 27 July, CA.

[6] *R v Davies* (2002) 166 JP 243, CA. See also *R v R* [1994] 4 All ER 260, CA, Ch 20.

[7] (1745) 1 Atk 21.

[8] In *Monroe v Twisleton* (1802) Peake Add Cas 219, followed in *O'Connor v Marjoribanks* (1842) 4 Man&G 435, it was held that a former spouse of a party to civil proceedings is incompetent following the termination of his or her marriage insofar as his or her evidence relates to events which occurred during the marriage. Reversal of the decision is long overdue.

Evidence Act 1898;[9] and in the case of the spouse of the accused, section 80 of the Police and Criminal Evidence Act 1984, whereby the spouse became competent as a witness for the accused, a co-accused or, except where jointly charged with the accused, the prosecution. The only remaining exceptions to the first limb of the general rule relate to the accused as a witness for the prosecution, children and persons of defective intellect. The only remaining exceptions to the second limb of the general rule relate to the accused, his or her spouse or civil partner, heads of sovereign states, diplomats, and, in certain circumstances, bankers.[10]

The accused

For the prosecution

Under section 53 of the Youth Justice and Criminal Evidence Act 1999 (the 1999 Act), the accused, whether charged solely or jointly, is incompetent as a witness for the prosecution. Section 53 provides as follows:

(1) At every stage in criminal proceedings all persons are (whatever their age) competent to give evidence.

(2) Subsection (1) has effect subject to subsections (3) and (4).

(3) A person is not competent to give evidence in criminal proceedings if it appears to the court that he is not a person who is able to—
(a) understand questions put to him as a witness, and
(b) give answers to them which can be understood.

(4) A person charged in criminal proceedings is not competent to give evidence in the proceedings for the prosecution (whether he is the only person, or is one of two or more persons, charged in the proceedings).

(5) In subsection (4) the reference to a person charged in criminal proceedings does not include a person who is not, or is no longer, liable to be convicted of any offence in the proceedings (whether as a result of pleading guilty or for any other reason).

Thus if the prosecution wish to call a co-accused to give evidence for them, they may only do so if, in effect, he has ceased to be a co-accused. This may happen, as section 53(5) indicates, as a result of pleading guilty. It may also happen in three other ways: the co-accused may be acquitted, for example where no evidence is offered against him or he makes a successful submission of no case to answer at the close of the prosecution case; an application to sever the indictment may succeed so that he is not tried with the other accused; or the Attorney General may enter a *nolle prosequi*, thereby putting an end to the proceedings against him. In any of these circumstances a former co-accused becomes both a competent and compellable witness for the prosecution.[11] Where a co-accused has pleaded guilty and proposes to give evidence for the prosecution, as a general rule he should be sentenced after the trial of the other accused.[12] However, the rule would appear to be one of practice only and the matter

---

[9] And the Statute Law (Repeals) Act 1981.

[10] The leave of the wardship court is not required to call a ward to give evidence at a criminal trial: *Re K (minors)* [1988] 1 All ER 214, Fam D; and *Re R (minors)* [1991] 2 All ER 193, CA. Concerning interviews with wards by the prosecution or police, see *Practice Direction (Criminal Proceedings: Consolidation)* [2002] 1 WLR 2870, para 5; and *Re R, Re G (minors)* [1990] 2 All ER 633, Fam D. As to interviews with wards by those representing the accused, see *Re R (minors)* [1991] 2 All ER 193, CA.

[11] If he is an accomplice, a care warning may be called for (see Ch 8).

[12] Per Boreham J in *R v Weekes* (1982) 74 Cr App R 161 at 166, CA. Contrast *R v Payne* [1950] 1 All ER 102, CCA. See also *R v Woods* (25 Oct 1977, unreported), CA and *R v Potter* (15 Sept 1977, unreported), CA.

remains within the discretion of the judge. The same may be said of the rule in *R v Pipe*[13] that an accomplice who is not an accused in the proceedings in question but against whom proceedings are pending should only be called by the prosecution if they have undertaken to discontinue the proceedings against him.[14]

For himself

The accused is a competent but not compellable witness for the defence in all criminal proceedings. As to competence, the authority is now to be found in section 53(1) of the 1999 Act. As to compellability, section 1(1) of the Criminal Evidence Act 1898 (the 1898 Act) provides that: 'A person charged in criminal proceedings shall not be called as a witness in the proceedings except upon his own application.'

The phrase, in section 53(1), 'at every stage in criminal proceedings', is most likely to be construed in the same way as was the phrase 'at every stage of the proceedings' in the original unamended version of section 1 of the 1898 Act, so as to allow the accused to give evidence on the *voir dire*[15] and, after conviction, in mitigation of sentence,[16] as well as during the trial proper. If the accused elects to give evidence, he may of course be cross-examined by the prosecution and, even if he has not given evidence against a co-accused, by any co-accused.[17] Indeed, having elected to give evidence, then subject to section 1(2) and (4) of the 1898 Act, and section 101 of the Criminal Justice Act 2003 (the 2003 Act), which are described in outline below, he will be treated like any other witness and his evidence will be evidence for all the purposes of the case. Thus the evidence of an accused in his own defence may be used against a co-accused whether such evidence was given in chief[18] or elicited in cross-examination. In *R v Paul*[19] an accused had confined his evidence in chief to an admission of his own guilt. A cross-examination of him, which had elicited evidence undermining the defence of a co-accused, was held by the Court of Criminal Appeal to have been properly permitted.[20]

Section 1(2) of the 1898 Act removes from the accused who testifies the privilege against self-incrimination in respect of any offence with which he is charged. It provides that 'Subject to section 101 of the 2003 Act (admissibility of evidence of defendant's bad character), a person charged in criminal proceedings who is called as a witness in the proceedings may be asked any question in cross-examination notwithstanding that it would tend to criminate him as to any offence with which he is charged in the proceedings.'[21] Section 101 of the 2003 Act sets out the only circumstances in which evidence of the bad character of the accused is admissible.[22] Section 1(4) of the 1898 Act provides that 'every person charged in criminal proceedings who is called as a witness in the proceedings shall, unless otherwise ordered by the court, give his evidence from the witness box or other place from which the other witnesses give their evidence'. The court may 'order otherwise' if the accused is too

---

[13] (1966) 51 Cr App R 17, CA.

[14] *R v Turner* (1975) 61 Cr App R 67, CA.

[15] *R v Cowell* [1940] 2 KB 49.

[16] *R v Wheeler* [1917] 1 KB 283.

[17] *R v Hilton* [1972] 1 QB 421, CA.

[18] See *R v Rudd* (1948) 32 Cr App R 138; cf *R v Meredith* (1943) 29 Cr App R 40.

[19] [1920] 2 KB 183.

[20] But see *Young v HM Advocate* 1932 JC 63, where the view was expressed that in these circumstances the judge should exercise his discretion to prevent such cross-examination.

[21] See also Ch 20, 593 under **The privilege against self-incrimination**.

[22] See further Ch 17, 463 under **Evidence of the bad character of the defendant**.

infirm to walk to the witness box or too violent to be controlled there.[23] Subject to exceptional circumstances of this kind, the proviso does not confer a discretion to direct where evidence should be given from, and it is improper to offer the accused a choice as to whether he wishes to give his evidence from the dock or witness box.[24] If an accused elects not to give evidence, it should be the invariable practice of counsel to record the decision and to cause the accused to sign the record, giving a clear indication that he has by his own will decided not to testify bearing in mind the advice, if any, given to him by his counsel.[25]

For a co-accused

It will be clear from section 53(1) of the 1999 Act and section 1(1) of the 1898 Act that an accused is a competent but not compellable witness for a co-accused. A person who has ceased to be an accused is both competent and compellable for a co-accused. This may happen where he has pleaded guilty,[26] where he has been acquitted (for example where no evidence has been offered against him, or he has made a successful submission of no case to answer at the close of the prosecution case),[27] or where an application to sever the indictment has succeeded so that he is not tried with the other accused.[28]

The spouse or civil partner of an accused

For the prosecution

Prior to the Police and Criminal Evidence Act 1984 (the 1984 Act), the spouse of the accused was generally incompetent as a witness for the prosecution. There were a number of common law and statutory exceptions, but in almost all of these cases the spouse, although competent, was not compellable for the prosecution. In its 11th Report, the Criminal Law Revision Committee considered to what extent the spouse of the accused should be competent and compellable for the prosecution. The problem was seen as a question of balancing the desirability that all available and relevant evidence should be before the court against (i) the objection on social grounds to disturbing marital harmony; and (ii) the harshness of compelling one spouse to give evidence against the other. The Committee felt that the older objections based on the theoretical unity of the spouses, the interest of the accused's spouse in the outcome of the proceedings, and the likelihood of a spouse being biased in favour of the accused, were of no contemporary value.[29] Concerning competence, the Committee concluded that the wife should be competent for the prosecution in all cases: 'If she is willing to give evidence, we think that the law would be showing excessive concern for the preservation of marital harmony if it were to say that she must not do so.'[30] This view was given effect by section 80(1) of the 1984 Act. Section 80(1) was repealed: the spouse of an accused is now competent for the prosecution under section 53(1) of the 1999 Act whereby, as we have seen, subject to section 53(3), in criminal proceedings all persons are competent to give evidence. As we have also seen, section 53(1) is also subject to section 53(4), whereby a

---

[23] *R v Symonds* (1924) 18 Cr App R 100 at 101.

[24] *R v Farnham Justices, ex p Gibson* [1991] Crim LR 642, DC.

[25] *R v Bevan* (1993) 98 Cr App R 354, CA.

[26] *R v Boal* [1965] 1 QB 402 at 414.

[27] *R v Conti* (1973) 58 Cr App R 387, CA.

[28] *R v Richardson* (1967) 51 Cr App R 381.

[29] Para 147 (Cmnd 4991) (1972).

[30] Para 148.

person charged in criminal proceedings is not competent to give evidence in the proceedings for the prosecution, whether he is the only person, or one of two or more, charged in the proceedings. Thus if a husband and wife are co-accused, whether charged jointly with the same offence or charged with different offences, neither is competent to give evidence for the prosecution. As section 53(5) indicates, the spouse may only become competent for the prosecution if he or she ceases to be a co-accused. This may happen if the spouse pleads guilty or is acquitted (because no evidence is offered against the spouse or the spouse makes a successful submission of no case to answer), or if one of the spouses makes a successful application to sever the indictment.

Concerning compellability, the Criminal Law Revision Committee was in favour of maintaining the common law rule, as it then stood, of compellability in the case of offences involving personal violence by the accused against his or her spouse. The reasons included the public interest in the punishment of those committing crimes of violence and the fact that compellability would make it easier for the accused's spouse to counter the effect of possible intimidation by the accused and persuade him or her to give evidence.[31] It was also proposed to make the spouse compellable in the case of offences of a violent or sexual nature against children under the age of 16 belonging to the same household as the accused. Among the reasons given by the Committee were: (i) the seriousness of some of these cases; (ii) the reluctance to testify of a wife in fear of her husband; (iii) the difficulties of proving such offences, especially in cases in which the child is unable to testify; and (iv) the fact that in some cases the spouse, although not prosecuted, is a party to or at least acquiesces in the offence committed.[32] Subsequent to the Committee's Report and prior to the 1984 Act, a majority of the House of Lords in *Hoskyn v Metropolitan Police Comr*[33] held that where an accused is charged with an offence of violence against his or her spouse, that spouse is competent but *not compellable* for the prosecution. The majority of their Lordships were reluctant to compel a wife to testify against her husband on a charge of violence, however trivial, and regardless of the consequences to herself, her family, and her marriage. Lord Edmund Davies, the sole dissentient, regarded as extremely unlikely prosecutions based on trivial violence and was of the opinion that cases of serious physical violence by one spouse against the other were too grave to depend upon the willingness of the injured spouse to testify and 'ought not to be regarded as having no importance extending beyond the domestic hearth'. Against this background of differing and strongly held opinion, Parliament not only adopted but extended the proposals of the Criminal Law Revision Committee. Section 80(2A)–(4A) of the 1984 Act provide as follows:

(2A) In any proceedings the wife or husband of a person charged in the proceedings shall, subject to subsection (4) below, be compellable
    (a) to give evidence on behalf of any other person charged in the proceedings but only in respect of any specified offence with which that other person is charged; or
    (b) to give evidence for the prosecution but only in respect of any specified offence with which any person is charged in the proceedings.
(3) In relation to the wife or husband of a person charged in any proceedings, an offence is a specified offence for the purposes of subsection (2A) above if

---

[31] Para 149.
[32] Para 150.
[33] [1979] AC 474.

(a) it involves an assault on, or injury or a threat of injury to, the wife or husband or a person who was at the material time under the age of 16;[34]

(b) it is a sexual offence alleged to have been committed in respect of a person who was at the material time under that age; or

(c) it consists of attempting or conspiring to commit, or of aiding, abetting, counselling, procuring or inciting the commission of, an offence falling within paragraph (a) or (b) above.[35]

(4) No person who is charged in any proceedings shall be compellable by virtue of subsection (2) or (2A) above to give evidence in the proceedings.

(4A) References in this section to a person charged in any proceedings do not include a person who is not, or is no longer, liable to be convicted of any offence in the proceedings (whether as a result of pleading guilty or for any other reason).

Section 80 applies in relation to a civil partner of an accused as it applies to a spouse of an accused.[36] The subsections apply 'in any proceedings', a phrase which encompasses criminal proceedings brought by one spouse against the other. Thus in the unlikely event of such proceedings being pursued by a spouse who declines to give evidence, then he or she may nonetheless be compellable in accordance with section 80(2A) and (3).

It is submitted that the words 'wife' and 'husband' refer to a married person whose marriage, wherever it was celebrated, would be recognized by English law.[37] In *R v Pearce*,[38] it was held, construing section 80 prior to its amendment by the 1999 Act, that the phrase 'wife or husband of the accused' does not cover the cohabitee of an accused and that the proper respect for private and family life envisaged by Article 8 of the European Convention on Human Rights does not require that such a person should not be a compellable witness.

The meaning of the phrase 'involves an assault on, or injury or a threat of injury to' is unclear. A purposive approach, having regard to some of the reasons advanced by the Criminal Law Revision Committee in favour of their recommendations, might support a broad construction so as to cover not only cases in which an assault, injury, or threat of injury is required to be proved by virtue of the way in which the offence in question is defined, but also cases in which that is not so, but nonetheless evidence is adduced to show that the offence did in fact involve an assault, injury or threat of injury.[39] The issue could arise, for example, in a case of reckless driving in which the evidence discloses that the spouse, or person under 16 years of age, sustained injuries as a passenger in the car driven by the accused. Similar reasoning could be used to conclude that 'threat of injury' does not relate to the state of mind of the accused, but means risk of injury.[40] In subsection (3)(b) 'sexual offence' means an offence under the Protection of Children Act 1978 or Part 1 of the Sexual Offences Act 2003.[41]

[34] Where the age of any person at any time is material for the purposes of s 80(3), his age at the material time shall 'be deemed to be or to have been that which appears to the court to be or to have been his age at that time': s 80(6).

[35] The reference to incitement has effect as a reference to (or to conduct amounting to) the offences of encouraging or assisting crime under Part 2 of the Serious Crime Act 2007 (s 63(1) and Sch 6 para 9 of the 2007 Act).

[36] Civil Partnership Act 2004, s 84(1).

[37] See, at common law, *R v Khan* (1987) 84 Cr App R 44, CA and *R v Yacoob* (1981) 72 Cr App R 313, CA.

[38] [2002] 1 WLR 1553, CA.

[39] Cf *R v McAndrew-Bingham* [1999] Crim LR 830, CA, a decision under s 32(2)(a) of the Criminal Justice Act 1988.

[40] Cf *R v Lee* [1996] 2 Cr App R 266, CA, another decision under s 32(2)(a) of the 1988 Act.

[41] Section 80(7).

Where the accused is charged with two or more offences in respect of only one of which the spouse is compellable, it seems from the wording of subsection (2A)(b) that the spouse is compellable to give evidence for the prosecution on the one offence, but not the other or others,[42] even where such a distinction is artificial because the evidence is relevant to the other or others. Let us suppose, for example, that in the course of a neighbourhood dispute that develops into a fracas, A assaults both B and B's 15-year-old son. It seems that A's wife would only be compellable to give evidence in relation to the assault on B's son, but her evidence would be likely to be relevant to both offences charged. Presumably, in such a case, A could apply for separate trials for each of the offences, or might apply to exclude the evidence of his wife relying upon section 78(1) of the 1984 Act or the common law discretion to exclude in order to ensure a fair trial. It may be doubted, however, that either application would have much prospect of success.[43]

There is no requirement, before interviewing a spouse who is competent but not compellable for the prosecution about the crime of which her husband is suspected, to tell her that she is not compellable.[44] An accused's spouse who is called as a competent but not compellable witness for the prosecution but proves adverse for the purposes of section 3 of the Criminal Procedure Act 1865,[45] may be treated as a hostile witness in the normal way. This was established prior to the 1984 Act in _R v Pitt_,[46] an authority which may be assumed to remain good law. The Court of Appeal held that the choice of a wife whether or not to give evidence, being a competent but not compellable witness for the prosecution, is not lost because she makes a witness statement or gives evidence at the committal proceedings. She retains the right of refusal up to the point when she takes the oath in the witness box, and waiver of her right of refusal is effective only if made with full knowledge of her right to refuse. However, if she knowingly waives her right of refusal, she becomes an ordinary witness and, having started her evidence, must complete it, unable to retreat behind the barrier of non-compellability. Accordingly, if the nature of her evidence warrants it, an application may be made to treat her as a hostile witness. For these reasons, the Court of Appeal thought it desirable that the judge should explain to the wife, in the absence of the jury and before she takes the oath, that she has the right to give evidence but that if she chooses to do so she may be treated like any other witness. In appropriate circumstances the Court of Appeal may upset a verdict if it feels that injustice may have occurred because a wife gave evidence without appreciating that she had a right to refuse to do so.

For the accused

Prior to the 1984 Act, the accused's spouse was competent but not compellable as a witness for the accused.[47] The Criminal Law Revision Committee had no doubt that the accused's spouse should be made competent and compellable for the accused in all cases,[48] a recommendation implemented by the 1984 Act. The wife or husband of an accused is now competent to give

---

[42] The issue was raised but not resolved in _R v L (R)_ [2008] 2 Cr App R 243, CA at [19]–[22].

[43] See Peter Creighton, 'Spouse Competence and Compellability' [1990] _Crim LR_ 34.

[44] _R v L (R)_ [2008] 2 Cr App R 243, CA.

[45] See Ch 6.

[46] [1982] 3 All ER 63.

[47] See s 1 of the Criminal Evidence Act 1898; _R v Boal_ [1965] 1 QB 402 at 416; s 30(3) of the Theft Act 1968; and s 39(1) of the Sexual Offences Act 1956.

[48] Para 153.

evidence on behalf of the accused under section 53(1) of the 1999 Act, and this remains the case even if the wife or husband is also charged in the same proceedings. As to compellability, section 80(2) provides as follows:

> (2) In any proceedings the wife or husband of a person charged in the proceedings shall, subject to subsection (4) below, be compellable to give evidence on behalf of that person.

The only exception to section 80(2) is in cases in which the spouses are both charged in the same proceedings.[49]

For a co-accused

Under the 1898 Act, the accused's spouse was, with the consent of the accused, competent but not compellable as a witness for any other person jointly charged with the accused.[50] The Criminal Law Revision Committee recommended that the spouse of an accused should be competent to give evidence on behalf of any co-accused whether or not the accused consents. This proposal was given effect by section 80(1) of the 1984 Act, which was repealed by the 1999 Act. The wife or husband of an accused is now competent to give evidence on behalf of any person jointly charged with the accused by virtue of section 53(1) of the 1999 Act, and this is the case even if the wife or husband is also charged in the same proceedings.

The more difficult question related to compellability on behalf of a co-accused. The interests of justice would seem to require that the co-accused should be able to compel the spouse if he or she is able to give relevant evidence in his defence. On the other hand, if the spouse is compelled to testify in such circumstances, the prosecution, in cross-examination of the spouse, may well elicit evidence incriminating the accused, a result which is inconsistent with the general rule that the prosecution may not compel a spouse to testify for them. Given these competing interests of the accused and the co-accused, the Committee proposed that the spouse should be compellable on behalf of a co-accused in any case where he or she would be compellable on behalf of the prosecution.[51] The substance of these proposals has been enacted in section 80(2A) and (3) of the 1984 Act, which provide that in any proceedings the spouse of the accused shall be compellable to give evidence on behalf of any other person charged in the proceedings, but only in respect of any specified offence with which that other person is charged.[52] The only exception is in cases in which the spouse is charged in the same proceedings.[53] Where co-accused A and B are charged with two or more offences in respect of only one of which the spouse of B is compellable to give evidence on behalf of A, then it seems from the wording of section 80(2A)(a) that the spouse of B is compellable to give evidence on behalf of A on that offence even if that evidence is also relevant to the other offence(s).

Former spouses

In criminal proceedings, a former spouse of an accused is competent under section 53(1) of the Youth Justice and Criminal Evidence Act 1999. Such a person is also compellable. Section 80(5) of the Police and Criminal Evidence Act 1984 provides that:

---

[49] Section 80(4), above.

[50] Section 1 and proviso (c) thereto.

[51] Para 155.

[52] The offences are set out in s 80(3), above.

[53] Section 80(4), above.

In any proceedings a person who has been but is no longer married to the accused shall be compellable to give evidence as if that person and the accused had never been married.

The effect of these two sections is to render former spouses, after their marriage has been dissolved, both competent and compellable to give evidence for either the defence or prosecution, whether the evidence relates to events which occurred before, during, or after the terminated marriage.[54] In section 80(5) of the 1984 Act the phrase 'in any proceedings' means any proceedings which took place after section 80(5) came into effect on 1 January 1986, and therefore an ex-spouse is competent and compellable to give evidence in such proceedings about any relevant matter whether it took place before or after that date.[55] The phrase 'is no longer married' is apt to apply where the spouses have been divorced and where their marriage, being voidable, has been annulled. If there is evidence to show that a marriage was void *ab initio*, a legally valid marriage never having existed, the parties to such a union are, in accordance with the general rules, both competent and compellable throughout. Spouses who are judicially separated, although often treated in law as the equivalent of divorced spouses, cannot be said to be 'no longer married' for the purposes of section 80(5). Likewise, the subsection has no application to spouses who are not cohabiting, whether without any arrangement or agreement, or pursuant to a separation agreement, non-cohabitation order, or informal arrangement. The Criminal Law Revision Committee considered whether to provide that judicially separated or non- cohabiting spouses should be treated for the purposes of competence and compellability as if they were unmarried. It is difficult to disagree with their conclusions against such a provision:[56]

if there is little prospect that they will become reconciled, the spouse in question is likely to be willing to give evidence; and if there is a prospect of reconciliation, it may be better to avoid the risk of spoiling this prospect by compelling the spouse to give evidence when he or she would not have been compellable in the ordinary case.

Children and persons of unsound mind—criminal cases

The competence of all witnesses to give evidence in criminal proceedings is governed by section 53(1)–(3) of the 1999 Act, which provide as follows:

(1) At every stage in criminal proceedings all persons are (whatever their age) competent to give evidence.
(2) Subsection (1) has effect subject to subsections (3) and (4).[57]
(3) A person is not competent to give evidence in criminal proceedings if it appears to the court that he is not a person who is able to—
    (a) understand questions put to him as a witness, and
    (b) give answers to them which can be understood.

In *R v MacPherson*[58] it was held that the words 'put to him as a witness' in subsection (3)(a) mean the equivalent of 'being asked of him in court' and therefore an infant who can only

---

[54] See *R v Mathias* [1989] Crim LR 64, CC.
[55] *R v Cruttenden* [1991] 3 All ER 242, CA.
[56] Para 156.
[57] As to s 53(4), see under **The accused**, at 117 above.
[58] [2006] 1 Cr App R 459, CA.

communicate in baby language with its mother will not ordinarily be competent but a child who can speak and understand basic English with strangers will be competent. The court in that case, rejecting a submission to the effect that a judge must decide whether a child appreciates the difference between truth and falsehood, also held that there is no requirement that the child be aware of his witness status and that questions of credibility and reliability are not relevant to competence but go to the weight of the evidence and thus may be considered on a submission of no case to answer. Equally, a child who has no recollection of an event may be a perfectly competent witness.[59] However, it is submitted that a person should be treated as unable to understand questions put to him as a witness, and unable to give answers to them which can be understood, if he is unable to distinguish truth from fiction or fact from fantasy.[60]

In the case of young children, obviously, the younger the child the more likely it is that he or she will be incapable of satisfying the test in section 53(3), and care clearly needs to be taken if the question of competence arises. However, a court cannot properly decide that a child is incapable of satisfying the test simply on the basis that he or she is of or below a certain age.[61] This accords with the views of Lord Lane CJ in *R v Z*,[62] disapproving *R v Wallwork*.[63] In the latter case, Lord Goddard CJ said that it was most undesirable to call a child as young as five years old, a dictum approved in *R v Wright, R v Ormerod*.[64] However, in *R v Z* Lord Lane CJ was of the opinion that the decision in *R v Wallwork* had been overtaken by events. Part of Lord Goddard's concern related to the presence of the child in court, a problem largely cured by the introduction of video links.[65] Furthermore, the repeal of the proviso to section 38(1) of the Children and Young Persons Act 1933, whereby an accused was not liable to be convicted on the uncorroborated unsworn evidence of a child, indicated 'a change of attitude by Parliament, reflecting in its turn a change of attitude by the public in general to the acceptability of the evidence of young children'.

In *R v Sed*,[66] which concerned the competence of an 81-year-old woman who suffered from Alzheimer's disease, it was said that, depending on the length and nature of the questioning and the complexity of the subject matter, section 53 may not always require 100 per cent, or near 100 per cent, mutual understanding between the questioner and the questioned and that the judge should also make allowance for the fact that the witness's performance and command of detail may vary according to the importance to him of the subject matter, how recent it was, and any strong feelings that it may have engendered.[67]

The question whether a witness is competent to give evidence in criminal proceedings may be raised either by a party to the proceedings or by the court of its own motion, but either

---

[59] *DPP v R* [2007] All ER(D) 176 (Jul).

[60] Cf *R v D* (1995) The Times, 15 Nov, CA.

[61] *R v MacPherson* [2006] 1 Cr App R 459, CA and *R v Powell* [2006] 1 Cr App R 468, CA.

[62] [1990] 2 All ER 971, CA at 974.

[63] (1958) 42 Cr App R 153.

[64] (1987) 90 Cr App R 91, CA.

[65] See s 24 of the Youth Justice and Criminal Evidence Act 1999, and now, other 'special measures directions', below.

[66] [2005] 1 Cr App R 55, CA at [45].

[67] The weight to be attached to the evidence given by a mentally handicapped person is for the jury: *R v Hill* (1851) 2 Den CC 254. A person suffering from a mental illness may be a reliable witness in relation to matters not affected by the condition: see *R v Barratt and Sheehan* [1996] Crim LR 495, CA (fixed belief paramoia). See also *R (B) v DPP* [2009] EWHC 106 (Admin).

way must be determined by the court in accordance with section 54 of the 1999 Act.[68] It is clear from this that a judge is only bound to investigate a witness's competence if he has, or is given, any reason to doubt it.[69] Under section 54(2), the burden is on the party calling the witness to satisfy the court, on a balance of probabilities, that the witness is competent. In determining whether the witness is competent, the court must treat the witness as having the benefit of any special measures directions under section 19 of the 1999 Act[70] which the court has given or proposes to give in relation to the witness.[71] Under section 54(4), any proceedings for the determination of the question shall take place in the absence of the jury (if there is one); under section 54(5), expert evidence may be received on the question (which is always likely to be required in the case of the mentally handicapped);[72] and under section 54(6), any questioning of the witness, where the court considers that necessary, shall be conducted by the court in the presence of the parties.

The issue of a child's competence should be decided before he or she is sworn, usually as a preliminary issue at the start of the trial when the judge should watch any videotaped interview of the child[73] and/or ask the child appropriate questions.[74] The questioning of children under section 54(6), it is submitted, is best conducted in the spirit suggested in *R v Hampshire*:[75]

> it should be a matter of the judge's perception of the child's understanding demonstrated in the course of ordinary discourse. It is submitted that there is also much to be said in favour of another proposition that derives from that case, namely that the judge's pre-trial view of the recording, if it has been properly conducted,[76] should normally enable him to form a view as to the child's competence, but if it has left him in doubt, he should conduct an investigation.

A decision that a child is competent should be kept under review and may need to be reconsidered when his or her evidence is complete. Thus although at the start of a trial a videotaped interview may indicate competence, a ruling to that effect should be reversed if the child is unable to understand questions or give answers which can be understood, which may be the result of a lapse of time and lack of memory.[77] There is a risk that the child will not have an accurate recollection of the events, and a further risk that if shown the video before or during the trial, may recollect only what was said on the video and be incapable of distinguishing that from the events themselves. Effective cross-examination, in such circumstances, would be virtually impossible.[78]

[68] Section 54(1).

[69] Where this is not the case, the judge may find it appropriate to remind a child, in the presence of the accused and jury, of the importance of telling the truth, by saying, eg: 'Tell us all you can remember of what happened. Don't make anything up or leave anything out. This is very important.' See per Auld J in *R v Hampshire* [1995] 2 All ER 1019, CA at 1029.

[70] See under **Witnesses in criminal cases**, at 140 below.

[71] Section 54(3).

[72] In *R v Barratt and Sheehan* [1996] Crim LR 495, CA it was held that the proper course is to adduce expert medical evidence so that it is not normally necessary to call the witness said to suffer from mental illness.

[73] See s 27 of the Youth Justice and Criminal Evidence Act 1999, under **Witnesses in criminal cases**, at 140 below.

[74] *R v MacPherson* [2006] 1 Cr App R 459, CA.

[75] [1995] 2 All ER 1019, CA.

[76] See *Achieving Best Evidence in Criminal Proceedings: Guidance for Vulnerable or Intimidated Witnesses, including Children* (2002).

[77] *R v Powell* [2006] 1 Cr App R 468, CA, applied in *R v Malicki* [2009] EWCA Crim 365.

[78] *R v Malicki*, ibid.

A witness who is competent to give evidence in criminal proceedings may be sworn for the purpose of giving his evidence on oath, or may give his evidence unsworn. Section 55(1)–(4) of the 1999 Act provides as follows:

(1) Any question whether a witness in criminal proceedings may be sworn for the purpose of giving evidence on oath, whether raised—
   (a) by a party to the proceedings, or
   (b) by the court of its own motion,
   shall be determined by the court in accordance with this section.
(2) The witness may not be sworn for that purpose unless—
   (a) he has attained the age of 14, and
   (b) he has a sufficient appreciation of the solemnity of the occasion and of the particular responsibility to tell the truth which is involved in taking an oath.
(3) The witness shall, if he is able to give intelligible testimony, be presumed to have a sufficient appreciation of those matters if no evidence tending to show the contrary is adduced (by any party).
(4) If any such evidence is adduced, it is for the party seeking to have the witness sworn to satisfy the court that, on a balance of probabilities, the witness has attained the age of 14 and has a sufficient appreciation of the matters mentioned in subsection (2)(b).

For the purposes of section 55(3), a person is able to give intelligible testimony if he is able to (a) understand questions put to him as a witness; and (b) give answers to them which can be understood.[79] This test is the same as that for testing competence in section 53(3). Thus a witness aged 14 or over who is competent as a witness must be presumed to satisfy the test set out in section 55(2)(b), provided that there is no evidence tending to show the contrary. Under section 55(5), any proceedings for the determination of the question whether a witness may be sworn for the purpose of giving his evidence on oath shall take place in the absence of the jury (if there is one); under section 55(6), expert evidence may be received on the question; and, under section 55(7), any questioning of the witness, where the court considers that necessary, shall be conducted by the court in the presence of the parties.

Section 56 (1)–(4) of the 1999 Act provides as follows:

(1) Subsections (2) and (3) apply to a person (of any age) who—
   (a) is competent to give evidence in criminal proceedings, but
   (b) (by virtue of s 55(2)) is not permitted to be sworn for the purpose of giving evidence on oath in such proceedings.
(2) The evidence in criminal proceedings of a person to whom this subsection applies shall be given unsworn.
(3) A deposition of unsworn evidence given by a person to whom this subsection applies may be taken for the purpose of criminal proceedings as if that evidence had been given on oath.
(4) A court in criminal proceedings shall accordingly receive in evidence any evidence given unsworn in pursuance of subsection (2) or (3).

Under the mandatory terms of section 56(2), therefore, the evidence of any child under the age of 14 who is competent to testify must be given unsworn; and the same applies to anyone who has attained that age and is competent to testify if (a) evidence is adduced that he does not have a sufficient appreciation of the solemnity of the occasion and of the particular

---

[79] Section 55(8).

responsibility to tell the truth which is involved in taking an oath; and (b) the party seeking to have him sworn fails to satisfy the court, on a balance of probabilities, that he has such an appreciation.

It is an offence for a person giving unsworn evidence in pursuance of section 56(2) and (3) wilfully to give false evidence in such circumstances that, had the evidence been given on oath, he would have been guilty of perjury;[80] but the mere fact that a child under the age of 10 cannot be prosecuted is not a reason to prevent him from giving unsworn evidence.[81]

Children and persons of unsound mind—civil cases

Children

At common law, a child who did not understand the nature of an oath was incompetent to testify and could not be called as a witness.[82] Section 96 of the Children Act 1989 now provides that:

(1) Subsection (2) applies where a child who is called as a witness in any civil proceedings does not, in the opinion of the court, understand the nature of an oath.
(2) The child's evidence may be heard by the court if, in its opinion—
    (a) he understands that it is his duty to speak the truth; and
    (b) he has sufficient understanding to justify his evidence being heard.

A child, for these purposes, is a person under the age of 18.[83] In deciding, under section 96(1), whether or not a child understands the nature of an oath, it is submitted that the court should be guided by the common law authorities which governed in criminal as well as civil cases prior to parliamentary intervention. The issue is for the court to decide and the judge should put preliminary questions in order to form an opinion.[84] Whether a child warrants such examination is a matter of discretion for the judge. There is no fixed age above which a child should be treated as competent and below which a child should be examined. In *R v Khan*,[85] however, it was held that although much depends on the type of child before the court, in the experience of all three members of the court, as a general working rule, inquiry is necessary in the case of a child under the age of 14. Originally, the competence of children to give sworn evidence depended on 'the sense and reason they entertain of the danger and impiety of falsehood'.[86] On this basis, judges would ask questions designed to discover whether the child was aware of the divine sanction of the oath, such as 'Do you have religious instruction at school?' and 'Do you know what I mean by God?' It was questioning of this kind that led the Court of Appeal in *R v Hayes*[87] to adopt a secular approach. Acknowledging that in the present state of society the divine sanction of the oath is probably not generally recognized amongst the adult population, it was held that the important consideration is:[88]

---

[80] Section 57 of the 1999 Act.
[81] See *R v N* (1992) 95 Cr App R 256, CA.
[82] *Baker v Rabetts* (1954) 118 JPN 303.
[83] Section 105.
[84] *R v Surgenor* (1940) 27 Cr App R 175.
[85] (1981) 73 Cr App R 190, CA. But see also *Bains v DPP* [1992] Crim LR 795, DC.
[86] *R v Brasier* (1779) 1 Leach 199.
[87] [1977] 1 WLR 234.
[88] [1977] 1 WLR 234 at 237.

whether the child has a sufficient appreciation of the solemnity of the occasion and the added responsibility to tell the truth, which is involved in taking an oath, over and above the duty to tell the truth which is an ordinary duty of normal social conduct.

The court, in *R v Hayes*, also appears to have accepted a concession made by counsel for the defence that 'the watershed dividing children who are normally considered old enough to take the oath and children normally considered too young to take the oath, probably falls between the ages of eight and ten'.

If, in civil proceedings, a child fails on the secular test in *R v Hayes*, his or her evidence may be given unsworn if, in the opinion of the court, the conditions in section 96(2)(a) and (b) are satisfied. It would appear that 'the duty to speak the truth' under section 96(2) (a) should be taken to mean the duty to tell the truth which is an ordinary duty of normal social conduct.

Persons of unsound mind

In civil proceedings, in deciding on the competence of a person of unsound mind, it is submitted that the courts should be guided by the common law authorities which governed in criminal as well as civil cases prior to parliamentary intervention. In *R v Hill*[89] a patient of a lunatic asylum, labouring under a delusion that he had a number of spirits about him which were continually talking to him, but with a clear understanding of the obligation of the oath, was held competent to give evidence for the Crown on a charge of manslaughter.[90] Three principles were established in the case:

1. If in the opinion of the judge a proposed witness, by reason of defective intellect, does not understand the nature and sanction of an oath, he is incompetent to testify.

2. A person of defective intellect who does understand the nature of an oath may give evidence and it will be left to the jury to attach such weight to his testimony as they see fit.

3. If his evidence is so tainted with insanity as to be unworthy of credit, the jury may properly disregard it.

Since *R v Hill* there has been one important development: the test to be applied by the judge should be the secular one adopted in *R v Hayes*. In *R v Bellamy*[91] it was held that the trial judge had, in the case of a woman aged 33 with a mental age of 10, unnecessarily embarked upon an inquiry into the extent of her belief in and knowledge of God; the proper test of the competence of a mentally handicapped person is whether that person has a sufficient appreciation of the seriousness of the occasion and a realization that taking the oath involves something more than the duty to tell the truth in ordinary day-to-day life. Resolution of the question calls for appropriate expert medical evidence: it will not normally be necessary to call the witness said to be suffering from mental illness.[92]

A witness unable to understand the nature of the oath, his intellect being temporarily impaired by reason of drink or drugs, may become competent after an adjournment of suitable length.

---

[89] (1851) 2 Den 254.

[90] Lord Campbell CJ was doubtless sobered by his observation that any rule to the contrary would have excluded the evidence of Socrates 'for he believed that he had a spirit always prompting him'.

[91] (1985) 82 Cr App R 222, CA.

[92] *R v Barratt and Sheehan* [1996] Crim LR 495, CA.

The Sovereign and diplomats

The Sovereign and heads of other sovereign states are competent but not compellable to give evidence. A number of statutes provide for varying degrees of immunity from compellability in the case of diplomats, consular officials, and certain officers of prescribed international organizations.[93]

Bankers

We shall see in Chapter 9 that, pursuant to the Bankers' Books Evidence Act 1879, copies of entries in bankers' books are, subject to certain safeguards, admissible as evidence of their contents. To protect bank personnel from the unnecessary inconvenience of either providing the originals of such books or appearing as witnesses, section 6 of the Act provides that:

> A banker or official of a bank shall not, in any legal proceedings to which the bank is not a party, be compellable to produce any banker's book the contents of which can be proved under this Act, or to appear as a witness to prove the matters, transactions, and accounts therein recorded, unless by order of a judge made for special cause.

Oaths and affirmations

Sworn evidence is evidence given by a witness who has either taken an oath or made an affirmation. The general rule in both civil and criminal proceedings is that the evidence of any witness should be sworn. In civil claims which have been allocated to the small claims track, the court need not take evidence on oath.[94] The exceptions in the case of certain children and those of unsound mind have already been considered. There are two other minor exceptions at common law. A witness called only to produce a document may give unsworn evidence provided that the identity of the document is either not disputed or can be established by another witness.[95] Counsel acting for one of two parties who have reached a compromise may give unsworn evidence of its terms.[96] Where a video-recording of an interview with a child is admitted in evidence, and the child is at that stage aged 14 or over, the oath should be administered before the start of the cross-examination.[97] However, under section 56(5) of the 1999 Act, where a witness who is competent to give evidence in criminal proceedings has given evidence in such proceedings unsworn, no conviction, verdict, or finding in those proceedings shall be taken to be unsafe, for the purposes of the grounds of appeal set out in sections 2(1), 13(1), or 16(1) of the Criminal Appeal Act 1968, by reason only that the witness was in fact a person falling within section 55(2) of the 1999 Act[98] and accordingly should have given his evidence on oath.

---

[93] See the Diplomatic Privileges Act 1964, Consular Relations Act 1968, International Organisations Act 1968, and State Immunity Act 1978.

[94] CPR r 27.8(4).

[95] *Perry v Gibson* (1834) 1 Ad&El 48.

[96] *Hickman v Berens* [1895] 2 Ch 638, CA.

[97] *R v Simmonds* [1996] Crim LR 816, CA, a decision under s 32A of the Criminal Justice Act 1988. See now s 27 of the Youth Justice and Criminal Evidence Act 1999, below.

[98] See under **Children and persons of unsound mind—criminal cases**, at 124 above.

The modern law of oaths and affirmations is governed by the Oaths Act 1978. Section 1(1) provides for the manner of administration of the oath in the case of Christians and Jews. Unless a person about to take the oath in this form and manner objects thereto, or is physically incapable of so taking the oath, it will be administered without inquiry on the part of the judge.[99] It is therefore incumbent on those of other religious beliefs or those who wish to affirm, to object to the taking of such an oath.[100] In the case of those of other religious beliefs, section 1(3) provides that the oath shall be administered 'in any lawful manner'. Such witnesses usually take the oath upon such holy book as is appropriate to their religious belief. Section 3 of the Act expressly permits a witness to be sworn with uplifted hand in the form and manner in which an oath is usually administered in Scotland. Whether an oath is administered in a 'lawful manner' under section 1(3) does not depend on the intricacies of the particular religion which is adhered to by the witness but on whether the oath is one which appears to the court to be binding on the conscience of the witness and, if so, whether it is an oath which the witness himself considers to be binding on his conscience. Both conditions were satisfied in *R v Kemble*,[101] in which a Muslim had taken the oath using the New Testament, whereas under the strict tenets of Islam, no oath taken by a Muslim is valid unless taken on a copy of the Koran in Arabic.

Any person who objects to the taking of an oath shall be permitted instead, the choice being his, to make a solemn affirmation.[102] An affirmation is of the same force and effect as an oath,[103] and if there is a real risk that the jury will attach less weight to the evidence of a witness of a particular faith because he has affirmed, rather than taken the oath on the relevant holy book, then the judge has a discretion to allow the witness to be questioned, in a sensitive manner, as to why he did not take the oath on the particular holy book.[104]

Occasionally, a court may find itself unequipped to administer an oath in the manner appropriate to a person's particular religious belief. Accordingly, it is provided that a person may be permitted, and indeed required, to affirm where 'it is not reasonably practicable without inconvenience or delay to administer an oath in the manner appropriate to his religious belief'.[105]

A person who has taken a duly administered oath could with relative ease subsequently allege that it was of no binding effect because at the time of taking it he had no religious belief. Section 4(2) avoids this possibility by providing that the fact that a person had, at the time of taking the oath, no religious belief 'shall not for any purpose affect the validity of the oath'.

A witness who, having taken an oath or made an affirmation, wilfully makes a statement material to the proceedings in question which he knows to be false or does not believe to be true, commits perjury and may be prosecuted accordingly.[106]

---

[99] Section 1(2).

[100] For the arguments against the continued use of religious oaths, see the eleventh report of the Criminal Law Revision Committee, *Evidence (General)* (Cmnd 4991) (1972), paras 279–81 and Lord Justice Auld's *Review of the Criminal Courts of England and Wales*, HMSO (2001) 598–600.

[101] [1990] 3 All ER 116, CA.

[102] Section 5(1). See *R v Bellamy* (1985) 82 Cr App R 222, CA.

[103] Section 5(4).

[104] See *R v Mehrban* [2002] 1 Cr App R 561, CA, where one of the accused, a Muslim, had affirmed because 'unclean', not having been able to wash himself in the appropriate way before swearing.

[105] Section 5(2) and (3).

[106] See s 1 of the Perjury Act 1911 and s 5(4) of the Oaths Act 1978, above.

Live links

In civil proceedings, CPR rule 32.3 provides that the court may allow a witness to give evidence 'through a video link or by other means'.[107] No defined limit or set of circumstances should be placed upon discretionary exercise of this power to permit video link evidence, which is not confined to cases of 'pressing need', as when a witness is too ill to attend in person. Relevant factors include whether failure to attend is an abuse or contemptuous or designed to obtain a collateral advantage, as well as considerations of cost, time, and inconvenience. The court should also have regard to Article 6 of the European Convention on Human Rights and the need to see that the parties are on an equal footing.[108] In *Polanski v Condé Nast Publications Ltd*[109] the House of Lords held, by a majority, that although special cases may arise, as a general rule a claimant's unwillingness to come to the UK because he is a fugitive from justice is a valid reason, and can be a sufficient reason, for making a video conferencing order, because such a person, despite his status, is entitled to invoke the assistance of the court and its procedures in protection of his civil rights. Since such a person can bring or defend proceedings without bringing the administration of justice into disrepute, it was difficult to see why it should be brought into disrepute by his making use of a procedural facility flowing from a technological development readily available to all litigants.

In criminal cases, there are three sets of rules governing the use that may be made of live links. First, section 32 of the Criminal Justice Act 1988, which provides that, in trials on indictment[110] or proceedings in youth courts,[111] a person other than the accused who is outside the United Kingdom may, with the leave of the court, give evidence through a live television link.[112] Secondly, under section 24 of the 1999 Act, a special measures direction may provide for a child or other vulnerable witness to give evidence by a live television link. Section 24 is considered, together with other special measures directions, separately, below. Thirdly, under Part 8 of the Criminal Justice Act 2003 (the 2003 Act) (sections 51–56) general provision is made for the use of live links in criminal cases.[113] There is no common law power to permit evidence to be given by live link: the statutory regime provides exclusively for the circumstances in which live link evidence may be used in the course of a criminal trial.[114]

Part 8 of the 2003 Act has been introduced without any indication as to the relationship between its general provisions and the provisions in the 1999 Act, except to state that Part 8 is without prejudice to 'any power of a court . . . to give directions . . . in relation to any witness'.[115]

---

[107] See also CPR PD 32, Annex 3, *Videoconferencing Guidance* and *Black v Pastouna* [2005] EWCA Civ 1389, The Independent, 2 Dec 2005.

[108] *Rowland v Bock* [2002] 4 All ER 370, QBD.

[109] [2005] 1 All ER 945, HL.

[110] Or an appeal to the Court of Appeal (Criminal Division) or the hearing of a reference of a case to the Court of Appeal under s 9 of the Criminal Appeal Act 1995.

[111] Or appeals to the Crown Court arising out of such proceedings or hearings of references under s 11 of the Criminal Appeal Act 1995 so arising.

[112] A statement made on oath by such a witness shall be treated for the purposes of s 1 of the Perjury Act 1911 as having been made in the proceedings in which it is given in evidence: s 32(3). However, it is not a condition of admissibility that the witness is in a country from which he can be extradited to stand trial for perjury: *R v Forsyth* [1997] 2 Cr App R 299, CA.

[113] See also the Crime (International Cooperation) Act 2003.

[114] *R (S) v Waltham Forest Youth Court* [2004] 2 Cr App R 335, DC at [86]–[89].

[115] Section 56(5)(a) of the Criminal Justice Act 2003.

Under section 51(1)–(3) of the 2003 Act, a court may, on the application of a party, or of its own motion, direct that a witness, other than the accused, give evidence through a live link in the following criminal proceedings: a summary trial, an appeal to the Crown Court arising out of such a trial, a trial on indictment, and an appeal to the criminal division of the Court of Appeal.[116] A 'live link' means a live television link or other arrangement by which a witness, while at a place in the United Kingdom which is outside the building where the proceedings are being held, is able both to see and hear a person at the place where the proceedings are being held and to be seen and heard by the accused, the judge, the justices, and the jury (if there is one), the legal representatives and any interpreter or other person appointed by the court to assist the witness.[117] Rules of court may make provision as to the procedure to be followed in connection with an application for a direction to give evidence through a live link and as to the arrangements or safeguards to be put in place in connection with the operation of the link.[118] Under section 51(4)(a), a direction may not be given unless the court is satisfied that it is in the interests of the efficient or effective administration of justice.[119] Under section 51(6), in deciding whether to give a direction, the court must consider all the circumstances. Section 51(7) provides that:

(7) Those circumstances include in particular—
    (a) the availability of the witness,
    (b) the need for the witness to attend in person,
    (c) the importance of the witness's evidence to the proceedings,
    (d) the views of the witness,
    (e) the suitability of the facilities at the place where the witness would give evidence through a live link,
    (f) whether a direction might tend to inhibit any party to the proceedings from effectively testing the witness's evidence.

If the court refuses an application for a direction, it must state its reasons in open court and, if it is a magistrates' court, must cause them to be entered in the register of its proceedings.

Where a direction has been given, the witness may not give evidence otherwise than through the link,[120] and therefore will also be subject to cross-examination and any re-examination through the link, but the court may rescind a direction if there has been a material change of circumstances since the direction was given.[121] Where the evidence is given through a live link, the court retains the power to exclude evidence at its discretion (whether by preventing questions from being put or otherwise),[122] and the judge may give the jury such direction as he thinks necessary to ensure that the jury gives the same weight to the evidence as if it had been given by the witness in the courtroom.[123]

---

[116] Also the hearing of a reference under s 9 or s 11 of the Criminal Appeal Act 1995, a hearing before a magistrates' court or the Crown Court which is held after the accused has entered a plea of guilty, and a hearing before the Court of Appeal under s 80 of the 2003 Act (application for retrial following acquittal): s 51(2).

[117] Section 56(2) and (3). For these purposes, the extent (if any) to which a person is unable to see or hear by reason of any impairment of eyesight or hearing is to be disregarded: s 56(4).

[118] Section 55.

[119] Also the Secretary of State must have notified the court that suitable facilities for receiving evidence through a live link are available in the area: s 51(4)(b).

[120] Section 52(2).

[121] Section 52(5) and (6).

[122] Section 56(5)(b).

[123] Section 54.

The time at which evidence should be adduced

In both civil and criminal proceedings, as a general rule of practice rather than law, a party should adduce all the evidence on which he intends to rely before the close of his case.[124] In a civil case, the claimant, after the close of the trial but before the judgment has been handed down, may introduce in evidence a document which ought to have been disclosed by the defendant and which the claimant could not have obtained by other means.[125]

Prosecution evidence

If, in a criminal case, evidence becomes available to the prosecution for the first time *after* the close of its case, the question of its admissibility should be referred to and decided by the judge.[126] The evidence may be admitted, even if not strictly of a rebutting character, but the court should take care, in the exercise of its discretion, in case injustice is done to the accused, and should consider whether to grant the defence an adjournment.[127]

Although, in criminal cases, the general rule applies not only to the adducing of evidence, but also to matters to be put in cross-examination of an accused,[128] it is confined to evidence probative of his guilt, rather than evidence going only to his credit.[129] If evidence capable of forming part of the affirmative case for the prosecution case did not form part of the evidence on which the accused was committed for trial, the practice is to give notice of the additional evidence to the defence before it is tendered.[130] The fact that the accused might then trim his evidence is not a reason for withholding the material until he gives evidence, because an accused needs to know in advance the case against him if he is to have a proper opportunity of answering that case to the best of his ability. He is also entitled to such knowledge when deciding whether to testify. It is better in the interests of justice that an accused is not induced, by thinking it is safe to do so, to exaggerate, embroider, or lie. To do so might be to ambush the accused.[131]

To the general rule of practice there are two exceptions and a 'wider discretion' to be exercised outside the two exceptions sparingly. As to the first exception, evidence is allowed in rebuttal of matters arising *ex improviso*, which no human ingenuity could have foreseen.[132] Under this exception, it is for the judge, in his discretion, to determine whether the relevance of the evidence could *reasonably* have been anticipated.[133] If the prosecution can reasonably foresee that the evidence is relevant to their case, it must be adduced as a part of that case and not to remedy defects in that case after it has been closed.[134] In *R v Milliken*,[135] the

[124] *R v Rice* (1963) 47 Cr App R 79, CCA.
[125] *Stocznia Gdanska SA v Latvian Shipping Co* (2000) LTL 19/10/2000, QBD.
[126] *R v Kane* (1977) 65 Cr App R 270, CA.
[127] *R v Doran* (1972) 56 Cr App R 429, CA and *R v Patel* [1992] Crim LR 739, CA; cf *R v Pilcher* (1974) 60 Cr App R 1, CA.
[128] *R v Kane* (1977) 65 Cr App R 270, CA.
[129] *R v Halford* (1978) 67 Cr App R 318, CA.
[130] *R v Kane* (1977) 65 Cr App R 270, CA.
[131] *R v Phillipson* (1989) 91 Cr App R 226, CA. See also *R v Sansom* [1991] 2 QB 130, CA.
[132] *R v Frost* (1839) 4 State Tr NS 85. The exception may be used by the prosecution to adduce evidence in rebuttal of not only defence *evidence*, but also matters unsupported by evidence but arising by implication from the defence closing speech: *R v O'Hadhmaill* [1996] Crim LR 509, CA.
[133] *R v Scott* (1984) 79 Cr App R 49, CA.
[134] *R v Day* (1940) 27 Cr App R 168.
[135] (1969) 53 Cr App R 330, CA.

accused, when giving evidence, for the first time accused officers of a conspiracy to fabricate evidence. Evidence in rebuttal was allowed, because it only became relevant when the accused gave evidence. Equally, the prosecution may rely on this exception where the evidence in question was not, at the outset, *clearly* relevant, but only marginally, minimally, or doubt-fully relevant[136] or constituted fanciful and unreal statements such as allegations which were obviously ridiculous and untrue.[137]

Under the second exception, the judge has a discretion to admit evidence which has not been adduced by reason of inadvertence or oversight. Although this exception is usually said to apply only in the case of evidence of a formal or uncontentious nature,[138] the cases show that the evidence may relate to a matter of substance.[139]

In *R v Francis*[140] the prosecution established where a man was standing at a group identi-fication, but failed to call evidence that the man in that position was the accused. After the close of their case, the prosecution were allowed to adduce such evidence. It was held that although the failure was not a mere technicality, but an essential if minor link in the chain of identification evidence, the discretion of the judge to admit evidence after the close of the prosecution case is not confined to the two well-established exceptions: there is a wider discretion, but it should only be exercised outside the two exceptions on the rarest of occa-sions. In *R v Munnery*[141] it was held that this last proposition could be expanded to include the words 'especially when the evidence is tendered after the case for the defendant has begun'. An example of evidence being admitted even at this late stage is *James v South Glamorgan County Council*.[142] In that case, in which the defence had not made a submission of no case to answer, the prosecution, after the accused had given his evidence-in-chief, were allowed to re-open their case to call their main witness, whose evidence was important, if not essential to their case, the witness having arrived late by reason of transport difficulties and genuine confusion about the location of the court house. *Jolly v DPP*,[143] a decision relating to a sum-mary trial, also supports a wider discretionary approach to admissibility. It was held that it was 'beyond argument' that there was a general discretion to permit the prosecution to call evidence after the close of their case, which, in a magistrates' court, extended up to the time when the bench retired. The court would look carefully at the interests of justice overall and in particular the risk of prejudice to the accused, as when the defence would have been con-ducted differently had the evidence been adduced as part of the prosecution case. Thus the discretion would be exercised sparingly, but it was doubted whether it assisted to speak in terms of 'exceptional circumstances'.[144]

[136] *R v Levy* (1966) 50 Cr App R 198.

[137] *R v Hutchinson* (1985) 82 Cr App R 51, CA.

[138] For example, failure to prove that leave of the Director of Public Prosecutions to bring proceedings has been obtained (*R v Waller* [1910] 1 KB 364, CCA, applied in *Price v Humphries* [1958] 2 All ER 725, DC) or failure to prove a statutory instrument by production of a Stationery Office copy (*Palastanga v Solman* [1962] Crim LR 334 and *Hammond v Wilkinson* [2001] Crim LR 323). See also *R v McKenna* (1956) 40 Cr App R 65.

[139] See, eg, *Piggott v Sims* [1973] RTR 15 (an analyst's certificate); *Matthews v Morris* [1981] Crim LR 495 (a statement by the owner of the property allegedly stolen); and *Middleton v Rowlett* [1954] 1 WLR 831 and *Smith v DPP* [2008] EWHC 771 (Admin) (evidence of identification).

[140] [1991] 1 All ER 225, CA.

[141] (1990) 94 Cr App R 164, CA.

[142] (1994) 99 Cr App R 321, DC. See also (applying *R v Francis*) *R v Jackson* [1996] 2 Cr App R 420, CA.

[143] [2000] Crim LR 471, DC.

[144] See also *Cook v DPP* [2001] Crim LR 321, DC.

In appropriate circumstances, rather than have the prosecution re-open its case, a judge may, in the interests of justice, admit evidence himself. In *R v Bowles*[145] it was held that a judge was justified in calling certain evidence to provide an answer to a question raised by the jury during the defence case: the defence had not closed their case, and the evidence, which was non-controversial and did not contradict that of the accused, helped the jury resolve an issue on the basis of known facts, rather than speculation. In the exercise of his discretion, the judge may also recall or permit the recall of a witness at any stage in the proceedings before the end of his summing-up.[146]

Defence evidence

A judge may permit an accused to be recalled to deal with matters which arose after he gave evidence if he could not reasonably have anticipated them and it appears to be in the interests of justice.[147] A judge may, as a matter of discretion and in the interests of justice, allow an accused to be recalled to clarify some feature of his evidence or to address a possible source of misunderstanding or to be given the opportunity to answer new allegations by a co-accused not put to him under cross-examination. However, it is difficult to imagine a situation in which an accused should be allowed to be recalled to advance a new account of facts contradicting his earlier evidence, which would normally constitute an abuse of process.[148]

Evidence after the retirement of the magistrates or jury

In the magistrates' court, evidence may be called even after the magistrates have retired, provided that there are special circumstances, as when the defence seek to ambush the prosecution by raising an issue for the first time in their closing speech.[149] In the Crown Court, once the jury has retired to consider their verdict on the conclusion of the summing-up, no further evidence may be admitted, whether by the calling or re-calling of witnesses,[150] and the jury must not be given any additional matter or material to assist them,[151] either at their own request, or in error.[152] However, this principle has been relaxed in the case of additional evidence put before the jury at the request of the accused because it assists his case.[153]

When the jury retire, an exhibit may be taken into the jury room for inspection. Where a silent film or video has been shown in court and the jury, after retirement, ask to see it again, they may do so, but it is better that they do so in open court.[154] Concerning tapes, if

---

[145] [1992] Crim LR 726, CA. See also *R v Aitken* (1991) 94 Cr App R 85, CA.

[146] *R v Sullivan* [1923] 1 KB 47; *R v McKenna* (1956) 40 Cr App R 65. The witness may be cross-examined on new evidence given: *R v Watson* (1834) 6 C&P 653.

[147] *R v Cook* [2005] EWCA Crim 2011 at [28].

[148] *R v Ikram* [2008] 2 Cr App R 347, CA.

[149] *Malcolm v DPP* [2007] 2 Cr App R 1, DC.

[150] *R v Owen* (1952) 36 Cr App R 16. In *R v Flynn* (1957) 42 Cr App R 15, evidence in rebuttal was called immediately before the summing-up. In *R v Sanderson* (1953) 37 Cr App R 32, fresh evidence was called after the summing-up but before the jury retired. The Criminal Law Revision Committee proposed that evidence be allowed to be given at any time prior to verdict: see 11th Report (Cmnd 499), paras 213–16.

[151] *R v Davis* (1975) 62 Cr App R 194. See also *R v Crees* [1996] Crim LR 830, CA, where the jury were improperly given a ruler which they wished to use as if it were a knife, for the purposes of a re-enactment.

[152] See *R v Gilder* [1997] Crim LR 668, CA.

[153] See *R v Hallam* [2007] EWCA Crim 1495 and *R v Khan* [2008] EWCA Crim 1112; and cf *R v Cadman* [2008] EWCA Crim 1418.

[154] *R v Imran* [1997] Crim LR 754, CA.

nothing turns on tone of voice, it will usually suffice for the jury to have a transcript, much of which should be summarized, but where tone of voice is all-important, then, subject to editing out inadmissible material, the jury should have the original tape.[155] If the tape is not played during the trial, the jury may listen to it after retirement, but if there is a risk that they may hear inadmissible material, the tape should be played in open court.[156] If the prosecution do not rely on parts of a tape, the jury may only hear it as edited.[157] However, if the tape, of which there is an agreed transcript, has already been played in court and does not contain inadmissible material, the judge has a discretion to permit the jury to play it in their retiring room.[158] In the case of a video-recording used as a child's evidence pursuant to section 27 of the 1999 Act, if the jury, after they have retired, wish to be reminded of *what* the witness said, the judge should remind them from the transcript or his own notes; but if they wish to be reminded of how the words were spoken, the judge may in his discretion allow the video, or relevant part, to be replayed, provided that the replay takes place in court.[159] Either way, the judge should warn the jury that by reason of hearing the evidence again they should guard against the risk of giving it disproportionate weight and bear well in mind the other evidence in the case, and the judge should remind the jury, from his notes, of the cross-examination and re-examination of the complainant.[160]

A jury request for equipment, such as weighing scales, to enable them to carry out unsupervised scientific experiments with exhibits, should not be met.[161]

Witnesses in civil cases

The witnesses to be called

Prior to the Civil Procedure Rules, a party to civil proceedings was under no obligation to call particular witnesses, could call such witnesses to support his case as he saw fit, and could call them in the order of his choice.[162] As to the judge, he had no right to call witnesses against the will of the parties,[163] except in cases of civil contempt,[164] but did have the power to recall

---

[155] *R v Emmerson* (1990) 92 Cr App R 284, CA.

[156] *R v Riaz* (1991) 94 Cr App R 339, CA.

[157] See *R v Hagan* [1997] 1 Cr App R 464, CA.

[158] *R v Tonge* [1993] Crim LR 876, CA.

[159] In normal circumstances it is inappropriate for the video to be replayed unless there has been a specific request to that effect from the jury: *R v M* [1996] 2 Cr App R 56, CA.

[160] See, in the case of a reminder from the transcript, *R v McQuiston* [1998] 1 Cr App R 139, CA and *R v Morris* [1998] Crim LR 416, CA; and see, in the case of a replay, *R v Rawlings* [1995] 1 All ER 580, CA, applied in *R v M* [1996] 2 Cr App R 56, CA and *R v B* [1996] Crim LR 499, CA. The principles, however, do not lay down an inflexible practice to be followed to the letter in every case: *R v Horley* [1999] Crim LR 488, CA. For example, it is unnecessary to remind the jury of the cross-examination if the judge dealt with it in detail in his summing up and the jury have declined an offer of further assistance in that regard: *R v Saunders* [1995] 2 Cr App R 313, CA.

[161] *R v Stewart, R v Sappleton* (1989) 89 Cr App R 273, CA; cf *R v Wright* [1993] Crim LR 607, CA. A magnifying glass, a ruler or a tape-measure do not normally raise the possibility of such an experiment: *R v Maggs* (1990) 91 Cr App R 243, CA.

[162] *Briscoe v Briscoe* [1966] 1 All ER 465; but cf *Bayer v Clarkson Puckle Overseas Ltd* [1989] NLJR 256.

[163] *Re Enoch and Zaretzky, Bock & Co's Arbitration* [1910] 1 KB 327, CA, where an arbitrator was held to be in the same position.

[164] *Yianni v Yianni* [1966] 1 WLR 120.

a witness called by a party.[165] CPR rule 32.1(1) now provides that the court may control the evidence by giving directions as to the nature of the evidence which it requires to decide the issues on which it requires evidence, and the way in which the evidence is to be placed before the court; and under rule 32.1(2) the court may use its power under the rule to exclude evidence that would otherwise be admissible. In exercising these powers, the judge must seek to give effect to the 'overriding objective' of the Civil Procedure Rules, which is to enable the court 'to deal with cases justly'.[166] It seems that CPR rule 32.1(1) does not empower the court to dictate to a litigant what evidence he should tender. Thus a party who has disclosed a witness statement in accordance with pre-trial directions cannot be ordered by the court to call the witness, although he should notify the other parties of his decision and whether he proposes to put the statement in as hearsay.[167] In appropriate circumstances, however, the judge may take the view that, in order to give effect to the overriding objective, he should give directions under CPR rule 32.1(1) as to the order in which witnesses should give their evidence, and as to those witnesses who are not required to decide the issues and whose evidence, therefore, although admissible, should not be heard.

Witness statements

The rules for the exchange of witness statements in civil cases have been designed to promote the fair disposal of proceedings and to save costs: they identify the real issues, encourage the parties to make appropriate admissions of fact, promote fair settlements, remove the element of surprise as to the witnesses each party intends to call and, give to the cross-examining party the advantage of knowing in advance what each witness will say in his examination-in-chief.

A witness statement is a written statement signed by a person which contains the evidence which that person would be allowed to give orally.[168] Under CPR rule 32.4(2), the court will order a party to serve on the other parties any witness statement of the oral evidence which the party serving the statement intends to rely on in relation to any issues of fact to be decided at the trial; and under rule 32.4(3) the court may give directions as to the order in which the statements are to be served.[169] The court will give directions for the service of witness statements when it allocates a case to the fast track[170] or multi-track.[171] Normally, the court will direct the simultaneous exchange of statements,[172] but sequential exchange may be appropriate where one party will not know fully or precisely the case he has to answer until he has had sight of his opponent's witness statements. If a party fails to serve witness statements, any

---

[165] *Fallon v Calvert* [1960] 2 QB 201, CA.

[166] See further Ch 2, 43 under **Exclusionary discretion**.

[167] *Society of Lloyd's v Jaffray* (2000) The Times, 3 Aug, QBD.

[168] CPR r 32.4(1). The statement, therefore, should not contain material which is irrelevant or otherwise inadmissible.

[169] Although CPR Pt 32 (except r 32.1) does not apply to claims which have been allocated to the small claims track (r 27.2(1)), in the case of many such claims directions for the exchange of witness statements will be given nonetheless: see r 27.4 and PD 27.

[170] Rule 28.2, r 28.3 and PD 28.

[171] Rule 29.2 and PD 29.

[172] PD 28, para 3.9 and PD 29, para 4.10.

other party may apply for an order to enforce compliance or for a sanction to be imposed,[173] and, ultimately, the court has the power to strike out the claim or defence.[174]

A witness statement should be dated.[175] It must, if practicable, be in the intended witness's own words and should be expressed in the first person.[176] It must also indicate which of the statements in it are made from the witness's own knowledge and which are matters of information or belief.[177] The statement is the equivalent of the oral evidence which the witness would, if called, give in evidence, and must include a statement of truth by the intended witness, ie a signed statement that he believes the facts in it are true.[178] If it is not verified by a statement of truth, then the court may direct that it shall not be admissible as evidence.[179] Equally, if it does not comply with CPR Part 32 or Practice Direction 32 in relation to its form, the court may refuse to admit it as evidence.[180]

CPR rule 32.5 provides as follows:

(1) If—
    (a) a party has served a witness statement; and
    (b) he wishes to rely at trial on the evidence of the witness who made the statement,
    he must call the witness to give oral evidence unless the court orders otherwise or he puts the statement in as hearsay evidence.
(2) Where a witness is called to give evidence under paragraph (1), his witness statement shall stand as his evidence in chief unless the court orders otherwise.
(3) A witness giving oral evidence at trial may with the permission of the court—
    (a) amplify his witness statement;
    (b) give evidence in relation to new matters which have arisen since the witness statement was served on the other parties.
(4) The court will give permission under paragraph (3) only if it considers that there is good reason not to confine the evidence of the witness to the contents of his witness statement.
(5) If a party who has served a witness statement does not—
    (a) call the witness to give evidence at trial; or
    (b) put the witness statement in as hearsay evidence, any other party may put the witness statement in as hearsay evidence.

As to rule 32.5(2), it is likely that the court, in deciding whether to order that the statement should not stand as the witness's evidence-in-chief, will have regard to such matters as the extent to which his evidence is likely to be controversial and to go to the heart of the dispute,

---

[173] See PD 28, para 5.1 and PD 29, para 7.1.

[174] See CPR r 3.4.

[175] Rule 32.8 and PD 32, para 17.2.

[176] Ibid para 18.1.

[177] Ibid para 18.2.

[178] PD 32, para 20.1 and CPR r 22.1(6). Proceedings for contempt of court may be brought against a person making a false statement in a document verified by a statement of truth without an honest belief in its truth: CPR r 32.14. In *Aquarius Financial Enterprises Inc v Certain Underwriters at Lloyd's* (2001) NLJ 694, QBD, where there was evidence that a witness statement had been obtained by bullying, inducements, and threats, it was held that it was part of the duty of solicitors to ensure, so far as lay within their power, that statements are taken either by themselves or, if that is not practicable, by somebody who can be relied upon to exercise the same standard as should apply when statements are taken by solicitors.

[179] Rule 22.3.

[180] PD 32, para 25.1.

and the extent to which his credibility will be in issue.[181] As to rule 32.5(4), the pertinent factors would seem to be the relevance of the evidence to the issues, any prejudice likely to be caused to the party against whom the evidence is to be used and, in the case of rule 32.5(3)a, the reason why the witness statement did not include the additional material.

Under rule 32.9, provision is made for a party who is unable to obtain a witness statement to apply for permission to serve a witness summary instead. Rule 32.9 covers cases where a party knows the name and address of a particular witness, but the witness is reluctant or unwilling to give evidence or, having indicated his willingness to give evidence, changes his mind. A typical example is the employee who is loath to give evidence, on behalf of an ex-employee, against his employer.[182] Rule 32.9 provides as follows:

(1) A party who—
   (a) is required to serve a witness statement for use at trial; but
   (b) is unable to obtain one, may apply, without notice, for permission to serve a witness summary instead.
(2) A witness summary is a summary of—
   (a) the evidence, if known, which would otherwise be included in a witness statement; or
   (b) if the evidence is not known, the matters about which the party serving the witness summary proposes to question the witness.
(3) Unless the court orders otherwise, a witness summary must include the name and address of the intended witness.
(4) Unless the court orders otherwise, a witness summary must be served within the period in which a witness statement would have had to be served.
(5) Where a party serves a witness summary, so far as practicable, rules 32.4 (requirement to serve witness statements for use at trial), 32.5(3) (amplifying witness statements), and 32.8 (form of witness statement) shall apply to the summary.

Under rule 32.10, if a witness statement or witness summary is not served in respect of an intended witness within the time specified by the court, then the witness may not be called to give oral evidence unless the court gives permission. In deciding whether to give permission, the relevant factors would appear to be the length of delay, whether there is a good reason for failure to serve the statement or it is a result of incompetence on the part of the legal advisers, the relevance of the evidence, including the risk of injustice to the party seeking to call the witness if permission is not given, and any prejudice likely to be caused to his opponent if permission is given.

Witnesses in criminal cases

Under rule 3.3 of the Criminal Procedure Rules 2005,[183] each party to criminal proceedings must (a) actively assist the court in fulfilling the court's duty to further the overriding objective (that criminal cases be dealt with justly) by actively managing the case, without or if necessary with a direction; and (b) apply for a direction if needed to further the overriding objective. Under rule 3.9, which applies to the parties' preparation for trial, each party, in fulfilling his duty under rule 3.3, must, inter alia, take every reasonable step to make sure his witnesses will

---

[181] See *Mercer v Chief Constable of the Lancashire Constabulary* [1991] 2 All ER 504, CA, a decision under an earlier version of the rules.
[182] See further Ch 6, 183 under **Unfavourable and hostile witnesses**.
[183] SI 2005/384.

attend when they are needed; and under rule 3.10, in order to manage the trial, the court may require a party to identify (a) which witnesses he intends to give oral evidence; (b) the order in which he intends those witnesses to give their evidence; (c) whether he requires an order compelling the attendance of a witness; and (d) what arrangements, if any, he proposes to facilitate the giving of evidence by a witness.

The witnesses to be called

In criminal proceedings, the choice as to which witnesses are called rests primarily with the parties. A trial judge also has the right to call a witness not called by either the prosecution or defence, and without the consent of either party if, in his opinion, this course is necessary in the interests of justice.[184] Justices have the same right in summary proceedings.[185] This right may be exercised by the judge even after the close of the case for the defence, but only where a matter has arisen *ex improviso*.[186] The prosecution is under an obligation to call certain witnesses and to have others available at court to be called by the defence. In the case of trials on indictment, the principles were set out in *R v Russell-Jones*:[187]

1. Generally speaking the prosecution must bring to court all the witnesses 'named on the back of the indictment', a phrase reflecting the old practice, nowadays meaning those whose statements have been served as witnesses on whom the prosecution intend to rely, if the defence want those witnesses to attend.[188]

2. The prosecution have a discretion to call, or to tender for cross-examination by the defence, any witness it requires to attend, but the discretion is not unfettered.

3. The discretion must be exercised in the interests of justice so as to promote a fair trial.

4. The prosecution should normally call or offer to call all the witnesses who can give direct evidence of the primary facts of the case, even if there are inconsistencies between one witness and another, unless for good reason, in any instance, the prosecutor regards the witness's evidence as unworthy of belief.[189] In *R v Oliva*,[190] for example, it was held that the prosecution were not obliged to call the victim of an offence who gave evidence at the committal proceedings first implicating and then exonerating the accused. The witness had proved himself unworthy of belief and, if called by the prosecution, would have confused the jury.[191] However, if the prosecution are of the view that part of a witness's evidence is capable

---

[184] *R v Chapman* (1838) 8 C&P 558 and *R v Holden* (1838) 8 C&P 606; cf *R v McDowell* [1984] Crim LR 486, CA. The power should rarely be exercised: *R v Grafton* (1993) 96 Cr App R 156, CA. If it is, an adjournment may be necessary to enable one of the parties to call evidence in rebuttal: see *R v Coleman* (1987) The Times, 21 Nov, CA.

[185] *R v Wellingborough Magistrates' Court, ex p François* (1994) 158 JP 813 and *R v Haringey Justices, ex p DPP* [1996] 2 Cr App R 119, DC.

[186] See *R v Cleghorn* [1967] 2 QB 584, CA; cf *R v Tregear* [1967] 2 QB 574, CA.

[187] [1995] 3 All ER 239, CA. See also *R v Brown and Brown* [1997] 1 Cr App R 112, CA. Similar principles apply to summary proceedings: see *R v Haringey Justices, ex p DPP* [1996] 2 Cr App R 119, DC.

[188] The prosecution are under no duty to call the makers of statements which have never formed part of the prosecution case because inconsistent with it and which have been served on the defence as unused material: *R v Richardson* (1993) 98 Cr App R 174, CA.

[189] Reading out the material parts of the statement of a witness may discharge the duty on the prosecution: see *R v Armstrong* [1995] Crim LR 831, CA.

[190] [1965] 1 WLR 1028. Cf *R v Witts and Witts* [1991] Crim LR 562, CA.

[191] See also *R v Nugent* [1977] 3 All ER 662 and *R v Balmforth* [1992] Crim LR 825, CA.

of belief, even though they do not rely on other parts of his evidence, they are entitled to exercise their discretion to call him, since it would be contrary to the interests of justice to deprive the jury of that part of his evidence which could be of assistance to them.[192]

5. It is for the prosecution to decide which witnesses can give direct evidence of the primary facts.

6. The prosecutor is also the primary judge of whether or not a witness to the material events is unworthy of belief.

7. A prosecutor properly exercising his discretion will not be obliged to proffer a witness merely in order to give the defence material with which to attack the credit of other witnesses on whom the Crown relies.

The order of witnesses

Although in criminal proceedings the parties are generally free to call their witnesses in the order of their choice, at common law the defence was required to call the accused before any of his witnesses: 'He ought to give his evidence before he has heard the evidence and cross-examination of any witness he is going to call.'[193] In *R v Smith*[194] the Court of Appeal approved this rule, subject to 'rare exceptions such as when a formal witness, or a witness about whom there is no controversy, is interposed before the accused person with the consent of the court in the special circumstances then prevailing'. The Criminal Law Revision Committee favoured retention of the rule but was of the opinion that the court should be given a discretion, wider than that stated in *R v Smith*, to call other witnesses before the accused.[195] Section 79 of the 1984 Act, implementing this recommendation, provides that:

> If at the trial of any person for an offence—
> (a) the defence intends to call two or more witnesses to the facts of the case; and
> (b) those witnesses include the accused,
> the accused shall be called before the other witness or witnesses unless the court in its discretion otherwise directs.

Evidence-in-chief by video-recording

In his *Review of the Criminal Courts of England and Wales*[196] Lord Justice Auld recommended that, further to the use of video-recorded evidence-in-chief for vulnerable witnesses,[197] video-recorded evidence should also be admissible for the witnesses of all serious crimes. The government, in adopting this proposal, recognized the two key advantages of allowing the video-recording to replace the witness's evidence-in-chief, namely the fact that the witness's recollection of the events in question is likely to have been better at the time of the recording, and the reduction in levels of stress when giving evidence on oath. The danger that the witness may, in the recording, make statements elicited in answer to leading questions, was

---

[192] *R v Cairns* [2003] 1 Cr App R 662, CA.

[193] Per Lord Alverstone CJ in *R v Morrison* (1911) 6 Cr App R 159 at 165.

[194] (1968) 52 Cr App R 224.

[195] 11th Report (Cmnd 4991), para 107. The Committee gave as an example a witness who is to speak of some event which occurred before the events about which the accused is to give evidence.

[196] HMSO, 2001, at 555.

[197] See below.

not thought to be serious given that it would be 'completely evident' whether the witness had been led. Under section 137 of the 2003 Act, therefore (i) where a prosecution witness, or a defence witness other than the accused, is called in proceedings for an offence triable only on indictment, or for an offence triable either way prescribed in an order made by the Secretary of State; (ii) he claims to have witnessed the offence or part of it, or other closely connected events; and (iii) a video-recording of his account of events has been made at a time when the events were fresh in his memory, the court may direct that the recording be admitted as his evidence-in-chief. Such a direction may only be given, however, if it appears to the court that his recollection of events is likely to have been significantly better at the time of the recording than it will be when he gives oral evidence and it is in the interests of justice for the recording to be admitted, having regard in particular to certain prescribed matters, such as factors that might affect the reliability of what the witness said. Under section 137(2), which effectively side-steps the hearsay rule, the statements in the recorded account are not treated as out-of-court statements admissible as evidence of the matters stated, but shall be treated as if made by the witness in his evidence if, or to the extent that, in his oral evidence he asserts the truth of them. Section 137 provides as follows:

(1) This section applies where—
    (a) a person is called as a witness in proceedings for an offence triable only on indictment, or for a prescribed offence triable either way,
    (b) the person claims to have witnessed (whether visually or in any other way)—
        (i) events alleged by the prosecution to include conduct constituting the offence or part of the offence, or
        (ii) events closely connected with such events,
    (c) he has previously given an account of the events in question (whether in response to questions asked or otherwise),
    (d) the account was given at a time when those events were fresh in the person's memory (or would have been, assuming the truth of the claim mentioned in paragraph (b)),
    (e) a video recording was made of the account,
    (f) the court has made a direction that the recording should be admitted as evidence in chief of the witness, and the direction has not been rescinded, and
    (g) the recording is played in the proceedings in accordance with the direction.
(2) If, or to the extent that, the witness in his oral evidence in the proceedings asserts the truth of the statements made by him in the recorded account, they shall be treated as if made by him in that evidence.
(3) A direction under subsection (1)(f)—
    (a) may not be made in relation to a recorded account given by the defendant;
    (b) may be made only if it appears to the court that—
        (i) the witness's recollection of the events in question is likely to have been significantly better when he gave the recorded account than it will be when he gives oral evidence in the proceedings, and
        (ii) it is in the interests of justice for the recording to be admitted, having regard in particular to the matters mentioned in subsection (4).
(4) Those matters are—
    (a) the interval between the time of the events in question and the time when the recorded account was made;
    (b) any other factors that might affect the reliability of what the witness said in that account;
    (c) the quality of the recording;

(d) any views of the witness as to whether his evidence in chief should be given orally or by means of the recording.

(5) For the purposes of subsection (2) it does not matter if the statements in the recorded account were not made on oath.

(6) In this section 'prescribed' means of a description specified in an order made by the Secretary of State.

Nothing in section 137 affects the admissibility of any video-recording which would be admissible apart from the section.[198]

Section 138(1), (2), and (3) of the 2003 Act provide as follows:

(1) Where a video recording is admitted under section 137, the witness may not give evidence in chief otherwise than by means of the recording as to any matter which, in the opinion of the court, has been dealt with adequately in the recorded account.

(2) The reference in subsection (1)(f) of section 137 to the admission of a recording includes a reference to the admission of part of the recording; and references in that section and this one to the video recording or to the witness's recorded account shall, where appropriate, be read accordingly.

(3) In considering whether any part of a recording should not be admitted under section 137, the court must consider—

(a) whether admitting that part would carry a risk of prejudice to the defendant, and

(b) if so, whether the interests of justice nevertheless require it to be admitted in view of the desirability of showing the whole, or substantially the whole, of the recorded interview.

Special measures directions for vulnerable and intimidated witnesses

Sections 16–33 of the 1999 Act introduced a range of 'special measures' which were proposed in *Speaking Up for Justice* (Home Office, 1998) and are designed to minimize the ordeal and trauma experienced by certain types of vulnerable and intimidated witnesses when giving evidence in criminal cases.[199] The provisions are sensible modifications to orthodox trial procedures designed to meet the real needs of children and other vulnerable witnesses and most applications for special measures succeed.[200] However, there are four failings. First, the new statutory scheme is needlessly complex, in parts almost impenetrable. Secondly, it is unduly inflexible and, in the case of children, makes a crude distinction between sexual offences and offences of physical violence. Thirdly, the provision relating to the video-recording of cross-examination and re-examination has simply not been brought into force.[201] Fourthly, more could be achieved, both in improving the processes

---

[198] Section 138(5).

[199] See also *Report of the Advisory Group on Video-Recorded Evidence* (Home Office, 1989) (the 'Pigot Report'), Law Commission Consultation Paper No 130, *Mentally Incapacitated and Other Vulnerable Adults: Public Law Protection*, and generally Professor Di Birch, 'A Better Deal for Vulnerable Witnesses?' [2000] *Crim LR* 223 and Laura Hoyano, 'Variations on a Theme by Pigot: Special Measures Directions for Child Witnesses' [2000] *Crim LR* 250 and 'Striking a Balance between the Rights of Defendants and Vulnerable Witnesses: Will Special Measures Directions Contravene Guarantees of a Fair Trial?' [2001] *Crim LR* 948.

[200] See Roberts et al, 'Monitoring success, accounting for failure: The outcome of prosecutors' applications for special measures directions under the Youth Justice and Criminal Evidence Act 1999' (2005) 9 *E&P* 269.

[201] See generally Cooper, 'Pigot Unfulfilled: Vide-recorded Cross-examination under section 28 of the Youth Justice and Criminal Evidence Act 1999' [2005] *Crim LR* 456.

for the identification of vulnerable and intimidated witnesses[202] and by the introduction of specific new measures such as improved assessment of individual need, the mandatory visual recording of initial interviews, and the curtailment of inappropriate questioning and cross-examination tactics.[203]

The judge may give a direction providing for the following special measures to apply to evidence given by vulnerable and intimidated witnesses: screening the witness; giving evidence by live link; giving evidence in private; the removal of wigs and gowns; admitting a video-recording of an interview of the witness as the evidence-in-chief of the witness; video-recording the cross-examination and re-examination of the witness and admitting such a recording as the evidence of the witness under cross-examination and on re-examination;[204] the examination of the witness through an intermediary; and the provision of appropriate aids to communication with the witness.

Special measures are only available to 'eligible witnesses', namely (i) witnesses other than the accused eligible for assistance on grounds of age or incapacity, for whom all the above special measures are available, and (ii) witnesses other than the accused eligible for assistance on grounds of fear or distress about testifying, for whom all but the last two of the above special measures are available.[205] It will be convenient to consider in more detail the nature of the special measures available and the above types of witness eligible for assistance before turning to consider the circumstances in which a special measures direction may or must be given. Finally, consideration will be given to the special position of the accused.

Special measures directions

Screens. Under section 23(1) of the 1999 Act, a special measures direction may provide for the witness while giving evidence or being sworn in court to be prevented by means of a screen or other arrangement from seeing the accused. However, the screen must not prevent the witness from being able to see, and to be seen by, the judge or justices, the jury (if there is one), legal representatives acting in the case, and any interpreter or other person appointed to assist the witness.[206]

Live link. Under section 24, a special measures direction may provide for the witness to give evidence by a live television link or other arrangement whereby the witness, while absent from the courtroom, is able to see and hear a person there and to be seen and heard by the judge or justices, the jury (if there is one), the legal representatives in the case, and any interpreter or other person appointed to assist the witness. Where a direction has been given providing for the witness to give evidence by live link, the court may later give permission for the witness to give evidence in some other way, if it appears to be in the interests of justice to do so.[207]

---

[202] See Burton et al, 'Implementing Special Measures for Vulnerable and Intimidated Witnesses: The Problem of Identification' [2006] *Crim LR* 229.

[203] See Burton et al, 'Vulnerable and intimidated witnesses and the adversarial process in England and Wales' (2007) 11 *E&P* 1.

[204] This special measure (see s 28) is unlikely to be introduced.

[205] See s 18(1).

[206] Section 23(2). See also, prior to the enactment of s 23, Home Office Circular 61/1990, *Use of Screens in Magistrates' Courts*; and *R v X, Y and Z* (1989) 91 Cr App R 36, CA; *R v Watford Magistrates' Court, ex p Lenman* [1993] Crim LR 388, DC; *R v Cooper and Schaub* [1994] Crim LR 531, CA; and *R v Foster* [1995] Crim LR 333, CA.

[207] Section 24(3).

Evidence in private.   Under section 25, a special measures direction may provide for the exclusion from the court, during the giving of the witness's evidence, of persons of any description specified in the direction other than the accused, legal representatives acting in the case, or any interpreter or other person appointed to assist the witness.[208] However, such a direction may only be given where the proceedings relate to a sexual offence[209] or it appears to the court that there are reasonable grounds for believing that any person other than the accused has sought, or will seek, to intimidate the witness in connection with testifying in the proceedings.[210]

Removal of wigs and gowns.   Under section 26, provision may be made for the wearing of wigs and gowns to be dispensed with during the giving of the witness's evidence.

Video-recorded evidence-in-chief.   Sections 27(1)–(3) provide as follows:

(1) A special measures direction may provide for a video recording of an interview of the witness to be admitted as evidence in chief of the witness.
(2) A special measures direction may, however, not provide for a video-recording, or part of such a recording, to be admitted under this section if the court is of the opinion, having regard to all the circumstances of the case, that in the interests of justice the recording, or that part of it, should not be so admitted.
(3) In considering, for the purposes of subsection (2) whether any part of a recording should not be admitted under this section, the court must consider whether any prejudice to the accused which might result from that part being so admitted is outweighed by the desirability of showing the whole, or substantially the whole, of the recorded interview.

Subsection (2) allows the court to direct that any part of the recording be excluded, in which case the party admitting the video must then edit it accordingly.[211] The effect of section 27(3) is not to extend the common law rules as to the admissibility of evidence so as to lead to the admission of otherwise inadmissible evidence, for example inadmissible evidence of bad character. Such evidence will normally be edited out. Section 27(3) is designed to cover unusual cases in which the evidence of the witness cannot be given in a way that is coherent and understandable to the listener without the inclusion of the inadmissible material.[212] In such cases, it is submitted, the judge will need to give a direction to the jury—which, in the circumstances, is likely to be difficult for them to comprehend—that the offending material is not evidence of the matters stated.

Where a recording (or part of it) is admitted, then: (a) the witness must be called by the party tendering it in evidence, unless either (i) a special measures direction provides for the witness's evidence on cross-examination to be given otherwise than by testimony in court, or (ii) the parties in the proceedings have agreed that there is no need for the witness to be available for cross-examination; and (b) the witness may not give evidence-in-chief otherwise

---

[208] Where the persons specified are representatives of the media, the direction shall be expressed not to apply to one named person nominated by one or more news gathering or reporting organizations: s 25(3).

[209] 'Sexual offence' is defined in s 62 of the 1999 Act as any offence under Part 1 of the Sexual Offences Act 2003 or any relevant superseded offence.

[210] Section 25(4).

[211] See *Practice Direction (Criminal Proceedings: Consolidation)* [2002] 1 WLR 2870, para 40, which also governs the procedure for production and proof of the recording.

[212] *R (on the application of the Crown Prosecution Service Harrow) v Brentford Youth Court* [2004] Crim LR 159 (DC).

than by means of the recording (or part of it) (i) as to any matter which in the opinion of the court has been dealt with adequately in the witness's recorded testimony (or part of it), or (ii) without the permission of the court, as to any other matter which, in the opinion of the court, is dealt with in that testimony (or part of it).[213] The court may give such permission if it appears to the court to be in the interests of justice to do so either (a) on an application by a party to the proceedings, if there has been a material change of circumstances since the time when the direction was given (or, if a previous application has been made, the time when the application or last application was made); or (b) of its own motion.[214] Where a special measures direction provides for a recording (or part of it) to be admitted under section 27, the court may nevertheless subsequently make a direction to the contrary if it appears to the court that (i) the witness will not be available for cross-examination (whether conducted in the ordinary way or in accordance with a special measures direction) and the parties have not agreed that there is no need for the witness to be so available, or (ii) any rules of court requiring disclosure of the circumstances in which the recording (or part of it) was made have not been complied with to the satisfaction of the court.[215] Nothing in section 27 affects the admissibility of any video-recording which would be admissible apart from the section.[216]

Video-recorded interviews with child witnesses should be conducted in accordance with the guidance given in 'Achieving Best Evidence in Criminal Proceedings: Guidance for Vulnerable or Intimidated Witnesses, Including Children' ('The Memorandum'),[217] a non-statutory code published by the Home Office, which deals with such matters as leading questions, previous statements, and the bad character of the accused. The guidance should be regarded as expert advice as to what will normally be the best practice to adopt in seeking to ensure that a child's evidence is reliable, and if it is not observed there are grounds for a judge or jury to consider with particular care whether the child is reliable.[218] In *R v K*[219] it was held that, in deciding whether to exclude evidence obtained in breach of the Memorandum, the starting point is the statutory wording and the strong presumption in favour of the use of special measures, and the test is 'Could a reasonable jury properly directed be sure that the witness has given a credible and accurate account notwithstanding the breaches?' The prime consideration is reliability, which will normally be assessed by reference to the interview itself, the conditions under which it was held, the age of the child, and the nature and extent of the breaches. There may be cases in which other evidence in the case demonstrates that the breaches did not undermine the credibility or accuracy of the interview, but references to other evidence should be undertaken with considerable caution.

In order to reach a decision under section 27(2), the judge, in most—if not all—cases, must watch the video-recording. In the case of interviews with some child witnesses, the court will need to decide upon the competence of the child.[220] If, on viewing the recording, he considers that the

---

[213] Section 27(5) and (6).

[214] Section 27(7) and (8). The court may, in giving permission, direct that the evidence in question be given by the witness by means of a live link: s 27(9).

[215] Section 27(4) and (6).

[216] Section 27(11).

[217] Available at <http://www.homeoffice.gov.uk>.

[218] *R v Dunphy* (1993) 98 Cr App R 393 at 395, CA, a decision under an earlier version of the Memorandum.

[219] [2006] 2 Cr App R 175, CA.

[220] In deciding, the court shall treat the witness as having the benefit of any directions under s 19 which the court has given, or proposes to give, in relation to the witness: s 54(3) of the 1999 Act.

child is incompetent to give evidence, the evidence should not be admitted; but if he concludes that the child is competent, there is no need to investigate the child's competence again at the trial before the playing of the recording. Nonetheless, he still has the power to exclude the evidence if, in the course of it, he forms the view that the child is, after all, incompetent.[221]

In a decision under section 32A of the Criminal Justice Act 1988, the statutory precursor to section 27, it was held that where a video-recording has been admitted and there is a transcript, the jury may be provided with copies, on three conditions: (i) the transcript must be likely to assist them in following the evidence, as when a child suffers from a speech disorder or poor articulation; (ii) the judge must make it clear that the transcript has been provided only for that limited purpose and that they should concentrate primarily on the oral evidence; and (iii) the judge should give them such directions as would be likely to be effective safeguards against the risk of disproportionate weight being given to the transcript.[222] It has also been held, however, that unless the defence consent, the jury should not normally be permitted to retire with the transcript.[223]

Video-recorded cross-examination or re-examination.   Under section 28(1), where a special measures direction provides for a video-recording to be admitted as evidence-in-chief of the witness under section 27, the direction may also provide for any cross-examination and any re-examination of the witness to be recorded by means of a video-recording and for such a recording, so far as it relates to any such cross-examination or re-examination, to be admitted as evidence of the witness under cross-examination or re-examination.[224] Under section 28(2), such a recording must be made in the presence of such persons as rules of court or the direction may provide, and in the absence of the accused, but in circumstances in which (a) the judge or justices (or both) and legal representatives acting in the proceedings are able to see and hear the examination of the witness and to communicate with those in whose presence the recording is being made; and (b) the accused is able to see and hear any such examination and to communicate with any legal representative acting for him.[225] Where a special measures direction provides for a recording to be admitted under section 28, the court may nevertheless subsequently make a direction to the contrary if any requirement of section 28(2) or rules of court or the direction itself has not been complied with to the satisfaction of the court.[226] Where in pursuance of section 28(1) a recording has been made, the witness may not be subsequently cross-examined or re-examined in respect of any evidence given by the witness (whether or not in any recording admissible under section 27 or section 28) unless the court gives a further special measures direction,[227] but such a further direction may only be given if it appears to the court (a) that the proposed cross-examination is sought by a party to the proceedings as a result of that party having become aware, since the time when the original recording was made, of a matter which that party could not with reasonable diligence have

---

[221] See *R v Hampshire* [1995] 2 All ER 1019, CA, a decision under s 32A of the Criminal Justice Act 1988.

[222] *R v Welstead* [1996] 1 Cr App R 59, CA.

[223] *R v Coshall* [1995] 12 LS Gaz R 34, CA. See also *R v N* [1998] Crim LR 886, CA.

[224] Section 28 has not been brought into force.

[225] Section 28 has no application in relation to any cross-examination of the witness by the accused in person: s 28(7).

[226] Section 28(4).

[227] Section 28(5).

WITNESSES IN CRIMINAL CASES

ascertained by then; or (b) that for any other reason it is in the interests of justice to give the further direction.[228]

Examination of witness through intermediary. Under section 29, a special measures direction may provide for any examination of the witness (however and wherever conducted) to be conducted through an interpreter or other intermediary approved by the court. The function of the intermediary is to communicate to the witness questions put to the witness, to communicate to the person asking such questions the answers given by the witness in reply, and to explain such questions or answers so far as necessary to enable them to be understood.[229] Any examination under section 29 must take place in the presence of such persons as rules of court or the direction may provide, but in circumstances in which (a) the judge or justices (or both) and legal representatives acting in the proceedings are able to see and hear the examination of the witness and to communicate with the intermediary; and (b) the jury, if there is one, are able to see and hear the examination of the witness (except in the case of a video-recorded examination).[230] A special measures direction may provide for a recording of an interview, conducted through an intermediary, to be admitted under section 27, provided that the intermediary has been approved by the court before the direction is given.[231]

Aids to communication. Under section 30, a special measures direction may provide for the witness, while giving evidence (whether in court or otherwise), to be provided with such device as the court considers appropriate with a view to enabling questions or answers to be communicated to or by the witness despite any disability or disorder or other impairment which the witness has or suffers from.

The witnesses eligible for assistance

Witnesses eligible for assistance on grounds of age or incapacity. Sections 16(1) and (2) of the 1999 Act provide as follows:

(1) . . . a witness in criminal proceedings (other than the accused) is eligible for assistance by virtue of this section—
   (a) if under the age of 17 at the time of the hearing; or
   (b) if the court considers that the quality of the evidence given by the witness is likely to be diminished by reason of any circumstances falling within subsection (2).
(2) The circumstances falling within this subsection are—
   (a) that the witness—
      (i) suffers from mental disorder within the meaning of the Mental Health Act 1983; or
      (ii) otherwise has a significant impairment of intelligence and social functioning;
   (b) that the witness has a physical disability or is suffering from a physical disorder.

---

[228] Section 28(6).

[229] Section 29(2). As to the extent to which s 29 will assist eligible witnesses to give their best evidence or promote more empathic communication during cross-examination, see L Ellison, 'The Mosaic Art?': cross-examination and the vulnerable witness' (2001) 21 *LS* 353 and 'Cross-examination and the Intermediary: Bridging the Language Divide?' [2002] *Crim LR* 114.

[230] Section 29(3).

[231] Section 29(6).

In section 16(1)(a), 'the time of the hearing', in relation to a witness, means the time when it falls to the court to decide whether to make a special measures direction.[232] In deciding whether a witness has a physical disability or is suffering from a physical disorder, the court must consider any views expressed by the witness.[233] References to the quality of a witness's evidence, in section 16 and in other sections relating to special measures directions, are to its quality in terms of completeness, coherence, and accuracy; and for this purpose 'coherence' refers to a witness's ability in giving evidence to give answers which address the questions put to the witness and can be understood both individually and collectively.[234]

Witnesses eligible for assistance on grounds of fear or distress about testifying.   Under section 17(1) of the Act, a witness other than the accused is eligible for assistance if the court is satisfied that the quality of evidence given by the witness is likely to be diminished by reason of fear or distress on the part of the witness in connection with testifying in the proceedings. In deciding whether a witness falls within section 17(1), the court must take into account, in particular: (a) the nature and alleged circumstances of the offence to which the proceedings relate; (b) the age of the witness; (c) such of the following matters as appear to the court to be relevant, namely (i) the social and cultural background and ethnic origins of the witness, (ii) the domestic and employment circumstances of the witness and (iii) any religious beliefs or political opinions of the witness; and (d) any behaviour towards the witness on the part of the accused, members of the family or associates of the accused, or any other person who is likely to be an accused or a witness in the proceedings.[235] In deciding, the court must also consider any views expressed by the witness.[236] A complainant in respect of a sexual offence[237] who is a witness in proceedings relating to that offence, or to that offence and any other offences, is automatically eligible for assistance unless he or she has informed the court of his or her wish not to be so eligible.[238]

The circumstances in which special measures directions are given
General.   A party to the proceedings may make an application for the court to give a special measures direction or the court of its own motion may raise the issue whether such a direction should be given.[239] Section 19(2) provides as follows:

> (2) Where the court decides that the witness is eligible for assistance by virtue of section 16 or 17, the court must then—
>
> (a) determine whether any of the special measures available in relation to the witness (or any combination of them), would, in its opinion, be likely to improve the quality of evidence given by the witness; and
>
> (b) if so—
>
> (i) determine which of those measures (or combination of them) would, in its opinion, be likely to maximise so far as practicable the quality of such evidence; and

---

[232] Section 16(3).
[233] Section 16(4).
[234] Section 16(5).
[235] Section 17(2).
[236] Section 17(3).
[237] See n 209.
[238] Section 17(4).
[239] Section 19(1).

(ii) give a direction under this section providing for the measure or measures so determined to apply to evidence given by the witness.

In deciding whether any special measure or measures would or would not be likely to improve, or to maximize so far as practicable, the quality of evidence given by the witness, the court must consider all the circumstances of the case, including in particular any views expressed by the witness and whether the measure or measures might tend to inhibit such evidence being effectively tested by a party to the proceedings.[240] Under section 20(1), as a general rule a special measures direction has binding effect from the time it is made until the proceedings for the purposes of which it is made are either determined or abandoned in relation to the accused or (if there is more than one) in relation to each of them. The court may discharge or vary a special measures direction if it appears to the court to be in the interests of justice to do so.[241] The court must state in open court its reasons for giving or varying, or refusing an application for, a special measures direction.[242]

Child witnesses.   Section 21 of the 1999 Act makes special provision in the case of child witnesses. In the case of witnesses under the age of 17, in effect it creates a presumption in favour of a special measures direction in accordance with section 27 (video-recorded evidence to be admitted as evidence-in-chief) and, in the case of any evidence given by such witnesses which is not given by means of a video-recording, in accordance with section 24 (evidence by live link). Section 21 also provides that in the case of child witnesses under the age of 17 'in need of special protection' (because the offence to which the proceedings relate is one of a number of specified offences), if a special measures direction is made in accordance with section 27, then it must also provide for the special measure available under section 28 (video-recorded cross-examination or re-examination). Section 21 provides as follows:

(1) For the purposes of this section—
   (a) a witness in criminal proceedings is a 'child witness' if he is an eligible witness by reason of section 16(1)(a) (whether or not he is an eligible witness by reason of any other provision of sections 16 or 17);
   (b) a child is 'in need of special protection' if the offence (or any other offences) to which the proceedings relate is—
      (i) an offence falling within section 35(3)(a) (sexual offences etc),[243] or
      (ii) an offence falling within section 35(3)(b), (c) or (d) (kidnapping, assaults etc);[244] and
   (c) a 'relevant recording', in relation to a child witness, is a video recording of an interview of the witness made with a view to its admission as evidence in chief of the witness.

---

[240] Section 19(3).

[241] Section 20(2).

[242] Section 20(5).

[243] Any offence under any of ss 33–36 of the Sexual Offences Act 1956, the Protection of Children Act 1978, or Part 1 of the Sexual Offences Act 2003.

[244] Kidnapping, false imprisonment, or an offence under s 1 or s 2 of the Child Abduction Act 1984, any offence under s 1 of the Children and Young Persons Act 1933, and any offence (other than the foregoing offences and those listed in n 243 above) 'which involves an assault on, or injury or a threat of injury to, any person'. This phrase was also used in s 32(2)(a) of the Criminal Justice Act 1988, which the current provisions have replaced. In *R v McAndrew-Bingham* [1999] Crim LR 830, CA, a decision under that subsection, it was held that the phrase should be given a broad purposive interpretation to protect children who were likely to be traumatized by confrontation with the accused, so as to cover offences which may, but do not necessarily, involve an assault, injury, or threat of injury. See also *R v Lee* [1996] 2 Cr App R 266, CA, another decision under s 32(2)(a), in which 'threat of injury' was held not to relate to the state of mind of the accused, but was taken to mean risk of injury.

(2) Where the court, in making a determination for the purposes of section 19(2), determines that a witness in criminal proceedings is a child witness, the court must—

(a) first have regard to subsections (3) to (7) below; and

(b) then have regard to section 19(2);

and for the purposes of section 19(2), as it then applies to the witness, any special measures required to be applied in relation to him by virtue of this section shall be treated as if they were measures determined by the court, pursuant to section 19(2)(a) and (b)(i), to be ones that (whether on their own or with any other special measures) would be likely to maximise, so far as practicable, the quality of his evidence.

(3) The primary rule in the case of a child witness is that the court must give a special measures direction in relation to the witness which complies with the following requirements—

(a) it must provide for any relevant recording to be admitted under section 27 (video recorded evidence in chief); and

(b) it must provide for any evidence given by the witness in the proceedings which is not given by means of a video recording (whether in chief or otherwise) to be given by means of a live link in accordance with section 24.

(4) The primary rule is subject to the following limitations—

(a) . . .

(b) the requirement contained in subsection (3)(a) . . . has effect subject to subsection 27(2); and

(c) the rule does not apply to the extent that the court is satisfied that compliance with it would not be likely to maximise the quality of the witness's evidence so far as practicable (whether because the application to that evidence of one or more other special measures available in relation to the witness would have the result or for any other reason).

(5) However, subsection (4)(c) does not apply in relation to a child witness in need of special protection.

(6) Where a child witness is in need of special protection by virtue of subsection (1)(b)(i), any special measures direction given by the court which complies with the requirement contained in subsection (3)(a) must in addition provide for the special measure available under s 28 (video-recorded cross-examination or re-examination) to apply in relation to—

(a) any cross-examination of the witness otherwise than by the accused in person, and

(b) any subsequent re-examination.

(7) The requirement contained in subsection (6) has effect subject to the following limitations—

(a) . . .

(b) it does not apply if the witness has informed the court that he does not want that special measure to apply in relation to him.

(8) Where a special measures direction is given in relation to a child witness who is an eligible witness by reason only of section 16(1)(a), then—

(a) subject to subsection (9) below, and

(b) except where the witness has already begun to give evidence in the proceedings, the direction shall cease to have effect at the time when the witness attains the age of 17.

(9) Where a special measures direction is given in relation to a child witness who is an eligible witness by reason only of section 16(1)(a) and

(a) the direction provides—

(i) for any relevant recording to be admitted under section 27 as evidence in chief of the witness, or

(ii) for the special measure available under section 28 to apply in relation to the witness, and

(b) if it provides for that special measure to so apply, the witness is still under the age of 17 when the video recording is made for the purposes of section 28, then, so far as it provides as mentioned in paragraph (a)(i) or (ii) above, the direction shall continue to have effect in accordance with section 20(1) even though the witness subsequently attains that age.[245]

In *R (D) v Camberwell Green Youth Court*[246] the House of Lords held that section 21(5) is compliant with Article 6 of the European Convention on Human Rights insofar as it prevents individualized consideration of the necessity for a special measures direction at the stage at which the direction is made and that there is nothing in the special measures provisions inconsistent with the principles set out by the European Court of Human Rights in *Kostovski v Netherlands*.[247] All the evidence is produced at the trial in the presence of the accused, some of it in pre-recorded form and some of it by contemporaneous television transmission. The accused can see and hear it all and has every opportunity to challenge and question the witnesses against him at the trial itself. A face-to-face confrontation is missing, but the Convention does not guarantee a right to such a confrontation. The court also has the opportunity to scrutinize the video-recorded interview at the outset and exclude all or part of it. Furthermore, at the trial it has the fallback of allowing the witness to give evidence in the court room or to expand upon the video-recording if the interests of justice require this.

The status of video-recorded evidence etc
Section 31(1)–(4) of the 1999 Act provide as follows:

(1) Subsections (2) to (4) apply to a statement[248] made by a witness in criminal proceedings which, in accordance with a special measures direction, is not made by the witness in direct oral testimony in court but forms part of the witness's evidence in those proceedings.[249]
(2) The statement shall be treated as if made by the witness in direct oral testimony in court; and accordingly—
   (a) it is admissible evidence of any fact of which such testimony from the witness would be admissible;
   (b) it is not capable of corroborating any other evidence given by the witness.
(3) Subsection (2) applies to a statement admitted under sections 27 or 28 which is not made by the witness on oath even though it would have been required to be made on oath if made by the witness in direct oral testimony in court.
(4) In estimating the weight (if any) to be attached to the statement, the court must have regard to all the circumstances from which an inference can reasonably be drawn (as to the accuracy of the statement or otherwise).

Section 32 of the 1999 Act provides that where, on a trial on indictment with a jury, evidence has been given in accordance with a special measures direction, the judge must give the jury such warning (if any) as the judge considers necessary to ensure that the fact that the direction

[245] See also s 22, which extends the provisions of s 21 to witnesses who were over the age of 17 at the time of the hearing, but who were under that age when a relevant recording was made, if the offence to which the proceedings relate is an offence falling within s 35(3)(a)–(d).
[246] [2005] 1 All ER 999, HL.
[247] (1990) 12 EHRR 434 at 447–8.
[248] 'Statement' includes any representation of fact, whether made in words or otherwise: s 31(8).
[249] Ie statements given in evidence by live television link or recorded in a video-recording admitted as evidence: see *R (S) v Waltham Forest Youth Court* [2004] 2 Cr App R 335 at [76].

was given in relation to the witness does not prejudice the accused. In the case of the use of screens, for example, it may suffice to say that they must not allow their use by witnesses to prejudice them in any way against the accused.[250]

The accused

Under section 33A of the 1999 Act, inserted by section 47 of the Police and Justice Act 2007, a court may permit an accused to give his oral evidence through a live link if the conditions in either subsection (4) or (5) are met and it is in the interests of justice to do so.[251] The conditions in subsection (4), which apply to an accused aged under 18, are that (a) his ability to participate effectively as a witness giving oral evidence in court is compromised by his level of intellectual ability or social functioning; and (b) use of a live link would enable him to participate more effectively.[252] The conditions in subsection (5), which apply where the accused has attained the age of 18, are that (a) he suffers from a mental disorder (within the meaning of the Mental Health Act 1983) or otherwise has a significant impairment of intelligence and social function; (b) he is for that reason unable to participate effectively as a witness giving oral evidence in court; and (c) use of a live link would enable him to participate more effectively.[253]

In *R (S) v Waltham Forest Youth Court*,[254] a decision prior to the amendment of the 1999 Act, it was held that since Parliament had sought to provide exclusively for the circumstances in which live link might be used in a criminal trial, there was no residual common law power to allow an accused to give evidence by live link. This approach was followed in *R v Ukpabio*,[255] a decision after the amendment but prior to its coming into force, but doubted by the House of Lords in *R (D) v Camberwell Green Youth Court*,[256] where it was held that the court had wide and flexible inherent powers to ensure that the accused is not at a substantial disadvantage compared with the prosecution and receives a fair trial, including a fair opportunity of giving the best evidence he can.[257] Baroness Hale was of the view that in exceptional circumstances special measures designed to shield a vulnerable or intimidated witness can apply in the case of the accused, giving as a possible example the use of live link by a younger child accused too scared to give evidence in the presence of her co-accused.

Witness anonymity

In some cases, witnesses will be in genuine and justified fear of serious consequences should their true identity become known. If such witnesses do not give evidence, criminals may walk free and the innocent may be convicted. To ensure the safety of such witnesses and induce them to give evidence, various measures can be taken, including the use of a pseudonym, the withholding from the defence of any particulars which might identify them, a ban of any

---

[250] See *R v Brown* [2004] Crim LR 1034, CA.

[251] Section 33A(2).

[252] Section 33A(4).

[253] Section 33A(5).

[254] [2004] 2 Cr App R 335, DC.

[255] [2008] 1 Cr App R 101, CA.

[256] [2005] 1 All ER 999.

[257] For example, the court can allow an accused with learning and communication difficulties to have the equivalent of an interpreter to assist with communication, and his written statement can be read to the jury so that they know what he wants to say: see *R v H* [2003] EWCA Crim 1208.

questions in cross-examination of the witnesses which might enable any of them to be identified, and the giving of evidence behind screens.[258] The obvious danger, however, is the potential or actual disadvantage to the accused, which has been likened to taking blind shots at a hidden target,[259] and the concomitant risk of an unfair trail. In *R v Davis*[260] the House of Lords held that the use of such measures, in the circumstances of the case, hampered the conduct of the defence in a manner and to an extent which was unlawful and rendered the trial unfair. Their Lordships were in agreement that it was a long established principle of the English common law that subject to certain exceptions and statutory qualifications, the accused should be confronted by his accusers in order that he may cross-examine them and challenge their evidence. Article 6(3)(d) of the European Convention, guaranteeing the accused the right to examine or have examined witnesses against him, had not added anything of significance to English law. The Strasbourg case law has established that no conviction should be based solely or to a decisive extent upon the statements or testimony of anonymous witnesses, because it results from a trial which cannot be regarded as fair. However, their Lordships did not doubt that the problem of witness intimidation was real and prevalent and might well call for urgent attention by Parliament.

The parliamentary response was swift and decisive, not least because the decision in *R v Davis* was bound to lead to the collapse of numerous trials, including a number of murder trials, in which applications had been or were being made for witness anonymity orders. The Criminal Evidence (Witness Anonymity) Act 2008 abolishes the common law rules and provides for the making of witness anonymity orders in relation to witnesses in criminal proceedings,[261] a witness for this purpose being any person called or proposed to be called to give evidence at the trial.[262] The remaining provisions of the Act may be summarized as follows.[263] The measures that can be taken under a witness anonymity order are (a) the withholding, and removal from materials disclosed to any party to the proceedings, of the witness's name and other identifying details; (b) use of a pseudonym; (c) not permitting the witness to be asked questions that might lead to his identification; (d) screening the witness, but not to the extent that the witness cannot be seen by the judge, jury, or any interpreter or other person appointed by the court to assist the witness; or (e) subjecting the witness's voice to modulation, but not to the extent that his natural voice cannot be heard by the judge, juror, etc.[264] Application for an order may be made by the prosecution or defence; where it is made by the prosecution, they must inform the court of the identity of the witness, but are not required to disclose either identity or information that may lead to identification to any other party to the proceedings or his lawyers; and where it is made by the defence, they must inform the court and the prosecutor of the identity of the witness, but are not required to disclose either identity or information that might lead to identification to any other accused

---

[258] The alternative or supplementary measure of secret relocation of witnesses and their families, which has found favour in the US, is costly and effectively penalizes the witness for doing his civic duty, as well as his family.

[259] *R v Davis* [2008] 3 All ER 461, per Lord Bingham at [32].

[260] Ibid.

[261] Section 1.

[262] Section 12.

[263] See also the Attorney General's guidelines on the prosecutor's role in applications for witness anonymity orders and the *Consolidated Criminal Practice Direction (Amendment No 21) (Criminal Proceedings: Witness Anonymity Orders; Forms)* [2009] 1 Cr App R 70.

[264] Section 2.

or his lawyers.[265] Every party must be given the opportunity to be heard on an application for an order, except that the court may hear one or more parties in the absence of an accused and his lawyers if it appears to the court appropriate to do so.[266] Under section 4 of the Act, the court may only make an order if satisfied that Conditions A to C are met. Condition A is that the measures to be specified in the order are necessary in order (a) to protect the safety of the witness or another or to prevent any serious damage to property (and in deciding the question of necessity in this respect, the court must have regard in particular to any reasonable fear on the part of the witness that, if identified, he or another would suffer death or injury or there would be serious damage to property); or (b) in order to prevent real harm to the public interest. Condition B is that, having regard to all the circumstances, the taking of those measures would be consistent with the accused receiving a fair trial. Condition C is that it is necessary to make the order in the interests of justice because it appears to the court that (a) it is important that the witness should testify; and (b) the witness would not testify without the order. When deciding whether Conditions A to C are met, the court must have regard to the considerations set out in section 5(2) and such other matters as the court considers relevant. The considerations in section 5(2) are:

(a) the general right of an accused to know the identity of a witness;

(b) the extent to which the credibility of the witness would be a relevant factor when assessing the weight of his evidence;

(c) whether the evidence given by the witness might be the sole or decisive evidence implicating the accused;

(d) whether the witness's evidence could be properly tested (on grounds of credibility or otherwise) without his identity being disclosed;

(e) whether there is any reason to believe that the witness (i) has a tendency to be dishonest, or (ii) has any motive to be dishonest in the circumstances of the case, having regard in particular to any previous convictions and to any relationship between him and the accused or any of his associates; and

(f) whether it would be reasonably practicable to protect the witness's identity by means other than by making an order specifying the measures under consideration by the court.

Under section 7 of the Act, in jury trials the judge must give the jury such warning as he considers appropriate to ensure that the fact that an order was made does not prejudice the accused.

R v Mayers[267] offers detailed guidance on the meaning and application of the new statutory provisions. It may be summarized as follows:

1. Save in the exceptional circumstances permitted by the Act, the ancient principle that the accused is entitled to know the identity of the witnesses who incriminate him is maintained.

2. The Act seeks to address the provisions of the European Convention and the relevant jurisprudence of the European Court by seeking to preserve the delicate balance between

---

[265] Section 3.

[266] Section 3(6) and (7).

[267] [2009] 2 All ER 145, CA.

the rights of the accused, including his entitlement to a fair trial and public hearing, and to examine or have the witnesses who inculpate him properly examined (Article 6) and the witness's right to life (Article 2) and physical security (Article 3) and the right to respect for his private life (Article 8).

3. Bearing in mind other provision such as special measures under the 1999 Act[268] and the admissibility of evidence under section 116 of the 2003 Act where a witness is unavailable,[269] an anonymity order should be regarded as a special measure of last practicable resort.

4. The principles which govern the use of special counsel for public interest immunity purposes[270] should be adapted when the use of such counsel arises in the context of witness anonymity, when the issue will be whether sufficient and complete investigation and consequential disclosure have taken place. A detailed investigation into the background of each potential anonymous witness will almost inevitably be required.

5. The judge should normally reflect both at the close of the prosecution and when the defence evidence is concluded, whether properly directed and in the light of the evidence as a whole, the case can safely be left to the jury.

6. The section 7 warning must be sufficient to ensure that the jury do not make any assumptions adverse to the accused or favourable to the witness and, in particular, do not draw an inference of guilt against the accused.

7. None of the section 5(2) considerations outweighs any of the others, none is conclusive on the question whether the individual accused will receive a fair trial, and none precludes the possibility of an order.

8. Section 5(2)(a) restates the common law principle that the accused is normally entitled to know the identity of any witness who gives incriminating evidence against him and section 5(2)(f) confirms that an order represents the last resort.

9. Concerning the considerations in section 5(2)(b)(d) and (e), the process of investigation and disclosure is crucial. The three considerations are distinct but linked and are likely to require an overall view of the potential impact of the witness on the trial. Thus, for example, there may be no reason to doubt the integrity or motive or credibility of a witness; the issue may be his accuracy, which may be fully tested without disclosure of his identity.

10. Concerning the consideration in section 5(2)(c), which addresses the jurisprudence of the European Court, the fact that a witness provides the sole or decisive evidence against the accused is not conclusive whether conditions A, B, and C are met, but does directly impinge on the question whether condition B may be met. Whether the evidence is sole or decisive raises two separate questions, but if the evidence is both sole and decisive condition B may be harder to meet. The court should examine whether the evidence is supported extraneously. The more facts independent of the witness which tend to support him (and which may derive from the conduct of the accused himself), the safer it is to admit anonymous evidence. Where there are number of anonymous witnesses

[268] See above.
[269] See Ch 10.
[270] See Ch 19.

who incriminate the accused, whether there is a link between them, and if so its nature, should be investigated, addressing any question of possible improper collusion or cross-contamination. Suspicion is less likely to be engendered about the integrity of witnesses who immediately or virtually immediately are identified or identify themselves, before a sufficient opportunity to engineer a sophisticated conspiracy, than witnesses who turn up late and 'out of the blue'.

11. Condition C should probably be addressed first. The order should not be made where the oral testimony of the witness is not potentially important or where the proposed anonymous evidence could be addressed by admissions or agreed facts or, subject to proper editing, is capable of being read. It must be clear that, notwithstanding the powers invested in the court in relation to contempt, the witness 'would not testify' without the order: it is insufficient that the witness might prefer not to testify or would be reluctant or unhappy at the prospect. However, the court may conclude that the witness would not testify if the circumstances of the offence justify the inference.

12. Condition A does not require the risk to the safety to the witness to be attributable to the action of the accused personally: the threat may come from any source. Under Condition A, the order must be necessary, which goes well beyond what may be described as desirable or convenient. A specific problem arises in relation to police witnesses, especially those working undercover, for there are often sound operational reasons for maintaining anonymity; the court would normally be entitled to follow the unequivocal assertion by an undercover officer that without an order he would not be prepared to testify. The witnesses may well be known to the accused by a false identity, and the accused may be able to advance criticisms of their evidence or conduct without being disadvantaged by ignorance of their true identities. Condition A covers a potentially very wide group, ranging from undercover officers working in areas of terrorism to test purchase officers. It is worth identifying the public interest which is involved in the deployment of these witnesses. At the most dangerous level, extreme measures might be taken to discover the identity of undercover officers who have penetrated criminal associations, not merely out of revenge, but to prevent their use as witnesses and compromise or damage sensitive covert techniques or to discourage them or others from continuing with their activities (all of which serve a valuable public interest).

13. Condition B appears to be focused on the *accused* receiving a fair trial, even when it is the accused seeking the anonymity order. Condition B is fact-specific. In the vast majority of cases, all of the section 5(2) considerations will require attention.

14. The 2008 Act is silent about the use of anonymous *hearsay* evidence, or evidence in the form of a statement by an unidentified witness. Sch evidence is not admissible under either section 114 or section 116 of the 2003 Act.[271]

The 2008 Act has a 'sunset' clause: it will expire on 31 December 2009 unless extended for another year.[272] Extension seems most likely given the number of orders that are likely to be made under the Act. As the Court of Appeal observed in *R v Powar*:[273] '. . . the calling of anonymous witnesses must not become a routine event in the prosecution of serious crime

---

[271] See Ch 10.
[272] Section 14.
[273] [2009] EWCA Crim 594.

but we reject the submission that witness anonymity orders should be confined to cases of terrorism or gangland killings. The intimidation of witnesses has become an ugly feature of contemporary life . . . '

Witness training and witness familiarization

The Court of Appeal in *R v Momodou*[274] has made it clear that in criminal proceedings, witness training or coaching is prohibited, but witness familiarization is permitted. The following reasons were given for the ban on training or coaching. It reduces the possibility that one witness may tailor his evidence in the light of what anyone else has said. Even if the training takes place one-to-one with someone completely remote from the facts of the case, the witness may come, even unconsciously, to appreciate which aspects of his evidence are not quite consistent with what others are saying or not quite what is required of him. An honest witness may alter the emphasis of his evidence. A dishonest witness will very rapidly calculate how his evidence may be 'improved'. Where a witness is jointly trained with other witnesses to the same events, the dangers dramatically increase: recollections change, memories are contaminated, and witnesses bring their respective accounts into what they believe to be better alignment with others. They may even collude deliberately.

The ban on witness training or coaching, however, does not preclude pre-trial arrangements, usually in the form of a visit to the court, to familiarize witnesses with the court layout, the likely sequence of events, and a balanced appraisal of the different responsibilities of the various participants. Such arrangements are welcomed because witnesses should not be disadvantaged by ignorance of the process nor, when they come to give evidence, be taken by surprise at the way it works. None of this involves discussions about proposed evidence. Equally, the ban does not prohibit the out-of-court training of expert and similar witnesses in, for example, the technique of giving comprehensive evidence of a specialist kind to a jury, both in examination-in-chief and in cross-examination, and developing the ability to resist the inevitable pressure of going further in evidence than matters covered by the witness's specific expertise. However, such training should not be arranged in the context of, nor be related to, any forthcoming trial.

It was also held in *R v Momoudou* that where arrangements are to be made for familiarization in the case of prosecution witnesses by outside agencies, the Crown Prosecution Service should be informed in advance and the proposals should be reduced into writing so that they can be amended if they breach the permitted limits. If the defence engage in the process, it is wise to seek counsel's advice in advance, and in any event the trial judge and the Crown Prosecution Service should be informed of any familiarization process organized using outside agencies. The familiarization process itself should normally be supervised or conducted by a solicitor or barrister, but no-one involved should have any personal knowledge of the matters in issue, none of the material should bear any similarity whatever to the issues in the trial, nothing in it should play on or trigger the witness's recollection of events, and if discussion of the trial begins, it must be stopped. Records should be maintained of all those present and the identity of those responsible for the process. All documents used in the process should be retained and handed to the Crown Prosecution Service or, in the case of defence witnesses, should be produced to the court.

[274] [2005] 2 All ER 571, CA.

ADDITIONAL READING

Birch, 'A Better Deal for Vulnerable Witnesses?' [2000] *Crim LR* 223.

Burton et al, 'Implementing Special Measures for Vulnerable and Intimidated Witnesses: The Problem of Identification' [2006] *Crim LR* 229.

Burton et al, 'Vulnerable and intimidated witnesses and the adversarial process in England and Wales' (2007) 11 *E&P* 1.

Creighton, 'Spouse Competence and Compellability' [1990] *Crim LR* 34.

Ellison, 'The Mosaic Art?: Cross-examination and the vulnerable witness' (2001) 21 *Legal Studies* 353.

Ellison, 'Cross-examination and the Intermediary: Bridging the Language Divide?' [2002] *Crim LR* 114.

Hoyano, 'Variations on a Theme by Pigot: Special Measures Directions for Child Witnesses' [2000] *Crim LR* 250.

Hoyano, 'Striking a balance between the Rights of Defendants and Vulnerable Witnesses: Will Special Measures Directions Contravene Guarantees of a Fair Trial?' [2001] *Crim LR* 948.

Hoyano, 'The Child Witness Review: Much Ado about Too Little' [2007] *Crim LR* 849.

Law Commission Consultation Paper No 130, *Mentally Incapacitated and Other Vulnerable Adults: Public Law Protection* (1993).

Plotnikoff and Woolfson, 'Making Best Use of the Intermediary Special Measure at Trial' [2008] *Crim LR* 91.

Report of the Advisory Group on Video-Recorded Evidence (the *Pigot Report*) (Home Office, 1989).

Spencer and Flin, *The Evidence of Children* (2nd edn, London, 1993).

Examination-in-chief

6

Key Issues

- What restrictions, if any, should be placed on the manner in which evidence is elicited from witnesses in their evidence-in-chief?

- Should a party calling a witness be permitted to ask questions which suggest the answer sought? If such questions are put, what is the evidential status of the evidence elicited?

- In what circumstances should a witness be permitted to refresh his memory from a record containing his earlier recollection of an event about which he is called to give evidence?

- What is the evidential status of a document used by a witness to refresh his memory?

- When and why should a party calling a witness be permitted to adduce evidence of a statement made by him on a previous occasion consistent with his testimony at trial?

- What steps should be open to a party calling a witness where the witness fails to come up to proof or gives evidence supporting another party?

- What steps should be open to a party calling a witness where the witness shows no desire to tell the truth?

The general rule, in both civil and criminal trials, is that any fact which needs to be proved by the evidence of witnesses is to be proved by their oral evidence, given in public.[1] The questioning of witnesses, which generally falls into three stages known as examination-in-chief, cross-examination, and re-examination, is central to the English adversary system of justice. The first stage, examination-in-chief, is the questioning of a witness by the party calling him. In examination-in-chief the party calling a witness, or counsel on his behalf, will seek to elicit evidence which supports his version of the facts in issue.[2] This chapter concerns the rules governing the manner in which this may be done. They are considered under the headings of 'Leading questions', 'Refreshing the memory', 'Previous consistent or self-serving statements', and 'Unfavourable and hostile witnesses'.

Leading questions

A party calling a witness and seeking to elicit evidence supporting his case often faces a witness who, although favourable, is not particularly forthcoming. The party calling him may be sorely tempted to put words into the witness's mouth and thereby explain what he wants him to say. In examination-in-chief, however, the general rule is that a witness may not be asked leading questions.[3] Evidence elicited by leading questions is not inadmissible but the weight to be attached to it may be reduced.[4] Leading questions are usually those so framed as to suggest the answer sought. Thus it would be a leading question if counsel for the prosecution, seeking to establish an assault, were to ask the victim, 'Did X hit you in the face with his fist?' The proper course would be to ask, 'Did X do anything to you?' and, if the witness then gives evidence of having been hit, to ask the questions 'Where did X hit you?' and 'How did X hit you?' Questions are also leading if so framed as to assume the existence of facts yet to be established. If evidence has yet to be given of the assault, it would be improper, for example, to ask, 'What were you doing immediately before X hit you?' The examples given are reasonably straightforward, but in practice the avoidance of leading questions often requires considerable skill and experience. An over-strict adherence to the rule against leading questions would render examination-in-chief extremely difficult. The question 'Did X do anything to you?', even if it does not suggest that X hit the witness, suggests that X did something, whereas in fact he might have been asleep at the relevant time. 'And what happened next?' is a solution often resorted to. However, the judge, and counsel for the other side, will not always demand strict adherence to the rule, and for good reason: ' "leading" is a relative, not an absolute term'.[5]

To the general prohibition on leading questions there are frequently recurring exceptions. A witness may be asked leading questions on formal and introductory matters, such as his name, address, and occupation. Leading questions are also permissible on facts which are not

[1] However, in civil cases this is subject to any provision to the contrary, whether in the Civil Procedure Rules or elsewhere, or to any order of the court: CPR r 32.2. A civil court, in exercise of its power under r 32.1 to control evidence, may direct that in order to decide a particular issue, it only requires evidence in written form.

[2] Excessive questioning of a witness by the judge may improperly interfere with the opportunity which counsel should be given to present the witness's evidence in the most impressive way he or she can devise: see *R v Gunning* (1994) 98 Cr App R 303, CA.

[3] Leading questions may be put in cross-examination: *Parkin v Moon* (1836) 7 C&P 408.

[4] *Moor v Moor* [1954] 1 WLR 927, CA.

[5] Best, *Law of Evidence* (12th edn, London, 1922) 562.

in dispute, and counsel for the other side may well indicate, in the case of any witness, those matters on which he has no objection to such questions being put. Leading questions may also be put to a witness called by a party who has been granted leave to treat him as hostile.[6]

Refreshing the memory

Witnesses often experience difficulty in recollecting the events to which their evidence relates, especially when the events took place a long time ago. In consequence, common law rules have evolved to allow a witness to refresh his memory from a document made or verified by him at an earlier time. The common law rules have been supplemented and, in part, superseded by, statutory provisions. However, the scope for use of the memory-refreshing rules has diminished by reason of the growth in the categories of admissible hearsay and the introduction of rules permitting a witness statement or a video-recorded account to stand as a witness's evidence-in-chief. Thus in civil proceedings a witness statement will normally stand as a witness's evidence-in-chief, unless the court orders otherwise,[7] and the previous documentary statement of a witness is admissible with the leave of the court as evidence of any facts contained in it pursuant to section 6(2)(a) of the Civil Evidence Act 1995.[8] In criminal proceedings, section 137 of the Criminal Justice Act 2003 (the 2003 Act) provides that, in the case of offences triable only on indictment and other serious offences, a video-recording of an account, given by a witness to the offence, may stand as his evidence-in-chief, provided that it was given at a time when the events were fresh in his memory, his recollection of the events is likely to have been significantly better at that time, and it is in the interests of justice to do so.[9] Furthermore, in criminal proceedings a previous statement made by a witness with personal knowledge of the matters dealt with, and contained in a document created or received by a person in the course of, inter alia, a trade, business, or profession, may be admitted as evidence of any facts contained in it, under section 117 of the 2003 Act; and under section 114(1)(d) of that Act, the court also has a discretionary power to admit a hearsay statement in the interests of justice.[10]

Refreshing the memory in court

The rules

At common law, a witness in either civil or criminal proceedings, in the course of giving his evidence, may refer to a document, such as a diary, log-book, or account-book, in order to refresh his memory. The conditions are that the document (i) was made or verified by him either contemporaneously with the events in question or so shortly thereafter that the facts were still fresh in his memory; (ii) is, in prescribed cases, the original; and (iii) is produced for inspection by either the court or the opposite party.

In criminal proceedings, this common law rule has not been repealed, but has in effect been replaced, and relaxed, by section 139(1) of the 2003 Act. Section 139(1) substitutes for the requirement of contemporaneity, or that the facts were still fresh in the

---

[6] See below at 183 under **Hostile witnesses**.
[7] See CPR r 32.5, Ch 5.
[8] See Ch 11.
[9] See Ch 5.
[10] See Ch 10.

memory, two different conditions. The first is that the witness testifies that the document records his recollection at the time when he made it. The second is that his recollection is likely to have been significantly better at that time than at the time of his oral evidence. The common law rule has also been supplemented by section 139(2), which provides for the refreshing of memory from a transcript of a sound recording, a provision designed to avoid the practical difficulties that would otherwise be encountered in refreshing the memory from the sound recording itself. Section 139 is in the following terms:

(1) A person giving oral evidence in criminal proceedings about any matter may, at any stage in the course of doing so, refresh his memory of it from a document made or verified by him at an earlier time if—
  (a) he states in his oral evidence that the document records his recollection of the matter at that earlier time, and
  (b) his recollection of the matter is likely to have been significantly better at that time than it is at the time of his oral evidence.
(2) Where—
  (a) a person giving oral evidence in criminal proceedings about any matter has previously given an oral account, of which a sound recording was made, and he states in that evidence that the account represented his recollection of the matter at that time,
  (b) his recollection of the matter is likely to have been significantly better at the time of the previous account than it is at the time of his oral evidence, and
  (c) a transcript has been made of the sound recording, he may at any stage in the course of giving his evidence, refresh his memory of the matter from that transcript.

An application for a witness to refresh his memory will normally be made by the party calling the witness, but it is a proper function of the judge, where the interests of justice so demand, to suggest that a witness, including in a criminal case, a witness for the prosecution, refresh his memory.[11] Both section 139(1) and (2) refer to 'a person giving oral evidence', ie any person giving oral evidence, and therefore apply, as does the common law rule, to any witness, including the accused.[12] Both subsections also permit the witness to refresh his memory 'at any stage' in the course of giving his evidence. Thus, as at common law, although a witness will normally refresh his memory in examination-in-chief, there is nothing wrong in principle in allowing him to do so during re-examination.[13]

In *R v McAfee*[14] it was held that the person in the best position to decide whether the condition in section 139(1)(b) is met is the trial judge, whose decision should be upheld unless obviously wrong, unreasonable, or perverse, but that the trial judge has a residual discretion to refuse an application under section 139 even if the statutory conditions are met.

In criminal proceedings for summary only offences, where a witness while giving evidence is permitted to use a document to refresh his memory, the party calling him may ask him to adopt all or part of that document as part of his evidence, but only if the parties agree and the court permits.[15]

---

[11] *R v Tyagi* (1986) The Times, 21 July, CA.
[12] See *R v Britton* [1987] 1 WLR 539, CA.
[13] *R v Harman* (1984) 148 JP 289, CA and *R v Sutton* (1991) 94 Cr App R 70, CA.
[14] [2006] All ER (D) 142 (Nov), [2006] EWCA Crim 2914.
[15] Part 37.4(4)(e) of the Criminal Procedure Rules 2005, SI 2005/384.

Present recollection revived and past recollection recorded

The common law rule on refreshing memory applies in the case of both 'present recollection revived' and 'past recollection recorded'.[16] 'Present recollection revived' is a phrase used to describe the genuine refreshing of memory on sight of the document. In the case of 'present recollection revived', both at common law and under section 139, it is the oral testimony of the witness whose memory has been refreshed, and not the document, which constitutes the evidence in the case. 'Past recollection recorded' refers to the situation in which the witness, although he has no current recollection of the events, his memory being a perfect blank, is prepared to testify as to the accuracy of the contents of the document. Thus in *Maugham v Hubbard*[17] a witness, called to prove that he had received a sum of money, looked at an unstamped acknowledgment signed by himself and thereupon gave evidence that he had no doubt that he had received the money although he had no recollection of having done so. It was held that the witness's oral evidence sufficed to establish receipt of the money, the written acknowledgment not being evidence in the case because it was unstamped.[18] It has always been inaccurate to describe the witness in such a case as having 'refreshed his memory'.[19] The term is equally inapposite in the case of the police officer who, with no recollection of the relevant events, simply reads from his notes. However, at common law, cases of 'past recollection recorded' are treated in the same way as cases of 'present recollection recorded' in that the oral evidence of the witness, and not the document, constitutes the evidence in the case.[20] The view that, in principle, it would be better to regard such out-of-court documentary statements as a variety of admissible hearsay,[21] has now been adopted in criminal proceedings. Under section 120 of the 2003 Act, in criminal proceedings, a previous statement of a witness, which may be a statement made orally or a statement made in a document, is admissible as evidence of any matter stated, provided that the witness testifies that to the best of his belief he made the statement and it states the truth, and that he does not remember the matters and cannot reasonably be expected to do so. Section 120(1), (4) and (6) of the 2003 Act provide as follows:

(1) This section applies where a person (the witness) is called to give evidence in criminal proceedings.

   ...

(4) A previous statement by the witness is admissible as evidence of any matter stated of which oral evidence by him would be admissible, if—
   (a) any of the following three conditions is satisfied, and
   (b) while giving evidence the witness indicates that to the best of his belief he made the statement, and to the best of his belief it states the truth.

(6) The second condition is that the statement was made by the witness when the matters stated were fresh in his memory but he does not remember them, and cannot reasonably be expected to remember them, well enough to give oral evidence of them in the proceedings.

---

[16] See J H Wigmore, *Evidence in Trials at Common Law*, vol 3 (rev J H Chadbourn) (Boston Mass, 1970) ch 28.

[17] (1828) 8 B&C 14.

[18] See also *R v Simmonds* [1969] 1 QB 685 CA.

[19] See per Hayes J in *Lord Talbot de Malahide v Cusack* (1864) 17 ICLR 213 at 220.

[20] See *Maugham v Hubbard* (1828) 8 B&C 14, but see also *R v Sekhon* (1987) 85 Cr App R 19 CA and *R v Virgo* (1978) 67 Cr App R 323, CA, both considered below.

[21] See, eg, the 5th edition of this book at 144.

Section 120(4) only applies in the case of a statement *made* by the witness, and has no application, therefore, in the case of a statement *verified* by him.

If, on a trial before a judge and jury, a statement made in a document is admitted in evidence under section 120, and the document or a copy of it is produced as an exhibit, the exhibit must not accompany the jury when they retire to consider their verdict unless the court considers it appropriate or all the parties to the proceedings agree that it should accompany the jury.[22]

The conditions

A document.   At common law a document includes a tape-recording,[23] but in criminal proceedings, for the purposes of section 139(1) of the 2003 Act, it means anything in which information of any description is recorded, but not including any recordings of sounds or moving images.[24]

Made or verified.   Both at common law and under section 139(1) of the 2003 Act, a witness may refresh his memory either from a document made by himself or by another, provided that, if made by another, the witness verified the document, ie checked the contents of the document, while the events were still fresh in his memory, and satisfied himself as to their accuracy.[25] For example, in *Anderson v Whalley*[26] it was held that entries in a ship's log-book made by the mate and verified by the captain about a week later could be used to refresh the memory of the latter. It is submitted that under section 139(1), as at common law, verification can be either visual or aural. In *R v Kelsey*,[27] H, a witness called for the prosecution, was allowed to refresh his memory as to the registration number of a car from a note which he had dictated to a police officer. The officer had read his note back aloud and H had confirmed that it was correct. Although H had seen the officer making the note, he had not read it himself. The officer gave evidence that the note used in court was the one that the witness saw him make. The Court of Appeal held that verification could be either visual or aural, the important matter being that the witness satisfies himself, while the matters are fresh in his mind, (i) that a record has been made; and (ii) that it is accurate. However, where a witness dictates a note to another, hears it read back, and confirms its accuracy without reading it himself, another witness must be called to prove that the note used in court is the one that was dictated and read back. The officer in the instant case having given evidence to that effect, Kelsey's appeal was dismissed.[28]

Contemporaneity.   At common law, but not under section 139 of the 2003 Act, the document, whether made or verified by the witness, 'must have been written either at the time of the transaction or so shortly afterwards that the facts were fresh in his memory'.[29] Commenting on this definition, the Court of Appeal has observed that it provides 'a measure of elasticity and

[22] Section 122 of the Criminal Justice Act 2003.
[23] *R v Bailey* [2001] All ER (D) 185 (Mar), [2001] EWCA Crim 733.
[24] Section 140.
[25] See *Burrough v Martin* (1809) 2 Camp 112 and *R v Langton* (1876) 2 QBD 296, CCR.
[26] (1852) 3 Car&Kir 54. See also *R v Sekhon* (1986) 85 Cr App R 19, CA and cf *R v Eleftheriou* [1993] Crim LR 947, CA.
[27] (1982) 74 Cr App R 213.
[28] Contrast *R v Mills* [1962] 1 WLR 1152, CCA at 1156, per Winn J, obiter. The officer's note, in *R v Kelsey*, would now be admissible as evidence of the matters stated under s 117 of the 2003 Act (business and other documents): see Ch 10.
[29] See *Phipson on Evidence* (11th edn, London, 1970) 634, para 1528.

should not be taken to confine witnesses to an over-short period'.[30] The question of whether a note is to be regarded as contemporaneous is a matter of fact and degree.[31] Thus the permitted gap between the date of the statement and that of the events to which it relates cannot be fixed with precision. The precedents are therefore of very limited value.[32]

Originals and copies. There is no requirement, either at common law or under section 139(1) of the 2003 Act, that the memory-refreshing document be the first or only document made or verified by the witness recording his recollection of the matters in question. A witness, therefore, may refresh his memory from a document which is based on original notes or a tape-recording made by him. In *A-G's Reference (No 3 of 1979)*[33] the Court of Appeal held that a police officer could refresh his memory from notes compiled, at a time when the facts were still fresh in his memory, from earlier brief jottings of an interview. In *R v Cheng*[34] the Court of Appeal held that a police officer was entitled to rely on a statement which was a partial but not exact copy of earlier notes from which it was prepared (and which were not available at the trial) on the grounds that the statement 'substantially' reproduced the notes. Similarly, in *R v Mills*[35] a police officer, who had heard and made a tape-recording of a conversation between two accused, was allowed to refer to his notes written up with the assistance of that tape-recording, which was not itself put in evidence. A witness may also refresh his memory from a copy of his original document, provided that the court is satisfied that the copy is accurate or substantially reproduces the contents of the original. Thus, in *Topham v McGregor*[36] the author of an article written some 14 years earlier was allowed to refresh his memory from a copy of the newspaper in which it had appeared, evidence being given of the destruction of the original and the accuracy of the copy. More recently, in *R v Chisnell*[37] an officer was allowed to use a statement made nine months after an interview and compiled on the basis of a contemporaneous note, the court being satisfied that the note, which had been lost, had been accurately transcribed into the statement. However, in cases of 'past recollection recorded' in which the original has *not* been lost or destroyed, then there is old authority that the original document must be used.[38]

Production of the document. A document used to refresh memory in court must be produced for inspection by the opposite party who may wish to cross-examine the witness on its contents.[39] At the request of the opposite party, the document may also be shown to the jury, if this is necessary to their determination of a point in issue in the case. In *R v Bass*[40] the only evidence against the appellant was a confession allegedly made to two police officers. They read identical accounts of the interview with the appellant but denied that they had been prepared in collaboration. The trial judge refused a defence application that the jury be allowed to examine

[30] *R v Richardson* [1971] 2 QB 484.
[31] *R v Simmonds* [1969] 1 QB 685, CA.
[32] *R v Woodcock* [1963] Crim LR 273, CCA (three-month gap treated as too long); *R v Graham* [1973] Crim LR 628, CA (one-month gap regarded as doubtful); *R v Fotheringham* [1975] Crim LR 710, CA (21-day gap accepted).
[33] (1979) 69 Cr App R 411.
[34] (1976) 63 Cr App R 20.
[35] [1962] 1 WLR 1152, CCA.
[36] (1844) 1 Car&Kir 320.
[37] [1992] Crim LR 507, CA.
[38] *Doe d Church and Phillips v Perkins* (1790) 3 Term Rep 749.
[39] *Beech v Jones* (1848) 5 CB 696.
[40] [1953] 1 QB 680, CCA; cf *R v Fenlon* (1980) 71 Cr App R 307, CA.

the notebooks. The Court of Criminal Appeal, allowing the appeal, held that the jury, by an inspection of the notebooks, might have been assisted in their evaluation of the credibility and accuracy of the officers.[41] Similarly, in cases in which the witness's evidence is long and involved, it may be convenient for the jury to use the document as an *aide memoire* as to that evidence, but care should be exercised in adopting this course in cases where the evidence is bitterly contested, because of the danger that the jury will improperly regard the document as constituting evidence in the case.[42]

Cross-examination on the document

In the majority of cases, the fact that there is cross-examination on the basis of a document used to refresh memory in court will neither entitle the jury to inspect the document nor make it evidence in the case.[43] Cross-examining counsel may inspect the document without thereby making it evidence[44] and may cross-examine on it without thereby making it evidence provided that his cross-examination goes no further than the parts which were used by the witness to refresh his memory. However, cross-examination on new matters deriving from other parts of the document not used by the witness to refresh his memory entitles the party calling the witness to put the document in evidence and to let the tribunal of fact see the document upon which such cross-examination is based.[45] Two other situations have been identified in which the document may be admitted in evidence.[46] First, where the nature of the cross-examination involves a suggestion that the witness has subsequently fabricated his evidence, which will usually involve the allegation that the record is concocted, the document is then admissible to rebut this suggestion and, if the document assists as to this, to show whether or not it has the appearance of being a contemporaneous record which has not subsequently been altered.[47] Secondly, where the document is inconsistent with the evidence, the document is then admissible as evidence of this inconsistency.

---

[41] The court also made it clear that it is not improper for two or more police officers to refresh their memories from notes in the making of which they have collaborated. See also *R (Saunders) v Independent Police Complaint Commission* [2009] 1 All ER 379 in which the Divisional Court, while acknowledging the risks of innocent contamination and deliberate collusion inherent in the practice, asserted that the pooling of recollections could also improve the accuracy of an officer's notes, for example, by reminding him of something which he had forgotten, correcting something which he had misstated, or helping him to make sense of confused recollections. Moreover, a prohibition on the practice would have serious operational disadvantages. However, as a general rule discussions between witnesses as to the evidence they will give should not take place: *R v Skinner* (1993) 99 Cr App R 212, CA. If they have taken place, each case should be dealt with on its own facts. If the discussion may have led to fabrication, it may be unsafe to leave any of the evidence to the jury. In other cases it may suffice to direct the jury on the implications of such conduct in relation to the reliability of the evidence. See *R v Arif* (1993) The Times, 17 June, CA.

[42] Per Woolf LJ in *R v Sekhon* (1986) 85 Cr App R 19 at 23, CA: the document may also be put before the jury where it is difficult for them to follow the *cross-examination* of the witness who has refreshed his memory without having the document before them. But cf *R v Dillon* (1983) 85 Cr App R 29, CA.

[43] Per Woolf LJ in *R v Sekhon* (1986) 85 Cr App R 19 at 22, CA.

[44] There is an obscure common law rule that a party calling for and inspecting a document in the possession of the other party which has *not* been used to refresh a witness's memory must put it in evidence if called upon so to do. See *Wharam v Routledge* (1805) 5 Esp 235 and *Stroud v Stroud* [1963] 1 WLR 1080 P, D and Admlty (see Ch 7).

[45] *Gregory v Tavernor* (1833) 6 C&P 280; *Senat v Senat* [1965] P 172 P, D and Admlty per Sir Jocelyn Simon P at 177; *R v Britton* [1987] 1 WLR 539, CA.

[46] *R v Sekhon* (1986) 85 Cr App R 19 at 22–3, CA.

[47] Cf *R v Fenlon* (1980) 71 Cr App R 307, CA and *R v Dillon* (1983) 85 Cr App R 29, CA.

Where, as a result of cross-examination, a memory-refreshing document is admitted in evidence in civil proceedings, it is admitted as evidence of any matter stated. Under section 1 of the Civil Evidence Act 1995 (the 1995 Act), in civil proceedings evidence shall not be excluded on the ground that it is hearsay. Section 6(4) and (5) of the 1995 Act provide as follows:

(4) Nothing in this Act affects any of the rules of law as to the circumstances in which, where a person called as a witness in civil proceedings is cross-examined on a document used by him to refresh his memory, that document may be made evidence in the proceedings.

(5) Nothing in this section shall be construed as preventing a statement of any description referred to above from being admissible by virtue of s 1 as evidence of the matters stated.

Although section 6(5) refers to 'a statement of any description referred to above' and section 6(4) makes no reference to a 'statement' as such, it seems reasonably clear that the parliamentary intention was to perpetuate the rule formerly stated with clarity in section 3(2) of the Civil Evidence Act 1968, ie that where a memory-refreshing document is made evidence in civil proceedings, any statement made in the document is admissible as evidence of any matter stated therein.

Where, as a result of cross-examination, a memory-refreshing document *made* by a witness is admitted in evidence in criminal proceedings, it is admitted as evidence of any matter stated. Section 120(1) and (3) of the 2003 Act provide as follows:

(1) This section applies where a person (the witness) is called to give evidence in criminal proceedings.
. . .
(3) A statement made by the witness in a document—
(a) which is used by him to refresh his memory while giving evidence,
(b) on which he is cross-examined, and
(c) which as a consequence is received in evidence in the proceedings,
is admissible as evidence of any matter stated of which oral evidence by him would be admissible.

Section 120(1) and (3) provide not for the circumstances in which a documentary statement may be received in evidence, but merely for the evidential status of a document where it is received in evidence.[48]

Section 120 does not apply in the case of a statement *verified* by a witness which, as a result of cross-examination, is admitted in evidence. In criminal proceedings, therefore, such a statement is not admitted as evidence of any of the matters stated in it, but as evidence of the witness's consistency or inconsistency, going only to his credit.

If, on a trial before a judge and jury, a statement made in a document is admitted in evidence under section 120, and the document or a copy of it is produced as an exhibit, the exhibit must not accompany the jury when they retire to consider their verdict unless the court considers it appropriate or all the parties to the proceedings agree that it should accompany the jury.[49]

Refreshing the memory out of court

It is a common practice, in both civil and criminal proceedings, for witnesses, before going into the witness box, to look at and refresh their memories from their own previous statements.

[48] *R v Pashmfouroush* [2007] All ER (D) 45 (Feb), [2006] EWCA Crim 2330.
[49] Section 122 of the Criminal Justice Act 2003.

Such a statement may have been made by a witness for some personal reason, may constitute a 'proof of evidence' made at the request of the solicitor for the party calling him or, in the case of a prosecution witness, may be a signed statement which he made to the police.[50] Whatever form it takes, however, it would appear that the conditions on which a witness may refresh his memory while giving evidence do not apply to the witness who refreshes his memory outside the witness box.[51] In *R v Richardson*[52] the Court of Appeal approved the following two observations of the Supreme Court of Hong Kong in *Lau Pak Ngam v R*:[53]

1. Testimony in the witness box becomes more a test of memory than of truthfulness if witnesses are deprived of the opportunity of checking their recollection beforehand by reference to statements or notes made at a time closer to the events in question.

2. Refusal of access to statements would tend to create difficulties for honest witnesses but be likely to do little to hamper dishonest witnesses.

However, it was also observed in *R v Richardson* that it would obviously be wrong for several witnesses to be handed statements in circumstances enabling one to compare with another what each had said. Equally, as a general rule, discussions between witnesses, particularly just before going into court to give evidence, should not take place, and statements or proofs should not be read to witnesses in each other's presence.[54] It is incumbent on prosecuting authorities and judges to ensure that witnesses are informed that they should not discuss cases in which they are involved.[55]

In *R v Da Silva*[56] it was held that it is open to the judge, in the exercise of his discretion and in the interests of justice, to permit a witness who has begun to give his evidence, to withdraw and refresh his memory from a statement made near to the time of the events in question, even if not 'contemporaneous', provided he is satisfied that: (i) the witness indicates that he cannot now recall the details of the events because of the lapse of time; (ii) he made a statement much nearer the time of the event,[57] the contents of which represented his recollection at the time he made it; (iii) he has not read the statement before giving evidence; and (iv) he wishes to read the statement before he continues to give evidence. It does not matter whether the witness withdraws from the witness box to read his statement or reads it in the witness box, but if the former course is adopted, no communication must be had with the witness other than to see that he can read the statement in peace. If either course is adopted, the statement must be removed from him when he continues to give his evidence and he should not be permitted to refer to it again. However, in criminal proceedings, the witness may be permitted to make further use of the document to refresh

---

[50] A circular issued in April 1969, with the approval of the Lord Chief Justice and the judges of the Queen's Bench Division, recognized that prosecution witnesses are normally entitled, if they so request, to copies of any statements taken from them by the police.

[51] Yet see *R v Thomas* [1994] Crim LR 745, CA, where, for reasons that are not disclosed, it was held to be undesirable for a child aged 8 to be shown her signed police statement. See also *Owen v Edwards* (1983) 77 Cr App R 191, DC, below.

[52] [1971] 2 QB 484.

[53] [1966] Crim LR 443.

[54] *R v Skinner* (1993) 99 Cr App R 212, CA at 216.

[55] *R v Shaw* [2002] All ER (D) 79 (Dec), [2002] EWCA Crim 3004.

[56] [1990] 1 WLR 31, CA.

[57] On the facts of the case, the statement was made one month after the events to which it related.

his memory in the witness box, provided that the conditions of section 139 of the 2003 Act are met.[58]

In *R v South Ribble Magistrates' Court, ex p Cochrane*[59] it was held that *R v Da Silva* does not lay down as a matter of law that all four conditions to which it refers must be satisfied, because the court has a 'real discretion', ie a choice free of binding criteria, whether to permit a witness to refresh his memory from a non-contemporaneous statement. In that case it was held that a witness who had read his statement before giving evidence, but who had not taken it in properly, and therefore did not satisfy condition (iii), had been properly permitted to refresh his memory. The discretion is a broad fact-sensitive discretion to be exercised in the interests of fairness and justice.[60]

The fact that a witness has refreshed his memory out of court and before entering the witness box may be relevant to the weight which can properly be attached to his evidence, so that in a criminal case injustice may be caused to the accused if the matter is not brought to the attention of the jury. For this reason, the Court of Appeal in *R v Westwell*[61] held that the prosecution, if aware that statements have been seen by their witnesses, should inform the defence. Informing the defence, however, is 'desirable but not essential' and 'if for any reason this is not done, the omission cannot of itself be a ground for acquittal'.[62] *R v Westwell* left undecided the question whether a party may call for, inspect, and cross-examine on a document which a witness called by the opposite party has used to refresh his memory outside court but has not used while giving evidence. The issue arose in *Owen v Edwards*.[63] A policeman, outside the court room and before giving evidence for the prosecution, refreshed his memory from a notebook which he did not use in the witness box. The Divisional Court held that defence counsel was entitled not only to inspect the notebook but also to cross-examine the witness upon relevant matters contained in it. It was further held that although defence counsel may cross-examine upon the material in the notebook from which the witness has refreshed his memory without the notebook being made evidence in the case, if he cross-examines on material in the notebook which has not been referred to by the witness, he runs the risk of the notebook being put in evidence. McNeill J said: 'the rules which apply to refreshing memory in the witness box should be the same as those which apply if memory has been refreshed outside the door of the court'.[64] As we have seen, in civil cases, the document will be admitted as evidence of the matters stated. The same applies in criminal cases, but only in the case of statements made, as opposed to verified, by the witness. The weight to be attached to the documentary evidence will obviously vary according to the precise circumstances, but a note made a long time after the events in question, may be viewed by the tribunal of fact with considerable caution, if not suspicion.

[58] See above.

[59] [1996] 2 Cr App R 544, DC.

[60] *R v Gordon* [2002] All ER (D) 99 (Feb), [2002] EWCA Crim 412, where a witness who was dyslexic and unable to read the statement himself, adopted it after it had been read out to him by counsel in the absence of the jury.

[61] [1976] 2 All ER 812. See also *Worley v Bentley* [1976] 2 All ER 449, DC.

[62] See also, *sed quaere*, *R v H* [1992] Crim LR 516, CA: child victims of sexual offences should only refresh their memory out of court with the *consent* of the defence.

[63] (1983) 77 Cr App R 191.

[64] Ibid at 195.

Previous consistent or self-serving statements

The general rule

There is a general common law rule that a witness may not be asked in examination-in-chief about former oral or written statements made by him and consistent with his evidence in the proceedings. Evidence of the earlier statement may not be given either by the witness who made it or by any other witness. The reason usually given for the rule is the danger of manufactured evidence.[65] A resourceful witness, minded to deceive the court, could with ease deliberately repeat his version of the facts to a number of people prior to trial with a view to showing consistency with the story he tells in the witness box, thereby bolstering his credibility.[66]

The rule also applies to re-examination. Thus the credibility of a witness may not be bolstered by evidence of a previous consistent statement merely because his testimony has been impeached in cross-examination.[67] This remains the case 'even if the impeachment takes the form of showing a contradiction or inconsistency between the evidence given at the trial and something said by the witness on a former occasion'.[68] However, the court does have a residual discretion to permit re-examination to show consistency by reference to a previous statement to ensure that the jury is not positively misled by the cross-examination as to the existence of some fact or the terms of an earlier statement.[69]

The rule is distinct from the common law rule against hearsay, whereby an out-of-court statement is inadmissible as evidence of the facts stated. A previous consistent or self-serving statement of a witness is excluded as evidence of his consistency. The distinction may be illustrated by the following two cases. In *Corke v Corke and Cook*[70] a husband petitioned for divorce on the ground of adultery. Late one night he had accused his wife of having recently committed adultery with a lodger. The Court of Appeal held that the wife, who denied adultery, had been improperly permitted to give evidence that some 10 minutes after the husband's accusation she had telephoned her doctor and asked him to examine herself and the lodger with a view to showing that there had been no recent sexual intercourse. In *R v Roberts*[71] the accused was convicted of the murder of a girl by shooting her. His defence was that the gun went off accidentally while he was trying to make up a quarrel with the girl. Evidence that two days after the event the accused had told his father that his defence would be accident was held by the Court of Criminal Appeal to have been properly excluded. In both of these cases the evidence in question was hearsay and inadmissible as evidence of the facts stated, that is to show in the one case that there was no sexual intercourse and in the other that the gun went off accidentally. But it was also inadmissible, by reason of the

---

[65] See, eg, per Humphreys J in *R v Roberts* [1942] 1 All ER 187, CCA at 191.

[66] But see *Fennell v Jerome Property Maintenance Ltd* (1986) The Times, 26 Nov, QBD: as a matter of principle, evidence produced by the administration of some mechanical, chemical, or hypnotic truth test on a witness is inadmissible to show the veracity (or otherwise) of that witness. See also *R v McKay* [1967] NZLR 139, NZCA: a psychiatrist is not permitted to give evidence of statements made by the accused while under the influence of a truth drug and consistent with his (the accused's) evidence.

[67] *R v Coll* (1889) 25 LR Ir 522.

[68] Per Holmes J (1889) 25 LR Ir 522 at 541. See also *R v Weekes* [1988] Crim LR 244, CA; *R v Beattie* (1989) 89 Cr App R 302, CA per Lord Lane CJ at 306–7; and *R v P (GR)* [1998] Crim LR 663, CA. Contrast, *sed quaere, Ahmed v Brumfitt* (1967) 112 Sol Jo 32, CA.

[69] *R v Ali* [2004] 1 Cr App R 501, CA.

[70] [1958] P 93.

[71] [1942] 1 All ER 187.

rule against previous consistent statements, to bolster the credibility of the witnesses in question by demonstrating their consistency.

Where a previous statement of a witness is admitted as hearsay, ie as evidence of the matters stated, it will also be received as evidence of consistency. Thus a decision such as *Corke v Corke and Cook* might be decided differently today, because in civil proceedings the previous statements of a witness may be admitted, with the leave of the court, both as evidence of the matters stated, and also, therefore, as evidence of consistency, under section 6(2) of the 1995 Act. The admissibility of such statements is considered in Chapter 11. Similarly, if a previous statement of a witness is admitted in criminal proceedings as evidence of the matters stated, under section 114(1)(c) of the 2003 Act, ie where all parties agree to it being admissible, or under section 114(1)(d) of that Act, ie where the court is satisfied that it is in the interests of justice for it to be admissible, then it will also be received as evidence of consistency.

To the rule against previous consistent statements, there are a number of common law exceptions. The statutory categories of admissible hearsay now embrace almost all of the varieties of statement admissible by way of the common law exceptions to the rule against previous consistent statements, in some cases expanding their scope. Such justification as there is for separate treatment of the common law exceptions stems from the fact that (a) the overlap is not total (wholly exculpatory statements made on accusation, for example, are not admissible as evidence of the matters asserted); (b) Parliament has elected not to repeal any of the common law exceptions; and (c) in some cases (statements admissible to rebut allegations of recent fabrication and statements in documents used to refresh the memory and received in evidence), Parliament, rather than give the common law exception a statutory formulation, has chosen to identify it as a category of hearsay by simply referring to the circumstances in which the statement may be admitted at common law.

The common law exceptions

Complaints in sexual cases

If, in cases of rape and other sexual offences, the complainant made a voluntary complaint shortly after the alleged offence, the person to whom the complaint was made may give evidence of the particulars of that complaint in order to show the consistency of that conduct with the complainant's evidence and, in cases in which consent is in issue, to negative consent. Section 120(7) of the 2003 Act has extended the principle to cover a previous statement by a person against whom *any* offence has been committed, provided that it is an offence to which the proceedings relate, that the statement consists of a complaint about conduct which would, if proved, constitute the offence, and the complainant, in giving evidence, indicates that to the best of his belief, he made the statement and it states the truth. A statement received under section 120(7) is admissible as evidence of the matters stated and, provided that the evidence is given by the person to whom the complaint was made,[72] also goes to the consistency of the witness. Section 120(7), which is considered in Chapter 10, is much wider than the common law exception. The common law exception, therefore, is likely to be invoked only rarely and falls to be considered in outline only.

---

[72] See *White v R* [1999] 1 Cr App R 153, PC.

The common law exception applies to written, as well as oral, complaints, and even extends to a written note given to a friend by mistake.[73] Where the exception applies, it is essential to direct the jury that the complaint is not evidence of the facts complained of, and cannot be independent confirmation of the complainant's evidence since it does not come from a source independent of her, but may assist in assessing her veracity.[74]

In *White v R*[75] it was held that if the person to whom the complaint was made does not give evidence, the complainant's own evidence that she made a complaint cannot assist in either proving her consistency or negativing consent because, without independent confirmation, her own evidence that she complained takes the jury nowhere in deciding whether she is worthy of belief. In that case, Lord Hoffmann held that although it does not follow that evidence that the complainant spoke to someone after the incident is inadmissible, the complainant should not be allowed to say that she had told people 'what had happened', because the jury will be bound to infer that she had made statements in terms substantially the same as her evidence. It was also held that where evidence is given of the bare fact that the complainant spoke to someone after the incident, it is incumbent on the judge to give the jury clear instructions that they are not entitled to treat the evidence as confirming the complainant's credibility.

Rape and other sexual offences. The common law exception applies only in the case of complaints of rape and other sexual offences, but is not restricted to sexual offences where absence of consent is among the facts in issue.[76] Nor is the exception confined to sexual offences against females.[77]

The fact and the particulars of the complaint. There is a two-stage test for the jury to follow, first to decide whether the recent complaint was in fact made and, if so, secondly to decide whether it is consistent with the complainant's evidence.[78] In *R v Lillyman*,[79] it was held that the person to whom the complaint had been made could give detailed evidence as to what the complainant had said. To limit evidence to the bare fact that the complaint was made would be to leave to the witness to whom the statement was made determination of the question whether a complaint really was made and thereby prevent the jurors from judging for themselves whether the complaint in question was consistent with the complainant's evidence.

Consistency is a question of degree. In *R v S*[80] it was held that evidence of a recent complaint will be admissible where it is sufficiently consistent that it can, depending on the view of the evidence taken by the jury, support or enhance the credibility of the complainant. Whether the complaint is sufficiently consistent must depend on the facts. It is not necessary that the complaint discloses the ingredients of the offence, but it is usually necessary that it discloses evidence of material and relevant unlawful sexual conduct on the part of the accused which can support the complainant's credibility. Thus it is not usually necessary that the complaint

[73] *R v B* [1997] Crim LR 220, CA.
[74] *R v Islam* [1999] 1 Cr App R 22, CA, applied in *R v NK* [1999] Crim LR 980, CA.
[75] [1999] 1 Cr App R 153, PC.
[76] *R v Osborne* [1905] 1 KB 551, CCR.
[77] *R v Camelleri* [1922] 2 KB 122, CCA. See also *R v Wannell* (1924) 17 Cr App R 53, CCA. Cf *R v Christie* [1914] AC 545 which must now be viewed as wrongly decided on this point.
[78] *R v Hartley* [2003] All ER (D) 208 (Oct), [2003] EWCA Crim 3027.
[79] [1896] 2 QB 167, CCR.
[80] [2004] 1 WLR 2940, CA.

describes the full extent of the unlawful sexual conduct alleged by the complainant in the witness box, provided that it is capable of supporting the credibility of the complainant's evidence. Differences may be accounted for by a variety of matters, including for example the complainant's reluctance to disclose the full extent of the conduct at the time of the complaint, but it is for the jury to assess such matters.

Voluntariness. It is a condition of the admissibility of a complaint in a sexual case that it should have been made voluntarily, and not in reply to questions of a suggestive, leading or intimidating character. In *R v Osbourne*[81] it was held that if the circumstances indicate that but for the questioning there probably would have been no voluntary complaint, the answer is inadmissible.

The time of complaint. A complaint is only admissible in evidence under the exception 'when it is made at the first opportunity after the offence which reasonably offers itself'.[82] In every case, the court must also be satisfied that the complaint was 'recent'.[83] Whether a complaint was made as soon as was reasonably practicable after the occurrence of the offence is a question of fact and degree to be decided by the judge in each case.[84] The answer will depend on the circumstances, including the character of the complainant and the relationship between the complainant and the person to whom she might have complained but did not do so. Victims often need time before they can bring themselves to tell what has happened, and whereas some will find it impossible to complain to anyone other than a parent or member of their family, others may feel it impossible to tell their parents or members of their family.[85] As to 'recency', in *R v Birks*[86] it was held, albeit reluctantly, that a complaint made at the earliest two months after the alleged offences, was inadmissible, notwithstanding that the complaint was made spontaneously, that the alleged offences began when the accused was only 5 or 6 years old, and that the accused had allegedly threatened her by saying that if she told her mother she would be put in a home.

Admissibility to show consistency. At common law, the complaint is not evidence of the facts complained of and may be used only as evidence of the consistency of the complaint with the testimony of the complainant and, in cases where consent is in issue, as evidence inconsistent with consent. Thus if the terms of the complaint are not ostensibly consistent with the terms of the complainant's testimony, the introduction of the complaint has no purpose.[87] Likewise, in cases where the complainant does not testify, there being no evidence with which the complaint may be consistent, the particulars of the complaint are inadmissible.[88] It is submitted that evidence of the mere fact of the complaint, inadmissible as evidence of the facts complained of, and clearly incapable of showing consistency, should similarly be excluded.[89]

---

[81] [1905] 1 KB 551, CCR at 556.

[82] Per Ridley J [1905] 1 KB 551, CCR at 561. See also *R v Cummings* [1948] 1 All ER 551, CCA. However, the fact that the complaint was not the first to be made is not, per se, sufficient to exclude it: *R v Wilbourne* (1917) 12 Cr App R 280, CCA.

[83] *R v Birks* [2003] 2 Cr App R 122, CA.

[84] A complaint made one week after the offence was admitted in *R v Hedges* (1910) 3 Cr App R 262, CCA.

[85] *R v Valentine* [1996] 2 Cr App R 213, CA.

[86] [2003] 2 Cr App R 122, CA.

[87] *R v Wright* and *R v Ormerod* (1987) 90 Cr App R 91, CA.

[88] See, eg, *R v Wallwork*, (1958) 42 Cr App R 153, CCA.

[89] See Cross (1958) 74 LQR 352. See also per Lord Hoffmann in *White v R* [1999] 1 AC 210, PC at 218.

Where evidence of a complaint is admitted but it is, in part, inconsistent with the evidence given by the complainant in the witness box, the judge should make clear to the jury the extent and significance of the inconsistency, drawing to their attention any reason given for the inconsistency and telling them that it is for them to take all these matters into account in deciding whether the complainant is telling the truth.[90]

Admissibility to negative consent.   In cases where consent is in issue, evidence of a complaint is admissible as evidence inconsistent with such consent. Australian authority suggests that the complaint is received as evidence relevant to the credibility of the victim who, in testifying, denies consent.[91]

Statements admissible to rebut allegations of recent fabrication

If, in cross-examination, it is suggested to a witness that his account of some incident or set of facts is a recent invention or fabrication, evidence of prior statements made by him to the same effect is admissible to support his credit.[92] 'Recent' in this context should not be confined within a temporal straightjacket but should be understood as an 'elastic' description which ought not extend to the exclusion of a previous consistent statement where there is a rational and cogent basis on which it could assist the tribunal of fact in determining where the truth lies.[93] Such prior statements will normally be put to the witness in re-examination. In *R v Oyesiku*[94] the accused was convicted of assaulting a police officer. In cross-examination, it was put to the accused's wife, who had given evidence that the police officer was the aggressor, that her evidence had been recently fabricated. The Court of Appeal held that the trial judge had improperly refused to admit evidence of a previous statement consistent with her testimony and made by her to a solicitor after her husband's arrest but before she had seen him. Karminski LJ, giving the judgment of the court, accepted as a correct statement of the law the judgment of Dixon CJ in *Nominal Defendant v Clement*,[95] from which the following propositions derive. The exception is brought into play where it is suggested in cross-examination that the witness's account 'is a late invention or has been recently reconstructed, even though not with conscious dishonesty'. The prior statement is admissible 'if it was made by the witness contemporaneously with the event or at a time sufficiently early to be inconsistent with the suggestion that his account is a late invention or reconstruction'. The judge, in determining whether the exception h as been brought into play, should exercise care to assure himself of the following three matters: (i) 'that the account given by the witness in his testimony is attacked on the ground of recent invention or reconstruction or that a foundation for such an attack has been laid'; (ii) 'that the contents of the statement are in fact to the like effect as his account given in his evidence'; and (iii) 'that having regard to the time and circumstances in which it was made, it (the statement) rationally tends to answer the attack'.

In both civil and criminal proceedings, the previous consistent statement is now admissible both to negative the suggestion of invention or reconstruction and thereby confirm

[90] *R v S* [2004] 1 WLR 2940, CA.

[91] *Kilby v R* (1973) 129 CLR 460, High Court of Australia.

[92] Evidence of a complaint in a sexual case may be admissible on this basis notwithstanding that it was not made at the first reasonably practicable opportunity (see above): *R v Tyndale* [1999] Crim LR 320, CA.

[93] *R v Athwal* [2009] 1 WLR 2430, CA at [58].

[94] (1971) 56 Cr App R 240. See also *R v Benjamin* (1913) 8 Cr App R 146, CCA; *Flanagan v Fahy* [1918] 2 IR 361, Ir KBD; and *Fox v General Medical Council* [1960] 1 WLR 1017, PC.

[95] (1961) 104 CLR 476, High Court of Australia. The extracts given in the text are at 479.

the witness's credit, and as evidence of the matters stated. Under section 1 of the 1995 Act, in civil proceedings evidence shall not be excluded on the ground that it is hearsay. Section 6(2) and (5) of the 1995 Act provide as follows:

> (2) A party who has called or intends to call a person as a witness in civil proceedings may not in those proceedings adduce evidence of a previous statement made by that person, except—
>
> . . .
>
> (b) for the purposes of rebutting a suggestion that his evidence has been fabricated.
>
> . . .
>
> (5) Nothing in this section shall be construed as preventing a statement of any description referred to above from being admissible by virtue of section 1 as evidence of the matters stated.

In criminal proceedings, section 120(1) and (2) of the 2003 Act provide as follows:

> (1) This section applies where a person (the witness) is called to give evidence in criminal proceedings.
> (2) If a previous statement by the witness is admitted as evidence to rebut a suggestion that his oral evidence has been fabricated, that statement is admissible as evidence of any matter stated of which oral evidence by the witness would be admissible.

Section 120(1) and (2) do not provide for the circumstances in which a previous statement by a witness may be received in evidence, but merely regulate the use to which such evidence, once admitted, may be put.[96] It follows that although section 120(2) omits reference to the recency of the fabrication, this omission does not, as one commentator has suggested,[97] mean that it is no longer a requirement for admissibility.

Statements made on accusation

Provided that the conditions of admissibility are satisfied, and subject to the exclusionary discretion of the court, an admission made by an accused is admissible, by way of exception to the general rule against hearsay, as evidence of the facts contained in it.[98] There is also, however, a well-established practice on the part of the prosecution, which has been approved by the Court of Appeal,[99] 'to admit in evidence all unwritten and most written statements made by an accused person to the police whether they contain admissions or whether they contain denials of guilt'. If such statements are wholly exculpatory, they are not admitted as evidence of the facts stated. In *R v Storey*,[100] the police having found a large quantity of cannabis in the accused's flat, she explained that it belonged to a man who had brought it there against her will. The Court of Appeal upheld the judge's rejection of a submission of no case to answer, at the close of the prosecution case, on the ground that the accused's statement was not evidence of the facts contained in it. The statement was admissible 'because of its vital relevance as showing the reaction of the accused when first taxed with the incriminating facts'.[101] It does not follow from these words, however, that the only statements admissible as evidence of reaction are those which the accused made on the first encounter with his accusers. In *R v Pearce*[102] the Court of Appeal decided that statements subsequently made are also admissible, although 'the longer the time that has elapsed after the first encounter the less the weight

---

[96] *R v T* [2008] EWCA Crim 484. See also *R v Athwal* [2009] 1 WLR 2430, CA.

[97] D Ormerod, '*R v Athwal*' (case comment) [2009] Crim LR 726. See also R Pattenden, '*R v Athwal*' (case comment) (2009) 13 E&P 342.

[98] See Ch 13.

[99] *R v Pearce* (1979) 69 Cr App R 365, CA at 368 and 370.

[100] (1968) 52 Cr App R 334.

[101] Per Widgery LJ at 337.

[102] (1979) 69 Cr App R 365 at 369.

which will be attached to the denial', a matter on which the judge may direct the jury. Thus, in that case it was held that a judge had improperly excluded self-serving statements made by the accused to the police after his arrest, which took place two days after he was first taxed by his employer's security officer with incriminating facts relating to handling stolen goods. However, this principle cannot be relied upon to admit a statement which adds nothing to evidence of reaction which has already been admitted. In *R v Tooke*[103] the accused made an exculpatory statement shortly after the time of the offence. Some 40 minutes later, he went to the police station and made a spontaneous exculpatory witness statement. The first statement was admitted, but the defence were not permitted to cross-examine a constable to prove the statement made at the station. The fact that it was a witness statement and not a statement in answer to a charge made no difference, because the same test applied. It was inadmissible because it added nothing to the evidence of reaction already before the jury.

Impromptu exculpatory statements made on accusation are admissible as evidence of consistency in the case of an accused who testifies. However, in a case where the accused gives no evidence, there is no duty on the judge to remind the jury of voluntary statements made by the accused to the police exonerating himself.[104] Moreover, the accused will not be permitted to take unfair advantage of the rule:

> Although in practice most statements are given in evidence even when they are largely self-serving, there may be a rare occasion when an accused produces a carefully prepared written statement to the police, with a view to it being made a part of the prosecution evidence. The trial judge would probably exclude such a statement as inadmissible.[105]

A careful distinction needs to be drawn between a purely exculpatory statement and a 'mixed' statement, that is a statement containing both inculpatory and exculpatory parts, such as 'I killed X. If I had not done so, X would certainly have killed me there and then.'[106] When the prosecution admits in evidence a statement relied upon as an admission, the whole statement, including qualifications, explanations, and other exculpatory parts of it favourable to the accused, becomes admissible. Any other course would be unfair and misleading.[107] The jury must decide whether the statement viewed as a whole constitutes an admission. As to the question whether the judge should then direct the jury (a) that the statement is not evidence of the facts contained in it except insofar as it constitutes an admission (the 'purist' approach); or (b) that the whole statement is evidence of the truth of the facts it contains (the 'common sense' approach), in *R v Duncan*[108] the Court of Appeal came down firmly in favour of the latter approach. The appellant, who elected not to testify, was convicted of murder. He had made a statement in which he admitted that he killed a woman but suggested that he must have lost his temper when she teased him. The trial judge held that insofar as his statements were self-serving, they were not evidence of the facts contained in them. Rejecting this reasoning as erroneous, Lord Lane CJ, in a

[103] (1989) 90 Cr App R 417, CA.

[104] *R v Barbery* (1975) 62 Cr App R 248, CA. Contrast *R v Donaldson* (1977) 64 Cr App R 59, CA at 69.

[105] *R v Pearce* (1979) 69 Cr App R 365, CA at 370. See, eg, *R v Newsome* (1980) 71 Cr App R 325, CA. Such a statement remains inadmissible notwithstanding that access to the solicitor is delayed by the police in exercise of their right to do so under s 58 of the Police and Criminal Evidence Act, 1984: *R v Hutton* (1988) The Times, 27 Oct, CA.

[106] See per Lord Lane CJ in *R v Duncan* (1981) 73 Cr App R 359, CA at 364.

[107] *R v Pearce* (1979) 69 Cr App R 365, CA at 369–70.

[108] (1981) 73 Cr App R 359.

dictum which has subsequently been applied by the Court of Appeal (*R v Hamand*[109]) and unanimously endorsed by the House of Lords (*R v Sharp*[110]), said:[111]

> Where a 'mixed' statement is under consideration by the jury in a case where the defendant has not given evidence, it seems to us that the simplest, and, therefore, the method most likely to produce a just result, is for the jury to be told that the whole statement, both the incriminating parts and the excuses or explanations, must be considered by them in deciding where the truth lies. It is, to say the least, not helpful to try to explain to the jury that the exculpatory parts of the statement are something less than evidence of the facts they state. Equally, where appropriate, as it usually will be, the judge may, and should, point out that the incriminatory parts are likely to be true (otherwise why say them?) whereas the excuses do not have the same weight.

The requirement that the judge direct the jury on how to approach the weight to be attached to the respective parts of a mixed statement is open to criticism. In *R v Rojas*[112] the Supreme Court of Canada refused to adopt the direction on the ground that in most circumstances expounding the rationale for an evidentiary rule may only serve to confuse the jury unnecessarily or risk encroaching unduly upon their role as fact finders. Such observations may be better left to the advocacy of counsel.

The principle established in *R v Duncan* applies whether the 'mixed' statement is a written statement or a record of questions and answers at an interview.[113] In the case of a suspect who asserts his innocence, his answers in interview will almost always contain *some* admissions of relevant fact, but statements will only be treated as 'mixed' for the purposes of the principle if they contain an admission of fact which is 'significant' in relation to an issue in the case, ie capable of adding some degree of weight to the prosecution case on an issue which is relevant to guilt.[114] The admission in interview of an ingredient of the offence will often constitute a significant admission.[115] However, there is no requirement that any act admitted be unlawful per se.[116] Whether a mixed statement is 'significant' in relation to an issue in the case can only be determined by reference to what happens at trial and, therefore, can only be finally resolved at the close of the evidence. In particular, the greater the reliance the prosecution place on the inculpatory parts of the statement at trial, the more likely it is that the jury should be told that the exculpatory parts are also evidence in the case.[117]

It remains unclear whether the principle applies if the statement is not relied on by the prosecution. On one view, the self-serving parts of the statement are only admissible for their truth if the prosecution elect to rely on the statement as containing an admission.[118] However, it is submitted that there are compelling reasons against any such additional requirement. As Butterfield J pointed out in *Western v DPP*,[119] whether a statement is mixed or not should not

---

[109] (1985) 82 Cr App R 65, CA.

[110] [1988] 1 WLR 7. See also *R v Aziz* [1995] AC 41, HL.

[111] (1981) 73 Cr App R 359 at 365. The appeal was dismissed, however, because on the facts nothing in the statements amounted to a claim of provocation.

[112] [2008] SCC 56; [2009] Crim LR 130.

[113] *R v Polin* [1991] Crim LR 293, CA.

[114] *R v Garrod* [1997] Crim LR 445, CA. See also *R v Papworth* [2008] 1 Cr App R 439, CA.

[115] *R v Papworth*, ibid.

[116] *R v McCleary* [1994] Crim LR 121, CA.

[117] *R v Papworth* [2008] 1 Cr App R 439, CA.

[118] See per Lord Steyn in *R v Aziz* [1995] AC 41, HL at 50.

[119] [1997] 1 Cr App R 474, DC at 484–5.

depend on the accident of what other evidence is available to the prosecution; and in cases in which the statement is *not* relied on by the prosecution, the view advanced would mean reviving the unintelligible direction, repudiated in *R v Duncan*, to the effect that although the admission is evidence of the facts stated, the self-serving parts of the statement are only evidence of reaction.[120]

The common law rule relating to the admissibility of mixed statements as evidence of the matters stated is among the common law rules preserved by section 118 of the 2003 Act.[121]

Statements made on discovery of incriminating articles

In cases of handling and theft, if it is shown that the accused was found in possession of recently stolen goods, but failed to give a credible innocent explanation, the jury *may* infer guilty knowledge or belief and return a finding of guilt.[122] Any explanation which is given by the accused is admissible, if the accused testifies to the same effect, as evidence of consistency.[123]

Previous identification

Where, in criminal proceedings, a witness gives evidence identifying the accused as the person who committed the offence charged, evidence of a previous identification of the accused by that witness may be given, either by the witness himself or by any other person who witnessed the previous identification,[124] for example a police officer who conducted a formal identification procedure such as a video identification or an identification parade, as evidence of consistency.[125] Section 120(5) of the 2003 Act, when read in conjunction with section 120(1) and (4) of the 2003 Act, has extended the principle to cover a previous statement of a witness which identifies *or describes* a person, *object or place*, provided that the witness, while giving evidence, indicates that to the best of his belief, he made the statement and it states the truth. A statement received under section 120(5) is admitted as evidence of any matter stated, and will also be evidence of the witness's consistency. Section 120(5) is considered in Chapter 10. The text which follows relates to the common law principle.

In *R v Christie*[126] the accused was convicted of indecent assault on a boy. The boy gave unsworn evidence in which he described the assault, and identified the accused, but made no reference to any previous identification. The House of Lords, by a majority of five to two, held that both the boy's mother and a constable had been properly allowed to give evidence

---

[120] See generally Di Birch, 'The Sharp End of the Wedge: Use of Mixed Statements by the Defence' [1997] Crim LR 416.

[121] Section 118(1) 5.

[122] See Ch 22, 653 under *The presumption of guilty knowledge*.

[123] See *R v Abraham* (1848) 3 Cox CC 430. For further authorities and discussion, see RN Gooderson 'Previous Consistent Statements' (1968) *CLJ* 64 at 70–3.

[124] For the difficulties which arise where the witness fails to identify the accused in court, having previously identified him outside court, see *R v Osbourne* and *R v Virtue* [1973] QB 678, CA and *R v Burke and Kelly* (1847) 2 Cox CC 295 (see Ch 10).

[125] The detailed rules governing the proper conduct of formal identification procedures, which are contained in the Code of Practice issued by the Home Secretary pursuant to s 66 of the Police and Criminal Evidence Act 1984, are beyond the scope of this book. Failure on the part of the police to observe the provisions may be taken into account by the court when deciding whether to exclude identification evidence and by the jury when assessing the weight of such evidence (see Ch 3).

[126] [1914] AC 545.

that shortly after the alleged act they saw the boy approach the accused, touch his sleeve, and identify him by saying, 'That is the man'. Evidence of the previous identification was admissible as evidence of the witness's consistency, 'to show that the witness was able to identify at the time' and 'to exclude the idea that the identification of the prisoner in the dock was an afterthought or mistake'.[127] Evidence that a witness previously identified the accused from a photograph is also admissible for these purposes provided that the photograph does not come from police files or, if it does, cannot be identified as such.[128] Thus, evidence of identification from a photograph which forms part of an album of police photographs[129] or which shows the accused wearing prison clothes[130] should be excluded, unless the jury have been or will be made aware of the accused's record for some other good reason.[131] The accused should not be prejudiced by the jury being informed or allowed to suspect that he has previous convictions.[132]

The admissibility of evidence of previous identification of the accused has been justified on the ground that:

> In cases where there has been a considerable lapse of time between the offence and the trial, and where there might be a danger of the witness's recollection of the prisoner's features having become dimmed, no doubt it strengthens the value of the evidence if it can be shown that in the meantime, soon after the commission of the offence, the witness saw and recognized the prisoner.[133]

The evidence of a witness who identifies the accused as the person who committed the offence charged is, in the absence of a previous identification, treated with considerable suspicion. There is the obvious danger stemming from delay. There is also the real risk of prejudice, because a witness, asked if he sees the person who committed the offence in court, might all too readily point to the person standing in the dock, overriding any doubts in his mind, especially in cases where he gave a description to the police, by the thought: 'Surely the police would not have brought the wrong person to court?' For these reasons, it is undesirable to invite a witness to make a 'dock identification', that is to identify the accused for the first time in court,[134] and the usual practice, in cases where there has been a prior out-of-court

---

[127] Per Viscount Haldane LC [1914] AC 545 at 551.

[128] Such a photograph may also be used to show that between commission of the offence and arrest, the accused had strikingly changed his appearance and thereby thwarted an attempt by the identifying witness to pick him out of an identification parade: *R v Byrne and Trump* [1987] Crim LR 689, CA.

[129] *R v Wainwright* (1925) 19 Cr App R 52, CCA.

[130] *R v Dwyer* and *R v Ferguson* [1925] 2 KB 799, CCA. See also *R v Varley* (1914) 10 Cr App R 125, CCA.

[131] See, eg, *R v Allen* [1996] Crim LR 426, CA.

[132] But see also *R v Governor of Pentonville Prison, ex p Voets* [1986] 1 WLR 470, QBD: such photographs are admissible in law and their exclusion discretionary. The police should not show photographs, including that of a suspect, to potential witnesses where the suspect is already under arrest: *R v Haslam* (1925) 19 Cr App R 59, CCA. Such witnesses should not be shown photographs of an accused whom they will be asked to identify in court: *R v Dwyer* and *R v Ferguson* [1925] 2 KB 799, CCA. However, the police, if in doubt as to the identity of a criminal, may show photographs to potential witnesses in order to discover who the offender is: *R v Palmer* (1914) 10 Cr App R 77, CCA. See also *R v Crabtree* [1992] Crim LR 65, CA: it is permissible for officers to identify the accused from photographs taken as part of a surveillance operation and shown to them before the offence was committed. As to the rules to be observed when a witness is shown photographs for identification purposes, see paras 3.3 and 3.28 of, and Annex E to, Code D, the Code of Practice on Identification issued pursuant to s 66 of the Police and Criminal Evidence Act 1984.

[133] Per Ferguson J in *R v Fannon* (1922) 22 SRNSW 427 at 430.

[134] *R v Cartwright* (1914) 10 Cr App R 219, CCA.

identification, is to elicit evidence on this *before* asking a question such as, 'Is that person in court today?'[135] The making of a dock identification is not, by its very nature, incompatible with the right to a fair trial in Article 6(1) of the European Convention on Human Rights, but may be incompatible depending on all the circumstances of the case.[136]

Although it has been held that it would be wrong to apply one approach to dock identifications for minor offences and another for more serious offences,[137] in *Barnes v Chief Constable of Durham*,[138] the Divisional Court held that dock identifications were customary in magistrates' courts, in relation to driving offences at least, and that if, in every case where the defendant did not distinctly admit driving there had to be a formal identification procedure, the whole process of justice in a magistrates' court would be severely impaired. This approach was followed in *Karia v DPP*,[139] a case of speeding and failing to produce insurance and other documents, where the court rejected a submission that *Barnes v Chief Constable of Durham* could be distinguished on the basis that in that case the defendant had been arrested and interviewed, whereas Karia was summonsed and had had no opportunity to explain that he was not the driver.

Statements admissible as part of the res gestae

The common law principle of *res gestae*, which is considered in Chapter 12, renders admissible all those events and statements which may be said to constitute a part of a transaction which is in issue. For example, in *R v Fowkes*[140] the accused, charged with murder, was commonly known, in the circumstances somewhat unfortunately it may be thought, as 'the butcher'. The son of the deceased gave evidence that he was sitting in a room with his father and a police officer, that a face appeared at the window through which a shot was fired, and that he thought the face was that of the accused. Both the son and the police officer, who had not seen the face, were allowed to give evidence that the son, on seeing the face, had shouted, 'There's Butcher'. A statement forming part of the *res gestae* is admissible at common law as evidence of the matters stated and also as evidence of consistency insofar as it confirms testimony given by the witness to the same effect. In criminal proceedings the common law rules in this regard have been preserved by the 2003 Act.[141] In civil proceedings, a previous statement forming part of the *res gestae* may only be adduced with the leave of the court.[142]

Statements in documents used to refresh the memory and received in evidence

As we have seen earlier in this chapter, where a party, or counsel on his behalf, cross-examines a witness on a document used by him to refresh his memory, and goes beyond the parts relied

---

[135] A dock identification is justified if the suspect has refused to take part in a formal identification procedure (*R v John* [1973] Crim LR 113, CA) or if the identifying witness claims to recognize the suspect as a person he already knows well (see para 3.12(ii) of Code D). However, a formal identification procedure is necessary where the witness has seen the suspect only once, or on a few occasions, before: *R v Fergus* [1992] Crim LR 363, CA. Where a dock identification is made but not solicited by the prosecution, it is insufficient for the judge merely to direct the jury that such an identification is abnormal and unfair—they should probably be told to disregard it altogether: see *R v Thomas* [1994] Crim LR 128, CA.

[136] *Holland v Her Majesty's Advocate* [2005] HRLR 25, PC. See also *Young v Trinidad* and *Tobago* [2008] UKPC 27.

[137] See *North Yorkshire Trading Standards Dept v Williams* (1994) 159 JP 383, DC.

[138] [1997] 2 Cr App R 505, DC.

[139] (2002) 166 JP 753, QBD.

[140] (1856) The Times, 8 Mar, Assizes.

[141] Section 118(1) 4.

[142] See s 6(2)(a) of the Civil Evidence Act 1995 (see Ch 11).

upon by the witness, the document may be received in evidence. As we have also seen, in civil proceedings, statements in the document are admitted as evidence of the matters stated; and the same applies in criminal proceedings, provided that the statement was made, as opposed to verified, by the witness. Where such statements are received in evidence, they may also go to the consistency of the witness.

Unfavourable and hostile witnesses

The rule against a party impeaching the credit of his own witness

A party seeking to elicit evidence in support of his version of the facts in issue may call a witness who fails to come up to proof or who gives evidence in support of the other party's version of the facts in issue. A party thus disappointed, in order to remedy the situation, may understandably wish to change course and attack the credibility of the witness. The general rule at common law, however, is that a party is not permitted to impeach the credit of a witness he calls: the party may neither question the witness about, nor call evidence concerning, his bad character,[143] convictions, prior inconsistent statements, or bias. In short, if the witness gives adverse evidence, the party may not turn round and cross-examine him as if he were a witness for the opposite party: 'It would be repugnant to principle, and likely to lead to abuse, to enable a party, having called a witness on the basis that he is at least in general going to tell the truth, to question him or call other evidence designed to show that he is a liar.'[144]

Unfavourable witnesses

An unfavourable witness may be defined as a witness who, although he displays no hostile animus to the party calling him, fails to come up to proof or gives evidence unfavourable to the case of that party. At common law a party is not permitted to impeach the credit of an unfavourable witness by any of the means outlined in the preceding paragraph but may call other witnesses to give evidence of those matters in relation to which the unfavourable witness failed to come up to proof. Thus in *Ewer v Ambrose*,[145] the defendant having called a witness to prove a partnership and the witness having testified to the contrary, it was held that while the defendant could not adduce general evidence to show that the witness was not to be believed on his oath, he was entitled to contradict him by calling other witnesses. If the rule were otherwise, undue importance would attach to the order in which witnesses are called. As Littledale J observed, 'if a party had four witnesses upon whom he relied to prove his case, it would be very hard that, by calling first the one who happened to disprove it, he should be deprived of the testimony of the other three'.

Hostile witnesses

A hostile witness may be defined as a witness who, in the opinion of the judge, shows no desire to tell the truth at the instance of the party calling him, to whom he displays a hostile

---

[143] It appears that a party is permitted to adduce evidence of the witness's bad character where the evidence is relevant to an issue in the case but does not discredit him or his credibility in relation to the discrete issue on which he gives evidence: *R v Ross* [2008] Crim LR 306, CA.

[144] 11th Report, Criminal Law Revision Committee (Cmnd 4991), para 162.

[145] (1825) 3 B&C 746. See also *Bradley v Ricardo* (1831) 8 Bing 57; cf Hamilton J in *Sumner and Leivesley v John Brown & Co* (1909) 25 TLR 745, Assizes.

animus.[146] In a civil case, it seems that a party may call a person even if he has shown signs that he is likely to be a hostile witness by refusing to make a statement.[147] Similarly, in a criminal case, the prosecution may call a person who has shown such signs, for example by retracting a statement, or making a second statement, prior to the trial,[148] but it appears that in cases in which the person refuses to assist the prosecution or court, or claims to be no longer able to remember anything, the judge has a discretion to hold a *voir dire* in order to decide whether to prevent him from being called at all.[149] However, although the question whether a witness is hostile is for the judge alone, the evidence and demeanour of the potentially hostile witness should usually be tested in the presence of the jury.[150] It is only in very exceptional cases that a *voir dire* should be held to decide whether or not a witness who has yet to be called might prove to be hostile.[151] Equally, once a witness has started to give his evidence, a *voir dire* before a decision on whether to treat him as hostile is only appropriate in exceptional circumstances, because the jury may see the witness apparently giving evidence in one frame of mind and then see a complete turn-around after events which have taken place in their absence.[152]

At common law a judge may allow cross-examination of a hostile witness by the party calling him.[153] An application to treat a witness as hostile may be made at any time during the witness's evidence, even at the late stage of re-examination.[154] The judge has a discretion whether to grant leave to cross-examine and his decision will seldom be challenged successfully on appeal.[155] In deciding whether a witness is not merely unfavourable but should be treated as hostile, the judge may take into account the attitude and demeanour displayed by the witness, his willingness to cooperate, and the extent to which any prior statement made by him is inconsistent with his testimony. If a hostile witness gives evidence contrary to an earlier statement, or fails to give the evidence expected, the party calling him and the trial judge should first consider inviting him to refresh his memory from material which it is legitimate to use for that purpose, and should not immediately proceed to treat him as hostile, unless he displays such an excessive degree of hostility that that is the only appropriate course.[156] In *R v Fraser* and *R v Warren*[157] Lord Goddard CJ went so far as to state, and it is perhaps best regarded as an over-statement, that if the prosecution have in their possession a previous statement 'in flat contradiction' of the witness's testimony, they are *entitled* to cross-examine and should apply for leave to do so. Be that as it may, if a witness is treated as hostile, the party calling him may ask leading questions[158] but may neither cross-examine him on his previous misconduct or

---

[146] See Stephen, *Digest of the Law of Evidence* (12th edn, London, 1948) Art 147.

[147] See CPR r 32.9, whereby a party unable to obtain a witness statement may seek permission to serve a witness summary instead (see Ch 4).

[148] See *R v Mann* (1972) 56 Cr App R 750, CA; *R v Vibert* (21 Oct 1974, unreported), CA; and *R v Dat* [1998] Crim LR 488, CA.

[149] *R v Honeyghon and Sayles* [1999] Crim LR 221, CA. See also *R v Dat* [1998] Crim LR 488, CA.

[150] *R v Darby* [1989] Crim LR 817, CA. Cf *R v Jones* [1998] Crim LR 579, CA.

[151] *R v Olumegbon* [2004] All ER (D) 60 (Aug), [2004] EWCA Crim 2337.

[152] *R v Khan* [2003] Crim LR 428, CA.

[153] It appears that the party calling the witness retains the right to *re-examine* him on any new matters arising out of cross-examination by the other party to the action: *R v Wong* [1986] Crim LR 683 (Crown Court).

[154] *R v Powell* [1985] Crim LR 592, CA.

[155] *Rice v Howard* (1886) 16 QBD 681 and *Price v Manning* (1889) 42 Ch D 372, CA.

[156] *R v Maw* [1994] Crim LR 841, CA.

[157] (1956) 40 Cr App R 160, CCA.

[158] *R v Thompson* (1976) 64 Cr App R 96, CA.

convictions, nor adduce evidence to show that he is not to be believed on oath. At common law, it was doubtful whether the party could prove prior statements made by the witness and inconsistent with his testimony, a matter which is now governed by section 3 of the Criminal Procedure Act 1865.[159] Section 3 provides that:

> A party producing a witness shall not be allowed to impeach his credit by general evidence of bad character, but he may, in case the witness shall, in the opinion of the judge, prove adverse, contradict him by other evidence, or, by leave of the judge, prove that he has made at other times a statement inconsistent with his present testimony; but before such last mentioned proof can be given the circumstances of the supposed statement, sufficient to designate the particular occasion, must be mentioned to the witness, and he must be asked whether or not he has made such statement.

Section 3 was not drafted with felicity.[160] In *Greenough v Eccles*[161] it was held that the word 'adverse' in the section means 'hostile' and not 'unfavourable'. Bearing this in mind, the section may be analysed in terms of three rules governing a party's entitlement to discredit his own witness. The first is that he is not entitled to impeach the witness's credit by general evidence of his bad character. In other words, he may neither cross-examine the witness on his previous misconduct or convictions nor adduce evidence of a general nature to show that the witness is not to be believed on oath. This rule applies to both unfavourable and hostile witnesses and amounts to no more than a statutory restatement of the common law. The second rule, that the party may contradict the witness by other evidence, applies under the statute only to hostile witnesses. The section suggests that this rule does not apply to unfavourable witnesses, but in *Greenough v Eccles*, Williams and Willes JJ held that the section has not affected the rule at common law that a party may contradict an unfavourable witness by calling other witnesses.[162] The third rule, that the party may prove that the witness made at other times a statement inconsistent with his present testimony, applies only in the case of hostile witnesses.[163] In this connection, it remains to note that section 3 has not removed the common law right of the judge, in his discretion, to allow cross-examination when a witness proves hostile. In *R v Thompson*[164] the accused was convicted of indecent assault and incest. His daughter, who had given a statement to the police implicating him, was called into the witness box but stood mute of malice, refusing to give evidence. The judge gave leave to treat her as a hostile witness, and she was then asked leading questions and her former statement was put to her. On appeal, it was argued that since the girl had given no 'testimony', the case

---

[159] Section 3 applies to both civil and criminal proceedings. In civil proceedings the prior statement of any witness may with the leave of the court be admitted as evidence of the facts contained in it: see s 6(2)(a) of the Civil Evidence Act 1995 (see Ch 11). The evidential status of a prior inconsistent statement of a hostile witness in civil proceedings is governed by s 6(3) of the same Act: see below.

[160] 'Section 3 of the 1865 Act certainly requires thorough revision': 11th Report, Criminal Law Revision Committee (Cmnd 4991), para 161. See also cl 11 of the draft Bill.

[161] (1859) 5 CBNS 786, a decision on the construction of s 22 of the Common Law Procedure (Amendment) Act 1856, which was repealed but re-enacted by s 3 of the 1865 Act.

[162] See *Ewer v Ambrose* (1825) 3 B&C 746. The Criminal Law Revision Committee was of the opinion that there is no need to make statutory provision for a party to be allowed to call evidence to contradict an unfavourable witness because this is allowed by common law: see 11th Report (Cmnd 4991), para 163. The attempt to deal with the matter in s 3 was 'the great blunder in the drawing of it': per Cockburn CJ in *Greenough v Eccles* (1859) 5 CBNS 786 at 806.

[163] Acceptance by the witness that he made some parts of the statement and signed it may constitute proof for these purposes: see *R v Baldwin* [1986] Crim LR 681, CA.

[164] (1976) 64 Cr App R 96, CA.

did not fall within section 3. Dismissing the appeal, Lord Parker CJ held it unnecessary to decide whether section 3 applied, since there was authority at common law for what the judge had done.[165]

If a hostile witness, on being cross-examined on a previous inconsistent statement, adopts and confirms the contents (or part of them), then what he says becomes part of his evidence and, subject to the assessment of his credibility by the tribunal of fact, it is capable of being accepted.[166] However, even if the witness does not admit the truth of the previous statement, it is admissible in both civil and criminal proceedings as evidence of the matters stated. Under section 1 of the 1995 Act, in civil proceedings evidence shall not be excluded on the ground that it is hearsay. Section 6(3) and (5) of the 1995 Act provide as follows:

(3) Where in the case of civil proceedings sections 3, 4 or 5 of the Criminal Procedure Act 1865 applies, which make provision as to—

(a) how far a witness may be discredited by the party producing him,

. . .

this Act does not authorise the adducing of evidence of a previous inconsistent or contradictory statement otherwise than in accordance with those sections.

. . .

(5) Nothing in this section shall be construed as preventing a statement of any description referred to above from being admissible by virtue of section 1 as evidence of the matters stated.

As to criminal proceedings, section 119 of the 2003 Act provides as follows:

(1) If in criminal proceedings a person gives oral evidence and—

(a) he admits making a previous inconsistent statement,[167] or

(b) a previous inconsistent statement made by him is proved by virtue of section 3, 4 or 5 of the Criminal Procedure Act 1865 (c. 18),

the statement is admissible as evidence of any matter stated of which oral evidence by him would be admissible.

In both civil and criminal cases, therefore, the tribunal of fact may now accept as the truth of the matter the previous statement of a witness who has been declared hostile. However, it is submitted that section 119 is of no application where the witness is declared hostile at common law, rather than under section 3 of the Criminal Procedure Act 1865, and does not admit making the previous inconsistent statement. Nor does it apply to a witness who, once sworn, stands mute of malice because the provision only applies where a witness 'gives oral evidence'.[168]

Section 119 of the 2003 Act, by allowing previous inconsistent statements to be admitted for the truth of the matter stated, has changed the landscape of the criminal trial. Protection for defendants is contained in the court's powers to exclude evidence,[169] to direct an acquittal

---

[165] Reliance was placed upon *Clarke v Saffery* (1824) Ry&M 126 and *Bastin v Carew* (1824) Ry&M 127. It remains unclear whether if, in circumstances such as those in *R v Thompson*, the witness denies making the previous statement, it can be proved at common law.

[166] *R v Maw* [1994] Crim LR 841, CA. See also *R v Gibbons* [2009] Crim LR 197, CA.

[167] The effect of s 119(1)(a) of the 2003 Act is to make a prior statement admissible for the truth of the matter stated where a witness admits having made the prior statement without an application having been made to treat him as hostile. See *R v Joyce* [2005] All ER (D) 309 (Jun), [2005] EWCA Crim 1785.

[168] However, in such circumstances it would be open to the court to admit the statement as evidence of the truth of the matter stated under s 114(1)(d) of the 2003 Act (see Ch 10).

[169] See, eg, *R v Coates* [2008] 1 Cr App R 52, CA.

or discharge the jury where the evidence provided by the statement is unconvincing,[170] and to give appropriate directions to the jury.[171]

As to how the judge should direct a jury in relation to a witness's evidence and any prior statement that is admitted in evidence, in *R v Golder*,[172] which was decided prior to the 2003 Act, Lord Parker CJ said: 'When a witness is shown to have made previous statements inconsistent with the evidence given by that witness at the trial, the jury should . . . be directed that the evidence given at the trial should be regarded as unreliable.' The statement has since been cited with approval[173] but it may be doubted whether it was ever intended to be regarded as a rigid formula or precise form of words to be recited to juries in every case. It has since been said that it is not always necessary or appropriate, as an inflexible rule, to direct the jury that the evidence of the witness should be treated as unreliable.[174] In some cases the evidence given by the witness may be regarded as reliable notwithstanding his prior inconsistent statement— for example when the witness is able to give a convincing explanation of the inconsistency. However, in *R v Joyce*,[175] which was decided under the 2003 Act, it was held that the jury may accept either what the witness said on the previous occasion or when giving evidence. As to that the strength of the direction on the weight to be attached to the witness's evidence or previous statement it is submitted that it should vary according to the particular circumstances of the case in question. The jury should not be directed that a previous statement is just as much evidence as the witness's testimony in court because the jury may take the direction to mean that they are obliged to give both the same evidential weight.[176] However, it is necessary for the jury to consider whether a hostile witness should be treated as creditworthy at all. The judge should give a clear warning about the dangers of a witness who has contradicted himself. It is insufficient to tell the jury to approach the evidence with great caution and reservation. Before the jury may rely on either the witness's evidence or prior statement as evidence of truth supporting the prosecution case, they must be sure that it is true. However, where it is exculpatory of the accused, it is sufficient if the jury are persuaded that it may be true.[177] Where a witness is declared hostile but subsequently proves not to be so, the trial judge is still obliged to warn the jury to approach his evidence with caution, the precise nature of the direction depending on the particular circumstances of the case.[178]

Under section 122 of the 2003 Act, if in a jury trial a statement made in a document is admitted under section 119 and produced as an exhibit, it must not accompany the jury when they retire to consider their verdict unless the court considers it appropriate or all parties agree that it should accompany them. The reason for the general rule in section 122 is the risk that the jury, by having the document in front of them, will place disproportionate weight

---

[170] Section 125 of the Criminal Justice Act 2003.

[171] See *R v Joyce* [2005] All ER (D) 309 (Jun), [2005] EWCA Crim 1798 and *R v Bennett* [2008] All ER (D) 208 (Jan), [2008] EWCA Crim 248.

[172] [1960] 1 WLR 1169, CCA at 1172–3. See also *R v Nyberg* (1922) 17 Cr App R 59, CCA and *R v Harris* (1928) 20 Cr App R 144, CCA.

[173] See *R v Oliva* [1965] 1 WLR 1028, CCA at 1036–7.

[174] *Driscoll v R* (1977) 137 CLR 517, High Court of Australia, a view supported by *R v Pestano* [1981] Crim LR 397, CA; *Alves v DPP* [1992] 4 All ER 787, HL; and *R v Goodway* [1993] 4 All ER 894, CA at 899. See also *R v Billingham* [2009] 2 Cr App R 341, CA.

[175] [2005] EWCA Crim 1785 at [29]-[30]; see Specimen Direction 28 for the model direction, available at <http://www.jsboard.co.uk/criminal_law/cbb/index.htm>.

[176] *R v Billingham* [2009] 2 Cr App R 341, CA.

[177] *R v Billingham* [2009] ibid; see also *R v Maw* [1994] Crim LR 841, CA.

[178] *R v Greene* (2009) The Times, 28 Oct.

on its contents as compared with the oral evidence. Normally, in the absence of some special feature of the document, it is sufficient for the judge to give a reminder in the summing-up of the contents of the statement and anything said by the witness about the document and the circumstances in which it was made. In cases where it is appropriate for the jury to take the document with them, the judge should not only give the general direction about a hostile witness, but also impress upon the jury the reason why they are being given the document and the importance of not attaching disproportionate weight to it simply because they have it before them.[179]

ADDITIONAL READING

Birch, 'The Sharp End of the Wedge: Use of Mixed Statements by the Defence' [1997] *Crim LR* 416.

Lewis, 'Delayed complaints in childhood sexual abuse prosecutions—a comparative evaluation of admissibility determinations and judicial warnings' (2006) 10 *E&P* 104.

[179] *R v Hulme* [2007] 1 Cr App R 334, CA.

Cross-examination and re-examination

7

Key Issues

- When and why should a party to litigation be entitled to cross-examine a witness called by his opponent or another party?

- Should an accused always be entitled to cross-examine a witness in person? If not, when should such cross-examination be prohibited?

- What is the object of cross-examination?

- What restrictions, if any, should be placed on the form of questioning in cross-examination?

- What are the consequences for a party to litigation who fails to cross-examine a witness called by another party?

- When and why is a party to litigation permitted to prove that a witness called by another party has made a prior inconsistent statement?

- When and why should questions or evidence concerning the previous sexual experiences of complainants in proceedings for sexual offences be allowed?

- When and why should a party to litigation be permitted to call further evidence with a view to contradicting a witness who denies a matter when under cross-examination?

- When and why should a witness who has been cross-examined be re-examined by the party calling him?

Cross-examination

Cross-examination is the questioning of a witness, immediately after his examination-in-chief, by the legal representative of the opponent of the party calling him, or by the opposing party in person, or by the legal representative of any other party to the proceedings or by any other party in person.[1] Thus if an accused elects to testify, he will be open to cross-examination not only by the prosecution but also by a co-accused; and the co-accused is entitled to cross-examine him whether he has given evidence unfavourable to the co-accused or has merely given evidence in his own defence.[2] The order of cross-examination where two or more are jointly indicted and separately represented is the order in which their names appear on the indictment.[3]

Liability to cross-examination

All witnesses are liable to be cross-examined. If a witness dies before cross-examination, his evidence-in-chief is admissible, though little weight may attach to it.[4] If a witness, during cross-examination, becomes incapable through illness of giving further evidence, the judge may allow the trial to continue on the basis of the evidence already given, subject to an appropriate direction to the jury to acquit if they feel that the truncated cross-examination prevented them from judging fairly the witness's credibility.[5]

To the general rule that all witnesses are liable to cross-examination, there are three minor exceptions in the case of: (i) a witness who is not sworn, being called merely to produce a document;[6] (ii) a witness called by mistake, because he is unable to speak as to the matters supposed to be within his knowledge, where the mistake is discovered before the examination-in-chief has begun but after the witness has been sworn;[7] and (iii) a witness called by the judge, in which case neither party is entitled to cross-examine him without the leave of the judge, although such leave should be given if the evidence is adverse to either party.[8]

---

[1] Concerning the extent to which the judge may intervene, see *R v Sharp* [1994] QB 261, CA and *R v Roncoli* [1998] Crim LR 584, CA. Interventions which may raise an eyebrow do not necessarily result in an unfair trial: *R v Denton* [2007] All ER (D) 492 (Apr), [2007] EWCA Crim 1111. However, interventions carry the risk of depriving the judge of the advantage of calm and dispassionate observation and lengthy interrogation may so hamper his ability properly to evaluate and weigh the evidence as to impair his judgment and render the trial unfair: *Southwark London Borough Council v Kofi-Adu* [2006] HLR 33, CA.

[2] *R v Hilton* [1972] 1 QB 421, CA.

[3] *R v Barber* (1844) 1 Car&Kir 434; *R v Richards* (1844) 1 Cox CC 62.

[4] *R v Doolin* (1882) 1 Jebb CC 123, IR.

[5] *R v Stretton* and *R v McCallion* (1986) 86 Cr App R 7, CA. See also *R v Wyatt* [1990] Crim LR 343, CA. However, if the only direct evidence on one important part of the prosecution case is given by a witness who, at the end of his examination-in-chief, is unable to give further evidence, it is at least doubtful whether any direction to the jury, however strongly expressed, can overcome the powerful prejudice of his evidence going wholly untested by cross-examination: see *R v Lawless* (1993) 98 Cr App R 342, CA.

[6] *Summers v Moseley* (1834) 2 Cr&M 477. Nor may such a witness be cross-examined if he was sworn unnecessarily: *Rush v Smith* (1834) 1 Cr M&R 94.

[7] However, if counsel seeks to withdraw a witness who can give relevant evidence because he might also reveal other inconvenient matters, the witness is liable to cross-examination: *Wood v Mackinson* (1840) 2 Mood&R 273.

[8] *Coulson v Disborough* [1894] 2 QB 316, CA; *R v Cliburn* (1898) 62 JP 232, CCC. See also *R v Tregear* [1967] 2 QB 574, CA at 580.

Cross-examination by accused in person

Cross-examination may be conducted by a legal representative or by a party in person. In criminal cases, as a general rule, an unrepresented accused is entitled to cross-examine in person any witness called by the prosecution. However, there are common law restrictions on this rule, as well as statutory exceptions to it. As to the former, the judge is not obliged to give an unrepresented accused his head to ask whatever questions, at whatever length, he wishes;[9] and although he should not descend into the arena on behalf of the accused, it is generally desirable for the judge to ask such questions as he sees fit to test the reliability and accuracy of the witness.[10] Sections 34–39 of the Youth Justice and Criminal Evidence Act 1999 (the 1999 Act) protect three categories of witness from cross-examination by an accused in person.[11] Under section 34, no person charged with a sexual offence[12] may cross-examine in person the complainant, either in connection with the offence, or in connection with any other offence (of whatever nature) with which that person is charged in the proceedings. Under section 35, no person charged with one of a number of specified offences[13] may cross-examine in person a 'protected witness', either in connection with the offence, or in connection with any other offence (of whatever nature) with which that person is charged in the proceedings. A 'protected witness' is a witness[14] who (a) is the complainant or is alleged to have been a witness to the commission of the offence; and (b) either is a child or falls to be cross-examined after giving evidence-in-chief (i) by means of a video-recording made for the purposes of section 27 of the 1999 Act (video-recorded evidence admitted as evidence-in-chief)[15] at a time when the witness was a child, or (ii) in any other way at any such time.[16]

Section 36 gives the court a general power, in a case where neither section 34 nor section 35 operates, to give a direction prohibiting the accused from cross-examining a witness in person.[17] An application for such a direction may be made by the prosecutor or the court may raise the issue of its own motion.[18] Under section 36(2), such a direction may be given if it appears to the

---

[9] *R v Brown* [1998] 2 Cr App R 364, CA.

[10] *R v De Oliveira* [1997] Crim LR 600, CA.

[11] As to the need for similar statutory protection in civil cases, see per Wood J in *H v L and R, Re* [2007] 2 FLR 162, Fam D.

[12] A 'sexual offence' is defined in s 62 as any offence under Part 1 of the Sexual Offences Act 2003 or any relevant superseded offence. 'Relevant superseded offence' means rape or burglary with intent to rape, an offence under any of ss 2 to 12 and 14 to 17 of the Sexual Offences Act 1956, an offence under s 128 of the Mental Health Act 1959, an offence under s 1 of the Indecency with Children Act 1960 (indecent conduct towards child under 14), and an offence under 54 of the Criminal Law Act 1977 (incitement of child under 16 to commit incest).

[13] The offences are any offence under any of ss 33 to 36 of the Sexual Offences Act 1956, the Protection of Children Act 1978, Part 1 of the Sexual Offences Act 2003, any of ss 1 to 32 of the Sexual Offences Act 1956, the Indecency with Children Act 1960, the Sexual Offences Act 1967 or s 54 of the Criminal Law Act 1977 (s 35(3)(a)); and kidnapping, false imprisonment, or an offence under s 1 or s 2 of the Child Abduction Act 1984, any offence under s 1 of the Children and Young Persons Act 1933, and any offence (not already listed) which involves an assault on, or injury, or a threat of injury to, any person (s 35(3)(b), (c), and (d)).

[14] A 'witness' includes a witness who is charged with an offence in the proceedings: s 35(5). Thus an accused may not cross-examine in person a 'protected witness' who is a co-accused: *R (S) v Waltham Forest Youth Court* [2004] 2 Cr App R 335, DC at [27].

[15] See Ch 5.

[16] Section 35(2). Child means, where the offence falls within s 35(3)(a), a person under the age of 17; or, where the offence falls within s 35(3)(b), (c) or (d), a person under the age of 14. See n 13, above.

[17] A 'witness', for these purposes, does not include any other person who is charged with an offence in the proceedings: s 36(4)(a).

[18] Section 36(1).

court (a) 'that the quality of evidence[19] given by the witness on cross-examination—(i) is likely to be diminished if the cross-examination . . . is conducted by the accused in person, and (ii) would be likely to be improved if a direction were given . . . ' and (b) it would not be contrary to the interests of justice. In deciding whether section 36(2)(a) applies, the court must have regard to various matters, including any views expressed by the witness, the nature of the questions likely to be asked, the accused's behaviour during the proceedings, any relationship (of any nature) between the witness and the accused, and any special measures direction[20] which the court has given or proposes to give in relation to the witness.[21] The accused should be given the opportunity to make representations in relation to these matters.[22] The court must state in open court its reasons for giving or refusing an application for a direction under section 36.[23]

Where an accused is prevented from cross-examining a witness in person under section 34, section 35, or section 36, the court must invite the accused to arrange for a legal representative to act for him for the purpose of the cross-examination, and if the invitation is not taken up, must consider whether it is necessary in the interests of justice for the witness to be cross-examined by a legal representative appointed to represent the interests of the accused.[24] If the court decides that it is necessary to do so, it will choose and appoint the representative, who will not be responsible to the accused.[25] In a trial on indictment with a jury in which an accused is prevented from cross-examining a witness in person under section 34, section 35 or section 36, the judge must give the jury such warning (if any) as is considered necessary to ensure that the accused is not prejudiced by any inferences that might be drawn from the fact that such cross-examination has been prevented or the fact that the cross-examination was carried out by a court-appointed legal representative.[26]

The permitted form of questioning in cross-examination

The permitted form of questioning in cross-examination is most conveniently considered by reference to the objects of cross-examination. These are twofold. The cross-examiner will seek (i) to elicit evidence which supports his version of the facts in issue; and (ii) to cast doubt upon the witness's evidence. Before giving further consideration to these objects of cross-examination, it will be useful to consider two general matters. First, it may be noted that a witness under cross-examination may be asked leading questions, even if he appears to be more favourable to the cross-examiner than to the party who called him, and whether the questions are directed to either the first or second of the two objects of cross-examination.[27] Secondly, it may be noted that all cross-examination is subject to an important general constraint which applies whether the questions to be put to the witness go to the matters in issue or to credit only. This is the discretion of the judge to prevent any questions which in his opinion are unnecessary, improper, or oppressive. Cross-examination, a powerful weapon

---

[19] 'The quality of evidence' is to be construed in accordance with s 16(5) (s 36(4)(b)): see Ch 5, 144 under **Special measures directions for vulnerable and intimidated witnesses.**

[20] See Ch 5.

[21] Section 36(3).

[22] *R (Hillman) v Richmond Magistrates' Court* [2003] All ER (D) 455 (Oct), [2003] EWHC 2580 (Admin).

[23] Section 37(4).

[24] Section 38(1)–(4).

[25] Section 38(4) and (5).

[26] Section 39.

[27] *Parkin v Moon* (1836) 7 C&P 408.

entrusted to counsel, should be conducted with restraint and with a measure of courtesy and consideration to the witness.[28] Thus counsel will be restrained from embarking on lengthy cross-examination on matters that are not really in issue[29] and from framing his questions in such a way as to invite argument rather than elicit evidence on the facts in issue.[30] In criminal cases, entitlement to a fair trial is not inconsistent with proper judicial control over the use of time as part of the judge's responsibility to manage the trial.[31] It should not become a routine feature of trial management to impose time-limits for cross-examination (or examination-in-chief), but if counsel indulges in prolix and repetitious questioning, judges are obliged to impose reasonable time-limits; counsel has a duty to put his client's case fearlessly but also to avoid wasting time.[32] In civil proceedings, CPR rule 32.1(3) bluntly provides that: 'The court may limit cross-examination.' When exercising this power, the judge must seek to give effect to the 'overriding objective',[33] which is to enable the court 'to deal with cases justly',[34] and in deciding how long cross-examination should last in the interests of justice, for both parties and for the witness, the judge may take into account any medical condition which the witness may have.[35]

Cross-examination as to matters in issue

The questions of the cross-examiner are not restricted to matters proved in examination-in-chief but may relate to any fact in issue or relevant to a fact in issue. This does not mean that evidence which is otherwise inadmissible can become admissible by being put to a witness in cross-examination: the ordinary rules relating to the inadmissibility of certain types of evidence operate to prevent such evidence from being elicited in cross-examination as well as in examination-in-chief. Thus in *R v Treacy*[36] the accused, charged with murder, was held by the Court of Criminal Appeal to have been improperly cross-examined upon certain inadmissible confessions made on arrest and inconsistent with his testimony.[37] Similarly, a party is unable to admit an inadmissible hearsay statement contained in a document by handing it to a witness under cross-examination and requiring him to read it aloud. Counsel may, of course, properly produce the document to the witness and ask him

---

[28] See per Sankey LC in *Mechanical & General Inventions Co Ltd v Austin* [1935] AC 346, HL at 360. See also the Code of Conduct of the Bar of England and Wales at para 708 and para 5.10, Written Standards for the Conduct of Professional Work.

[29] *R v Kalia* [1975] Crim LR 181, CA and *Mechanical & General Inventions Co Ltd v Austin* [1935] AC 346 at 359, HL.

[30] See per Lord Hewart CJ in *R v Baldwin* (1925) 18 Cr App R 175, CCA. Thus counsel should not put to a witness what somebody else has said or is expected to say (at 178–9). Nor should the judge put such questions: *R v Wilson* [1991] Crim LR 838, CA.

[31] *R v Chaaban* [2003] Crim LR 658, CA and see now the Criminal Procedure Rules, SI 2005/384, paras 1.1(2)(e), 3.2(2)(e), and 3.2(3).

[32] *R v B* [2006] Crim LR 54, CA. See also para 6(v) (Controlling prolix cross-examination), Protocol for the control and management of heavy fraud and other complex criminal cases [2005] 2 All ER 429.

[33] CPR r 1.2.

[34] CPR r 1.1(1). See further Ch 2, 43 under **Exclusionary discretion,** *Civil cases.*

[35] *Three Rivers District Council v Bank of England* [2005] CP Rep 46, CA.

[36] [1944] 2 All ER 229.

[37] See also *R v Thomson* [1912] 3 KB 19, CCA and *R v Windass* (1988) 89 Cr App R 258, CA (inadmissible hearsay); *Re P* [1989] Crim LR 897, CA (inadmissible complaint in a sexual case); and *R v Gray* [1998] Crim LR 570, CA (interview with a co-accused inadmissible as against the accused). In civil proceedings, see *Beare v Garrod* (1915) 85 LJKB 717, CA and *Sharp v Loddington Ironstone Co Ltd* (1924) 132 LT 229, CA.

if he accepts the contents as true,[38] and, if the witness does, the contents of the document become evidence in the case. However, if the witness does not accept the contents as true, it would be improper for counsel to request the witness to read aloud from the document, the contents of which remain inadmissible hearsay evidence.[39]

The principle laid down in *R v Treacy* that a person solely accused cannot be cross-examined by the *prosecution* in such a way as to reveal that he made a confession which has been ruled inadmissible, also obtains in favour of any co-accused of the maker of such a confession.[40] However, where an accused has made a confession statement which has been ruled inadmissible but which is relevant to the defence of a co-accused, then if the accused gives evidence which is inconsistent with his statement, he may be cross-examined on it by the *co-accused*, provided that the judge directs the jury not to treat it as evidence of its maker's guilt.[41]

Cross-examination as to credit

Concerning the second object of cross-examination, at common law there is a wide variety of ways in which the cross-examining party may seek to cast doubt upon the witness's evidence-in-chief and to show that the witness ought not to be believed on his oath. He may cross-examine him about omissions or inconsistencies in previous statements, if the omission or inconsistency will affect his likely standing with the tribunal of fact;[42] he may question him about his means of knowledge of the facts to which he has testified; he may challenge the quality of his memory[43] and his powers of perception; he may ask him about his unreliability by reason of any physical or mental disability; and he may ask him to explain any delay in reporting the offence[44] as well as any omissions, mistakes, or inconsistencies in his evidence insofar as they militate against his veracity or plausibility. As to omissions, for example, where an accused is charged with a sexual offence and asserts fabrication on the part of the complainant, he may be cross-examined as to what facts are known to

---

[38] He should not, however, describe the nature or contents of the document to the court: see *R v Yousry* (1914) 11 Cr App R 13, CCA.

[39] *R v Gillespie* and *R v Simpson* (1967) 51 Cr App R 172, CA, applied in *R v Cooper* (1985) 82 Cr App R 74, CA; and *R v Cross* (1990) 91 Cr App R 115, CA.

[40] Per Winn J in *R v Rice* [1963] 1 QB 857, CCA at 868–9.

[41] *R v Rowson* [1986] QB 174, CA, followed in *Lui-Mei Lin v R* [1989] AC 288, PC and *R v Corelli* [2001] Crim LR 913, CA. See also *R v O'Boyle* (1990) 92 Cr App R 202, CA. The co-accused may also cross-examine prosecution witnesses on the confession if to do so will affect the cogency of the prosecution evidence against him: *R v Beckford* (1991) 94 Cr App R 43, CA. See also *R v Myers* [1998] AC 124, HL (see Ch 13).

[42] He may do so even if evidence of the making of the statement would not be allowed because it is not 'relative to the subject matter of the indictment or proceeding' for the purposes of s 4 of the Criminal Procedure Act 1865: *R v Funderburk* [1990] 1 WLR 587, CA. Section 4 of the 1865 Act is considered below.

[43] For a consideration of issues relating to memory as they arise in legal proceedings see The British Psychological Society Memory and the Law Working Party, *Guidelines on Memory and the Law: Recommendations from the Scientific Study of Human Memory* (British Psychological Society, 2008).

[44] In *R v D* [2009] Crim LR 591, CA. The Court of Appeal recognized that the trauma of serious sexual assault may cause feelings of shame and guilt which might inhibit a person from making a complaint. The judge is therefore entitled to direct the jury as to how to approach the complainant's evidence so as to prevent them from coming to an unjustified conclusion as to her credibility, but he must be careful to do so in a measured and balanced way.

him that might explain why the complainant would make a false accusation against him.[45] Questions about omissions or inconsistencies in previous statements, often relating to matters of less than central importance, are the stock-in-trade of cross-examination with a view to discrediting a witness by implying his unreliability or untruthfulness. However, as to omissions, research shows that in the case of stressful events central details are more likely to be remembered than peripheral details; equally, as to inconsistency, research shows that variability of memory is the norm, and can be exacerbated both by the impact of trauma such as that experienced by victims of sexual assaults and, in the case of children, by under-developed communication skills.[46]

The cross-examining party may also ask questions about the witness's bad character and previous misconduct, including questions about previous convictions and questions with a view to showing his prejudice or bias. However, section 99 of the Criminal Justice Act 2003 (the 2003 Act) abolishes the common law rules governing the admissibility of evidence of 'bad character' in criminal proceedings and the intention appears to be to abolish not only the rules as to the introduction of such evidence, but also the rules governing cross-examination about conduct that comes within the statutory definition of 'bad character' in section 98 of the 2003 Act. The effect is that in criminal cases such cross-examination is only permitted if it comes within one of a number of specified categories of admissibility set out in section 100 (non-defendant's bad character) or section 101 (defendant's bad character). Evidence of bad character, for the purposes of these provisions, is evidence of, or of a disposition towards, misconduct, other than evidence which 'has to do' with the alleged facts of the offence charged or evidence of misconduct in connection with the investigation or prosecution of that offence. Section 108 of the 2003 Act imposes an additional restriction in relation to offences committed by the accused when a child. Finally, under section 41 of the 1999 Act, in the case of sexual offences, except with the leave of the court, no question may be asked in cross-examination about any sexual behaviour of the complainant. The restrictions in the 2003 Act are considered in Chapter 17. The restriction in section 41 of the 1999 Act is considered below.

Hobbs v Tinling[47] and *R v Sweet-Escott*[48] set out the general principles as to the propriety of cross-examining a witness as to his credit which are applicable generally in civil proceedings but in criminal proceedings are now limited to cross-examination as to the witness's credit about conduct which falls short of the statutory definition of 'bad character' in section 98 of the 2003 Act. In *Hobbs v Tinling* Sankey LJ held that the court, in the exercise of its discretion to disallow questions as to credit in cross-examination, should have regard to the following considerations:[49]

1. Such questions are proper if they are of such a nature that the truth of the imputation conveyed by them would seriously affect the opinion of the court as to the credibility of the witness on the matter to which he testifies.

---

[45] *R v B* [2003] 1 WLR 2809, CA, preferring *R v T* [1998] 2 NZLR 257 (New Zealand Court of Appeal) to *R v Palmer* (1998) 193 CLR 1 (Australian High Court).

[46] See Ellison, 'Closing the credibility gap; The prosecutorial use of expert witness testimony in sexual assault cases' (2006) 9 *E&P* 239 at pp 241–8, which cross-refers to much of the psychological and other research literature.

[47] [1929] 2 KB 1 at 51, CA.

[48] (1971) 55 Cr App R 316, Assizes.

[49] The principles derive from s 148 of the Indian Evidence Act (I of 1872).

2. Such questions are improper if the imputation which they convey relates to matters so remote in time, or of such a character, that the truth of the imputation would not affect, or would affect in a slight degree, the opinion of the court as to the credibility of the witness on the matter to which he testifies.

3. Such questions are improper if there is a great disproportion between the importance of the imputation made against the witness's character and the importance of his evidence.

In *R v Sweet-Escott* Lawton J posed the question: 'How far back is it permissible for advocates when cross-examining as to credit to delve into a man's past and to drag up such dirt as they can find there?' It was held that:

> Since the purpose of cross-examination as to credit is to show that the witness ought not to be believed on oath, the matters about which he is questioned must relate to his likely standing after cross-examination with the tribunal which is trying him or listening to his evidence.[50]

The effect of a party's failure to cross-examine

A party may decide that there is no need to cross-examine at all, especially if the witness in question has proved to be unfavourable or even hostile to the party calling him. A party's failure to cross-examine, however, has important consequences. It amounts to a tacit acceptance of the witness's evidence-in-chief. A party who has failed to cross-examine a witness upon a particular matter in respect of which it is proposed to contradict his evidence-in-chief or impeach his credit by calling other witnesses, will not be permitted to invite the jury or tribunal of fact to disbelieve the witness's evidence on that matter.[51] A cross-examiner who wishes to suggest to the jury that the witness is not speaking the truth on a particular matter must lay a proper foundation by putting that matter to the witness so that he has an opportunity of giving any explanation which is open to him.[52] The rule, however, is not absolute or inflexible. Thus if it is proposed to invite the jury to disbelieve a witness on a matter, it is not always necessary to put to him explicitly that he is lying, provided that the overall tenor of the cross-examination is designed to show that his account is incapable of belief.[53] In other cases, the story told by a witness may be so incredible that the matter upon which he is to be impeached is manifest, and in such circumstances it is unnecessary to waste time in putting questions to him upon it.[54] The most effective cross-examination in such a situation would be, in the words of Lord Morris, 'to ask him to leave the box'. The rule has also been held to be unsuitable in the case of proceedings in magistrates' courts.[55] It could be argued[56] that the rule should not apply in any criminal case, because there is no obligation on the accused to put his case by adducing evidence, but there is no authority to that effect.

[50] (1971) 55 Cr App R 316, Assizes at 320.

[51] Evidence to contradict a witness which was not put to the witness in cross-examination, may still be admitted, provided that the witness is recalled and cross-examination of him re-opened in order to put the new evidence to him: *R v Cannan* [1998] Crim LR 284, CA.

[52] *Browne v Dunn* (1893) 6 R 67, HL. See also *R v Hart* (1932) 23 Cr App R 202, CCA; *R v Bircham* [1972] Crim LR 430, CA; and *R v Fenlon* (1980) 71 Cr App R 307, CA.

[53] *R v Lovelock* [1997] Crim LR 821, CA.

[54] *Browne v Dunn* (1893) 6 R 67, HL.

[55] *O'Connell v Adams* [1973] Crim LR 313, DC. See also *Wilkinson v DPP* [2003] All ER (D) 294 (Feb), [2003] EWHC 865 (Admin).

[56] As in *R v Livistis* [2004] NSWCCA 287.

Cross-examination on documents

In civil proceedings, where a witness is called to give evidence at trial, he may be cross-examined on his witness statement,[57] whether or not the statement or any part of it was referred to during his evidence-in-chief.[58] Cross-examining counsel may also put to an opposing witness a statement taken on behalf of the cross-examiner's own client, but may not, it seems, cross-examine a witness called by an opposing party by reference to a statement of another witness who may or may not be called in the future by that opposing party or by someone other than the party on whose behalf the cross-examination is being conducted.[59]

The law relating to the cross-examination of a witness upon a previous statement made by him relative to the subject matter of the indictment or proceeding and inconsistent with his testimony, the proof of such a statement, and the evidential use to which it may be put, is governed by sections 4 and 5 of the Criminal Procedure Act 1865 (the 1865 Act), which are considered later in this chapter. The common law and statutory rules on the cross-examination of a witness upon a document used by him to refresh his memory, the circumstances in which such a document may be put in evidence, and the evidential effect of so doing, are considered in Chapter 6.

So far as other documents are concerned, there is an obscure common law rule that, where a party calls for and inspects a document in the possession of another party, that other party may require him to put it in evidence. This rule was applied in *Stroud v Stroud*.[60] A doctor was called as a witness on behalf of a wife petitioning for divorce on the ground of cruelty. Counsel for the husband, in the course of cross-examining the doctor, called for and read certain medical reports made by other doctors and in the possession of the witness. It was held that, as a result of this conduct, the wife could require that the reports be put in evidence. It is submitted that the rule in *Stroud v Stroud* is obsolete in civil proceedings, given the combined effect of the modern law on disclosure and the provisions of the Civil Evidence Act 1995 (the 1995 Act), and should be abolished. Although Wrangham J clearly envisaged that the rule might apply to criminal proceedings, this would appear never to have happened. The Criminal Law Revision Committee recommended abolition of the rule in criminal proceedings on the grounds that (i) it may be impossible, or difficult to find out who supplied the information contained in the document, or what his authority was for doing so; and (ii) the information may have come from someone incompetent to give evidence to the same effect as the information.[61] For these reasons, and given the general obscurity of the rule, it is submitted that in criminal proceedings, also, it should be abolished.

Previous inconsistent statements

If it is put to a witness, in cross-examination, that he has made a previous oral or written statement inconsistent with his testimony, and the witness admits that he has made such a statement, no further proof of the making of the statement is needed or permitted.[62] However, if the witness denies making the statement, or does not distinctly admit that he

---

[57] See Ch 5.
[58] CPR r 32.11.
[59] *Fairfield-Mabey Ltd v Shell UK Ltd* [1989] 1 All ER 576, QBD, a decision on an earlier version of the rules.
[60] [1963] 1 WLR 1080, P, D and Admlty relying on *Calvert v Flower* (1836) 7 C&P 386.
[61] See para 223 and cl 29 of the draft Bill (Cmnd 4991).
[62] *R v P (GR)* [1998] Crim LR 663, CA.

made it, and the statement is 'relative to the subject matter of the indictment', then it may be proved against him. The proof of such a statement in both civil and criminal proceedings is governed by sections 4 and 5 of the 1865 Act. Section 5 applies only to written statements, whereas section 4 applies to both oral and written statements.[63] Section 4 provides that:

> If a witness, upon cross-examination as to a former statement made by him relative to the subject matter of the indictment or proceeding, and inconsistent with his present testimony, does not distinctly admit that he has made such a statement, proof may be given that he did in fact make it; but before such proof can be given, the circumstances of the supposed statement, sufficient to designate the particular occasion, must be mentioned to the witness, and he must be asked whether or not he has made such statement.

This section assumes, correctly, the existence of a common law right to cross-examine a witness about a former inconsistent statement. It is not confined to previous statements made on oath.[64] The section refers to a witness who 'does not distinctly admit' his previous statement and accordingly applies not only to a witness who clearly denies the statement but also to a witness who, neither denying nor admitting the statement, is equivocal, asserts that he has no recollection of it, or refuses to answer.

Whether a statement is 'relative to the subject matter of the indictment or proceeding' is a matter within the discretion of the judge.[65] In *R v Funderburk*[66] F was charged with counts of sexual intercourse with a girl of 13. She gave evidence of a number of acts of intercourse with F, and her evidence of the first act clearly described the loss of her virginity. The defence claimed that she was lying and in order to explain how a girl of her age, if lying, could have given such detailed and varied accounts of the acts of intercourse, wished to show that she was sexually experienced and had either transposed to F experiences with others or fantasized about experiences with F. They wished (a) to put to her that she had told a Miss P that, before the first incident complained of, she had had sexual intercourse with two men; and (b) if she denied making this previous inconsistent statement, to call P to prove the conversation. As to (a), it was held that the proper test for cross-examination as to credit was not the test set out in the 1865 Act, but that suggested by Lawton LJ in *R v Sweet-Escott*,[67] and that the cross-examination should have been allowed because the jury might then have wished to reappraise the girl's evidence about the loss of her virginity. As to (b), it was held that the conversation, if denied, could have been proved, because the previous statement did not merely go to credit but was also 'relative to the subject matter of the indictment': where the disputed issue is a sexual one between two persons in private, the difference between questions going to credit and questions going to the issue is reduced to vanishing-point.[68]

Unlike section 4, section 5 applies only to previous written statements and constitutes a considerable departure from, and improvement on, the rules at common law.[69] It provides that:

> A witness may be cross-examined as to previous statements made by him in writing or reduced into writing relative to the subject-matter of the indictment or proceeding, without such writing

---

[63] *R v Derby Magistrates' Court, ex p B* [1996] AC 487, HL, per Lord Taylor CJ at 498.

[64] *R v Hart* (1957) 42 Cr App R 47, CCA; *R v O'Neill* [1969] Crim LR 260, CA.

[65] See per Veale J in *R v Bashir and Manzur* [1969] 1 WLR 1303, Assizes at 1306.

[66] [1990] 1 WLR 587, CA. Cf, *sed quaere*, *R v Gibson* [1993] Crim LR 453, CA.

[67] (1971) 55 Cr App R 316, CA, above.

[68] See also *R v Nagrecha* [1997] 2 Cr App R 401, CA; and cf *R v Neale* [1998] Crim LR 737, CA.

[69] See *Queen Caroline's Case* (1820) 2 Brod&Bing 284.

being shown to him; but if it is intended to contradict such witness by the writing, his attention must, before such contradictory proof can be given, be called to those parts of the writing which are to be used for the purpose of so contradicting him; provided always, that it shall be competent for the judge, at any time during the trial, to require the production of the writing for his inspection, and he may thereupon make such use of it for the purposes of the trial as he may think fit.

A witness under cross-examination is often taken by surprise when, without being shown a previous written statement made by him, he is asked by counsel whether he has ever said something inconsistent with his present testimony. Section 5 expressly permits the cross-examination of a witness about a previous statement contained in a document without that document being shown to him, but because the judge, pursuant to section 5, may require production of the document and make such use of it as he may think fit, the cross-examining party must have the document with him even if he does not intend to contradict the witness with it.[70]

If that party wishes to contradict the witness, he should, without reading the contents of the document aloud, hand it to the witness, direct his attention to the relevant part of its contents, ask him to read that part of the document to himself and then inquire whether he still wishes to stand by the evidence which he has given. If the witness adopts the previous statement, it becomes part of his evidence, which has therefore changed, and to that extent his credibility will have been impeached. If the witness adheres to his original evidence, there is no obligation on the cross-examining party to put the document in evidence, a course which he may well wish to avoid if the discrepancy is minor or the document, taken as a whole, tends to confirm rather than contradict the witness.[71] The cross-examining party, therefore, may simply accept the answer given and move on to some other matter. However, if the cross-examining party does wish to contradict the witness, he must then prove the document and put it in evidence.[72] After reading aloud the relevant parts of the previous statement, or inviting the witness to do so, the cross-examining party will put it to the witness that the truth of the matter is contained in the earlier statement as opposed to his evidence. Once the document has been put in evidence, the tribunal of fact may inspect it in its entirety, looking at those passages, if any, which are consistent, as well as those which are inconsistent with the evidence given by the witness. However, although the *whole* document may be put before the jury, because under section 5 the judge may 'make such use of it for the purposes of the trial as he may think fit', he has a discretion to permit the jury to see only those parts on which the cross-examination was based, and not other parts relating to other unconnected matters.[73]

Where a prior inconsistent statement has been put in evidence under section 4 or section 5 of the 1865 Act, in both civil and criminal proceedings it is admissible not merely as evidence of inconsistency going to credit, but also as evidence of the matters stated. Under section 1 of the 1995 Act, in civil proceedings evidence shall not be excluded on the ground that it is hearsay. Section 6(3) and (5) of the 1995 Act provide as follows:

---

[70] *R v Anderson* (1930) 21 Cr App R 178, CCA.

[71] For an example of a case where the admission of a prior inconsistent statement must have been, at best, a mixed blessing, see *R v Askew* [1981] Crim LR 398, CA, where defence counsel cross-examined the victim of an alleged rape on a statement made to the police in which she had incriminated the appellant. But see *R v Beattie* (1989) 89 Cr App R 302, CA, below.

[72] Per Channell B in *R v Riley* (1866) 4 F&F 964; *R v Wright* (1866) 4 F&F 967.

[73] *R v Beattie* (1989) 89 Cr App R 302, CA.

(3) Where in the case of civil proceedings section . . . 4 or 5 of the Criminal Procedure Act 1865 applies, which make provision as to—

. . .

(b) the proof of contradictory statements made by a witness, and

(c) cross-examination as to previous statements made in writing,

this Act does not authorise the adducing of evidence of a previous inconsistent or contradictory statement otherwise than in accordance with those sections. ...

(5) Nothing in this section shall be construed as preventing a statement of any description referred to above from being admissible by virtue of s 1 as evidence of the matters stated.

As to criminal proceedings, section 119(1) of the 2003 Act, which is considered further in Chapter 10, provides as follows:

(1) If in criminal proceedings, a person gives oral evidence and—

(a) he admits making a previous inconsistent statement, or

(b) a previous inconsistent statement made by him is proved by virtue of section 3, 4 or 5 of the Criminal Procedure Act 1865,

the statement is admissible as evidence of any matter stated of which oral evidence by him would be admissible.

In both civil and criminal cases, therefore, the tribunal of fact will have to decide whether the truth is to be found in what the witness said on oath, in what he said in the previous statement but denied on oath, or is to be found elsewhere because neither version can be accepted as the truth of the matter.[74] By allowing a previous inconsistent statement to be put before the tribunal of fact for the truth of the matter stated, section 119 of the 2003 Act has introduced a significant change to criminal proceedings which can operate unfairly to the prejudice of the accused. Protection is contained in the court's powers to exclude evidence,[75] to direct an acquittal or discharge the jury where the evidence provided by the statement is unconvincing,[76] and to give appropriate directions to the jury[77].

Complainants in proceedings for sexual offences

In cases of rape and other sexual offences, whether, and to what extent, evidence may be adduced, or the complainant cross-examined, by or on behalf of the accused, about her or his sexual experience with the accused or any other person, is now governed by sections 41–43 of the 1999 Act. These provisions, which restrict the use that the accused can make of evidence of the complainant's sexual history, reflect a recognition that it is bad for society if victims of sexual crimes do not complain, for fear that they will be harassed unfairly at trial by questions about their previous sexual experiences, because in consequence the guilty may escape justice. However, the intention underlying the provisions is also to counter what in the Canadian jurisprudence has been described as the twin myths

---

[74] In criminal proceedings, before the jury may rely on either the witness's evidence or prior statement as evidence of truth supporting the prosecution case, they must be sure that it is true. Where it is exculpatory of the defendant, it is sufficient if the jury are persuaded that it may be true. See *R v Billingham* [2009] 2 Cr App 341, CA.

[75] See, eg, *R v Coates* [2008] 1 Cr App R 52, CA.

[76] Section 125 of the Criminal Justice Act 2003.

[77] See *R v Joyce* [2005] All ER (D) 309 (Jun), [2005] EWCA Crim 1798 and *R v Bennett* [2008] EWCA Crim 248.

that unchaste women are more likely to consent to intercourse and in any event are less worthy of belief.[78] Lord Steyn, in the leading case of *R v A (No 2)*, said:[79]

> Such generalized, stereotyped and unfounded prejudices ought to have no place in our legal system. But even in the very recent past such defensive strategies were habitually employed. It resulted in an absurdly low conviction rate in rape cases. It also inflicted unacceptable humiliation on complainants in rape cases.

Prior to the 1999 Act, a distinction was drawn between evidence of previous sexual experiences with the accused, which was admissible as rendering it more likely that the complainant consented on the occasion under investigation, and evidence of previous sexual experiences with others, which, under section 2 of the Sexual Offences (Amendment) Act 1976 (the 1976 Act), now repealed, was only admissible if the judge was satisfied that it would be unfair to the accused to refuse its admission. No such distinction exists under the 1999 Act, but a number of new and difficult distinctions have been introduced and have given rise to lively academic debate.[80] However, their impact on the use of sexual history evidence appears to have been limited and the conviction rate for rape continued to fall after their implementation; there is certainly scope for strengthening the legislation.[81]

The restriction

Section 41(1) of the 1999 Act provides as follows:

(1) If at a trial a person is charged with a sexual offence, then, except with the leave of the court—
   (a) no evidence may be adduced, and
   (b) no question may be asked in cross-examination, by or on behalf of any accused at the trial, about any sexual behaviour of the complainant.

Section 41 applies to a number of other proceedings, as it applies to a trial, including any hearing held, between conviction and sentencing, for the purposes of deciding matters relevant to the court's decision as to how the accused is to be dealt with, and the hearing of an appeal; and references in section 41 to a person charged with an offence accordingly include a person convicted of an offence.[82] Under section 62, a 'sexual offence', for the purposes of section 41, means any offence under Part 1 of the Sexual Offences Act 2003[83] or any 'relevant superseded offence'.[84] 'Sexual behaviour' is defined in section 42(1)(c), which provides as follows:

---

[78] See per McLachlin J in *R v Seaboyer* [1991] 2 SCR 577 (Supreme Court of Canada) at 604 and per Lords Steyn and Hutton in *R v A (No 2)* [2002] 1 AC 45, HL at [27] and [147] respectively.

[79] Ibid at [27].

[80] See Neil Kibble, 'The Sexual History Provisions: Charting a course between inflexible legislative rules and wholly untrammelled judicial discretion?' [2000] *Crim LR* 274 and 'Judicial Perspectives on the Operation of s 41 and the Relevance and Admissibility of Prior Sexual History Evidence: Four Scenarios' [2005] *Crim LR* 190; Jennifer Temkin, 'Sexual History Evidence—Beware the Backlash' [2003] *Crim LR* 217; Di Birch, 'Rethinking Sexual History Evidence: Proposals for Fairer Trials' [2002] *Crim LR* 531 and 'Untangling Sexual History Evidence: A Rejoinder to Professor Temkin' [2003] *Crim LR* 370; and Mike Redmayne, 'Myths, relationships and coincidences: The new problems of sexual history' (2003) 7 *E&P* 75.

[81] For an evaluation of the impact of s 41 and recommendations for improvement, see the study commissioned by the Home Office, Kelly et al, *Section 41: an evaluation of new legislation limiting sexual history evidence in rape trials*, Home Office Online Report 20/06. Cf David Wolchover and Anthony Heaton-Armstrong, 'Debunking rape myths' (2008) 158 *NLJ* 117.

[82] Section 42(3).

[83] See also s 42(1)(d) and (2).

[84] See n 12, above.

(c) 'sexual behaviour' means any sexual behaviour or other sexual experience, whether or not involving any accused or other person, but excluding (except in s 41(3)(c)(i) and (5)(a)) anything alleged to have taken place as part of the event which is the subject matter of the charge against the accused.

Such a definition, it is submitted, covers not only physical advances of a sexual nature, but also verbal advances.[85] The definition also covers sexual behaviour or sexual experience even if it does not involve any other person. Leave would be required, for example, to introduce evidence of the possession of a vibrator, which could be relevant as evidence of the possible cause of the ruptured state of a complainant's hymen.[86] Whether behaviour or experience is 'sexual' cannot depend upon the perception of the complainant, because that would result in many vulnerable people, including children and those with learning difficulties, losing the protection of section 41.[87]

In *R v B*[88] it was held that there is no difference in substance between questions of a female complainant about her suggested sexual habits or promiscuity or frequency of casual sexual engagement and questions of a male complainant about his suggested homosexuality and casual homosexual encounters. In each case the questions are predicated on the proposition that previous consent is evidence of present consent and fall squarely within the restriction in section 41(1).

In *R v T*[89] it was held that normally, questions, or evidence about the complainant's past false statements about sexual assaults, or about a failure to complain about the assault which is the subject matter of the charge at the time when she complained about sexual assaults by others, are not 'about' any sexual behaviour of the complainant, because they relate not to her sexual behaviour but to her past statements or her past failure to complain, and the purpose of the 1999 Act was not to exclude such evidence. However, it was also held, *per curiam*, that if the defence wish to put questions about previous false complaints, they should seek a ruling from the judge that section 41 does not exclude them. It would be improper to put such questions as a device to smuggle in evidence about the complainant's past sexual behaviour. In any such case the defence must have a proper evidential basis for asserting that the previous statement was both made and untrue. Without such a basis, the questions are not about lies but about sexual behaviour within the meaning of section 41(1).[90] In *R v M*[91] it was held that a 'proper evidential basis' is less than a strong factual foundation for concluding that the previous complaint was false, but must comprise some material from which that conclusion could properly be reached. The basis may, depending on the circumstances, derive from the complainant's subsequent failure to cooperate with the police,[92] but presumably not where there is evidence to establish reasons for non-cooperation other than fabrication, such as fear of the criminal process itself. Where there is a proper evidential basis, there is an additional

[85] See *R v Hinds* [1979] Crim LR 111 (Crown Court) and *R v Viola* [1982] 1 WLR 1138, CA, both decided under the 1976 Act.

[86] Cf *R v Barnes* [1994] Crim LR 691, CA.

[87] *R v E* [2005] Crim LR 227, CA.

[88] [2007] Crim LR 910, CA.

[89] [2002] 1 WLR 632, CA.

[90] Applied in *R v E* [2005] Crim LR 227, CA.

[91] [2009] EWCA Crim 618; See also *R v Garaxo* [2005] Crim LR 883, CA.

[92] *R v V* [2005] All ER (D) 404 (Jul), [2006] EWCA Crim 1901 and *R v Garaxo* [2005] Crim LR 883, CA.

hurdle: leave is required under section 100(1) of the 2003 Act,[93] because questioning about previous false complaints would relate to the bad character of the complainant.[94]

The principle established in *R v T* has no application where an accused seeks to adduce evidence of the fact that a statement was made by the complainant about her previous sexual experience simply to show that the statement was made, rather than that it was false, as when it is argued that it is relevant to a defence of belief in consent: such evidence falls within section 41(1).[95] Nor does the principle apply to evidence or questions about the complaint's false denials concerning her previous sexual experiences because the falsity of the denial can only be exposed if the complainant's sexual behaviour is established.[96]

Section 41 only applies to evidence to be adduced or questions to be put 'by or on behalf of any accused at the trial'. In appropriate circumstances, therefore, evidence of the complainant's sexual behaviour may be adduced by the prosecution, as in *R v Soroya*,[97] where the evidence was relevant to the issue of consent because it showed that the complainant had *falsely* told the accused that she was a virgin in the hope that this might cause him to desist from the assault on her. The court rejected the argument that because such evidence cannot be introduced by the defence, its admission infringes the principle of equality of arms between the defence and prosecution in breach of the right to a fair trial under Article 6 of the European Convention on Human Rights, observing that where appropriate section 78 of the Police and Criminal Evidence Act 1984 can be deployed.

When the restriction may be lifted

Under section 41(2) of the 1999 Act, the court may not give leave in relation to any evidence or question unless satisfied (a) that the evidence or question is of the kind specified in section 41(3) or (5) and (b) a refusal of leave might render unsafe a conclusion of the jury or court on any 'relevant issues in the case', ie any issue falling to be proved by the prosecution or defence in the trial of the accused.[98] Subsection (3) covers evidence or questions relating to a relevant issue in the case and draws an important distinction between cases in which that issue is not an 'issue of consent' and cases in which it is. An 'issue of consent', for these purposes, means any issue whether the complainant in fact consented to the conduct constituting the offence with which the accused is charged (and accordingly does not include any issue as to the belief of the accused that the complainant so consented).[99] Subsection (5) covers evidence or questions to rebut or explain evidence adduced by the prosecution about any sexual behaviour of the complainant.

Section 41(2) to (8) provide as follows:

(2) The court may give leave in relation to any evidence or question only on an application made by or on behalf of an accused, and may not give such leave unless it is satisfied—

    (a) that subsection (3) or (5) applies; and

    (b) that a refusal of leave might have the result of rendering unsafe a conclusion of the jury or (as the case may be) the court on any relevant issue in the case.

---

[93] See Ch 17.
[94] *R v V* [2006] EWCA Crim 1901.
[95] *R v W* [2005] Crim LR 965, CA.
[96] *R v Winter* [2008] Crim LR 971, CA.
[97] [2007] Crim LR 181, CA.
[98] Section 42(1)(a).
[99] Section 42(1)(b).

(3) This subsection applies if the evidence or question relates to a relevant issue in the case and either—

    (a) that issue is not an issue of consent; or

    (b) it is an issue of consent and the sexual behaviour of the complainant to which the evidence or question relates is alleged to have taken place at or about the same time as the event which is the subject matter of the charge against the accused; or

    (c) it is an issue of consent and the sexual behaviour of the complainant to which the evidence or question relates is alleged to have been, in any respect, so similar—

        (i) to any sexual behaviour of the complainant which (according to evidence adduced or to be adduced by or on behalf of the accused) took place as part of the event which is the subject matter of the charge against the accused, or

        (ii) to any other sexual behaviour of the complainant which (according to such evidence) took place at or about the same time as that event,

    that the similarity cannot reasonably be explained as a coincidence.

(4) For the purposes of subsection (3) no evidence or question shall be regarded as relating to a relevant issue in the case if it appears to the court to be reasonable to assume that the purpose (or main purpose) for which it would be adduced or asked is to establish or elicit material for impugning the credibility of the complainant as a witness.

(5) This subsection applies if the evidence or question—

    (a) relates to any evidence adduced by the prosecution about any sexual behaviour of the complainant; and

    (b) in the opinion of the court, would go no further than is necessary to enable the evidence adduced by the prosecution to be rebutted or explained by or on behalf of the accused.

(6) For the purposes of subsections (3) and (5) the evidence or question must relate to a specific instance (or specific instances) of alleged sexual behaviour on the part of the complainant (and accordingly nothing in those subsections is capable of applying in relation to the evidence or question to the extent that it does not so relate).

(7) Where this section applies in relation to a trial by virtue of the fact that one or more of a number of persons charged in the proceedings is or are charged with a sexual offence—

    (a) it shall cease to apply in relation to the trial if the prosecutor decides not to proceed with the case against that person or those persons in respect of that charge; but

    (b) it shall not cease to do so in the event of that person or those persons pleading guilty to, or being convicted of, that charge.

(8) Nothing in this section authorizes any evidence to be adduced or any question to be asked which cannot be adduced or asked apart from this section.

Before leave can be granted, the test in section 41(2)(b) must always be met. It would seem that 'a refusal of leave might have the result of rendering unsafe a conclusion of the jury . . . on any relevant issue' (which typically, in a rape case, will be the issue of consent or mistaken belief in consent), where to disallow the evidence or question would prevent the jury (or court) from hearing (taking into account) something which might cause them to change their minds on that issue. This hurdle, therefore, is not particularly high: the court need only be satisfied that a refusal of leave *might* have the consequence specified, not that such a consequence is probable or even likely. The last point is of particular significance where section 41(3)(a) applies, ie where the evidence or question relates to a relevant issue in the case other than whether the complainant in fact consented, because in such cases section 41(2)(b) is the *only* condition to be met.

The operation of section 41 involves, not the exercise of judicial discretion, but making a judgment whether to admit evidence said by the defence to be relevant. If it is relevant, then subject to section 41(4), and assuming that the criteria for admitting it are established, all of it may be adduced. The judge must ensure that a complainant is not unnecessarily humiliated or cross-examined with inappropriate aggression, and is treated with proper courtesy, but this does not permit him, by way of general discretion, to exclude evidence admissible under section 41 merely because it comes in a stark, uncompromising form.[100]

The following examples may be given of issues falling within section 41(3)(a): (i) the defence of reasonable belief in consent; (ii) that the complainant was biased against the accused or had a motive to fabricate the evidence; (iii) that there is an alternative explanation for the physical conditions on which the Crown relies to establish that intercourse took place; and (iv) especially in the case of young complainants, that the detail of their account must have come from some other sexual activity before or after the event which provides an explanation for their knowledge of that activity.[101] As to (i), in *R v Barton*[102] it was stressed that, when considering the effect of the complainant's past sexual behaviour on the accused's belief in consent, whereas evidence of his belief that the complainant was consenting to intercourse is relevant, evidence of his belief that the complainant would consent if advances were made is irrelevant. Although *R v Barton* was a decision under section 2 of the 1976 Act relating to a defence of *mistaken* belief in consent, the distinction was subsequently approved by the Court of Appeal in *R v Winter*[103] in relation to a decision under section 41 of the 1999 Act relating to a defence of *reasonable* belief in consent under the Sexual Offences Act 2003.

In *R v Mokrecovas*,[104] a case of rape in which the defence was consent, the issue was whether it was open to the defence under section 41(3)(a) to cross-examine the complainant about an allegation that she had had consensual sexual intercourse with the accused's brother on two occasions in the 12 hours before the alleged rape. It was submitted that the cross-examination did not go to the issue of consent but to the separate issue of the complainant's motive for lying to her father when she first complained of rape. The foundations for the allegation of this motive were that the rape had occurred when the complainant had stayed away from home without the permission of her parents, that she had drunk to excess, and that she had stayed in the flat of the two brothers and her parents may well have thought that she had been guilty of sexual behaviour of which they would disapprove. It was held that cross-examination about sexual intercourse with the accused's brother would add nothing to these foundations for the allegation.

Subsections (3)(b) and (c) were designed to reverse the decision in *R v Riley*:[105] in a rape case, leave will not be granted in relation to evidence or questions about sexual behaviour of the complainant simply because the behaviour in question is previous voluntary sexual intercourse with the accused. In many cases, however, the jury will be likely to infer such behaviour by virtue of the other evidence in the case, as when evidence is introduced that the accused and the complainant are married or have cohabited for a period of time, and in this situation, it is submitted, the judge, rather than simply ignore the likelihood of such an inference being drawn, should direct the jury that any such inference can have no bearing on the issues to be decided.

[100] *R v F* [2005] 1 WLR 2848, CA (videotapes of the complainant stripping and masturbating).
[101] See per Lord Hope in *R v A (No 2)* [2002] 1 AC 45 at [79]. As to (i), Lord Hope referred to the defence of 'honest' belief in consent, but see now ss 1(1)(c) and 75–77 of the Sexual Offences Act 2003.
[102] (1986) 85 Cr App R 5, CA.
[103] [2008] Crim LR 971, CA.
[104] [2002] 1 Cr App R 226, CA.
[105] (1887) 18 QBD 481, CCR.

To come within section 41(3)(b), the evidence or question must relate to sexual behaviour alleged to have taken place at or about the same time as the event which is the subject matter of the charge, other than anything alleged to have taken place as part of that event.[106] The distinction between sexual behaviour which took place at the same time as the event, and sexual behaviour which took place as part of the event, is not readily apparent. The meaning of 'the event which is the subject matter of the charge' is also unclear, but seems designed to embrace more than 'the conduct constituting the offence'.[107] The phrase 'at or about the same time as the event', although it provides a degree of elasticity, is a narrow temporal restriction and prima facie prohibits questions both as to a continuous period of cohabitation or sexual activity, and as to individual events more than a very limited period before or after the 'event', generally no more than 24 hours before or after the offence.[108] Section 41(3)(b) could cover behaviour such as any sexual advances made by the complainant towards the accused or other men shortly before or after 'the event' and other behaviour relevant to the issue of consent. An example would be an allegation that the complainant invited the accused to have sexual intercourse with her earlier in the evening.[109] However, the example furnished by *R v Mukadi*[110] seems hard to justify.

Subsection (3)(c) covers the sexual behaviour of the complainant with the accused (or another man) on another occasion, provided that it is sufficiently similar in nature to her behaviour during, or shortly before or after, the event which is the subject matter of the charge. It was included in the Act in response to the *Romeo and Juliet* scenario advanced by Baroness Mallalieu.[111] She envisaged a complainant in a rape case who says that the accused climbed up onto her balcony and into her bedroom, but who, on occasions both before and after the alleged rape—but not 'at or about the same time as the event' under section 41(3)(b)—invited men to re-enact the *Romeo and Juliet* balcony scene prior to consensual sexual intercourse. An example, provided by Lord Steyn in *R v A (No 2)*,[112] would be, in a rape case in which the accused says that after consensual intercourse the complainant tried to blackmail him by alleging rape, evidence of a previous occasion when she similarly tried to blackmail him.[113] Such evidence is introduced under section 41(3)(c) not so much to show that history has been repeated as to indicate a state of mind on the part of the complainant which is potentially highly relevant to her state of mind on the occasion in question.[114] A comparison can be made

---

[106] Section 42(1)(c).

[107] A phrase also used in s 42(1): see s 42(1)(b).

[108] *R v A (No 2)* [2002] 1 AC 45, per Lords Slynn, Steyn, and Hope at [9], [40], and [82] respectively. But see also per Lord Clyde at [132], who was of the view that it is undesirable to prescribe any test in terms of days or hours, while accepting that it may be difficult to extend the period to 'several days'.

[109] Ibid, per Lord Steyn at [40].

[110] [2004] Crim LR 373, CA.

[111] House of Lords Committee Stage, Hansard, 1 Feb 1999, col 45.

[112] [2002] 1 AC 45 at [42].

[113] See also *R v T* [2004] 2 Cr App R 32, CA, where the alleged rape took place in a climbing frame in a park and there was evidence that three to four weeks earlier the accused and the complainant had had consensual intercourse in the same climbing frame and had adopted the same positions (both standing and the complainant facing away from the accused); and *R v Harris* [2010] Crim LR 54, where the Court of Appeal stated that *R v T* was an easy case, the similarity being so clear that it was not disputed. In more difficult cases the court indicated that it would not interfere where the judge adopted a view on similarity which was open to him within the margin of judgement open to a decision maker.

[114] Per Lord Clyde in *R v A (No 2)* at [133].

between the wording of section 41(3)(c) and the concept of similar fact evidence as formulated by Lord Salmon in *DPP v Boardman:*[115] 'The similarity would have to be so unique or striking that common sense makes it inexplicable on the basis of coincidence.' However, as Lord Clyde said in *R v A (No 2)*[116] the phrase 'striking similarity' is not used in section 41(3)(c)—the standard is something short of a striking similarity. Elaborating on this, Lord Clyde said:[117]

> It is only a similarity that is required, not an identity. Moreover the words 'in any respect' deserve to be stressed. On one view any single factor of similarity might suffice to attract the application of the provision, provided that it is not a matter of coincidence. That the behaviour was with the same person, the defendant, must be at least a relevant consideration. But if the identity of the defendant was alone sufficient as the non-coincidental factor that would seem to open the way in almost every case for a complete inquiry into the whole of the complainant's sexual behaviour with the defendant at least in the recent past, and that can hardly have been the intention of the provision. What must be found is a similarity in some other or additional respect. Further the similarity must be such as cannot reasonably be explained as coincidence. To my mind that does not necessitate that the similarity has to be in some rare or bizarre conduct.

However, in *R v A (No 2)* the House of Lords also recognized that as a matter of common sense a prior sexual relationship between the accused and the complainant may, depending on the circumstances, be relevant to the issue of consent, as a species of prospectant evidence which, although it cannot prove consent on the occasion in question, may throw light on the complainant's state of mind.[118] Recognizing further that section 41 is therefore prima facie capable of preventing an accused from putting forward relevant evidence which may be critical to his defence, whether one of consent or belief in consent, the House was of the unanimous view that it is possible under section 3 of the Human Rights Act 1998 (the 1998 Act) to read section 41 of the 1999 Act, and in particular section 41(3)(c), as subject to the implied provision that evidence or questioning which is required to ensure a fair trial under Article 6 of the European Convention on Human Rights should not be treated as inadmissible. The result is that sometimes logically relevant evidence of sexual experience between a complainant and an accused may be admitted under section 41(3)(c). Lord Steyn said:[119] 'section 3 of the 1998 Act requires the court to subordinate the niceties of the language of section 41(3)(c) of the 1999 Act, and in particular the touchstone of coincidence, to broader considerations of relevance judged by logical and commonsense criteria of time and circumstances.' Members of the House were agreed as to the effect of its decision, namely that:

> under s 41(3)(c) of the 1999 Act, construed where necessary by applying the interpretative obligation under s 3 of the 1998 Act, and due regard always being paid to the importance of seeking to protect the complainant from indignity and from humiliating questions, the test of admissibility is whether the evidence (and questioning in relation to it) is nevertheless so relevant to the issue of consent that to exclude it would endanger the fairness of the trial under art 6 of the Convention. If this test is satisfied, the evidence should not be excluded.[120]

---

[115] [1975] AC 421, HL at 462.
[116] [2002] 1 AC 45 at [133].
[117] Ibid at [135].
[118] See, eg, per Lord Steyn at [31].
[119] At [45].
[120] Per Lord Steyn at [46].

Thus where there has been a recent close and affectionate relationship between the complainant and the accused, it is probable that the evidence will be relevant and admissible, not to prove consent, but to show the complainant's specific mindset towards the accused, namely her affection for him. But where, as in *R v A (No 2)* itself, there have only been some isolated acts of intercourse, even if fairly recently, without the background of an affectionate relationship, it is probable that the evidence will not be relevant. It is not possible to state with precision where the line is to be drawn—it will depend on the facts of the individual case as assessed by the trial judge.[121] *R v A (No 2)* was applied in *R v R*[122] where it was held that permission should have been given to the defence to cross-examine the complainant about both a previous consensual sexual relationship with the accused and consensual sexual intercourse with the accused occurring some 11 months after the alleged offence.

It is very much more difficult to show relevance to the issue of consent in the case of evidence of the complainant's sexual behaviour with men other than the accused than in the case of evidence of sexual behaviour with the accused himself.[123] In *R v White*,[124] W denied rape and said that the complainant had asked him for money which he had refused to give her, and that after consensual intercourse he had woken up to find her with his wallet. It was held that the judge had properly refused an application to cross-examine the complainant on her previous and ongoing activities as a prostitute. A prostitute was as entitled as any other person to say 'no' to sex and the fact that the complainant was a prostitute did not mean that she was more ready than any other to say 'yes'. The bare fact that the complainant was a prostitute was therefore irrelevant to the issue of consent. There had to be something about the specific circumstances that satisfied the test in section 41(3)(c). *R v A (No 2)*, it was held, could be distinguished, since it did not concern the introduction of evidence of sexual behaviour with men other than the accused, and it would take a very special case to admit such evidence in circumstances where it could not be admitted by an ordinary reading of section 41.

Section 41(4) operates where 'the purpose' or the 'main purpose' for adducing the evidence or asking the question is to impugn the credibility of the complainant. In *R v Martin,*[125] a case of indecent assault involving enforced oral sex, M alleged that the complainant had fabricated her evidence because he had rejected her advances. It was held that the defence should have been allowed to question her about his allegation that two days earlier she had not merely pestered him for sex, but had performed an act of oral sex upon him, after which he had rejected her. It was held that although one purpose of the questioning was to impugn the credibility of the complainant, it also went to the accused's credibility and strengthened the defence case of fabrication, because the jury might have interpreted a rejection after the performance of oral sex as more hurtful than rejection after mere verbal advances.

Following *R v Martin*, it has been observed that merely because evidence may impugn the complainant's credibility, it does not follow that the purpose or main purpose for deploying it is to do so.[126] However, section 41(4), construed literally, would mean that where the purpose or main purpose is to impugn the complainant's credibility, the evidence or question cannot be regarded as relating to a relevant issue in the case, even where it plainly does relate to such an issue and

---

[121] Per Lord Hutton at [152].
[122] [2003] All ER (D) 346 (Oct), [2003] EWCA Crim 2754 .
[123] See per Lord Clyde at [125]–[127].
[124] [2004] All ER (D) 103 (Mar), [2004] EWCA Crim 946,
[125] [2004] 2 Cr App R 354, CA.
[126] Per Judge LJ in *R v F* [2005] 1 WLR 2848, CA at [27].

where to refuse leave to adduce the evidence or ask the question, might have the result, to use the words of section 41(2)(b), 'of rendering unsafe a conclusion of the jury . . . on any relevant issue in the case'. Such a construction, however, would in very large measure seem to defeat the purposes of section 41(3)(b) and (c), because when the issue is consent and the sexual behaviour of the complainant is relevant to that issue, in many if not most cases it will satisfy the test in section 41(2)(b) on the basis that the jury will hear something which will cause them to change their minds about the complainant's evidence in relation to the issue of consent, which all too often, of course, will be to impugn the credibility of the complainant. For these reasons, it is submitted, section 41(4) should be taken to mean that no evidence or question shall be regarded as relating to a relevant issue if the purpose (or main purpose) is to suggest nothing more than that the complainant, by reason of her sexual behaviour, ought not to be believed on oath.

Subsection (4) applies only for the purposes of subsection (3) and not for the purposes of subsection (5), which concerns evidence, or a question, in rebuttal or explanation of evidence adduced by the prosecution about *any* sexual behaviour of the complainant, including anything alleged to have taken place as part of the event which is the subject matter of the charge.[127] Thus, in *R v F*[128] where the complainant gave evidence that she had been raped by her mother's partner, that she had subsequently become pregnant but had not been sexually active with anyone else at the time, the Court of Appeal held that the accused ought to have been permitted to ask questions about the complainant's medical notes which recorded that to her doctor she had attributed her pregnancy to a 'condom accident' with her boyfriend and that she subsequently been prescribed oral contraceptives. However, in *R v Winter*,[129] where the complainant, who claimed that she had been raped by the accused, sought to give evidence that at the time of the alleged offence she was in a happy long-term relationship with her partner, the statement was held not to be so misleading that evidence of an affair with another man was admissible in rebuttal. 'Evidence adduced by the prosecution' refers to evidence placed before the jury by prosecution witnesses in the course of their evidence-in-chief and by other witnesses in the course of cross-examination by prosecuting counsel and, where it is necessary to ensure a fair trial, may also include something said by a prosecution witness in cross-examination about the complainant's sexual behaviour which was not deliberately elicited by defence counsel and is potentially damaging to the accused's case.[130] The subsection only allows the defence to rebut *evidence* adduced by the prosecution about the sexual behaviour of the complainant, and not, it seems, inferences about her sexual behaviour that may reasonably be drawn from evidence adduced by the prosecution.

Section 41(6) would rule out, for example, evidence or questions revealing the complainant to be, for example, a prostitute or of a promiscuous nature. Nor will the requirements of section 41(6) be met, in the case of a prostitute, by the information contained in a list of previous convictions for prostitution.[131] However, in some cases, of course, evidence or questions relating to specific instances may well allow the jury to infer that the complainant was a prostitute or promiscuous, as would happen, for example, if evidence were to be introduced that the accused had on a number of previous occasions agreed to sleep with men for money.

[127] See s 42(1)(c).
[128] [2008] EWCA Crim 2859
[129] [2008] Crim LR 971, CA.
[130] *R v Hamadi* [2008] Crim LR 635, CA.
[131] *R v White* [2004] All ER (D) 103 (Mar), [2004] EWCA Crim 946.

The procedure on applications under section 41

Where the defence wish to make use of section 41, they must apply in writing pre-trial, identifying the issue to which the sexual behaviour is relevant and the exception to the general prohibition on which they rely and giving particulars of the evidence they want to introduce or the questions they want to ask; and a party who wishes to make representations about such an application must also do so in writing.[132] An application for leave under section 41 shall be heard in private and in the absence of the complainant.[133] After the court has reached its decision, it must state in open court, but in the absence of the jury (if there is one), its reasons for giving or refusing leave and, if it gives leave, the extent to which evidence may be adduced or questions asked in pursuance of the leave.[134]

Finality of answers to collateral questions

The rule

A party eliciting from a witness under cross-examination evidence unfavourable to his case, may understandably seek to adduce evidence in rebuttal. To allow that party to adduce such evidence without restriction, however, would lead to a multiplicity of issues, some of which might be of minimal relevance to the facts in issue in the case, and thereby prolong the trial unnecessarily. As a general rule, therefore, the answers given by a witness under cross-examination to questions concerning collateral matters, that is, matters which are irrelevant to the issues in the proceedings, must be treated as final. Finality for these purposes does not mean that the tribunal of fact is obliged to accept the answers as true, but simply that the cross-examining party is not permitted to call further evidence with a view to contradicting the witness.

Whether a question is collateral is not always easy to decide. According to the often cited test formulated by Pollock CB in *A-G v Hitchcock*,[135] if the witness's answer is a matter on which the cross-examining party would be allowed to introduce evidence-in-chief, because of its connection with the issues in the case, then the matter is not collateral and may be rebutted.[136] Relevance, however, is a question of degree, the answer to which may turn on whether the matter which the cross-examining party seeks to prove is a single fact which is easy of proof or a broad issue which will require the jury to embark on a difficult and complex task.[137] Questions which go merely to the credit of the witness are clearly collateral. However, where the disputed issue is a sexual one between two persons in private, the difference between questions going to credit and questions going to the issue is reduced to vanishing-point because sexual intercourse, whether or not consensual, most often takes place in private and leaves few visible traces of having occurred, so that the evidence is often effectively limited to that of the parties, and much is likely to depend upon the balance

---

[132] See Part 36 of the Criminal Procedure Rules 2005, SI 2005/384.

[133] Section 43(1).

[134] Section 43(2). A magistrates' court must also cause such matters to be entered in the register of its proceedings: s 43(2).

[135] (1847) 1 Exch 91 at 99.

[136] The test seems to be circular, but its utility may lie in the fact that the answer is an instinctive one, based on the sense of fair play of the prosecutor and the court rather than any philosophic or analytic process: per Henry J in *R v Funderburk* [1990] 1 WLR 587, CA at 598. But see also per Evans LJ in *R v Neale* [1998] Crim LR 737, CA: the decision is ultimately a matter of common sense and logic.

[137] *R v S* [1992] Crim LR 307, CA.

of credibility between them.[138] This principle, however, is not confined to cases involving sexual intercourse.[139]

Whether cross-examination goes merely to credit or can be said to be relevant to the issue in the proceedings is clearly a question of some difficulty. The nicety of the distinction is apparent in the authorities, some of which are difficult to reconcile. In *R v Burke*[140] an Irish witness who gave evidence through an interpreter and was cross-examined about his knowledge of English, denied that he was able to speak the language. The witness's ability to speak English being irrelevant to any matter directly in issue in the proceedings, it was held that evidence in rebuttal was inadmissible. In *A-G v Hitchcock*[141] a maltster was charged with the use of a cistern in breach of certain statutory requirements. A prosecution witness, who gave evidence that the cistern had been used, was asked in cross-examination whether he had not said to one Cook that the Excise officers offered him £20 to give evidence that the cistern had been used. The witness denied this allegation and it was held that counsel for the defence was not permitted to call Cook to give evidence in rebuttal of what the witness had said. Pollock CB said:[142]

> it is totally irrelevant to the matter in issue, that some person should have thought fit to offer a bribe to the witness to give an untrue account of a transaction, and it is of no importance whatever, if that bribe was not accepted.

Some of the criminal authorities as to the application of the rule, such as *R v Edwards*,[143] must be treated with caution insofar as they involved questioning the witness about his previous misconduct or disposition towards such misconduct. As previously noted, in criminal proceedings, the asking of questions about a witness's bad character is governed by sections 100 and 101 of the 2003 Act, which are considered in Chapter 17.

The exceptions

To the general rule on the finality of answers to collateral questions there are three exceptions, although it may be that the categories of exception are not closed.[144]

Previous convictions.   Under section 6 of the 1865 Act:

> If, upon a witness being lawfully questioned as to whether he has been convicted of any felony or misdemeanour, he either denies or does not admit the fact, or refuses to answer, it shall be lawful for the cross-examining party to prove such conviction.[145]

Section 6 applies to both civil and criminal proceedings. In criminal proceedings, a witness will only be 'lawfully questioned' as to his previous convictions where the questions are lawful having regard to the relevant provisions of the 2003 Act, namely section

[138] Per Henry J in *R v Funderburk* [1990] 1 WLR 587, CA at 597, citing *Cross on Evidence* (6th edn, London, 1985) 295.
[139] See *R v Nagrecha* [1997] 2 Cr App R 401, CA, a case of indecent assault, and *R v David R* [1999] Crim LR 909, CA; but see also s 41 of the Youth Justice and Evidence Act 1999.
[140] (1858) 8 Cox CC 44.
[141] (1847) 1 Exch 91; cf *R v Phillips* (1936) 26 Cr App R 17, CCA, below.
[142] (1847) 1 Exch 91 at 101.
[143] [1991] 1 WLR 207, CA. See also *R v Clancy* [1997] Crim LR 290, CA and *R v Irish* [1995] Crim LR 145, CA.
[144] *R v Funderburk* [1990] 1 WLR 587, CA, per Henry J at 599.
[145] However, if the witness accepts the conviction but claims his innocence, the cross-examining party may be prevented from adducing evidence in rebuttal: see *R v Irish* [1995] Crim LR 145, CA.

100 in the case of the previous convictions of a non-defendant and section 101 in the case of the previous convictions of the defendant. These provisions are considered in Chapter 17. In civil proceedings, cross-examination of any witness about 'spent' convictions is prohibited by section 4(1) of the Rehabilitation of Offenders Act 1974,[146] unless the judge is satisfied that it is not possible for justice to be done except by admitting the convictions.[147] This section does not apply in criminal proceedings, but under a *Practice Direction* issued by the Lord Chief Justice in 1975 no reference should be made to a spent conviction if that 'can reasonably be avoided'.[148] However, according to *R v Corelli*,[149] the *Practice Direction* does not operate to remove an unfettered statutory entitlement of a co-accused to cross-examine another co-accused on his previous convictions.[150] Subject to *R v Corelli*, the effect of the *Practice Direction* is to give the judge a wide discretion with the exercise of which the Court of Appeal will be loath to interfere. Thus in *R v Lawrence*,[151] where the trial judge refused the defence permission to question the victim of a wounding in detail on his 20 previous spent convictions, most of which were for offences of dishonesty, but did allow questions on four more recent offences, the Court of Appeal held that although it might have exercised the discretion differently and permitted cross-examination on one of the spent convictions, which involved perverting the course of justice, the judge had not erred in principle. In *R v Evans*,[152] on the other hand, a case of wounding with intent, the defence being self-defence, it was held that the judge should have allowed cross-examination of the victim on her previous but spent convictions for dishonesty and violence because, evidentially speaking, there was a head-on collision between the accused and the victim.

There is authority to suggest that, in civil proceedings, subject to section 4(1) of the Rehabilitation of Offenders Act 1974, section 6 permits a witness to be cross-examined about his convictions irrespective of their relevance to his credibility or the issues in the case.[153] It seems clear, however, that cross-examination about a witness's previous convictions is subject to the general power of the judge to restrain unnecessary, irrelevant, or unduly oppressive questions in cross-examination.[154] In civil proceedings, a judge may use the general exclusionary discretion under CPR rule 32[155] to limit cross-examination on previous convictions to the convictions of offences of dishonesty, although where sitting with a jury should be more hesitant in exercising the discretion.[156] It remains to mention that, in criminal proceedings,

[146] Exceptions to the applicability of s 4(1) are to be found in Sch 3 to the Rehabilitation of Offenders Act (Exceptions) Order 1975 (SI 1975/1023) and in s 189 of the Financial Services Act 1986.

[147] Section 7(3). Evidence of the conviction may be admitted under s 7(3) not only if relevant to an issue in the case, but also if relevant merely to the credit of the witness, but the judge should weigh its relevance and its prejudicial effect and only admit it if satisfied that otherwise the parties would not have a fair trial or the witness's credit could not be fairly assessed: *Thomas v Metropolitan Police Comr* [1997] QB 13, CA.

[148] See now *Practice Direction (Criminal Proceedings: Consolidation)* [2002] 1 WLR 2870, para 6. See also s 108 of the Criminal Justice Act 2003 (Ch 17).

[149] [2001] Crim LR 913, CA.

[150] The statutory entitlement in the case arose under s 1(3)(iii) of the Criminal Evidence Act 1898. See now s 101(1)(e) of the Criminal Justice Act 2003 (Ch 17).

[151] [1995] Crim LR 815, CA.

[152] [1992] Crim LR 125, CA.

[153] *Clifford v Clifford* [1961] 1 WLR 1274 P, D and Admlty at 1276.

[154] See, eg, per Lawton J in *R v Sweet-Escott* (1971) 55 Cr App R 316, Assizes.

[155] See Ch 2.

[156] *Watson v Chief Constable of Cleveland Police* [2001] All ER (D) 193 (Oct), [2001] EWCA Civ 1547.

section 101(1)(g) of the 2003 Act operates as a powerful disincentive to the use of section 6 by defence counsel in cross-examination of prosecution witnesses. We shall see in Chapter 17 that, under section 101(1)(g), the accused, by making an attack on another person's character, thereby renders admissible evidence of his own bad character.

Bias. 'It has always been permissible to call evidence to contradict a witness's denial of bias or partiality towards one of the parties and to show that he is prejudicial so far as the case being tried is concerned.'[157] Thus where a female servant of the claimant is called as his witness and denies in cross-examination that she is his kept mistress, the defendant may call evidence to contradict her.[158] Under s 99 of the 2003 Act, this common law principle has been abolished in criminal proceedings to the extent that it allows the introduction of evidence of the witness's bad character, ie evidence of, or of a disposition towards, misconduct on his part. However, much evidence of bias is likely to remain admissible at common law, because outside the statutory definition of evidence of bad character in section 98 of the 2003 Act, which excludes 'evidence of, or of a disposition towards misconduct . . . which has to do with the alleged facts of the offence with which the defendant is charged, or is evidence of misconduct in connection with the investigation or prosecution of that offence'. Alternatively, to the extent that the evidence is not admissible on that basis, it is likely to be admitted under section 100(1)(b) of the 2003 Act, ie as evidence of the bad character of a person other than the defendant which has substantial probative value in relation to a matter which is in issue in the proceedings and of substantial importance in the context of the case as a whole.[159] Thus the *outcome* in each of the following examples of the common law doctrine is likely to remain the same.

In *R v Shaw*[160] it was held that the accused may call evidence to contradict a prosecution witness who, in cross-examination, denies having threatened to be revenged on the accused following a quarrel with him. In *R v Mendy*,[161] during a trial for assault, and while a detective was giving evidence, a man in the public gallery was observed to be taking notes. The man was seen to leave the court and hold a conversation, apparently concerning the detective's evidence, with the accused's husband, who, as a prospective witness, had been kept out of court in accordance with the normal practice. The husband subsequently gave evidence and under cross-examination denied that he had spoken to the man in question. The Court of Appeal held that the trial judge had properly allowed evidence to be given in rebuttal. The jury were entitled to know that, in order to deceive them and help the accused, the witness was prepared to cheat.

The line dividing questions put to a witness in cross-examination concerning facts tending to show prejudice or bias, and those concerning collateral facts on which the witness's answers must be treated as final, is often a very fine one. Although in *A-G v Hitchcock*,[162] as we have seen, it was held that the witness's denial of an alleged statement by him that he had been *offered* a bribe, being a collateral matter, could not be contradicted, the court acknowledged that where a witness denies *acceptance* of a bribe to testify, a matter tending to show his

---

[157] Per Geoffrey Lane LJ in *R v Mendy* (1976) 64 Cr App R 4, CA at 6.
[158] *Thomas v David* (1836) 7 C&P 350.
[159] Sections 99 and 100 of the 2003 Act are considered in Ch 17.
[160] (1888) 16 Cox CC 503, Assizes.
[161] (1976) 64 Cr App R 4.
[162] (1847) 1 Exch 91.

partiality, evidence in rebuttal is admissible. *R v Phillip*[163] also falls to be contrasted with the actual decision in *A-G v Hitchcock*. The accused was charged with incest. His defence was that the principal prosecution witnesses, his two daughters, had been 'schooled' by their mother into giving false evidence. In cross-examination, the girls denied that their testimony was no more than a repetition of what their mother had told them to say. The girls also denied that on separate occasions each of them had admitted to another person that their evidence in previous criminal proceedings against their father for indecent assault had been false. The trial judge refused to allow defence counsel to call two women to whom these admissions were alleged to have been made. The Court of Criminal Appeal, quashing the conviction, held that this evidence was admissible on the grounds that the questions were directed not to the credibility of the two girls but went to the very foundation of the accused's defence.

In *R v Busby*[164] police officers were cross-examined on the basis that they had made up statements attributed to the accused and indicative of his guilt, and had threatened W, a potential witness for the defence, to stop him giving evidence. The allegations were denied. The trial judge ruled that W, who was subsequently called for the defence, could not give evidence that he had been threatened by the officers, because this would go solely to their credit. The Court of Appeal, allowing the appeal against conviction, held that the judge had erred: W's evidence was relevant to an issue which had to be tried, in that, if true it showed that the police were prepared to go to improper lengths in order to secure a conviction, and this would have supported the accused's case that the statements attributed to him had been fabricated. In *R v Funderburk*[165] *R v Busby* was treated as having created a new exception to the rule against finality, but in *R v Edwards*[166] it was held that the facts came within the exception of bias and that if the case could not be explained on that basis, it was inconsistent with the general rule itself.

Evidence of physical or mental disability affecting reliability.   The credibility of a witness may be impeached by expert medical evidence which shows that he suffers from some physical or mental disability that affects the reliability of his evidence.[167]

> If a witness purported to give evidence of something which he believed that he had seen at a distance of 50 yards, it must surely be possible to call the evidence of an oculist to the effect that the witness could not possibly see anything at a greater distance than 20 yards, or the evidence of a surgeon who had removed a cataract from which the witness was suffering at the material time and which would have prevented him from seeing what he thought he saw. So, too, must it be allowable to call medical evidence of mental illness which makes a witness incapable of giving reliable evidence, whether through the existence of delusions or otherwise.

These examples were given by Lord Pearce in *Toohey v Metropolitan Police Comr.*[168] Toohey was convicted with others of an assault with intent to rob. The defence was that the alleged victim had been drinking and that while they were trying to help him by taking him home, he became hysterical and accused them of the offence charged. The trial judge held that, although a doctor called for the defence could give evidence that when he examined the

---

[163] (1936) 26 Cr App R 17.

[164] (1981) 75 Cr App R, CA.

[165] [1990] 1 WLR 587, CA at 591.

[166] [1991] 1 WLR 207, CA at 215.

[167] For a critique of the use of psychiatric evidence in rape trials, see Ellison, 'The use and abuse of psychiatric evidence in rape trials' [2009] 13 *E&P* 28.

[168] [1965] AC 595 at 608. See also *R v Eades* [1972] Crim LR 99, Assizes.

victim he was hysterical and smelt of alcohol, he could not give evidence that in his opinion drink could exacerbate hysteria and that the alleged victim was more prone to hysteria than a normal person. The Court of Criminal Appeal dismissed the appeal, but the House of Lords, quashing the convictions, held that the doctor's evidence had been improperly excluded.[169] Lord Pearce, in a speech with which the other members of the House concurred, held that the evidence was admissible not only because of its relevance to the facts in issue, regardless of whether or not it affected the credibility of the alleged victim as a witness, but also to show that the evidence of the alleged victim was unreliable.

> Medical evidence is admissible to show that a witness suffers from some disease or defect or abnormality of mind that affects the reliability of his evidence. Such evidence is not confined to a general opinion of the unreliability of the witness but may give all the matters necessary to show, not only the foundation of and reasons for the diagnosis, but also the extent to which the credibility of the witness is affected.[170]

Expert opinion evidence is admissible in relation to matters requiring special knowledge or expertise, not matters within the ordinary experience and knowledge of the tribunal of fact. Thus expert medical evidence on the reliability of a witness will only be admissible if the disability from which the witness suffers is a proper subject of such evidence. As Lord Pearce observed in *Toohey v Metropolitan Police Comr*:[171]

> Human evidence ... is subject to many cross-currents such as partiality, prejudice, self-interest and above all, imagination and inaccuracy. Those are matters with which the jury, helped by cross-examination and common sense, must do their best. But when a witness through physical (in which I include mental) disease or abnormality is not capable of giving a true or reliable account to the jury, it must surely be allowable for medical science to reveal this vital hidden fact to them.

In *R v MacKenney*[172] the accused were convicted of murder. At their trial, they had alleged that the chief prosecution witness had fabricated his evidence and wished to call a psychologist by whom the witness had refused to be examined. The psychologist had watched the witness give his evidence and as a result had formed the opinion that he was a psychopath who was likely to be lying and whose mental state was such that his demeanour and behaviour when giving evidence would not convey the usual indications to the jury as to when he was lying. The evidence of the psychologist was ruled inadmissible. The convictions were upheld on appeal. On referral to the Court of Appeal by the Criminal Cases Review Commission, there was fresh evidence from a psychiatrist. He, too, had not examined the witness. His opinion was very similar to that of the psychologist who had attended the trial. It was held that the evidence of the psychologist would today be admissible and that the absence of an examination by the expert went to the weight to be attached to his opinion, not its admissibility. Deciding the reference on the fresh evidence, the conviction was quashed.

---

[169] The Court of Criminal Appeal was bound by the case of *R v Gunewardene* [1951] 2 KB 600, CCA which the House of Lords overruled.

[170] [1965] AC 595 at 609.

[171] [1965] AC 595 at 608.

[172] [2004] 2 Cr App R 32, CA.

In *R v Robinson*[173] it was held that although a party, A, cannot call a witness of fact, W, and then, without more, call a psychologist or psychiatrist to give reasons why the jury should regard W as reliable, if the other party, B, proposes to call an expert to say that W should be regarded as unreliable due to some mental abnormality outside the jury's experience, then A may call an expert in rebuttal or even, anticipating B's expert, as part of his own case. Where B does not call an expert, but puts a case in cross-examination that W is unreliable by reason of mental abnormality, this may also be open to rebuttal by expert evidence, although much may depend on the nature of the abnormality and of the cross-examination. If such expert evidence is admitted, it must be restricted to the specific challenge, and should not extend to 'oath-helping'. Thus on the facts of that case, since B had not called evidence impugning W's reliability and had not put a specific case in cross-examination that W was peculiarly suggestible or liable to fantasize as a result of her mental impairment, expert evidence to suggest the opposite was inadmissible.

R v Robinson was distinguished in *R v S*,[174] where it was held that the judge had not erred in allowing an expert to make a general observation that it would be unlikely for an autistic person, as the victim was, to have invented such an account as that given by her, leaving it to the jury to decide whether the victim was capable of belief.

The rule against 'oath-helping', however, will not necessarily prevent a non-expert from giving evidence as to the good character of a witness from which his likely reliability may be inferred. In *R v Tobin*,[175] a case of indecent assault on a girl, the defence claimed that the sexual activity had been initiated by the girl. The accused gave evidence that he was a married man with no previous convictions for sexual offences and called five character witnesses. The girl's mother was allowed to give evidence that she had never had problems with her daughter, who had done well at school, got on well with her siblings, was very polite and quiet, and had been brought up to respect people. It was held that the evidence did go to boost the claimant's credibility, but since full evidence had been given about the accused's character, the court's sense of fair play was not offended by admission of the evidence as to the complainant's character.

Re-examination

A witness who has been cross-examined may be re-examined by the party who called him.[176] The object of re-examination is, in broad terms, to repair such damage as has been done by the cross-examining party insofar as he has elicited evidence from the witness supporting his version of the facts in issue and cast doubt upon the witness's evidence-in-chief.

The cardinal rule of re-examination is that it must be confined to such matters as arose out of the cross-examination.[177] Thus although the witness may be asked to clarify or explain any matters, including evidence of new facts, which arose in cross-examination, questions on other matters may only be asked with the leave of the judge. In *Prince v Samo*[178] Lord

---

[173] [1994] 3 All ER 346, CA. See also *R v Beard* [1998] Crim LR 585, CA.

[174] [2006] EWCA Crim 2389.

[175] [2003] Crim LR 408, CA.

[176] Even a hostile witness, apparently, may be re-examined by the party who called him (on any new matters which arose out of cross-examination by the other party to the action): *R v Wong* [1986] Crim LR 683 (Crown Court).

[177] The rule applies in the case of a witness whose name was 'on the back of the indictment' and who was called by the prosecution merely to allow the defence to cross-examine him: *R v Beezley* (1830) 4 C&P 220.

[178] (1838) 7 Ad&El 627. See also *Queen Caroline's Case* (1820) 2 Brod&Bing 284.

Denman CJ held that where a witness under cross-examination has given evidence of part of a conversation, evidence may not be given in re-examination about everything that was said in that conversation, but only about so much of it as is in some way connected with the evidence given in cross-examination. For example, the witness may be re-examined about things said which qualify or explain the statement on which he was cross-examined, but not about things said on other distinct and unrelated matters.

Evidence which was not admissible in examination-in-chief may become admissible in re-examination as a result of the nature of the cross-examination. Thus although in criminal proceedings an earlier statement of a witness which is consistent with his testimony on a particular matter is generally inadmissible in chief, it will become admissible in re-examination if, in cross-examination, it is suggested to him that his evidence on that matter is a recent fabrication.[179] It remains to note that leading questions may be asked in re-examination to the same limited extent as in examination-in-chief.

ADDITIONAL READING

Birch, 'Rethinking Sexual History Evidence: Proposals for Fairer Trials' [2002] *Crim LR* 531.

Birch, 'Untangling Sexual History Evidence: A Rejoinder to Professor Temkin' [2003] *Crim LR* 370.

Cohen, 'Errors of Recall and Credibility: Can omissions and discrepancies in successive statements reasonably be said to undermine credibility of testimony?' (2001) *Med Leg J* vol 96, pt I, 25–34.

Kibble, 'The Sexual History Provisions: Charting a course between inflexible legislative rules and wholly untrammelled judicial discretion?' [2000] *Crim LR* 274.

Kibble, 'Judicial Perspectives on the Operation of s 41 and the Relevance and Admissibility of Prior Sexual History Evidence: Four Scenarios' [2005] *Crim LR* 190.

Office for Criminal Justice Reform, 'Convicting Rapists and Protecting Victims—Justice for Victims of Rape' <www.homeoffice.gov.uk>.

Redmayne, 'Myths, relationships and coincidences: The new problems of sexual history' [2003] 7 *E&P* 75.

Saward and Green, *Rape—My Story* (London, 1990).

Temkin, 'Sexual History Evidence—Beware the Backlash' [2003] *Crim LR* 217.

Temkin and Krahé, *Sexual Assault and the Justice Gap: A Question of Attitude* (Oxford, 2008).

Ward, 'Usurping the role of the jury? Expert evidence and witness credibility in English criminal trials' [2009] 13 *E&P* 83.

---

[179] See, eg, *R v Oyesiku* (1971) 56 Cr App R 240, CA (see Ch 6).

Corroboration and care warnings

8

Key Issues

- Where a witness gives evidence in a criminal trial in order to prove the guilt of the accused, why might it be desirable to have additional independent evidence by way of confirmation or support?

- Where a witness gives evidence that he saw or heard the accused committing a crime, why should his testimony be treated with caution?

- What should a judge do in order to give effect to the need for such caution?

- Where a potential witness to a crime states that he can identify the perpetrator by his distinctive voice, should the police be required to conduct a 'voice identification procedure', ie a procedure whereby the witness is called on to pick out the voice of the perpetrator from among the voices of other innocent parties who might sound like him?

- Where a witness who is mentally handicapped confesses that he has committed a crime (a) why should evidence of his confession be treated with care; and (b) what should a judge do to ensure that the confession is treated with care?

'Any risk of the conviction of an innocent person is lessened if conviction is based upon the testimony of more than one acceptable witness.'[1] In civil, as well as criminal cases, it would not be unreasonable to expect a general rule requiring a party who seeks to prove certain facts by the testimony of a single witness, to adduce additional independent evidence, by way of confirmation or support, so that the tribunal of fact is double-sure before it makes a particular finding, or gives judgment, in that party's favour. Although this is the case in most civil law jurisdictions, there is no general rule to this effect in English law. Thus in a criminal trial, provided that the jury is satisfied beyond all reasonable doubt of the guilt of the accused, a conviction may be based on the testimony of a single prosecution witness who swears that he saw the accused commit the crime in question, and this remains the case even if part or all of his evidence is contradicted by the testimony of one or more witnesses called by the defence.[2] A party is, of course, free to adduce evidence which corroborates or supports the other evidence that he has tendered,[3] and to the extent that this would strengthen an otherwise weak case, as a matter of common sense he would be well advised to do so. As a general rule, however, there is (a) no requirement that evidence be corroborated; and (b) no requirement that the tribunal of fact be warned of the danger of acting on uncorroborated evidence.

This chapter is concerned with the exceptions to the general rule. There are three categories of exception. The first is where corroboration (probably in a technical sense) is required as a matter of law. In cases falling within this category, the ambit of which is clearly defined, comprising as it does four cases governed by statute (speeding, perjury, treason, and attempts to commit such offences), a conviction cannot be based on uncorroborated evidence and, if it is, will be reversed on appeal. Thus in the absence of such corroboration, the judge should direct an acquittal. Depending on the statute in question, the corroboration may be required to take a particular form, such as the evidence of another witness, or may be permitted to take any form, whether testimony, real evidence, or documentary evidence.

In the second category, which comprises a miscellany of different cases, neither corroboration in a technical sense nor supportive evidence is required as a matter of law, but in appropriate circumstances the tribunal of fact should be warned to exercise caution before acting on the evidence of certain types of witness, if unsupported. The witnesses in question include: (i) accomplices giving evidence for the prosecution; (ii) complainants in sexual cases; (iii) other witnesses whose evidence may be tainted by an improper motive; (iv) children; and (v) anonymous witnesses. Whether a warning is given at all is a matter of judicial discretion dependent on the circumstances of the case, and therefore failure to give a warning will not necessarily furnish a good ground of appeal. Where a warning is given, the strength of the warning and the extent to which the judge should elaborate upon it, for example by referring to the potentially supportive material, also depends upon the particular circumstances of the case.

The third category comprises five cases in which corroboration in a technical sense is not required as a matter of law, and there is no obligation to warn the tribunal of fact of the danger of acting on the evidence in question *simply* by reason of the fact that it is uncorroborated or unsupported, but there is a special need for caution which has led to requirements analogous

---

[1] Per Lord Morris in *DPP v Hester* [1973] AC 296, HL at 315.

[2] However, a conviction in such circumstances may be set aside where it is unsafe: see *R v Cooper* [1969] 1 QB 267 at 271, CA. In civil cases, a new trial may be ordered where the verdict of the jury is against the weight of the evidence: see per Lord Selborne in *Metropolitan Rly Co v Wright* (1886) 11 App Cas 152, HL at 153.

[3] Subject to the inherent power of the court to prevent, for reasons of cost and time, the admission of superfluous evidence.

to, but distinct from, those relating to the first two categories. The five cases are confessions by mentally handicapped persons, identification evidence, lip-reading evidence, cases of Sudden Infant Death Syndrome (colloquially 'cot deaths'), and unconvincing hearsay. The last of these cases is governed by section 125 of the Criminal Justice Act 2003, which requires a judge to direct an acquittal or discharge the jury if satisfied that the case against the accused is based wholly or partly on a hearsay statement and the evidence provided by the statement is so unconvincing that the accused's conviction would be unsafe. It is convenient to consider section 125 in Chapter 10, 'Hearsay in criminal cases'.[4]

Corroboration required by statute

At common law a trial judge was required as a matter of law to warn the jury of the danger of acting on certain types of evidence if uncorroborated. Corroboration, for these purposes, bore a technical meaning. Corroboration, where required by statute, probably bears the same technical meaning. This appears to have been the view of Lord Reading CJ in *R v Baskerville*.[5] Moreover, corroboration in the technical sense *is* required in the case of the statutory provision relating to perjury;[6] and although, as we shall see, neither the perjury provision nor the provisions relating to speeding and treason expressly require 'corroboration', section 2(2)(g) of the Criminal Attempts Act 1981 (the 1981 Act) has been drafted on the assumption that that is exactly what they require. It is necessary to consider first, therefore, the meaning of corroboration in the technical sense.

To be capable of amounting to corroboration in the technical sense, evidence must be (i) relevant, (ii) admissible, (iii) credible, (iv) independent, and (v) evidence which implicates the accused in the way that the specific statute requires. The first two requirements[7] apply to evidence generally and need no further explanation in the present context. As to the third requirement: 'Corroboration can only be afforded … by a witness who is otherwise to be believed. If a witness's testimony falls of its own inanition, the question of his … being capable of giving corroboration does not arise.'[8] Under the fourth requirement, independence, the evidence must emanate from a source other than the witness who is to be corroborated.[9] The fifth requirement, implication, is best explored by reference to the statutory provisions themselves. Before turning to them, it remains to note the respective functions of the judge and jury.[10] Where a judge does give a direction to the jury on corroboration, he must explain what it is. No particular form of words is necessary and there is no need even to use the word 'corroboration' provided that the requirements of credibility, independence, and implication are made clear.[11] The judge should also indicate what evidence is (and is not) capable of being

---

[4] See Ch 10, 312 under **Other safeguards**, *Stopping the case where the evidence is unconvincing*.

[5] [1916] 2 KB 658 at 667.

[6] See para 3.9, Law Commission Working Paper No 115 (1990), citing *R v Hamid* (1979) 69 Cr App R 324.

[7] See per Scarman LJ in *R v Scarrott* [1978] QB 1016, CA at 1021.

[8] Per Lord Hailsham in *DPP v Kilbourne* [1973] AC 729 at 746. See also per Lord Morris in *DPP v Hester* [1973] AC 296 at 315 ('Corroborative evidence will only fill its role if it itself is completely credible') and *R v Thomas* (1985) 81 Cr App R 331, CA.

[9] See, eg, *R v Whitehead* [1929] 1 KB 99, CCA.

[10] It is submitted that the authorities that follow, which mainly related to common law corroboration requirements, also apply where corroboration is required by statute.

[11] See *R v Fallon* [1993] Crim LR 591, CA.

corroboration.[12] Having directed the jury as to what evidence is capable in law of amounting to corroboration, the judge should explain that it falls to them, as the tribunal of fact, to decide whether the evidence does in fact constitute corroboration.[13]

Speeding

The opinion evidence of non-experts is generally inadmissible.[14] One of the exceptions to this rule is opinion evidence relating to speed. Section 89(2) of the Road Traffic Regulation Act 1984, in recognition of the danger of such evidence being inaccurate, provides that a person charged with an offence of driving a motor vehicle on a road at an excessive speed 'shall not be liable to be convicted solely on the evidence of one witness to the effect that in the opinion of the witness the person prosecuted was driving the vehicle at a speed exceeding a specified limit'. The opinion evidence of two or more people that a vehicle was exceeding the speed limit is sufficient to justify a conviction under this provision provided that their evidence relates to the speed of the vehicle at the same place and time.[15] The provision only applies to evidence of mere opinion and not to evidence of fact.[16] Speedometers and other similar devices[17] will be presumed, in the absence of evidence to the contrary, to have been working properly at the material time and to be capable of providing evidence of fact.

In *Crossland v DPP*[18] Bingham LJ said: 'It is plain . . . that the subsection is intended to prevent the conviction of a defendant on evidence given by a single witness of his unsupported visual impression of a defendant's speed.' An expert in accident reconstruction testified that he had inspected the scene of a road traffic accident, including skid marks and damage to the defendant's car, carried out speed and braking tests on the car, and calculated that its speed had been not less than 41 mph. It was held that this was not just the opinion evidence of one witness: the expert had also described the objectively determined phenomena on which his opinion was based.

Perjury

The rationale for the requirement of corroboration in relation to offences of perjury is not entirely clear. Historically, perjury was first punished in the Star Chamber, which usually required a second witness. Prior to the statutory provisions, the requirement at common law was held to be justified 'else there is only oath against oath'.[19] This argument did not seem strong to the Criminal Law Revision Committee 'as there may be more than oath against oath when the falsity of the accused's evidence is corroborated although not by a second witness'.

---

[12] *R v Charles* (1976) 68 Cr App R 334n; *R v Cullinane* [1984] Crim LR 420, CA; and *R v Webber* [1987] Crim LR 412, CA. If the judge fails to do so, this is unlikely to result in a successful appeal if there was in fact ample corroboration and the Court of Appeal is in no doubt that if a proper direction had been given, the jury would still have convicted: see *R v McInnes* (1989) 90 Cr App R 99, CA.

[13] *R v Tragen* [1956] Crim LR 332; *R v McInnes* (1989) 90 Cr App R 99, CA.

[14] See Ch 18.

[15] *Brighty v Pearson* [1938] 4 All ER 127.

[16] See *Nicholas v Penny* [1950] 2 KB 466 where it was held that magistrates could convict on the evidence of a police officer who had checked his speedometer and driven at an even distance behind the accused's car

[17] See *Collinson v Mabbott* (1984) The Times, 10 Oct, DC (corroboration by radar gun); and *Burton v Gilbert* [1984] RTR 162, DC (corroboration by radar speed meter).

[18] [1988] 3 All ER 712 at 714.

[19] *R v Muscot* (1713) 10 Mod Rep 192.

Furthermore, 'there are many cases where corroboration is not required but the decision depends on the choice between two pieces of sworn evidence'. However, a majority of the Committee felt that to make a prosecution for perjury too easy might discourage persons from giving evidence and create the danger of a successful party to litigation, his evidence having been preferred, seeking to have his adversary, or his adversary's witnesses, prosecuted for perjury.[20]

Section 13 of the Perjury Act 1911 (the 1911 Act) provides that:

> A person shall not be liable to be convicted of any offence against this Act, or of any other offence declared by any other Act to be perjury or subornation of perjury, or to be punishable as perjury or subornation of perjury, solely upon the evidence of one witness as to the falsity of any statement alleged to be false.

The judge is therefore required to direct the jury that, before a conviction of perjury can be recorded, there must be evidence before them, which they accept, of more than one witness, ie either evidence of at least one other witness or some other supporting evidence, by way of confession or otherwise, which supplements that of a single witness.[21]

The section requires corroboration not only in relation to the offence of perjury in judicial proceedings, but also in relation to the many other offences under the Perjury Act of making false statements, on oath, in statutory declarations or otherwise, but not in judicial proceedings.[22] The corroboration need relate only to the *falsity* of the statement in question. Thus, if the accused admits that the statement was untrue, the prosecution need call no evidence to prove this fact and section 13 does not apply.[23] Nor does the section apply to certain allegations of perjury contrary to section 1(1) of the 1911 Act, which provides that if any person lawfully sworn as a witness wilfully makes a statement material in the proceedings which he knows to be false *or does not believe to be true*, he shall be guilty of an offence.[24]

Treason

Section 1 of the Treason Act 1795 requires corroboration in the form of evidence given by a second witness. It provides that a person charged with the offence of treason by compassing the death or restraint of the Queen or her heirs shall not be convicted except on 'the oaths of two lawful and credible witnesses'. The Criminal Law Revision Committee recommended the repeal of this provision.[25]

---

[20] Paras 178 and 190, 11th Report (Cmnd 4991).

[21] See *R v Hamid* (1979) 69 Cr App R 324, CA and *R v Carroll* (1993) 99 Cr App R 381, CA. Failure to direct the jury in accordance with s 13 may afford grounds for a successful appeal: see *R v Rider* (1986) 83 Cr App R 207, CA.

[22] The Criminal Law Revision Committee and the Law Commission (para 45, Published Working Paper No 33, *Perjury and Kindred Offences*) saw no need to preserve the latter requirement.

[23] *R v Rider* (1986) 83 Cr App R 207, CA.

[24] Ibid. Section 13 will not apply because the truth or falsehood of the statement forms no part of the prosecution case. Note that the requirements of s 13 will be satisfied by two witnesses hearing the the accused admit the falsity of the statement on the same occasion: *R v Peach* [1990] 2 All ER 966, CA. See also *R v Threlfall* (1914) 10 Cr App R 112: a letter suborning another to commit perjury in relation to the same matter in respect of which the false statement was made may constitute corroboration.

[25] Para 195, 11th Report (Cmnd 4991).

Attempts

Under section 2(2)(g) of the 1981 Act, any provision whereby a person may not be convicted on the uncorroborated evidence of one witness (including any provision requiring the evidence of not less than two credible witnesses) shall have effect with respect to an offence under section 1 of the Act of attempting to commit an offence as it has effect with respect to the offence attempted.

Care warnings

Accomplices testifying for the prosecution and complainants in sexual cases

The background

Prior to the Criminal Justice and Public Order Act 1994 (the 1994 Act), there existed at common law a category of exception to the general rule under which, although corroboration (in the technical sense) was not required as a matter of law, the tribunal of fact had to be warned, as a matter of law, of the danger of acting on evidence if not corroborated (in the technical sense). This obligatory warning was required in respect of the evidence of (a) accomplices testifying on behalf of the prosecution;[26] and (b) complainants in sexual cases.[27] As to the former, accomplices were defined as: (i) parties to the offence in question; (ii) handlers of stolen goods, in the case of thieves from whom they receive, on the trial of the latter for theft; and (iii) parties to another offence committed by the accused in respect of which evidence is admitted under the similar fact evidence doctrine.[28] Whether a particular witness was an accomplice was a question usually answered by the witness himself, by confessing to participation, by pleading guilty to it, or by being convicted of it. If not answered by the witness himself, the question whether he was in fact an accomplice was for the jury (provided that there was evidence on which a reasonable jury could have concluded that the witness was an accomplice).[29] As to complainants in sexual cases, the warning was required in respect of the victims, whether male or female,[30] of sexual offences.[31]

There were only two exceptions to the requirement that a warning be given. A warning was not required where an accomplice gave evidence, on behalf of the prosecution, which was mainly favourable to the accused and more harm would have been done to the accused by giving the warning than by not giving it.[32] Nor was a warning required in sexual

---

[26] But see *Galler v Galler* [1954] P 252: in divorce proceedings 'an adulterer who gives evidence of his own adultery is in the same position as an accomplice in a criminal case'. See also *Fairman v Fairman* [1949] P 341.

[27] The need for such a warning was not confined to criminal proceedings. In *Mattouk v Massad* [1943] AC 588, a civil suit, the Privy Council was of the opinion that to accept the uncorroborated evidence of a girl aged 15 in charging a man with sexual intercourse was very dangerous and required great caution.

[28] *Davies v DPP* [1954] AC 378, HL. An accomplice, for these purposes, also included a thief from whom a handler has received goods, on the trial of the latter for receiving (*R v Vernon* [1962] Crim LR 35) but not an *agent provocateur* (*R v Mullins* (1848) 3 Cox CC 526), a child victim of a sexual offence (*R v Pitts* (1912) 8 Cr App R 126), or a woman upon whose immoral earnings the accused was charged with having lived (per Lord Reading CJ in *R v King* (1914) 10 Cr App R 117, CCA) unless, on the facts, there was evidence of aiding and abetting the accused, eg evidence of collecting money on behalf of the accused from other prostitutes (as in *R v Stewart* (1986) 83 Cr App R 327, CA).

[29] *Davies v DPP* [1954] AC 378.

[30] *R v Burgess* (1956) 40 Cr App R 144, CCA.

[31] The rule did not apply to other kinds of offence, even if their commission was allegedly accompanied by some form of sexual activity on the part of the accused: *R v Simmons* [1987] Crim LR 630, CA.

[32] See *R v Royce-Bentley* [1974] 1 WLR 535, CA.

cases in which identification was in issue, but not the commission of the offence itself.[33] Subject to these exceptions, failure to give the warning furnished a good ground of appeal. The warning to be given to the jury became known as the 'full' warning, which comprised four parts:

1. The warning itself, ie that it was dangerous to convict on the uncorroborated evidence of the 'suspect' witness but that if they, the jury, were satisfied of the truth of such evidence, they might none the less convict.

2. An explanation of the meaning of corroboration in the technical sense.

3. An indication of what evidence was (and was not) capable in law of amounting to corroboration.

4. An explanation that it fell to the jury, as the tribunal of fact, to decide whether that evidence did in fact constitute corroboration.

By reason of section 32 of the 1994 Act, full warnings are no longer required. In order to understand the effect of section 32, it is important to consider first both the justification for the rules requiring a full warning and the reasons for their abolition. The justification given for the requirement of a warning in the case of an accomplice giving evidence for the prosecution was that such a witness may have a purpose of his own to serve: he may give false evidence against the accused out of spite, to exaggerate or even invent the accused's role in the crime, or with a view to minimizing the extent of his own culpability. Concerning sexual offences (as in procuration cases), the requirement of a warning stemmed from an assumption that such a charge is easy to make but difficult to refute. There is also 'the danger that the complainant may have made a false accusation owing to sexual neurosis, jealousy, fantasy, spite or a girl's refusal to admit that she consented to an act of which she is now ashamed'.[34] Such a danger may be hidden, yet the nature of the evidence may well make jurors sympathetic to the complainant and so prejudice them against the accused.

The reasons in favour of the abolition of mandatory corroboration warnings were compelling.[35] The first and most serious objection was that the rules applied on a class basis, ie irrespective of the circumstances of the particular case and the credibility of the particular witness. Thus even if there was no danger of the 'suspect' witness giving false evidence, the judge still had to give the warning. Secondly, since many sexual offences are committed in circumstances in which corroboration is difficult if not impossible to obtain, the requirement was capable of resulting in the acquittal of the guilty. In cases involving the sexual abuse of children, the mandatory warning simply compounded the difficulty of securing a conviction.[36] Thirdly, the full warning had become extremely complex, not least because of the technical rules on what constituted corroboration, and this often led to successful appeals. Fourthly, there was an element of self-contradiction in directing jurors that it was 'dangerous' to convict on uncorroborated evidence and then proceeding to direct them

[33] See *R v Chance* [1988] 3 All ER 225, CA.
[34] Para 186, 11th Report, Criminal Law Revision Committee (Cmnd 4991).
[35] See generally paras 183–6, 11th Report, Criminal Law Revision Committee (Cmnd 4991); Law Commission Working Paper No 115 (1990); Law Commission Report No 202 (Cm 1620) (1991); and Ch 8, Royal Commission on Criminal Justice (Cm 2263) (1993). Although note the Canadian case of *R v Khela* 2009 SCC 4, in which views to the contrary were expressed. For comment on this case, see Pattenden, 'Case Commentaries' (2009) 13 *E&P* 243.
[36] See para 5.17, *Report of the Advisory Group on Video Evidence* (Home Office, 1989).

that they could nonetheless do so. Finally, there was some evidence to suggest that where a warning was given, far from operating as a safeguard for the accused, the jury were more likely to convict.[37]

Section 32 of the Criminal Justice and Public Order Act 1994

Section 32 of the 1994 Act provides as follows:

1. Any requirement whereby at a trial on indictment it is obligatory for the court to give the jury a warning about convicting the accused on the uncorroborated evidence of a person merely because that person is—
   (a) an alleged accomplice of the accused, or
   (b) where the offence charged is a sexual offence, the person in respect of whom it is alleged to have been committed,
   is hereby abrogated. . . .
2. Any requirement that—
   (a) is applicable at the summary trial of a person for an offence, and
   (b) corresponds to the requirement mentioned in subsection (1) above . . .
   is hereby abrogated.

Thus in cases involving the evidence of an alleged accomplice or of a complainant in a sexual case, section 32 has simply abrogated any requirement whereby it was *obligatory* for the tribunal of fact to be given a full warning—the judge still has a discretion to give some form of warning whenever he considers it necessary to do so. The leading authority on section 32 is *R v Makanjuola*,[38] in which Lord Taylor CJ summarized the relevant principles:[39]

1. Section 32(1) abrogates the requirement to give a corroboration direction in respect of an alleged accomplice or a complainant of a sexual offence simply because a witness falls into one of those categories.
2. It is a matter for the judge's discretion what, if any, warning he considers appropriate in respect of such a witness, as indeed in respect of any other witness in whatever type of case. Whether he chooses to give a warning and in what terms will depend on the circumstances of the case, the issues raised, and the content and quality of the witness's evidence.
3. In some cases, it may be appropriate for the judge to warn the jury to exercise caution before acting upon the unsupported evidence of a witness. This will not be so simply because the witness is a complainant of a sexual offence nor will it necessarily be so because a witness is alleged to be an accomplice There will need to be an evidential basis for suggesting that the evidence of the witness may be unreliable. An evidential basis does not include mere suggestions by cross-examining counsel.
4. If any question arises as to whether the judge should give a special warning in respect of a witness, it is desirable that the question be resolved by discussion with counsel in the absence of the jury before final speeches. (The judge will often consider that no special warning is required at all. Where, however, the witness has been shown to be unreliable, he or she may consider it necessary to urge caution.[40] In a more extreme case, if the witness is shown to have lied, to have made previous false complaints, or to bear the defendant some grudge, a stronger

---

[37] See paras 2.9 and 2.18, Law Commission Working Paper No 115 and *Vetrovec v R* (1982) 136 DLR (3d) 89 at 95.

[38] [1995] 3 All ER 730, CA.

[39] [1995] 3 All ER 730 at 733. See also Lewis, 'A Comparative Examination of Corroboration and Care Warnings in Prosecutions of Sexual Offences' [2006] *Crim LR* 889.

[40] Eg, when a complainant's evidence is internally inconsistent or there are previous inconsistent statements: see *R v Walker* [1996] Crim LR 742, CA.

warning may be thought appropriate and the judge may suggest it would be wise to look for some supporting material before acting on the impugned witness's evidence.[41] We stress that these observations are merely illustrative of some, not all, of the factors which judges may take into account in measuring where a witness stands in the scale of reliability...)[42]

5. Where the judge does decide to give some warning in respect of a witness, it will be appropriate to do so as part of the judge's review of the evidence and his comments as to how the jury should evaluate it rather than a set-piece legal direction.

6. Where some warning is required, it will be for the judge to decide the strength and terms of the warning. It does not have to be invested with the whole florid regime of the old corroboration rules.

7. It follows that we emphatically disagree with the tentative submission [that if a judge does give a warning, he should give a full warning and should tell the jury what corroboration is in the technical sense and identify the evidence capable of being corroborative]. Attempts to re-impose the straitjacket of the old corroboration rules are strongly to be deprecated.

8. Finally, this court will be disinclined to interfere with a judge's exercise of his discretion save in a case where that exercise is unreasonable in the *Wednesbury* sense.[43]

'Supporting material'

Following *R v Makanjuola*, if there is an evidential basis for suggesting that the witness may be unreliable, and the trial judge therefore decides to direct the jury that it would be wise to look for some 'supporting material', the judge is no longer required to identify for the jury what evidence is and is not capable of being corroboration in the technical sense. However, once such a direction is given, it has been held that it is then incumbent on the judge to identify any 'independent supporting evidence'.[44] It seems reasonably clear that such evidence may be furnished by the accused himself, as when evidence is given of an out-of-court confession or the accused makes a damaging admission in the course of giving his evidence.[45] It seems equally clear that it may be furnished by (i) the accused's lies, whether told in or out of court; (ii) his silence; (iii) his refusal to consent to the taking of samples; or (iv) his misconduct. It will be convenient to consider, briefly, these examples before turning to some items of evidence which, arguably, cannot constitute 'supporting material'.

Lies by the accused may amount to 'supporting material' depending on the nature of the lie and the nature of the other evidence in the case. It is submitted that the criteria for determining whether a lie constitutes 'supporting material' are the same as those previously employed for determining whether a lie amounted to corroboration in the technical sense. Those criteria, applicable to lies whether told in or out of court, were established in *R v Lucas*:[46]

> To be capable of amounting to corroboration the lie ... must first of all be deliberate.[47] Secondly it must relate to a material issue. Thirdly the motive for the lie must be a realisation of guilt and

---

[41] Delay in complaining will not, by itself, require either the 'stronger direction' or the urging of 'caution': see *R v R* [1996] Crim LR 815, CA and *R v Fallis* [2004] EWCA Crim 923.

[42] The bracketed material is set out in an earlier part of the judgment (at 732).

[43] See *Associated Provincial Picture Houses Ltd v Wednesbury Corpn* [1948] 1 KB 223. This is a heavy burden for an appellant to discharge: see *R v R* [1996] Crim LR 815, CA.

[44] *R v B (MT)* [2000] Crim LR 181, CA.

[45] See *R v Dossi* (1918) 13 Cr App Rep 158, CCA: on a charge of indecently assaulting a girl, an admission by the accused, in court, that he had innocently fondled her, is some corroboration of her evidence.

[46] [1981] QB 720, CA at 724.

[47] A lie being an *intentional* false statement, the meaning of the first requirement is obscure.

a fear of the truth. The jury should in appropriate cases be reminded that people sometimes lie, for example, in an attempt to bolster up a just cause, or out of shame or out of a wish to conceal disgraceful behaviour from their family. Fourthly the statement must clearly be shown to be a lie by evidence other than that of the [witness] who is to be corroborated, that is to say by admission or by evidence from an independent witness.

Thus where an accused, charged with a sexual offence, tells the police that on the evening in question he did not leave his house, but subsequently admits that this statement was false, his lie may be used to support the evidence of the victim that the offence had taken place near to the accused's home,[48] because 'a false statement . . . may give to a proved opportunity a different complexion from what it would have borne had no such false statement been made'.[49] *R v Lucas* itself concerned the fourth criterion. The appeal was allowed because the jury had been invited to prefer the evidence of an accomplice to that of the accused and then to use their disbelief of the accused as corroboration of the accomplice. The direction was erroneous because the 'lie' told by the accused was not shown to be a lie by evidence other than that of the accomplice who was to be corroborated.[50]

Where a person is accused of a crime, by a person speaking to him on even terms, in circumstances such that it would be natural for him to reply, evidence of his silence may be admitted, at common law, to show that he admits the truth of the charge made[51] and may constitute 'supporting material'.[52] Such material, it is submitted, may also be derived from inferences properly drawn from (i) the accused's failure to mention facts when questioned by a constable or on being charged with an offence; (ii) his silence at trial; (iii) his failure or refusal to account for objects, substances, marks, or presence at a particular place;[53] or (iv) his refusal to consent to the taking of 'intimate samples'.[54] Supporting material may also take the form of evidence of the accused's misconduct on some other occasion admitted under the similar fact evidence doctrine as evidence relevant to the question of guilt on the charge before the court.[55]

Whether a given item of evidence is capable of amounting to 'supporting material' is not always as easy as the above examples might suggest. For example, in a case of rape in which the complainant is shown to have made previous false complaints and a warning is properly given, should any of the following items be treated as 'supporting material', and in any event, how should the judge direct the jury in their regard: (i) evidence of recent complaint;[56] (ii) evidence of the distressed condition of the complainant; and (iii) medical evidence showing that someone had had intercourse with the complainant at a time consistent with her evidence? There are compelling reasons to suggest that each of these items, by itself, should not be treated as 'supporting material' and the judge should direct the jury accordingly. As to a recent

[48] See *Credland v Knowler* (1951) 35 Cr App R 48, DC. For an example of a lie told in court, see *Corfield v Hodgson* [1966] 2 All ER 205.

[49] Per Lord Dunedin in *Dawson v McKenzie* (1908) 45 SLR 473.

[50] See also per Lord MacDermott in *Tumahole Bereng v R* [1949] AC 253 at 270.

[51] See *R v Mitchell* (1892) 17 Cox CC 503; *R v Chandler* [1976] 3 All ER 105, CA; *Parkes v R* [1976] 1 WLR 1251; and generally Ch 13.

[52] See *R v Cramp* (1880) 14 Cox CC 390, a decision on corroboration in the technical sense.

[53] See Criminal Justice and Public Order Act 1994, ss 34–7 (Ch 14).

[54] See *R v (Robert William) Smith* (1985) 81 Cr App R 286, CA and Police and Criminal Evidence Act 1984, s 62(10) (Ch 14).

[55] See Ch 17.

[56] See s 120 of The Criminal Justice Act 2003.

complaint, the trial judge should, at the least, explain to the jury that the evidence emanates from the complainant herself.[57] As to evidence of distress, the same point could be made, but such a direction would be inappropriate if, for example, the distress was witnessed shortly after the offence, the complainant was unaware that she was being observed, and there is nothing to suggest that she put on an act and simulated distress.[58] However, in appropriate cases the jury should now be alerted to the very real risk that distress may have been feigned.[59] Concerning medical evidence of intercourse, the trial judge might sensibly direct the jury that it does not, by itself, show that intercourse took place without consent or that the accused was a party to it.[60] It is to be hoped that commonsensical guidance and helpful directions of this kind will not be regarded as 'attempts to re-impose the straitjacket of the old corroboration rules'. It would be a pity if the baby of common sense were to be thrown out with the corroboration bath water.

Sexual cases in which identification is in issue

There is nothing to suggest that the principles established in *R v Makanjuola* should not apply to sexual cases in which identification is in issue. If the identity of the offender is in issue, but the fact that someone committed the offence is not in issue, either because formally admitted by the accused or, if not formally admitted, because there has been no suggestion by the defence that there is any doubt as to the commission of the offence, it will normally suffice to direct the jury, in accordance with *R v Turnbull*,[61] about the need for caution before convicting on identification evidence; a further warning about the complainant's evidence as to the *offence* is only required where there is an evidential basis for suggesting that her evidence in that regard is unreliable.[62]

Other witnesses whose evidence may be tainted by an improper motive

There are a number of common law authorities to the effect that the jury should be warned to exercise caution before acting on the evidence of a witness who may have a purpose of

---

[57] Such evidence was not corroboration in the technical sense because not independent of the witness requiring to be corroborated: see *R v Whitehead* [1929] 1 KB 99, CCA.

[58] Evidence of distress *could* amount to corroboration in the technical sense, but juries had to be warned that except in special circumstances little weight should be given to it: see per Lord Parker CJ in *R v Knight* [1966] 1 WLR 230 at 233. For examples, see *R v Redpath* (1962) 46 Cr App R 319, CCA; *R v Chauhan* (1981) 73 Cr App R 232, CA; and *R v Dowley* [1983] Crim LR 168, CA.

[59] *R v Romeo* [2004] 1 Cr App R 417, CA. Conversely, an issue that has not uncommonly arisen in sexual cases has been a complainant's apparent lack of distress, inferred from such things as delay in reporting, demeanour after the offence and demeanour in the witness box. Where such points are made as part of an accused's defence, a careful direction should be given to the jury that the trauma of a serious sexual assault means that there is no one classic response. See *R v Doody* [2008] EWCA Crim 2394, [2009] Crim LR 591.

[60] For these reasons, such evidence was not corroboration in the technical sense: *James v R* (1970) 55 Cr App R 299, PC. However, if there was *also* evidence that the accused alone had been with the complainant at the relevant time, and evidence that her underclothing was torn and that she had injuries to her private parts, the combined effect of all the evidence was capable of amounting to corroboration: see per Lord Lane CJ in *R v Hills* (1987) 86 Cr App R 26, CA at 31. In a case in which the only issue is consent, it would seem that evidence of injuries is, by itself, capable of supporting the complainant's assertion of lack of consent. However, where two or more accused are charged with successive acts of rape, the question whether the material can support the complainant's case against more than one of them will turn on the particular circumstances of the case: see *R v Pountney* [1989] Crim LR 216, CA and *R v Franklin* [1989] Crim LR 499, CA, decisions on corroboration in the technical sense. See also *R v Ensor* [1989] 1 WLR 497, CA.

[61] [1977] QB 224, CA (see below).

[62] Cf *R v Chance* [1988] 3 All ER 225, CA, a decision on corroboration in the technical sense.

his own to serve. These authorities are considered in the paragraphs that follow. Some of the authorities preceding *R v Makanjuola* suggested that in some circumstances, at any rate, the warning was obligatory. It is now clear, from the decision in *R v Muncaster*,[63] that all such authorities need to be looked at afresh in the light of *R v Makanjuola*. It was held that the guidance in *R v Makanjuola* must be read as applying generally to all cases in which a witness may be suspect because he falls into a certain category.

An accomplice who is a co-accused may incriminate another co-accused when giving evidence in his own defence. Because, in these circumstances, an accomplice may be regarded as having some purpose of his own to serve, it has been held that it is desirable, but only as a matter of practice, to warn the jury of the danger of acting on his unsupported evidence, and that every case must be looked at in the light of its own facts.[64] In *R v Cheema*,[65] following a full review of the authorities, Lord Taylor CJ said:

> although a warning in suitable terms as to the danger of a co-defendant having an axe to grind is desirable, there is no rule of law or practice requiring a full corroboration direction . . . what is required when one defendant implicates another in evidence is simply to warn the jury of what may very often be obvious—namely that the defendant witness may have a purpose of his own to serve.[66]

Following *R v Makanjuola*, it is clear that whether a warning is given, and if so, its strength, remain matters of judicial discretion dependent on the circumstances of the case.[67] In *R v Jones*[68] it was held that in the case of cut-throat defences, including mirror-image cut-throat defences, a warning should normally be considered and given and, if given, should at least warn the jury to examine the evidence of each accused with care because each has or may have an interest of his own to serve.[69] There is a particular need for some such warning where, as in *R v Jones* itself, one of the accused has refused to answer questions in interview and is therefore able, if he wishes, to tailor his defence to the facts in evidence. It was further held that, subject to what justice demands on the particular facts of each case, in many or most cases a judge might consider four points to put to the jury: (1) to consider the case for and against each accused separately; (2) to decide the case on all the evidence, including the evidence of each co-accused; (3) when considering the evidence of each co-accused, to bear in mind that he may have an interest to serve or 'an axe to grind'; and (4) to assess the evidence of co-defendants in the same way as the evidence of any other witness in the case.[70]

---

[63] [1999] Crim LR 409, CA.

[64] *R v Prater* [1960] 2 QB 464, CCA at 466. See also *R v Knowlden* (1983) 77 Cr App R 94, CA; *R v Stannard* [1964] 1 All ER 34 at 40, per Winn J; and *R v Whitaker* (1976) 63 Cr App R 193, CA at 197, per Lord Widgery. However, if the evidence incriminates the accused in one material respect but otherwise exonerates him, there is no need for a warning (which could operate to the *disadvantage* of the accused): see *R v Perman* [1995] Crim LR 736, CA.

[65] [1994] 1 All ER 639, CA at 647–9.

[66] See also *R v Sargent* [1993] Crim LR 713, CA: the defendant witness may well have a 'row of his own to hoe'.

[67] *R v Muncaster* [1999] Crim LR 409, CA.

[68] [2004] 1 Cr App R 60, CA.

[69] Contrast *R v Burrows* [2000] Crim LR 48, CA, where, according to *R v Jones*, the court was heavily influenced by the particular facts.

[70] *R v Jones* was followed in *R v Petkar* [2004] 1 Cr App R 270, CA. However, in *Petkar*, Rix LJ voiced two concerns about Jones which are worth noting. The first concerned the fact that the warning could devalue the evidence of both co-accused in the eyes of the jury. The second concerned the fact that point (3) in *Jones* did not appear to lie easily with point (4).

There are no special conditions of admissibility for cell confessions, and no requirement that they be corroborated.[71] However, in *Pringle v R*[72] it was held that a judge must always be alert to the possibility that the evidence of one prisoner against another is tainted by an improper motive, especially where a prisoner who has yet to face trial gives evidence that the other prisoner has confessed to the crime for which he is being held in custody. The indications that the evidence may be tainted by an improper motive must be found in the evidence—described as 'not an exacting test'—and the surrounding circumstances may justify the inference that his evidence is so tainted. This approach was followed in *Benedetto v R*,[73] where the Privy Council observed that the prisoners giving the evidence will almost always have strong reasons of self-interest for seeking to ingratiate themselves with those who may be in a position to reward them for volunteering the evidence, and that the accused is always at a disadvantage because he has none of the usual protections against the inaccurate recording or invention of words when interviewed by the police, and if the informer has a bad character, it may be difficult for him to obtain all the information needed to expose it fully. However, a much more flexible approach was adopted in *R v Stone*[74], where the Court of Appeal held as follows.

1. Not every case involving a cell confession requires the detailed directions discussed in *Pringle v R* and *Benedetto v R*. Such cases prompt the most careful consideration by the trial judge, but that consideration is not trammelled by fixed rules; the trial judge is best placed to decide the strength of any warning and any accompanying analysis.

2. In the case of a 'standard two-line confession', there would generally be a need to point out that such confessions are often easy to concoct and difficult to disprove and that experience has shown that prisoners may have many motives to lie. Further, if the informant has a significant criminal record or history of lying, this should usually be pointed out, explaining why it gives rise to a need for great care.

3. However, a summing-up should be tailored to the circumstances of the particular case. Where an alleged confession would not be easy to invent, it would be absurd to give a direction on the ease of concoction. Similarly, where the defence deliberately do not cross-examine the complainant about the motive of hope of obtaining advantage, there is no requirement to tell the jury that the informant being a prisoner, there might, intrinsically, have been such a motive.

4. There will be cases where the prisoner has witnessed the acts constituting the offence in which it will be appropriate to treat him as an ordinary witness about whose evidence nothing out of the usual needs to be said.

5. Indications that the prison informant's evidence may be tainted by an improper motive have to be found in the evidence.

In *R v Beck*[75] it was argued that an accomplice warning should be given in cases where a witness has a substantial interest of his own for giving false evidence even though there is no material to suggest any involvement by the witness in the crime. Although rejecting the argument,

---

[71] For an analysis of the issues, see Jeremy Dein, 'Non Tape Recorded Cell Confession Evidence—On Trial' [2002] *Crim LR* 630.

[72] [2003] All ER (D) 236 (Jan), 2003 UKPC 9.

[73] [2003] 1 WLR 1545, PC.

[74] [2005] Crim LR 569, CA.

[75] [1982] 1 WLR 461, CA.

Ackner LJ said that the court did not wish to detract from 'the obligation on a judge to advise a jury to proceed with caution where there is material to suggest that a witness's evidence may be tainted by an improper motive', continuing, 'and the strength of that advice must vary according to the facts of the case'.[76] Thus a warning may be given where there is evidence to suggest that a witness is acting out of spite or malevolence, has a financial or other personal interest in the outcome of the proceedings, or is otherwise biased or partial.[77] Where a witness, awaiting sentence, gives evidence for the prosecution in another case in circumstances in which he knows that at the very least by doing so he stands a chance of having his sentence reduced, it has been held that the potential fallibility of his evidence should be put squarely before the jury.[78] In *R v Asghar*[79] a group of men became involved in a fight in which someone was fatally stabbed. A was charged with murder. Three others from the group pleaded guilty to affray and gave evidence for the prosecution against A. It was held that the judge should have exercised his discretion to direct the jury on the danger of convicting A on the evidence of the other three without some independent supporting evidence because: (i) the defence case was that the three had put their heads together with others to fabricate a story incriminating A in order to protect one of their number; (ii) this suggested motive for their alleged lies was directly linked with the murder charge and did not arise from some unconnected cause; and (iii) the three were not on trial with A and not at risk, their position being akin to those of accomplices in the strict sense.[80]

R v Spencer, R v Smails[81] may be regarded as a further example. In that case, nursing staff at a secure hospital were charged with ill-treating patients convicted of crimes and suffering from mental disorders. The prosecution case consisted of the evidence of patients who were characterized as being mentally unbalanced, of bad character, anti-authoritarian, and prone to lie or exaggerate and who could have had old scores to settle. The House of Lords held that where the only evidence for the prosecution is that of a witness who, by reason of his particular mental condition and criminal connection, fulfils criteria analogous to those which (formerly) justified a full corroboration warning (accomplices testifying for the prosecution and complainants in sexual cases), the judge should warn the jury that it is dangerous to convict on his uncorroborated evidence, but such a warning need not amount to the full warning.[82] Thus while it may often be convenient to use the words 'danger' or 'dangerous', the use of such words is not essential to an adequate warning, so long as the jury is made fully aware of the dangers of convicting on such evidence, and the extent to which the judge should refer to the corroborative material, if any exists, depends on the facts of each case.[83] It may be doubted whether 'corroborative material', for these purposes, was ever intended to

---

[76] [1982] 1 WLR 461 at 469. See also *R v Witts and Witts* [1991] Crim LR 562, CA.

[77] A warning is unnecessary, however, if it would do more harm than good, as when it is obvious to the jury, from the circumstances of the case, that a witness is suspect: *R v Lovell* [1990] Crim LR 111, CA.

[78] *Chan Wai-Keung v R* [1995] 2 All ER 438, PC.

[79] [1995] 1 Cr App R 223, CA.

[80] Although the final reason is no longer compelling (see s 32 of the Criminal Justice and Public Order Act 1994, above), it is submitted that in such a case the need for some form of warning remains. See further, the judgment of Lord Reading CJ in *R v King* (1914) 10 Cr App R 117; and cf *R v Hanton* (1985) The Times, 14 Feb, CA; and *R v Evans* [1965] 2 QB 295.

[81] [1986] 2 All ER 928, HL.

[82] Overruling, in this respect, *R v Bagshaw* [1984] 1 All ER 971, CA.

[83] See also, concerning confessions made by the mentally handicapped, *R v Bailey* [1995] Crim LR 723, CA and Police and Criminal Evidence Act 1984, s 77, below.

mean corroboration in the strict sense; and it is submitted that, notwithstanding the analogy drawn with cases which (formerly) justified a full corroboration warning (which, in the light of section 32 of the 1994 Act, would suggest that a warning is no longer obligatory), a warning of the kind indicated in *R v Spencer, R v Smails* should still be given in respect of witnesses sharing the same unfortunate characteristics as the witnesses in that case. Following *R v Makanjuola*, however, it is clear that where a warning is given, its terms will depend on the precise circumstances of the particular case.[84]

Children

Under the proviso to section 38(1) of the Children and Young Persons Act 1933, where the unsworn evidence of a child was given on behalf of the prosecution, the accused was not liable to be convicted unless that evidence was corroborated by some other material evidence implicating him; and at common law, the sworn evidence of a child required a corroboration warning as a matter of law.[85] Section 38(1) has been repealed[86] and section 34(2) of the Criminal Justice Act 1988[87] provides that: 'Any requirement whereby at a trial on indictment it is obligatory for the court to give the jury a warning about convicting the accused on the uncorroborated evidence of a child is abrogated.' The rationale underlying the proviso to section 38(1) and the common law rule was the danger that the evidence of a child, especially if unsworn, but even if sworn, may be unreliable by reason of childish imagination, suggestibility, or fallibility of memory. These dangers remain, and although in *R v Pryce*[88] it was held that a direction to treat the evidence of a 6-year-old girl with caution was not required, because this would amount to a re-introduction of the abrogated rule, it is clear, following *R v Makanjuola*, that judges do retain a discretionary power to give such a direction, but whether such a direction should be given, and if so, its precise terms, are matters dependent on the circumstances of the case.[89] In the case of children, the relevant factors include the age and intelligence of the child, whether the evidence is given on oath, and, if the evidence is unsworn, how well the child in question understands the duty of speaking the truth. In *R v Pryce* itself, the Court of Appeal thought that it was sufficient for the trial judge to have told the jury to take into account the fact that the witness was a child. In other cases, a stronger direction will be called for.

Anonymous witnesses

In criminal cases witnesses may give evidence anonymously under the Criminal Evidence (Witness Anonymity) Act 2008, provided certain express pre-conditions are satisfied.[90] Prior to the Act, the Court of Appeal had held in *R v Davis* [91] that where the prosecution rely on the evidence of anonymous witnesses, the judge 'would probably' suggest that the jury should consider whether there is any independent, supporting evidence tending to confirm their

---

[84] See *R v Causley* [1999] Crim LR 572, CA.

[85] See, eg, *R v Cleal* [1942] 1 All ER 203, CCA.

[86] Criminal Justice Act 1991, s 101(2) and Sch 13.

[87] As amended by Criminal Justice and Public Order Act 1994, s 32(2).

[88] [1991] Crim LR 379, CA.

[89] See *R v L* [1999] Crim LR 489, CA.

[90] See Ch 5 at 154, **Witness anonymity**.

[91] [2006] 4 All ER 648, CA, per Sir Igor Judge, P, at [61]. The decision was overturned by the House of Lords (see *R v Davis* [2008] 1 AC 1128). See also *R v Myers and others* [2009] 2 All ER 145, 1 Cr App R 30.

credibility and the incriminating evidence that they have given. Under section 7 of the Act, the judge is required to give the jury a 'judicial warning' to ensure that an accused is not prejudiced by the fact that a witness has given evidence anonymously.[92] It is submitted that such a warning also 'would probably' suggest that the jury should consider the existence or absence of independent supporting evidence.

Matrimonial cases

Where a matrimonial 'offence' is alleged, whether in proceedings in the High Court or in a summary court, the gravity of the consequences of proof of such an allegation and the risk of a miscarriage of justice in acting on the uncorroborated evidence of a spouse have led the courts to acknowledge the desirability of corroboration. Corroboration is sought as a matter of practice rather than as a matter of law. Thus the court may act on the uncorroborated evidence of a spouse if in no doubt where the truth lies.[93] However, in cases where sexual misconduct is alleged, or the evidence of adultery is that of a willing participant,[94] the appellate court will intervene unless the trial court expressly warned itself of the danger of acting on uncorroborated evidence.[95]

Section 4 of the Affiliation Proceedings Act 1957 provides that in affiliation proceedings the court shall not adjudge the defendant to be the putative father of the child, in a case where evidence is given by the mother, unless her evidence is corroborated in some material particular. Under section 17 of the Family Law Reform Act 1987, the 1957 Act shall cease to have effect. Despite the abolition of affiliation proceedings, the question of paternity will, of course, continue to arise in family and other proceedings. What corroboration requirement, if any, remains? The justification for the corroboration requirement in section 4, which was the comparative ease with which a false allegation as to paternity could be made, and the difficulty of rebutting it, is no longer entirely convincing. Section 20 of the Family Law Reform Act 1969 provides that, in any civil proceedings in which the parentage of any person falls to be determined, the court may direct the taking of blood samples of that person, the mother of that person, and any party alleged to be the father of that person. Presumably, although there is no longer any requirement for corroboration, or even a warning, it is likely that the courts will be aware of the need for caution, if only in those cases in which, no direction having been given under section 20, the mother adduces no material in support of her allegation.

Claims against the estate of a deceased person

Where a claim is advanced by a person against the estate of a deceased person, it is natural to look for corroboration in support of the claimant's evidence, but there is no rule of law which prevents the court from acting on the claimant's uncorroborated evidence, if it is convincing.[96]

---

[92] According to the Explanatory Notes of the 2008 Act at [42], s 7 is based on s 32 of the Youth Justice and Criminal Evidence Act 1999 which provides for jury warnings in cases where special measures have been enacted for vulnerable witnesses. See Ch 5, 153, *The status of video-recorded evidence etc.*

[93] See *Curtis v Curtis* (1905) 21 TLR 676.

[94] See *Galler v Galler* [1954] P 252, CA and *Fairman v Fairman* [1949] P 341.

[95] However, see also *Joseph v Joseph* [1915] P 122 and *Alli v Alli* [1965] 3 All ER 480.

[96] *Re Hodgson, Beckett v Ramsdale* (1885) 31 Ch D 177, CA; *Re Cummins* [1972] Ch 62, CA.

Confessions by the mentally handicapped

In *R v MacKenzie*[97] Lord Taylor CJ, applying the guidance given in *R v Galbraith*[98] to cases involving confessions by the mentally handicapped, held that where (i) the prosecution case depends wholly on confessions; (ii) the defendant suffers from a significant degree of mental handicap; and (iii) the confessions are unconvincing to a point where a jury properly directed could not properly convict on them, then the judge, assuming he has not excluded the confessions earlier, should withdraw the case from the jury. It was held that confessions may be unconvincing, for example, because they lack the incriminating details to be expected of a guilty and willing confessor, because they are inconsistent with other evidence, or because they are otherwise inherently improbable. In a case which is not withdrawn from the jury, the fact that the confession was made by a mentally handicapped person may be taken into account by the judge not only for the purpose of deciding whether it should be excluded as a matter of law (under section 76 of the Police and Criminal Evidence Act 1984 (the 1984 Act)), but also in deciding whether to exercise his discretion to exclude (under section 82(3) or section 78(1) of that Act).[99] Thus in *R v Moss*[100] it was held that confessions made by an accused on the borderline of mental handicap, in the absence of a solicitor or any other independent person, in the course of nine interviews held over nine days, should have been excluded under section 76(2)(b).

Where the confession of a mentally handicapped person *is* admitted in evidence, section 77 of the 1984 Act imposes on the court a duty, in certain circumstances, to warn the tribunal of fact of the dangers of convicting such a person in reliance on his confession. It provides that:

1. Without prejudice to the general duty of the court at a trial on indictment with a jury to direct the jury on any matter on which it appears to the court appropriate to do so, where at such a trial—
    (a) the case against the accused depends wholly or substantially on a confession by him; and
    (b) the court is satisfied—
       (i) that he is mentally handicapped; and
       (ii) that the confession was not made in the presence of an independent person,
    the court shall warn the jury that there is a special need for caution before convicting the accused in reliance on the confession, and shall explain that the need arises because of the circumstances mentioned in paragraphs (a) and (b) above.
2. In any case where at the summary trial of a person for an offence it appears to the court that a warning under subsection (1) above would be required if the trial were on indictment with a jury, the court shall treat the case as one in which there is a special need for caution before convicting the accused on his confession.[101]

Concerning the 'general duty' referred to in section 77(1), in *R v Bailey*[102] it was held that in cases where the accused is significantly mentally handicapped and the prosecution would not have a case in the absence of the accused's confessions, the judge should give a full and proper statement of the accused's case against the confessions being accepted by the jury as true and

---

[97] [1993] 1 WLR 453, CA.
[98] [1981] 2 All ER 1060 (Ch 2).
[99] See generally Ch 13.
[100] (1990) 91 Cr App R 371, CA. See also *R v Cox* [1991] Crim LR 276, CA and *R v Wood* [1994] Crim LR 222, CA.
[101] Section 2A makes the warning under s 77(1) a requirement in trials on indictment without a jury.
[102] [1995] Crim LR 723, CA.

accurate, which should include not only the points made on the accused's behalf, but also any points which appear to the judge to be appropriate. The matters which in *that* case should have been put before the jury[103] included: (i) that the experience of the courts has shown that people with significant mental handicap do make false confessions for a variety of reasons; (ii) the various possible reasons for the accused having made false confessions; and (iii) that without the confessions, there was no case against the accused.

Concerning section 77(1)(a), the word 'substantially' should not be given a restricted meaning: section 77 is not confined to cases where either the whole or 'most of the case' depends on the confession.[104] In deciding whether a case depends 'substantially' on the confession, the test to be applied is whether the case for the Crown is substantially less strong without the confession, a test which may not be satisfied if there is other prosecution evidence such as identification evidence and evidence of another confession which was made in the presence of an independent adult.[105]

Although paragraph (a) of section 77(1), unlike paragraph (b), does not expressly state that it is for the court to be satisfied of the circumstances mentioned therein, it seems clear that the need for a direction to the jury can only arise where the *judge* is satisfied as to the circumstances mentioned in paragraph (a) as well as paragraph (b),[106] since the judge, when a warning is given, must explain that the need for caution arises because of the circumstances mentioned in both paragraphs. Accordingly, the judge should not direct the jury that a special need for caution *may* arise if *they* are satisfied of the circumstances mentioned in the paragraphs, but that there is a special need for caution which has arisen because the case against the accused *does* depend wholly or substantially on a confession, the accused is mentally handicapped, and the confession *was not* made in the presence of an independent person.

In *R v Campbell*[107] it was held that, as to the 'warning', the judge does not have to follow any specific form of words, but would be wise to use the phrase 'special need for caution', and as to the 'explanation', the judge should explain that persons who are mentally disordered or mentally handicapped may, without wishing to do so, provide information which is unreliable, misleading, or self-incriminating. The explanation should be tailored to the particular evidence in the case, for example evidence that the accused is particularly suggestible or prone to acquiesce, comply or give in to pressure. The judge should then explain that the function of the appropriate adult is designed to minimize the risk of the accused giving unreliable information by seeing that the interview is conducted properly and fairly and facilitating, if need be, communication between the police and the suspect.

A person is mentally handicapped if 'he is in a state of arrested or incomplete development of mind which includes significant impairment of intelligence and social functioning'.[108] An 'independent person' is defined negatively as not including a police officer or a person employed for, or engaged on, 'police purposes'[109] and could include, for example, a relative or

---

[103] The court held that nothing in its judgment was to be taken as of general application.

[104] *R v Bailey* [1995] Crim LR 723, CA.

[105] See *R v Campbell* [1995] 1 Cr App R 522, CA.

[106] However, concerning para (b), see also, *sed quaere*, *R v Lamont* [1989] Crim LR 813, CA: the trial judge should have directed the jury to exercise the caution called for if *they* accepted the evidence of mental handicap.

[107] [1995] 1 Cr App R 522, CA.

[108] Section 77(3).

[109] Section 77(3). 'Police purposes' has the meaning assigned to it by s 64 of the Police Act 1964, which defines such purposes as including 'the purposes of special constables appointed for that area, of police cadets undergoing

friend of the accused or his solicitor.[110] Should a dispute arise on the issue whether the accused is mentally handicapped (or whether his confession was made in the presence of an independent person) evidence, if necessary expert medical evidence, may be adduced to enable the judge to come to a decision. In these circumstances, the section is silent as to the incidence of the burden of proof. Presumably, the onus is on the defence to prove the circumstances mentioned in section 77(1)(b) on a balance of probabilities, rather than on the prosecution to prove their non-existence beyond reasonable doubt.

The number of cases in which a section 77 warning will be required is likely to be very small. The possibilities of withdrawing the case from the jury or excluding the confession under sections 76, 78, or 82(3) have already been mentioned. It should also be noted that, under Code C, a person who is mentally handicapped must not be interviewed in the absence of an 'appropriate adult' (a concept which in large measure overlaps with that of an 'independent person' for the purposes of section 77)[111] unless an officer of the rank of superintendent or above considers that delay would be likely (a) to lead to (i) interference with or harm to evidence, or (ii) interference with or physical harm to other people, or (iii) serious loss of or damage to property; (b) to lead to the alerting of other people suspected of having committed an offence but not yet arrested for it; or (c) to hinder the recovery of property obtained in consequence of the commission of an offence.[112] Thus it seems that section 77 is confined to cases in which the confession was made either in an interview conducted in breach of the Code or in an 'urgent interview'.[113] In the rare cases in which section 77 does apply, however, failure to warn the jury as required is grounds for a successful appeal.[114]

Identification cases

Visual identification by witnesses

In *R v Turnbull*[115] Lord Widgery CJ, giving the judgment of the Court of Appeal, laid down important guidelines relating to evidence of allegedly mistaken visual identification of the accused.[116] Mistaken identification of the accused, especially in cases of visual identification,

---

training with a view to becoming members of the police force maintained for that area and of civilians employed for the purposes of that force or of any such special constables or cadets'.

[110] Although the definition of an 'independent person' suggests that s 77 only applies in the case of questioning by police officers, in *R v Bailey* [1995] Crim LR 723, CA it was held that a s 77 warning should have been given in respect of a confession made to a member of the public.

[111] It is defined to include, inter alia, a relative, guardian, or other person responsible for his care or custody: see para 1.7(b), Code C. See also *R v Lewis* [1996] Crim LR 260, CA.

[112] Paras 11.15 and 11.18 and Annex E, Code C.

[113] See per Taylor LJ in *R v Moss* (1990) 91 Cr App R 371, CA at 377.

[114] See *R v Lamont* [1989] Crim LR 813,CA where it was held that such a direction was not a matter of prudence, but an essential part of a fair summing-up. However, also see *R v Qayyum* [2007] Crim LR 160, CA, where it was held that giving a formal warning would have made no difference to the jury's approach.

[115] [1977] QB 224.

[116] Other aspects of visual identification evidence are considered elsewhere: the exclusion of such evidence, if obtained in breach of Code D, under s 78 of the Police and Criminal Evidence Act 1984 (Ch 3); the admissibility of evidence of previous identification, and dock identifications (Ch 6); identification by samples (Ch 14); identification by photographs, films, photofits, and sketches (Ch 9); and expert evidence on identification by voice (Ch 18). As to the importance of pre-trial procedures relating to identification evidence, see Roberts, 'The problem of mistaken identity: Some observations on process' (2004) 8 *E&P* 100.

may be regarded as the greatest cause of wrong convictions.[117] The guidelines in *R v Turnbull* were designed to lessen this danger. The Court of Appeal attempted to follow the recommendations in the Report of the Committee on Evidence of Identification in Criminal Cases chaired by Lord Devlin.[118] The Committee had recommended the enactment of a general rule precluding a conviction in any case in which the prosecution relies wholly or mainly on evidence of visual identification by one or more witnesses, but the guidelines fall considerably short of the Committee's proposals.

Failure to follow the guidelines is likely to result in a conviction being quashed if, on all the evidence, the verdict is unsafe.[119] It will be otherwise, however, if the Court of Appeal is convinced that had the jury been directed correctly, they would nevertheless have come to the same conclusion.[120] Privy Council authority is to the same effect, so that in 'exceptional circumstances' a conviction based on unsupported identification evidence might be upheld even though a *Turnbull* direction was not given.[121] In *Freemantle v R*[122] the trial judge failed to give a *Turnbull* direction. The identification, which was by way of recognition evidence, was of exceptionally good quality: both identification witnesses had more than a fleeting glance of the accused and one of them said to the accused that he recognized him, to which the accused had replied in a way which appeared to acknowledge that he had been correctly identified. The Board was of the opinion that 'exceptional circumstances' include the fact that the evidence of identification is of exceptionally good quality and accordingly held that application of a proviso similar in its terms to section 2(1) of the Criminal Appeal Act 1968 was justified.

It is advisable, in every case in which a *Turnbull* direction may be required, for there to be a discussion between the judge and counsel, prior to the closing speeches and the summing-up, as to how identification issues will be addressed.[123]

The *Turnbull* guidelines are extensive. It will be convenient to consider separately seven extracts from the judgment of the Court of Appeal, together with subsequent developments in relation to each.

The special need for caution

First, whenever the case against an accused depends wholly or substantially on the correctness of one or more identifications of the accused which the defence alleges to be mistaken, the judge should warn the jury of the special need for caution before convicting the accused in reliance on the correctness of the identification or identifications. In addition he should instruct them as to the reason for the need for such a warning and should make some reference to the possibility that a mistaken witness can be a convincing one and that a number of such witnesses can all be mistaken. Provided that this is done in clear terms, the judge need not use any particular form of words.

---

[117] See para 196, 11th Report, Criminal Law Revision Committee (Cmnd 4991).

[118] Cmnd 338 (1976).

[119] *R v Kane* (1977) 65 Cr App R 270, CA. See also *R v Tyson* [1985] Crim LR 48, CA.

[120] *R v Hunjan* (1978) 68 Cr App R 99, CA, where the conviction was in fact quashed; and cf *R v Clifton* [1986] Crim LR 399, CA, where the prosecution case was exceptionally strong.

[121] See *Reid v R* (1989) 90 Cr App R 121 at 130, PC and also the judgment of Lord Griffiths, in *Scott v R* [1989] 2 All ER 305 at 314–15, PC. However, see also Lord Ackner in *Reid v R* (1989) 90 Cr App R 121 at 130.

[122] [1994] 3 All ER 225, PC.

[123] *R v Stanton* (2004) The Times, 28 Apr, [2004] EWCA Crim 490.

Although Lord Widgery CJ himself said that *Turnbull*'s case 'is intended primarily to deal with the ghastly risk run in cases of fleeting encounters . . . ',[124] the warning should be given even if the opportunities for observation were good and the identifying witness is convinced that he has correctly identified the accused.[125] A warning must also be given notwithstanding that the identifying witness has picked out the accused at a formal identification procedure such as a video identification procedure .[126] It is of the utmost importance to give a warning where the sole evidence of identification is contained in the deposition of a deceased witness and the identification may have been based on a fleeting glance.[127]

Where identification is in issue and there is strong prosecution evidence that the accused was with some other person at the relevant time, then the evidence identifying that other, unless unchallenged by the defence, should normally be the subject of a *Turnbull* direction.[128]

According to *R v Slater*,[129] where there is no issue as to the presence of the accused at or near the scene of the offence, but the issue is as to what he was doing, whether a *Turnbull* direction is necessary will depend on the circumstances of the case. It was held that it will be necessary where, on the evidence, the possibility exists that the identifying witness may have mistaken one person for another, for example because of similarities in face, build, or clothing between two or more people present,[130] but where there is no possibility of such a mistake, there is no need to give a *Turnbull* direction. On the facts, the accused was six foot six inches tall and there was no evidence to suggest that anyone else present was remotely similar in height. It was therefore held that there was no basis for any mistake: the issue in the case was not identification, but what the accused did, and accordingly a *Turnbull* direction was not required. The court observed that in some cases, where presence is admitted but conduct disputed, it would be contrary to common sense to require a *Turnbull* direction, as when a black man and a white man are present and the complainant says that it was the white man.[131]

It has also been said that a full direction is not required if none of the identifying witnesses purports to identify the accused, their evidence merely serving to provide a description which is not inconsistent with the appearance of the accused and forming only one part, albeit a very important part, of all the evidence, because such a case does not depend wholly or substantially upon the correctness of their evidence.[132] In *R v Constantinou*,[133] where none of the witnesses purported to identify the accused but merely gave descriptions which might have

---

[124] *R v Oakwell* (1978) 66 Cr App R 174 at 178.

[125] *R v Tyson* [1985] Crim LR 48, CA.

[126] Per Lord Griffiths in *Scott v R* [1989] 2 All ER 305 at 314, PC. Where the witness picks out a volunteer, there is no obligation to give a 'reverse *Turnbull* direction', ie that the witness may be honest but mistaken in identifying the volunteer, because the purpose of the *Turnbull* direction is to lessen the danger of a wrongful conviction, not a wrongful acquittal: see *R v Trew* [1996] Crim LR 441, CA. For the special issues that arise where there has been a qualified identification, see *R v George* [2003] Crim LR 282, CA and Andrew Roberts, 'The perils and possibilities of qualified identification: *R v George*' (2003) 7 E&P 130.

[127] *Scott v R* [1989] 2 All ER 305 at 314–15.

[128] *R v Bath* [1990] Crim LR 716, CA. Note that a *Turnbull* direction is not required in relation to the identification of cars: *R v Browning* (1991) 94 Cr App R 109, CA.

[129] [1995] 1 Cr App R 584, CA.

[130] See, eg, *R v Thornton* [1995] 1 Cr App R 578, CA, where the appellant and others were similarly dressed.

[131] See also *R v Conibeer* [2002] EWCA Crim 2059 and cf *R v O'Leary* [2002] EWCA Crim 2055, CA.

[132] *R v Browning* (1991) 94 Cr App R 109. Cf *R v Andrews* [1993] Crim LR 590, CA.

[133] (1989) 91 Cr App R 74, CA.

been consistent with his appearance, and a photofit was admitted which also might have been consistent with his appearance, it was held that no *Turnbull* warning was required in respect of the photofit. This decision, it is submitted, is in need of review.

In a case where identification is in issue but the defence is that the identifying witness is lying, rather than mistaken, a *Turnbull* direction may not be required. In *R v Courtnell*[134] the defence was one of alibi and it was alleged that the purported identification, by someone who had known the accused for a week, was a fabrication. It was held that the trial judge had properly withdrawn the issue of mistaken identity from the jury: the sole issue was the veracity of the identifying witness and therefore a *Turnbull* direction would only have confused the jury.[135]

As to the terms of the direction, *R v Turnbull* is not a statute and does not require an incantation of a formula or set form of words: provided that the judge complies with the sense and spirit of the guidance given, he has a broad discretion to express himself in his own way.[136] Thus as to the reason for the warning, failure to use the word 'convincing' ('a mistaken witness can be a convincing one') need not be fatal to the summing-up.[137] Indeed, even prefacing the warning with advice to guard against 'allowing an oversophisticated approach to evidence relating to identification to become…a "mugger's charter"' was not fatal because, in the round, the judge did set out the direction sufficiently.[138] Nonetheless, to depart from the standard form of the direction was 'singularly unwise' and the use of the words 'mugger's charter' was plainly inappropriate.[139] In relation to the general risk of mistaken identification, it is insufficient merely to say that 'even an honest witness may be mistaken': the judge should explain that evidence of visual identification is a category of evidence which experience has shown to be particularly vulnerable to error, in particular by honest and impressive witnesses, and that this has been known to result in wrong convictions.[140] There is a requirement to make clear that the need for special caution is rooted in the court's actual experience of miscarriages of justice.[141]

The circumstances of the identification and specific weaknesses in the identification evidence
Secondly, the judge should direct the jury to examine closely the circumstances in which the identification by each witness came to be made. How long did the witness have the accused under observation? At what distance? In what light? Was the observation impeded in any way, as for example by passing traffic or a press of people? Had the witness ever seen the accused before? How often? If only occasionally, had he any special reason for remembering the accused? How long a time elapsed between the original observation and the subsequent

---

[134] [1990] Crim LR 115, CA.

[135] See also, applying *R v Courtnell*, *R v Cape* [1996] 1 Cr App R 191, CA and *R v Beckles and Montague* [1999] Crim LR 148, CA; and *R v Ryder* [1994] 2 All ER 859, CA, *Capron v R* [2006] UKPC 34 and *R v Giga* [2007] Crim LR 571, CA, cases of recognition. But see further *Beckford v R* (1993) 97 Cr App R 409, PC, applied in *Shand v R* [1996] 1 All ER 511, PC, below.

[136] Per Lord Steyn in *Mills v R* [1995] 3 All ER 865, PC at 872.

[137] See *Rose v R* [1995] Crim LR 939, PC.

[138] *R v Shervington* [2008] EWCA Crim 658; [2008] Crim LR 581.

[139] Ibid at [25] and [28].

[140] Per Lord Ackner in *Reid v R* (1989) 90 Cr App R 121 at 134–5.

[141] *R v Nash* [2005] Crim LR 232, CA. However, it has also been held that failure to refer to past miscarriages of justice is not fatal: *R v Tyler* [1993] Crim LR 60, CA. Indeed, in jurisdictions in which there is no history of well-publicized miscarriages of justice, eg Jamaica, such a reference would be unnecessary and unhelpful: *Amore v R* (1994) 99 Cr App R 279, PC.

identification to the police? Was there any material discrepancy between the description of the accused given to the police by the witness when first seen by them and his actual appearance? If in any case the prosecution have reason to believe that there is such a material discrepancy, they should supply the accused or his legal advisers with particulars of the description the police were first given. In all cases, if the accused asks to be given particulars of such descriptions, the prosecution should supply them. Finally, he should remind the jury of any specific weaknesses which had appeared in the identification evidence.

Simply paying lip service to the guidelines, without reference to the particular circumstances relevant to the accuracy of the identification will not suffice.[142] Nor is it sufficient for the judge simply to invite the jury to take into account what counsel for the defence has said about 'specific weaknesses': the judge must fairly and properly summarize for the jury any such weaknesses which can arguably be said to have been exposed in the evidence.[143] However, provided that the judge does identify all the specific weaknesses, there is no obligation to do so in a particular way, for example by bringing them together and listing them, rather than by dealing with them in context when reviewing the evidence in the case.[144] Equally, in the case of minor discrepancies between what the identifying witnesses have said, it is a matter for the judge's discretion whether simply to refer to them in his review of the evidence, or to categorize them specifically as potential weaknesses.[145]

The same rules apply to police officers as to other identifying witnesses, but sometimes an officer, because an officer, pays particular attention to the identity of a person, even in a fleeting glance type case, and the judge should then specifically direct the jury as to the likelihood of the officer being correct, when a 'mere casual observer' might not be, because an officer has a greater appreciation of the importance of identification, is trained, and is less likely to be affected by the excitement of the situation.[146]

Where evidence of a formal identification procedure at which the accused was identified is central to the prosecution case but the judge, notwithstanding breaches of Code D, properly decides not to exercise his discretion under section 78 of the Police and Criminal Evidence Act 1984 to exclude it, then in his summing-up he should make specific references to the breaches and leave it to the jury to consider what their approach should be in the light of them.[147]

Recognition

Recognition may be more reliable than identification of a stranger; but even when the witness is purporting to recognize someone whom he knows, the jury should be reminded that mistakes in recognition of close relatives and friends are sometimes made.

Many people experience seeing someone in the street whom they know, only to discover that they are wrong. The expression 'I could have sworn it was you' indicates the sort of warning which a judge should give, because that is exactly what a witness does—he swears that it

---

[142] *R v Graham* [1994] Crim LR 212, CA, applied in *R v Allen* [1995] Crim LR 643, CA, where the trial judge took no steps to remove the possible prejudice resulting from an improper refusal to hold an identification parade. See also *R v I* [2007] 2 Cr App R 316, CA. Cf *R v Doldur* [2000] Crim LR 178, CA.

[143] *R v Fergus* (1993) 98 Cr App R 313, CA.

[144] *R v Mussell* [1995] Crim LR 887, CA; *R v Barnes* [1995] 2 Cr App R 491, CA; and *R v Qadir* [1998] Crim LR 828, CA. Cf *R v Pattinson* [1996] 1 Cr App R 51, CA.

[145] *R v Barnes* [1995] 2 Cr App R 491 at 500, CA.

[146] *R v Ramsden* [1991] Crim LR 295, *CA*; *R v Tyler* [1993] Crim LR 60, CA. Cf per Lord Ackner in *Reid v R* (1989) 90 Cr App R 121 at 137: 'experience has undoubtedly shown that police identification can be just as unreliable [as that of an ordinary member of the public].'

[147] *R v Quinn* [1995] 1 Cr App R 480, CA.

was the person he thinks it was. In the field of recognition, there are degrees of danger, but perhaps less where the parties have known each other for many years or where there is no doubt that the person identified was at the scene at the time. Even here, it is at least advisable to alert the jury to the possibility of honest mistake and to the dangers, and the reasons why such dangers exist.[148] In *Beckford v R*[149] the Privy Council held as follows. (1) A general warning on *Turnbull* lines *must* normally be given in recognition cases and failure to do so will nearly always *by itself* suffice to invalidate a conviction substantially based on identification evidence. (2) Such a warning should be given even if the sole or main thrust of the defence is directed to the issue of the identifying witness's credibility, ie whether his evidence is true or false as distinct from accurate or mistaken. The first question for the jury is whether the witness is honest, and if the answer to that question is Yes, the next question is whether he could be mistaken. (3) This 'strong general rule' is subject to only very rare exceptions:

> If, for example, the witness's identification evidence is that the accused was his workmate whom he has known for 20 years and that he was conversing with him for half an hour face to face in the same room and the witness is sane and sober, then, if credibility is the issue, it will be the only issue.[150]

However, in *Capron v R*[151] the Privy Council deprecated the use of phrases such as 'wholly exceptional' or 'very rare' to describe the situations in which the court can dispense with a *Turnbull* direction on the basis that the sole or main issue is the credibility of the identification witness or witnesses; what matters, it was said, is the nature of the identification evidence in each case. In *R v Giga*,[152] the Court of Appeal, affirming this approach, held that each case must turn on its own facts.

Nonetheless, where evidence of recognition is adduced, failure to warn the jury of its inherent dangers *will* nearly always be fatal to a conviction. In *R v Ali*,[153] a case involving a 'steaming' robbery whereby a train passenger was surrounded by a group and robbed, the accused was identified as a participant by the passenger. Evidence was also given by a police officer that he recognized the accused from a recording by closed-circuit television of a group of males on the platform. Whilst the judge provided a *Turnbull* warning in respect of the complainant's identification, none was provided in respect of the police officer's recognition. In quashing the conviction, the Court of Appeal remarked that even with recognition, the risk of mistaken identification remains and a direction is required which brings home fully to the jury that an identifying witness can make a mistake when purporting to recognize someone he knows.[154]

In *Ali* it was held that the recognition evidence by a police officer from a closed-circuit television recording was not admissible on the facts of the case, but there is no general rule excluding police recognition evidence by police officers including recognition evidence based on a viewing of a video tape of the crime recorded by a security camera. This is the case even though the jury may then infer that the accused has previously been in trouble with the

---

[148] *R v Bentley* (1991) 99 Cr App R 342, CA; *R v Bowden* [1993] Crim LR 379, CA. Cf *R v Curry* [1983] Crim LR 737 and *R v Oakwell* (1978) 66 Cr App R 174, CA.

[149] (1993) 97 Cr App R 409, PC.

[150] (1993) 97 Cr App R 409 at 415, applied in *Shand v R* [1996] 1 All ER 511, PC. Contrast *R v Courtnell* [1990] Crim LR 115, CA and *R v Ryder* [1994] 2 All ER 859, CA, both above.

[151] [2006] UKPC 34.

[152] [2007] Crim LR 571, CA.

[153] [2008] EWCA Crim 1522.

[154] Ibid at [35].

police, because the fact of the officers' knowledge is of critical significance to the quality of the identification, and to exclude the evidence would unfairly advantage those with criminal records.[155] As to pre-trial procedure applicable to identification by police officers from CCTV images, it has been questioned whether Code D is directly applicable.[156] However, whether it applies or not, some record should be kept which would enable an accused to test the reliability of the identification. This could include a record of the officer's reactions to viewing the images, noting, for example, whether or not he failed to recognize the suspect in a first viewing or the words he used when recognizing the suspect.[157]

Identification evidence of good quality

When the quality [of the identification evidence] is good, as for example when the identification is made after a long period of observation, or in satisfactory conditions by a relative, a neighbour, a close friend, a workmate and the like, the jury can safely be left to assess the value of the identifying evidence even though there is not other evidence to support it: provided always, however, that an adequate warning has been given about the special need for caution.

Where the quality of the identification evidence is such that the jury can be safely left to assess its value, even though there is no other evidence to support it, then the judge is fully entitled, if so minded, to direct the jury that an identification by one witness can constitute support for the identification by another, *provided* that he warns them in clear terms that even a number of honest witnesses can all be mistaken.[158]

Identification evidence of poor quality

When, in the judgment of the trial judge, the quality of the identifying evidence is poor, as for example when it depends solely on a fleeting glance or on a longer observation made in difficult conditions, the situation is very different. The judge should then withdraw the case from the jury and direct an acquittal unless there is other evidence which goes to support the correctness of the identification. This may be corroboration in the sense that lawyers use that word; but it need not be so if its effect is to make the jury sure that there has been no mistaken identification.

Under this guideline, a case is withdrawn from the jury not because the judge considers that the witness is lying, but because the evidence, even if taken to be honest, has a base which is so slender that it is unreliable and therefore insufficient to found a conviction. The jury is protected from acting upon the type of evidence which, even if believed, experience has shown to be a possible source of injustice.[159]

---

[155] See *R v Crabtree* [1992] Crim LR 65, CA and *R v Caldwell* (1993) 99 Cr App R 73, CA; and cf *R v Fowden and White* [1982] Crim LR 588, CA. The defence then face difficulties in challenging the extent of the officers' knowledge of the accused. In *R v Caldwell* the Court of Appeal thought the difficulty was 'manageable', approving the sensitive ruling of the trial judge that the officers should not refer to any convictions or criminal associations of the accused, their families, etc.

[156] *R v Smith* [2009] 1 Cr App R 521, CA. See also *R v Chaney* [2009] 1 Cr App R 512, CA.

[157] *R v Smith* ibid, at [68]–[69]. For comment on Code D and pre-trial procedure for CCTV recognition evidence, see Roberts, 'Commentary' [2009] *Crim LR* 437.

[158] Per Lord Lane CJ in *R v Weeder* (1980) 71 Cr App R 228, CA at 231. In *R v Breslin* (1984) 80 Cr App R 226, CA it was held that this direction (and warning) should be given in all identification cases to which it applies.

[159] Per Lord Mustill in *Daley v R* [1993] 4 All ER 86 at 94, PC.

Even in the absence of a submission, the judge is under a duty to invite submissions when, in his view, the identification evidence is poor and unsupported.[160] Moreover, *R v Turnbull* plainly contemplates that the position must be assessed not only at the end of the prosecution case, but also at the close of the defence case.[161] In exceptional cases, a ruling can be made even before the close of the prosecution case, on the depositions, but apparently in any event a *voir dire* should not be held.[162] A judge should not direct a jury that he would have withdrawn the case from them on a submission of no case to answer, had he thought that there was insufficient identification evidence, because the jury may mistakenly take this to mean that the evidence is sufficiently strong for them to convict.[163]

Supporting evidence

The trial judge should identify to the jury the evidence which he adjudges is capable of supporting the evidence of identification. If there is any evidence or circumstances which the jury might think was supporting when it did not have this quality, the judge should say so. A jury, for example, might think that support could be found in the fact that the accused had not given evidence before them. An accused's absence from the witness box cannot provide evidence of anything and the judge should tell the jury so.[164] But he would be entitled to tell them that, when assessing the quality of the identification evidence, they could take into consideration the fact that it was uncontradicted by any evidence coming from the accused himself.

It is essential for the judge to make clear to the jury that although he has adjudged that certain evidence is capable of supporting the evidence of identification, it is for them to decide, if they accept it, whether it does in fact support the evidence of identification.[165] The support may be provided by evidence of the accused's association with other suspects who have been identified[166] or by evidence that the identifying witness correctly identified another suspect seen with the accused at the relevant time.[167] There is some authority to the effect that the correct identification by a witness of one accused in difficult circumstances may be capable of providing support for the correctness of the identification of another accused by the same witness at the same time. The inference which may be drawn by the jury is that the circumstances which permitted the correct identification of one suspect were not so difficult as to make the same witness's identification of the other suspect unreliable.[168]

---

[160] *R v Fergus* (1993) 98 Cr App R 313, CA.

[161] Ibid, citing *R v Turnbull* [1977] QB 224 at 228–9.

[162] See *R v Flemming* (1987) 86 Cr App R 32, CA and cf *R v Beveridge* [1987] Crim LR 401, CA.

[163] *R v Smith and Doe* (1986) 85 Cr App R 197, CA. See also *R v Akaidere* [1990] Crim LR 808, CA: a judge should not direct the jury that the identification evidence is so poor that he would have stopped the case if it had stood alone.

[164] Failure to give such a direction will found a successful appeal. This remains the case, where the failure may have led the jury to believe that the accused's absence from the witness box was supportive, even if the quality of the identification evidence was good and there was evidence supportive of it: *R v Forbes* [1992] Crim LR 593, CA. But see now Criminal Justice and Public Order Act 1994, s 35 (Ch 14).

[165] *R v Akaidere* [1990] Crim LR 808, CA.

[166] *R v Penny* (1991) 94 Cr App R 345, CA.

[167] *R v Castle* [1989] Crim LR 567, CA and *R v Jones (Terence)* [1992] Crim LR 365, CA. See also *R v Brown* [1991] Crim LR 368, CA.

[168] See Archbold, *Criminal Evidence Pleading and Practice* (2009) at 14-23a and *R v Hussain* [2004] EWCA 1064 where it was held that it was perfectly proper for a judge to direct a jury in this way.

In a case of purported recognition in circumstances such that, had it been a case of identi-fication by a stranger, the quality of the evidence would have been poor, the fact that it was a recognition may itself form part of the evidence in support.[169] However, it is doubtful that recognition of a suspect by a police officer would be supporting evidence for another witness's identification where the officer was not an expert and his recognition was based on viewing recorded images in which the suspect's face was partially hidden.[170] Further, it has been held that the physical appearance of an accused, however singular, and however closely it corre-sponds with the evidence of a witness describing the criminal, cannot amount without more to corroboration of that evidence because it does not establish the reliability of the witness's evidence that the criminal had such an appearance.[171]

It is for the jury to decide whether evidence is in fact supportive of the identification, and although there may be cases where in the light of the evidence that has unfolded the jury should be directed not to convict on the identification evidence alone, there is no general requirement to give such a direction.[172]

False alibis

Care should be taken by the judge when directing the jury about the support for an identifica-tion which may be derived from the fact that they have rejected an alibi. False alibis may be put forward for many reasons: an accused, for example, who has only his own truthful evi-dence to rely on may stupidly fabricate an alibi and get lying witnesses to support it out of fear that his own evidence will not be enough. Further, alibi witnesses can make genuine mistakes about dates and occasions like any other witnesses can. Only when the jury is satisfied that the sole reason for the fabrication was to deceive them and there is no other explanation for its being put forward can fabrication provide any support for identification evidence. The jury should be reminded that proving the accused has told lies about where he was at the material time does not by itself prove that he was where the identifying witness says he was.

Such a direction should be given even if the prosecution has not relied on the collapse of the alibi as part of the material supporting its case.[173]

Visual identification by the jury

In a case in which the jurors themselves are asked to 'identify' the accused, whom they have seen in court, from a photograph or video-recording of the offender committing the offence,[174] they should be warned of the risk of mistaken identity and of the need to exercise particular

---

[169] *R v Turnbull* [1977] QB 224. See also *R v Ryan* [1990] Crim LR 50, CA: it is rare for the court to feel concern about the rightness of a conviction based on evidence of recognition.

[170] See *R v Ali* [2008] EWCA Crim 1522, CA. However, see also *R v Clare, R v Peach* [1995] 2 Cr App R 333, CA: an officer could acquire special knowledge which the court did not possess obtained by, for example, spending a long time analysing material from the crime scene.

[171] *R v Willoughby* (1988) 88 Cr App R 91, CA. However, see *R v McInnes* (1989) 90 Cr App R 99, CA, where a kidnapping victim's detailed knowledge of the inside of the alleged kidnapper's car was independent corroboration. See also *R v Nagy* [1990] Crim LR 187, CA.

[172] *R v Ley* [2007] 1 Cr App R 25, CA.

[173] See *R v Duncan* (1992) The Times, 24 July, CA and *R v Pemberton* (1993) 99 Cr App R 228, CA.

[174] In *Attorney General's Reference (No 2 of 2002)* [2003] 1 Cr App R 21, CA, the Court of Appeal suggested circum-stances where the jury might make an identification this way. These included where the image was clear enough to make a comparison with the accused, where the accused was recognized in the image by someone who knew him sufficiently well, or where the accused has been identified in the image by an expert in facial mapping or with some other relevant expertise.

care in any identification which they make. One factor which they must take into account is whether the appearance of the accused has changed since the visual recording was made, but a full *Turnbull* direction is inappropriate because the process of identifying a person from a photograph is a commonplace and everyday event and some things are obvious from the photograph itself. For example, the jury does not need to be told that the photograph is of good quality or poor, nor whether the person is shown in close-up or was distant from the camera, or was alone or part of a crowd.[175] However, an accused who has elected not to testify is under no obligation to meet a jury request that he stand up and turn around, in order that they may be given a better view of him.[176]

Voice identification

Unlike visual identification, in the case of aural or voice identification, little judicial thought has been given to the danger of mistakes being made or to the safeguards necessary to lessen the danger. Moreover Code D all but ignores the subject and simply states that the Code does not preclude the police from making use of aural identification procedures, such as a 'voice identification parade', where they judge that appropriate.[177] Such a parade was held in *R v Hersey*, [178] where 11 volunteers and the accused, H, read out a passage of text from an unrelated interview with H. This was listened to by the 'earwitness' who had heard considerable speech by two masked robbers during the robbery of his shop. On a *voir dire* an expert gave evidence that 12 voices was too many, that almost all of the volunteers' voices were of a pitch higher than that of H, and only H had read the passage in a way which made sense. He also gave evidence of the effect of stress on pitch. The trial judge decided not to exclude the identification evidence under section 78 of the 1984 Act, and ruled that the evidence of the expert was not admissible before the jury. The Court of Appeal held that evidence of the parade had been properly admitted and that the jurors did not require the assistance of the expert, who had dealt with matters which were within their own experience and competence.[179] It was also held that a warning based on the guidelines in *Turnbull* should be given, but tailored for the purposes of voice identification and recognition.

The Court of Appeal has since acknowledged, in *R v Roberts*,[180] that according to the expert research that has been done, voice identification is more difficult than visual identification, especially in the case of a stranger, and therefore should attract an even more stringent warning than that given in the case of visual identification. It is also clear that where a tape-recording, including a covert tape-recording, of a voice alleged to be that of the accused is admitted in evidence, the opinion evidence of an expert in phonetics is admissible on the question whether the voice matches that of the accused. Indeed, in *R v Chenia*[181] it was held that without such

---

[175] *R v Blenkinsop* [1995] 1 Cr App R 7, CA, approving *R v Downey* [1995] 1 Cr App R 547, CA. Cf *R v Dodson and Williams* (1984) 79 Cr App R 220, CA; and see also *Taylor v Chief Constable of Cheshire* [1987] 1 All ER 225, DC (Ch 10). Research, however, shows that there are difficulties and dangers: see Bruce, 'Fleeting Images of Shade' (1998) *The Psychologist* 331 and Henderson et al 'Matching the Faces of Robbers Captured on Video' (2001) 15 *Applied Cognitive Psychology* 445.

[176] *R v McNamara* [1996] Crim LR 750, CA.

[177] Para 1.2. See also para 18, Annex B, which deals with the situation in which a witness at a visual identification parade wishes to hear any parade member speak.

[178] [1998] Crim LR 281, CA.

[179] See *R v Turner* [1975] QB 834, CA, Ch 18.

[180] [2000] Crim LR 183, CA.

[181] [2004] 1 All ER 543, CA at [106] and [107]. See also *R v O'Doherty* [2003] 1 Cr App R 77, Ch 18.

expert assistance the jury should not be asked to compare what they hear on a recording with either what they hear on another recording or the voice of the accused when giving evidence. However, this must now be considered in the light of *R v Flynn*[182], where the Court of Appeal concluded that apart from *Chenia*, there was no other authority for the proposition that juries could only make such a comparison with expert assistance. Accordingly, it was held that it was wrong to direct the jury not to make their own comparison between the voices heard on a covert recording and the voices of the accused when they gave evidence where, during the trial, recognition evidence identifying the accused had been given by police officers as 'lay listeners'. Such a comparison *was* permissible provided the jury had received guidance from *either* experts or lay listeners. Nonetheless, the court stated that the increasing use of police officers to conduct 'lay listener' identifications of voice recordings was to be treated with 'great care and caution'.[183] Further guidance is clearly needed on aural dock identifications which, it is submitted, are no less dangerous than visual dock identifications.[184] Further detailed guidance is also required on the dangers of mistaken voice identification, and on the relevant factors to be taken into account by a judge in assessing the quality of voice identification so that he may properly decide (i) whether it is of such poor quality that he should withdraw the case from the jury and, if not; (ii) how he may adequately warn the jury about the special need for caution. Such factors are likely to include, for example, distinctive vocal features, duration of speech, and the effect of stress or of an attempt to disguise a voice.[185]

As to the pre-trial procedure, it has been made clear since *R v Hersey* that there is no duty to hold a voice identification procedure under Code D, which relates only to visual identification, and that the matter is properly dealt with by a suitably adapted *Turnbull* warning.[186] However, it is submitted that there is an obvious need for a pre-trial procedure and not one crudely modelled on the procedures used in the case of visual identification, because that would be to duck important issues of the kind raised by the expert in *R v Hersey*, for example questions relating to the number of voices that should be heard, the nature of the text that should be used, and the method by which the police should select those whose voices, so far as possible, resemble that of the accused.[187] In *R v Flynn*[188] the Court of Appeal did provide some 'minimal safeguards' in respect of pre-trial procedure for 'lay listener' voice identification, but much more is needed.[189] The 'minimum safeguards' were as follows.

1. The evidence gathering procedure should be properly recorded, in particular the amount of time spent in contact with the accused should be recorded as it is highly relevant to the issue of the officer's familiarity with the accused when identifying his voice.

---

[182] [2008] Cr App R 20 at [56]

[183] Ibid at [63].

[184] See Ch 6, 180 under **Previous consistent or self-serving statements**, *Previous identification*.

[185] See generally R Bull and B Clifford, 'Earwitness Testimony' in Heaton-Armstrong et al (eds), *Analysing Witness Testimony* (London, 1999), ch 13.

[186] *R v Gummerson and Steadman* [1999] Crim LR 680, CA.

[187] For an analysis of the dangers of using voice identification and recognition evidence and possible safeguards for its use both before and at the trial, see David Ormerod, 'Sounds Familiar?—Voice Identification Evidence' [2001] *Crim LR* 595.

[188] Ibid at [53].

[189] See D Warburton and T Lewis, 'Opinion evidence; admissibility of ad hoc expert voice recognition evidence: *R v Flynn*' (2009) 13 E&P 50.

2. The date and time spent by the police officer compiling a transcript of a covert recording must be noted and annotated with the officer's views as to who is speaking on the recording.

3. Before attempting to make a voice identification the police officer should not be supplied with a copy of a transcript bearing another officer's annotations of who he believes is speaking.

4. A voice identification should be carried out by someone other than an officer involved in investigating the case because of the risk that the identification might be influenced by knowledge already gained in the course of the investigation.

Given that the courts recognized as long ago as 2000[190] that the risk of an unreliable voice identification may be more severe than a visual identification, it is submitted that it is unsatisfactory that, at the time of writing, not even minimal safeguards of the kind suggested in *Flynn* appear in Code D.

Lip-reading evidence

An expert lip-reader who has viewed a video or CCTV recording of a person talking, may give expert opinion evidence as to what was said, notwithstanding that such evidence is always, to some extent, unreliable, because not all words can be identified by vision alone, single syllabus words with little context are very difficult to interpret, and even when the words are presented in clearly spoken sentences, the best lip-readers can only achieve up to 80 per cent correctness. In *R v Luttrell*[191] the Court of Appeal considered two issues: when such evidence should be excluded; and, where such evidence is admitted, the nature of the special warning that the judge must give to the jury. As to the former, Rose LJ said:[192]

> The decision in each case is likely to be highly fact sensitive. For example, a video may be of such poor quality or the view of the speaker's face so poor that no reliable interpretation is possible. There may also be cases where the interpreting witness is not sufficiently skilled. A judge may properly take into account: whether consistency with extrinsic facts confirms or inconsistency casts doubt on the reliability of an interpretation; whether information provided to the lip reader might have coloured the reading; and whether the probative effect of the evidence depends on the interpretation of a single word or phrase or on the whole thrust of the conversation. In the light of such considerations, (which are not intended to be exhaustive) a judge may well rule on the *voir dire* that any lip-reading evidence proffered should not be admitted before the jury.

The court was in no doubt that where the evidence is admitted, it requires a warning from the judge as to its limitations and the concomitant risk of error, not least because the expert may fall significantly short of complete accuracy. Rose LJ said:[193]

> As with any 'special warning', its precise terms will be fact-dependent, but in most, if not all cases, the judge should spell out to the jury the risk of mistakes as to the words that the lip reader believes were spoken; the reasons why the witness may be mistaken; and the way in which a convincing, authoritative and truthful witness may yet be a mistaken witness. Furthermore, the

---

[190] *R v Roberts* [2000] Crim LR 183, CA.
[191] [2004] 2 Cr App R 520, CA. For case comment, see *Rees and Roberts* [2004] Crim LR 939.
[192] At [38].
[193] At [44].

judge should deal with the particular strengths and weaknesses of the material in the instant case, carefully setting out the evidence, together with the criticisms that can properly be made of it because of other evidence. The jury should be reminded that the quality of the evidence will be affected by such matters as the lighting at the scene, the angle of the view in relation to those speaking, the distances involved, whether anything interfered with the observation, familiarity on the part of the lip-reader with the language spoken, the extent of the use of single syllable words, any awareness on the part of the expert witness of the context of the speech and whether the probative value of the evidence depends on isolated words or phrases or the general impact of long passages of conversation.

However, the court was also of the view that there was no reason in principle why lip-reading evidence adduced by the prosecution should not establish a prima facie case, although in reaching this conclusion the court may have been influenced by its own—and, it is submitted, questionable—observation that it is highly unlikely that lip-reading evidence will ever stand alone.

Sudden infant death syndrome

Infant deaths are attributed to Sudden Infant Death Syndrome (SIDS), known colloquially as 'cot deaths', where the immediate cause of death is apnoea, loss of breath or cessation of breathing occurring naturally, the underlying cause or causes being as yet unknown. Infant deaths cannot be attributed to SIDS, therefore, if they are clinically explicable or consequent on demonstrable trauma.

In *R v Cannings*[194] the appellant had been convicted of the murder of two of her four children, J who had died six weeks after his birth and M who had died eighteen weeks after his birth. Her eldest child, G, had died thirteen weeks after her birth. The Crown's case, for which there was no direct evidence, was that the accused had smothered all three of the children and that the deaths of J and M formed part of an overall 'pattern'. Their case depended on expert evidence that the conclusion of smothering could be drawn from the extreme rarity of three separate infant deaths in the same family. The appellant's case was that the deaths were attributable to SIDS and at the appeal she relied on fresh expert evidence to the effect that infant deaths occurring in the same family can and do occur naturally, even when unexplained. Allowing the appeal, it was held that where three infant deaths have occurred in the same family, each apparently unexplained, and for each of which there is no evidence extraneous to the expert evidence that harm was or must have been inflicted—for example, indications or admissions of violence or a pattern of ill-treatment—the proper approach is to start with the fact that three unexplained deaths in the same family are indeed rare, but to proceed on the basis that if there is nothing to explain them, in our current state of knowledge they remain unexplained and, despite the known fact that some parents do smother their infant children, possible natural deaths. Whether there are one, two, or even three deaths, the exclusion of currently known natural causes of infant death does not establish that the death or deaths resulted from the deliberate infliction of harm. If, on examination of all the evidence, every possible cause has been excluded, the cause remains unknown. It was further held that, for the time being, where a full investigation into two or more sudden unexplained infant deaths in the same family is followed by a serious disagreement between reputable experts about the cause of death, and a body of such expert opinion concludes that natural causes,

[194] [2004] 1 WLR 2607, CA.

whether explained or not, cannot be excluded as a reasonable (and not a fanciful) possibility, a prosecution for murder should not be started or continued unless there is additional cogent evidence, extraneous to the expert evidence tending to support the conclusion that one of the infants was deliberately harmed, such as indications or admissions of violence or a pattern of ill-treatment.

The impact of the decision in *R v Cannings* in care proceedings was considered in *In re U (a Child) (Serious Injury: Standard of Proof)*.[195] It was held that although *R v Cannings* had provided a useful warning to judges in care proceedings against ill-considered conclusions or conclusions resting on insufficient evidence, a local authority should not refrain from proceedings or discontinue proceedings in any case where there is a substantial disagreement among the medical experts. However, there were considerations emphasized by the judgment in *R v Cannings* that were of direct application in care proceedings: (i) the cause of an injury or episode that cannot be explained scientifically remains equivocal; (ii) recurrence is not of itself probative; (iii) particular caution is necessary where medical experts disagree, with one opinion declining to exclude a reasonable possibility of natural cause; (iv) the court has to be on its guard against the over-dogmatic expert, an expert whose reputation or amour propre is at stake or one who has developed a scientific prejudice; and (v) it should never be forgotten that today's medical certainty may be discarded by the next generation of experts or that scientific research will throw light into corners that are, at present, dark.

ADDITIONAL READING

Bruce, 'Fleeting Images of Shade' (1988) *The Psychologist* 331.

Bull and Clifford, 'Earwitness Testimony' in Heaton-Armstrong et al (eds), *Analysing Witness Testimony* (London, 1999), Ch 13.

Costigan, 'Identification from CCTV: The Risk of Injustice' [2007] *Crim LR* 591.

Cutler and Penrod, *Mistaken Identification—The Eyewitness, Psychology and the Law* (Cambridge, 1995).

Dein, 'Non Tape Recorded Cell Confession Evidence—On Trial' [2002] *Crim LR* 630.

Henderson et al., 'Matching the Faces of Robbers Captured on Video' (2001) 15 *Applied Cognitive Psychology* 445.

Lewis, 'A Comparative Examination of Corroboration and Caution Warnings in Prosecutions of Sexual Offences' [2006] *Crim LR* 889.

Ormerod, 'Sounds Familiar?—Voice Identification Evidence' [2001] *Crim LR* 595.

Ormerod, 'Sounding Out Expert Voice Identification' [2002] *Crim LR* 771.

Report to the Secretary of State for the Home Department of the Departmental Committee on Evidence of Identification in Criminal Cases (HMSO, 1976).

[195] [2005] Fam 134, CA.

Documentary and real evidence

9

Key Issues

- Where a party to litigation wishes to adduce in evidence a statement contained in a document, (a) should it be open to proof—as an alternative to proof by production of the document itself—by production of a copy and, if so, (b) in what circumstances and subject to what safeguards?

- Where a party to litigation wishes to admit a document in evidence, (a) should he be required to establish that it was written, signed, or attested by the person or persons by whom it purports to be written, signed or attested, and if so, (b) how should these matters be established?

- When should material objects be admissible in evidence and why do they need to be accompanied by oral testimony?

- When, and subject to what safeguards, should a court inspect a place or object out of court?

Documentary evidence

Statements contained in documents, like oral statements, are subject to the general rules of evidence on admissibility which are considered elsewhere in this book.[1] This chapter concerns two additional requirements relating to the proof of documents on the contents of which a party seeks to rely. The first relates to proof of the contents, the essential question being whether the party relying on the document must produce primary evidence, for example the original, as opposed to secondary evidence, for example a copy of the original. The second relates to proof of the fact that the document was properly executed.[2]

In *R v Daye*[3] Darling J defined a document as 'any written thing capable of being evidence', whether the writing is on paper, parchment, stone, marble or metal. Nowadays, it would be reasonable to assume that the word bears an even wider meaning. Today's equivalent of paper is often a disc, memory stick, tape, or film and conveys information by symbols, diagrams, and pictures as well as by words and numbers. It is clear from the modern authorities, however, that the definition of a document varies according to the nature of the proceedings and the particular context in question. Concerning proof of a document in criminal proceedings, the word has been narrowly defined. In *Kajala v Noble*[4] Ackner LJ, referring to the rule that if an original document is available in a party's hands, that party must produce it and cannot give secondary evidence by producing a copy, concluded: 'the old rule is limited and confined to written documents in the strict sense of the term, and has no relevance to tapes or films.'[5]

In civil proceedings, by contrast, 'document', for the purposes of the rules on the disclosure and inspection of documents, means 'anything in which information of any description is recorded',[6] a definition wide enough to cover not only documents in writing, but also maps, plans, graphs, drawings, discs, audio-tapes, sound-tracks, photographs, negatives, videotapes, and films. The same definition is used in relation to documents, including computer-produced documents, containing hearsay statements admissible under the Civil Evidence Act 1995 (the 1995 Act) or the Criminal Justice Act 2003 (the 2003 Act).[7]

Proof of contents

Proof of the contents of a document on which a party seeks to rely is now largely governed, in criminal cases, by section 133 of the 2003 Act and section 71 of the Police and Criminal Evidence Act 1984, and in civil cases by sections 8 and 9 of the 1995 Act.[8] Section 133 of the 2003 Act provides that:

---

[1] Principal among these, in criminal cases, is the rule against hearsay. The admissibility of documentary statements as evidence of the truth of the facts contained in them is considered in Chs 10–12.

[2] A third issue, relating to the admissibility of extrinsic evidence for the purpose of explaining, contradicting, varying, or adding to the terms of a document, is beyond the scope of the present work.

[3] [1908] 2 KB 333 at 340.

[4] (1982) 75 Cr App R 149, CA.

[5] (1982) 75 Cr App R 149 at 152. As an authority on the *proof of contents* in a criminal case, this decision should now be read subject to s 133 of the Criminal Justice Act 2003, below.

[6] CPR r 31.4.

[7] Civil Evidence Act 1995, s 13 and Criminal Justice Act 2003, s 134(1).

[8] In the case of tape recordings and transcripts of police interviews sought to be introduced in criminal proceedings, s 133 of the 2003 Act must be read in conjunction with the Code of Practice on Tape Recording of Interviews with Suspects (Code E) and para 43, *Practice Direction (Criminal Proceedings: Consolidation)* [2002] 1 WLR 2870.

Where a statement in a document is admissible as evidence in criminal proceedings, the statement may be proved by producing either—

(a) the document, or

(b) (whether or not the document exists) a copy of the document or of the material part of it, authenticated in whatever way the court may approve.[9]

Under section 71 of the Police and Criminal Evidence Act 1984, in any criminal proceedings the contents of a document may (whether or not the document is still in existence) be proved by the production of an enlargement of a microfilm copy of that document or the material part of it, authenticated in such manner as the court may approve.

Section 8 of the 1995 Act is cast in terms similar to those of section 133 of the 2003 Act. Under section 9(1) and (2) of the 1995 Act, a document which is certified as forming part of the records of a business or public authority may be received in evidence in civil proceedings without further proof; and under section 9(3) of that Act, the *absence* of an entry in the records of a business or public authority may be proved by the affidavit of an officer of the business or authority.[10]

Section 133 of the 2003 Act and section 8 of the 1995 Act appear to be of general application, ie to apply to *any* statement contained in a document, and thus not confined to hearsay statements in documents admissible under the 2003 Act or the 1995 Act. Likewise, section 9 of the 1995 Act appears to apply to *any* document forming part of the records of a business or public authority and not merely documents containing hearsay statements admissible under the 1995 Act. On this reading, these provisions have reversed completely the general rule at common law that a party seeking to rely on the contents of a document must adduce primary evidence (usually the original). Pending a definitive ruling to that effect, the general common law rule, considered below, may continue to apply in the case of non-hearsay, a conclusion that has been described as 'absurd'.[11] In any event, section 133 of the 2003 Act is permissive as to the means of proof and therefore cannot be taken to have overridden (i) the common law rule that where secondary evidence of the contents of a private document is admissible, it may take the form of *oral* evidence (use of which is not sanctioned by section 133);[12] (ii) a number of statutory provisions, mainly relating to public documents, which provide for proof of their contents by copies which are required to take a particular form, such as an examined copy (ie a copy proved by oral evidence to correspond with the original) or a certified copy (ie a copy certified to be accurate by an official who has custody of the original); or (iii) the Bankers' Books Evidence Act 1879, whereby provision is made for the admission of copies of entries in a banker's book, but only subject to the fulfilment of certain conditions, one of which is that some person proves that he has examined the copy with the original and that it is correct.[13] The same may be said, concerning civil cases, of sections 8 and 9 of the 1995 Act. Section 14 of that Act provides that nothing in the Act affects (i) the proof of documents by means other than those specified in sections 8

---

[9] For the meaning of the words 'statement', 'document', and 'copy', see s 115(2) and s 134(1) of the 2003 Act, Ch 10.

[10] See further Ch 11.

[11] R Pattenden, 'Authenticating 'things' in English law: principles for adducing tangible evidence in common law jury trials' (2008) 12 *E&P* 273 at 294.

[12] *R v Nazeer* [1998] Crim LR 750, CA.

[13] All three matters are considered below.

or 9;[14] or (ii) the operation of certain statutory provisions governing the means of proving certain public and official documents.[15]

The general rule at common law—primary evidence

The general rule is that a party seeking to rely upon the contents of a document must adduce primary evidence of those contents. The rule, often regarded as the only remaining instance of the 'best evidence rule',[16] under which a party must produce the best evidence that the nature of the case will allow, may be justified as a means of reducing the risks of fraud, mistake, and inaccuracy which might result from proof by either production of a copy of a document or oral evidence of its contents.

There are three recognized categories of primary evidence of the contents of a document: the original, copies of enrolled documents, and admissions made by parties. The best kind of primary evidence is the original document in question. Although the original is usually identifiable with ease, some cases do occasion difficulty. Where documents are produced in duplicate, each of them may constitute an original. Thus the duplicates of a deed which have been executed by all parties are all originals.[17] A copy of a document, however, whether produced by carbon, duplicator, or photocopying machine, is not original unless signed or otherwise duly executed. In the case of telegrams, the original, if tendered against the receiver, is the message he received; the original, if tendered against the sender, is the message that was handed in or recorded at the Post Office.[18] A counterpart lease executed by the lessee alone is the original if tendered against him, whereas the other part is the original if tendered against the lessor.[19] Where a private document is required to be enrolled, that is officially filed either in a court or some other public office, a copy issued by the court or office in question is treated as an original. Thus where executors obtain a grant of probate, the probate copy of the will is treated as primary evidence of the contents of the will.[20] Where a party to litigation has made an informal admission concerning the contents of a document, his admission constitutes primary evidence of the contents and is admissible in evidence against him. Thus, in *Slatterie v Pooley*[21] an action on a deed by which the defendant covenanted to indemnify the plaintiff against certain debts contained in the schedule to another deed, which was inadmissible because not duly stamped, an oral admission by the defendant that a particular debt was included in the schedule was held to be admissible against him.[22]

---

[14] Section 14(2).

[15] Section 14(3). It is unclear, however, why only some of the many statutory provisions governing the proof of various types of document have been specified. Those referred to in s 14(3) include the Documentary Evidence Act 1868, s 2 and the Documentary Evidence Act 1882, s 2 (see 257 below under **Public documents**); the Evidence (Colonial Statutes) Act 1907, s 1 (see Ch 18); and the Evidence (Foreign, Dominion and Colonial Documents) Act 1933, s 1 (see Chs 2 and 12).

[16] In fact it pre-dates the best evidence rule.

[17] *Forbes v Samuel* [1913] 3 KB 706.

[18] *R v Regan* (1887) 16 Cox CC 203.

[19] *Doe d West v Davis* (1806) 7 East 363.

[20] If a question arises concerning construction of the will, however, the court may examine the original: see *Re Battie-Wrightson, Cecil v Battie-Wrightson* [1920] 2 Ch 330.

[21] (1840) 6 M&W 664.

[22] But see now Civil Evidence Act 1995, s 7(1) (Ch 11).

The general rule applies in any case where a party seeks to rely upon the actual contents of a document. Thus in *MacDonnell v Evans*[23] the defendant's counsel was not allowed to cross-examine a witness as to whether a certain letter, which was produced, was written by him in answer to another letter, which was not produced, charging him with forgery. This amounted to an attempt to admit the contents of the other letter without producing it. Maule J said: 'it is a general rule . . . that, if you want to get at the contents of a written document, the proper way is to produce it, if you can.' However, in cases where it is unnecessary to place reliance upon the contents of a document because the fact or matter in issue, even if recorded in a document, can be proved by other evidence, the general rule has no application. Thus, whereas proof of the length of a tenancy, or the amount of rent due thereunder, requires production of the lease, proof of the existence or fact of a tenancy, albeit created by a lease, may be proved by other evidence. In *Augustien v Challis*,[24] an action against a sheriff alleged to have negligently withdrawn a writ of *fi fa*, his defence was that a claim of the debtor's landlord, in respect of rent due, had priority over the plaintiff's claim. Evidence given by the landlord that the rent was payable under a lease was held to be inadmissible on the grounds that the amount of rent due could not be proved without producing the original of the lease.[25] In *R v Holy Trinity, Hull (Inhabitants)*,[26] by contrast, the fact of a tenancy, created by a lease which defined its terms, could be proved without production of that lease; oral evidence, such as evidence on the payment of the rent, sufficed.[27] Likewise, the rule has no application where reference is made to a document merely for the purpose of establishing the bare fact of its existence. In *R v Elworthy*[28] the accused, a solicitor, was charged with perjury. It was alleged that he had falsely sworn that there was no draft of a certain statutory declaration which he had prepared. The Court for Crown Cases Reserved held that although secondary evidence of the contents of the draft and of certain alterations made in it was inadmissible, the prosecution could properly adduce oral evidence that such a draft existed and was in the possession of the accused.[29] It remains to note that the general rule does not apply when the contents of a document are referred to merely in order to identify it. Thus it has been said that 'in an action of trover for a promissory note, the contents of the promissory note may be stated verbally by a witness'.[30]

Although both the general rule and the common law exceptions to it are well established, in *Springsteen v Flute International Ltd*[31] the Court of Appeal favoured a more generalized discretionary approach to admissibility. It held as follows. (1) The best evidence rule, long on its deathbed, had finally expired. (2) In every case where a party seeks to adduce secondary evidence of the contents of a document, it is a matter for the court to decide, in the light of all the circumstances of the case, what, if any, weight to attach to the evidence. (3) Where such a party can readily adduce the document, it may be expected that, absent

---

[23] (1852) 11 CB 930.

[24] (1847) 1 Exch 279.

[25] See also *Twyman v Knowles* (1853) 13 CB 222 (the length of a tenancy).

[26] (1827) 7 B&C 611.

[27] See also *Alderson v Clay* (1816) 1 Stark 405 (proof of the fact of a partnership).

[28] (1867) LR 1 CCR 103.

[29] The Crown had not given notice to the accused to produce the original. Had they done so, secondary evidence of the contents of the draft would have been admissible (see below).

[30] Per Martin B in *Boyle v Wiseman* (1855) 11 Exch 360 at 367, citing *Whitehead v Scott* (1830) 1 Mood&R 2.

[31] [2001] EMLR 654, CA.

some special circumstances, the court will decline to admit the secondary evidence on the ground that it is worthless. (4) At the other extreme, where such a party genuinely cannot produce the document, it may be expected that, absent some special circumstances, the court will admit the secondary evidence and attach such weight to it as it considers appropriate. (5) In cases falling between these two extremes, it is for the court to make a judgment as to whether in all the circumstances any weight should be attached to the secondary evidence.[32]

The exceptions—secondary evidence

Public documents, which constitute one of the exceptions to the general rule, are considered later in this chapter. In the case of private documents, secondary evidence of their contents, where admissible, may take the form of a copy, a copy of a copy,[33] or oral evidence. Where a copy is produced, proof is required that it is a true copy of the original. In *R v Collins*[34] the accused, who had cashed a cheque on his bank account which he knew to have been closed, was convicted of obtaining money by false pretences. Having been called upon to produce a letter sent to him informing him that the account was closed, which he had failed to do, secondary evidence of the contents of the letter became admissible.[35] Accordingly, at the trial the prosecution called a manager of the bank to produce a copy of a carbon-copy of the letter. The Court of Criminal Appeal held that the copy produced, in the absence of proof that it was not only a true copy of the carbon-copy, but also in the same terms as the original, had been improperly admitted.

Where secondary evidence is admissible, there is a general rule that 'there are no degrees of secondary evidence'.[36] Thus although less weight may attach to inferior forms of secondary evidence, there is no obligation to tender the 'best' copy, rather than an inferior copy or a copy of a copy, and oral evidence of the contents is admissible even if a copy or some other more satisfactory type of secondary evidence is available. To this general rule there is a variety of exceptions. The contents of a will admitted to probate may not be proved by oral evidence if the original or probate copy exists. Judicial documents and bankers' books[37] are generally proved not by oral evidence but by office copies and examined copies respectively. Finally, many public documents may be proved by oral evidence only if examined, certified, or other copies are unavailable.[38]

Hearsay statements admissible by statute. Where the contents of a document are admissible hearsay under the 2003 Act, they may be proved in accordance with section 133 of that Act and section 71 of the Police and Criminal Evidence Act 1984; and where the contents of a document are admissible hearsay under the 1995 Act, they may be proved in accordance with sections 8 and 9 of that Act.[39]

---

[32] See also *Post Office Counters Ltd v Mahida* [2003] EWCA Civ 1583, (2003) The Times, 31 Oct, Ch 2.

[33] *Lafone v Griffin* (1909) 25 TLR 308; *R v Collins* (1960) 44 Cr App R 170. Contrast *Everingham v Roundell* (1838) 2 Mood&R 138.

[34] (1960) 44 Cr App R 170; cf *R v Wayte* (1982) 76 Cr App R 110, CA.

[35] See below.

[36] Per Lord Abinger CB in *Doe d Gilbert v Ross* (1840) 7 M&W 102.

[37] See below.

[38] See below.

[39] See generally above and Chs 10 and 11.

Failure to produce after notice.   A party seeking to rely upon a document may prove its contents by secondary evidence if the original is in the possession or control of another party to the proceedings who, having been served with a notice to produce it, has failed to do so. The purpose of serving such a notice is not to notify the other party that reliance will be placed on a document so that he can prepare evidence to explain or confirm it, but merely to give him sufficient opportunity to produce it if he wishes or, if he does not, to enable the first party to adduce secondary evidence. Thus it has been held that where the original is in court, secondary evidence is admissible even where a party fails to comply with a notice to produce served during the course of the trial.[40]

It is assumed that the foregoing principles remain good law notwithstanding that the Civil Procedure Rules make no provision for formal service of a notice to produce.[41]

A notice to produce has never *compelled* production of a document. A party to civil proceedings who wishes to rely at the trial on the original of a document, should serve a witness summons requiring a witness to produce the document to the court.[42]

A stranger's lawful refusal to produce.   Secondary evidence of the contents of a document may be given when the original is in the possession of a stranger to the litigation who, having been served with a *subpoena duces tecum* (now known as a witness summons requiring a witness to produce a document),[43] has lawfully refused to produce it, for example by reason of a claim to privilege[44] or diplomatic immunity[45] or because he is outside the jurisdiction and therefore cannot be compelled to produce it.[46] However, if the stranger, in unlawful disobedience of the summons, refuses to produce the original, secondary evidence is inadmissible because he is bound to produce it and is punishable for contempt if he refuses to do so.[47] The effect of these rules is to cast a duty upon the party seeking to rely upon the document to compel the stranger to produce the original, thereby eliminating the risk of unreliable secondary evidence being admitted in consequence of their collusion.

Lost documents.   Secondary evidence of the contents of a document is admissible on proof that the original has been destroyed or cannot be found after due search. The quality of evidence required to show the loss or destruction varies according to the nature and value of the document in question. In *Brewster v Sewell*[48] the plaintiff was unable to produce a policy of insurance against loss by fire on which a claim had been paid. Subsequent to the fire, which had occurred some years before the proceedings, a fresh policy had been issued. Evidence was given of a thorough but unsuccessful search for the earlier policy. It was held that, in the circumstances, the original policy had become 'mere waste paper' and that sufficient evidence of due search had been given to allow proof of its contents by secondary evidence. Bayley J said:[49]

---

[40] *Dwyer v Collins* (1852) 21 LJ Ex 225.

[41] See, formerly, RSC Ord 24, r 10.

[42] See CPR r 34.2.

[43] See CPR r 34.2.

[44] *Mills v Oddy* (1834) 6 C&P 728.

[45] *R v Nowaz* [1976] 3 All ER 5, CA.

[46] *Kilgour v Owen* (1889) 88 LT Jo 7.

[47] *R v Llanfaethly (Inhabitants)* (1853) 2 E&B 940.

[48] (1820) 3 B&Ald 296. See also *R v Wayte* (1982) 76 Cr App R 110, CA.

[49] (1820) 3 B&Ald 296 at 300.

There is a great distinction between useful and useless papers. The presumption of law is that a man will keep all those papers which are valuable to himself, and which may, with any degree of probability, be of any future use to him. The presumption on the contrary is that a man will not keep those papers which have entirely discharged their duty, and which are never likely to be required for any purpose whatever.

Production of original impossible. Secondary evidence is admissible where production of the original is either physically impossible, for example because it is an inscription upon a tombstone or wall,[50] or legally impossible, for example because the document in question is a notice which is required by statute to be constantly affixed at a factory or workshop.[51]

Public documents. At common law, secondary evidence of the contents of a wide variety of public documents is admissible on the grounds that production of the originals would entail a high degree of public inconvenience.[52] Under the modern law, there is a large number of statutes which also provide for the proof of public documents by secondary evidence. Secondary evidence for these purposes is usually required to take the form of an examined, authenticated, certified, office, Queen's Printer's or Stationery Office copy. Under section 7 of the Evidence Act 1851, for example, the contents of all proclamations, treaties, and other acts of state of any foreign state or of any British colony, and all judgments, decrees, orders, and other judicial proceedings of any court of justice in any foreign state or in any British colony may be proved by an examined copy, which is a copy proved by oral evidence to correspond with the original, or by copies authenticated with the seal of the foreign state, British colony, or foreign or colonial court, as the case may be.[53] Certified copies are copies certified to be accurate by an official who has custody of the original.[54] They are employed to prove byelaws and records kept in the Public Record Office.[55] They are also used to prove a birth or death,[56] an adoption,[57] and a marriage[58] or civil partnership.[59] Under section 14 of the Evidence Act 1851, certified or examined copies may be used to prove the contents of any document provided that it is of such a public nature that it is admissible in evidence on production from proper custody and no other statute provides for proof of its contents by means of a copy. Office copies, which are prepared by officials who have custody of original

---

[50] Per Alderson B in *Mortimer v M'Callan* (1840) 6 M&W 58. See also, *sed quaere*, *R v Hunt* (1820) 3 B&Ald 566 (inscriptions on flags or banners).

[51] *Owner v Bee Hive Spinning Co Ltd* [1914] 1 KB 105, DC. See also *Alivon v Furnival* (1834) 1 Cr M&R 277 (document in custody of foreign court).

[52] See, eg, *Mortimer v M'Callan* (1840) 6 M&W 58 (books of the Bank of England).

[53] As to sealed copies, see also n 54, below. In the case of a foreign conviction, it remains necessary to establish that the examined copy relates to the person said to have been convicted, which may be achieved by the admission of any relevant evidence, including, eg, fingerprint evidence: *R v Mauricia* [2002] 2 Cr App R 377, CA.

[54] Where a statute provides for proof of a document by a certified, sealed, or stamped copy, the copy, provided it purports to be signed, sealed, or stamped, is admissible without any proof of the sign, seal or stamp, as the case may be: Evidence Act 1845, s 1.

[55] Local Government Act 1972, s 238 (the clerk to the local authority) and Public Records Act 1958, s 9 (the Keeper of Public Records).

[56] Births and Deaths Registration Act 1953, s 34.

[57] Adoption and Children Act 2002, s 77(4).

[58] Marriage Act 1949, s 65(3).

[59] Civil Partnership (Registration Provisions) Regulations 2005, SI 2005/3176, regs 13(4) and 14(4).

judicial documents and are authenticated with the seal of the court,[60] may be used to prove judgments, orders, and other judicial documents. Queen's Printer's copies are used to prove private Acts of Parliament and journals of either House of Parliament,[61] royal proclamations, orders, and statutory instruments.[62]

Bankers' books.   In both civil and criminal proceedings, it is often necessary to adduce evidence of the contents of bankers' books. In order to avoid the inconvenience that production of the originals would entail, the Bankers' Books Evidence Act 1879 (the 1879 Act) provides for the admission of copies. Section 3, an exception to the rule against hearsay, reads as follows:

> Subject to the provisions of this Act, a copy of an entry in a banker's book shall in all legal proceedings be received as prima facie evidence of such entry, and of the matters, transactions, and accounts therein recorded.

'Banker' is defined as a 'deposit-taker' or the National Savings Bank.[63] 'Bankers' books' were originally defined to include 'ledgers', 'day books', 'cash books' and 'account books'. The definition has since been extended to include, in addition, 'other records used in the ordinary business of the bank, whether those records are in written form or are kept on microfilm, magnetic tape, or any other form of mechanical or electronic data retrieval mechanism'.[64] 'Other records used in the ordinary business of the bank' has to be read *eiusdem generis* with 'ledgers, day books cash books', and 'account books', which are the means by which banks record day-to-day financial transactions, and therefore do not cover bank records of conversations between its employees and customers or others, or internal memoranda.[65] Paid cheques and paying-in slips retained by a bank after the conclusion of a banking transaction to which they relate have been held not to be bankers' books on the same basis or on the grounds that even if bundles of such documents can be treated as 'records used in the ordinary business of the bank', the addition of an individual cheque or paying-in slip cannot be regarded as making an 'entry' in those records.[66]

---

[60] See n 53 above.

[61] Evidence Act 1845, s 3 and Documentary Evidence Act 1882, s 2. Stationery Office copies may also be used. The Interpretation Act 1978, s 3 provides that: 'Every Act is a public Act to be judicially noticed as such, unless the contrary is expressly provided by the Act.' This section applies to all Acts passed after 1850. At common law, judicial notice is taken of earlier enactments, if public (see Ch 22).

[62] Evidence Act 1845, s 3 and Documentary Evidence Act 1868, s 2. Such documents may also be proved by a copy of the Gazette containing them or by a copy certified to be true by the appropriate official. However, where a photocopy from a commercial publication is produced instead, and there is no suggestion of any inaccuracy in the version before the court, an appeal may not succeed: *R v Koon Cheung Tang* [1995] Crim LR 813, CA. An 'order' under s 2 of the 1868 Act covers any executive act of government performed by the bringing into existence of a public document for the purpose of giving effect to an Act of Parliament (*R v Clarke* [1969] 2 QB 91 at 97). See also *West Midlands Probation Board v French* [2008] EWHC 2631 (a licence issued by the governor of a prison on behalf of the Secretary of State for the Home Office).

[63] Section 9(1). A 'deposit taker' will normally be someone with permission under Part 4 of the Financial Services and Markets Act 2000 to accept deposits: see s 9(1A)–(1C).

[64] Section 9(2).

[65] *Re Howglen Ltd* [2001] 1 All ER 376, Ch D.

[66] *Williams v Williams* [1987] 3 All ER 257, CA. In civil proceedings, if such documents relate to the bank account of the other party to the action, an order for disclosure may be made and the bank, as agent holding the documents on that party's behalf, may then be required to disclose them. In other cases, the party seeking disclosure of specific documents may be able to make use of CPR r 31.17, which provides for disclosure by a person who is not a party to the proceedings or CPR r 34.2, which empowers the court to issue a witness summons requiring a witness to produce documents to the court.

The same reasoning may be used to justify the decision, reached prior to the extension of the definition of 'bankers' books', that copies of letters written by a bank and contained in a file of its correspondence do not constitute bankers' books.[67]

A copy is only admissible under section 3 of the 1879 Act if: (i) a partner or officer of the bank proves, by oral evidence or affidavit, that the book was at the time of the making of the entry one of the ordinary books of the bank, the entry was made in the usual and ordinary course of business, and the book is in the custody or control of the bank;[68] and (ii) some person proves, by oral evidence or affidavit, that he has examined the copy with the original and that it is correct.[69] Section 7 provides for any party to legal proceedings to apply to a court[70] or judge for an order to be at liberty to inspect and take copies of entries in bankers' books for the purposes of those proceedings. The order may be made without summoning the bank or any other party and shall be served on the bank three clear days before it is to be obeyed, unless the court or judge otherwise directs.[71] An order may be made under section 7 to inspect the account of a person who is not a party to the proceedings, even if that person is not compellable as a witness,[72] but in criminal cases, such an order should be made only in exceptional circumstances and where the private interest in keeping a bank account confidential is outweighed by the public interest in assisting a prosecution.[73]

In civil proceedings, an application under section 7 to inspect entries in the bank account of a third party will only be granted if (i) the court is satisfied that the account is in fact the account of the other party to the action or an account with which he is so much concerned that items in it would be evidence against him; and (ii) the applicant shows very strong grounds for suspicion, almost amounting to certainty, that there are items in the account which would be material evidence against the other party.[74] A foreign bank which is not a party to the proceedings, even if it carries on business within the jurisdiction, should not, save in exceptional circumstances, be ordered to produce documents which are outside the jurisdiction and concern business transacted outside the jurisdiction, because an order under the 1879 Act is an exercise of sovereign authority to assist in the administration of justice, and foreign banks owe their customers a duty of confidence regulated by the law of the country where the documents are kept.[75] Although in criminal proceedings an order will not be refused on the grounds that it

---

[67] *R v Dadson* (1983) 77 Cr App R 91, CA. See also *Barker v Wilson* [1980] 1 WLR 884, DC.

[68] Section 4.

[69] Section 5.

[70] Justices constitute a court for these purposes: *R v Kinghorn* [1908] 2 KB 949.

[71] Although the Act allows an application to be made without notice, there is much to be said for notice being given: per Widgery LJ in *R v Marlborough Street Magistrates' Court, ex p Simpson* (1980) 70 Cr App R 291, DC at 294. In the case of an application in respect of accounts of a person who is not a party to the proceedings, the order should either not be made until the account owner has been informed and given an opportunity to be heard or should be made in the form of an order *nisi*, allowing a period for the person affected to show cause why the order should not take effect: per Oliver LJ in *R v Grossman* (1981) 73 Cr App R 302 at 309, CA.

[72] *R v Andover Justices, ex p Rhodes* [1980] Crim LR 644, DC.

[73] *R v Grossman* (1981) 73 Cr App R 302 at 307, CA.

[74] *South Staffordshire Tramways Co v Ebbsmith* [1895] 2 QB 669, CA (a pre-trial application) and *D B Deniz Nakliyati TAS v Yugopetrol* [1992] 1 All ER 205, CA (an application against a judgment debtor).

[75] *MacKinnon v Donaldson Lufkin and Jenrette Securities Corpn* [1986] 1 All ER 653, Ch D, applying *R v Grossman* (1981) 73 Cr App R 302, CA (a decision acknowledged to have been given *per incuriam*, the proceedings in the case being criminal and the Court of Appeal, therefore, having no jurisdiction). However, a party seeking to obtain documents from a foreign bank in these circumstances may apply to a master under CPR r 34.13 for the issue of letters of request to the courts of the country in question specifying the documents to be produced, or may apply directly to

incriminates the party against whom it is made,[76] it is a serious interference with the liberty of the subject and the court should satisfy itself that the application is more than a mere fishing expedition by considering whether the prosecution has other evidence to support the charge.[77] In *R v Nottingham City Justices, ex p Lynn*[78] an order made by justices against an accused charged with drug smuggling for the inspection of accounts over a three-year period, was reduced by the Divisional Court to cover a period of six months, there being insufficient evidence to link the accused with offences during most of the three years.

An order under section 7 is not a necessary pre-condition of producing evidence under section 3; an order enables bankers' books to be inspected and copied despite the duty of confidentiality owed by banker to customer and is clearly unnecessary if the customer waives the right to confidentiality and the bank agrees to the inspection and copying.[79]

Proof of due execution

The general rule, in both civil and criminal proceedings, is that a document will only be admitted in evidence on proof of due execution. An exception exists in the case of public documents covered by statutes of the kind referred to earlier in this chapter, most of which not only provide for the proof of contents by secondary evidence, but also exempt from proof of due execution. In the case of a private document, proof of due execution may be admitted or presumed, but otherwise usually involves proof of handwriting or a signature and, in some cases, proof of attestation. In some cases, documents are required to be stamped for the purposes of stamp duty. Each of these matters now falls to be considered further.

Proof of handwriting

Proof of the due execution of a private document usually involves showing that it was written or signed by the person by whom it purports to have been written or signed. For these purposes, direct oral evidence that the signatory signed in a particular name may be given by the signatory himself or by any other person who witnessed the execution of the document. Proof may also be effected by admissible hearsay assertions to the same effect; or by the opinion evidence of someone who, although not a witness to the execution of the document, is acquainted with the handwriting of the person in question. In *Doe d Mudd v Suckermore*[80] Coleridge J said:

> either the witness has seen the party write on some other occasion, or he has corresponded with him, and transactions have taken place between them, upon the faith that letters purporting to have been written or signed by him have been so written or signed.

It is clear, however, that the weight to be attached to such opinion evidence will vary according to the circumstances in question.

---

a court in that country under the relevant local provisions, having first obtained the permission of the English court on an application with notice.

[76] In civil proceedings the Act may not be used to compel disclosure of incriminating material: see *Waterhouse v Barker* [1924] 2 KB 759, CA and *Re Bankers' Books Evidence Act 1879, R v Bono* (1913) 29 TLR 635.

[77] *Williams v Summerfield* [1972] 2 QB 512, DC.

[78] [1984] Crim LR 554.

[79] *Wheatley v Commissioner of Police of the British Virgin Islands* [2006] 1 WLR 1683, PC, a decision under the equivalent statutory provisions of the British Virgin Islands.

[80] (1837) 5 Ad&El 703 at 705.

A final method of proving handwriting or a signature is by comparison of the document in question with another document which is proved or admitted to have been written by the person in question. Section 8 of the Criminal Procedure Act 1865 provides that:

> Comparison of a disputed writing with any writing proved to the satisfaction of the judge to be genuine shall be permitted to be made by witnesses;[81] and such writings, and the evidence of witnesses respecting the same, may be submitted to the court and jury as evidence of the genuineness or otherwise of the writing in dispute.

The section applies to both civil and criminal proceedings but whereas in the former the court must be satisfied as to the genuineness of the specimen handwriting only on a balance of probabilities, proof beyond reasonable doubt is the appropriate standard for the prosecution in criminal cases.[82] The tribunal of fact, in comparing the disputed and specimen handwriting, may be assisted by the evidence of someone who, although not an expert, is familiar with the handwriting in question[83] or by the opinion evidence of an expert in handwriting, whether his skill has been acquired professionally or otherwise.[84] As a general rule in criminal cases, the jury should not be left to draw their own unaided conclusion from a comparison without the assistance of an expert.[85] However, where an expert is called, it is his function to point out similarities or differences between the documents, leaving it to the tribunal of fact to draw their own conclusion.[86] In cases where the documents are placed before the jury as exhibits or for some proper purpose other than that of making a comparison and an expert is not called, the jury should be warned very carefully not to make a comparison.[87]

Any of the above forms of proof of handwriting may be used in the case of a document which, although not required by law to be attested, was in fact attested. Section 7 of the Criminal Procedure Act 1865 provides that such a document may be proved 'as if there had been no attesting witness thereto'.

Proof of attestation

Proof of due execution sometimes requires evidence of attestation. It will be convenient to consider first the proof of wills and other testamentary documents. Except where probate is sought in common form, in order to prove the due execution of a will, one of the attesting witnesses, if available, must be called. Witnesses to the execution of a will are treated as the court's witnesses and may be cross-examined by the party seeking to prove due execution.[88] If the witness denies the execution[89] or refuses to give evidence,[90] other evidence becomes admissible. If all of the attesting witnesses are dead, insane, beyond the jurisdiction, or untraceable, secondary evidence of attestation by proof of the handwriting of one of the attesting witnesses is required. If, despite every effort to do so, it is impossible to prove the

---

[81] A witness who has not seen the original 'disputed writing' (because, eg, it is lost) may use a photocopy of it to make the comparison: *Lockheed-Arabia Corpn v Owen* [1993] 3 All ER 641, CA.

[82] *R v Ewing* [1983] 2 All ER 645, CA (Ch 4).

[83] *Fitzwalter Peerage Claim* (1844) 10 Cl&Fin 193, HL.

[84] *R v Silverlock* [1894] 2 QB 766.

[85] *R v Tilley* [1961] 1 WLR 1309, CCA; *R v Harden* [1963] 1 QB 8, CCA.

[86] *Wakeford v Bishop of Lincoln* (1921) 90 LJPC 174.

[87] *R v O'Sullivan* [1969] 1 WLR 497, CA.

[88] *Oakes v Uzzell* [1932] P 19.

[89] *Bowman v Hodgson* (1867) LR 1 P&D 362.

[90] *Re Oven's Goods* (1892) 29 LR Ir 451.

handwriting of one of the attesting witnesses, other evidence of due execution is admissible, for example that of a non-attesting witness to the execution.[91]

Although at one time it was necessary in the case of any document required by law to be attested to call one of the attesting witnesses (unless they were all unavailable), section 3 of the Evidence Act 1938 provides that, except in the case of a will or other testamentary document, any document required by law to be attested 'may, instead of being proved by an attesting witness, be proved in the manner in which it might be proved if no attesting witness were alive'. Thus documents, other than testamentary documents, which require attestation may, but need not, be proved by the evidence of an attesting witness. Proof may be effected by evidence of the handwriting of an attesting witness or, if this is unobtainable, by other evidence.

Admissions and presumptions

In practice, due execution is frequently admitted or presumed, thereby rendering proof of handwriting and attestation unnecessary. Due execution may be formally admitted both in civil proceedings and, under section 10 of the Criminal Justice Act 1967, in criminal proceedings. Under CPR rule 32.19(1) a party shall be deemed to admit the authenticity of a document disclosed to him under Part 31 of the rules (disclosure and inspection of documents) unless he serves notice that he wishes the document to be proved at trial. Proof of due execution is also unnecessary when the document in question is in the possession of an opponent who refuses to comply with a notice to produce it.[92]

A document which is more than 20 years old[93] and comes from proper custody is presumed to have been duly executed. Although proper custody, for these purposes, does not mean that the document should be found in 'the best and most proper place of deposit', if the document is found in some other place, the court must be satisfied that such custody was 'reasonable and natural' in the circumstances of the case. This was the view of Tindal CJ in *Meath (Bishop) v Marquis of Winchester*,[94] who accordingly held that certain documents relating to a bishopric had been produced from proper custody despite having been found among the papers of a deceased bishop rather than in the custody of his successor, which was the best place of deposit.

There are four other presumptions relating to documents. They are: (i) that a document was made on the date which it bears;[95] (ii) that an alteration or erasure in a deed was made before execution, in a will after execution (on the grounds that a deed, but not a will, would be invalidated if presumed to have been altered after execution);[96] and (iii) that a deed was duly sealed.[97]

Stamped documents

Certain documents are required to be stamped for the purposes of stamp duty. Although in criminal proceedings such a document is admissible if unstamped, in civil proceedings

---

[91] *Clarke v Clarke* (1879) 5 LR Ir 47.

[92] *Cooke v Tanswell* (1818) 8 Taunt 450.

[93] At common law, the period was 30 years. The period of 20 years was substituted by the Evidence Act 1938, s 4.

[94] (1836) 3 Bing NC 183, HL; cf *Doe d Lord Arundel v Fowler* (1850) 14 QB 700.

[95] *Anderson v Weston* (1840) 6 Bing NC 296.

[96] Per Lord Campbell CJ in *Doe d Tatum v Catomore* (1851) 16 QB 745. An alteration in a will is only valid and effective if executed in like manner as is required for the execution of the will: Wills Act 1837, s 21.

[97] *Sed quaere*: see *Re Sandilands* (1871) LR 6 CP 411.

a document requiring a stamp shall not be given in evidence unless it is duly stamped in accordance with the law in force at the time when it was first executed or, the court having objected to the omission or insufficiency of the stamp, and the document being one which may be legally stamped after its execution, payment is made of the amount of unpaid duty, together with any penalty payable on stamping, and a further sum of one pound.[98] The parties cannot waive these rules.[99] If a document requiring a stamp cannot be found or is not produced after notice to do so, it is presumed to have been duly stamped. However, if there is evidence to show that the document was not duly stamped, it is presumed, in the absence of evidence to the contrary, that this remained the case.[100]

Real evidence

Real evidence usually takes the form of some material object examined by the tribunal of fact as a means of proof. This and other varieties of real evidence are considered separately as follows.

Material objects

Where the existence, condition, or value of some material object is in issue or relevant to an issue, it may be produced for inspection by the tribunal of fact. Thus where a purchaser alleges that certain goods do not answer the vendor's description, the goods in question may be produced to the judge so that he may act on his own perception. Likewise, a jury may inspect a knife alleged to have been used in the commission of a murder. Although the tribunal of fact may attach considerable weight to such evidence, this would be rare in the absence of accompanying testimony. Thus in the examples given, the goods would require to be identified and the knife, as an item of evidence, would be of limited value in the absence not only of some testimony connecting it with the accused, for example evidence that it was found in his possession, but also of expert testimony that it was capable of causing the injuries sustained by the victim.[101]

There is no rule of law that unless a material object is produced, or its non-production excused, oral evidence respecting it is inadmissible. Thus in *Hocking v Ahlquist Bros Ltd*,[102] the issue concerning the method by which certain garments had been made, it was held that although the garments were not produced at the trial, the evidence of witnesses who had seen them and could speak to their condition was not inadmissible. However, non-production of the object in question may go to the weight of the oral evidence adduced[103] and give rise to an inference adverse to the party failing to produce. Thus, in *Armory v Delamirie*[104] an action in trover against a goldsmith who failed to produce certain stones which he had removed from a jewel found by a chimney sweeper's boy, Pratt CJ directed the jury to assess damages on the basis that the stones were of the first water.

---

[98] Stamp Act 1891, s 14.

[99] *Bowker v Williamson* (1889) 5 TLR 382.

[100] *Closmadeuc v Carrel* (1856) 18 CB 36.

[101] In some cases the tribunal of fact may not draw its own unaided conclusion without the assistance of an expert witness: *R v Tilley* [1961] 1 WLR 1309 (comparison of handwriting), above. See also *Anderson v R* [1972] AC 100, PC.

[102] [1944] KB 120. See also *R v Uxbridge Justices, ex p Sofaer* (1986) 85 Cr App R 367.

[103] Per Lord Coleridge CJ in *R v Francis* (1874) LR 2 CCR 128 at 133.

[104] (1722) 1 Stra 505.

The appearance of persons and animals

Real evidence may take the form of a person's physical appearance. Thus it may be relevant, for identification or some other purpose, to have regard to a person's physical characteristics such as his height or colour of eyes or the fact that he is left-handed or bears some scar or other distinguishing feature. His accent, as opposed to the actual words he utters, also constitutes real evidence. Personal injuries may be examined on a question of causation or quantum of damages. Although in many cases little weight should be attached to it, the facial resemblance of a child to its alleged father and mother may be relevant to the issue of legitimacy.[105] For the purposes of contempt of court, a person's misconduct in court may constitute real evidence. Real evidence may also take the form of an animal, as in *Line v Taylor*,[106] where a dog of allegedly vicious disposition was brought into court and examined by the jury.

The demeanour of witnesses

The way in which a witness gives his evidence is often just as important as what he actually says. While some witnesses may appear to be forthright and frank, others may present themselves as hesitant, equivocal, or even hostile. Whatever form it takes, the demeanour and attitude of a witness in the course of giving his evidence is real evidence which is relevant to his credit and the weight to be attached to the evidence he gives.[107]

Lip-reading and facial mapping

Where an expert lip-reader, after viewing a CCTV recording of a person talking, gives opinion evidence as to what that person said, he is providing expert assistance to the jury in their interpretation of a species of real evidence.[108] Expert opinion evidence of facial mapping may be regarded in the same way.[109]

Documents

A document may be tendered in evidence for a variety of purposes. If it is produced by a party relying upon the statements it contains, whether that party is relying upon them as evidence of their truth, by way of exception to the hearsay rule, or simply as original evidence, for example to show that they were made,[110] it constitutes documentary evidence and is subject to the rules considered earlier in this chapter.[111] However, if the document is tendered in evidence as a material object, regardless of the words contained in it, for instance to show the bare fact of its existence, the substance of which it is made (eg whether parchment or paper), or the condition that it is in (eg whether crumpled or torn), it constitutes real evidence.[112]

---

[105] *C v C* [1972] 3 All ER 577; cf *Slingsby v A-G* (1916) 33 TLR 120, HL at 122–3.

[106] (1862) 3 F&F 731.

[107] For a critical analysis of demeanour as a test of credibility, see Paul Ekman *Telling Lies* (1986) and Marcus Stone 'Instant Lie Detection? Demeanour and Credibility in Criminal Trials' [1991] *Crim LR* 821.

[108] *R v Luttrell* [2004] 2 Cr App R 520, CA at [37].

[109] *R v Clarke* [1995] 2 Cr App R 425 at 429.

[110] See Ch 10.

[111] But this is not the case if the contents are referred to merely for the purpose of identifying the document: see above.

[112] But see *R v Rice* [1963] 1 QB 857, CCA (Ch 10).

Tape-recordings, films, and photographs

Tape-recordings, films, and photographs are, as we have seen earlier in this chapter, sometimes treated as documentary evidence. By playing over a tape-recording in court, a statement recorded on it may be admitted as evidence of the truth of its contents, by way of exception to the hearsay rule,[113] or as original evidence, for example merely to show that it was made. To the extent, however, that the recording also reveals the way in which the person in question spoke, his accent, accentuation, tone, intonation, etc, it is real evidence.[114]

In *The Statue of Liberty*,[115] an action concerning a collision between two ships, the plaintiff sought to admit in evidence a cinematograph film of radar echoes recorded by a shore radar station. The defendants argued that the evidence, having been produced mechanically and without human intervention, was inadmissible hearsay. Rejecting this submission, Sir Jocelyn Simon P said:[116]

> If tape-recordings are admissible, it seems that a photograph of radar reception is equally admissible—or indeed, any other type of photograph. It would be an absurd distinction that a photograph should be admissible if the camera were operated manually by a photographer, but not if it were operated by a trip or clock mechanism. Similarly, if evidence of weather conditions were relevant, the law would affront commonsense if it were to say that those could be proved by a person who looked at a barometer from time to time, but not by producing a barograph record. So, too, with other types of dial recording. Again, cards from clocking-in-and-out machines are frequently admitted in accident cases.[117]

It is tempting, on the basis of these words of Sir Jocelyn Simon P, to conclude that photographs and films, the relevance of which can be established by the testimony of someone with personal knowledge of the circumstances in which they were taken or made, are admissible as items of real evidence and can never give rise to problems of a hearsay nature. If the evidence of a witness to certain events is admissible, it may be reasoned, then photographs or films recording those same events should be no less admissible. Thus in *R v Dodson; R v Williams*[118] the Court of Appeal entertained no doubt that photographs taken by security cameras installed at a building society office at which an armed robbery was attempted, were admissible in evidence, being relevant to the issues of both whether an offence was committed and, if so, who committed it.[119] As to the latter issue, the jury were entitled to compare the photographic images with the accused sitting

---

[113] As in *R v Senat; R v Sin* (1968) 52 Cr App R 282, CA, where tape-recordings of incriminating telephone conversations were held to have been properly admitted. See also *R v Maqsud Ali* [1966] 1 QB 688, CCA at 701: provided the jury are guided by what they hear, there is no objection to a properly proved transcript being put before them. As to tape-recordings and transcripts of police interviews sought to be adduced in criminal proceedings, see also *R v Rampling* [1987] Crim LR 823, CA, the Code of Practice on Tape Recording of Interviews with Suspects (Code E) and para 43, *Practice Direction (Criminal Proceedings: Consolidation)* [2002] 1 WLR 2870.

[114] See, eg, *R v Emmerson* (1990) 92 Cr App R 284, CA (tone of voice). Before it is played over to the jury, the judge must satisfy himself that there is a prima facie case that it is both original and authentic: see *R v Stevenson* [1971] 1 WLR 1 and *R v Robson; R v Harris* [1972] 1 WLR 651 (Ch 4).

[115] [1968] 1 WLR 739.

[116] [1968] 1 WLR 739 at 740.

[117] Cf *R v Wood* (1982) 76 Cr App R 23, CA: a computer print-out is an item of real evidence and not hearsay if the computer in question is used as a calculator, a tool which does not contribute its own knowledge but merely does calculations which can be performed manually (see Ch 10).

[118] (1984) 79 Cr App R 220, CA.

[119] See also *Kajala v Noble* (1982) 75 Cr App R 149, CA, *R v Thomas* [1986] Crim LR 682, and *Taylor v Chief Constable of Cheshire* [1987] 1 All ER 225, DC (Ch 10).

in the dock; and that the jury can do this will not prevent the calling of a witness who was not present at the scene of the crime, but who knows the person shown in the photograph, video, or film, to give evidence as to his identity.[120] It is clear, however, that a photograph or film is as capable of containing an out-of-court statement as a tape or a document made of paper. Both the 1995 Act, and the 2003 Act operate on this assumption by catering for the admissibility of a statement contained in a 'document', which is defined as 'anything in which information of any description is recorded',[121] a definition wide enough to cover not only audio-tapes, but also photographs, videotapes, and films. Indeed, the film in *The Statue of Liberty*, which may be regarded as having constituted a statement as to the paths taken by the two ships, would now be admissible for the truth of its contents under the 1995 Act. In cases falling outside these statutory provisions, however, it would seem that a photograph or film, even if it contains, or can itself be treated as the equivalent of, an out-of-court statement, will, if relevant, be admitted as an item of real evidence rather than excluded as hearsay. Indeed, in *R v Cook*[122] Watkins LJ went so far as to state that the photograph, together with the sketch and the photofit, are in a class of evidence of their own to which neither the rule against hearsay nor the rule against previous consistent or self-serving statements applies.

For the purposes of disclosure in civil proceedings, a video, film, or recording is a document within the extended meaning contained in CPR rule 31.4 and therefore a party proposing to use it is subject to all the rules as to disclosure and inspection of documents contained in CPR rule 31. Equally, if it is disclosed in accordance with rule 31, the other party will be deemed to admit its authenticity unless notice is served that he wishes it to be proved at trial.[123] If he does serve such notice, the first party will be obliged to serve a witness statement by the person who took the video, film, or recording in order to prove its authenticity. If authenticity is not challenged, in the absence of any ruling by the court to the contrary, it is available for use by the first party, which includes using it in cross-examination of the other party and his witnesses.[124]

Views and demonstrations

A view is an inspection out of court of the *locus in quo* or of some object which it is inconvenient or impossible to bring to court.[125] There is some dispute whether out-of-court demonstrations or re-enactments are properly to be regarded as real evidence or as the equivalent of testimonial evidence. If the latter, it is arguable that the demonstrator should take the oath and thereby offer himself for cross-examination. On balance, the authorities would appear to favour the former view. In *Buckingham v Daily News Ltd*,[126] a negligence action concerning a machine, the judge

---

[120] See *R v Fowden and White* [1982] Crim LR 588, CA, *R v Grimer* [1982] Crim LR 674, CA, and *Attorney General's Reference (No 2 of 2002)* [2003] 1 Cr App R 21, CA. See also *R v Clare and Peach* [1995] 2 Cr App R 333, CA, where a witness who did *not* know the people shown in a video-recording, but had spent time analysing the photographic images, thereby acquiring special knowledge that the jury lacked, was permitted to identify them as the same people shown in a film and still photographs of the accused; and *R v Clarke* [1995] 2 Cr App R 425, CA, where the witness was an expert in facial identification who, using the technique of video superimposition, had compared photographs of a bank robber taken by an automatic camera with police identification photographs of the accused.

[121] Civil Evidence Act 1995, s 13 and Criminal Justice Act 2003, s 134(1).

[122] [1987] 1 All ER 1049 at 1054, CA. See also, in the case of photofits, *R v Constantinou* (1989) 91 Cr App R 74, CA.

[123] See CPR r 32.19(1).

[124] *Rall v Hume* [2001] 3 All ER 248, CA at [16].

[125] See, eg, *London General Omnibus Co Ltd v Lavell* [1901] 1 Ch 135, CA (an omnibus).

[126] [1956] 2 QB 534, CA.

inspected the machine and watched the plaintiff demonstrate what he had done. Judgment was given for the defendants. On appeal, it was argued that the judge had acted improperly by substituting his own opinion, based on the impression which he had gained at the view, for the plaintiff's oral evidence. Rejecting this argument, the Court of Appeal held that what the judge had seen was as much a part of the evidence as if the machine had been brought into the well of the court and the plaintiff had there demonstrated what took place.[127]

It is critical, before a court embarks upon a view, that there is clarity about precisely what is to happen, who is to stand where, what, if any, objects should be placed where, and who will do what. None of this should happen at the scene of the view, which should be conducted without discussion.[128] As a general rule, a view should be attended by the judge, the tribunal of fact, the parties, and counsel. In civil proceedings, each of the parties must be given the opportunity of being present at a view and a failure to do so may result in a retrial.[129] In a summary trial, as a general rule a view by magistrates of the scene of the alleged offence should take place before the conclusion of the evidence and in the presence of the parties or their representatives so as to afford them an opportunity of commenting on any feature of the locality which has altered since the time of the incident or any feature not previously noticed by the parties which impresses the magistrates.[130] The presence of the accused at a view is important because he may be able to point out some important matter of which his legal adviser is ignorant or about which the magistrates are making a mistake.[131] In a criminal trial by jury, the judge should always be present at a view, whether or not any witness is present for the purposes of a demonstration,[132] in order to control the proceedings. In particular, he should take precautions to prevent any witnesses who are present from communicating, except by way of demonstration, with the jury.[133] Because the jury should remain together at all times when evidence is being received, it is improper for one juror to attend a view and report back to the others what he observed.[134]

ADDITIONAL READING

Ekman, *Telling Lies* (3rd edn, 2002).

Hollander, *Documentary Evidence* (9th edn, 2006).

Stone, 'Instant Lie Detection? Demeanour and Credibility in Criminal Trials' [1991] *Crim LR* 821.

---

[127] The court approved, in this respect, the views of Denning LJ in *Goold v Evans & Co* [1951] 2 TLR 1189, CA. But contrast per Hodson LJ in the same case at 1191–2 and per Barwick CJ in *Railway Comr v Murphy* (1967) 41 ALJR 77 at 78, HC of A.

[128] *M v DPP* [2009] EWHC 752 (Admin).

[129] *Goold v Evans & Co* [1951] 2 TLR 1189, CA. But see per Widgery LJ in *Salsbury v Woodland* [1970] 1 QB 324, CA, a civil appeal, at 343–4: although a judge attending a demonstration at which the events in question are reconstructed or simulated should be accompanied by representatives of both parties, he may visit the *locus in quo* in order to see that which has previously been represented to him in court by plan and photograph on his own and without reference to the parties at all.

[130] *Parry v Boyle* (1986) 83 Cr App R 310, DC.

[131] *R v Ely Justices, ex p Burgess* [1992] Crim LR 888, DC.

[132] *R v Hunter* [1985] 2 All ER 173, CA. Contrast *Tameshwar v R* [1957] AC 476, PC. See also *R v Turay* [2007] EWCA Crim 2821, where there was no disadvantage to the defence.

[133] *R v Martin* (1872) LR 1 CCR 378; *Karamat v R* [1956] AC 256, PC.

[134] *R v Gurney* [1976] Crim LR 567, CA.

Hearsay in criminal cases

10

Key Issues

- If a statement is made out of court and tendered as evidence of the facts asserted (hearsay), when and why should it be excluded or admitted in criminal proceedings?

- If a statement is made out of court and tendered for some relevant purpose other than as evidence of the facts asserted (original evidence), when and why should it be admitted?

- Should the definition of hearsay evidence encompass:

  (a) assertions that may be inferred from a person's out-of-court statement but which she did not intend to communicate;

  (b) out-of-court statements tendered as evidence of the non-existence of a fact; and

  (c) statements produced by computers or other machines?

- To what extent is the admission of hearsay evidence compatible with Article 6 of the European Convention on Human Rights?

- Where hearsay evidence is admissible, what safeguards may be needed to address any risk of unfair prejudice?

Background and rationale

This chapter covers the meaning of hearsay in criminal proceedings. It also deals with all but one of the categories of hearsay admissible by statute in such proceedings. The exceptional category, confessions, merits the discrete treatment given to it in Chapter 13. It is also convenient to consider separately the subsisting common law rules governing the admissibility of hearsay evidence in criminal proceedings. They are considered in Chapter 12.

Under the common law rule against hearsay, any assertion, other than one made by a person while giving oral evidence in the proceedings, was inadmissible if tendered as evidence of the facts asserted.[1] The rule operated to prevent counsel from eliciting such evidence from any witness, whether in examination-in-chief or cross-examination[2] and applied to assertions in documents as well as oral assertions. The rule is perhaps best explained by way of example. Let us suppose that A, who witnessed an act of dangerous driving, some weeks later said to B that the car in question was blue and at that time also made a written note to the same effect. B reported to C what A had said to him. If A is subsequently called as a witness in proceedings concerned with the incident in question, he may of course make a statement from the witness box in the course of giving his evidence to the effect that the colour of the car he saw was blue. However, evidence may not be given by A, B, or C, for the purpose of establishing the colour of the car, of the oral statement made by A out of court. Likewise, the written statement made by A is inadmissible for that purpose. This is a simple example, but the common law rule against hearsay was highly complex, technical, difficult to describe with accuracy and of unclear scope.

The common law rule was subject to a variety of common law and statutory exceptions, and these too were often complex and technical in nature, some of them ill-considered and subject to frequent amendment. For example, the Criminal Evidence Act 1965, designed to admit hearsay in trade and business records, was passed as an interim measure, but few could have foreseen that the broader provisions set out in sections 68–72 of the Police and Criminal Evidence Act 1984 (the 1984 Act) relating to documentary hearsay by which it was replaced, would in turn be replaced only four years later by sections 23–28 of the Criminal Justice Act 1988 (the 1988 Act), provisions which unfortunately contained serious drafting errors. Sections 23–28 of the 1988 Act have now been repealed.[3] In criminal cases, the meaning of hearsay and the circumstances in which it is admissible, are now governed by Chapter 2 of Part 11 of the Criminal Justice Act 2003 (the 2003 Act).

A number of reasons have been advanced to justify the rule against hearsay, including the danger of manufactured evidence and, in the case of oral hearsay, especially multiple oral hearsay (X testifies as to what Y told him Z had said, for example), the danger of inaccuracy or mistake by reason of repetition. The principle rationale of the common law rule was summarized by Lord Bridge in *R v Blastland*:[4]

> Hearsay evidence is not excluded because it has no logically probative value ... The rationale of excluding it as inadmissible, rooted as it is in the system of trial by jury, is a recognition of the great difficulty, even more acute for a juror than for a trained judicial mind, of assessing what,

---

[1] Per Lord Havers in *R v Sharp* [1988] 1 WLR 7, HL and per Lords Ackner and Oliver in *R v Kearley* [1992] 2 AC 228, HL at 255 and 259 respectively. The rule also extended to out-of-court statements of otherwise admissible *opinion* (see Ch 18).

[2] For the application of the rule in cross-examination, see *R v Thomson* [1912] 3 KB 19, CCA (Ch 7).

[3] Section 136 of the Criminal Justice Act, 2003.

[4] [1986] AC 41, HL at 53 and 54.

if any, weight can properly be given to a statement by a person whom the jury have not seen or heard and who has not been subject to any test of reliability by cross-examination . . . The danger against which this fundamental rule provides a safeguard is that untested hearsay evidence will be treated as having a probative force which it does not deserve.

On the other hand, evidence of virtually unquestionable reliability has been excluded under the rule; cross-examination has been said to be arguably the poorest technique employed in the common law courts to elicit accurate testimony;[5] and there are dangers in deciding veracity on the basis of demeanour.[6] That the danger to which Lord Bridge referred can be overstated was recognized in the Report of the Royal Commission of Criminal Justice.[7] A reference to the Law Commission led to a consultation paper[8] and a final report.[9] The Commission, rejecting a range of other options, favoured retention of the rule but proposed a statutory formulation of both the rule and some of the exceptions to it, an expansion of the exceptions, and a 'safety valve' discretion to admit sufficiently reliable hearsay evidence not covered by any of the exceptions.[10] Subsequently, the Auld Report[11] recommended an alternative approach, that hearsay should be admissible if the original source or 'best evidence' is not available. This approach would have placed much greater trust in the fact finders to give hearsay evidence the weight it deserves. 'Many are of the view that both [judges and magistrates] are already more competent than we give them credit for assessing the weight of the evidence, including hearsay evidence.'[12] Greater trust in the fact finders would also have followed if the government had accepted the plea, made during the passage of the Criminal Justice Act through the House of Lords, for a simple rule giving judges a wide discretionary power. Lord Ackner referred to a paper, written by Lord Chief Justice Woolf and supported by all the judges of the criminal division of the Court of Appeal, in which he said:[13]

> If we have got to the stage where it is considered that it is safe to allow juries to hear hearsay evidence, then we must be accepting that they can be trusted to use that evidence in accordance with the directions of the judge. Instead of the detailed and complex provisions which are contained in Chapter 2, what is needed is a simple rule putting the judge in charge of what evidence is admissible and giving him the responsibility of ensuring that the jury use the evidence in an appropriate manner.

The Government rejected both this plea and the approach favoured by Lord Justice Auld. The provisions relating to hearsay in Chapter 2 of Part 11 of the 2003 Act are, in very large measure, based on the proposals of the Law Commission.[14]

---

[5] Australian Law Reform Commission Research Paper No 8 (1982), *Manner of Giving Evidence* ch 10, para 5. See also Law Commission Consultation Paper No 138 (1995), *Evidence in Criminal Proceedings: The Hearsay Rule and Related Topics* paras 6.49 and 6.62.

[6] See Law Commission Consultation Paper No 138 paras 6.22 and 6.27.

[7] Cm 2263 (1993).

[8] See n 5 above.

[9] Law Com No 245 (1997), *Evidence in Criminal Proceedings: Hearsay and Related Topics*, Cm 3670.

[10] For a critique of the Report, see C Tapper, 'Hearsay in Criminal Cases: An Overview of Law Commission Report No 245' [1997] *Crim LR* 771.

[11] *Review of the Criminal Courts of England and Wales* (2001).

[12] Ibid para 98, ch 11.

[13] *Hansard* HL vol 654 cols 752–3 (4 Nov 2003).

[14] For a critique of the statutory framework, see D Birch, 'Criminal Justice Act 2003 (4) Hearsay: Same Old Story, Same Old Song?' [2004] *Crim LR* 556.

Admissibility of hearsay under the Criminal Justice Act 2003

General

The statutory scheme

The only heads under which hearsay is admissible in criminal proceedings are set out in section 114(1) of the 2003 Act. Section 114(1), which is subject to discretionary powers to exclude hearsay,[15] provides as follows:

> (1) In criminal proceedings[16] a statement not made in oral evidence in the proceedings is admissible as evidence of any matter stated if, but only if—
>
> (a) any provision of this Chapter or any other statutory provision makes it admissible,
> (b) any rule of law preserved by s 118 makes it admissible,
> (c) all parties to the proceedings agree to it being admissible, or
> (d) the court is satisfied that it is in the interests of justice for it to be admissible.

Concerning the first part of section 114(1)(a), the categories of hearsay rendered admissible under the provisions of Chapter 2 of Part 11 of the 2003 Act are (i) statements made by persons who are not available as witnesses; (ii) statements in business and other documents; (iii) certain inconsistent and other previous statements of witnesses; (iv) statements on which an expert will in evidence base an opinion; and, by virtue of section 128(1) of the 2003 Act (v) confessions admissible on behalf of a co-accused.[17] Concerning the second part of section 114(1)(a), whereby hearsay may be admitted by virtue of 'any other statutory provision', 'statutory provision' means any provision contained in, or in an instrument made under, the 2003 Act or any other Act, including any Act passed after the 2003 Act.[18] These statutory provisions are considered at the end of this chapter, except in the case of confessions, which are considered in Chapter 13.

As to section 114(1)(b), the rules of law preserved by section 118 are most, but not all, of the common law rules providing for the admissibility of various categories of hearsay.[19] With the exception of the rules preserved by section 118, the common law rules governing the admissibility of hearsay evidence in criminal proceedings are abolished.[20] The statute abolishes the common law rule as well as the exceptions which it does not preserve.[21] Some of the rules preserved by section 118—statements in public documents, works of reference, evidence of age, evidence of reputation, and statements forming part of the *res gestae*—are considered in Chapter 12 (Hearsay admissible at common law). It is convenient to consider the remainder of the preserved rules in other parts of this work: mixed statements in Chapter 6 (Examination-in-chief); confessions, admissions by agents, and statements made by a party to a common

---

[15] See s 126, considered at 313 below, under **Other safeguards**, *Discretion to exclude*.

[16] 'Criminal proceedings' means criminal proceedings in relation to which the strict rules of evidence apply: s 134(1). These include proceedings under s 4A of the Criminal Procedure (Insanity) Act 1964: *R v Chal* [2008] 1 Cr App R 18, CA.

[17] Section 128(2) provides that, subject to s128(1), nothing in Chapter 2 makes a confession by an accused admissible if it would not be admissible under s 76 of the Police and Criminal Evidence Act 1984.

[18] Section 134(1).

[19] The rule permitting the admissibility of dying declarations, a rule that has never been easy to justify, has been abandoned. Declarations by persons, since deceased, either against interest or in the course of duty, have also been abandoned.

[20] Section 118(2).

[21] *R v Singh* [2006] 1 WLR 1564, CA.

enterprise in Chapter 13 (Confessions); and the rule whereby an expert may draw on the body of expertise relevant to his field in Chapter 18 (Opinion evidence).

Section 114(1)(c) permits hearsay to be admissible where the prosecution, the accused, and any co-accused agree to it being admissible. Finally, section 114(1)(d) provides for the admissibility of hearsay which it would be in the interests of justice to admit, ie hearsay admissible by exercise of the inclusionary discretion.

Under section 114(3):

> Nothing in this Chapter affects the exclusion of evidence of a statement on grounds other than the fact that it is a statement not made in oral evidence in the proceedings.

Thus if hearsay evidence falls to be excluded because it is irrelevant or inadmissible on grounds of public policy, privilege or any other exclusionary rule of evidence, it will still fall to be excluded notwithstanding that it is otherwise admissible hearsay.

Article 6 of the European Convention on Human Rights
Article 6 of the European Convention on Human Rights provides:

> (3) Everyone charged with a criminal offence has the following minimum rights:
>
> ...
>
> (d) to have examined witnesses against him and to obtain the attendance and examination of witnesses on his behalf under the same conditions as witnesses against him.

The leading authority on the relationship between the statutory provisions and Article 6 is *R v Horncastle*.[22] In that case, the Court of Appeal undertook a thorough review of the Strasbourg jurisprudence, from which it derived the following principles.

1. The admissibility of evidence is a matter for the national court.

2. The ordinary rule, sometimes known as the right to confrontation, is that witnesses must be examined in court.

3. The expression 'witness' has an autonomous meaning for the purposes of Article 6, which includes a person who has given information to the police which is relied on in the trial process.

4. The right in Article 6(3)(d) is not absolute or unqualified and there may be circumstances which justify a departure from it. Thus, to use as evidence witness statements or depositions obtained at the pre-trial stage, whether by the police or an investigating judge, is not in itself inconsistent with Article 6(1) and (3)(d).

5. In departing from the Article 6(3)(d) right, the Convention rights of witnesses are engaged and material. Contracting States should organize their criminal proceedings in such a way that those rights are not unjustifiably imperiled.

6. Departure from the right to confrontation must not be taken without careful thought and analysis of (a) the circumstances in which the statements are to be relied upon were made; and (b) the reasons for the witness not being called and made available for examination. Any departure from the right must then be justified.

---

[22] [2009] 4 All ER 183, CA.

7. Where evidence is relied upon which is not given orally by the witness who is available to be examined by the accused, the rights of the defence must be respected. There is a requirement for 'counterbalancing measures' sufficient to compensate for the restrictions placed on the defence. However, at least where the evidence in question is only a part of the evidence relied upon there need be no counterbalancing measures.

A difficult question that has confronted the courts is whether there will be a breach of Article 6 if a conviction is based solely or to a decisive degree on depositions or statements made by someone whom the accused has had no opportunity to question. In *Al-Khawaja and Tahery v UK*[23] the Strasbourg court, relying on *Luca v Italy*[24] asserted that Article 6(3)(d) is a minimum right which constitutes an express guarantee that must be accorded to anyone who is charged with a criminal offence and, in principle, requires that the accused must be given a proper and adequate opportunity to challenge and question a witness against him either when the witness statement was made or at a later stage. The court held that, absent a witness being kept from giving evidence through fear induced by the defendant,[25] an exception previously recognized by the Court of Appeal in *R v Sellick*,[26] it was doubtful whether any counterbalancing factors would be sufficient to justify the introduction of evidence of an untested statement which was the sole or decisive basis for a conviction.

However, the Court of Appeal in *R v Horncastle*[27] declined to follow *Al-Khawaja*, holding that *Luca*, in failing to properly distinguish between absent and anonymous witnesses, went further than the previously decided Strasbourg case law. The Article 6(3)(d) right is not absolute and can be restricted, provided that the trial is still fair. The court stated that Part 11, Chapter 2 of the 2003 Act contains a crafted code intended to ensure that evidence is admitted only when it is fair that it should be. The Act allows the defence to test the credibility of evidence[28] and contains an overriding safeguard in the power of the judge to stop a trial where the evidence is unconvincing.[29] The Act concluded that, provided the provisions of the 2003 Act are observed, there is therefore no breach of Article 6 and in particular Article 6(3)(d), even if the conviction is based solely or to a decisive degree on hearsay evidence admitted under the 2003 Act.[30]

Section 114 is not restricted to the admission of a hearsay statement the maker of which is not available for cross-examination. Where hearsay evidence takes the form of a statement made by a person who is also called to give evidence at trial, for example, because it is admitted under section 119 or 120,[31] and is therefore available for questioning, it is submitted that there can be no question of its admission being in breach of Article 6(3)(d).[32]

---

[23] (2009) 49 EHRR 1.

[24] (2003) 36 EHRR 807.

[25] In such circumstances the accused has denied himself the opportunity of examining the witness: *R v Sellick* [2005] 1 WLR 3257, CA and *R v M (KJ)* [2003] 2 Cr App R 322, CA.

[26] Ibid.

[27] [2009] 4 All ER 183, CA.

[28] Section 124. See at 310 under **Other safeguards**, *Credibility*.

[29] Section 125. See below at 312 under **Other safeguards**, *Stopping the case where the evidence is unconvincing*.

[30] See also *R v Xhabri* [2006] 1 All ER 776, CA.

[31] See below under **Previous inconsistent statements of witnesses** at 303 and **Other previous statements of witnesses** at 304.

[32] See, eg, *R v Xhabri* [2006], ibid at [44].

In none of the decided cases has the expression 'witness' been extended beyond persons who have provided statements to the authorities as part of the prosecutorial process, and so it is doubtful whether the admission of statements less formal than a witness statement, deposition, or business documents would infringe the rights of the accused under Article 6(3)(d). The jurisprudence on Article 6(3)(d) is therefore of principal relevance where the prosecution seek to admit hearsay evidence under section 116 or 114(1)(d).[33]

Before considering in detail the various categories of hearsay admissible under the 2003 Act, it is necessary to consider first the way in which hearsay is defined in the Act.

The meaning of hearsay in the Criminal Justice Act 2003

As we have seen from section 114(1), hearsay is 'a statement not made in oral evidence in the proceedings ... admissible as evidence of any matter stated'. This formulation covers not only 'out-of-court' statements as such, but also statements made in previous criminal or civil proceedings. 'Oral evidence', for the purposes of section 114(1) and other provisions relating to hearsay in the 2003 Act, includes evidence which, by reason of any disability, disorder, or other impairment, a person called as a witness gives in writing or by signs or by way of any device.[34]

'A statement'

'A statement', for the purposes of the provisions relating to hearsay in the 2003 Act, is 'any representation of fact or opinion made by a person by whatever means; and it includes a representation made in a sketch, photofit or other pictorial form'.[35] This is a very wide definition. It covers a statement of opinion, provided that it is admissible opinion of course,[36] as well as a statement of fact.[37] The statement may have been made unsworn or on oath by any person, whether or not a person called as a witness in the proceedings in question. The representation, however, must have been made by a person—statements in computer-generated documents are not covered. The admissibility of computer-generated documents is considered separately, below.

The phrase 'any representation ... by whatever means' clearly covers statements made orally as well as statements made in writing, whether by hand, or by means of a typewriter, word processor, computer, or other similar device. A common law example of oral hearsay, which will continue to be hearsay under the 2003 Act is *R v Rothwell*,[38] a case of supplying heroin. The prosecution sought to rely on evidence that the accused was seen on several occasions passing small packages to various people, coupled with the evidence of a drugs squad officer that the recipients were known to him as heroin users. It was held that, insofar as the officer's evidence was based on statements made to him by others, for example the alleged recipients, then the evidence would be inadmissible hearsay; but that it would not be hearsay insofar as it was based on the recipients' convictions for possession of heroin[39] or, for example, the officer's personal observation of needle marks on the recipients' forearms or his personal knowledge of

[33] See, eg, *R v L* [2009] 1 WLR 626, CA.

[34] Section 134(1).

[35] Section 115(2).

[36] See s 114(3), above.

[37] See also s 30 of the Criminal Justice Act 1988, considered below at 318, under **Expert reports**.

[38] (1994) 99 Cr App R 388, CA.

[39] Admissible under the Police and Criminal Evidence Act 1984, s 74: see Ch 2.

the recipients being in possession of heroin or receiving treatment for heroin addiction. *Patel v Comptroller of Customs*[40] provides an example of written hearsay. The appellant was convicted of making a false declaration in an import entry form concerning certain bags of seed. The appellant had declared that the country of origin of the seed was India. Evidence was admitted that the bags of seed bore the words 'Produce of Morocco'. The Privy Council held that the evidence was inadmissible hearsay and advised that the conviction be quashed.[41]

The phrase 'any representation ... by whatever means' is also wide enough to embrace statements made by conduct or signs and gestures, and statements made partly orally and partly by conduct or signs and gestures. A common law example of the last is *R v Gibson*,[42] a trial for malicious wounding in which the prosecutor gave evidence that after he had been hit by a stone, a woman, pointing to the door of a house, had said, 'The person who threw the stone went in there.' The occupant of the house was convicted. The conviction was quashed on the ground that evidence of the woman's statement was inadmissible.[43] *Chandrasekera v R*[44] provides an example of a hearsay statement made solely by signs or gestures. The appellant was charged with murder. At the trial evidence was admitted that the victim, whose throat had been cut, had made certain signs, the apparent effect of which was to indicate the accused. Asked whether it was the appellant who had cut her throat, she replied by nodding her head. Lord Roche was of the opinion that the case resembled that of a dumb person able to converse by means of finger alphabet, and held that the woman had effectively stated that the accused had cut her neck. The hearsay statement was nevertheless held to be admissible under an exception contained in the Ceylon Evidence Ordinance 1895. The evidence would now be admissible under section 116(1) and (2)(a) (a statement made by a person since deceased).[45]

The inclusion, within the definition of 'a statement', of 'a representation made in a sketch, photofit or other pictorial form' reflects a principled approach which was lacking in some of the common law authorities.[46] Photographs and films are excluded from the definition and continue to be admissible, at common law, as a variety of real evidence, if relevant to the issues, including the important issues of whether an offence was committed and who committed it.[47]

[40] [1966] AC 356, PC.

[41] See also *R v Sealby* [1965] 1 All ER 701 (Crown Court) and *R v Brown* [1991] Crim LR 835, CA (evidence of a name on an appliance inadmissible to establish its ownership); and cf *R v Rice* [1963] 1 QB 857, below.

[42] (1887) LR 18 QBD 537, CCR.

[43] The Court for Crown Cases Reserved gave no express reason as to why the evidence was inadmissible, but the decision has been cited subsequently in cases expressly concerned with the rule against hearsay: see, eg, *R v Saunders* [1899] 1 QB 490, CCR.

[44] [1937] AC 220, PC.

[45] If a policeman employs an interpreter to question a suspect whose language he does not understand, the translated answers may be given in evidence by the translator but not by the policeman: see *R v Attard* (1958) 43 Cr App R 90, where the police officer's evidence of what the accused had said was held to be inadmissible hearsay. In consequence of this decision, the Home Office issued a circular to the police which points to the necessity of ensuring that the interpreter is available to give evidence. Whenever practicable, the interpreter should make his own notes of the interview or, failing this, he should initial the police record which he may then use to refresh his memory.

[46] See *R v Cook* [1987] QB 417, CA, in which it was held that photofits, together with sketches and photographs, are in a class of evidence of their own to which neither the rule against hearsay nor the rule against previous consistent statements is applicable. *R v Cook* was applied, in the case of a photofit, in *R v Constantinou* (1989) 91 Cr App R 74, CA. See also *R v Percy Smith* [1976] Crim LR 511, CA (a sketch made by a police officer under the direction of an identification witness).

[47] See, eg, *R v Dodson; R v Williams* (1984) 79 Cr App R 220, CA (photographs) and *R v Roberts* [1998] Crim LR 682, CA, considered in Ch 9.

As to whether 'representation' refers only to what is expressly represented or also includes implied representations, it is submitted that the legislative framework suggests the broader interpretation. This would accord with Parliament's intention that section 115(3) should be the mechanism by which implied assertions[48] are kept outside the scope of the rule, while still allowing for declarations to be classified as hearsay where the purpose of the maker was to cause another to believe the matter stated or to cause another to act or a machine to operate on the basis that the matter is as stated, even if the declaration contains no express representation of fact or opinion.[49]

Original evidence

Under section 114(1) of the 2003 Act, hearsay is a statement not made in oral evidence in the proceedings 'admissible as evidence of any matter stated'. Hearsay falls to be distinguished from original evidence, which may be defined as a statement not made in oral evidence in the proceedings which is admissible for any relevant purpose other than that of establishing any matter stated. This is a difficult distinction, but an important one, because whereas hearsay is admissible only under the heads set out in section 114(1), original evidence is admissible provided only that it is sufficiently relevant. Examples of original evidence may be classified according to whether they are admitted (i) simply to show that the statement was made, because that is a fact in issue in the proceedings; or (ii) because of their relevance to some other fact in issue in the proceedings.

The making of the statement as a fact in issue.   If the making of a certain statement is itself a fact in issue in the proceedings, that statement, even if inadmissible as evidence of any matter stated, may be admitted as evidence of the fact that it was made.[50] For example, on a charge of making a threat to kill, the victim may give evidence of the fact that the accused said to her 'I am going to kill you.'[51] *R v Chapman*[52] provides an instructive example. Following a road traffic accident, the accused was taken to a hospital where a breath test was administered. He was subsequently convicted of driving a motor vehicle with excess alcohol. Section 2(2)(b) of the Road Safety Act 1967 provided that a hospital patient shall not be required to provide a specimen of breath if the medical practitioner in charge of his case 'objects' on the grounds that it would be prejudicial to the proper care or treatment of the patient. At the trial, a police officer gave evidence that the doctor in question had not objected to the provision of a specimen. It was argued on appeal that this evidence was inadmissible hearsay. Rejecting the

---

[48] See below at 278 under **The meaning of hearsay in the Criminal Justice Act 2003, Implied assertions**.

[49] But see *R v Leonard* [2009] Crim LR 802 at [34]–[38]; and *R v K* (2008) 172 JP 538, CA at [12] and [17].

[50] But see *West Midlands Probation Board v French* [2009] 1 WLR 1715, a case concerning proceedings under s 40A(4) for the breach of a licence issued to a serving prisoner on his release from imprisonment, in which the Divisional Court held that the licence was hearsay. It is submitted that this decision was incorrect as the licence was adduced not as evidence of the matters stated but simply as evidence that the matters were stated. Section 40A(4) provides that 'If the person fails to comply with such conditions as may for the time being be specified in the licence, he shall be liable on summary convictions to [penalties specified]'. For further criticism of this decision see D Ormerod, '*West Midlands Probation Board v French*' (case comment) at [2009] *Crim LR* 283.

[51] In *R v Rizwan Mawji* (2003) LTL 16/10/2003, CA, where such a threat was contained in an e-mail which had been sent from the accused's e-mail address, it was held that whether the jury accepted the e-mail as genuine was a matter manifestly for them.

[52] [1969] 2 QB 436, CA.

argument, the Court of Appeal held that the evidence had been properly adduced to establish that the doctor had made no objection.

The statement as evidence relevant to some other fact in issue.   A statement may be admissible as a fact relevant to a fact in issue in the proceedings notwithstanding that it is inadmissible as evidence of any matter stated. Examples that may be given are many and various. In some cases the statement is admitted as evidence of the state of mind of its maker. Thus a man's assertion in 2009 that he is Napoleon, Emperor of France, may be tendered for the purpose of showing his insanity.

In *Ratten v R*[53] Ratten was convicted of the murder of his wife by shooting her. His defence was that a gun went off accidentally while he was cleaning it. The evidence established that the shooting, from which the wife had died almost immediately, took place between 1.12 pm and about 1.20 pm. A telephonist from the local exchange gave evidence that at 1.15 pm she had received a telephone call from Ratten's house made by a sobbing woman who in an hysterical voice had said, 'Get me the police please.' The Privy Council held that there was no hearsay element in this evidence, which was relevant (i) in order to show that, contrary to the evidence of Ratten, who denied that any telephone call had been made by his wife, a call had been made; and (ii) as possibly showing that the wife was in a state of emotion or fear at an existing or impending emergency, which was capable of rebutting Ratten's defence that the shooting was accidental.[54] *Ratten*'s case was held to be clearly distinguishable in *R v Blastland*.[55] In that case, the House of Lords held that the accused, convicted of buggery and murder, had been properly disallowed to adduce evidence of statements made by a third party indicating *his* knowledge of the murder before the body was found, because the only issue was whether the accused had committed the crimes and what was relevant to that issue was not the third party's knowledge but how he had acquired it; since he could have done so in a number of different ways, there was no rational basis on which the jury could infer that he, rather than the accused, was the murderer.[56]

In some cases, the statement is admitted as evidence of the state of mind of the person who heard or read it, ie to show what the person who heard or read it, knew, thought, or believed. If A is charged with the murder of B, evidence of a statement by C to A that B was having an adulterous relationship with A's spouse, even if not admissible as evidence of the adulterous relationship, has an obvious relevance on the question of A's motive. In *Subramaniam v Public Prosecutor*[57] the accused was convicted of being in unlawful possession of ammunition. His defence was that he had been threatened by terrorists and had acted under duress. Evidence of what the terrorists had said was excluded by the trial judge as inadmissible hearsay. Quashing the conviction, the Privy Council held that the trial judge had erred. Statements could have

---

[53] [1972] AC 378.

[54] See also *R v Gilfoyle* [1996] 3 All ER 883, CA (suicide notes admissible as evidence of a woman's suicidal frame of mind and further statements made by her which showed that when she wrote the notes she had no intention of taking her own life) and *R v Gregson* [2003] 2 Cr App R 521, CA (evidence that G had expressed concerns about how to dispose of a quantity of ecstasy tablets he had purchased admissible in relation to his intent to supply, the defence case being that he believed he was acquiring a much smaller amount).

[55] [1986] AC 41.

[56] An out-of-court statement made by the *accused* and disclosing his possession of certain knowledge which tends to incriminate him may be admitted, by way of statutory exception to the hearsay rule, as a confession: see Police and Criminal Evidence Act 1984, s 76 and Ch 13.

[57] [1956] 1 WLR 965. See also *R v Willis* [1960] 1 WLR 55, CCA and *R v Madden* [1986] Crim LR 804, CA.

been made by the terrorists which, even if not admissible as evidence of any matter stated, might reasonably have induced in the accused, if he believed them, an apprehension of instant death if he failed to conform to their wishes. The statements were accordingly admissible as potentially cogent evidence of duress.[58]

A statement may be admitted as original evidence where it is tendered for the purpose of allowing the tribunal of fact to conclude that its contents are false and to draw inferences from the falsity of those contents. In *A-G v Good*[59] the demonstrably false statement of a debtor's wife that her husband was not at home was admissible for the purpose of showing her husband's intention to defraud his creditors. If an unreasonable time had intervened between the demand for entrance and the opening of the door, that would have been a fact relevant to the issue, and the untrue statement of the wife was relevant in the same way. In *Mawaz Khan v R*[60] the appellants were convicted of murder. At the trial the prosecution had relied upon the fact that each of them had in his statement to the police sought to set up a joint alibi, many of the details of which were demonstrated to be false by other evidence. The Privy Council held that the trial judge had properly directed the jury that although a statement made by one of the accused in the absence of another was not evidence against the other, they were entitled to compare the statements of the two accused and, if they concluded that they were false, to draw the inference that the accused had cooperated after the alleged crime and jointly concocted the story out of a sense of guilt.[61]

In *Woodhouse v Hall*[62] the manageress of a sauna and massage parlour was charged with acting in the management of a brothel. Plain clothes police officers, who had entered the premises as customers, alleged that they had been offered masturbation by the manageress and other women employed there. At the trial, the justices held that the police officers' evidence of the offers made to them was inadmissible hearsay. The information was dismissed. On the prosecutor's appeal by way of case stated, Donaldson LJ held that the evidence had been wrongly excluded: 'There is no question of the hearsay rule arising at all. The relevant issue was did these ladies make these offers?'[63] The very fact that such offers had been made was relevant to the central fact in issue, namely whether the premises were being used as a sauna and massage parlour or a brothel. As Lord Ackner pointed out in *R v Kearley*,[64] 'in order to establish that the premises are being used as a brothel it is sufficient to prove that at the premises more than one woman *offers* herself as a participant in physical acts of indecency for the sexual gratification of men'.[65]

Implied assertions

At common law a question which gave rise to considerable difficulty was whether the hearsay rule applied to implied assertions, an area of evidence law which has been characterized as a

---

[58] See also *R v Davis* [1998] Crim LR 659, CA (evidence of a solicitor's advice to the accused may be admissible for the purpose of establishing the accused's reason for not answering questions in interview).

[59] (1825) M'Cle&Yo 286.

[60] [1967] 1 AC 454.

[61] See also *R v Binham* [1991] Crim LR 774, CA, where evidence of B's previous statements in support of his alibi defence, together with evidence as to their falsity, was admissible as original evidence.

[62] (1981) 72 Cr App R 39, DC.

[63] Ibid at 42. Cf, *sed quaere*, *R v Lawal* [1994] Crim LR 746, CA.

[64] [1992] 2 AC 228, HL at 257.

[65] See *Kelly v Purvis* [1983] QB 663, DC.

legalistic backwater which is 'the home of sophistry and the graveyard of common sense'.[66] An implied assertion is an assertion, whether made orally, in writing, or by conduct, from which it is possible to infer a particular matter. To take a simple example, if Harry, walking down the street, and not using a mobile telephone, says, 'Hello, Bill', it is possible to infer that Bill was in Harry's presence. The common law authorities treated as hearsay implied assertions made orally or in writing (or by a combination of an oral or written statement and conduct). Under the statutory formulation of hearsay, as we have seen, section 114(1) refers to a statement not made in oral evidence in the proceedings which is admissible as evidence of any 'matter stated'. Under 115(3):

> (3) A matter stated is one to which this Chapter applies if (and only if) the purpose, or one of the purposes, of the person making the statement appears to the court to have been—
>   (a) to cause another person to believe the matter, or
>   (b) to cause another person to act or a machine to operate on the basis that the matter is as stated.

The effect of section 115(3) is to narrow the ambit of section 114 so that it applies to render hearsay admissible as evidence of any matter stated under one of the heads set out in section 114(1) if and only if the purpose, or one of the purposes, of the person making the statement, was of the kind described in either subsection (3)(a) or (b). Under subsection (3)(a), the purpose, or one of the purposes, in making the statement is to cause another to believe the matter, ie to accept that matter as true, whereas under subsection (3)(b) the purpose, or one of the purposes, in making the statement, is simply to cause another to act on the basis that the matter is as stated, ie to act on the basis that the matter is true (or to cause a machine to operate on the basis that the matter is as stated). There appears to be a considerable overlap between the two subsections, in that if the purpose is to cause another to act on the basis that a certain matter is as it has been stated, then whether or not that is the truth of the matter, the purpose, in many situations, will also be to cause the other to believe the matter. Subsection (3)(b) will apply, but not subsection (3)(a), where the purpose is to cause another to do no more than to act on the basis that the matter is as stated, and not to cause the other to believe the matter, perhaps because, for example, the maker of the statement is aware that the matter is not as stated or is unsure as to the truth of the matter.

The Explanatory Notes to the 2003 Act state that the purpose of section 115(3) is 'to overturn the ruling in *Kearley*[67] that "implied assertions" are covered by the hearsay rule and therefore prima facie inadmissible'. This is misleading in two respects. First, section 115(3) will operate to exclude from the ambit of section 114 some express as well as implied assertions. For example, if an express assertion is made by a person who is talking to himself and unaware that he is being overheard, or is contained in a memorandum which is kept for purely personal purposes,[68] then plainly it is not among the purposes of the maker of the statement to cause another to believe the matter stated. Such statements are therefore not covered by, or subject to, section 114 of the Act. They would now appear to be admissible, provided that they are relevant, and, if tendered by the prosecution, subject to the discretionary powers of exclusion. At first blush, it might be thought that section 115(3) will also operate to exclude from

---

[66] D Birch, 'Criminal Justice Act 2003 (4) Hearsay: Same Old Story, Same Old Song?' [2004] *Crim LR* 556 at 564.

[67] *R v Kearley* [1992] 2 AC 228, HL, considered below.

[68] See, eg, *R v N* (2007) 171 JP 158, CA.

the ambit of section 114 an express assertion made with the purpose of causing another to *disbelieve* the matter stated, as when the maker says, for example, 'Of course X was present ... and pigs were flying!' However, such a statement would surely be treated as a statement made with the purpose of causing another to believe that X was absent.

Secondly, it is submitted that section 115(3) will not operate to exclude all implied assertions from the ambit of section 114. It will overturn the ruling in the leading case of *R v Kearley*, and operate to admit many implied assertions which would formerly have been excluded. However, although in *R v Singh*[69] it was baldly asserted that 'when sections 114 and 118 are read together they ... create ... a new rule against hearsay which does not extend to implied assertions'[70] it is submitted that some implied assertions will continue to be classified as hearsay. In each case the court will need to consider the purpose or purposes of a person in making the particular statement in question and, in cases in which it concludes that the statement does amount to hearsay, it will need to go on to consider whether it falls under any of the heads of admissibility set out in section 114.

The application of section 115(3) in the case of implied assertions is perhaps best explored by reference to the facts of some of the common law authorities.

Oral assertions. In *R v Kearley* the police found drugs in K's flat, but not in sufficient quantities to raise the inference that he was a dealer. The police remained there for several hours and intercepted 10 telephone calls in which the callers asked to speak to K and asked for drugs. Seven other people arrived at the flat, some with money, also asking for K and asking to be supplied with drugs, but at all relevant times K was either absent or not within earshot. At K's trial for possession with intent to supply, the officers who had intercepted the calls or received the visitors gave evidence of the conversations. The House of Lords, by a majority of three to two, allowed the appeal against conviction. It was held: (i) that evidence of the requests made by the callers and visitors was irrelevant because it could only be evidence of the state of mind or belief of those making the requests, which was not a relevant issue at the trial, the issue being whether K intended to supply drugs; and (ii) applying *Wright v Doe d Tatham*[71] and approving *R v Harry*,[72] that insofar as the evidence was relevant to the issue of K's intent to supply, ie as an implied assertion that K was a supplier, it was inadmissible hearsay, and it made no difference that there were a large number of such requests all made at the same place on the same day. The decision is open to criticism on the basis that the evidence could have been admitted as circumstantial evidence, ie evidence from which K's intent to supply could be inferred.[73] In any event, section 115(3) operates to reverse the decision. It seems most unlikely that it was among the purposes of the callers and visitors to cause others to believe that K was a supplier. Their purpose was to contact K in order to be supplied with drugs. The evidence, therefore, would now be admissible as direct evidence of the fact that there was a ready market for the supply of drugs from the premises, from which could be inferred an intention by an occupier to supply drugs.[74]

---

[69] [2006] 1 WLR 1564, CA.

[70] At [14].

[71] (1837) 7 Ad&El 313.

[72] (1987) 86 Cr App R 105, CA.

[73] See Taylor, 'Two English hearsay heresies' (2005) 9 *E&P* 110.

[74] *R v Singh* [2006] 1 WLR 1564, CA per Rose LJ at [14]. See also *R v K* (2008) 172 JP 538, CA in which an inquiry about the availability and price of specific drugs made by a person during a telephone call to the defendant was held

In *Teper v R*[75] the accused was convicted of arson of a shop belonging to his wife. His defence was one of alibi. In order to establish his presence within the vicinity of the shop, a policeman gave evidence that, some 25 minutes after the fire had begun, an unidentified woman bystander had shouted to a motorist, who resembled the accused, 'Your place burning and you going away from the fire.' The Privy Council, quashing the conviction, held that this assertion which, by implication, established Teper's presence, was inadmissible hearsay.[76] It is not clear that section 115(3) operates to reverse this decision. It would turn upon whether it appears to the court that one of the purposes of the unidentified woman, in making her statement, was to cause one or more of the bystanders to believe that Teper was present but departing.

Written assertions. In *Wright v Doe d Tatham*,[77] which concerned, inter alia, the mental competence of a testator, it was held that the trial judge had properly disallowed the production in evidence of a number of letters written to the testator by certain of his acquaintances in terms from which it could legitimately be inferred that they regarded him as sane. As evidence of the truth of the implied assertion that the testator was sane, they constituted inadmissible hearsay. If the same issue were to arise in a criminal context, section 115(3) would operate to reverse this decision. It would be most unlikely to appear to the court that one of the purposes of the testator's acquaintances was to cause others to believe that the testator was sane. The principal and probably only purpose in writing was to convey to the testator the contents of their letters.

R v Lydon[78] and *R v Rice*[79] are cases which highlight the difficult borderline that exists between circumstantial evidence and implied assertions. In *R v Lydon* the appellant, whose first name was Sean, was convicted of robbery. His defence was one of alibi. About one mile from the scene of the robbery, on the verge of the road which the getaway car had followed, were found a gun and, nearby, two pieces of rolled paper on which someone had written 'Sean rules' and 'Sean rules 85'. Ink of similar appearance and composition to that on the paper was found on the gun barrel. The Court of Appeal held that evidence relating to the pieces of paper had been properly admitted as circumstantial evidence: if the jury were satisfied that the gun was used in the robbery and that the pieces of paper were linked to the gun, the references to Sean could be a fact which would fit in with the appellant having committed the offence. The references were not hearsay because they involved no assertion as to the truth of the contents of the pieces of paper, ie they were not tendered to show that Sean ruled anything. The outcome, it is submitted, should be the same under the 2003 Act, because the prosecution would not be relying upon the pieces of paper as 'evidence of any matter stated', ie that 'Sean rules' or that 'Sean rules 85', and that insofar as the statements can be treated as statements which, by implication, in some way linked Lydon with the offence, then for the purposes of section 115(3), it was unlikely to have been among the purposes of Lydon, in making the statements, to cause others to believe this.[80]

---

to have been correctly admitted as evidence from which it could properly be inferred that the defendant was a person concerned in the supply of drugs.

[75] [1952] AC 480.

[76] It was also held that the statement did not form part of the *res gestae* (see Ch 12).

[77] (1837) 7 Ad&El 313, Ex Ch.

[78] (1987) 85 Cr App R 221, CA.

[79] [1963] 1 QB 857, CCA.

[80] See also *R v McIntosh* [1992] Crim LR 651, CA (calculations as to the purchase and sale prices of 12 oz of an unnamed commodity, not in M's handwriting but found concealed in the chimney of a house where he had been

In *R v Rice* the accused were convicted of conspiracy. Part of the prosecution case involved proving that two of them, Rice and Hoather, had taken a certain flight to Manchester. A used airline ticket, which bore the name of Rice and of another accused, Moore, was admitted in evidence against Rice. The Court of Criminal Appeal held that although the ticket was inadmissible hearsay if tendered for the purposes of speaking its contents, that is to show that the booking was effected by Rice or even by any man of that name, it had been properly admitted. Winn J said:[81]

> The relevance of that ticket in logic and its legal admissibility as a piece of real evidence both stem from the same root, viz., the balance of probability recognized by common sense and common knowledge that an air ticket which has been used on a flight and which has a name upon it has more likely than not been used by a man of that name or by one of two men whose names are upon it.

The ticket was only relevant, it is submitted, because it allowed the jury to conclude that Rice had taken a certain flight to Manchester, a conclusion that could only be drawn on the basis that the ticket contained an implied assertion that Rice would take that flight. Whether the ticket would now be treated as containing a hearsay statement would turn upon whether it appears to the court that one of the purposes of the person who put Rice's name on the ticket was to cause others to believe that Rice would be using it.

R v Rice was a decision that it was difficult, if not impossible, to reconcile with *R v Van Vreden*.[82] At a trial for obtaining by deception, which was alleged to have involved the use of a Barclaycard issued in South Africa to a Miss Lang, the application form relating to that card, upon which the account number had been entered, was held by the Court of Appeal, to have been improperly admitted, on the basis that its production at the trial effected the same result as the production of a statement made by a named clerk in South Africa asserting that he had issued a card to Miss Lang bearing the number which he had entered as the account number. Under section 115(3), the application form would also be treated as hearsay, because there can be little doubt that the purpose of the clerk, in entering the account number, was to cause others who had occasion to refer to the form, to believe that Miss Lang's card bore that number.

Assertions by conduct.   Concerning implied assertions by conduct alone, there were few common law authorities. In *Chandrasekera v R*,[83] as we have seen, the signs used by the victim to identify her assailant were treated as hearsay, and section 115(3) operates to preserve the decision, the very purpose of the victim's conduct having been to cause others to believe that the accused had cut her throat. In *Wright v Doe d Tatham* Parke B expressed the obiter view that, on a question of the seaworthiness of a vessel, evidence of the conduct of a deceased captain who, after examining every part of the vessel, embarked in it with his family, would constitute hearsay. It would be very difficult to uphold such a view now, because it seems most unlikely, without

---

living, admissible as circumstantial evidence tending to connect him with drug-related offences) and *Roberts v DPP* [1994] Crim LR 926, DC (documents found at R's offices and home, including repair and gas bills and other accounts relating to certain premises, admissible as circumstantial evidence linking R with those premises, on charges of assisting in the management of a brothel and running a massage parlour without a licence) and cf *R v Horne* [1992] Crim LR 304, CA.

[81] [1963] 1 QB 857 at 871.
[82] (1973) 57 Cr App R 818, CA.
[83] [1937] AC 220, PC.

more, that one of the purposes of the captain, in examining the vessel, was to cause another to believe that the vessel was seaworthy. In *Manchester Brewery Co Ltd v Coombs*,[84] a case concerning an alleged breach by a brewer to supply a publican with good beer, it was held, obiter, that evidence would be admissible that certain customers ordered the beer, tasted it, did not finish it, and then either left it or threw it away. Section 115(3) operates to uphold this view because of the unlikelihood, without more, that one of the purposes of the customers, in behaving as they did, was to cause another to believe that the beer was no good.

There can be little doubt that section 115(3) will operate to render admissible much evidence that was previously excluded as hearsay. Underlying this development of the law was the opinion that 'as a class, implied assertions are more reliable than assertions made for the purpose of communicating information'.[85] There are two compelling reasons, however, why such evidence will often need to be treated with caution. The first stems from the fact that it is often possible to draw different inferences from the same conduct and, depending on the precise circumstances, this will reduce the weight to be attached to the evidence. For example, the conduct of the captain could have been a search for a stowaway, and the customers who rejected the beer could all have been French and unfamiliar with the taste of English beer. Secondly, there will be the risk, in some cases, of error or malicious concoction, the degree of risk varying according to the precise circumstances. For example, in *R v Kearley*, it was most unlikely that, without more, 17 callers were all mistaken or all set out with the deliberate intention of deceiving the police into believing that the accused was a dealer, but if there had been only one or two callers, there would have been at least some risk of mistake or malice.[86]

Negative hearsay

Under the 2003 Act, as at common law, an oral out-of-court statement will amount to hearsay whether it is tendered as evidence of the existence or non-existence of a fact. Thus if the presence of A at a certain place on a certain date is in issue, evidence by B as to what he heard C say on the matter is hearsay, whether C said that he saw or did not see A on the occasion in question. At common law, however, the hearsay rule did not operate to prevent proof of the non-existence of a fact by a combination of (i) evidence of the absence of a recording of the fact in a written record; and (ii) testimony of an appropriate person to the effect that having regard to the method of compilation and custody of the record, one would have expected the fact, had it existed, to have been recorded. In *R v Patel*[87] the accused was charged, inter alia, with assisting the illegal entry of one Ashraf into the UK. In order to prove that Ashraf was an illegal immigrant, the prosecution called Mr Stone, an immigration officer at Manchester airport, who gave evidence that Ashraf's name was not in certain Home Office records of persons entitled to a certificate of registration in the UK and that at the material time Ashraf was therefore an illegal entrant. The Court of Appeal held that evidence relating to the Home Office records was inadmissible hearsay. However, Bristow J said:[88]

---

[84] (1901) 82 LT 347, Ch D at 349.

[85] See Law Com No 245 (1977) *Evidence in Criminal Proceedings: Hearsay and Related Topics*, Cm 3670.

[86] See per Lord Griffiths, one of the minority, at 349 and 353.

[87] [1981] 3 All ER 94. Cf *R v Muir* (1983) 79 Cr App R 153, CA.

[88] [1981] 3 All ER 94 at 96.

an officer responsible for their compilation and custody should have been called to give evidence that the method of compilation and custody is such that if Ashraf's name is not there, he must be an illegal entrant. It is not suggested that Mr Stone is such an officer.

This dictum was applied in *R v Shone*.[89] The appellant was convicted of receiving three vehicle springs which bore numbers which enabled them to be identified as having been dispatched by the manufacturers to L Ltd. Their arrival at L Ltd was recorded on stock record cards. The prosecution called two employees of L Ltd responsible for these records, who gave evidence that the cards were marked to indicate when the spare parts were sold or used and that the cards in respect of the three springs bore no such marks. On appeal, it was argued that the absence of a mark on the cards amounted to an inadmissible hearsay statement that the springs had been neither sold nor used by L Ltd. The Court of Appeal held that the evidence of the employees in explaining the significance of the absence of the marks was not hearsay evidence but direct evidence from which the jury were entitled to draw the inference that all three springs were stolen.

It is submitted that evidence of the kind admitted in *R v Shone* will remain admissible as direct evidence and is not covered by the 2003 Act simply because no statement has been made for the purposes of section 114. However, according to the Explanatory Notes to the 2003 Act,[90] the situation is governed by section 115(3):[91] 'where the assertion relates to a failure to record an event, sometimes known as negative hearsay, it will not be covered by Chapter 2 [Hearsay evidence] if it was not the purpose of the person who failed to record the event to cause anyone to believe that the event did not occur.' On that analysis, the evidence could now amount to hearsay on the basis that it was the purpose of the employees with responsibility for the cards, in not marking them, to cause anyone who had reason to inspect them, to believe that the springs in question had not been sold or used. However, it does not follow that the cards would be inadmissible: they could be admitted as business documents under section 117 of the Act or by exercise of the court's inclusionary discretion, ie on the basis that it is in the interests of justice for them to be admitted.

Statements produced by computers and mechanical and other devices
As we have seen, a 'statement', according to section 115(2), is any representation of fact or opinion 'made by a person' by whatever means. Thus, as the Explanatory Notes to the Act make clear:

> Subsection (2) preserves the present position whereby statements which are not based on human input fall outside the ambit of the hearsay rule. Tapes, films or photographs which directly record the commission of an offence and documents produced by machines which automatically record a process or event or perform calculations will not therefore be covered by Chapter 2 [Hearsay evidence].[92]

However, in *R v Cochrane*,[93] it was held that before the judge can decide whether computer printouts are admissible, whether as real evidence or as hearsay, it is necessary to call appropriate authoritative evidence to describe the function and operation of the computer. Where

---

[89] (1982) 76 Cr App R 72.
[90] Para 401.
[91] See above at 278, under **The meaning of hearsay in the Criminal Justice Act 2003**, *Implied assertions*.
[92] Para 402.
[93] [1993] Crim LR 48, CA.

a statement generated by a computer or other machine is based on information supplied by a person, for example a printout which is a copy of a letter or a record of other information supplied by a person, then under section 129 of the 2003 Act it will not be admissible as evidence of any fact stated unless it is proved that the information was accurate. Section 129 provides as follows:

> (1) Where a representation of any fact—
>   (a) is made otherwise than by a person, but
>   (b) depends for its accuracy on information supplied (directly or indirectly) by a person,
> the representation is not admissible in criminal proceedings as evidence of the fact unless it is proved that the information was accurate.
> (2) Subsection (1) does not affect the operation of the presumption that a mechanical device has been properly set or calibrated.[94]

The common law principle in effect preserved by section 115(2) was described by Lord Lane CJ in *R v Wood*[95] in the following terms.

> Witnesses, and especially expert witnesses, frequently and properly give factual evidence of the results of a physical exercise which involves the use of some equipment, device or machine. Take a weighing machine; the witness steps on the machine and reads a weight off the dial, receives a ticket printed with the weight, or even hears a recorded voice saying it. None of this involves hearsay evidence. The witness may have to be cross-examined as to whether he kept one foot on the ground; the accuracy of the machine may have to be investigated. But this does not alter the character of the evidence which has been given.

Other examples may be readily imagined. A witness gives evidence that a certain event occurred at a certain time because at that time he had consulted his wristwatch. A motorist gives evidence that, according to the speedometer of his car, he was travelling at a certain speed. A forensic scientist testifies that certain of his findings involved the use of an electronic calculator. In *R v Wood*[96] the appellant was convicted of handling stolen metal. In order to prove that metal found in his possession and metal retained from the stolen consignment had the same chemical composition, samples were subjected to an X-ray spectrometer and a neutron transmission monitor. The figures thus produced were then subjected to a laborious mathematical process in order that the percentage of the various metals in the samples could be stated as figures. That process was undertaken by a computer operated by chemists. At the trial, detailed evidence was given as to how the computer had been programmed and used. The Court of Appeal held that the trial judge had properly allowed evidence of the computer results to be admitted. The computer was used as a calculator, a tool which did not contribute its own knowledge but merely did a sophisticated calculation which could have been done manually. Lord Lane CJ said that the computer printout was not hearsay but more properly to be treated as a piece of real evidence, the actual proof and

---

[94] The common law presumption is normally cast in wider terms, namely that mechanical instruments that are usually in working order, were in working order at the time when they were used: see Ch 22, 654 under *Presumptions without basic facts*.

[95] (1982) 76 Cr App R 23, CA at 26.

[96] (1982) 76 Cr App R 23. See also *The Statue of Liberty* [1968] 1 WLR 739. Contrast *R v Pettigrew* (1980) 71 Cr App R 39, CA, a decision under the now repealed Criminal Evidence Act 1965.

relevance of which depended upon the evidence of the chemists, computer programmer, and other experts involved.[97]

The principle applies not only where the device in question processes information supplied to it, but also where the device itself gathers information. Thus in *R v Spiby*[98] a printout from a computerized machine used to monitor telephone calls and automatically record such information as the numbers from and to which the calls were made and the duration of the calls, was admitted as real evidence. It was held that where information is recorded by mechanical means without the intervention of a human mind, the record made by the machine is admissible.[99] *R v Governor of Brixton Prison, ex p Levin*[100] is to similar effect. The issue was whether L had used a computer terminal to gain unauthorized access to the computerized fund transfer service of a bank and to make fraudulent transfers of funds from accounts of clients of the bank to accounts which he controlled. Each request for transfer was processed automatically and a record of the transaction was copied to the computer's historical records. The House of Lords held that the printouts of screen displays of these records were admissible to prove the transfers of funds they recorded. Lord Hoffmann said: 'They do not assert that such transfers took place. They record the transfers ... The evidential status of the printouts is no different from that of a photocopy of a forged cheque.'[101]

Taylor v Chief Constable of Cheshire,[102] which involved out-of-court use of a video cassette recording, is perhaps best regarded as an example of the same principle. The recording had been made by a security camera and showed a person in a shop picking up an item and putting it inside his jacket. The recording was subsequently played to police officers who identified Taylor as the person shown. The recording was returned to the shop where, by accident, it was erased from the cassette. The officers were allowed to give evidence of what they had seen on the video and Taylor was convicted of theft. On appeal it was argued that, although the recording itself would have been admissible, the evidence of the officers was hearsay because they had not witnessed the theft personally or directly. The appeal was dismissed on the grounds that what the officers saw on the video was no different in principle from the evidence of a bystander who had actually witnessed the incident by direct vision. The evidence was admissible, although its weight and reliability had to be assessed carefully and, because identification was in issue, by reference to the usual criteria laid down in the form of guidelines in the case of *R v Turnbull*.[103] Those criteria, according to McNeill J, had to be

---

[97] See also *Castle v Cross* [1984] 1 WLR 1372, DC (an Intoximeter 3000 breath-test machine machine was a tool, albeit a sophisticated one, and that in the absence of any evidence that it was defective, the printout, the product of a mechanical device, fell into the category of real evidence).

[98] (1990) 91 Cr App R 186, CA.

[99] Cf *R v Shephard* (1991) 93 Cr App R 139, CA (till rolls not treated as real evidence because much of the information recorded on them was supplied by cashiers).

[100] [1997] AC 741, HL.

[101] See also *R (on the application of O'Shea) v Coventry Magistrates Court* [2004] ACD 50, DC.

[102] [1986] 1 WLR 1479. Cf *R v Fowden and White* [1982] Crim LR 588, CA, Ch 9. See also *R v Maqsud Ali* [1966] 1 QB 688, CCA (evidence of translators who had listened to a tape together with a transcript of their translation).

[103] [1977] QB 224, CA (see Ch 8). See also *R v Smith* [2009] 1 Cr App R 521, CA in which it was held that although it is not clear whether Code D applies, the safeguards which the Code is designed to put in place are as important in such cases as they are for other identifying witnesses. Accordingly, a record must be kept of the police officer's initial reactions, including what it is about the image that is said to have triggered any identification. However, in *R v Chaney* [2009] 1 Cr App R 512, CA, a failure by the officer to identify the features that led to his identification of the defendant from a photograph did not render the conviction unsafe, the Court of Appeal acknowledging that it

applied not only in relation to the camera itself, but also in relation to the visual display unit or recorded copy and to the officers who had watched the video-recording. In *R v Chaney,*[104] the Court of Appeal held that as the identification of an accused by a police officer from CCTV footage is an issue of recognition, rather than identification, a full Turnbull direction is inappropriate, although the judge should still make reference to the need for caution.

Under section 16(1)(a) of the Road Traffic Offenders Act 1988,[105] in proceedings for an offence of driving when unfit through drink or driving after consuming excess alcohol, evidence of the proportion of alcohol in a breath specimen may be given by a statement automatically produced by the device used to measure such proportion, together with a certificate, signed by a constable, that the statement relates to a specimen provided by the accused. In *Garner v DPP*[106] it was held that the purpose of this provision is to enable the facts to be established without the need to call anybody and therefore, if the certificate is defective, the printout remains admissible as real evidence[107] and can be linked to the accused by oral evidence. However, oral evidence of the reading, in the absence of the automatically produced statement, does not come up to the required standard of proof.[108]

Evasion

Given that the hearsay rule, at common law, could operate to exclude highly cogent evidence, and that a majority of the House of Lords in *Myers v DPP*[109] confirmed that it was for the legislature and not the judiciary to add to the classes of exception to the hearsay rule, it is perhaps not altogether surprising that both bar and bench employed a variety of devices with a view to evasion of the rule. One such device employed by counsel involved asking what a conversation or document was about, rather than what was said in the conversation or written in the document. Another involved asking a witness about certain acts which were of relevance only insofar as they gave rise to an inference as to the contents of an out-of-court statement. Thus counsel would ask, for example: 'Did you go to X?', 'As a result of something he said, did you then do something?', 'What did you do?' Both devices were held to be objectionable[110] and will remain equally objectionable in the case of hearsay which is inadmissible under the 2003 Act.

Judicial evasion of the rule was apparent in a number of cases, especially those in which the rule would otherwise operate to exclude apparently reliable identification evidence[111] or evidence which assisted in proving a negative.[112] Hopefully, now that judges have the

---

may be difficult to identify those features of a person that enable one to recognize him. For an evaluation of the law relating to identification from image evidence in light of the psychology research see R Costigan, 'Identification from CCTV: the risk of injustice' (2007) *Crim LR* 591.

[104] [2009] 1 Cr App R 512.

[105] Formerly s 10(3)(a) of the Road Traffic Act 1972.

[106] (1990) 90 Cr App R 178, DC.

[107] See 99n.

[108] *Owen v Chesters* [1985] RTR 191, DC.

[109] [1965] AC 1001.

[110] See per Lord Devlin in *Glinski v McIver* [1962] AC 726, HL at 780–1 and *R v Turner* [1975] QB 834, CA at 840. See also *R v Saunders* [1899] 1 QB 490, CCR.

[111] See, eg, *R v Osbourne, R v Virtue* [1973] QB 678, CA.

[112] See, eg, *R v Muir* (1983) 79 Cr App R 153, CA.

discretionary power under section 114(1)(d) to admit otherwise inadmissible hearsay if satisfied that it is the interests of justice to do so, they will no longer need to evade the rules.

Cases where a witness is unavailable

General

Under section 116 of the 2003 Act, first-hand hearsay statements, whether made orally or in a document, are admissible, on behalf of the prosecution or defence, subject to three conditions: first, that oral evidence given in the proceedings by the maker of the statement would be admissible as evidence of the matter stated, secondly, that the maker of the statement is identified, and thirdly, that the maker of the statement does not give oral evidence for one of a number of specified reasons, which include, for example, his unfitness to be a witness and fear. There is a fourth condition, the leave of the court, but this is imposed only where the maker of the statement does not give oral evidence through fear. This reflects the view of the Law Commission that whereas a general leave requirement would result in inconsistent and arbitrary decision-making, always allowing judges opposed to hearsay to find reasons to exclude it, a requirement of leave in the case of the statements of witnesses not giving oral evidence through fear was necessary to avoid the danger of witnesses making statements in the knowledge that they could later claim to be frightened and thereby avoid cross-examination.[113]

A statement which is admissible under section 116 may be excluded by the court in the exercise of its discretionary powers of exclusion, including the power to exclude evidence on which the prosecution propose to rely under section 78 of the 1984 Act. Section 78 is likely to take on a particular importance, in the case of evidence which is admissible under section 116 without the leave of the court, as the only means of excluding evidence to ensure that the accused receives a fair trial in accordance with Article 6 of the European Convention on Human Rights. Section 78 and the other statutory provisions relating to the discretion to exclude (and also those provisions which relate to the question of proof and to the capability and credibility of the maker of the statement) apply to hearsay admissible not only under section 116 but also under other sections of the Act, and for this reason they are considered separately, below.[114]

Section 116(1), (2), (3) and (5) provide as follows:

(1) In criminal proceedings a statement not made in oral evidence in the proceedings is admissible as evidence of any matter stated if—
   (a) oral evidence given in the proceedings by the person who made the statement would be admissible as evidence of that matter,
   (b) the person who made the statement (the relevant person) is identified to the court's satisfaction, and
   (c) any of the five conditions mentioned in subsection (2) is satisfied.
(2) The conditions are—
   (a) that the relevant person is dead;
   (b) that the relevant person is unfit to be a witness because of his bodily or mental condition;
   (c) that the relevant person is outside the United Kingdom and it is not reasonably practicable to secure his attendance;

---

[113] See paras 4.28 et seq and para 8.58.
[114] See below at 313, under **Other safeguards**, *Discretion to exclude.*

(d) that the relevant person cannot be found although such steps as it is reasonably practicable to take to find him have been taken;

(e) that through fear the relevant person does not give (or does not continue to give) oral evidence in the proceedings, either at all or in connection with the subject matter of the statement, and the court gives leave for the statement to be given in evidence.

(3) For the purposes of subsection (2)(e) 'fear' is to be widely construed and (for example) includes fear of the death or injury of another person or of financial loss.

...

(5) A condition set out in any paragraph of subsection (2) which is in fact satisfied is to be treated as not satisfied if it is shown that the circumstances described in that paragraph are caused—

(a) by the person in support of whose case it is sought to give the statement in evidence, or

(b) by a person acting on his behalf,

in order to prevent the relevant person giving oral evidence in the proceedings (whether at all or in connection with the subject matter of the statement).

Concerning the opening words of section 116(1), 'criminal proceedings', 'statement', and 'matter stated' bear the same meaning as in section 114 of the Act and call for no additional comment in the present context. The purpose of section 116(1)(a) is to prevent section 116 from being used to admit evidence which, if the maker of the statement were to be called as a witness, would be inadmissible because, for example, he has no personal knowledge of the facts,[115] or the evidence constitutes expert opinion evidence which the maker is not qualified to give, or the evidence is simply irrelevant to the facts in issue.

Section 116 applies to both oral and written statements. Having regard to the requirements of section 116(1)(a), (b), and (c), it is plainly very important, in the case of statements made in writing, to identify correctly the person who made the statement (the 'relevant person'), and for this purpose valuable guidance is provided by the decisions reached under section 23 of the 1988 Act. If A makes an oral statement within the hearing of B, who writes down what A says, and A reads and signs the document, then clearly A is the relevant person. Similarly, if A dictates the statement to B and checks that what B has written down is an accurate record of what he said (by reading it or having it read back to him) then, even without his signature, A is the relevant person.[116] It would be otherwise, however, if B made a written record of A's oral statement which was not agreed to or approved or accepted by A because in these circumstances A has made an oral statement, not a statement in a document.[117] B has made a statement in a document, but his statement would not be admissible under section 116 because the condition in section 116(1)(a) cannot be met—oral evidence by B would not be admissible of the matter stated because B has no direct or personal knowledge of those matters.

Section 116(1)(b) reflects the view that the risk of unreliability in the case of hearsay statements made by unidentified individuals is high and ensures that where a statement is admitted, the opposing party is in a position to impugn the credibility of the maker of the statement.[118]

The reasons for not calling the maker of the statement to give evidence
Section 116(2)(a) to (e) of the 2003 Act have been cast in words similar, but not identical, to those employed in section 23(2)(a), (b), and (c) of the 1988 Act and, subject to the significant

---

[115] See *R v JP* [1999] Crim LR 401, CA, a decision under s 23 of the Criminal Justice Act 1988.

[116] *R v McGillivray* (1992) 97 Cr App R 232, CA.

[117] Cf *Re D (a minor)* [1986] 2 FLR 189 Fam D.

[118] See below at 310, under **Other safeguards**, *Credibility*.

alterations to some of the wording, the decisions interpreting the earlier provisions provide very useful guidance as to the way in which the provisions of the 2003 Act are likely to be construed.

Relevant person unfit to be a witness because of his bodily or mental condition.   Unlike its statutory precursor, which referred to a person who was 'unfit to attend as a witness', section 116(2)(b) refers to a person who is 'unfit to be a witness'. However, it is submitted that subsection (2)(b) is likely to cover a person physically unable to get to court 'to be a witness' as well as a person able to attend court but unfit to give evidence, such as a witness who, by reason of his mental condition, is unable to recall the events in question.[119] Ordinarily, a witness who is not competent to give evidence because of lack of mental capacity will also be 'unfit to be a witness because of his ... mental condition' for the purposes of section 116(2)(b).[120]

Relevant person outside the United Kingdom and it is not reasonably practicable to secure his attendance.   The requirement in section 116(2)(c) is likely to be treated, as before, as a requirement of a strictly territorial nature and therefore will not be satisfied if the person who made the statement is a consul or embassy official in the UK.[121] The word 'attendance' was treated as capable of including the giving of evidence through a live television link from outside the United Kingdom under section 32 of the 1988 Act, but not examination of a witness on commission by a court in his country of residence.[122]

The question whether it is reasonably practicable to secure the attendance of the maker of the statement should be examined not at the time when the trial opens, but against the whole background to the case. Thus in *R v Bray*[123] an argument that it was not reasonably practicable to secure the attendance of a person because it was only when the trial started that it was realized that he was overseas, was rejected by the Court of Appeal: since the person had been overseas for some seven months before the trial began, it had not been shown that it was not reasonably practicable to secure his attendance at the trial. In *R v C*[124] it was held that what is reasonably practicable in section 116(2)(c) should be judged on the basis of the steps taken or not taken by the party seeking to ensure the attendance of the witness. This accords with the decision under the 1988 Act in *R v Maloney*[125] that the word 'practicable' is not equivalent to physically possible and must be construed in the light of the normal steps which would be taken to arrange the attendance of a witness at trial; and that the word 'reasonably' involved a further qualification of the duty, to secure attendance by taking the reasonable steps which a party would normally take to secure a witness's attendance having regard to the means and resources available to the parties. Thus the relevant factors, in deciding whether it is reasonably practicable to secure the attendance of a witness, include such matters as the cost of travel,[126] whether an offer was made to pay the fare, the reason for any refusal to attend, and

---

[119] See *R v Setz-Dempsey* (1994) 98 Cr App R 23, CA.

[120] *DPP v R* [2007] All ER (D) 176 (Jul), [2007] EWHC 1842. However, see also s 123(1), considered below at 309 under **Other safeguards**, *Capability*.

[121] *R v Jiminez-Paez* (1994) 98 Cr App R 239, CA.

[122] *R v Radak* [1999] 1 Cr App R 187, CA.

[123] (1988) 88 Cr App R 354, CA. This was a decision under s 68(2)(a)(ii) of the Police and Criminal Evidence Act 1984, the statutory precursor to s 23(2)(b) of the 1988 Act. The wording of the two provisions was identical.

[124] [2006] Crim LR 637, CA.

[125] [1994] Crim LR 525, CA.

[126] *R v Case* [1991] Crim LR 192, CA. See also *R v Castillo* [1996] 1 Cr App R 438, CA.

whether an approach was made to the person's employer or the British Embassy.[127] The fact that it is possible for a witness to attend does not on its own settle whether his attendance is reasonably practicable.[128] The test may be satisfied notwithstanding that (i) practicable arrangements have been made for the witness to attend and he has stated an intention to attend (because circumstances may occur at short notice which render it impracticable to secure his attendance on the day in question);[129] (ii) the witness chooses not to attend court (because the test is not whether it is reasonably practicable for the witness to attend);[130] or (iii) if there were to be an adjournment, the witness might attend at some future date (because there is no necessity to look to the future).[131]

Relevant person does not give oral evidence through fear. Section 116(2)(e) has been cast in very wide terms. It covers not only cases in which, through fear, the maker of the statement does not give (or continue to give) evidence in connection with the subject matter of the hearsay statement in question, but also cases in which, through fear, the maker of the statement does not give oral evidence at all or, having started to give oral evidence, 'dries up'. It covers, therefore, not only the potential witness who has been intimidated, but also those who are scared of the process—in some cases the ordeal—of going to court and giving evidence.[132] The question of fear or otherwise has to be judged at the time when the witness would be expected to give his evidence orally. However, there has to be a degree of sensible give and take. Sometimes, for example, the appropriate ruling will be sought before the trial to enable counsel for the prosecution to decide how the case should be opened to the jury. Equally, it may suffice to show continuing fear and that the witness has disappeared.[133]

Subsection (3) makes clear that 'fear' is to be widely construed, and it is equally clear from the examples given in the subsection, that it is not confined to fear arising out of threats or intimidation directed at the maker of the statement himself. Nonetheless, the subsection rather begs the question as to just *how* widely 'fear' is to be construed. Does it extend, for example, to the witness whose testimony is such that it will expose him to public humiliation or disgrace? If the authorities on section 23(3) of the 1988 Act—the statutory precursor to section 116(2)(e)—are any guidance, then the word will be construed very widely indeed. In *R v Acton Justices, ex p McMullen; R v Tower Bridge Magistrates' Court, ex p Lawlor*[134] the Divisional Court held that: 'Fear of what and whether that is relevant is a matter for the court's consideration in the given circumstances.' In that case, it was submitted that: (i) the test of fear is objective, not subjective; (ii) the fear should be based on reasonable grounds; and (iii) it is insufficient if there is fear in the absence of threats, interference, or intimidation after the commission of the offence. Rejecting these submissions, it was held: 'It will be sufficient that the court on the evidence is sure that the witness is in fear as a consequence of the commission

[127] *R v Gonzales de Arango* (1991) 96 Cr App R 399, CA, a decision under s 68(2) of the Police and Criminal Evidence Act 1984.
[128] *R v Castillo* [1996] 1 Cr App R 438, CA, followed in *R v Yu* [2006] Crim LR 643, CA.
[129] *R v Hurst* [1995] 1 Cr App R 82, CA.
[130] *R v French* (1993) 97 Cr App R 421, CA.
[131] *R v French*, ibid. But in the case of a *pre-trial* application, the court will obviously need to look to the future to see whether it would be practicable for the witness's attendance to be secured at the date of the trial: *R v Hurst* [1995] 1 Cr App R 82 at 92, CA.
[132] See generally paras 8.63–8.66, Law Com No 245.
[133] *R v H* [2001] Crim LR 815, CA.
[134] (1990) 92 Cr App R 98 at 105.

of the material offence or of something said or done subsequently in relation to that offence and the possibility of the witness testifying to it.' However, even this modest qualification of the statutory wording was rejected in *R v Martin*,[135] where the witness said he was fearful for his family, having been approached by a silent stranger whom he had previously seen outside his door. It was held that the court has no power, or reason, to qualify the statutory wording, which was wide enough to cover not only genuine witness intimidation, but also cases of fear based on mistake or misunderstanding.[136]

In *R v Horncastle*,[137] a decision under the 2003 Act, the Court of Appeal noted that fear includes the fear of being seen to give evidence and fear to which a police officer has contributed, although it ought not to extend to fear based upon inappropriate assurances by police officers given to a witness regarding the likelihood that his evidence will be read at trial.[138] Fear of the consequences for the accused also falls outwith the ambit of the statutory wording.[139]

The effect of section 116(5) is that a party cannot rely on section 116 where he, or someone acting on his behalf has, in order to prevent the maker of the statement giving oral evidence, brought about one of the conditions set out in section 116(2). This would be the case, for example, if the party in question had murdered the maker of the statement (section 116(2)(a)) or falsely imprisoned the witness at a secret location (section 116(2)(d)). Presumably, it is for the party resisting admissibility of the statement to establish such conduct.

The requirement of leave where the maker of the statement does not give oral evidence through fear

Leave may only be given under section 116(2)(e) if the court considers that the statement ought to be admitted in the interests of justice, having regard to the factors set out in section 116(4). Section 116(4) provides as follows:

> (4) Leave may be given under subsection (2)(e) only if the court considers that the statement ought to be admitted in the interests of justice, having regard—
> (a) to the statement's contents,
> (b) to any risk that its admission or exclusion will result in unfairness to any party to the proceedings (and in particular to how difficult it will be to challenge the statement if the relevant person does not give oral evidence),
> (c) in appropriate cases, to the fact that a direction under s 19 of the Youth Justice and Criminal Evidence Act 1999 (special measures for the giving of evidence by fearful witnesses etc) could be made in relation to the relevant person, and
> (d) to any other relevant circumstances.

Subsection (4)(c) in effect requires the court to consider whether the statement ought not to be admitted in the interests of justice because a special measures direction can be given under section 19 of the Youth Justice and Criminal Evidence Act 1999. Such a direction may be made, for example, to admit a video-recording of an interview of the witness as his evidence-in-chief,

---

[135] [1996] Crim LR 589, CA.

[136] See also *R v Fairfax* [1995] Crim LR 949, CA (all that needs to be proved is that the witness does not give evidence through fear) and *R v Arnold* [2005] Crim LR 56, CA.

[137] [2009] 4 All ER 183, CA.

[138] Ibid at [84], [86] and [88].

[139] See *R v L* [2009] 1 WLR 626, CA, in which the trial judge refused to admit the complainant's statement on this basis. The point was not considered on appeal.

and to admit a video-recording of the cross-examination and re-examination of the witness as his evidence under cross-examination and on re-examination.[140]

Subsection (4)(a), (b), and (d) are closely modelled on section 26(i), (ii), and (iii) of the Criminal Justice Act 1988, which set out the factors to which the court was to have regard in deciding whether to grant leave to admit a statement which had been prepared for the purposes of pending or contemplated litigation or of a criminal investigation and was admissible under either section 23 or section 24 of that Act. The significant differences are that the precursor to subsection 116(4)(b) referred to any risk of unfairness to 'the accused', and referred to the difficulty of 'controverting', rather than 'challenging' the statement. It is submitted that, subject to these differences, the following principles established in decisions reached under section 26 of the 1988 Act provide useful guidance as to the way in which the courts should approach their task under section 116(4) of the 2003 Act.

It is for the party seeking to admit the evidence to show that it should be admitted in the interests of justice, a test which involves considerations of fairness both to the defence and to the prosecution.[141] In *R v Cole*[142] it was held that a 'complex balancing exercise' is involved: 'the weight to be attached to the inability to cross-examine and the magnitude of any consequential risk that admission of the statement will result in unfairness to the accused, will depend in part on the court's assessment of the quality of the evidence shown by the contents of the statement.'[143] It was also held that the court should consider how far any potential unfairness arising from the inability to cross-examine on the statement may be effectively counterbalanced by a warning to the jury about the limitations of reading out a statement, ie the absence of opportunity to judge the maker's reliability and credibility in examination and cross-examination.[144] The court will also consider whether, having regard to other evidence available to the party seeking to admit the statement, the interests of justice will be properly served by excluding it.[145] *R v Cole* was applied in *R v Fairfax*[146] to admit statements whose makers did not give oral evidence through fear. Although the statements were the foundation of the case against the accused and without them the prosecution case was bound to have failed, it was held that they contained evidence of good quality and could be controverted by the accused himself. In *R v Kennedy*,[147] it was held that where a statement is admitted and the judge directs the jury on the disadvantages of not having the maker of the statement before them, it would not be proper to direct them to pay less attention to his evidence than to that of the live witnesses: it is for the jury alone to decide what weight they place on the evidence.[148]

[140] See Ch 5.

[141] *R v Patel* (1992) 97 Cr App R 294, CA.

[142] [1990] 1 WLR 866 at 877, CA.

[143] See, eg, *R v Thompson* [1999] Crim LR 747, CA, where a statement was admitted notwithstanding that its maker suffered from long-term alcohol-related problems and depression.

[144] There is no fixed rule as to the terms in which such a warning should be given: *R v Batt and Batt* [1995] Crim LR 240, CA. However, it is inappropriate to direct the jury that the statement is of less worth than the evidence of the witnesses in the case: *R v Greer* [1998] Crim LR 572, CA.

[145] *R v Cole* [1990] 1 WLR 866 at 877.

[146] [1995] Crim LR 949, CA.

[147] [1992] Crim LR 37, CA.

[148] Cf *R v Kennedy* [1994] Crim LR 50, CA.

The importance or otherwise of the contents of the statement to the issues in the case is a matter to be taken into account.[149] The fact that the statement goes to the crucial issues in the case does not necessarily count against its admission—it may be, for that reason, all the more important that it should be admitted.[150] Thus in *R v Setz-Dempsey*[151] it was held that where identification is in issue, neither the fact that the statement contains identification evidence, nor the fact that it is the only evidence against the accused, nor the inability to cross-examine will of itself be sufficient to justify exclusion—the quality of the evidence in the statement is the crucial factor.[152] However, in that case it was also held that, although not determinative, inability to probe evidence of identification by cross-examination is of the utmost significance and therefore the court should be cautious about admitting such evidence, especially where there are grounds for believing that, if the evidence had been given in person, it might have been significantly undermined by cross-examination. It is submitted that the court should be astute to examine all the circumstances in which the observation was made, such as the duration of the observation, the distance from which it was made, whether it was impeded in any way, the length of time between the observation and the time at which the statement was made, and so on.

If the evidence is tendered by the prosecution, its *admission* could result in unfairness to the accused; if it is tendered by an accused, its *exclusion* could result in unfairness to the accused but its *admission* could result in unfairness to a co-accused, in which case it seems that the court should conduct a balancing exercise which may result in the exclusion of the evidence on the basis that the damage done to the co-accused outweighs the benefit to the accused.[153] However, such an outcome would hardly be 'in the interests of justice' in a case in which, had the accused been tried separately, the evidence would have been of such benefit to him that it would have been admitted.[154]

In considering the risk of unfairness to the accused, particular regard must be had to the possible difficulty of controverting—under the 2003 Act, 'challenging'—the statement in the absence of its maker. The judge, in coming to a conclusion on the matter, should not embark on a detailed comparison between what might have happened if the maker of the statement had given oral evidence and had been cross-examined, and what might happen if his statement is admitted without him attending.[155] In *R v Cole*[156] it was held that the judge, in considering whether it was likely to be possible to controvert the statement, had properly taken into account not only the availability of prosecution witnesses for cross-examination, but also the availability of the accused or other witnesses to give evidence for the defence. Thus although the court cannot require to be told whether the accused intends to give evidence or to call witnesses, it is not required to assess the possibility of controverting the statement on the basis

---

[149] *R v French* (1993) 97 Cr App R 421, CA at 428.

[150] *R v Patel* (1992) 97 Cr App R 294, CA. See also *R v Batt and Batt* [1995] Crim LR 240, CA.

[151] (1994) 98 Cr App R 23, CA at 30, applying the principles enunciated by Lord Griffiths in *Scott v R* [1989] AC 1242, PC.

[152] See also *R v Dragic* [1996] 2 Cr App R 232, CA, although in that case the evidence was evidence of recognition and was challenged on the basis that the maker of the statement was either unreliable, possibly because of drink, or had lied.

[153] As in *R v Gregory and Mott* [1995] Crim LR 507, CA, a decision under s 25(2)(d) of the 1988 Act.

[154] *R v Duffy* [1999] QB 919, CA.

[155] *R v Radak* [1999] 1 Cr App R 187, CA.

[156] [1990] 1 WLR 866, CA.

that the accused will not give evidence or call witnesses.[157] In *R v Gokal*[158] it was submitted that the statutory provisions should be so construed as to exclude, as a means of controverting the statement, the possibility of the accused himself giving evidence in rebuttal, having regard to the right to silence and the entitlement to a fair hearing under Article 6 of the European Convention on Human Rights. The Court of Appeal rejected the submission and approved *R v Cole*. Noting that the possibilities for controverting the statement are wide, and include putting in issue the credibility of the maker of the statement,[159] the court held that although admission of the statement may make it more difficult for the accused to exercise his right of silence, the right is not abrogated. It was also held, after consideration of judgments of the European Commission and European Court of Human Rights, that, since the whole basis of the exercise of the discretion is to assess the interests of justice by reference to the risk of unfairness to the accused, 'our procedures appear to us to accord fully with our treaty obligations'.

In considering the risk of unfairness, it may also be relevant to consider whether the party against whom the statement is tendered had any opportunity of interviewing or making inquiries of the maker of the statement, but in any event this is another relevant circumstance (see now section 116(4)(d)).[160] 'Other relevant circumstances', for the purposes of section 116(4)(d), are also likely to include the circumstances in which the statement was made, including any attempts made to get the maker to make the statement in the way most favourable to the party seeking to rely upon it, the fact that the maker of the statement made prior inconsistent statements, whether oral or written,[161] and other facts or matters affecting his credibility. Thus, as to the last, although it may be in the interests of justice to admit the statement of a person even if he is of bad character, particularly when that bad character can readily be demonstrated, it should be excluded where he is so dishonest that the absence of an opportunity for the jury to assess him as a witness, to observe his demeanour and the manner in which he gives his evidence, would result in potential unfairness.[162] In *R v D*[163] the victim of an attempted rape was an 81-year-old woman whose police interview was recorded on video, at a time when she would have been competent as a witness. However, by the time of the preparatory hearing she was not mentally fit enough to give live evidence. The judge granted the prosecution leave to admit the video under sections 23 and 26 of the 1988 Act, taking the view that since he had concluded that it was in the interests of justice to admit the video, having balanced the interests of justice as between victim and defendant, then it was unlikely that there would be a breach of Article 6. On appeal it was held that the judge had adopted the right approach. Prima facie, the complainant had a right to have her complaint put before a jury, and the accused's rights would be protected because

---

[157] See also *R v Price* [1991] Crim LR 707, CA (notes of a conversation between the accused and another were properly admitted notwithstanding that the only way in which P could controvert the statement was by giving evidence himself, which he could not be required to do). See also *R v Samuel* [1992] Crim LR 189, CA and *R v Moore* [1992] Crim LR 882, CA.

[158] [1997] 2 Cr App R 266.

[159] See below at 310, under **Other safeguards**, *Credibility*.

[160] *R v Patel* (1993) 97 Cr App R 294, CA.

[161] *R v Sweeting and Thomas* [1999] Crim LR 75, CA, in which it was also held that if the statement is admitted, the logical course is to admit the inconsistent statement. See now under s 124(2)(c) of the 2003 Act, considered below at 310, under **Other safeguards**, *Credibility*.

[162] See *R v Lockley* [1995] 2 Cr App R 554, CA, a decision under s 25 of the Criminal Justice Act 1988, where the maker of the statement had demonstrated and indeed boasted about his remarkable ability to deceive.

[163] [2003] QB 90, CA.

he could call medical evidence to challenge the complainant's capacity to remember, understand, and say what happened. Furthermore, if it was in the interests of justice to admit the video, it was unlikely to be unfair under section 78 of the 1984 Act.

As we have already noted,[164] as a *general rule*, Article 6(1) and (3)(d) require an accused to be given a proper and adequate opportunity to challenge and question witnesses. However, the right set out in Article 6(3)(d) is not absolute but can be qualified provided that there is adherence to the overriding principle that a criminal trial must be fair to the accused and his rights respected. Thus, it is not necessarily incompatible with Article 6(1) and (3)(d) for a witness statement to be read where there has been no opportunity to question the witness at any stage of the proceedings. In *R v Sellick*[165] it was held that while the provisions in the 2003 Act should not be abused, where the court can be *sure* that an identified witness has been kept away by the accused and provided that (a) the quality of the evidence is compelling; (b) firm steps are taken to draw the jury's attention to aspects of the witness's credibility; and (c) a clear direction is given to the jury to exercise caution, there will be no breach of Article 6; the accused himself has denied himself the opportunity of examining the witness.[166] Where the court believes to a high degree of probability that an identified witness is being intimidated by or on behalf of the accused and is sure that the witness cannot be traced and brought before the court, there is no absolute rule that where his evidence is compelling and the only or decisive evidence, its admission will automatically lead to a breach of Article 6.[167] In *R v Horncastle*,[168] the Court of Appeal observed that Part 11, Chapter 2 of the 2003 Act contains a crafted code intended to ensure that evidence is admitted only when it is fair that it should be. Therefore, provided the provisions of the 2003 Act are observed, there is no breach of Article 6 and in particular Article 6(3)(d), even if the conviction is based solely or to a decisive degree on hearsay evidence admitted under the 2003 Act.

Business and other documents

Section 117 of the 2003 Act, which provides for the admissibility of hearsay statements contained in business and other documents, is modelled on section 24 of the 1988 Act, which it replaces, but there are a number of significant differences. Under section 117, statements contained in documents are admissible as evidence of any matter stated on five conditions. The first is that oral evidence would be admissible as evidence of the matter stated. The second is that the document was created or received by a person in the course of a trade, business, profession, or other occupation or as the holder of a paid or unpaid office. The third is that the person who supplied the information, who may be the same person as the creator or receiver of the document, had or may reasonably be supposed to have had personal knowledge of the matters dealt with. The fourth, which is only imposed if the information was supplied indirectly, is that each person through whom it was supplied, received it in the course of a trade, business, profession, or other occupation or as the holder of a paid or unpaid office. The fifth condition, which is imposed only where the statement was prepared for the

---

[164] See above at 272, under **General**, *Article 6 of the European Convention of Human Rights*.
[165] [2005] 1 WLR 3257, CA.
[166] Approving *R v M (KJ)* [2003] 2 Cr App R 322, CA.
[167] See also, following *R v Sellick*, *Grant v The State* [2006] 2 WLR 835, PC.
[168] [2009] 4 All ER 183, CA.

purpose of pending or contemplated criminal proceedings, or for a criminal investigation, is that the supplier of the information does not give oral evidence for one of the reasons set out in section 116(2)[169] or because he cannot reasonably be expected to have any recollection of the matters dealt with in the statement. A statement admissible under section 117 may be excluded by the court in the exercise of its discretionary powers of exclusion.[170]

Section 117 provides as follows:

(1) In criminal proceedings a statement contained in a document is admissible of any matter stated if—

   (a) oral evidence given in the proceedings would be admissible as evidence of that matter,

   (b) the requirements of subsection (2) are satisfied, and

   (c) the requirements of subsection (5) are satisfied, in a case where subsection (4) requires them to be.

(2) The requirements of this subsection are satisfied if—

   (a) the document or the part containing the statement was created or received by a person in the course of a trade, business, profession or other occupation, or as the holder of a paid or unpaid office,

   (b) the person who supplied the information contained in the statement (the relevant person) had or may reasonably be supposed to have had personal knowledge of the matters dealt with, and

   (c) each person (if any) through whom the information was supplied from the relevant person to the person mentioned in paragraph (a) received the information in the course of a trade, business, profession or other occupation, or as the holder of a paid or unpaid office.

(3) The persons mentioned in paragraphs (a) and (b) of subsection (2) may be the same person.

(4) The additional requirements of subsection (5) must be satisfied if the statement—

   (a) was prepared for the purposes of pending or contemplated criminal proceedings, or for a criminal investigation, but

   (b) was not obtained pursuant to a request under section 7 of the Crime (International Co-operation) Act 2003 or an order under paragraph 6 of Schedule 13 to the Criminal Justice Act 1988 (which relate to overseas evidence).[171]

(5) The requirements of this subsection are satisfied if—

   (a) any of the five conditions mentioned in section 116(2) is satisfied (absence of relevant person etc), or

   (b) the relevant person cannot reasonably be expected to have any recollection of the matters dealt with in the statement (having regard to the length of time since he supplied the information and all other circumstances).

(6) A statement is not admissible under this section if the court makes a direction to that effect under subsection (7).

(7) The court may make a direction under this subsection if satisfied that the statement's reliability as evidence for the purpose for which it is tendered is doubtful in view of—

   (a) its contents,

   (b) the source of the information contained in it,

   (c) the way in which or the circumstances in which the information was supplied or received, or

   (d) the way in which or the circumstances in which the document concerned was created or received.

---

[169] See above at 288, under **Cases where a witness is unavailable**.

[170] See below at 313, under **Other safeguards**, *Discretion to exclude*.

[171] These provisions relate to the issue of letters of request.

As to the opening words of section 117(1), 'criminal proceedings', 'statement', and 'matter stated' bear the same meaning as in section 114 of the Act and call for no additional comment in the present context. The words of section 117(1)(a) bear the same meaning as in section 116(1)(a) of the Act but whereas under section 116(a) the test is whether oral evidence 'given ... by the person who made the statement' would be admissible, under section 117(1)(a) the test is simply whether oral evidence would be admissible, ie oral evidence given by anyone. A 'document' is defined by section 134(1) as 'anything in which information of any description is recorded', a description wide enough to include, inter alia, maps, plans, graphs, drawings, photographs, discs, audio-tapes, video-tapes, films, microfilms, negatives, and computer-generated print-outs. Under section 117(2)(a), the document (or part) containing the statement must be 'created or received' by a person in the course of a trade (or business etc). A document, given its wide definition, may be created in a number of different ways: by writing or typing (a document in writing); by drawing (a map or plan); by development (a photograph); or by recording (discs, tapes, sound-tracks, etc). A document may be received by hand, by post, by facsimile machine, by e-mail, or by linked computers. Whatever the means by which the document is created or received, the act of creation or receipt must be in the course of a trade (or business etc).[172] Under section 117(2)(b), the information contained in the document must have been supplied by a person who had, 'or may reasonably be supposed to have had', personal knowledge of the matters dealt with,[173] wording which allows the court, in appropriate circumstances, to infer personal knowledge on the part of the supplier.[174] Section 117(3) makes clear that the creator of the document and the supplier of the information may be one and the same person; judged in terms of potential reliability, it would be odd if a hearsay statement contained in a trade, business, or related document were to be admissible *only* if at least second-hand.

Under section 117(2)(c), if the information contained in the document was supplied indirectly, each intermediary through whom it was supplied must have received it in the course of a trade (or business etc). It is the act of *receiving*, as opposed to the act of supplying, which must have been performed in the course of a trade (or business etc). Thus, if A, a businessman and an intermediary (under section 117(2)(c)), supplies information to B, another businessman and intermediary, then provided that both A and B receive the information in the course of their respective businesses, it matters not that A is not acting in the course of his business when he supplies the information to B. The trade (or business etc) of one intermediary need not be the same trade (or business etc) as that of either another intermediary or the creator or receiver of the document.

Under section 117(4) and (5), unlike section 116, the requirement that the person who supplied the information be unable to give oral evidence for one of the specified reasons (section 116(2)(a)–(e)), is imposed only in the case of 'a statement ... prepared for the purposes of pending or contemplated criminal proceedings, or for a criminal investigation'. This phrase is wide enough to include a witness statement taken by a police officer, a statement from

---

[172] The fact that a document created by a company's officer effects a corrupt payment does not prevent it from being a document 'created ... in the course of a ... business': see *R v Foxley* [1995] 2 Cr App R 523 at 538, CA. See also *R v Gray* [2007] EWCA Crim 2658.

[173] See *R v Humphris* (2005) 169 JP 441, followed in *R v Ainscough* [2006] Crim LR 635, CA (officers lacking knowledge of the details of offences in police records of convictions).

[174] See *R v Foxley* [1995] 2 Cr App R 523 at 536. See also *R v Schreiber and Schreiber* [1988] Crim LR 112, CA, a decision under s 1 of the Criminal Evidence Act 1965.

a potential witness recorded by a police officer in his notebook, a statement of a potential witness, an attendance note of an interview with a potential witness made by an accused's solicitor,[175] and a custody record.[176] The expression 'statement prepared for the purposes of contemplated criminal proceedings' has been construed to include a statement made in the course of criminal proceedings, so that a transcript of the evidence of a witness at a previous trial is admissible provided that the maker of the statement is unable to give evidence for one of the reasons specified.[177] Another difference from section 116 is the additional reason set out in section 117(5)(b), namely that the supplier of the information cannot reasonably be expected to have any recollection of the matters dealt with in the statement.[178] The word 'statement' in section 117(5)(b) bears the same meaning as in section 114 and other sections of Chapter 2 of Part 11 of the 2003 Act[179] and does not mean the entire contents of the document. Thus if the supplier cannot reasonably be expected to have any recollection of matters dealt with in only some of the statements contained in a document, those statements may be admitted notwithstanding that he can recollect matters dealt with in other statements contained in the document.[180]

Where the requirements of section 117(1), (2), and (5) are met, the court may use section 117(6) and (7) to direct that the statement in question is nonetheless inadmissible, if satisfied that it is of doubtful reliability. It may reach this conclusion having regard to (a) its contents, which, for example, may be internally inconsistent, or inconsistent with a prior statement from the same source; (b) the source of the information, who, for example, may be shown to be dishonest or unreliable; and (c) the mode and circumstances of the supply or receipt of the information; or (d) the mode and circumstances of the creation or receipt of the document, either of which may demonstrate the likelihood of inaccuracy in the contents of the statement.

Admissibility in the interests of justice

The Law Commission was of the view that, in order to prevent injustice, there should be an inclusionary discretion to render admissible reliable hearsay which would not otherwise be admitted. It recognized that such a discretion, or 'safety valve', would introduce the risks of inconsistency and unpredictability, but believed that without such a discretion its proposed reforms would be too rigid. Some 'limited flexibility' needed to be incorporated. It therefore proposed that a hearsay statement should be admitted if 'despite the difficulties there may be in challenging the statement, its probative value is such that the interests of justice require it to be admissible'.[181] However, the inclusionary discretion in the 2003 Act has been cast more broadly and therefore relaxes the hearsay rule to a greater degree. Under section 114(1)(d) of the 2003 Act, it will be recalled, a statement not made in oral evidence in the proceedings is

---

[175] Per Kennedy J, obiter, in *R v Cunningham* [1989] Crim LR 435, CA, a decision under s 68 of the Police and Criminal Evidence Act 1984.

[176] *R v Hogan* [1997] Crim LR 349, CA.

[177] *R v Lockley* [1995] 2 Cr App R 554, CA. However, the expression does not extend to a licence issued to a serving prisoner on his release from imprisonment: *West Midlands Probation Board v French* [2009] 1 WLR 1715, DC.

[178] This reason cannot be established if the supplier has some other document on the basis of which he can refresh his memory in court: per Buxton LJ in *R v Derodra* [2000] 1 Cr App R 41, CA at 44.

[179] See above.

[180] *R v Carrington* (1993) 99 Cr App R 376, CA.

[181] Cl 9, Draft Bill, Law Com No 245.

admissible as evidence of any matter stated if 'the court is satisfied that it is in the interests of justice for it to be admissible'.

Section 114(1)(d) is open to use by both the prosecution and defence.[182] It applies to both oral and written statements and can be used to admit first-hand, second-hand, or multiple hearsay. Although it is likely to be used as a last resort, in the sense that it will only be relied upon if the statement in question is not admissible under some other provision of the 2003 Act, some other statutory provision, or one of the preserved common-law rules, there is nothing in the section which suggests that section 114(1)(d) is a limited inclusionary discretion to be used only exceptionally. Thus, the Divisional Court has observed, it is inappropriate to describe it as 'safety valve'.[183] It follows that the provision cannot be read so as to subordinate it to the other exceptions.[184] Nevertheless, the section must not be lightly applied and the Court of Appeal has emphasized that that the greatest care must be taken before admitting an out-of-court statement under section 114(1)(d).[185] Moreover, the inclusionary discretion should not be applied so as to render section 116 nugatory and the Court of Appeal has shown a reluctance to admit statements by witnesses who are not 'unavailable' for one of the statutory reasons contained in section 116(2),[186] although the admission of evidence relating to an *uncontentious* matter has been held to be 'plainly in the interests of justice' even where the party calling the witness had taken such inadequate steps to find him that it was unable to satisfy the provisions of section 116(2)(d). Section 114(1)(d) obviously should not be used if, having regard to Article 6 of the European Convention on Human Rights, this would result in an unfair trial.[187]

The Court of Appeal will only interfere with a decision of a trial judge under section 114(1)(d) if it was outwith the range of reasonable decisions, because the trial judge is best placed to assess accurately the fairness of admitting evidence in the context of the trial as a whole.[188] In deciding whether to exercise the power contained in section 114(1), the trial judge must have regard to the non-exhaustive list of factors set out in section 114(2).[189] Section 114(2) provides as follows:

(2) In deciding whether a statement not made in oral evidence should be admitted under subsection (1)(d), the court must have regard to the following factors (and to any others it considers relevant)—

---

[182] The interests of justice will not necessarily point in the same direction for both the prosecution and the defence. Moreover, Since the burden of proving the case is on the prosecution, very considerable care will need to be taken in any case in which a hearsay statement would provide the prosecution with a case, when otherwise it would have none: *R v Y* [2008] 1 WLR 1683, CA at [59]. The test to be applied to a defendant on a serious criminal charge will often be less exacting than that which would apply to the prosecution but the interests of justice are synonymous not with the interests of the defendant but with the public interest in arriving at the right conclusion in the case: *R v Marsh* [2008] All ER (D) 338 (Jul), [2008] EWCA Crim 1816.

[183] *Sak v CPS* (2008) 172 JP 89 at [26].

[184] See *R v Y* [2008] 1 WLR 1683, CA at [47].

[185] *R v Y* [2008] ibid.

[186] See *R v O'Hare* [2006] EWCA Crim 2512 at [30]; *R v Y* [2008] 1 WLR 1683, CA at [60]; *R v Marsh* [2008] All ER (D) 338 (Jul), [2008] EWCA Crim 1816; and *R v Sadiq* (2009) 173 JP 471, CA at [24]; *R v Z* [2009] 3 All ER 1015, CA at [20] and [24].

[187] See above at 272 under **General**, *Article 6 of the European Convention on Human Rights*.

[188] *R v Musone* [2007] 1 WLR 2467, CA at [20]. See also *R v Finch* [2007] 1 WLR 1645 at [23].

[189] The Court of Appeal will be more willing to interfere with a judge's decision under s 114(1)(d) where a judge fails to take into account, or fails to show that he has taken into account, the factors set out in s 114(2): *R v Z* [2009], 3 All ER 1015, CA.

(a) how much probative value the statement has (assuming it to be true) in relation to a matter in issue in the proceedings, or how valuable it is for the understanding of other evidence in the case;

(b) what other evidence has been, or can be, given on the matter or evidence mentioned in paragraph (a);

(c) how important the matter or evidence mentioned in paragraph (a) is in the context of the case as a whole;

(d) the circumstances in which the statement was made;

(e) how reliable the maker of the statement appears to be;

(f) how reliable the evidence of the making of the statement appears to be;

(g) whether oral evidence of the matter stated can be given and, if not, why it cannot;

(h) the amount of difficulty involved in challenging the statement;

(i) the extent to which that difficulty would be likely to prejudice the party facing it.

As to section 114(2)(a), evidence of considerable importance that would undermine the defence and point powerfully to a conviction makes the other factors even more significant, and in particular section 114(2)(g).[190] The Court of Appeal has stressed that section 114(2)(g) refers to the inability of a witness to give evidence rather than their reluctance to do so and it will be rare that potentially prejudicial evidence will be admitted under section 114(1)(d) where a witness is available, although reluctant, and the reluctance is not due to fear.[191] The correct approach to section 114(2)(h) is to focus on the difficulty in assessing the veracity of the declarant's statement and not the difficulties of challenging the witness who reports the statement,[192] which ought to be taken into account under section 114(2)(f).

In *R v Taylor*[193] two prosecution witnesses named T as a participant in an attack, having been told his name by someone else. The trial judge admitted this evidence under section 114(1)(d), although he was unable to reach a conclusion on a number of the factors set out in section 114(2), such as the circumstances in which the informant's statement was made, his reliability, and whether he could give oral evidence. The Court of Appeal held that section 114(2) requires an exercise of judgment in the light of the factors identified and does not require an investigation, resulting in some cases in the hearing of evidence, in order that the judge may reach a conclusion established by reference to each or any of the factors. On that basis, it was held that the judge's approach could not be challenged. The decision is somewhat surprising. As one commentator has submitted:[194]

Surely the judge should engage in some degree of investigation and, in cases where the hearsay evidence is of great importance, this might involve receiving evidence. As to the outcome, and the value of the case as a precedent in that respect, it is important to note that that the court seems to have been heavily influenced by the 'considerable body of evidence' against T apart from the naming of him by the two witnesses.[195]

---

[190] *R v Z* [2009], ibid at [24].

[191] *R v Z* [2009], ibid. See also *R v Y* [2008] 1 WLR 1683 at [60] and *R v Khan* [2009] EWCA Crim 86 at [15].

[192] *R v Marsh* [2008] All ER (D) 338 (Jul), [2008] EWCA Crim 816, at [19].

[193] [2006] 2 Cr App R 222, CA.

[194] D Ormerod, '*R v Taylor*' (case comment) at [2006] *Crim LR* 640.

[195] See also *Maher v DPP* (2006) 170 JP 441, DC, considered below in the context of multiple hearsay.

The Law Commission gave three examples of how its 'safety valve' might be used. The first two examples, based on the facts of *Sparks v R*[196] and *R v Thomas*[197] are not entirely convincing.[198] The third example was based on the facts of *R v Cooper*.[199] Charged with assault, the accused was not allowed to introduce a hearsay statement made by a third party, of similar appearance to the accused, to a friend of his, that he had committed the assault. Subsequent authorities confirmed that an out-of-court confession, by a third party, to the offence with which the accused is charged, is inadmissible,[200] decisions which have been justified on the grounds that, since it is for the legislature, not the judiciary, to create new exceptions to the hearsay rule,[201] to hold otherwise 'would be to create a very significant and, many might think, a dangerous new exception'.[202] The obvious danger is the ease with which a third party confession may be manufactured or fabricated coupled with the fact that such a confession, by itself, could lead the jury to entertain 'a reasonable doubt'. However, each case will now involve the court in a complex balancing exercise, having regard to the factors set out in section 114(2) in the context of the particular facts of the case. It is not without significance, for instance, that in the example given by the Law Commission, the third party was of similar appearance to the accused. *R v Finch*[203] concerned a confession by D2, who pleaded guilty, exonerating D1, D2 being 'reluctant' to give evidence for reasons that were not compelling. The trial judge concluded that the interests of justice did not call for the evidence to be admitted on behalf of D1. Although it was plainly of substantial probative value and without it there was only the evidence of D1 himself, and therefore it was of considerable importance in the context of the case as a whole, oral evidence could be given by D2, his reliability was open to question if he was not prepared to support in the witness box what he had said to the police, and there would be difficulties for the prosecution in challenging his statement in his absence. The principal factor was that D2 was compellable, and therefore could have been called and subjected to cross-examination.[204] The Court of Appeal upheld the decision, observing that section 114(2) calls for the exercise of judgment by the trial judge with which it should only interfere if it was exercised on wrong principles or if the conclusion reached was outside the band of legitimate decisions available.

While each case turns upon its own facts the following are illustrative of circumstances in which the Court of Appeal has approved the use of section 114(1)(d) to admit otherwise inadmissible hearsay evidence. A wife having made a witness statement undermining her husband's defence to a charge of raping his daughter, having subsequently retracted it and, not being compellable by virtue of section 80 of the 1984 Act, having refused to testify, the

---

[196] [1964] AC 964, PC.

[197] [1994] Crim LR 745, CA.

[198] For a critique, see the 6th edition of this work at 314.

[199] [1969] 1 QB 267, CA.

[200] *R v Turner* (1975) 61 Cr App R 67, CA. See also *R v Callan* (1994) 98 Cr App R 467, CA. As to the admissibility, for an accused, of a confession made by a *co-accused*, see s 76A, Police and Criminal Evidence Act 1984, Ch 13.

[201] See *Myers v DPP* [1965] AC 1001, HL.

[202] Per Lord Bridge in *R v Blastland* [1985] [1986] AC 41at 53, HL. Contrast *Chambers v Mississippi* 410 US 295 (1973) (US Sup Court): the exclusion of the confessions of a third party deprives the accused of a fair trial.

[203] [2007] 1 WLR 1645, CA.

[204] See also *R v Marsh* [2008] All ER (D) 338 (Jul), [2008] EWCA Crim 1816, in which it was stated per Hughes LJ at [25] that there ought to be pause before admitting hearsay evidence when the declarant is available to be seen by the jury and his stance in relation to the assertion which it is sought to prove can be discovered.

prosecution were permitted to adduce the statement.[205] Where the victim of an attempted murder, and a crucial witness for the prosecution, sustained horrific injuries during the offence, as a result of which he was incapable of giving evidence other than through an intermediary, the transcript of his evidence at the first trial was admissible at a retrial.[206] Where an accused charged with murder made admissions to his girlfriend, the prosecution were permitted to adduce the confession at the trial of the accomplice as evidence of his involvement in the offence.[207] Where an accused refused to agree the circumstances of a conviction admissible under the provisions of the 2003 Act relating to the admission of evidence of bad character, the prosecution were permitted to adduce a summary of the content of his police interviews and the evidence he gave at the trial for that offence.[208]

Previous inconsistent statements of witnesses

Under section 3 of the Criminal Procedure Act 1865 (the 1865 Act), a party calling a witness who proves to be hostile may, by leave of the judge, prove that he has made at other times a statement inconsistent with his testimony.[209] Under section 4 of the 1865 Act, if a witness, upon cross-examination as to a previous inconsistent statement, does not distinctly admit that he made such a statement, proof may be given by the cross-examining party that he did in fact make it. Proof of the statement is governed by both sections 4 and 5 of the 1865 Act, section 4 applying to both oral and written statements, and section 5 applying to written statements only.[210] If the hostile witness, or the witness under cross-examination, adopts the contents of the previous statement, then they become part of his evidence and will be evidence of the matter stated. However, as the law stood prior to the coming into force of section 119(1) of the 2003 Act, if, in criminal cases, the witness did not admit to making the statement and it was proved that he did in fact make it, the statement was not introduced as evidence of the matter stated, but went merely to his credit. Under section 119(1), the statement is admitted as evidence of any matter stated of which oral evidence by the witness would be admissible. The reasoning of the Law Commission was that if the tribunal of fact is trusted to decide that the witness lacks credibility and his testimony should be disregarded, they should also be free to accept the previous statement as reliable.[211] Section 119(1) provides as follows:

(1) If in criminal proceedings, a person gives oral evidence and—
    (a) he admits making a previous inconsistent statement, or
    (b) a previous inconsistent statement made by him is proved by virtue of section 3, 4 or 5 of the Criminal Procedure Act 1865,
the statement is admissible as evidence of any matter stated of which oral evidence by him would be admissible.

Section 119(1) has the merit of removing from the tribunal of fact, in this particular context, the difficult concept of a previous statement being admitted not as evidence of the matters

---

[205] *R v L* [2009] 1 WLR 626, CA.

[206] *R v Sadiq* (2009) 173 JP 471, CA.

[207] *R v Y* [2008] 1 WLR 1683, CA. See also *R v McLean* [2008] 1 Cr App R 156, CA, *R v Ibrahim* [2008] 4 All ER 208 and *R v B* [2008] All ER (D) 108 (Jul), [2008] EWCA Crim 365.

[208] *R v Steen* [2008] 2 Cr App R 380, CA.

[209] See Ch 6, 183, under **Unfavourable and hostile witnesses**.

[210] See Ch 7, 197, under **Cross-examination**, **Previous inconsistent statements**.

[211] Para 10.89, Law Com No 245.

stated but as evidence to undermine the credibility of its maker as a witness in the case. It is a radical change in the law and is a powerful tool in relation to hostile witnesses.[212] Section 119(1) is subject to the discretionary powers to exclude evidence on which the prosecution propose to rely; and, in jury trials in which the case against the accused is based wholly or partly on such a statement, the court has the power under section 125 of the Act to direct the jury to acquit if the evidence provided by the statement is so unconvincing that the conviction of the accused would be unsafe.[213] In cases where the statement is left before the jury, and the witness maintains that it is untrue, a careful direction is called for.[214]

Other previous statements of witnesses

At common law, the general rule against previous consistent statements prevents a witness from being asked in examination-in-chief about a former out-of-court statement made by him and consistent with his testimony. Under the general rule, such a statement is excluded as evidence of consistency and is also inadmissible hearsay, except to the extent that it is admissible under the 2003 Act.[215] As with other types of hearsay, there is the usual danger of manufactured evidence, and to allow a witness to give evidence of a previous statement which is consistent with his testimony is to encourage the reception of superfluous evidence. On the other hand, one of the main justifications of the hearsay rule, the impossibility of cross-examining the maker of the statement, does not apply. Furthermore, an out-of-court statement made shortly after the events to which it relates, and while those events are fresh in the memory, is likely to be more reliable than testimony at a trial which takes place some months or years later. Under section 120 of the 2003 Act, a provision of compromise, the previous statements of a witness only become admissible as evidence of the matters stated in five situations, four of which are plainly based upon, and in some cases expanded versions of, the rather technical common law exceptions to the rule against previous consistent or self-serving statements. It provides as follows.

(1) This section applies where a person (the witness) is called to give evidence in criminal proceedings.
(2) If a previous statement by the witness is admitted as evidence to rebut a suggestion that his oral evidence has been fabricated, that statement is admissible as evidence of any matter stated of which oral evidence by the witness would be admissible.
(3) A statement made by the witness in a document—
    (a) which is used by him to refresh his memory while giving evidence,
    (b) on which he is cross-examined, and
    (c) which as a consequence is received in evidence in the proceedings,
    is admissible as evidence of any matter stated of which oral evidence by him would be admissible.
(4) A previous statement by the witness is admissible as evidence of any matter stated of which oral evidence by him would be admissible, if
    (a) any of the following three conditions is satisfied, and
    (b) while giving evidence the witness indicates that to the best of his belief he made the statement, and that to the best of his belief it states the truth.

---

[212] See Ch 6.
[213] See below at 312, under **Other safeguards**, *Stopping the case where the evidence is unconvincing*.
[214] See *R v Joyce* [2005] All ER (D) 309 (Jun), [2005] EWCA Crim 1785; and see Specimen Direction 28 for the model direction, available at <http://www.jsboard.co.uk/criminal_law/cbb/index.htm>.
[215] See Ch 6.

(5) The first condition is that the statement identifies or describes a person, object or place.

(6) The second condition is that the statement was made by the witness when the matters stated were fresh in his memory but he does not remember them, and cannot reasonably be expected to remember them, well enough to give oral evidence of them in the proceedings.

(7) The third condition is that—

    (a) the witness claims to be a person against whom an offence has been committed,

    (b) the offence is one to which the proceedings relate,

    (c) the statement consists of a complaint made by the witness (whether to a person in authority or not) about conduct which would, if proved, constitute the offence or part of the offence,

    (d) the complaint was made as soon as could reasonably be expected after the alleged conduct,

    (e) the complaint was not made as a result of a threat or promise, and

    (f) before the statement is adduced the witness gives oral evidence in connection with its subject matter.

(8) For the purposes of subsection (7) the fact that the complaint was elicited (for example, by a leading question) is irrelevant unless a threat or a promise was involved.

Statements in rebuttal of allegations of recent fabrication

Under section 120(2), a previous oral or written statement of a witness is admissible as evidence of any matter stated of which oral evidence by him would be admissible 'if ... admitted as evidence to rebut a suggestion that his oral evidence has been fabricated', ie if admitted under the exception to the rule against previous consistent statements which arises when, in cross-examination of the witness, it is suggested to him that the account given by him in his testimony is a recent invention or fabrication.[216]

Statements in documents used to refresh the memory

Section 120(3), which mirrors an exception to the rule against previous consistent statements, applies where the witness is cross-examined on a memory-refreshing document and, as a consequence, it 'is received in evidence in the proceedings', ie where the whole document is received in evidence at common law. This happens when a party, or counsel on his behalf, in cross-examining the witness on the memory-refreshing document, asks questions about matters derived from parts of the document not used by the witness to refresh his memory.[217]

Statements identifying or describing a person, object, or place

Under section 120(5), when read in conjunction with section 120(4), a previous oral or written statement of a witness identifying or describing a person, object, or place, will be admissible as evidence of any matter stated of which oral evidence by him would be admissible if, in evidence, he indicates that to the best of his belief he made the statement and it states the truth. Section 120(5) is based on the exception to the rule against previous consistent statements in the case of previous *identification of the accused* but, in accordance with the recommendation of the Law Commission, extends the principle to the identification, or description, of any person, object, or place.[218]

---

[216] See further Ch 6, 172, under **Previous consistent or self-serving statements.**

[217] See further Ch 6, 163, under **Refreshing the memory.**

[218] See further Ch 6, 172, under **Previous consistent or self-serving statements.**

Statements made when the matters were fresh in the memory

Section 120(6) operates to abolish the common law fiction that when a witness does not remember certain matters, or does not remember them well enough to give evidence about them, and therefore 'refreshes his memory' by reference to a statement made by him when the matters stated were fresh in his memory, it is the oral testimony of the witness which constitutes the evidence in the case. Many commentators over many years have submitted that it would be more principled to regard the statement as a variety of admissible hearsay. This is achieved by section 120(6), which applies to previous statements whether made orally or in a document, provided that the witness gives the indications required by section 120(4).[219]

Statements consisting of a complaint about the alleged offence

Section 120(7) is based on the exception to the rule against previous consistent statements in the case of recent complaints in sexual cases.[220] However, the new statutory provisions do not codify the law, but are freestanding and provide their own criteria.[221] As stated in the fifth edition of this book,[222] what is curious is not that the common law exception had survived, but that for no good reason it had been confined to sexual cases. Section 120(7), in accordance with the recommendations of the Law Commission[223] and, long before that, the Criminal Law Revision Committee,[224] extends the principle to a previous statement, whether oral or written, made by a person against whom *any* offence has been committed, provided that it is an offence to which the proceedings relate, and that the statement consists of a complaint about conduct which would, if proved, constitute the offence or part of the offence to which the proceedings relate.[225]

There are a number of other conditions to be met, in addition to the requirement that the witness give the indications required by section 120(4). Section 120(7)(d) requires that the complaint was made as soon as could reasonably be expected after the alleged conduct. This requirement reflects the requirement at common law that a recent complaint in a sexual case is only admissible by way of exception to the rule against previous consistent statements 'when it is made at the first opportunity after the offence which reasonably offers itself'.[226] The common law authorities are likely to offer valuable guidance to the way in which section 120(7)(d) is applied. It has been held, for example, that whether a complaint was made as soon as was reasonably practicable after the occurrence of the offence is a question of fact and degree to be decided by the judge in each case and that the answer will depend on the circumstances, including the character of the complainant and the relationship between the complainant and the person to whom she might have complained but did not do so. Victims often need time before they can bring themselves to tell what has happened, and whereas some will find it impossible to complain to anyone other than a parent or member of their family,

---

[219] See further Ch 6, 163, under **Refreshing the memory.**

[220] See Ch 6, 172, under **Previous consistent or self-serving statements**.

[221] *R v O* [2006] 2 Cr App R 405, CA.

[222] At 153.

[223] Paras 10.53–10.61, Law Com No 245 (1997).

[224] Para 232, 11th report, Cm 4991 *Evidence (General)* (1972).

[225] *R v T* [2008] EWCA Crim 484: s 120(7) is restricted to complaints about offences which are on the indictment and does not include complaints about other offences, eg, offences admitted as evidence of the defendant's bad character.

[226] Per Ridley J [1905] 1 KB 551, CCR at 561. See also *R v Cummings* [1948] 1 All ER 551, CCA.

others may feel it impossible to tell their parents or members of their family.[227] As at common law, the statute allows more than one complaint to be admitted, but there is a need in fairness to restrict evidence of 'complaint upon complaint', which may be self-serving, although not where a complaint has a relevance over and above an earlier complaint.[228] Section 120(7) contains no requirement of 'recency' as such, and it is submitted that the test in section 120(7)(d) is therefore broader than the common law test and, depending on all the circumstances, allows for the admissibility of complaints made months or, as in *R v O*,[229] even years after the offence.[230] This a welcome development: there is an assumption that those who are truly the victims of sexual offences complain immediately, which is flawed given the many possible reasons for a delayed complaint, including belief that the abuse is normal, threats from the abuser, and fear of the effect of disclosure for the victim and within his or her family.[231]

Section 120(7)(e) requires that the complaint was not made as a result of a threat or promise, and under section 120(8), which does not follow the approach taken in the common law authorities relating to a recent complaint in a sexual case, the fact that the complaint was elicited, for example, by a leading question, is irrelevant unless a threat or promise was made. Thus it is not only irrelevant to admissibility if the complaint was made in answer to a non-leading question such as 'What is the matter?', but also if it was made in answer to a leading question such as 'Did X (naming the accused) assault you?' Although a complaint elicited by way of a leading question is bound to affect the weight to be attached to it, so far as admissibility is concerned, the issue is whether it was made voluntarily in the sense that it was not obtained by a threat or promise.

Finally, section 120(7)(f) requires that before the statement is introduced in evidence, the witness 'gives oral evidence in connection with its subject matter', words which suggest that this requirement will be met provided only that the complainant gives some evidence in relation to the conduct referred to in her complaint, even if the evidence does not replicate the complaint or is not wholly consistent with it.

Multiple hearsay

Multiple hearsay, as when X testifies as to what Y told him Z had said, gives rise to problems of both reliability and proof. As to reliability, business and other written records which have passed through many hands may be no less reliable than first-hand hearsay, but there are obvious risks in the case of multiple oral hearsay: in addition to the fact that the maker of the original statement may be unavailable for cross-examination, and the usual risk of manufactured or fabricated evidence, there is scope for error or distortion in the transmission or repeated transmission of information.[232] As to proof, section 121 of the 2003 Act provides as follows:

---

[227] *R v Valentine* [1996] 2 Cr App R 213, CA.

[228] *R v O* [2006] 2 Cr App R 405, CA.

[229] *R v O*, ibid.

[230] See also per Rix LJ in *R v Birks* [2003] 2 Cr App R 122 at [27]–[29] and per Pill LJ in *R v K* [2008] EWCA Crim 434 at [55]–[57].

[231] See further Lewis, 'Delayed complaints in childhood sexual abuse prosecutions—a comparative evaluation of admissibility determinations and judicial warnings' (2006) 10 *E&P* 104. See also the Home Office consultation paper, *Convicting Rapists and Protecting Victims—Justice for Victims of Rape*, 2006, which proposes, inter alia, admitting complaints whenever made.

[232] See paras 8.16 et seq, Law Com No 245.

(1) A hearsay statement is not admissible to prove the fact that an earlier hearsay statement was made unless—
  (a) either of the statements is admissible under section 117, 119 or 120,
  (b) all parties to the proceedings so agree, or
  (c) the court is satisfied that the value of the evidence in question, taking into account how reliable the statements appear to be, is so high that the interests of justice require the later statement to be admissible for that purpose.
(2) In this section 'hearsay statement' means a statement, not made in oral evidence, that is relied on as evidence of a matter stated in it.

The purpose of section 121(1)(a) appears to be to allow a party to prove the fact that the 'earlier statement' was made by a 'hearsay statement' provided that either (i) the earlier statement is admissible under one of sections 117, 119, or 120; or (ii) the hearsay statement is admissible under one of those sections. *R v Xhabri*[233] provides an example of the former. The victim's complaint of false imprisonment was relayed by two unidentified informants to a police constable. It was held that the constable could give evidence of the informant's hearsay statement to prove the victim's earlier statement, because that earlier statement was admissible under section 120(4) and (7). The court held that the complaint was also admissible under section 121(1)(c). As to the latter, let us suppose that D is charged with assaulting E; that H, a witness to the assault, made an out-of-court statement to his wife, W, that D assaulted E; that H is now dead, and therefore the statement is admissible under section 116. Let us now consider three additional but alternative developments.

1. By the time of the trial, W is also dead, and therefore cannot prove what H said. However, before her death, she made a written statement to the police, recording the fact that H had told her that D had assaulted E. H's statement is now admissible as evidence of the matters he stated, because in this situation W's statement is admissible under section 117 to prove the fact that H's hearsay statement was made.

2. W told X that H had told her that D had assaulted E. W is called by the prosecution to prove what H said. In giving her evidence, she shows no desire to tell the truth, is treated as a hostile witness, and flatly denies that H made any statement to her that D had assaulted E. W's statement to X is then proved, by calling X to give evidence of it, by virtue of section 3 of the 1865 Act. H's statement is again admissible as evidence of the matters he stated, in this situation because evidence of W's previous inconsistent statement is admissible under section 119(1)(b) of the 2003 Act to prove the fact that H's hearsay statement was made.

3. Very shortly after H made his statement to W, and while the fact that he had made the statement was fresh in W's memory, she wrote a letter to Y in which she recorded that H had told her that D had assaulted E. W is called by the prosecution to prove what H said but does not remember the fact that H made the statement which he did, and in all the circumstances, including the state of her memory and the time that has elapsed, she cannot reasonably be expected to remember the matter well enough to give oral evidence of it. However, when she is shown a copy of her letter to Y, she indicates that to the best of her belief she made the statement in the letter and to the best of her belief it states the truth. H's statement is again admissible as evidence of the matters he stated, in this

[233] [2006] 1 All ER 776, CA.

situation because evidence of W's previous statement is admissible under section 120(4) and (6) to prove the fact that H's hearsay statement was made.

Section 121(1)(b) is self-explanatory.

Section 121(1)(c) permits the court to admit a hearsay statement to prove that another hearsay statement was made, even if the later statement is not otherwise admissible hearsay and the parties to the proceedings do not agree to its admission. The test is whether the court is satisfied that the value of the evidence in question, taking into account how reliable the statements appear to be, is so high that the interests of justice require the later statement to be admissible for the purpose of proving that the earlier statement was made. Section 121(1)(c) is plainly designed to be a stringent test and should not be invoked where, having regard to Article 6 of the European Convention on Human Rights, it would result in an unfair trial. The Court of Appeal will only interfere with a trial judge's decision under section 121(1)(c) if it falls outside the range of reasonable decisions.[234] An example of the application of section 121(1)(c) is provided by *Maher v DPP*.[235] The issue was whether M had carelessly driven her car into another parked car. A witness, D, wrote down the number of M's car on a piece of paper and put it under the wiperblade of the parked car. The girlfriend of the owner of the parked car, McD, phoned the police and read the number from the piece of paper—later lost or destroyed—to a police clerk, who recorded it in a log. M admitted to the police that she had driven in the car park at the material time, but denied any collision. It was held that although the log could not be used under section 121(1)(a) to prove D's 'earlier statement', because it was not admissible under sections 117, 119 or 120, it was admissible under section 121(1)(c), or sections 114(1)(d) and 114(2) (admissibility in the interests of justice), having regard to the likely reliability of the identification of the number of the car and of its transmission via McD to the police log, given the magnitude of the precise coincidence with the number of D's car that was in the car park at the relevant time. However, *R v Walker*[236] establishes that, although section 121(1)(c) imposes a higher threshold than sections 114(1)(d) and 114(2), it is not an alternative to the establishment of admissibility under those sections. Thus if reliance is placed on a hearsay statement to prove 'an earlier hearsay statement' admissible under sections 114(1)(d) and 114(2), section 121(1)(c) is an additional test to be met.

Other safeguards

Capability

Under section 123(1) of the 2003 Act, a hearsay statement cannot be admitted under section 116 (cases where a witness is unavailable), section 119 (inconsistent statements), or section 120 (other previous statements of witnesses) if its maker did not have the 'required capability' at the time when he made the statement. 'Required capability', for these purposes, means the capability of understanding questions put to him about the matters stated and giving answers to such questions which can be understood, a test reflecting the test for competence in criminal cases set out in section 53 of the Youth Justice and Criminal Evidence Act 1999. Under section 123(2) of the 2003 Act, a hearsay statement cannot be admitted under section 117 (business and other documents) if any person who supplied or received the information, or

---

[234] *R v Musone* [2007] 1 WLR 2467, CA at [20].
[235] (2006) 170 JP 441, DC.
[236] [2007] EWCA Crim 1698.

created or received the document, did not have the 'required capability' at the time of supply or receipt etc or, if any such person cannot be identified, 'cannot reasonably be assumed to have had the required capability at that time'. The procedure to be followed in the event of a dispute as to whether any person had the 'required capability' is governed by section 123(4). Section 123 provides as follows:

(1) Nothing in section 116, 119 or 120 makes a statement admissible as evidence if it was made by a person who did not have the required capability at the time when he made the statement.

(2) Nothing in section 117 makes a statement admissible as evidence if any person who, in order for the requirements of section 117(2) to be satisfied, must at any time have supplied or received the information concerned or created or received the document or part concerned—
   (a) did not have the required capability at that time, or
   (b) cannot be identified but cannot reasonably be assumed to have had the required capability at that time.

(3) For the purposes of this section a person has the required capability if he is capable of—
   (a) understanding questions put to him about the matters stated, and
   (b) giving answers to such questions which can be understood.

(4) Where by reason of this section there is an issue as to whether a person had the required capability when he made a statement—
   (a) proceedings held for the determination of the issue must take place in the absence of the jury (if there is one);
   (b) in determining the issue the court may receive expert evidence and evidence from any person to whom the statement in question was made;
   (c) the burden of proof on the issue lies on the party seeking to adduce the statement, and the standard of proof is the balance of probabilities.

Credibility

The general purpose of section 124 of the 2003 Act is to enable the parties to attack or support the credibility of the maker of a hearsay statement who is not called as a witness as if he had been so called. In the case of a statement in a document admitted under section 117 (business and other documents), the person who supplied or received the information contained in the statement, or who created or received the document, if not called as a witness, is also to be treated as 'the maker of the statement' for the purposes of the section. Section 124 provides as follows:

(1) This section applies if in criminal proceedings—
   (a) a statement not made in oral evidence in the proceedings is admitted as evidence of a matter stated, and
   (b) the maker of the statement does not give oral evidence in connection with the subject matter of the statement.

(2) In such a case—
   (a) any evidence which (if he had given such evidence) would have been admissible as relevant to his credibility as a witness is so admissible in the proceedings;
   (b) evidence may with the court's leave be given of any matter which (if he had given such evidence) could have been put to him in cross-examination as relevant to his credibility as a witness but of which evidence could not have been adduced by the cross-examining party;
   (c) evidence tending to prove that he made (at whatever time) any other statement inconsistent with the statement admitted as evidence is admissible for the purpose of showing that he contradicted himself.

(3) If as a result of evidence admitted under this section an allegation is made against the maker of a statement, the court may permit a party to lead additional evidence of such description as the court may specify for the purposes of denying or answering the allegation.

(4) In the case of a statement in a document which is admitted as evidence under section 117 each person who, in order for the statement to be admissible, must have supplied or received the information concerned or created or received the document or part concerned is to be treated as the maker of the statement for the purposes of subsections (1) to (3) above.

Section 124(2)(a), (b), and (c) are largely concerned with situations which, if the maker had been called as a witness, would have been governed by the rule of finality of answers on collateral issues, by the exceptions to that rule,[237] or by section 100 of the 2003 Act (non-defendant's bad character).[238] Under the rule of finality, the answers given by a witness under cross-examination to questions concerning collateral matters, including questions which go merely to the credit of the witness, must be treated as final in the sense that the cross-examining party is not permitted to call further evidence with a view to contradicting the witness. Sub-paragraph (a) allows evidence attacking the credibility of the maker to be given where such evidence, had he been called as a witness, would have been admissible either under an *exception* to the rule of finality or, with the leave of the court, under section 100 of the 2003 Act. Accordingly, for example, evidence admissible under sub-paragraph (a) may include evidence that the maker is unfit to be believed because of some physical or mental disability,[239] one of the exceptions to the rule against finality, or, with the leave of the court under section 100 of the 2003 Act, evidence that he has been convicted of an offence.[240] The sub-paragraph may also be used to admit evidence to support the credibility of the maker. At common law a witness's previous consistent statement is exceptionally admissible in order to rebut a suggestion that his evidence has been fabricated.[241] Thus if the party against whom the hearsay statement is admitted suggests that it was fabricated by the maker, evidence to show that before making the statement in question he made a statement, whether written or oral, consistent with it, would be admissible to support his credibility under sub-paragraph (a).

Sub-paragraph (b) applies to situations which, if the maker had been called as a witness, would have been governed by the *rule* of finality of answers on collateral issues, that is situations in which, if the maker had been cross-examined about a matter in order to attack his credibility as a witness but had denied the matter put, evidence in rebuttal would *not* have been admissible. Under sub-paragraph (b), evidence of the matter which could have been put to the maker in cross-examination, had he been called as a witness, for example the fact that whereas he is giving his evidence through an interpreter he is able to speak English,[242] may be adduced with the leave of the court. The reasoning underlying this provision, and the statutory precursors to it on which it is closely modelled, is that since, if the maker of the statement had given evidence, he might have admitted the matter put, or his denial might not have been believed, the party against whom the hearsay statement is given in evidence might be put at an unfair disadvantage because unable to cross-examine the maker of the statement. In deciding whether to grant leave, it would seem that the judge should balance the risk of such

[237] See Ch 7.
[238] See Ch 17.
[239] *Toohey v Metropolitan Police Comr* [1965] AC 595, HL.
[240] See also s 6 of the Criminal Procedure Act 1865, Ch 7.
[241] See Ch 6.
[242] See *R v Burke* (1858) 8 Cox CC 44, Ch 7.

unfairness against the fact that to allow evidence to the discredit of the absent maker to be given without restriction, might be unfair to him and might lead to an undue prolongation of the trial.[243]

Sub-paragraph (c) allows evidence tending to prove that the maker of the hearsay statement made another statement inconsistent with it to be admitted for the purpose of showing that he contradicted himself. The inconsistent statement may have been made orally or in writing and either before or after the hearsay statement. Under section 119(2) of the Act, if evidence of an inconsistent statement by any person is given under section 124(2)(c), the statement is admissible as evidence of any matter stated in it of which oral evidence by that person would be admissible.

Under section 124(3), where as a result of evidence admitted under section 124(2), an allegation is made against the maker of the statement, the court may permit additional specified evidence to be adduced in rebuttal.

Stopping the case where the evidence is unconvincing

In *R v Galbraith*[244] it was held that a submission of no case to answer should fail where the Crown's case is such that its strength or weakness depends on the view to be taken of a witness's reliability, or other matters which are, generally speaking, within the jury's province, and where on one view of the facts there is evidence on which a jury could properly conclude that the accused is guilty. The Law Commission was of the view that a derogation from *R v Galbraith* could be justified in the case of hearsay evidence on the same basis as in identification cases. In identification cases, 'the case is withdrawn from the jury not because the judge considers that the witness is lying, but because the evidence even if taken to be honest has a base which is so slender that it is unreliable and therefore not sufficient to found a conviction'.[245] Similarly, in the case of hearsay, 'even though the (absent) declarant may be honest, his or her evidence, being hearsay, may be so poor that a conviction would be unsafe'.[246] Section 125 of the 2003 Act, based on clause 14 of the Law Commission's draft bill, provides as follows:

(1) If on a defendant's trial before a judge and jury for an offence the court is satisfied at any time after the close of the case for the prosecution that—
   (a) the case against the defendant is based wholly or partly on a statement not made in oral evidence in the proceedings, and
   (b) the evidence provided by the statement is so unconvincing that, considering its importance to the case against the defendant, his conviction of the offence would be unsafe,
   the court must either direct the jury to acquit the defendant of the offence or, if it considers that there ought to be a retrial, discharge the jury.
(2) Where—
   (a) a jury is directed under subsection (1) to acquit a defendant of an offence, and
   (b) the circumstances are such that, apart from this subsection, the defendant could if acquitted of that offence be found guilty of another offence,
the defendant may not be found guilty of that other offence if the court is satisfied as mentioned in subsection (1) in respect of it.

---

[243] See generally 11th Report, Criminal Law Revision Committee (Cmnd 4991), para 263.
[244] [1981] 1 WLR 1039, CA (see Ch 2).
[245] See per Lord Mustill in *Daley v R* [1994] 1 AC 117, PC at 129 (see Ch 8).
[246] Law Com No 245 (1997), Cm 3670.

While the judge may exercise the power under section 125 at 'any time after the close of the case for the prosecution' he ordinarily ought not do so until the close of all the evidence.[247] The same duty to direct an acquittal or discharge the jury also applies in cases in which a jury is required to determine under the Criminal Procedure (Insanity) Act 1964 whether the accused did the act or made the omission charged.[248] Section 125 is without prejudice to any other power a court may have to direct an acquittal or discharge a jury.[249]

Discretion to exclude

Section 126 of the Act provides as follows:

> (1) In criminal proceedings the court may refuse to admit a statement as evidence of a matter stated if—
>   (a) the statement was made otherwise than in oral evidence in the proceedings, and
>   (b) the court is satisfied that the case for excluding the statement, taking account of the danger that to admit it would result in undue waste of time, substantially outweighs the case for admitting it, taking account of the value of the evidence.
> (2) Nothing in this Chapter prejudices—
>   (a) any power of a court to exclude evidence under section 78 of the Police and Criminal Evidence Act 1984 (exclusion of unfair evidence), or
>   (b) any other power of a court to exclude evidence at its discretion (whether from preventing questions from being put or otherwise).

As we have seen, there is a discretion to admit hearsay under section 114(1)(d) if it is 'in the interests of justice'. The same phrase is used in two other provisions: under section 116(4), leave may be given to admit the hearsay statement of someone who does not give oral evidence through fear only if the court considers that the statement ought to be admitted in the interests of justice; and under section 121(1)(c), which relates to multiple hearsay, a hearsay statement is not admissible to prove the fact that an earlier hearsay statement was made unless the interests of justice require it to be admissible for that purpose. Although strictly speaking, where a court has admitted a hearsay statement under section 114(1)(d), section 116(4), or section 121(1)(c), it may proceed to consider use of one of its three discretionary powers of exclusion, this is likely to be a pointless exercise given that it is of the opinion that it is in the interests of justice to admit the evidence. Furthermore, in the case of section 114(1)(d) and section 116(4), the court, in considering whether it is in the interests of justice, shall have regard, in addition to the matters listed in section 114(2)(a)–(i) and section 116(4)(a)–(c), to any other relevant factors or circumstances, which could, of course, include any of the factors or circumstances relevant to the exercise of any of the discretionary powers to exclude. It is for reasons of this kind, presumably, that it has been observed that the test in section 78 of the 1984 Act is unlikely to produce a different result from that of 'the interests of justice' in sections 114(1)(d) and 116(4).[250]

Section 126(1), which has been described as a 'general' discretion to exclude,[251] creates a discretionary power to exclude otherwise admissible hearsay, whether tendered by the prosecution

---

[247] *R v Horncastle* [2009] 4 All ER 183, CA at [74].

[248] Section 125(3).

[249] Section 125(4).

[250] See, in the case of s 114(1)(d), *R v Cole* [2008] 1 Cr App R 81, CA; and, in the case of s 116(4), *R v D* [2002] 2 Cr App R 601, CA.

[251] *R v C* [2006] Crim LR 637, CA.

or defence. Under the balancing exercise described in section 126(1)(b), regard must be had, on the one hand, to the case for exclusion, taking account not of the danger of waste of time—the risk of *some* waste of time is plainly acceptable—but of the danger of *undue* waste of time. This has to be weighed against the case for admission of the evidence, taking account of its 'value', a word which appears to embrace not only its probative value, or its value in understanding other evidence in the case, but also its value in the sense of its reliability or weight. It is only if the court is satisfied that the case for exclusion *substantially* outweighs the case for admission, that the discretion should be exercised. This is likely to occur, for example, where the hearsay statement is of minimal probative value and wholly or to a very large extent superfluous, because other evidence has been or will be given on the matters stated.

Section 126(2) preserves the two pre-existing powers of the court to exclude otherwise admissible hearsay. The first is the power in section 78 of the 1984 Act under which evidence on which the prosecution proposes to rely may be excluded where in all the circumstances, including those in which the evidence was obtained, it would have such an adverse effect on the fairness of the proceedings that the court ought not to admit it. The second is the common law power to exclude prosecution evidence on the basis that its prejudicial effect outweighs its probative value.

Under Article 6(1) of the European Convention on Human Rights, the accused is entitled to a fair hearing and under Article 6(3)(d) the accused has the right to examine or have examined witnesses against him. As we have seen, it is not necessarily incompatible with Article 6(1) and (3)(d) for depositions or witness statements to be read, even if there has been no opportunity to question the witness at any stage of the proceedings as long as there is a legitimate justification for the admission of the witness statement and, where appropriate, sufficient counterbalancing measures, the adequacy of which is to be determined by the fairness of the trial as a whole.

In *R v Cole*[252] Lord Phillips CJ stated that once one moves away from the proposition that there is an absolute rule that evidence of a statement cannot be adduced in evidence unless the defendant has an opportunity to examine the maker, there can only be one governing criterion, namely whether the admission of the evidence is compatible with a fair trial and it is that question alone with which Article 6 is concerned. Factors that are likely to be of concern to the court are identified in section 114(2) of the Act, namely the probative value of the statement, what other evidence can be given of the matter in issue, how important the matter in issue is, the circumstances in which the statement was made etc.[253]

Rules of court

Under section 132 of the Act, rules of court may be made providing for the procedural conditions to be followed by a party proposing to tender a hearsay statement in evidence. The rules may require such a party to serve on the other party or parties notice and particulars of the evidence[254] and may provide that the evidence is admissible if a notice has been served but there has been no service of a counter-notice objecting to the admission of the evidence.[255] The rules applicable in magistrates' courts and crown courts are set out in Part 34 of the Criminal Procedure Rules 2005.[256] If a party proposing to tender evidence fails to comply

---

[252] [2008] 1 Cr App R 81, CA at [20]–[21].
[253] See s 114(2) above.
[254] Section 132(3).
[255] Section 132(4).
[256] SI 2005/384.

with a prescribed requirement, the evidence is not admissible except with the court's leave.[257] Where the defendant seeks to adduce hearsay evidence but fails to comply, leave should be granted where any unfairness to the prosecution or co-accused may be cured, for example by an adjournment, and where the interests of justice otherwise require the evidence to be admitted, but not where to admit the evidence would cause incurable unfairness.[258] Where leave is given the court or jury may draw such inferences from a failure to comply with a prescribed requirement as appear proper.[259] However, a person is not to be convicted of an offence solely on the basis of such an inference.[260]

The direction to the jury

A trial judge should give the jury a careful direction on the correct approach to hearsay. The following guidance was given in *Grant v The State*.[261] The jury should be told that a hearsay statement has not been verified on oath nor its author tested by cross-examination. The judge should point out the potential risk of relying on a statement by someone whom the jury have not been able to assess and should invite them to scrutinize the evidence with particular care. It is proper to direct the jury to give the statement such weight as they think fit. Finally, it is desirable to direct them to consider the statement in the context of the other evidence, drawing attention to any discrepancies between the statement and the oral evidence of other witnesses.[262]

Questions of proof

Proof of conditions of admissibility

It is submitted that many of the principles established in the cases concerning proof of the conditions of admissibility contained in sections 23 and 24 of the 1988 Act (and other repealed statutory precursors to the hearsay provisions of the 2003 Act) remain valid. Thus where it is sought to admit a hearsay statement under section 116 (or to comply with the requirement of section 117(5)(a)), because the maker of the statement is unable to give oral evidence for one of the reasons set out in section 116(2), the court should make a finding of fact, based on admissible evidence, that such a reason exists.[263] If necessary, the matter should be decided on a *voir dire*,[264] at which the party against whom the evidence is tendered is entitled to cross-examine witnesses relied on to establish the necessary facts.[265] The *voir dire* is of particular importance in cases covered by section 116(2)(e), ie where the maker of the statement does not give oral evidence through fear: it is highly desirable that any investigation of his reasons should be conducted in the absence of the jury and that some innocuous form of words should be used to explain his

---

[257] Section 132(5).

[258] *R v Musone* [2007] 1 WLR 2467, CA at [37].

[259] Section 132(5).

[260] Section 132(7).

[261] [2006] 2 WLR 835, PC.

[262] See Specimen Direction 35 for the model direction, available at <http://www.jsboard.co.uk/criminal_law/cbb/index.htm>.

[263] See *R v Wood and Fitzsimmons* [1998] Crim LR 213, CA; and *R v Feest* [1987] Crim LR 766, CA, a decision on s 68(2)(a)(iii) of the 1984 Act. See also *R v T* (2009) 173 JP 425, CA, a decision under s 116(2)(d), in which the court stated that given the importance of the right to confrontation, it is impermissible to proceed with an application under s 116(2)(d) informally; if the facts cannot be agreed, evidence must be called and the judge must make findings of fact.

[264] See *R v Minors; R v Harper* [1989] 1 WLR 441, CA.

[265] See *R v Wood and Fitzsimmons* [1998] Crim LR 213, CA.

absence to the jury[266] and prevent the jury from speculating that the accused may be responsible for the absence.[267] However, there is no requirement that the judge should test statements of fear through video link or tape-recording, particularly as to the reasons for the fear; courts should not test the basis of fear by calling witnesses before them, since that may create the very situation which section 116(2)(e) was designed to avoid.[268] As to the standard of proof, the prosecution must satisfy the court beyond reasonable doubt,[269] the defence on a balance of probabilities.[270] Evidence to establish one of the reasons may take the form of either direct testimony or admissible hearsay (including a statement itself admissible under the statutory provisions)[271] but cannot be furnished by the contents of the very statement sought to be introduced, because prima facie they are inadmissible hearsay.[272] In order to establish that the maker of a statement does not give oral evidence through fear, reliance may be placed on his sworn evidence,[273] his demeanour[274] (which may be particularly important if he does not state his fear explicitly),[275] and medical evidence.[276] Alternatively, use may be made of his out-of-court written statement of fear,[277] whether or not contained in the very statement sought to be admitted, on the basis that it constitutes original evidence admissible to prove state of mind[278] or, if it is treated as hearsay, is admissible under the *res gestae* principle which covers statements concerning the maker's contemporaneous state of mind.[279] This principle is among the common law categories of admissibility preserved by section 118 of the 2003 Act.

According to *R v Foxley*[280] evidence of the requirements contained in section 24(1) of the 1988 Act, which were broadly similar to the requirements set out in section 117(2)(a) and (b) of the 2003 Act, was often desirable, but not always essential. In that case the trial judge was entitled to infer from the documents themselves and from the method or route by which they had been produced before the court that the requirements were satisfied. The purpose of section 24 was to enable the document to speak for itself, a purpose that would be defeated if oral evidence were to be required in every case from the creator or keeper of the document or the supplier of the information it contained.[281]

---

[266] See *R v Jennings* [1995] Crim LR 810, CA.

[267] See *R v Wood and Fitzsimmons* [1998] Crim LR 213, CA. If the jury ask why the maker has not been called to give evidence, the judge should simply say that he cannot answer the question: *R v Churchill* [1993] Crim LR 285, CA.

[268] *R v Davies* [2007] 2 All ER 1070, CA.

[269] See *R (Meredith) v Harwich Magistrates' Court* (2007) 171 JP 249, DC a decision under the Criminal Justice Act 2003, s 116(2)(b) (unfit to be a witness because of bodily or mental condition).

[270] See *R v Mattey, R v Queeley* [1995] 2 Cr App R 409, CA.

[271] See *R v Castillo* [1996] 1 Cr App R 438, CA.

[272] See *R v Case* [1991] Crim LR 192, CA and *R v Mattey, R v Queeley* [1995] 2 Cr App R 409, CA.

[273] Although in *R v Greer* [1998] Crim LR 572, CA reliance was placed on unsworn evidence, technically he should be sworn: see *R v Jennings* [1995] Crim LR 572, CA.

[274] See *R v Waters* [1997] Crim LR 823, CA.

[275] See *R v Ashford Magistrates' Court, ex p Hilden* [1993] QB 555, DC.

[276] See *R v Waters* [1997] Crim LR 823, CA.

[277] See *R v Rutherford* [1998] Crim LR 490, CA.

[278] See *R v Fairfax* [1995] Crim LR 949, CA, relying on *R v Blastland* [1986] AC 41, HL.

[279] See *R v Fairfax* [1995] Crim LR 949 (citing *Neill v North Antrim Magistrates' Court* [1992] 1 WLR 1220, HL: see per Lord Mustill, obiter at 1228) and *R v Wood and Fitzsimmons* [1998] Crim LR 213, CA. But see also *R v Belmarsh Magistrates' Court, ex p Gilligan* [1998] 1 Cr App R 14, DC, in which neither possible means of admissibility was even mentioned, and Astill J pointed out that in *R v Fairfax* there had been a great deal of oral evidence of fear.

[280] [1995] 2 Cr App R 523, CA.

[281] See also, applying *R v Foxley, R v Ilyas and Knight* [1996] Crim LR 810, CA.

Proof of a statement contained in a document

Section 133 of the 2003 Act provides that:

> Where a statement in a document is admissible as evidence in criminal proceedings, the statement may be proved by producing either—
> (a) the document, or
> (b) (whether or not the document exists) a copy of the document or of the material part of it, authenticated in whatever way the court may approve.

The word 'document' means anything in which information of any description is recorded,[282] a definition wide enough to include, for example, audio-tapes, films, and video-tapes. 'Copy', in relation to a document, means anything on to which information recorded in the document has been copied, by whatever means, and whether directly or indirectly,[283] a definition which would cover, among other things, a transcript of an audio-tape as well as reproductions or still reproductions of the images embodied in films and video-tapes, whether enlarged or not. 'Producing' would seem to refer not to counsel handing the document to the court, but to a witness who is qualified to do so in accordance with the rules of evidence producing the document and saying what it is.[284] The reference to authentication appears to relate to the authentication of a copy of a document as a true copy of the original, and not to proof of the original.[285] Section 133 is considered further at 251 under **Documentary evidence** in Chapter 9.

Evidence by video-recording

In the case of offences triable only on indictment and prescribed offences triable-either way, where a person, other than the accused, is called as a witness, having witnessed the events constituting the offence or part of it, or events closely connected with it, and having previously given a video-recorded account of those events at a time when they were fresh in his memory, section 137 of the 2003 Act permits the court to direct that the recording be admitted as his evidence-in-chief. Section 137 is considered in Chapter 5.

Expert evidence: preparatory work

In many cases, a witness giving expert opinion evidence will have no personal or first-hand knowledge of the facts, or all of the facts, upon which his opinion is based. For example, a surgeon may express his expert opinion as to whether the wounds of a deceased person were self-inflicted, basing his opinion on someone else's description of the wounds. Similarly, an expert may give his expert opinion on the basis of preparatory work, such as scientific tests, carried out by assistants. The facts upon which the expert opinion is based, sometimes referred to as 'primary facts', must be proved by the person with personal or first-hand knowledge of them.[286] Section 127 of the 2003 Act permits such facts to be proved by the hearsay statement of such a person, unless, on an application by a party to the proceedings, that is not in the interests of justice. Section 127 provides as follows:

---

[282] Section 134(1).

[283] Section 134(1).

[284] As under the Civil Evidence Act 1968, s 6(1) (see now the Civil Evidence Act 1995, s 8): per Staughton LJ in *Ventouris v Mountain (No 2)* [1992] 1 WLR 887, CA (see Ch 11).

[285] Cf *Ventouris v Mountain (No 2)* [1992] 1 WLR 887, CA (see Ch 11).

[286] See Ch 18, 525, under **Expert opinion evidence**.

(1) This section applies if—

    (a) a statement has been prepared for the purposes of criminal proceedings,

    (b) the person who prepared the statement had or may reasonably be supposed to have had personal knowledge of the matters stated,

    (c) notice is given under the appropriate rules that another person (the expert) will in evidence given in the proceedings orally or under s 9 of the Criminal Justice Act 1967[287] base an opinion or inference on the statement, and

    (d) the notice gives the name of the person who prepared the statement and the nature of the matters stated.

(2) In evidence given in the proceedings the expert may base an opinion or inference on the statement.

(3) If evidence based on the statement is given under subsection (2) the statement is to be treated as evidence of what it says.

(4) This section does not apply if the court, on an application by a party to the proceedings, orders that it is not in the interests of justice that it should apply.

(5) The matters to be considered by the court in deciding whether to make an order under subsection (4) include—

    (a) the expense of calling as a witness the person who prepared the statement;

    (b) whether relevant evidence could be given by that person which could not be given by the expert;

    (c) whether that person can reasonably be expected to remember the matters stated well enough to give oral evidence of them.

(6) Subsections (1) to (5) apply to a statement prepared for the purposes of a criminal investigation as they apply to a statement prepared for the purposes of criminal proceedings, and in such a case references to the proceedings are to criminal proceedings arising from the investigation.

Under subsection (4), it appears that the court may only disapply the section on the application of a party and not of its own motion. Subsection (5) provides a short non-exhaustive list of the factors to be considered by the court in deciding whether to disapply the section. Absent from the list are, it is submitted, the most important factors: the extent to which the matters stated are in dispute—if they are not in dispute, then there should be no application under subsection (4)—and the risk, having regard to how difficult it will be to challenge the statement if its maker is not called as a witness, that its admission or exclusion will result in unfairness.

Nothing in section 127 affects the common law rule under which an expert witness may draw on the body of expertise relevant to his field.[288] That rule is among the common-law categories of admissibility preserved by section 118 of the Act.

Expert reports

Section 30(1) of the 1988 Act provides that an expert report, that is a written report by a person dealing wholly or mainly with matters on which he is (or would if living be) qualified to give expert evidence,[289] shall be admissible as evidence in criminal proceedings whether or not the person making it attends to give oral evidence in those proceedings. The

---

[287] See below at 319, under **Written statements under section 9 of the Criminal Justice Act 1967**.

[288] See *R v Abadom* [1983] 1 WLR 126, CA, Ch 18.

[289] Section 30(5).

report, when admitted, shall be evidence of any fact or opinion of which the person making it could have given oral evidence.[290] However, if it is proposed that the person making the report shall not give oral evidence, the report shall only be admissible with the leave of the court.[291] In deciding whether to give leave, the court shall have regard to (i) the contents of the report; (ii) the reasons why it is proposed that the person making the report shall not give oral evidence; (iii) any risk, having regard in particular to whether it is likely to be possible to controvert statements in the report if the person making it does not attend to give oral evidence, that its admission or exclusion will result in unfairness to the accused or, if there is more than one, to any of them; and (iv) any other circumstances that appear to the court to be relevant.[292]

If any party to a criminal trial proposes, pursuant to section 30(1), to put an expert report in evidence at the trial, then whether or not the person making the report attends to give oral evidence in the proceedings, that party, in accordance with rule 24 of the Criminal Procedure Rules 2005,[293] shall as soon as practicable furnish the other party or parties with a statement in writing of any finding or opinion which he proposes to adduce by way of such evidence. Rule 24, the exceptions to it, and certain related rules are set out and considered in Chapter 18, which concerns opinion evidence generally.[294]

Written statements under section 9 of the Criminal Justice Act 1967

Under section 9 of the 1967 Act, in summary trials and trials on indictment, a written statement (with or without exhibits) by any person shall be admissible as evidence 'to the like extent as oral evidence to the like effect by that person'. The principal conditions of admissibility are that (i) the statement is signed by its maker; (ii) it contains a declaration that it is true; (iii) before the hearing a copy of it is served by the party proposing to tender it on each of the other parties; and (iv) none of the other parties or their solicitors, within seven days from the service of the copy, serves a notice objecting to the statement being tendered in evidence.[295] The last two conditions do not apply if the parties agree before or during the hearing that the statement shall be so tendered.[296] Under section 9(4), notwithstanding that a statement may be admissible by virtue of section 9, the party who served a copy of it may call its maker to give evidence and the court may, either of its own motion or on the application of any party to the proceedings, require its maker to attend court and give oral evidence. An application under section 9(4) would be appropriate, for example, where a party disputes the evidence contained in the statement but failed to serve a notice of objection in accordance with the section. Such an application may be made before the hearing.[297] Where a section 9 statement is admitted in evidence, it should normally be read out aloud.[298]

---

[290] Section 30(4).

[291] Section 30(2).

[292] Section 30(3).

[293] SI 2005/384.

[294] See below at 552 under **Expert opinion evidence, Restrictions on, and disclosure of, expert evidence in criminal cases**.

[295] There must be strict compliance with the terms of s 9: see *Paterson v DPP* [1990] Crim LR 651, DC.

[296] Section 9(2).

[297] Section 9(5).

[298] Section 9(6). Reading aloud the statement, or a summary of the relevant parts, is obligatory in a magistrates' court: Part 37.5 of the Criminal Procedure Rules 2005, SI 2005/384.

Where the prosecution tenders written statements under section 9, it is frequently not only proper, but also necessary for the orderly presentation of the evidence, for the statements to be edited. This may be either because a witness has made more than one statement whose contents should conveniently be reduced into a single comprehensive statement or because a statement contains inadmissible, prejudicial, or irrelevant material. Such editing should be carried out by a Crown Prosecutor, and not by a police officer, in accordance with paragraph 24 of the *Practice Direction (Criminal Proceedings: Consolidation).*[299]

Depositions of children and young persons under section 43 of the Children and Young Persons Act 1933

Under section 42 of the 1933 Act, where a magistrate is satisfied by the evidence of a qualified medical practitioner that the attendance before a court of any child or young person in respect of whom any of certain specified offences is alleged to have been committed would involve serious danger to his life or health, the magistrate may take a deposition from him out of court. The offences specified include offences under the Offences Against the Person Act 1861, the 1933 Act itself, the Protection of Children Act 1978, and the Sexual Offences Act 2003, and any other offences involving bodily injury to a child or young person. Under section 43, a deposition taken under section 42 shall be admissible in evidence in any proceedings either for or against the accused provided, in the latter case, that it is proved that reasonable notice of the intention to take the deposition was served upon the accused and he or his legal representative had an opportunity of cross-examining the deponent.

ADDITIONAL READING

Birch, 'Criminal Justice Act 2003 (4) Hearsay: Same Old Story, Same Old Song?' [2004] *Crim LR* 556.

Choo, *Hearsay and Confrontation in Criminal Trials* (Oxford, 1996).

Law Commission, *Evidence in Criminal Proceedings: Hearsay and Related Topics* (Law Com No 245, London, 1997).

Lewis, 'Delayed complaints in childhood sexual abuse prosecutions—a comparative evaluation of admissibility determinations and judicial warnings' (2006) 10 *E&P* 104.

Spencer, *Hearsay Evidence in Criminal Proceedings* (Oxford, 2008).

Tapper, 'Hearsay in Criminal Cases: An Overview of Law Commission Report No 245' [1997] *Crim LR* 771.

Taylor, 'Two English hearsay heresies' (2005) 9 *E&P* 110.

Worthen, 'The Hearsay Provisions of the Criminal Justice Act 2003: so far, not so good?' (2008) *Crim LR* 431.

---

[299] [2002] 1 WLR 2870. The principles set out do not apply to documents which are exhibited (including statements under caution and signed contemporaneous notes). Nor, as a general rule, do they apply to oral statements of an accused which are recorded in the witness statements of interviewing police officers. Such material should remain in its original state and any editing left to prosecuting counsel at the Crown Court: see para 24.6.

Hearsay admissible by statute in civil proceedings

11

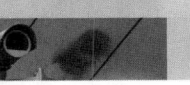

Key Issues

- When and why should a statement made out of court and tendered as evidence of the facts asserted (hearsay) be admissible in civil proceedings?

- If admissible, should the party tendering the evidence be required to apply for leave to adduce it? If so, when should leave be granted?

- Should the party be required to give notice of intention to adduce the evidence? If so, what should the notice requirements be?

- Should the other party be permitted to call the maker of the statement with a view to cross-examining him? If the maker is not called for cross-examination, what opportunities should the other party have to impeach his credibility?

- How much weight should be given to hearsay evidence in civil proceedings?

- If a hearsay statement is contained in a document, how may it be proved?

The background

As we have seen in Chapter 10, under the common law rule against hearsay, any assertion, other than one made by a person while giving oral evidence in the proceedings, was inadmissible if tendered as evidence of the facts asserted. The Civil Evidence Act 1968 (the 1968 Act) constituted a major assault upon the common law rule in civil proceedings. Although it did not abolish the rule, it made provision for the admissibility of both oral and written hearsay (including statements contained in documents which were or formed part of a record) subject to certain conditions, principally (i) notification of the other parties to the litigation; and (ii) either calling the maker of the statement as a witness (in which case the statement could not be given in evidence without the leave of the court) or establishing one of a number of reasons for not calling the maker of the statement as a witness. The 1968 Act also provided for the admissibility of statements contained in computer-produced documents and gave express statutory force to a number of the pre-existing common law exceptions, including informal admissions and facts contained in public documents.

In June 1988 the Civil Justice Review recommended an inquiry by a law reform agency into the usefulness of the hearsay rule in civil proceedings and the machinery for rendering it admissible. The matter was referred to the Law Commission. The response to its Consultation Paper[1] identified three major reasons for change.

1. The regime under the 1968 Act was unwieldy and the law outmoded and unnecessarily difficult to understand. In particular, the rules as to notification were too complicated so that in practice compliance was the exception.

2. The statutory regime lagged behind developments in the law and practice of civil litigation which pointed to a new approach in which (a) the main emphasis is upon ensuring that, so far as possible, and subject to considerations of reliability and weight, all relevant evidence is adduced;[2] and (b) litigation is conducted in a more open climate, with more emphasis on identifying and refining the issues in advance of the trial.

3. Intelligent witnesses and litigants were confused by, and dissatisfied with, rules which sometimes operated to prevent them from giving evidence of matters which they rightly perceived as relevant and cogent.[3]

Guided by two major principles, that the law should be simplified to the greatest degree consistent with the proper functioning of the law of evidence, and that, as a general rule, all evidence should be admissible unless there is good reason for it to be treated as inadmissible,[4] the Commission recommended abolition of the hearsay rule in civil proceedings subject to safeguards such as a new simplified notice provision and statutory guidelines to assist courts to assess the weight to be attached to hearsay evidence. The main recommendations of the Commission, in summary, were as follows:

1. In civil proceedings the hearsay rule should be abolished.

2. A party calling a person as a witness should not adduce evidence of a previous statement made by that person except with the leave of the court.

---

[1] *The Hearsay Rule in Civil Proceedings* (1991) Consultation Paper No 117.
[2] See per Balcombe LJ in *Ventouris v Mountain (No 2)* [1992] 1 WLR 887, CA at 899.
[3] See *The Hearsay Rule in Civil Proceedings*, Law Commission Report No 216 (Cm 2321) (1993), paras 1.4–1.6.
[4] Law Com No 216 (Cm 2321), para 4.2.

3. A party intending to rely on hearsay should be under a duty to give notice of that fact where this is reasonable and appropriate, according to the particular circumstances of the case. Although failure to give notice should not render the evidence inadmissible, it may detract from the weight that will be placed on it or lead to the imposition of costs sanctions.

4. There should be power for a party to call a witness for cross-examination on his hearsay statement.

5. Courts should be given guidelines to assist them in assessing the weight of hearsay evidence.

6. For business and other records there should be no additional safeguards, beyond those applicable to all other hearsay statements, and the procedure for proving such records should be simplified.

All of these recommendations were put into effect by the Civil Evidence Act 1995 (the 1995 Act).

Before considering the detail of the Act, it is important to note that it contains no special conditions of admissibility or other specific safeguards in the case of statements in computer-produced documents. The 1968 Act contained elaborate precautions in this regard, including requirements to prove that the document was produced in the normal course of business and in an uninterrupted course of activity. Requirements of this kind reflected a fundamental mistrust and fear of the potential for error and mechanical failure. However, as the Law Commission observed, since 1968 technology has developed to an extent where computers and computer-generated documents are relied on in every area of business. It also thought that it was at least questionable whether the requirements of the 1968 Act provided any real safeguard in relation to the reliability of the hardware or software concerned, and noted that in any event they provided no protection against the inaccurate inputting of data. The Commission recognized that, as confidence in the inherent reliability of computers had grown, so had concern over the potential for misuse, through the capacity to hack, corrupt, or alter information in a manner which is undetectable, but could see no reason for maintaining a different regime for the admission of computer-generated documents. It considered that the potential for misuse was best dealt with by concentrating upon the weight to be attached to such evidence, rather than by the reformulation of complex and inflexible rules of admissibility.[5]

Admissibility of hearsay under the Civil Evidence Act 1995

Abolition of the rule against hearsay

Section 1 of the 1995 Act provides as follows:

(1) In civil proceedings evidence shall not be excluded on the ground that it is hearsay.
(2) In this Act—
   (a) 'hearsay' means a statement made otherwise than by a person while giving oral evidence[6] in the proceedings which is tendered as evidence of the matters stated; and
   (b) references to hearsay include hearsay of whatever degree.

[5] See generally Law Com No 216 (Cm 2321), paras 3.14–3.21 and 4.43.
[6] 'Oral evidence' includes evidence which, by reason of a defect of speech or hearing, a person called as a witness gives in writing or by signs: s 13.

'In civil proceedings'

The phrase 'civil proceedings' is defined by section 11 as 'civil proceedings, before any tribunal, in relation to which the strict rules of evidence apply, whether as a matter of law or by agreement of the parties'. Thus the Act applies to civil proceedings in any of the ordinary courts of law and in both tribunals and arbitrations in which the strict rules of evidence are applied, but not to the wardship jurisdiction of the High Court,[7] the Court of Protection, or Coroners' Courts. The strict rules of evidence do not apply to all civil proceedings in magistrates' courts. For example, the Act does not apply to magistrates when considering whether there is reasonable cause to suspend a private hire vehicle licence under the Local Government (Miscellaneous Provisions) Act 1976.[8] In *Savings and Investment Bank Ltd v Gasco Investments (Netherlands) BV (No 2)*,[9] a decision under the equivalent provision of the 1968 Act, it was held that an application to commit for contempt founded on the breach of an order made in civil proceedings was itself a civil proceeding, notwithstanding the criminal standard of proof appropriate to such an application[10] and its possible penal consequences.

'Shall not be excluded'

Under section 1(1) of the 1995 Act, 'evidence shall not be excluded on the ground that it is hearsay'. The subsection needs to be considered alongside section 14(1) of the Act, which provides that:

> Nothing in this Act affects the exclusion of evidence on grounds other than that it is hearsay.

> This applies whether the evidence falls to be excluded in pursuance of any enactment or rule of law, for failure to comply with rules of court or an order of the court, or otherwise.

Thus hearsay cannot be excluded because it is hearsay but will only be admissible if it does not fall to be excluded on some ground other than that it is hearsay. For example, hearsay opinion evidence which is inadmissible under the Civil Evidence Act 1972 (the 1972 Act)[11] falls to be excluded in pursuance of an enactment; hearsay which is irrelevant or inadmissible on grounds of public policy or privilege falls to be excluded in pursuance of a rule of law; and the hearsay opinion of an expert may fall to be excluded if a party fails to comply with CPR rule 35.13, ie if he fails to disclose the expert's report.

'Hearsay'

The purpose of the statutory definition of hearsay in section 1(2) is to identify the type of evidence which would have formerly been excluded by virtue of the common law rule against hearsay, ie first-hand, second-hand, or multiple hearsay, and to which the safeguards and supplementary provisions of the Act apply. However, there is likely to continue to be reference to the common law authorities in cases in which the boundary of the definition is unclear.[12] Section 13 provides that 'statement' means 'any representation of fact or opinion, however made'. Thus the Act covers a statement of opinion, provided that it is admissible under the 1972 Act, as well as a statement of fact, whether the statement was

---

[7] See *Official Solicitor to the Supreme Court v K* [1965] AC 201, HL.
[8] *Westminster City Council v Zestfair Ltd* (1989) 88 LGR 288, DC; *Leeds City Council v Hussain* [2003] RTR 13, DC.
[9] [1988] 2 WLR 1212, CA.
[10] See Ch 4.
[11] See Ch 18.
[12] Law Com No 216 (Cm 2321), para 4.6.

made orally, in writing (whether hand-written, type-written, or produced by computer), or by conduct. It may be doubted, however, whether a written statement in an affidavit is covered by the Act.[13]

Original evidence. Under section 1(2)(a), hearsay is defined as a statement made otherwise than by a person while giving oral evidence in the proceedings which is 'tendered as evidence of the matter stated' and falls to be distinguished from original evidence, ie a statement made otherwise than by a person while giving oral evidence in the proceedings which is tendered for any relevant purpose other than that of establishing any matter stated. The distinction between hearsay and original evidence is important because whereas hearsay is only admissible subject to the conditions and safeguards set out in the 1995 Act, original evidence, if sufficiently relevant, is admissible without more. In some cases, original evidence is introduced simply to show that the statement in question was made, because that is among the facts in issue in the case. Thus in defamation proceedings in which it is in issue whether the allegedly defamatory statement was made, a witness may give evidence of the making of the statement, including its terms. So-called 'operative words' provide a further illustration. The utterance of such words binds the speaker under the substantive law because a reasonable person, on hearing them, would believe that the speaker intended to be bound. Thus if the parties dispute whether a contract was entered into, evidence of the terms of the contractual offer are admissible because under the law of contract the words spoken are of legal effect if a reasonable person in the position of the offeree would have believed that the offeror intended to be bound. Likewise, words of gift accompanying a transfer of property may be admitted as original evidence. In other types of case, original evidence is introduced because the statement in question is relevant to a fact in issue, typically the state of mind of the person who heard or read it, to show what he knew, thought or believed. Thus P may tender evidence of a certain alleged misrepresentation made to him by Q for the purpose of showing that he was thereby misled. If X brings an action against Y for malicious prosecution, then Y, in order to show the reasonableness of his conduct in the prosecution of X, may tender evidence of a statement made to him by Z that X had committed a criminal offence.[14] Almost all of the reported examples of original evidence have arisen in criminal cases and the topic is considered more fully in Chapter 10.[15]

Implied assertions. An implied assertion is an assertion, whether made orally, in writing or by conduct, from which it is possible to infer a particular matter. For example, in *Wright v Doe d Tatham*,[16] one of the issues being the mental competence of a testator, it was held that the trial judge had properly excluded a number of letters written to the testator by certain of his acquaintances in terms from which it could legitimately be inferred that they regarded him as sane. As evidence of the truth of the implied assertion that the testator was sane, they constituted inadmissible hearsay. As to implied assertions by conduct, Parke B was of the obiter opinion that on the question of the seaworthiness of a vessel, evidence of the conduct of a deceased captain in examining every part of the vessel and then embarking on it with his family would also amount to hearsay. On the other hand, in *Manchester Brewery*

---

[13] In *Rover International Ltd v Cannon Film Sales Ltd (No 2)* [1987] 1 WLR 1597, Ch D at 1603 Harman J doubted whether affidavits were 'documents' for the purposes of the 1968 Act.

[14] See *Perkins v Vaughan* (1842) 4 Man & G 988.

[15] See 276 under **The meaning of hearsay in the Criminal Justice Act 2003**, *Original evidence.*

[16] (1837) 7 Ad&El 313, Ex Ch.

Co Ltd v Coombs,[17] which concerned an alleged breach by a brewer to supply good beer, it was held, obiter, that evidence could be given that customers ordered the beer, tasted it, did not finish it, and then either left it or threw it away. Further examples, together with the cases which highlight the difficult grey area that lies between implied assertions and circumstantial evidence, are considered in Chapter 10.[18] In *criminal* proceedings, an implied assertion is treated as hearsay only if the purpose, or one of the purposes of the person making the assertion, was to cause another person to believe the matter asserted or to cause another to act (or a machine to operate) on the basis that the matter is as asserted.[19] There is no equivalent provision in the 1995 Act and it is unclear whether a 'representation' covers an implied assertion. In the case of conduct, the Law Commission took the view that the question whether assertive or non-assertive conduct should come within the statutory definition of hearsay was 'a matter for judicial consideration and development'.[20] However, it seems that such consideration and development is also called for in the case of implied assertions made orally or in writing.

Evidence admissible apart from section 1

Section 1(3) and (4) of the 1995 Act provides as follows:

(3) Nothing in this Act affects the admissibility of evidence admissible apart from this section.

(4) The provisions of sections 2 to 6 (safeguards and supplementary provisions relating to hearsay evidence) do not apply in relation to hearsay evidence admissible apart from this section, notwithstanding that it may also be admissible by virtue of this section.

Various statutory provisions, apart from section 1 of the 1995 Act, provide for the admissibility of particular types of hearsay and the purpose of section 1(3) is to preserve their effect. An example is the Births and Deaths Registration Act 1953, section 34 of which provides for the admissibility of a certified copy of an entry in the register of births as evidence of the facts contained in it. Similarly, the same section provides for the proof of death, where there is evidence identifying the person named in the certificate with the person in question, by reliance on a death certificate.[21] Other important statutory provisions include the orders made under section 96 of the Children Act 1989,[22] whereby in civil proceedings[23] before the High Court or a county court, in family proceedings in a magistrates' court,[24] and in proceedings under the Child Support Act 1991, evidence given in connection with the upbringing, maintenance or welfare of a child shall be admissible notwithstanding any rule of law relating to hearsay.[25]

---

[17] (1901) 82 LT 347, Ch D at 349.

[18] See 278 under **The meaning of hearsay in the Criminal Justice Act 2003**, *Implied assertions*.

[19] Section 115(3) of the Criminal Justice Act 2003: see Ch 10.

[20] Law Com No 216 (Cm 2321), para 4.35.

[21] See also the Bankers' Books Evidence Act 1879 (Ch 9), the Marriage Act 1949, s 65(3) (Ch 12), and the Solicitors Act 1974, s 18 (Ch 22).

[22] See SI 1993/621.

[23] 'Civil proceedings' has the same meaning as it has under the 1995 Act (by virtue of s 11): see s 96(7) of the 1989 Act.

[24] The order extends not only to all the proceedings defined as 'family proceedings' by s 8(2) of the 1989 Act, but also to other proceedings which are part of the magistrates' courts' family proceedings jurisdiction by virtue of s 92(2) of the 1989 Act: *R v Oxfordshire County Council* [1992] 3 WLR 88 Fam D.

[25] The party seeking to adduce the evidence must show that it has a substantial connection with the upbringing etc of the child.

Article 6(1) of the European Convention on Human Rights

In *Clingham v Kensington and Chelsea London Borough Council*[26] the Divisional Court held that there was nothing in the Human Rights Act 1998, nor in the jurisprudence of the European Court of Human Rights, which led to the automatic exclusion of hearsay evidence in civil proceedings, and that there was no requirement to give the 1995 Act any meaning which it did not naturally bear. The court also held that the admission of hearsay evidence, without the possibility of cross-examination, does not automatically result in an unfair trial under Article 6(1) of the Convention.[27]

Conditions of admissibility

Competence

As previously noted, hearsay admissible under section 1 of the 1995 Act must be evidence which is otherwise admissible. However, section 1 does not make clear whether hearsay may be admitted if the maker of the statement would not have been competent to give evidence at the time he made it. It is also unclear whether his statement, if admissible, may be proved by the statement of another who, at the time when he made his statement, would not have been competent as a witness. For example, if A makes an oral statement within the hearing of B, and A would have been competent to give evidence at that time, may A's statement be proved by B's written record as to what he said, the record having been made at a time when B would not have been competent? Section 5(1) of the Act renders explicit the competence requirements. It provides as follows:

> Hearsay evidence shall not be admitted in civil proceedings if or to the extent that it is shown to consist of, or to be proved by means of, a statement made by a person who at the time he made the statement was not competent as a witness.

> For this purpose 'not competent as a witness' means suffering from such mental or physical infirmity, or lack of understanding, as would render a person incompetent as a witness in civil proceedings; but a child shall be treated as competent as a witness if he satisfies the requirements of section 96(2)(a) and (b) of the Children Act 1989 (conditions for reception of unsworn evidence of child).[28]

The burden of proof, under section 5(1), is borne by the party seeking to exclude the evidence.[29]

The requirement of leave

Section 1 of the 1995 Act, if unqualified, would permit a party to adduce, as evidence of the matters stated, the previous out-of-court statement of a person called as a witness. The Law Commission took the view that, in the case of previous consistent statements, a leave requirement was necessary in order to prevent the pointless proliferation of superfluous evidence, which would needlessly prolong trials and increase costs.[30] Section 6 of the Act provides as follows:

> (1) Subject as follows, the provisions of this Act as to hearsay evidence in civil proceedings apply equally (but with any necessary modifications) in relation to a previous statement made by a person called as a witness in the proceedings.

---

[26] (2001) 165 JP 322, DC.
[27] See also *R (McCann) v Crown Court at Manchester* [2003] 1 AC 787, HL at [35].
[28] See Ch 5.
[29] *JC v CC* [2001] EWCA Civ 1625.
[30] See Law Com No 216 (Cm 2321), para 4.30.

(2) A party who has called or intends to call a person as a witness in civil proceedings may not in those proceedings adduce evidence of a previous statement made by that person, except—

    (a) with the leave of the court, or

    (b) for the purpose of rebutting a suggestion that his evidence has been fabricated.[31]

This shall not be construed as preventing a witness statement (that is, a written statement of oral evidence which a party to the proceedings intends to lead) from being adopted by a witness in giving evidence or treated as his evidence.[32]

Leave is required under section 6(2)(a) whether the previous statement is a previous *consistent* statement or relates to matters other than those dealt with in the testimony of the witness, but the concluding words of section 6(2) make it clear that it is not intended that a witness statement which stands as a witness's evidence-in-chief under CPR rule 32.5(2) should be regarded as a 'previous statement' for the purposes of the provision.

At common law, previous statements of a witness were generally excluded both as evidence of the truth of the facts they contained and as evidence of consistency.[33] The questions naturally arise as to what considerations the court should take into account in deciding whether to grant leave, and whether leave should be granted only exceptionally. As to the former, it is submitted that, in deciding whether to grant leave, the judge should consider the importance of the previous statement in relation to the facts in issue, the reliability and weight of the statement, including all the circumstances in which it was made, and whether admission would be unjust to the other parties to the proceedings. As to the latter, it is submitted that leave should be granted not only where the witness is incapable of giving direct evidence on the matter in question because, for example, he has no recollection of the matter (in which case, the statement would not be a previous *consistent* statement), but also where, although he is capable of giving direct evidence of the matter, it is of questionable reliability or unintelligible by reason of partial loss of memory, lapse of time, age, or illness. Such an approach would accord with the spirit of *Morris v Stratford-on-Avon RDC*,[34] a decision under the equivalent leave requirement in the 1968 Act.[35] That was an action against the council for damages for the alleged negligence of one of their employees. The trial began some five years after the cause of action arose and the employee gave confused and inconsistent evidence. After his examination-in-chief, counsel for the defendants was granted leave to admit in chief a written statement made by the employee and given to the defendants' insurers some nine months after the accident. The Court of Appeal held that the trial judge had not erred in allowing the evidence to be admitted.

Where leave is given, there is no restriction in section 6 as to when the previous statement may be given in evidence. Thus according to the circumstances, the statement may be given in

---

[31] Section 6(2)(b) is considered in Ch 6, 172, under **Previous consistent or self-serving statements.**

[32] Pursuant to s 6(3), the Act does not authorize the adducing of evidence of previous *inconsistent* statements otherwise than in accordance with ss 3, 4, and 5 of the Criminal Procedure Act 1865; and, pursuant to s 6(4), the Act does not affect the common law rules whereby a memory-refreshing document may be rendered admissible as a result of cross-examination. Section 6(3) is considered in Ch 6 (under **Hostile witnesses** at 183) and Ch 7 (under **Previous inconsistent statements** at 197); and s 6(4) is considered in Ch 6 (under **Refreshing the memory** at 163).

[33] The exceptions, in effect preserved by s 6(2)(b) and (4) of the 1995 Act, relate to statements admissible to rebut allegations of recent fabrication (see n 31, above) and memory-refreshing documents rendered admissible as a result of cross-examination (see n 32, above).

[34] [1973] 1 WLR 1059.

[35] Section 2(2).

evidence before or during the witness's examination-in-chief (which would seem appropriate if likely to improve the intelligibility of his evidence), rather than at the conclusion of his examination-in-chief. Equally, there is no restriction as to *who* may prove the statement: the court may allow evidence of the making of the previous statement to be given by someone other than its maker.

Safeguards

The requirement to give advance notice

The notice provisions of the 1995 Act are simpler and more flexible than those in operation under the 1968 Act. The objectives of the earlier provisions were that all issues arising out of the adduction of hearsay evidence should be dealt with pre-trial and that there should be no surprises at trial. The Law Commission endorsed these objectives but believed that they could be met by a notice provision which (i) requires a party to give notice of the fact that he or she proposes to adduce hearsay; and (ii) puts the onus on the receiving party to demand such particulars as he requires in order to be able to make a proper assessment of the weight and cogency of the hearsay in question and to be in a position to respond adequately to it. The Commission also appreciated that circumstances can arise in litigation rendering compliance with a notice requirement impracticable. For example, some hearings need to be arranged urgently and in other cases advance notification may carry a real risk of danger to the witness or some other person. For reasons of this kind, it recommended that allowance should be made for the possibility that, in some circumstances, it would be unreasonable and impracticable to give any notice at all. With a view to further maximizing flexibility, it also recommended that the notice provisions should be subject to rules of court to allow them to be disapplied in respect of certain classes of proceedings if, as experience is gained, that is felt to be appropriate; and that the parties should also be free to agree to exclude the notice provisions.[36] Reflecting these recommendations, section 2 of the Act provides as follows:

(1) A party proposing to adduce hearsay evidence in civil proceedings shall, subject to the following provisions of this section, give to the other party or parties to the proceedings—
   (a) such notice (if any) of that fact, and
   (b) on request, such particulars of or relating to the evidence,
   as is reasonable and practicable in the circumstances for the purpose of enabling him or them to deal with any matters arising from its being hearsay.
(2) Provision may be made by rules of court—
   (a) specifying classes of proceedings or evidence in relation to which subsection (1) does not apply, and
   (b) as to the manner in which (including the time within which) the duties imposed by that subsection are to be complied with in the cases where it does apply.
(3) Subsection (1) may also be excluded by agreement of the parties; and compliance with the duty to give notice may in any case be waived by the person to whom notice is required to be given.

The relevant rules of court are CPR rule 33.2 and 33.3.[37]

[36] See generally Law Com No 216 (Cm 2321), paras 4.9 and 4.10.
[37] CPR r 33 does not apply to claims which have been allocated to the small claims track: CPR r 27.2.

33.2 Notice of intention to rely on hearsay evidence

(1) Where a party intends to rely on hearsay evidence at trial and either—
   (a) that evidence is to be given by a witness giving oral evidence; or
   (b) that evidence is contained in a witness statement of a person who is not being called to give oral evidence;

   that party complies with section 2(1)(a) of the Civil Evidence Act 1995 by serving a witness statement on the other parties in accordance with the court's order.[38]

(2) Where paragraph (1)(b) applies, the party intending to rely on the hearsay evidence must, when he serves the witness statement—
   (a) inform the other parties that the witness is not being called to give oral evidence; and
   (b) give the reason why the witness will not be called.

(3) In all other cases where a party intends to rely on hearsay evidence at trial, that party complies with section 2(1)(a) of the Civil Evidence Act 1995 by serving a notice on the other parties which—
   (a) identifies the hearsay evidence;
   (b) states that the party serving the notice proposes to rely on the hearsay evidence at trial; and
   (c) gives the reason why the witness will not be called.

(4) The party proposing to rely on the hearsay evidence must—
   (a) serve the notice no later than the latest date for serving witness statements; and
   (b) if the hearsay evidence is to be in a document, supply a copy to any party who requests him to do so.

33.3 Circumstances in which notice of intention to rely on hearsay evidence is not required

Section 2.1 of the Civil Evidence Act 1995 (duty to give notice of intention to rely on hearsay evidence) does not apply—
   (a) to evidence at hearings other than trials;
   (aa) to an affidavit or witness statement which is to be used at trial but which does not contain hearsay evidence;
   (b) to a statement which a party to a probate action wishes to put in evidence and which is alleged to have been made by the person whose estate is the subject of the proceedings; or
   (c) where the requirement is excluded by a practice direction.

Section 2(4) of the 1995 Act provides as follows:
   (4) A failure to comply with subsection (1), or with rules under subsection (2)(b), does not affect the admissibility of the evidence but may be taken into account by the court—
   (a) in considering the exercise of its powers with respect to the course of proceedings and costs, and
   (b) as a matter adversely affecting the weight to be given to the evidence in accordance with section 4.

This subsection reflects the view of the Law Commission that if a party does not give notice, where it would have been reasonable and practicable in all the circumstances for him to have done so, the court should *not* be allowed to refuse to admit evidence.[39] Instead, under section 2(4)(a), the court, in exercise of its inherent powers to control the conduct of the proceedings,

---

[38] See Ch 5.

[39] The Commission was of the view that such a sanction could have the effect of simply re-introducing the rule against hearsay.

may grant an adjournment (to compel a party to perfect an inadequate notice or to allow the recipient time to deal with the effect of late notification) and/or may impose a costs sanction; and under section 2(4)(b), the court may take the non-compliance as a matter reducing the weight to be attached to the evidence.[40]

The power to call witnesses for cross-examination

Where a party adduces hearsay evidence of a statement but does not call the maker of the statement as a witness, and the other party to the proceedings wishes to challenge the statement, it is an obvious safeguard to allow the other party to call the maker with a view to cross-examining him as to both the accuracy of the statement and his credibility as a witness. The other party is allowed to do so under section 3 of the 1995 Act, but only with the leave of the court. Section 3 provides that:

> Rules of court may provide that where a party to civil proceedings adduces hearsay evidence of a statement made by a person and does not call that person as a witness, any other party to the proceedings may, with the leave of the court, call that person as a witness and cross-examine him on the statement as if he had been called by the first-mentioned party and as if the hearsay statement were his evidence in chief.

The relevant rule is CPR rule 33.4, which provides as follows:

(1) Where a party—
    (a) proposes to rely on hearsay evidence; and
    (b) does not propose to call the person who made the original statement to give oral evidence, the court may, on the application of any other party, permit that party to call the maker of the statement to be cross-examined on the contents of the statement.
(2) An application for permission to cross-examine under this rule must be made not more than 14 days after the day on which a notice of intention to rely on the hearsay evidence was served on the applicant.

If the court considers that the maker of the statement, even if overseas, should attend and be cross-examined at court in person, but the party proposing to rely on the evidence refuses to obey the order of the court, then the consequence will ordinarily be that the party will not be entitled to rely upon the evidence. In such a case, the court has ample powers to exclude the statement under CPR rule 32.1.[41]

Rule 33.4 normally applies when a party, having served a witness statement, proposes to rely upon it as hearsay and does not propose to call its maker as a witness. It also applies when, in the event, such a party does not put the statement in as hearsay evidence or call the witness to give evidence at the trial, and the other party, in reliance upon CPR rule 32.5(5)(b),[42] then puts the statement in as hearsay evidence. In these circumstances, the first party may apply to the court for permission to call the maker of the statement to be cross-examined on its contents.[43]

---

[40] In *TSB (Scotland) plc v James Mills (Montrose) Ltd (in receivership)* 1992 SLT 519, a decision under the Civil Evidence (Scotland) Act 1988, it was held that in certain circumstances the courts may declare the evidence wholly unreliable, in effect according it no weight.

[41] *Polanski v Condé Nast Publications Ltd* [2004] 1 WLR 387, CA at [22] to [23] and [62]. As to CPR r 32.1, see Ch 2.

[42] See above at 138, under **Witnesses in civil cases, Witness statements.**

[43] *Douglas v Hello! Ltd* [2003] EWCA Civ 332, [2003] EMLR 633, CA.

Weighing hearsay evidence

The statutory guidelines on weighing hearsay evidence do not impose any new obligation on the courts but simply indicate the more important factors which a court should bear in mind when it performs its usual function of weighing the evidence before it. The Law Commission recommended such guidelines for two reasons. First, having abolished the exclusionary rule, it wished to place extra emphasis on the need for courts to be vigilant in testing the reliability of such evidence. Secondly, it thought that it was important to deter the parties from abusing abolition of the rule, for example by deliberately failing to give notice or by giving late and inadequate notice,[44] by relying on hearsay evidence in preference to calling a dubious witness to give direct evidence of a fact,[45] or by attempting to conceal an essential witness in a case by amassing hearsay statements on a point.[46] Section 4 provides that:

(1) In estimating the weight (if any) to be given to hearsay evidence in civil proceedings the court shall have regard to any circumstances from which any inference can reasonably be drawn as to the reliability or otherwise of the evidence.
(2) Regard may be had, in particular, to the following—
    (a) whether it would have been reasonable and practicable for the party by whom the evidence was adduced to have produced the maker of the original statement as a witness;
    (b) whether the original statement was made contemporaneously with the occurrence or existence of the matters stated;
    (c) whether the evidence involves multiple hearsay;
    (d) whether any person involved had any motive to conceal or misrepresent matters;
    (e) whether the original statement was an edited account, or was made in collaboration with another or for a particular purpose;
    (f) whether the circumstances in which the evidence is adduced as hearsay are such as to suggest an attempt to prevent proper evaluation of its weight.

The phrase 'the original statement', which is used in subsection (2)(a), (b), and (e), is defined as 'the underlying statement (if any) by—(a) in the case of evidence of fact, a person having personal knowledge of that fact, or (b) in the case of evidence of opinion, the person whose opinion it is'.[47]

Section 4(2) will be of particular importance in cases in which hearsay carries inherent dangers, making it difficult for the judge to assess the truth in the absence of the original maker of the statement, as when a defendant to a claim for a possession or anti-social behaviour order is faced in court with serious complaints made by anonymous or absent witnesses about matters that took place, if at all, many months earlier.[48]

Concerning section 4(2)(a), it seems that if it would have been reasonable and practicable for the party by whom the evidence was adduced to have produced the maker of the original statement as a witness, an inference as to unreliability may be drawn, a very strong inference indeed if, had the maker been called as a witness, the court would not have granted leave

[44] See s 4(2)(f).
[45] See s 4(2)(a).
[46] See Law Com No 216 (Cm 2321), para 4.19.
[47] Section 13.
[48] *Moat Housing Group South Ltd v Harris* [2006] QB 606, CA, applied in *R (Cleary) v Highbury Corner Magistrates' Court* [2007] 1 WLR 1272, DC.

under section 6(2) to adduce evidence of the statement. It also seems that such inferences may be drawn whether or not the maker is called for cross-examination by any other party to the proceedings under section 3, although it may be that such inferences are less likely to be drawn where the other party or parties have *not* applied for leave to call and cross-examine the maker under that section.

As to section 4(2)(d), the obscure phrase 'any person involved' may be taken to include (i) the maker of the 'original statement'; (ii) the 'receiver' of the statement, ie the person who claims to have heard or otherwise perceived the statement and/or to have recorded it in a document; and (iii) in the case of multiple hearsay, ie in cases in which the information contained in the original statement is not supplied to the 'receiver' directly, any intermediaries through whom it was supplied indirectly.

Under section 4(2)(e), whether the 'original statement' was made 'for a particular purpose' (and more importantly, if it was, what that purpose was) has an obvious bearing on its likely reliability. To take an extreme example, the express purpose of the 'original statement' may have been to mislead or deceive. On the other hand, the fact that the 'original statement' was made under an important statutory or other duty may well give rise to a strong inference as to the truth of its contents.

Impeaching credibility

Section 5(2) of the 1995 Act provides that:

> Where in civil proceedings hearsay evidence is adduced and the maker of the original statement, or of any statement relied upon to prove another statement, is not called as a witness—
>
> (a) evidence which if he had been so called would be admissible for the purpose of attacking or supporting his credibility as a witness is admissible for that purpose in the proceedings; and
>
> (b) evidence tending to prove that, whether before or after he made the statement, he made any other statement inconsistent with it is admissible for the purpose of showing that he had contradicted himself.
>
> Provided that evidence may not be given of any matter of which, if he had been called as a witness and had denied that matter in cross-examination, evidence could not have been adduced by the cross-examining party.

The general purpose of section 5(2) is to ensure that evidence relating to the credibility of certain persons not called as witnesses is as admissible as if those persons had been called as witnesses. The persons in question are (i) 'the maker of the original statement' and (ii) 'the maker . . . of any statement relied upon to prove another statement'. As to the former, it seems that where the maker of the 'original statement', although not called, is available as a witness, evidence is admissible for the purpose of attacking credibility notwithstanding that the party adducing it has elected not to call and cross-examine him (with the leave of the court) under section 3. As to the latter, the meaning of 'another statement' is not clear, but presumably will be taken to mean not 'a statement other than the original statement' but 'either the original statement or any other statement'. Let us suppose that A makes an oral statement (the 'original statement') within the hearing of B; B tells C what A said; C makes a written record of his conversation with B; A, B, and C are all unavailable to give evidence; and C's written record is used to prove A's oral statement. In these circumstances, evidence relating to the credibility of A and C is clearly admissible and, it is submitted, evidence relating to the credibility of B should also be admissible.

Concerning section 5(2)(a), evidence admissible for the purpose of attacking credibility would include evidence of bias or previous convictions. Concerning section 5(2)(b), it seems that whereas in civil proceedings a prior inconsistent statement of a *witness* is not only admissible to attack his credibility but, by virtue of section 6(3) and (5) of the 1995 Act, is also admissible as evidence of any matter stated therein, a prior inconsistent statement introduced under section 5(2)(b) goes to consistency only.[49] The proviso to section 5(2) ensures that the rule on finality of answers on collateral issues[50] operates to restrict the evidence admissible under section 5(2) in the same way as it applies in relation to *witnesses*.

Where a party, in reliance on section 5(2), intends to attack the credibility of the maker of the original statement, he must give notice of his intention to do so, to the party who proposes to give the hearsay statement in evidence, not more than 14 days after the day on which a notice of intention to rely on the hearsay evidence was served on him.[51]

Proof of statements contained in documents[52]

The provisions of the 1995 Act governing the proof of statements contained in documents draw a distinction between (i) documents generally; and (ii) documents which are shown to form part of the records of a business or public authority.

Documents generally

Section 8 of the 1995 Act provides that:

(1) Where a statement contained in a document is admissible as evidence in civil proceedings, it may be proved—
   (a) by the production of that document, or
   (b) whether or not that document is still in existence, by the production of a copy of that document or of the material part of it, authenticated in such manner as the court may approve.
(2) It is immaterial for this purpose how many removes there are between a copy and the original.

A 'document' for these purposes means 'anything in which information of any description is recorded',[53] a definition covering documents in any form and therefore wide enough to include maps, plans, graphs, drawings, photographs, discs, audio-tapes, videotapes, films, microfilms, negatives, and computer-generated printouts. A 'copy', in relation to a document, means 'anything onto which information recorded in the document has been copied, by whatever means and whether directly or indirectly',[54] a definition wide enough to cover, inter alia, a transcript of an audio-tape as well as reproductions or still reproductions of the images embodied in films and videotapes etc, whether enlarged or not.

---

[49] Although the Law Commission thought it important to preserve the position under the 1968 Act in this regard, cf s 7(5) of the 1968 Act.

[50] See Ch 7.

[51] CPR r 33.5.

[52] See also Ch 9, 251, under **Documentary evidence.**

[53] Section 13.

[54] Section 13.

Concerning section 8(1)(a), 'production' refers not to counsel handing the document to the court, but to a witness who is qualified to do so in accordance with the rules of evidence producing the document and saying what it is.[55] However, although such direct oral evidence is preferable and will carry greater weight, it would seem that the document may also be proved by another hearsay statement admissible under the 1995 Act. Thus, where a statement has been deliberately tape-recorded but its maker is unavailable to produce the tape and give direct evidence that it is the tape he made, it seems that his out-of-court statements to the same effect could be used to prove the tape.[56]

The reference to 'authentication' at the end of section 8(1) appears to relate to the authentication of copies of a document as true copies of the original, and not to proof of the original.[57]

Section 8(2) makes clear that copies of copies may be received in evidence (subject to authentication in such manner as the court may approve).

Records of a business or public authority

Although at one time records of a business or public authority were kept manually and responsibility could often be attributed to an individual record keeper, nowadays record keeping within an organization has been largely taken over by technology and there is often unlikely to be a witness who can give direct evidence of all or any aspects of the compilation of the records kept. For these reasons, the Law Commission recommended that documents certified as forming part of the records of a business or public authority should be capable of being received in evidence without further proof.[58] Section 9 of the 1995 Act provides that:

(1) A document which is shown to form part of the records of a business or public authority may be received in evidence in civil proceedings without further proof.
(2) A document shall be taken to form part of the records of a business or public authority if there is produced to the court a certificate to that effect signed by an officer of the business or authority to which the records belong.
For this purpose—
    (a) a document purporting to be a certificate signed by an officer of a business or public authority shall be deemed to have been duly given by such an officer and signed by him; and
    (b) a certificate shall be treated as signed by a person if it purports to bear a facsimile of his signature.

The precise scope of section 9(1) is unclear because the word 'records', said to mean 'records in whatever form',[59] is not otherwise defined. Hopefully, the word will not be construed as narrowly as it was under the 1968 Act, where it was taken to mean 'records which a historian would regard as original or primary sources, that is documents which either give effect to a transaction itself or which contain a contemporaneous register of information supplied by those with direct knowledge of the facts'. Accordingly, copies of documents consisting of summaries of the results of research into a drug and articles and letters about the drug published

[55] Per Staughton LJ in *Ventouris v Mountain (No 2)* [1992] 1 WLR 887 at 901, CA, a decision under s 6(1) of the 1968 Act.
[56] *Ventouris v Mountain (No 2)* [1992] 1 WLR 887, CA.
[57] Ibid.
[58] See Law Com No 216 (Cm 2321), paras 3.12 and 4.39.
[59] Section 9(4).

in medical journals were held not to be records, but merely a digest or analysis of records.[60] On this test, it was said, a bill of lading or cargo manifest,[61] a tithe map,[62] or a transcript of criminal proceedings[63] would rank as a record, but not a file of correspondence[64] or an anonymous document setting out a summary of legal proceedings taken or contemplated against a company.[65] In *Savings and Investment Bank Ltd v Gasco Investments (Netherlands) BV*[66] it was held that a report of inspectors appointed by the Secretary of State for Trade on the affairs and ownership of a company was not a record: it fell short of a compilation of the information supplied because it contained only a selection of that information, and went beyond such a compilation because it also contained the opinions of the inspectors.[67]

Under section 9(4), 'business' includes 'any activity regularly carried on over a period of time, whether for profit or not, by any body (whether corporate or not) or by an individual'; and 'public authority' includes 'any public or statutory undertaking, any government department and any person holding office under Her Majesty'. The wide definition of 'business' reflects the Law Commission's view that it is the quality of regularity that lends a business record its reliability, not the existence of a profit motive or the judicial nature of the person carrying on the activity. A business defined in this way may not have 'officers' in the strict sense of that word and, accordingly, under section 9(4), 'officer' includes 'any person occupying a responsible position in relation to the relevant activities of the business or public authority or in relation to its records'.

Unless the court orders otherwise, a document which may be received in evidence under section 9(1) shall not be receivable at trial unless the party intending to put it in evidence has given notice of his intention to the other parties; and where he intends to use the evidence as evidence of any fact, then he must give notice not later than the latest date for serving witness statements.[68] Where a party has given such notice, he must also give every other party an opportunity to inspect the document and to agree to its admission without further proof.[69]

The Law Commission considered that the absence of an entry in a record should be capable of being formally proved, despite the fact that proving a negative (and drawing inferences from it) is rarely possible by reference to any human source.[70] The most appropriate method of doing this was thought to be by way of affidavit. Section 9(3) provides that:

> The absence of an entry in the records of a business or public authority may be proved in civil proceedings by affidavit of an officer of the business or authority to which the records belong.

---

[60] *H v Schering Chemicals Ltd* [1983] 1 All ER 849, QBD.

[61] See *R v Jones; R v Sullivan* [1978] 1 WLR 195, CA, a decision under the Criminal Evidence Act 1965 (Ch 10).

[62] See *Knight v David* [1971] 1 WLR 1671, Ch D.

[63] See *Taylor v Taylor* [1970] 1 WLR 1148, CA.

[64] See *R v Tirado* (1974) 59 Cr App R 80, CA, a decision under the Criminal Evidence Act 1965. Cf *R v Olisa* [1990] Crim LR 721, CA: for the purposes of s 68 of the Police and Criminal Evidence Act 1984, three application forms completed by a customer of a bank did 'form part of a record' compiled by the bank officials.

[65] See *Re Koscot Interplanetary (UK) Ltd, Re Koscot AG* [1972] 3 All ER 829.

[66] [1984] 1 WLR 271, Ch D.

[67] See also *Re D (a minor)* [1986] 2 FLR 189, Fam D, where notes of an interview between a solicitor and his client fell short of being a complete record of what was said. They were treated as a selective and necessarily subjective *aide memoire*, in that the solicitor put down what he thought was relevant for the purpose of preparing a pleading, affidavit or other legal document.

[68] CPR r 33.6(2), (3), and (4).

[69] CPR r 33.6(8).

[70] See *R v Patel* [1981] 3 All ER 94, CA; *R v Shone* (1983) 76 Cr App R 72, CA; and generally Ch 10, 283, under **The meaning of hearsay in the Criminal Justice Act 2003**, *Negative hearsay*.

Presumably, the contents of the affidavit constitute hearsay and are therefore subject to the usual safeguards relating to notice, power to call for cross-examination, and weight.

The Law Commission recognized that, although business and other records have long been treated as belonging to a class of evidence which can be regarded as likely to be reliable, there are bound to be exceptions, and it therefore recommended a specific discretion, allowing courts to disapply the certification provisions.[71] Section 9(5) provides that:

> The court may, having regard to the circumstances of the case, direct that all or any of the above provisions of this section do not apply in relation to a particular document or record, or description of documents or records.

Evidence formerly admissible at common law

General

Section 9 of the 1968 Act preserved and gave statutory force to a number of common law exceptions to the hearsay rule (informal admissions, published works dealing with matters of a public nature, and public documents and records) without purporting to amend the law in relation to those exceptions. Subject to one important difference, this state of affairs is perpetuated by the 1995 Act. The important difference relates to informal admissions. The Law Commission considered that there was no longer any need to preserve this common law exception and recommended that the general provisions of the Act, including the notice and weight provisions, should apply to informal admissions as they apply to other hearsay statements.[72] Section 7(1) of the 1995 Act gives statutory effect to this recommendation and is considered further below. Concerning published works dealing with matters of a public nature, and public documents and records, however, the Commission recommended preserving the relevant common law rules because: (a) some of the statutory provisions which it believed should not be affected by its proposals presuppose the existence of the common law rules about public registers;[73] (b) it was not the policy of the Commission to add the procedural burden of the notice procedure where no such burden already existed; and (c) it would be rare for the weight to be attached to such evidence to be a matter for debate.[74] Section 7(2) gives statutory effect to this recommendation. The common law rules effectively preserved by the 1995 Act are considered in Chapter 12.

Informal admissions

Under section 7(1) of the 1995 Act, 'the common law rule effectively preserved by section 9(1) and (2)(a) of the 1968 Act (admissibility of admissions adverse to a party) is superseded by the provisions of this Act'. As noted above, the purpose of the subsection is to give effect to the Law Commission's recommendation that the general provisions of the Act should apply to informal admissions.[75]

---

[71] Law Com No 216 (Cm 2321), para 4.42.

[72] Law Com No 216 (Cm 2321), paras 4.32 and 4.33.

[73] Evidence (Foreign, Dominion and Colonial Documents) Act 1933, s 1 (see Chs 2 and 12) and the Oaths and Evidence (Overseas Authorities and Countries) Act 1963, s 5.

[74] Law Com No 216, (Cm 2321), para 4.33.

[75] Section 3, however, could hardly apply to an informal admission made by a party to legal proceedings (as opposed to someone in privity with him): it would involve that party calling and cross-examining himself!

The application of section 1 of the 1995 Act (admissibility)
At common law an informal admission was a statement by a party to the proceedings (or someone in privity with him) made other than while testifying in those proceedings and adverse to his case. Any such statement is now covered by section 1(1) of the Act and, by reason of the wide statutory definition of statement ('any representation of fact or opinion, however made'), an admission may be admitted whether made orally, in writing, or by conduct, demeanour, or even silence. Thus as at common law, a person may make an oral admission when talking either to another[76] or to himself.[77] Similarly, in the case of written admissions, the admission may be contained in a communication, such as a letter, or in a diary or other private memorandum.[78] A common law example of an admission by conduct is *Moriarty v London, Chatham and Dover Rly Co*,[79] where evidence of the plaintiff's conduct in suborning witnesses was admitted as an admission by him of the weakness and falsity of his claim. Where an out-of-court accusation is made against a party, his answer, whether given by words or conduct, may constitute an admission insofar as it amounts to an acknowledgment of the truth of the whole or part of the accusation made. Presumably, even silence, by way of reply, will amount to a 'statement' where the accusation is made in circumstances such that it would be reasonable to expect some explanation or denial. At common law, in *Wiedemann v Walpole*[80] Lord Esher MR said that, in the case of a letter written upon a matter of business, the court could take notice of the ordinary course adopted by men of business to answer letters the contents of which they do not intend to admit, so that a failure to reply to such a letter could be taken as some evidence of the truth of the statements contained in it, but that a man could not reasonably be expected to reply to a letter charging him with some offence or impropriety because 'it is the ordinary and wise practice of mankind not to answer such letters'.[81]

The application of section 4 of the Act (weight)
Section 4 of the 1995 Act applies to informal admissions as it applies to other hearsay statements. However, there are a number of special considerations which are relevant to the weighing of admissions. Some of these are of a general character, but there are also two specific considerations: whether the admission relates to facts of which its maker had no personal knowledge, and whether the admission was vicarious, ie made by someone in privity with a party to legal proceedings.

General considerations.   The weight to be attached to an informal admission depends upon its precise contents, the circumstances in which it was made (for example whether it was made as a result of some threat or inducement), and any contradictory or other evidence adduced by its maker at the trial with a view to explaining it away. In some cases, the tribunal of fact will need to consider carefully whether the statement is, in fact, adverse to the case of its maker, and for this purpose regard should be had to the whole statement, including any passages favourable to its maker which qualify, explain, or even nullify so much of the statement as is relied upon

[76] See *Rumping v DPP* [1964] AC 814, HL (the maker's wife).
[77] See per Alderson B in *R v Simons* (1834) 6 C&P 540.
[78] See *Bruce v Garden* (1869) 18 WR 384.
[79] (1870) LR 5 QB 314. See also *Alderson v Clay* (1816) 1 Stark 405.
[80] [1891] 2 QB 534, CA.
[81] Cf *Bessela v Stern* (1877) 2 CPD 265, CA.

as an admission. Although it may be that less weight may be attached to the favourable or self-serving parts of the statement,[82] it is clear that under the 1995 Act they are as much evidence of the facts they state as the passages relied upon as constituting an admission.[83]

Personal knowledge. An informal admission may be admitted under the 1995 Act notwithstanding that it relates to facts of which its maker has no personal knowledge[84] or amounts to no more than an expression of opinion or belief.[85] The weight to be attached to such evidence will vary according to the circumstances. For example, an admission by a party as to his age, although obviously based on hearsay, concerns a matter as to which it is reasonable to expect that he has been accurately informed.[86] On the other hand, in *Comptroller of Customs v Western Lectric Co Ltd*,[87] the Privy Council was of the view that an admission concerning the countries of origin of certain imported goods, made in reliance on the fact that the goods bore marks and labels indicating that they came from those countries, was evidentially worthless.[88]

Vicarious admissions. The rationale of the common law exception was the presumed unlikelihood of a person speaking falsely against his own interest, a rationale reflected in the rule that an informal admission could only be received in evidence if it was made directly (ie by a party to the legal proceedings) or vicariously (ie by someone in privity with a party). 'Privity' in this context usually denoted some common or successive interest in the subject matter of the litigation or some other relationship between the party and the privy, for example that of principal and agent, whereby the latter had actual or imputed authority to speak on behalf of the former. Under the 1995 Act, an out-of-court statement adverse to the case of a party may be received in evidence whether made by that party or by *anyone else*. However, the weight to be attached to an admission made by someone who, at common law, would have been in privity with a party is generally likely to be greater than an admission made by anyone else.

Those in privity included: (i) a predecessor in title of a party to proceedings (provided that the admission concerned title to the property in question and was made at a time when he had an interest in the property);[89] (ii) a partner (an admission or representation made by any partner concerning the partnership affairs and in the ordinary course of its business being evidence against the firm);[90] (iii) referees;[91] and (iv) agents. At common law, an admission by an agent could only be received against his principal if (a) it was made at a time when the agency existed (a matter which, apparently, could be inferred from the statements and conduct of the alleged agent himself);[92] (b) the communication in which it was made was authorized,

[82] See *Smith v Blandy* (1825) Ry&M 257.
[83] See *Harrison v Turner* (1847) 10 QB 482.
[84] Under s 1(2)(b), 'references to hearsay include hearsay of whatever degree'.
[85] Under s 13, a 'statement' is defined to include 'any representation of opinion'.
[86] See, at common law, *R v Turner* [1910] 1 KB 346, CCA and *Lustre Hosiery Ltd v York* (1936) 54 CLR 134, High Court of Australia.
[87] [1966] AC 367.
[88] See per Lord Hodson at 371.
[89] *Woolway v Rowe* (1834) 1 Ad&El 114. See also *Smith v Smith* (1836) 3 Bing NC 29.
[90] See the Partnership Act 1890, s 15, giving statutory force to a common law principle to the same effect. See also *Jaggers v Binnings* (1815) 1 Stark 64 and *Wood v Braddick* (1808) 1 Taunt 104.
[91] *Williams v Innes* (1808) 1 Camp 364, KB, where Lord Ellenborough CJ said (at 365): 'If a man refers another upon any particular business to a third person, he is bound by what this third person says or does concerning it, as much as if that had been said or done by himself.'
[92] See, *sed quaere*, *Edwards v Brookes (Milk) Ltd* [1963] 1 WLR 795, QBD.

whether expressly or by implication, by the principal;[93] and (c) it was made in the course of a communication with some third party as opposed to the principal himself.[94] Under the 1995 Act, failure to establish these three matters will not affect admissibility, but is likely to affect adversely the weight to be attached to the 'admission'.

The weight to be attached to an 'admission' made by someone who at common law would not have been in privity with a party is generally likely to be less than an admission made by that party himself or someone who would have been in privity with him. At common law there was no privity between (i) spouses, merely by virtue of their relationship of husband and wife; (ii) a parent and a child, merely by virtue of that relationship;[95] (iii) co-parties, ie co-plaintiffs or co-defendants (or, in divorce proceedings, a respondent and a co-respondent);[96] or (iv) a witness and the party calling him.[97]

Ogden tables

Section 10 of the 1995 Act provides that:

> The actuarial tables (together with explanatory notes) for use in personal injury and fatal accident cases issued from time to time by the Government Actuary's Department are admissible in evidence for the purpose of assessing, in an action for personal injury, the sum to be awarded as general damages for future pecuniary loss.

ADDITIONAL READING

Law Commission, *The Hearsay Rule in Civil Proceedings* (Law Com No 216, London, 1993).

---

[93] *Wagstaff v Wilson* (1832) 4 B&Ad 339; *G (A) v G (T)* [1970] 2 QB 643, CA; and *Johnson v Lindsay* (1889) 53 JP 599, DC. See also *Burr v Ware RDC* [1939] 2 All ER 688, CA and cf *Beer v W H Clench (1930) Ltd* [1936] 1 All ER 449, DC.

[94] See *Re Devala Provident Gold Mining Co* (1883) 22 Ch D 593, Ch D and cf *The Solway* (1885) 10 PD 137, P, D and Admlty.

[95] *G (A) v G (T)* [1970] 2 QB 643, CA.

[96] *Morton v Morton, Daly and McNaught* [1937] P 151, P, D and Admlty and *Myatt v Myatt and Parker* [1962] 1 WLR 570, P, D and Admlty.

[97] See *British Thomson-Houston Co Ltd v British Insulated and Helsby Cables Ltd* [1924] 2 Ch 160, CA and cf *Richards v Morgan* (1863) 4 B&S 641.

Hearsay admissible at common law

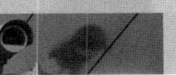

12

Key Issues

- If a statement is made out of court and tendered as evidence of the facts asserted (hearsay), why should it be admissible when:

    (a) it was made in a public document, eg a public register;

    (b) it was made in a work of reference dealing with a matter of a public nature, eg histories and maps;

    (c) it was made by a person who, at the time, was emotionally overpowered by an event, eg a victim of a serious assault; or

    (d) it relates to the contemporaneous physical sensation or mental state of its maker?

Under the common law rule against hearsay, any assertion, other than one made by a person while giving oral evidence in the proceedings, was inadmissible if tendered as evidence of the facts asserted. As we have seen in Chapters 10 and 11, the circumstances in which hearsay is admissible in criminal proceedings is now governed by Chapter 2 of Part 11 of the Criminal Justice Act 2003 (the 2003 Act), and in civil proceedings hearsay is admissible subject to compliance with the conditions of admissibility set out in the Civil Evidence Act 1995 (the 1995 Act). The categories of hearsay considered in this chapter—statements in public documents, works of reference, evidence of age, evidence of reputation, and statements forming part of the *res gestae*—share two common features: all of them were established at common law as exceptions to the rule against hearsay and all of them have been preserved by statute. All of the cases considered, apart from evidence of age and *res gestae* statements, have been expressly preserved and given statutory force in both criminal proceedings (by section 118(1) of the 2003 Act) and civil proceedings (by section 7(2) and (3) of the 1995 Act). The categories relating to evidence of age and statements forming part of the *res gestae* have been preserved in criminal but not civil proceedings. However, evidence formerly admissible in these cases at common law will now be admissible in civil proceedings under the general provisions of the 1995 Act.

It is convenient to consider the common law rules separately, here, under the rubric of hearsay admissible at common law, because neither section 118 of the 2003 Act nor section 7 of the 1995 Act purports to amend the rules to which they have given statutory force. Section 7(4) of the 1995 Act provides that the words in which a rule of law mentioned in the section is described 'are intended only to identify the rule and shall not be construed as altering it in any way'; and although there is no express equivalent in section 118 of the 2003 Act, it is plain that it too is designed to identify rules of law rather than alter them. Furthermore, where evidence is admissible under one of the preserved rules, it is not subject to other statutory conditions of admissibility and safeguards. However, the common law exceptions have been narrowly construed, and much evidence failing to meet all of the common law conditions of admissibility may well be admissible in civil proceedings under the general provisions of the 1995 Act (subject to compliance with the statutory conditions) and in criminal proceedings under statutory provisions of a general nature such as sections 116 and 117 of the 2003 Act (cases where a witness is unavailable and business and other documents).

Statements in public documents

Section 7(2)(b) and (c) of the 1995 Act preserve any rule of law whereby in civil proceedings—

- (b) public documents (for example, public registers, and returns made under public authority with respect to matters of public interest) are admissible as evidence of the facts stated in them, or
- (c) records (for example, the records of certain courts, treaties, Crown grants, pardons and commissions) are admissible as evidence of facts stated in them.

Section 118(1)1(b) and (c) of the 2003 Act preserve the same rules in criminal proceedings.

General

At common law, statements made in most public documents are admissible in both civil and criminal cases as evidence of the matters stated.[1] The admissibility of such evidence may be justified on the grounds of reliability and convenience. Where a record has been compiled by a person acting under a public duty to inquire into the truth of some matter and to record his findings so that the public may refer to them, the contents of that document may be presumed to be true.[2] Proof of the facts stated in the document by direct evidence would clearly be preferable, but in many cases the public official in question will be dead, otherwise unavailable or unable to remember the facts recorded because of the time which has elapsed. The common law principles relating to public documents, though not unimportant, are of comparatively minor significance, mainly because of the existence of a wide variety of statutory provisions which cater for the admissibility of particular classes of public document in both criminal and civil proceedings. Under section 34 of the Births and Deaths Registration Act 1953, for example, a certified copy of an entry purporting to be sealed or stamped with the seal of the General Register Office, shall be received as evidence of the birth or death to which it relates.[3]

Examples

The terms of section 7(2)(b) and (c) of the 1995 Act give some idea of the different classes of public document admissible under this head. The exception applies to a variety of public papers, official registers, surveys, assessments, inquisitions, returns, and other documents made under public authority in relation to matters of public concern. Examples include: recitals in public Acts of Parliament and royal proclamations;[4] entries relating to acts of state and public matters in parliamentary journals and governmental Gazettes;[5] entries in parish registers of baptisms, marriages, and burials;[6] extracts from foreign registers kept under the sanction of public authority as to matters properly and regularly recorded in them;[7] entries in the public books of a corporation relating to matters of public interest;[8] the contents of a file from the Companies Register containing the statutory returns made by a company in compliance with the Companies Act 1948;[9] the conditions of the licence on which a prisoner

---

[1] Concerning proof of the contents of a public document upon which a party seeks to rely, see Ch 9.

[2] See per Parke B in *Irish Society v Bishop of Derry* (1846) 12 Cl&Fin 641, HL.

[3] See also the Marriage Act 1949, s 65(3) (proof of the celebration of a marriage by the production of a certified copy of an entry kept at the General Register Office).

[4] *R v Sutton* (1816) 4 M&S 532.

[5] *A-G v Theakston* (1820) 8 Price 89; *R v Holt* (1793) 5 Term Rep 436.

[6] Entries in such registers of the particulars of birth and death would appear to be inadmissible because outside the actual knowledge of the person making the entries: see per Geoffrey Lane LJ in *R v Halpin* [1975] QB 907 CA, at 914; cf per Lord Blackburn in *Sturla v Freccia* (1880) 5 App Cas 623 at 644, HL.

[7] For example, foreign registers of baptisms and marriages: see per Lord Selborne in *Lyell v Kennedy* (1889) 14 App Cas 437 at 448–9, HL. See also the Evidence (Foreign, Dominion and Colonial Documents) Act 1933, whereby an Order in Council may provide that registers of a foreign country are documents of such a public nature as to be admissible as evidence of matters regularly recorded therein.

[8] *Shrewsbury v Hart* (1823) 1 C&P 113.

[9] *R v Halpin* [1975] QB 907, CA, below. See now the Companies Act 2006. Other documentary records relating to companies, such as the certificate of incorporation, the register of members and minutes of proceedings of meetings, are rendered admissible by the Act itself.

serving a term of imprisonment is released from custody;[10] statements in coastguards' books on weather conditions;[11] entries in university records relating to degrees conferred;[12] entries in Domesday Book;[13] records of assessment by commissioners of land tax;[14] inquisitions and surveys of Crown lands;[15] inquisitions in lunacy;[16] findings of professional misconduct by the General Medical Council;[17] and statements in a bishop's return to a writ from the Exchequer relating to vacancies and advowsons in his diocese.[18]

Conditions of admissibility

Given the multiplicity of public documents to which the exception applies, it is perhaps not surprising that the conditions of admissibility vary, to some extent, according to the particular type of document in question. Generally speaking, however, it seems that a public document is only admissible as evidence of the truth of its contents if (a) it concerns a public matter, (b) it was made by a public officer acting under a duty to inquire and record the results of such inquiry, and (c) it was intended to be retained for public reference or inspection.[19]

A public matter

In *Sturla v Freccia*[20] Lord Blackburn expressed the opinion that 'public', in this context, should not be taken to mean the whole world: the matter in question may concern either the public at large or a section of the public. Thus an entry in the books of a manor may be public as concerning all the people interested in the manor[21] and an entry in a corporation book concerning a corporate matter or something in which all the corporation is concerned may be public in the same sense.[22]

A public officer acting under a duty to inquire and record

A statement in a public document is only admissible if it was made by a public officer, as opposed to some private individual,[23] acting in discharge of a strict duty to inquire into and satisfy himself of the truth of the facts recorded.[24] Thus whereas a certificate of the registrar of births, deaths, and marriages is admissible as prima facie—but not conclusive—evidence of

---

[10] *West Midlands Probation Board v French* [2009] 1 WLR 1715. However, it has been doubted whether the conditions of such a licence are hearsay evidence at all: see D Ormerod, 'West Midlands Probation Board v French' (case comment) [2009] *Crim LR* 283.

[11] *The Catherina Maria* (1866) LR 1 A&E 53.

[12] *Collins v Carnegie* (1834) 1 Ad&El 695.

[13] *Duke of Beaufort v John Aird & Co* (1904) 20 TLR 602.

[14] *Doe d Strode v Seaton* (1834) 2 Ad&El 171.

[15] *Duke of Beaufort v Smith* (1849) 4 Exch 450.

[16] *Faulder v Silk* (1811) 3 Camp 126; *Harvey v R* [1901] AC 601, PC.

[17] *Hill v Clifford* [1907] 2 Ch 236, CA.

[18] *Irish Society v Bishop of Derry* (1846) 12 Cl&Fin 641, HL.

[19] See generally per Lord Blackburn in *Sturla v Freccia* (1880) 5 App Cas 623, HL at 643–4.

[20] (1880) 5 App Cas 623, HL.

[21] See, eg, *Heath v Deane* [1905] 2 Ch 86, Ch D (manorial rolls).

[22] But see *Hill v Manchester and Salford Waterworks Co* (1833) 5 B&Ad 866. See also *R v Sealby* [1965] 1 All ER 701, (Crown Court).

[23] *Daniel v Wilkin* (1852) 7 Exch 429 (a survey undertaken by a private individual).

[24] *Doe d France v Andrews* (1850) 15 QB 756; *Thrasyvoulos Ioannou v Papa Christoforos Demetriou* [1952] AC 84, PC; *White v Taylor* [1969] 1 Ch 150, Ch D.

the fact and date of a birth, death, or marriage,[25] it would appear, according to the obiter view of Swinfen Eady MR in *Bird v Keep*,[26] that information concerning the cause of death contained in a death certificate and based on information supplied by a coroner is inadmissible as evidence of the cause of death. This conclusion has been justified on the grounds that the registrar is *bound* to record the verdict of the coroner's jury and is under no duty to state the results of his own personal inquiry according to his own judgment.[27] Under the modern law, however, it seems that strict compliance with the requirement of personal knowledge on the part of a public official of the matters which he puts on file or records is no longer necessary. In *R v Halpin*[28] the appellant was convicted of conspiracy to cheat and defraud a council by making bogus claims for certain work allegedly carried out by a company. In order to prove that the appellant was a director of the company at the relevant time and therefore that any fraud that had been perpetrated must have been with his knowledge or connivance, the prosecution adduced in evidence at the trial a file from the Companies Register containing the annual returns made by the company under the Companies Act 1948. On appeal, it was argued that the file was inadmissible as a public document because the relevant official at the Companies Register has no duty to inquire and satisfy himself as to the truth of the recorded facts. Geoffrey Lane LJ, giving the judgment of the Court of Appeal, was satisfied that under the common law authorities it was a condition of admissibility that the official making the record should either have had personal knowledge of the matters recorded or should have inquired into the accuracy of the facts. However, although satisfied that on the facts the official in the Companies Registry had no personal knowledge of the matters which he had put on file or recorded, his Lordship said:[29]

> The common law as expressed in the earlier cases which have been cited were plainly designed to apply to an uncomplicated community where those charged with keeping registers would, more often than not, be personally acquainted with the people whose affairs they were recording and the vicar, as already indicated, would probably himself have officiated at the baptism, marriage or burial which he later recorded in the presence of the churchwardens on the register before putting it back in the coffers. But the common law should move with the times and should recognize the fact that the official charged with recording matters of public import can no longer in this highly complicated world, as like as not, have personal knowledge of their accuracy.
>
> What has happened now is that the function originally performed by one man has had to be shared between two: the first having the knowledge and the statutory duty to record that knowledge and forward it to the Registrar of Companies, the second having the duty to preserve that document and to show it to members of the public under proper conditions as required.

---

[25] See *Wilton & Co v Phillips* (1903) 19 TLR 390, KBD; *Brierley v Brierley and Williams* [1918] P 257, P, D and Admlty. However, a birth certificate by itself is insufficient to establish the fact of marriage between the parents of the child in question because it does not identify the persons it mentions. Such a certificate, in conjunction with other evidence, may suffice as proof of the fact of marriage between the parents: *Re Stollery, Weir v Treasury Solicitor* [1926] Ch 284, CA. See also *R v Clapham* (1829) 4 C&P 29: a statement in a parish register of baptisms that the person baptized was born on a particular day is not admissible as evidence of the date of birth, the record being admissible on the question of baptism not birth.

[26] [1918] 2 KB 692, CA at 697, 698 and 701.

[27] See per Scrutton LJ in *Re Stollery, Weir v Treasury Solicitor* [1926] Ch 284, CA at 322. But see also per Sargent LJ at 327: since the verdict of the coroner's jury is itself inadmissible as evidence of the truth of the facts on which it is based, it follows that the short note made of that verdict in the death certificate is also inadmissible.

[28] [1975] QB 907. See also *R v Sealby* [1965] 1 All ER 701 (Crown Court) at 703–4; cf *White v Taylor* [1969] 1 Ch 150, Ch D.

[29] [1975] QB 907 at 915.

Accordingly, it was held that where a duty is cast upon a company by statute to make accurate returns of company matters to the Registrar of Companies so that those returns can be filed and inspected by members of the public, all statements on the return are prima facie proof of the truth of their contents.

The statement in the public document must have been made by the official whose duty it was to inquire and record. Thus an entry in a register of baptisms made by the minister of the parish is admissible, but not a private memorandum made by the parish clerk.[30] At one time it appears that an entry in a register was only admissible if made promptly.[31] However, in *R v Halpin*, where the entries in the files from the Companies Register were acknowledged to be very much out of time, Geoffrey Lane LJ said that this was a matter which might go to their weight, but not to their admissibility.[32] Likewise, the fact that an entry was made by an interested party may affect its weight but will not, of itself, render it inadmissible. Thus, in *Irish Society v Bishop of Derry*,[33] statements in a bishop's return to a writ from the Exchequer relating to advowsons in his diocese were held to be admissible notwithstanding that some of the advowsons belonged to the bishop himself.

Retention for public reference

A public document, to be admissible as such, must have been brought into existence as a document of record to be retained indefinitely: a document intended to be of temporary effect[34] or designed to serve only temporary purposes[35] is inadmissible. Additionally, the document should have been prepared for the purposes of the public making use of it and must be available for public inspection.[36] In *Lilley v Pettit*[37] it was held that the regimental records of a serving soldier were not admissible as public documents, since they were kept for the information of the Crown and executive as opposed to members of the public, who had no right of access to them. Similarly, in *R v Sealby*,[38] a car registration book was ruled to be inadmissible as evidence of its contents, for example the chassis and engine numbers, on the grounds that it is a private document issued to a car owner who is under no obligation to produce it for inspection by anyone except a police officer or a local taxation officer.

Works of reference

Section 7(2)(a) of the 1995 Act preserves any rule of law whereby in civil proceedings—

---

[30] *Doe d Warren v Bray* (1828) 8 B&C 813.

[31] (1828) 8 B&C 813, where the minister made an entry in the register of the baptism of a child which had taken place before he had any connection with the parish and in respect of which he had acted on information from the parish clerk.

[32] [1975] QB 907 at 916, CA.

[33] (1846) 12 Cl&Fin 641, HL.

[34] *White v Taylor* [1969] 1 Ch 150, Ch D (a draft document).

[35] *Mercer v Denne* [1905] 2 Ch 538, CA.

[36] Per Lord Blackburn in *Sturla v Freccia* (1880) 5 App Cas 623 HL, at 648; *Thrasyvoulos Ioannou v Papa Christoforos Demetriou* [1952] AC 84, PC.

[37] [1946] KB 401, DC.

[38] [1965] 1 All ER 701 (Crown Court).

(a) published works dealing with matters of a public nature (for example, histories, scientific works, dictionaries and maps) are admissible as evidence of facts of a public nature stated in them . . .

Section 118(1)1(a) of the 2003 Act preserves the same rule in criminal proceedings.

Under the common law rule, authoritative published works of reference dealing with matters of a public nature are admissible to prove, or to assist the court in deciding whether to take judicial notice of, facts of a public nature stated in them.[39] Examples include: historical works concerning ancient public facts;[40] standard medical texts concerning the nature of a disease;[41] engineers' reports within the common knowledge of engineers and accepted by them as accurate on the nature of certain soil;[42] Carlisle Tables, which set out the average life expectancy of persons;[43] dictionaries, on the meaning of English words;[44] and published maps and plans generally offered for sale to the public, even if not prepared by someone acting under a public duty, concerning facts of geographical notoriety.[45]

Evidence of age

Section 118(1)1(d) of the 2003 Act preserves the following rule of law in criminal proceedings:

(d) evidence relating to a person's age or date or place of birth may be given by a person without personal knowledge of the matter.

Since the date of a person's birth is contained in his or her birth certificate, the normal way of proving a person's age is to produce a certified copy of an entry in the register of births, which is admissible under section 34 of the Births and Deaths Registration Act 1953 as evidence of the matters stated, accompanied by some evidence to identify the person whose age is in question with the person named in the certificate. At common law, the accompanying evidence of identification may be given by a person without personal knowledge of the matter, such as the evidence of a grandmother who, although present at the birth of her grandchild, was not present at the registration.[46] Similarly, the courts have acted on evidence as to age given by the person whose age is in question[47] or by another who has made enquiries as to his or her age.[48]

---

[39] On judicial notice generally, see Ch 22.

[40] *Read v Bishop of Lincoln* [1892] AC 644, PC. But not facts of a private or local nature: *Stainer v Droitwich (Burgesses)* (1695) 1 Salk 281. See also *Evans v Getting* (1834) 6 C&P 586 and *Fowke v Berington* [1914] 2 Ch 308, Ch D.

[41] *McCarthy v The Melita (Owners)* (1923) 16 BWCC 222, CA.

[42] *East London Rly Co v Thames Conservators* (1904) 90 LT 347, Ch D.

[43] *Rowley v London and North Western Rly Co* (1873) LR 8 Exch 221, Ex Ch.

[44] *Marchioness of Blandford v Dowager Duchess of Marlborough* (1743) 2 Atk 542 (a law dictionary); *R v Agricultural Land Tribunal, ex p Benney* [1955] 2 QB 140, CA (Fowler's *Modern English Usage*).

[45] See *R v Orton* (1873) and *R v Jameson* (1896) *Stephen's Digest of the Law of Evidence* (10th edn) 48.

[46] *R v Weaver* (1873) LR 2 CCR 85 CCR. See also *Wilton & Co v Phillips* (1903) 19 TLR 390, KBD.

[47] *Re Bulley's Settlement* [1886] WN 80, Ch D.

[48] *R v Bellis* (1911) 6 Cr App R 283, CCA.

Evidence of reputation

Section 7(3)(a) and (b) of the 1995 Act provide as follows:

> The common law rules . . . whereby in civil proceedings
>
> (a) evidence of a person's reputation is admissible for the purpose of establishing his good or bad character, or
> (b) evidence of reputation or family tradition is admissible—
>> (i) for the purpose of proving or disproving pedigree or the existence of a marriage,[49] or
>> (ii) for the purpose of proving or disproving the existence of any public or general right or of identifying any person or thing,
>
> shall continue to have effect in so far as they authorise the court to treat such evidence as proving or disproving that matter.
>
> Where any such rule applies, reputation or family tradition shall be treated for the purposes of this Act as a fact and not as a statement or multiplicity of statements about the matter in question.

As to the concluding part of section 7(3), it is born of a recognition that evidence of reputation or family tradition, if tendered to establish the facts reputed or the facts according to family tradition, is necessarily composed of a multiplicity of hearsay statements and therefore, if treated as such in civil proceedings, would render impossible application of the notice and weighing provisions of the 1995 Act.[50] The effect of treating such evidence as evidence of fact, in contrast, is that the party proposing to adduce the evidence will not be expected to give to the other party to the proceedings particulars of the person who had personal knowledge of the matter in question and of all the intermediaries through whom the information was conveyed to the declarant;[51] and the court, in assessing the weight of the evidence, will not be expected to have regard to a factor such as whether the person with personal knowledge made the 'original statement' contemporaneously with the occurrence or existence of the matters stated.[52]

Section 118(1)2 and 3 of the 2003 Act preserve, in criminal proceedings, the same rules as those identified in section 7(3)(a) and (b) of the 1995 Act. They also make clear that the rules are preserved in criminal proceedings only insofar as they allow the court to treat such evidence as proving the matter concerned. Thus if the matter concerned should not be open to proof of any kind, because that would be to introduce, for example, inadmissible evidence of bad character, then plainly the matter cannot be proved under any of the preserved common law rules.

Evidence of reputation for the purpose of establishing good or bad character requires no further explanation. The other preserved common law rules are technical and complex and are, perhaps, best considered under two headings, declarations as to pedigree and declarations as to public and general rights.

---

[49] The rule preserved by s 7(3)(b)(i) for the purpose of proof or disproof of the existence of a marriage applies in an equivalent way for the purpose of proof or disproof of the existence of a civil partnership: see the Civil Partnership Act 2004, s 84(5).

[50] Law Com No 216 (Cm 2321), para 4.34.

[51] See s 2 of the 1995 Act (Ch 11).

[52] See s 4 of the 1995 Act (Ch 11).

Declarations as to pedigree

At common law, a declaration concerning pedigree is admissible, after its maker's death, as evidence of the truth of its contents. This exception to the hearsay rule has been justified on the grounds that such declarations are often the only evidence that can be obtained concerning facts which may have occurred many years before the trial.[53] Matters of pedigree concern the relationship by blood or marriage between persons and therefore include, for example, the fact and date of births, marriages, and deaths, legitimacy, celibacy, failure of issue, and intestacy. Pedigree declarations may be oral, for example, declarations by deceased parents that one of their children, whose legitimacy is in issue, was born before their marriage; in writing, for example an entry in a family Bible, an inscription on a tombstone or a pedigree hung up in the family home; or by conduct, as when parents always treat one child as illegitimate and introduce and treat another child as the heir of the family.[54] There are three conditions of admissibility. First, the declaration is only admissible in proceedings in which a question of pedigree is directly in issue.[55] Secondly, the declaration must have been made by a blood relation or the spouse of a blood relation as opposed to, for example, relations in law,[56] domestic servants, or intimate acquaintances.[57] There is no requirement, however, of personal knowledge on the part of the declarant as to the facts stated, which may amount to no more than family tradition or reputation handed down from one generation to another.[58] Thirdly, the declaration must have been made *ante litem motam*, that is before any controversy arose upon the matter in question.[59] The controversy may create a bias in the minds of members of the family rendering their declarations unreliable. However, provided that the declaration was made *ante litem motam*, the fact that the declarant had an interest in establishing the relationship in question would appear to go only to weight and not admissibility.[60]

Declarations as to public and general rights

At common law, an oral or written statement concerning the reputed existence of a public or general right is admissible, after its maker's death, as evidence of the existence of that right. The primary justification for the admissibility of such evidence is the fact that other evidence, especially in the case of ancient rights, is usually unavailable. The declaration must concern a public or general and not a private right,[61] unless the private right coincides with a public right. Thus when a question arises as to the boundary of a private estate that is conterminous with a hamlet, evidence of reputation concerning the boundary of the latter is admissible to

---

[53] See per Best CJ in *Johnston v Lawson* (1824) 2 Bing 86 at 89 and generally per Lord Mansfield CJ in the *Berkeley Peerage Case* (1811) 4 Camp 401, HL.

[54] Per Lord Mansfield CJ in *Goodright d Stevens v Moss* (1777) 2 Cowp 591. See also *Vowles v Young* (1806) 13 Ves 140 (engravings upon rings).

[55] *Haines v Guthrie* (1884) 13 QBD 818, CA.

[56] *Shrewsbury Peerage Case* (1858) 7 HL Cas 1.

[57] *Johnson v Lawson* (1824) 2 Bing 86.

[58] *Davies v Lowndes* (1843) 6 Man&G 471; *Doe d Banning v Griffin* (1812) 15 East 293.

[59] *Berkeley Peerage Case* (1811) 4 Camp 401, HL; *Shedden v A-G* (1860) 2 Sw&Tr 170; and *Butler v Mountgarret* (1859) 7 HL Cas 633.

[60] *Doe d Tilman v Tarver* (1824) Ry&M 141; *Doe d Jenkins v Davies* (1847) 10 QB 314. But see *Plant v Taylor* (1861) 7 H&N 211.

[61] *Lonsdale v Heaton* (1830) 1 You 58.

prove the boundary of the former.[62] Public rights are those common to the public at large, such as rights to use paths,[63] highways,[64] ferries,[65] or landing-places on the banks of a river.[66] General rights are those common to a section of the public or a considerable class of persons, such as the inhabitants of a parish or the tenants of a manor.[67] In the case of a public right, it seems that any person is competent to make a declaration as to its reputed existence, because it concerns everyone, and the fact that the declarant has no knowledge of the subject goes only to weight, not admissibility. A declaration as to general rights, however, is only admissible if it was made by a person with some connection with or knowledge of the matter in question.[68] There are two further conditions of admissibility and these apply whether the declaration concerns public or general rights. First, as in the case of declarations as to pedigree, the declaration must have been made *ante litem motam*.[69] Secondly, the declaration must concern the reputed existence of the right in question and not particular facts tending to support or negative the existence of that right.[70]

Statements forming part of the *res gestae*

'Res gestae', it has been said, is 'a phrase adopted to provide a respectable legal cloak for a variety of cases to which no formula of precision can be applied'.[71] The words themselves simply mean a transaction. Under the inclusionary common law doctrine of *res gestae*, a fact or a statement of fact or opinion which is so closely associated in time, place, and circumstances with some act, event, or state of affairs which is in issue that it can be said to form a part of the same transaction as the act or event in issue, is itself admissible in evidence. The justification given for the reception of such evidence is the light that it sheds upon the act or event in issue: in its absence, the transaction in question may not be fully or truly understood and may even appear to be meaningless, inexplicable, or unintelligible. Despite judicial dicta to the contrary,[72] it is clear from the authorities that such statements have been received by way of exception to the common law rule against hearsay as evidence of the matters asserted. The multiplicity of cases in which hearsay statements have been received under the doctrine were usefully subdivided, by the late Sir Rupert Cross, into the following categories: (i) statements by participants in or observers of events or, as they would more accurately be described in the light of subsequent developments, statements by persons emotionally overpowered by an event; (ii) statements accompanying the maker's performance of an act;

---

[62] *Thomas v Jenkins* (1837) 6 Ad&El 525. See also *Stoney v Eastbourne RDC* [1927] 1 Ch 367, CA.

[63] See *Radcliffe v Marsden* UDC (1908) 72 JP 475 Ch D.

[64] See *R v Bliss* (1837) 7 Ad&El 550. See now Highways Act 1980, s 32, above.

[65] *Pim v Curell* (1840) 6 M&W 234.

[66] *Drinkwater v Porter* (1835) 7 C&P 181.

[67] *Nicholls v Parker* (1805) 14 East 331. However, numerous private rights of common of the several tenants of a manor do not amount to one public right: see *Earl of Dunraven v Llewellyn* (1850) 15 QB 791. See also *White v Taylor* [1969] 1 Ch 150, Ch D (individual rights of pasturage for sheep).

[68] See *Berkeley Peerage Case* (1811) 4 Camp 401, HL; *Rogers v Wood* (1831) 2 B&Ad 245; and *Crease v Barrett* (1835) 1 Cr M&R 919.

[69] *Berkeley Peerage Case* (1811) 4 Camp 401, HL. See also *Moseley v Davies* (1822) 11 Price 162.

[70] *Mercer v Denne* [1905] 2 Ch 538, CA. See also *R v Bliss* (1837) 7 Ad&El 550.

[71] Per Lord Tomlin in *Homes v Newman* [1931] 2 Ch 112, Ch D at 120.

[72] See, eg, per Lord Atkinson in *R v Christie* [1914] AC 545, HL at 553 and per Dixon J in *Adelaide Chemical and Fertilizer Co Ltd v Carlyle* (1940) 64 CLR 514 (High Court of Australia) at 531.

(iii) statements relating to a physical sensation; and (iv) statements relating to a mental state. The same categorization has been used in the 2003 Act to identify the common law rules preserved and put on a statutory footing.

In *R v Callender*[73] the Court of Appeal said that *res gestae* is a single principle and that a statement can only be admitted under the *res gestae* exception to the hearsay rule if the trial judge is satisfied that there is no real possibility of concoction or distortion. This dictum, it is submitted, has been made *per incuriam*. The requirement referred to only applies to *res gestae* statements in the first of the categories set out above.

Statements by persons emotionally overpowered by an event

Section 118(1)4(a) of the 2003 Act preserves the following rule of law in criminal proceedings:

> Any rule of law under which in criminal proceedings a statement is admissible as evidence of any matter stated if—
> (a) the statement was made by a person so emotionally overpowered by an event that the possibility of concoction or distortion can be disregarded.

Statements made concerning an event in issue in circumstances of such spontaneity or involvement in the event that the possibility of concoction, distortion, or error can be disregarded, are admissible as evidence of the truth of their contents. One of the earliest illustrations of the principle is to be found in *Thompson v Trevanion*,[74] where 'what the wife said immediate upon the hurt received and before that she had time to devise or contrive anything for her own advantage' was held to be admissible in evidence. In *R v Foster*,[75] on a charge of manslaughter by reckless driving, a statement made by the deceased immediately after he had been run down was admitted to show the cause of the accident.[76]

To the extent that some of the earlier cases were decided without regard to the likelihood of concoction, distortion, or error, but merely on the basis of whether the statement was spontaneous in the sense that it could be regarded as part of the event in question, they must be treated with considerable caution. Thus it has been said that *R v Bedingfield*,[77] one of the most famous cases on the subject, 'is more useful as a focus for discussion than for the decision on the facts'.[78] Bedingfield was charged with the murder of a woman. The deceased, her throat cut, came out of a room where she had been with the accused and immediately exclaimed 'Oh dear, Aunt, see what Bedingfield has done to me!' Cockburn CJ held that although statements made while the act is being done, such as 'Don't, Harry!' are admissible, the victim's statement could not be received in evidence because 'it was something stated by her after it was all over, whatever it was, and after the act was completed'. Commenting upon this decision in *Ratten v R*,[79] Lord Wilberforce said: 'though in a historical sense the emergence of the victim could be described as a different "*res*" from the cutting

---

[73] [1998] Crim LR 337, CA.

[74] (1693) Skin 402.

[75] (1834) 6 C&P 325 (Central Criminal Court).

[76] See also *Davies v Fortior Ltd* [1952] 1 All ER 1359, QBD where the statement in question would now be admissible under the Civil Evidence Act 1995.

[77] (1879) 14 Cox CC 341, Assizes; cf *R v Fowkes* (1856) The Times, 8 Mar (Ch 6).

[78] Per Lord Wilberforce in *Ratten v R* [1972] AC 378, PC at 390.

[79] [1972] AC 378, PC.

of the throat, there could hardly be a case where the words uttered carried more clearly the mark of spontaneity and intense involvement.' It follows, of course, that *R v Bedingfield* would be decided differently today.[80]

In *Ratten v R*, Ratten was convicted of the murder of his wife by shooting her. His defence was that a gun went off accidentally while he was cleaning it. The evidence established that the shooting of the wife, from which she died almost immediately, must have taken place between 1.12 pm and about 1.20 pm. A telephonist from the local exchange gave evidence that at 1.15 pm she had received a telephone call from Ratten's house made by a sobbing woman who in an hysterical voice had said, 'Get me the police please.' The Privy Council held that the telephonist's evidence was not hearsay and had been properly admitted because of its relevance to the issues.[81] However, the Privy Council then proceeded to consider the admissibility of the evidence on the assumption that it *did* contain a hearsay element, ie that the words used by the wife did involve an assertion of the truth of some fact, for example that she was being attacked by her husband. On this assumption, it was held that the evidence would have been admissible as part of the *res gestae* because not only was there a close association in place and time between the statement and the shooting, but also the way in which the statement came to be made, in a call for the police, and the tone of voice used, showed intrinsically that the statement was being forced from the wife by an overwhelming pressure of contemporary events. In *R v Newport*,[82] on the other hand, it was held that evidence of the contents of a telephone call made by the victim of a murder to her friend 20 minutes before she was stabbed had been improperly admitted: the call was not a spontaneous and unconsidered reaction to an immediately impending emergency.

In *Ratten v R*, Lord Wilberforce, delivering the reasons of the Board, said:[83]

> the test should be not the uncertain one whether the making of the statement was in some sense part of the event or transaction. This may often be difficult to establish: such external matters as the time which elapses between the events and the speaking of the words (or vice versa), and differences in location being relevant factors but not, taken by themselves, decisive criteria. As regards statements made after the event it must be for the judge, by preliminary ruling, to satisfy himself that the statement was so clearly made in circumstances of spontaneity or involvement in the event that the possibility of concoction can be disregarded. Conversely, if he considers that the statement was made by way of narrative of a detached prior event so that the speaker was so disengaged from it as to be able to construct or adapt his account, he should exclude it. And the same must in principle be true of statements made before the event. The test should be not the uncertain one, whether the making of the statement should be regarded as part of the event or transaction. This may often be difficult to show. But if the drama, leading up to the climax, has commenced and assumed such intensity and pressure that the utterance can safely be regarded as a true reflection of what was unrolling or actually happening, it ought to be received.

Lord Wilberforce's test was applied by the Court of Appeal in *R v Nye, R v Loan*,[84] and *R v Turnbull*,[85] and has been affirmed, by the House of Lords, in *R v Andrews*.[86] In *R v Nye, R v Loan*,

---

[80] Per Lord Ackner in *R v Andrews* [1987] AC 281, HL.

[81] See Ch 10.

[82] [1998] Crim LR 581, CA.

[83] [1972] AC 378, PC at 389.

[84] (1977) 66 Cr App R 252, CA.

[85] (1984) 80 Cr App R 104, CA.

[86] [1987] AC 281, HL.

Loan was convicted of assault. Following a collision between two cars, Loan, the passenger from one of the cars assaulted Lucas, the driver of the other, by punching him in the face. Somewhat shaken, Lucas sat in his car waiting to regain full possession of his faculties. The police were summoned and arrived shortly afterwards, the police station being only a few yards away. Lucas then made a statement identifying Loan, as opposed to the *driver* of the other car, as his assailant. The Court of Appeal, adding what was described as a gloss on Lord Wilberforce's test, namely 'was there any real possibility of error?',[87] was satisfied that there had been no opportunity for concoction and no chance of error and accordingly held that Lucas' statement had been properly admitted under the *res gestae* principle as a spontaneous identification. Lawton LJ said:[88]

> Was there an opportunity for concoction? The interval of time was very short indeed. During part of that interval Mr Lucas was sitting down in his car trying to overcome the effects of the blows which had been struck. Commonsense and experience of life tells us that in that interval he would not be thinking of concocting a case against anybody.

In *R v Turnbull* Ronald Turnbull was convicted of murder. At about 8.30 pm on the day in question the victim, who had been stabbed about 100 yards from a public house, staggered into the bar and collapsed on the floor. An ambulance was sent for and arrived at 8.33 pm. On a number of occasions, after he had arrived in the bar and while in the ambulance, the victim was asked to identify his assailant. The victim, who had a powerful Scottish accent and had been drinking heavily during the day, answered variously 'Tommo', 'Ronnie Tommo', and 'Ronnie'. The prosecution case was that the victim had been attempting to refer to Ronald Turnbull. The Court of Appeal held that the evidence had been properly admitted by the trial judge under the *res gestae* principle as explained by Lord Wilberforce in *Ratten v R*.

In *R v Andrews* Donald Andrews was convicted of manslaughter and aggravated burglary. Andrews and another man, O'Neill, with a blanket covering their heads, knocked on the door of the victim's flat and, when he opened it, stabbed him. Then, no longer covered by the blanket, they stole property from the flat. Minutes later, the victim, bleeding profusely from a deep stomach wound, went to the flat below for assistance. Again, within a matter of minutes, the police arrived. One of the constables asked the victim how he had received his injuries. In reply, the victim referred to one of his assailants as a man known to him as 'Donald'. The other constable present, who was making a note of this statement, heard and wrote down the name 'Donavon'. There was evidence that the victim had a Scottish accent, had drunk to excess, and had a motive to fabricate or concoct, namely a malice against the accused because he believed that on a previous occasion O'Neill, accompanied by Andrews, had attacked and damaged his house. The House of Lords held that the victim's statement to the police had been properly admitted under the *res gestae* doctrine. Lord Ackner summarized the relevant principles to be applied by the trial judge as follows:[89]

> (1) The primary question which the judge must ask himself is: can the possibility of concoction or distortion be disregarded? (2) To answer that question the judge must first consider the circumstances in which the particular statement was made, in order to satisfy himself that the event was so unusual or startling or dramatic as to dominate the thoughts of the victim,

---

[87] But see further, *R v Andrews* [1987] AC 281, HL, below.

[88] (1977) 66 Cr App R 252 at 256.

[89] [1987] AC 281 at 300–1.

so that his utterance was an instinctive reaction to that event, thus giving no real opportunity for reasoned reflection. In such a situation the judge would be entitled to conclude that the involvement or pressure of the event would exclude the possibility of concoction or distortion, providing that the statement was made in conditions of approximate but not exact contemporaneity. (3) In order for the statement to be sufficiently 'spontaneous' it must be so closely associated with the event which has excited the statement that it can fairly be stated that the mind of the declarant was still dominated by the event. Thus the judge must be satisfied that the event which provided the trigger mechanism for the statement was still operative. The fact that the statement was made in answer to a question is but one factor to consider under this heading. (4) Quite apart from the time factor, there may be special features in the case, which relate to the possibility of concoction or distortion. In the instant appeal the defence relied on evidence to support the contention that the deceased had a motive of his own to fabricate or concoct, namely a malice . . . The judge must be satisfied that the circumstances were such that, having regard to the special feature of malice, there was no possibility of any concoction or distortion to the advantage of the maker or the disadvantage of the accused. (5) As to the possibility of error in the facts narrated in the statement, if only the ordinary fallibility of human recollection is relied on, this goes to the weight to be attached to and not to the admissibility of the statement and is therefore a matter for the jury. However, here again there may be special features that may give rise to the possibility of error. In the instant case there was evidence that the deceased had drunk to excess . . . Another example would be where the identification was made in circumstances of particular difficulty or where the declarant suffered from defective eyesight. In such circumstances the trial judge must consider whether he can exclude the possibility of error.

R v Andrews was applied in *R v Carnall*,[90] where the victim, P, badly beaten and stabbed, took an hour to crawl for help before then naming Carnall, first to two witnesses who saw him in the street, bleeding heavily and asking for help, and later to a police officer, in an ambulance. The Court of Appeal held the evidence to have been properly admitted. Despite the time lapse and the fact that P had only named his assailant in response to questions, the trial judge was satisfied that his thoughts were so dominated by what had happened as to be unaffected by ex post facto reasoning or fabrication; and although P was known to have acted dishonestly in the past, the judge had properly taken the view that, in the context of the situation, there was nothing to make one think that he would do otherwise than tell the first person he saw who had inflicted his appalling injuries.

In *R v Andrews* Lord Ackner said that while he accepted that the doctrine admits hearsay statements not only where the declarant is dead or otherwise not available but also when he is called as a witness, he would strongly deprecate any attempt in criminal prosecutions to use the doctrine as a device to avoid calling the maker of the statement, when available.[91] This dictum, which does not prevent the admission of a *res gestae* statement made by someone who, served with a witness summons, fails to attend the trial,[92] was applied in *Tobi v Nicholas*.[93] However, it is clear from *Attorney General's Reference (No 1 of 2003)*[94] that it is not to be treated as an extra bar, in law, to admissibility. In that case, W was charged with a serious assault on his mother. The prosecution proposed to call witnesses to give evidence that they found

---

[90] [1995] Crim LR 944, CA.
[91] [1987] AC 281, HL at 302.
[92] *Edwards and Osakwe v DPP* [1992] Crim LR 576, DC.
[93] [1987] Crim LR 774, DC.
[94] [2003] 2 Cr App R 453, CA.

Mrs W lying by the steps of her house in great distress and that she had implicated her son, saying, among other things, 'He's gone bonkers. He threw me downstairs and set me on fire. Phone the police and the ambulance.' The prosecution did not intend to call the mother because they believed that she would give untruthful evidence and exculpate her son. She had declined to make a witness statement but had made a deposition in which she said that she was not prepared to attend court to give evidence against her son. The judge held that the evidence of the witnesses was inadmissible. As a result, the prosecution offered no evidence and not guilty verdicts were entered. The Court of Appeal held that once evidence is within the *res gestae* exception to the hearsay rule it is admissible and there is no rider, in law, that it is not to be admitted if better evidence is available or because the maker of the statement is available to give evidence. However, the judge should have been prepared to entertain an application by the defence under section 78 of the Police and Criminal Evidence Act 1984 (the 1984 Act). If the purpose of the Crown is that the *res gestae* evidence should be given without any opportunity for the defence to cross-examine the mother, the court may well conclude that the evidence will have an adverse effect on the fairness of the proceedings and refuse to admit it. As a general principle, it cannot be right that the Crown should be permitted to rely on such part of a victim's evidence as they considered reliable, without being prepared to tender the victim to the defence, so that the defence can challenge that part of the victim's evidence on which the Crown seeks to rely and elicit that part of her evidence on which the defence might seek to rely. Applying these principles to the facts of the case, the Court of Appeal concluded that it had effectively come to the same conclusion as the judge, the difference being that whereas the judge had erroneously added an extra legal bar to admissibility, their Lordships would have excluded the evidence in exercise of the discretion to exclude under section 78 of the 1984 Act.

The *res gestae* doctrine under discussion applies whether the statement was made by the victim of the offence, a bystander, or even, in appropriate circumstances, the accused himself. In *R v Glover*[95] a man assaulted J and was forcibly restrained. In anger, he then uttered the words 'I am David Glover … ', followed by a threat to shoot J and his family. Despite the possibility that the assailant was not Glover but deliberately pretending to be him, the words were held to be admissible on the basis that the opportunity for concoction or distortion was so unlikely that it could be disregarded.

Concerning the nature of the proof required to establish that a statement was made in such conditions of involvement or pressure that the possibility of concoction or error can be ruled out, it would appear that although the trial judge may, for these purposes, refer to the contents of the statement itself, the necessary connection between the statement and the event cannot be shown *solely* by reference to those contents because 'otherwise the statement would be lifting itself into the area of admissibility'.[96]

Concerning the summing-up, in *R v Andrews* it was held that the judge should make it clear to the jury that it is for them to decide what was said and that they should be sure that the witnesses were not mistaken in what they believed to have been said. The jury should also be satisfied that the declarant did not concoct or distort and, if there is material to raise the issue, that he was not activated by malice or ill-will. Further, the jury's attention should be drawn to any special features that bear on the possibility of mistake. In some cases judges

---

[95] [1991] Crim LR 48, CA.
[96] Per Lord Wilberforce in *Ratten v R* [1972] AC 378, PC at 391. See also *R v Taylor* 1961 (3) SA 614.

may think it appropriate to alert the jury to the need for extra caution because the evidence cannot be tested by cross-examination, but failure to do so, by itself, will not amount to a misdirection.[97]

Statements accompanying the maker's performance of an act

Section 118(1)4(b) of the 2003 Act preserves the following rule of law in criminal proceedings:

> Any rule of law under which in criminal proceedings a statement is admissible as evidence of any matter stated if—
>> (b) ... the statement accompanied an act which can properly be evaluated as evidence only if considered in conjunction with the statement.

Statements explaining an act in issue or relevant to an issue made by a person contemporaneously with his performance of that act are admissible as evidence of the truth of their contents. The best person to explain the significance of an act is often the person who performed it and the requirement of contemporaneity affords some guarantee of reliability. Typical examples are a bankrupt's statement as to his intention in going or remaining abroad[98] and, on a question of domicile, a statement of a person who has lived abroad as to whether he intends to live there permanently or only temporarily.[99] There are three conditions of admissibility. First, the statement must explain or otherwise relate to the act in question. In *R v Bliss*,[100] the issue being whether a certain road was public or private, evidence of a declaration made by a deceased owner of adjoining land, on planting a willow, that he was planting it to mark the boundary of the road and his estate, was held to be inadmissible. The declaration—which in any event was irrelevant, the question being not of boundary but as to the public or private character of the road—was said to have no connection with the act performed. Secondly, the statement must be more or less contemporaneous with the act performed. In the case of continuing acts, it suffices if the statement was made during their continuance, albeit some considerable time after their commencement. Thus in *Rawson v Haigh*,[101] where the question was whether a debtor had gone overseas with the intention of avoiding his creditors, letters indicating such an intention written subsequent to the act of departure were held to be admissible on the grounds that departing the realm is a continuing act and the letters were written during its continuance. Thirdly, the statement must be made by the person performing the act and not, for example, by someone witnessing it. In *Howe v Malkin*,[102] an action for trespass, evidence of a statement concerning the position of a boundary made by the plaintiff's father while certain work was being carried out on the land by builders was excluded. Grove J said:

> no act was shown to have been done by the plaintiff's father at the time of making the alleged statement, so that the declaration was by one person, and the accompanying act by another. That does not appear to me to come within the rule.

---

[97] *R v Carnall* [1995] Crim LR 944, CA.

[98] *Rawson v Haigh* (1824) 2 Bing 99; *Rouch v Great Western Rly Co* (1841) 1 QB 51.

[99] *Bryce v Bryce* [1933] P 83. See also *Scappaticci v A-G* [1955] P 47, P, D and Admlty (declarations concerning domicile of choice).

[100] (1837) 7 Ad&El 550.

[101] (1824) 2 Bing 99. See also *Homes v Newman* [1931] 2 Ch 112, Ch D.

[102] (1878) 40 LT 196, DC.

Under this head of *res gestae*, the statement is usually admissible to explain the declarant's reasons for, or intention in, performing some independent physical act. However, in *R v McCay*,[103] in which a witness was unable to remember the number of the man he had picked out at an identification parade carried out from behind a two-way mirror, an officer who had been present at the parade was allowed to give evidence that the witness had said 'It is number eight'. It was held that the physical activity of looking at the suspect, and the intellectual activity of recognizing him, were together sufficient to amount to a relevant act in respect of which the accompanying words were admissible. The difficulty with the decision is that even if there had been a physical act, such as pointing to or touching the suspect, earlier authority has clearly assumed that accompanying words of identification are *not* covered by the *res gestae* exception.[104] However, in *R v Lynch*[105] the Court of Appeal confirmed that the interpretation of the doctrine in *R v McCay* does accurately reflect the *res gestae* exception to the hearsay rule but noted that the concept of words spoken being part and parcel of an act implies a very limited scope and so a description of the role played by a suspect during an alleged offence is not admissible under the exception.

Statements relating to a physical sensation or a mental state

Section 118(1)4(c) of the 2003 Act preserves the following rule of law in criminal proceedings:

> Any rule of law under which in criminal proceedings a statement is admissible as evidence of any matter stated if—
>
> (c) ... the statement relates to a physical sensation or a mental state (such as intention or emotion).

Statements relating to a physical sensation

Statements of contemporaneous physical sensation experienced by a person are admissible as evidence of the existence of that sensation, if it is in issue or relevant to an issue, but not as evidence of its possible causes. Thus a statement made by an ill workman to the effect that his illness was caused by an accident in his employment and is causing him certain bodily or mental pain is admissible to prove the sensation of pain but not the cause of the illness.[106] One of the earliest illustrations of the principle is *Aveson v Lord Kinnaird*,[107] which concerned the truth or falsity of a statement, made when a policy of life insurance was taken out by a husband on the life of his wife, that she was then in a good state of health. It was held that statements of bodily symptoms made by her when lying in bed, apparently ill, were admissible to show her bad state of health at the time when the policy was effected. The authorities indicate that the exception is not confined to statements of sensation experienced at the actual moment when the maker is speaking, the requirement of contemporaneity being a question of degree.[108]

---

[103] [1990] 1 WLR 645, CA.

[104] See, eg, *R v Christie* [1914] AC 545, HL, in which a child touched the sleeve of the accused and said 'That is the man'; and *R v Gibson* (1887) 18 QBD 537, in which a woman pointed to the door of a house and said 'The person who threw the stone went in there.'

[105] [2008] 1 Cr App R 338, CA.

[106] *Gilbey v Great Western Rly Co* (1910) 102 LT 202, CA. See also *R v Johnson* (1847) 2 Car&Kir 354; *R v Conde* (1867) 10 Cox CC 547; *R v Gloster* (1888) 16 Cox CC 471; and contrast *R v Black* (1922) 16 Cr App R 118, CCA.

[107] (1805) 6 East 188.

[108] See per Salter J, *arguendo*, in *R v Black* (1922) 16 Cr App R 118, CCA at 119; *Aveson v Lord Kinnaird* (1805) 6 East 188; and contrast per Charles J in *R v Gloster* (1888) 16 Cox CC 471 (Central Criminal Court).

Statements relating to a mental state

Statements made by a person concerning his contemporaneous state of mind or emotion are admissible as evidence of the existence of his state of mind or emotion at that time, if it is in issue or relevant to an issue, but not as evidence of any other fact or matter stated. Thus where a bankrupt makes a payment which is alleged to be a fraudulent preference, evidence of a statement by him that he knew he was insolvent is admissible to prove his knowledge of that fact at the time when the payment was made, but not to prove the insolvency.[109] Statements may be admitted under this head to prove such diverse matters as political opinion,[110] marital affection,[111] fear,[112] and dislike of a child.[113] It seems reasonably clear that a statement made by a person as to his intention is also admissible under this exception as evidence of the existence of such intention at the time when the statement was made.[114] The admissibility of such a statement, however, gives rise to two further questions: first, whether it can support an inference that the intention also existed at a date prior or subsequent to the date on which the statement was made and, secondly, in the case of a statement of intention to do a certain act, whether it is admissible to prove that such an act was done. Concerning the first question, the authorities support an affirmative answer[115] except in the case of a party's self-serving statements of intention, which, it has been said, cannot support an inference that the speaker's intention also existed at some later (or earlier) time than the date on which the statement was made, because 'otherwise it would be easy for a man to lay grounds for escaping the consequences of his wrongful acts by making such declarations'.[116] Concerning the second question, the authorities conflict.[117] In *R v Buckley*[118] the accused was charged with the murder of a police officer on a certain night. On the crucial issue of whether it was the accused who had committed the offence, Lush J admitted a statement made by the deceased to a senior officer on the morning of the day in question to the effect that he intended to watch the movements of the accused that night. Similarly, in *R v Moghal*,[119] a more recent murder trial in which M was charged with aiding and abetting S, his mistress, who had already been tried separately and acquitted, M's defence being that S had committed the offence and that he was no more than a terrified spectator, the Court of Appeal expressed the opinion that a tape-recorded statement by S made some six months before the murder to the effect that she intended to kill the victim would have been

---

[109] *Thomas v Connell* (1838) 4 M&W 267.

[110] *R v Tooke* (1794) 25 State Tr 344.

[111] *Trelawney v Coleman* (1817) 1 B&Ald 90; *Willis v Bernard* (1832) 8 Bing 376.

[112] *R v Vincent, Frost and Edwards* (1840) 9 C&P 275; *R v Gandfield* (1846) 2 Cox CC 43; and *Neill v North Antrim Magistrates' Court* [1992] 1 WLR 1220 HL, at 1228-9.

[113] *R v Hagan* (1873) 12 Cox CC 357. See also per Mahon J in *Customglass Boats Ltd v Salthouse Bros Ltd* [1976] 1 NZLR 36 (New Zealand Supreme Court).

[114] See per Mellish LJ in *Sudgen v Lord St Leonards* (1876) 1 PD 154 CA, at 251.

[115] See per Cozens-Hardy MR in *Re Fletcher, Reading v Fletcher* [1917] 1 Ch 339, CA at 342 (proof of earlier intention) and per Lord Ellenborough in *Robson v Kemp* (1802) 4 Esp 233 (proof of subsequent intention).

[116] Per Crampton J in *R v Petcherini* (1855) 7 Cox CC 79. See also *R v Callender* [1998] Crim LR 337, CA.

[117] For a consideration of this aspect of the doctrine of *res gestae* (and what it means to 'preserve' a disputed rule of common law) see: Munday, 'Legislation that would "preserve" the common law: the case of the declaration of intention' [2008] LQR 46.

[118] (1873) 13 Cox CC 293, Assizes.

[119] (1977) 65 Cr App R 56, CA.

admissible on the accused's behalf.[120] In *R v Wainwright*,[121] on the other hand, Cockburn CJ ruled that evidence of a statement made by the victim of a murder on leaving her lodgings that she was going to the accused's premises was inadmissible because 'it was only a statement of intention which might or might not have been carried out'. *R v Thomson*[122] is to the same effect. The defence to a charge of using an instrument on a woman in order to procure a miscarriage was that the woman, who had died before the trial, had operated on herself. The Court of Criminal Appeal held that evidence, in support of the defence, that the woman had made a statement some weeks before her miscarriage that she intended to operate on herself (and had said, one week after the miscarriage, that she had done so) had been properly excluded as inadmissible hearsay.[123]

ADDITIONAL READING

Munday, 'Legislation that would "preserve" the common law: the case of the declaration of intention" [2008] *LQR* 46.

[120] It has been doubted, however, whether the evidence was of any relevance to the issue, namely whether M was a willing accomplice or an unwilling spectator: per Lord Bridge in *R v Blastland* [1986] AC 41, HL at 59–60.

[121] (1875) 13 Cox CC 171 (Central Criminal Court). See also *R v Pook* (1871) 13 Cox CC 172.

[122] [1912] 3 KB 19, CCA.

[123] But see also the much discussed decision of the United States' Supreme Court in *Mutual Life Insurance Co v Hillman* 145 US 285 (1892).

Confessions

13

Key Issues

- Why should a confession made by an accused be admissible in evidence to prove what he admitted?

- Having regard to the ways in which a confession made by an accused may be obtained, when should the prosecution be prevented from relying upon a confession?

- When should a confession made by an accused be admissible for a co-accused?

- Should the trial judge have discretion to exclude a confession, even if it is admissible in law, and if so, on what basis (a) where the prosecution rely on the confession; (b) where a co-accused relies upon the confession?

- When a confession is given in evidence by the prosecution and implicates both its maker and a co-accused, when, if at all, should it be used against the co-accused?

- In what circumstances may a statement made in the presence of the accused be treated as a confession made by him?

- If a confession is inadmissible, should it prevent the admissibility in evidence of incriminating facts discovered in consequence of the confession (as when, for example, a confession to theft includes a statement that the stolen goods are in the accused's home, where they are subsequently found)?

Admissibility

The background

The Police and Criminal Evidence Act 1984 (the 1984 Act) brought about major changes in the law relating to the admissibility of confessions. It will be useful, however, before examining the statutory provisions, to summarize briefly the position at common law. At common law an informal admission (ie an out-of-court statement made by an accused against his interest), was admissible by way of exception to the hearsay rule, as evidence of the truth of its contents, on the basis that what a person says against himself is likely to be true. An informal admission made by an accused person prior to his trial to a person in authority was known as a confession, an expression which included not only a full admission of guilt but also any incriminating statement.[1] A person in authority, generally speaking, was anyone who had authority or control over the accused or over the proceedings or the prosecution against him.[2] In most cases, the person in authority was the police officer investigating the case or interrogating the accused. A confession could not be given in evidence by the prosecution unless shown by them to be a voluntary statement in the sense that it was not obtained from the accused by fear of prejudice or hope of advantage exercised or held out by a person in authority[3] or by oppression.[4] If the admissibility of the confession was in dispute, the issue fell to be determined by the trial judge on a *voir dire* in the absence of the jury. The prosecution bore the legal burden of proving beyond reasonable doubt that the confession was voluntary.[5] If the prosecution failed to discharge this burden, the confession was inadmissible. However, even if satisfied beyond reasonable doubt that it was made voluntarily, the trial judge could exclude it, in the exercise of his discretion, on the grounds that (i) its prejudicial effect outweighed its probative value; (ii) it was obtained by improper or unfair means;[6] or (iii) it was obtained in breach of the Judges' Rules.[7]

Confessions defined

Section 82(1) of the 1984 Act adopts the inclusive definition of the word recommended by the Criminal Law Revision Committee.[8] It provides that:

In this . . . Act—
'confession' includes any statement wholly or partly adverse to the person who made it, whether made to a person in authority or not and whether made in words or otherwise;

The definition, by making no distinction between a statement wholly or partly adverse to the accused, preserves the effect of Lord Reid's dictum, at common law, in *Customs and Excise Comrs v Harz and Power*,[9] that there is no difference, in relation to admissibility, between a confession

[1] See per Lord Reid in *Customs and Excise Comrs v Harz and Power* [1967] 1 AC 760 at 817–18.
[2] Per Viscount Dilhorne in *Deokinanan v R* [1969] 1 AC 20, PC at 33.
[3] Per Lord Sumner in *Ibrahim v R* [1914] AC 599, PC at 609. In *DPP v Ping Lin* [1976] AC 574 at 597, Lord Hailsham said that he thought Lord Sumner had really said, not 'exercised', but 'excited'.
[4] Per Lord Parker CJ in *Callis v Gunn* [1964] 1 QB 495, DC at 501 and per Edmund Davies LJ in *R v Prager* [1972] 1 WLR 260 at 266, CA.
[5] *R v Thompson* [1893] 2 QB 12, CCR.
[6] See *R v Sang* [1980] AC 402, HL.
[7] Per Lord Goddard CJ in *R v May* (1952) 36 Cr App R 91 at 93 and per Edmund Davies LJ in *R v Prager* [1972] 1 WLR 260 at 265–6, CA.
[8] 11th Report (Cmnd 4991) paras 58 and 66.
[9] [1967] 1 AC 760 at 817–18.

and an admission falling short of a full confession.[10] Section 82(1) is wide enough to cover a plea of guilty. Thus if an accused pleads guilty but is subsequently granted leave to vacate the plea, the guilty plea, together with the basis of the plea, may be admitted in evidence at his trial as a confession statement.[11] In suitable cases, for example where the evidence is admissible on behalf of the prosecution under section 76 of the 1984 Act and the accused, at the time of entering the guilty plea was unrepresented or misunderstood the nature of the charge, it seems that the judge, as at common law, can exclude the evidence in the exercise of his discretion;[12] but if the evidence is admissible on behalf of a co-accused under section 76A of the Act, there is no residual discretion to exclude it in the interests of a fair trial.[13]

Section 82(1) covers 'mixed' statements, that is statements which are both inculpatory and exculpatory in nature.[14] However, in *R v Hasan*,[15] the House of Lords, approving *R v Sat-Bhambra*,[16] held that the subsection does not cover a statement intended by its maker to be wholly exculpatory or neutral, and which appears to be so on its face, but which becomes damaging to him at the trial because, for example, its contents can then be shown to be evasive or false or inconsistent with the maker's evidence on oath. It was further held, distinguishing *Saunders v United Kingdom*[17] that section 76(1) (and section 82(1)) were compatible with Article 6 of the European Convention on Human Rights given the unrestricted capability of section 78 to avoid injustice by excluding any evidence obtained by unfairness, including wholly exculpatory or neutral statements obtained by oppression. However, the effect is that it will be for the accused to convince the judge that the evidence was so obtained and not for the prosecution, on a *voir dire*, to disprove the matter beyond reasonable doubt. This approach is in contrast to that adopted in the United States[18] and Canada.[19]

Section 82(1) abolishes the rule at common law that a threat or inducement only operates to exclude a resulting confession if it was made or held out by 'a person in authority'. A confession, for the purposes of the Act, can be made to anyone. The assumption is that the risk of an inducement resulting in an untrue confession is similar whether or not the inducement comes from a person in authority.[20]

The phrase 'whether made in words or otherwise' means that a confession can be made not only in words, whether oral or written, but also by conduct. The Criminal Law Revision Committee gave as an example the accused nodding his head in reply to an accusation.[21] Presumably, as at common law, the accused may also accept the accusation of another, so as to make all or part of it a confession statement of his own, by other conduct, by his

[10] Per Lord Havers in *R v Sharp* [1988] 1 All ER 65, HL at 68.

[11] *R v Johnson* [2007] EWCA Crim 1651.

[12] *R v Rimmer* [1972] 1 WLR 268, CA. See also *R v Hetherington* [1972] Crim LR 703, CA and generally below at 376, under **The discretion to exclude**.

[13] *R v Johnson*, ibid.

[14] See per Lord Steyn in *R v Aziz* [1995] 3 All ER 149, HL at 155; *R v Sharp* [1988] 1 All ER 65, HL and, generally, Ch 6.

[15] [2005] 2 AC 467, HL.

[16] (1988) 88 Cr App R 55, CA.

[17] (1997) 2 BHRC 358.

[18] See per Chief Justice Warren in *Miranda v Arizona* (1975) 384 US 436, US Supreme Court, at 477.

[19] See *Piché v R* (1970) 11 DLR (3d) 709, Supreme Court of Canada. See further Roderick Munday, 'Adverse Denial and Purposive Confession' [2003] *Crim LR* 850.

[20] See per Viscount Dilhorne in *Deokinanan v R* [1969] 1 AC 20, PC at 33. See also 11th Report, Criminal Law Revision Committee (Cmnd 4991) para 58.

[21] 11th Report (Cmnd 4991) Annex 2 at 214.

demeanour, or even by his silence at the time when the accusation was made. It will be convenient to consider this topic and the common law authorities in that regard later in this chapter.[22] A confession can also be made otherwise than in words by a re-enactment by the accused of the crime committed. In *Li Shu-ling v R*[23] the accused, two days after he had confessed to murder by strangulation, agreed to re-enact the crime. He was reminded that he was still under caution and told that he was not obliged to re-enact the crime. The Privy Council held that a video-recording made of the re-enactment, accompanied by a running commentary by the accused explaining his movements, had properly been admitted in evidence as a confession. By way of safeguard, it was held that: the video-film should be made reasonably soon after the oral confession; the accused should be warned that he need not take part and, if he agrees to take part, should do so voluntarily; and the video-recording should be shown to the accused as soon as practicable after it has been completed so that he has an opportunity to make and have recorded any comments he wishes to make about the film.

It was also acknowledged that there are some crimes which it would be wholly inappropriate to attempt to re-enact on video, such as a killing committed in the course of an affray involving many people.

The conditions of admissibility

Section 76 of the 1984 Act provides that:

(1) In any proceedings[24] a confession made by an accused person may be given in evidence against him in so far as it is relevant to any matter in issue in the proceedings and is not excluded by the court in pursuance of this section.

(2) If, in any proceedings where the prosecution proposes to give in evidence a confession made by an accused person, it is represented to the court that the confession was or may have been obtained—

    (a) by oppression of the person who made it; or

    (b) in consequence of anything said or done which was likely, in the circumstances existing at the time, to render unreliable any confession which might be made by him in consequence thereof,

the court shall not allow the confession to be given in evidence against him except in so far as the prosecution proves to the court beyond reasonable doubt that the confession (notwithstanding that it may be true) was not obtained as aforesaid.

(3) In any proceedings where the prosecution proposes to give in evidence a confession made by an accused person, the court may of its own motion require the prosecution, as a condition of allowing it to do so, to prove that the confession was not obtained as mentioned in subsection (2) above.

Section 76(1) only applies to a confession 'made by an accused'. Thus where there is no dispute that a confession was made, but the identity of the maker is disputed, the prosecution must prove that the maker was the accused, although it seems that this may be inferred if the confession contains information about the accused which, even if known by others, is

---

[22] See below at 399, under **Statements made in the presence of the accused**.

[23] [1988] 3 All ER 138, PC.

[24] 'Proceedings' means criminal proceedings, including proceedings in the UK or elsewhere before a court-martial or the Courts-Martial Appeal Court, and proceedings before a Standing Civilian Court: s 82(1).

best known by the accused himself. In *R v Ward*[25] the prosecution admitted evidence of an admission by W as to his presence in a particular car on three occasions. On each occasion, an officer had stopped the car and one of the passengers had identified himself as W and given W's correct date of birth and address, but the officer could not identify the passenger as W. It was held, in effect, that it could be inferred from the correct information provided by the passenger that he was W, but that the jury should be given a clear direction that they should only rely on the statement as a confession if they were sure, from the contents of the statement and such surrounding evidence as there was, that W made the statement. Similar reasoning was employed in *Mawdesley v Chief Constable of the Cheshire Constabulary*.[26] M was sent a note of intended prosecution for speeding and a form asking him to provide information under section 172 of the Road Traffic Act 1988 as to the identity of the driver. The form was returned with the number of M's driving licence and his name and address in the relevant boxes, but with the space for his signature left blank. It was held that the form could amount to a confession because it was open to the court to infer from the fact that the notice had been sent to M's address and had been returned bearing the information that it did, that the entries had been made by M.

It has been held that a confession can only be given in evidence, pursuant to section 76(1), by the prosecution,[27] although in *R v Myers*[28] Lord Slynn's view was that this was a question still subject to debate. However, an accused's confession, if it could have been but was not introduced by the prosecution, may be introduced by a co-accused, being admissible at common law as an admission by a party against his interest.[29] In *R v Myers*[30] the House of Lords held that where the prosecution do not seek to admit a confession made by a co-accused, because there have been breaches of the Codes of Practice, another co-accused may elicit evidence of the confession, provided that it is relevant to his defence or undermines the prosecution case against him, either in cross-examination of the officers to whom it was made or by calling them on his behalf. It was suggested, however, that the outcome may be different if the confession has been obtained in the circumstances referred to in section 76(2) of the 1984 Act, on the basis that such a confession is worthless, whoever it is who seeks to rely on it.[31] Further to the recommendation of the Law Commission, the matter is now governed by statute. Under section 76A of the 1984 Act, a section inserted by the Criminal Justice Act 2003, confessions may be given in evidence for a co-accused, and the conditions of admissibility are the same as those which apply in the case of confessions adduced on behalf of the prosecution, except that the co-accused need only prove that the confession was not obtained by oppression or

---

[25] [2001] Crim LR 316, CA.

[26] [2004] 1 WLR 1035, Admin Court.

[27] *R v Beckford; R v Daley* [1991] Crim LR 833, CA, where it was also held that if the co-accused is convicted, the conviction may be set aside as unsafe and unsatisfactory. A conviction will not be set aside where the confession is made not by a co-accused but by a third party who could have been called by the defence: *R v Callan* (1993) 98 Cr App R 467, CA.

[28] [1998] AC 124, HL.

[29] *R v Campbell and Williams* [1993] Crim LR 448, CA.

[30] [1998] AC 124.

[31] It was also noted that there is no discretion to exclude, at the request of one co-accused, evidence tendered by another (see *Lobban v R* [1995] 2 All ER 602, PC, Ch 2), although Lord Hope did not wish to be taken as being of the view that a request by a co-accused to introduce evidence of a confession obtained in breach of a Code should be acceded to in all circumstances ([1997] 4 All ER 314 at 333–4). See also *R v Lawless* [2003] All ER (D) 183 (Feb), CA.

'in consequence of anything said or done . . . ' on the balance of probabilities. Section 76A provides as follows:

(1) In any proceedings a confession made by an accused person may be given in evidence for another person charged in the same proceedings (a co-accused) in so far as it is relevant to any matter in issue in the proceedings and is not excluded by the court in pursuance of this section.

(2) If, in any proceedings where a co-accused proposes to give in evidence a confession made by an accused person, it is represented to the court that the confession was or may have been obtained—

(a) by oppression of the person who made it; or

(b) in consequence of anything said or done which was likely, in the circumstances existing at the time, to render unreliable any confession which might be made by him in consequence thereof,

the court shall not allow the confession to be given in evidence for the co-accused except in so far as it is proved to the court on the balance of probabilities that the confession (notwithstanding that it may be true) was not so obtained.

(3) Before allowing a confession made by an accused person to be given in evidence for a co-accused in any proceedings, the court may of its own motion require the fact that the confession was not obtained as mentioned in subsection (2) above to be proved in the proceedings on the balance of probabilities.

The purpose of section 76A is to ensure that where a co-accused proposes to rely upon a confession made by an accused, the accused has a protection against unfairness similar to that which he has when the prosecution propose to rely upon a confession. Thus if the confession is admissible against the accused and undermines the defence of a co-accused, but in law is inadmissible against the co-accused, the prejudice is thought to be cured by a clear direction to the jury that the confession is no evidence against the co-accused and section 76A cannot be used to challenge its admissibility.[32]

Section 76A only operates in the case of co-accused. Thus a confession made by D1 cannot be given in evidence under section 76A for D2 if D1 pleads guilty, because D1 will then cease to be an accused and D2 will then no longer be 'charged in the same proceedings' as D1.[33] On the same reasoning, it is submitted, section 76A has no application where D1 is acquitted (either because no evidence is offered against him or he makes a successful submission of no case to answer) or he makes a successful application to sever the indictment. In such circumstances, however, D1's confession may be admissible, depending on the circumstances, under section 114(1)(d) of the Criminal Justice Act 2003.[34]

More controversial is the question whether the section 82(1) definition of a confession will be applied strictly in the context of section 76A so as to cover only that part of a statement adverse to its maker or will extend to those parts of the statement going beyond the confession and serving the interests of a co-accused.[35] Plainly, not everything said at the same time as a confession will fall within the definition, but it is submitted that it would be artificial, misleading, and unfair to adopt a strict approach to statements such as 'I did it *alone*' or 'I did it, *not D2*' and that there is a strong case for going beyond this and using section 76A to admit anything that could fairly be said to form a part of D1's confession which is relevant to D2's defence or undermines the prosecution case against him.

[32] *R v Ibrahim* [2008] 2 Cr App R 311, CA.

[33] *R v Finch* [2007] 1 Cr App R 439, CA.

[34] See Ch 10.

[35] The question was raised, but not answered, in *R v Finch*, ibid.

A confession admitted in evidence under section 76 or section 76A is admitted as evidence of the matters stated. At common law, an admissible confession was sufficient to warrant a conviction even in the absence of other evidence implicating the accused.[36] However, where a conviction was based on a confession which was equivocal or otherwise of poor quality, it could be quashed on appeal.[37] Similar principles should operate, it is submitted, in the case of confessions admitted under section 76 and section 76A.[38]

Under section 76(2) (and section 76A(2)) the defence may raise the question of admissibility merely by representing to the court, without adducing any evidence in support of such a representation, that the confession was or may have been obtained by the methods described in that subsection. However, even if the defence have not raised the question, the court of its own motion may require the prosecution to prove that the confession was not obtained by the methods described, in exercise of the power conferred on it by section 76(3) (and section 76A(3)). In either event, the question will then be determined in the absence of the jury on a *voir dire* at which the prosecution will bear the burden of proving beyond reasonable doubt (or the co-accused will bear the burden of proving on a balance of probabilities) that the conditions of admissibility have been satisfied. If this burden is not discharged, the court has no *inclusionary* discretion, but *shall not* allow the confession to be given in evidence, even if satisfied that its contents are true.

Although the 1984 Act and the Codes of Practice issued thereunder contain a wide variety of provisions regulating, inter alia, the arrest, detention, treatment, and questioning of suspects, the fact that a confession was obtained in breach of the Act or Codes will not necessarily mean that it was obtained by the methods described in section 76(2) (and section 76A(2)).[39] However, evidence of non-compliance with the Act or Codes, either alone or together with other evidence, may show that the confession was obtained by such methods or, failing that, in a case in which the *prosecution* proposes to adduce evidence of the confession, ie under section 76, may nonetheless result in the confession being excluded by the court in the exercise of its discretion. Under section 67(11) of the Act, the Codes are admissible in evidence and if any provision of the Codes appears to the court to be relevant to any question arising in the proceedings, it shall be taken into account in determining that question.

Oppression

Under section 76(2)(a) (and section 76A(2)), a confession, in order to be admissible, must not have been obtained by oppression. Broadly speaking, this reflects the views of both the Criminal Law Revision Committee[40] and the Royal Commission on Criminal Procedure[41] that a confession obtained by oppression of a suspect should be automatically excluded in view of society's

---

[36] See *R v Sullivan* (1887) 16 Cox CC 347 and *R v Mallinson* [1977] Crim LR 161, CA and contrast per Cave J in *R v Thompson* [1893] 2 QB 12.

[37] See *R v Barker* (1915) 11 Cr App R 191; *R v Schofield* (1917) 12 Cr App R 191; and *R v Pattinson* (1973) 58 Cr App R 417, CA.

[38] See also, in the case of confessions by mentally handicapped persons, s 77 (see Ch 8).

[39] Some of the more important provisions of the Act and Codes are considered below at 376, under **The discretion to exclude.**

[40] 11th Report (Cmnd 4991) para 60.

[41] (Cmnd 8092) para 4.132. The Commission proposed exclusion on this ground only if the confession was obtained from the suspect by torture, violence, the threat of violence, or inhuman or degrading treatment.

abhorrence of the use of such methods during interrogation. Before considering the meaning of 'oppression', four matters of a general nature may be noted. First, a confession obtained by oppression will be excluded whether or not it is unreliable and notwithstanding that it may be true. Secondly, the confession must not have been 'obtained by' oppression: there must be a causal link. Thus a confession will not be excluded under section 76(2)(a) where the accused confessed *before* he was subjected to some form of oppression. Equally, there will be no causal link between an interview not complying with the 1984 Act and a subsequent confession freely and voluntarily made.[42] Thirdly, although section 76(2) refers to oppression 'of the person who made it (the confession)', ie the accused, in appropriate circumstances the oppression of another could also amount to oppression of the accused (or constitute conduct likely to render unreliable any confession which might be made by him for the purposes of section 76(2)(b)). Fourthly, it would appear that a confession excluded under section 76(2)(a) will, in most if not all cases, also fall to be excluded under section 76(2)(b). It is difficult to envisage a case in which, the confession having been obtained by oppression, it was not made in consequence of anything said or done which was likely, in the then existing circumstances, to have rendered unreliable any confession which might have been made in consequence thereof.

Concerning the meaning of oppression, although, as we shall see, it is an exercise of only limited value, it is convenient to examine first the way in which the word was defined at common law. Prior to the 1984 Act, oppression was taken to mean 'something which tends to sap and has sapped that free will which must exist before a confession is voluntary'[43] or, in the context of interrogation, 'questioning which by its nature, duration or other attendant circumstances (including the fact of custody) excites hopes (such as the hope of release) or fears, or so affects the mind of the suspect that his will crumbles and he speaks when otherwise he would have stayed silent'.[44] Whether or not there was oppression in any particular case involved a consideration of a wide variety of factors, including the length of time of any period of questioning, whether the accused had been given proper refreshment, and the characteristics of the accused in question. This last factor was of particular relevance: what might have been oppressive in the case of a child, an invalid, an old man, or someone inexperienced in the ways of the world[45] might not have been oppressive in the case of a person of a tough character or a professional criminal.[46]

Section 76(8) (and section 76A(7)) defines 'oppression' as including 'torture, inhuman or degrading treatment, and the use or threat of violence (whether or not amounting to torture)'. The phrase 'torture or inhuman or degrading treatment' derives from Article 3 of the European Convention on Human Rights and it may be that the English courts will be guided by the decisions of the European Court of Human Rights and the European Commission of Human Rights. In the *Greek Case*,[47] for example, the Commission defined 'degrading treatment' as that

---

[42] *R v Parker* [1995] Crim LR 233, CA.

[43] Per Sachs J in *R v Priestley* (1965) 51 Cr App R 1n at 1–2; applied in *R v Prager* [1972] 1 WLR 260, CA.

[44] Lord MacDermott in an address to the Bentham Club (1968) 21 *CLP* 10.

[45] See, eg, *R v Westlake* [1979] Crim LR 652, CC. Cf *R v Rennie* [1982] 1 All ER 385, CA and *R v Miller* [1986] 3 All ER 119, CA. See also *R v Hudson* (1980) 72 Cr App R 163, CA.

[46] See, eg, *R v Dodd* (1981) 74 Cr App R 50. Cf *R v Gowan* [1982] Crim LR 821, CA.

[47] (1969) 12 Yearbook 1, EComHR at 186. See also *Ireland v United Kingdom* (1978) 2 EHRR 25, para 167 (torture and inhuman treatment) and *Campbell and Cosans v United Kingdom* (1982) 4 EHRR 293. Assistance may also be derived from the decisions under s 8(2) of the Northern Ireland (Emergency Provisions) Act 1978. See also the definition of 'torture' contained in Art 1 of the Draft United Nations Convention against Torture and Other Cruel, Inhuman or Degrading Treatment or Punishment.

which grossly humiliates a person before others or drives a person to act against his will or conscience. Concerning the meaning of 'torture', assistance may be derived from the way in which the offence of torture is defined in section 134 of the Criminal Justice Act 1988.[48] The inclusive nature of the definition in section 76(8) indicates that the varieties of oppression it contains do not constitute a comprehensive list.

There was no reference to section 76(8) in *R v Fulling*,[49] the first case to come before the Court of Appeal on the meaning of oppression for the purposes of the 1984 Act. The appellant, Ruth Fulling, was convicted of obtaining property by deception. After her arrest she was taken into custody and interviewed twice on that day and once on the following day. Despite persistent questioning, she exercised her right to remain silent, but after a break in the interview on the second day, she made a confession. According to her evidence on the *voir dire*, she made the confession because during the break in that interview one of the officers told her that for the last three years her lover had been having an affair with another woman who was presently in the cell next to hers. The appellant said that these revelations so distressed her that she could not stand being in the cells any longer and thought that by making a statement she would be released. The police denied that they had made the revelations suggested. The defence submitted that the confession was or may have been obtained by oppression. The judge ruled that, even on the assumption that the accused's version of events was the true one, there was no oppression because oppression meant something above and beyond that which is inherently oppressive in police custody and must import some oppression actively applied in an improper manner by the police.

The Court of Appeal upheld this ruling and dismissed the appeal. It was held, applying the principles set out in *Bank of England v Vagliano Bros*,[50] that since the 1984 Act was a codifying Act, rather than a consolidating Act or an Act declaratory of the common law, the court should give to the words used in it their natural meaning, uninfluenced by any considerations derived from the previous state of the law. Accordingly, the word 'oppression' was given its ordinary dictionary definition, namely, 'exercise of authority or power in a burdensome, harsh, or wrongful[51] manner; unjust or cruel treatment of subjects, inferiors, etc; the imposition of unreasonable or unjust burdens'. Lord Lane CJ, delivering the judgment of the court, pointed out that, according to one of the quotations given in the *Oxford English Dictionary*, 'There is not a word in our language which expresses more detestable wickedness than *oppression*.' His Lordship found it hard to envisage any circumstances in which oppression thus defined would not entail some impropriety on the part of the interrogator. It was held that although section 76(2)(b) is wide enough to cover some of the circumstances which were embraced by the 'artificially wide' definition of oppression at common law, and although a confession may be excluded, under section 76(2)(b), where there is no suspicion of impropriety, the

---

[48] The intentional infliction by act or omission of severe physical or mental pain or suffering by (a) a public official, or a person acting in an official capacity, in the performance or purported performance of his official duties; or (b) by some other person at the instigation or with the consent or acquiescence of a public official, or person acting in an official capacity, performing or purporting to perform his official duties when he instigates the commission of the offence or consents to or acquiesces in it.

[49] [1987] 2 All ER 65, CA.

[50] [1891] AC 107 at 144–5, HL.

[51] The word 'wrongful' should be understood in the context of the rest of the definition, particularly the words which precede and follow it, otherwise any breach of the Code, which might be said to be 'wrongful', could be said to amount to oppression, which clearly is not so: *R v Parker* [1995] Crim LR 233, CA.

remarks alleged to have been made by the officer were not likely to have made unreliable any confession which the appellant might have made.

The decision in *R v Fulling* calls for comment in a number of respects. First, the first two parts of the definition of oppression given would appear to apply only in the case of someone vested with some authority, power, or control over the accused, someone akin to a person who, at common law, would have been regarded as a 'person in authority'. Secondly, concerning impropriety, the decision, although not explicit on the point, suggests strongly that it must be deliberate or intentional. This would accord with the former decision at common law in *R v Miller*,[52] in which it was held that although it could amount to oppression if questions, addressed to a suspect suffering from paranoid schizophrenia, were skilfully and deliberately asked with the intention of triggering off hallucinations and flights of fancy, the mere fact that questions put to such a suspect did produce such a disordered state of mind would not, by itself, be indicative of oppression. Thirdly, however, although oppression normally requires deliberate impropriety, not all deliberate impropriety amounts to oppression. Sometimes it will be a question of degree. Thus if an interrogator is rude and discourteous, raising his voice and using bad language, this does not constitute oppression;[53] but bullying and hectoring by officers adopting a highly hostile and intimidatory approach will amount to oppression,[54] as will a deliberate misstatement of the evidence in order to pressurize the suspect.[55] Trickery, per se, will not necessarily constitute oppression. Thus it does not amount to oppression to make a covert tape-recording of an incriminating conversation between two suspects sharing a police cell.[56]

Fourthly, it seems clear that, as at common law, regard should be had to the personal characteristics of the accused, which may be of critical relevance in deciding not only whether the confession was *obtained* by oppression, but also whether particular conduct was 'burdensome', 'harsh' or 'cruel'. Thus account may be taken of the fact that the suspect is, for example, intelligent, sophisticated, and an experienced professional person,[57] or a person of below normal intelligence on the borderline of mental handicap.[58] The will of a particular suspect may be so affected by oppression in an interview that a confession made in a subsequent but properly conducted interview should be excluded.[59]

A final matter concerns the relevance of the common law authorities to section 76(2)(b). Paragraph (b) is considered wide enough to cover only *some* of the circumstances embraced

---

[52] [1986] 3 All ER 119, CA.

[53] *R v Emmerson* (1990) 92 Cr App R 284, CA. See also *R v Heaton* [1993] Crim LR 593, CA.

[54] *R v Paris* (1992) 97 Cr App R 99, CA, where the accused, who was of limited intelligence, had denied his involvement over 300 times. But see also *R v L* [1994] Crim LR 839, CA, a decision under s 76(2)(b), in which although similar methods were employed, *R v Paris* was distinguished on the grounds, inter alia, that L was of normal intelligence and the length of the interviews not excessive.

[55] *R v Beales* [1991] Crim LR 118, CC.

[56] *R v Parker* [1995] Crim LR 233, CA.

[57] *R v Seelig* [1991] 4 All ER 429, CA at 439, where it was held not to be oppressive for DTI inspectors conducting an investigation of a company's affairs, to question such a person, notwithstanding that (a) in conformity with normal practice, no caution was given; and (b) refusal to answer such questions could result in committal for contempt under s 436 of the Companies Act 1985. It was also held that the confession made did not fall to be excluded under s 76(2)(b) or s 78. Concerning s 78, it was held that although the accused were subject to an inquisitorial process and therefore worse placed than the average man questioned as to crime, a fundamental countervailing consideration was the fact that the legislature had deliberately decided that they should be treated less favourably than the average man.

[58] *R v Paris* (1992) 97 Cr App R 99, CA.

[59] See *R v Ismail* (1990) 92 Cr App R 92, CA and cf *Y v DPP* [1991] Crim LR 917, DC.

by the common law definition of oppression. The facts of *R v Fulling* itself are instructive in this regard because, although at common law a strong argument could have been advanced to the effect that in all the circumstances of the case what the officer said, assuming that he did in fact say it, had sapped the free will of the accused or so affected her mind that her will crumbled and she spoke when otherwise she would have remained silent, the court was satisfied that, for the purposes of section 76(2)(b), what was said was not likely, in the circumstances, to have rendered unreliable any confession which she might have made in consequence.

Unreliability

The background

Section 76(2)(b) in large measure reflects the recommendations of the Criminal Law Revision Committee.[60] In order to appreciate the significance of the reliability test, it will be useful to summarize the Committee's reasons for changing the rules at common law. At common law, as we have seen, the fundamental condition of the admissibility of a confession was that it should have been made voluntarily. Two reasons have been given for that rule: the first, the reliability principle, is that an involuntary confession may not be reliable because an accused subjected to threats, inducements, or oppression may 'confess' falsely; the second, the disciplinary principle, is that the police must be discouraged from using improper methods to obtain a confession by being deprived of the advantage of the confession for the purposes of obtaining a conviction. A majority of the Committee was in favour of accepting the mixture of these two principles as the basis of the law. However, although they were also in favour of preserving the law in general, they proposed a relaxation of the strict rule that any threat or inducement, however mild or slight, should render inadmissible any resulting confession. In *R v Northam*[61] the accused, while on bail in respect of charges of housebreaking, was questioned by the police about another housebreaking. Before confessing to the latter offence, the accused had asked an officer whether, instead of being tried for it separately, it could be taken into consideration at his forthcoming trial, and the officer said the police would have no objection. In the event, however, he was tried separately for the other offence and convicted of it, but the Court of Appeal, albeit reluctantly, quashed the conviction on the grounds that the confession had been obtained by an inducement. The decision was followed in *R v Zaveckas*.[62] The accused was convicted of larceny. At the trial, evidence was given of a confession made after he had asked an officer 'If I make a statement, will I be given bail now?' and had received an answer in the affirmative. The Court of Appeal, with some regret, quashed the conviction on the grounds that the confession should have been excluded as it followed upon an inducement.[63] Cases such as these, in the opinion of the Committee, showed that the common law rule was too strict. Accordingly, cases of oppression apart, they recommended that a confession should only be rendered inadmissible if made as a result of a threat or inducement of a kind likely to produce an unreliable confession.

---

[60] 11th Report (Cmnd 4991) paras 53–69. The Government rejected the proposals relating to confessions made by The Royal Commission on Criminal Procedure (Cmnd 8092).

[61] (1967) 52 Cr App R 97.

[62] (1970) 54 Cr App R 202.

[63] See also *R v Smith* [1959] 2 QB 35, C-MAC and *R v Cleary* (1963) 48 Cr App R 116, CCA.

The test

The word 'unreliable' is the keynote to section 76(2)(b) (and section 76A(2)(b)). It is not defined in the Act, but means 'cannot be relied upon as being the truth'.[64] Section 76(2)(b), by its express incorporation of the reliability principle, offers less scope for exclusion than existed at common law. However, it offers greater scope for exclusion than would have been the case under clause 2(2)(b) of the draft Bill annexed to the 11th report of the Criminal Law Revision Committee because although it closely resembles the clause, it is different in one significant respect: the phrase 'anything said or done' has been substituted for 'any threat or inducement'.[65]

In reaching a decision under section 76(2)(b), a trial judge must examine all the relevant circumstances of the interrogation, both before and after what was 'said' or 'done', and take into account the nature and effect of what was said or done, the seriousness of the offence in question and, if necessary, the terms of the confession, which may throw light on the facts concerning the interrogation.[66] The test of reliability is hypothetical: it applies not to the confession made by the accused, but to 'any confession which might be made by him'.[67] However, as Mance LJ said in *Re Proulx*, the test cannot be satisfied by postulating some entirely different confession:[68]

> The word 'any' must . . . be understood as indicating 'any such', or 'such a', confession as the applicant made. The abstract element involved also reflects the fact that the test is not whether the actual confession was untruthful or inaccurate. It is whether whatever was said or done was, in the circumstances existing as at the time of the confession, *likely* to have rendered such a confession unreliable, whether or not it may be seen subsequently (with hindsight and in the light of all the material available at trial) that it did or did not actually do so.

The phrase 'anything said or done' has been given a wide interpretation. It includes omissions to say, or do, certain things.[69] It is not restricted to things said or done by persons in authority. However, advice properly given to the accused by his solicitor will not normally provide a basis for excluding a subsequent confession, even when, as it sometimes ought to be, it is robust and, for example, points to the advantages which may derive from an acceptance of guilt or the corresponding disadvantages of a 'no comment' interview, but it may do so in the case of a particularly vulnerable accused.[70]

The phrase 'anything said or done' requires something external to the accused which was likely to have some influence on him. Thus a confession cannot be excluded on the basis that it may have been obtained in consequence of anything said or done by the accused himself which was likely to render unreliable any confession which he might have made in consequence thereof. An example is *R v Wahab*,[71] where W instructed his solicitor to approach the police to see if members of his family might be released from custody if he

---

[64] Per Stuart-Smith LJ in *R v Crampton* (1990) 92 Cr App R 369 at 372, CA.

[65] See *R v Harvey* [1988] Crim LR 241, CC, below.

[66] (Cmnd 4991) para 65.

[67] *R v Barry* (1991) 95 Cr App R 384, CA. The test is objective, but all the circumstances should be taken into account, including those affecting the accused, including his desires etc: ibid.

[68] [2001] 1 All ER 57, DC at [46]. But see also *R v Cox* [1991] Crim LR 276, CA, *R v Crampton* (1990) 92 Cr App R 369 at 372, CA and *R v Kenny* [1994] Crim LR 284, CA.

[69] See, eg, *R v Doolan* [1988] Crim LR 747, CA: failure to caution, to keep a proper record of the interview, and to show that record to the suspect.

[70] *R v Wahab* [2003] 1 Cr App R 232, CA at [42].

[71] Ibid.

admitted his guilt, but was uninfluenced by anything said or done by anyone else. In *R v Goldenberg*[72] the suspect, a heroin addict, while in police custody, requested an interview. The admissions he made were alleged by the defence to be an attempt by him to obtain bail and to be released in order to feed his addiction. It was held that the case fell outside section 76(2)(b). In *R v Crampton*[73] a heroin addict made admissions at interviews in the police station after he had been undergoing withdrawal symptoms. It was sought to distinguish *R v Goldenberg* on the grounds that the interviews held were not at the request of the accused, but conducted by the police at their own convenience. The Court of Appeal, however, doubted whether the mere holding of an interview, at a time when the suspect is undergoing withdrawal symptoms, is something 'done' under section 76(2), the wording of which seemed to postulate some 'words spoken' or 'acts done'.

Section 76(2)(b), by imposing on the prosecution the burden of proving that the confession was not obtained 'in consequence' of anything said or done, clearly requires a causal connection between what was said or done and the confession made. This reflects the position at common law. In *DPP v Ping Lin*[74] the accused, suspected of a drugs offence, attempted to make a deal with the police whereby they would release him and in return he would disclose the name of his supplier. When told that this could not be done, he admitted that he had been dealing in heroin but made two more attempts to effect some sort of bargain. An officer then said: 'If you show the judge that you have helped the police to trace bigger drug people, I am sure he will bear it in mind when he sentences you.' Subsequently, the accused disclosed the name of his supplier. The House of Lords held that the accused's statements were voluntary because there was no question of any threat or inducement being held out to him *before* he confessed. The accused may have hoped to obtain immunity or lenience, but that hope was entirely self-generated. Similarly, in *R v Tyrer*,[75] a decision under section 76(2)(b) in which the trial judge ruled that things were said and done which were likely to render a partial confession unreliable, the prosecution satisfied him that it was not obtained in consequence of what was said or done and it was therefore ruled admissible. In *R v Weeks*[76] the trial judge was satisfied of the same matter on the basis of the evidence and demeanour of the accused on the *voir dire*—he came across as a very astute young man who had previous experience of being interviewed at a police station.

In *R v Rennie*,[77] a common law authority, the accused was convicted of conspiracy to obtain a pecuniary advantage by deception. The co-accused, his sister, had pleaded guilty to obtaining a pecuniary advantage by deception and a charge of conspiring with her brother was allowed to lie on the file. After his arrest, the accused at first denied any part in the offence but when a detective sergeant revealed the strength of the evidence known to him and asked 'This was a joint operation by your family to defraud the bank, wasn't it?', the accused replied, 'No, don't bring the rest of the family into this, I admit it was my fault.' On the *voir dire*, the detective sergeant denied that he had told the accused that he would involve other members of his family but admitted that the accused was frightened of this happening. He said 'I think he made the confession in the hope that I would terminate my inquiries into members

---

[72] (1988) 88 Cr App R 285, CA.
[73] (1990) 92 Cr App R 369, CA.
[74] [1976] AC 574, HL.
[75] (1989) 90 Cr App R 446 at 449, CA.
[76] [1995] Crim LR 52, CA.
[77] [1982] 1 WLR 64, CA.

of his family . . . '. The judge ruled that the evidence was admissible. The Court of Appeal, observing that the evidence as to the motives of the accused should not have been admitted, because the drawing of inferences was a matter for the judge and not witnesses, nonetheless acted on the assumption that the accused confessed because he hoped that inquiries would cease into the part played by his family, and posed the following question:[78]

> How is this principle[79] to be applied where a prisoner, when deciding to confess, not only realizes the strength of the evidence known to the police and the hopelessness of escaping conviction but is conscious at the same time of the fact that it may well be advantageous to him or . . . to someone close to him, if he confesses? How, in particular, is the judge to approach the question when these different thoughts may all, to some extent at least, have been prompted by something said by the police officer questioning him?

The answer, it was held, was not to be found from any refined analysis of the concept of causation. The judge should approach the question much as would jurors if it were for them, understanding the principle and the spirit behind it and applying common sense. Dismissing the appeal on the grounds that the approach of the trial judge had been flawless, Lord Lane CJ said:[80]

> Very few confessions are inspired solely by remorse. Often the motives of an accused are mixed and include a hope that an early admission may lead to an earlier release or a lighter sentence. If it were the law that the mere presence of such a motive, even if prompted by something said or done by a person in authority, led inexorably to the exclusion of a confession, nearly every confession would be rendered inadmissible. This is not the law. In some cases the hope may be self-generated. If so, it is irrelevant, even if it provides the dominant motive for making the confession. In such a case the confession will not have been obtained by anything said or done by a person in authority. More commonly the presence of such a hope will, in part at least, owe its origin to something said or done by such a person. There can be few prisoners who are being firmly but fairly questioned in a police station to whom it does not occur that they might be able to bring both their interrogation and their detention to an earlier end by confession.

This dictum was approved and applied in *R v Crampton*,[81] a decision under section 76(2)(b): the mere fact that the accused had been undergoing withdrawal symptoms and may have had a motive for making a confession did not mean that the confession was necessarily unreliable.

The question of causation poses particular problems when a confession made at an improperly conducted interview is repeated at a subsequent but properly conducted interview. In *R v McGovern*[82] it was held that a confession made in an interview in consequence of an improper denial of access to a solicitor was likely to be unreliable and should have been excluded. It was also held that a confession made in a properly conducted second interview on the following day was also inadmissible because the first interview tainted the second and the very fact that the suspect had already made a confession was likely to have had an effect on her in the second interview.[83]

[78] [1982] 1 WLR 64 at 70.
[79] Ie the common law principle of voluntariness.
[80] [1982] 1 WLR 64 at 69.
[81] (1990) 92 Cr App R 369, CA. See also *R v Wahab* [2003] 1 Cr App R 232, CA at [44]–[45].
[82] (1990) 92 Cr App R 228, CA.
[83] See also *R v Blake* [1991] Crim LR 119, CC; and cf *R v Ismail* (1990) 92 Cr App R 92, CA.

The physical condition and mental characteristics of the accused are a part of the 'circumstances existing at the time' for the purposes of section 76(2)(b). Thus, in *R v Everett*[84] it was held that these circumstances obviously included the mental condition of a 42-year-old with a mental age of 8, and the material consideration was not what the police thought about his mental condition, but the nature of that condition itself. Similarly, in *R v McGovern*[85] it was held that the particular vulnerability and physical condition of the suspect at the time of her interview—she was borderline mentally subnormal, six months pregnant, and in a highly emotional state—formed the background for the submission that her confession should be excluded. However, the mental characteristics which may have a bearing on the question of reliability are not confined to cases of 'mental impairment' or 'impairment of intelligence or social functioning': any mental or personality abnormalities may be of relevance.[86]

The judge must consider the likely effect of what was 'said or done' on the mind of the particular accused. Thus it may be that in some cases the things said or done may be unjustified, improper, illegal, or in breach of the Act or Codes of Practice yet not of a kind likely to render unreliable any confession which might be made by an accused who, for the sake of argument, is an experienced professional criminal with a tough character or who is otherwise capable of coping with even a vigorous interrogation.[87] In *R v Alladice*,[88] for example, it was held that although the accused, who was charged with robbery of £29,000 in cash, had been refused access to a solicitor in contravention of section 58 of the 1984 Act,[89] and this was relevant to the question of whether to exclude his confession under section 76(2)(b), it was not only doubtful whether the confession had been obtained as a result of the refusal of access, but in all the circumstances there was no reason to believe that that refusal was likely to render unreliable any confession which the accused might have made. The circumstances showed that the police had acted with propriety, apart from the breach of section 58, and that the accused was well able to cope with the interviews, understood the cautions that he had been given, at times exercising his right to silence, and was aware of his rights so that, had the solicitor been present, his advice would have added nothing to the knowledge of his rights which the accused already had.[90] On the other hand, it is easy to imagine cases where, although it would be impossible to criticize the propriety of what was 'said or done', any confession which might be made by the accused would be likely to be unreliable in all the circumstances because the accused is, for example, of previous good character and highly suggestible, easily intimidated, of very low intelligence or mentally handicapped.[91] In *R v Harvey*[92] the accused, a woman of low intelligence suffering from a psychopathic disorder, was charged with murder. Her confession was excluded under section 76(2)(b) on the

---

[84] [1988] Crim LR 826, CA.

[85] (1990) 92 Cr App R 228, CA.

[86] *R v Walker* [1998] Crim LR 211, CA.

[87] In *R v Gowan* [1982] Crim LR 821, CA, O'Connor LJ, although not sanctioning improper or unfair questioning on the part of the police, said: 'serious and experienced professional criminals . . . must, and do, expect that their interrogation by trained and experienced police officers will be vigorous.'

[88] (1988) 87 Cr App R 380, CA.

[89] See below.

[90] For these reasons it was also held that the confession should not be excluded under s 78 (see Ch 3).

[91] See generally Gisli Gudjohnsson, *The Psychology of Interrogations, Confessions and Testimony* (London, 1992). In the case of confessions by mentally handicapped persons, see also s 77 (Ch 8).

[92] [1988] Crim LR 241, CC.

grounds that it may have been obtained as a result of hearing a confession made by her lover. There was psychiatric evidence that her state of mind at the relevant time could have been such that, on hearing her lover's confession, she confessed to protect the lover in a child-like attempt to try to take the blame. It may be noted that there was no threat or inducement; there was no impropriety or illegality; what was said (done) was not said (done) by a person in authority; and the crucial factor, in deciding whether what was said was likely to render unreliable any confession which she might have made, was her own state of mind.[93]

In some cases, of course, the confession will be excluded on the basis of *both* unjustified police behaviour *and* the personal nature and characteristics of the accused. *R v Delaney*[94] was a case of indecent assault on a girl aged three. The whole basis of the prosecution case was an admission made by the accused at the very end of a one-and-a-half hour interview which, until that point in time, had consisted of a series of denials. The police, in breach of the Codes of Practice, had failed to make a contemporaneous note of the interview, thereby depriving the court of the most cogent evidence as to what did induce the confession. Moreover, there was evidence from a psychologist that the accused, who was aged 17, was educationally subnormal, of low IQ, and poorly equipped to cope with sustained interrogation. The Court of Appeal held that, had the trial judge paid proper attention to this combination of factors, he would and should have excluded the confession. The Court of Appeal reached a similar conclusion in *R v Moss*.[95] The suspect, who was on the borderline of mental handicap, was kept in custody for nine days, interviewed nine times without an independent person being present, and improperly refused access to a solicitor.

It is clear from cases such as *R v Fulling*[96] and *R v Harvey*[97] that a confession may be excluded under section 76(2)(b) if there is not even a suspicion of impropriety. Equally, as we have seen, confessions obtained as a result of even serious breaches of the provisions of the 1984 Act and the Codes of Practice will not necessarily result in exclusion. Nonetheless, exclusion in many of the reported cases has been based wholly or mainly on such breaches, including the following: failure to caution, to keep a proper record of the interview or to show it to the suspect;[98] an offer of bail and numerous breaches of Code C, including a failure to keep a proper record of the interviews held;[99] questioning before allowing access to a solicitor, failure to record the admissions immediately and failure to show the note of the interview to the suspect;[100] asking a question after the suspect has been charged which is not for the purpose of clearing up an ambiguity;[101] and conducting an interview with a juvenile without an 'appropriate adult',[102] the adult present having a low IQ, being virtually illiterate and probably incapable of appreciating the gravity of the juvenile's situation[103] or

---

[93] See also *R v Sat-Bhambra* (1988) 88 Cr App R 55, CA, where evidence of a confession was excluded on the basis that the accused may have been affected at the time by valium given to him by the police doctor to calm his nerves.

[94] (1988) 88 Cr App R 338, CA. See also *R v Waters* [1989] Crim LR 62, CA.

[95] (1990) 91 Cr App R 371, CA.

[96] [1987] 2 All ER 65, CA, above.

[97] [1988] Crim LR 241, CC, above.

[98] See paras 10, 11.7, and 11.11, Code C and *R v Doolan* [1988] Crim LR 747, CA.

[99] *R v Barry* (1991) 95 Cr App R 384, CA.

[100] See s 58(4) of the 1984 Act, paras 11.7 and 11.11, Code C and *R v Chung* (1990) 92 Cr App R 314, CA.

[101] See para 16.5, Code C and *R v Waters* [1989] Crim LR 62, CA.

[102] See para 11.15, Code C.

[103] See *R v Morse* [1991] Crim LR 195.

being a person with whom the juvenile has no empathy (her estranged father whom she did not wish to attend).[104]

Section 105 of the Taxes Management Act 1970

Concerning the admissibility of confessions in any criminal proceedings against a person for any form of fraudulent conduct in relation to tax, section 76 of the 1984 Act must be read in conjunction with section 105 of the Taxes Management Act 1970, which operates in such proceedings to prevent the exclusion of statements made or documents produced in so-called 'Hansard interviews', ie interviews at which the accused is informed of the practice of HM Revenue & Customs to take into account the cooperation of the taxpayer in deciding whether to bring any prosecution for fraud.[105] The precursor to section 105[106] was introduced to reverse the decision in *R v Barker*.[107] Section 105(1) is in the following terms:

> Statements made or documents produced by or on behalf of a person shall not be inadmissible . . . by reason only that it has been drawn to his attention that—
>
> (a) pecuniary settlements may be accepted instead of a penalty being determined, or proceedings being instituted, in relation to any tax,
> (b) though no undertaking can be given as to whether or not the Board will accept such a settlement in the case of any particular person, it is the practice of the Board to be influenced by the fact that a person has made a full confession of any fraudulent conduct to which he has been a party and has given full facilities for investigation,
>
> and that he was or may have been induced thereby to make the statements or produce the documents.

Section 105 does not prevent reliance upon section 78 of the 1984 Act where the interview has been conducted in breach of Code C, but it is relevant to exercise of the discretion under section 78 that Parliament expected statements made at Hansard interviews to be admissible in evidence.[108]

The discretion to exclude

If the prosecution fails to discharge the burden of proving that a confession was not obtained by the methods described in section 76(2), the court, as we have seen, shall not allow the confession to be given in evidence and has no discretion to admit it, even if satisfied that it is true. It does not follow from this, however, that the confession *must* be admitted if the prosecution succeeds in proving that the confession was not obtained by those methods: section 76(1) provides that a confession *may* be given in evidence if not excluded under the section. In such cases the trial judge may exclude the confession in the exercise of his discretion pursuant to

---

[104] See *DPP v Blake* (1989) 89 Cr App R 179, DC, now reflected in Note 1B, Code C; and cf *R v Jefferson* [1994] 1 All ER 270, CA: robust interventions by a father, sometimes joining in the questioning of his son and challenging his exculpatory account of certain incidents, were not such as to render unreliable any confession made as a result. See generally Jacqueline Hodgson, 'Vulnerable Suspects and the Appropriate Adult' [1997] *Crim LR* 785.

[105] Section 105 also applies to any proceedings for the recovery of any tax due from him and any proceedings for a penalty: s 105(2).

[106] Section 34 of the Finance Act 1942.

[107] [1941] 2 KB 381.

[108] *R v Gill* [2004] 1 WLR 49, CA at [45].

section 82(3) or section 78(1). Although these two provisions overlap to a considerable extent, it will be convenient to consider them separately.

Section 82(3) of the Police and Criminal Evidence Act 1984

Section 82(3) provides that:

> Nothing in this Part of this Act (ss 73–82) shall prejudice any power of a court to exclude evidence (whether by preventing questions from being put or otherwise) at its discretion.

The effect of this subsection is, in the present context, to preserve any discretion to exclude an otherwise admissible confession that the court possessed at common law prior to the 1984 Act. At common law, a trial judge, even if satisfied that a confession was made voluntarily, could exclude it as a matter of discretion on a number of different albeit overlapping grounds. Two of the grounds were made clear by the House of Lords in *R v Sang*.[109] First, as a part of his function at a criminal trial to ensure that the accused receives a fair trial, the judge has a discretion to refuse to admit evidence where, in his opinion, its prejudicial effect outweighs its probative value. Secondly, the judge has a discretion to exclude an otherwise admissible confession obtained by improper or unfair means. A third ground was that the confession was obtained in contravention of the Judges' Rules[110] or the statutory provisions governing the detention and treatment of suspects.

The discretion, in so far as it may be exercised on the first ground—that is where the prejudicial effect of the confession so outweighs its probative value that it would be unfair to the accused to admit it—was of particular use in the case of confessions made by accused suffering from mental disability.[111] In *R v Miller*[112] the Court of Appeal held that a confession may be excluded, as a matter of discretion, if it comes from an irrational mind or is the product of delusions and hallucinations. On the facts of the case, a murder trial in which there was evidence that part of the interrogation of the accused, who suffered from paranoid schizophrenia, may have triggered off hallucinations and flights of fancy, the Court of Appeal went on to hold that the trial judge had not erred in his decision to admit the confession. However, in *R v Stewart*[113] a trial judge exercised his discretion on this ground to exclude confessions made by an accused who suffered from a severe mental disability, having the mental age of a five-and-a-half-year-old and the comprehension level of a three-and-a-half-year-old. Similarly, it has been held that the discretion may be exercised to exclude a confession obtained at a time when the mental state of the accused was so unbalanced as to render his statements wholly unreliable.[114] Thus in *R v Davis*[115] a confession, obtained at a time when the accused may still have been influenced by a drug, pethidine, was excluded as a matter of discretion on the grounds of its potential unreliability. The facts of that

---

[109] [1980] AC 402.

[110] The Judges' Rules were rules of practice, not law, originally drawn up by the judges of the King's Bench Division in 1912 for the guidance of the police, and designed to regulate the interrogation and treatment of suspects.

[111] On confessions by mentally handicapped persons, see also s 77 of the 1984 Act (Ch 8).

[112] [1986] 3 All ER 119, CA.

[113] (1972) 56 Cr App R 272, CCC.

[114] Per Lord Widgery CJ in *R v Isequilla* [1975] 1 WLR 716, CA, approving a passage from *Cross on Evidence* (3rd edn, London 1967) 450–1. In that case, however, it was held that the mental state of the accused, who was frightened and hysterical, was not such as to render it unsafe to act upon his statements.

[115] [1979] Crim LR 167, CC.

case, however, would now support a submission that the confession should be excluded as a matter of law under section 76(2)(b).[116]

Most of the reported cases in which the exclusionary discretion was exercised on either the second or the third ground, were cases involving some breach of the Judges' Rules. It should be emphasized, however, that a voluntary confession could be admitted notwithstanding a breach of the rules.[117] Such a breach merely enabled a submission to be made that an otherwise admissible confession should, as a matter of discretion, be excluded.[118] In the exercise of that discretion (which was rarely reversed on appeal) the trial judge could examine, in addition to the breaches alleged, all the circumstances of the case, including in particular the probative value of the confession and the nature and seriousness of the offence charged. The Judges' Rules, and many of the old statutory provisions governing the detention and treatment of suspects, have now been replaced by a wide variety of provisions contained in the 1984 Act and the Codes of Practice which have been issued pursuant to the Act. The Codes do not apply only to police officers: under section 67(9) of the 1984 Act they also apply to other persons 'charged with the duty of investigating offences or charging offenders'.[119] This phrase covers those charged with a legal duty of the kind in question, whether imposed by statute or by the common law or by contract.[120] It covers Customs and Excise officers,[121] but is not restricted to government officials and others acting under statutory powers.[122] Whether a person satisfies the test is a question of fact in each case[123] or, more accurately, a question of mixed law and fact, involving an examination of the statute, contract, or other authority under which a person carries out his functions, as well as a consideration of his actual work.[124] Thus the test will not necessarily be satisfied by line managers conducting disciplinary interviews,[125] Department of Trade Inspectors investigating a company's affairs[126] or by those supervising a bank on behalf of the Bank of England under the Banking Act 1987,[127] but may be satisfied by commercial investigators such as company investigators,[128] store detectives,[129] and investigators employed by the Federation against Copyright Theft.[130] The test is met by officers of the Special Compliance Office, HM Revenue & Customs' investigation branch charged with investigating serious tax fraud, because such fraud inevitably involves the commission of an offence or offences.[131]

[116] See *R v Sat-Bhambra* (1988) 88 Cr App R 55, CA, above.
[117] *R v Prager* [1972] 1 WLR 260.
[118] See per Lord Goddard CJ in *R v May* (1952) 36 Cr App R 91 at 93.
[119] The principles of fairness enshrined in Code C may have an even wider application: see *R v Smith* (1993) 99 Cr App R 233, CA (Ch 3).
[120] *Joy v Federation against Copyright Theft Ltd* [1993] Crim LR 588, DC.
[121] *R v Sanusi* [1992] Crim LR 43, CA.
[122] *R v Bayliss* (1993) 98 Cr App R 235, CA at 237–8.
[123] Per Watkins LJ in *R v Seelig* [1991] 4 All ER 429 at 439, CA.
[124] Per Neill LJ in *R v Bayliss* (1993) 98 Cr App R 235 at 238–9 and in *R v Smith* (1993) 99 Cr App R 233, CA.
[125] *R v Welcher* [2007] Crim LR 804, CA.
[126] See *R v Seelig* [1991] 4 All ER 429, CA.
[127] See *R v Smith* (1993) 99 Cr App R 233, CA.
[128] *R v Twaites; R v Brown* (1990) 92 Cr App R 106, CA.
[129] *R v Bayliss* (1993) 98 Cr App R 235, CA.
[130] *Joy v Federation against Copyright Theft Ltd* [1993] Crim LR 588, DC. In the case of an investigation by the Director of the Serious Fraud Office into a suspected offence involving serious or complex fraud, the general provisions of Code C yield to the inquisitorial regime established by the Criminal Justice Act 1987: see *R v Director of Serious Fraud Office, ex p Smith* [1992] 3 All ER 456, HL, and Ch 14.
[131] *R v Gill* [2004] 1 WLR 49, CA.

Codes A to F relate to the following matters—A: the exercise by police officers of statutory powers of stop and search; B: the searching of premises by police officers and the seizure of property found by police officers on persons or premises; C: the detention, treatment, and questioning of persons by police officers; D: the identification of persons by police officers; E: the audio recording of interviews with suspects;[132] and F: the visual recording with sound of interviews with suspects. It is convenient at this stage, therefore, to consider some of these provisions, first in so far as they relate to the requirement to administer a caution, and then more generally. Before doing so, however, it should be stressed that compliance with the Act and Codes will not necessarily result in a confession being admitted; if it cannot be proved that it was not obtained by the methods described in section 76(2) then, as we have seen, it *shall not* be given in evidence. Conversely, non-compliance with the Act or Codes will not necessarily lead to the exclusion of an otherwise admissible confession: the decision whether to exclude remains entirely a matter of discretion.

The caution

Under the Judges' Rules, the police, in a number of different situations, were required to administer a caution to a suspect. In this respect, rules II and III were of particular importance. They provided as follows:

II. As soon as a police officer has evidence which would afford reasonable grounds for suspecting that a person has committed an offence, he shall caution that person or cause him to be cautioned before putting to him any questions, or further questions, relating to that offence . . .

III.

(a) Where a person is charged with or informed that he may be prosecuted for an offence he shall be cautioned . . .

(b) It is only in exceptional cases that questions relating to the offence should be put to the accused person after he has been charged or informed that he may be prosecuted . . .

These rules have now been replaced by paragraphs 10 and 16 of Code C, the Code of Practice for the Detention, Treatment and Questioning of Persons by Police Officers. They provide as follows:

10.1 A person whom there are grounds to suspect of an offence must be cautioned before any questions about an offence, or further questions if the answers provide the grounds for suspicion, are put to them if either the accused's answers or silence (ie failure or refusal to answer or answer satisfactorily) may be given in evidence to a court in a prosecution. A person need not be cautioned if questions are for other necessary purposes, e.g.:

---

[132] The Code on Tape Recording applies to interviews held at police stations of persons suspected of committing indictable offences (except certain terrorism offences). See also para 43, *Practice Direction (Criminal Proceedings: Consolidation)* [2002] 1 WLR 2870, which deals with such matters as the practice to be followed for: (a) amending a transcript of an interview (or editing a tape) by agreement; (b) notification of intention to play a tape in court; (c) notification of objection to production of a tape; and (d) proof of a tape. Concerning video-recorded interviews with children (see Ch 5), departure from the guidance on interviewing contained in 'Achieving Best Evidence in Criminal Proceedings: Guidance for Vulnerable or Intimidated Witnesses, Including Children' ('The Memorandum') will probably be treated as the equivalent of a breach of one of the Codes of Practice. Account has been taken of a failure to conform to the recommendations contained in the report of Butler Sloss LJ, the *Inquiry into Child Abuse in Cleveland* (1987) (Cm 412): see *R v H* [1992] Crim LR 516, CA. See also *R v Dunphy* (1993) 98 Cr App R 393, CA, a decision on the precursor to The Memorandum.

(a) solely to establish their identity or ownership of any vehicle;

(b) to obtain information in accordance with any relevant statutory requirement[133] . . . ;

(c) in furtherance of the proper and effective conduct of a search, e.g. to determine the need to search in the exercise of powers of stop and search or to seek cooperation while carrying out a search;

(d) to seek verification of a written record as in paragraph 11.13;[134] or

. . .

10.4 A person who is arrested, or further arrested, must also be cautioned unless:

(a) it is impracticable to do so by reason of their condition or behaviour at the time;

(b) they have already been cautioned immediately prior to arrest as in paragraph 10.1.

10.5 The caution which must be given on:

(a) arrest;

(b) all other occasions before a person is charged or informed that they may be prosecuted, (see section 16),

should, unless the restriction on drawing adverse inferences from silence applies, (see Annex C), be in the following terms:

'You do not have to say anything. But it may harm your defence if you do not mention when questioned something which you later rely on in Court. Anything you do say may be given in evidence.'

. . .

10.7 Minor deviations from the words of any caution given in accordance with this Code do not constitute a breach of this Code, provided the sense of the relevant caution is preserved . . .

10.8 After any break in questioning under caution, the person being questioned must be made aware they remain under caution. If there is any doubt the relevant caution should be given again in full when the interview resumes . . .

16.1 When the officer in charge of the investigation reasonably believes that there is sufficient evidence to provide a realistic prospect of . . . conviction for the offence . . . they shall without delay, and subject to the following qualification, inform the custody officer who will be responsible for considering whether the detainee should be charged . . . When a person is detained in respect of more than one offence it is permissible to delay informing the custody officer until the above conditions are satisfied in respect of all the offences . . .

. . .

16.2 When a detainee is charged with or informed they may be prosecuted for an offence, [see Note 16B], they shall, unless the restriction on drawing adverse inferences from silence applies, (see Annex C), be cautioned as follows:

'You do not have to say anything. But it may harm your defence if you do not mention now something which you later rely on in court. Anything you do say may be given in evidence.' . . . [135]

---

[133] For example, under the Road Traffic Act 1988.

[134] Para 11.13 relates to records of comments made by a suspect outside the context of an interview.

[135] Where a person wishes to make a written statement under caution, he shall first be asked to write out and sign: 'I make this statement of my own free will. I understand that I do not have to say anything but that it may harm my defence if I do not mention when questioned something which I later rely on in court. This statement may be given in evidence': see para 2, Annex D, Code C. See also *R v Pall* (1991) 156 JP 424, CA and cf *R v Hoyte* [1994] Crim LR 215, CA.

Although paragraph 10.1, unlike rule II, does not include a requirement that the grounds to suspect be reasonable, this is implicit, because the grounds must be assessed objectively.[136] In *R v Osbourne, R v Virtue*[137] the question arose as to the point in time at which a caution under rule II should be administered. Lawton LJ, delivering the judgment of the Court of Appeal, said:[138]

> The rules contemplate three stages in the investigations leading up to somebody being brought before a court for a criminal offence. The first is the gathering of information, and that can be gathered from anybody, including persons in custody provided they have not been charged. At the gathering of information stage no caution of any kind need be administered. The final stage, the one contemplated by rule III of the Judges' Rules, is when the police officer has got enough (and I stress the word 'enough') evidence to prefer a charge . . . But a police officer when carrying out an investigation meets a stage in between the mere gathering of information and the getting of enough evidence to prefer the charge. He reaches a stage where he has got the beginnings of evidence. It is at that stage that he must caution. In the judgment of this court, he is not bound to caution until he has got some information which he can put before the court as the beginnings of a case.

Under paragraph 10.4 of the Code, as a general rule a caution must be administered to a person upon arrest. Where the accused is not arrested, the phrase 'grounds to suspect' in paragraph 10.1 has been interpreted in a manner similar to the interpretation given to the phrase 'evidence which would afford reasonable grounds for suspecting' in *R v Osbourne; R v Virtue.* Thus in *R v Shah*[139] it was held that a mere hunch or sixth sense, or the simple fact that the questioner is suspicious, will not suffice to bring paragraph 10.1 into play; paragraph 10.1 sets out an objective test in that there must be grounds for suspicion before the need to caution arises and although they may well fall short of evidence supportive of a prima facie case of guilt, they must exist and be such as to lead both to a suspicion that an offence has been committed and that the person being questioned has committed it.[140] In *R v Hunt*,[141] where officers saw H in someone else's garden putting a flick-knife in his pocket, searched him and found the knife, it was held that at that stage the officers had ample evidence on which to suspect the commission of an offence and should have cautioned him. The answers to the questions then put, without a caution, should have been excluded under section 78. However, if a person is cautioned in respect of one offence and minutes later the police have grounds to suspect another offence, it seems that there is no requirement to caution again, under either paragraph 10.1 or paragraph 10.8, before putting questions about the other offence.[142]

A caution is not required under paragraph 10.1, in respect of a person whom there are grounds to suspect of an offence, if questions are not put to him regarding his involvement or suspected involvement in that offence, but for other purposes. However, if the questions

---

[136] *R v James* [1996] Crim LR 650, CA. *R v James* and other authorities in the ensuing text and footnotes are decisions on an earlier version of Code C.

[137] [1973] QB 678, CA.

[138] [1973] QB 678 at 688.

[139] [1994] Crim LR 125, CA.

[140] See also, and cf *R v Nelson and Rose* [1998] 2 Cr App R 399, CA.

[141] [1992] Crim LR 582, CA. Cf *R v Purcell* [1992] Crim LR 806, CA.

[142] *R v Oni* [1992] Crim LR 183, CA.

are put for two purposes, partly regarding his involvement or suspected involvement in an offence, and partly for other purposes, then a caution should be given.[143]

Paragraph 10.1 and other requirements of the Code were not intended to apply to a conversation between a suspect and officers who adopt an undercover pose or disguise, because there can be no question of pressure or intimidation by the officers as persons actually in authority or believed to be so. However, it is wrong for officers to adopt such a pose or disguise to ask questions about an offence uninhibited by the provisions of the Code and with the effect of circumventing it, and if they do so, the questions and answers may be excluded under section 78.[144]

Paragraph 16.2 of the Code is designed to apply to that stage in the course of an interrogation when there is sufficient evidence to prosecute and for the prosecution to succeed. At that point in time, and subject to exceptions, questioning should cease.[145] Concerning rule III, it was held that the word 'charged' means formally charged[146] but that when a person is told 'you will be charged' it is the same as saying that a charge has in fact already been preferred.[147] The phrase 'informed that he may be prosecuted', it has been said, is designed to cover a case where, during interrogation of a suspect (who has not been arrested) the time comes when the police contemplate that a summons may be issued against him.[148] It may be assumed that paragraph 16.2 of the Code, in these respects, will be interpreted in the same way.

Provisions governing procedural fairness

A detailed analysis of the relevant provisions of the 1984 Act and the various Codes of Practice issued thereunder is well beyond the scope of this work. However, two provisions of particular significance in the present context, sections 56 and 58, do merit close consideration. They relate to the right to have someone informed when arrested and what has been called 'one of the most important and fundamental rights of a citizen',[149] namely the right of access to legal advice.[150] Section 56(1) provides that:

> Where a person has been arrested and is being held in custody in a police station or other premises, he shall be entitled, if he so requests, to have one friend or relative or other person who is known to him or who is likely to take an interest in his welfare told, as soon as is practicable except to the extent that delay is permitted by this section, that he has been arrested and is being detained there.[151]

[143] *R v Nelson and Rose* [1998] 2 Cr App R 399, CA.

[144] See *R v Christou* [1992] QB 979, CA (see Ch 3).

[145] See para 16.5, Code C and *R v Bailey* [1993] 3 All ER 513, CA. Where a suspect is charged by the police and then required by the Serious Fraud Office to attend for an interview, the Director is not required to caution him, because the Criminal Justice Act 1987 showed a parliamentary intention to establish an inquisitorial regime in relation to serious or complex fraud in which the Director could obtain by compulsion answers which might be self-incriminating. Under s 2(13), a person who without reasonable excuse fails to answer questions or provide relevant information is liable to imprisonment, a fine, or both. But see also s 2(8): subject to minor exceptions, statements made by the suspect cannot be used in evidence against him.

[146] *R v Brackenbury* [1965] 1 WLR 1475n.

[147] *Conway v Hotten* [1976] 2 All ER 213, DC.

[148] *R v Collier; R v Stenning* [1965] 1 WLR 1470, CCA.

[149] Per Hodgson J in *R v Samuel* [1988] 2 All ER 135, CA at 147.

[150] See also paras 5 and 6, Code C.

[151] The rights conferred are exercisable whenever the person detained is transferred from one place to another: s 56(8).

Section 58 provides that:

(1) A person arrested and held in custody in a police station or other premises[152] shall be entitled, if he so requests, to consult a solicitor[153] privately at any time.

(2) Subject to subsection (3) below, a request under subsection (1) above and the time at which it was made shall be recorded in the custody record.

(3) Such a request need not be recorded in the custody record of a person who makes it at a time while he is at a court after being charged with an offence.

(4) If a person makes such a request, he must be permitted to consult a solicitor as soon as is practicable except to the extent that delay is permitted by this section.[154]

Many of the subsections of sections 56 and 58 are cast in identical or very similar terms. In any case the person in custody must be permitted to exercise the rights conferred within 36 hours from the 'relevant time',[155] which is usually either the time at which the person arrives at the police station or the time 24 hours after the time of arrest, whichever is the earlier.[156] Delay is only permitted if four conditions are met. The first is that the person detained is in police detention for an indictable offence. The second is that the delay is authorized by an officer of at least the rank of inspector or superintendent.[157] The third condition is that the person in

[152] The intention behind these words, which are also used in s 56(1), is to limit the application of the section to a person whose detention in custody has been authorized, ie an arrested person taken to a police station in respect of whom the custody officer is satisfied that the statutory conditions for detention are made out. Thus a person arrested while committing burglary is *in custody* on premises, but is not *held* in custody, and is therefore outside the terms of ss 56 and 58: see *R v Kerawalla* [1991] Crim LR 451, CA. Although s 58(1) does not apply to a person in custody after being remanded by a magistrates' court, such a person has a common law right to be permitted on request to consult a solicitor as soon as is reasonably practicable: *R v Chief Constable of South Wales, ex p Merrick* [1994] Crim LR 852, DC.

[153] 'Solicitor' means a solicitor who holds a current practising certificate and an accredited or probationary representative included on the register of representatives maintained by the Legal Services Commission: see para 6.12, Code C. If a solicitor wishes to send a non-accredited or probationary representative to provide advice on his behalf, that person shall be admitted to the police station for this purpose unless an officer of the rank of inspector or above considers that such a visit will hinder the investigation of crime and directs otherwise: para 6.12A, Code C. In exercising his discretion, the officer should take into account in particular whether the identity and status of the representative have been satisfactorily established; whether he is of suitable character to provide legal advice (a person with a criminal record is unlikely to be suitable unless the conviction was for a minor offence and not recent); and any other matters in any written letter of authorization provided by the solicitor on whose behalf he is attending: para 6.13, Code C, reflecting the decision in *R v Chief Constable of Avon and Somerset Constabulary, ex p Robinson* [1989] 2 All ER 15, DC. The discretion cannot be used to make a blanket direction that a representative should not be admitted to any police station in a particular area, and although senior officers may give general advice, the responsibility rests with the officer concerned with the investigation in question as to whether that particular investigation will be hindered: *R (Thompson) v Chief Constable of the Northumberland Constabulary* [2001] 1 WLR 1342, CA.

[154] Section 58 does not entitle a person, suspected of committing an offence of driving when unfit through drink or drugs or driving after consuming excess alcohol, to consult a solicitor *before* supplying a specimen for analysis; and the refusal of the police to permit such a consultation does not amount to a 'reasonable excuse' for failing to provide a specimen when required to do so: *DPP v Billington* [1988] 1 All ER 435, DC. Procedures undertaken under s 7 of the Road Traffic Act 1988 (ie questions and answers leading to the giving of a specimen) do not constitute interviewing for the purposes of Code C: see *DPP v D; DPP v Rous* (1992) 94 Cr App R 185, DC and para 11.1A, Code C.

[155] Sections 56(3) and 58(5).

[156] Section 41(2).

[157] Sections 56(2)(b) and 58(6)(b) respectively. The authorization may be oral, in which case it shall be confirmed in writing as soon as possible: ss 56(4) and 58(7). The authorization under s 58(6)(b) may also be given by an officer of the rank of chief inspector if he has been authorized to do so by an officer of at least the rank of chief superintendent: s 107(1). The holder of an acting rank may be treated for the purpose of these provisions as the holder of the substantive rank: *R v Alladice* (1988) 87 Cr App R 380, CA.

detention has not yet been charged with an offence, that is any offence, whether or not the one in respect of which he was originally arrested.[158] The fourth condition, contained in sections 56(5) and 58(8), is that the officer must have:

> reasonable grounds for believing that telling the named person of the arrest (exercise of the right . . . [to consult a solicitor] at the time when the person detained desires to exercise it) (a) will lead to interference with or harm to evidence connected with an indictable offence or interference with or physical injury to other persons or (b) will lead to the alerting of other persons suspected of having committed such an offence but not yet arrested for it or (c) will hinder the recovery of any property obtained as a result of such an offence.[159]

If a delay is authorized, the detainee shall be told the reason for it, which shall be noted on his custody record.[160] Once the reason for authorizing delay ceases to subsist, there may be no further delay in permitting the exercise of the rights conferred.[161] This may occur, for example, if the police succeed in recovering the property obtained as a result of an indictable offence or arrest the other persons suspected of having committed such an offence.[162]

The occasions for properly authorizing delay under section 58(8) will be infrequent[163] and the task of satisfying a court that reasonable grounds existed at the time when the decision was made will prove formidable.[164] In *R v Samuel* Hodgson J said:[165]

> a court which has to decide whether denial of access to a solicitor was lawful has to ask itself two questions: 'Did the officer believe?', a subjective test; and 'Were there reasonable grounds for that belief?', an objective test.
>
>   What it is the officer must satisfy the court that he believed is this: that (1) allowing consultation with a solicitor (2) will (3) lead to or hinder one or more of the things set out in paragraphs (a) to (c) of s 58(8). The use of the word 'will' is clearly of great importance. There were available to the draftsman many words or phrases by which he could have described differing nuances as to the officer's state of mind, for example 'might', 'could', 'there was a risk', 'there was a substantial risk' etc. The choice of 'will' must have been deliberately restrictive.
>
>   Of course, anyone who says that he believes that something will happen, unless he is speaking of one of the immutable laws of nature, accepts the possibility that it will not happen, but the use of the word 'will' in conjunction with belief implies in the believer a belief that it will very probably happen.

---

[158] Para A1, Annex B, Code C and *R v Samuel* [1988] 2 All ER 135, CA.

[159] It is not an adequate ground for the authorization of delay under s 58(8) that access to a solicitor might 'prejudice inquiries' or result in advice to the suspect to remain silent (*R v McIvor* [1987] Crim LR 409, CC) or to refuse to answer any more questions (*R v Samuel* [1988] 2 All ER 135, CA). See also para A4, Annex B, Code C. Sections 56(5) and 58(8) are expressed to be subject to ss 56(5A) and 58(8A) respectively. These latter subsections provide that an officer may also authorize delay where he has reasonable grounds for believing that—(a) the person detained for the indictable offence has benefited from his criminal conduct; and (b) the recovery of the value of the property constituting the benefit will be hindered by telling the named person of the arrest (the exercise of the right to consult a solicitor).

[160] Sections 56(6) and 58(9). These duties shall be performed as soon as is practicable: ss 56(7) and 58(10).

[161] Sections 56(9) and 58(11).

[162] As in *R v (Eric) Smith* [1987] Crim LR 579, CC.

[163] Per Lord Lane CJ in *R v Alladice* (1988) 87 Cr App R 380, CA.

[164] Per Hodgson J in *R v Samuel* [1988] 2 All ER 135, CA at 144.

[165] [1988] 2 All ER 135 at 143.

Furthermore, it was held that the circumstances in which delay may be authorized necessarily involve conduct, on the part of the solicitor, which is either deliberate and criminal or inadvertent. As to the former, the number of times that a police officer could genuinely believe that a solicitor, an officer of the court, would commit a criminal offence would be rare, and in any event the grounds put forward to justify the delay would have to have reference to a specific solicitor and could never be advanced in relation to solicitors generally. As to inadvertent conduct, solicitors were intelligent, professional people whereas persons detained were frequently not very clever; the expectation that one of the events in paras (a) to (c) would be brought about by such conduct contemplated a degree of intelligence and sophistication in persons detained and perhaps a naïvety and lack of common sense in solicitors which was of doubtful occurrence; and the grounds put forward would have to have reference to the specific person detained, the archetype being a sophisticated criminal who was known or suspected to be a member of a gang of criminals.

The facts of *R v Samuel* revealed that the solicitor in question was highly respected, very experienced, and unlikely to be hoodwinked by the suspect, who was 24 years old. Accordingly, it was held that there could have been no reasonable grounds for the belief that section 58(8) required.[166] Similarly, in *R v Alladice*,[167] a case of robbery in which access had been denied on the grounds that one of the suspects was still at large, none of the proceeds of the robbery had been recovered, and a gun which had been used in the crime had not been located, Lord Lane CJ, giving the reserved judgment of the Court of Appeal, held that although their Lordships did not share the scepticism expressed in *R v Samuel* as to solicitors being used as unwitting channels of communication, there had been a breach of section 58 because the suspect still at large had already been alerted by events, there was no reason to believe that access to a solicitor would impede recovery of the stolen money or gun, there was no suggestion that the solicitor requested would involve himself in any dishonesty or malpractice, and the suspect could not be classed as a sophisticated criminal.

Section 78(1) of the Police and Criminal Evidence Act 1984

Section 78(1) provides that:

> In any proceedings the court may refuse to allow evidence on which the prosecution proposes to rely to be given if it appears to the court that, having regard to all the circumstances, including the circumstances in which the evidence was obtained, the admission of the evidence would have such an adverse effect on the fairness of the proceedings that the court ought not to admit it.

Many of the most important cases on section 78(1) have concerned confessions, to which the subsection clearly applies,[168] and some of these have already been considered, as part of the general consideration of the subsection, in Chapters 2 and 3. Although section 78 operates without prejudice to the common law discretion to exclude,[169] section 78 has in very large measure superseded the common law power.

---

[166] Cf *Re Walters* [1987] Crim LR 577, DC, an application for habeas corpus following extradition proceedings, where it was held that there were reasonable grounds for believing that the applicant would use the solicitor as an innocent agent to get a message out and thereby alert other suspects.

[167] (1988) 87 Cr App R 380, CA. See also *R v Parris* (1988) 89 Cr App R 68, CA.

[168] *R v Mason* [1987] 3 All ER 481, CA.

[169] *R v O'Leary* (1988) 87 Cr App R 387, CA and *Matto v Crown Court at Wolverhampton* [1987] RTR 337, DC.

A confession may be excluded under section 78(1) in the absence of any breaches of the 1984 Act or Codes of Practice. Thus if an interview is held with a suspect who does not appear to have hearing difficulties, but it is subsequently established that his hearing was so impaired that it would be unfair for his answers to be admitted in evidence, the answers will be excluded under section 78(1).[170] However, the chief importance of section 78(1), in relation to confessions, lies in its potential for the exclusion of confessions obtained illegally or improperly. As we saw in Chapter 3, although breaches of the Act or Codes will not necessarily result in exclusion, it is implicit in the wording of the subsection that the circumstances in which the evidence was obtained may have such an adverse effect that it should be excluded.[171] As we also saw, the purpose of the subsection is not disciplinary, but protective, and therefore although mala fides or deliberate misconduct may render exclusion more likely, the determinative factor is the extent to which the defendant has been denied the right of a fair trial by reason of breaches of the provisions governing procedural fairness.[172]

Before considering some examples of such breaches, it will be convenient to consider first the procedure to be adopted when the defence seeks to exclude a confession obtained in such circumstances. In *R v Keenan*[173] Hodgson J identified three different situations: (a) breaches of a code may be apparent from the custody record (as when an order has been made by an officer of insufficient rank) or the witness statements; (b) there may be a prima facie breach which, if objection is taken, must be justified by evidence adduced by the prosecution (eg an order refusing access to a solicitor can only be justified by compelling evidence from the senior officer who made the order); and (c) there may be breaches which can probably only be established by the evidence of the accused himself (eg cases involving persons at risk, such as the mentally handicapped).[174] The procedure appropriate in each case may vary. In (a), it may be that all that is necessary is an admission by the police, followed by argument. However, the prosecution will not often be content to take this course in cases where they wish to show how or why the breaches occurred and to submit that the evidence should be adduced despite the breaches. In (b), the prosecution clearly have to call evidence to justify the order made and the defence may wish to call evidence from eg the solicitor to whom access was sought, or the accused himself. Cases under (c) are likely to be rare. It is unlikely that, in (a) and (b), the accused will be called. If the proper procedures have, on the face of the record, been observed, the contentions of the accused, for example that a properly recorded interview is inaccurate, would be unlikely to succeed. But if the breaches are obvious, the trial judge has no means of knowing what will ensue after he has made his ruling. If he excludes, the accused may exercise his right not to testify. To admit the evidence of the interview may therefore effectively deprive the accused of a right he otherwise had. And if the evidence is admitted, the accused may then give evidence that the interview never took place, or that it did take place but the questions and answers were fabricated or inaccurately recorded, or that it did take place and the record is accurate. Although it seems unjust that evidence should be excluded under section 78 when, if all the facts and the defence response were known, it would be clear that the evidence should not be excluded under the section, the difficulty cannot be avoided: the decision has to be made at a stage when

---

[170] See *R v Clarke* [1989] Crim LR 892, CA and para 13.5, Code C.

[171] Per Woolf LJ in *Matto v Crown Court at Wolverhampton* [1987] RTR 337, DC.

[172] See *R v Alladice* (1988) 87 Cr App R 380, CA and *R v Walsh* (1989) 91 Cr App R 161 at 163, CA.

[173] [1989] 3 All ER 598, CA at 604–5, 606, and 608.

[174] See paras 11.15 and 11.17–11.20, Code C.

the judge does not know the full facts. In *R v Dunford*,[175] a case involving denial of access to a solicitor, it was held that the trial judge was entitled (i) to take account of the accused's previous convictions; and (ii) to look at the contents of the record of the interview, including the terms of the confession, in order to help him to decide whether the presence of a solicitor might have made it less likely that the accused would confess. However, it was also said that it may not be right to refer to or rely on the record where evidence has been adduced on the *voir dire* and there is a root and branch challenge to its contents.

Denial of access to a solicitor contrary to section 58 of the 1984 Act will, prima facie, have an adverse effect on the fairness of the proceedings.[176] In *R v Samuel*[177] Hodgson J held that had the trial judge decided, as he should have done, that the accused had been improperly denied 'one of the most important and fundamental rights of a citizen', he might well have concluded that the refusal of access and consequent unlawful interview compelled him to find that admission of the confession would have had an adverse effect on the fairness of the proceedings. Similarly, where, in breach of Code C,[178] an arrested person is not properly informed, both orally and in writing, of his right to consult a solicitor, this may well result in exclusion, especially in the case of a foreigner with no previous convictions who is unfamiliar with the rights of a suspect at interview,[179] and such breaches will not necessarily be cured if he is later asked whether he agrees to be interviewed without a solicitor, and replies in the affirmative.[180] However, breach of section 58 or the accompanying provisions of the Code is no guarantee of exclusion.[181] Thus where a suspect is kept incommunicado, contrary to section 58, but after interview says that the absence of a solicitor made no difference and, following a belated granting of access to a solicitor, signs the notes of the interview, the evidence is admissible.[182] Similarly, if a suspect who has agreed to be interviewed without a solicitor present, changes his mind, and the police improperly continue to interview him without allowing him to receive legal advice,[183] although this is a serious inroad into his rights, admissions subsequently made are admissible if the solicitor would have added nothing to his knowledge of his rights.[184]

In *R v Kirk*[185] it was held that where the police, having arrested a suspect in respect of one offence, propose to question him in respect of another more serious offence, they must first either charge him with the more serious offence, as envisaged by section 37 of the 1984 Act, or ensure that he is aware of the true nature of the investigation: that is the thrust and purport of paragraph 10.1 of Code C. The accused can then give proper weight to the nature of the investigation when deciding whether or not to exercise his right to obtain free legal advice under the Code and when deciding how to respond to the questions which the police propose to ask. The Act and the Codes, it was held, proceed

[175] (1990) 91 Cr App R 150, CA.

[176] Per Saville J in *R v Walsh* (1989) 91 Cr App Rep 161 at 163, CA. See also *R v Parris* (1988) 89 Cr App R 68, CA (see Ch 3).

[177] [1988] 2 All ER 135, CA.

[178] See paras 3.1, 3.2, and 3.5.

[179] *R v Sanusi* [1992] Crim LR 43, CA.

[180] *R v Beycan* [1990] Crim LR 185, CA.

[181] See *R v Alladice* (1988) 87 Cr App R 380, CA and *R v Dunford* (1990) 91 Cr App R 150, CA (Ch 3). See J Hodgson, 'Tipping the Scales of Justice' [1992] *Crim LR* 854.

[182] *R v Findlay; R v Francis* [1992] Crim LR 372, CA.

[183] See para 6.6, Code C.

[184] *R v Oliphant* [1992] Crim LR 40, CA. See also *R v Anderson* [1993] Crim LR 447, CA.

[185] [1999] 4 All ER 698, CA.

on the assumption that a suspect in custody will know why he is there and, when being interviewed, will know at least in general terms the level of offence in respect of which he is suspected; and if he does not know, and as a result does not seek legal advice and gives critical answers which he might not otherwise have given, the evidence should normally be excluded under section 78, because its admission will have a seriously adverse effect on the fairness of the proceedings.

In *R v Keenan*[186] it was held that if there have been serious and substantial breaches of the 'verballing' provisions of the Code (whereby, for example, an accurate contemporaneous record of an interview should be made), evidence so obtained should be excluded.[187] Thus confessions have been excluded on the basis of the following breaches: interviewing a juvenile in the absence of an 'appropriate adult';[188] interviewing a suspect before he has arrived at the police station and been informed of his right to free legal advice;[189] failure to tell a suspect that he is not under arrest coupled with failure to make a contemporaneous record of an interview;[190] failure to caution and to make such a record;[191] failure to give the suspect the opportunity to read and sign it as correct or to indicate the respects in which he considers it inaccurate;[192] failure to record a statement made other than in English in the language used and failure to give the opportunity to read a record and check its accuracy;[193] in a case in which the accused denied making a confession allegedly made *after* a taped interview with him, failure to give the suspect such an opportunity;[194] and undue pressure, by threatening a number of charges, instead of only two, if the suspect continued to deny

[186] [1989] 3 All ER 598, CA (see Ch 3).

[187] Under para 11.1A, Code C, an interview is the questioning of a person regarding his involvement or suspected involvement in a criminal offence or offences which, under para 10.1 of Code C, must be carried out under caution. Whether there is an interview primarily turns on the nature of the questioning, rather than the number of questions or their length. Thus if an officer asks a single question directly relating to the crime, his motive being to clarify an ambiguity in a comment made by the suspect on arrest, that question and the answer to it may constitute an interview, although the officer's motive may be very relevant to the question of exclusion under s 78: *R v Ward* (1993) 98 Cr App R 337, CA. If an accused, under arrest, voluntarily offers to provide information and officers, without asking any questions, accede to that request and make a record of that information, that is not an interview, but nothing said at such a meeting can be produced in evidence at any subsequent trial: *R v Menard* [1995] 1 Cr App R 306, CA.

[188] *R v Weekes* (1993) 97 Cr App R 222, CA (para 11.15, Code C).

[189] *R v Cox* (1992) 96 Cr App R 464, CA (para 11.1; also paras 3.1, 3.2, and 10.1).

[190] *R v Joseph* [1993] Crim LR 206, CA (paras 10.2 and 11.7, Code C). Cf *Watson v DPP* [2003] All ER (D) 132 (Jun), DC.

[191] See *R v Sparks* [1991] Crim LR 128, CA (paras 10.1 and 11.7, Code C) and *R v Bryce* [1992] 4 All ER 567, CA (paras 10.8 and 11.7, Code C). See also *R v Okafor* [1994] 3 All ER 741, CA, where there was *also* a failure to remind of the right to legal advice (para 11.2, Code C).

[192] See *R v Foster* [1987] Crim LR 821, CC (para 11.11, Code C) and *R v Weerdesteyn* [1995] 1 Cr App R 405, CA, where there was also a failure to caution. Cf *R v Courtney* [1995] Crim LR 63, CA, where failure to give the suspect an opportunity to read and sign a record of comments outside the context of an interview (in breach of para 11.13, Code C) was treated as 'insubstantial'. See also *R v Park* (1993) 99 Cr App R 270, CA: if answers to exploratory questions give rise in due course to a well-founded suspicion that an offence has been committed, what has started out as an inquiry may have become an interview and if it does, the requirements of the Code must be followed in relation to both the earlier and later questioning. Thus, although a contemporaneous note is no longer possible, a record should be made as soon as practicable of the earlier questions and answers, the reason for the absence of a contemporaneous note should be recorded, and the suspect should be given the opportunity to check the record.

[193] *R v Coelho* [2008] EWCA Crim 627 (paras 13.4 and 11.13, Code C).

[194] *R v Scott* [1991] Crim LR 56, CA, where it was held that by admitting the confession, the judge effectively compelled the accused to give evidence. Cf *R v Matthews, R v Dennison, and R v Voss* (1989) 91 Cr App R 43, CA.

the charge.[195] However, relatively trivial breaches, such as a failure to record the reason why an interview record was not completed in the course of an interview,[196] or such a breach coupled with a failure to record the time when an interview record was made,[197] have not resulted in exclusion. Moreover, even serious breaches of the 'verballing' provisions may be 'cured' by the presence of a solicitor or his clerk. In *R v Dunn*[198] D denied making a confession, allegedly made *after* his interview, during the signing of the interview notes, and in the presence of his solicitor's clerk. The 'conversation' in which the confession was made was not recorded contemporaneously and no note of it was shown to D. It was held that, despite these serious breaches, the evidence was admissible because the clerk was present to protect D's interests: she could have intervened to prevent the accused from answering, her presence would have inhibited the police from fabricating the conversation, and, if they were to fabricate, it would not simply be a question of their evidence against that of D, because she would also be able to give evidence for the accused.

If a confession is excluded under section 78 by reason of a breach of the Code, a confession made in a subsequent, but properly conducted interview *may* be tainted by the earlier breach and therefore also fall to be excluded under section 78. The question of exclusion is a matter of fact and degree which is likely to depend on whether the objections leading to the exclusion of the first interview were of a fundamental and continuing nature and, if so, if the arrangements for the subsequent interview gave the accused a sufficient opportunity to exercise an informed and independent choice as to whether he should repeat or retract what he said in the first interview or say nothing.[199] In *R v Canale*,[200] where the first two interviews were not contemporaneously recorded and no record was shown to the accused for verification, it was held that these breaches had affected subsequent admissions which therefore should have been excluded under section 78. However, in *R v Gillard and Barrett*[201] it was held that breaches of the Code (similar to those in *R v Canale*) in earlier interviews had not tainted confessions made in subsequent but properly conducted interviews. *R v Canale* was distinguished on the basis that in that case there was a nexus between the earlier and later interviews: the accused claimed that he had been induced by promises to make the admissions in the first interview and these promises may have continued to affect answers in the later interviews. The length of time separating the interviews is clearly relevant,[202] but the critical factor, it seems, is whether there is any suggestion of oppression, inducement, stress, or pressure in the earlier interview which might continue to exert a malign influence during the later interview.[203]

[195] *R v Howden-Simpson* [1991] Crim LR 49, CA (para 11.5, Code C). See also *R v De Silva* [2003] 2 Cr App R 74, CA, where the confessions were made, after being cautioned, in telephone calls to other suspects which the police had induced the accused to make by the promise of a reduced sentence, if convicted.

[196] See *R v White* [1991] Crim LR 779, CA and para 11.10, Code C.

[197] See *R v Findlay; R v Francis* [1992] Crim LR 372, CA and para 11.9, Code C.

[198] (1990) 91 Cr App R 237, CA. See also D Roberts, 'Questioning the Suspect' [1993] *Crim LR* 368 and J Baldwin, 'Legal Advice at the Police Station' [1993] *Crim LR* 371.

[199] *R v Neil* [1994] Crim LR 441, CA, applied in *R v Nelson and Rose* [1998] 2 Cr App R 399, CA.

[200] [1990] 2 All ER 187, CA (see Ch 3). See also *R v Blake* [1991] Crim LR 119, CC.

[201] (1990) 92 Cr App R 61, CA.

[202] See *R v Conway* [1994] Crim LR 838, CA, where account was taken of the fact that only 20 minutes separated the interviews.

[203] See per Taylor LJ in *Y v DPP* [1991] Crim LR 917, DC. See also *R v Glaves* [1993] Crim LR 685, CA; *R v Wood* [1994] Crim LR 222, CA; and generally Peter Mirfield, 'Successive Confessions and the Poisonous Tree' [1996] *Crim LR* 554.

As noted earlier in this chapter, the application of the Codes is confined to police officers and others charged with the duty of investigating offences or charging offenders. However, where a confession has been made in the course of an interview with some other person, for example a doctor or psychiatrist, the court, in deciding whether to exercise the section 78 discretion, is entitled to take into account the fact that the accused did not have the benefit of the safeguards provided by the Codes. In *R v Elleray*[204] it was held that, given the need for frankness in the exchanges between a probation officer and an offender, the prosecution should only rely upon a confession made to a probation officer if it is in the public interest to do so, but where they do rely on such a confession, the court, in deciding whether to exclude it under section 78, is entitled to take into account not only the need for frankness, but also the reliability of the record of what was said, that the offender was not cautioned, and that he did not have the benefit of legal representation. On the facts of the case, the confessions, which were of rape, were held to have been properly admitted.[205]

The *voir dire*

If either (i) the prosecution rely on oral statements and the defence case is simply that the interview never took place or that the incriminating statements were never made; or (ii) the prosecution rely on written statements and the defence case is that they are forgeries, no question of admissibility falls for the judge's decision. The issue of fact whether or not the statement was made by the accused is for the jury. However, if the accused denies authorship of the written statement and claims that he signed it involuntarily, or claims that his signature to what in fact was a confession statement was obtained by the fraudulent misrepresentation that he was signing a document of an entirely different character, he puts in issue the admissibility of the statement on which the judge must rule and, if the judge admits the statement, all issues of fact as to the circumstances of the making and signing of the statement should then be left for the jury to consider and evaluate.[206]

Subject to the foregoing, if the prosecution proposes to admit evidence of a confession, the defence has two options. It may represent[207] to the court that the confession was or may have been obtained by the methods set out in section 76(2) (or in any event should be excluded by the judge in the exercise of his discretion) and the question of admissibility must then be determined on the *voir dire*.[208] The defence have no right to insist on the presence of the jury at the *voir dire*: the judge, after listening to the views of the defence, has the final word on whether the jury should remain in court.[209] Alternatively, the defence may choose not to dispute the admissibility of the confession, in which case, assuming that the court does not exercise its own powers under section 76(3) to require the prosecution to prove that the confession was not

---

[204] [2003] 2 Cr App R 165, CA.

[205] See also *R v McDonald* [1991] Crim LR 122, CA, Ch 3.

[206] Per Lord Bridge in *Ajodha v The State* [1981] 2 All ER 193, PC at 201–2, applied in *R v Flemming* (1987) 86 Cr App R 32, CA.

[207] A suggestion, in cross-examination, that a confession was obtained improperly does not amount to a representation for the purposes of s 76(2): per Russell LJ, expressly confining his rulings to summary trials, in *R v Liverpool Juvenile Court, ex p R* [1987] 2 All ER 668, DC at 673.

[208] Concerning summary trials, see Ch 2, 34, under **The functions of the judge and jury, The *voir dire*, or trial within a trial**.

[209] *R v Hendry* (1988) 153 JP 166, CA, applied in *R v Davis* [1990] Crim LR 860, CA.

obtained by the methods set out in section 76(2), the confession may be given in evidence.[210] At common law, prior to the 1984 Act, there was a third option, namely to allow the jury to hear the evidence of the confession and subsequently, when all the evidence had been heard, to submit to the judge that, if he doubted the admissibility of the statement, he should direct the jury to disregard it.[211] It would appear, however, that this option has not survived the 1984 Act: on its wording, section 76 only permits the question of legal admissibility to be raised where the prosecution 'proposes' to give a confession in evidence. Similarly, section 78 refers to evidence on which the prosecution 'proposes' to rely. Accordingly, it has been said that if an accused wishes to exclude a confession under section 76, the time to make such a submission is before the confession is put in evidence and not afterwards.[212] This would also appear to be the time at which a submission based on section 78 should be made.[213]

In cases in which defence counsel intends to make a submission that a confession should be excluded, his intention will be conveyed to prosecuting counsel at the Plea and Case Management Hearing or immediately before the trial commences, so that the confession is not referred to in the presence of the jury, whether in the prosecution opening speech or otherwise.[214] The prosecution will adduce their evidence in the normal way but at that point in time when the confession would otherwise be admitted, counsel will intimate to the court that a point of law has arisen which falls to be determined in the absence of the jury.[215] At the *voir dire*, the prosecution will bear the burden of proving beyond reasonable doubt that the confession was not obtained by the methods described in section 76(2). Witnesses, in the usual case police officers, will be called to give evidence of the confession and the circumstances in which it was made and will be open to cross-examination by defence counsel. The accused may then give evidence and call any witnesses who can support his version of events. The defence witnesses will also be open to cross-examination. The judge may also take into account any relevant evidence already given in the main trial, because the issue of admissibility cannot be tried in total isolation from the whole background of the case.[216] After speeches from counsel, the judge gives his ruling. If the confession is excluded, then nothing more should be heard of it.[217] If the confession is admitted, it may be put in evidence before the jury. Either way, however, in modern English practice the judge's decision is never revealed to the jury.[218]

[210] However, any resulting conviction may be quashed if the prosecution failed to disclose material which would have provided the defence with an informed opportunity to seek a *voir dire*: *R v Langley* [2001] Crim LR 651, CA.

[211] See per Lord Bridge in *Ajodha v The State* [1981] 2 All ER 193 at 202–3.

[212] See *R v Sat-Bhambra* (1988) 88 Cr App R 55, CA, below. See also *R v Millard* [1987] Crim LR 196, CC and *R v Davis* [1990] Crim LR 860, CA. For the position in summary trials, see *R v Liverpool Juvenile Court, ex p R* [1987] 2 All ER 668, DC (Ch 2).

[213] But see, in the case of summary trials, per Russell LJ in *R v Liverpool Juvenile Court, ex p R* [1987] 2 All ER 668 at 672–3.

[214] *R v Cole* (1941) 165 LT 125. In the trial of an unrepresented accused, it may be prudent, if the judge has any reason to suppose that the admissibility (voluntariness) of a statement proposed to be put in evidence by the prosecution is likely to be in issue, to explain to the accused his rights in the matter before the trial begins: per Lord Bridge in *Ajodha v The State* [1981] 2 All ER 193 at 203, PC.

[215] Occasionally it is convenient to determine admissibility immediately after the jury has been empanelled, as when the evidence of the confession is so important to the prosecution case that without reference to it they cannot even open their case: see *R v Hammond* [1941] 3 All ER 318.

[216] *R v Tyrer* (1989) 90 Cr App R 446, CA.

[217] *R v Treacy* [1944] 2 All ER 229, CCA. But see also *R v Rowson* [1985] 2 All ER 539, CA (see Ch 7); and *R v Myers* [1997] 4 All ER 314, HL, above.

[218] Per Lord Steyn in *Mitchell v R* [1998] 2 Cr App R 35, PC at 42.

The case of *Wong Kam-Ming v R*[219] gave rise to three important questions concerning the *voir dire*. They were: (i) during cross-examination of an accused on the *voir dire*, whether questions may be put as to the truth of the confession; (ii) whether the prosecution is permitted, on the resumption of the trial proper, to adduce evidence of what the accused said on the *voir dire*; and (iii) whether the prosecution is permitted, in the trial proper, to cross-examine the accused upon what he said on the *voir dire*. The accused was charged with murder at a massage parlour. The only evidence against him was a signed confession in which he admitted that he was present at the parlour at the relevant time, had a knife in his hand and 'chopped' someone. The admissibility of the confession was challenged on the ground that it was not made voluntarily. Under cross-examination on the *voir dire*, the accused was asked questions about the contents of the confession statement which were directed at establishing their truth. In answer, the accused admitted that he was present at the parlour and involved in the incident in question. The trial judge ruled that the confession statement was inadmissible. Before the jury, the judge allowed the prosecution to establish the accused's presence at the parlour by calling the shorthand writers to produce extracts from the transcript of the cross-examination on the *voir dire*. After the accused had given his evidence-in-chief before the jury, the prosecution were also permitted to cross-examine him on inconsistencies between that evidence and his evidence on the *voir dire* as recorded in the shorthand transcript. The accused was convicted and the Court of Appeal of Hong Kong dismissed his appeal. The Privy Council allowed the appeal on three grounds. First, it was held by a majority that the accused had been improperly cross-examined on the *voir dire* as to the truth of his confession statement because the sole issue on the *voir dire* was whether the statement had been made involuntarily, an issue to which its truth or falsity was irrelevant.[220] Secondly, it was held that the prosecution had been improperly permitted to adduce before the jury evidence of the answers given by the accused on the *voir dire*. In the opinion of their Lordships, such evidence should not be adduced, regardless of whether the confession is excluded or admitted, because a clear distinction should be maintained between the issue of voluntariness, which is alone relevant to the *voir dire*, and the issue of guilt which falls to be decided in the main trial.[221] Thirdly, it was held that the prosecution had been improperly permitted to cross-examine the accused on inconsistencies between his evidence before the jury and his statements on the *voir dire* because such a course is only permitted where the *voir dire* results in the admission of the confession and the accused gives evidence before the jury on some matter other than the voluntariness of the confession, which is no longer in issue, and in so doing gives answers which are inconsistent with his testimony on the *voir dire*.[222]

---

[219] [1980] AC 247.

[220] Lord Hailsham, dissenting, was of the opinion that in many cases the truth or falsity of the alleged confession could be relevant to the question at issue on the *voir dire* or to the credibility of either the defence or prosecution witnesses. See also *R v Hammond* [1941] 3 All ER 318, CCA, where it was held that prosecuting counsel was entitled, when cross-examining the accused on the *voir dire*, to ask him whether a statement, alleged by the accused to have been extorted by gross maltreatment, was in fact true. The accused's answer was in the affirmative. The question was held to be relevant to the issue of whether the evidence as to the gross maltreatment given by the accused on the *voir dire*, was true or false. The majority in *Wong Kam-Ming v R* took the view that *R v Hammond* was wrongly decided.

[221] See also *R v Brophy* [1982] AC 476, HL, below.

[222] Cf s 4 of the Criminal Procedure Act 1865, which provides that 'if a witness, upon cross-examination as to a former statement made by him . . . does not distinctly admit that he has made such statement, proof may be given that he did in fact make it . . . ': see Ch 7. Section 13 of the Hong Kong Evidence Ordinance is to the same effect. Lord Edmund Davies said at 259: 'But these statutory provisions have no relevance if the earlier statements cannot be put in evidence'.

What is the status of the decision in *Wong Kam-Ming v R* in the light of the Police and Criminal Evidence Act 1984? Concerning the first part of the decision, the law remains the same under the Act. The truth of the confession is as irrelevant to the issue of 'oppression' or 'unreliability' as it was to the issue of 'voluntariness'. Section 76(2), it will be recalled, requires the prosecution to prove that the confession, 'notwithstanding that it may be true', was not obtained by the methods it describes.[223] The second and third parts of the decision, insofar as they prohibit the prosecution from leading evidence on or cross-examining the accused about what he said on the *voir dire*, continue to represent the law under the Act but only, it would appear, in relation to statements made by the accused on the *voir dire* which are not 'adverse' to him. Section 82(1) defines a confession to include *any* statement wholly or partly adverse to the person who made it. Thus if, on the *voir dire*, the accused makes an inculpatory statement relevant to his guilt on the offence charged, which can hardly be said to have been obtained by oppression or in circumstances such as to render unreliable any confession which he might have made, then regardless of whether the extra-judicial confession is excluded or admitted, the statement may be given in evidence by the prosecution under section 76(1) and the accused may be cross-examined on any inconsistencies between that statement and the evidence he gives before the jury.[224] If this is correct, it presents the accused with an unenviable choice. An accused seeking to challenge the admissibility of a confession is virtually obliged to testify on the *voir dire* if his challenge is to have any chance of succeeding. If he elects to contest admissibility, then to the extent that evidence given by him on the *voir dire* is admissible in evidence at the trial, he is in effect deprived of the right to choose not to give evidence before the jury. If he elects to preserve that right, however, he deprives himself of the right to challenge the admissibility of the confession.[225] An accused deprived of his rights in this manner, it has been said, would not receive a fair trial.[226] The solution, it is submitted, is for the judge to exercise his discretion under section 78 of the 1984 Act to exclude the statements made by the accused on the *voir dire* on the grounds that they would have such an adverse effect on the fairness of the proceedings that the court ought not to admit them.

The issue of discretion, in this context, arose in *R v Brophy*.[227] The accused was tried by a judge sitting without a jury under the Northern Ireland (Emergency Provisions) Act 1978 on an indictment containing 49 counts including counts of murder, causing explosions, and belonging to a proscribed organization, namely the IRA (count 49). The only evidence connecting him with the crimes was a number of oral and written statements made to the police. The accused challenged the admissibility of the statements on the grounds that they had been obtained by torture and inhuman or degrading treatment. The trial judge, after a *voir dire*, excluded evidence of the statements. The accused, in his evidence-in-chief on the *voir dire*, said that he had been a member of the IRA during most of the period charged in count 49. When the trial resumed, the prosecution called the shorthand writer to prove the statements of the accused as to his membership of the IRA. The accused was acquitted of the first 48 counts,

---

[223] *Wong Kam Ming v R* is strong persuasive authority that the accused should not be cross-examined as to the truth of his confession on the *voir dire*: *R v Davis* [1990] Crim LR 860, CA.

[224] See Peter Mirfield, 'The Future of the Law of Confessions' [1984] *Crim LR* 63 at 74.

[225] See generally per Lord Hailsham in *Wong Kam-Ming v R* [1980] AC 247 at 261 and per Lord Fraser in *R v Brophy* [1982] AC 476 at 481. For views different to those expressed, see P Murphy [1979] *Crim LR* 364 and R Pattenden (1983) 32 *ICLQ* 812.

[226] Per Lord Fraser in *R v Brophy* [1982] AC 476 at 482.

[227] [1982] AC 476.

which were unsupported by any evidence, but convicted on count 49. The Court of Appeal in Northern Ireland allowed the appeal and the appeal to the House of Lords was dismissed. It was held that the accused's membership of the IRA was relevant to the issue on the *voir dire* because the police would probably have known this and therefore would not only have been more hostile to him but also would have expected him to have received instruction on how to avoid succumbing to the normal techniques of interrogation not involving physical ill-treatment. It was further held that, in any event, the evidence-in-chief given by an accused on the *voir dire* should be treated as relevant, unless clearly and obviously irrelevant, with the accused being given the benefit of any reasonable doubt.[228] The House concluded that the relevance of the evidence in question to the issue at the *voir dire* having been established, the consequence was that it was inadmissible in the substantive trial. In answer to a submission by counsel for the prosecution that if the evidence on the *voir dire* were admissible in the trial proper, the accused would be adequately safeguarded if the judge had a discretion to exclude any such evidence which would prejudice him unfairly, Lord Fraser said:[229]

> The right of the accused to give evidence at the *voir dire* without affecting his right to remain silent at the substantive trial is in my opinion absolute and is not to be made conditional on an exercise of judicial discretion.

Now that the actual decision in this case would appear to have been reversed by the 1984 Act, it is submitted that evidence given on the *voir dire* should be excluded from the trial proper by exercise of the discretion under section 78.[230]

The trial

Once the trial judge has ruled that a confession is admissible, the weight to be attached to it, which depends upon its content and all the circumstances in which it was obtained, is entirely a question of fact for the jury.[231] On the resumption of the trial proper, therefore, the defence is fully entitled to adduce evidence and cross-examine prosecution witnesses with a view to impeaching the credibility of the person to whom the confession was allegedly made and showing, for example, that the confession was fabricated, in whole or in part, or made in circumstances different from those alleged by the prosecution. Although, as we have seen, the truth of the confession is irrelevant on the *voir dire*, it is a crucial issue for the jury to consider.[232] The judge, pursuant to section 67(11) of the 1984 Act, may refer the jury to any relevant breaches of the Codes.[233] Moreover, the House of Lords in *R v Mushtaq*,[234] disapproving *Chan Wei Keung v R*,[235] held by a majority that where the judge has ruled that

[228] However, if the accused goes out of his way to boast of having committed the crimes charged or uses the witness box as a platform for a political speech, such evidence will almost certainly be irrelevant to the issue at the *voir dire*: per Lord Fraser [1982] AC 476 at 481.

[229] [1982] AC 476 at 483.

[230] However, concerning Lord Fraser's reference to the 'right to remain silent at the substantive trial', see now s 35 of the Criminal Justice and Public Order Act 1994 (Ch 14) and generally P Mirfield, 'Two Side-Effects of Sections 34 to 37 of the Criminal Justice and Public Order Act 1994' [1995] *Crim LR* 612.

[231] Per Lord Parker CJ in *R v Burgess* [1968] 2 QB 112 at 117–18, CA. But see s 77 (Ch 8).

[232] *R v Murray* (1950) 34 Cr App R 203 at 207.

[233] See *R v Kenny* [1992] Crim LR 800, CA.

[234] [2005] 1 WLR 1513, HL.

[235] [1967] 2 AC 160, PC.

a confession was not obtained by oppression nor in consequence of anything said or done which was likely to render unreliable any confession, but there is some evidence before the jury that the confession may have been so obtained, and they conclude that the alleged confession was or may have been so obtained, they must disregard it. If the jury reach such a conclusion, to permit them to rely upon the confession would be to fly in the face of the policy considerations said to underlie section 76(2), namely that the rejection of an improperly obtained confession is dependent not only upon possible unreliability, but also upon the principle that a man cannot be compelled to incriminate himself and upon the importance that attaches in a civilized society to proper behaviour by the police towards those in their custody. The judge should therefore direct the jury that unless they are satisfied beyond reasonable doubt that the confession was not obtained by the means set out in section 76(2)(a) and (b), they should disregard it.[236] Furthermore, permission to rely upon the confession in these circumstances would also be an invitation to the jury to act in a way that was incompatible with the accused's right against self-incrimination under Article 6(1) of the European Convention on Human Rights.

The trial judge, once he has determined that a confession is admissible under section 76 of the 1984 Act, has no power, at some later stage in the trial, to reconsider its admissibility as a matter of *law*. In *R v Sat-Bhambra*[237] a confession was ruled to be admissible after a trial within a trial in which a doctor had given expert evidence to the effect that the accused, who suffered from a mild form of diabetes, could have been affected by hypoglycaemia at the time of his interrogation. When the doctor was called in the trial proper, his evidence on the issue came out more in favour of the accused. The trial judge, however, declined to reconsider his decision on admissibility on the grounds that he was precluded from so doing by the terms of section 76. The Court of Appeal held that the trial judge had acted properly. Section 76 refers to a confession which the prosecution 'proposes to give in evidence' and which the court 'shall not allow . . . to be given in evidence' and therefore, once the judge has ruled that a confession is admissible, section 76 ceases to have effect. Section 78, which, similarly, refers to evidence on which the prosecution 'proposes to rely', also ceases to have effect.[238] The judge, however, is not powerless: if, in the light of the evidence given in the trial proper, he concludes that his previous decision on admissibility has been invalidated, he may, in the exercise of his discretion to exclude under section 82(3), direct the jury to disregard the confession.[239] Alternatively, and depending on the circumstances of the case, he may either point out to the jury the evidence which affects the weight of the confession and leave the matter in their hands or, if he thinks that the matter is not capable of remedy by any form of direction, discharge the jury from giving a verdict. The same options, presumably, would be open to a judge when a confession is put in evidence and the accused *then* gives evidence to the effect that it was obtained by one of the methods described in section 76(2).[240]

---

[236] *R v Pham* [2008] ALL ER(D) 96 (Dec), CA.

[237] (1988) 88 Cr App R 55, CA.

[238] Cf per Russell LJ in *R v Liverpool Juvenile Court, ex p R* [1987] 2 All ER 668 at 672–3, dealing with similar issues in relation to summary trials (see Ch 2).

[239] Section 82(3) is the source of the power, but the judge is likely to re-apply the s 78 criteria in the light of the new evidence: see *R v Hassan* [1995] Crim LR 404, CA.

[240] It may also be assumed that the judge has a discretion, in this situation, to require the relevant prosecution witnesses to be recalled for further cross-examination: see per Lord Bridge in *Ajodha v The State* [1981] 2 All ER 193, PC at 202–3, a case decided under the law as it stood prior to the 1984 Act.

Confessions implicating co-accused

If an accused goes into the witness box and gives evidence implicating a co-accused, then what he says becomes evidence for all purposes of the case and accordingly may be used by the jury as evidence against the co-accused.[241] However, subject to three exceptions, which are considered below, where a confession is given in evidence by the prosecution and implicates both its maker and a co-accused, it is no evidence against the co-accused because a confession is admissible as evidence of the truth of its contents only as against its maker. In these circumstances, therefore, the judge is duty bound to impress upon the jury that the confession cannot be used against the co-accused.[242] It may be doubted, however, whether such a direction, even if clear and emphatic, can ever fully remove the prejudice likely to be caused to the co-accused.[243] In one case it was said that it would require mental gymnastics of Olympic standards for the jury to approach their task without prejudice.[244] One obvious solution is to order separate trials for the accused, but although the Court of Appeal in *R v Lake*[245] recognized that exceptionally this can be done, it nevertheless upheld a trial judge's refusal to order a separate trial for the accused. Another solution is to edit the confession, for example by replacing the names of any co-accused with letters of the alphabet or expressions such as 'another person' or 'someone'.[246] Alternatively, counsel for the prosecution may agree not to read those parts of a confession statement which implicate a co-accused but have no real bearing on the case against its author. However, if the reference to the co-accused is exculpatory of the maker of the statement, he is entitled to have the statement read out in its entirety. As Lord Goddard CJ observed in *R v Gunewardene*,[247] in a passage approved by the Privy Council in *Lobban v R*:[248]

> It not infrequently happens that a prisoner, in making a statement, though admitting his guilt up to a certain extent, puts greater blame upon the co-prisoner, or is asserting that certain of his actions were really innocent and it was the conduct of the co-prisoner that gave them a sinister appearance or led to the belief that the prisoner making the statement was implicated in the crime. In such a case that prisoner would have a right to have the whole statement read and could complain if the prosecution picked out certain passages and left out others . . .

In three exceptional situations, a confession may be admitted not only as evidence against its maker but also as evidence against a co-accused. The first exception was established in *R v Hayter*,[249] where the House of Lords held, by a majority, that in a joint trial of two or more accused for a joint offence, a jury is entitled to consider first the case in respect of accused A which is solely based on his own out-of-court admissions, and then to use their findings of A's guilt as a

[241] See per Humphreys J in *R v Rudd* (1948) 32 Cr App R 138.

[242] *R v Gunewardene* [1951] 2 KB 600, CCA. See also *R v Blake* [1993] Crim LR 133, CA and per Lord Steyn in *Lobban v R* [1995] 2 All ER 602, PC at 613.

[243] See, eg, *R v Williams; R v Davis* (1992) 95 Cr App R 1, CA. See also Peter Thornton, 'The Prejudiced Defendant: Unfairness Suffered by a Defendant in a Joint Trial' [2003] *Crim LR* 433.

[244] *R v Silcott* [1987] Crim LR 765, CC.

[245] (1976) 64 Cr App R 172.

[246] As suggested in *R v Silcott* [1987] Crim LR 765, CC. See also *R v Rogers and Tarran* [1971] Crim LR 413 and *R v Mathias* [1989] Crim LR 64, CC. However, insofar as *R v Silcott* and *R v Mathias* suggest that a judge has a discretionary power at the request of one accused to exclude evidence tending to support the defence of another, they do not correctly reflect the law: per Lord Steyn in *Lobban v R* [1995] 2 All ER 602, PC at 613 (see Ch 2).

[247] [1951] 2 KB 600 at 610–11.

[248] [1995] 2 All ER 602 at 612 (see Ch 2).

[249] [2005] 1 WLR 605, HL.

fact to be used evidentially in respect of co-accused B, and further that where proof of A's guilt is necessary for there to be a case to answer against B, there will be a case to answer against him notwithstanding that the only evidence of A's guilt is his own out-of-court admissions. A's confession, however, can only be admitted against B on two conditions: first, that the jury are sufficiently sure of its truthfulness to decide that on that basis alone they can safely convict A; and secondly, that the jury are expressly directed that when deciding the case against B they must disregard entirely anything said out of court by A which might otherwise be thought to incriminate B. In reaching this conclusion, the majority were heavily influenced by the policy considerations underlying section 74 of the 1984 Act, whereby the fact that someone other than the accused has been convicted of an offence is admissible to prove, where to do so is relevant to an issue in the proceedings, that that person committed the offence. If there had been separate trials and A had been convicted, evidence of the conviction would have been admissible under section 74 of the 1984 Act in a subsequent trial of B. *R v Hayter* was distinguished in *Persad v State of Trinidad and Tobago*[250] where (i) the co-accused was *not* jointly liable for the offence; and (ii) it *was* sought to rely on A's statement insofar as it incriminated B.

The second exception is where the co-accused by his words or conduct accepts the truth of the statement so as to make all or part of it a confession statement of his own.[251]

The third exception, which is perhaps best understood in terms of implied agency, applies in the case of conspiracy: statements (or acts) of one conspirator which the jury is satisfied were said (or done) in the execution or furtherance of the common design are admissible in evidence against another conspirator, even though he was not present at the time, to prove the nature and scope of the conspiracy, provided that there is some independent evidence to show the existence of the conspiracy and that the other conspirator was a party to it.[252] Thus in *R v Blake and Tye*,[253] where the accused were charged with conspiracy to pass goods through the Custom House without paying duty, it was held that whereas a false entry by T in a counterfoil of a cheque, by which he received his share of the proceeds of the crime, was not admissible against B because it was not made in pursuance of the conspiracy, but simply as a matter of record and convenience, another false entry by T in a day book could be used in evidence against B since it was made in the execution or furtherance of their common design. It does not matter in what order the evidence of the statements (or acts) of the conspirator and the 'independent evidence' is adduced.[254] Thus evidence of the statements (or acts) may be admitted conditionally, ie conditional upon some other evidence of the common design being adduced; if it transpires that there is no other evidence of common design, then the statements (or acts) should be excluded.[255]

[250] [2008] 1 Cr App R 140, PC.
[251] See generally below at 399, under **Statements made in the presence of the accused**.
[252] *R v Shellard* (1840) 9 C&P 277, *R v Meany* (1867) 10 Cox CC 506, *R v Walters*, *R v Tovey* (1979) 69 Cr App R 115, and *R v Jenkins* [2003] Crim LR 107, CA. However, if there are two conspiracies, what A does in pursuance of the first is not admissible against B in respect of his involvement in the second: *R v Gray* [1995] 2 Cr App R 100, CA at 131. For a comparative examination of this exception to the hearsay rule, including an evaluation of its possible rationale, see Spencer, 'The common enterprise exception to the hearsay rule' (2007) 11 *E&P* 106.
[253] (1844) 6 QB 126.
[254] *R v Governor of Pentonville Prison, ex p Osman* [1989] 3 All ER 701, QBD at 731.
[255] *R v Donat* (1985) 82 Cr App R 173, CA. See also *R v Platten* [2006] Crim LR 920, CA, where it is suggested that the decision whether there is sufficient other evidence of the common design is for the judge alone, and not the judge and also, thereafter, the jury. Cf *R v Williams* [2002] EWCA Crim 2208.

R v Blake and Tye was applied in *R v Devonport*,[256] in which the prosecution were allowed to rely on a document, dictated by one accused, which showed the proposed division of the proceeds of the conspiracy among all five accused.[257] The following elaborations on the principle derive from *R v Platten*.[258] (1) The exception does not cover narrative after the conclusion of the conspiracy describing past events. (2) It covers statements made during a conspiracy and as part of the natural process of making the arrangements to carry it out, which are admissible not just as to the nature and extent of the conspiracy, but also as to the participation in it of persons absent when the statements were made. (3) Such statements can be admitted against all the conspirators even if made by one conspirator to a non-conspirator. (4) Statements about a conspirator having 'second thoughts' would be made in furtherance of the common design, because it is typical of a conspiracy for one conspirator to have doubts and to be persuaded by his co-conspirators to forget them. (5) Statements made before a conspirator was alleged to have joined the agreement can only be evidence of the origin of the conspiracy, not evidence of his part in it.

The third exception has been extended so that when, although a conspiracy is not charged, two or more people are engaged in a common enterprise, the acts and declarations of one in pursuance of the common purpose are admissible against another.[259] This principle applies to the commission of a substantive offence or series of offences by two or more people acting in concert, but is limited to evidence which shows the involvement of each accused in the commission of the offence or offences.[260] However, it cannot be extended to cases where individual defendants are charged with a number of separate substantive offences and the terms of a common enterprise are not proved or are ill-defined.[261] The rule is that the acts and declarations of one, in furtherance of a sufficiently defined common design, are admissible to prove a substantive offence committed by another alone, but in pursuance of the same common design.[262]

The foregoing common law exceptions have been preserved by statute. Section 118(1) of the Criminal Justice Act 2003 preserves: '5 Any rule of law relating to the admissibility of confessions . . . in criminal proceedings' and '7 Any rule of law under which in criminal proceedings a statement made by a party to a common enterprise is admissible against another party to the enterprise as evidence of any matter stated.'

Editing

Where a confession is given in evidence, the whole statement, including qualifications, explanations, or other exculpatory parts of it should be admitted so that the jury can fairly decide whether the statement, viewed as a whole, incriminates the accused.[263] However, where a confession statement contains inadmissible matter prejudicial to the accused, such as a reference to his previous convictions or bad character, it should be edited so as to

---

[256] [1996] 1 Cr App R 221, CA.

[257] See also *R v Ilyas and Knight* [1996] Crim LR 810, CA.

[258] [2006] Crim LR 920, CA.

[259] See, eg, *R v Jones* [1997] 2 Cr App R 119, CA.

[260] *R v Gray* [1995] 2 Cr App R 100, CA. See also *Tripodi v R* (1961) 104 CLR 1, HC of A.

[261] *R v Murray* [1997] 2 Cr App R 136, CA, per Otton LJ at 148.

[262] *R v Williams* [2002] All ER (D) 200 (Oct), [2002] EWCA Crim 2208, approving *R v Murray*, ibid.

[263] *R v Pearce* (1979) 69 Cr App R 365 at 369–70. How the judge should properly direct the jury in relation to a statement containing both inculpatory and exculpatory parts is considered in Ch 6, 172, under **Previous consistent or self-serving statements**.

eliminate the offending material.[264] Counsel may confer on the matter and, if necessary, the judge can take his part in ensuring that the statement is edited properly and to the right degree.[265] Although the rule is one of practice rather than law, a failure to edit may result in a conviction on indictment being quashed.[266] If the confession and the offending material are so interwoven as to be inseparable, or the removal of the latter would seriously alter the sense and meaning of the former so that they stand or fall together, the judge may, in the exercise of his discretion, exclude the entire statement on the grounds that its prejudicial effect outweighs its probative value.[267]

Statements made in the presence of the accused

Under section 82(1) of the 1984 Act, a confession, as we have seen, includes any statement adverse to the person who made it 'whether made in words or otherwise'. It would seem, therefore, that under the Act, as at common law, the accused may accept the accusation of another so as to make it wholly or in part a confession statement of his own, not only by his words but also, in appropriate circumstances, by his conduct, demeanour, or even silence. An alternative basis for the same conclusion is the inclusive nature of the statutory definition. Either way, if this construction is correct, it would enable the accused, in appropriate circumstances, to make a representation under section 76(2) (or section 76A(2)) and thereby oblige the prosecution (or co-accused) to prove that such a confession was not obtained by the methods described in that subsection. If such a confession is admitted under section 76 (or section 76A), the common law authorities will provide guidance to the judge as to how he should direct the jury; and the common law principle of conditional admissibility will still apply (so that, in appropriate circumstances, the judge may direct the jury to disregard the evidence). The common law rules relating to statements made in the presence of the accused, which now fall to be considered in more detail, have been preserved by section 118 of the Criminal Justice Act 2003. Section 118 preserves '5 Any rule of law relating to the admissibility of confessions . . . in criminal proceedings.'[268]

In *R v Norton*[269] the accused was convicted of having sexual intercourse with a girl under 13. Evidence was admitted of a statement made by the girl and directed at the accused, in which she identified him as the offender, and of his replies thereto. The conviction was quashed on the grounds that there was no evidence that the accused had accepted the truth of the statement. Pickford J, giving the judgment of the Court of Criminal Appeal,

---

[264] When a suspect is interviewed about more offences than are eventually made the subject of committal charges, a fresh statement should be prepared and signed omitting all questions and answers about the uncharged offences unless either they might appropriately be taken into consideration or evidence about them is admissible on the charges preferred (eg as similar fact evidence). It may, however, be desirable to replace the omitted questions and answers with a phrase such as: 'After referring to some other matters, I then said . . . ', so as to make it clear that part of the interview has been omitted: see para 24.4(b), *Practice Direction (Criminal Proceedings: Consolidation)* [2002] 1 WLR 2870.

[265] *R v Weaver* [1968] 1 QB 353, CA.

[266] *R v Knight; R v Thompson* (1946) 31 Cr App R 52; *Turner v Underwood* [1948] 2 KB 284, DC.

[267] See s 82(3), above.

[268] As to inferences that may be drawn pursuant to *statute* from an accused's silence on being questioned under caution by a constable or on being charged, see ss 34, 36, 37, and 38 of the Criminal Justice and Public Order Act 1994 (Ch 14).

[269] [1910] 2 KB 496.

made a number of important observations which may be summarized in terms of four propositions:

1. Statements made in the presence of the accused upon an occasion on which he might reasonably be expected to make some observation, explanation or denial are admissible in evidence if the judge is satisfied that there is evidence fit to be submitted to the jury that the accused by his answer to them, whether given by word or conduct, including silence, acknowledged the truth of the whole or part of them.

2. Although if there is no such evidence fit to be left to the jury, the contents of the statements should be excluded, they may be given in evidence even when they were denied by the accused as it is possible that a denial may be given under such circumstances and in such a manner as to constitute evidence from which an acknowledgment may be inferred.[270]

3. If the statements are admitted, the question whether the accused's answer, by words or conduct, did or did not in fact amount to an acknowledgment of them should be left to the jury.

4. The judge should direct the jury that if they conclude that the accused acknowledged the truth of the whole or any part of the statement, they may take the statement or part of it into consideration as evidence, but that without such an acknowledgment they should disregard the statement altogether.[271]

In *R v Christie*[272] the accused was convicted of indecent assault on a boy, who gave unsworn evidence. The boy's mother and a constable gave evidence to the effect that shortly after the alleged act, the boy approached the accused, identified him by saying, 'That is the man', and described the assault. They also gave evidence that the accused then said, 'I am innocent.' The Court of Criminal Appeal quashed the conviction on the grounds that, the accused having denied the truth of the boy's statement, the evidence of the mother and constable had been improperly admitted. The House of Lords affirmed the order quashing the conviction on a different ground, that there had been a misdirection on corroboration. However, the House approved the approach taken in *R v Norton* but regarded the principles enunciated by Pickford J as valuable rules of guidance rather than strict rules of law.

When a person is accused of a crime in circumstances such that it would be reasonable to expect some explanation or denial from him, whether the accused's silence can give rise to an inference that he accepted the truth of the charge would appear to depend upon whether it was made by a police officer or some other person in authority or charged with the investigation of the crime as opposed to some other person with whom the accused can be said to have been 'on even terms'. In *Hall v R*[273] the question arose whether the silence of the accused *before* being cautioned could give rise to an inference that he accepted the truth of an accusation made by or through a police officer. The accused was convicted of unlawful

---

[270] The denial may also give rise to such an inference if inconsistent with statements subsequently made by him or inconsistent with his defence at the trial, as when he denies an assault but at his trial pleads self-defence: see per Lord Moulton in *R v Christie* [1914] AC 545 at 560. See further *R v Z* (2003) 1 WLR 1489, CA, at 361 above under **Admissibility, Confessions defined**.

[271] Contrast *R v Black* (1922) 16 Cr App R 118.

[272] [1914] AC 545.

[273] [1971] 1 WLR 298.

possession of drugs which were found in premises occupied by him and two co-accused. A police officer told the accused that one of the co-accused had said that the drugs belonged to him, that is the accused. The accused, who at that stage had not been cautioned, remained silent. All of the accused were convicted. The Privy Council advised that the accused's conviction be quashed. Lord Diplock, delivering the judgment of the Board, said:[274]

> It is a clear and widely known principle of the common law in Jamaica, as in England, that a person is entitled to refrain from answering a question put to him for the purpose of discovering whether he has committed a criminal offence. *A fortiori* he is under no obligation to comment when he is informed that someone else has accused him of an offence. It may be that in very exceptional circumstances an inference may be drawn from a failure to give an explanation or a disclaimer, but in their Lordships' view silence alone on being informed by a police officer that someone else has made an accusation against him cannot give rise to an inference that the person to whom this information is communicated accepts the truth of the accusation . . .
>
> The caution merely serves to remind the accused of a right which he already possesses at common law. The fact that in a particular case he has not been reminded of it is no ground for inferring that his silence was not in exercise of that right, but was an acknowledgment of the truth of the accusation.

Where there are two suspects and one of them answers a question put by an officer to both of them by telling a lie, similar principles apply to the issue whether the other of them, by his silence, adopted the answer of the first.[275]

In *Parkes v R*[276] the appellant was convicted of murder. At the trial, the victim's mother gave evidence that, having found her daughter injured, she went to the appellant and accused him twice of stabbing her daughter. The appellant said nothing and, when the mother threatened to detain him while the police were sent for, drew a knife and attempted to stab her. On these facts the Privy Council applied the following dictum of Cave J in *R v Mitchell*:[277]

> Undoubtedly, when persons are speaking on even terms, and a charge is made, and the person charged says nothing, and expresses no indignation, and does nothing to repel the charge, that is some evidence to show that he admits the charge to be true.

Accordingly, it was held that the trial judge had not erred in instructing the jury that the appellant's reactions to the accusations, including his silence, were matters from which they could, if they saw fit, infer that he had accepted the truth of the accusation.[278] *Hall v R* was distinguished on the grounds that, in that case, the person by whom the accusation was communicated was a police officer and there was no evidence of the accused's reaction other than his silence.

It seems that the accuser and the accused may be regarded as being on even terms notwithstanding that the police have brought them together and are present when the accusation is made. In *R v Horne*,[279] shortly after an assault, the police took the accused to the scene of the crime and sat him down opposite the victim. It was held that the accused's silent reaction to

---

[274] [1971] 1 WLR 298 at 301.

[275] *R v Collins* [2003] 2 Cr App R 199, CA.

[276] [1976] 1 WLR 1251, PC.

[277] (1892) 17 Cox CC 503 at 508.

[278] For a further example, see *R v Coll* [2005] EWCA Crim 3675.

[279] [1990] Crim LR 188, CA.

an accusation then made by the victim, but unprompted by the officers present, was capable of amounting to an acceptance of the accusation made.

The dictum of Cave J in *R v Mitchell* was also applied in *R v Chandler*.[280] The accused was convicted of conspiracy to defraud, the only evidence against him being an interview with a detective sergeant in the presence of his solicitor when, both *before* and *after* being cautioned, he answered some questions and remained silent or refused to answer others. The jury were directed that it was for them to decide whether the accused had remained silent before the caution in exercise of his common law right or because he thought that had he answered he might have incriminated himself. The Court of Appeal, satisfied that the accused and the detective sergeant were speaking on equal terms, since the former had his solicitor present to advise him and, if needed, subsequently to testify as to what had been said, held that some comment on the accused's lack of frankness before he was cautioned was justified. The conviction was quashed, however, on the grounds that the trial judge had short-circuited the proper intellectual process, which involved directing the jury to determine, first, whether the accused's silence amounted to an acceptance by him of what was said and, secondly, if satisfied that he did accept what was said, whether guilt could reasonably be inferred from what he had accepted. The importance of the decision lies in the reservations expressed about the dicta of Lord Diplock in *R v Hall*. Lawton LJ was of the opinion that they seemed to conflict with *R v Christie* and the earlier authorities and said:[281]

> The law has long accepted that an accused person is not bound to incriminate himself; but it does not follow that a failure to answer an accusation or question when an answer could reasonably be expected may not provide some evidence in support of an accusation. Whether it does will depend on the circumstances.

In a later passage, his Lordship said:[282]

> We do not accept that a police officer always has an advantage over someone he is questioning . . . A young detective questioning a local dignitary in the course of an inquiry into alleged local government corruption may be very much at a disadvantage. This kind of situation is to be contrasted with that of a tearful housewife accused of shoplifting or of a parent being questioned about the suspected wrongdoing of his son.

It remains to be seen, however, whether this flexible approach will prevail over Lord Diplock's view that silence alone, on being accused by or through a police officer, cannot give rise to an inference that the accused accepts the truth of the accusation made.

Facts discovered in consequence of inadmissible confessions

At common law, the fact that a confession was inadmissible did not affect the admissibility of any incriminating facts discovered in consequence of that confession. In *R v Warickshall*[283] a woman was charged, as an accessory after the fact, with receiving stolen property. In consequence of a confession made by her, the property was found concealed in her bed at her lodgings. The confession was excluded on the grounds that it had been obtained by promises

[280] [1976] 1 WLR 585.
[281] [1976] 1 WLR 585 at 589.
[282] [1976] 1 WLR 585 at 590.
[283] (1783) 1 Leach 263.

of favour. Counsel for the defence argued that evidence of the fact of finding the stolen property in her custody should also be excluded since it was obtained in consequence of the inadmissible evidence. Rejecting this argument, it was said:

> Confessions are received in evidence, or rejected as inadmissible, under a consideration whether they are or are not entitled to credit . . . This principle respecting confessions has no application whatever as to the admission or rejection of facts, whether the knowledge of them be obtained in consequence of an extorted confession, or whether it arises from any other source; for a fact, if it exists at all, must exist invariably in the same manner, whether the confession from which it is derived be in other respects true or false.[284]

The Criminal Law Revision Committee was in no doubt that this rule should be preserved on the grounds that to prevent the police from using any 'leads' obtained from an inadmissible confession would interfere unduly with justice and the detection of crime.[285] The rule is preserved by section 76(4) and by section 76A(4) of the 1984 Act, both of which provide that:

> The fact that a confession is wholly or partly excluded in pursuance of this section shall not affect the admissibility in evidence—
>
> (a) of any facts discovered as a result of the confession; . . .

If an interviewee, in consequence of some promise, inducement, or threat to produce documentary evidence, hands over an incriminating document, it is unclear whether the document itself constitutes a confession and therefore may fall to be excluded under section 76, or is evidence of fact, admissible in law albeit open to discretionary exclusion under section 78. On one view, if the promise, inducement, or threat expressly relates to the production of documentary evidence, any incriminating document then produced should be treated as a confession,[286] even if does not readily appear to be a 'statement' for the purposes of the section 82(1) definition of a confession ('any statement wholly or partly adverse to the person who made it . . . and whether made in words or otherwise').

Where incriminating facts discovered in consequence of an inadmissible confession are admitted in evidence, the question arises whether, notwithstanding that the confession itself must be excluded, evidence is admissible to show that the discovery of the facts in question was made as a result of the confession statement. For example, if an inadmissible confession of theft includes a statement that the stolen goods are hidden in a particular place, and they are found there, can the prosecution give evidence not only that they found the goods at that place but also that they found them as a result of something which the accused said? The importance of this question lies in the fact that proof that the stolen goods were hidden in a particular place, without reference to the confession, will do little or nothing to advance the prosecution case unless, as it happens, there is some link between the accused and the goods because, for example, they were found in a place frequented by him, such as his house or place of work, or bore his fingerprints. The cases at common law were in conflict.[287] The Criminal

---

[284] See also, in relation to evidence of facts discovered as a result of an illegal search, *Kuruma v R* [1955] AC 197 at 203–5 and *King v R* [1969] 1 AC 304.

[285] 11th Report (Cmnd 4991) para 68.

[286] See *R v Barker* [1941] 2 KB 381, CCA at 384–5, a decision at common law reversed by s 105 of the Taxes Management Act 1970 (see above) but in any event since disapproved by the House of Lords: see per Lord Hutton in *R v Allen (No 2)* [2001] 4 All ER 768 at [33]–[35].

[287] See *R v Griffin* (1809) Russ&Ry 151, CCR, *R v Gould* (1840) 9 C&P 364, CCC and *R v Garbett* (1847) 2 Car&Kir 474, Ex Ch; and cf *R v Warickshall* (1783) 1 Leach 263 and *R v Berriman* (1854) 6 Cox CC 388, Assizes.

Law Revision Committee was opposed to the admissibility of any part of the confession on the grounds that this would involve a decision on the part of the judge as to whether, in his opinion, the confession or part of it was likely to be true, an opinion which, although not binding on the jury, would be difficult for them not to be impressed by. The majority was in favour of allowing evidence to be given that the discovery of the incriminating facts was made 'as a result of a statement made by the accused'. The minority dissented on the grounds that the jury should not be informed indirectly of something of which the interests of justice require that they should not be informed directly.[288] Subject to cases in which the *defence* choose to give evidence as to how the incriminating facts were discovered, the minority view is reflected in section 76(5) and (6) and in section 76A(5) and (6) of the 1984 Act, which provide that:

(5) Evidence that a fact to which this subsection applies was discovered as a result of a statement made by an accused person shall not be admissible unless evidence of how it was discovered is given by him or on his behalf.
(6) Subsection (5) above applies—
  (a) to any fact discovered as a result of a confession which is wholly excluded in pursuance of this section; and
  (b) to any fact discovered as a result of a confession which is partly so excluded, if the fact is discovered as a result of the excluded part of the confession.

Thus where part of a confession to murder, the entirety of which is excluded because extracted by police brutality, indicates the location of the murder weapon, that part remains inadmissible even if later shown to be reliable by the discovery of the weapon in the place indicated.[289]

The Committee was also of the opinion that where something in a confession statement shows that the accused speaks, writes, or expresses himself in a particular manner and this serves to identify him with the offender, so much of the confession as is necessary to show such characteristics should be admissible for that purpose.[290] The point was illustrated by reference to *R v Voisin*.[291] The accused was convicted of murdering a woman whose body was found in a parcel together with a piece of paper bearing the handwritten words 'Bladie Belgiam'. The accused, without being cautioned, was asked by the police to write down 'Bloody Belgian'. He wrote down 'Bladie Belgiam' and this writing was admitted in evidence at his trial. The accused appealed on the grounds, inter alia, that he should have been cautioned before being asked to write the words in question. The appeal failed. Although the case did not concern an inadmissible confession, the Committee was of the view that, had the words been written in an inadmissible confession, that part of it should have been admissible, not as evidence of the truth of its contents, but for the purpose of identifying the accused with the offender. Section 76(4) and section 76A(4) of the 1984 Act both provide that:

The fact that a confession is wholly or partly excluded in pursuance of this section shall not affect the admissibility in evidence—

(b) where the confession is relevant as showing that the accused speaks, writes or expresses himself in a particular way, of so much of the confession as is necessary to show that he does so.

---

[288] 11th Report (Cmnd 4991) para 69.
[289] See *Lam Chi-ming v R* [1991] 3 All ER 172, PC.
[290] 11th Report (Cmnd 4991) para 69.
[291] [1918] 1 KB 531.

ADDITIONAL READING

Baldwin, 'Legal Advice at the Police Station' [1993] *Crim LR* 371.

Gudjohnsson, *The Psychology of Interrogations, Confessions and Testimony* (Chichester, 1992).

Mirfield, 'Two Side-Effects of Sections 34 to 37 of the Criminal Justice and Public Order Act 1994' [1995] *Crim LR* 612.

Mirfield, 'Successive Confessions and the Poisonous Tree' [1996] *Crim LR* 554.

Mirfield, *Silence, Confessions and Improperly Obtained Evidence* (Oxford, 1997).

Roberts, 'Questioning the Suspect' [1993] *Crim LR* 368.

Spencer, 'The common enterprise exception to the hearsay rule' (2007) 11 *E&P* 106.

Thornton, 'The Prejudiced Defendant: Unfairness Suffered by a Defendant in a Joint trial' [2003] *Crim LR* 433.

Statutory inferences from an accused's silence or conduct

14

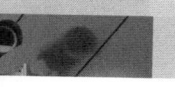

Key Issues

- What adverse inferences, if any, should be drawn against an accused, and why, from:

  (a) his failure to testify;

  (b) his failure, when questioned or charged, to mention facts which he could reasonably have been expected to have mentioned at that time and which he later relies on in his defence at trial;

  (c) his failure, on arrest, to account for any object, substance, or mark that the police reasonably believe may be attributable to his participation in the commission of an offence;

  (d) his refusal to consent to the police taking an intimate sample, such as a sample of blood, semen, or urine; and

  (e) his failure to provide advance disclosure of the defence case, the nature of his defence or the facts on which he takes issue with the prosecution?

- In the case of (b), if the accused remained silent on legal advice, should the answer be the same?

Inferences from silence

The 'right to silence'

The so-called 'right to silence' formerly comprised two 'rights', the privilege against self-incrimination, ie the freedom of an accused from the compulsion to incriminate himself, and the 'right' not to have adverse inferences drawn from his silence. More narrowly examined, the 'right to silence' encompassed a number of specific 'rights', more accurately rules, including the following.

1. A suspect is under no legal obligation to assist the police with their inquiries.[1]

2. An accused is not obliged to give advance notice of the evidence in support of his defence; and it is wrong to make adverse comments about the fact that an accused, having been cautioned by the police, (a) remained silent;[2] (b) declined to answer some questions;[3] or (c) failed to reveal his defence.[4]

3. An accused is not a compellable witness.[5]

4. The failure of an accused to testify shall not be made the subject of any comment by the prosecution.[6]

5. Although in appropriate circumstances a judge may invite a jury to draw adverse inferences from failure to testify, they should be directed not to assume guilt from such a failure.[7]

Prior to the Criminal Justice and Public Order Act 1994 (the 1994 Act), few statutory provisions operated to curtail the 'right to silence' to any significant degree. Two important examples may be given. First, rule 24 of the Criminal Procedure Rules 2005[8] provides that an accused shall not without the leave of the court adduce expert evidence unless he has given to the prosecution a written statement of the finding or opinion which he proposes to adduce.[9] Secondly, under the Criminal Justice Act 1987, in cases of serious or complex fraud, although an accused may depart from the case which he disclosed in pursuance of a requirement imposed by the court at a preparatory hearing, if he does so depart, or if he fails to comply with such a requirement, the judge or, with the leave of the judge, any other party, may make such comment as appears to the judge to be appropriate, and the jury or, in the case of a trial without jury, the judge, may draw such inferences as appear proper.[10]

---

[1] *Rice v Connolly* [1966] 2 QB 414.

[2] *R v Leckey* [1944] KB 80.

[3] *R v Gilbert* (1977) 66 Cr App R 237, CA; *R v Raviraj* (1986) 85 Cr App R 93, CA; and *R v Henry* [1990] Crim LR 574.

[4] *R v Lewis* (1973) 57 Cr App R 860, CA; *R v Foster* [1974] Crim LR 544, CA; and *R v Gilbert* (1977) 66 Cr App R 237. As to inferences from silence where an accused and his accuser are on 'even terms', see *R v Norton* [1910] 2 KB 496 etc (Ch 13). As to inferences from refusal to provide samples, see below.

[5] Section 1 of the Criminal Evidence Act 1898 and s 53 of the Youth Justice and Criminal Evidence Act 1999 (Ch 5).

[6] Section 1(b) of the Criminal Evidence Act 1898, now repealed: see below.

[7] *R v Bathurst* [1968] 2 QB 99, CA and *R v Taylor* [1993] Crim LR 223, CA.

[8] SI 2005/384.

[9] See Ch 18. Advance notice must also be given to the prosecution of certain defences available to charges that consumer goods failed to comply with the general safety requirements: see s 39 of the Consumer Protection Act 1987.

[10] See ss 7, 9, and 10.

Compared to these two statutory provisions, sections 34–38 of the 1994 Act, constitute a major curtailment of the 'right to silence'. Thus although the accused retains his 'right' to remain silent both at the trial and under interrogation, 'proper' inferences may be drawn from (i) his failure to give evidence or his refusal, without good cause, to answer any question at the trial (section 35); (ii) his failure to mention certain facts when questioned under caution or on being charged (section 34); and (iii) his failure or refusal to account for objects, substances or marks (section 36) or his presence at a particular place (section 37).[11]

Failure to testify

Section 35 of the 1994 Act provides as follows:

(1) At the trial of any person for an offence, subsections (2) and (3) below apply unless—
  (a) the accused's guilt is not in issue; or
  (b) it appears to the court that the physical or mental condition of the accused makes it undesirable for him to give evidence;
but subsection (2) below does not apply if, at the conclusion of the evidence for the prosecution, his legal representative informs the court that the accused will give evidence or, where he is unrepresented, the court ascertains from him that he will give evidence.

(2) Where this subsection applies, the court shall, at the conclusion of the evidence for the prosecution, satisfy itself (in the case of proceedings on indictment with a jury, in the presence of the jury) that the accused is aware that the stage has been reached at which evidence can be given for the defence and that he can, if he wishes, give evidence and that, if he chooses not to give evidence, or having been sworn, without good cause refuses to answer any question, it will be permissible for the court or jury to draw such inferences as appear proper from his failure to give evidence or his refusal, without good cause, to answer any question.

(3) Where this subsection applies, the court or jury, in determining whether the accused is guilty of the offence charged,[12] may draw such inferences as appear proper from the failure of the accused to give evidence or his refusal, without good cause, to answer any question.

(4) This section does not render the accused compellable to give evidence on his own behalf, and he shall accordingly not be guilty of contempt of court by reason of a failure to do so.

(5) For the purposes of this section a person who, having been sworn, refuses to answer any question shall be taken to do so without good cause unless—
  (a) he is entitled to refuse to answer the question by virtue of any enactment, whenever passed or made, or on the ground of privilege; or
  (b) the court in the exercise of its general discretion excuses him from answering it.

There must be an evidential basis for a defence application that section 35(1)(b) applies. If there is, the judge should decide the matter in a *voir dire*, but if there is not, it is not incumbent on him to order a *voir dire* of his own volition.[13] There must also be an evidential basis for the finding of the court under section 35(1)(b). The fact that the accused may have some difficulty

---

[11] As to the effect of the abolition of the right to silence in England and in Northern Ireland, see respectively T Bucke, R Street, and D Brown, *The Right of Silence: The Impact of the Criminal Justice and Public Order Act 1994* (Home Office Research Study No 199, 2000) and J Jackson, M Wolfe, and K Quinn, *Legislating Against Silence: The Northern Ireland Experience* (Northern Ireland Office, 2000). See also J Jackson, 'Silence and Proof: extending the boundaries of criminal proceedings in the United Kingdom' (2001) 5 *E&P* 145.

[12] Or any other offence of which the accused could lawfully be convicted on that charge: s 38(2).

[13] *R v A* [1997] Crim LR 883, CA. See also *R v Anwoir* [2008] 4 All ER 582, CA.

giving evidence is insufficient to justify a finding that it is undesirable for him to give evidence; and although such a finding does not always need to be based on expert medical evidence, such evidence will be necessary in some cases, as when it is said that the accused's depression makes it undesirable for him to give evidence.[14] However, expert evidence will not necessarily be determinative.[15] In *R v Friend*[16] it was said that for the purposes of section 35(1)(b) a 'physical condition' might include one involving a risk of an epileptic attack, and a 'mental condition' might include latent schizophrenia where the experience of evidence might trigger a florid state. It was also said that the language of the subsection was such as to give a wide discretion to the trial judge, whose decision can only be impugned if *Wednesbury* unreasonable.[17] In *R v Friend* the accused had a mental age of 9, but it was held that the trial judge had not erred in declining to rule that it was 'undesirable for him to give evidence'.

Section 35(2) places a mandatory requirement on the court to satisfy itself of the matters set out therein and the court can only do this by asking either the accused or his representative.[18] By inference, counsel has to be asked in a situation where it is possible to take instructions from the accused, which will not be possible where the accused has absconded.[19]

Under section 35(1) the court is not required to satisfy itself of the matters specified in section 35(2) if, at the end of the prosecution case, the accused's representative informs the court that the accused will give evidence. According to para 44.2 of the *Practice Direction (Criminal Proceedings: Consolidation)*,[20] this should be done in the presence of the jury and, if the representative indicates that the accused will give evidence, the case should proceed in the usual way. Somewhat bizarrely, therefore, if a represented accused indicates that he will testify, there is no obligation on the *court* to ascertain whether he is aware of the potential consequence of refusing without good cause to answer any question. It has been held that if, in the event, such an accused does refuse to answer any question without good cause, the judge may then tell him, in an unoppressive way, of the potential consequences.[21] It is submitted that in these circumstances, such a warning should be mandatory.

The *Practice Direction* continues as follows:

44.3 If the court is not so informed, or if the court is informed that the accused does not intend to give evidence, the judge should in the presence of the jury inquire of the representative in these terms:
'Have you advised your client that the stage has now been reached at which he may give evidence and, if he chooses not to do so or, having been sworn, without good cause refuses to answer any question, the jury may draw such inferences as appear proper from his failure to do so?'

44.4 If the representative replies to the judge that the accused has been so advised, then the case shall proceed. If counsel replies that the accused has not been so advised then the judge shall direct the representative to advise his client of the consequences set out in paragraph 44.3 and should adjourn briefly for this purpose before proceeding further.

---

[14] *R (DPP) v Kavanagh* [2006] Crim LR 370, DC, approved in *R v Tabbakh* [2009] EWCA Crim 464.
[15] See *R v Ullah* [2007] All ER (D) 156 (Mar) (psychiatric evidence of 'severe social phobia').
[16] [1997] 1 WLR 1433, CA.
[17] *Associated Provincial Picture Houses Ltd v Wednesbury Corpn* [1948] 1 KB 223, CA.
[18] *R v Cowan* [1996] 1 Cr App R 1, CA, at 9.
[19] *R v Gough* [2002] Cr App R 121, CA.
[20] [2002] 1 WLR 2870.
[21] *R v Ackinclose* [1996] Crim LR 74, CA.

44.5 If the accused is not represented, the judge shall at the conclusion of the evidence for the prosecution and in the presence of the jury say to the accused:

'You have heard the evidence against you. Now is the time for you to make your defence. You may give evidence on oath, and be cross-examined like any other witness. If you do not give evidence or, having been sworn, without good cause refuse to answer any question the jury may draw such inferences as appear proper. That means they may hold it against you. You may also call any witness or witnesses whom you have arranged to attend court. Afterwards you may also, if you wish, address the jury by arguing your case from the dock. But you cannot at that stage give evidence. Do you now intend to give evidence?'

Although section 35 is expressly without prejudice to the accused's right not to testify on his own behalf (section 35(4)), under section 35(3) the court or jury may draw 'proper' inferences from his failure to testify or his refusal, without good cause, to answer any question. Section 35(5) creates a conclusive presumption: an accused who has been sworn and refuses to answer any question will be deemed to have so refused without good cause unless either (a) he is entitled to refuse by reason of an enactment[22] or on the ground of privilege (eg legal professional privilege);[23] or (b) the court excuses him from answering in the exercise of its general discretion.

Under section 38(3):

A person shall not . . . be convicted of an offence solely on an inference drawn from such a failure as is mentioned in section . . . 35(3) . . .

However, as we shall see, in *Condron v United Kingdom*[24] the European Court of Human Rights has held that it is incompatible with the right to silence to base a conviction solely *or mainly* on the accused's silence or refusal to answer questions or give evidence.

In *R v Cowan*[25] the Court of Appeal rejected as contrary to the plain words of section 35, a submission that the operation of section 35(3) should be confined to exceptional cases. In answer to the first argument in support of the submission, that the section constituted an infringement of the accused's right to silence, the court stressed that the 'right of silence' had not been abolished by the section, but expressly preserved by section 35(4). Secondly, it was argued that the section had watered down the burden of proof and in effect put a burden on the accused to testify in order to avoid conviction. Lord Taylor CJ held that this argument was misconceived because (i) the prosecution have to establish a prima facie case before any question of the accused testifying is raised;[26] (ii) the court or jury is prohibited from convicting solely because of an inference drawn from silence (section 38(3)); and (iii) the burden of proving guilt beyond reasonable doubt remains on the prosecution throughout. Thus although the effect of section 35 is that the court or jury may regard the inference drawn from silence as, in effect, a further evidential factor in support of the prosecution case, it cannot be the only factor to justify a conviction: the totality of the evidence must prove guilt beyond reasonable doubt.

---

[22] The phrase 'entitled to refuse' was probably used because of the wording of s 1(3) of the Criminal Evidence Act 1898 (now repealed). Section 1(3) provided that an accused, if asked a question relating to his previous convictions or bad character, 'shall not be required' to answer it. See now s 101 of the Criminal Justice Act 2003, Ch 17.

[23] See Ch 20.

[24] (2001) 31 EHRR 1, ECHR.

[25] [1995] 4 All ER 939.

[26] The Domestic Violence, Crime and Victims Act 2004, s 6, creates an exception in the case of an accused charged in the same proceedings with murder or manslaughter and with an offence, in respect of the same death, under s 5 of the Act (causing or allowing the death of a child or vulnerable adult).

A third argument in support of the submission was that an inference should only be drawn where there is no reasonable possibility of an innocent explanation for the accused's silence; that an inference should not be drawn where there are 'good reasons' for silence consistent with innocence, for example (a) where there is other defence evidence to contradict the prosecution case; (b) where an accused is nervous, inarticulate, or unlikely to perform well in the witness box; (c) where an accused is under duress or fear for his or another's safety; or (d) where—as in two of the cases before the court—an accused has attacked prosecution witnesses and decided not to give evidence because it would expose him to cross-examination on his previous convictions; and that counsel may properly advance such reasons without the need for evidence. This argument was also rejected. The court accepted that, apart from the mandatory exceptions in section 35(1), it is open to the court to decline to draw an adverse inference and for a judge to direct or advise a jury against drawing such an inference if the circumstances of the case justify such a course, but held that there needs to be either some evidential basis for declining to draw an adverse inference[27] or some exceptional factors in the case making that a fair course to take—it is improper for defence counsel to give to the jury reasons for his client's silence at trial in the absence of evidence to support such reasons.[28] The court stressed that the inferences permitted are only such 'as appear proper', a phrase intended to leave a broad discretion to a trial judge to decide in all the circumstances whether any proper inference is capable of being drawn by the jury. If not, he should tell them so; otherwise, it is for the jury to decide whether in fact an inference should properly be drawn.

The court also rejected the specific submission that an inference should not be drawn where an accused seeks to avoid cross-examination on his record. It was pointed out that to hold otherwise would lead to the bizarre result of an accused with previous convictions being in a more privileged position than an accused with a clean record. *R v Cowan* was endorsed, in this respect, in *R v Becouarn*,[29] where the House of Lords gave two reasons for rejecting a submission that in these circumstances the judge should at least give a direction along the lines that there may be various possible other reasons why the accused did not give evidence: first, that such a direction would either signal to the jurors that the accused *does* have previous convictions, or set them off on a trail of unfounded speculation about the existence of other imaginary reasons; and secondly, that although fear of allowing in his convictions may be an element in a decision not to testify, reluctance to face cross-examination may be another and much more predominant element.

The Judicial Studies Board has suggested the following specimen direction.

> The defendant has not given evidence. That is his right. But, as he has been told, the law is that you may draw such inferences as appear proper from his failure to do so. Failure to give evidence on its own cannot prove guilt but depending on the circumstances, you may hold his failure against him when deciding whether he is guilty. [There is evidence before you on the basis of which the defendant's advocate invites you not to hold it against the defendant that he has not given evidence before you namely . . . If you think that because of this evidence you should not hold it against the defendant that he has not given evidence, do not do so. But if the evidence he

---

[27] Presumably it is open to the judge to hear such evidence on a *voir dire*, a course that would seem to be particularly important in cases in which the reasons for silence can only be established, in effect, by the accused himself.

[28] No examples were given of the kind of 'evidential basis' or 'exceptional factors' which might lead a judge to conclude that an inference should not be drawn. In *R v Napper* [1996] Crim LR 591, CA, it was held that the fact that the police failed to interview the accused while the alleged frauds were reasonably fresh in his mind did not warrant such a conclusion.

[29] [2005] 1 WLR 2589, HL. See also *R v Taylor* [1999] Crim LR 77, CA.

relies on presents no adequate explanation for his absence from the witness box then you may hold his failure to give evidence against him. You do not have to do so.] What proper inferences can you draw from the defendant's decision not to give evidence before you? If you conclude that there is a case for him to answer, you may think that the defendant would have gone into the witness box to give you an explanation for or an answer to the case against him. If the only sensible explanation for his decision not to give evidence is that he has no answer to the case against him, or none that could have stood up to cross-examination, then it would be open to you to hold against him his failure to give evidence. It is for you to decide whether it is fair to do so.

In *R v Cowan* the Court of Appeal considered the specimen direction to be, in general terms, a sound guide. It held that although it may be necessary to adapt or add to it in the particular circumstances of an individual case, there were certain essentials.

1. The judge must direct the jury that the burden remains on the prosecution throughout and must direct them as to the required standard of proof.

2. The judge should make clear that the accused is entitled to remain silent: it is his right and his choice.

3. The jury must be told that an inference from failure to give evidence cannot on its own prove guilt (section 38(3)).[30]

4. The jury must be satisfied that the prosecution have established a case to answer before drawing any inferences from silence.[31] Although the judge must have thought that there was a case to answer, the jury may not believe the witnesses whose evidence the judge considered sufficient to raise a prima facie case. It must therefore be made clear that they must find that there is a case to answer on the prosecution evidence before drawing an adverse inference from silence.[32]

5. The jury should also be directed that if, despite any evidence relied upon to explain the accused's silence, or in the absence of such evidence, they conclude that the silence can only sensibly be attributed to his having no answer, or none that would stand up to cross-examination, they may draw an adverse inference.[33]

The court further held that it is not possible to anticipate all the circumstances in which a judge might think it right to direct or advise a jury against drawing an adverse inference. Noting that it would not be wise even to give examples, as each case must turn on its own facts, the court cited with approval the following dictum of Kelly LJ in *R v McLernon*:[34]

---

[30] Cowan's appeal was allowed on the basis that the jury had not been directed in accordance with 3 (and 5, below).

[31] 'Inescapable logic' and fairness demand that this fourth 'essential' direction be given: see *R v Birchall* [1999] Crim LR 311, CA. See also *R v El-Hannachi* [1998] 2 Cr App R 226, CA. In both cases, failure to give the direction resulted in a successful appeal against conviction. But see further footnote 26 above.

[32] See further per Lord Slynn in *Murray v DPP* (1994) 99 Cr App R 396, HL, below. Presumably, the jury will need specific guidance on the concept of 'a case to answer'. The task of deciding that matter, at the end of the trial, but on the basis of the prosecution evidence alone, would seem to be particularly onerous.

[33] Where there is no evidence to explain the accused's silence, it is not incumbent on a judge to embark on, or to invite the jury to embark on, possible speculative reasons consistent with innocence which might theoretically prompt an accused to remain silent: per Lord Taylor CJ, [1995] 4 All ER 939 at 949.

[34] [1992] NIJB 41, a decision on the equivalent provision in Art 4 of the Criminal Evidence (NI) Order 1988, SI 1988/1987 (NI 120).

the court has then a complete discretion as to whether inferences should be drawn or not. In these circumstances it is a matter for the court in any criminal case (1) to decide whether to draw inferences or not; and (2) if it decides to draw inferences what their nature, extent and degree of adversity, if any, may be. It would be improper and indeed quite unwise for any court to set out the bounds of either steps (1) or (2). Their application will depend on factors peculiar to the individual case . . .

Finally, the court in *R v Cowan* stressed that the Court of Appeal will not lightly interfere with a judge's exercise of discretion to direct or advise the jury as to the drawing of inferences from silence and as to the nature, extent, and degree of such inferences. As long as the judge gives the jury adequate directions of law of the kind indicated above, and leaves the decision to them, the Court of Appeal will be slow to substitute its own view.

In some cases, failure to go into the witness box is unlikely to have any real bearing on the issues in the case, as when the facts are not in dispute and the only issue is whether they fall within the offence charged[35] and as when an accused charged with murder admits the assault on the victim but denies causation, an issue which is then resolved on the basis of the expert witnesses called.[36] It seems equally clear, however, that in other cases it may be perfectly proper to draw a strong adverse inference. Typically, such an inference is likely to be drawn where the uncontested or clearly established facts point so strongly to the guilt of the accused as to call for an explanation,[37] or where the defence case involves alleged facts which are at variance with the prosecution evidence or additional to it and exculpatory and must, if true, be within the accused's knowledge.[38] However, it does not follow that inferences may only be drawn in respect of specific facts: in appropriate circumstances, it may be proper to draw a general inference that by reason of his silence, the accused is guilty of the offence charged. In *Murray v DPP*,[39] a decision under the equivalent provision in the Criminal Evidence (NI) Order 1988,[40] M was convicted of attempted murder and possession of a firearm with intent to endanger life. There was evidence to link the accused with the attack, but he gave no evidence at the trial. The trial judge said that it seemed to him remarkable that the accused had not given evidence and that it was only common sense to infer 'that he is not prepared to assert his innocence on oath because that is not the case'. The House of Lords, upholding the conviction, held that having regard to the cumulative effect of all the circumstantial evidence against the accused, the trial judge was entitled as a matter of common sense to infer that there was no innocent explanation to the prima facie case that he was guilty. Lord Slynn said:[41]

> The accused cannot be compelled to give evidence but he must risk the consequences if he does not do so. Those consequences are not simply . . . that specific inferences may be drawn from specific facts. They include in a proper case the drawing of an inference that the accused is guilty . . .
>
> This does not mean that the court can conclude simply because the accused does not give evidence that he is guilty. In the first place the prosecutor must establish a prima facie case—a case for him to answer. In the second place in determining whether the accused is guilty the judge or

[35] *R v McManus* [2002] 1 Arch News 2, [2001] EWCA Crim 2455.
[36] See Wasik and Taylor, *Blackstone's Guide to the Criminal Justice and Public Order Act 1994* (London, 1995) 65.
[37] See, at common law, *R v Mutch* [1973] 1 All ER 178, CA. See also *R v Corrie* (1904) 20 TLR 365.
[38] See, at common law, *R v Martinez-Tobon* [1994] 2 All ER 90, CA; and in cases where the accused bears the burden of proof, *R v Bathurst* [1968] 2 QB 99 at 107, CA.
[39] (1994) 99 Cr App R 369.
[40] Art 4, SI 1988/1987 (NI 120).
[41] (1993) 99 Cr App R 369 at 405.

jury can draw only 'such inferences from the refusal as appear proper'. As Lord Diplock said in *Haw Tua Tau v Public Prosecutor*:[42]

'What inferences are proper to be drawn from an accused's refusal to give evidence depend upon the circumstances of the particular case, and is a question to be decided by applying ordinary common sense.'

There must thus be some basis derived from the circumstances which justify the inference.

If there is no prima facie case shown by the prosecution there is no case to answer. Equally, if parts of the prosecution case had so little evidential value that they called for no answer, a failure to deal with those specific matters cannot justify an inference of guilt.

On the other hand, if aspects of the evidence taken alone or in combination with other facts clearly call for an explanation which the accused ought to be in a position to give, if an explanation exists, then a failure to give any explanation may as a matter of common sense allow the drawing of an inference that there is no explanation and that the accused is guilty.[43]

Under proviso (b) to section 1 of the Criminal Evidence Act 1898, the failure of any person charged with an offence to give evidence shall not be made the subject of any comment by the prosecution. Section 1(b) has been repealed by the 1994 Act.[44] Comment is now permissible. However, if the trial judge is minded to direct or advise a jury against drawing an adverse inference, it is submitted that it would be good practice for him to inform prosecuting counsel of this before closing speeches, so that counsel refrains from comment. Conversely, if the judge is minded to direct the jury that they may draw proper inferences, it is submitted that prosecuting counsel should adhere to the kind of comment suggested (for the judge) in the Judicial Studies Board specimen direction and in *R v Cowan*.

Failure to mention facts when questioned or charged

Background

In its 11th Report, the Criminal Law Revision Committee proposed that where an accused fails to mention any fact relied on in his defence which he could reasonably have been expected to mention either (i) before he was charged on being questioned by the police; or (ii) on being charged, the court should be entitled to draw such inferences as appear proper, and the caution should be replaced by a notice explaining the potentially adverse effect of silence.[45] These proposals attracted widespread criticism at the time, but in 1976 were adopted in Singapore[46] and in 1988 were adopted in Northern Ireland.[47] There was also strong judicial comment in favour of their adoption in England and Wales. In *R v Alladice*[48] Lord Lane CJ, giving the reserved judgment of the Court of Appeal, observed that the effect of section 58 of the Police

---

[42] [1982] AC 136 at 153.

[43] The drawing of adverse inferences from silence in *Murray v DPP* did not violate the European Convention on Human Rights: *Murray v United Kingdom* (1996) 22 EHRR 29, European Court of Human Rights, but see also Roderick Munday, 'Inferences from Silence and European Human Rights Law' [1996] *Crim LR* 370.

[44] Section 168(3) and Sch 11.

[45] Paras 28–52 and cl 11 of the draft Bill (Cmnd 4991).

[46] See Meng Heong Yeo, 'Diminishing the Right of Silence: The Singapore Experience' [1983] *Crim LR* 89 and Alan Khee-Jin Tan, 'Adverse Inferences and the Right to Silence: Re-examining the Singapore Experience' [1997] *Crim LR* 471.

[47] See SI 1988/1987 (NI 120) and JD Jackson 'Curtailing the Right of Silence: Lessons from Northern Ireland' [1991] *Crim LR* 404.

[48] (1988) 87 Cr App R 380.

and Criminal Evidence Act 1984 (The 1984 Act)[49] was that in many cases a detainee who would otherwise have answered the questions of the police would be advised by his solicitor to remain silent and weeks later, at the trial, would not infrequently produce an explanation of, or a defence to, the charge, the truthfulness of which the police would have had no chance to check. Thus despite the fact that the explanation or defence, if true, could have been disclosed at the outset, and despite the advantage which the accused had gained by those tactics, no comment could be made to the jury to that effect. The effect of section 58, it was said, was such that the balance of fairness between prosecution and defence could not be maintained unless proper comment was permitted on silence in such circumstances.

The report of the Working Group set up by the Home Secretary in 1988 expressed the view that failure to answer police questions, even before the accused is brought to the police station, should be admissible evidence against him to show that his defence is untrue and to undermine his credibility, and he should be warned of the possibility at the outset.[50] The majority recommendation of the Royal Commission on Criminal Justice, in contrast, was that no inferences should be drawn from silence at the police station, but that when the prosecution case has been disclosed, an accused should be required to disclose his case, at the risk of adverse comment by the judge on any new defence then disclosed or any departure from the defence previously disclosed.

Section 34 of the 1994 Act reflects the recommendations of the Criminal Law Revision Committee, and not those of the Royal Commission on Criminal Justice.[51] In *R v Hoare*[52] Auld LJ said: 'The whole basis of section 34, in its qualification of the otherwise general right of an accused to remain silent and require the prosecution to prove its case, is an assumption that an innocent defendant—as distinct from one who is entitled to require the prosecution to prove its case—would give an early explanation to demonstrate his innocence.'

Section 34 provides that:

(1) Where, in any proceedings against a person for an offence, evidence is given that the accused—
    (a) at any time before he was charged with the offence, on being questioned under caution by a constable trying to discover whether or by whom the offence had been committed, failed to mention any fact relied on in his defence in those proceedings; or
    (b) on being charged with the offence or officially informed that he might be prosecuted for it, failed to mention any such fact,
being a fact which in the circumstances existing at the time the accused could reasonably have been expected to mention when so questioned, charged or informed, as the case may be, subsection (2) below applies.

(2) Where this subsection applies—
    (a) [repealed];
    (b) a judge, in deciding whether to grant an application made by the accused under paragraph 2 of Schedule 3 to the Crime and Disorder Act 1998;[53]

---

[49] See Ch 13.

[50] See AAS Zuckerman, 'Trial by Unfair Means—The Report of the Working Group on the Right of Silence' [1989] *Crim LR* 855. See also S Greer, 'The Right of Silence: A Review of the Current Debate' (1990) 53 *MLR* 709.

[51] See generally D Birch, 'Suffering in Silence: A Cost–Benefit Analysis of Section 34' [1999] *Crim LR* 769 and R Leng, 'Silence pre-trial, reasonable expectations and the normative distortion of fact-finding' (2001) 5 *E&P* 240.

[52] [2005] 1 Cr App R 355, CA at [53].

[53] Ie an application by an accused to dismiss the charge or any of the charges in respect of which he has been sent to the Crown Court under s 51 of the Crime and Disorder Act 1998. Under s 51, an adult brought before a magistrates' court charged with an offence triable only on indictment shall be sent forthwith to the Crown Court.

(c) the court, in determining whether there is a case to answer; and

(d) the court or jury, in determining whether the accused is guilty of the offence charged,[54] may draw such inferences from the failure as appear proper.

(2A) Where the accused was at an authorised place of detention[55] at the time of the failure, subsections (1) and (2) above do not apply if he had not been allowed an opportunity to consult a solicitor prior to being questioned, charged or informed as mentioned in subsection (1) above.

'On being questioned under caution . . . or on being charged'

Section 34(1)(a) only applies in the case of an accused 'on being questioned under caution'. Thus it has no application in the case of an accused who simply refuses to leave the police cell in which he is being detained in order to be interviewed by the police, but section 34(1)(b) will apply if such an accused, on being subsequently charged, fails to mention any fact relied on in his defence.[56] Paragraph 10.5 of Code C (the Code of Practice for the Detention, Treatment and Questioning of Persons by Police Officers) provides that the caution given before a person is charged or informed he may be prosecuted should be in the following terms:

You do not have to say anything. But it may harm your defence if you do not mention when questioned something which you later rely on in court. Anything you do say may be given in evidence.

Paragraph 10.7 provides that:

Minor deviations from the words of any caution given in accordance with this Code do not constitute a breach of this Code, provided the sense of the relevant caution is preserved.

Under Note 10D of the Code:

If it appears a person does not understand the caution, the person giving it should explain it in their own words.

Under para 11.4 of the Code, where a 'significant silence' (a silence which might give rise to an inference under the 1994 Act) has occurred before the start of the interview at the police station, then at the start of the interview, the interviewer, after cautioning the suspect, shall put the earlier 'significant silence' to the suspect and ask him whether he confirms or denies it and if he wants to add anything.

Section 34 applies in relation to questioning not only by constables, but also 'by persons (other than constables) charged with the duty of investigating offences or charging offenders' and in section 34(1) 'officially informed' means informed by a constable or any such person.[57] Under section 67(9) of the 1984 Act, which also refers to 'persons charged with the duty of investigating offences or charging offenders',it has been held, somewhat unsatisfactorily, that whether a person satisfies the test is a question of fact in each case.[58]

---

[54] Or any other offence of which the accused could lawfully be convicted on that charge: s 38(2).

[55] 'Authorised place of detention' means a police station or other place prescribed by order made by the Secretary of State: s 38(2A).

[56] *R v Johnson* [2006] Crim LR 567, CA.

[57] Section 34(4).

[58] See *R v Seelig* [1991] 4 All ER 429, CA etc (Ch 13).

Section 34(1)(a) applies to questioning under caution by a constable 'trying to discover whether or by whom the offence had been committed'. Where there is sufficient evidence for a suspect to be charged and the interview should be brought to an end,[59] but questioning continues and is met with silence from which adverse inferences may be drawn, evidence of the silence may be excluded.[60] However, it has also been held that the sufficiency of evidence can normally only be judged after the suspect has been given an opportunity to volunteer an explanation, and that further questioning will not be in breach of the Code if the officer is still open-minded about the possibility of an explanation which might prevent the suspect from being charged,[61] in which case the officer will still be 'trying to discover whether or by whom the offence has been committed'.[62]

Section 34(1)(b) applies when the accused is 'charged with the offence or officially informed that he might be prosecuted for it', at which stage paragraph 16.2 of Code C requires that the caution should be in the following terms:

> You do not have to say anything. But it may harm your defence if you do not mention now something which you later rely on in court. Anything you do say may be given in evidence.

Given this wording, there is no requirement—in order to rely on section 34(1)(b)—that an officer should go further and, for example, invite the detainee to give any explanation he may have for his conduct.[63]

An inference may be drawn from silence on being questioned under section 34(1)(a), or from silence on being charged under section 34(1)(b), or from both. Thus although in most cases it will add nothing to invite the jury to consider drawing an additional inference at the later stage, in some cases it may be possible to draw a stronger inference then, as when a suspect, after interview, is bailed to come back to the police station a week later, when he is charged, having had a long time to think back over the events. These principles derive from *R v Dervish*,[64] where it was held that if no inference can be drawn under section 34(1)(a)— the interviews in that case were inadmissible by reason of breaches of the Codes of Practice—then subject to any issue of unfairness, the trial judge may leave to the jury the possibility of drawing an inference under section 34(1)(b). However, the court added that the trial judge should not permit the jury to draw such an inference if to do so would nullify the safeguards of the 1984 Act and Codes, or if there was bad faith by the police deliberately breaching the safeguards with a view to falling back on section 34(1)(b).

'Failed to mention any fact relied on in his defence'

Where an accused, in interview after arrest, gives to the police a prepared statement and thereafter refuses to answer questions, he has not 'failed to mention' the facts set out in his statement. Thus in *R v Knight*,[65] where the prepared statement was wholly consistent with the defence evidence at trial, an adverse inference could not be drawn. The court held that the

---

[59] See paras 11.6 and 16.1 of Code C.

[60] See *R v Pointer* [1997] Crim LR 676, CA and *R v Gayle* [1999] Crim LR 502, CA.

[61] *R v McGuinness* [1999] Crim LR 318, CA and *R v Ioannou* [1999] Crim LR 586, CA.

[62] *R v Odeyemi* [1999] Crim LR 828, CA. But see also s 37(7) of the Police and Criminal Evidence Act 1984 and generally Ed Cape, 'Detention Without Charge; What Does "Sufficient Evidence to Charge" Mean' [1999] *Crim LR* 874.

[63] *R v Goodsir* [2006] EWCA Crim 852.

[64] [2002] 2 Cr App R 105, CA.

[65] [2004] 1 WLR 340, CA. See also *T v DPP* [2007] EWHC 7193 (Admin).

purpose of section 34(1)(a) was early disclosure of a suspect's account and not, separately and distinctly, the subjection of that account to the test of police cross-examination. However, as the court went on to stress, giving a prepared statement is not of itself an inevitable antidote to later adverse inferences because the statement may be incomplete in comparison with the accused's later account at trial. As was pointed out in *R v Turner*,[66] the submission of a prepared statement is a dangerous course for an innocent person, who may subsequently discover at trial that something significant was omitted. In that case it was held that the judge must identify any fact not mentioned in the prepared statement, which should be the subject of a specific direction. The court also noted that inconsistencies between the prepared statement and the accused's evidence do not necessarily amount to reliance on a fact not previously mentioned; and that where there are differences between the statement and the evidence given at trial, then depending on the precise circumstances, it may be better to direct the jury to consider the difference as constituting a previous lie,[67] rather than the foundation for a section 34 inference.

Inferences can only be drawn under section 34 where the accused has failed to mention 'any fact', as opposed to some speculative possibility, relied on in his defence. In *R v Nickolson*[68] N, charged with sexual offences against the complainant in his house, denied in interview that anything indecent had ever occurred, but said that he was in the habit of masturbating in the bathroom. Subsequently, seminal stains were found on the complainant's nightdress and, at the trial, when asked if he could provide an explanation, N suggested that the complainant could have entered the bathroom after he had masturbated there. It was held that section 34 did not apply because N had not asserted as a fact that the complainant had visited the bathroom, but had proffered it as an explanation, something more in the nature of a theory, a possibility, or speculation. Section 34 will apply, however, if such speculation is based on a fact and the accused could reasonably have been expected to mention both the speculation and the factual basis for it.[69]

It seems clear that an inference may be drawn under section 34 from an accused's failure to mention a fact not only when the fact is first disclosed at trial, but also when the accused, having initially failed to mention a fact on being questioned under caution, disclosed it at a later stage of police questioning or in a written statement to the police.[70] In any event, however, the fact that the accused failed to mention must be relied on in his defence. In *R v Moshaid*,[71] in which the accused did not give or call any evidence, it was held that section 34 did not bite. It does not follow, however, that the relevant fact may be established only by the accused or a defence witness: it may also be established by a prosecution witness, either in cross-examination or examination-in-chief.[72] Thus section 34 does apply where defence counsel puts or suggests the fact to a prosecution witness in cross-examination and the witness accepts it.[73] It can also apply even if the witness under cross-examination does not accept

[66] [2004] 1 All ER 1025, CA.

[67] See *R v Lucas* [1981] QB 720, CA etc, Ch 2.

[68] [1999] Crim LR 61, CA.

[69] *R v B (MT)* [2000] Crim LR 181, CA.

[70] See *R v McLernon* (1990) Belfast CC, 20 Dec, a decision under Art 3 of the Criminal Evidence (NI) Order 1988, SI 1988/1987 (NI 120).

[71] [1998] Crim LR 420, CA.

[72] *R v Bowers* [1998] Crim LR 817, CA.

[73] See *R v McLernon* [1992] NIJB 41, CA.

the fact put or suggested. In *R v Webber*[74] the House of Lords held that an accused relies on a fact in his defence when counsel, acting on his instructions, puts a specific and positive case to a prosecution witness, as opposed to asking questions intended to probe or test the prosecution case,[75] even if the witness rejects the case being put. Two reasons were given. First, although questions only become evidence if accepted by the witness, where specific positive suggestions have been made, the jury may for whatever reason distrust the witness's evidence and ask themselves whether the version put for the accused may not be true. Secondly, since section 34(2)(c) permits the court to draw proper inferences when determining whether there is a case to answer, ie at a stage when the accused has had no opportunity to give or adduce evidence, it would be surprising if subsection (2)(c) were intended to apply only when, unusually, specific suggestions put to a prosecution witness are *accepted* by him. It was further held that where defence counsel adopts on behalf of his client in closing submissions evidence given by a co-accused, this may also amount to reliance on facts for the purposes of section 34.

In *R v Betts*[76] it was held that the bare admission at trial of a fact asserted by the prosecution cannot amount to reliance on a fact, but where explanation for the admitted fact is advanced by reliance on other facts, those facts may give rise to an inference if they were not mentioned on being questioned or charged. The court gave an example: if an accused admits for the first time at trial that a fingerprint was his and offers no explanation for it being found where it was, he relies on no fact, but it will be different if he also puts forward an explanation for the finding of the fingerprint. The court gave two reasons for its conclusion. The first was that a bare admission of a prosecution fact adds no fact to the case. As has been observed, however, the same can be said of a mere denial.[77] The second and compelling reason was that to draw an inference against an accused who did not make an admission in interview but did make it at trial would effectively be to remove his right of silence in breach of Article 6 of the European Convention on Human Rights. A further compelling reason was given in *R v Webber*. In that case, Lord Bingham approved earlier unreported authorities to the effect that rarely if ever can a section 34 direction be appropriate on failure to mention at interview an admittedly true fact, because the adverse inference to be drawn under the section is that the fact not mentioned at interview but relied on in his defence is likely to be *untrue*.

'A fact which . . . the accused could reasonably have been expected to mention'

The fact relied on must be 'a fact which in the circumstances existing at the time the accused could reasonably have been expected to mention when . . . questioned, charged, or informed, as the case may be'. If the accused gives evidence, his reason for not putting forward any fact relied on should be explored.[78] In deciding the matter, the jury will be very much concerned with the truth or otherwise of any explanation given by the accused for not mentioning the fact, because if they accept an exculpatory explanation as true, or possibly so, it will be obviously unfair to draw any adverse inference.[79]

---

[74] [2004] 1 WLR 404.

[75] If the judge is in doubt whether counsel is testing the prosecution evidence or advancing a positive case, he should ask counsel in the absence of the jury: ibid at [36].

[76] [2001] 2 Cr App R 257, CA.

[77] See D Birch [2001] *Crim LR* at 757.

[78] *T v DPP* [2007] EWHC 1793 (Admin).

[79] Per Lord Bingham in *R v Webber* [2004] 1 WLR 404, HL at [29].

In *R v Argent*[80] it was held that the expression 'in the circumstances' is not to be construed restrictively: account may be taken of such matters as time of day, the accused's age, experience, mental capacity, state of health, sobriety, tiredness, knowledge, personality, and legal advice. 'The accused', it was said, refers not to some hypothetical reasonable accused of ordinary phlegm and fortitude, but to the actual accused, with such qualities, apprehensions, knowledge, and advice as he is shown to have had at the time. Sometimes, therefore, the jury may conclude that it was reasonable for the accused to have held his peace because, for example, he was tired, ill, frightened, drunk, drugged, unable to understand what was going on, suspicious of the police, afraid that his answer would not be fairly recorded, worried at committing himself without legal advice, or acting on legal advice. In other cases the jury may conclude that the accused could reasonably have been expected to mention the fact in issue. In *R v Howell*[81] Laws LJ said:

> we do not consider the absence of a written statement from the complainant to be good reason for silence (if adequate oral disclosure of the complaint has been given), and it does not become good reason merely because a solicitor has so advised. Nor is the possibility that the complain-ant may not pursue his complaint good reason, nor a belief by the solicitor that the suspect will be charged in any event whatever he says. The kind of circumstance which may most likely justify silence will be such matters as the suspect's condition (ill-health, in particular mental disability; confusion; intoxication; shock, and so forth—of course we are not laying down an authoritative list), or his inability genuinely to recollect events without reference to documents which are not to hand, or communication with other persons who may be able to assist his recollection.

In deciding whether a fact is one that the accused could reasonably have been expected to mention, another relevant factor, it is submitted, is the importance of the fact to the defence in question, whether central to that defence or of only peripheral importance, because an accused cannot reasonably be expected to mention every fact, for example every last detail of an alibi as opposed to the key facts relating to where he was, when, and with whom (if any-body). The nature of the fact itself may also be highly relevant, especially if of a kind likely to embarrass the accused or compromise his personal or professional life, for example the fact, in support of an alibi, that at the time of the alleged offence he was not at the scene of the crime but elsewhere, in bed with a prostitute. It would be equally relevant, to take another example, if the fact in question were of a kind likely to create a danger of reprisals against the accused, his family, or friends. Account also needs to be taken of the accused's knowledge of the case against him, and his understanding of (a) the nature of the offence in question; and (b) the facts which might go to show his innocence of that offence.

Section 34(3) of the 1994 Act provides that:

> Subject to any directions by the court, evidence tending to establish the failure may be given before or after evidence tending to establish the fact which the accused is alleged to have failed to mention.

In *R v Condron and Condron* the Court of Appeal, while stressing that no hard and fast procedure should be laid down, gave the following guidance:

---

[80] [1997] 2 Cr App R 27, CA.
[81] [2005] 1 Cr App R 1, CA at [24].

In the ordinary way . . . it would seem appropriate for prosecuting counsel to adduce evidence limited to the fact that after the appropriate caution the accused did not answer questions or made no comment. Unless the relevance of a particular point has been revealed in cross-examination, it would not seem appropriate to spend time at this stage going through the questions asked at interview.

If and when the accused gives evidence and mentions facts which, in the view of prosecuting counsel, he can reasonably have been expected to mention in interview, he can be asked why he did not mention them. The accused's attention will then no doubt be drawn to any relevant and pertinent questions asked at interview. The accused's explanation for his failure can then be tested in cross-examination. It will not generally be necessary to call evidence in rebuttal, unless there is a dispute as to the relevant contents of the interview.

Silence on legal advice

In *R v Condron and Condron*[82] the question arose whether an adverse inference can be drawn if the accused remained silent on legal advice. The accused, both heroin addicts, were convicted of offences relating to the supply of heroin. On their arrest, although a police doctor considered that they were fit for interview, a view of which they were aware, their solicitor considered that they were unfit to be interviewed because of their drug withdrawal symptoms. The solicitor therefore advised them not to answer questions, also advising them of the potential consequences, and making it plain that it was entirely their choice. At their trial, they gave detailed innocent explanations in relation to the prosecution evidence, which could have been given in answer to specific questions by the police in their interview. The Court of Appeal held that the trial judge had properly directed the jury that it was for them to decide whether any adverse inference should be drawn, but that it would have been *desirable* if he had given an additional direction to the effect that an adverse inference may be drawn if, despite any evidence relied on to explain the silence at interview, or in the absence of such evidence, they conclude that the silence can only sensibly be attributed to the accused having fabricated the evidence subsequently. However, the European Court of Human Rights has held that a direction along these lines is mandatory.[83] The Condrons complained that their right to a fair trial under Article 6 of the Convention had been violated. The European Court held as follows: (1) The right to silence could not be considered as an absolute right and the fact that the issue was left to the jury could not of itself be considered incompatible with Article 6. (2) The right was at the heart of the notion of a fair procedure under Article 6 and particular caution was required before a domestic court could invoke an accused's silence against him. It was incompatible with the right to base a conviction solely or mainly on the accused's silence or refusal to answer questions, or give evidence, but where a situation called for an explanation from an accused, then his silence could be taken into account in assessing the persuasiveness of the evidence against him. (3) The judge had not reflected the balance between the right to silence and the circumstances in which an adverse inference could be drawn. The judge's direction was such that the jury may have drawn an adverse inference even if satisfied with the accused's explanation of the silence. As a matter of fairness, the jury should have been directed that if they were satisfied that the accused's silence at interview could not sensibly be attributed to their having no answer or none that would stand up to cross-examination, then they should not draw an adverse inference.

[82] [1997] 1 WLR 827, CA.
[83] *Condron v United Kingdom* (2001) 31 EHRR 1.

The direction of the kind suggested by the Court of Appeal in *R v Condron and Condron* does not have to be geared only to the inference of subsequent fabrication, but may deal with the different inference that the accused, by the time of the interview, had already invented a false story, in whole or in part, but did not want to reveal it, because of the risk that the police might then be able to expose its falsity.[84]

In *R v Condron and Condron* it was also held that the bare assertion, by an accused, that he did not answer questions because he was advised by his solicitor not to do so, is unlikely to prevent an adverse inference from being drawn:[85] it is necessary, if the accused wishes to invite the court not to draw an adverse inference, to go further and give the basis or reason for the advice. However, as the court pointed out, whereas a 'bare assertion' will not amount to a waiver of the legal professional privilege that attaches to communications between an accused and his solicitor prior to a police interview,[86] once the basis or reason for the advice is stated, this will amount to a waiver entitling the prosecution to ask the accused or, if the solicitor is also called, the solicitor, whether there were any other reasons for the advice, and the nature of the advice given, so as to explore whether the advice may also have been given for tactical reasons. It is desirable, therefore, that the judge warn counsel or the accused that the privilege may be lost.[87] In *R v Bowden*[88] it was held that if the defence reveal the basis or reason for the solicitor's advice to the accused not to answer questions, this amounts to a waiver of privilege, whether the revelation is made by the accused or by the solicitor acting as his authorized agent, and whether it is made during pre-trial questioning, in evidence before the jury, or in evidence in a *voir dire* which is not repeated before the jury.

The courts have stressed that the jury is not concerned with the correctness of the solicitor's advice, nor with whether it complies with the Law Society's guidelines, but with the reasonableness of the accused's conduct in all the circumstances, including the giving of the advice.[89] Such conduct is likely to be regarded as reasonable in some cases, for example where there is evidence that the interviewing officer disclosed to the solicitor little or nothing of the nature of the case against the accused, so that the solicitor could not usefully advise the client, or where the nature of the offence or the material in the hands of the police is so complex, or relates to matters so long ago, that no sensible immediate response is feasible.[90] However, if an accused has stayed silent on legal advice and his silence is objectively unreasonable, it will not become reasonable merely because the solicitor's advice was ill-judged or bad,[91] which has

---

[84] See, eg, *R v Taylor* [1999] Crim LR 77, CA, where T, who had given the 'bare bones' of his alibi to his solicitor, failed to mention it in interview, only furnishing the details of it in his alibi notice.

[85] See, eg, *R v Roble* [1997] Crim LR 449, CA.

[86] See Ch 20.

[87] It was also said that an accused (or his solicitor) who gives evidence of what was said to the solicitor in response to a prosecution allegation of recent fabrication does not thereby waive privilege. The reason is that there is no way of dealing with the allegation other than by revealing what was said, whereas when an accused volunteers information about what was said, which may enable an allegation of fabrication to be made, that is the consequence of the voluntary provision: per Hooper LJ in *R v Loizou* [2006] EWCA Crim 1719 at [84].

[88] [1999] 4 All ER 43, CA.

[89] See per Lord Bingham CJ in *R v Argent* [1997] 2 Cr App R 27, CA at 35–6 and per Rose LJ in *R v Roble* [1997] Crim LR 449, CA.

[90] Per Rose LJ in *R v Roble* [1997] Crim LR 449, CA.

[91] *R v Connolly and McCartney* (1992) Belfast CC, 5 June.

led one commentator to observe that, if that is the law, then it punishes the accused for the failings of his solicitor.[92]

In *R v Betts*,[93] applied in *R v Chenia*,[94] it was said that it is not the *quality* of the decision not to answer questions that matters, but the genuineness of the decision, whereas in *R v Howell*,[95] approved, obiter, in *R v Knight*,[96] the Court of Appeal rejected the notion that once it is shown that the advice, of whatever quality, has genuinely been relied on as the reason for silence, adverse comment is thereby disallowed. However, as was pointed out in *R v Hoare*,[97] there is no real inconsistency in the authorities, because it is plain from the judgment in *R v Betts* that even where an accused has genuinely relied on legal advice to remain silent, an adverse inference may still be drawn if the jury is sure that the true reason for silence is that he had no or no satisfactory explanation consistent with innocence to give. In other words, the jury must consider whether the accused relied on the legal advice to remain silent both genuinely and reasonably. In *R v Beckles*,[98] Lord Woolf CJ said:

> in a case where a solicitor's advice is relied upon by the defendant, the ultimate question for the jury remains under s 34 whether the facts relied on at trial were facts which the defendant could reasonably have been expected to mention at interview. If they were not, that is the end of the matter. If the jury consider that the defendant genuinely relied on the advice, that is not the end of the matter. It may still not have been reasonable of him to rely on the advice, or the advice may not have been the true explanation for his silence.
>
> In *R v Betts* . . . at [54] Kay LJ . . . says:
>
> 'A person, who is anxious not to answer questions because he has no or no adequate explanation to offer, gains no protection from his lawyer's advice because that advice is no more than a convenient way of disguising his true motivation for not mentioning facts.'
>
> If, in the last situation, it is possible to say that the defendant genuinely acted upon the advice, the fact that he did so because it suited his purpose may mean he was not acting reasonably in not mentioning the facts. His reasonableness in not mentioning the facts remains to be determined by the jury. If they conclude that he was acting unreasonably they can draw an adverse inference from the failure to mention the facts.

The legal test, therefore, now requires both genuine and reasonable reliance. It is submitted that to direct the jury in such terms is both potentially misleading and needlessly complex. Ultimately, what matters is the reasonableness of the accused in relying on the advice. A lack of genuine reliance is no more than an example—and there are many examples—of unreasonableness: if an accused has relied on the advice, but not genuinely, the reliance is a sham or pretence, and the accused will not have acted reasonably in following it.[99] It is submitted that it would be better to remove any reference to genuineness from the jury direction.

---

[92] See Rosemary Pattenden, 'Inferences from Silence' [1995] *Crim LR* 602. See also *R v Kinsella* (1993) Belfast CC, Dec.

[93] [2001] 2 Cr App R 257, CA at [53].

[94] [2004] 1 All ER 543, CA. See also *R v Compton* [2002] All ER (D) 149 (Dec), [2002] EWCA Crim 2835.

[95] [2005] 1 Cr App R 1.

[96] [2004] 1 WLR 340, CA.

[97] [2005] 1 Cr App R 355, CA at [51].

[98] [2005] 1 All ER 705, CA at [46].

[99] See, to similar effect, Fitzpatrick, 'Commentary' [2005] *Crim LR* 562 and Cooper, 'Legal advice and pre-trial silence—unreasonable developments' (2006) 10 *E&P* 60. See also Malik, 'Silence on legal advice: Clarity but not justice?: R v Beckles' (2005) 9 *E&P* 211.

Directing the jury on the inferences that may be drawn

Even if the conditions for drawing an inference set out in section 34 are satisfied, it does not necessarily follow that the section should be invoked. In *Brizzalari v R*[100] the Court of Appeal noted that the mischief at which section 34 was primarily aimed was the positive defence following a no comment interview and/or the ambush defence. The court counselled against 'the further complicating of trials and summings-up by invoking this statute, unless the merits of the individual case require that it should be done', adding that 'if the section is not relied on in a particular case, it may well be sensible for the judge to raise with counsel whether a direction not to draw any adverse inference is desirable or necessary'. Thus there may be no point in invoking the section, even if it applies, if the direction of the judge will be substantially the same whether or not the section is invoked, as in *R v Maguire*,[101] where M gave one account in interview and another, different, account at trial so that in any event the Crown case was that the evidence was untruthful and the judge would have directed the jury that it was for them to decide whether to draw such a conclusion.

On one view, an inference may not be drawn under section 34 where the jury can only logically draw an inference by first concluding that the accused is guilty. In *R v Mountford*[102] the police entered W's flat and saw M drop from a window a package later found to contain heroin. On being interviewed, M made no comment. W pleaded guilty to permitting his premises to be used for the purposes of supplying heroin and, at M's trial on a charge of possession of heroin with intent to supply, gave evidence against him. M's evidence was that he was at the flat to buy heroin from W, who was the dealer, and that when the police had arrived, W had thrown him the heroin which he had dropped from the window. His reason for not volunteering this information on interview was that he did not know what W had said and did not want to get him into trouble. It was held that inferences could not be drawn under section 34 because the jury could only be sure that this explanation was true if they were to conclude that W was the dealer, not M, and conversely could only be sure that this explanation was false if they were to conclude that M was the dealer, and not W. This element of circularity, it was held, could only be resolved by a verdict founded in no way upon an inference under section 34, but on the other evidence in the case. The same conclusion was reached in *R v Gill*,[103] but it has since been held that *R v Mountford* was concerned with its own set of specific facts and was not intended to have a general application[104] and that it will only be in rare cases of the simplest and most straightforward kind that the *Mountford* approach is appropriate.[105] In *R v Daly*[106] the Court of Appeal cast doubt on the decision in *R v Mountford* on the basis that although it accepted that the fact not mentioned was closely related to the issue in the case, it could find nothing in the statutory wording which requires that the section 34 issue be capable of resolution as a separate issue in the case. In *R v Gowland-Wynn*[107] the Court of Appeal went further, Lord Woolf CJ being of the view that although it may be that *R v Mountford* and *R v Gill* can be confined to their special facts, they had the effect of

[100] (2004) The Times, 3 Mar, [2004] EWCA Crim 310.
[101] [2008] EWCA Crim 1028.
[102] [1999] Crim LR 575, CA.
[103] [2001] 1 Cr App R 160 (CA).
[104] *R v Hearne* 4 May 2000, unreported, CA, followed in *R v Milford* [2001] Crim LR 330, CA.
[105] *R v Chenia* [2004] 1 All ER 543, CA at [34]–[35].
[106] [2002] 2 Cr App R 201.
[107] [2002] 1 Cr App R 569.

emasculating and defeating the very purpose of section 34, and should be consigned to oblivion and should not be followed. Similarly in *R v Webber*[108] the House of Lords, while not expressly overruling *R v Mountford*, expressed the view that section 34 did apply to the case.

In cases where a direction under section 34 is called for, then subject to the facts of the particular case, juries should be directed in accordance with the Judicial Studies Board specimen direction,[109] which was approved by the European Court of Human Rights in *Beckles v UK*[110] in the context of the accused's silence on legal advice. The trial judge must remind the jury of the words of the caution given to the accused.[111] The judge must also direct the jury to the effect that an adverse inference can only be drawn if, despite any evidence relied upon by the accused, they conclude that the silence can only sensibly be attributed to the accused having no answer or no answer that would stand up to questioning and investigation.[112] The alternative in the last sentence is worth stressing. Section 34 is not limited to cases of recent invention, ie where the jury may conclude that the facts were invented after the interview, but also covers cases where they may conclude that the accused had the facts in mind at the time of the interview but did not believe that they would stand up to scrutiny at that time.[113] The judge must clearly identify for the jury the inferences which they may properly draw.[114] Contrary to the ruling of the Court of Appeal in *R v Doldur*,[115] the trial judge must also make clear to the jury that they must be satisfied that the prosecution have established a case to answer before drawing any inference.[116] The jury should be told that, if an inference is drawn, they should not convict 'wholly or mainly on the strength of it'. The first of those alternatives, 'wholly', is a clear way of putting the need for the prosecution to be able to prove a case to answer, otherwise than by means of an inference drawn. The second alternative, 'mainly', buttresses that need.[117]

The latest specimen direction emphasizes the desirability of any proposed direction being discussed with counsel before closing speeches and suggests that the discussion should start by a consideration whether any direction under section 34 should be given. In both respects, the specimen direction has been strongly endorsed by the Court of Appeal.[118] However, it does not necessarily follow from a failure to give a proper direction that there has been a breach of Article 6 of the Convention or that a conviction is unsafe. The Court of Appeal will have regard to the particular facts of the case. Factors which may count against the accused, depending on the precise nature of the misdirection or non-direction, may include the strength of the case to answer, the strength of the prosecution evidence, the fact that the accused declined to answer questions himself, rather than on legal advice, and the fact that a clear and accurate

---

[108] [2004] 1 WLR 404.

[109] *R v Chenia* [2004] 1 All ER 543, CA at [47].

[110] [2001] 31 EHRR 1.

[111] *R v Chenia* [2004] 1 All ER 543, CA at [49]–[51].

[112] See *Condron v UK* [2001] 31 EHRR 1 at para 61, *R v Betts* [2001] 2 Cr App R 257, CA, *R v Daly* [2002] 2 Cr App R 201, CA, and *R v Petkar* [2004] 1 Cr App R 270, CA.

[113] *R v Milford* [2001] Crim LR 330, CA. See also *R v Daniel* (1998) 2 Cr App R 373, CA at 382–3 and *R v Argent* [1997] 2 Cr App R 27, CA at 34 and 36.

[114] *R v Petkar* [2004] 1 Cr App R 270, CA at [51].

[115] [2000] Crim LR 178, CA.

[116] See *R v Milford* [2001] Crim LR 330, CA, *Beckles v UK* [2001] 31 EHRR 1 and *R v Chenia* [2004] 1 All ER 543, CA.

[117] *R v Petkar* [2004] 1 Cr App R 270, CA, at [51], citing *Murray v UK* (1996) 22 EHRR 29 at 60, para 47.

[118] See *R v Chenia* [2004] 1 All ER 543 at [36] and *R v Beckles* [2005] 1 All ER 705, CA at [34].

direction was given under section 35 of the 1994 Act.[119] Thus in a case involving legal advice to remain silent, failure to say anything about having to be sure that the accused remained silent not because of the legal advice, but because he had no answer to give, is likely to be fatal;[120] but failure to direct the jury to consider whether there was a case to answer will not render the trial unfair or the conviction unsafe where, on the facts, no jury could have concluded that there was no case to answer.[121]

The trial judge, in directing the jury, must take care to identify the specific facts relied on at trial which were not mentioned on being questioned or charged:[122] section 34 does not apply simply because the accused made no comments at interview.[123] In *R v Argent*[124] it was made clear that under section 34 the following matters are all questions of fact for the jury: (i) whether there is some fact which the accused has relied on in his defence; (ii) whether the accused failed to mention it on being questioned or charged; and (iii) whether it is a fact which in the circumstances existing at the time he could reasonably have been expected to mention when questioned or charged. It was also held that the 'proper' inferences that the jurors are permitted to draw means such inferences as appear proper to them. However, although (i) and (ii) above are questions of fact for the jury, in *R v McGarry*[125] it was held that there will plainly be cases in which it is appropriate for the judge to decide as a matter of law whether there is any evidence on which a reasonable jury properly directed could conclude that either or both of those requirements has been satisfied. Thus if the prosecution accept that those requirements have not been satisfied, and the judge considers that this is a proper view, no question of inviting the jury to draw inferences from the failure of the accused to answer some of the questions put to him can arise. In *R v Argent* it was held that although the question whether the fact was one which the accused could reasonably have been expected to mention is an issue on which the judge should give appropriate directions, ordinarily the issue should be left to the jury to decide, and that only rarely should the judge direct that they should, or should not draw the appropriate inference. As to the latter direction, in *R v McGarry*[126] it was held that where the jury are aware that the accused failed to answer questions and the judge rules that there is no evidence on which they can properly conclude that he failed to mention any fact relied on in his defence, then there should be a specific direction not to draw any adverse inference.[127] However, such a specific direction is plainly not called for where the accused gives a no comment interview and gives no evidence at trial, thereby attracting a direction under section 35 of the 1994 Act, because in such a case it would be fanciful to suggest that an inference of the kind permitted by section 34 might be drawn by the jury in the absence of a direction not to do so.[128]

---

[119] See *R v Chenia* ibid at [59]–[65].

[120] See *R v Bresa* [2006] Crim LR 179, CA.

[121] *R v Chenia* ibid at [53]–[55].

[122] *R v Webber* [2004] 1 WLR 404, HL at [27] and *R v Chenia* ibid at [29] and [87].

[123] *R v Argent* [1997] 2 Cr App R 27, CA and *T v DPP* [2007] EWHC 1793 (Admin).

[124] [1997] 2 Cr App R 27, CA at 32.

[125] [1999] 1 Cr App R 377, CA at 382–3.

[126] [1999] 1 Cr App R 377, CA.

[127] But failure to give such a direction will not necessarily render a conviction unsafe: *R v Bowers* [1998] Crim LR 817, CA. See also *R v Bansal* [1999] Crim LR 484, CA.

[128] *R v La Rose* [2003] All ER (D) 24 (May), [2003] EWCA Crim 1471.

Under section 34(2) the inferences that may be drawn are 'such inferences from the failure as appear proper'. The breadth of this phrase is such that it could be construed to permit a general inference that the accused is guilty of the offence charged, a construction supported, arguably, by section 38(3) of the Act.[129] In fact the logical inference to be drawn is narrower and more precise, that the facts relied on in the accused's defence are not true, on the basis that, if they were true, the accused could reasonably have been expected to have mentioned them in interview or on being charged, but did not do so because of the risk that the police might then be able to expose their falsity or because he had yet to invent them, or all of them.

The extent to which an inference drawn under section 34 will assist the prosecution in establishing a case to answer, or in proving the guilt of the accused, will obviously turn on the nature of the fact relied on in the defence and its importance to that defence. However, section 38(3) and (4) of the 1994 Act provide that:

(3) A person shall not have the proceedings against him transferred to the Crown Court for trial, have a case to answer or be convicted of an offence solely on an inference drawn from such a failure or refusal as is mentioned in section 34(2), 35(3), 36(2) or 37(2).

(4) A judge shall not refuse to grant such an application as is mentioned in section 34(2)(b), 36(2)(b) and 37(2)(b) solely on an inference drawn from such a failure as is mentioned in section 34(2), 36(2) or 37(2).

These provisions, in relation to section 34(2), appear to be otiose. It is true that in cases of confession and avoidance, as when the accused admits an assault but raises a defence of self-defence, rejection of that defence may result in a finding of guilt. However, since the worst possible inference that can be drawn is that the fact relied upon in the defence is untrue, then, as the example given illustrates, such an inference could not *by itself* justify a conviction (or a decision that there is a case to answer). The purpose of section 38(3) in the present context seems to be twofold. First, it requires the judge to remind himself that he is not entitled to decide that there is a case to answer solely on the basis that the relevant facts relied on by the accused in his defence are untrue. Secondly, it requires him to direct the jury that they are not entitled to convict solely—or, in the light of *Condron v United Kingdom*, mainly—on the basis that such facts are untrue.

The discretion to exclude evidence of failure to mention facts
Section 38(6) provides that:

Nothing in sections 34, 35, 36 or 37 prejudices any power of a court, in any proceedings, to exclude evidence (whether by preventing questions being put or otherwise) at its discretion.

In appropriate circumstances, therefore, the court could exclude evidence of the accused's failure to mention any fact on the basis of either section 78 of the 1984 Act or the common law discretion to exclude.[130] This might be appropriate, for example, in cases where it would be unfair to make use of the accused's silence by reason of breach of the provisions of the 1984 Act or the Codes, especially those relating to the caution, interrogation, and access to a solicitor (for example, failure to caution) or because the accused's silence was brought about by some other improper or unfair means (for example, threatening to beat up the accused unless he remains silent). However, it was held in *R v Condron and Condron* that if the defence

---

[129] See below.
[130] See Ch 2.

objection is simply that the jury should not be invited to draw any adverse inference, it will seldom be appropriate to invite the judge to rule on this before the conclusion of all the evidence, because it will not be apparent until then what are the material facts that were not disclosed or the reason for non-disclosure. It was said that only in the most exceptional case could it be appropriate to make such a submission before the introduction of the evidence by the Crown, eg where the accused is of very low intelligence and understanding and has been advised by his solicitor to say nothing.

Acceptance of the accusation of another by silence

Section 34(5) of the 1994 Act provides that:

> This section does not—
>
> (a) prejudice the admissibility in evidence of the silence or other reaction of the accused in the face of anything said in his presence relating to the conduct in respect of which he is charged, in so far as evidence thereof would be admissible apart from this section; or
> (b) preclude the drawing of any inference from any such silence or other reaction of the accused which could properly be drawn apart from this section.

The effect of this subsection is to preserve the common law authorities whereby, in appropriate circumstances, the accused, by his conduct, demeanour, or silence, may be treated as having accepted the accusation of another so as to make it a confession statement of his own.[131]

Failure or refusal to account for objects, substances, marks, etc

Sections 36 and 37 of the 1994 Act, which are based on sections 18 and 19 of the Irish Criminal Justice Act 1984, fall to be considered together.

Section 36 of the 1994 Act provides that:

> (1) Where—
> (a) a person is arrested by a constable, and there is—
>   (i) on his person; or
>   (ii) in or on his clothing or footwear; or
>   (iii) otherwise in his possession; or
>   (iv) in any place[132] in which he is at the time of his arrest,
>   any object, substance or mark, or there is any mark on any such object; and
> (b) that or another constable investigating the case reasonably believes that the presence of the object, substance or mark may be attributable to the participation of the person arrested in the commission of an offence specified by the constable;[133] and
> (c) the constable informs the person arrested that he so believes, and requests him to account for the presence of the object, substance or mark; and
> (d) the person fails or refuses to do so,
> then if, in any proceedings against the person for the offence so specified, evidence of those matters is given, subsection (2) below applies.

---

[131] See *R v Norton* [1910] 2 KB 496; *Parkes v R* [1976] 1 WLR 1251 etc (Ch 13). See further Peter Mirfield, 'Two Side-Effects of Sections 34 to 37 of the Criminal Justice and Public Order Act 1994' [1995] *Crim LR* 612, who argues that it may now be permissible to draw an inference that a suspect who has been cautioned but remains silent in the face of police accusations accepts the truth of the accusations.

[132] For the purposes of both s 36 and s 37 'place' includes any building or part of a building, any vehicle, vessel, aircraft or hovercraft and any other place whatsoever: s 38(1).

[133] Ie not necessarily the offence for which arrested. Cf s 37(1)(b), below.

(2) Where this subsection applies—

    (a) [repealed];

    (b) a judge, in deciding whether to grant an application made by the accused under paragraph 2 of Schedule 3 to the Crime and Disorder Act 1998;[134]

    (c) the court, in determining whether there is a case to answer; and

    (d) the court or jury, in determining whether the accused is guilty of the offence charged,[135] may draw such inferences from the failure or refusal as appear proper.

(3) Subsections (1) and (2) above apply to the condition of clothing or footwear as they apply to a substance or mark thereon.

(4) Subsections (1) and (2) above do not apply unless the accused was told in ordinary language by the constable when making the request mentioned in subsection (1)(c) above what the effect of this section would be if he failed or refused to comply with that request.

(4A) Where the accused was at an authorised place of detention[136] at the time of the failure or refusal, subsections (1) and (2) above do not apply if he had not been allowed an opportunity to consult a solicitor prior to the request being made.

(5) This section applies in relation to officers of customs and excise as it applies in relation to constables.[137]

(6) This section does not preclude the drawing of any inference from a failure or refusal of the accused to account for the presence of an object, substance or mark or from the condition of clothing or footwear which could properly be drawn apart from this section.

Section 37 of the 1994 Act provides that:

(1) Where—

    (a) a person arrested by a constable was found by him at a place at or about the time the offence for which he was arrested is alleged to have been committed; and

    (b) that or another constable investigating the offence reasonably believes that the presence of the person at that place and at that time may be attributable to his participation in the commission of the offence; and

    (c) the constable informs the person that he so believes, and requests him to account for that presence; and

    (d) the person fails or refuses to do so,

then if, in any proceedings against the person for the offence, evidence of those matters is given, subsection (2) below applies.

(2) [Identical, in its terms, to s 36(2).]

(3) [Identical, in its terms, to s 36(4).]

(4) [Identical, in its terms, to s 36(5).]

(3A) Where the accused was at an authorised place of detention[138] at the time of the failure or refusal, subsections (1) and (2) do not apply if he had not been allowed an opportunity to consult a solicitor prior to the request being made.

    . . .

(5) This section does not preclude the drawing of any inference from a failure or refusal of the accused to account for his presence at a place which could properly be drawn apart from this section.

---

[134] See note to s 34(2)(b), above.

[135] Or any other offence of which the accused could lawfully be convicted on that charge: s 38(2).

[136] See note to s 34(2A), above.

[137] Arrest by others charged with the duty of investigating offences and charging offenders will not suffice. Cf s 34, above.

[138] See note to s 34(2A), above.

It has been held that under section 36, the jury must be satisfied that the accused failed (or refused) to account for the object, substance, or mark; and that section 36(1)(b) does not require the constable to specify in precise terms the offence in question.[139]

Sections 36 and 37 contain no proviso, analogous to that contained in section 34(1), whereby an inference may only be drawn if the accused could reasonably have been expected to account for the object, substance, etc at the time when questioned about it. Notwithstanding this omission, it is submitted that the trial judge should give a clear direction to the jury that, in deciding whether to draw an inference, and if so the strength of the inference to be drawn, they should take into account the nature and personal characteristics of the accused, including, as appropriate, his age, intelligence, language, and literacy and his physical, mental, and emotional state at the time when he was questioned. The nature and strength of any inference drawn under section 36 will also depend on the nature of the object, substance, etc, the extent to which evidence of its presence supports the prosecution case and the other circumstances of the case. For example, if the accused, on arrest for murder by stabbing, is found with a blood-stained knife in his pocket, his failure or refusal to account for its presence is likely to result in a highly damaging adverse inference. However, if the stabbing takes place in a very crowded pub and the blood-stained knife is found on the floor,[140] the accused's failure to account for its presence is unlikely, without more, to result in any adverse inference. Similar considerations apply to section 37.

The scope of both section 36 and section 37 has been fixed somewhat arbitrarily. For example, if a person, suspected of murder by stabbing, fails to explain why the jacket he is wearing on arrest is blood-stained, an adverse inference may be drawn under section 36. But if such a suspect, having abandoned his blood-stained jacket at the scene of the crime, where it is found by the police, is then arrested by them on his way home and fails to explain why his jacket is blood-stained (or even why he abandoned it), no adverse inference may be drawn.

Inferences under section 36 and section 37 can only be drawn where evidence is given of the presence of the object, substance, etc, or of the presence of the accused, at a place at or about the time of the offence. Clearly, in some cases, that evidence, either taken alone or together with the adverse inference that can be drawn under the statutory provisions, will be sufficient to establish a case to answer or, indeed, to convict, as when a drug courier is arrested carrying a large package of heroin. Presumably, as in the case of section 34, the purpose of section 38(3)[141] in relation to section 36(2) and section 37(2), is simply to require the judge to direct the jury (or himself) that they are not entitled to convict (he is not entitled to decide that there is a case to answer) solely or, in the light of *Condron v United Kingdom*, mainly, on the basis of the inference drawn.

Under section 38(6), as we have seen,[142] nothing in section 36 or section 37 prejudices any power of a court to exclude evidence at its discretion. There is obvious potential for discretionary exclusion where the evidence of the matters specified in section 36(1) and section 37(1) was obtained illegally, improperly, or unfairly.

---

[139] *R v Compton* [2002] All ER (D) 149 (Dec), [2002] EWCA Crim 2835.
[140] See s 36(1)(a)(iv).
[141] See under s 34, above.
[142] Ibid.

Inferences from refusal to consent to the taking of samples

In appropriate circumstances, an adverse inference may be drawn from a suspect's refusal, without good cause, to consent to the taking of 'intimate samples' from his body. Under section 65 of the 1984 Act, an intimate sample is defined as (a) a sample of blood, semen, or any other tissue fluid, urine, or pubic hair; (b) a dental impression; and (c) a swab taken from any part of a person's genitals (including pubic hair) or from a person's body orifice other than the mouth. Section 62 of the 1984 Act provides that:

(1) Subject to section 63B[143] an intimate sample may be taken from a person in police detention only—
   (a) if a police officer of at least the rank of inspector authorises it to be taken; and
   (b) if the appropriate consent is given.[144]

(1A) An intimate sample may be taken from a person who is not in police detention but from whom, in the course of the investigation of an offence, two or more non-intimate samples[145] suitable for the same means of analysis have been taken which have proved insufficient—
   (a) if a police officer of at least the rank of inspector authorises it to be taken; and
   (b) if the appropriate consent is given.

(2) An officer may only give an authorisation under subsection (1) or (1A) above if he has reasonable grounds—
   (a) for suspecting the involvement of the person from whom the sample is to be taken in a recordable offence;[146] and
   (b) for believing that the same will tend to confirm or disprove his involvement.

(10) Where the appropriate consent to the taking of an intimate sample from a person was refused without good cause, in any proceedings against that person for an offence—
   (a) the court, in determining . . .
      (ii) whether there is a case to answer; and . . .
   (b) the court or jury, in determining whether that person is guilty of the offence charged,
   may draw such inferences from the refusal as appear proper.

Before a person is asked to provide an intimate sample, he must be warned that if he refuses without good cause, his refusal may harm his case if it comes to trial.[147] Whether consent was refused 'without good cause' is a question of fact. In appropriate circumstances, a person's bodily or mental condition may amount to good cause. However, whether a refusal out of embarrassment or on the grounds of some deeply held personal conviction is capable of constituting good cause is less clear.

There is no equivalent to section 62(10) in the case of 'non-intimate samples' because, subject to compliance with the statutory conditions, such samples may be taken without

---

[143] Section 63B provides for the taking of a urine or non-intimate sample to test for the presence of a Class A drug.

[144] 'Appropriate consent' means, in relation to a person aged 17 or over, the consent of that person; in relation to a person aged 14 or over but under 17, the consent of that person and his parent or guardian; and in relation to a person aged under 14, the consent of his parent or guardian: s 65. The consent must be given in writing: s 62(4).

[145] See below.

[146] A 'recordable offence' is defined to include all offences punishable with imprisonment and a number of other specified offences: see the National Police Records (Recordable Offences) Regulations 1985, SI 1985/1941, as amended.

[147] Para 6.3 and Note 6D, Code D.

consent. Under section 65 of the 1984 Act, a non-intimate sample means: (a) a sample of hair other than pubic hair; (b) a sample taken from a nail or from under a nail; (c) a swab taken from any part of a person's body other than a part from which a swab taken would be an intimate sample; (d) saliva; and (e) a skin impression (which means any record (other than a fingerprint) which is a record (in any form and produced by any method) of the skin pattern and other physical characteristics or features of the whole or any part of a foot or any other part of a body). Section 63 of the Act provides that:

> (2A) A non-intimate sample may be taken from a person without the appropriate consent if two conditions are satisfied.
> (2B) The first is that the person is in police detention in consequence of his arrest for a recordable offence.
> (2C) The second is that—
>> (a) he has not had a non-intimate sample of the same type and from the same part of the body taken in the course of the investigation of the offence by the police, or
>> (b) he has had such a sample taken but it proved insufficient.
> (3) A non-intimate sample may be taken from a person without the appropriate consent if—
>> (a) he is being held in custody by the police on the authority of a court; and
>> (b) an officer of at least the rank of superintendent authorises it to be taken without the appropriate consent.
> (3A) A non-intimate sample may be taken from a person (whether or not he is in police detention or held in custody by the police on the authority of a court) without the appropriate consent if—
>> (a) he has been charged with a recordable offence or informed that he will be reported for such an offence; and
>> (b) either he has not had a non-intimate sample taken from him in the course of the investigation of the offence by the police or he has had a non-intimate sample taken from him but either it was not suitable for the same means of analysis or, though so suitable, the sample proved insufficient.
> (3B) A non-intimate sample may be taken from a person without the appropriate consent if he has been convicted of a recordable offence.
> (3C) A non-intimate sample may also be taken from a person without the appropriate consent if he is a person to whom section 2 of the Criminal Evidence (Amendment) Act 1997 applies (persons detained following acquittal on grounds of insanity or finding of unfitness to plead).
> (4) An officer may only give an authorisation under subsection (3) above if he has reasonable grounds—
>> (a) for suspecting the involvement of the person from whom the sample is to be taken in a recordable offence; and
>> (b) for believing that the sample will tend to confirm or disprove his involvement.
>> . . .
> (9A) Subsection (3B) above shall not apply to any person convicted before 10th April 1995 unless he is a person to whom section 1 of the Criminal Evidence (Amendment) Act 1997 applies (persons imprisoned or detained by virtue of pre-existing conviction for sexual offence etc).

Section 61 of the 1984 Act makes similar provision for fingerprints of a person to be taken without his consent.

Inferences from failure to provide advance disclosure of the defence case

Trials on indictment

Under the rules of primary prosecution disclosure in section 3 of the Criminal Procedure and Investigations Act 1996 (the 1996 Act), the prosecutor must disclose to the accused previously undisclosed material which might reasonably be considered capable of undermining the case for the prosecution against the accused or of assisting the case for the accused, or give the accused a written statement that there is no such material. Section 5(5) of the Act is to the effect that where a person is charged with an offence for which he is sent for trial to a Crown Court and the prosecutor complies or purports to comply with section 3, the accused must give a defence statement to the court and the prosecutor.[148] The defence statement must be served during a prescribed 'relevant period' (within 14 days of primary prosecution disclosure).[149] The contents of the defence statement are prescribed by section 6A, which provides as follows:

(1) ... a defence statement is a written statement—
  (a) setting out the nature of the accused's defence, including any particular defences on which he intends to rely,
  (b) indicating the matters of fact on which he takes issue with the prosecution,
  (c) setting out, in the case of each such matter, why he takes issue with the prosecution, and
  (d) indicating any point of law (including any point as to the admissibility of evidence or an abuse of process) which he wishes to take, and any authority on which he intends to rely for that purpose.
(2) A defence statement that discloses an alibi must give particulars of it, including—
  (a) the name, address and date of birth of any witness the accused believes is able to give evidence in support of the alibi, or as many of those details as are known to the accused when the statement is given;
  (b) any information in the accused's possession which might be of material assistance in identifying or finding any such witness in whose case any of the details mentioned in paragraph (a) are not known to the accused when the statement is given.
(3) For the purposes of this section evidence in support of an alibi is evidence tending to show that by reason of the presence of the accused at a particular place or in a particular area at a particular time he was not, or was unlikely to have been, at the place where the offence is alleged to have been committed at the time of its alleged commission.

In *R v Wheeler*[150] it was held that as a matter of good practice a defence statement should be signed by the accused as an acknowledgment of its accuracy to obviate error and dispute of the kind which had arisen in that case, where part of the defence statement was contrary to the original instructions given by the accused to his solicitors.

Under section 6B(1) of the 1996 Act, where an accused has given a defence statement, he must also give to the court and the prosecutor, during a prescribed 'relevant period', either

---

[148] Although there is no obligation on an accused to give a defence statement to a co-accused, if the prosecutor forms the view that a defence statement of one co-accused might reasonably be expected to assist the defence of another, it should be disclosed to the other on secondary prosecution disclosure: *R v Cairns* [2003] 1 Cr App R 38, CA.

[149] See s 5(9), s 12, and reg 2 of the Criminal Procedure and Investigations Act 1996 (Defence Disclosure Time Limits) Regulations 1997, SI 1997/684.

[150] [2001] Crim LR 745, CA.

(a) an updated defence statement (which must comply with the requirements imposed by section 6A by reference to the state of affairs at the time when it is given);[151] or (b) a statement of the kind mentioned in section 6B(4), namely a written statement stating that he has no changes to make to the initial defence statement. Finally, under section 6C, there is an obligation on the defence, during a prescribed 'relevant period', to give notification of intention to call defence witnesses. Section 6C(1) provides as follows:

> (1) The accused must give to the court and the prosecutor a notice indicating whether he intends to call any persons (other than himself) as witnesses at his trial and, if so—
>   (a) giving the name, address and date of birth of each such proposed witness, or as many of those details as are known to the accused when the notice is given;
>   (b) providing any information in the accused's possession which might be of material assistance in identifying or finding any such proposed witness in whose case any of the details mentioned in paragraph (a) are not known to the accused when the notice is given.

Under section 11(5) of the 1996 Act, where an accused fails to comply with the disclosure requirements of sections 5, 6A, 6B, or 6C, the court or any other party may make appropriate adverse comment and the court or jury, in deciding the question of guilt, may draw proper adverse inferences. If it appears to the court at a pre-trial hearing that an accused has failed to comply fully with section 5, 6B, or 6C, so that there is a possibility of comment being made or inferences being drawn under section 11(5), he shall warn the accused accordingly.[152] Section 11 provides as follows:

> (1) This section applies in the cases set out in subsections (2), (3), and (4).
> (2) The first case is where section 5 applies and the accused—
>   (a) fails to give an initial defence statement,
>   (b) gives an initial defence statement but does so after the end of the . . . relevant period for section 5,
>   (c) is required by section 6B to give either an updated defence statement or a statement of the kind mentioned in subsection (4) of that section but fails to do so,
>   (d) gives an updated defence statement or a statement of the kind mentioned in section 6B(4) but does so after the end of the . . . relevant period for section 6B,
>   (e) sets out inconsistent defences in his defence statement,[153] or
>   (f) at his trial—
>   (i) puts forward a defence which was not mentioned in his defence statement or is different from any defence set out in the statement,
>   (ii) relies on a matter which in breach of the requirements imposed by or under section 6A, was not mentioned in his defence statement,
>   (iii) adduces evidence in support of an alibi[154] without having given particulars of the alibi in his defence statement, or
>   (iv) calls a witness to give evidence in support of an alibi without having complied with section 6A(2)(a) or (b) as regards the witness in his defence statement.

---

[151] Section 6B(3).

[152] Section 6E(2).

[153] A reference simply to an accused's 'defence statement' is a reference (i) where he has given only an initial defence statement, or an initial defence statement and a statement under s 6B(4), to the initial defence statement; and (ii) where he has given an initial and an updated defence statement, to the updated statement: s 11(12)(c).

[154] A reference to 'evidence in support of an alibi' shall be construed in accordance with s 6A(3): s 11(12)(d).

(3) The second case is . . . [155]

(4) The third case is where the accused—

    (a) gives a witness notice but does so after the end of . . . the relevant period for section 6C, or

    (b) at his trial calls a witness (other than himself) not included, or not adequately identified, in a witness notice.

(5) Where this section applies—

    (a) the court or any other party may make such comment as appears appropriate;

    (b) the court or jury may draw such inferences as appear proper in deciding whether the accused is guilty of the offence concerned.

(6) Where—

    (a) this section applies by virtue of subsection (2)(f)(ii) . . . , and

    (b) the matter which was not mentioned is a point of law (including any point as to the admissibility of evidence or an abuse of process) or an authority,

comment by another party under subsection 5(a) may be made only with the leave of the court.

(7) Where this section applies by virtue of subsection (4), comment by another party under subsection (5)(a) may be made only with the leave of the court.

(8) Where the accused puts forward a defence which is different from any defence set out in his defence statement, in doing anything under subsection (5) or in deciding whether to do anything under it the court shall have regard—

    (a) to the extent of the difference in the defences, and

    (b) to whether there is any justification for it.

(9) Where the accused calls a witness whom he has failed to include, or to identify adequately, in a witness notice,[156] in doing anything under subsection (5) or in deciding to do anything under it the court shall have regard to whether there is any justification for the failure.

(10) A person shall not be convicted of an offence solely on an inference drawn under subsection (5).

(11) Where the accused has given a statement of the kind mentioned in section 6B(4), then, for the purposes of subsections (2)(f)(ii) and (iv), the question as to whether there has been a breach of the requirements imposed by or under section 6A or a failure to comply with section 6A(2)(a) or (b) shall be determined—

    (a) by reference to the state of affairs at the time when that statement was given, and

    (b) as if the defence statement was given at the same time as that statement.

Under section 11(5)(b), proper inferences may be drawn only in deciding whether the accused is guilty of the offence charged, and not in deciding whether there is a case to answer.[157]

Three important matters were established in *R v Tibbs*.[158] First, section 11 does not disallow or require leave for cross-examination of an accused on differences between his defence at trial and his defence statement—it precludes comment or invitation to the jury to draw an inference from the differences unless the court gives leave. Secondly, the word 'defence' in section 11 is not restricted to its general legal description (eg 'self-defence' or 'mistaken identification'), but includes the facts and matters to be relied on in the defence, otherwise there would be little, if any, scope for comparing the extent of the difference in the defences under section 11(8)(a)—on the restrictive interpretation the defence put forward would either be the same as or different from the defence in the defence statement. Third,

---

[155] The second case relates to failure to disclose prior to summary trial: see below.

[156] 'Witness notice' means a notice given under s 6C: s 11(12)(e).

[157] Cf ss 34(2), 36(2), and 37(2) of the Criminal Justice and Public Order Act 1994, above.

[158] [2000] 2 Cr App R 309, CA.

failure to warn the jury in accordance with section 11(10) that they cannot convict solely from drawing an adverse inference will not necessarily result in a successful appeal against conviction. The issue will turn on the particular circumstances, including the strength of the prosecution case.

In some cases, the defence statement may be relied on by the Crown, or may be used by the jury, as a lie by the accused indicative of a consciousness of his guilt, in which case the jury will need to be directed in accordance with *R v Goodway*.[159]

Summary trials

Section 6 of the 1996 Act is to the effect that where a person is charged with an offence in respect of which the court proceeds to summary trial and the prosecutor complies or purports to comply with section 3, then the accused *may* give a defence statement to the prosecutor, and, if he does so, must also give such a statement to the court, and must give the statement during a prescribed 'relevant period'. The magistrates' court may permit appropriate comment and draw proper inferences in the same circumstances as such comment may be permitted and such inferences may be drawn in a trial on indictment (late disclosure, inconsistent defences, etc), with the obvious exception of failure to give a defence statement.[160] As in trials on indictment, in summary cases a person shall not be convicted of an offence solely on an inference drawn under section 11(5).[161]

Preparatory hearings

Under section 29 of the 1996 Act, a Crown Court judge may order a preparatory hearing where it appears to him that the indictment reveals a case of such complexity, a case of such seriousness, or a case whose trial is likely to be of such length that substantial benefits are likely to accrue from such a hearing.[162] Section 31(4) provides that at the preparatory hearing the judge may order the prosecutor to give the court and the accused a case statement of such matters as the facts of the case for the prosecution, the witnesses who will speak to them, and relevant exhibits. Under section 31(6), where the prosecutor has complied with such an order, the judge may order the accused to give the court and prosecutor written notice of any objections that he has to the case statement. If he does so, he shall warn the accused of the possible consequences under section 34 of the Act of not complying with his order.[163]

Section 34 provides as follows:

(1) Any party may depart from the case he disclosed in pursuance of a requirement imposed under section 31.

(2) Where—
   (a) a party departs from the case he disclosed in pursuance of a requirement imposed under section 31, or
   (b) a party fails to comply with such a requirement,

---

[159] [1993] 4 All ER 894, CA (see Ch 2).

[160] Section 11(3).

[161] Section 11(10).

[162] Separate but similar provision is made for cases of serious or complex fraud—see ss 7, 9, and 10 of the Criminal Justice Act 1987.

[163] Section 31(8).

the judge or, with the leave of the judge, any other party may make such comment as appears to the judge or the other party (as the case may be) to be appropriate and the jury or, in the case of a trial without a jury, the judge, may draw such inferences as appear proper.

(3) In doing anything under subsection (2) or in deciding whether to do anything under it the judge shall have regard—

    (a) to the extent of the departure or failure, and

    (b) to whether there is any justification for it.

(4) Except as provided by this section, in the case of a trial with a jury no part—

    (a) of a statement given under section 31(6)(a), or

    (b) of any other information relating to the case for the accused or, if there is more than one, the case for any of them, which was given in pursuance of a requirement imposed under section 31,

may be disclosed at a stage in the trial after the jury have been sworn without the consent of the accused concerned.

ADDITIONAL READING

Birch, 'Suffering in Silence: A Cost-Benefit Analysis of Section 34' [1999] *Crim LR* 769.

Buckle et al, *The Right of Silence: The Impact of the Criminal Justice and Public Order Act 1994* (Home Office Research Study No 199, 2000).

Cooper, 'Legal advice and pre-trial silence—unreasonable developments' (2006) 10 *E&P* 60.

Greer, 'The Right of Silence: A Review of the Current Debate' (1990) 53 *MLR* 709.

Jackson, 'Silence and Proof: Extending the boundaries of criminal proceedings in the United Kingdom' (2001) 5 *E&P* 145.

Jackson et al, *Legislating Against Silence: The Northern Ireland Experience* (Northern Ireland Office, 2000).

Khee-Jin Tan, 'Adverse Inferences and the Right to Silence: Re-examining the Singapore Experience' [1974] *Crim LR* 471.

Leng, 'Silence pre-trial, reasonable expectations and the normative distortion of fact-finding' (2001) 5 *E&P* 240.

Meng Heong Yeo, 'Diminishing the Right of Silence: The Singapore Experience' [1983] *Crim LR* 89.

Mirfield, 'Two Side-Effects of Sections 34 to 37 of the Criminal Justice and Public Order Act 1994' [1995] *Crim LR* 612.

Munday, 'Inferences from Silence and European Human Rights Law' [1996] *Crim LR* 370.

Pattenden, 'Inferences from Silence' [1995] *Crim LR* 602.

Zuckerman, 'Trial by Unfair Means—The Report of the Working Group on the Right of Silence' [1989] *Crim LR* 855.

Evidence of character: evidence of character in civil cases

15

Key Issues

- Should evidence be admitted in civil proceedings to show the disposition of the claimant or defendant towards good conduct?

- When and why should evidence be admitted in civil proceedings to show the disposition of the defendant towards misconduct?

- Why might it be more acceptable in a civil case than in a criminal case to admit evidence of the disposition of the defendant towards misconduct?

This chapter, together with Chapters 16 and 17 of this book, consider the admissibility of evidence of character. The admissibility of character evidence is governed by a number of factors which it will be useful to summarize before considering the law in detail. Two obvious considerations are whether the proceedings are civil or criminal and whether the evidence relates to the character of a party or non-party. Additionally, it is necessary to consider the nature of the character evidence in question. It may relate to either good or bad character and, in either event, may constitute evidence of a person's actual disposition, that is his propensity to act, think, or feel in a given way, or evidence of his reputation, that is his *reputed* disposition or propensity to act, think, or feel in a given way. Thus the character of a person may be proved by evidence of general disposition, by evidence of specific examples of his conduct on other occasions (including, in the case of bad conduct, evidence of his previous convictions), or by evidence of his reputation among those to whom he is known. The final important consideration is the purpose for which the character evidence in question is sought to be adduced or elicited in cross-examination. There are three possibilities. First, it may be adduced because the character of a person is itself in issue in the proceedings. Secondly, it may be adduced because of its relevance to a fact in issue, that is because of its tendency to prove that a person did a certain act, whether he did that act being in issue in the proceedings. Thirdly, evidence of the character of a party or witness may be adduced because of its relevance to his credibility.

Character in issue or relevant to a fact in issue

In civil proceedings, evidence of the character of a party or non-party is admissible if it is in issue or of relevance to a fact in issue. The law of defamation provides a number of examples. Thus on the question of liability in an action for defamation in which justification is pleaded, the claimant's character will obviously be in issue. If, for example, the defendant has alleged that the claimant is a thief, evidence of the claimant's convictions for theft may be admitted to justify the allegation.[1] Similarly, the claimant, in order to rebut a defence of fair comment, may adduce evidence of his good reputation at the time of publication of the allegedly defamatory material.[2] The character of a claimant in an action for defamation is also of direct relevance, if he succeeds, to the quantum of recoverable damages, the damage sustained being dependent on the estimation in which he was previously held.

Evidence of the disposition of the parties towards good conduct

It is submitted that evidence of the disposition of the parties to civil proceedings towards good conduct on other occasions should be admitted if it meets the ordinary requirement of relevance. However, according to the few reported decisions on the topic, such evidence has been treated as irrelevant to the facts in issue and accordingly excluded.

[1] Section 13 of the Civil Evidence Act 1968 provides that in libel or slander actions in which the question whether a person committed a criminal offence is relevant to an issue in the action, proof of his conviction shall be conclusive evidence that he committed the offence: see Ch 21.
[2] See *Cornwell v Myskow* [1987] 2 All ER 504, CA.

As to good conduct on the part of the defendant, in *A-G v Bowman*,[3] at the trial of an information for keeping false weights, a civil suit, Eyre CB held that the evidence of a witness to character called by the defendant was inadmissible because the proceedings were not criminal. Similarly in *A-G v Radloff*[4] the rule was justified on the basis that whereas there is a fair and just presumption that a person of good character would not commit a crime, no presumption fairly arises in most civil cases, from the good character of the defendant, that he did not commit the breach of contract or civil duty alleged against him.

As to the claimant, in *Hatton v Cooper*,[5] a case involving a collision between two cars in which there was an unusual dearth of relevant evidence, it was held that the trial judge, on the question of liability, had improperly relied on evidence from the claimant's employer that the claimant was an excellent driver, calm, assured, and composed, who never took risks. Jonathan Parker LJ said that in the context of this collision, the opinion of a third party as to the driving ability of either party was 'completely worthless'.

Evidence of the disposition of the parties towards bad conduct

In civil proceedings, evidence of the disposition of the defendant towards wrongdoing or the commission of a particular kind of civil wrong may be admissible if it is of sufficient relevance or probative value in relation to the facts in issue. Such evidence, which relates to particular acts of misconduct on other occasions, whether occurring before or after the occurrence of the facts in issue,[6] is designated 'similar fact evidence'.

Whereas in criminal proceedings the rules relating to the admissibility of similar fact evidence have reflected a paramount concern to safeguard the accused from the admission of unduly prejudicial evidence, in civil proceedings, where trial is seldom by jury, the emphasis has been on probative value rather than prejudicial effect. To this extent, in civil cases, the principle of admissibility has tended to approximate to the ordinary test of relevance and accordingly similar fact evidence has been admitted more readily. In *Hales v Kerr*,[7] a negligence action in which the plaintiff alleged that he had contracted ringworm from a dirty razor used by the defendant, a hairdresser, evidence was admitted that two other customers shaved by the defendant had also contracted ringworm. In *Joy v Phillips, Mills & Co Ltd*[8] a claim was made for workmen's compensation by the father of a deceased stable boy. The boy was kicked by a horse and found nearby holding a halter. Evidence that the boy had previously teased horses with a halter was held to be admissible in rebuttal of the applicant's allegation that the accident had occurred in the course of the boy's employment. More recently, in *Jones v Greater Manchester Police Authority*,[9] civil proceedings for a sex offender order under section 2 of the Crime and Disorder Act 1998, it was held that evidence of propensity to commit sexual offences against young males was relevant and admissible because the purpose of the proceedings was to seek to predict the extent to

---

[3] (1791) 2 Bos&P 532n.

[4] (1854) 10 Exch 84 at 97.

[5] [2001] RTR 544, CA.

[6] *Desmond v Bower* [2009] EWCA Civ 667.

[7] [1908] 2 KB 601.

[8] [1916] 1 KB 849. See also *Barrett v Long* (1851) 3 HL Cas 395; *Osborne v Chocqueel* [1896] 2 QB 109; and *Sattin v National Union Bank* (1978) 122 Sol Jo 367, CA.

[9] [2001] EWHC Admin 189, [2002] ACD 4, DC.

which past events gave rise to reasonable cause for believing that an order was necessary to protect the public from serious harm; and that the admission of such evidence did not breach either Article 6 or Article 8 of the European Convention on Human Rights and did not render the proceedings unfair.

In *Mood Music Publishing Co Ltd v De Wolfe Publishing Ltd*,[10] similar fact evidence was admitted in an action for infringement of copyright. The defendants admitted the similarity between the musical work in which the plaintiffs owned the copyright and the work which they had produced, but alleged that the similarity was coincidental. Evidence was admitted to show that on other occasions the defendants had produced musical works bearing a close resemblance to musical works which were the subject of copyright. The Court of Appeal held that the evidence had been properly admitted to rebut the allegation of coincidence.

The leading authority is *O'Brien v Chief Constable of South Wales Police*.[11] The claimant had been convicted of murder. After serving eleven years in prison, his case had been referred to the Criminal Cases Review Commission and his appeal had been allowed. He then brought proceedings against the Chief Constable for misfeasance in public office and malicious prosecution, alleging that he had been 'framed' by a Detective Inspector L and a Detective Chief Superintendent C, who was said to have approved some aspects of the misconduct alleged against L. The House of Lords held that evidence had properly been admitted to show that L had behaved with similar impropriety on two other occasions and that C had done so on one other occasion. The House of Lords held that the test of admissibility in civil cases was different from that which applied in criminal cases. The test in criminal cases, as propounded in *R v P*[12] and the Criminal Justice Act 2003, required an enhanced relevance or substantial probative value because, if the evidence was not cogent, the prejudice that it would cause to the accused might render the proceedings unfair. That test led to the exclusion of evidence which was relevant on the grounds that it was not sufficiently probative. (The test, as described, is as propounded in *R v P*, but is *not* as now set out in the Criminal Justice Act 2003.[13]) There was no warrant for the automatic application of such a test in a civil suit. To do so would be to introduce an inflexibility which was inappropriate and undesirable. Lord Phillips said:[14]

> I would simply apply the test of relevance as the test of admissibility of similar fact evidence in a civil suit. Such evidence is admissible if it is potentially probative of an issue in the action. That is not to say that the policy considerations that have given rise to the complex rules . . . in sections 100 to 106 of the 2003 Act have no part to play in the conduct of civil litigation. They are policy considerations which the judge who has the management of the civil litigation will wish to keep well in mind. CPR r 1.2 requires the court to give effect to the overriding objective of dealing with cases justly. This includes dealing with the case in a way which is proportionate to what is involved in the case, and in a manner which is expeditious and fair. CPR r 1.4 requires the court actively to manage the case in order to further the overriding objective. CPR r 2.1 gives the court the power to control the evidence. This power expressly enables the court to exclude evidence that would otherwise be admissible and to limit cross-examination.

[10] [1976] Ch 119; cf *EG Music v SF (Film) Distributors* [1978] FSR 121. See also *Berger v Raymond & Son Ltd* [1984] 1 WLR 625.
[11] [2005] 2 WLR 2038, HL.
[12] [1991] 3 All ER 337, HL.
[13] See Ch 17.
[14] At [53]–[56].

Similar fact evidence will not necessarily risk causing any unfair prejudice to the party against whom it is directed . . . It may, however, carry such a risk. Evidence of impropriety which reflects adversely on the character of a party may risk causing prejudice that is disproportionate to its relevance, particularly where the trial is taking place before a jury. In such a case the judge will be astute to see that the probative cogency of the evidence justifies this risk of prejudice in the interests of a fair trial.[15]

Equally, when considering whether to admit evidence, or permit cross-examination, on matters that are collateral to the central issues, the judge will have regard to the need for proportionality and expedition. He will consider whether the evidence in question is likely to be relatively uncontroversial, or whether its admission is likely to create side issues which will unbalance the trial and make it harder to see the wood from the trees.

Character relevant to credit

In civil proceedings, any person who gives evidence, whether or not a party to the proceedings, is liable to cross-examination as to his credibility as a witness.[16] However, as a general rule, the cross-examining party is not allowed to adduce evidence to contradict a witness's answer to a question concerning credit. The rule, and the exceptions to it, are considered in detail in Chapter 7.

ADDITIONAL READING

Munday, 'Case management, similar fact evidence in civil cases, and a divided law of evidence' (2006) 10 *E&P* 81.

---

[15] Experimental data suggest that judges are no better than jurors at excluding from their calculations prejudicial and inadmissible evidence. For a review, prompted by Lord Phillips' dicta, see Munday, 'Case management, similar fact evidence in civil cases, and a divided law of evidence' (2006) 10 *E&P* 81.

[16] See Ch 7, 194, under *Cross-examination as to credit.*

Evidence of character: evidence of the good character of the accused

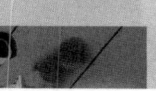

16

Key Issues

- Why should an accused be allowed to call evidence of his previous good character?

- Where an accused has previous convictions, in what circumstances might it be acceptable for a judge to tell a jury that they should consider the accused as a person of good character?

- Where an accused has no previous convictions, in what circumstances might it be acceptable for a judge to refuse to tell a jury that they should consider the accused as a person of good character?

This chapter concerns the circumstances in which, in criminal proceedings, evidence of the good character of the accused may be adduced because of its relevance either to a fact in issue or to his credibility.[1]

The evidence admissible

In criminal proceedings, the accused is allowed to adduce evidence of his good character. It may be proved either in chief, by the evidence of the accused himself or other defence witnesses, or in cross-examination of witnesses called for the prosecution. In *R v Rowton*[2] the accused, charged with indecent assault on a boy, called witnesses to his character. It was held that such evidence should be confined to evidence of the reputation of the accused amongst those to whom he is known and should not include evidence of specific credit-able acts of the accused nor evidence of the witness's opinion of his disposition. Although this case was decided prior to the Criminal Evidence Act 1898, section 1 of which made the accused a competent witness for the defence in all criminal cases,[3] the rule would appear to apply even when the evidence of good character is given by the accused himself. Thus not-withstanding that in the normal case the accused would be much better qualified to give evidence of his disposition as revealed by specific acts of creditable conduct, as opposed to evidence of his reputation, strictly speaking he must confine himself to the latter. However, although *R v Rowton* has never been expressly overruled, nowadays it is not, in practice, strictly adhered to. In *R v Redgrave*,[4] a case of importuning for immoral purposes in which the Court of Appeal held that the accused was not entitled to produce documents and photographs to show that he had had relationships of a heterosexual nature, because this amounted to calling evidence of particular facts to show that he was of a disposition which made it unlikely that he would have committed the offence charged, the court also said that an accused, in such a case, was entitled to give evidence of a normal sexual relation-ship with his wife or girlfriend.

The common law rule under which in criminal proceedings evidence of a person's reputation is admissible for the purpose of proving his good (or bad) character has been preserved and put on a statutory basis by section 118(1) of the Criminal Justice Act 2003 (the 2003 Act).

The direction to the jury

The leading authority on how to direct the jury about evidence of the good character of the accused is *R v Vye*.[5] Prior to *R v Vye*, the law was unclear as to (a) whether a judge is under a duty to direct the jury about evidence of the good character of the accused; and (b) if so, whether he should direct them not only that the evidence is relevant to credibility (the first

---

[1] Other aspects of the subject are more conveniently considered under 'Examination-in-chief' and 'Cross-examination': see **The rule against a party impeaching the credit of his own witness** (Ch 6, 183) and **Cross-examination as to credit** and **Finality of answers to collateral questions** (Ch 7, 194 and 210). In criminal cases, the character of a person who is neither a party nor a witness is rarely relevant to a fact in issue: for an example, see *R v Murray* [1994] Crim LR 927, CA.

[2] (1865) Le&Ca 520, CCR.

[3] See now s 53(1) of the Youth Justice and Criminal Evidence Act 1999 (Ch 5).

[4] (1981) 74 Cr App R 10, CA.

[5] [1993] 1 WLR 471.

limb of the direction) but also that it has a probative value in relation to the issue of guilt, in that a person of good character is less likely to have committed the offence (the second limb). Lord Chief Justice Taylor, giving the reserved judgment of the Court of Appeal, laid down the following three principles.

1. If the accused testifies, the judge should give a first limb direction. If the accused does not give evidence at trial but relies on pre-trial answers or statements, that is, exculpatory statements made to the police or others, the judge, who is entitled to make observations about the way the jury should approach such evidence in contrast to evidence given on oath, should give a first limb direction by directing the jury to have regard to the accused's good character when considering the credibility of those statements.[6] If the accused does not give evidence and has given no pre-trial answers or statements, no issue as to his credibility arises and a first limb direction is not required.

2. A second limb direction should be given, whether or not the accused has testified or made pre-trial answers or statements.[7] It is for the judge in each case to decide how he tailors the direction to the particular circumstances. He would probably wish to indicate, as is commonly done, that good character cannot amount to a defence.

3. Where an accused of good character is jointly tried with an accused of bad character, principles 1 and 2 still apply: the accused of good character is entitled to a full direction.[8] As to any direction concerning the accused of bad character, in some cases the judge may think it best to tell the jury that there has been no evidence about his character and they must not speculate or take the absence of such information as any evidence against him. In other cases, the judge may think it best to say nothing about the absence of such information. The course to be taken depends on the circumstances of the individual case, including how great an issue was made of character during the evidence and speeches.

Where good character directions are required in accordance with *R v Vye*, it is not necessary for judges to use any particular form of words, but they may be wise to avoid saying that the jury are 'entitled' to take the evidence into account, which suggests that the jury has a choice whether or not to take it into account for the purposes in question.[9] Similarly, it is a serious misdirection to tell the jury that they can put good character into the scales[10] or, in the case of the first limb, that good character 'might assist' them on the question of credibility.[11] Equally, character directions should not be given in the form of a question or rhetorical question (eg 'Is it more likely that he is telling you the truth because he is a man of good character?'), but in the form of an affirmative statement, as in the Judicial Studies Board guideline direction for the first limb ('it is a factor which you should take into account when deciding whether you believe his evidence').[12]

---

[6] See also *R v Chapman* [1989] Crim LR 60, CA.

[7] Improper disclosure that the accused had previously been arrested for an offence of the same type as the offence charged will undermine a second limb direction and effectively deprive the accused of the good character direction: *Arthurton v R* [2004] 2 Cr App R 559, PC.

[8] It was held that the suggestion of Lord Lane CJ in *R v Gibson* (1991) 93 Cr App R 9, CA, that the judge may decide to say little if anything about the good character of the one accused, was not satisfactory and ought not to be followed. *R v Vye*, in this respect, was applied in *R v Houlden* (1993) 99 Cr App R 244, CA.

[9] *R v Miah* [1997] 2 Cr App R 12, CA.

[10] *R v Boyson* [1991] Crim LR 274, CA.

[11] *R v Gray* [2004] 2 Cr App R 498, CA.

[12] *R v Lloyd* [2000] 2 Cr App R 355, CA and *R v Scranage* [2001] All ER (D) 185 (Apr), [2001] EWCA Crim 1171, CA.

In *R v Vye* it was held that if the judge gives both limbs of the direction, the Court of Appeal will be slow to criticize any qualifying remarks based on the facts of the individual case. Such remarks, however, must be justified.[13]

In *R v Aziz*[14] the House of Lords has made clear that the phrase 'pre-trial answers or statements', as used in the first principle in *R v Vye*, refers not to wholly exculpatory statements, but only to 'mixed' statements, ie statements containing inculpatory as well as exculpatory material which are, for that reason, tendered as evidence of the truth of the facts they contain.[15] Thus an accused who does not give evidence but relies on wholly exculpatory statements is not entitled to a first limb direction. It was further held in *R v Aziz* that an accused who is entitled to directions as to good character in accordance with *R v Vye* will not lose that entitlement by mounting an attack on a co-accused such as a cut-throat defence.[16]

As to the third principle in *R v Vye*, relating to directions about the accused of 'bad character', that phrase appears to cover both an accused in respect of whom there is no evidence of character, one way or the other, and an accused of bad character whose bad character is not revealed in evidence, but not an accused whose bad character is revealed in evidence.[17]

A good character direction will be of some value in every case in which it should be given[18] and therefore, although a failure to give the direction will not necessarily render a conviction unsafe, with each case to be reviewed in the light of its own facts,[19] it will rarely be possible for an appellate court to say that such a failure could not have affected the outcome of the trial.[20] However, the good character of the accused must be distinctly raised, by defence evidence or in cross-examination of prosecution witnesses, and it is the duty of defence counsel to ensure that a direction is obtained; if the issue is not raised by the defence, the judge is under no duty to raise it himself.[21]

In *R v Campbell*,[22] an appeal concerning a direction relating to an accused's *bad* character, Lord Phillips CJ, in a passage which borders on suggesting that the common law rules relating to directions to the jury on the *good* character of the accused have been modified by the 2003 Act[23] referred to both limbs of the good character direction and observed that although

---

[13] See *R v Fitton* [2001] EWCA Crim 215, CA where the judge misdirected the jury in a qualification to the standard directions to the effect that a doorman's good character was of less relevance and weight given that the offence he was alleged to have committed was spontaneous. See also *R v Handbridge* [1993] Crim LR 287, CA, where the judge was wrong and unfair to have directed the jury to ignore good character unless the rest of the evidence left them in doubt about guilt.

[14] [1995] 3 All ER 149, HL.

[15] See *R v Duncan* (1981) 73 Cr App R 359, CA and *R v Sharp* [1988] 1 All ER 65, HL. A statement is only 'mixed' if it contains an admission of fact which is 'significant' in relation to an issue in the case: see *R v Garrod* [1997] Crim LR 445, CA and generally Ch 6.

[16] [1995] 3 All ER 149 at 158.

[17] See *R v Cain* [1994] 2 All ER 398, CA, where the evidence relating to the character of three co-accused was different: there was evidence of positive good character of A, no evidence in relation to the character of B and evidence of the previous convictions of C. Only A was covered by *Vye*.

[18] *R v Fulcher* [1995] 2 Cr App R 251, CA at 260.

[19] *Singh v The State* [2006] 1 WLR 146, PC.

[20] *R v Kamar* (1999) The Times, 14 May.

[21] *Thompson v The Queen* [1998] AC 811, affirmed in *Teeluck v The State* [2005] 2 Cr App R 378, PC.

[22] [2007] 1 WLR 2798, CA at [20]–[23].

[23] See also *R v Doncaster* (2008) 172 JP 202 per Rix LJ at [42]: 'Although there is no ... abolition of the common law rules as to good character, it is difficult to think that the new law (as to bad character) has no impact for the old law (as to good character).'

the second limb was no more than common sense that one might have expected a jury to be capable of applying without assistance, failure to give either limb of the direction automatically resulted in the quashing of a conviction. His Lordship described this as a 'lamentable state of affairs' and said: 'Failure to give a direction that is no more than assistance in applying common sense to the evidence should not automatically be treated as a ground of appeal, let alone a reason to allow an appeal'. It is submitted that these obiter remarks, made without any reference to the relevant jurisprudence, should not be used to reverse the earlier authorities that clearly indicate an entitlement to a second limb direction.[24]

The meaning of 'good character'

As to what 'good character' means for the purposes of the principles established in *R v Vye*, there is no simple answer.[25] For example, previous convictions will not necessarily prevent an accused from being treated as of previous good character, particularly if they are spent or convictions for minor offences which have no relevance to credibility and took place a long time ago.[26] In these circumstances, the judge has a discretion whether or not to give directions in accordance with *R v Vye*, and if so in what terms, but he should give directions in *unqualified* terms if the previous convictions can only be regarded as irrelevant or of no significance in relation to the offence charged.[27] In *R v M (CP)*[28] the accused was tried for assaulting and raping a child under 13 (his niece). He had two old previous convictions for criminal damage which were spent. It was held that the judge had erred in not giving the 'full direction on good character' which she herself had clearly decided the accused was entitled to. Firstly, by simply telling the jury it was 'a factor that [they] should take into account, she had failed to make it sufficiently clear that his good character and his credibility were factors *in his favour*.[29] Secondly, and more strikingly, she failed to mention explicitly the fact that he had never shown any propensity to commit offences of a sexual nature.

However, it does not follow from this that a direction will be given automatically to those whose bad character is not of sufficient probative value or relevance to be admitted against them, and still less should it be given to those whose bad character is excluded as a matter of discretion; a good character direction is appropriate in the case of those who the judge rules may be treated as if they are without known bad character at all.[30]

---

[24] See *R v Garnham* [2008] All ER (D) 50 (May) where it was held that the judge was wrong to withhold a modified good character direction in favour of a modified bad character direction.

[25] See generally R Munday 'What Constitutes a Good Character?' [1997] *Crim LR* 247.

[26] See, eg, *R v Goss* [2005] Crim LR 61, CA (on a charge of possessing a firearm, a previous conviction for driving a motor vehicle without car insurance, in the absence of evidence to show that the accused had deliberately flouted road traffic law).

[27] *R v Durbin* [1995] 2 Cr App R 84, citing *R v Herrox* (5 Oct 1993, unreported), CA and *R v Heath* [1994] 13 LS Gaz R 34, CA. But contrast *R v Nye* (1982) 75 Cr App R 247, CA, as understood by the Court of Appeal in *R v O'Shea* [1993] Crim LR 951: an accused with previous but spent convictions may not be put forward as being of good character without qualifications but may be referred to as of good character 'without relevant convictions' because although, so far as possible, the judge should exercise the discretion favourably towards the accused, the jury must not be misled or told lies.

[28] [2009] 2 Cr App R 3, CA. See also *R v Nye* (1982) 75 Cr App R 247, CA and *R v Lloyd* [200] 2 Cr App R 355, CA.

[29] Ibid at [11].

[30] Per Hughes LJ in *R v Lawson* [2007] 1 Cr App R 178, CA at [40].

An unqualified direction will be appropriate where, although there is evidence of previous misconduct on the part of the accused, it is disputed, and its potential for distracting the jury from the main issues in the case outweighs any benefit to be had from a qualified direction.[31] By the same token, there will be cases where the accused is not of absolutely good character and the fact of the previous conviction or other character blemish is known to the jury, but where the only proper course is to give a qualified direction, which is likely to mean that careful consideration should be given to the distinction between the two limbs of credibility and propensity.[32] In *R v Gray*,[33] a murder trial in which the accused denied being present at the killing and volunteered that he had been convicted of driving with excess alcohol and without a licence or insurance, it was held that he was entitled to an ordinary first limb direction and a modified second limb direction.[34] In *R v Garnham*[35] the accused was charged with rape and volunteered evidence of his single previous conviction for assault occasioning actual bodily harm. Under cross-examination he conceded that in respect of the previous conviction, his defence of self-defence had been rejected by the jury. It was held that the judge had been wrong to withhold a modified good character direction on the basis that the accused had been disbelieved in his trial for assault and this showed a propensity to be untruthful. The judge had fallen into error in his approach[36] and the appellant was entitled to a modified good character direction, although the Court of Appeal did not indicate what form it should have taken.

An accused without previous convictions is not necessarily of good character, for he may have been dishonest or guilty of other criminal behaviour even if not convicted of any offence in that respect. In *R v Durbin*[37] the accused was charged with the unlawful importation of cannabis. When interviewed, he gave a false account of his movements on the Continent prior to his arrival in the UK; at the trial he admitted having misled two prosecution witnesses in relation to his dealings with his co-accused; and in both interview and in evidence he admitted that in the course of the visit to the Continent which gave rise to the charge, he had knowingly engaged in smuggling computer parts across European frontiers in order to avoid customs duties. The Court of Appeal rejected the idea that in these circumstances it was a matter of discretion for the trial judge to decide what direction, if any, should be given: the accused was *entitled* to qualified *Vye* directions. It was held that where an accused is of previous good character then he is entitled to the good character direction (both limbs if his credibility is in issue, the second limb only if it is not), notwithstanding that he may have admitted telling lies in interview[38] and may have admitted other offences or disreputable conduct in relation to the subject matter of the charge, but the terms of the direction should be modified to take account of the circumstances of the case, including all facts known to the

---

[31] *R v Butler* [1999] Crim LR 835, CA.

[32] *R v Durbin* [1995] 2 Cr App R 84. See also *R v Aziz* [1995] 3 All ER 149, HL at 152–3; *R v Timson* [1993] Crim LR 58, CA; *R v H* [1994] Crim LR 205, CA; and *R v Mentor* [2005] Crim LR 472, CA; and cf *R v Hickmet* [1996] Crim LR 588, CA, where it was held that a direction would have had no significant effect and may have simply confused the jury. There are obvious difficulties in the way of a qualified direction, as when the accused admits that he has lied (credibility) or set out with a criminal intent (propensity): see *R v Burnham* [1995] Crim LR 491, CA.

[33] [2004] 2 Cr App R 498, CA.

[34] Cf *R v Payton* [2006] Crim LR 997, CA.

[35] [2008] All ER (D) 50 (May).

[36] The principle that propensity to untruthfulness may be established by evidence that an accused has been disbelieved on oath was proposed in *R v Hanson* [2005] 1 WLR 3169. See Ch. 17.

[37] [1995] 2 Cr App R 84, CA.

[38] Citing *R v Kabariti* (1990) 92 Cr App R 362.

jury, either as regards credibility or propensity or both.[39] *R v Durbin* was not brought to the attention of the House of Lords in *R v Aziz*.[40] In that case two of the accused, charged with conspiracy to cheat the public revenue of VAT, pleaded not guilty and relied on the fact that they had no previous convictions, but also gave evidence of previous misconduct, including evidence of making false mortgage applications, telling lies during interview, and not declaring full earnings for Inland Revenue purposes. Lord Steyn, acknowledging that this was an area in which generalizations are hazardous, and that a wide spectrum of cases must be kept in mind, held as follows:

1. A trial judge has a residual discretion to decline to give *Vye* directions in the case of an accused without previous convictions if he considers it an insult to common sense to give such directions. A judge should never be compelled to give meaningless or absurd directions. Cases occur where an accused with no previous convictions is shown beyond doubt to have been guilty of serious criminal behaviour similar to the offence charged. A judge is not compelled to go through the charade of giving *Vye* directions where the accused's claim to good character is spurious.
2. This discretionary power is narrowly circumscribed.
3. Prima facie the directions must be given. The judge will often be able to place a fair and balanced picture before the jury by giving *Vye* directions and then adding words of qualification concerning the proved or possible misconduct.
4. Whenever a judge proposes to give a direction not likely to be anticipated by counsel, he should invite submissions on his proposed directions.

On the facts, it was held that the two accused had not lost the right to *Vye* directions, but it would have been proper for the judge to have qualified them by reference to the admitted misconduct.

In *R v Doncaster*,[41] the accused was charged with cheating the public revenue (although not on the scale of the accused in *Aziz*) and two offences of false accounting. He had only one conviction which was 30-years old and irrelevant, but evidence of misconduct from two separate tax enquiries into his failure to declare income was adduced under the bad character provisions of the 2003 Act. The judge declined to give a good character direction. It was held that, although the judge should have reminded the jury about the lack of convictions, he was entitled to exercise his residual discretion to withhold a *Vye* direction. Distinguishing *R v Aziz*, Lord Justice Rix[42] stated that the misconduct in that case was trivial by comparison with the massive conspiracy with which the accused were charged , whereas in *R v Doncaster* the misconduct was persistent, serious, and similar to the offences charged. In any case, according to Rix LJ, the judge was entitled to conclude, as per Lord Steyn in *R v Aziz*, that a good character direction should not be given because it would have been a charade or spurious, or an insult to common sense. It is submitted that this must be correct since the jury were bound to receive a *bad* character direction explaining how the misconduct revealed

---

[39] See also, *R v Zoppola- Barraza* [1994] Crim LR 833, CA. See also *R v Buzalek* [1991] Crim LR 115, CA.
[40] [1995] 3 All ER 149, HL.
[41] (2008) JP 202
[42] At [42]

in the tax enquiries could be held against the accused in terms of showing a propensity to commit offences and undermining his credibility.[43]

Other problems arise when an accused pleads guilty to only some counts on the indictment. It is clear from *R v Teasdale*[44] that if an accused pleads guilty to an offence which is an alternative to that on which he is being tried, and the facts are such that, if he is convicted on the greater offence then the guilty plea on the lesser offence will have to be vacated, a good character direction should be given, tailored to take into account the guilty plea. However, in *R v Challenger*[45] it was held that in all other cases in which an accused pleads guilty to another count on the indictment, he ceases to be a person of good character and the full character direction becomes inappropriate.[46]

ADDITIONAL READING

Munday, 'What Constitutes a Good Character?' [1997] *Crim LR* 247.

---

[43] Rix LJ suggested obiter at [43] that one approach to directing a jury where an accused had no previous convictions (or none that were relevant) but there was evidence of misconduct, could be a modified bad character direction, the modification being to add that the accused has no previous convictions and would have been entitled to a good character direction but for the misconduct. The jury should then be told to consider which counted more with them—the absence of previous convictions or the evidence of bad character. If they considered the former counted more, that could be taken into account in the accused's favour. If the latter counted more, then that could be taken into account against him. It is submitted that a bad character direction which refers the jury to a good character direction that the accused might have been but was not entitled to, has an obvious potential to confuse.

[44] [1993] 4 All ER 290, CA.

[45] [1994] Crim LR 202, CA.

[46] It was further held that it would be misleading to tell a jury that an accused was of good character where they had not been made aware of his guilty plea. However, if an accused gives evidence of his guilty plea then the judge may remind the jury about any argument made to the effect that, by virtue of his admission of guilt on one count, greater weight should be attached to his assertions of innocence on the remaining counts. Note also *R v Shepherd* [1995] Crim LR 153, CA, where formal admissions went some way towards informing the jury that S had pleaded guilty to other counts. It was held that if the defence had grasped the nettle and brought out in evidence that S, apart from the matters covered by the admissions, had no other convictions, then it might have been appropriate for the judge to have directed the jury that, apart from attaching such weight as they saw fit to the admissions, S was entitled to ask them to consider his case on the basis of previous good character.

Evidence of character: evidence of bad character in criminal cases

17

Key Issues

- How might evidence of an accused's past misconduct (a) prove that he is guilty of the crime with which he is charged; and (b) show that he should not be believed when he says he is not guilty of the crime?

- Should the law of evidence generally permit the prosecution to adduce evidence of an accused's past misconduct? If not, in what circumstances should the law permit such evidence to be adduced?

- When should the prosecution or an accused be permitted to adduce evidence of the bad character of someone other than an accused?

- In what circumstances should an accused be permitted to introduce evidence of the bad character of a co-accused?

- Where the accused's bad character is admissible in evidence, should the judge nonetheless have a discretion to prevent it going before the jury?

Introductory

The background to the Criminal Justice Act 2003

The admissibility of evidence of bad character in criminal cases is governed, almost exclusively, by Chapter 1 of Part 11 of the Criminal Justice Act 2003 (the 2003 Act). However, it is necessary first to consider in outline the applicable rules before the scheme introduced by the 2003 Act, most of which have been repealed but some of which have survived.

Before the new statutory provisions, there were both common law and statutory rules. Under section 3 of the Criminal Procedure Act 1865, which remains in force, a party is not entitled to impeach the credit of his own witness by general evidence of his bad character.[1] At common law a witness other than the accused could be *cross-examined* about his previous misconduct in order to impugn his credibility.[2] However, under the rule of finality of answers to collateral questions, answers given by the witness to questions on his previous misconduct, insofar as they could properly be regarded as questions on collateral matters, were final, in the sense that the cross-examining party could not call further evidence with a view to contradicting the witness. The exceptions to the rule, ie the cases in which evidence in rebuttal was admissible, included cases of denial of previous convictions, admissible under section 6 of the Criminal Procedure Act 1865, and, at common law, denial by the witness of his bias or his reputation for untruthfulness.

As to the accused, the law was, as it was put in an earlier edition of this work, 'complex, unprincipled and riddled with anomalies'. The general rule was exclusionary. The prosecution were not permitted either to adduce evidence of the accused's bad character, other than that relating directly to the offence charged, or to cross-examine witnesses for the defence with a view to eliciting such evidence. The rule prevented the prosecution from introducing evidence of previous convictions, previous misconduct, and disposition towards wrongdoing or misconduct, the principal rationale of the rule being that the prejudice created by such evidence outweighed any probative value it might have.

At common law, there were only two exceptions to the general rule: first, where the evidence in question was so-called 'similar fact evidence', including so-called 'background evidence', and second where the defence raised the issue of the accused's character. As to the former, similar fact evidence, which could be admitted by the prosecution or on behalf of a co-accused, was evidence of the disposition of the accused towards wrongdoing or specific acts of misconduct on other occasions judged to be of sufficient probative force in relation to the facts in issue in the case to make it just to admit it notwithstanding its prejudicial effect. As to the latter, the prosecution were entitled to adduce evidence of the bad character of the accused in rebuttal of evidence of his good character adduced by the defence.

The most important statutory exception to the general rule was contained in section 1(3) of the Criminal Evidence Act 1898 (the 1898 Act). The first part of section 1(3) armed an accused with what was often referred to as a 'shield' against cross-examination about his bad character, and the latter part of the subsection set out certain situations in which the shield could be lost, including the following: (i) where the accused asserted his good character; (ii) where the nature or conduct of the defence was such as to involve imputations on the character of

---

[1] See Ch 6.

[2] Subject to restrictions on cross-examination of complainants in proceedings for sexual offences: see ss 41–3 of the Youth Justice and Criminal Evidence Act 1999: see Ch 7.

witnesses for the prosecution or the deceased victim of the alleged crime; and (iii) where the accused gave evidence against any other person charged in the same proceedings.

Chapter 1 of Part 11 of the 2003 Act (sections 98–113) all but codifies the law governing the admissibility of evidence of bad character in criminal cases, abolishing the common law rules,[3] amending section 6 of the Criminal Procedure Act 1865[4] to ensure that cross-examination on a witness's previous convictions is governed by the new statutory rules, and repealing section 1(3) of the 1898 Act.[5] In general terms, the Government's approach to reform has been informed by Lord Justice Auld's *Review of the Criminal Courts of England and Wales*[6] and the Law Commission Report *Evidence of Bad Character in Criminal Proceedings*.[7] There are, however, substantial differences between the proposals of both the Review and the Commission and the measures subsequently enacted.

The Review made no firm recommendations about character evidence but was highly critical of the law, as it then stood, and did recommend that the law of criminal evidence should, in general, move away from technical rules of admissibility to trusting judicial and lay fact finders to give relevant evidence the weight it deserves.[8] The Government's proposals were also said to be underpinned by the concept that the criminal justice system should be more trusting of fact finders to assess relevant evidence. However, the Government did not opt for an approach based on the general admissibility of all evidence of bad character.

The Law Commission was also highly critical of the law as it then stood. Fundamental to the scheme recommended by the Commission was the idea that in any trial there is a central set of facts about which any party should be free to adduce relevant evidence, including evidence of bad character, without restraint. Such evidence 'has to do' with the offence charged or is evidence of misconduct connected with the investigation or prosecution of the offence. The Commission recommended that evidence of bad character falling outside this category should only be admissible with leave or if all parties agree to its admission or it is evidence of the accused's bad character and he wishes to adduce it. Witnesses and the accused were both to be protected against allegations of misconduct extraneous to the events which are the subject of the trial and which have only marginal relevance to the facts of the case.[9] Under the recommended scheme, and under the scheme as enacted, evidence is only admissible if it falls within one of a number of specified categories of admissibility, many of which replicate the cases in which evidence of bad character was admissible at common law. However, whereas the Law Commission recommended in effect an exclusionary rule subject to exceptions under which bad character evidence could be admitted with the leave of the court, overall the Government's approach is designed to be more inclusionary,[10] and under the new provisions evidence of the bad character of the accused falling within one of the categories of admissibility may be introduced without leave, subject, in some cases, to a discretion to exclude.

---

[3] Section 99(1).

[4] Section 331 and para 79, Sch 36.

[5] Section 331 and para 80(b), Sch 36.

[6] HMSO, 2001.

[7] Law Com No 273, Cm 5257 (2001). For critiques of the Report, see M Redmayne, 'The Law Commission's character convictions' (2002) 6 *E&P* 71 and P Mirfield, 'Bad character and the Law Commission' (2002) 6 *E&P* 141.

[8] Para 78.

[9] See paras 1.12 and 1.13.

[10] See Hansard, HL, vol 654, col 739 (4 Nov 2003) and para 365 of the Home Office Explanatory Notes to the 2003 Act.

Unfortunately, the scheme contained in the 2003 Act, as we shall see, is not simple and is in parts unclear, some of the key provisions being open to widely differing interpretations. A former Lord Chief Justice described section 1 of the Criminal Evidence Act 1898, with justification, as 'a nightmare of construction'.[11] The same is likely to be said of some of the new statutory provisions, especially those governing admissibility of the bad character of the accused. It would not be unfair to describe them, to be colloquial, as something of a dog's breakfast.

Abolition of the common law rules

Section 99 of the 2003 provides as follows:

(1) The common law rules governing the admissibility of evidence of bad character in criminal proceedings[12] are abolished.
(2) Subsection (1) is subject to section 118(1) in so far as it preserves the rule under which in criminal proceedings a person's reputation is admissible for the purposes of proving his bad character.

Although section 99(1) refers only to the rules governing the admissibility of evidence of bad character and not to the common law rules governing cross-examination of a witness other than the accused about his bad character, it is submitted that the intention is to cover both. As to the questioning of witnesses on matters covered by the exceptions to the rule of finality of answers to collateral questions, the common law rules can certainly be said to 'govern' the admissibility of evidence of bad character, because the matters are put to the witness with a view to eliciting such evidence and, if the matters are denied, they can be proved. The common law rules permitting the questioning of witnesses on their bad character in relation to matters not covered by the exceptions to the rule of finality may also be said to 'govern' the admissibility of evidence of bad character in that they too are questions put with a view to eliciting such evidence and notwithstanding that if the witness denies the matters put, they cannot be proved.

It would seem that the general common law discretion to exclude prosecution evidence where its prejudicial effect outweighs its probative value[13] may continue to be exercised in respect of evidence of bad character. It is submitted that the phrase 'common law rules governing . . . admissibility' is not apt to cover a common law *discretion* to exclude.

'Bad character' defined

Under section 98 of the 2003 Act:

References in this Chapter to evidence of a person's 'bad character' are to evidence of, or of a disposition towards, misconduct on his part, other than evidence which—
(a) has to do with the alleged facts of the offence with which the defendant is charged, or
(b) is evidence of misconduct in connection with the investigation or prosecution of that offence.

The definition of bad character in section 98 applies in the case of both the accused and non-defendants and appears to cover misconduct occurring, or disposition towards misconduct

---

[11] Lord Lane CJ in *R v Anderson* [1988] QB 678 at 686.

[12] 'Criminal proceedings', for the purposes of the provisions of the 2003 Act relating to evidence of bad character, means criminal proceedings in relation to which the strict rules of evidence apply: s 112(1).

[13] See Ch 2.

existing, either before or after the offence with which the accused is charged. The definition covers circumstantial as well as direct evidence of bad character, notwithstanding that when dealing with circumstantial evidence the question is begged whether the evidence goes to show misconduct until the inference is drawn.[14] 'Bad character' has been defined broadly by section 98, a definition that generally reflects the common law concept. The broad definition is designed to prevent evidence which, under the pre-existing law, would have been excluded, from falling outside the statutory scheme and thereby becoming admissible.[15] Although the definition does not include a person's reputation for misconduct, the common law rule under which a person's reputation is admissible for the purpose of proving his bad character, has been preserved by section 118(2).

'Misconduct', for the purposes of the definition, means 'the commission of an offence or other reprehensible behaviour',[16] 'offence' in its turn being defined to include a service offence.[17] Evidence of bad character under the Act therefore covers evidence of a person's misconduct whether or not unlawful; if unlawful, whether or not it resulted in a prosecution; and where it did result in a prosecution, whether within the jurisdiction or overseas, and whether it resulted in a conviction or an acquittal. As to acquittals, the definition in effect preserves the decision of the House of Lords in *R v Z*[18] that where evidence of misconduct on the part of the accused is relevant and otherwise admissible prosecution evidence, it does not fall to be excluded because it shows or tends to show that the accused was guilty of an offence of which he was previously acquitted. The definition also covers evidence of misconduct in respect of which a trial is pending, evidence of an accused's misconduct which relates to other charges on the indictment, and allegations that have never been tried, for example because of a stay for abuse of process,[19] but not arrest on suspicion followed by release without charge,[20] nor, it seems, an allegation made but later withdrawn[21] Although the definition does not cover, by itself, evidence that someone has been suspected or informally charged with misconduct, evidence concerning such suspicions and accusations is generally irrelevant and therefore inadmissible on that basis.[22] Likewise, although the definition does not cover evidence of the bare fact that someone has been formally charged with an offence, such evidence is generally inadmissible because irrelevant, the fact that a man has been charged with an offence being

[14] *R v Wallace* [2008] 1 WLR 572, CA. Circumstantial evidence from three robberies and an attempted robbery charged as separate counts on the same indictment came *technically* within the definition in s 98 and so, strictly speaking, fell to be admitted as evidence of bad character which was cross-admissible from one count to another. A further question is begged whether a judge should give a jury a 'bad character' direction in respect of circumstantial evidence which falls within the definition of bad character. The Court of Appeal remarked that no bad character direction would be needed and indeed references to 'bad character' would not have been necessary (at [44]). It may well be that, in spite of the deliberately broad definition in s 98, the bad character provisions were not intended to capture such a case (at [41]).

[15] See Hilary Benn MP, HC Committee, 23 Jan 2003, col 545.

[16] See R Munday, 'What Constitutes "Other Reprehensible Behaviour" under the Bad Character Provisions of the Criminal Justice Act 2003?' [2005] *Crim LR* 24.

[17] Section 112(1).

[18] [2002] 2 AC 483.

[19] *R v Edwards* [2006] 1 WLR 1524, CA at [78] and [81].

[20] *R v Weir* [2006] 1 WLR 1885, CA at [118].

[21] *R v Bovell* [2005] 2 Cr App R 401, CA at [21]. Although a *number* of 'strikingly similar' allegations, made and then withdrawn, could be covered. See *R v Ladds* [2009] EWCA Crim 1249.

[22] See *Stirland v DPP* [1944] AC 315, HL, a decision under the Criminal Evidence Act 1898.

no proof that he committed it and having no bearing on his credibility as a witness.[23] Nor does the definition cover the bare fact that someone has been convicted where that conviction has been quashed. In *R v Hussain*,[24] an accused's previous conviction for murder had been quashed and at a retrial his plea of guilty to a lesser offence of assault occasioning actual bodily harm was accepted. It was held that the definition covered only the lesser offence, the quashed conviction being no more than an unproven charge.[25]

The word 'reprehensible' carries with it some element of culpability or blameworthiness,[26] but whether conduct is 'reprehensible' is not determined by an exercise in moral judgment. So in *R v Fox*[27] where the accused was charged with sexual offences against children, the keeping of a private notebook recording what Scott Baker LJ called 'dirty' sexual thoughts was judged, although with caution, not to be a disposition towards reprehensible behaviour. Whether particular lawful behaviour involves culpability or blameworthiness will depend on the particular circumstances and is a question on which views are likely to differ.[28] In *R v Weir*[29] the appellant M was convicted of indecently assaulting A. At the time of the offences, M was 39 and A was 13. It was held that evidence was admissible of an earlier sexual relationship with another girl B, who was 16, M then being 34. There was no feature of this lawful relationship to make it reprehensible, such as evidence of grooming. However, since evidence of the relationship was not 'evidence of bad character', and therefore the abolition of the common law rules governing the admissibility of 'evidence of bad character' by section 99(1) did not apply, it was admissible at common law as demonstrating a sexual interest in early- or mid-teenage girls much younger than M and therefore bore on the truth of his case of a truly supportive asexual interest in A.[30]

If evidence of bad character does fall within the statutory definition it can only be admitted in evidence if it satisfies the further conditions of admissibility in section 100 (non-defendant's bad character) or section 101 (defendant's bad character). Where the evidence to be adduced is evidence of the bad character of an accused who disputes the facts relied upon to establish his bad character, then a *voir dire* may also be required.[31]

---

[23] See *Maxwell v DPP* [1935] AC 309, HL, a decision under the Criminal Evidence Act 1898. See also *R v Renda* [2006] 1 WLR 2984, CA at [46], on the different and, it is submitted, unconvincing reasoning that in the circumstances there was 'a bare allegation, itself wholly unproved'.

[24] [2008] EWCA Crim 1117.

[25] Ibid at [13]. However, it was held that the evidence should have been admitted on the basis that it was relevant to a co-accused's defence of duress.

[26] *R v Renda* [2006] 1 WLR 2948, CA at [24], where the court held that the mere fact that the appellant was found unfit to plead some 18 months after an apparent incident of gratuitous violence did not, by itself, extinguish culpability at the time of the offence.

[27] [2009] EWCA Crim 653 at [30].

[28] Verbal aggression is not necessarily reprehensible: see *R v Osbourne* [2007] Crim LR 712, CA. Possession of rap lyrics personally altered to include a vague threat could be reprehensible when combined with possession of photographs of victims of a violent assault: see *R v Saleem* [2007] All ER (D) 349 (Jul). It is doubtful that exaggeration to fellow pupils about being pushed by a teacher after everyday classroom misbehaviour is reprehensible: see *R v V* [2006] All ER (D) 404 (Jul). It is not reprehensible to have recently taken a drugs overdose: see *R v Hall-Chung* [2007] All ER (D) 429 (Jul).

[29] [2006] 1 WLR 1885, CA.

[30] It was also held that a person's refusal, without reasons, to give a witness statement when a victim of crime is not reprehensible behaviour. However, it is submitted that this could be affected by the motive of the victim, for example, where the motive was to protect the criminal.

[31] See *R v Wright* [2000] Crim LR 851, CA, a decision under the Criminal Evidence Act 1898.

The admissibility of evidence of bad character 'to do with' the facts of the offence or in connection with its investigation or prosecution

Section 99(1) of the 2003 Act, as we have seen, abolishes the common law rules governing admissibility of evidence of bad character as defined by section 98. It follows, of course, that the common law rules continue to operate insofar as they permit evidence to be adduced which, looking to the wording of section 98(a) 'has to do with the alleged facts of the offence' or, looking to the wording of section 98(b) 'is evidence of misconduct in connection with the investigation or prosecution of that offence'. Section 98(a) covers such prosecution evidence, other than evidence of previous misconduct or evidence of disposition towards misconduct, as tends to show that the accused is guilty of the offence charged, such as evidence of witnesses to the crime and fingerprint evidence. Provided that there is some 'nexus in time',[32] it also covers misconduct other than the offence charged, for example an assault or criminal damage committed by the accused in the course of the burglary with which he is charged. Similarly, it may cover misconduct that was the subject of another count originally in the indictment but subsequently severed.[33] Section 98(a) can also cover misconduct on the part of someone other than the accused, for example evidence in support of a defence of self-defence that the victim was the aggressor. In *R v Machado*,[34] it was held that on a charge of robbery, evidence was admissible that the victim had offered to supply drugs to the appellant and that he had said that he had taken an ecstasy tablet. However, the court appears to have overlooked the basic requirement of relevance. That the victim had taken drugs may well have been relevant because there was a suggestion that rather than being pushed to the ground, he fell over, but his alleged offer to supply drugs had no obvious relevance to any of the issues in the case.

Evidence admissible by virtue of section 98(a) falls to be distinguished from so-called 'background evidence', which is evidence of bad character potentially admissible under section 101(1)(c), a distinction which is likely to be difficult to draw in some cases.[35] However, if section 98(a) applies, then the evidence is admissible without more ado,[36] subject of course to the requirement of relevance and the discretion to exclude.

Section 98(b) covers, for example: evidence that during the investigation the police obtained evidence unlawfully or unfairly, for instance by fabricating a confession or planting evidence on the accused or in his premises; evidence that during interview the accused told lies; and evidence that during the investigation or proceedings the prosecution or the accused had sought to intimidate potential witnesses.

The role of the trial judge and the court of appeal

Provided that a trial judge has not erred in principle, the Court of Appeal will be loath to interfere with a judge's ruling in relation to the admissibility of evidence of bad character, whether

---

[32] *R v Tirnaveanu* [2007] 1 WLR 3049.

[33] *R v Edwards* [2006] 1 WLR 1524, CA at [23].

[34] (2006) 170 JP 400.

[35] See under s 101(1)(c) below.

[36] *R v Edwards* [2006] 1 WLR 1524, CA at [1](i). See also *R v Leonard* (2009) 173 JP 366 at [11]: text messages sent to the accused which implied that he had been dealing in drugs had to do with the alleged facts of the offence of possession of controlled drugs with intent to supply and did not fall to be adduced as evidence of bad character but were deemed to be inadmissible hearsay. See Ch 10.

of the accused or of someone other than the accused, under the Criminal Justice Act 2003. In *R v Renda*,[37] Sir Igor Judge P said:

> The circumstances in which this court would interfere with the exercise of a judicial discretion are limited. The principles need no repetition.[38] However, we emphasise that the same general approach will be adopted when the court is being invited to interfere with what in reality is a fact-specific judgment . . . the trial judge's 'feel' for the case is usually the critical ingredient of the decision at first instance which this court lacks. Context therefore is vital . . . This legislation has now been in force for nearly a year. The principles have been considered by this court on a number of occasions. The responsibility for their application is not for this court but for the trial judge.

In the last edition of this text it was submitted that the last three sentences of this passage should not be taken to mean that after less than one year there were unlikely to be new points of principle for the appellate courts to consider or, worse, that if there were , appellate courts might side-step them by deferring to the 'feel' of the trial judge in the context of the specific case. Two years on, the appellate courts continue to generate and refine points of principle at what could be fairly described as an 'industrial rate'.[39]

Evidence of the bad character of a person other than the defendant

Section 100 of the Criminal Justice Act 2003

At common law a witness could be cross-examined about his previous misconduct with a view to impugning his credibility. He could be cross-examined, for example, about acts of dishonesty or immorality on his part, about lies he told or false allegations he made, about his drink or drug abuse, and so on. However, as we have already seen, insofar as the questions could properly be said to be on collateral matters and the witness denied them, evidence was admissible in rebuttal only exceptionally. The exceptions covered previous convictions, bias and general reputation for untruthfulness.

In *R v Edwards*[40] it was held that subject to the limits laid down in *Hobbs v Tinling*,[41] a witness could be cross-examined about any improper conduct of which he may have been guilty, for the purpose of testing his credit. The following three principles were established in *Hobbs v Tinling*.[42]

1. Questions as to credit in cross-examination are proper if of such a nature that the truth of the imputation conveyed by them would seriously affect the opinion of the court as to the credibility of the witness on the matters to which he testifies.

2. Such questions are improper if the imputation which they convey relates to matters so remote in time or of such a character that the truth of the imputation would not affect, or would affect in a slight degree, the opinion of the court as to the credibility of the witness on the matter to which he testifies.

---

[37] [2006] 1 WLR 2948, CA at [3].

[38] See Ch 2, 42, under **Judicial Discretion**.

[39] See *Court of Appeal Criminal Division Review of the Legal Year 2007–2008*, <http://www.hmcourts-service.gov.uk/cms/files/Criminal_Division_Review_2007–08_web.pdf> [3.8].

[40] [1991] 1 WLR 207.

[41] [1929] 2 KB 1, CA.

[42] Ibid at 51.

3. Such questions are improper if there is a great disproportion between the importance of the imputation made against the witness's character and the importance of his evidence.

The Law Commission was of the view that further restraints were necessary. Three reasons were given: the power of evidence of bad character to distort the fact-finding process; the need to encourage witnesses to give evidence; and the need for courts 'to control gratuitous and offensive cross-examination of little or no purpose other than to intimidate or embarrass the witness or muddy the waters'.[43] Balancing these factors against the need not to prejudice a fair trial, the Commission recommended a test based on the degree of relevance of bad character evidence to the issues in the case. Evidence of only trivial relevance would be excluded. The views of the Commission are reflected in the terms of section 100 of the 2003 Act. Section 100(1) provides as follows:

> (1) In criminal proceedings evidence of the bad character of a person other than the defendant is admissible if and only if—
> (a) it is important explanatory evidence,
> (b) it has substantial probative value in relation to a matter which—
>   (i) is a matter in issue in the proceedings, and
>   (ii) is of substantial importance in the context of the case as a whole, or
> (c) all parties to the proceedings agree to the evidence being admissible.

Section 100 may be used by the prosecution, the accused, or any co-accused. The meaning of 'bad character' has already been considered. A 'person other than the defendant' may or may not be a witness in the case. Although, on its face, section 100 governs only the admissibility of evidence of bad character and does not, in terms, govern the asking of questions about bad character in cross-examination,[44] it is submitted that the intention is to cover both. This would be consistent with the interpretation of section 99(1) of the Act that it abolishes the common law rules relating not only to the admissibility of evidence of bad character but also to cross-examination of witnesses about bad character.[45]

Threshold conditions for admissibility

Important explanatory evidence
Section 100(2) provides as follows:

> (2) For the purposes of subsection (1)(a) evidence is important explanatory evidence if—
> (a) without it, the court or jury would find it impossible or difficult properly to understand other evidence in the case, and
> (b) its value for understanding the case as a whole is substantial.

Section 100(2) covers evidence of or a disposition towards misconduct on the part of someone other than the accused, without which the prosecution (or defence) account would be incomplete or incoherent.[46] Thus if the matter to which the evidence relates is largely comprehensible without the explanatory evidence, the evidence will be inadmissible. The wording of section 100(2)(a) is a slightly different formulation of the common law rule permitting the

---

[43] Law Com No 273, op cit at para 9.35
[44] Cf, in this regard, s 41 of the Youth Justice and Criminal Evidence Act 1999.
[45] See above at 454, under **Abolition of the common law rules**.
[46] Law Com No 273, op cit, para 9.13.

use of background evidence, notwithstanding that it reveals the bad character or criminal disposition *of the accused*, where it is part of a continual background or history which is relevant to the offence charged and without the totality of which the account placed before the jury would be incomplete or incomprehensible.[47] The first option, 'incomplete', is probably best ignored: in the nature of things the account will be incomplete. The Explanatory Notes to the Act give an example of section 100(2)(a) arising in a case which involves the abuse by one person of another over a long period of time: 'For the jury to understand properly the victim's account of the offending and why they (sic) did not seek help from, for example, a parent or other guardian, it might be necessary for evidence to be given of a wider pattern of abuse involving that other person.'[48]

Explanatory evidence, to be admissible, must also satisfy section 100(1)(b), ie its value for understanding the case as a whole must be 'substantial', as opposed to minor or trivial.[49]

Evidence of substantial probative value

Under section 100(1)(b), evidence of the bad character of a person other than the accused is admissible if it has substantial probative value in relation to a matter which—(i) is a matter in issue in the proceedings; and (ii) is of substantial importance in the context of the case as a whole. The probative value must be 'substantial'—evidence of only minor probative force should not be admitted. A 'matter in issue in the proceedings' means any matter in issue, whether an issue of disputed fact or an issue of credibility, and credibility as an issue for the purposes of section 100 is wider than a propensity to be untruthful.[50] In order to be admissible, however, the evidence must also be of substantial importance in the context of the case as a whole—evidence which goes only to some minor or trivial issue should not be admitted.

Section 100(3) sets out a non-exhaustive list of the factors to which the court must have regard in assessing the probative value of the evidence. It provides as follows:

(3) In assessing the probative value of evidence for the purposes of subsection (1)(b) the court must have regard to the following factors (and to any others it considers relevant)—
  (a) the nature and number of the events, or other things, to which the evidence relates;
  (b) when those events or things are alleged to have happened or existed;
  (c) where—
    (i) the evidence is evidence of a person's misconduct, and
    (ii) it is suggested that the evidence has probative value by reason of similarity between that misconduct and other alleged misconduct,
the nature and extent of the similarities and dissimilarities between each of the alleged instances of misconduct;
  (d) where—
    (i) the evidence is evidence of a person's misconduct,
    (ii) it is suggested that that person is also responsible for the misconduct charged, and
    (iii) the identity of the person responsible for the misconduct charged is disputed, the extent to which the evidence shows or tends to show that the same person was responsible each time.

---

[47] Per Purchas LJ in *R v Pettman,* 2 May 1985, CA, unreported.

[48] Para 360. For an exploration of the dangers of using the Explanatory Notes as an aid to construction, see Munday, 'Bad Character Rules and Riddles: "Explanatory Notes" and True Meanings of s. 103(1) of the Criminal Justice Act 2003' [2005] *Crim LR* 337.

[49] Law Com No 273, op cit, para 9.1.

[50] *R v S* [2006] 2 Cr App R 437, CA at [7] and [10]. See also *R v Weir* [2006] 1 WLR 1885, CA at [73].

As to section 100(3)(a), if, for example, a key witness has previous convictions or has been guilty of improper conduct in the past, the nature and number of the offences committed or of the incidents of misconduct will have an obvious bearing in deciding its probative value in relation to the issue of his credibility as a witness. A conviction for perjury will have a probative force normally lacking in a conviction for, say, a minor motoring offence. Similarly, evidence of previous false accusations may have a probative value not to be found in, say, evidence of cruelty to animals. However, previous convictions which do not involve either the making of false statements or the giving of false evidence are also capable of having substantial probative value in relation to the credibility of a non-defendant.[51] Each case will turn on its own facts. In *R v S*,[52] S, charged with indecent assault, was of good character. He claimed that the claimant, a prostitute, had agreed to sexual activities for £10 and that when, afterwards, he refused her demand for more money, she threatened to accuse him of rape and tried to grab a gold chain he was wearing. It was held that S should have been allowed to cross-examine her on her convictions for going equipped for theft, handling, and burglary, because they showed a propensity to act dishonestly and possessed substantial probative value on the issues whether, in effect, she had demanded money with menaces and had tried to take S's property. By contrast, in *R v Garnham*[53] it was held that the accused, tried for rape, was properly prevented from cross-examining the complainant about any of her 65 previous convictions for theft. It was held that the judge had been correct in his conclusion that in the circumstances a propensity to dishonesty was not the same as a propensity to untruthfulness and that the complainant's previous convictions were not of substantial probative value in relation to her credibility.

However, it is difficult, without more, to justify the conclusion in *R v Renda*[54] that a defence witness's conviction for a violent offence was of substantial probative value in relation to the issue of his credibility, being 'particularly germane' to the question whether a robbery had occurred or been fabricated by the complainant. One possible explanation is that it was a conviction after a not guilty plea, which can operate to impugn credibility.[55]

As to section 100(3)(b), evidence of misconduct occurring many years ago is usually likely to have less probative value than more recent misconduct, although plainly very serious misconduct in the past may have much greater probative value than recent but relatively minor misconduct. Misconduct capable of having substantial probative value includes misconduct after the commission of the offence charged in the proceedings. So, for example, where an accused seeks to blame another person who was previously a suspect but not charged, misconduct by that person after the offence could be probative of whether he rather than the accused committed the offence. In such a case, the more time that has elapsed since the offence, the less probative the misconduct is likely to be. This can be further affected by factors such as the person's age at the time of the offence and his age at the time of the trial. In *R v Ross*,[56] the Court of Appeal held that the trial judge was correct to exclude previous convictions of a former suspect, N, whom the accused sought to blame for the murder of an old lady in her

---

[51] *R v Stephenson* [2006] EWCA Crim 2325.

[52] [2006] 2 Cr App R 437, CA.

[53] [2008] All ER (D) 50 (May).

[54] [2006] 1 WLR 2948, CA at [59].

[55] See *R v Renda*, ibid, but in the case of another appellant, *Razaq*, at [73]. Although this may remain the position in respect of witnesses *other* than an accused, in respect of an accused, it is questionable whether a conviction after a not guilty plea can impugn credibility in the light of *R v Campbell* [2007] 1 WLR 2798 (considered later in this chapter).

[56] [2009] EWCA Crim 1165. See [24].

home some 13 years previously. N's convictions included burglary, housebreaking, rape, and violence committed between two and nine years *after* the date of the murder. During the trial the jury had heard highly probative hearsay evidence implicating N and it was held that the convictions added little. Also, considering that N was 15 years old at the time the murder, some of the convictions for violence committed as an adult could not be probative to show a propensity for using severe violence as a 15-year-old during a burglary.

Section 100(3)(c) relates to evidence of a person's misconduct, the probative value of which, in relation to a matter in issue in the proceedings, derives from its similarity to other misconduct on his part. Thus if the accused alleges that the case against him has been fabricated by a police officer who has threatened a potential witness for the defence—evidence of which would be admissible under section 98(b)—and there is evidence that in other cases the officer has also gone to improper lengths to secure a conviction, in assessing the probative value of the evidence the court should have regard to the nature and extent of the similarities, for example, whether in some of the cases he had also threatened potential defence witnesses.

Section 100(3)(d) relates to evidence, in cases in which the identity of the offender is in dispute, suggesting that a person other than the accused is responsible for the offence charged. Such evidence will often take the form of evidence of similar facts. For example, if the accused is charged with a sexual assault in a public park, the prosecution case being that the crime was committed by someone wearing eccentric clothes, and the defence being one of mistaken identity, and there is evidence that X, the resident of a house overlooking the park has previously committed sexual assaults in the park, then in assessing the probative value of the evidence, the court must have regard to the extent to which the evidence shows or tends to show that X was responsible for each of the offences, for example whether the evidence shows that X wore eccentric clothing or the same eccentric clothing on each occasion.

Evidence admitted by agreement

Under section 100(1)(c) evidence of the bad character of a person other than the accused may be admitted by agreement of 'all parties to the proceedings', ie the prosecution, the accused, and any co-accused. Under section 100(4), evidence may be admitted under section 100(1)(c) without the leave of the court.

The requirement of leave

Section 100(4) of the 2003 Act provides that 'Except where subsection (1)(c) applies, evidence of the bad character of a person other than the defendant must not be given without the leave of the court.' Thus evidence admissible under section 100(1)(a) or (b) must not be adduced without leave. Unfortunately, however, the subsection gives no guidance as to what factors, if any, should be taken into account in deciding whether or not to grant leave, over and above the factors set out in section 100(2) and (3).

On one view, section 100(4) also applies to evidence of bad character of complainants admissible under section 41 of the Youth Justice and Criminal Evidence Act 1999. If that is so, then in this context also the purpose of the subsection is elusive, because it is unclear what factors, if any, should be taken into account in deciding whether or not to grant leave, over and above the matters that have to be taken into account in deciding whether to grant leave under section 41 itself. The further question arises as to what kinds of sexual behaviour on the part of the complainant should be treated as 'bad character' as defined in the 2003 Act. An alternative and preferable view, it is submitted, is that when evidence of bad character is admitted under section 41, there will of necessity be compliance with section 100(4) of the 2003 Act because of the leave requirement in section 41 itself.

Discretion to exclude

It is submitted that the general common law discretionary power to exclude evidence where its prejudicial effect outweighs its probative value may be exercised in respect of *prosecution* evidence of bad character admissible under section 100.[57] As to whether the general discretionary power to exclude prosecution evidence under section 78 of the Police and Criminal Evidence Act 1984[58] applies in the case of prosecution evidence of bad character otherwise admissible under the 2003 Act, the case law tends to suggest an affirmative answer.[59] If it does apply, then it will be open to the defence to submit that evidence admissible under section 100 of the 2003 Act upon which the prosecution propose to rely should be excluded where, having regard to all the circumstances, its admission would have such an adverse effect on the fairness of the proceedings that the court ought not to admit it. The arguments for and against the application of section 78 are more conveniently set out in the context of section 101(3), which is considered in the next section of this chapter.

Evidence of the bad character of the defendant

Evidence admitted through inadvertence

At common law, as we have seen, the general rule was that the prosecution were not permitted either to adduce evidence of the accused's bad character or to cross-examine witnesses for the defence with a view to eliciting such evidence, the rationale of the rule being the risk of the tribunal of fact becoming biased against an accused. The importance that English law attached to the rule was such that in cases where none of the exceptions to it applied but the bad character of the accused was inadvertently revealed to the jury, whether by a witness or counsel, the judge could exercise his discretion to discharge the whole jury from giving a verdict and order a retrial.[60] It is submitted that the principles established at common law to deal with the problem of disclosure of the accused's bad character by inadvertence will continue to provide valuable guidance. Thus, as at common law, much is likely to depend on how explicit the reference to bad character was, the extent to which, if at all, the defence was to blame, and whether a direction to the jury is capable of neutralizing the prejudice to the accused.[61] The question for the judge, in exercising the discretion, is likely to remain whether there is a real danger of injustice occurring because the jury, having heard the prejudicial matter, may be biased.[62] Thus in appropriate circumstances, as when the effect on the jury appears to be

[57] See above at 454, under **Abolition of the common law rules**.
[58] See Ch 2.
[59] See *R v Highton* [2005] 1 WLR 3472; *R v Weir* [2006] 1 WLR 1885; *R v Tirnaveanu* [2007] 1 WLR 3049; and *R v O'Dowd* [2009] 2 Cr App R 280, CA.
[60] See, eg, *R v Tyrer* (1988) The Times, 13 Oct, CA. See generally Roderick Munday, 'Irregular Disclosure of Evidence of Bad character' [1990] *Crim LR* 92.
[61] *R v Weaver* [1968] 1 QB 353, CA.
[62] *R v Docherty* [1999] 1 Cr App R 274, CA.

minimal, the trial may properly continue.[63] The starting point is not that the jury should be discharged; nor is there a sliding scale whereby the burden on an accused seeking a discharge increases according to the weight or length of the case or the stage it has reached when the point arises for determination.[64]

In summary proceedings in which the magistrates become aware of the bad character of the accused, either by inadvertence, or deliberately, as when called upon to decide on the admissibility of evidence of bad character, procedural and evidential problems can arise, because magistrates must perform the combined role of tribunal of law and tribunal of fact.[65]

The background to section 101 of the Criminal Justice Act 2003

Before the coming into force of the 2003 Act, evidence of the bad character of the accused was admissible only exceptionally and a sharp distinction was drawn between evidence adduced because of its relevance to the issue of guilt, and evidence elicited in cross-examination of the accused and bearing upon his credibility as a witness. The approach under section 101 of the 2003 Act is radically different. It is not one of inadmissibility subject to exceptions, but of admissibility if certain criteria are met.[66] Section 101 sets out seven gateways through which evidence of the bad character of the accused can be admitted. Collectively, these grounds for admissibility are much wider than those which they have replaced. Under the section, (a) no distinction is drawn between evidence introduced as a part of the prosecution's case and evidence elicited in cross-examination of the accused; (b) evidence is admissible irrespective of whether the accused gives evidence; and (c) there are no explicit limitations on the purpose for which the evidence is adduced.

The provisions in the 2003 Act relating to evidence of the bad character of the accused provoked much controversy during their parliamentary passage, especially in the House of Lords, where some members voiced the opinion that section 101 undermined the presumption of innocence.[67] A major criticism of the statutory scheme is that although it is based on the proposals of the Law Commission, each of the safeguards contained in the Law Commission framework and designed to protect the accused from the introduction of prejudicial evidence has been either abandoned or diluted.[68] For example, under the Commission's proposals, in each of the four situations in which evidence of bad character of the accused was admissible, leave was required and in three of those situations there was a condition that the interests of justice required the evidence to be admissible, even taking account of its potentially prejudicial effect. Under section 101, however, leave is not required and instead of an 'interests of justice' condition, there is a discretionary power to exclude, but only on the application of the defence and only in respect of evidence admissible under two of the seven 'gateways'. The breadth of section 101, coupled with the absence of the much tighter restrictions on admissibility contained in the Law Commission's proposals, are such as to allow evidence

---

[63] See *R v Coughlan* and *R v Young* (1976) 63 Cr App R 33, CA and *R v Sutton* (1969) 53 Cr App R 504, CA. See also *R v Wilson* [2008] 2 Cr App R 39, where there was minimal prejudice from the risk of the jury having seen the accused's name on a Crown Court list for another unspecified matter pending.

[64] *R v Lawson* [2007] 1 Cr App R 277, CA at [65].

[65] See Martin Wasik, 'Magistrates: Knowledge of Previous Convictions' [1996] *Crim LR* 851, where the cases are reviewed.

[66] *R v Weir* [2006] 1 WLR 1885, CA at [35].

[67] See, eg, Lord Alexander and Lord Kingsland, *Hansard*, HL, Vol 654, cols 729, 731, and 741 (4 Nov 2003).

[68] See generally C Tapper, 'Criminal Justice Act 2003 (3) Evidence of Bad Character' [2004] *Crim LR* 533.

of the accused's bad character to be admitted more readily than in the past. The effect, it is submitted, will be to oblige judges to make much greater use of their discretionary powers to exclude such evidence.

It does not follow from the foregoing that the prosecution should apply as a matter of routine to admit evidence of the accused's bad character. In *R v Hanson*,[69] the first Court of Appeal decision on the new provisions, it was held that the starting point should be for judges and practitioners to bear in mind that Parliament's purpose was to assist in the evidence-based conviction of the guilty, without putting those who are not guilty at risk of conviction by prejudice, and that it was accordingly to be hoped that prosecution applications to adduce evidence of an accused's bad character will not be made routinely, simply because an accused has previous convictions, but will be based on the particular circumstances of each case. It was held in that case that if a judge has directed himself correctly, the Court of Appeal will be very slow to interfere with a ruling as to admissibility[70] and will not interfere unless the judge's judgment as to the capacity of prior events to establish propensity is plainly wrong or discretion has been exercised unreasonably in a *Wednesbury* sense.[71] It was also held that if, following a ruling that evidence of bad character is admissible, an accused pleads guilty, it is highly unlikely that an appeal against conviction will be entertained.

Section 101 of the Criminal Justice Act 2003

Section 101 provides as follows:

  (1) In criminal proceedings evidence of the defendant's[72] bad character is admissible if, but only if
    (a) all parties to the proceedings agree to the evidence being admissible,
    (b) the evidence is adduced by the defendant himself or is given in answer to a question asked by him in cross-examination and intended to elicit it,
    (c) it is important explanatory evidence,
    (d) it is relevant to an important matter in issue between the defendant and the prosecution,
    (e) it has substantial probative value in relation to an important matter in issue between the defendant and a co-defendant,[73]
    (f) it is evidence to correct a false impression given by the defendant, or
    (g) the defendant has made an attack on another person's character.
  (2) Sections 102 to 106 contain provision supplementing subsection (1).
  (3) The court must not admit evidence under subsection (1)(d) or (g) if, on an application by the defendant to exclude it, it appears to the court that the admission of the evidence would have such an adverse effect on the fairness of the proceedings that the court ought not to admit it.
  (4) On an application to exclude evidence under subsection (3) the court must have regard, in particular, to the length of time between the matters to which that evidence relates and the matters which form the subject of the offence charged.

---

[69] [2005] 1 WLR 3169, CA.

[70] Or as to the consequences of non-compliance with the regulations for giving notice of intention to rely on bad character evidence: *R v Malone* [2006] All ER (D) 32 (Jun) CA and *R v Spartley* [2007] All ER (D) 233 (May).

[71] *Wednesbury Corpn v Ministry of Housing and Local Government* [1965] 1 WLR 261, CA. The position is the same when the Divisional Court is considering an appeal against a decision of a magistrates' court: *DPP v Chard* [2007] EWHC 90 (Admin).

[72] 'Defendant', in relation to criminal proceedings, means a person charged with an offence in those proceedings: s 112(1).

[73] 'Co-defendant', in relation to a defendant (see footnote 63 above), means a person charged with an offence in the same proceedings: s 112(1).

Although section 101(1) governs only the admissibility of evidence of bad character and does not explicitly deal with the asking of questions about bad character in cross-examination, the intention is to cover both. The phrase 'prosecution evidence' is defined to include evidence which a witness is to be invited to give (or has given) in cross-examination by the prosecution;[74] the 'only evidence' admissible under section 101(1)(e) includes evidence which a witness is invited to give (or has given) in cross-examination by the co-defendant;[75] and the rules of court to be made under the 2003 Act may, and where the party in question is the prosecution, must, require a party to serve notice on the defendant where it is proposed to cross-examine a witness with a view to eliciting evidence of the accused's bad character.[76]

There are seven 'gateways' under section 101(1) through which evidence of the bad character of the accused may be admitted. Section 101(1)(a) provides for the admissibility of such evidence by consent of the parties. Under section 101(1)(b), such evidence may be admitted at the election of the accused and without the agreement of the other parties. Speaking generally, section 101(1)(c) is designed to admit evidence which would have been admissible at common law as so-called 'background evidence'. Section 101(1)(d) covers prosecution evidence relevant to an important matter, ie a matter of substantial importance in the context of the case as a whole, which is in issue between the prosecution and the defence. Subsections (1) (e), (f), and (g) broadly correspond to and widen pre-existing grounds of admissibility. Broadly speaking, section 101(1)(e) relates to evidence formerly admissible on behalf of a co-accused on one of two grounds, either on the basis of its relevance to the guilt of the accused or, in cases where the nature or conduct of the defence of the accused undermines the defence of the co-accused, to attack the credibility of the accused; section 101(1)(f) relates to prosecution evidence formerly admissible in rebuttal of evidence of good character adduced by an accused; and section 101(1)(g) is designed to admit prosecution evidence in cases where the accused has cast an imputation on the character of another.

Before considering further each of the 'gateways', it is convenient first to consider some issues of general importance relating to admissibility, use, leave, and discretionary exclusion.

Admissibility and use

Parties are well advised to reflect, at the time of the application to admit evidence of bad character, as to the use to which such evidence is likely to be put and be in a position to assist the judge in this regard.[77] Lord Woolf CJ made clear in *R v Highton*[78] that the use to which the evidence may be put depends upon the matters to which it is relevant rather than the gateway through which it was admitted. The reasoning that leads to the admission of evidence under section 101(1)(d) may also determine the matter to which the evidence is relevant or primarily relevant once admitted. This is because, as we shall see, that provision deals separately with the accused's propensity to commit offences of the kind with which he is charged (section 103(1)(a)) and his propensity to be untruthful (section 103(1)(b)). However, under other gateways, which make no reference to the use to which the bad character evidence may be put, for example under section 101(1)(g), where admissibility depends on the accused having made an attack on another person's character, the evidence may, depending on the particular facts, be

---

[74] Section 112(1).

[75] Section 104(2)(b).

[76] Section 111(2)(b).

[77] *R v Edwards* [2006] 1 WLR 1524, CA at [1](ii).

[78] [2006] 1 Cr App R 125, CA.

relevant not only to credibility but also to propensity to commit offences of the kind charged. The full implications of Lord Woolf's reasoning became explicit in *R v Campbell*.[79] In that case it was submitted that in directing the jury as to the relevance of bad character evidence, the judge should have regard only to the gateway through which the evidence was introduced, unless the evidence could have been introduced through an additional gateway, in which case the jury could be directed as to its additional relevance under that gateway. Lord Phillips CJ rejected the submission on the basis that to direct the jury to have regard to bad character evidence for some purposes and disregard its relevance in other respects 'would be to revert to the unsatisfactory practices that prevailed under the old law'. This was an explicit reference to the fact that under section 1(f) of the Criminal Evidence Act 1898 it was often the case that the judge was required to direct the jury that the previous conviction was relevant only to the accused's credibility, not guilt. As Lord Phillips CJ says, this was contrary to common sense where the previous convictions showed propensity to commit the type of offence with which the accused was charged. However, with respect it is no justification for his rejection of the submission made because in such a case, under the 2003 Act, insofar as the evidence is relevant to propensity to commit the offence charged, it is admissible under section 101(1)(d), provided it meets the requirements of that gateway, in addition to any other gateway through which it is admissible and relevant to credit. The consequence of the view adopted by the Lord Chief Justice is that, for example, evidence of propensity to commit offences of the kind charged can now be admitted under section 101(1)(g) (making an attack on another person's character) even if it is not relevant to an important matter in issue between the prosecution and the defence (a requirement under section 101(1)(d), but not under section 101(1)(g)) or does not have substantial probative value in relation to an important matter in issue between the accused and a co-accused (a requirement under section 101(1)(e), but not under section 101(1)(g)). It seems most unlikely that this is what Parliament intended.[80]

It will be clear, from the foregoing, that the judge must exercise care when summing up. He will need to warn the jury against placing undue reliance on previous convictions, which cannot by themselves prove guilt, and also explain why they have heard the evidence and the ways in which it is relevant to and may help their decision.[81] Where bad character evidence is admitted and thereafter 'the ground shifts', the judge may need to direct the jury that, given the course taken by the trial, the evidence is of little weight.[82] In appropriate circumstances, which may arise when evidence of previous convictions is adduced by the accused himself under section 101(1)(b), the judge may even be required to direct the jury that the evidence does not assist on either propensity or untruthfulness.[83]

In *R v Campbell*, Lord Phillips CJ set out the following general principles governing the way in which juries should be directed about evidence admitted under section 101.

1. The changes introduced by the 2003 Act should be the occasion for simplifying the directions to juries in relation to evidence of the accused's bad character.

---

[79] [2007] 1 WLR 2798, CA.

[80] For further implications and a powerful critique of *R v Highton*, ibid, see Munday, 'The Purposes of Gateway (g): Yet Another Problematic of the Criminal Justice Act 2003' [2006] *Crim LR* 300.

[81] See per Rose LJ in *R v Edwards* [2006] 1 WLR 1524, CA at [3].

[82] *R v Edwards*, ibid, at [1](iv).

[83] *R v Edwards*, ibid at [87]–[104].

2. Decisions in this field before the 2003 Act came into force are unhelpful and should not be cited.

3. The jury should be given assistance as to the relevance of bad character evidence that is tailored to the facts of the individual case.

4. Relevance can normally be deduced by the application of common sense. The summing-up that assists the jury with the relevance of bad character evidence will accord with common sense and assist them to avoid prejudice that is at odds with this.

5. Once evidence has been admitted through a gateway it is open to the jury to attach significance to it in any respect in which it is relevant. There is no rule to the effect that in directing the jury as to relevance, the judge shall have regard only to the gateway through which the evidence was introduced or any other gateway through which it could have been introduced.

6. The extent of the significance to be attached to previous convictions is likely to depend upon a number of variables, including their number, their similarity to the offence charged, how recently they were incurred, and the nature of the defence.

7. In considering the inference to be drawn from bad character the courts have in the past distinguished propensity to offend and credibility. This distinction is usually unrealistic. If the jury learn that an accused has shown a propensity to commit criminal acts they may well also conclude that it is more likely that he is guilty and that he is less likely to be telling the truth when he says that he is not. It will be comparatively rare for the case of an accused who has pleaded not guilty not to involve some element that the prosecution suggest is untruthful.

8. Reciting the statutory wording of the gateway by which the evidence was admitted is unlikely to be helpful. The jury should be told in simple language and with reference, where appropriate, to the particular facts of the case, why the bad character may be relevant.

9. Where evidence of a crime or other blameworthy act on the part of the accused is adduced because it bears on a particular issue of fact and the evidence has no bearing on the accused's propensity to commit the offence charged,[84] this should be made plain to the jury.

10. It is highly desirable that the jury should be warned against attaching too much weight to bad character evidence, let alone concluding that he is guilty simply because of his bad character.[85]

Leave

As we have seen section 100(4) of the 2003 Act expressly states that evidence of the bad character of a *non-defendant* 'must not be given without the leave of the court'. There is no equivalent in relation to evidence of the bad character of an *accused* admissible under section 101(1)(c) to (g). However, whether any of the requirements for admissibility in those sub-paragraphs has been met is a question of law for the judge to decide, in appropriate cases only after holding a *voir dire*, and it is submitted that given the potentially irremediable harm of

---

[84] See 487 below, under *Other types of misconduct*.

[85] As to the further principles enunciated and relating to s 103(1)(b) of the Act, see 493 below, under *Bad character evidence under section 101(1)(d) relevant to the credibility of the accused*. The current Judicial Studies Board specimen direction 24 reflects these principles: <http://www.jsboard.co.uk/criminal_law/cbb/index.htm>.

the jury hearing evidence which is later ruled inadmissible, counsel for the prosecution or, as appropriate, the co-accused, before introducing the evidence, will need to satisfy the judge that the statutory requirements are met.

Discretion to exclude

Turning to the issue of discretionary exclusion, in the case of evidence meeting the requirements of either section 101(1)(d) or (g), the court has the discretionary power to exclude it under section 101(3) on the basis of its adverse effect on the fairness of the proceedings. Provided that the judge, in exercising the discretion, has in mind the time factor in section 101(4), the Court of Appeal will not ordinarily interfere with his decision unless there has been some error in principle.[86] If the evidence is inherently incredible, that is likely to be a strong factor against admitting it, but whilst the judge will have regard to the potential weight of the evidence, he should not usurp the jury's function of deciding what evidence is accepted and what rejected.[87] If the evidence is based on information received by a witness from unidentified third parties, by its nature it will be difficult for the accused to meet and therefore should be excluded.[88] It is not an error in principle to admit allegations of misconduct in respect of which the accused was told that he would not be prosecuted.[89]

Section 101(3) is brought into play 'on an application by the accused to exclude' the evidence, wording which seems to preclude the court from exercising the power under the subsection of its own motion. However, bearing in mind the provisions of Article 6 of the European Convention on Human Rights, a judge should if necessary encourage an application to exclude if it appears that admission of the evidence may have such an adverse effect on the fairness of the proceedings that it ought not to admit it.[90] Where the trial judge has used section 101(3) to exclude evidence potentially admissible under section 101(1)(d), that will not prevent him later in the trial from admitting the evidence under section 101(1)(g), because the fairness of the proceedings and the impact on it of admitting the evidence has to be gauged at the time at which the application is made and by reference to the gateway under which admissibility is sought.[91]

The fact that section 101(3) does not apply to section 101(1)(a), (b), and (e) makes perfect sense. In the case of both section 101(1)(a) and (b), there is no need for a discretion to exclude—the accused already has control over whether the evidence is admitted or not. As to section 101(1)(e), which relates to evidence admissible on behalf of a co-accused, the good reason for the absence of a discretionary power to exclude is that a co-accused should be free to adduce any evidence relevant to his case whether or not it prejudices any other accused. The principle was the same, before the coming into force of section 101, in the case of both 'similar fact evidence' tendered by a co-accused and cross-examination of an accused by a co-accused under the 1898 Act.[92]

---

[86] *R v Edwards* [2006] 1 WLR 1524, CA at [75]. See also *R v Malone* [2006] All ER (D) 32 (Jun) CA and *R v Spartley* [2007] All ER (D) 233.

[87] *R v Edwards*, ibid at [82].

[88] *R v Weir* [2006] 1 WLR 1885, CA at [40].

[89] *R v Edwards*, ibid at [76]. See also *R v Nguyen* (2008) 2 Cr App 99, CA, where it was held that it was not unfair to admit evidence of previous assaults which the Crown had decided not to prosecute.

[90] *R v Weir*, ibid.

[91] *R v Edwards*, ibid at [14].

[92] See *Lobban v R* [1995] 2 All ER 602, PC approving the description of this principle appearing in the 3rd edition of this book. However, in rare cases the evidence may now be excluded for failure to comply with the requirement to give notice: see *R v Musone* [2007] 1 WLR 2467, CA 517 below, under **Rules of Court**.

However, the fact that section 101(3) does not apply to section 101(1)(c) and (f) is difficult to justify and raises the question whether evidence otherwise admissible under those sub-paragraphs can be excluded using common law discretionary power or section 78 of the Police and Criminal Evidence Act 1984.[93] As to the former, it is submitted that the general common law discretionary power to exclude prosecution evidence where its prejudicial effect outweighs its probative value may be exercised in respect of evidence of bad character admissible under section 101(1)(c) (if it is to be adduced by the prosecution) and section 101(1)(f) (under which only prosecution evidence is admissible).[94] As noted, when considering section 100 of the 2003 Act, it is unclear whether section 78 of the 1984 Act applies in the case of prosecution evidence of bad character otherwise admissible under the 2003 Act. Two strong arguments support the view that the parliamentary intention was to exclude the operation of section 78. First, there is express provision in Chapter 2 of Part 11 of the 2003 Act, which concerns hearsay evidence, that nothing in that chapter prejudices any power of a court to exclude evidence under section 78.[95] Secondly, if section 78 does apply, section 101(3), the critical words of which mirror those to be found in section 78, is otiose.[96] On the other hand, section 78 is plainly a provision of general application, applying to any evidence on which the prosecution propose to rely, and, it may be argued, should not be taken to cease to apply to particular types of prosecution evidence without express provision to that effect. The balance of case law falls in favour of this position. In *R v Highton*[97] Lord Woolf CJ expressed a preliminary but not concluded view that reliance can be placed on section 78. It was said that pending a ruling to the contrary, judges might make use of section 78, as appropriate, which would avoid any risk of injustice to the accused, and that to do so would be consistent with the result to which the court would come if it complied with its obligations under section 3 of the Human Rights Act 1998 to construe sections 101 and 103 of the 2003 Act in accordance with the European Convention on Human Rights. Although it was observed in *R v Davis*[98] that the operation of section 78 to exclude evidence of an accused's bad character was 'possibly controversial', in *R v O'Dowd*,[99] it was held that section 78 should be considered where section 101(3) was not available. This is consistent with an increasing number of other authorities.[100]

Section 101(1)(a)—evidence admitted by agreement of all the parties

Evidence of the accused's bad character may be admitted under section 101(1)(a) with the consent of all the parties, ie the prosecution, accused, and any co-accused, and without the leave of the court.[101]

---

[93] See Ch 2.

[94] See above at 454, under **Abolition of the common law rules.**

[95] Section 126(2).

[96] Although it has been said that a 'significant difference' is to be found in the mandatory opening words of s 101(3) and s 78 (per Kennedy LJ in *R v Weir* [2006] 1 WLR 1885, CA at [46]), this is a distinction without a difference, as under s 78 a court has no discretion once the condition is, in its view, satisfied: per Thomas LJ in *R v Tirnaveanu* [2007] 1 WLR 3049, at [28].

[97] [2006] 1 Cr App R 125, CA.

[98] [2009] 2 Cr App R 306, CA at [36].

[99] [2009] All ER (D) 103 (May), at [31].

[100] *R v Weir* [2006] 1 WLR 1885; *R v Tirnaveanu* [2007] 1 WLR 3049; *R v B* [2008] EWCA 1850 at [17]. See also *R v Fox* [2009] EWCA Crim 653 at [28].

[101] See *R v Hussain* [2008] EWCA Crim 1117: both an accused and co-accused, running cut-throat defences, had convictions for dishonesty. These were admitted by agreement because, realistically, they were bound to have been admitted in the absence of agreement.

Section 101(1)(b)—evidence admitted by the defendant himself

Section 101(1)(b) permits evidence of the accused's bad character to be admitted by the accused himself without the leave of the court. This option is of limited if any value in cases in which the prosecution have already adduced the evidence by virtue of one of the other sub-paragraphs of section 101(1). However, where the evidence is not admissible as a part of the prosecution case, there are two situations in which the accused may sensibly elect to admit it himself. First, if it is evidence of comparatively minor misconduct, he may adduce it on the basis that otherwise the jurors, especially if they have gained some experience by serving in other cases, might speculate that his character is worse than it is. The second is where he adduces evidence attacking another person's character and therefore brings into play section 101(1)(g), when it may be tactically wiser for him to be frank with the jury and give evidence of his bad character himself, rather than allow the prosecution to elicit evidence on the matter in cross-examination. This may be a particularly sensible course of action where the previous convictions were all based on guilty pleas because however the judge directs the jury about the bad character evidence, there is obvious scope for the defence to say to the jury, in their closing submissions, that the fact that the accused has for the first time pleaded not guilty indicates that his denial on oath ought to be believed.

Under section 101(1)(b), the evidence may be either adduced by the accused himself or may be given in answer to a question asked by the defence in cross-examination, provided that the question was intended to elicit it. Thus if the witness under cross-examination volunteers the evidence of bad character, it is inadmissible and the judge will need to direct the jury to ignore it or, if no direction is capable of neutralizing the prejudice to the accused and there is therefore a real risk of injustice occurring, exercise his discretion to discharge the jury and order a re-trial.[102]

Section 101(1)(c)—important explanatory evidence

Under section 101(1)(c), which may be used by either the prosecution or a co-accused, evidence of the accused's bad character is admissible if it is 'important explanatory evidence'. Section 102 provides that:

> For the purposes of section 101(1)(c) evidence is important explanatory evidence if—
> (a) without it, the court or jury would find it impossible or difficult properly to understand other evidence in the case, and
> (b) its value for understanding the case as a whole is substantial.

Section 101(c) is closely based on the recommendation of the Law Commission except that it lacks the safeguard contained in the Commission's draft clause that the court be satisfied either that the evidence carries no risk of prejudice to the accused or that the value of the evidence for understanding the case as a whole is such that, taking account of the risk of prejudice, the interests of justice nevertheless require it to be admissible.

This definition in section 102 is the same as that contained in section 100(2)(a), which applies in relation to evidence of a non-defendant's bad character. As noted in that context, the definition is a slightly different formulation of the common law rule permitting the use of background evidence, notwithstanding that it reveals the bad character or criminal disposition of the accused, where it is part of a continual background or history which is relevant to the

---

[102] See 463 above under **Evidence admitted through inadvertence**.

offence charged and without the totality of which the account placed before the jury would be incomplete or incomprehensible.[103] If the matter to which the evidence relates is largely comprehensible without the explanatory evidence, the evidence will be inadmissible. Explanatory evidence, to be admissible, must also satisfy section 102(b), ie its value for understanding the case as a whole must be 'substantial', as opposed to minor or trivial. In *R v Edwards*,[104] a case of robbery and possession of an imitation firearm, the statement of an identification witness that she was able to recognize the accused because she had brought heroin from him every other day for a year or so, was held to have been properly admitted as important explanatory evidence in relation to the basis of her identification. However, no convincing reason was given for rejecting the submission that, given the prejudice arising from the allegation of heroin dealing, the statement should have been edited so as to disclose the frequency of the encounters, but not the reason for them.

In *R v D*,[105] it was emphasized that the test for admissibility under section 101(1)(c) should be applied cautiously where it was also possible to argue that evidence showed propensity. The accused was charged with murdering his common law wife whom he had accused of having an affair. Using section 101(1)(c), the prosecution adduced the evidence of a former girlfriend that some 20 years previously he had acted with jealous aggression and made threats to kill. The Court of Appeal held that the evidence did not have a substantial value for understanding the case, and indeed could have undermined the jury's understanding of the accused's relationship with his wife and the events leading up to her death. The evidence was really evidence of propensity and it should not have been allowed to 'slide in' as explanatory evidence. However, the decision in *R v D*[106] should not be taken to mean that evidence capable of showing propensity will not be admitted under section 101(1)(c). In *R v Ladds*[107] the accused stabbed her partner, F, and was convicted of wounding with intent. Her defence was that F had inflicted the wounds on himself. The Court of Appeal held that evidence of previous 'strikingly similar' incidents where F had suffered injuries and reported that they had been inflicted by the accused was properly admissible as important explanatory evidence.[108]

Since section 101(1)(c) in effect gives statutory force to a doctrine established at common law, it is submitted that the common law authorities will continue to provide valuable guidance, notwithstanding that they reveal an occasional tendency to admit evidence with a high risk of prejudice but providing comparatively limited assistance to the jury in understanding the other evidence in the case. The authorities show that the evidence often relates to other acts done or statements made by the accused revealing his desire to commit, or reason for committing, the offence charged.[109] Similarly in *R v Ball*[110] Lord Atkinson was of the view that in an ordinary prosecution for murder evidence is admissible of previous acts or words of the accused to show that he entertained feelings of enmity towards the deceased, and although

---

[103] Per Purchas LJ in *R v Pettman*, 2 May 1985, CA, unreported.

[104] [2006] 1 WLR 1524, CA.

[105] (2008) 172 JP 358.

[106] Ibid.

[107] [2009] EWCA Crim 1249 at [12]–[15].

[108] It would have been 'positively misleading' for the jury not to have heard about these incidents since the accused had adduced evidence of F having attempted suicide in support of her defence that he had inflicted the injuries on himself.

[109] See, for example, *R v Bond* [1906] 2 KB 389.

[110] [1911] AC 47, HL at 68.

R v Ball was disapproved in *R v Berry*,[111] it was affirmed in *R v Williams*[112] and reaffirmed in *R v Phillips*.[113] In *R v Phillips*,[114] the accused denied being the murderer of his wife and evidence was admitted of the unhappy state of the marriage over a number of years.[115]

However, evidence will not be admitted under the principle if it relates to events so distant in time from the crime as to be of little if any probative value. For example in *R v Phillips* it was held that it would have been quite wrong to have admitted the evidence of a stormy relationship eight years before the crime was committed, especially if thereafter it was a happy marriage.[116] Similarly in *R v Dolan*,[117] where the accused was charged with the murder of his baby son by shaking him forcefully, it was held to be irrelevant that in the past he had lost his temper and shown violence towards inanimate objects. The touchstones of the principle, said the court, were relevance and necessity.[118] In that case it was also made clear that background evidence needs to be distinguished from so-called 'similar fact evidence'[119] and should not be used as a vehicle for smuggling in otherwise inadmissible similar fact evidence. Equally, where background evidence is properly admitted, the jury will often need to be directed carefully as to the use to which the evidence may and may not be put. *R v Sawoniuk*[120] furnishes a good example. The accused was convicted of the murder of Jews in Belarus in 1942. The Court of Appeal upheld the decision of the trial judge to admit evidence of his participation in a 'search and kill' operation against Jewish survivors of an earlier massacre. The evidence was relevant to the identification evidence in the case, but it was also held to be admissible as background evidence because, as Lord Bingham CJ put it, 'criminal charges cannot fairly be judged in a factual vacuum'.[121] The court noted that the evidence was not similar fact evidence and that the trial judge had adequately directed the jury not to follow a forbidden line of reasoning, ie that by reason of his earlier actions the accused was more likely to have committed the offences with which he was charged.

The point has already been made that evidence of misconduct 'which has to do with the alleged facts of the offence' and is therefore admissible by virtue of section 98(a) will often be difficult to distinguish from background evidence admissible under section 101(1)(c). The overlap will typically arise where the misconduct and the facts of the offence are part of one continuous transaction. *R v Ellis*[122] is an old but good example. A shop assistant was charged with stealing six marked shillings from a till. Evidence was given that on several occasions on the day in question

---

[111] (1986) Cr App R 7, CA.

[112] (1986) 84 Cr App R 299, CA.

[113] [2003] 2 Cr App R 528, CA per Dyson LJ at 534. See also *R v Campbell*, 20 Dec 1984, CA, unreported; *R v Giannette* [1996] Crim LR 722, CA; and *R v Williams* (1986) 84 Cr App R 299, CA. Cf also *R v Berry* (1986) 83 Cr App R 7, CA.

[114] [2003] 2 Cr App R 528, CA.

[115] See also *R v Asif* (1985) 82 Cr App R 123, CA, concerning the failure to comply with statutory VAT requirements. For further examples, see *R v Carrington* [1990] Crim LR 330, CA; *R v Sidhu* (1993) 98 Cr App R 59, CA; *R v Fulcher* [1995] 2 Cr App R 251, CA; and *R v Shaw* [2003] Crim LR 278. See also, *sed quaere*, *R v Underwood* [1999] Crim LR 227, CA.

[116] [2003] 2 Cr App R 528 at 536. See also *R v Butler* [1999] Crim LR 835, CA, where the events had taken place three years before the offence charged.

[117] [2003] 1 Cr App R 281, CA.

[118] Ibid at 285–6.

[119] See also *R v M (T)* [2000] 1 WLR 421, CA.

[120] [2002] 2 Cr App R 220, CA.

[121] At 234.

[122] (1826) 6 B&C 145.

he was seen to take money from the till and that, on his arrest, he was found in possession of a sum of money equal to that missing from the till and made up of the six marked shillings and some other unmarked money. The evidence, insofar as it tended to show that the assistant had stolen unmarked money as well as the marked money, was held to be admissible on the grounds that it went to show the history of the till from the time when the marked money was put into it up to the time when it was found in the possession of the accused. Bayley J said:

> Generally speaking it is not competent to a prosecutor to prove a man guilty of one felony, by proving him guilty of another unconnected felony; but where several felonies are connected together, and form part of one entire transaction, then the one is evidence to show the character of the other.[123]

Since the test in section 101(1)(c) does not require the court to balance the value of the evidence to be admitted against the prejudice to the accused, then when the *prosecution* seek to admit evidence under the sub-paragraph, as will usually be the case, there is obvious scope for use of the common law discretionary power to exclude, assuming, as submitted earlier, that that power subsists in relation to prosecution evidence admissible under section 101.[124] The court should exercise the discretion where the prejudicial effect of the evidence is out of all proportion to its probative value, as when it relates to particularly serious misconduct on the part of the accused and without it the jury would find it difficult, but perhaps not especially difficult, properly to understand other evidence in the case.

Section 101(1)(d)—prosecution evidence relevant to an important matter in issue between the defendant and the prosecution

Under the carefully wrought proposals of the Law Commission, there were separate clauses governing admissibility of evidence of the bad character of the accused going to the issue of his guilt and admissibility of evidence of his bad character going to the issue of his credibility.[125] This distinction was borne of a recognition that the two issues usually arise at different stages of the trial and that the relevant factors for the purpose of deciding the admissibility of each type of evidence are different. Under the Commission's proposals, evidence of the bad character of the accused would have been admissible on the issue of guilt if (i) it had 'substantial probative value' in relation to a matter of substantial importance in the context of the case as a whole; and (ii) if the court was satisfied that (a) the evidence carried no risk of prejudice to the accused; or (b) that, taking into account the risk of prejudice, the interests of justice nevertheless required the evidence to be admissible in view of its degree of probative value in relation to the matter in issue, any other evidence that could be given on the matter, and how important the matter was in the context of the case as a whole. In assessing the probative value of the evidence, the court also had to have regard to a variety of other specified factors. Concerning evidence of bad character going to the issue of the credibility of the accused, it was only to be admitted where an attack had been made on the truthfulness of another. In this context also, the factors to be taken into consideration were set out in detail.

Section 101(1)(d) of the 2003 Act reflects a markedly different and less sophisticated approach. It is a single 'gateway' providing for the admissibility of prosecution evidence going

---

[123] See also *R v Rearden* (1864) 4 F&F 76.
[124] See 465 above, under **Section 101 of the Criminal Justice Act 2003.**
[125] Law Com No 273 (2001) Draft Bill, cl 8 and cl 9.

to the guilt of the accused as well as evidence going to his credibility. Under subsection (1)(d), prosecution evidence of the accused's bad character is admissible if 'it is relevant to an important matter in issue between the defendant and the prosecution'.[126] The test is one of simple relevance or probative value.[127] There is no requirement of enhanced relevance or 'substantial probative value' as there is under section 101(1)(e) and, in relation to the bad character of someone other than the accused, under section 100(1)(b). The evidence, however, must be relevant to an important matter in issue between the accused and the prosecution. The matters in issue between the accused and the prosecution are, of course, the disputed facts and issues of credit or credibility. In a sense, all such matters in issue between the accused and the prosecution are important, but 'important matter' is defined in the Act as 'a matter of substantial importance in the context of the case as a whole',[128] a definition which, it is submitted, will only operate to exclude evidence relevant to matters in issue which are of minor or marginal significance. The overall effect of section 101(1)(d), therefore, is to permit the introduction of prosecution evidence of the bad character of the accused whenever it is relevant to any of the main matters in issue between the prosecution and the defence, and is not limited to propensity. In a case of possession with intent to supply Class A drugs, for example, where the matter in issue is the accused's knowledge of the drugs, a previous conviction for importing such drugs could be relevant to rebut his defence.[129] Similarly, in a case of dangerous driving where the issue is whether a police officer has correctly recognized an accused, previous convictions for driving whilst disqualified could be relevant to the issue.[130] The breadth of the new provision means that the prosecution will seek to admit much bad character evidence that in the past would have been inadmissible. In consequence, defence applications to exclude under section 101(3) will become a regular feature of most trials.[131]

Section 101(1)(d) is supplemented by section 103, which makes it clear that 'matters in issue' between the accused and the prosecution can include (a) the question whether the accused has a propensity to commit offences of the kind with which he is charged and (b) the question whether he has a propensity to be untruthful. For the purposes of exposition, it will be convenient to consider these two issues separately, albeit, in the case of the former, as part of the wider issue of bad character relevant to the guilt of the accused.

Bad character evidence under section 101(1)(d) relevant to the guilt of the accused

Evidence of propensity under section 103 of the Criminal Justice Act 2003. Section 103(1) and (2) of the 2003 Act provides as follows:

(1) For the purposes of section 101(1)(d) the matters in issue between the defendant and the prosecution include—

---

[126] Only prosecution evidence is admissible under s 101(1)(d): s 103(6).

[127] *R v Weir* [2006] 1 WLR 1885, CA at [36].

[128] Section 112(1).

[129] *R v Colliard* [2008] All ER (D) 127 (Jun). See also *R v Jordan* [2009] All ER (D) 210, where convictions for robbery and possession of a firearm were relevant to the issue of whether the accused knew about the presence of a gun in the car in which he was travelling or was an innocent passenger.

[130] *R v Spittle* [2009] RTR 14.

[131] For a study of the number and characteristics of bad character applications in selected Crown Courts and magistrates' courts see Morgan Harris Burrows LPP for the Office of Criminal Justice Reform, *Research into the impact of bad character provisions*, <https://www.justice.gov.uk/publications/research.htm>.

    (a) the question whether the defendant has a propensity to commit offences of the kind with which he is charged, except where his having such a propensity makes it no more likely that he is guilty of the offence;

    (b) the question whether the defendant has a propensity to be untruthful, except where it is not suggested that the defendant's case is untruthful in any respect.

(2) Where subsection (1)(a) applies, a defendant's propensity to commit offences of the kind with which he is charged may (without prejudice to any other way of doing so) be established by evidence that he has been convicted of—

    (a) an offence of the same description as the one with which he is charged, or

    (b) an offence of the same category as the one with which he is charged.

(3) Subsection (2) does not apply in the case of a particular defendant if the court is satisfied, by reason of the length of time since the conviction or for any other reason, that it would be unjust for it to apply in his case.

(4) For the purposes of subsection (2)—

    (a) two offences are of the same description as each other if the statement of the offences in a written charge or indictment would, in each case, be in the same terms;

    (b) two offences are of the same category as each other if they belong to the same category of offences prescribed for the purposes of this section by an order made by the Secretary of State.

(5) A category prescribed by an order under subsection 4(b) must consist of offences of the same type.

(6) Only prosecution evidence is admissible under s 101(1)(d).

The inclusionary nature of section 103(1) indicates that the matters in issue to which evidence of bad character may be relevant are not confined to those specified in the subsection.

As to section 103(1)(a), it is conceptually confusing and its meaning is, in part, obscure. It is conceptually confusing because propensity of the kind to which it refers has never before been treated as a matter in issue. In the past, propensity, or to be more accurate, admissible evidence of propensity, has been the means of establishing the matters in issue. Under the subsection, in any case in which the prosecution seek to rely upon section 101(1)(d) in relation to the issue of guilt, propensity will always be deemed to be a matter in issue, provided that it is of the kind referred to in the subsection. However, the prosecution will still need to establish that the propensity in question is an 'important' matter in issue, ie 'a matter of substantial importance in the context of the case as a whole'[132] because section 103 is not free-standing but operates 'for the purposes of section 101(1)(d)'. If the prosecution can establish such importance, then subject to section 101(3) and, it is submitted, the common law discretion to exclude on the basis of prejudicial effect outweighing probative value, the propensity may be established under section 103(2) by evidence of a relevant conviction or in 'any other way'. Insofar as section 103(2) permits proof by evidence of a conviction, it is submitted that it too is a deeming provision, in the sense that evidence of the conviction is to be treated as, in the words of section 101(1)(d), 'evidence of the defendant's bad character' that 'is relevant to an important matter in issue', ie the propensity.

The meaning of the exception within section 103(1)(a)—'except where his having such a propensity makes it no more likely that he is guilty of the offence'—is obscure, given that all too often evidence of propensity to commit offences of the kind charged will make it more probable that the accused committed the offence charged, albeit that in many cases it will

---

[132] Section 112(1).

have only limited or very limited probative force. The Explanatory Notes to the Act furnish only one illustration: where there is no dispute about the facts of the case and the question is whether those facts constitute the offence, 'for example, in a homicide case, whether the defendant's actions caused death'.[133]

Questions of proof. Section 103(2) provides that where the matter in issue is whether the accused has a propensity to commit offences of the kind with which he is charged, the propensity can be proved by evidence that he has been convicted of an offence of the kind referred to in either section 103(2)(a) or (b). This is subject to section 103(3), whereby evidence of the conviction should not be given if the court is satisfied that it would be unjust to do so 'by reason of the length of time since the conviction or for any other reason'. Bearing in mind that section 103 exists 'for the purposes of section 101(1)(d)', that any evidence admissible under section 101(1)(d) is subject to the discretionary power to exclude contained in section 101(3) and (4), and that those subsections contain a test for exclusion similar to, but obviously cast in different language from, the test in section 103(3), there appears to be a large degree of unnecessary overlap between those subsections and section 103(3).

The wording of section 103(2) indicates that in at least some cases, at any rate, proof of the mere fact of the conviction or convictions may be used to establish propensity. In other cases, however, the propensity will be established not simply by the fact of the conviction, but by evidence of the conduct which resulted in the conviction. In the latter type of case, the prosecution will doubtless use section 103(2) in conjunction with section 74(3) and section 75 of the Police and Criminal Evidence Act 1984.[134] Under section 74(3), as amended by the 2003 Act, where evidence of the fact that the accused has committed an offence is admissible and proof is given that he has been convicted of the offence, there is a rebuttable presumption that he committed the offence. Under section 75, where evidence of a conviction is admissible by virtue of section 74, then without prejudice to the admissibility of any other evidence for the purpose of identifying the facts on which the conviction was based, the contents of, inter alia, the information or indictment shall be admissible for that purpose. Where reliance is placed on specific facts relating to modus operandi beyond those contained in the information or indictment, and they are disputed, then they need to be established by calling a witness to give first-hand evidence or by adducing admissible hearsay evidence in that regard.[135] However, this runs the risk of 'satellite litigation' during a trial, which could distract from the real issues and unnecessarily lengthen proceedings.[136]

Section 103(2) permits propensity to be proved by evidence of a conviction of an offence falling within either section 103(2)(a) or (b). Subsection (2)(a) refers to an offence of the same description as the one with which the accused is charged. Section 103(4)(a) makes clear that an offence will only be 'of the same description' if the statement of the offence in a written charge or indictment would, in each case, be the same. Thus, as it says in the Explanatory Notes to the Act, the test relates to the particular law that has been broken, rather than the circumstances

---

[133] Para 371.

[134] See Ch 21. See, in the case of s 74(3), *R v O'Dowd* [2009] All ER (D) 103 (May), CA at [71].

[135] *R v Humphris* (2005) 169 JP 441, CA and *R v Ainscough* [2006] Crim LR 635, CA.

[136] *R v O'Dowd*, ibid. See *R v McKenzie* [2008] RTR 277, where the Court of Appeal deprecated the admission of evidence of collateral issues which could add to the length and cost of a trial and complicate the issues the jury had to decide. See also *R v McAllister* (2009) 1 Cr App R 10.

in which it was committed.[137] Section 103(2)(b) refers to an offence of the same category as the one with which the accused is charged. By reason of section 103(4)(b) and section 103(5), an offence will be 'of the same category' if it falls within a category consisting of offences of the same type drawn up by the Secretary of State in secondary legislation. Two categories have been drawn up, a 'Theft Category' and a 'Sexual Offences (persons under the age of 16) Category'.[138] The first includes offences of theft, robbery, burglary, handling stolen goods, etc. The second includes offences of rape of a person under the age of 16, assault by penetration of a person under the age of 16, sexual assault on a person under the age of 16, etc.[139]

For the purposes of sections 101 and 103, evidence of propensity may relate to events that occurred after the offence charged and not just those that occurred before it.[140]

According to *R v Chopra*,[141] whereas at common law evidence of the accused's propensity to offend in the manner charged was prima facie inadmissible, under the 2003 Act it is prima facie admissible. In *R v Hanson*[142] the Court of Appeal laid down the following important principles relating to the admissibility of evidence of propensity under section 103.

1. Where propensity to commit the offence is relied upon by reference to section 101(1)(d) and section 103(1)(a), there are three questions to be considered: (i) whether the history of conviction(s) establishes a propensity to commit offences of the kind charged; (ii) whether that propensity make it more likely that the accused committed the offence charged; and (iii) whether it is unjust to rely on the conviction(s) of the same description or category and, in any event, whether the proceedings will be unfair if they are admitted.

2. In referring to offences of the same description or category, section 103(2) is not exhaustive of the types of misconduct which may be relied upon to show evidence of propensity to commit offences of the kind charged.[143] Nor, however, is it necessarily sufficient in order to show such propensity that a conviction is of the same description or type as that charged.

3. There is no minimum number of events necessary to demonstrate such a propensity. The fewer the number of convictions, the weaker the evidence of propensity is likely to be. A single previous conviction for an offence of the same description or category will often not show propensity, but may do so where, for example, it shows a tendency to unusual behaviour, or where its circumstances demonstrate probative force in relation to the offence charged.

4. Circumstances demonstrating probative force are not confined to those sharing striking similarity, but if the modus operandi has significant features shared by the offence charged, it may show propensity. When considering what is just under section

---

[137] Para 373.

[138] See Criminal Justice Act 2003 (Categories of Offences) Order 2004, SI 2004/3346.

[139] Both categories also include an offence of (a) aiding, abetting, counselling, procuring or inciting the commission of an offence specified; or (b) attempting to commit an offence specified.

[140] *R v Adenusi* [2006] Crim LR 929, CA.

[141] [2007] 1 Cr App R 225, CA.

[142] [2005] All ER (D) 380, CA.

[143] See *R v Johnson* [2009] 2 Cr App Rep 101: conspiracy to burgle is not an offence of the same description or category as the substantive offence of burglary, but may be admissible to show evidence of propensity.

103(3), and the fairness of the proceedings under section 101(3), the judge may, along with other factors, take into consideration the degree of similarity between the previous conviction and the offence charged (albeit that they are both within the same description or prescribed category). This does not mean, however, that what used to be referred to as striking similarity must be shown before convictions become admissible.

5. The judge may also take into consideration the respective gravity of the past and present offences.[144]

6. The judge must also consider the strength of the prosecution case. If there is no, or very little, other evidence against an accused, it is unlikely to be just to admit his previous convictions, whatever they are.

7. In principle, if there is a substantial gap between the dates of the commission of, and conviction for, earlier offence(s), the date of commission is, generally, to be regarded as being of more significance than the date of conviction when assessing admissibility. Old convictions with no special features shared with the offence charged are likely seriously to affect the fairness of proceedings adversely unless, despite their age, it can properly be said that they show a continuing propensity.

8. It will often be necessary, before determining admissibility, and even when considering offences of the same description or category, to examine each individual conviction rather than merely to look at the nature of the offence or at the accused's record as a whole.

9. The sentence passed will not normally be probative or admissible at the behest of the Crown.

10. Where past events are disputed, the judge must take care not to permit the trial unreasonably to be diverted into an investigation of matters not charged on the indictment.

11. The Crown needs to have decided, at the time of giving notice of the application, whether it proposes to rely simply on the fact of conviction or also upon the circumstances of it. It is to be expected that the relevant circumstances of previous convictions will, generally, be capable of agreement, and that, subject to the trial judge's ruling as to admissibility, they will be put before the jury by way of admission. Even where the circumstances are genuinely in dispute, it is to be expected that the minimum indisputable facts will thus be admitted. It will be very rare indeed for it to be necessary for the judge to hear evidence before ruling on admissibility under the Act.

12. In any case in which evidence of bad character is admitted to show propensity, whether to commit offences or to be untruthful, the judge in summing-up should warn the jury clearly against placing undue reliance on previous convictions. Evidence of bad character cannot be used simply to bolster a weak case or to prejudice the minds of the jury against the defendant. Without purporting to frame a specimen direction, in particular, a jury should be directed: (i) that they should not conclude that an accused is guilty or untruthful merely because he has previous convictions; (ii) that, although

[144] Sometimes, therefore, a ruling on admissibility should be deferred until all of the prosecution evidence has been adduced: *R v Gyima* [2007] Crim LR 890, CA.

the convictions may show a propensity, this does not mean that he committed the offence charged or has been untruthful in the case; (iii) that whether they in fact show a propensity is for them to decide; (iv) that they must take into account what an accused has said about his previous convictions; and, (v) that, although they are entitled, if they find propensity is shown, to take this into account when determining guilt, propensity is only one relevant factor and they must assess its significance in the light of all the other evidence in the case.

The principles in paragraphs (3) and (7) were refined and developed in *R v M*,[145] where it was held that on a charge of possession of a firearm with intent to cause fear of violence, the issue being the correctness of the identification of the accused, evidence of a previous conviction, some 20 years before, for possession of a firearm without a certificate, had been improperly admitted under section 101(1)(d). It was held that whilst there might be cases where the factual circumstances of a single previous conviction, even as long ago as 20 years, might be relevant to showing a propensity, such cases would be rare and would be those where the previous conviction showed some very special and distinctive feature, such as a predilection on the part of the accused for a highly unusual form of sexual activity, or some arcane or highly specialized knowledge relevant to the offence charged. Where there were less distinctive features in common, some evidence of the propensity manifesting itself in the intervening period would be necessary in order to render the previous conviction admissible as evidence of a continuing propensity.

Section 103(2) states that it is without prejudice to other ways of establishing an accused's propensity to commit offences of the kind with which he is charged. Thus propensity may be established by evidence of an offence other than an offence 'of the same description' or 'of the same category' within section 103(2); the purpose of that subsection is simply to make it easier to admit evidence of convictions of the kind to which it refers.[146] It may also be established by evidence of misconduct or disposition towards misconduct that did not result in a conviction, in which case it may be proved, subject to the rules of evidence generally, in the same way as any other relevant facts. Concerning misconduct, there are three types of case. The first is where the misconduct did not result in a prosecution, including cases in which the accused was formally cautioned or previously asked to have offences taken into consideration.[147] The second is where the misconduct did result in a prosecution, but the outcome was an acquittal.[148] The third arises out of section 112(2) of the 2003 Act, which provides that:

(2) Where a defendant is charged with two or more offences in the same criminal proceedings, this Chapter (except section 101(3)) has effect as if each offence were charged in separate proceedings; and references to the offence with which the defendant is charged are to be read accordingly.

In *R v Chopra*[149] it was held that this subsection means that where an accused faces two or more counts on an indictment, the evidence which goes to suggest that he committed count

---

[145] [2007] Crim LR 637, CA.

[146] *R v Weir* [2006] 1 WLR 1885, CA at [7].

[147] *R v Weir*, ibid at [7].

[148] See *R v Z* [2002] 2 AC 483, HL, considered at 454 above, under **'Bad character' defined** and *R v L* [2007] All ER (D) 81 (Jul).

[149] [2007] 1 Cr App R 225, CA.

2 is, so far as count 1 is concerned, bad character evidence and can be admitted in relation to count 1 if, but only if, it passes through one of the section 101 gateways; and that the same applies vice versa and however many counts there may be. A similar principle applies where no single piece of evidence is enough to convict the accused of any of the offences charged, and the important matter in issue is not whether the accused had a propensity to commit offences or to be untruthful, but whether the circumstantial evidence linking him to the offences, when viewed as a whole, points to his guilt of each offence.[150]

It remains to stress that even in cases where the misconduct did result in a conviction, in some such cases, as already indicated, propensity can only be established by going beyond the fact of the conviction and introducing evidence of the misconduct which resulted in the conviction. Where, in such a case, the conviction was based on a guilty plea, it is submitted that under the Act, as at common law, it would not be unfair for the prosecution to prove the plea, together with confessions made by the accused in police interviews. Although this denies the accused the opportunity to cross-examine the victim or other witnesses to the offence of which he stands convicted, it is fairer to the accused to adduce only what he admitted rather than to call the victim or other witnesses, who may give additional prejudicial evidence.[151]

As at common law,[152] if evidence of the accused's misconduct is admissible on the issue of his guilt, it is no bar to its admissibility that it is disputed and that the jury may, in the event, reject it. Thus although bad character evidence may take the form of conclusive or indisputable evidence, it may also take the form of unproved allegations, as when, as we have seen, propensity is advanced by way of multiple counts none of which has been proved, their proof being a question for the jury.[153] Equally, however, it is submitted that the evidence must be cogent enough to lead a reasonable jury to conclude, as a possibility, that the misconduct did in fact occur. In *Harris v DPP*,[154] a common law authority, the evidence was insufficiently cogent for these purposes. H, a police constable, charged and tried on an indictment containing eight counts of larceny, was acquitted on the first seven but convicted on the eighth. The offences occurred in May, June, and July 1951 and the evidence showed that on each occasion someone had entered, by the same method, the same office in Bradford market and stolen only part of the money which could have been taken. On the first seven counts, the only evidence connecting H with the offences was that none of them had occurred when he was on leave and on each occasion he might have been on solitary duty in the vicinity of the market. Concerning the eighth count, H was on duty in the market at the relevant time and was found by detectives near the office shortly after the sounding of a burglar alarm. The stolen money was found hidden in a nearby bin. The House of Lords quashed the conviction because the judge had failed to warn the jury that the evidence on the first seven counts could not confirm the eighth charge. As Lord Morton observed, H was not proved to have been near the office or even in the market at the time when the first seven thefts occurred.[155] The need

[150] *R v Wallace* [2008] 1 WLR 572, CA. See also *R v Freeman* [2009] 1 Cr App R 137, CA, where evidence relating to two or more counts in the same indictment was 'cross-admissible'.
[151] See *R v Bedford* (1990) 93 Cr App R 113, CA.
[152] See *R v Rance and Herron* (1975) 62 Cr App R 118, CA.
[153] *R v Chopra* [2007] 1 Cr App R 225, CA at [15].
[154] [1952] AC 694.
[155] Cf *R v Mansfield* (1977) 65 Cr App R 276, CA. See also *R v Lunt* (1986) 85 Cr App R 241, CA (similar fact evidence provided by an accomplice) and *R v Seaman* (1978) 67 Cr App R 234, CA.

for a sufficient degree of cogency is also illustrated by *R v McKenzie*.[156] On a charge of causing death by dangerous driving, evidence was admitted as 'indicative of a propensity to drive in a chancy way'. This included evidence from his driving instructor that, five years before, his driving was generally aggressive and overconfident. It was held that this evidence should not have been admitted as it was very general in character when the accused was a 20-year-old learner driver. However, other evidence was sufficiently cogent to be admissible, including evidence from his former girlfriend that he habitually drove fast and had once overtaken a long line of traffic following a tractor, cut in front of the tractor and immediately made a sharp left turn. This showed a propensity to drive aggressively and in a manner which involved taking dangerous risks.

Examples of evidence of propensity to commit the offence charged.   In *R v Brima*[157] it was made clear that the task of the judge is not to determine whether misconduct does establish propensity, an issue for the jury, but whether it has the capacity to do so. That question, together with the issue whether the propensity makes it more likely that the accused committed the offence charged, is fact-specific. In *R v Brima* itself, a case of murder by stabbing, it was held that evidence of B's two previous convictions, one for assault occasioning actual bodily harm involving a stabbing, another for robbery involving the holding of a knife to the throat of the victim, were capable of establishing propensity to commit offences of the kind charged and did make it more likely that B had committed the offence charged. In *R v Highton*[158] in the case of one appellant it was held that previous convictions, including convictions for offences of violence and the possession of offensive weapons provided evidence of propensity to commit offences of the kind charged, which included kidnapping and robbery; but in the case of another appellant it was said that evidence of heroin use was not admissible under section 101(1)(d) on a charge of cultivating a controlled drug, the critical issue in the case being whether the appellant was engaged in cultivation of the drug. In *R v Beverley*[159] a case of conspiracy to import cocaine, where the issue was whether B, in driving the car in which the drugs were found, was a knowing participant, it was doubted whether B's two previous convictions, assuming that they established propensity, made it more likely that B committed the offence charged. One was for simple possession of cannabis. The other was for possession of cannabis with intent to supply, a crime committed a long time earlier and which concerned a form of dealing different in nature and scale from the conspiracy charged. In *R v Lawson*[160] it was not disputed that a previous conviction for wounding was incapable of showing a propensity to commit manslaughter because, on the facts, the manslaughter was a different kind of misconduct and was recklessly dangerous rather than aggressive.[161]

Similar fact cases.   Evidence of misconduct may derive its probative force on the basis that the similarities in the evidence of the prosecution witnesses are such that, in the absence of collusion or contamination, they must be telling the truth, such is the unlikelihood of them telling the same untruth.

[156] [2008] RTR 277.
[157] [2007] 1 Cr App R 316, CA.
[158] [2006] 1 Cr App R 125, CA.
[159] [2006] Crim LR 1064, CA.
[160] [2007] 1 Cr App R 178, CA.
[161] For examples of evidence of propensity from the authorities decided prior to the 2003 Act, see *R v Straffen* [1952] 2 QB 911 and *R v Ball* [1911] AC 47, HL.

In *R v Chopra*[162] the indictment alleged that C, a dentist, had indecently touched three teenage patients. In each case the complainant alleged that C had deliberately placed his hand on her breast and squeezed it and in each case C denied that he had done any such thing. The Court of Appeal upheld the judge's ruling that the evidence of each complainant could be used by the jury to support that of another, providing that the possibility of collusion or contamination between them was excluded.[163] It was held that the evidence was cross-admissible under section 101(1)(d), being relevant, in the case of each count, to the important matter in issue whether there was an offence committed by C or no offence at all. The critical question in such a case is whether the evidence of each complainant is capable of establishing propensity to commit offences of the kind charged. Not all evidence of other misbehaviour will do so; there has to be a sufficient similarity or connection between the facts of the several allegations to make it more likely that each allegation is true; and, as at common law, the likelihood or unlikelihood of innocent coincidence will be a relevant and sometimes critical test. For example, one kind of assault may fail to be capable of establishing a propensity to commit a different kind of assault. However, the answer to the question will not *necessarily* be the same as it would have been before the common law rules were abolished, because the test now is the simple test of relevance; there is no requirement of enhanced probative value. In the instant case, it was held that there was sufficient connection and similarity between the allegations to make them capable of establishing a propensity occasionally to molest young female patients in the course of examination and to make it more likely that each allegation was true.[164] In response to C's contention that in the case of a dentist it is interference with the breasts which is likely to be alleged if false accusations of indecency are made, since that is the area to which his hands are nearest, the Court of Appeal made two points. First, that when considering admissibility, the judge is required to assume that the evidence is truthful unless no jury could reasonably believe it.[165] Secondly, propensity to commit an offence remains so even in the case of a common offence or one which can readily be imagined by someone bent on making a false allegation. As the court observed, even before the 2003 Act the suggestion that similar fact evidence had to go beyond the so-called stock in trade of the sexual offender had been discredited.[166]

In *R v Chopra*[167] the court observed that the right way to deal with the new law was not first to ask what would have been the position under the old. However, it went on to say that it had no doubt that some, perhaps many, of the considerations of relevance and fairness relevant at common law in the 'similar fact' cases would continue to arise and that some of the answers might be the same. It is instructive, therefore, to consider, if only in outline, some of the relevant principles established at common law.

At common law evidence of misconduct was admissible where relevant to the question whether the acts constituting the crime were designed or accidental or to rebut a defence

---

[162] [2007] 1 Cr App R 225, CA.

[163] In cases in which no collusion is suggested, it may still be important to direct the jury about the dangers of innocent contamination of the evidence of the complainants, as when, eg, they have talked together about their encounters with the accused: *R v Lamb* [2007] EWCA Crim 1766.

[164] See also, at common law, *R v Sims* [1946] KB 531, CCA; *R v Bedford* (1990) 93 Cr App R 113, CA at 116; and *R v Venn* [2003] All ER (D) 207 (Feb) at [35].

[165] See s 109 under **Rules of Court** at 517 below.

[166] See *R v P* [1991] 3 All ER 337, HL.

[167] Ibid at [12].

which was fairly open to the accused.[168] Much of the evidence admitted was similar fact evidence properly so called, ie evidence of facts bearing a similarity to the facts to be established by the prosecution in order to prove the offence with which the accused was charged. In some of the cases the similar facts were *strikingly* similar either to the facts of the offence or to the circumstances surrounding the commission of the offence. One of the best-known examples of evidence of facts bearing a *striking* similarity to the facts of the offence charged is *R v Smith*,[169] the case of the 'brides in the bath'. Smith was convicted of the murder of a woman with whom he had recently gone through a ceremony of marriage. He sought to explain that the death had resulted from an epileptic fit. Evidence was admitted of the subsequent deaths of two other women with whom he had gone through a ceremony of marriage. The following similarities existed in the evidence relating to the three deaths: in each case Smith stood to gain financially by the woman's death; he had informed a doctor that the woman suffered from epileptic fits; the bathroom door would not lock; and the woman was found drowned in the bath. The Court of Criminal Appeal held that the evidence had been properly admitted. Lord Reading CJ approved the following direction of the trial judge as to why the evidence was admissible:[170]

> If you find an accident which benefits a person and you find that the person has been sufficiently fortunate to have that accident happen to him a number of times, benefiting him each time, you draw a very strong, frequently irresistible inference that the occurrence of so many accidents benefiting him is such a coincidence that it cannot have happened unless it was design.

Many of the cases involved indictments with two (or more) counts, the issue being whether the prosecution evidence on one of the counts was strikingly similar to the prosecution evidence on the other and therefore could be treated as evidence relevant to guilt on the other. The leading authority in this respect was *DPP v Boardman*.[171] The appellant, the headmaster of a boarding school for boys, was convicted of attempted buggery with S, a pupil aged 16, and of inciting H, a pupil aged 17, to commit buggery with him. The similarities between the allegations made by the two boys were that they were woken up in the school dormitory and spoken to in a low voice, invited to commit the offence in the appellant's sitting room, and requested to play the active role in the act of buggery. The defence was that the boys were lying and that the incidents had never occurred. The trial judge held that the evidence of each boy in relation to the count concerning him was admissible on the count concerning the other. The appeal was dismissed by both the Court of Appeal and House of Lords.

The test for admissibility in cases of the kind before the House was described in a variety of ways by their Lordships, but the common theme was probative value derived from a striking similarity between the facts testified to by the several witnesses. Lord Wilberforce said:[172] 'This [strong degree of] probative force is derived, if at all, from the circumstances that the facts testified to by the several witnesses bear to each other such a striking similarity that they must, when judged by experience and common sense, either all be true, or have arisen from a cause common to the witnesses or from pure coincidence.' Lord Salmon said:

---

[168] See Lord Herschell LC's celebrated formulation of the rule in *Makin v A-G for New South Wales* [1894] AC 57, PC at 65.

[169] (1915) 11 Cr App R 229, CCA.

[170] (1915) 11 Cr App R 229 at 233.

[171] [1975] AC 421.

[172] [1975] AC 421 at 444.

if the crime charged is committed in a uniquely or strikingly similar manner to other crimes committed by the accused the manner in which the other crimes were committed may be evidence upon which a jury could reasonably conclude that the accused was guilty of the crime charged. The similarity would have to be so unique or striking that common sense makes it inexplicable on the basis of coincidence.[173]

At common law similar fact evidence was capable of possessing the requisite degree of probative value if it was evidence of facts which were strikingly similar not to the facts of the offence charged but to the *circumstances* surrounding the commission of that offence. In *R v Scarrott*[174] Scarman LJ said:

Plainly some matters, some circumstances may be so distant in time or place from the commission of an offence as not to be properly considered when deciding whether the subject matter of similar fact evidence displays striking similarities with the offence charged. On the other hand, equally plainly one cannot isolate, as a sort of laboratory specimen, the bare bones of a criminal offence from its surrounding circumstances and say that it is only within the confines of that specimen, microscopically considered, that admissibility is to be determined. Indeed in one of the most famous cases of all dealing with similar fact evidence, 'the brides in the bath case', *R v Smith*, the court had regard to the facts that the accused man married the women and that he insured their lives. Some surrounding circumstances have to be considered in order to understand either the offence charged or the nature of the similar fact evidence which it is sought to adduce and in each case it must be a matter of judgment where the line is drawn. One cannot draw an inflexible line as a rule of law.

The principle under discussion can operate even if the evidence does not disclose the commission of an offence of the same kind as the offence charged or indeed the commission of any offence at all. In *R v Barrington*,[175] the appellant was convicted of indecently assaulting three young girls. The girls gave evidence that he had induced them to go into his house on the pretext that they were required as baby-sitters but that once inside he had shown them pornographic pictures, asked them to pose for photographs in the nude, and committed the offences charged. The defence was that each of the girls had a private motive to tell lies and that they had put their heads together to concoct a false story against him. Three other girls were allowed to give evidence that they had been induced to go into the house on the pretext of baby-sitting, and that they had been shown pornographic pictures and had been asked to pose for photographs in the nude. On appeal, it was argued that the evidence of these girls was inadmissible as similar fact evidence because it included no evidence of indecent assault or of any other offence similar to those with which the appellant was charged. The Court of Appeal, following the reasoning of Scarman LJ in *R v Scarrott*, held that the evidence had been properly admitted. Referring to the similar facts, Dunn LJ, who gave the judgment of the court, said:[176]

That they did not include evidence of the commission of offences similar to those with which the appellant was charged does not mean that they are not logically probative in determining the

---

[173] [1975] AC 421 at 462.
[174] [1991] 2 All ER 796, CA at 1025.
[175] [1981] 1 WLR 419, CA. See also *R v Horry* [1949] NZLR 791.
[176] [1981] 1 WLR 419 at 430. Compare the case of *R v Tricoglus* (1976) 65 Cr App R 16, CA. The accused was convicted of raping a woman who had accepted a lift from him. Evidence from another witness who had accepted a lift from him and was raped was admissible because it bore a striking similarity. However, evidence from two witnesses that they had been offered but refused lifts from him should not have been admitted as similar fact evidence as it showed no more than a propensity to 'kerb crawl'.

guilt of the appellant. Indeed we are of the opinion that taken as a whole they are inexplicable on the basis of coincidence and that they are of positive probative value in assisting to determine the truth of the charges against the appellant, in that they tended to show that he was guilty of the offences with which he was charged.

In *R v P*[177] the House of Lords held that in cases where the similar fact evidence to be adduced is to be given by another alleged victim of the accused, striking similarity is not an essential element. The accused was convicted of counts of rape and incest. The victims were his two daughters. The trial judge found striking similarities between the various offences in (i) the extreme discipline exercised over the daughters; (ii) abortions carried out on each girl paid for by P; and (iii) the acquiescence of the mother in P's sexual attentions to the daughters. The Court of Appeal allowed the appeal on the grounds that the similarities did not go beyond what was described as 'the incestuous father's stock-in-trade'. Thus it held that, with the possible exception of (ii), the similarities did not relate to P's modus operandi and could not be described as unusual features rendering the account of one girl more credible because mirrored in the statement of the other. The House of Lords restored the conviction. Lord Mackay LC, with whom the rest of the House concurred, after extensive citations from *DPP v Boardman*, held that, from all that was said in that case, 'the essential feature of evidence which is to be admitted is that its probative force in support of the allegation that an accused person committed a crime is sufficiently great to make it just to admit the evidence, notwithstanding that it is prejudicial to the accused in tending to show that he was guilty of another crime'.[178]

Whether the evidence has sufficient probative value to outweigh its prejudicial effect must in each case be a question of degree. Insofar as some authorities had held that similar fact evidence is inadmissible in the absence of some feature of similarity going beyond 'the pederast's or the incestuous father's stock-in-trade',[179] they were overruled. Turning to the facts, it was held that certain circumstances, when taken together, gave a sufficient probative force to the evidence of each of the girls in relation to the incidents involving the other. Those circumstances included the prolonged course of conduct in relation to each girl, the force used against each girl, the general domination of the girls and of the wife, and P's involvement in the payment for the abortions.

R v P, in making clear that probative value may but need not be derived from 'unusual characteristics', necessarily lowered the standard for admissibility.[180] Section 101(1)(d) has lowered the standard even further in that the test has become one of mere relevance, provided only that the evidence of misconduct is relevant to a matter in issue that is 'important'. It follows that evidence formerly admissible as similar fact evidence will now be admissible as 'relevant' evidence under section 101(1)(d).[181] It also follows that evidence which would not have satisfied

[177] [1991] 2 AC 447.

[178] [1991] 2 AC 447 at 460.

[179] *R v Inder* (1977) 67 Cr App R 143; *R v Clarke* (1977) 67 Cr App R 398; *R v Tudor* (18 July 1988, unreported); and *R v Brooks* (1990) 92 Cr App R 36, CA.

[180] See, eg, *R v Roy* [1992] Crim LR 185, CA; *R v Simpson* (1993) 99 Cr App R 48, CA; and *R v Gurney* [1994] Crim LR 116, CA.

[181] In *R v Stephenson* [2006] EWCA Crim 2325, a case which considered s 100, Hughes LJ observed at [27] that '…the same degree of caution which is applied to a Crown application when considering relevance and discretion does not fall to be deployed when what is at stake is a defendant's right to deploy relevant material to defend himself against a criminal charge'. This is not easy to reconcile with the wording of the respective provisions: under s 101(1)(d) the test is one of simple relevance whereas s 100 sets a test of 'substantial probative value' with a further requirement of leave.

the test in *R v P may* also be admissible under section 101(1)(d). However, since such evidence was excluded at common law if it had insufficient probative value to outweigh its prejudicial effect, in these circumstances there will now be obvious scope for a defence argument that the court should exclude the evidence, either in exercise of its common law discretion to exclude on this basis (assuming, as has been submitted, the discretion survives in this context)[182] or in reliance on section 101(3), ie on the basis that admission of the evidence would have such an adverse effect on the fairness of the proceedings that the court ought not to admit it.

Other types of misconduct. Evidence of bad character relevant to the guilt of the accused and admissible under section 101(1)(d) is not confined to evidence of propensity to commit the offence charged and similar fact evidence properly so called. At common law, other types of misconduct were admissible to establish a particular and essential part of the prosecution's case or to rebut the accused's defence. If, for example, the accused denies being in the neighbourhood where the crime was committed at the relevant time, evidence may be admitted that he committed another crime in that area shortly before or after the time of the offence charged.[183] Such evidence is admitted not for the purpose of concluding that the accused, because of his criminal disposition, is a person likely to have committed the offence charged, nor as similar fact evidence, but to establish that part of the prosecution case which is denied, namely presence in the neighbourhood at the relevant time. An English example is *R v Salisbury*.[184] A postman was charged with the larceny of a letter which contained bank notes belonging to another. It was part of the prosecution case that these bank notes had been inserted in another letter, the contents of which had been removed and which were in the possession of the accused. Evidence of the interception of this letter was held admissible to establish a link in the chain of events necessary to prove the larceny charged. Cases of this kind, it seems clear, would be decided in exactly the same way, although in cases like *R v Salisbury*, it is arguable that the evidence is 'evidence which has to do with the alleged facts of the offence', under section 98(a), and admissible on that basis.[185]

It has also been held, in decisions which were probably much more borderline than the courts have been prepared to acknowledge, that when, on a charge of importing controlled drugs, the accused denies any knowledge of how the drugs came to be concealed in his luggage or in his vehicle, which carries the implication that he is the innocent victim of some other person who concealed them, evidence showing that he is connected with the same kind of drugs inside the UK, for example evidence of finding such drugs in his home, is relevant and admissible, because the jury are entitled to consider such a coincidence, which may go to rebut the defence raised.[186] The principle, however, is not confined to drug couriers, but extends to others alleged to have been involved in the illegal importation. In *R v Yalman*[187] Y met his father at an airport on his arrival in England. Y senior was carrying a suitcase containing heroin. The prosecution case was that it was a family-organized importation, but Y said that he was unaware of the

---

[182] See 469 above, under **Section 101 of the Criminal Justice Act 2003**, *Discretion to exclude.*

[183] See *R v Ducsharm* [1956] 1 DLR 732.

[184] (1831) 5 C&P 155. See also *R v Voke* (1823) Russ&Ry 531; *R v Cobden* (1862) 3 F&F 833; and *R v Rearden* (1864) 4 F&F 76.

[185] See also *R v Anderson* [1988] 2 All ER 549, CA and *R v Kidd* [1995] Crim LR 406, CA.

[186] *R v Willis* (29 Jan 1979, unreported), CA. The principle holds good even if the drugs found in the UK are of a different kind, but there could be cases where they are of such a different kind that the evidence could not be said to be relevant: *R v Peters* [1995] 2 Cr App R 77, CA.

[187] [1998] 2 Cr App R 269, CA.

drugs. It was held, applying *R v Groves*,[188] that once there was a prima facie case for Y to answer, then evidence that he had used heroin, and that drugs paraphernalia had been found at his home, was admissible on the issue whether he was *knowingly* involved in the importation, as tending to rebut his assertion that his presence at the airport was entirely innocent.[189]

Categories of relevance and the nature of the defence.   It is submitted that the following important common law principles, relating to categories of relevance and the nature of the defence, will continue to operate in relation to the admissibility of evidence relevant to the issue of guilt under section 101(1)(d).

1. At common law the notion that 'similar fact' evidence, in order to be admissible, had to fall within a closed list of defined categories of relevance, such as 'proof of identity', 'rebutting accident', or 'rebutting innocent association', was firmly rejected in *Harris v DPP*.[190]

2. An associated notion, that similar fact evidence could never be used in rebuttal of particular kinds of defence, was also rejected.[191]

3. At common law evidence relevant to the issue of guilt could be admitted not only to rebut a defence which the accused had actually raised but also to rebut a defence which, even if not raised by the accused, was fairly open to him, on the basis that otherwise a submission of no case to answer might succeed when evidence properly available to support the prosecution case had been withheld.[192]

4. At common law it was always essential for the court, in considering a disputed issue as to the admissibility of 'similar fact' evidence, to consider the question not in the abstract but in the light of all the other evidence and the particular issue in respect of which the evidence was tendered.[193] In many cases, the particular issue on which the evidence had a bearing was the defence.[194]

5. There is no general rule to the effect that similar fact evidence is inadmissible where the accused simply denies the charge. Although in *R v Chandor*[195] and *R v Flack*[196] it was suggested that similar fact evidence might be admissible to rebut a defence such as mistaken identity, absence of intent and innocent association, but not a defence of complete denial, both cases were criticized in *DPP v Boardman*.[197] Lord Cross, while prepared to accept that the decision in each case might well have been correct, was unable to agree with the reasoning underlying such a distinction:[198]

---

[188] [1998] Crim LR 200, CA.

[189] However, the jury should also be directed to disregard the evidence if it does not assist them on the issue of knowledge or involvement: *R v Barner-Rasmussen* [1996] Crim LR 497, CA.

[190] [1952] AC 694, HL at 705.

[191] See, eg, *R v Wilmot* (1988) 89 Cr App R 341, CA (consent) and *R v Beggs* (1989) 90 Cr App R 430, CA at 438 (self-defence).

[192] See *Harris v DPP* [1952] AC 694, HL.

[193] See per Steyn LJ in *R v Clarke* [1995] 2 Cr App R 425, CA at 434–5.

[194] For an example, in relation to a defence actually raised, see *R v Anderson* [1988] 2 All ER 549, CA; and for an example in relation to a defence which was fairly open to the accused (and in the event raised), see *R v Lunt* (1986) 85 Cr App R 241, CA.

[195] [1959] 1 QB 545, CCA.

[196] [1969] 2 All ER 784, CA.

[197] [1975] AC 421, HL.

[198] [1975] AC 421 at 458.

If I am charged with a sexual offence why should it make any difference to the admissibility or non-admissibility of similar fact evidence whether my case is that the meeting at which the offence is said to have been committed never took place or that I committed no offence in the course of it? In each case I am saying that my accuser is lying.

The distinction was redrawn in *R v Lewis*,[199] but the evidence admitted in that case was evidence of propensity and not evidence of similar facts.

Identification cases. Much care is needed before admitting evidence of bad character in order to prove the identity of the accused as the offender, not least because where reliance is placed on evidence of similar facts, in many cases the evidence, without more, will usually only show that the same person committed both offences and not that that person is the accused. It is submitted that the following principles, established at common law, will remain instructive for the purposes of section 101(1)(d).

1. According to the dictum of Lord Mackay LC in *R v P*,[200] as construed by Hooper J in *R v W (John)*,[201] identity can be established where the only evidence of any substance against the accused is similar fact evidence which affords something in the nature of a personal hallmark or signature or other very striking similarity. *R v Mullen*[202] provides an example and shows that even if the hallmark is not peculiar to the accused it may still be admissible if of sufficient probative force. In that case M pleaded not guilty to three burglaries in the north-east of England, but admitted three other burglaries. In all of the burglaries the method of entry involved use of a blowtorch to crack glass. Only six offenders from the north or north-east of England were known to have used such a method. Evidence of the burglaries to which M had admitted was held to have been properly adduced.[203] However, where such evidence is adduced, it is submitted that it should be accompanied by a very clear warning to the jury that they need to be sure that the crime was committed by the accused and not by one of the others known to commit the crime in the same strikingly similar or unusual way.

2. Identity can also be established in the absence of evidence affording something in the nature of a personal hallmark or signature. In *R v W (John)*[204] W was convicted of false imprisonment of, and indecent assault on, C in Aldershot (counts 1 and 2) and of false imprisonment of S in Farnham two weeks later (count 3). The issue in both cases was identity, but the evidence revealed no signature or other special feature. W appealed on the basis that the trial judge had failed to make it clear that the evidence on counts 1 and 2 was not admissible on count 3 and vice versa. The Court of Appeal held that the evidence on the Aldershot counts and the Farnham counts did not need to be strikingly similar or of the nature of a signature. The court went on to identify the proper test in a case of the kind before it:[205] evidence tending to show that a defendant has committed

---

[199] (1982) 76 Cr App R 33.
[200] [1991] 2 AC 447, at 462 .
[201] [1998] 2 Cr App R 289, CA.
[202] [1992] Crim LR 735, CA.
[203] See also *R v Ruiz* [1995] Crim LR 151, CA and *R v West* [1996] 2 Cr App R 374 and cf *R v Johnson* [1995] 2 Cr App R 41, CA.
[204] [1998] 2 Cr App R 289, CA.
[205] [1998] 2 Cr App R 289 at 303.

an offence charged in count A may be used to reach a verdict on count B and vice versa, if the circumstances of both offences (as the jury would be entitled to find them) are such as to provide sufficient probative support for the conclusion that the defendant committed both offences, and it would therefore be fair for the evidence to be used in this way notwithstanding the prejudicial effect of so doing. On the facts of the case, this test was satisfied: most (but not all) of the descriptions of the attacker fitted the appellant; the descriptions of some of the attacker's clothes fitted the clothes that the appellant was known to be wearing; the appellant lived near both attacks, having moved from Aldershot to Farnham in the period between the time of the two attacks; the attacks took place within a short time of each other; and the attacks bore certain similarities.

3. In similar fact cases in which identity is in issue, in directing the jury a careful distinction needs to be drawn between the similar fact evidence and the other evidence in the case. There are two different types of situation, one calling for a 'sequential approach' and the other for a 'cumulative approach'.[206] The first is where, in deciding whether the accused committed offence A, the jury can have regard to evidence that he also committed offence B. This sequential approach involves proof not only of similarity, but also that the accused did in fact commit offence B. *R v McGranaghan*[207] is an illustration. M was convicted of three separate aggravated burglaries of homes and rapes or indecent assaults on the women occupants. M denied having had anything to do with any of the offences. The appeal was allowed on the grounds that although, on the evidence at the time of the trial, the similarities in the features of the offences rendered the evidence on each admissible in relation to the others, the jury should have been directed to consider first whether, disregarding the similarity of the facts, the other evidence in the case was sufficient to make them sure that M committed at least one of the offences. Only if they were so sure, could they then use the similarity to prove that the accused committed the other offences. Glidewell LJ said:[208] 'The similar facts go to show that the same man committed both offences, not that the defendant was that man. There must be some evidence to make the jury sure that on at least one offence the defendant was that man.'[209]

4. The cumulative approach applies where there is evidence, other than the evidence of visual identification, on the basis of which the jury can conclude that offences A and B were committed by the same man, but that evidence, by itself, falls short of proving that that man was the accused in either case. In this situation, once the jury is satisfied that the 'other' evidence shows both offences to have been committed by the same man, the identification evidence of the victims can be used cumulatively in deciding whether that man was the accused. In *R v Barnes*[210] the accused was convicted of three separate offences, indecent assaults on two females and the wounding of a third. Evidence was

---

[206] *R v Barnes* [1995] 2 Cr App R 491, CA, relying upon *R v Downey* [1995] 1 Cr App R 547, CA.

[207] [1995] 1 Cr App R 559n, CA.

[208] [1995] 1 Cr App R 559 at 572.

[209] See also *R v Rubin* [1995] Crim LR 332, CA. The principle is confined to cases in which identification is in issue: see *R v S* [1993] Crim LR 293, CA. It is probably also confined to cases in which the indictment contains two or more counts and it is the evidence on each which is potentially admissible, in relation to the other or others, as similar fact evidence. Thus it does not extend to a case in which there is also similar fact evidence relating to an offence of which the accused already stands convicted: see *R v Black* [1995] Crim LR 640, CA. See also *R v Mullen* [1992] Crim LR 735, CA.

[210] [1995] 2 Cr App R 491, CA.

admitted of three other similar incidents. There was no dispute that the six incidents were sufficiently similar to be admitted in order to show that all of the offences were committed by the same man. It was held that the identification evidence of the three victims could be considered cumulatively in deciding whether that man was the accused.[211]

5. The cumulative approach may also be used where offences A and B bear the hallmark or signature of the same gang, of which the accused is alleged to be a member. The danger, however, is that membership of the gang may alter after the commission of the first offence, and there may be nothing in the hallmark or signature which identifies the accused as opposed to the gang. For reasons of this kind, in *R v Brown*[212] it was held that the issue for the jury, once they were satisfied that the same gang committed both offences, was whether the prosecution had established on all the evidence that the accused was a member of the gang and whether the totality of the evidence had established beyond reasonable doubt that he was a member of the gang on both occasions.[213]

Sexual cases. Common law developments were such that by the mid-1970s it was established that there were no special rules of admissibility for sexual offences or sexual offences against men, boys, or children of either sex. In sexual cases, therefore, the admissibility of 'similar fact' evidence was decided by applying the same principles as in any other type of case. It is submitted that the position is the same under the statutory scheme and that there are no special rules in sexual cases in which evidence of bad character is sought to be admitted on the basis of its relevance to the issue of guilt under section 101(1)(d).

In the case of evidence of sexual disposition, the threshold issue, under the Act, is whether it amounts to evidence of a disposition towards, 'misconduct'[214] which, it will be recalled, means 'the commission of an offence or other reprehensible behaviour'.[215] If there is evidence of the commission of a sexual offence of the kind with which the accused is charged, then the prosecution will rely upon section 103(1)(a) and, if it resulted in a conviction, section 103(2).[216] However, in the case of sexual disposition which has not involved the commission of any offence, a disposition towards, say, paedophilia, incest, or bestiality will be regarded as evidence of disposition towards 'reprehensible behaviour', but it seems most unlikely that a homosexual disposition, any more than a heterosexual disposition, could properly be so regarded. The admissibility of evidence of homosexual or heterosexual disposition, therefore, is not governed by the Act and will simply turn on whether it is relevant and, if so, whether it should be excluded by virtue of the common law discretion to exclude where its prejudicial effect outweighs its probative value. Such evidence, it is submitted, will very often be irrelevant or unduly prejudicial, but obviously each case will turn on its own facts. Thus if the accused, charged with a sexual offence against a man, were to assert his heterosexual disposition, then evidence of his homosexual disposition would be plainly relevant to the issue.

---

[211] See also *R v Grant* [1996] 2 Cr App R 272, CA and *R v Wallace* [2008] 1 WLR 572.
[212] [1997] Crim LR 502, CA.
[213] See also *R v Lee* [1996] Crim LR 825, CA.
[214] Section 98, above.
[215] Section 112(1).
[216] See 477 above, under *Questions of proof.*

The common law authorities have provided examples of the approach taken by the courts to evidence of a homosexual disposition. In *DPP v Boardman*[217] the House of Lords decisively rejected the suggestion that there is a special rule for sexual offences or sexual offences against men or boys. Views expressed in a previous decision of the House in *Thompson v R*,[218] that a homosexual disposition could be regarded as an 'abnormal propensity' and could be relevant to identifying the perpetrator of sexual offences against men or boys, were repudiated. In the words of Lord Wilberforce:[219] 'In matters of experience it is for the judge to keep close to current mores. What is striking in one age is normal in another: the perversions of yesterday may be the routine or the fashions of tomorrow.'

Evidence of homosexual disposition, however, has been admitted on account of its *particular* relevance in disproving a defence of innocent association. In *R v King*,[220] a decision of dubious authority reached prior to *DPP v Boardman*, the appellant was convicted of a number of sexual offences against boys. His defence, in relation to some of the incidents, was innocent association. He admitted that he had met two boys in a public lavatory and asked them to spend the night in his room and also that one had slept on the floor while the other had shared his bed, but he denied the offence charged. In cross-examination he confirmed that he was a homosexual. The Court of Appeal held that this evidence fell within the principle in *Thompson v R* and had been properly admitted. *R v King* may be compared with *R v Horwood*,[221] where the appellant was convicted of attempted gross indecency with a boy. The boy's evidence was that they drove to a wood, got out to look for rabbits, that the offence took place and that he then ran away and was chased by the appellant. The appellant admitted that he had driven the boy to a wood but said that he had got out of the car to urinate and had returned to find that the boy had vanished. During police interrogation, the appellant said that he used to be a homosexual but had been cured and now went out with girls. The Court of Appeal, quashing the conviction, held that the evidence of homosexual propensity had been improperly admitted. O'Connor LJ held that it was only in exceptional circumstances that such evidence could be admitted to rebut innocent association and that *R v King* was such a case because the evidence could properly be said to be relevant to an issue before the jury. It would appear that *R v King* was distinguished on the basis of the greater degree of admitted intimacy in that case. The nature of the admitted association in the instant case (taking a boy for a drive in a car in broad daylight) was contrasted with that in *R v King* (taking a boy home and getting into bed with him).[222]

Incriminating articles.   At common law, evidence of the possession of articles of the kind used in the commission of the offence charged, albeit not used in the commission of the offence charged, could be admitted in order to identify the accused as the offender. Evidence of the possession of such articles is likely to be treated as evidence of a disposition towards misconduct for the purposes of section 98 of the 2003 Act, or evidence of propensity to commit

---

[217] [1975] AC 421. But see *Reza v General Medical Council* [1991] 2 All ER 796, PC.

[218] [1918] AC 221, HL.

[219] [1975] AC 421 at 444.

[220] [1967] 2 QB 338, CA. In *Thompson v R*, it could be argued that the accused's homosexual disposition could have been admitted because of its *particular* relevance to the question of whether he had been mistakenly identified offences of gross indecency with boys in a public lavatory.

[221] [1970] 1 QB 133, CA.

[222] See also *R v King* (7 Apr 1982, unreported), CA. The appellant provided boys with inducements (games and bicycles) to come to his flat.

offences of the kind with which the accused is charged for the purposes of section 103(1)(a), and to be admitted under section 101(1)(d) because of its relevance in identifying the accused as the offender. In *R v Reading*,[223] Reading, alleged to have hijacked a lorry, was convicted of robbery and taking a motor vehicle. The Court of Criminal Appeal held that evidence of his possession of articles, including a walkie-talkie radio set and a police-type uniform capable of being used in the type of robbery charged, albeit not proved to have been used in the commission of the offence charged, was admissible to rebut his defence of alibi and mistaken identity. In reaching this conclusion, the court distinguished *R v Taylor*.[224] In that case, Taylor's conviction for shopbreaking was quashed on the ground that evidence had been improperly admitted that a jemmy had been found in his possession. The reasoning of the court was that there being no evidence that a jemmy had been used to break open the door in question, and Taylor's defence being that the door had been broken accidentally, the evidence was tendered for the sole purpose of showing him to be of a criminal disposition and likely not to have been in the doorway for an innocent purpose. The evidence in question, it is submitted, would now be likely to be admitted under section 101(1)(d).

Bad character evidence under section 101(1)(d) relevant to the credibility of the accused
Under section 101(1)(d), as we have seen, prosecution evidence of the accused's bad character is admissible if 'it is relevant to an important matter in issue between the defendant and the prosecution' and although the test is one of simple rather than enhanced relevance, the requirement of relevance to an 'important matter' is a requirement of relevance to a matter in issue 'of substantial importance in the context of the case as a whole'.[225] Insofar as section 101(1)(d) may be used to attack the credibility of the accused, it is supplemented by section 103(1)(b), which provides as follows:

(1) For the purposes of section 101(1)(d) the matters in issue between the defendant and the prosecution include—

. . .

(b) the question whether the defendant has a propensity to be untruthful, except where it is not suggested that the defendant's case is untruthful in any respect.

The effect of section 103(1)(b) is that in any case in which the prosecution seek to rely upon section 101(1)(d) to attack the credibility of the accused, his propensity to be untruthful will always be deemed to be a matter in issue, except in the very rare cases in which it is not suggested that his case is untruthful in any respect. The exception would apply, for example, when the defence do not dispute the facts established by the prosecution and the only question is whether the judge should stop the case on the basis that the prosecution evidence, taken at its highest, is such that the jury, properly directed, could not convict on it.[226] The meaning of 'defendant's case' is undefined and unclear, but it appears to refer to the defendant's case at trial, rather than what he said during police questioning or in his disclosed defence statement but which he does not rely on at trial, albeit that in many cases the prosecution case will be that the accused is not telling the truth about a particular matter at trial having regard to what

---

[223] [1966] 1 WLR 836, CCA.

[224] (1923) 17 Cr App R 109. See also *R v Manning* (1923) 17 Cr App R 85 and *Thompson v R* (1968) 42 ALJR 16, HC of A. *R v Reading* [1966] 1 WLR 836, CCA, was followed in *R v Mustafa* (1976) 65 Cr App R 26, CA.

[225] Section 112(1).

[226] See *R v Galbraith* [1981] 1 WLR 1039, CA, Ch 2.

he did or did not say to the police or in his defence statement. It is submitted that a plea of not guilty, by itself, cannot lead to the conclusion that the accused's case will be untruthful in some respect, because the plea simply puts the prosecution to proof.

The scope for use of section 103(1)(b) appears to be very limited, having regard to the views of Lord Phillips CJ in *R v Campbell*.[227]

> It will be comparatively rare for the case of a defendant who has pleaded not guilty not to involve some element that the prosecution suggest is untruthful. It does not, however, follow that, whenever there is an issue as to whether the defendant's case is truthful evidence can be admitted to show that he has a propensity to be untruthful.
>
> The question whether a defendant has a propensity for being untruthful will not normally be described as an important matter in issue between the defendant and the prosecution. A propensity for untruthfulness will not, of itself, go very far to establishing the commission of a criminal offence. To suggest that a propensity for untruthfulness makes it more likely that a defendant has lied to the jury is not likely to help them. If they apply common sense they will conclude that a defendant who has committed a criminal offence may well be prepared to lie about it, even if he has not shown a propensity for lying whereas a defendant who has not committed the offence charged will be likely to tell the truth, even if he has shown a propensity for telling lies. In short, whether or not a defendant is telling the truth to the jury is likely to depend simply on whether or not he committed the offence charged. The jury should focus on the latter question rather than on whether or not he has a propensity for telling lies.
>
> For these reasons, the only circumstances in which there is likely to be an important issue as to whether a defendant has a propensity to tell lies is where telling lies is an element of the offence charged. Even then, the propensity to tell lies is only likely to be significant if the lying is in the context of committing criminal offences, in which case the evidence is likely to be admissible under section 103(1)(a).

This reasoning, it is respectfully submitted, is flawed. It may well be that whether or not an accused is telling the truth is likely to depend on whether or not he committed the offence, but it simply does not follow that a propensity for untruthfulness is unlikely to be an important matter in issue or that evidence of such propensity is unlikely to assist the jury. As to the former, in many cases there is a direct conflict between the evidence of the accused and that of the prosecution witnesses and the question is which side is lying as opposed to mistaken, which will be a matter of importance, if not the most important matter, in the context of the case as a whole. As to the latter, in such a case it is submitted that it will plainly assist the jury to know that the accused has a propensity for untruthfulness, especially if the prosecution witnesses do not, and that this is so whether or not telling lies is an element of the offence charged.

Lord Phillip's reasoning is also difficult to reconcile with the fact that under section 101(1)(e) it has been readily recognized that evidence of propensity to untruthfulness is capable of having substantial probative value in relation to the credibility of the accused.[228] If the reasoning is adopted, it would narrow the ambit of section 101(1)(d) to such an extent that it will rarely be used to admit evidence other than evidence of propensity to commit offences of the kind charged.

According to the Explanatory Notes, section 103(1)(b) 'is intended to enable the admission of a limited range of evidence such as convictions for perjury or other offences involving deception

---

[227] [2007] 1 WLR 2798, CA at [29]–[31].

[228] See *R v Lawson* [2007] 1 Cr App R 178, CA and *R v Jarvis* [2008] EWCA Crim 488.

(for example, obtaining property by deception) as opposed to the wider range of evidence that will be admissible where the defendant puts his character in issue by, for example, attacking the character of another person', ie under section 101(1)(g).[229] However, the range of evidence admissible under section 101(1)(d) is neither as clear nor as limited as the Notes suggest. As to the former, for example, interesting questions are likely to arise as to which offences, other than 'perjury or other offences involving deception' will also be characterized as offences showing 'a propensity to be untruthful'. In *R v Hanson*[230] it was held that propensity to untruthfulness is not the same as propensity to dishonesty. Thus it may be that offences of benefit fraud show a propensity to be untruthful but offences of theft by shoplifting may show no more than propensity to dishonesty.[231] As to the limits on the range of evidence admissible under section 101(1)(d), it is not confined to evidence of convictions, but may relate to instances of untruthfulness which did not amount to criminal behaviour, or which did amount to criminal behaviour, but did not result, or by the time of the trial in question had not resulted, in a conviction. Equally, propensity to be untruthful may be established by reference to convictions for offences other than, and not necessarily similar to, 'perjury or other offences involving deception', where it is clear that the jury rejected the accused's version of events. An example would be previous convictions for sexual offences, the accused having run an unsuccessful defence of alibi in each case. In *R v Hanson*[232] it was held that previous convictions, whether for offences of dishonesty or otherwise, are only likely to be capable of showing a propensity to be untruthful where, in the present case, truthfulness is in issue and, in the earlier case, either there was a plea of not guilty and the accused gave an account (on arrest, in interview or in evidence) which the jury must have disbelieved, or the way in which the offence was committed shows a propensity for untruthfulness, for example by the making of false representations.[233] It was also made clear that the court's observations as to the number of previous convictions in relation to section 103(1)(a)[234] apply equally in relation to section 103(1)(b).

Where evidence is admissible under section 101(1)(d) by virtue of section 103(1)(b), the court has a discretionary power to exclude it either under section 101(3) or in reliance on the common law power to exclude on the basis that its prejudicial effect outweighs its probative value (assuming, as has been submitted earlier, that the common law discretion subsists in relation to prosecution evidence admissible under section 101).[235] In cases in which evidence is admissible only to go to truthfulness or credit, there is a danger that the jury may even subconsciously and despite careful direction be influenced by the evidence on the question of propensity and thus guilt, and for this reason it has been said that 'a cautious test of admissibility' should be applied, whether on examination of the test of relevance under section 101(1)(d) or, which seems more apposite, on application of the discretion under section 101(3).[236]

---

[229] Para 374.

[230] [2005] 1 WLR 3169, CA.

[231] *R v Edwards* [2006] 1 WLR 1524, CA at [33]. See also *R v Garnham* [2008] All ER (D) 50 (May), CA.

[232] [2005] 1 WLR 3169, CA.

[233] See *R v Gumbrell* [2009] EWCA Crim 550: evidence of past false representations by the accused as to his competence and qualifications as a builder was properly admitted to show a propensity to make false representations. See also *R v Foster* [2009] All ER (D) 85 (Feb) at [17], where the trial judge was held to have wrongly directed the jury that they could take previous robbery convictions into account in deciding the accused's truthfulness.

[234] See above.

[235] See 469 above under **Section 101 of the Criminal Justice Act 2003**, *Discretion to exclude*.

[236] See per Hughes LJ in *R v Lawson* [2007] 1 Cr App R 178, CA at [33].

Section 101(1)(e)—evidence of substantial probative value in relation to an important issue between the defendant and a co-defendant

Section 101(1)(e), like section 101(1)(d), is a single gateway providing for the admissibility of evidence going to the guilt of the defendant as well as evidence going to his credit or propensity to be untruthful. It can only be used by a co-defendant. However, simply because an application to admit evidence of bad character is made by a co-defendant, the judge is not bound to admit it; the gateway in section 101(1)(e) must be gone through.[237] Under section 101(1)(e), evidence of the defendant's bad character is admissible if 'it has substantial probative value in relation to an important matter in issue between the defendant and a co-defendant'. According to the Explanatory Notes, the requirement that the probative value of the evidence be 'substantial' will have the effect of excluding evidence of no more than marginal or trivial value.[238] An 'important matter' is 'a matter of substantial importance in the context of the case as a whole',[239] and not, according to the Explanatory Notes, a matter of 'marginal or trivial' importance in that context;[240] and because it is the context of the case as a whole that matters, in determining an application under section 101(1)(e), analysis with a fine toothcomb is unlikely to be helpful.[241] In *R v Lawson*[242] it was said that 'the feel' of the trial judge will often be critical on the question whether evidence is capable of having substantial probative value under section 101(1)(e) and that the Court of Appeal is unlikely to interfere unless the judge was plainly wrong or *Wednesbury* unreasonable.[243]

Evidence is only admissible under section 101(1)(e) on behalf of the co-defendant. The prosecution cannot rely upon section 101(1)(e), nor can another co-defendant, unless the evidence is also of substantial probative value in relation to an important matter in issue between the defendant and that other co-defendant. Section 104(2) provides that:

(2) only evidence—
   (a) which is to be (or has been) adduced by the co-defendant, or
   (b) which a witness is to be invited to give (or has given) in cross-examination by the co-defendant,
   is admissible under section 101(1)(e).

Because evidence admissible under section 101(1)(e) is only admissible on behalf of a co-defendant, there is no discretionary power to exclude it.[244] As noted previously, a co-defendant should be free to adduce any evidence relevant to his case, whether or not it prejudices the defendant, a principle established at common law and which applied in relation both to evidence going to the guilt of the defendant and to cross-examination of the defendant in order to impugn his credibility.

It will be convenient to consider separately evidence admissible under subsection (1)(e) which is relevant to the guilt of the accused and evidence admissible under the subsection which is relevant to his credibility.

---

[237] *R v Edwards* [2006] 1 WLR 1524, CA at [1](v).
[238] Para 375.
[239] Section 112(1).
[240] Para 375.
[241] *R v Edwards*, ibid at [1](v).
[242] [2007] 1 Cr App R 178, CA.
[243] *Associated Provincial Picture Houses Ltd v Wednesbury Corpn* [1948] 1 KB 223, CA.
[244] *R v Assani* [2008] All ER (D) 188 (Nov) at [10].

Bad character evidence under section 101(1)(e) relevant to the guilt of the accused

R v Edwards[245] illustrates how section 101(1)(e) may be used by a co-accused to introduce evidence of the bad character of the accused which is relevant to the issue of his guilt. That was a case of wounding in which each of the accused told an entirely different story as to what had occurred and each was saying that he was not involved in the violence. It was held that the previous convictions for violence of D1 had substantial probative value on the issue between him and D2, evidence of D1's propensity to commit offences of violence being relevant to the issue of which of D1 and D2 was more likely to have been the assailant.

The leading authority at common law was the decision of the House of Lords in *R v Randall*.[246] In that case, R and G were tried together on a charge of murder. Each raised a cut-throat defence, blaming the other for the infliction of the fatal injuries. Both thereby lost the protection of section 1 of the 1898 Act and were asked questions about their previous convictions and bad character. R had relatively minor convictions. G had a bad record, including convictions for burglary, when he had armed himself with a screwdriver. G also admitted that he had been involved in a robbery in which all the robbers had been armed with knives. The House of Lords held that in the particular circumstances of the case the evidence of G's propensity to use and threaten violence was relevant not only in relation to the truthfulness of his evidence, but also because the imbalance between that history and the antecedent history of R tended to show that the version of events put forward by R was more probable than that put forward by G. Lord Steyn said:[247]

> Postulate a joint trial involving two accused arising from an assault committed in a pub. Assume it to be clear that one of the two men committed the assault. The one man has a long list of previous convictions involving assaults in pubs. It shows him to be prone to fighting when he has consumed alcohol. The other man has an unblemished record. Relying on experience and common sense one may rhetorically ask why the propensity to violence of one man should not be deployed by the other man as part of his defence that he did not commit the assault. Surely such evidence is capable, depending on the jury's assessment of all the evidence, of making it more probable that the man with the violent disposition when he had consumed alcohol committed the assault. To rule that the jury may use the convictions in regard to his credibility but that convictions revealing his propensity to violence must otherwise be ignored is to ask the jury to put to one side their common sense and experience. It would be curious if the law compelled such an unrealistic result.

Later, Lord Steyn said:[248]

> For the avoidance of doubt I would further add that in my view where evidence of propensity of a co-accused is relevant to a fact in issue between the Crown and the other accused it is not necessary for a trial judge to direct the jury to ignore that evidence in considering the case against the co-accused. Justice does not require that such a direction be given. Moreover, such a direction would needlessly perplex juries.

This passage, however, is open to differing interpretations. *R v Randall* was followed in *R v Price*,[249] a murder trial where one accused, another, *or both*, had committed the offence.

---

[245] [2006] 3 All ER 882, CA at [51]–[52].
[246] [2004] 1 WLR 56. See also DW Elliott, 'Cut Throat Tactics: the freedom of an accused to prejudice a co-accused' [1991] *Crim LR* 5.
[247] At [22].
[248] At [35].
[249] [2005] Crim LR 304. See also *R v Robinson* [2006] 1 Cr App R 480, CA.

It was held that the propensity of D2 to be aggressive was relevant to the question whether, had only one person killed the deceased, that person was D1, and did not become irrelevant simply because, if the jury answered no to that question, they still had to decide whether D1 had been a party to the attack. It was further held that the evidence was relevant to determination of the Crown's case against D2 and could be taken into account by the jury against D2 'as they thought appropriate'. *R v Randall* was distinguished in *R v B (C)*,[250] where there was no joint charge, no cut-throat defence, no attempt to support the credibility of D1 by reference to the evidence of D2's previous misconduct, and that evidence, therefore had no relevance to D1's defence. As to Lord Steyn's dictum 'for the avoidance of doubt', the court was of the view that where D2's propensity becomes relevant as between D1 and the Crown, no distinction is to be attempted in viewing the position as between D2 and the Crown ('the Crown becomes the beneficiary'), but added that the jury should be warned to be cautious before using propensity as a guide to guilt. In *R v Mertens*,[251] on the other hand, it was held that the 'evidence of propensity' to which Lord Steyn had referred was evidence of disposition admissible on behalf of the Crown and that where the evidence of D2's misconduct is not admissible on that basis, although it can be relied upon by D1 in his case against the Crown with a view to showing that D2 was more likely to have committed the offence, it should be disregarded in considering the case against D2.[252] However, as Hooper LJ observed in *R v Robinson*,[253] if the evidence was, in any event, admissible at the behest of the Crown, then there was no need for Lord Steyn to address the issue.

In *R v Miller*,[254] A, B and C were charged with conspiracy to evade customs duties. B's defence was that he was not concerned in the illegal acts but that C masqueraded as him (B) and used his (B's) office for their commission. In furtherance of that defence, B's counsel asked a prosecution witness whether C was not in prison during a period when no illegal importations had occurred. Devlin J held that whereas in the case of the prosecution there is a duty to exclude questions tending to show the previous commission of some crime if its prejudicial effect outweighs its probative value, no such limitation applies to a question asked by counsel for a co-accused, whose duty is to adduce any evidence relevant to his case whether or not it prejudices any other accused. The evidence was relevant to B's case and accordingly was admissible.[255] The dicta of Devlin J in *R v Miller* were affirmed in *R v Neale*,[256] a decision on the other side of the line. N and B were charged with arson and manslaughter. Counsel for N sought to adduce evidence, either by cross-examining prosecution witnesses or by calling evidence himself, that B had admitted that he had started fires by himself on four other occasions. The Court of Appeal upheld the ruling of the trial judge that the evidence was inadmissible: it was

---

[250] [2004] 2 Cr App R 570, CA.

[251] [2005] Crim LR 301, CA.

[252] See also *R v Murrell* [2005] Crim LR 869, CA: it is perfectly possible to describe the Crown's case against D2 without referring to the evidence admissible in support of D1, before making clear the relevance of that evidence.

[253] [2006] 1 Cr App R 480, CA at [71].

[254] [1952] 2 All ER 667, Winchester Assizes.

[255] See also *R v Bracewell* (1978) 68 Cr App R 44 per Ormrod LJ at 50: 'The problem generally arises in connection with evidence tendered by the Crown, so that marginal cases can be dealt with by the exercise of the discretion. "When in doubt, exclude", is a good working rule in such cases. But where the evidence is tendered by a co-accused, the test of relevance must be applied, and applied strictly . . .'

[256] (1977) 65 Cr App R 304. See also *R v Campbell and Williams* [1993] Crim LR 448, CA and *R v Myers* [1997] 4 All ER 314, HL (Ch 13).

evidence only of B's propensity to commit wanton and unaided arson and contained nothing of relevance to N's defence, which was that at the relevant time he was elsewhere and asleep in bed.[257] In *R v Randall*[258] the House of Lords considered that *R v Neale* was a borderline decision and 'wondered' how the case would have been decided if N had admitted that he was on the scene.

R v Miller was also referred to and approved by the Privy Council in *Lowery v R*,[259] for a long time regarded as an unusual case which was decided on its own special facts,[260] but approved by the House of Lords in *R v Randall*. L and K were charged with the murder of a girl. It was clear that one or both of them must have committed the offence. L emphasized his good character and said that because of his fear of K he had been unable to prevent the murder. K said that he had been under the influence of drugs and powerless to prevent L from killing the victim. K was allowed to call a psychologist to give evidence that L was aggressive, lacked self-control, and was more likely to have committed the offence than K. The Privy Council held that this evidence had been properly admitted. It seems that the evidence was admitted as relevant to prove K's innocence because L had already put his character in issue by testifying to the effect that he was not the sort of man to have committed the offence.

In *R v Douglass*[261] it was held that where a cut-throat defence is being run by two accused jointly charged with an offence and evidence of the bad character of one of them is relevant to the guilt or innocence of the other, the evidence is admissible whether they are alleged to have committed the offence by way of joint enterprise or by separate but contributory means. D and P were charged with causing death by reckless driving. The prosecution alleged that D had been drinking and was trying to prevent P from overtaking and that P, in vying for position, had collided with an oncoming car. P did not testify, but his counsel cross-examined P's girlfriend to elicit from her that P had never drunk alcohol in the two years that she had known him. The clear purpose was to suggest that P, unlike D, was unlikely to have been affected by alcohol so as to have driven badly. Applying *Lowery v R*, *R v Bracewell*, and *R v Miller*, it was held that where one accused adduces evidence of his own lack of propensity and this goes to the issue of a co-accused's guilt, the co-accused may call contradictory evidence. Accordingly, D should have been allowed to adduce evidence of P's previous convictions for motoring offences, including two drink-driving offences.

In both *Lowery v R* and *R v Douglass* the evidence was admitted against an accused who had put his character in issue.[262] However in *R v Randall* the House of Lords, while approving *Lowery v R*, was confident that 'there must be cases in which the propensity of one accused may be relied on by the other, irrespective of whether he has put his character in issue'.[263]

Bad character evidence under section 101(1)(e) relevant to the credibility of the accused
Insofar as section 101(1)(e) permits a co-accused to introduce evidence of the bad character of the accused which is relevant to his credibility, it is qualified by section 104(1), which provides as follows:

---

[257] See also *R v Nightingale* [1977] Crim LR 744 and *R v Knutton* (1992) 97 Cr App R 115, CA.
[258] [2004] 1 WLR 56, HL.
[259] [1974] AC 85, PC.
[260] Per Lawton LJ in *R v Turner* [1975] QB 834, CA.
[261] (1989) 89 Cr App R 264, CA. Cf *R v Kennedy* [1992] Crim LR 37, CA.
[262] See also *R v Sullivan* (2003) The Times, 18 Mar and *R v Rafiq* [2005] Crim LR 963, CA.
[263] [2004] 1 WLR 56, per Lord Steyn at [29]. See also *R v Robinson* [2006] 1 Cr App R 480, CA.

(1) Evidence which is relevant to the question whether the defendant has a propensity to be untruthful is admissible on that basis under section 101(1)(e) only if the nature or conduct of his defence is such as to undermine the co-defendant's defence.

One might have supposed that the phrase 'propensity to be untruthful' would bear the same restrictive meaning in section 104(1) as it is said to bear in section 103(1)(b)[264] and that generally it would be as unlikely to assist the jury as is thought to be the case under section 103(1)(b).[265] However, in *R v Lawson*[266] the court, while accepting that an offence of dishonesty will not necessarily be capable of establishing a propensity for untruthfulness, held that it did not follow that previous convictions not involving the making of false statements or the giving of false evidence are incapable of having substantial probative value in relation to the credibility of an accused. The court was also of the view that 'unreliability'—and it is possible that the court fell into error at this point by departing from the statutory wording of 'propensity to be untruthful'—was capable of being shown by conduct which did not involve an offence of untruthfulness, ranging from large-scale drug- or people-trafficking via housebreaking to criminal violence; but that whether in a particular case conduct is in fact capable of having the requisite probative value is for the trial judge to decide on all the facts. On the facts of the case before it, it was held that the trial judge was entitled to conclude that a previous conviction for wounding did have the requisite probative value in relation to the credibility of the accused who was charged with manslaughter. Unfortunately, however, no reasons are given—it was felt to be sufficient to defer to 'the feel of the trial judge'.[267] In *R v Jarvis*,[268] the Court of Appeal made a broad statement that section 104(1) did not bear the restrictive meaning of section 103(1)(b).

> We are quite satisfied that there is no warrant in the statute for restricting bad character evidence going to a propensity to untruthfulness to evidence of past untruthfulness of a witness. That would very largely and quite unwarrantably restrict the admission of very relevant evidence. If a witness or defendant in the case has a proven history of untruthful dealing with other people, serial lying and the like, that is plainly relevant and ought to be admitted, so long of course, as it has substantial probative value on an issue arising between the parties.

The words 'nature or conduct of his defence' in section 104(1) make clear that the defence of the co-accused may be undermined not only by the evidence of the accused or witnesses called on his behalf, but also in cross-examination of witnesses called by the prosecution or co-accused. The phrase 'nature or conduct' was also used in section 1(3)(ii) of the Criminal Evidence Act 1898, under which the accused could lose his shield and be cross-examined on his bad character when the nature or conduct of the defence was such as to involve imputations on the character of, among others, witnesses for the prosecution. For the purposes of section 1(3)(ii) of the 1898 Act it was held in *R v Jones*[269] that answers given by an accused under cross-examination were generally to be treated as part of the cross-examiner's case and therefore prima facie should not be taken into account, and that the shield should not be lost

---

[264] See *R v Hanson* [2005] 1 WLR 3169, CA, above.

[265] See *R v Campbell* [2007] 1 WLR 2789, CA, above.

[266] [2007] 1 Cr App R 178, CA.

[267] For a general exploration of the difficulties of construction posed by section 104, see Munday, 'Cut-throat Defences and the "Propensity to be Untruthful" under s. 104 of the Criminal Justice Act 2003' [2005] *Crim LR* 624.

[268] [2008] EWCA Crim 488 per Hughes LJ at [30]. See also, comment on *Jarvis* at [2008] Crim LR 266.

[269] (1909) 3 Cr App R 67, CCA.

where the accused was trapped into making an imputation by the form of the question put.[270] On the other hand, it was held that the shield could be lost where the imputation was not necessary in answer to the question put[271] or was voluntary and gratuitous.[272] These principles, it is submitted, are likely to remain valid, in the context of section 104, in relation to cross-examination of the accused, whether at the hands of the prosecution or a co-accused.

Under section 1(3)(iii) of the 1898 Act an accused could lose his shield where he had 'given evidence against' a co-accused. In the leading case of *Murdoch v Taylor*[273] the House of Lords held that 'evidence against' included evidence which either supported the prosecution's case in a material respect or which 'undermined the defence' of a co-accused. *Murdoch v Taylor* and some of the subsequent decisions provide much valuable guidance as to the way in which section 104(1) is likely to be interpreted, both generally and in relation to the phrase 'to undermine the co-defendant's defence'.

In *Murdoch v Taylor* it was held that section 1(3)(iii) does not refer only to evidence given by one accused against another with hostile intent, that it is the effect of the evidence upon the minds of the jury which is material and not the state of mind of the person who gives it, and that the test to be applied is therefore objective and not subjective. The same may be said, it is submitted, in relation to section 104(1). However, section 104(1) of the 2003 Act is narrower in its scope than section 1(3)(iii) of the 1898 Act, as interpreted in *Murdoch v Taylor*, in that the former is not triggered by evidence which does no more than support the prosecution case. Thus although in many cases evidence which supports the prosecution case will also undermine the defence of the co-accused, if the evidence supports the prosecution case but does not undermine the defence of the co-accused, because for example he has not raised a defence, evidence of the accused's bad character will not be admissible to attack his credibility under section 101(1)(e).[274] Such evidence will also be inadmissible, it is submitted, where the accused gives evidence to the same effect as the prosecution on a factual matter on which there is no issue between the Crown and the co-accused, because such evidence will not undermine the defence of the co-accused.[275] However, it would seem that if a co-accused has only a scintilla or iota of a defence, as when his defence is almost completely undermined by his own testimony which, although he declines to change his plea, amounts to an admission of guilt, there is still the possibility of undermining it.[276]

The meaning of undermining the defence of the co-accused gave rise to some difficulty in cases in which the accused appeared merely to have contradicted the evidence given by a co-accused or to have denied participation in a joint venture. In *R v Bruce*[277] it was held that evidence which undermined a co-accused's defence would only trigger section 1(3)(iii) if it made his acquittal less likely.[278] Eight accused were charged with robbery, one of whom, M, admitted

[270] See also and cf *R v Britzman; R v Hall* [1983] 1 WLR 350, CA.
[271] *R v Jones*, ibid.
[272] *R v Courtney* [1995] Crim LR 63, CA.
[273] [1965] AC 574, HL.
[274] Cf *R v Adair* [1990] Crim LR 571, CA.
[275] Cf *R v Crawford* [1998] 1 Cr App R 338, CA.
[276] *R v Mir* [1989] Crim LR 894, CA.
[277] [1975] 1 WLR 1252, CA. Cf *R v Hatton* (1976) 64 Cr App R 88, CA. A denied that there was a plan to steal scrap metal. H gave evidence that both he and A had been parties to a plan to steal but denied that either of them had acted dishonestly. It was held that H had given evidence against A.
[278] Per Stephenson LJ [1975] 1 WLR 1252 at 1259.

that there had been a plan to commit robbery but said that he had not been a party to its execution. Another accused, B, testified that there had been no plan to rob. Counsel for M was then permitted to cross-examine B about his previous convictions. B, acquitted of robbery but convicted of theft, appealed. The Court of Appeal held that section 1(3)(iii) had not been triggered because although B had contradicted M, his evidence was more in M's favour than against him in that it provided him with a different and possibly better defence.[279] It remains to be seen whether section 104(1) of the 2003 Act will be interpreted in the same way.

It seems clear, however, from the decisions in *R v Davis*[280] and *R v Varley*,[281] that evidence which on its face amounts to no more than a denial of participation in a crime or which appears merely to contradict something said by a co-accused, may, in appropriate circumstances, undermine the defence of a co-accused. In *R v Davis*, D and O were jointly charged with the theft of certain items in circumstances such that the offence had been committed either by one or both of them. D, having denied the theft of one of the items, was cross-examined under section 1(3)(iii). He appealed on the ground that a mere denial did not amount to giving evidence against a co-accused. The Court of Appeal held that as only D, O, or both of them could have stolen the items in question, D's denial that he had done so necessarily meant that O had, and the appeal was dismissed.[282] In *R v Varley*, V and D were jointly charged with robbery. D's defence was that he did take part but was forced to do so by threats on his life by V. V gave evidence that he had not taken part in the robbery and that D's evidence was untrue. D's counsel was given leave to cross-examine V as to his previous convictions. V was convicted and appealed. Dismissing the appeal, it was held that a mere denial of participation in a joint venture is not of itself sufficient to trigger section 1(3)(iii)—for section 1(3)(iii) such denial 'must' lead to the conclusion that if the one accused did not participate then it must have been the other who did. It was further held that where one accused asserts a view of the joint venture which is directly contradicted by the other, such contradiction may be evidence against the co-accused. Applying these principles to the facts of the case, V's evidence was against D because it amounted to saying not only that D was telling lies, but also that D was a participant on his own and not acting under duress.

In *R v Crawford*[283] the victim of a robbery alleged that she had been alone in the lavatories of a restaurant with three other women, all of whom had committed the offence. The three were the accused C, her co-accused A, and a third woman, L. C's evidence was to the effect that A and L were in the lavatories at the material time, but that she, C, was not. A's evidence, which was put to C during cross-examination, was that C and L had committed the robbery while she, A, was merely an innocent bystander. It was held that the trial judge had properly allowed A to cross-examine C on her previous convictions, because if the jury accepted C's evidence that only A and L were in the lavatories at the material time, that was very damaging to the credibility of A and made it much less likely that A was simply a passive bystander.[284] It was submitted on appeal that this outcome was in conflict with the proposition in *R v Varley* to the effect that, for section 1(3)(iii) to apply, a mere denial of participation in a joint venture 'must' lead to the conclusion that if the accused did not participate, then it must have been

---

[279] The appeal was dismissed because of the overwhelming evidence of guilt.

[280] [1975] 1 WLR 345, CA.

[281] [1982] 2 All ER 519, CA.

[282] Cf *R v Hendrick* [1992] Crim LR 427, CA.

[283] [1998] 1 Cr App R 338, CA.

[284] Cf *R v Kirkpatrick* [1998] Crim LR 63, CA.

the co-accused who did: this was not a case where it was either C or A who had committed the offence, and if it was not C therefore it must have been A. Rejecting this submission, the Court of Appeal held that, insofar as the proposition from *R v Varley* had been cast in mandatory terms, it went too far: the word 'may' was more appropriate.

In *R v Edwards*[285] it was held, referring to *R v Varley*, that whether an accused's stance amounts to no more than a denial of participation or gives rise to an important matter in issue between a defendant and a co-defendant under section 101(1)(e) will inevitably turn on the facts of the individual case.

It is submitted that in appropriate circumstances, evidence of a conviction admissible under section 101(1)(e) to impugn the credibility of the accused need not be confined to the fact of the previous conviction but may extend to the details of the offence. This would reflect the position in relation to section 1(3)(iii) of the 1898 Act.[286]

Section 101(1)(f)—prosecution evidence to correct a false impression given by the defendant

Under section 101(1)(f), prosecution evidence of the defendant's bad character is admissible if 'it is evidence to correct a false impression given by the defendant'.[287] Section 101(1)(f), together with section 105, by which it is supplemented, are based upon the recommendations of the Law Commission, but lack the Commission's important safeguards. These included a requirement of enhanced relevance, ie *substantial* probative value in correcting the false impression, a requirement to consider a number of detailed factors and, in the case of evidence of prejudicial effect, a requirement that admissibility be in the interests of justice.[288] Furthermore, although it is submitted that evidence admissible under section 101(1)(f) is subject to the common law discretion to exclude on the basis that its prejudicial effect outweighs its probative value, it is not subject to the exclusionary discretion in section 101(3).

Section 105 of the 2003 Act provides as follows:

(1) For the purposes of section 101(1)(f)—
   (a) the defendant gives a false impression if he is responsible for the making of an express or implied assertion which is apt to give the court or jury a false or misleading impression about the defendant;
   (b) evidence to correct such an impression is evidence which has probative value in correcting it.
(2) A defendant is treated as being responsible for the making of an assertion if—
   (a) the assertion is made by the defendant in the proceedings (whether or not in evidence given by him),
   (b) the assertion was made by the defendant—
      (i) on being questioned under caution, before charge, about the offence with which he is charged, or
      (ii) on being charged with the offence or officially informed that he might be prosecuted for it, and evidence of the assertion is given in the proceedings,
   (c) the assertion is made by a witness called by the defendant,

---

[285] [2006] 1 WLR 1524 at [1](vi).

[286] See also *R v Reid* [1989] Crim LR 719, CA. Cf *R v McLeod* [1994] 3 All ER 254, CA, below.

[287] See *R v Assani* [2008] All ER (D) 188 (Nov), which makes it clear that the gateway in s 101(1)(f) and in (g), which will be considered shortly, are restricted to prosecution evidence and are not available to a co-defendant.

[288] Clause 10, Law Commission Draft Bill.

    (d) the assertion is made by any witness in cross-examination in response to a question asked by the defendant that is intended to elicit it, or is likely to do so, or

    (e) the assertion was made by any person out of court, and the defendant adduces evidence of it in the proceedings.

(3) A defendant who would otherwise be treated as responsible for the making of an assertion shall not be so treated if, or to the extent that, he withdraws it or disassociates himself from it.

(4) Where it appears to the court that a defendant, by means of his conduct (other than the giving of evidence) in the proceedings, is seeking to give the court or jury an impression about himself that is false or misleading, the court may if it appears just to do so treat the defendant as being responsible for the making of an assertion which is apt to give that impression.

(5) In subsection (4) 'conduct' includes appearance or dress.

(6) Evidence is admissible under section 101(1)(f) only if it goes no further than is necessary to correct the false impression.

(7) Only prosecution evidence is admissible under section 101(1)(f).

Section 101(1)(f), as supplemented by section 105, reflects but is wider than the pre-existing common law and statutory rules. At common law, if the accused adduced evidence of his good character, the prosecution were permitted to call evidence in rebuttal, and under section 1(3)(ii) of the Criminal Evidence Act 1898, if the accused questioned witnesses for the prosecution with a view to establishing his good character, or gave evidence of his good character, he could be cross-examined on his bad character.

Whether the accused has given a false impression is obviously a question for the judge. That question and the question whether there is evidence which may properly serve to correct the false impression, are fact-specific.[289] It is submitted that the risk of prejudice, where corrective evidence is admitted only to be subsequently ruled inadmissible, is such that in many cases the question of admissibility will need to be the subject of a ruling by the judge in the absence of the jury. Indeed, where the accused denies that the impression conveyed is false and disputes the corrective evidence on which the prosecution seek to rely, it would seem that the judge could only properly decide the matter by holding a *voir dire*.

Express assertions, implied assertions, and assertions by conduct

A simple denial of the offence cannot be treated as either an express or implied false impression for the purposes of section 101(1)(f).[290] 'Express' false assertions, for the purposes of section 105(1)(a), would cover, for example, false assertions that the accused is of good character or a religious man or a man who earns an honest living or who would never use violence. 'Implied' false assertions would cover false assertions relating to the accused's conduct or behaviour from which it can be implied that he is of good character or honest. *R v Samuel*,[291] a decision under section 1(3)(ii) of the 1898 Act, provides a good example. In that case, the accused, charged with larceny, gave evidence of previous occasions on which he had restored lost property to its owner and was held to have been properly cross-examined about his previous convictions for theft. Section 105(1)(a) is also apt to cover false assertions by the accused about his bad character. If, for example, the accused, charged with a sexual offence, falsely asserts that he has only one previous conviction, also for a sexual offence,

---

[289] *R v Renda* [2006] 1 WLR 2948, CA at [19].
[290] *R v Weir* [2006] 1 WLR 1885, CA at [43].
[291] (1956) 40 Cr App R 8, CCA.

then corrective evidence would be admissible that in fact he also has previous convictions for offences of dishonesty. *R v Spartley*[292] provides an example of where evidence of *misconduct* was admitted to correct a false impression. The accused was charged with conspiracy to import ecstasy and possession of cannabis with intent to supply. In his police interview he stated that he had never been involved in the supply of drugs. It was held that evidence from an interview with Dutch police some seven years earlier, in which he had admitted being a cannabis courier between Spain and Holland, was admissible under section 101(1)(f) to correct the false impression.

An example of a false or misleading impression conveyed by conduct, for the purposes of section 105(4) and (5), would be an accused who, not being a priest, appears in the proceedings wearing a clerical dog-collar. However, an accused with many previous convictions for dishonesty does not make a false assertion as to his good character by simply taking the oath or reminding the jury of the oath that he has sworn on the bible and, on that reasoning, nor will he do so by his conduct in holding and gesticulating with a bible while in the witness box.[293]

Under section 105(4), the court will only treat the accused as being responsible for the making of an assertion by means of his conduct 'if it appears just to do so', a hurdle presumably designed to prevent overuse or abuse of the subsection. For example, many accused will dress up for their court appearance, wearing outfits which they would normally wear only on very special occasions. Section 105 should not cover, it is submitted, the case of the plumber or plasterer who appears in court in his best suit. It would be otherwise, however, if he were to sport a regimental tie or blazer, never having served in the army.

Corrective evidence

Evidence to correct the false impression must have probative value in correcting it,[294] but must go no further than is necessary to correct it.[295] Thus if the accused expressly asserts that he 'earns an honest living', the corrective evidence may include evidence of his previous convictions for crimes of dishonesty, but not evidence of his previous convictions for, say, assault or driving with excess alcohol. However, problems are likely to be encountered, in some cases, in identifying precisely what the false or misleading impression is. For example, if an accused is charged with inflicting grievous bodily harm in an 'off the ball' incident during the course of a rugby match, and gives evidence that he has no previous convictions, is evidence admissible to show his disciplinary record of violent play on the rugby field.[296] The same problem exists in the case of implied assertions or assertions by conduct. The accused wearing a clerical collar presumably conveys the impression not only that he is a priest, but also that he behaves as a priest should, and therefore the corrective evidence should not be confined to evidence which goes to show that he is not a priest, or has been defrocked, but should extend to general evidence of his misconduct or disposition to misconduct.

---

[292] [2007] All ER (D) 233 (May). A conviction in Holland would also have been admissible (in accordance with the Crime (International Co-operation) Act 2003, ss 7 and 8).

[293] See *R v Robinson* [2001] Crim LR 478, CA, a decision under s 1(3)(ii) of the 1898 Act.

[294] Section 105(1)(b).

[295] Section 105(6).

[296] In *R v Marsh* [1994] Crim LR 52, CA, from which these facts are taken, it was held that the evidence was admissible in cross-examination under s 1(3)(ii) of the Criminal Evidence Act 1898.

Withdrawal or disassociation from an assertion

Under section 105(2)(d), an accused is treated as being responsible for the making of an assertion made by a witness cross-examined by (or, presumably, on behalf of) him, but only if the
assertion was in response to a question intended to elicit it or which was likely to elicit it.
Thus if the witness volunteers a false impression about the accused, the accused will not be
treated as being responsible for the making of the volunteered assertion and evidence will
be admissible to correct it. In contrast, under section 105(2)(c) an accused is treated as being
responsible for the making of an assertion made by a witness called by him, and corrective
evidence will be admissible in this situation where the witness volunteers a false impression
as much as when he asserts it in answer to a question intended to elicit it or which was likely
to elicit it. However, in this situation it seems that the accused can prevent the introduction
of corrective evidence by disassociating himself from the assertion made by the witness, in
reliance upon section 105(3). An accused who no longer stands by a false assertion made by
him and introduced in evidence under section 105(2)(b) by the prosecution, would also be
well advised to withdraw it. In cases in which the accused himself makes, or adduces evidence
of, a false assertion, section 105(3) also provides him with the opportunity to embark upon a
damage limitation exercise. For example, if the accused makes, or adduces evidence of, a false
assertion to the effect that he is of good character, but then withdraws or disassociates himself
from the assertion, he will thereby prevent the admission of corrective evidence of, say, his
previous convictions, but the jury will by then be aware that he is not of good character and
also, in cases in which the assertion was made by him in giving his evidence, that he is not
always a reliable witness. However, an accused must take the initiative if he wishes to rely on
section 105(3); a concession extracted in cross-examination will not normally amount to a
withdrawal or disassociation for the purposes of section 105(3).[297]

Corrective evidence as to guilt or credibility of the accused

Given the breadth of provision for the admissibility of evidence of disposition under section
101(1)(d), presumably such evidence will only rarely be admitted as corrective evidence
under section 101(1)(f). Where such evidence is admitted under section 101(1)(f), however, then it seems clear that it is evidence that will go not only to the credibility of the
accused but also to the likelihood of his guilt, and that the jury should be directed accordingly. It remains to be seen whether the position will be the same in the case of corrective
evidence of misconduct, ie evidence of the commission of an offence or other reprehensible
behaviour. However, it is submitted that there is much force in the argument that where an
accused makes, or adduces evidence of, a false assertion as to his good character, he generally does so for the purpose of showing that it is unlikely that he committed the offence
charged, and the corrective evidence is introduced to show the contrary, and not merely to
attack his credibility.[298]

Discretionary exclusion

If, as has been submitted, prosecution evidence admissible under section 101 may be excluded
in reliance upon the common law discretionary power to exclude prosecution evidence the

---

[297] *R v Renda* [2006] 2 All ER 553, CA at [21].

[298] For dicta to this effect in relation to evidence admissible in cross-examination of an accused who had put his
character in issue, under s 1(3)(ii) of the Criminal Evidence Act 1898, see per Viscount Sankey in *Maxwell v DPP*
[1935] AC 309 at 319 and per Lord Goddard CJ in *R v Samuel* (1956) 40 Cr App R 8 at 12.

prejudicial effect of which outweighs its probative value, there may well be limited scope for the exercise of the discretion in relation to evidence admissible under section 101(1)(f) because to exclude such evidence may seriously mislead the jury.[299]

Section 101(1)(g)—prosecution evidence where the defendant has made an attack on another person's character

Under section 101(1)(g) of the 2003 Act, prosecution evidence of the accused's bad character is admissible if 'the defendant has made an attack on another person's character'. Where section 101(1)(g) is triggered, evidence of the accused's bad character is admissible even if he elects not to testify.[300] The purpose of the gateway was explained by Underhill J in *R v Lamaletie*:[301]

> The conception underlying [the] gateway…is that where a defendant has impugned the character of a prosecution witness the jury will be assisted in deciding who to believe by knowing the defendant's character.

Section 101(1)(g), as supplemented by section 106, is in some measure based on the recommendations of the Law Commission but, as in the case of section 101(1)(f), lacks the Commission's important safeguards, including the requirement of enhanced relevance, the requirement to consider a number of detailed factors and, in the case of evidence of prejudicial effect, the requirement that admissibility be in the interests of justice.[302] The statutory provisions also depart from the recommendation of the Law Commission that evidence of the bad character of the defendant should not be admissible where he makes an attack on another person using evidence of his bad character which 'has to do with the alleged facts of the offence with which the defendant is charged, or is evidence of misconduct in connection with the investigation or prosecution of that offence',[303] as when the accused asserts that the offence was committed by another or that another has invented the allegation against him.

An attack on another person's character

Section 106 of the 2003 Act provides as follows:

(1) For the purposes of section 101(1)(g) a defendant makes an attack on another person's character if—
  (a) he adduces evidence attacking the other person's character,
  (b) he (or any legal representative appointed under section 38(4) of the Youth Justice and Criminal Evidence Act 1999 to cross-examine a witness in his interests) asks questions in cross-examination that are intended to elicit such evidence, or are likely to do so, or
  (c) evidence is given of an imputation about the other person made by the defendant—
    (i) on being questioned under caution, before charge, about the offence with which he is charged, or
    (ii) on being charged with the offence or officially informed that he might be prosecuted for it.

---

[299] See *R v Marsh* [1994] Crim LR 52, CA, above.

[300] At common law, if the accused did not give evidence but attacked witnesses for the prosecution, then, without more, evidence of the accused's bad character could not be introduced: *R v Butterwasser* [1948] 1 KB 4, CCA.

[301] [2008] EWCA Crim 314 at [15]. Lord Devlin's explanation in *R v Cook* [1959] 2 QB 340 at 347 of the same principle underlying the old law, was cited with approval.

[302] Clause 9, Law Commission Draft Bill.

[303] Clause 9(2), ibid.

(2) In subsection (1) 'evidence attacking the other person's character' means evidence to the effect that the other person—

(a) has committed an offence (whether a different offence from the one with which the defendant is charged or the same one), or

(b) has behaved, or is disposed to behave, in a reprehensible way;

and 'imputation about the other person' means an assertion to that effect.

(3) Only prosecution evidence is admissible under section 101(1)(g).

Under section 106, the circumstances in which a defendant makes an attack on another person's character are different from the circumstances under section 105 in which the accused is treated as being responsible for the making of a false assertion. Thus section 106 appears not to apply where an attack on another person's character is made by the accused while being cross-examined at the hands of either the prosecution or any co-accused. However, although matters are not spelt out in the way that they are in section 105, it seems reasonably clear that section 106(1)(a) does cover an attack on another person's character when either made by a witness called by the accused or contained in a hearsay statement adduced by the accused. Evidence 'given' under section 106(1)(c) may be 'given' by the prosecution, provided that it is relevant to the issues in the case and otherwise admissible, as opposed to merely providing a basis for satisfying gateway (g);[304] and because section 106 contains no equivalent of section 105(3), this will trigger section 101(1)(g) even if the accused wishes to withdraw the out-of-court statement on which the prosecution rely or to disassociate himself from it.

The definition of 'evidence attacking the other person's character' in section 106(2) must be read together with section 100 of the Act. Under section 100, it will be recalled, except where all parties agree to the admissibility of evidence of the bad character of a person other than the accused, such evidence is only admissible with the leave of the court and such leave can only be granted if the evidence is either (a) important explanatory evidence; or (b) has substantial probative value in relation to a matter which is in issue in the proceedings and is of substantial importance in the context of the case as a whole. Thus evidence to attack another person's character which does not meet the requirements of section 100 will be inadmissible.

It is clear from section 106 that 'another person' may or may not be a witness in the case. Thus an attack may be made on a victim who dies by reason of the crime, for example a victim of murder, manslaughter, or causing death by dangerous driving, a victim of an offence of violence who, by reason of the injuries sustained, is unable to be called as a witness, a victim who does not give evidence by reason of threats, interference, or intimidation, a person whose hearsay statement is in evidence in the proceedings, and so on. However, it is also reasonably clear that 'another person' must be an identified individual. The definition of 'evidence attacking the other person's character' in section 106(2) clearly envisages that the identity of that person is known.

Section 106(2)(a) covers cases in which the evidence is to the effect that the person has committed either the very offence with which the accused is charged or some other offence. Section 106(2)(b), which refers to evidence to the effect that the other person has behaved or is disposed to behave in a reprehensible way, will typically cover evidence of misconduct on the part of the police or prosecution witnesses which amounted to 'imputations' for the purposes of section 1(3)(ii) of the 1898 Act. Examples included allegations that the prosecutor or a witness for the prosecution invented the crime alleged,[305] obtained

---

[304] *R v Nelson* [2007] Crim LR 709, CA. See also *R v Renda* [2006] 1 WLR 2948, CA at [29]–[38].

[305] *Selvey v DPP* [1970] AC 304, HL.

a confession by bribes,[306] deliberately held the accused on remand after remand in order to concoct evidence,[307] manufactured a confession statement,[308] completely fabricated part of his evidence,[309] or asked a relative to have a quiet word with the accused to get him to talk and admit the offence.[310] Looking at section 106(2) as a whole, there is no doubt that, subject to discretionary exclusion, evidence of the bad character of the accused will be admissible under section 101(1)(g) notwithstanding that the attack on another person's character is a necessary or justifiable part of his defence.

In *R v Hanson*[311] it was held that pre-2003 Act authorities will continue to apply when assessing whether an attack has been made on another person's character under section 101(1)(g), to the extent that they are compatible with section 106.

Assertions of innocence and denials of guilt

Under section 1(3)(ii) of the 1898 Act, it was held that mere assertions of innocence by the accused, or his emphatic denials of guilt, did not result in a loss of the shield and were to be distinguished from attacks on the veracity of the prosecutor or a prosecution witness, which did have that result.[312] It is submitted that such a distinction remains valid for the purposes of section 101(1)(g). The distinction, however, is difficult and narrow, as is apparent in an early and classic example given by Lord Hewart CJ in *R v Jones*:[313]

> It was one thing for the appellant to deny that he had made the confession; but it is another thing to say that the whole thing was an elaborate and deliberate concoction on the part of the inspector.

The difficulty and narrowness lies in the fact that, in some cases, to deny that the confession was made necessarily means, by implication, that the police have fabricated evidence, and although section 106, unlike section 105, does not refer to implied as well as express assertions, it is submitted that an accused will trigger section 101(1)(g) where an attack on another person's character is made by necessary implication, rather than in terms. Under section 1(3)(ii) of the 1898 Act, it was said that 'each case falls to be determined upon the exact facts, the exact circumstances, the exact language used',[314] but some of the authorities were very difficult to reconcile.[315] In *R v Britzman; R v Hall*[316] the Court of Appeal set out guidelines. In that case, police officers gave evidence of admissions made by the appellant during a lengthy interview, of which there was a written record, and in the course of a shouting-match between Britzman and Hall in the cells. The appellant denied that the interview and the shouting-match had ever taken place and, in cross-examination of the officers, this was suggested to

---

[306] *R v Wright* (1910) 5 Cr App R 131.

[307] *R v Jones* (1923) 17 Cr App R 117.

[308] *R v Clark* [1955] 2 QB 469.

[309] *R v Levy* (1966) 50 Cr App R 238. See also *R v Dunkley* [1927] 1 KB 323, CCA.

[310] *R v Courtney* [1995] Crim LR 63, CA.

[311] [2005] 1 WLR 3169, CA.

[312] See per Lord Goddard CJ in *R v Clark* [1955] 2 QB 469 at 478, applied in *R v St Louis and Fitzroy Case* (1984) 79 Cr App R 53, CA.

[313] (1923) 17 Cr App R 117 at 120.

[314] Per Lord Parker CJ in *R v Levy* (1966) 50 Cr App R 238 at 241.

[315] See, eg, *R v Rouse* [1904] 1 KB 184 and cf *R v Rappolt* (1911) 6 Cr App R, 156, CCA; and see *R v Tanner* (1977) 66 CR App R 56, CA and cf *R v Nelson* (1978) 68 Cr App R 12, CA.

[316] [1983] 1 WLR 350.

them by counsel for the appellant. The Court of Appeal, noting that it was not a case of a denial of a single answer and that there was no suggestion of mistake or misunderstanding, held that the nature and conduct of the defence did involve imputations on the character of the prosecution witnesses. To deny that the conversations took place at all necessarily meant by implication that the police officers had given false evidence which they had made up for the purposes of a conviction. It was held that a distinction could not be drawn between a defence so conducted as to make specific allegations of fabrication and one in which such allegations arose by way of necessary and reasonable implication.[317] It is submitted that some of the guidelines set out by Lawton LJ, giving the judgment of the court, are likely to remain valid for the purposes of section 101(1)(g). His Lordship said:

> the exercise of discretion in favour of defendants . . . should be used if there is nothing more than a denial, however emphatic or offensively made, of an act or even a short series of acts amounting to one incident or in what was said to have been a short interview . . . The position would be different however if there were a denial of evidence of a long period of detailed observation extending over hours and . . . where there were denials of long conversations . . . cross-examination should only be allowed if the judge is sure that there is no possibility of mistake, misunderstanding or confusion and that the jury will inevitably have to decide whether the prosecution witnesses have fabricated evidence. Defendants sometimes make wild allegations when giving evidence. Allowance should be made for the strain of being in the witness box and the exaggerated use of language which sometimes results from such strain or lack of education or mental stability.[318]

Discretionary exclusion

Evidence admissible under section 101(1)(g) is open to discretionary exclusion under section 101(3) if it appears to the court that the admission of the evidence would have such an adverse effect on the fairness of the proceedings that the court ought not to admit it. Such evidence, it is submitted, is also open to exclusion in reliance upon the common law discretion to exclude prosecution evidence the prejudicial effect of which outweighs its probative value.[319]

The likely grounds for discretionary exclusion are considered under the following headings.

An attack on the character of a non-witness non-victim.   To admit evidence of the accused's bad character under section 101(1)(g) by reason of an attack on the character of someone who is neither a witness nor a victim of the offence, will *normally* have such an adverse effect on the fairness of the proceedings that the court ought not to admit it; an exception would be, for example, where there is an attack on the witness victim that he conspired with the non-witness non-victim to fabricate the allegation, because the attack on the character of the non-witness may influence the jury in their view of the victim's evidence.[320]

Evidence of bad character irrelevant or disproportionate to the bad character of the other person.   As noted earlier, evidence admissible under section 101(1)(g) may be relevant not only to credibility but also to propensity to commit offences of the kind charged.[321] However, it is submitted that bad character evidence that has little or no bearing on the credibility of the accused

---

[317] See also *R v Owen* (1985) 83 Cr App R 100, CA.
[318] [1983] 1 WLR 350 at 355.
[319] See 469 above, under *Discretion to exclude*.
[320] *R v Nelson* [2007] Crim LR 709, CA.
[321] See 466 above, under *Admissibility and use*.

or his defence and does not show his propensity to commit offences of the kind charged, even if admissible in law, should be excluded by the exercise of discretion. For example, in a case of fraud, a previous conviction for fraud may be relevant to both credibility and propensity, but evidence of the accused's disposition towards sexual misconduct or cruelty to animals could serve no purpose but prejudice.[322] Equally, it is submitted, there is scope for exercise of the discretion where the bad character of the accused is disproportionate to the bad character of the person whose character has been attacked. In *R v Burke*,[323] Ackner LJ, rehearsing the cardinal principles set out in *Selvey v DPP*[324] upon which the discretion to exclude was exercised under section 1(3)(ii) of the 1898 Act, said that in the ordinary and normal case the trial judge may feel that if the credit of the prosecutor or his witnesses has been attacked, it is only fair that the jury should have before them material on which they can form their judgment whether the accused is any more worthy of belief than those he has attacked. Earlier, however, he said:

> The trial judge must weigh the prejudicial effect of the questions against the damage done by the attack on the prosecution's witnesses, and must generally exercise his discretion so as to secure a trial that is fair both to the prosecution and the defence . . .
>
> Cases must occur in which it would be unjust to admit evidence of a character gravely prejudicial to the accused, even though there may be some tenuous grounds for holding it technically admissible . . .

Attacks which are a necessary or justifiable part of the defence.   It is clear that under section 101(3), impact on the fairness of the proceedings must be assessed by reference to matters other than what the motive or intention of the accused was in making an attack on another's character.[325] However, in some cases it will be obvious that the attack was necessary to enable him to establish his defence and although, as we have seen, this will not prevent the admissibility in law of his bad character, and although the discretion to exclude should not invariably or even generally be exercised in these circumstances, because that would amount to a qualification to section 101(1)(g) under the guise of discretion, it is submitted that the discretion should be exercised, as necessary, to prevent too severe an application of section 101(1)(g). As the House of Lords observed in *Selvey v DPP*,[326] in relation to exercise of the discretion on this basis to prevent cross-examination of the accused under section 1(3)(ii) of the 1898 Act, the discretion is unfettered, its exercise being dependent on the circumstances of each case and the overriding duty of the judge to ensure a fair trial.

Similarities between the facts of previous offences and the offence charged.   As previously noted, evidence of the accused's bad character is admissible under section 101(1)(g) because of the bearing it has on the credibility of the defence case and, it is submitted, a judge should direct the jury accordingly and, in cases in which the bad character is not also admissible as propensity evidence, should further direct the jury that the evidence does not show propensity to commit the offence charged. It does not follow from this that the exclusionary discretion

---

[322] But see *R v Highton* [2006] 1 Cr App R 125, where the Court of Appeal could see no grounds to challenge the judge's refusal to exclude, under s 101(3), two drink-related driving offences, failure to provide a specimen and driving with excess alcohol.

[323] (1985) 82 Cr App R 156, CA.

[324] [1970] AC 304, HL.

[325] *R v Bovell* [2005] 2 Cr App R 401, CA at [32].

[326] [1970] AC 304, HL.

should always be exercised to prevent cross-examination which would lead the jury to infer that the accused is guilty of the offence charged, as when the accused is cross-examined on previous offences of a type similar to that charged, but the nature of that offence and the extent to which it resembles the offence charged, are certainly relevant matters for the judge to take into account. In deciding whether and how to exercise the discretion in respect of evidence admissible under section 101(1)(g), valuable guidance is likely to be derived from the decisions reached in relation to exercise of the discretion to prevent cross-examination under section 1(3)(ii) of the 1898 Act.

In *R v McLeod*[327] M was convicted of an armed robbery which involved the use of a number of stolen cars. At interview he made a confession, but in evidence he said he had nothing to do with the robbery and that the police had created a false case against him and fabricated his confession. Anticipating cross-examination on previous convictions, his counsel asked M about them briefly during his examination-in-chief. In cross-examination on the previous convictions under section 1(3)(ii),[328] M was asked about: (i) a robbery, following a not guilty plea and a defence of alibi; (ii) another robbery in which the victim had been locked in an understairs cupboard; (iii) theft of a car involving a change of the plates to a false registration; and (iv) handling of a car with false registration plates. On appeal it was submitted that the questions should not have been asked. Stuart-Smith LJ, giving the judgment of the court, set out the following principles:

1. The primary purpose of cross-examination as to previous convictions and bad character of the accused is to show that he is not worthy of belief, not to show that he has a disposition to commit the type of offence with which he is charged.[329] But the mere fact that the offences are of a similar type to that charged or because of their number and type have the incidental effect of suggesting a tendency or disposition to commit the offence charged will not make them improper.[330]

2. It is undesirable that there should be prolonged or extensive cross-examination in relation to previous offences, because it will divert the jury from the principal issue in the case, the guilt of the accused on the instant offence, and not the details of earlier ones. Unless the earlier ones are admissible as similar fact evidence, prosecuting counsel should not seek to probe or emphasize similarities between the underlying facts of previous offences and the instant offence.[331]

3. Similarities of defences which have been rejected by juries on previous occasions, for example false alibis or the defence that the incriminating substance has been planted and whether or not the accused pleaded guilty or was disbelieved having given evidence on oath, may be a legitimate matter for questions. These matters do not show a disposition to commit the offence in question but are clearly relevant to credibility.

---

[327] [1994] 1 WLR 1500, CA.

[328] Strictly speaking, the case is not an authority on s 1(3)(ii) because the jury were already aware of the previous convictions: see *Jones v DPP* [1962] AC 635, HL, above. However, there seems little doubt that whether the evidence of bad character was introduced under s 1(3)(ii) or at common law, the principles relating to discretionary exclusion were the same.

[329] *R v Vickers* [1972] Crim LR 101, CA.

[330] See *R v Powell* [1986] 1 All ER 193, CA; *Selvey v DPP* [1970] AC 304, HL, above; and *R v Wheeler* [1995] Crim LR 312, CA. See also *R v Davison-Jenkins* [1997] Crim LR 816, CA.

[331] See, eg, the subsequent decision in *R v Davison-Jenkins* [1997] Crim LR 816, CA.

4. Underlying facts that show particularly bad character over and above the bare facts of the case are not necessarily to be excluded. However, the judge should be careful to balance the gravity of the attack on the prosecution with the degree of prejudice to the defence which will result from the disclosure of the facts in question. Details of sexual offences against children are likely to be regarded by the jury as particularly prejudicial to an accused and may well be the reason why in *R v Watts*[332] the court thought the questions impermissible.

Applying those principles to the facts, the appeal against conviction was dismissed. The questions were not unduly prolonged or extensive. Concerning the first offence, there was nothing wrong in asking about the plea and the rejected defence of alibi. As to the victim of the second offence being locked under the stairs, it merely showed that the offence was somewhat more ruthless than may normally be the case in a robbery where, by definition, violence or the threat of it, is used. As to the other two offences, it was fanciful to contend that the facts elicited were designed to show a propensity to commit armed robbery, merely because the use of stolen vehicles with false registration plates is the stock in trade of armed robbery.[333]

Discretionary exclusion of evidence described in section 106(1)(c). In cases in which the prosecution seek to rely on evidence falling within section 106(2), ie evidence of an imputation made by the accused on being questioned under caution or on being charged with the offence,[334] then insofar as the accused can show that the evidence was obtained illegally, improperly, or unfairly, whether by virtue of breaches of the codes of practice or otherwise, there will be obvious scope for discretionary exclusion of the evidence, which in turn could prevent section 101(1)(g) from being triggered. The authorities in relation to the discretionary exclusion of prosecution evidence obtained illegally, improperly, or unfairly, are considered in Chapter 3. There may also be scope for discretionary exclusion of evidence of an imputation made by the accused on being questioned or charged where the accused wishes to withdraw or disassociate himself from the imputation at the trial This may require more from the accused than simply not repeating it in evidence.[335]

Offences committed by defendant when a child

Section 108(2) and (3) of the 2003 Act, which replace section 16(2) and (3) of the Children and Young Person's Act 1963, provide as follows:

(2) In proceedings for an offence committed or alleged to have been committed by the defendant when aged 21 or over, evidence of his conviction for an offence when under the age of 14 is not admissible unless—
(a) both of the offences are triable only on indictment, and
(b) the court is satisfied that the interests of justice require the evidence to be admissible.
(3) Subsection (2) applies in addition to section 101.

[332] (1983) 77 Cr App R 126.
[333] Cf *R v Barsoum* [1994] Crim LR 194, CA. Although note, *R v Barrat* [2000] Crim LR 847, CA where the accused should not have been cross-examined on an old spent conviction which had little impact on credibility.
[334] See *R v Ball*, the conjoined appeal in *R v Renda* [2006] 1 WLR 2948, where the attack was made in a police interview. See also *R v Lamaletie* [2008] EWCA Crim 314.
[335] See *R v Ball*, the conjoined appeal in *R v Renda* [2006] 1 WLR 2948.

General

Assumption of truth in the assessment of relevance or probative value

By virtue of section 109 of the 2003 Act, a court, when considering the relevance or probative value of evidence of bad character under section 100 (non-defendant) or section 101 (defendant) in order to decide whether it is admissible, should operate on the assumption that the evidence is true, but need not do so if no reasonable court or jury could reasonably find it to be true. Section 109 provides as follows:

(1) Subject to subsection (2), a reference in this Chapter to the relevance or probative value of evidence is a reference to its relevance or probative value on the assumption that it is true.

(2) In assessing the relevance or probative value of an item of evidence for any purpose of this Chapter, a court need not assume that the evidence is true if it appears, on the basis of any material before the court (including any evidence it decides to hear on the matter), that no court or jury could reasonably find it to be true.

Section 109 applies to section 101(e) (evidence of substantial probative value in relation to an important matter in issue between the defendant and a co-defendant) and to 101(1)(f), as supplemented by section 105 (evidence to correct a false impression given by the defendant). Its chief importance, however, is likely to be in relation to the assessment of the probative value of 'similar fact evidence' properly so called under section 101(1)(d) (evidence of the defendant's bad character relevant to an important matter in issue between the defendant and the prosecution) and under section 100(3)(c) and (d) (evidence of a non-defendant's bad character of substantial probative value). The probative value of similar fact evidence often arises out of the nexus between the spontaneous and independent accounts of two or more witnesses. That probative value disappears, therefore, if there is also evidence to suggest that the witnesses have deliberately concocted false evidence by conspiracy or collaboration or, which is more common, the evidence of each of them has been innocently contaminated by knowledge of the account of the other, whether acquired directly, ie in discussion with the other,[336] or indirectly, from a third person,[337] or as a result of media publicity.[338] In *R v H*[339] the House of Lords considered whether evidence carrying a real risk of collusion or contamination should be excluded by the judge or should be left to the jury with an appropriate warning. *R v H* was a case of sexual offences against a daughter and a step-daughter between whom, the parties agreed, there existed a risk of collusion. It was held that save in very rare cases, the question of collusion goes not to the admissibility of similar fact evidence, but to its credibility, an issue for the jury, and that it would be wrong for the judge to decide whether there is a risk of collusion because he would inevitably be drawn into considering whether the evidence is untrue and hence whether there is a real possibility that the accused is innocent, the very question which the jury has to decide. The following principles derive from the judgments given.

---

[336] See *R v W* [1994] 2 All ER 872, CA.

[337] See *R v Ananthanarayanan* [1994] 1 WLR 788, CA.

[338] See per Lord Wilberforce in *DPP v Boardman* [1975] AC 421, HL at 444 and per Stuart-Smith LJ in *R v Bedford* (1990) 93 Cr App R 113, CA at 116.

[339] [1995] 2 AC 596, HL.

1. Normally, where there is an application to exclude similar fact evidence carrying a risk of collusion or contamination, the judge should approach the question of admissibility on the basis that the similar facts alleged are true.

2. In very exceptional cases, evidence of collusion or contamination may be taken into account and in such cases the judge would be compelled to hold a *voir dire*.

3. If the evidence is admitted and it becomes apparent that no reasonable jury could accept it as free from collusion, the judge should direct the jury that it cannot be used for any purpose adverse to the defence.

4. Where this is not so, but the question of collusion has been raised, the judge must draw the importance of collusion to the attention of the jury and direct then that if they are not satisfied that the evidence can be relied upon as free from collusion, they cannot rely upon it for any purpose adverse to the defence.

Although section 109 is clearly based on the common law rules it replaces, there are two significant differences. First, as we have seen, it is much wider in its ambit in that it applies for the purpose of assessing the relevance or probative value of the bad character of the non-defendant as well as the defendant. Secondly, there is nothing to suggest that section 109(2) should be invoked only exceptionally. However, section 109(2), as drafted, is a somewhat curious provision in that where it appears to the court on the basis of the material before it, including any evidence given in a *voir dire*, that no court or jury could find the facts in question to be true, then the court 'need not assume' that those facts are true. It is submitted that the unstated but more obvious action that the court needs to take, once it has concluded that no court or jury could find the facts in question to be true, is to exclude the evidence. It remains to be seen whether the courts will adopt such a robust approach and also whether different approaches will be adopted depending upon whether the evidence is relied upon by the defence or the prosecution. In any event, it is submitted that the third and fourth principles derived from *R v H* as set out above remain good law.

Stopping the case where evidence contaminated

Under section 107 of the 2003 Act, which applies only to trials before a judge and jury, if evidence of the bad character of the accused has been admitted under any of paragraphs (c) to (g) of section 101(1), and the court is satisfied, at any time after the close of the prosecution case, that the evidence is so contaminated that the accused's conviction of the offence would be unsafe, the court must either direct the jury to acquit or, if there ought to be a retrial, discharge the jury. Section 107 of the 2003 Act provides as follows:

(1) If on a defendant's trial before a judge and jury for an offence—
   (a) evidence of his bad character has been admitted under any of paragraphs (c) to (g) of section 101(1), and
   (b) the court is satisfied at any time after the close of the case for the prosecution that—
      (i) the evidence is contaminated, and
      (ii) the contamination is such that, considering the importance of the evidence to the case against the defendant, his conviction of the offence would be unsafe,
   the court must either direct the jury to acquit the defendant of the offence or, if it considers that there ought to be a retrial, discharge the jury.

(2) Where—

    (a) a jury is directed under subsection (1) to acquit a defendant of an offence, and

    (b) the circumstances are such that, apart from this subsection, the defendant could if acquitted of that offence be found guilty of another offence,

the defendant may not be found guilty of that other offence if the court is satisfied as mentioned in subsection (1)(b) in respect of it.

    . . . [340]

(4) This section does not prejudice any other power a court may have to direct a jury to acquit a person of an offence or to discharge a jury.

(5) For the purposes of this section a person's evidence is contaminated where—

    (a) as a result of an agreement or understanding between the person and one or more others, or

    (b) as a result of the person being aware of anything alleged by one or more others whose evidence may be, or has been, given in the proceedings,

the evidence is false or misleading in any respect, or is different from what it would otherwise have been.

Subsection (5)(a) covers cases of conspiracy and collaboration, whereas subsection (5)(b) seems designed to cover cases of innocent contamination and has been cast in sufficiently wide terms, it is submitted, to cover cases in which a person became aware of the allegation of another not only directly, but also indirectly, through some third person or as a result of media coverage.

It appears that section 107 may be brought into play either on an application by the accused or by the court of its own motion. However, according to the Explanatory Notes to the Act, the test in section 107(1)(b)(ii) is designed to be a high test so that if the judge were to consider that a jury direction along the lines described in *R v H*[341] would be sufficient to deal with any potential difficulties, then the question of the safety of the conviction would not arise and the case should not be withdrawn.[342]

The following propositions relating to section 107 derive from *R v C*:[343]

1. Contamination may result from deliberate collusion, or the exercise of improper pressure, but equally may arise innocently or through inadvertence.

2. Contamination issues extend to evidence of bad character in the broad sense, as well as to unequivocal evidence of bad character arising from unchallenged evidence of previous convictions.

3. Whether the evidence of a witness is false or misleading or different from what it would have been if it had not been contaminated, requires the judge to form his own assessment, or judgment, of matters traditionally regarded as questions of fact for the jury.

4. The effect of section 107 is to reduce the risk of a conviction based on over-reliance on evidence of previous misconduct: the dangers inherent in contamination may be obscured by the evidence of bad character.

---

[340] Section 107(3) is cast in terms similar to s 107(1) and is to the same effect, but applies not to a trial but to a jury determination under s 4A(2) of the Criminal Procedure (Insanity) Act 1964 whether a person charged on indictment did the act or made the omission charged.

[341] [1995] 2 AC 596, HL. See principles 3 and 4, at 515 above, under **Assumption of truth in the assessment of relevance or probative value.**

[342] Paras 384 and 385.

[343] [2006] 1 WLR 2994, CA.

5. If the judge is satisfied of the matters in section 107(1)(b), then what follows is not a matter of discretion.

6. An order for retrial would not normally be susceptible to a subsequent appplication based on an asserted abuse of process.

In *R v C* there was a two-count indictment, the first alleging sexual assault on one child, V1, and the second alleging sexual assault on another child, V2, and the prosecution evidence on count one was admissible evidence of bad character relevant to the issue of guilt on count 2. In such circumstances, it is submitted, if the court is satisfied that by reason of the contamination of V1's evidence, there should be an acquittal on count 2, then the court may also be compelled, depending on the circumstances, to direct an acquittal on count one.[344] However, the question of whether evidence has been contaminated is highly fact sensitive. Unless there is a clear misdirection or a clear failure to consider material evidence, appellate courts will not overturn a decision of the trial judge, who is considered to be in the best position to make the assessment required by section 107.[345]

Court's duty to give reasons for rulings

Section 110 of the 2003 Act gives effect to the Law Commission's proposal that there should be a duty on the court to give reasons for its rulings. The section applies not only to rulings on whether an item of evidence is evidence of bad character, but also to rulings on admissibility under section 100 (non-defendant's bad character), section 101 (defendant's bad character), and section 107 (stopping the case where the evidence is 'contaminated'). Section 110 provides as follows:

(1) Where the court makes a relevant ruling—
   (a) it must state in open court (but in the absence of the jury, if there is one) its reasons for the ruling;
   (b) if it is a magistrates' court, it must cause the ruling and the reasons for it to be entered in the register of the court's proceedings.
(2) In this section 'relevant ruling' means—
   (a) a ruling on whether an item of evidence is evidence of a person's bad character;
   (b) a ruling on whether an item of such evidence is admissible under section 100 or 101 (including a ruling on an application under section 101(3);[346]
   (c) a ruling under section 107.

Despite the mandatory nature of section 110(1), it seems likely that a failure to give reasons for a relevant ruling is, by itself, unlikely to render a conviction unsafe: the appellate court is likely to concentrate on whether the ruling itself was wrong.

Rules of court

Under section 111(1) of the 2003 Act, rules of court may make such provision as appear to be necessary or expedient for the purposes of the Act. Under section 111(2) of the 2003 Act:

---

[344] See Richardson, 'Commentary' [2006] *Crim LR* 1060.

[345] *R v K* [2008] EWCA Crim 3177. See also *R v Lamb* [2007] EWCA Crim 1766.

[346] Under s 101(3), the court has a discretionary power to exclude evidence otherwise admissible under either s 101(1)(d) or s 101(1)(g).

(2) The rules may, and, where the party in question is the prosecution, must, contain provisions requiring a party who—
(a) proposes to adduce evidence of a defendant's bad character, or
(b) proposes to cross-examine a witness with a view to eliciting such evidence,
to serve on the defendant such notice, and such particulars of or relating to the evidence, as may be prescribed.

The rules applicable in magistrates' courts and crown courts are set out in rule 35 of the Criminal Procedure Rules 2005.[347] Under rule 35, where a party wants to introduce evidence of an accused's bad character, there is a requirement to give notice, whether that party is the prosecution[348] or a co-accused.[349] Where notice has not been given, the judge has a discretion to permit notice to be given orally or in a different form to that prescribed and he has power to shorten the time-limit or to extend it after it has expired.[350] The time-limits must be observed, but the discretion to extend the time-limit is not fettered by a requirement that it should be exercised only in exceptional circumstances. The court should take account of the overriding objective, the reason for failure to comply, when relevant inquiries were initiated, why they were not completed in time, and whether the accused's position has been prejudiced.[351] The judge can shorten the time-limit to any degree and thus dispense with the notice requirement altogether.[352] Where a co-accused proposes to adduce bad character evidence, he should always alert counsel for the other accused to his intentions, even in a case where notice has not or could not be given.[353] There is no provision in rule 35 to the effect that where a party fails to give notice, the evidence is only admissible with leave, but in *R v Musone*[354] the Court of Appeal, relying on the overriding objective in rule 1.1, including in particular its recognition of the right to a fair trial under Article 6 of the European Convention on Human Rights, held that the court does have power to exclude the evidence. The court emphasized that it would be rare to exclude evidence of substantial probative value on this basis, and acknowledged that the judge should also consider the possibility of discharging the jury, but held that in some cases exclusion will be the only way of ensuring fairness, as in the case before it, where an accused, relying on section 101(1)(e), had deliberately sought to ambush a co-accused by giving him no opportunity of dealing properly with the allegation made. In *R v Bullen*,[355] a murder case, an issue that arose concerned a change, without notice, to the basis for an application to admit previous convictions for relatively low level violence. The original application was made to rebut an anticipated defence of self-defence, but when the accused pleaded guilty to manslaughter the issue became one of specific intent. Without rethinking or adapting the notice, the Crown applied to admit the convictions to show a propensity for violence.

---

[347] SI 2005/384.
[348] Rule 35.4.
[349] Rule 35.5.
[350] Rule 35.8.
[351] *R (Robinson) v Sutton Coldfield Magistrates' Court* [2006] 4 All ER 1029, DC.
[352] *R v Lawson* [2007] 1 Cr App R 178, CA at [18].
[353] *R v Lawson*, ibid at [41].
[354] [2007] 1 WLR 2467, CA.
[355] [2008] 2 Cr App R 75, CA. On notice requirements, see also *R v Jarvis* [2008] Crim LR 632 where key considerations when dealing with late applications included whether the target of the application would simply be unable to deal with it and the risk of 'satellite litigation'. On the separate issue of general violence and specific intent, see also *R v Swellings* [2009] EWCA Crim 3249.

The Court of Appeal, quashing the conviction, held that this was where matters started to go wrong. The previous convictions were for crimes of *basic* intent and the issue of *specific* intent was the sole substantive issue in the trial.[356] Insufficient consideration had been given in the renewed application to the relevance of a propensity to violence to specific intent.

Other provisions governing the admissibility of evidence of bad character

In addition to the provisions of the 2003 Act, various other provisions have a bearing on the admissibility or exclusion of evidence of bad character. Thus as to admissibility, there are a number of statutory provisions whereby the conviction of, or sentence for, one offence is an essential ingredient of another. For example, under section 103 of the Road Traffic Act 1988, it is an offence to obtain a licence or drive a vehicle on a road 'while disqualified for holding or obtaining a licence'. Similarly under section 21 of the Firearms Act 1968, 'a person who has been sentenced to imprisonment for a term of three years or more' shall not at any time have a firearm or ammunition in his possession.[357] Evidence of conviction or sentence for the purposes of such statutes is probably best categorized as evidence 'which has to do with the alleged facts of the offence with which the defendant is charged' within section 98(b) of the 2003 Act.[358] As to the exclusion of evidence of bad character, nothing in the scheme under the 2003 Act affects the exclusion of evidence under either (a) the rule in section 3 of the Criminal Procedure Act 1865,[359] which prevents a party from impeaching the credit of his own witness by general evidence of bad character; or (b) section 41 of the Youth Justice and Criminal Evidence Act 1999,[360] which restricts evidence or questions about the complainant's sexual history in proceedings for sexual offences.[361]

In this final section of this chapter consideration is given to three other provisions. The first two, section 27(3) of the Theft Act 1968 and section 1(2) of the Official Secrets Act 1911, provide for the admissibility of the accused's disposition towards certain kinds of wrongdoing. The third, paragraph 6 of the *Practice Direction (Criminal Proceedings: Consolidation)*,[362] provides for the exclusion of spent convictions.

Section 27(3) of the Theft Act 1968

It will be seen in Chapter 22 that where an accused is found in possession of recently stolen goods, an explanation is called for which, if not forthcoming, will entitle the jury to presume guilty knowledge or belief on a charge of receiving stolen goods. The task of the prosecution in proving guilty knowledge or belief is further assisted by section 27(3), which provides that:

[356] *R v Bullen*, ibid at [27]

[357] Previous convictions may also be admitted, after a verdict of guilty, if directly relevant to the question of sentence and, unless the accused denies them, formal proof is not required. Evidence of a conviction, if disputed, is also admissible where the accused pleads *autrefois convict* to prevent the prosecution proceeding against him in respect of an offence of which he has already been convicted.

[358] See 457 above, under **The admissibility of evidence of bad character 'to do with' the facts of the offence or in connection with its investigation or prosecution.**

[359] See Ch 6.

[360] See Ch 7.

[361] Section 112(3) of the 2003 Act.

[362] [2002] 1 WLR 2870.

Where a person is being proceeded against for handling stolen goods (but not for any offence other than handling stolen goods), then at any stage of the proceedings, if evidence has been given of his having or arranging to have in his possession the goods the subject of the charge, or of his undertaking or assisting in, or arranging to undertake or assist in, their retention, removal, disposal or realisation, the following evidence shall be admissible for the purpose of proving that he knew or believed the goods to be stolen goods:

    (a) evidence that he has had in his possession, or has undertaken or assisted in the retention, removal, disposal or realisation of, stolen goods from any theft taking place not earlier than twelve months before the offence charged; and

    (b) (provided that seven days' notice in writing has been given to him of the intention to prove the conviction) evidence that he has within the five years preceding the date of the offence charged been convicted of theft or of handling stolen goods.

Where evidence is introduced under section 27(3)(a), strict regard must be had to its terms: it was not designed to allow evidence to be given of what is in effect another offence of handling committed before the offence charged and does not permit the introduction of details of the transaction as a result of which the earlier property came into the possession of the accused.[363] However, under section 27(3)(a), providing a description of the stolen goods appears to be unavoidable.[364] Subsection 3(b) has to be read with section 73 of the Police and Criminal Evidence Act 1984, whereby the fact of a conviction may be proved by producing a certificate of conviction giving 'the substance and effect (omitting the formal parts) of the indictment and of the conviction',[365] wording which renders admissible not only the fact, date and place of the conviction, but also a description of the stolen goods.[366] In cases in which there are a number of counts of handling on some of which the accused denies possession, the judge should warn the jury that evidence admitted under section 27(3) is relevant only to those counts in which guilty knowledge is involved and not those in which possession is the only or primary issue.[367]

It is no answer to an application to admit evidence under section 27(3)(b) to say that the previous convictions are for theft or handling of a different kind or have no bearing on a specific prosecution argument based on a system or modus operandi, because the very purpose of the subsection is to admit evidence of the general disposition of the accused to be dishonest.[368] Nevertheless, it is well-established that the judge does have a discretion to exclude evidence admissible under section 27(3) where it would only be of minimal assistance to the jury or, as it is put, its prejudicial effect would outweigh its probative value.[369] In *R v Hacker*,[370] a trial for handling the bodyshell of an Escort RS Turbo motor car, in which the accused denied that the goods had been stolen and also denied guilty knowledge or belief, it was held that the judge

---

[363] *R v Bradley* (1979) 70 Cr App R 200, applied in *R v Wood* [1987] 1 WLR 779, CA. Possession of the earlier property may be proved by evidence of an admission made by the accused under caution, in a written statement to the police, provided that the statement is edited so as to disclose only the bare fact of such possession.

[364] *R v Fowler* (1987) 86 Cr App R 219 at 226, CA.

[365] See Ch 2.

[366] *R v Hacker* [1995] 1 All ER 45, HL.

[367] *R v Wilkins* [1975] 2 All ER 734, CA.

[368] *R v Perry* [1984] Crim LR 680, CA.

[369] See *R v List* [1965] 3 All ER 710; *R v Herron* [1967] 1 QB 107 (decided under s 43(1) of the Larceny Act 1916, re-enacted, with some modification, in s 27(3)); *R v Knott* [1973] Crim LR 36, CA; and *R v Perry* [1984] Crim LR 680, CA. See also *R v Rasini* (1986) The Times, 20 Mar, CA.

[370] [1995] 1 All ER 45, HL.

was entitled, in his discretion, to admit evidence of a previous conviction of receiving a Ford RS Turbo motor car, evidence said to be highly relevant to the issue of knowledge.

Section 1(2) of the Official Secrets Act 1911

Under section 1(1) of the Official Secrets Act 1911, it is an offence to commit various acts of espionage 'for any purpose prejudicial to the safety or interests of the State'. Evidence of disposition to commit such acts is admissible under section 1(2), which provides that:

> (2) On a prosecution under this section, it shall not be necessary to show that the accused person was guilty of any particular act tending to show a purpose prejudicial to the safety or interests of the State, and notwithstanding that no such act is proved against him, he may be convicted if, from the circumstances of the case, or his conduct, or his known character as proved, it appears that his purpose was a purpose prejudicial to the safety or interests of the State . . .

Paragraph 6 of the Practice Direction (Criminal Proceedings: Consolidation)

The Rehabilitation of Offenders Act 1974 provides that in civil proceedings no evidence shall be admissible to prove that a 'rehabilitated' person has committed, been charged with, prosecuted for, convicted of, or sentenced for any offence which was the subject of a 'spent' conviction[371] unless the judge is satisfied that in the circumstances justice cannot be done in the case except by admitting such evidence.[372] The Act does not apply to criminal proceedings[373] but under paragraph 6 of the *Practice Direction (Criminal Proceedings: Consolidation)*[374] in criminal proceedings, 'both court and advocates should give effect to the general intention of Parliament by never referring to a spent conviction when such reference can reasonably be avoided . . . '. It also provides that 'No one should refer in open court to a spent conviction without the authority of the judge, which authority should not be given unless the interests of justice so require.' A conviction becomes 'spent' on the expiry of a 'rehabilitation period', which runs from the date of conviction, varies according to the sentence imposed and is reduced by half for persons under 18 years old at the date of conviction.[375] Certain sentences are excluded from rehabilitation under the Act and these include imprisonment for life or for a term exceeding 30 months and a sentence of detention during Her Majesty's pleasure.[376]

ADDITIONAL READING

Elliott, 'Cut Throat Tactics: the Freedom of an Accused to Prejudice a Co-accused' [1991] *Crim LR* 5.

Fortson and Ormrod, 'Bad Character Evidence and Cross-Admissibility' [2009] *Crim LR* 313.

---

[371] Section 4(1)(a).

[372] Section 7(3). See also *Thomas v Metropolitan Police Comr* [1997] 1 All ER 747, CA. As to the procedure to be adopted by licensing justices in deciding whether to admit the spent convictions of the person applying for the licence, see *Adamson v Waveney District Council* [1997] 2 All ER 898, DC.

[373] Section 7(2)(a).

[374] [2002] 1 WLR 2870.

[375] See Tables A and B under s 5(2).

[376] Section 5(1). As to how a jury should be directed on the character of an accused with previous but spent convictions, see Ch 16.

Goudkamp, 'Bad Character' (2008) *E & P* 116.

Law Commission, *Evidence of Bad Character in Criminal Proceedings* (Law Com No 273, London, 2001).

Lloyd-Bostock, 'The Effects on Juries of Hearing that the Defendant has a Previous Conviction' [2000] *Crim LR* 734.

Lloyd-Bostock, 'The Effects on Lay Magistrates of hearing that the Defendant is of "Good Character", Being Left to Speculate, or Hearing that he has a Previous Conviction' [2006] *Crim LR* 189.

Mirfield, 'Bad character and the Law Commission' (2002) 6 *E&P* 141.

Mirfield, 'Character and Credibility' [2009] *Crim LR* 135.

Munday, 'Irregular Disclosure of Evidence of Bad Character' [1990] *Crim LR* 92.

Munday, 'Cut-throat Defences and the "Propensity to be Untruthful" under s.104 of the Criminal Justice Act 2003' [2005] *Crim LR* 624.

Munday, 'What Constitutes "Other Reprehensible Behaviour" under the Bad Character Provisions of the Criminal Justice Act 2003?' [2005] *Crim LR* 24.

Munday, 'The Purposes of Gateway (g): Yet Another Problematic of the Criminal Justice Act 2003' [2006] *Crim LR* 300.

Redmayne, 'The Law Commission's character convictions' (2002) 6 *E&P* 71.

Tapper, 'Criminal Justice Act 2003 (3) Evidence of Bad Character' [2004] *Crim LR* 533.

Wasik, 'Magistrates: Knowledge of Previous Convictions' [1996] *Crim LR* 851.

Opinion evidence

18

Key Issues

- When and why should experts be allowed to give expert opinion evidence on facts in issue?

- When and why should non-experts be allowed to give non-expert opinion evidence on facts in issue?

- What are the dangers of allowing experts to give expert opinion evidence?

- What safeguards can be used against such dangers?

- What duties to the court should an expert witness have?

- If two or more parties to litigation wish to submit expert evidence on an issue, when should the court direct that the evidence on the issue be given by a single joint expert?

- Why should the parties disclose their expert opinion evidence before the trial?

As a general rule, opinion evidence is inadmissible: a witness may only speak of facts which he personally perceived, not of inferences drawn from those facts. To this general rule there are two exceptions: (i) an appropriately qualified expert may state his opinion on a matter calling for the expertise which he possesses; and (ii) a non-expert witness may state his opinion on a matter not calling for any particular expertise as a way of conveying the facts which he personally perceived. There are two main reasons for the general rule. First, it has been said that, whereas any fact that a witness can prove is relevant, his opinion is not.[1] The opinion of a non-expert has no probative value in relation to a subject calling for expertise and is usually insufficiently relevant to a subject not calling for any particular expertise. Secondly, the general rule prevents witnesses from usurping the role of the tribunal of fact. The tribunal of fact, although free to reject any opinions proffered, might be tempted simply to accept those opinions rather than draw its own inferences from the facts of the case.

The first exception assumes that a distinction can easily be drawn between a person who gives evidence of expert opinion as opposed to evidence of fact, but that is not always so.[2] The exception stems from an acknowledgment that in some cases the tribunal of fact, in the absence of opinion evidence, may be unable properly to reach a conclusion. Expert opinion evidence is admitted because the drawing of certain inferences calls for an expertise which the tribunal of fact simply does not possess. This rationale is essentially flawed: if the tribunal of fact lacks the relevant expertise, it will often be unlikely to be able to evaluate the cogency or reliability of the expert evidence.[3] In any event, and as already noted, there is a danger that the tribunal of fact may blindly defer to the opinion given. The danger is particularly acute in the case of opinions expressed by expert witnesses, whose dogmatic views, on subjects in respect of which scientific knowledge may be limited or incomplete, may occasion miscarriages of justice. Following the successful appeal of Angela Cannings in the 'cot death' case of *R v Cannings*,[4] the Attorney General announced a review of 258 convictions relating to homicide or infanticide of a baby under 2 years old by a parent, and a similar review in civil cases was ordered by the Children's Minister. The risks of miscarriage of justice are increased by the current absence of any scheme of compulsory accreditation or registration for expert witnesses and any scheme of mandatory practical training for judges and practitioners in understanding expert evidence and in assessing its likely reliability.[5]

The duties and responsibilities of the expert are governed, in criminal litigation, by Part 33 of the Criminal Procedure Rules 2005, and in civil litigation by CPR rule 35, as supplemented by a Protocol for the Instruction of Experts to Give Evidence in Civil Claims, designed to help experts and those instructing them in all cases where the CPR apply.

The second non-expert exception stems from a recognition that the fundamental assumption upon which the general rule is based, that it is possible to distinguish between fact and

---

[1] Per Goddard LJ in *Hollington v Hewthorn & Co Ltd* [1943] KB 587 at 595, CA.

[2] The distinction is of considerable procedural significance, especially in civil cases, where expert witnesses are subject to strict case management compared to witnesses of fact: see D Dwyer, 'The effect of the fact/opinion distinction on CPR r.35.2: *Kirkman v Euro Oxide Corporation; Gall v Chief Constable of the West Midlands*' (2008) 12 *E&P* 141. See also *Multiplex Construction (UK) Ltd v Cleveland Bridge UK Ltd* [2008] All ER (D) 04 (Oct), TCC: in construction litigation, if an engineer, being an expert in his field, is called as a witness of *fact*, he may also give expert opinion reasonably related to the facts within his knowledge.

[3] See P Roberts and A Zuckerman, *Criminal Evidence* (Oxford, 2004) at 294–5.

[4] [2004] 1 WLR 2607, CA, Ch 8.

[5] For an analysis of the need for forensic science training, and specific recommendations, see the House of Commons Science and Technology Committee, *Forensic Science on Trial*, HC 96-I 2005.

opinion, is false.[6] The words of a witness testifying as to perceived facts are always coloured, to some extent, by his opinion as to what he perceived. The separation of an inference or value judgment from the facts on which it is based is often extremely difficult and sometimes impossible. In criminal proceedings, for example, a witness may identify the accused as the culprit, saying, 'He is the man I saw.' It is evidence of opinion, not fact. The witness means: 'He so resembles the man I saw that I am prepared to say that they are one and the same.' He could confine himself to a description of the man he saw and leave it to the jury to decide whether the description fits the accused. In cases of this kind, the opinion expressed conveys the facts perceived. The witness, in such cases, is allowed to give his evidence in his own way which is often, although not invariably, the most natural and comprehensible way in which to convey to the tribunal of fact the facts as he perceived them.

Expert opinion evidence[7]

Matters calling for expertise

Examples

The opinion evidence of an expert is only admissible on a matter calling for expertise. The field of expertise is large and ever-expanding.[8] It embraces subjects as diverse as accident investigation and driver behaviour,[9] the age of a person,[10] ballistics, battered women's syndrome,[11] blood tests, breath tests, blood-alcohol levels and back-calculations thereof,[12] ear-print identification,[13] facial mapping[14] or facial identification by video superimposition,[15] fingerprint identification, voice identification,[16] DNA or genetic fingerprinting,[17] indented

---

[6] 'In a sense all testimony to matter of fact is opinion evidence; ie it is a conclusion formed from phenomena and mental impressions': Thayer, *A Preliminary Treatise on Evidence at the Common Law* (Boston, 1898) 524.

[7] This section of the chapter concerns expert *evidence*. Civil actions without a jury in the High Court may be tried by a judge sitting with assessors. The function of assessors, who are principally used in the Admiralty Court in cases concerning collisions between vessels, is to assist the judge on matters of fact calling for specialized knowledge: see s 70 of the Supreme Court Act 1981, s 63 of the County Courts Act 1984, and CPR r 35.15.

[8] *The Expert Witness Directory 2006* claims coverage of over 1,800 specialisms.

[9] See *R v Dudley* [2004] All ER (D) 374 (Nov).

[10] *R (I) v Secretary of State for the Home Department* [2005] EWHC 1025 (Admin) and *N (a child) (residence order), Re* [2006] EWHC 1189 (Fam).

[11] See *R v Hobson* [1998] 1 Cr App R 31, CA.

[12] Ie calculation of the amount of alcohol eliminated in the period between driving and providing a specimen in order to show that a person's alcohol level was above the prescribed limit at the time of driving. See *Gumbley v Cunningham* [1989] 1 All ER 5, HL.

[13] *R v Dallagher* [2003] 1 Cr App R 195, C; *R v Kempster (No 2)* [2008] 2 Cr App R 256, CA.

[14] *R v Stockwell* (1993) 97 Cr App R 260, CA. It is open to the jury in a criminal trial to convict on the basis of such expert evidence: *R v Mitchell* [2005] All ER (D) 182 (Mar).

[15] *R v Clarke* [1995] 2 Cr App R 425, CA.

[16] *R v Robb* (1991) 93 Cr App R 161, CA.

[17] For a basic description of the method by which DNA profiling is carried out, see *R v Gordon* [1995] 1 Cr App R 290 at 293–4, CA. The technique may be used not only to identify criminal suspects but also to decide questions of pedigree. In evaluating DNA evidence, use should not be made of Bayes Theorem, or any similar statistical method of analysis, because it plunges the jury into inappropriate and unnecessary realms of theory and complexity: *R v Adams* [1996] 2 Cr App R 467, CA. As to the procedure to be adopted when DNA evidence is introduced, see *R v Doheny and Adams* [1997] 1 Cr App R 369, CA. See also Mike Redmayne, 'The DNA Database: Civil Liberty and Evidentiary Issues' [1995] *Crim LR* 437 and C Jowett, 'Sittin' in the Dock with the Bayes' (2001) *NLJ* 201. For the controversy about the use of Low Copy Number DNA analysis, following the concerns expressed in *R v Hoey* [2007] NICC 49, see C Foster, 'Untwining the strands' (2008) *NLJ* 157 and S Burns, 'Low copy DNA on trial' [2008] *NLJ* 919.

impressions left on one document as a result of writing on another,[18] insanity, lip reading,[19] Sudden Infant Death Syndrome (SIDS),[20] the genuineness of works of art, and the state of public opinion.[21] Frequently recurring examples of matters upon which expert evidence is admissible include medical, scientific, architectural, engineering, and technological issues and questions relating to standards of professional competence, market values, customary terms of contracts, and the existence of professional and trade practices. Handwriting may be proved either by a non-expert familiar with the handwriting in question[22] or by a qualified expert, but an expert should be called in criminal cases tried by jury when, pursuant to section 8 of the Criminal Procedure Act 1865, disputed handwriting is compared with a specimen sample of handwriting proved to the satisfaction of the court to be genuine.[23] Expert opinion is admissible on questions of a literary or artistic nature, for example in relation to the defence of 'public good' under section 4 of the Obscene Publications Act 1959, which provides that:

(1) A person shall not be convicted of an offence ... if it is proved that publication of the article in question is justified as being for the public good on the ground that it is in the interests of science, literature, art or learning, or of other objects of general concern.

(2) It is hereby declared that the opinion of experts as to the literary, artistic, scientific or other merits of an article may be admitted in any proceedings under this Act either to establish or to negative the said ground.

A final example, calling for special attention, is a point of foreign law, which, as we have seen in Chapter 2, is a question of fact to be decided on the evidence by the judge. Foreign law is usually proved by the evidence, including opinion evidence, of an expert[24] who may refer to foreign statutes, decisions, and textbooks.[25] If the evidence of the experts conflicts, the judge is bound to look at the sources of knowledge from which the experts have drawn, in order to decide between the conflicting testimony.[26] However, he is not at liberty to conduct his own

[18] The impressions may be detected by the use of Electrostatic Detection Apparatus (ESDA). ESDA has been useful not only in dating documents and determining the origin of anonymous communications, but also in showing whether pages were written in sequence and whether there were subsequent additions to the contents: see *R v Wellington* [1991] Crim LR 543, CA and generally Audrey Giles, 'Good Impressions' (1991) *NLJ* 605.

[19] *R v Luttrell* [2004] 2 Cr App R 520, CA.

[20] See *R v Cannings* [2004] 1 WLR 2607, CA, Ch 8.

[21] Eg on the issue of reputation in passing-off actions. See *Sodastream Ltd v Thorn Cascade Co Ltd* [1982] RPC 459 and *Lego Systems A/S v Lego M Lemelstrich Ltd* [1983] FSR 155. Cf *Reckitt & Colman Products v Borden Inc (No 2)* [1987] FSR 407.

[22] *Doe d Mudd v Suckermore* (1837) 5 Ad&El 703.

[23] *R v Harden* [1963] 1 QB 8, CCA: see generally Ch 9.

[24] An exception exists in the case of the construction of provisions of foreign legislation admitted in evidence under the Evidence (Colonial Statutes) Act 1907: see the authorities cited in *Jasiewicz v Jasiewicz* [1962] 1 WLR 1426. Under s 1 of the 1907 Act, copies of Acts, ordinances, and statutes passed by the legislature of any part of Her Majesty's dominions exclusive of the UK and of orders, regulations, and other instruments issued or made under the authority of any such Act, ordinance, or statute, if purporting to be printed by the government printer of the possession shall be received in evidence by all courts in the UK without proof that copies were so printed. See also s 6 of the Colonial Laws Validity Act 1865. The British Law Ascertainment Act 1859 permits English courts to state a case on a point of foreign law for the opinion of a superior court in another part of Her Majesty's dominions. The opinion pronounced is admissible in evidence on the point of foreign law in question. See also the Foreign Law Ascertainment Act 1861.

[25] It may also be proved by the witness statement of an expert (if admissible) or by a statement of agreed facts pursuant to s 10 of the Criminal Justice Act 1967: *R v Ofori (No 2)* (1993) 99 Cr App R 223, CA.

[26] Per Lord Langdale MR in *Nelson (Earl) v Lord Bridport* (1845) 8 Beav 527 at 537 and per Scarman J in *Re Fuld's Estate (No 3), Hartley v Fuld* [1968] P 675 at 700–3.

research into those sources and to rely on material not adduced in evidence in order to reject the expert evidence.[27]

At common law, the consequence of treating foreign law as a question of fact is that where there has been an English decision on a particular point of foreign law and the same point subsequently arises again, it must be decided afresh on new expert evidence.[28] This remains the position where a point of foreign law arises in English criminal proceedings. The position in civil proceedings, however, has now been altered by section 4 of the Civil Evidence Act 1972 (the 1972 Act). Section 4(2)(a) of that Act provides that a previous determination by an English court of superior status, whether civil or criminal, on a point of foreign law shall, if reported in citable form,[29] be admissible in evidence in civil proceedings. Section 4(2)(b) provides that except where there are two or more previous determinations which are in conflict, the foreign law on the point in question shall be taken to be as previously determined unless the contrary is proved.[30] Subsection (2)(b) raises a presumption that the earlier decision is correct. However, the court which has to consider the question for a second time decides for itself what weight to attach to the previous decision and, although it is desirable to reach consistent conclusions, the subsection is not to be construed as laying down a general rule that the presumption can only be displaced by particularly cogent evidence.[31]

Matters within the experience and knowledge of the tribunal of fact

Where the triers of fact can form their own opinion without the assistance of an expert, the matter in question being within their own experience and knowledge, the opinion evidence of an expert is inadmissible because unnecessary.[32] Thus leave should not be granted to call a professor of psychology or other medical evidence to demonstrate the likely deterioration of the memory of an ordinary witness.[33] On the other hand, although a witness's ability to remember events will ordinarily be well within the experience of jurors, in rare cases in which a witness gives evidence of an event said to have occurred during 'the period of childhood amnesia', which extends to the age of about seven, and the evidence is very detailed and contains a number of details that are extraneous to the central feature of the event, an appropriately qualified expert may give evidence that it should be treated with caution and may be unreliable because recall of events during that period will be fragmented, disjointed, and idiosyncratic rather than a detailed

---

[27] Per Lord Chelmsford in *Duchess Di Sora v Phillipps* (1863) 10 HL Cas 624 at 640 and per Purchas LJ in *Bumper Development Corpn Ltd v Metropolitan Police Comr* [1991] 4 All ER 638 at 643–6, CA.

[28] *M'Cormick v Garnett* (1854) 23 LJ Ch 777.

[29] Ie where the report, if the question had been as to the law of England and Wales, could have been cited as an authority in legal proceedings in England and Wales: s 4(5).

[30] Notice of intention to rely on the previous determination must be given to the other parties: s 4(3) and CPR r 33.7.

[31] *Phoenix Marine Inc v China Ocean Shipping Co* [1999] 1 Lloyd's Rep 682, QBD.

[32] Per Lawton LJ in *R v Turner* [1975] QB 834 at 841. In some cases, however, a jury may properly receive assistance on a matter within their own experience and knowledge on the basis that the witness has had more time and better facilities to consider the matter than it would be practicable to afford to them. Such a witness, in reality a non-expert, may be regarded as 'sufficiently expert ad hoc': see *R v Howe* [1982] 1 NZLR 618 at 627. Thus in *R v Clare and Peach* [1995] 2 Cr App R 333, CA an officer who had viewed a video-recording about 40 times, examining it in slow motion, frame by frame, was permitted to give evidence as to whether persons on the recording were the accused. However, research suggests that the accuracy of identification is not significantly enhanced by repeated replay: Bruce et al 'Face Recognition in Poor Quality Video Evidence from Security Surveillance' (1999) 10 *Psychological Science* 243. See also Munday, 'Videotape Evidence and the Advent of the Expert Ad Hoc' (1995) 159 *JP* 547.

[33] *R v Browning* [1995] Crim LR 227, CA.

narrative account.[34] Similarly, expert evidence may be admitted as to the dangers of evidence produced by hypnotherapy, not to express an opinion on the witness's truthfulness, but to criticize the techniques of the hypnotherapist and express an opinion about the danger that *if* the witness's recollection was falsely engendered, the witness would regard it as genuine memory.[35]

Expert evidence is inadmissible on the question whether an unidentified person shown in a photograph is under the age of 16.[36] It is also inadmissible on a trial for posting packets containing indecent articles, on the ordinary meaning of the words 'indecent or obscene'.[37] Similarly, in the ordinary case, the issue of obscenity in prosecutions under the Obscene Publications Act 1959 falls to be tried without the assistance of expert evidence.[38] *DPP v A & B C Chewing Gum Ltd*,[39] was not an 'ordinary case', but 'a very special case'[40] which should be regarded as 'highly exceptional and confined to its own circumstances'.[41] The accused was charged with publishing for gain obscene battle cards which were sold together with packets of bubble gum. The Divisional Court held that the magistrates had improperly refused to admit the evidence of experts in child psychiatry concerning the likely effect of the cards on children. Lord Parker CJ was of the opinion that, whereas expert opinion evidence as to whether a publication tends to deprave or corrupt may be unnecessary when considering its effect on an adult, it was admissible when considering its effect on children of various ages from five upwards because then 'any jury and any justices need all the help they can get'.

The distinction between matters calling for expertise and matters within the experience and knowledge of the jury is also illustrated by cases concerning a person's mental state. As we shall see, many of the decisions reflect the view that expertise is only called for in the case of a person suffering from a mental illness, a view which, it is submitted, is unnecessarily inflexible. As Farquharson LJ observed in *R v Strudwick*:[42]

> The law is in a state of development in this area. There may well be other mental conditions about which a jury might require expert assistance in order to understand and evaluate their effect on the issues in a case.

Expert psychiatric evidence is a practical necessity in order to establish insanity[43] or diminished responsibility.[44] In *R v Smith*[45] the accused was convicted of murder by stabbing. His

---

[34] *R v H (JR) (Childhood Amnesia)* [2006] 1 Cr App R 195, CA. The ambit of the decision should not be widened and care should be taken in the case of a narrative which has become 'polished' simply as a part of the process of the police questioning a witness and then drafting his statement: *R v S; R v W* [2007] 2 All ER 974, CA.

[35] *R v Clark* [2006] EWCA Crim 231.

[36] *R v Land* [1998] 1 Cr App R 301, CA.

[37] *R v Stamford* [1972] 2 QB 391.

[38] *R v Anderson* [1972] 1 QB 304 per Lord Widgery CJ at 313. Cf *R v Skirving; R v Grossman* [1985] 2 All ER 705, where the jury needed expert evidence on the characteristics of cocaine and the different effects of the various methods of ingesting the drug on the user and abuser in order to decide whether a book had a tendency to deprave and corrupt.

[39] [1968] 1 QB 159.

[40] Per Ashworth J in *R v Stamford* [1972] 2 QB 391, CA at 397.

[41] Per Lord Widgery CJ in *R v Anderson* [1972] 1 QB 304 at 313. See also the doubts expressed about the case by Lord Dilhorne in *DPP v Jordan* [1977] AC 699, HL at 722.

[42] (1993) 99 Cr App R 326, CA at 332.

[43] See s 1(1) of the Criminal Procedure (Insanity and Unfitness to Plead) Act 1991, below.

[44] See *R v Byrne* [1960] 2 QB 396 at 402, applied in *R v Dix* (1981) 74 Cr App R 306, CA. See also *R v Chan-Fook* [1994] 2 All ER 552, CA, applied in *R v Morris* [1998] 1 Cr App R 386, CA: where psychiatric injury is relied on as the basis for a charge of assault occasioning actual bodily harm and is not admitted by the defence, the Crown should call expert evidence.

[45] [1979] 1 WLR 1445, CA.

defence was automatism while asleep. The Court of Appeal held that psychiatric evidence adduced by the prosecution as to whether the evidence of the accused was consistent with his defence had been properly admitted, the type of automatism in question not being within the realm of the ordinary juryman's experience. Concerning the defence of duress by threats, expert medical evidence is admissible for the purposes of the subjective (but not the objective) test, provided that the mental condition or abnormality in question is relevant and its effects are outside the knowledge and experience of laymen.[46] However, according to *R v Walker*[47] psychiatric evidence may be admissible to show that an accused was suffering from some mental illness, mental impairment, or recognized psychiatric condition, provided persons generally suffering from such a condition might be more susceptible to pressure and threats, and thus to assist the jury in deciding whether a reasonable person suffering from such a condition might have been impelled to act as the accused did, but evidence is not admissible that an accused who was not suffering from such an illness, impairment or condition, was especially timid, suggestible or vulnerable to pressure and threats.

Except where the accused comes into the class of mental defective or is afflicted by some medical condition affecting his mental state, expert medical or psychiatric evidence is not admissible on the question of *mens rea*.[48] In *R v Wood*,[49] W, charged with murder, raised the partial defence under section 4 of the Homicide Act 1957 of unsuccessful execution of a suicide pact. Once the killing was proved, the questions were whether there was such a pact and whether W was acting in pursuance thereof and had the settled intention of dying in pursuance thereof. It was held that psychiatric evidence that W had a personality which to some extent was abnormal and liable to give way to excesses of behaviour under stress had been properly excluded, the matter not being outside the ordinary experience of the average juror. Similarly, in *R v Masih*,[50] in which the appellant, who was convicted of rape, suffered from no psychiatric illness but had an intelligence quotient of only 72, just above the level of subnormality, it was held that on the question of whether he knew that the complainant was not consenting or was reckless as to whether she consented or not, expert psychiatric evidence about his state of mind, intelligence, and ability to appreciate the situation had been properly excluded. The Court of Appeal held that, generally speaking, if an accused comes into the class of mental defective, with an IQ of 69 or below, then insofar as that defectiveness is relevant to an issue, expert evidence may be admitted, provided that it is confined to an assessment of the accused's IQ and an explanation of any relevant abnormal characteristics, to enlighten the jury on a matter that is abnormal and *ex hypothesi* outside their experience; but where an accused is within the scale of normality, albeit at the lower end, as the appellant was, expert evidence should generally be excluded.[51]

---

[46] *R v Hegarty* [1994] Crim LR 353, CA. See also *R v Horne* [1994] Crim LR 584, CA; and cf *R v Hurst* [1995] 1 Cr App R 82, CA.

[47] [2003] All ER (D) 64 (Jun).

[48] *R v Chard* (1971) 56 Cr App R 268, CA. See also *R v Reynolds* [1989] Crim LR 220, CA and, in the case of adolescents, *R v Coles* [1995] 1 Cr App R 157, CA.

[49] [1990] Crim LR 264, CA.

[50] [1986] Crim LR 395, CA. See also *R v Hall* (1987) 86 Cr App R 159, CA and *R v Henry* [2006] 1 Cr App R 118, CA and contrast *Schultz v R* [1982] WAR 171 (Supreme Court of Western Australia). In *R v Lupien* (1970) 9 DLR (3d) 1 (Supreme Court of Canada) it was held that psychiatric evidence is admissible to show a person's lack of capacity to form intent.

[51] However, as Hodgson J stated in *R v Silcott* [1987] Crim LR 765 (see [1988] Crim LR 293): 'To draw a strict line at 69/70 does seem somewhat artificial.' For a critical analysis of the notion that there is a clear line dividing normality

In *R v Toner*,[52] a case of attempted murder in which a doctor gave evidence that T may have been suffering from a minor hypoglycaemic state caused by eating after a 41-day fast, it was held that the defence should have been permitted to cross-examine him as to whether the effect of such an attack could have negatived T's special intent to kill and to cause serious bodily harm. The Court of Appeal could see no distinction between such medical evidence and medical evidence as to the effect of a drug on intent: both matters were outside the ordinary experience of jurors. Similarly in *R v Huckerby*[53] it was held that evidence that the accused was suffering from post-traumatic stress disorder, a recognized mental condition with which the jury would not be expected to be familiar, was admissible because relevant to an essential issue bearing upon his guilt or innocence, namely whether it caused him to panic and cooperate with criminals in circumstances where he would otherwise not have done so.

Expert evidence is generally inadmissible on the issue of a witness's credibility.[54] In *Re S (a child) (adoption: psychological evidence)*,[55] an appeal against a care order, the judge at first instance had relied on the results of a personality questionnaire, including a 'Lie-Scale' measuring the mother's willingness to distort her responses in order to create a good impression. Allowing the appeal, it was held that the results of personality or psychometric tests should only rarely have any place in such cases because it is for judges to decide questions of credibility.

In its consultation paper *Convicting Rapists and Protecting Victims—Justice for Victims of Rape* (2006), the Government proposed that prosecutors should be able to present general expert evidence about the psychological impact of sexual offences upon victims. This impact is not necessarily within the understanding of the average juror and expert evidence is capable of dispelling popular myths and misconceptions and explaining behaviour which might otherwise be thought to be puzzling, including, for example, delay in making a complaint.[56] The Government's proposal has, in the light of the responses to the consultation paper, been replaced by a proposal to provide information packs or videos for jurors or to give them special warnings. The original proposal, however, reflected an assumption that expert evidence concerning the behavioural symptoms typical of victims of sexual abuse is currently not admissible because it relates to their credibility. The assumption is erroneous, it is submitted, because such evidence, if general in nature and if it does not include an opinion on the credibility of the victim, simply provides the tribunal of fact with relevant information by which it may better evaluate the witness's evidence.[57]

---

and subnormality, see R D Mackay, 'Excluding Expert Evidence: a tale of ordinary folk and common experience' [1991] *Crim LR* 800.

[52] (1991) 93 Cr App R 382, CA.

[53] [2004] EWCA Crim 3251, [2004] All ER (D) 364 (Dec).

[54] See *R v Henry* [2006] 1 Cr App R 118, CA (the credibility of the accused) and *R v Joyce* [2005] NTS 21 (the credibility of a prosecution witness) and cf *R v S* [2006] EWCA Crim 2389, Ch 7.

[55] [2004] EWCA Civ 1029, [2004] All ER (D) 593 (Jul). As to credibility, see also *R v Robinson* [1994] 3 All ER 346, CA and, in the case of children, *G v DPP* [1997] 2 All ER 755 at 759–60, CA.

[56] For a comparative review of the admissibility of expert evidence to explain delay, see Lewis, 'Expert evidence of delay in complaint in childhood sexual abuse prosecutions' (2006) 10 *E&P* 157.

[57] But see the response to the consultation by the Council of Circuit Judges: '…general expert evidence that cannot focus on the credibility of the individual case would be of limited real value'. For an examination of some of the credibility barriers confronting victims of sexual offences, the use of expert witness testimony in the USA, and the potential admissibility of such evidence in England and Wales, see Ellison, 'Closing the credibility gap: The prosecutorial use of expert witness testimony in sexual assault cases' (2005) 9 *E&P* 239. See also Dempsey, *The Use of Expert Testimony in the Prosecution of Domestic Violence* (CPS London, 2004).

Expert evidence is generally inadmissible to establish that an accused was likely to have been provoked. In *R v Turner*[58] the accused was convicted of murder by battering a girl 15 times with a hammer. His defence was provocation, that he was deeply in love with the girl, who, he thought, was pregnant by him, and that he had struck her when she told him with a grin that while he had been in prison she had been sleeping with other men, that she could make money in this way, and that the child she was carrying was not his. The accused appealed on the ground that the trial judge had refused to admit psychiatric evidence on the issues of credibility and provocation. The psychiatrist intended to say, inter alia, that the accused had a deep emotional relationship with the girl which was likely to have caused an explosive release of blind rage when she confessed her infidelity to him and that, subsequent to the killing, he had behaved like someone suffering from profound grief. The Court of Appeal held that the jury needed no expert assistance in deciding either what reliance they could put upon the accused's evidence or the likelihood of his having been provoked, a matter which was well within ordinary human experience.[59] *R v Turner* is not easily reconciled with the earlier decision of the Privy Council in *Lowery v R*.[60] L and K were charged with murder, the circumstances being such that one or both of them must have committed the offence. There was no apparent motive for the murder. The Privy Council held that the trial judge had properly permitted K to call a psychologist to give evidence that L was aggressive, lacking in self-control, and more likely to have committed the offence than K. However, even if evidence of L's disposition was properly admissible,[61] it is unclear why it was given by an expert. In *R v Turner* Lawton LJ said:[62]

> We adjudge *Lowery v R* to have been decided on its special facts. We do not consider that it is an authority for the proposition that in all cases psychologists and psychiatrists can be called to prove the probability of the accused's veracity.[63]

Lowery v R was relied upon by the House of Lords in *R v Randall*[64] as a precedent for the proposition that in appropriate cases the propensity to violence of an accused may be relevant to the issues between the prosecution and the co-accused tendering such evidence, but the House expressly declined to explore any doubts about the admissibility of *expert* evidence on propensity.[65]

The expert evidence of a psychiatrist or psychologist is admissible on the issue of the reliability or truth of a confession.[66] It has been said that such evidence will not be admissible before the jury on the issue of the truth of a confession made by an accused who, although he may have an abnormal personality, does not suffer from mental illness and is not below normal intelligence.[67] This is misleading because the evidence admissible is not confined to evidence

---

[58] [1975] QB 834.

[59] See also per Lord Simon in *R v Camplin* [1978] AC 705, HL at 727.

[60] [1974] AC 85.

[61] See Ch 17.

[62] [1975] QB 834, CA at 842.

[63] See also *Toohey v Metropolitan Police Comr* [1965] AC 595, HL; *R v MacKenney* [2004] 2 Cr App R 32, CA; and *R v Robinson* [1994] 3 All ER 346 (all in Ch 7); *R v Bracewell* (1978) 68 Cr App R 44; and *R v Rimmer and Beech* [1983] Crim LR 250, CA.

[64] [2004] 1 All ER 467, HL.

[65] See Per Lord Steyn at [30].

[66] See *R v Walker* [1998] Crim LR 211, CA and *R v Ward* [1993] 1 WLR 619, CA.

[67] *R v Weightman* (1990) 92 Cr App R 291, CA.

of personality disorders so severe as properly to be categorized as mental disorders. The test is not whether the abnormality fits into a recognized category such as anti-social personality disorder. That is neither necessary nor sufficient. There are two requirements. First, the abnormal disorder must be of the type which might render the confession unreliable, and in this respect there must be a very significant deviation from the norm. Secondly, there should be a history pre-dating the making of the confession, based not solely on what the accused says, which points to or explains the abnormality. When such evidence is admitted at trial, the jury should be directed that they are not obliged to accept it, but may consider it as throwing light on the personality of the accused and bringing to their attention aspects of it of which they might otherwise have been unaware.[68] The evidence of a psychologist is also admissible to show the likely unreliability of a confession made by someone not suffering from any abnormal disorder if it is a 'coerced compliant confession', that is a confession brought about by fatigue and inability to control what is happening, which may induce a vulnerable individual to experience a growing desire to give up resisting the suggestions put to him so that eventually he is overwhelmed by the need to achieve the immediate goal of ending the interrogation.[69]

Expert witnesses

Expertise

A witness is competent to give expert evidence only if, in the opinion of the judge, he is properly qualified in the subject calling for expertise.[70] In rare cases it will be necessary to hold a *voir dire* to decide whether a purported expert should be allowed to give evidence, but in the vast majority of cases the judge will be able to make the decision on the basis of written material. The judge, during the trial, also has the power, should the need arise, to remove a witness's 'expert' status and limit his evidence to factual matters.[71]

An expert may have acquired his expertise through study, training, or experience. Thus an engineer who understands the construction of harbours, the causes of their destruction and how remedied, may express his opinion on whether an embankment caused the decay of a harbour;[72] a police officer with qualifications and experience in accident investigation may give expert opinion evidence on how a road accident occurred;[73] and someone with no medical qualifications but with experience and knowledge of drug abuse through charitable work, drug projects, and personal research may give expert opinion evidence as to what quantities of ecstasy are consistent with personal use and how users acquire an increasing tolerance of the drug.[74] On the other hand, a medical orderly experienced in the treatment of cuts is not

---

[68] *R v O'Brien* [2000] Crim LR 676, CA, applied in *R v Smith* [2003] EWCA Crim 927, [2003] All ER (D) 28 (Apr).

[69] *R v Blackburn* [2005] 2 Cr App R 440, CA.

[70] But see s 1(1) of the Criminal Procedure (Insanity and Unfitness to Plead) Act 1991: a jury shall not acquit on the ground of insanity except on the evidence of two or more registered doctors, at least one of whom is approved by the Secretary of State as having appropriate expertise. An expert, if competent to testify, is also compellable, even where having inadvertently advised both parties, he is loath to appear on behalf of one of them: *Harmony Shipping Co SA v Saudi Europe Line Ltd* [1979] 1 WLR 1380, CA.

[71] *R v G* [2004] 2 Cr App R 638, CA.

[72] *Folkes v Chadd* (1782) 3 Doug KB 157.

[73] *R v Oakley* (1979) 70 Cr App R 7, CA; *R v Murphy* [1980] QB 434, CA. Cf *Hinds v London Transport Executive* [1979] RTR 103, CA. See also *R v Hodges* [2003] 2 Cr App R 247, CA, below. See also, *sed quaere*, *R v Somers* [1963] 1 WLR 1306, CCA.

[74] *R v Ibrahima* [2005] Crim LR 887, CA. Cf *R v Edwards* [2001] EWCA Crim 2185, below.

sufficiently qualified to express an opinion on whether a cut to the forehead was caused by a blunt instrument or a head-butt.[75] There is no requirement that the witness should have acquired his expertise professionally or in the course of his business. Thus in *R v Silverlock*[76] the Court for Crown Cases Reserved held that a solicitor who had studied handwriting for 10 years, mostly as an amateur, had properly been allowed to give his opinion as to whether certain disputed handwriting was that of the accused.

Many of the cases concern the competence of a witness to give expert opinion evidence on a point of foreign law. A person has been held to be suitably qualified for these purposes if he is a practitioner in the foreign jurisdiction in question,[77] a former practitioner,[78] a person who has not practised in the jurisdiction but is qualified to do so,[79] or a person who has acquired the appropriate expertise other than by practice, whether by academic study,[80] as an embassy official,[81] or in the course of some non-legal profession or business such as banking[82] or trading.[83] Although at common law there is authority that a practitioner in the jurisdiction in question should *always* be called,[84] in civil proceedings section 4(1) of the 1972 Act now declares that:

> a person who is suitably qualified to do so on account of his knowledge or experience is competent to give expert evidence as to the law of any country or territory outside the United Kingdom, or of any part of the United Kingdom other than England and Wales, irrespective of whether he has acted or is entitled to act as a legal practitioner there.

Independence

As we shall see, the role of an expert witness is special because he owes a duty to the court which he must discharge notwithstanding the interest of the party calling him.[85] A conflict of interest does not automatically disqualify an expert, because the key question is whether his evidence is independent, but if the conflict is material or significant, which is a question for the court and not the parties, the evidence should be excluded or ignored, and therefore a party who wishes to call an expert with a potential conflict of interests of any kind should disclose the details to the other party and to the court at the earliest possible opportunity.[86] In *Liverpool Roman Catholic Archdiocesan Trustees Inc v Goldberg (No 3)*[87] the expert was a good friend of the defendant on whose behalf he was called. The expert said that his personal sympathies were engaged to a greater degree than would probably be normal with an expert witness. It was held that this admission rendered the evidence unacceptable on grounds of policy: that

[75] *R v Inch* (1989) 91 Cr App R 51, C-MAC.

[76] [1894] 2 QB 766.

[77] *Baron de Bode's Case* (1845) 8 QB 208.

[78] *Re Duke of Wellington, Glentanar v Wellington* [1947] Ch 506.

[79] *Barford v Barford and McLeod* [1918] P 140.

[80] *Brailey v Rhodesia Consolidated Ltd* [1910] 2 Ch 95 (Reader in Roman-Dutch Law to the Council of Legal Education).

[81] *Dost Aly Khan's Goods* (1880) 6 PD 6.

[82] *de Beéche v South American Stores* [1935] AC 148, HL; *Ajami v Comptroller of Customs* [1954] 1 WLR 1405, PC.

[83] *Vander Donckt v Thellusson* (1849) 8 CB 812.

[84] *Bristow v Sequeville* (1850) 5 Exch 275.

[85] See per Cresswell J in *National Justice Cia Naviera SA v Prudential Assurance Co Ltd, The Ikarian Reefer* [1993] 2 Lloyd's Rep 68.

[86] *Toth v Jarman* [2006] EWCA Civ 1028.

[87] [2001] 1 WLR 2337, Ch D.

justice must be seen to be done as well as done. While accepting that there was no statutory or other authority expressly excluding the expert evidence of a friend of one of the parties, it was held that where there is a relationship between them which a reasonable observer might think was capable of affecting the views of the expert so as to make him unduly favourable to the party calling him, his evidence should not be admitted, however unbiased his conclusions might probably be.[88] However, it has also been held that an employee of a party can be an independent expert, provided that the party can demonstrate that the employee has not only the relevant experience but also an awareness of his overriding duty, as an expert witness, to the court.[89] Similarly, in the case of an expert who is an employee of a third party, it has been held that an acknowledged risk of a subliminal but not conscious bias or lack of objectivity goes to weight and not admissibility.[90]

Reliability

On a number of occasions, English judges have cited with approval the test for the admissibility of expert evidence as propounded in *R v Bonython*[91] where, in addition to the issues of whether the subject matter of the opinion calls for expertise and whether the witness has the requisite expertise, reference is also made to 'whether the subject matter of the opinion forms part of a body of knowledge or experience which is sufficiently organized or recognized to be accepted as a reliable body of knowledge or experience, a special acquaintance with which by the witness would render his opinion of assistance to the court'. However, English law, with notable exceptions, shows a general reluctance to apply any such condition of admissibility, which is curious given the obvious dangers, especially in criminal trials, of allowing the tribunal of fact to rely on 'expert' testimony of questionable reliability.[92]

R v Gilfoyle,[93] one of the exceptions, was a murder trial in which the only other possible explanation for the death was suicide. The Court of Appeal refused to hear the fresh evidence of a psychologist who had carried out a 'psychological autopsy' of the deceased. One of the reasons given for this conclusion was that the expert had identified no criteria by reference to which the court could test the quality of his opinions: there was no database comparing real and questionable suicides and there was no substantial body of academic writing approving his methodology. Another reason was the Canadian and United States authority pointing against the admission of such evidence. The court was of the view that the English approach accorded with the guiding principle in the United States, as stated in *Frye v United States*,[94] and to the effect that expert evidence based on novel or developing scientific techniques that are not generally accepted by the scientific community should be excluded. In fact, the test in *Frye* is no longer the guiding principle in the United States. In *Daubert v Merrell Dow Pharmaceuticals*[95]

---

[88] The decision has since been doubted: see *Admiral Management Services Ltd v Para-Protect Europe Ltd* [2002] 1 WLR 272, Ch D at [33].

[89] *Field v Leeds City Council* [2001] CPLR 129.

[90] *R v Stubbs* [2006] EWCA Crim 2312, CA at [59].

[91] (1984) 38 SASR 45.

[92] See generally M Redmayne, *Expert Evidence and Criminal Justice* (Oxford, 2001), ch 5, WE O'Brian Jr, 'Court scrutiny of expert evidence: Recent decisions highlight the tensions' (2003) 7 E&P 172 and the report of the House of Commons Science and Technology Committee, *Forensic Science on Trial*, HC 96–1 2005, which recommends the establishment of a Forensic Science Advisory Council to develop a gate-keeping test for expert evidence.

[93] [2001] 2 Cr App R 57, CA.

[94] 293 F 1013 (DC Cir, 1923).

[95] 509 US 579 (1993).

the Supreme Court held that in federal courts the test had been superseded by rule 702 of the Federal Rules of Evidence 1975; that the courts must ensure the reliability, as well as the relevance, of scientific evidence before admitting it; and that reliability is to be determined having regard to a number of factors, including whether the technique can be and has been tested, whether it has been the subject of publication and peer review, its error rate, and whether it is generally accepted.

In *R v Dallagher*,[96] where identity was in issue, evidence was received from two experts who had examined ear prints. The expertise of ear print comparison is in its relative infancy, and after the trial it emerged that other forensic scientists had misgivings about the extent to which ear print evidence alone can, in the present state of knowledge, safely be used to identify a suspect. It was held that the expert evidence had been properly admitted, but the appeal was allowed and a retrial ordered on the basis that the fresh evidence, if given at trial, might reasonably have affected the approach of the jury to the identification evidence of the experts and thus affected their decision to convict.[97] In reaching its decision that the expert evidence had been properly admitted, the court appeared to accept that the English approach is analogous to that to be found in rule 702 of the Federal Rules of Evidence and also referred to *Daubert*. However, it had no regard to the factors listed in that case, none of which, if considered, would have supported the case for admission. Instead, it simply approved a passage from *Cross and Tapper on Evidence*[98] which, after a reference to the *Frye* approach, states:

> The better, and now more widely accepted, view is that so long as a field is sufficiently well-established to pass the ordinary tests of relevance and reliability, then no enhanced test for admissibility should be applied, but the weight of the evidence should be established by the same adversarial forensic techniques applicable elsewhere.

The same passage was also approved in *R v Luttrell*[99] where the court, while accepting that the reliability of expert evidence can be relevant to the issue of admissibility, rejected the argument that lip-reading evidence as to what was said by someone talking on a CCTV recording should not be admitted unless it could be seen to be reliable because the methods used were sufficiently explained to be tested in cross-examination and so to be verifiable or falsifiable.

The dangers of this relaxed approach are highlighted by the decisions in *R v Robb*[100] and *R v O'Doherty*.[101] In *R v Robb* a lecturer in phonetics was held to be well qualified by his academic training and practical experience to express an opinion as to the identity of a voice, notwithstanding that his auditory technique, which was to pay close attention to voice quality, pitch, and pronunciation, was not generally respected by other experts in the field because it was not supplemented and verified by acoustic analysis based on physical measurements of resonance, frequency, etc. In *R v O'Doherty* the prosecution expert at the trial gave evidence based on the same technique as the expert in *R v Robb*. On appeal the Court of Appeal for Northern Ireland received fresh expert evidence to the effect that auditory techniques, unless supplemented and verified by acoustic analysis, were an unreliable basis of speaker identification, and that, based on an acoustic analysis, the voice on the tape was not that of the

---

[96] [2003] 1 Cr App R 195, CA.
[97] See also *R v Kempster (No 2)* [2008] 2 Cr App R 256, CA.
[98] 9th edn, London, 1999, 523.
[99] [2004] 2 Cr App R 520, CA.
[100] (1991) 93 Cr App R 161, CA.
[101] [2003] 1 Cr App R 77, CA (NI).

accused. Allowing the appeal, the court observed that since *R v Robb*, 'time has moved on'. It was held that in the present state of scientific knowledge, no prosecution should be brought in Northern Ireland in which one of the planks is voice identification given by an expert which is solely confined to auditory analysis. There should also be expert evidence of acoustic analysis.[102] However, in *R v Flynn*[103] it has since been stated, but without any specific amplification, that it is 'neither possible nor desirable' to go as far as the Northern Ireland Court of Appeal in this respect.

Reliability tests of the kind set out in *Frye* and *Daubert* raise additional and complex questions and issues: whether particular scientific techniques have been generally accepted;[104] identification of the scientific community by which there may have been such general acceptance, which could be a community reflecting a broad or narrow field of expertise; whether scientific techniques may be reliable even if not, or not yet, accepted by a scientific community;[105] and whether reliance on general acceptance by a scientific community amounts to a usurpation of the role of the trial judge.[106] The Law Commission, in its consultation paper on the admissibility of expert evidence in criminal proceedings,[107] proposes that there should be an explicit 'gate-keeping' role for the trial judge involving a determination whether the proffered evidence is sufficiently reliable to be admitted. It is proposed that it is for the party wishing to rely on the expert evidence, whether the prosecution or the accused, to show that it is sufficiently reliable. The test would be whether the evidence is predicated on sound principles, techniques, and assumptions that have been properly applied to the facts of the case and is supported by those principles, techniques, and assumptions as applied to the facts of the case. It is also proposed that in deciding the issue, the court should have regard to guidelines such as, in the case of scientific expert evidence, whether the principles etc have been properly tested, the margin of error associated with their application, and whether they are regarded as sound in the scientific community.[108] The Commission also sought views on another possible development in which it saw merit, namely that a judge, in determining the question of sufficient reliability in cases in which the evidence or field is particularly difficult, should be permitted to call upon an independent expert assessor for assistance or guidance. The Commission envisages such an assessor being called upon only exceptionally, but cases of difficulty are probably much more common than the Commission presupposes.[109]

In the context of medical expert evidence on the cause of injury or death, particular caution is needed where the scientific knowledge is or may be incomplete and also where the expert opinion evidence is not relied upon as additional material in support of a prosecution, but

---

[102] The court made three exceptions to its general statement: where the voices of a known group are being listened to and the issue is which voice has spoken which words, or where there are rare characteristics which render a speaker identifiable, or the issue relates to the accent or dialect of the speaker.

[103] [2008] 2 Cr App R 266, CA at 281.

[104] See the pre-publication summary of the report of the US National Academy of Sciences, available on its website: see Pattenden, Noticeboard, (2009) 13 *E&P* 252.

[105] See, eg, the concern expressed in *R v Hoey* [2007] NICC 49 about the absence of validation guidelines for LCN DNA tests compared to the 'normal' SGM+ DNA tests.

[106] A Roberts, 'Drawing on Expertise: Legal Decision-making and the Reception of Expert Evidence' [2008] *Crim LR* 443 at 455–7.

[107] Consultation Paper No 190 (2009), <http://www.lawcom.gov.uk/1155.htm>.

[108] For critical commentary, see A Roberts, 'Rejecting General Acceptance, Confounding the Gate-keeper: the Law Commission and Expert Evidence' [2009] *Crim LR* 551.

[109] See A Roberts, [2008] *Crim LR* 443 at 460.

is fundamental to it.[110] In *R v Cannings*[111] Judge LJ, delivering the judgment of the Court of Appeal, said:

> Experts in many fields will acknowledge the possibility that later research may undermine the accepted wisdom of today. 'Never say never' is a phrase which we have heard in many different contexts from expert witnesses. That does not normally provide a basis for rejecting the expert evidence, or indeed for conjuring up fanciful doubts about the possible impact of later research.

However, the court went on to say that in the case of two or more sudden unexplained infant deaths in the same family, in many important respects we are still at the frontiers of knowledge. It was held that, for the time being, where a full investigation is followed by a serious disagreement between reputable experts about the cause of death and a body of such expert opinion concludes that natural causes cannot be excluded as a reasonable and not a fanciful possibility, the prosecution of a parent or parents for murder should not be started or continued in the absence of additional cogent evidence extraneous to the expert evidence and tending to support the conclusion of deliberate harm.[112]

R v Cannings was distinguished in *R v Kai-Whitewind*.[113] K-W was convicted of the murder of her infant son. She had had difficulty bonding with the child and there was evidence that shortly after he was born she had felt like killing the child. The child died while in her sole care. On the day of his death, she had sought medical advice after the child had developed a spontaneous nosebleed, an extremely rare occurrence in the case of an infant. Post-mortem examinations revealed new and old blood in the lungs. According to the prosecution experts, this was consistent with two distinct episodes of upper airway obstruction, but the views of the defence experts were that death by natural causes was more probable than unnatural death or that the cause of death was unascertained. The appeal against conviction was dismissed. It was held that *R v Cannings* concerned inferences based upon coincidence, or the unlikelihood of two or more infant deaths in the same family, or one death where another child or other children in the family had suffered from unexplained 'Apparent Life Threatening Events'. There was essentially no evidence beyond the inferences based upon coincidence which the prosecution experts were prepared to draw but as to which other reputable experts in the same specialist field took a different view. Hence the need for additional cogent evidence. It did not follow from this that whenever there was a conflict between expert witnesses, the case for the prosecution had to fail unless the conviction was justified by evidence independent of the expert witnesses. In the instant case there was a single death, it was not suggested that any inference should be drawn against the accused from any previous incident involving any of her children, and the evidence about the child's condition found on the post-mortem examination was evidence of fact and precisely the kind of material which was sought and could not be found in *R v Cannings*. The dispute between experts about the interpretation of the findings at the post-mortem did not extinguish the findings themselves, and the jury had been entitled to evaluate the expert evidence, taking account of the facts found at the post-mortem and bearing in mind in addition, for example, that they related to an infant whose mother had spoken about killing him, had made a comment about smothering another child, who might have delayed reporting his death, and who had elected not to give evidence.

---

[110] *R v Holdsworth* [2009] Crim LR 195, CA.

[111] [2004] 1 All ER 725 at [178].

[112] The case is considered in more detail in Ch 8.

[113] (2005) The Times, 11 May, CA.

Some commentators are troubled by the decision in *R v Kai-Whitewind* on the basis that it allows juries to convict notwithstanding that eminent experts are of the view that such a conclusion would be unjustified or even wrong.[114] However, assuming that this is not a veiled criticism of trial by jury, as the court itself observes, it would be inappropriate, whenever there is a genuine conflict of opinion between reputable experts, that the prosecution should not proceed or should be stopped, or that the evidence of the prosecution experts should be disregraded. A less radical solution would be to introduce some form of corroboration requirement, if only to direct the jury to exercise caution in the absence of any independent supporting prosecution evidence.

The duty of the expert

In civil proceedings, under CPR r 35.1, it is the duty of the expert to help the court on the matters within his expertise, a duty that overrides any obligation to the person from whom he has received instructions or by whom he is paid. In similar vein, rule 33.2 of the Criminal Procedure Rules provides that in criminal proceedings an expert has a duty to the court to help it to achieve the overriding objective by giving objective unbiased opinion on matters within his expertise, a duty that overrides any obligation from the person by whom he is instructed or paid and that includes an obligation to inform all parties and the court if his opinion changes from that contained in a report served as evidence or given in a statement under Part 24 of the Rules (disclosure of expert evidence) or Part 29 of the Rules (expert evidence in connection with special measures directions). The duty of the expert as described in these rules builds on and, to an extent, overlaps with, the descriptions of the obligations of an expert set out by Cresswell J in *National Justice Cia Naviera SA v Prudential Assurance Co Ltd, The Ikarian Reefer*[115] and the guidance for experts giving evidence involving children provided by Wall J in *In re AB (Child Abuse: Expert Witnesses)*.[116] In *R v Harris*[117] it was held that these descriptions were also very relevant in criminal proceedings. Some of the factors set out by Cresswell J in *The Ikarian Reefer* were summarized in *R v Harris*[118] as follows:

1. Expert evidence presented to the court should be and be seen to be the independent product of the expert uninfluenced as to form or content by the exigencies of litigation.

2. An expert witness should provide independent assistance to the court by way of objective unbiased opinion in relation to matters within his expertise. An expert witness in the High Court should never assume the role of advocate.

3. An expert witness should state the facts or assumptions on which his opinion is based. He should not omit to consider material facts which detract from his concluded opinion.

4. An expert should make it clear when a particular question or issue falls outside his expertise.

---

[114] See, eg, Hirst, 'Blackstone's Criminal Practice Bulletin', Issue 2, Jan 2006 at 13.
[115] [1993] 2 Lloyd's Rep 68 at 81.
[116] [1995] 1 FLR 181.
[117] [2006] 1 Cr App R 55, CA.
[118] At [271].

5. If an expert's opinion is not properly researched because he considers that insufficient data is available then this must be stated with an indication that the opinion is no more than a provisional one.

6. If, after exchange of reports, an expert witness changes his view on material matters, such changes of view should be communicated to the other side without delay and when appropriate to the court.

In *In re AB (Child Abuse: Expert Witnesses)* Wall J, referring to cases in which there is a genuine disagreement on a scientific or medical issue or where it is necessary for a party to advance a particular hypothesis to explain a given set of facts, said:[119]

> Where that occurs, the judge [in a criminal case, jury] will have to resolve the issue which is raised. Two points must be made. In my view, the expert who advances such a hypothesis owes a very heavy duty to explain to the court that what he is advancing is a hypothesis, that it is controversial (if it is) and to place before the court all material which contradicts the hypothesis. Secondly, he must make all his material available to the other experts in the case. It is the common experience of the courts that the better the experts the more limited their areas of disagreement, and in the forensic context of a contested case relating to children, the objective of the lawyers and the experts should always be to limit the ambit of disagreement on medical issues to the minimum.[120]

In *R v Harris* the court emphasized[121] that developments in scientific thinking should not be kept from the court simply because they remain at the stage of a hypothesis, but that it is of the first importance that the true status of the expert's evidence is frankly indicated to the court. In cases involving allegations of child abuse, it was said that the judge should be prepared to give directions in respect of expert evidence, taking into account the guidance to which the court had referred.

R v Puaca[122] illustrates the importance of compliance with the obligations on an expert. In that case, in which a murder conviction was quashed because the conclusions of the Crown's pathologist could not safely be relied on, it was held that it is wholly wrong for a pathologist carrying out the first post-mortem at the request of the police or the coroner to leave it to the defence to instruct a pathologist to prepare a report setting out contrary arguments.

Evidence of facts upon which an opinion is based
In many—probably most—cases, the expert will have no personal or first-hand knowledge of the facts upon which his opinion is based. For example, in *Beckwith v Sydebotham*[123] shipwrights expressed their opinion on the seaworthiness of a ship which they had not examined. In such a case, the expert should state the *assumed* facts upon which his opinion is based and examination-in-chief and cross-examination should take the form of *hypothetical* questions. The facts upon which the expert's opinion is based, sometimes referred to as 'primary facts', must be proved by admissible evidence.[124] The primary facts may be proved by calling the person with personal or first-hand knowledge of them to give direct evidence of them. Thus in *R v Mason*,[125] a murder

[119] At 192.
[120] See also CPR r 35.12 and r 33.5 of the Criminal Procedure Rules, both considered below.
[121] At [270].
[122] [2005] EWCA Crim 3001.
[123] (1807) 1 Camp 116.
[124] Per Lawton LJ in *R v Turner* [1975] QB 834 at 840, CA.
[125] (1911) 7 Cr App R 67, CCA.

trial in which a witness who had seen the deceased's body was called to describe the wounds, a surgeon, who had not seen the body, was asked whether the deceased had died from natural causes or in consequence of his wounds and whether the wounds could have been self-inflicted. Alternatively, under section 127 of the Criminal Justice Act 2003, the primary facts may be proved by the hearsay statement of the person with personal or first-hand knowledge of them, unless, on an application by a party to the proceedings, that is not in the interests of justice.[126] In some cases, the expert will have personal or first-hand knowledge of the facts in question, as when he examines an exhibit or visits the *locus in quo*, and in such a case he may testify as to both fact and opinion. In any event the expert should be asked in examination-in-chief to state the facts or assumed facts upon which his evidence is based so that the court can assess the value of his opinion.[127] 'If the expert has been misinformed about the facts or has taken irrelevant facts into consideration or has omitted to consider relevant ones, the opinion is likely to be valueless.'[128]

In criminal cases, although an expert cannot *prove* facts upon which his opinion is based but of which he has no personal or first-hand knowledge, because that would be a breach of the rule against hearsay,[129] he is entitled to rely upon such facts as a part of the process of forming an opinion and, in this sense, is not subject to the rule against hearsay in the same way as a non-expert or witness of fact. *English Exporters (London) Ltd v Eldonwall Ltd*,[130] which must now be read subject to the Civil Evidence Act 1995, provides an instructive example. In that case, landlords applied for the determination of a reasonable interim rent under the Landlord and Tenant Act 1954. Megarry J held that although a professional valuer, called as an expert witness to give his opinion as to the value of the property, could not give evidence of comparable rents of which he had no personal knowledge in order to establish those rents as matters of fact, because that would amount to inadmissible hearsay, he was entitled to express opinions that he had formed as to values even though substantial contributions to the formation of those opinions had been made by matters of which he had no first-hand knowledge but had learned about from sources such as journals, reports of auctions and other dealings, and information, relating to both particular and more general transactions, obtained from professional colleagues and others. Similarly, in *R v Bradshaw*,[131] a case of murder where the only issue at the trial was that of diminished responsibility, it was held that although doctors called by the defence could not state what the accused had told them about past symptoms as evidence of the existence of those symptoms, because that would infringe the rule against hearsay, they could give evidence of what the patient had told them in order to explain the grounds upon which they came to a conclusion with regard to his condition.[132]

---

[126] See Ch 10.

[127] But it seems that where an expert expresses an opinion based on primary facts derived from his use of a computer, for example the printout of a machine used by him to analyse the chemical constituents of a substance believed to be a particular drug, there is no *obligation* to produce the printout: see *R v Golizadeh* [1995] Crim LR 232, CA.

[128] Per Lawton LJ in *R v Turner* [1975] QB 834 at 840. In a case where the real factual issues between the parties will emerge with clarity only after all the factual evidence has been given, and the views of the experts will be of the greatest value if given in the light of that evidence, in the Commercial Court at least, the High Court has power to order that all the factual evidence be given by both sides before any expert evidence is received: *Bayer v Clarkson Puckle Overseas Ltd* [1989] NLJR 256, QBD.

[129] See, eg, *R v Jackson* [1996] 2 Cr App R 420, CA

[130] [1973] Ch 415. See also *Ramsay v Watson* (1961) 108 CLR 642.

[131] (1985) 82 Cr App R 79, CA.

[132] Per Lord Lane CJ, (1985) 82 Cr App R 79 at 83, citing *Cross on Evidence* (5th edn, London, 1979) 446.

Under the same doctrine, the expert may fortify his opinion by referring not only to any relevant research, tests, or experiments which he has personally carried out, whether or not expressly for the purposes of the case, but also to works of authority, learned articles, research papers, letters, and other similar material written by others and comprising part of the general body of knowledge falling within the field of expertise of the expert in question.[133] In *H v Schering Chemicals Ltd*,[134] Bingham J said:

> If an expert refers to the results of research published by a reputable authority in a reputable journal the court would, I think, ordinarily regard those results as supporting inferences fairly to be drawn from them, unless or until a different approach was shown to be proper.[135]

In *R v Abadom*[136] the accused was convicted of robbery. The prosecution case rested on evidence that he had broken a window during the robbery and that fragments of glass embedded in his shoes had come from the window. An expert gave evidence that, as a result of a personal analysis of the samples, he found that the glass from the window and the glass in the shoes bore an identical refractive index. He also gave evidence that he had consulted unpublished statistics compiled by the Home Office Central Research Establishment which showed that the refractive index in question occurred in only 4 per cent of all glass samples investigated. He then expressed the opinion that there was a very strong likelihood that the glass in the shoes came from the window. On appeal it was argued that the evidence of the Home Office statistics was inadmissible hearsay because the expert had no knowledge of the analysis on which the statistics had been based. The appeal was dismissed on the grounds that once the 'primary facts' on which an opinion is based have been proved by admissible evidence, the expert is entitled to draw on the work of others as part of the process of arriving at his conclusion. The primary facts in the instant case, that is the refractive indices of the glass from the window and the glass in the shoes, had been proved by admissible evidence (as it happened by the evidence of the expert himself on the basis of his own analysis). Accordingly the expert was entitled to refer to the Home Office statistics and this involved no infringement of the hearsay rule. Experts, it was said, should not limit themselves to drawing on material which has been published in some form: part of their experience and expertise lies in their knowledge and evaluation of unpublished material. The only proviso is that they should refer to such material in their evidence so that the cogency and probative value of their conclusions can be tested and evaluated by reference to it.[137]

R v Abadom was applied in *R v Hodges*,[138] a case of conspiracy to supply heroin, in which a very experienced drugs officer gave evidence partially deprived from what he had been told by others, including other officers, informants, and drug users, as to the usual method of supplying heroin, its purchase price in a particular place at the time, and what weight was more than

---

[133] *Davie v Edinburgh Magistrates* 1953 SC 34, Court of Session; *Seyfang v GD Searle & Co* [1973] QB 148 at 151. However, the court is only entitled to make use of those parts of the material which have been relied upon by the expert or upon which he has been cross-examined: see *Collier v Simpson* (1831) 5 C&P 73.

[134] [1983] 1 All ER 849.

[135] [1983] 1 All ER 849 at 853.

[136] [1983] 1 All ER 364, CA.

[137] Cf *R v Bradshaw* (1985) 82 Cr App R 79, CA, above, where it was held that if the doctors' opinions had been based entirely upon the 'hearsay' statements of the accused as to his past symptoms and the accused had elected not to testify and thus not provided any direct evidence as to such symptoms, the judge would have been justified in telling the jury that the defence case was based upon a flimsy or non-existent foundation.

[138] [2003] 2 Cr App R 247, CA.

would have been for personal use alone. The relevant primary facts were the observations of the activities of the accused, the finding of 14 grams of heroin in the possession of one of them, and the finding of other drugs paraphernalia in his house. The court distinguished *R v Edwards*.[139] In that case, the issue was whether the accused intended to supply the ecstasy tablets found in his possession or whether they were for personal consumption. Witnesses for both the prosecution and defence, neither of whom had any medical or toxicological qualification, were not allowed to give evidence, based on what they had been told by drugs users, rather than any academic materials, as to the personal consumption rates of ecstasy tablet users, and the impact of use in terms of developing tolerance or suffering serious harm. The evidence was held to have been properly excluded on the basis that the witnesses lacked the appropriate expertise to exempt their opinions from the rule against hearsay.[140]

The common law doctrine under discussion has been preserved, in criminal proceedings, by statute. Section 118(1)8 of the Criminal Justice Act 2003 preserves 'Any rule of law under which in criminal proceedings an expert witness may draw on the body of expertise relevant to his field'.

Evidence on ultimate issues

Historically, the courts have striven to prevent any witness from expressing his opinion on an ultimate issue, that is one of the very issues which the court has to determine. In *Haynes v Doman*,[141] for example, the issue being the reasonableness of a covenant in restraint of trade, Lord Lindley MR held that affidavits from persons in the trade expressing their views on the reasonableness of the clause on which the case turned were out of place and inadmissible. The justification of the rule is that insofar as such evidence might unduly influence the tribunal of fact, it prevents witnesses from usurping the function of the court: witnesses are called to testify, not to decide the case. The rule is open to criticism on a number of levels.[142] The objection of undue influence makes no allowance for cases in which the tribunal of fact is a professional judge rather than a jury, overlooks the frequency of conflicts in expert testimony, and is largely incompatible with the very justification for admitting expert evidence, that the drawing of inferences from the facts in question calls for an expertise which the tribunal of fact does not possess. However, in practice the rule is often of no more than semantic effect: the expert is allowed to express his opinion provided that the diction employed is not noticeably the same as that which will be used when the matter is subsequently considered by the court![143] Whatever its merits, in civil proceedings the rule has been abolished. Section 3(1) of the 1972 Act provides that:

> Subject to any rules of court made in pursuance of this Act, where a person is called as a witness in any civil proceedings, his opinion on any relevant matter on which he is qualified to give expert evidence shall be admissible in evidence.

Section 3(3) reads:

> In this section 'relevant matter' includes an issue in the proceedings in question.

---

[139] [2001] EWCA Crim 2185, [2001] All ER (D) 271 (Oct).

[140] Cf *R v Ibrahima* [2005] Crim LR 887, CA, above.

[141] [1899] 2 Ch 13, CA.

[142] See generally the 17th Report of the Law Reform Committee, *Evidence of Opinion and Expert Evidence* (Cmnd 4889) paras 266–71; 11th Report, Criminal Law Revision Committee (Cmnd 4991); and RD Jackson, 'The Ultimate Issue Rule: One Rule Too Many' [1984] *Crim LR* 75.

[143] See, eg, *Rich v Pierpont* (1862) 3 F&F 35 and per Lord Parker CJ in *DPP v A & B C Chewing Gum Ltd* [1968] 1 QB 159 at 164.

In family law cases involving suspected child abuse, expert evidence may relate to the presence and interpretation of physical, mental, behavioural, and emotional signs, but often necessarily includes a view as to the likely veracity of the child. In this context, in *Re M and R (minors)*,[144] it was held that it is 'plainly right' that 'issue' in section 3(3) *can* include an issue of credibility and that when dealing with children the court needs 'all the help it can get'.[145] In the normal case, as we have seen, expert evidence of credibility will be inadmissible because unnecessary, being a matter on which the tribunal of fact can form its own opinion unaided.

Technically, the ultimate issue rule still operates in criminal proceedings, but in relation to expert witnesses is in practice largely ignored.[146] In *R v Hookway*,[147] for example, it was recognized that expert evidence of 'facial mapping' is sufficient, by itself, to establish the identity of the accused; in *R v Mason*,[148] as we have seen, a surgeon was asked for his opinion whether a person died in consequence of his wounds and whether they could have been self-inflicted; and in *R v Holmes*[149] the Court of Criminal Appeal held that it was not improper to cross-examine a doctor called by the accused in a murder trial about whether the accused's conduct after the offence indicated that he knew the nature of the act and that it was contrary to the law of the land, both issues, of course, being central to the defence of insanity within the M'Naghten rules.[150] In *DPP v A & B C Chewing Gum Ltd*[151] Lord Parker CJ, although of the opinion that in a prosecution under the Obscene Publications Act 1959 it would be wrong to ask an expert directly whether a publication tended to deprave and corrupt, later observed that more and more inroads had been made into the rule against opinion evidence on ultimate issues:[152]

> Those who practise in the criminal courts see every day cases of experts being called on the question of diminished responsibility, and although technically the final question 'Do you think he was suffering from diminished responsibility?' is strictly inadmissible, it is allowed time and time again without any objection.

Weight

In cases in which expert opinion evidence is properly adduced, the weight to be attached to it is a matter entirely for the tribunal of fact. The duty of experts, it has been said, 'is to furnish the judge or jury with the necessary scientific criteria for testing the accuracy of their conclusions, so as to enable the judge or jury to form their own independent judgment by the application

---

[144] [1996] 4 All ER 239, CA.

[145] [1996] 4 All ER 239 at 249.

[146] In its 11th Report, the Criminal Law Revision Committee was of the opinion that the rule probably no longer existed: para 268 (Cmnd 4991). See also per Lord Taylor CJ in *R v Stockwell* (1993) 97 Cr App R 260 at 265: the rule has become 'a matter of form rather than substance'. Contrast, *sed quaere*, *R v Jeffries* [1997] Crim LR 819, CA.

[147] [1999] Crim LR 750, CA.

[148] (1911) 7 Cr App R 67, CCA. See also *R v Smith* [1979] 1 WLR 1445, CA, above; and *R v Silcott* [1987] Crim LR 765, CC, where the educational subnormality of one accused was described by the experts as 'very likely' and 'significantly likely' to render 'unreliable' a confession allegedly made by him. See s 76(2)(b) of the Police and Criminal Evidence Act 1984, Ch 13.

[149] [1953] 1 WLR 686. Contrast *R v Wright* (1821) Russ&Ry 456.

[150] See also *R v Udenze* [2001] EWCA Crim 1381 (in a rape case, expert evidence as to the effects of alcohol on the complainant's ability to give informed consent); and *R v Hodges* [2003] 2 Cr App R 247, above (in a case of supplying drugs, expert evidence that the amount found was more than would have been for personal use alone).

[151] [1968] 1 QB 159.

[152] [1968] 1 QB 159 at 164.

of these criteria to the facts proved in evidence'.[153] Thus, in the civil context, although lay evidence should not be preferred to expert evidence without good reason,[154] it has been held that there is no principle of law preventing a judge from preferring the evidence of lay claimants whom he finds to be honest over the evidence of a jointly instructed expert with whose evidence he can find no fault.[155] Similarly, on the question whether or not a will was forged, a court may prefer the evidence of non-expert attesting witnesses to that of a handwriting expert.[156] Equally, in the criminal context, it has been held that it is incumbent on magistrates to approach expert evidence critically, even if no expert is called on the other side and to be willing to reject it if it leaves questions unanswered.[157] In Crown Court cases in which expert opinion evidence is given on an ultimate issue, the judge should make clear to the jury that they are not bound by the opinion, and that the issue is for them to decide.[158] The same applies where the evidence does not relate to an ultimate issue, but there is no inflexible requirement that the warning take any particular form.[159] It is a misdirection to tell the jury that expert evidence should be accepted if uncontradicted[160] or in the absence of reasons for rejecting it.[161] However, it has also been held to be wrong to direct a jury that they may disregard expert opinion evidence when the only evidence adduced dictates one answer.[162] In an attempt to reconcile the authorities, in *R v Sanders*,[163] a case concerning the defence of diminished responsibility, it was held that if there are no other circumstances to consider, unequivocal, uncontradicted medical evidence favourable to an accused should be accepted by a jury and they should be so directed; but where there are other circumstances to consider (including, presumably, the nature of the killing, the conduct of the accused before, at the time of and after it, and any history of mental abnormality), then the medical evidence, though unequivocal and uncontradicted, must be assessed in the light of those circumstances.

If there is conflicting expert evidence, the tribunal of fact is obviously forced to make a choice. For these purposes, no less than when deciding whether to accept the evidence of even a single expert witness, the tribunal of fact may take into account an expert's qualifications and how they were acquired, his credibility, the degree of reliability of his opinion, and the extent to which, if at all, his evidence-in-chief was based on assumed facts which do not accord with those ultimately established.

[153] Per Lord President Cooper in *Davie v Edinburgh Magistrates* 1953 SC 34 at 40, Court of Session. Thus concerning voice identification, the jury, in forming their own judgment on the opinions of the experts, are entitled to know the features of the voice to which they paid attention (*R v Robb* (1991) 93 Cr App R 161 at 166) and to hear the tapes which they analysed (*R v Bentum* (1989) 153 JP 538, CA).

[154] See *Re B (a minor)* [2000] 1 WLR 790, CA.

[155] *Armstrong v First York Ltd* (2005) The Times, 19 Jan. See also *Stevens v Simons* [1988] CLY 1161, CA.

[156] *Fuller v Strum* (2000) The Times, 14 Feb 2001.

[157] *DPP v Wynne* (2001) The Independent, 19 Feb, DC.

[158] Per Lord Taylor CJ in *R v Stockwell* (1993) 97 Cr App R 260.

[159] *R v Fitzpatrick* [1999] Crim LR 832, CA.

[160] *Davie v Edinburgh Magistrates* 1953 SC 34 at 40.

[161] Per Diplock LJ in *R v Lanfear* [1968] 2 QB 77, CA.

[162] *Anderson v R* [1972] AC 100, PC. See also *R v Matheson* [1958] 1 WLR 474, CCA: in a murder trial, if there are no facts or circumstances to displace or throw a doubt on unchallenged medical evidence of diminished responsibility, a verdict of guilty will not be in accordance with the evidence; and *R v Bailey* (1977) 66 Cr App R 31n, CCA: although juries are not bound to accept such expert medical evidence, they must act on it, and if there is nothing before them to cast doubt on it, cannot reject it. But see also *Walton v R* [1978] AC 788, PC, followed in *R v Kiszko* (1978) 68 Cr App R 62, CA.

[163] (1991) 93 Cr App R 245, CA.

Restrictions on, and disclosure of, expert evidence in civil cases

In *Access to Justice, Final Report*,[164] Lord Woolf regarded expert evidence as one of the major generators of unnecessary cost in civil litigation, operating against the principles of proportionality and access to justice. He also reiterated concerns about the lack of impartiality of experts, or what has been called 'hired gun syndrome': 'it is often quite surprising to see with what facility and to what extent, their views can be made to correspond with the wishes or the interests of the parties who call them'.[165] As one commentator has observed: 'The court hears not the most expert opinions, but those favourable to the respective parties.'[166] Lord Woolf's Final Report made a number of recommendations which formed the basis of the new rules to be found in Part 35 of the Civil Procedure Rules and its accompanying Practice Direction.[167] In the case of testifying experts, ie those who have been instructed to prepare or give expert *evidence*, in addition to imposing an overriding duty to the court,[168] they create a duty to restrict the amount of expert evidence, and introduce new requirements as to the form in which expert evidence shall be given and as to advance disclosure. They do not apply, however, to an 'advising expert', ie an expert retained by a party for the purpose of advising that party, who owes no duty to the court and whose advice, if given in contemplation of legal proceedings, will be privileged against disclosure. The use of advising experts is quite common in relation to commercial litigation.

The duty and power to restrict expert evidence
The duty to restrict expert evidence is governed by rule 35.1.

> 35.1 Expert evidence shall be restricted to that which is reasonably required to resolve the proceedings.

The court's power to restrict expert evidence is governed by rule 35.4, which provides as follows:

(1) No party may call an expert or put in evidence an expert's report without the court's permission.
(2) When a party applies for permission under this rule he must identify—
   (a) the field in which he wishes to rely on expert evidence; and
   (b) where practicable the expert in that field on whose evidence he wishes to rely.
(3) If permission is granted under this rule it shall be in relation only to the expert named or the field identified under paragraph (2).
(4) The court may limit the amount of the expert's fees and expenses that the party who wishes to rely on the expert may recover from any other party.

Where, for no good reason, an application for permission to call an expert under rule 35.4 is not made in good time, it is unlikely to be granted if made so shortly before the trial that it would work a significant injustice to the other side.[169]

---

[164] HMSO (1996).

[165] Taylor, *Treatise on the Law of Evidence* (12th edn, London, 1931) 59.

[166] John Basten 'The Court Expert in Civil Trials, a Comparative Appraisal' (1977) 40 *MLR* 174.

[167] Excepting rr 35.1, 35.3, 35.7, and 35.8, Part 35 does not apply to claims which have been allocated to the small claims track: CPR r 27.2(1)e.

[168] See above.

[169] *Calenti v North Middlesex NHS Trust* (2001) LTL 10 Apr 2001, QBD.

Written reports

Under the new rules, there is a presumption—in the case of claims on the fast track, a strong presumption—that if expert evidence is permitted, it should be given by means of an expert's written report, rather than by calling the expert as a witness. Rule 35.5 provides as follows:

(1) Expert evidence is to be given in a written report unless the court directs otherwise.

(2) If a claim is on the fast track, the court will not direct an expert to attend a hearing unless it is necessary to do so in the interests of justice.

The single joint expert

Rule 35.7 challenges the notion that where both parties wish to adduce expert evidence, there is a need for two experts: it permits the court to direct that the evidence should be given by a single joint expert. As we shall see, the parties themselves may agree to such a direction, which the court may then approve. Indeed, as a general rule, good practice will require a party to attempt to agree a joint expert with his opponent rather than to instruct his own expert. This practice is promoted by the pre-action protocols: see, eg, paragraph 2.11 of the Notes of Guidance in the Pre-Action Protocol for Personal Injury Claims. Of course, there is nothing in the Civil Procedure Rules to prevent a party from instructing his own expert, and this may well be thought to be appropriate in a case in which a claimant needs expert assistance in order to decide whether he has a valid claim at all. However, where a party obtains an expert's report without the approval of the court, there is a real risk that he will not recover his costs in this respect: under rule 35.4, the court may refuse permission to admit the report or call the expert, and under rule 35.7 may direct the use of a jointly instructed expert.

Rule 35.7 does not create a presumption in favour of a direction that there should be one expert only, but in many cases, such a direction will give effect to the 'overriding objective', especially in saving expense and putting the parties on an equal footing. However, much may turn on the value and complexity of the litigation: single joint experts are not commonly appointed in Commercial Court cases, and there is a greater willingness to permit two experts in multi-track cases, which are typically more complex than fast track claims. It can be wrong to appoint a single joint expert on a medical issue on which there are different schools of thought.[170] In *Peet v Mid Kent Healthcare Trust*,[171] a claim of medical negligence, it was said that whereas in the great majority of cases non-medical evidence dealing with quantum should be given by a single expert rather than by experts called on behalf of each party, it is sometimes difficult to restrict the medical evidence because of the difficult issues as to the appropriate form and standard of treatment required. In *ES v Chesterfield & North Derbyshire Royal Hospital NHS Trust*[172] the claimant alleged negligence on the part of an obstetric registrar and his consultant, the value of the claim being about £1.5 million. The claimant appealed a direction limiting the expert evidence to one expert obstetrician on each side. The Court of Appeal, having regard to both the 'overriding objective' and the terms of rule 35.1, allowed the appeal and permitted the claimant to call two expert obstetricians. Relevant factors taken into account included the value and complexity of the case and the fact that the obstetric registrar and his consultant were both able to give evidence of their actions based on their professional expertise.

---

[170] *Oxley v Penwarden* [2001] Lloyds Rep Med 347, CA. See also *Casey v Cartwright* [2007] 2 All ER 78, CA.

[171] [2002] 1 WLR 210, CA at [6]–[7].

[172] (2003) EWCA Civ 1284.

Rule 35.7 provides as follows:

(1) Where two or more parties wish to submit expert evidence on a particular issue, the court may direct that the evidence on that issue is to be given by one expert only.
(2) The parties wishing to submit the expert evidence are called 'the instructing parties'.
(3) Where the instructing parties cannot agree who should be the expert, the court may—
    (a) select the expert from a list prepared or identified by the instructing parties; or
    (b) direct that the expert be selected in such other manner as the court may direct.

In most cases, it is likely that the court will expect the parties to be able to agree who the expert should be. Given the overriding duty of the expert to the court, it may be difficult for a party to object to a particular expert, even if it is known that he has previously been instructed extensively or exclusively by the firm of solicitors representing the other party, or has previously acted only on behalf of, say, defendant employers or insurance companies.

Where the court has directed that the evidence on a particular issue should be given by one expert only, but there are a number of disciplines relevant to that issue, a leading expert in the dominant discipline should be used, who should prepare the general part of the report and be responsible for annexing or incorporating the contents of any reports from experts in the other disciplines.[173]

Rule 35.8 deals with the instructions to be given to a single joint expert:

(1) Where the court gives a direction under rule 35.7 for a single joint expert to be used, each instructing party may give instructions to the expert.
(2) When an instructing party gives instructions to the expert he must, at the same time, send a copy of the instructions to the other instructing parties.
(3) The court may give directions about—
    (a) the payment of the expert's fees and expenses; and
    (b) any inspection, examination or experiments which the expert wishes to carry out.
(4) The court may, before an expert is instructed—
    (a) limit the amount that can be paid by way of fees and expenses to the expert; and
    (b) direct that the instructing parties pay that amount into court.
(5) Unless the court otherwise directs, the instructing parties are jointly and severally liable for the payment of the expert's fees and expenses.

In cases in which one party has exclusive access to information about the basic facts on which expert opinion will need to be based, it will be difficult if not impossible for the other party to properly instruct an expert without access to that information. Rule 35.9 therefore empowers the court to direct the one party to provide such information to the other:

Where a party has access to information which is not reasonably available to the other party, the court may direct the party who has access to the information to—
    (a) prepare and file a document recording the information; and
    (b) serve a copy of that document on the other party.

Where the court makes such a direction, the document to be prepared should set out sufficient details of any facts, tests, or experiments which constitute the information to enable the other party to assess and understand its significance.[174]

[173] PD 35, para 6.
[174] PD 35, para 3.

Where the parties have instructed a single joint expert, it is not permissible for one party to have a conference with the expert in the absence of the other, without the latter's prior written consent. A conclusion to the contrary would be inconsistent with the concept of a jointly instructed expert owing an equal duty of openness and confidentiality to both parties.[175]

Where a court has directed that evidence on an issue be given by a single joint expert and the parties agree who the expert should be, a party who is unhappy with the expert's report will be refused permission to call a further expert unless such refusal would be unjust having regard to the 'overriding objective'.[176] The discretion may be exercised against the party if there is only a modest amount at stake and therefore it would be disproportionate to adduce further expert evidence.[177] Other relevant factors to be taken into account include the nature and importance of the issues, their number, the reasons for requiring another expert, the effect of adducing the additional evidence, and any delay likely to be caused.[178]

Under paragraph 3.14 of the Pre-Action Protocol for Personal Injury Claims, before any party instructs an expert, he should give the other party the name(s) of one or more experts whom he considers suitable to instruct. Under paragraph 3.16, the other party may object to one or more of the named experts and the first party should then instruct a mutually acceptable expert. Such an expert needs to be distinguished from a single joint expert. The latter is instructed by both parties, both are liable for his fees and both have an equal right to see his report. A mutually acceptable expert is instructed on behalf of one party, who is usually liable to pay his fees, and his report is protected by litigation privilege, unless the instructing party chooses to waive it. Thus although the Protocol encourages and promotes the voluntary disclosure of medical reports, it does not require it.[179]

Written questions to experts

In cases in which the expert evidence takes the form of a written report, whether prepared by a single joint expert or an expert instructed by a party, there will obviously be no opportunity to question him on oath in order either to clarify any part of his report or to challenge him on such matters as his methodology, the reasons for his opinion, any expert literature upon which he has relied, opposing expert opinion, and so on. For reasons of this kind, provision has been made to allow written questions to be put to the expert before the trial. A party is entitled to put such questions, if they are for the purpose only of clarification of the report; but if they are for some other purpose, they may only be asked if the court gives permission or the other party agrees. Rule 35.6 provides as follows:

(1) A party may put to—
    (a) an expert instructed by another party; or
    (b) a single joint expert appointed under rule 35.7, written questions about his report.[180]

---

[175] *Peet v Mid Kent Healthcare Trust* [2002] 1 WLR 210, CA.

[176] *Daniels v Walker* [2001] 1 WLR 1382, CA.

[177] Ibid.

[178] *Cosgrave v Pattison* [2001] CPLR 177, Ch D.

[179] *Carlson v Townsend* [2001] 3 All ER 663, CA. Cf *Beck v Ministry of Defence* [2004] PIQR 1, below.

[180] If the questions are sent direct, a copy of the questions should, at the same time, be sent to the other party or parties: PD 35, para 5.2.

(2) Written questions under paragraph (1)—
   (a) may be put once only;
   (b) must be put within 28 days of service of the expert's report; and
   (c) must be for the purpose only of clarification of the report; unless in any case,
      (i) the court gives permission; or
      (ii) the other party agrees.
(3) An expert's answers to questions put in accordance with paragraph (1) shall be treated as part of the expert's report.
(4) Where—
   (a) a party has put a written question to an expert instructed by another party in accordance with this rule; and
   (b) the expert does not answer that question,
      the court may make one or both of the following orders in relation to the party who instructed the expert—
      (i) that the party may not rely on the evidence of that expert; or
      (ii) that the party may not recover the fees and expenses of that expert from any other party.

Rule 35.6(2)(c) allows a party, with the permission of the court or other party, to ask about matters not covered in the expert's report, provided that they are within his expertise, and thereby renders the expert akin to a court expert.[181] The fact that experts can be required to answer written questions normally means that there is no need for a single joint expert's evidence to be amplified or tested by cross-examination of the expert. The court has a discretion to permit such amplification or cross-examination, but this should be restricted as far as possible.[182] If, exceptionally, the expert is to be subject to cross-examination, then he should know in advance what topics are to be covered, and where fresh material is to be adduced for his consideration, this should be done in advance of the hearing.[183]

The contents of the expert's report

An expert's report must comply with the requirements set out in Practice Direction 35,[184] which provides that a report must give details of the expert's qualifications; give details of any literature or other material relied on; set out the substance of all facts and instructions given to him which are material to the opinions expressed or upon which those opinions are based; make clear which facts in the report are within his own knowledge; say who carried out any test, or experiment which he has used for the report and whether or not it was carried out under his supervision; give the qualifications of the person who carried out any such test, or experiment; where there is a range of opinion on the matters dealt with in the report, summarize it and give reasons for his own opinion; contain a summary of his conclusions; if he is not able to give his opinion without qualification, state the qualification; and state that he understands his duty to the court and has complied and will continue to comply with that duty.[185] His report must also be verified by a statement of truth.[186]

---

[181] *Mutch v Allen* [2001] CPLR 200, CA.
[182] *Peet v Mid Kent Healthcare Trust* [2002] 1 WLR 210, CA at [28].
[183] *Popek v National Westminster Bank plc* [2002] EWCA Civ 42.
[184] CPR r 35.10(1).
[185] PD 35, para 2.2.
[186] PD 35, para 2.3.

Under rule 35.10(2), at the end of the expert's report there must be a statement that he understands his duty to the court and has complied with it. Rule 35.10(3) and (4) provide as follows:

(3) The expert's report must state the substance of all material instructions, whether written or oral, on the basis of which the report was written.
(4) The instructions referred to in paragraph (3) shall not be privileged against disclosure but the court will not, in relation to those instructions—
    (a) order disclosure of any specific document; or
    (b) permit any questioning in court, other than by the party who instructed the expert,
unless it is satisfied that there are reasonable grounds to consider the statement of instructions given under paragraph (3) to be inaccurate or incomplete.

Paragraph 4 of Practice Direction 35 states that cross-examination of the expert on the contents of his instructions will not be allowed unless the court permits it (or unless the party who gave the instructions consents to it). Paragraph 4 also states that if the court is satisfied that there are 'reasonable grounds' under rule 35.10(4)(b), then it will allow the cross-examination where it appears to be in the interests of justice to do so.

The intention behind rule 35.10(4) is to encourage the setting out fully of material instructions and facts, including, for example, witness statements provided to the experts and the previous report of another expert. However, the obligation under rule 35.10(3) is not to set out all the information and material supplied to the expert, but to disclose the 'substance of all material instructions'. Ordinarily the expert is to be trusted to comply with rule 35.10(3), and under rule 35.10(4) the party on the other side may not as a matter of course call for disclosure: there must be some concrete fact giving rise to the 'reasonable grounds' to which rule 35.10(4) refers.[187]

The requirements of PD 35 are intended to focus the mind of the expert on his responsibilities in order that litigation may progress in accordance with the overriding principles in CPR Part 1. If an expert demonstrates that he has no conception of those requirements, as when he fails to include in his report statements that he understands his duty to the court and has complied with it, and statements setting out the substance of all material instructions, then he may properly be debarred from acting as an expert witness in the case.[188] Moreover, in appropriate circumstances, the court may make a costs order against an expert who, by his evidence, has caused significant expense to be incurred, and has done so in flagrant and reckless disregard of his duties to the court.[189]

Discussions between experts

Rule 35.12 is another provision designed to save court time and reduce costs. It allows the court, at any stage, in cases in which the parties have been permitted to use competing experts, to direct a 'without prejudice'[190] discussion between the experts for the purpose of requiring them to identify the issues in the proceedings and, where possible, to reach agreement on an issue. The court may specify the issues which the experts must discuss. It may also direct that following the discussion the experts must prepare a statement for the court showing the issues on which they agreed and the issues on which they disagreed with a summary of their reasons

---

[187] *Lucas v Barking, Havering and Redbridge Hospitals NHS Trust* [2003] 4 All ER 720, CA.
[188] *Stevens v Gullis* [2000] 1 All ER 527, CA.
[189] *Phillips v Symes* [2005] 4 All ER 519 (Ch).
[190] See Ch 20.

for disagreeing.[191] Such a statement is not an admission and does not bind the parties, but is not privileged, even if made with an eye to assisting a mediation which, in the event, is unsuccessful.[192] However, the content of the *discussion* between the experts shall not be referred to at the trial unless the parties agree; and where the experts do agree on an issue, their agreement will not bind the parties unless they expressly agree to be bound by it.

If a party is dissatisfied with the revised opinion of his own expert following a discussion between experts, permission to call a further expert should only be granted where there is good reason to suppose that the expert modified his opinion or agreed with the expert instructed by the other side for reasons which cannot properly or fairly support his revised opinion, such as stepping outside his expertise or otherwise showing himself to be incompetent.[193]

Disclosure, non-disclosure, and inspection
Rules 35.11 and 35.13 provide as follows:

> 35.11 Where a party has disclosed an expert's report, any party may use that expert's report as evidence.
>
> . . .
>
> 35.13 A party who fails to disclose an expert's report may not use the report at the trial or call the expert to give evidence orally unless the court gives permission.

Where an expert has been asked to prepare a report, the dominant purpose being to use it in relation to anticipated or pending litigation, the report will be the subject of litigation privilege.[194] Neither the 1972 Act nor the Civil Procedure Rules compel the disclosure of privileged documents. However, under rule 35.13 a party will normally only be allowed to introduce an expert report in evidence, or to call its maker, if he has disclosed the report. Although the court may give permission for the evidence to be adduced notwithstanding failure to disclose the report, it is submitted that the new cards-on-the-table approach to civil litigation, which the courts will generally expect of the parties, is such that permission will rarely be granted, and then only in very exceptional circumstances.

Rule 35.13 does not provide a power to order disclosure of drafts of experts' reports, prepared for the purpose of discussion with a party's advisers prior to the completion of the expert's final report, and protected by litigation privilege. The specific and limited exemption from privilege of the material instructions pursuant to rule 35.10(4)[195] shows that there was no intention to abrogate the privilege attaching to draft expert reports.[196] However, where a party is dissatisfied with an expert's report and seeks permission to rely on a second, substitute expert's report, permission may be conditional upon disclosure of the final report of the first expert[197] or, in cases where the first expert did not complete a final report, any draft interim report containing the substance of his opinion on the various issues in the case.[198]

---

[191] In heavy fraud and other complex criminal cases, a direction should generally be made requiring the experts to meet and prepare such a statement: para 3(viii), Protocol for the control and management of heavy fraud and other complex criminal cases [2005] 2 All ER 429, CA.

[192] *Aird v Prime Meridian Ltd* (2007) The Times, 14 Feb.

[193] *Stallwood v David* [2007] 1 All ER 206, QBD.

[194] See Ch 20.

[195] See above.

[196] *Jackson v Marley Davenport Ltd* (2004) The Times, 7 Oct.

[197] *Beck v Ministry of Defence* [2004] PIQR 1.

[198] Per Dyson LJ, obiter, in *Vasiliou v Hajigeorgiou* [2005] 3 All ER 17, CA.

The effect of rule 35.11 is that where a party has been given permission to use an expert and has disclosed his expert's report, then the opposing party may use it as evidence at the trial, and this remains the case even if the first party has changed his mind and no longer intends to rely upon it.

Under rule 33.6, a party intending to introduce evidence, such as a plan, photograph, or model, which forms part of expert evidence but is not contained in an expert's report, must give notice of his intention when the expert report is served on the other party, and must give the other party an opportunity to inspect it and to agree to its admission without further proof.[199]

Directions and agreed directions

When a court allocates a case to the fast track, the directions it gives for the management of the case will include directions on expert evidence. If the parties have filed agreed directions, the court may approve them. Agreed directions may include a direction that no expert evidence is required; or directions for a single joint expert, or the exchange and agreement of expert evidence and without prejudice meetings of experts.[200] There are similar provisions for cases allocated to the multi-track.[201]

Under rule 35.14, an expert may file a written request for directions to assist him in carrying out his function as an expert. This may be done without giving notice to any party, although the court, when it gives directions, may direct that a party be served with a copy of the request and the directions. Rule 35.14 provides a useful safeguard for the expert in need of further guidance as to what is being asked of him, especially in cases where to take further instructions from a party may be regarded as a breach of his overriding duty to help the court.

Restrictions on, and disclosure of, expert evidence in criminal cases

The contents of the expert's report

In criminal proceedings, the required contents of an expert's report are set out in rule 33.3 of the Criminal Procedure Rules 2005,[202] are based on the guidance given in *R v B (T)*[203] and mirror those required in civil proceedings under Practice Direction 35, which have been considered earlier in this chapter. The only material differences from the civil rules are that there is no requirement to set out any instructions given to the expert and the report must be verified not by a statement of truth but by the same declaration of truth as for a witness statement. Under rule 33.4, a party who serves on another party or on the court an expert report must at once inform the expert of that fact.

Pre-hearing discussions

Under rule 33.5 of the Criminal Procedure Rules, where more than one party wants to introduce expert evidence, the court may direct the experts to discuss the expert issues and prepare a statement for the court of the matters on which they agree and disagree, giving their reasons. The contents of the discussion must not otherwise be referred to without the court's permission.[204]

---

[199] In medical negligence claims, there is also a standard direction dealing with disclosure of unpublished literature and lists of published literature on which an expert proposes to rely: see *Wardlaw v Farrar* [2003] 4 All ER 1358, CA.
[200] See CPR r 28.2 and 28.3 and PD28 paras 3.5–3.9.
[201] See CPR r 29.2 and 29.4 and PD29 paras 4.7–4.13.
[202] SI 2005/384.
[203] [2006] 2 Cr App R 22, CA.
[204] Rule 33.5(3).

Single joint experts

Under rule 33.7 of the Criminal Procedure Rules, where more than one accused wants to introduce expert evidence on an issue, the court may direct that the evidence on that issue be given by one expert only. If the co-accused cannot agree who the expert should be, the court may select the expert from a list prepared or identified by them or direct that the expert be selected in such other manner as it may direct. Where the court gives a direction under rule 33.7 for a single joint expert to be used, each of the co-accused may give instructions to the expert and, at the same time, send a copy of his instructions to the other co-accused.[205] The court may also give directions about any examination, measurement, test, or experiment which the expert wishes to carry out.[206]

Disclosure

At common law, the prosecution at a trial on indictment are not permitted to take the defence by surprise by adducing any evidence of which they have not given advance notice to the defence; and where such notice has not been given, the accused may apply for an adjournment.[207] The Royal Commission on Criminal Procedure proposed the introduction of an additional requirement of pre-trial disclosure in the case of defences depending on medical or expert scientific evidence, where the element of surprise involves some risk of the trial being adjourned, so that the prosecution may evaluate the evidence, undertake further inquiries and, if necessary, call its own experts in rebuttal.[208] The recommendation was adopted. Rule 24 of the Criminal Procedure Rules provides as follows:

24.1 (1) ... if any party to ... [criminal] proceedings proposes to adduce expert evidence (whether of fact or opinion) in the proceedings (otherwise than in relation to sentence) he shall as soon as practicable, unless in relation to the evidence in question he has already done so or the evidence is the subject of an application for leave to adduce such evidence in accordance with section 41 of the Youth Justice and Criminal Evidence Act 1999—
   (i) furnish the other party or parties[209] and the court with a statement in writing of any finding or opinion which he proposes to adduce by way of such evidence and notify the expert of this disclosure; and
   (ii) where a request in writing is made to him in that behalf by any other party, provide that party also with a copy of (or if it appears to the party proposing to adduce the evidence to be more practicable, a reasonable opportunity to examine) the record of any observation, test, calculation or other procedure on which such finding or opinion is based and any document or other thing or substance in respect of which any such procedure has been carried out.
  (2) A party may by notice in writing waive his right to be furnished with any of the matters mentioned in paragraph (1) and, in particular, may agree that the statement mentioned in paragraph (1)(i) may be furnished to him orally and not in writing.
  (3) In paragraph (1), 'document' means anything in which information of any description is recorded.
24.2 (1) If a party has reasonable grounds for believing that the disclosure of any evidence in compliance with the requirements imposed by rule 24.1 might lead to the intimidation,

---

[205] Rule 33.8(1) and (2).
[206] Rule 33.8(3).
[207] *R v Wright* (1934) 25 Cr App R 35, CCA.
[208] Para 8.22 (Cmnd 8092).
[209] Ie co-accused.

or attempted intimidation, of any person on whose evidence he intends to rely in the proceedings,[210] or otherwise to the course of justice being interfered with, he shall not be obliged to comply with those requirements in relation to that evidence.

(2) Where, in accordance with paragraph (1), a party considers that he is not obliged to comply with the requirements imposed by rule 24.1 with regard to any evidence in relation to any other party, he shall give notice in writing to that party to the effect that the evidence is being withheld and the grounds for doing so.

24.3 A party who seeks to adduce expert evidence in any proceedings and who fails to comply with rule 24.1 shall not adduce that evidence in those proceedings without the leave of the court.

The phrase 'expert evidence (whether of fact or opinion)', in rule 24.1(1), is wide enough to apply not only to evidence to be given by an expert witness, but also to an expert report which, whether or not the person making it attends to give oral evidence in the proceedings, it is proposed to adduce, by way of exception to the hearsay rule, under section 30(1) of the Criminal Justice Act 1988. Section 30(1) is considered in Chapter 10.

Section 11 of the Criminal Justice Act 1967 contained a provision similar in effect to rule 24.3 but applicable to particulars of an alibi defence. Under section 11, it was held that as a general rule, the mere fact that the necessary information was not given within the prescribed period was not, per se, a justification for refusing leave to admit the evidence because the discretion of the court had to be exercised judicially. Thus if, despite notice having been given outside the prescribed period, the prosecution had nevertheless had an opportunity to investigate the information provided, or could be given such an opportunity by means of an adjournment, leave to admit the evidence was granted.[211] It seems likely that rule 24.3 will be interpreted in a similar fashion.

In *R v Ward*[212] the Court of Appeal held that the rules (strictly, the original version of the rules) are helpful, but not exhaustive: they do not in any way supplant or detract from the prosecution's general duty of disclosure in respect of scientific evidence, a duty which exists irrespective of any request by the defence. That duty is not limited to documentation on which the opinion or finding of an expert is based, but extends to anything which may arguably assist the defence. It is a positive duty which, in the case of scientific evidence, obliges the prosecution to make full and proper inquiries from forensic scientists to ascertain whether there is discoverable material. Moreover, an expert witness who has carried out or knows of experiments or tests which tend to cast doubt on the opinion he is expressing is under a clear obligation to bring the records of such experiments or tests to the attention of the solicitor instructing him (so that it may be disclosed to the defence)[213] or the expert advising the defence. The importance of these principles was starkly illustrated in *R v Clark*,[214] where, on a reference back to the Court of Appeal by the Criminal cases Review Commission, Sally Clark's convictions for the murder of her two infant sons were quashed, a forensic pathologist having failed to disclose that in the case of one of the infants, a form of potentially lethal bacteria, which could not be excluded as the possible cause of death, had been isolated.

[210] Ie either the expert or any other potential witness.

[211] See per Salmon LJ in *R v Sullivan* [1971] 1 QB 253 at 258, CA. But see also *R v Jacks* [1991] Crim LR 611, CA, where the trial judge refused leave to admit the evidence and declined to adjourn. On the facts, admission of the evidence would have involved a clear risk of disadvantage to the Crown.

[212] [1993] 2 All ER 577 at 628.

[213] See also per Stuart-Smith LJ in *R v Maguire* [1992] 2 All ER 433 at 447, CA.

[214] [2003] All ER (D) 223 (Apr), [2003] EWCA Crim 1020.

Under section 6D of the Criminal Procedure and Investigations Act 1996, if the accused instructs a person with a view to his providing any expert opinion for possible use as evidence at his trial, he must give to the court and the prosecutor, within a prescribed 'relevant period', a notice specifying the person's name and address. Such a notice need not be given if the expert's name and address have already been given under section 6C of the 1996 Act, which requires the accused to give notice of his intention to call witnesses at the trial.[215]

Non-expert opinion evidence

A non-expert witness, as we have seen, may give opinion evidence on matters in relation to which it is impossible or virtually impossible to separate his inferences from the perceived facts on which those inferences are based. In these circumstances, the witness is permitted to express his opinion as a compendious means of conveying to the court the facts he perceived. The admissibility of non-expert opinion evidence is largely a question of degree and the matters open to proof by such evidence defy comprehensive classification. Examples include the identification of persons,[216] voices,[217] objects[218] and handwriting,[219] speed,[220] temperature, weather, and the passing of time. A non-expert may describe the condition of objects, using adjectives such as 'good', 'new', 'worn', and 'old'. Similarly, non-expert opinion evidence is admissible as to the value of objects. In *R v Beckett*,[221] a non-expert expressed the opinion that a plate-glass window was worth more than five pounds. However, although the point was not canvassed in the case, it seems clear that non-expert opinion evidence of value is only admissible in respect of commonplace objects, of which a plate glass window is perhaps best regarded as a borderline example, as opposed to works of art, antiques and other objects the valuation of which obviously calls for specialized skill or knowledge. A non-expert may also give opinion evidence of a person's age,[222] health, bodily or emotional state, or reaction to an event or set of circumstances. Although a person's sanity is a matter calling for expertise, it would appear that a close acquaintance may express his opinion as a convenient way of conveying the results of his observations of that person's behaviour.[223] A similar distinction was drawn in *R v Davies*.[224] It was held that on a charge of driving when unfit through drink, whereas the fitness of the accused to drive is a matter calling for expert evidence, a non-expert may properly give his general impression as to whether the accused had 'taken drink', provided that he describes the facts upon which his impression was based. Similarly, and

---

[215] See Ch 14.

[216] *R v Tolson* (1864) 4 F&F 103.

[217] *R v Robb* (1991) 93 Cr App R 161, CA; *R v Deenik* [1992] Crim LR 578, CA. The key to the admissibility of lay listener evidence is the degree of familiarity of the witness with the voice. If the prosecution call police officers to give such evidence, it should be treated with caution and it is desirable that an expert give an opinion on its veracity: *R v Flynn* [2008] 2 Cr App R 266 at 281, considered in Ch 8.

[218] *Lucas v Williams & Sons* [1892] 2 QB 113 (a picture); *Fryer v Gathercole* (1849) 13 Jur 542 (a pamphlet).

[219] *Doe d Mudd v Suckermore* (1837) 5 Ad&El 703: see Ch 9.

[220] Section 89(2) of the Road Traffic Regulation Act 1984: see Ch 8.

[221] (1913) 8 Cr App R 204.

[222] *R v Cox* [1898] 1 QB 179.

[223] Per Parke B in *Wright v Doe d Tatham* (1838) 4 Bing NC 489 at 543–4. But in criminal cases, expert psychiatric evidence is necessary in order to establish insanity: s 1(1) of the Criminal Procedure (Insanity and Unfitness to Plead) Act 1991, above.

[224] [1962] 1 WLR 1111, C-MAC.

subject to the same proviso, a non-expert may give his opinion as to whether an accused was 'drunk'.[225] In *R v Hill*[226] it was held that scientific evidence is not always required to identify a prohibited drug, but police officers' descriptions of a drug must be sufficient to justify the inference that it is the drug alleged.

At common law, as we have seen, the courts were opposed to any witness expressing his opinion on an ultimate issue, that is one of the very issues which the judge or jury has to decide. In civil proceedings the rule has been abolished. Section 3(2) of the 1972 Act declares that—

> where a person is called as a witness in any civil proceedings, a statement of opinion by him on any relevant matter on which he is not qualified to give expert evidence, if made as a way of conveying relevant facts personally perceived by him, is admissible as evidence of what he perceived.

Section 3(3) reads:

> In this section 'relevant matter' includes an issue in the proceedings in question.

Concerning non-expert opinion evidence in criminal proceedings, the rule may subsist.[227] In *R v Davies*[228] Lord Parker CJ held that although the witness could properly state the impression he formed as to whether the accused driver had taken drink, his opinion as to whether as a result of that drink he was fit or unfit to drive a car was inadmissible, being 'the very matter which the court itself has to determine'.[229] However, the rule is easily evaded by a careful use of words, and sometimes it is simply ignored. In *R v Beckett*,[230] it will be recalled, a witness valued a window at more than five pounds, yet that was exactly the issue to be determined by the court.

ADDITIONAL READING

Basten, 'The Court Expert in Civil Trials, a Comparative Appraisal' (1977) 40 *MLR* 174.

Bruce et al, 'Face Recognition in poor Quality Video Evidence from Security Surveilance' (1999) 10 *Psychological Science* 243.

Ellison, 'Closing the credibility gap: The prosecutorial use of expert witness testimony in sexual assault cases' (2005) 9 *E&P* 239.

Giles, 'Good Impressions' (1991) *NLJ* 605.

Jackson, 'The Ultimate Issue Rule: One Rule Too Many' [1984] *Crim LR* 75.

Jowett, 'Sittin in the Dock with the Bayes' (2001) *NLJ* 201.

Lewis, 'Expert evidence of delay in complaint in childhood sexual abuse prosecutions' (2006) 10 *E&P* 157.

Mackay, 'Excluding Expert Evidence: A Tale of Ordinary Folk and Common Experience' [1991] *Crim LR* 800.

---

[225] *R v Tagg* [2002] 1 Cr App R 22, CA.

[226] (1992) 96 Cr App R 456, CA.

[227] But see 11th Report, Criminal Law Revision Committee (Cmnd 4991), para 270. The Committee, recommending the enactment for criminal proceedings of provisions similar to those contained in s 3 of the 1972 Act, said: 'we have no doubt that this is the present law, but it seems desirable for the statute to be explicit.'

[228] [1962] 1 WLR 1111, C-MAC. See also *Sherrard v Jacob* [1965] NI 151, NICA.

[229] In Eire, the witness has been allowed to express an opinion on both matters: see *A-G (Rudely) v James Kenny* (1960) 94 ILTR 185.

[230] (1913) 8 Cr App R 204, CCA.

Munday, 'Videotape Evidence and the Advent of the Expert Ad Hoc' (1995) 159 *JP* 547.

O'Brian Jr, 'Court scrutiny of expert evidence: Recent decisions highlight the tensions' (2003) 7 *E&P* 172.

Redmayne, 'The DNA Database: Civil Liberty and Evidentiary Issues' [1995] *Crim LR* 437.

Redmayne, *Expert Evidence and Criminal Justice* (Oxford, 2001).

Roberts, 'Drawing on Expertise: Legal Decision-making and the Reception of Expert Evidence' [2008] *Crim LR* 443.

Roberts, 'Rejecting General Acceptance, Confounding the Gate-keeper: the Law Commission and Expert Evidence' [2009] *Crim LR* 551.

Public policy

Key Issues

- What types of relevant and otherwise admissible evidence should be excluded on the basis that disclosure would not be in the public interest (public interest immunity)?

- Should ultimate decisions on public interest immunity be taken by the courts or the executive?

- How can the interests of the accused be safeguarded when the prosecution apply to the court for immunity from disclosure in the public interest?

- Should evidence be withheld from disclosure solely on the basis that it was given in confidence, eg information given by a patient to a doctor?

- Should courts have power to require a journalist to disclose the source of information contained in a publication, and if so, in what circumstances?

- Where evidence is protected by public interest immunity, in what circumstances, if any, should it be possible to waive such immunity?

A party to litigation has an obvious interest in the admission of any item of evidence which supports his own case or defeats that of his opponent. Such an interest coincides with a public interest that justice should be done between litigants by the reception of all relevant evidence. The public interest in efficient and fair trials may also be seen as underlying the rules of disclosure in civil litigation, whereby a litigant is obliged to make pre-trial disclosure of, inter alia, the documents on which he relies and the documents which adversely affect his own case or adversely affect, or support, another party's case, even though such documents may not be admissible evidence at the trial.[1] There is also a public interest, however, in enabling material to be withheld where its disclosure would harm the nation or the public service. Where these two kinds of public interest clash and the latter prevails over the former, relevant and otherwise admissible evidence is excluded at trial and relevant documents are exempted from the duty to allow inspection on discovery. Such material is said to be withheld by reason of 'public interest immunity'.[2] This chapter begins by considering the development of the modern law in both civil and criminal cases. This is followed by an examination of the heads of public interest which the courts have recognized as being capable of leading to the exclusion of relevant material. Finally consideration is given to a variety of essentially procedural issues, including the procedural aspects, in civil proceedings, of the judicial task of striking a balance between the conflicting public interests.

The development of the modern law

Civil cases

Judicial reluctance to expose material, disclosure of which might harm the nation or the public service, was taken to extremes in *Duncan v Cammell Laird & Co Ltd*.[3] Departing from earlier authority that judges may call for and inspect documents in respect of which public interest immunity is claimed in order to satisfy themselves of the merits of such a claim,[4] Lord Simon held that where a minister decides against disclosure of a document on the grounds that it would be injurious to national defence or good diplomatic relations or because it belongs to a class of documents which it is necessary to keep secret for the proper functioning of the public service, his decision is binding upon the courts. This decision gave rise to considerable judicial criticism because it enabled executive claims to public interest immunity to succeed notwithstanding that disclosure involved only the smallest probability of injury to the public service and non-disclosure involved the gravest risk of injustice to a litigant.[5] By 1956, the tide began to turn. In that year, the Lord Chancellor announced that public interest immunity would not

---

[1] See generally CPR Pt 31. Where the Crown is a party to civil litigation in the High Court or in a county court, s 28 of the Crown Proceedings Act 1947 provides that the Crown may be required by the court to make discovery of documents, produce documents for inspection, and answer interrogatories, 'provided that this section shall be without prejudice to any rule of law which authorises or requires the withholding of any document or the refusal to answer any question on the ground that the disclosure of the document or the answering of the question would be injurious to the public interest'.

[2] The expression 'Crown privilege' has been judicially disapproved on the ground that there is no question of any privilege in the ordinary sense of the word: see per Lord Reid in *Rogers v Home Secretary* [1973] AC 388 at 400, HL; but cf per Lord Scarman in *Science Research Council v Nassé* [1980] AC 1028 at 1087.

[3] [1942] AC 624, HL.

[4] See, eg, *Robinson v South Australia State (No 2)* [1931] AC 704, PC and *Spigelman v Hocken* (1933) 50 TLR 87.

[5] See, eg, *Ellis v Home Office* [1953] 2 QB 135, CA and *Broome v Broome* [1955] P 190.

be claimed in respect of certain classes of document including, for example, medical reports of prison doctors in negligence actions against doctors or the Crown and documents relevant to the defence in criminal proceedings.[6] In the same year, the House of Lords held that, contrary to its understanding of the matter as expressed in *Duncan v Cammell Laird & Co Ltd*, in Scotland the courts had always had an inherent power to override the Crown's objection to the production of documents.[7] In 1964 the Court of Appeal held that the English courts also had a residual power, in appropriate cases, to inspect documents and form their own opinion as to the public interest.[8] In *Conway v Rimmer*[9] the Court of Appeal reverted to the rule laid down in *Duncan v Cammell Laird & Co Ltd* but the House of Lords, while in no doubt that the actual decision in that case was correct—because disclosure might have affected national security by assisting a foreign power, at a time when the country was at war, to understand the structure and design of a submarine—was also of the unanimous opinion that whether relevant evidence should be withheld in the public interest is ultimately a question for the decision of the courts and not the executive.

In *Conway v Rimmer* the plaintiff, a former probationary police constable who had been charged with but acquitted of stealing a torch, brought an action against his former superintendent claiming damages for malicious prosecution. The Home Secretary objected to the production of five reports, four relating to the plaintiff's conduct as a probationer and the fifth leading to his prosecution for theft, on the grounds that they belonged to classes of documents, namely police reports to senior officers and reports on criminal investigations, the production of which would be injurious to the public interest. The House of Lords held that a minister's affidavit or certificate is not final, public interest immunity being a question of law for the determination of the court, and that although an objection to production by the Crown was entitled to the greatest weight, the court could ask for a clarification or amplification of the objection and had the power to inspect the documents privately and order their production notwithstanding the minister's objection.[10] Concerning the test to be applied in deciding whether the objection should be upheld, their Lordships held that the court should balance two public interests, that of the state or public service in non-disclosure and that of the proper administration of justice in the production of the documents. A distinction, however, was drawn between a 'contents' claim, that is a claim that it would be against the public interest to disclose the contents of a particular document, and a 'class' claim, that is a claim that a document, whether or not it contains anything the disclosure of which would be against the public interest, belongs to a class of documents which ought to be withheld. In the case of 'contents' claims, Lord Reid said:[11]

> However wide the power of the court may be held to be, cases would be very rare in which it could be proper to question the view of the responsible Minister that it would be contrary to the public interest to make public the contents of a particular document.

---

[6] See 197 HL Deb (1956) col 741. Further concessions were made in 1962: 237 HL Deb (1962) col 1191.

[7] *Glasgow Corpn v Central Land Board* 1956 SC (HL) 1.

[8] *Re Grosvenor Hotel, London (No 2)* [1965] Ch 1210. See also *Merricks v Nott-Bower* [1965] 1 QB 57; *Wednesbury Corpn v Ministry of Housing and Local Government* [1965] 1 WLR 261.

[9] [1968] AC 910.

[10] But not, apparently, where there is a risk to national security demonstrated by an appropriate certificate: see *Balfour v Foreign and Commonwealth Office* [1994] 2 All ER 588, CA, below.

[11] [1968] AC 910 at 943. See also per Lord Upjohn at 993.

In the case of 'class' claims, however, although certain classes of document of a high level of public importance, such as Cabinet minutes and documents concerned with policy making within government departments, should hardly ever be disclosed, whatever their contents might be, because such disclosure 'would create or fan ill-informed or captious public or political criticism' or 'would be quite wrong and entirely inimical to the proper functioning of the public service',[12] there was a wide difference between such documents and routine reports. 'There may be special reasons for withholding some kinds of routine reports, but the proper test to be applied is to ask . . . whether the withholding of a document because it belongs to a particular class is really "necessary for the proper functioning of the public service".'[13] The House was especially critical of the argument that whole classes of documents should be withheld on the grounds of candour and uninhibited freedom of expression with and within the public service.

Turning to the documents in the case before them, their Lordships were of the opinion that whereas they might be of vital importance to the litigation in question, they were of a routine nature and it was most improbable that their disclosure would prejudice the public interest. The documents were ordered to be produced for inspection. Subsequently, the House itself read the documents and, having done so, ordered that they be made available to the plaintiff.

In *Conway v Rimmer* Lord Reid said:[14] 'I do not doubt that there are certain classes of documents which ought not to be disclosed whatever their contents may be.'[15] However, a contrary view was taken in *Burmah Oil Co Ltd v Bank of England*,[16] where Lord Keith said:[17]

> The courts are ... concerned with the consideration that it is in the public interest that justice should be done and should be publicly recognized as having been done. This may demand, . . . in a very limited number of cases, that the inner workings of government should be exposed to public gaze, and there may be some who would regard this as likely to lead, not to captious or ill-informed criticism, but to criticism calculated to improve the nature of that working as affecting the individual citizen.

That the court should be prepared, where appropriate, to require the disclosure of even high-level government papers was reasserted, in principle, in *Air Canada v Secretary of State for Trade (No 2)*,[18] where Lord Fraser said:[19]

> I do not think that even Cabinet minutes are completely immune from disclosure in a case where, for example, the issue in a litigation involves serious misconduct by a Cabinet minister. Such cases have occurred in Australia (see *Sankey v Whitlam*)[20] and in the United States

---

[12] Per Lords Reid and Upjohn at 952 and 993 respectively.

[13] Per Lord Reid at 952, citing Lord Simon in *Duncan v Cammell Laird & Co Ltd* [1942] AC 624 at 642. See also per Lord Reid in *Rogers v Secretary of State for the Home Department* [1973] AC 388, HL at 400–1.

[14] At 952.

[15] See also per Lords Hodson, Pearce and Upjohn at 973, 987, and 993 respectively.

[16] [1980] AC 1090.

[17] At 1134.

[18] [1983] 2 AC 394, HL. See also *Williams v Home Office* [1981] 1 All ER 1151, QBD and *Re HIV Haemophiliac Litigation* [1990] NLJR 1349.

[19] At 432. The quotation makes explicit what is probably implicit in other cases, namely that the weight of the public interest in the administration of justice (which is weighed against the public interest in non-disclosure) depends not only on the importance of the material to the litigation in hand but also on the public importance of the litigation itself. See also per Ackner LJ in *Campbell v Tameside Metropolitan Borough Council* [1982] QB 1065 at 1076; and generally TRS Allan (1985) 101 *LQR* 200.

[20] (1978) 21 ALR 505.

(see *Nixon v United States*)[21] but fortunately not in the United Kingdom: see also the New Zealand case of *Environmental Defence Society Inc v South Pacific Aluminium Ltd (No 2)*.[22] But, while Cabinet documents do not have complete immunity, they are entitled to a high degree of protection against disclosure.

In 1996 the Lord Chancellor announced that the division between class and content claims would be brought to an end and that in future ministers would focus on the damage that disclosure would cause, only claiming immunity when they believed that disclosure would cause real damage or harm to the public interest. It was said that damage will normally have to take the form of direct or immediate threat to the safety of an individual or the nation's economic interests or relations with a foreign state, although in some cases, such as damage to a regulatory process, the anticipated damage might be indirect or longer term. In any event the nature of the harm will need to be clearly explained and ministers will no longer be able to claim immunity for internal advice or national security by reference to the general nature of the document. Non-governmental bodies claiming immunity are not bound by the statement, but it is submitted that it would be desirable if the same approach were to be taken across the board.

It remains to note that there is no absolute bar to a claim for public interest immunity where the claim, if successful, would prevent the disclosure of evidence of serious criminal misconduct by officials of the state, even in the case of torture, cruel, inhuman or degrading treatment or other war crimes.[23]

Criminal cases

In criminal proceedings, as we shall see, the rule against the disclosure of sources of police information was established some 200 years ago. In remarkable contrast, it is only very recently that the English courts have given any detailed consideration to the applicability to criminal proceedings of the doctrine of public interest immunity. The question appears to have arisen for the first time in *R v Governor of Brixton Prison, ex p Osman*.[24] Noting that the seminal cases make no reference to criminal proceedings, Mann LJ held that the civil principles do apply in criminal cases, but involve a different balancing exercise: although the judge should balance the public interest in non-disclosure against the interests of justice in the particular case, the weight to be attached to the interests of justice in a criminal case touching and concerning liberty, and very occasionally life, is plainly very great indeed.[25] In *R v Clowes*[26] Phillips J held that he did not find easy the concept of balancing the nature of the public interest against the degree and potential consequences of the risk of a miscarriage of justice, but equally refused to accept readily that proportionality between the two could never be of relevance. In *R v Keane*[27] Lord Taylor CJ held that when the court is seised of the material, the judge should balance the weight of the public interest in non-disclosure against the importance of the documents to the issues of interest to the defence, present and potential, so far as they have been disclosed

---

[21] 418 US 683 (1974).

[22] [1981] 1 NZLR 153.

[23] *R (Mohamed) v Secretary of State for Foreign and Commonwealth Affairs* [2009] EWHC 152.

[24] [1992] 1 All ER 108, QBD.

[25] Approved in *R v Keane* [1994] 2 All ER 478, CA.

[26] [1992] 3 All ER 440, CCC.

[27] [1994] 2 All ER 478, CA.

to him or he can foresee them. However, as we shall see, the House of Lords has since made clear in *R v H*[28] that the golden rule is full prosecution disclosure and that although some derogation from the golden rule can be justified, it should always be to the minimum necessary to protect the public interest and it should never imperil the overall fairness of the trial. It was also held that if it does imperil the overall fairness of the trial, then fuller disclosure should be ordered even if this leads or may lead the prosecution to discontinue the proceedings so as to avoid having to make disclosure. Furthermore, the judge's initial ruling is not necessarily final. He is under a continuous duty to keep his initial decision under review—issues may emerge at a later stage so that the public interest in non-disclosure may be eclipsed by the defendant's need for access.[29] In deciding whether or not to order disclosure, the judge is not confined to admissible evidence but may take into account hearsay material.[30]

In *R v Ward*[31] it was held that the decision as to what should be withheld from disclosure is for the court, not the prosecution, the police, the DPP, or counsel.[32] A prosecution decision to withhold relevant evidence without notifying the judge would be a violation of Article 6 of the European Convention on Human Rights.[33] The prosecution cannot be judge in their own cause and if they are not prepared to let the court decide, the prosecution will have to be abandoned. However, in exceptional cases, the CPS may voluntarily disclose to the defence documents in a class covered by public interest immunity without referring the matter to the court for a ruling, subject to the safeguard of first seeking the written approval of the Treasury Solicitor. The CPS should submit to him copies of the documents, identify the public interest immunity class into which they fall, and indicate the materiality of the documents to the proceedings in which it is proposed to disclose them. The Treasury Solicitor should consult any other relevant government department and satisfy himself that the balance falls clearly in favour of disclosure. He will have regard to the class of documents involved, their materiality to the proceedings, and the extent to which disclosure will damage the public interest in the integrity of the class claim. He should be more ready to approve disclosure of documents likely to assist the defence than those which the CPS wish to disclose with a view to furthering the interests of the prosecution. Before approving disclosure of class documents sought to be used by the prosecution, he should consider not only their importance to the prosecution's case, but also the importance of the prosecution itself: it may be preferable to abandon the case rather than damage the integrity of the class claim. He should also maintain a permanent record of all approvals so that any court, ruling on disclosure, knows the extent to which the integrity of the class claim has been weakened by previous voluntary disclosure.[34]

The rule in *R v Ward*[35] that it is for the *court* to decide what material should be withheld, is now reflected in the statutory rules relating to pre-trial disclosure in Part 1 of the Criminal Procedure and Investigations Act 1996. Section 21(2) preserves the common law rules as to whether disclosure is in the public interest. Under paragraph 41 of the *Attorney General's*

---

[28] [2004] 2 AC 134, HL.

[29] *R v H* [2004] 2 AC 134, HL at [36]. See also *R v Bower* [1994] Crim LR 281, CA; *R v Brown (Winston)* [1994] 1 WLR 1599, CA; and ss 14 and 15 of the Criminal Procedure and Investigations Act 1996.

[30] *R v Law* (1996) The Times, 15 Aug.

[31] [1993] 1 WLR 619, CA.

[32] See also, in the case of a co-accused, *R v Adams* [1997] Crim LR 292, CA.

[33] *Rowe and Davis v UK* (2000) 30 EHRR 1. See also *Dowsett v UK* [2003] Crim LR 890.

[34] *R v Horseferry Road Magistrates, ex p Bennett (No 2)* [1994] 1 All ER 289, DC.

[35] [1993] 1 WLR 619, CA.

Guidelines: Disclosure of Information in Criminal Proceedings, before making an application to the court to withhold material in the public interest, a prosecutor should aim to disclose as much material as he properly can, by giving the defence redacted or edited copies or summaries. Under paragraph 42 of the *Guidelines*, prior to or at the hearing the court must be provided with full and accurate information. The Court of Appeal has stressed that where an *ex parte* hearing is held, it is imperative in all cases that the Crown is scrupulously accurate in the information provided.[36] Where a trial judge or the Court of Appeal learns that prosecution witnesses, in the course of a public interest immunity hearing, lied in their evidence, the prosecution is likely to be tainted beyond redemption, however strong the evidence against the accused otherwise was.[37] Paragraph 42 of the *Guidelines* also provides that the prosecution advocate must examine all material which is the subject matter of the application and make any necessary enquiries of the prosecutor and/or investigator.[38]

The procedure to be adopted where the prosecution apply for immunity from disclosure is set out in the Crown Court (Criminal Procedure and Investigations Act 1996) (Disclosure) Rules[39] and the Magistrates' Court (Criminal Procedure and Investigations Act 1996) (Disclosure) Rules,[40] which in effect reproduce the following principles laid down by Lord Taylor CJ in *R v Davis*.[41] Whenever possible, which will be in most cases, the prosecution must notify the defence of the application, indicating the category of material in question, so that the defence have the opportunity of making representations to the court. If to disclose even the category would be to reveal too much, the prosecution should notify the defence that an *ex parte* application will be made. In highly exceptional circumstances where to reveal even the fact of an *ex parte* application would be to reveal too much, an *ex parte* application may be made without notice. However if, in any case, the judge takes the view that the defence should be aware of the category of material and should have the opportunity of making representations, or at any rate should have notice of the application, he may so order.

The *ex parte* procedure is contrary to the general principles of open justice in criminal trials and should only be adopted on the application of the Crown for the specific purpose of enabling the court to test a claim that immunity or sensitivity justifies non-disclosure.[42] Thus, a *defence* application, such as an application for details of an informer to be disclosed, should not be heard *ex parte*.[43] An *ex parte* application on the part of the prosecution will not necessarily amount to a violation of Article 6 of the European Convention on Human Rights, whether the application is made at the trial[44] or in the Court of Appeal,[45] but unfairness caused at the trial by an improper failure to disclose material to the judge will not necessarily be remedied by an *ex parte* examination of the material by the Court of Appeal.[46]

---

[36] *R v Jackson* [2000] Crim LR 377, CA.

[37] *R v Early* [2003] 1 Cr App R 288, CA.

[38] See also *R v Menga* [1998] Crim LR 58, CA.

[39] SI 1997/698.

[40] SI 1997/703.

[41] [1993] 1 WLR 613, CA.

[42] *R v Keane* [1994] 2 All ER 478 at 483. See also *R v Smith* [1998] 2 Cr App R 1, CA.

[43] *R v Turner* [1995] 3 All ER 432, CA; *R v Tattenhove* [1996] 1 Cr App R 408, CA.

[44] *Jasper v UK* (2000) 30 EHRR 441. See also *Atlan v UK* [2002] 34 EHRR 833 and *R v Lawrence* [2002] Crim LR 584, CA.

[45] *R v Botmeh* [2002] 1 WLR 531, CA.

[46] *Rowe and Davis v UK* (2000) 30 EHRR 1. See also *Atlan v UK* [2002] 34 EHRR 833.

It is wrong and contrary to Article 6(1) for a judge to make use of information immune from disclosure to the defence in reaching a decision on the admissibility of evidence. In *Edwards v UK*[47] the applicant was charged with a drugs offence following an undercover operation. On an *ex parte* application to withhold material, the judge ruled against disclosure. On a subsequent unsuccessful defence application under section 78 of the Police and Criminal Evidence Act 1984 to exclude the evidence of the only undercover officer to be called by the prosecution, on the basis of entrapment, the judge ruled that he had seen nothing in the course of the *ex parte* application that would have assisted the defence in their application under section 78. The European Court, finding a violation of Article 6(1), held that since the public interest immunity evidence may have related to facts connected with the section 78 application, the defence were not able fully to argue the case on entrapment. However certain the trial judge was that the evidence did not assist the defence, this overlooked the possibility that the defence could have countered the evidence or shown it to be mistaken or otherwise unreliable. The denial of that opportunity on an issue so fundamental to the trial was a failure to comply with the requirements to provide adversarial proceedings and equality of arms and to incorporate adequate safeguards to protect the interests of the accused.[48]

In *Edwards v UK* the court referred to the recommendation, in Sir Robin Auld's *Review of the Criminal Courts of England and Wales*[49] that special independent counsel be introduced to represent the interests of the accused in those cases at first instance and on appeal where the court considers prosecution applications in the absence of the defence.[50] In *R v H*[51] it was argued that it is a violation of Article 6 for a trial judge to rule on a claim to immunity, in the absence of adversarial argument on behalf of the accused, where the material in question is or may be relevant to a disputed issue of fact which the judge has to decide in order to rule on an application which will effectively determine the outcome of the proceedings, and it was also argued that the *Edwards v UK* principle applies whenever the defence relies on entrapment as a basis for staying the case as an abuse of process or excluding prosecution evidence. It was held that to adopt such an approach would be to put the judge in a straitjacket. Lord Bingham laid down the following governing principles. The golden rule is full disclosure to the defence of any material held by the prosecution which weakens its case or strengthens that of the defence. In circumstances where such material cannot be disclosed, fully or at all, without the risk of serious prejudice to an important public interest, some derogation from the rule can be justified, but should always be to the minimum necessary to protect the public interest, and should never imperil the overall fairness of the trial. If prosecution claims for public interest immunity were operated with scrupulous attention to these principles, and with continuing regard to the proper interests of the accused, there should be no violation of Article 6. The appointment of special counsel raises ethical problems, since the lawyer cannot disclose to his client the material which is the basis of the application and cannot take full instructions from him, as well as practical problems of delay, expense, and continuing review.[52] None of these problems should deter the court from appointing

---

[47] (2003) 15 BHRC 189.

[48] See also *R v H* [2004] 2 AC 134, HL, overruling *R v Smith* [2001] 1 WLR 1031; and *R v Ali* [2008] EWCA Crim 146.

[49] HMSO 2001 at paras 193–7.

[50] See also *Jasper v UK* (2000) 30 EHRR 441.

[51] [2004] 2 AC 134, HL.

[52] See per Lord Bingham at [22].

an approved advocate as special counsel[53] where it is necessary, in the interests of justice, to secure protection of an accused's right to a fair trial. However, such appointments would be exceptional and should not be ordered unless and until the trial judge is satisfied that no other course will adequately meet the overriding requirement of fairness to the accused.

Edwards v UK was distinguished in *R v May*[54] where the judge, in confiscation proceedings under the Criminal Justice Act 1988, stated that he had ignored anything attracting immunity that had been revealed to him in earlier *ex parte* public interest immunity proceedings. The Court of Appeal rejected a submission, made in reliance on *Edwards v UK*, that since the judge may have been influenced by the material he had seen, however much he had tried to put it out of his mind, he should have recused himself or at least appointed special counsel. *Edwards v UK* was distinguished on the grounds that the Strasbourg court had proceeded on the basis that the trial judge *had* taken into account the material that the accused had been denied an opportunity to counter. It was held that if a judge is of the view that despite his best efforts he is unlikely to be able to ignore the undisclosed material, to the detriment of the accused, then he should consider the appointment of special counsel, but that in many cases the judge can be relied upon to put such material out of his mind.

Where a magistrates' court, whether made up of a stipendiary magistrate or lay justices, hears an application for non-disclosure on the grounds of public interest immunity and rules that the material in question is inadmissible, ordinarily it should proceed to hear the case itself, because of the court's duty of continuing review, and should exercise its discretion to order the case to be tried by a different bench only in exceptional circumstances, as when material was introduced at the non-disclosure hearing which was prejudicial and irrelevant to the question of admissibility.[55] Magistrates, in deciding an application for non-disclosure, should apply the same principles that apply in proceedings on indictment, but where it is known that a contested issue as to the disclosure of sensitive material is likely to arise, and the magistrates have discretion to send the case to the crown court for trial, they would be well advised to commit.[56] For this reason the occasions on which it will be appropriate to appoint special counsel in the magistrates' court will be even rarer than in the Crown Court.[57]

The scope of exclusion on grounds of public policy

Conway v Rimmer reasserted the courts' control over the scope of public interest immunity, but it also paved the way for a generalization of the principles of public policy, which has led to a widening of the heads of public interest which the courts will recognize. Thus it is now clear that documents, to be protected, need not relate to the workings of central government at all—the public also has an interest in the effective working of non-governmental bodies

---

[53] The Attorney General approves the list of counsel judged suitable to act as special advocates.

[54] [2005] 1 WLR 2902, CA.

[55] *R v Stipendiary Magistrate for Norfolk, ex p Taylor* [1998] Crim LR 276, DC. See also *R v Bromley Magistrates' Court, ex p Smith* [1995] 4 All ER 146 (and cf *R v South Worcestershire Magistrates, ex p Lilley* [1995] 4 All ER 186, DC); *R (DPP) v Acton Youth Court* [2001] 1 WLR 1828; *R v H* [2004] 2 AC 134, HL at [43]–[44]; and s 14 of the Criminal Procedure and Investigations Act 1996.

[56] See generally *R v Bromley Magistrates' Court, ex p Smith* [1995] 4 All ER 146, DC, distinguishing *R v DPP, ex p Warby* [1994] Crim LR 281, DC on the basis that it concerned committal proceedings.

[57] *R v H* [2004] 2 AC 134, HL.

and agencies performing public functions such as local authorities,[58] the Gaming Board,[59] the National Society for the Prevention of Cruelty to Children (NSPCC),[60] and the Law Society.[61] It is tempting to generalize the principles completely and to say that evidence will be excluded whenever a public interest in its non-disclosure is asserted which outweighs the importance of receiving the evidence in the particular case. This was an argument put forward in *D v NSPCC*[62] in answer to the proposition that public interest immunity is restricted to the effective functioning of departments or organs of central government. Both propositions were rejected by the House of Lords in favour of the middle view that although 'the categories of the public interest are not closed and must alter from time to time whether by restriction or extension as social conditions and social legislation develop',[63] nevertheless the court can proceed only by analogy with interests which have previously been recognized by the authorities.[64]

In that case, the NSPCC, a body established by royal charter and given statutory power, along with the police and local authorities, to bring care proceedings, sought to honour a promise given to an informant that his identity would not be revealed. The plaintiff claimed damages for the injury to her health caused by the negligence of the NSPCC in pursuing the allegations of the informant that she had maltreated her child, allegations which proved groundless. The House of Lords upheld the NSPCC's application to withhold from discovery documents disclosing the identity of the informant. Their Lordships held that the value of the NSPCC's work was indicated by statutory recognition of its function, by evidence that informants were more willing to approach the NSPCC than the police or local authorities, and by other statutory and common law authority acknowledging the importance of providing for the welfare of children. Relying on the analogy of judicial refusal to compel disclosure of sources of police information, they held that in both situations the public interest in the uninhibited flow of information justified the refusal to order disclosure since otherwise the sources of information would be expected to dry up.[65] Although the actual result of the case was

---

[58] *Re D (Infants)* [1970] 1 WLR 599, CA and *Gaskin v Liverpool City Council* [1980] 1 WLR 1549, CA (childcare records). But see also per Ralph Gibson LJ in *Brown v Matthews* [1990] 2 All ER 155 at 164–5, CA, doubting whether these cases are true examples of the application of the principle of public interest immunity. Where an authority applies for a care order in wardship proceedings, there is no absolute right against disclosure. See *Re A (minors)* [1992] 1 All ER 153, Fam Div; *Re M (a minor)* (1990) 88 LGR 841, CA; and *B v B* [1991] 2 FLR 487, Fam Div. The report of a court welfare officer is confidential to the parties and to the court, which may give permission for the information contained in it to be used in other proceedings: *Brown v Matthews* [1990] 2 All ER 155. As to the use in other proceedings of information confidential to child welfare proceedings, see *Re R (MJ) (an infant)* [1975] 2 All ER 749; *Re F (minors)* [1989] Fam 18, CA at 26; *Re X (minors)* [1992] 2 All ER 595 (Fam Div); *Re Manda* [1993] 1 All ER 733, CA; *Oxfordshire County Council v P* [1995] 2 All ER 225, Fam Div; *Cleveland County Council v F* [1995] 2 All ER 236, Fam Div; *Re K (minors)* [1994] 3 All ER 230, Fam Div; *Re G (a minor)* [1996] 2 All ER 65, CA; and *Re W (minors)* [1998] 2 All ER 801, CA.

[59] *Rogers v Secretary of State for the Home Department* [1973] AC 388, HL, below.

[60] *D v NSPCC* [1978] AC 171, HL (name of informant who prompted NSPCC inquiry).

[61] *Buckley v Law Society (No 2)* [1984] 1 WLR 1101, Ch D (names of informants whose complaints led to the Law Society's inquiry into a solicitor's conduct). See also *Medway v Doublelock Ltd* [1978] 1 WLR 710: an affidavit of means supplied in divorce proceedings can be withheld in subsequent litigation on grounds of public policy.

[62] [1978] AC 171, HL. See per Lord Diplock at 219–20 where the arguments are summarized.

[63] Per Lord Hailsham at 230.

[64] Per Lord Simon at 240, Lord Diplock at 219, and Lord Hailsham (with whom Lord Kilbrandon agreed) at 226.

[65] Cf *R v Bournemouth Justices, ex p Grey* [1987] 1 FLR 36, DC: it was difficult to envisage a father being dissuaded from admitting parentage to an adoption society on the basis of his knowledge that a later denial of such parentage might result in the earlier admission being used against him.

no doubt desirable, the reasoning by which that result was achieved is open to criticism. In particular, reliance on the arbitrary constraint of precedent seems an unsatisfactory means of containing the undesirable effect of an overgeneralized principle. If the constraint is applied, it must result in arbitrary distinctions. In practice, it has often been the generalized principle rather than the constraint that has been remembered by the lower courts. The relevance of statutory recognition must also be questioned: activities conducted without statutory provision or regulation can also be of great public importance.

It is convenient to consider the cases in which a claim to public interest immunity has been made under the heads of 'National security, diplomatic relations and international comity', 'Information for the detection of crime', 'Judicial disclosures', 'The proper functioning of the public service', and 'Confidential relationships'. In considering these cases, it needs to be remembered that there are always four variables capable of affecting the outcome, namely: (i) the importance of the public function in question; (ii) the extent to which disclosure would prejudice the effective exercise of that function; (iii) the importance of the material in question to the just determination of the litigation; and (iv) the public importance of that litigation.

National security, diplomatic relations, and international comity

Evidence will almost certainly be excluded in the interests of national security, good diplomatic relations and international comity. In *Asiatic Petroleum Co Ltd v Anglo-Persian Oil Co Ltd*[66] the defendants, acting on instructions from the Board of Admiralty, objected to the production of a letter to their agents containing information concerning the government's plans in respect of its campaign in Persia during the First World War. The Court of Appeal upheld the objection, not because the document was confidential or official, but because the information which it contained could not be disclosed without injury to the public interest. Similarly, in *Duncan v Cammell Laird & Co Ltd*, the defendants succeeded in their objection to the production of documents which might have given valuable information on the design of a new submarine to an agent of a foreign power at a time when the country was at war. Other examples under this head include a report of a military court of inquiry concerning the conduct of an officer,[67] communications between the governor of a colony and the colonial secretary,[68] or between the commander-in-chief of forces overseas and the government[69] and diplomatic despatches.[70]

Concerning national security, it now seems that a ministerial certificate will be conclusive. In *Balfour v Foreign and Commonwealth Office*[71] B, dismissed from his post as Vice-Consul in Dubai, complained to an industrial tribunal of unfair dismissal and sought disclosure of documents in the possession of the Foreign Office. Immunity was claimed on the grounds that disclosure of material in the documents relating to the security and intelligence services would be contrary to the public interest. Both the Foreign and Home Secretary signed certificates particularizing the nature and content of the material attracting immunity and the reasons for the claim. The Court of Appeal upheld the decision to refuse disclosure. Taking the view that *Conway v Rimmer*

[66] [1916] 1 KB 822, CA.
[67] *Home v Bentinck* (1820) 2 Brod&Bing 130; *Beatson v Skene* (1860) 5 H&N 838.
[68] *Hennessy v Wright* (1888) 21 QBD 509.
[69] *Chatterton v Secretary of State for India in Council* [1895] 2 QB 189, CA.
[70] *M Isaacs & Sons Ltd v Cook* [1925] 2 KB 391.
[71] [1994] 2 All ER 588, CA.

disposed of the appeal, it was held that although there must always be vigilance by the courts to ensure that public interest immunity of whatever kind is raised only in appropriate circumstances and with appropriate particularity, once there is an actual or potential risk to national security demonstrated by an appropriate certificate, the court should not exercise its right to inspect. In reaching its decision, the court approved and applied the dictum of Lord Diplock in *Council of Civil Service Unions v Minister for the Civil Service*[72] (when dealing with the question of national security in a completely different context):

> National security is the responsibility of the executive government; what action is needed to protect its interests is . . . a matter on which those on whom the responsibility rests, and not the courts of justice, must have the last word. It is par excellence a non-justiciable question. The judicial process is totally inept to deal with the sort of problems which it involves.

It is also in the public interest of the United Kingdom that the contents of confidential documents addressed to, or emanating from, foreign sovereign states, or concerning the interests of such states in relation to international territorial disputes between them, should not be ordered by the courts of this country to be disclosed by a private litigant without the consent of the states in question, because to order disclosure in such cases may be against the public interest in the maintenance of international comity and an English court should not be seen to be forcing the disclosure of such documents for the ostensible purpose of pronouncing, albeit indirectly, on the merits of such a dispute, the resolution of which is a question of politics.[73] The comity of nations also justifies an English court, in the exercise of its discretion, in refusing to authorize the issue of letters of request inviting the courts of a friendly foreign state to use their powers to assist in the obtaining of evidence, from witnesses resident in that or another friendly state, in order to show that the motives of the government of the friendly foreign state, in promulgating a particular law, were such that the law is unenforceable in the United Kingdom.[74]

Information for the detection of crime

If a witness called at trial is a police informer in relation to the crime charged, the court should be told and, unless there is a very strong countervailing interest not to do so, his status should be revealed.[75] However, it is in the public interest to protect the identity of informers, not only for their own safety, but also to ensure that the supply of information about criminal activities does not dry up. Accordingly, there is a rule, established since at least the late eighteenth century, that a witness in civil or criminal proceedings may not be asked to disclose the name of a police informer.[76] Likewise, no order for discovery will be made which

---

[72] [1985] AC 374, HL at 412.

[73] See per Brightman and Donaldson LJJ in *Buttes Gas & Oil Co v Hammer (No 3)* [1981] QB 223, CA.

[74] *Settebello Ltd v Banco Totta and Acores* [1985] 2 All ER 1025, CA. See also *Fayed v Al-Tajir* [1987] 2 All ER 396 per Mustill and Kerr LJJ, CA at 480 and 410 respectively: international comity requires that an inter-departmental memorandum prepared and circulated in the London embassy of a friendly foreign state should not be admitted as the foundation of an action for libel.

[75] *R v Patel* [2002] Crim LR 304.

[76] *R v Hardy* (1794) 24 State Tr 199. In principle, the rule should prevent disclosure of not only the name of the informer but also any information that will enable him to be identified: see *R v Omar* 2007 ONCA 117. See also s 17 of the Regulation of Investigatory Powers Act 2000, which renders inadmissible telephone-tap evidence, if lawfully obtained. See P Mirfield, 'Regulation of Investigatory Powers Act 2000 (2): Evidential Aspects' [2001] *Crim LR* 91.

will have that effect. Even if the party entitled to object does not invoke the rule, the judge is nonetheless obliged to apply it.[77] However, the rule will be overridden where, in a criminal trial, strict enforcement would be likely to cause a miscarriage of justice, ie where the accused can show good reason to expect that disclosure of the name of the informant will assist him in establishing his innocence.[78] In *Marks v Beyfus*[79] the plaintiff claimed damages for malicious prosecution. In the course of the trial, he asked the Director of Public Prosecutions to name his informants, but the judge disallowed the question. This ruling was upheld by the Court of Appeal on the ground 'that this was a public prosecution, ordered by the Government (or by an official equivalent to the Government) for what was considered to be a public object, and that therefore the information ought not, on grounds of public policy, to be disclosed'.[80] Lord Esher said:[81]

> I do not say it is a rule which can never be departed from; if upon the trial of a prisoner the judge should be of opinion that the disclosure of the name of the informant is necessary or right in order to show the prisoner's innocence, then one public policy is in conflict with another public policy, and that which says that an innocent man is not to be condemned when his innocence can be proved is the policy that must prevail. But, except in that case, this rule of public policy is not a matter of discretion; it is a rule of law . . .

Although it has been suggested that the possibility of a miscarriage of justice *dictates* disclosure,[82] it seems that a balancing exercise should be performed, even though, if the disputed material may prove the accused's innocence or avoid a miscarriage of justice, the balance will come down resoundingly in favour of disclosure.[83] Nonetheless, it has been held that judges need to scrutinize applications for disclosure of details about informants with very great care. They should be astute to see that assertions of a need to know such details (because essential to the running of a defence) are justified. In some cases the informant is an informant and no more; in others he may have participated in the events constituting, surrounding or following the crime. Even when the informant has participated, the judge will need to consider whether his role so impinges on an issue of interest to the defence, present or potential, as to make disclosure necessary.[84]

In *R v Agar*[85] the prosecution case was that A, on arrival at the house of X, found police officers present and, when he ran off, threw away a packet containing drugs. A alleged that the police had entered into an arrangement with X, an informer, to ask him to go to X's house and that the drugs allegedly found had been planted by the police. It was held that although an accused cannot discover the identity of an informer by pretending that something is part of his case when in truth it adds nothing to it, and although it *may* be that a defence which is manifestly frivolous and doomed to failure must be sacrificed to the general rule protecting informers,

---

[77] See per Lord Esher MR in *Marks v Beyfus* (1890) 25 QBD 494, CA at 500 and per Mann J in *R v Rankine* [1986] 2 All ER 566, CA at 569.

[78] Per Lawton LJ in *R v Hennessey* (1978) 68 Cr App R 419, CA at 426. See also *R v Hallett* [1986] Crim LR 462, CA.

[79] (1890) 25 QBD 494, CA.

[80] Per Lord Esher MR at 496–7. It would seem that bodies authorized by statute to bring prosecutions may claim the immunity, but not an individual prosecuting in a private capacity.

[81] (1890) 25 QBD 494, CA at 498.

[82] Per Mann LJ in *R v Governor of Brixton Prison, ex p Osman* [1992] 1 All ER 108 at 118.

[83] Per Lord Taylor CJ in *R v Keane* [1994] 2 All ER 478, CA at 484.

[84] Per Lord Taylor CJ in *R v Turner* [1995] 3 All ER 432, CA.

[85] [1990] 2 All ER 442, CA.

on the facts the defence should have been permitted to elicit that X had told the police that A would be coming to his house (which would have identified him as an informer)—such evidence was necessary to enable A to put forward his defence that he had been set up by X and the police acting in concert.[86]

In *R v Rankine*[87] it was held that the rule is not confined to the identification of police informers but also prevents the identification of premises used for police surveillance and the owners and occupiers of such premises. However, if the accused alleges that disclosure of the identification of such premises is necessary in order to establish his innocence, the prosecution must provide a sufficient evidential base to enable the trial judge properly to determine whether to afford the protection sought. In *R v Johnson*[88] the Court of Appeal held that the minimal evidential requirements for these purposes are twofold. First, the officer in charge of the observations, who normally should be of at least the rank of sergeant, should give evidence that he visited the premises to be used and ascertained the attitude of the occupiers to the use to be made of the premises and the possible disclosure thereafter of the use made and of facts which could lead to the identification of both premises and occupiers. He may additionally inform the court of any difficulties encountered in the particular locality in obtaining assistance from the public. Secondly, an officer of at least the rank of chief inspector should give evidence that immediately before the trial he visited the premises and ascertained whether the occupiers were still the same and, whether they were or not, what their attitude was to the possible disclosure of the use made of the premises and of facts which could lead to the identification of both premises and occupiers.[89]

Johnson was convicted of supplying drugs. The police alleged that he had been seen selling the drugs in a particular street by officers situated in buildings in the locality. The prosecution argued that the evidence which their witnesses should be compelled to give should not go further than revealing that all the observation points were within a given maximum distance from the scene of the offence. Defence counsel submitted that this would enable officers to cover up inconsistencies in their evidence and gravely embarrass him in his efforts to test in cross-examination precisely what they could see from their various locations having regard to the layout of the street and the objects in it, including trees. In the jury's absence, the police gave evidence as to the difficulty of obtaining assistance from the public for observation purposes and revealed that the occupiers, all of whom were also occupiers at the material time, did not wish their names and addresses to be disclosed because they feared for their safety. The judge ruled that the officers should not reveal the location of the premises used. The appeal was dismissed: although the conduct of the defence was to some extent affected by this restraint, it had led to no injustice.[90]

In *R v Brown, R v Daley*[91] the Court of Appeal emphasized that the extension of the exclusionary rule established in *R v Rankine* was based on the protection of the owner or occupier

---

[86] Applied in *R v Langford* [1990] Crim LR 653, CC. See also *R v Vaillencourt* [1993] Crim LR 311, CA and *R v Reilly* [1994] Crim LR 279, CA, where the identity of the informer would have contributed little or nothing to the defence being run, and *R v Menza and Marshalleck* [1998] Crim LR 58, CA.

[87] [1986] 2 All ER 566, CA.

[88] [1989] 1 All ER 121, CA.

[89] These guidelines do not require a threat of violence before protection can be afforded to the occupier—it suffices if he is in fear of harassment: *Blake v DPP* (1992) 97 Cr App R 169, DC.

[90] *R v Johnson* was applied in *R v Hewitt; R v Davis* (1991) 95 Cr App R 81, CA. See also *R v Grimes* [1994] Crim LR 213, CA.

[91] (1987) 87 Cr App R 52, CA.

of the premises and not on the identity, *simpliciter*, of the observation post. The accused were convicted of theft from a parked car. The chief prosecution witnesses were two officers who gave evidence that they had witnessed the commission of the offence as part of a surveillance operation conducted from an unmarked police vehicle. The defence was that their evidence had been fabricated. The judge allowed the prosecution to withhold information relating to the surveillance and the colour, make, and model of the police vehicle. The appeal was allowed. It was held that evidence of police methods and techniques, if relevant, was admissible. Even if public interest immunity could be successfully invoked to exclude evidence of sophisticated methods of criminal investigation, a possibility which the court was not prepared to rule out, the prosecution, in applying to exclude evidence on such a basis, would have to identify with precision the evidence to be excluded, give reasons for exclusion, and support the application by the independent evidence of senior officers. On the facts, this had not been done.

Disclosure to show that an accused is innocent of a criminal offence is not, as was once intimated,[92] the sole exception to a general rule against disclosure. The courts have softened the rigidity of this approach so as to permit a balance of competing public interests in a case specific manner as part of a wider jurisprudential move away from near absolute protection of various categories of public interest in non-disclosure. In *Chief Constable of Greater Manchester Police v McNally*,[93] civil proceedings for, inter alia, malicious prosecution, the trial judge had ordered the Chief Constable to disclose whether an individual, X, who had allegedly threatened a prosecution witness at the criminal trial, was a police informer. The Court of Appeal held that judges in civil cases are entitled to balance the public interest in the protection of an informer against the public interest in a fair trial but are required to give very considerable weight to the former interest and to reduce the weight of the latter, given that it is a civil trial at which liberty is not at stake. However, there were no grounds for interfering with the ruling of the judge who had properly given significant weight to three factors: that the evidence could have been decisive of the outcome of the case; that although the claimant's liberty was not at stake, he was seeking redress for wrongful deprivation of liberty for over ten months while in custody awaiting trial; and that although X had not consented to disclosure of information that he was an informer, the scope for protecting him was limited by the fact that both sides knew who he was.[94]

In *Savage v Chief Constable of Hampshire*[95] it was held that if a police informer wishes to sacrifice his own anonymity, he may do so, because in such circumstances the primary justification for non-disclosure, that disclosure would endanger his safety, disappears. In appropriate circumstances, however, it may be that notwithstanding the wishes of the informer, there remains a significant public interest which would be damaged by disclosure, as when disclosure might assist others involved in crime, reveal police methods of operation, or hamper police operations.

---

[92] See per Lord Diplock in *D v NSPCC* [1978] AC 171 at 218.

[93] [2002] 2 Cr App R 617, CA.

[94] See also *Re W (children) (care proceedings: disclosure)* [2004] 1 All ER 787, Fam D, which concerned information received by a local authority from the police, the disclosure of which in care proceedings, in the form in which it was provided, would have prejudiced covert police operations and enabled an informant to be identified.

[95] [1997] 2 All ER 631, CA.

Judicial disclosures

There are restrictions on the extent to which those involved in the conduct of a trial can be called to give evidence of the proceedings. The rationale of these restrictions probably stems from the need for efficiency in, and the finality of, litigation. They differ from the other heads of public policy in that although they prevent certain people being called to prove certain facts, for the most part they do not prevent proof of those facts by other means. These rules, which might equally well be considered under the heading of competence and compellability, or privilege, have played little, if any, part in the general development of public interest immunity.

A litigant may wish to prove what was said in earlier litigation. The court record and a properly proved transcript, where available, will usually be the best means, but in principle anyone who witnessed the proceedings may be called. However, a judge, including a master of the Supreme Court, cannot be compelled to give evidence of those matters of which he became aware relating to and as a result of the performance of his judicial functions, as opposed to some collateral matter, eg a crime committed in the face of the court. Nonetheless the judge is competent to give evidence, and if a situation arises where his evidence is vital, he should be able to be relied on not to assert his non-compellability.[96]

A jury's verdict cannot be questioned on the ground of anything that happened in the jury room.[97] Accordingly, the Court of Appeal in *R v Thompson*[98] refused to hear evidence to the effect that a juror had read a list of the accused's previous convictions, which had not been revealed in evidence. No doubt it is in the public interest to ensure finality of litigation and uninhibited discussion among jurors by holding that once they have clearly acquiesced in a verdict, the basis for their findings should not be questioned. However, the decision in *R v Thompson* seems to take this principle too far.

The proper functioning of the public service

Public interest immunity has been successfully claimed in respect of a variety of state interests on the grounds that protection is necessary for the proper functioning of the public service.[99] It is quite clear, for example, that subject to the court's assessment of the strength of the claim for immunity in each case and the importance of the material to the litigation, immunity may be claimed for communications to and from ministers and high-level government officials regarding the formulation of government policy.[100] In *Conway v Rimmer* itself it was recognized that internal communications of the police force (quite apart from those relating to the investigation of crime) would in appropriate cases qualify for immunity on the ground

---

[96] *Warren v Warren* [1996] 4 All ER 664, CA.

[97] See, eg, *R v Roads* [1967] 2 QB 108, in which a juror was not allowed to prove that she disagreed with the verdict.

[98] [1962] 1 All ER 65. See also per Lord Atkin in *Ras Behari Lal v R* (1933) 102 LJPC 144; *R v Bean* [1991] Crim LR 843, CA (an allegation of undue judicial pressure to reach a verdict); and *R v Lucas* [1991] Crim LR 844, CA (an allegation of undue pressure on one juror by the others). Cf *R v Newton* (1912) 7 Cr App R 214.

[99] At one time 'class' claims succeeded on this ground even in the case of documents of a relatively routine nature. See, eg, *Re Joseph Hargreaves* [1900] 1 Ch 347; *Anthony v Anthony* (1919) 35 TLR 559; *Ankin v London & North Eastern Rly Co* [1930] 1 KB 527; *Ellis v Home Office* [1953] 2 QB 135; and *Broome v Broome* [1955] P 190. All of these decisions pre-date *Conway v Rimmer* [1968] AC 910, and it is most unlikely that they would be followed today.

[100] See, eg, *Burmah Oil Co Ltd v Bank of England* [1980] AC 1090, and *Air Canada v Secretary of State for Trade (No 2)* [1983] 2 AC 394, above; cf *Williams v Home Office* [1981] 1 All ER 1151, CA.

that the public have an interest in the proper functioning of the police force which, though not a government department, 'carries out essential functions of government'. Concerning communications which do relate to the investigation of crime, it has been held that public interest immunity attaches to documents and information upon the strength of which search warrants have been obtained[101] and also to reports sent by the police to the Director of Public Prosecutions, even if the prosecution has been completed, whether successfully or not.[102] In the latter case it was held that it is important for the proper functioning of the criminal process of prosecution that there should be freedom of communication between police forces and the DPP in seeking his legal advice, without fear that the documents will be subject to inspection, analysis, and investigation in subsequent civil proceedings. There is also a clear public interest in the non-disclosure of international communications between police forces or prosecuting authorities, essentially so as not to divulge information useful to criminals and not to inhibit the fullest co-operation between such authorities in different jurisdictions.[103]

In *R v Lewes Justices, ex p Home Secretary*[104] an unsuccessful applicant for a gaming licence sought disclosure, in libel proceedings against the police, of a letter sent by the police to the Gaming Board which had requested information in the course of its statutory duty to investigate the applicant's suitability for a licence. The House of Lords refused the application, being clearly impressed by the importance of the Board's function in controlling the social evils which might otherwise have been expected to follow in the wake of the newly legalized activity of gaming. Lord Reid said:[105]

> I do not think that 'the public service' should be construed narrowly. Here the question is whether the withholding of this class of documents is really necessary to enable the board adequately to perform its statutory duties. If it is, then we are enabling the will of Parliament to be carried out.

An analogy was drawn with the principle relating to police informers: although the risk of disclosure might not inhibit the police, it would affect the wells of voluntary information. The plaintiff was thus, in effect, deprived of his cause of action.[106]

In *Lonrho plc v Fayed (No 4)*[107] the question arose whether, in the absence of consent to disclosure by a taxpayer, public interest immunity attaches to documents relating to his tax affairs in the hands of the Inland Revenue. A majority of the Court of Appeal, noting Parliament's clear intention (subject to specified exceptions) to prohibit disclosure by the Revenue of a

---

[101] *Taylor v Anderton* (1986) The Times, 21 Oct, Ch D.

[102] *Evans v Chief Constable of Surrey* [1989] 2 All ER 594, QBD.

[103] *R v Horseferry Road Magistrates, ex p Bennett (No 2)* [1994] 1 All ER 289, DC, although in that case the balance favoured disclosure, the documents being relevant to the issue whether B had been unlawfully returned to the jurisdiction.

[104] [1973] AC 388, also referred to as *Rogers v Secretary of State*. See also *Lonrho Ltd v Shell Petroleum* [1980] 1 WLR 627, HL where immunity was granted, in subsequent litigation, for evidence given to the Bingham inquiry into the operation of sanctions against Rhodesia: although the inquiry had powers to compel evidence to be given, its effectiveness depended on a voluntary supply of information which in turn required a valid guarantee of confidentiality. Cf *Hamilton v Naviede* [1994] 3 All ER 814, HL.

[105] [1973] AC 388 at 401. See also per Lord Morris at 405.

[106] It is important to distinguish public interest immunity and evidential privileges (see Ch 20) from privilege as a defence to libel proceedings. However, the policy considerations affecting these different issues can overlap to a surprising degree. See, eg, *Fayed v Al-Tajir* [1987] 2 All ER 396, CA.

[107] [1994] 1 All ER 870, CA.

taxpayer's affairs,[108] answered the question in the affirmative on the grounds that as a matter of public policy, the state should not by compulsory powers obtain information from a citizen for one purpose and then use it for another. Thus the confidentiality of such documents will only be overridden if the party seeking disclosure shows very strong grounds for concluding that on the facts of the particular case the public interest in the administration of justice outweighs the public interest in preserving the confidentiality. The court also held, unanimously, that no public interest immunity attaches to documents relating to tax affairs held by the taxpayer himself (or his agents).

The statutory functions of keeping import records for the purposes of Customs and Excise legislation (see *Norwich Pharmacal Co v Customs and Excise Comrs*)[109] and inquiring into the true nature of a person's trade in order to make a proper assessment to tax (see *Alfred Crompton Amusement Machines Ltd v Customs and Excise Comrs (No 2)*)[110] are both in principle capable of attracting public interest immunity. In the *Norwich Pharmacal* case, however, it was held that there was no serious risk that importers would be less likely to comply with their statutory duty to give the necessary information simply because of the possibility of that information being disclosed in civil proceedings, whereas in the *Alfred Crompton* case the information to be supplied by third parties about a trader's activities, even though supplied under statutory compulsion, was sufficiently sensitive to justify the fear that the Commissioners' functions would be hampered unless they were able to give an effective guarantee. Disclosure was thus required in the former case but denied in the latter.[111]

In *Science Research Council v Nassé*[112] the House of Lords firmly rejected a claim to immunity in relation to routine confidential employers' reports on employees seeking promotion.[113] *D v NSPCC*[114] was applied: public interest immunity can be extended only by analogy with previous authority. Lord Edmund-Davies[115] noted that public interest immunity had thus far been limited to bodies exercising statutory functions or duties in respect of which an analogy could be drawn with the principle relating to police informers. Lord Scarman said:[116]

> I regret the passing of the currently rejected term 'Crown privilege'. It at least emphasized the very restricted area of public interest immunity . . . The immunity exists to protect from disclosure only information the secrecy of which is essential to the proper working of the government of the state.

[108] See s 6 and Sch 1 of the Taxes Management Act 1970.

[109] [1974] AC 133, HL.

[110] [1974] AC 405, HL.

[111] Immunity can attach to evidence taken in a Department of Trade investigation under s 165 of the Companies Act 1948 (per Lord Widgery CJ, obiter, in *R v Cheltenham Justices, ex p Secretary of State for Trade* [1977] 1 WLR 95) and also to a report to the Secretary of State following a DTI inquiry into the activities of a company (see *Day v Grant* [1987] 3 All ER 678 at 680, CA). The former case was distinguished in *London and County Securities v Nicholson* [1980] 1 WLR 948, on the grounds that the importance of the evidence tipped the scales the other way. See also *Multi Guarantee Co Ltd v Cavalier Insurance Co Ltd* (1986) The Times, 24 June, Ch D, below: the immunity attaching to notes recording information given in confidence to officials of the DTI is capable of 'evaporating'. Concerning statutes requiring the disclosure of information and governing the extent to which it can be used in other proceedings, see generally Eagles, 'Public interest immunity and statutory privilege' (1983) 42 *CLJ* 118.

[112] [1980] AC 1028, HL.

[113] But also held that if discovery was not necessary for fairly disposing of the proceedings, it could be refused on the grounds of breach of confidence. See below.

[114] [1978] AC 171, HL.

[115] [1980] AC 1028 at 1073–4, approving the dicta of Browne LJ in the Court of Appeal.

[116] At 1087–8.

Defence, foreign relations, the inner workings of government at the highest levels where ministers and their advisers are formulating national policy, and the prosecution process in its pre-trial stage are the sensitive areas where the Crown must have the immunity if the government of the nation is to be effectually carried on. We are in the realm of public law, not private right. The very special case of *D v NSPCC* is not to be seen as a departure from this well-established principle.

In the case of statements obtained for the purposes of an investigation of a complaint against the police under Part IX of the Police and Criminal Evidence Act 1984, a class claim to immunity would tend to be largely self-defeating. Thus although it would be possible to justify immunity on the basis of (i) a candour argument (witnesses might be inhibited by the possibility of disclosure in subsequent litigation); and (ii) the underlying public interest in the maintenance of a law-abiding and uncorrupt police force, the consequences of immunity include preventing the complainant from seeing the relevant documents in any subsequent proceedings brought against the police. For reasons of this kind, in *R v Chief Constable of the West Midlands Police, ex p Wiley*[117] the House of Lords, overruling *Neilson v Laugharne*[118] (and the cases in which it was subsequently applied), held that there is no public interest immunity for such documents on the basis of a class claim.[119] It also held, however, that a claim to immunity may succeed on the basis of the contents of a particular document. Thus a claim could succeed in the case of a document containing, for example, police material on policy or operational matters or the identity of an informant. It was held that any contents claim should be decided in the proceedings in which the documents are relevant, such as a subsequent civil action in respect of the alleged misconduct (rather than in any collateral proceedings), because the conflicting public interests for and against disclosure will vary from case to case and the relationship between the conflicting interests may vary as the case proceeds to trial and even during the trial.[120]

The House of Lords in *ex p Wiley* left open the question whether reports prepared by the investigating officers form a class which is entitled to immunity. Subsequently, the Court of Appeal in *Taylor v Anderton*[121] answered the question in the affirmative, both as to working papers as well as such reports, holding that production of such material should only be ordered, therefore, where the public interest in disclosure of their contents outweighs the public interest in preserving their confidentiality. In reaching this decision, Sir Thomas Bingham MR was particularly influenced by (i) the fundamental public interest in ensuring that those responsible for maintaining law and order are themselves law-abiding and honest; and (ii) the need for investigating officers to feel free to report on professional colleagues or members of the public without the undesirably inhibiting apprehension that their opinions may become known to such persons.

Public interest immunity does not attach to statements made in a police grievance procedure, initiated by an officer, alleging racial or sexual discrimination.[122]

---

[117] [1994] 3 All ER 420.

[118] [1981] QB 736, CA.

[119] There is no immunity for written complaints prompting investigations against the police: *Conerney v Jacklin* [1985] Crim LR 234, CA.

[120] See also *Peach v Metropolitan Police Comr* [1986] 2 All ER 129, a decision prior to *ex p Wiley* in which *Neilson v Laugharne* was distinguished, and *Ex p Coventry Newspapers Ltd* [1993] 1 All ER 86, CA.

[121] [1995] 2 All ER 420, CA.

[122] *Metropolitan Police Comr v Locker* [1993] 3 All ER 584, EAT.

Confidential relationships

There are many important relationships which depend on the assumption that confidences will be respected. Examples include the relationship between doctor and patient, journalist and source, and priest and penitent. In *Alfred Crompton Amusement Machines Ltd v Customs and Excise Comrs (No 2)*[123] it was emphasized that confidentiality is never a sufficient ground of immunity, even though it is often a necessary condition. Thus at common law, in the absence of some additional consideration, as when the person claiming immunity is exercising a statutory function the effective performance of which would be impeded by disclosure, a claim to public interest immunity will not succeed.[124] An example of such an additional consideration is provided by *Re Barlow Clowes Gilt Managers Ltd*.[125] It was held that the liquidators of a company are under no duty to assist its directors, in defending criminal charges, by providing them with information obtained by the liquidators from third parties in circumstances of confidentiality and by assurances, express or implied, that it would be used only for the purpose of the liquidation, because if there comes to be a generally perceived risk of such disclosure, there is an obvious danger that professional men will no longer cooperate with liquidators on a voluntary basis, which would jeopardize the proper and efficient functioning of the process of compulsory liquidation.[126]

The question will often arise on disclosure, which under the Rules of Supreme Court was known as discovery. RSC Ord 24, rule 8 provided that the court should refuse to order discovery 'if and so far as it is of opinion that discovery is not necessary either for disposing fairly of the cause or matter or for saving costs'. In *Science Research Council v Nassé*[127] it was held that this provision provided the test to be used by an industrial tribunal, in discrimination proceedings, in deciding whether to order the discovery of confidential reports on employees and applicants for employment. The following propositions derive from the judgment of Lord Wilberforce:

1. There is no principle in English law by which documents are protected from discovery by reason of confidentiality alone, but, in the exercise of its discretion to order discovery, a tribunal may have regard to the fact that disclosure will involve a breach of confidence.

2. Relevance, though necessary, is not automatically a sufficient ground for ordering discovery.

---

[123] [1974] AC 405, HL.

[124] See *Lonrho Ltd v Shell Petroleum* [1980] 1 WLR 627, HL, above. See also *Lonrho plc v Fayed (No 4)* [1994] 1 All ER 870, CA, above; *R v Umoh* (1986) 84 Cr App R 138, CA (immunity for discussions between a prisoner and a legal aid officer); *R v K* (1993) 97 Cr App R 342, CA (an interview with a child victim of a sexual offence, conducted for therapeutic purposes, should not be disclosed unless the interests of justice so require, but if the liberty of the subject is an issue, and disclosure may be of assistance to an accused, a claim for disclosure will often be strong); and *Morrow v DPP* [1994] Crim LR 58, DC (having regard to the purpose of the Abortion Act 1967 to encourage the use of safe and controlled procedures, rather than resort to illegal abortions (a purpose reflected in the statutory restrictions on the disclosure of information furnished under the Abortion Regulations 1968), immunity may be claimed for confidential documents relating to abortions carried out under the Act). The matrimonial reconciliation cases considered in Ch 20 may also be regarded as a limb of public interest immunity—see, eg, per Lords Hailsham and Simon in *D v NSPCC* [1978] AC 171 at 226 and 236–7 respectively. Private privilege is available to protect certain types of communication between a lawyer and his client: see Ch 20.

[125] [1991] 4 All ER 385, Ch D.

[126] However, if the information is 'material evidence' for the purposes of a witness summons in the criminal proceedings, then the criminal court must balance the competing interests for and against disclosure and, as we have seen, in the case of very serious criminal charges at least, this may well result in disclosure: see *R v Clowes* [1992] 3 All ER 440, CCC, above.

[127] [1980] AC 1028, HL.

3. The ultimate test is whether discovery is necessary for disposing fairly of the proceedings: if it is, then discovery must be ordered notwithstanding confidentiality, but where the court is impressed with the need to preserve confidentiality, it will consider carefully whether the necessary information can be obtained by other means not involving a breach of confidence.

4. In order to decide whether discovery is necessary notwithstanding confidentiality, a tribunal should inspect the documents; it will also consider whether justice can be done by 'covering up', substituting anonymous references for specific names or, in rare cases, a hearing *in camera*. On the facts, the tribunals in question not having inspected the documents, the cases were remitted so that the documents could be examined and a decision taken as to which, if any, should be disclosed.

Science Research Council v Nassé remains the leading authority when courts are faced with an application for disclosure of confidential documents, but in deciding on such applications under the Civil Procedure Rules, account must be taken of the overriding objective. In particular, it is necessary to deal with cases justly, which includes saving expenses and dealing with cases with proportionality, and it is not proportionate to make an order for the supply of documents that will result in duplication.[128]

In *British Steel Corpn (BSC) v Granada Television Ltd*[129] Granada had received from a BSC employee copies of secret documents from BSC's files. Some of the documents were then used in a programme on the national steel strike. Granada had promised the informant that his identity would not be disclosed. BSC applied for an order that Granada disclose the identity of the informant. They relied upon the principle in *Norwich Pharmacal Co v Customs and Excise Comrs*,[130] namely that a person who becomes involved in the tortious acts of another, even if innocently, is under a duty to assist a person injured by those acts by disclosing the identity of the tortfeasor. The House of Lords ordered Granada to disclose the identity of the informant. It was accepted, however, that where possible, judges will respect the confidence:[131]

> Courts have an inherent wish to respect this confidence, whether it arises between doctor and patient, priest and penitent, bankers and customer, between persons giving testimonials to employees, or in other relationships . . . But in all these cases the court may have to decide, in particular circumstances, that the interest in preserving this confidence is outweighed by other interests to which the law attaches importance.

On the facts, Lord Wilberforce concluded that 'to confine BSC to its remedy against Granada and to deny it the opportunity of a remedy against the source would be a significant denial of justice'.[132] His Lordship approved the dictum of Lord Denning MR in *A-G v Mulholland*,[133] applying similar principles in relation to cross-examination at trial:

> The judge will respect the confidences which each member of these honourable professions receives in the course of it, and will not direct him to answer unless not only it is relevant

---

[128] *Simba-Tola v Elizabeth Fry Hospital* [2001] EWCA Civ 1371, LTL 30 July 2001.

[129] [1981] AC 1096, HL.

[130] [1974] AC 133.

[131] Per Lord Wilberforce [1981] AC 1096 at 1168.

[132] [1981] AC 1096 at 1175.

[133] [1963] 2 QB 477 at 489–90. See also *A-G v Lundin* (1982) 75 Cr App R 90, DC: there is no liability for contempt for refusal to answer unless the question is both relevant and necessary.

but also it is a proper and, indeed, necessary question in the course of justice to be put and answered. A judge is the person entrusted, on behalf of the community, to weigh these conflicting interests—to weigh on the one hand the respect due to confidence in the profession and on the other hand the ultimate interest of the community in justice being done. . . . If the judge determines that the journalist must answer, then no privilege will avail him to refuse.

Disclosure of the source of information contained in a publication is now governed by statute. Section 10 of the Contempt of Court Act 1981 was enacted to bring domestic law in this respect into line with Article 10 of the European Convention on Human Rights, which provides:

1. Everyone has the right to freedom of expression . . .
2. The exercise of these freedoms, since it carries with it duties and responsibilities, may be subject to such formalities, conditions, restrictions or penalties as are prescribed by law and are necessary in a democratic society, in the interests of national security, territorial integrity or public safety, for the prevention of disorder or crime, for the protection of health or morals, for the protection of the reputation or rights of others, for preventing the disclosure of information received in confidence, or for maintaining the authority and impartiality of the judiciary.

Section 10 of the Contempt of Court Act 1981 provides:

No court may require a person to disclose, nor is any person guilty of contempt of court for refusing to disclose, the source of information contained in a publication[134] for which he is responsible, unless it be established to the satisfaction of the court that disclosure is necessary in the interests of justice or national security or for the prevention of disorder or crime.

In *Ashworth Hospital Authority v MGN Ltd*[135] it was held that section 10 gives effect to the general requirements of Article 10 in the narrow context of the protection of the sources of information of the press; that Article 10 permits the right of freedom of expression to be circumscribed where necessary in a democratic society to achieve a number of specified 'legitimate aims'; and that the approach to the interpretation of section 10 should, insofar as possible (i) equate the specific purposes for which disclosure of sources is permitted under section 10 with the 'legitimate aims' under Article 10; and (ii) apply the same test of necessity to that applied by the European Court of Justice when considering Article 10.

The construction of section 10 was considered by the House of Lords for the first time in *Secretary of State for Defence v Guardian Newspapers Ltd*.[136] The House was of the firm view that section 10 substitutes for the discretionary protection which existed at common law a rule of wide and general application subject only to the four exceptions specified:[137] the prohibition does not differentiate between disclosure in interim proceedings for discovery prior to trial and disclosure at the trial itself and is not qualified by the nature of the proceedings or of the claim

---

[134] Section 10 applies to the publication of photographs as well as written information. Photographs communicate information visually, writing does it through words, but in either case what is contained in the publication is information: per Sir Nicolas Browne-Wilkinson V-C in *Handmade Films (Productions) Ltd v Express Newspapers* [1986] FSR 463, Ch D at 468.

[135] [2002] 1 WLR 2033, HL. The dicta cited are those of Lord Phillips MR, whose judgment in the Court of Appeal ([2001] 1 WLR 515) was expressly endorsed by the House of Lords.

[136] [1984] 3 All ER 601, HL.

[137] Per Lord Scarman at 615.

in respect of which the proceedings are brought.[138] Accordingly, it is sufficient to attract the protection of the section that an order of a court *may*, but not necessarily *will*, have the effect of disclosing a source of information.[139] Moreover, where a person seeks delivery up of a document which is his property in order to identify the informant from it, a judge, in exercising his discretion to order up delivery of goods under section 3(3) of the Torts (Interference with Goods) Act 1977, should have regard, when appropriate, to section 10, and should not make such an order unless the case falls within one of the four exceptions. It was also held that it is a question of fact, not discretion, whether a particular case falls within one of the exceptions, the burden being on the party seeking disclosure to prove on a balance of probabilities that disclosure is 'necessary'.[140] However, if a party seeks disclosure on an interim application, the court should be careful not to order disclosure unless the evidence before it establishes that the inference of necessity is unlikely to be displaced when all the evidence is produced and tested at trial.[141] Section 10 requires actual necessity to be established: expediency, however great, is not enough.[142]

Concerning 'justice', in the interest of which disclosure may be necessary, Lord Diplock, in *Secretary of State for Defence v Guardian Newspapers Ltd*, said that the word is used in the sense of the administration of justice in the course of legal proceedings in a court of law or tribunal.[143] This approach was adopted in *Maxwell v Pressdram Ltd*,[144] where it was held to be essential to identify and define the issue in the legal proceedings. Similarly, in *Handmade Films (Productions) Ltd v Express Newspapers*[145] it was held that although a claim for discovery based on the *Norwich Pharmacal* principle may come within 'the interests of justice', the claimant must show that he needs the name of the unknown wrongdoer because he intends to sue him—it is insufficient that an action *may* be brought.

Lord Diplock's definition, however, was rejected as too narrow in the leading English case, *X Ltd v Morgan-Grampian Ltd*.[146] The plaintiffs, X Ltd, two private companies, prepared a business plan in order to negotiate a bank loan to raise additional working capital. A copy of the plan was stolen. The next day, an unidentified source gave G, a journalist, information about the planned loan. G decided to write an article about X Ltd. X Ltd obtained an injunction against the defendant publishers, M-G Ltd, restraining publication of information derived from the plan, and applied under section 10 for an order disclosing the name of the source, their intention being to bring proceedings against him for recovery of the plan, an injunction to prevent further publication, and damages. The House of Lords held that, by reason of the *Norwich Pharmacal* principles, the court had jurisdiction to order M-G Ltd to disclose G's notes; that although the information obtained from the source had not been 'contained in a

---

[138] Per Lord Diplock at 603 and 606.

[139] See, eg, per Lord Roskill at 623.

[140] Per Lords Diplock and Scarman at 607 and 618 respectively.

[141] Per Lord Scarman at 618. See also *Handmade Films (Productions) Ltd v Express Newspapers* [1986] FSR 463, Ch D.

[142] Per Lord Diplock at 607, applied in *Handmade Films (Productions) Ltd v Express Newspapers* [1986] FSR 463, Ch D. Cf per Lord Griffiths in *Re an inquiry under the Company Securities (Insider Dealing) Act 1985* [1988] 1 All ER 203 at 208–9, HL: 'I doubt if it is possible to go further than to say that "necessary" has a meaning that lies somewhere between "indispensable" on the one hand and "useful" or "expedient" on the other, and to leave it to the judge to decide towards which end of the scale of meaning he will place it on the facts of any particular case.'

[143] [1984] 3 All ER 601 at 607.

[144] [1987] 1 All ER 656 at 665, CA.

[145] [1986] FSR 463, Ch D.

[146] [1990] 2 All ER 1, HL.

publication', the information having been received for the purposes of publication, it should be subject to section 10, since the purpose underlying the statutory protection of sources is as much applicable before as after publication; but, applying section 10, that disclosure of G's notes was necessary in the interests of justice.

The following propositions derive from the judgment of Lord Bridge, with which three other members of the House concurred:

1. Where a judge asks himself the question 'Can I be satisfied that disclosure of the source of *this* information is necessary to serve *this* interest?', he has to engage in a balancing exercise.

2. He starts with three assumptions: that the protection of sources is itself a matter of high public importance; that nothing less than necessity will suffice to override it; and that the necessity can only arise out of concern for another matter of high public importance, one of the four interests listed in section 10.

3. The public interests of national security and the prevention of crime are of such overriding importance that once it is shown that disclosure will serve one of those interests, the necessity of disclosure follows almost automatically (although a judge might properly refuse disclosure if the crime to be prevented is of a trivial nature).

4. The question whether disclosure is necessary 'in the interests of justice' gives rise to a more difficult problem of weighing one public interest against another. Lord Diplock's definition of justice was too narrow: it is 'in the interests of justice' that persons should be enabled to exercise important legal rights and to protect themselves from serious legal wrongs, whether or not resort to legal proceedings in a court of law is necessary to obtain those objectives. Thus if an employer is suffering grave damage from the activities of an unidentified disloyal employee, it is in the interests of justice that he should be able to identify him to end his contract of employment, notwithstanding that no legal proceedings may be necessary to do so.

5. It is only if the judge is satisfied that disclosure in the interests of justice is of such preponderating importance as to override the statutory privilege that the threshold of necessity will be reached.

6. This is a question of fact, but calls for the exercise of discriminating and sometimes difficult value judgments, to which many factors will be relevant on both sides of the scale. In favour of disclosure there will be a wide spectrum within which the particular case must be located. For example, if the party seeking disclosure shows that his very livelihood depends on it, the case will be near one end of the spectrum, but if what he seeks to protect is a minor interest in property, the case will be at or near the other end. On the other side, there is also a wide spectrum. One important factor is the nature of the information: the greater the legitimate public interest in it, the greater the importance of protecting the source. Another significant factor is the manner in which the information was obtained by the source: the importance of protecting the source will be enhanced if the information was obtained legitimately, but will be diminished if obtained illegally, unless counterbalanced by a clear public interest in publication, as when the source acts in order to expose iniquity.

Applying those principles to the facts, it was held that disclosure of X Ltd's plan during their refinancing negotiations would involve a threat of severe damage to their business, and consequently to the livelihood of their employees, which could only be defused by identification of the source, either as the thief or as the means of identifying the thief, which would then allow X Ltd to bring proceedings to recover the plan. On the other hand, the source was involved in a gross breach of confidentiality which was not counterbalanced by any legitimate interest in publication of the information.

In *Ashworth Hospital Authority v MGM Ltd*[147] it was said that the wider interpretation of the 'interests of justice' in *X Ltd v Morgan-Grampian Ltd* accords more happily with the scheme of Article 10 than the interpretation of Lord Diplock in *Secretary of State for Defence v Guardian Newspapers Ltd*. Confirming that 'interests of justice' in section 10 means interests that are justiciable, it was also observed that it is difficult to envisage any such interest that would not fall within one or more of the Article 10 'legitimate aims'.

The leading case in the European Court of Human Rights is *Goodwin v UK*,[148] which dealt with the same facts as those which had been the subject of the House of Lords decision in *X Ltd v Morgan-Grampian Ltd*, but under Article 10 of the European Convention on Human Rights. The tests which the European Court and the House of Lords applied were substantially the same,[149] but the European Court came to the opposite conclusion. This, however, is not as surprising as it might initially seem. As Thorpe LJ pointed out in *Camelot Group plc v Centaur Communications Ltd*,[150] the making of a value judgment on competing facts is very close to the exercise of a discretion based on those facts, and there was a lapse of six years between the decisions in London and Strasbourg, a period in which standards fundamental to the performance of the balancing exercise may change materially. In the *Camelot Group* case, the plaintiff company, which was authorized to run the National Lottery, intended to publish its 1997 final accounts on 3 June. An unidentified employee of the company leaked a copy of the draft accounts to a journalist, who published an article disclosing their contents. The company sought an order which would effectively result in the disclosure of the identity of the source of the leaked information. The Court of Appeal held that a court, in assessing whether it is necessary to order disclosure in the interests of justice, may take account of an employer's wish to identify a disloyal employee so as to end his employment, and that in certain cases this factor alone may be strong enough to outweigh the public interest in the protection of the anonymity of press sources. On the facts, it held that the necessity for an order for disclosure of the source had been established: there was unease and suspicion among the company's employees which inhibited good working relationships, and there was a continuing threat of disclosure of further information, a risk that the employee might prove untrustworthy in some new respect in the future, by revealing, for example, the name of a public figure who had won a large prize. On the other hand, it did not significantly further the public interest to secure the publication of the accounts a week earlier than planned.

In *Ashworth Hospital Authority v MGN Ltd*[151] the House of Lords accepted the approach of the European Court in *Goodwin v UK* that as a matter of general principle the 'necessity' for any restriction of freedom of expression must be convincingly established and that limitations on the confidentiality of journalistic sources call for the most careful scrutiny by the court. It was

---

[147] [2002] 1 WLR 2033, HL. The dicta cited are those of Lord Phillips MR, whose judgment in the Court of Appeal ([2001] 1 WLR 515) was expressly endorsed by the House of Lords.

[148] (1996) 22 EHRR 123, ECtHR

[149] See *Camelot Group v Centaur Communications Ltd* [1998] 1 All ER 251 at 259 and 262, CA.

[150] [1998] 1 All ER 251 at 262.

[151] [2002] 1 WLR 2033, HL.

also held that any restriction on the right to freedom of expression must meet two further requirements: (i) the exercise of the disclosure jurisdiction because of Article 10(2) should meet a 'pressing social need' and (ii) the restriction should be proportionate to the 'legitimate aim' which is being pursued.

In *Saunders v Punch Ltd*[152] the court refused to make an order to disclose the identity of a source of information the nature of which suggested that he had seen records of meetings between the plaintiff and his lawyers which were protected by legal professional privilege. It was held that although the privilege is of massive importance in the administration of justice, it will not inevitably and always preponderate in the balancing exercise which the court must carry out in deciding whether disclosure is in the interests of justice. The question in each case is 'Are the interests of justice so pressing as to require the ban on disclosure to be overridden?', a question which on the facts of the case was answered in the negative.

Secretary of State for Defence v Guardian Newspapers Ltd, which concerned the second exception, national security, turned on the quality of evidence relied on by the claimant. A copy of a secret Ministry of Defence memorandum concerning the handling of publicity relating to the instal-lation of nuclear weapons, had been 'leaked' to the *Guardian* newspaper. The Crown sought its return in order to identify the informant from markings made on the document. The House of Lords was unanimous in its view that where the Crown seeks an interim order for disclosure under this exception, the supporting affidavits should spell out, with the utmost particularity, all relevant material as to why disclosure is necessary. The House divided, however, on whether the evidence on which the Crown relied was sufficient to discharge the onus of proving necessity. A majority was satisfied that it was. The risk to national security lay not in the publication of the particular document but in the possibility that the person who had leaked it might in future leak other classified documents relating to the deployment of nuclear weapons, the disclosure of which would have much more serious consequences on national security.

Concerning the final exception, 'the prevention of crime', disclosure may be ordered if necessary for the prevention of crime generally rather than a particular identifiable future crime or crimes. Accordingly, in *Re an inquiry under the Company Securities (Insider Dealing) Act 1985*[153] the House of Lords held that a journalist who had made use of confidential price-sensitive information about takeover bids, leaked to him by a source inside one of the relevant government departments, was not entitled to the protection of section 10 because although inspectors appointed by the Secretary of State to investigate suspected leaks of this kind, and who had requested the journalist to reveal his source, were unable to show that they would take steps to prevent the commission of a particular future crime, nonetheless they needed the information for the purpose of exposing the leaking of official information and criminal insider trading and preventing such behaviour in the future. However, as in the case of the other exceptions, a claim will only succeed on the basis of the prevention of crime, if there is clear and specific evidence to prove 'necessity'. In *X v Y*[154] employees of the plaintiffs, a health authority, had supplied a national newspaper with information obtained from hospital records identifying two doctors who were carrying on general practice despite having contracted AIDS. The defendants had paid for the informa-tion. The plaintiffs sought disclosure by the defendants of their sources on the grounds that

[152] [1998] 1 All ER 234, Ch D.
[153] [1988] 1 All ER 203, HL.
[154] [1988] 2 All ER 648, QBD.

this was necessary for the prevention of crime.[155] The claim failed through lack of proof: although appropriate deterrent action could take a variety of forms—such as warning the culprits, dismissal, or criminal investigation—the plaintiffs had adduced no evidence as to what security procedures existed, what inquiries had been made to identify the sources, whether they had referred the matter to the police. and whether criminal investigation was the intended or likely consequence.

Procedural issues

Taking the objection

In civil litigation, a claim to public interest immunity usually arises at the disclosure stage. Under CPR rule 31.19, a party to litigation (or someone who has received an application for non-party disclosure) may apply, without notice, for an order permitting him to withhold disclosure of a document on the grounds that disclosure would damage the public interest. Under rule 31.19(6) the court, for the purposes of deciding such an application, may require the person seeking to withhold disclosure to produce the document to the court and may invite any person, whether or not a party, to make representations. Where a government department is a party to the litigation, it will make the application.[156] In other cases, the application may be made by the party possessing the documents on its own initiative or at the request of the relevant department, as in *Burmah Oil Co Ltd v Bank of England*.[157] If necessary, the head of the department or the Attorney General may intervene to prevent documents being disclosed. The claim must usually be supported by affidavit evidence from the relevant minister or head of department, identifying the documents and the grounds for withholding them in as much detail as possible. In the case of a ministerial objection, a certificate signed by the minister may suffice. Concerning information or documents to be disclosed by a witness, the issue will often be raised before the judge at trial (in a criminal case in the absence of the jury, of course). In any case, the judge himself should take the point if necessary for if there is a public interest to be protected it must be protected regardless of party advantage.[158]

If a party to civil litigation holds documents in a class prima facie immune, he should (save perhaps in a very exceptional case) assert that the documents are immune and decline to disclose them, since the ultimate judge of where the balance of public interest lies is not him but the court.[159] If, in a criminal case, the prosecution wish to claim the immunity for documents helpful to the defence, they are duty bound to give notice to the defence of the claim so that, if necessary, the court can be asked to rule on its legitimacy. It is incompatible with an accused's absolute right to a fair trial to allow the prosecution to be judge in their own cause on the asserted claim. If the prosecution are not prepared to have the issue determined by the court, the inevitable result is that the prosecution will have to be abandoned.[160]

---

[155] Under the Public Bodies Corrupt Practices Act 1889 and the Prevention of Corruption Act 1906.

[156] See s 28 of the Crown Proceedings Act 1947, above.

[157] [1980] AC 1090, HL.

[158] See, eg, Viscount Simon LC in *Duncan v Cammell Laird & Co Ltd* [1942] AC 624 at 642, citing *Chatterton v Secretary of State for India* [1895] 2 QB 189 at 195.

[159] Per Bingham LJ in *Makanjuola v Metropolitan Police Comr* [1992] 3 All ER 617 at 623.

[160] *R v Ward* [1993] 2 All ER 577 at 633, CA.

Waiver and secondary evidence[161]

Whether public interest immunity can be waived appears to turn on a variety of factors, including: the time (whether before or after a ruling by the court); whether or not immunity is claimed at all; whether the decision on waiver is being made by a relevant Secretary of State on behalf of his department, an ordinary litigant or the maker and recipient of the document in question; the nature of the document; and the extent to which 'the cat is already out of the bag'.

It is often said that public interest immunity cannot be waived. This was asserted by Lord Simon in *R v Lewes Justices, ex p Home Secretary*,[162] where it led to disapproval of the term 'Crown Privilege'—it is the duty of a party to assert the immunity, even if it is to his disadvantage in the litigation. The principle was forcefully reasserted by Bingham LJ in *Makanjuola v Metropolitan Police Comr*:[163] a party claiming immunity is not claiming a right but observing a duty and therefore the immunity cannot be waived—although one can waive rights, one cannot waive duties. Neither of these two dicta, however, is of general application. As Lord Woolf pointed out in *R v Chief Constable of the West Midlands Police, ex p Wiley*,[164] Lord Simon was referring to the situation *after* the court has determined that the public interest against disclosure outweighs that of disclosure, and the *Makanjuola* case was not one involving a department of state. As far as the contents of documents are concerned, Lord Woolf thought it most unlikely that the principle of public interest immunity can be used to prevent a department of state from disclosing documents which it considers it appropriate to disclose. Equally, as to class claims, it was doubted whether the courts would ever interfere, after the event, with governmental decisions in favour of disclosure. It is not clear, however, whether a Secretary of State is under a *duty*, before objecting to discovery of any particular documents of a class prima facie entitled to public interest immunity, to consider whether the public interest in non-disclosure of those particular documents is outweighed, on the facts of the particular case, by the public interest in those documents being available in the administration of justice. The proposition, it has been said, is 'at least arguable'.[165]

Concerning waiver by ordinary litigants, where a party other than a government department is in possession of documents in respect of which the courts have already established that class immunity applies, the court may intervene to prevent disclosure, but if the party in question has consulted the Attorney General or other appropriate minister, who has endorsed the party's decision to disclose, the court, if the matter comes before it, will act on their views. In a situation of doubt, however, the question of disclosure should normally be left to the court.[166]

Concerning waiver by the maker and recipient of confidential documents, however, the authorities are not clear. In *Science Research Council v Nassé*[167] inability to waive the immunity was among the reasons given for resisting its extension: if the immunity applied, it could

---

[161] The ensuing text concerns civil cases. As to voluntary disclosure by the CPS in criminal cases, see *R v Horseferry Road Magistrates, ex p Bennett (No 2)* [1994] 1 All ER 289, DC, above.

[162] [1973] AC 388 at 407.

[163] [1992] 3 All ER 617 at 623.

[164] [1994] 3 All ER 420 at 438–9.

[165] Per Rattee J in *Bennett v Metropolitan Police Comr* [1995] 2 All ER 1, Ch D at 13.

[166] Per Lord Woolf [1994] 3 All ER 420 at 438–9. See also per Lawton LJ in *Hehir v Metropolitan Police Comr* [1982] 1 WLR 715 at 722: if the reason for the immunity is the need to protect the public interest, individuals should be unable to waive it for their own purposes.

[167] [1980] AC 1028, per Lords Wilberforce and Fraser at 1066–7 and 1082 respectively.

not be waived either by the employer or by the employer with the consent of the subject of a report and its author, which would be unnecessarily restrictive.[168] However, a different approach was taken in *Campbell v Tameside Metropolitan Borough Council*.[169] That was a personal injury action arising out of an assault by a pupil on a teacher in which immunity was refused for psychiatric reports on the pupil obtained by the school in pursuance of its statutory duty. Lord Denning reasserted, obiter, a distinction he had drawn in *Neilson v Laugharne*:[170] in the case of documents in a higher category, including all those which must be kept top secret because their disclosure would be injurious to national defence, diplomatic relations, or the detection of crime, the immunity cannot be waived; but in the case of documents within a lower category, including documents which are kept confidential in order that subordinates should be frank and candid in their reports, or for any other good reason, immunity can be waived by the maker and recipients of the confidential document.[171] A similar approach was also taken in *Multi Guarantee Co Ltd v Cavalier Insurance Co Ltd*.[172] The plaintiffs sought certain declaratory and other relief against the defendant company, which was in liquidation. Notes of a confidential meeting between the directors of the defendant company and officials of the Department of Trade and Industry had, with certain passages blacked out, been disclosed by the Department to the liquidator. The liquidator, with the consent of the defendant company, had disclosed the notes in the course of discovery, and orders of *subpoena duces tecum* and *subpoena ad testificandum* had been made against officials of the Department, requiring them to produce the notes recording the information given to them in confidence, and to testify. The Department intervened and applied for the orders to be discharged. The court, having examined the documents in private, refused to set the orders aside. It was held that although public interest immunity cannot be waived, it is capable of evaporating if those involved in the giving and receiving of the information consent to its disclosure. The fact that the partial disclosure had already significantly eroded the immunity was a relevant consideration in balancing the public interest in non-disclosure against the interest of the proper administration of justice in disclosure. Knox J, while acknowledging that it was a matter of degree in any particular case, said that if the cat had got all four legs out of the bag, there was little point in holding on to its tail.

In *R v Governor of Brixton Prison, ex p Osman*[173] certain documents protected by public interest immunity had been disclosed in a previous application for habeas corpus, although they had not been read in open court. It was held that prior disclosure of a document is a matter to be taken into account in the balance: if there has been publication to the whole world, then the public interest in non-disclosure must collapse. On the facts, however, the small degree of publication that had occurred could not upset the balance, which came down heavily in favour of immunity.

---

[168] See also per Lord Donaldson MR in *Makanjuola v Metropolitan Police Comr* [1992] 3 All ER 617 at 621, CA.

[169] [1982] QB 1065, CA.

[170] [1981] QB 736, CA.

[171] See also per Lord Cross in *Alfred Crompton Amusement Machines Ltd v Customs and Excise Comrs (No 2)* [1974] AC 405 at 434 and per Brightman LJ in *Hehir v Metropolitan Police Comr* [1982] 1 WLR 715 at 723, whose approach was endorsed by Lord Woolf in *R v Chief Constable of the West Midlands Police, ex p Wiley* [1994] 3 All ER 420 at 440: 'If the purpose of the immunity is to obtain the co-operation of an individual to the giving of a statement, I find it difficult to see how that purpose will be undermined if the maker of the statement consents to it being disclosed.'

[172] (1986) The Times, 24 June, Ch D.

[173] [1992] 1 All ER 108 at 118.

Similar considerations presumably apply in relation to secondary evidence. Obviously, the submarine plans in *Duncan v Cammell Laird & Co Ltd*[174] could not be proved by any means; in *R v Lewes Justices, ex p Home Secretary*[175] a copy of the allegedly libellous letter had somehow been obtained by the person to whom it referred, but because public interest immunity applied he was not able to prove that letter by any means. However, if information is freely available to the public, the fact that that information also forms the subject matter of a protected communication will surely not prevent proof of the information from the public sources. In each case, it is submitted, the question should be whether, on the particular facts, the public interest really does require non-disclosure; if there has been limited disclosure, immunity may still be justified, especially if the disclosure was wrongful.

Disclosure, production, and inspection

Disclosure involves two stages, disclosure of the existence of a document and production of that document for inspection. Before any question of public interest immunity can be raised, the document has to be one which should be disclosed within the rules normally applicable in civil litigation.[176] Under CPR rule 31.6, standard disclosure requires a party to disclose only (a) the documents on which he relies; (b) the documents which adversely affect his own case, adversely affect another party's case or support another party's case; and (c) the documents he is required to disclose by a relevant practice direction. If the party seeking disclosure falls at this hurdle, the question of public interest immunity will simply not arise.[177] Moreover, the court, in deciding whether to dispense with or limit standard disclosure, or whether to make an order for specific disclosure or specific inspection under rule 31.12, must seek to give effect to the 'overriding objective' of enabling it to deal with the case justly, which includes saving expense and ensuring that it is dealt with expeditiously and fairly etc.[178] If the party seeking disclosure falls at these hurdles, again the question of immunity will simply not arise.[179]

If these hurdles are surmounted, but public interest immunity is claimed, the judge will have to ask first whether the head of public interest on which reliance is placed is at least 'analogous' to those which have already been recognized by authority. He will also have to assess the strength of the objector's reasons for saying that disclosure will prejudice that public interest. If a prima facie claim to immunity is thus made out, the person seeking disclosure must establish that the public interest in the administration of justice in the case 'tips the scales decisively in his favour'.[180] In some cases it will be obvious from the description of the documents and the nature of the litigation that the claim to immunity is either

---

[174] [1942] AC 624, HL.

[175] [1973] AC 388, HL.

[176] Per Wood J in *Evans v Chief Constable of Surrey* [1989] 2 All ER 594, QBD at 597–8, citing Lord Scarman in *Burmah Oil Co Ltd v Bank of England* [1980] AC 1090 at 1141 and Lord Edmund-Davies in *Air Canada v Secretary of State for Trade (No 2)* [1983] 2 AC 394 at 441.

[177] See *Evans v Chief Constable of Surrey* [1989] 2 All ER 594, a decision under the Rules of Supreme Court, now replaced by the CPR.

[178] See Ch 2, 43, under **Exclusionary discretion.**

[179] See per Lord Woolf in *R v Chief Constable of the West Midlands Police, ex p Wiley* [1994] 3 All ER 420, HL at 430 and per Sir Thomas Bingham MR in *Taylor v Anderton* [1995] 2 All ER 420, CA at 432–5, all decisions under the Rules of Supreme Court.

[180] Per Lord Edmund-Davies in *Burmah Oil Co Ltd v Bank of England* [1980] AC 1090 at 1127, citing Lord Cross in *Alfred Crompton Amusement Machines Ltd v Customs and Excise Comrs (No 2)* [1974] AC 405 at 434.

groundless or unanswerable. In other cases a more detailed assessment of the content of the documents is needed. In *Conway v Rimmer*[181] Lord Reid said:

> If [the judge] decides that on balance the documents probably ought to be produced, I think that it would generally be best that he should see them before ordering production and if he thinks that the Minister's reasons are not clearly expressed he will have to see the documents before ordering inspection.

Various objections to judicial inspection have been put forward. In *Duncan v Cammell Laird & Co Ltd*[182] the House of Lords regarded it as a wrongful communication between the judge and one party to the exclusion of the other. This reasoning was firmly rejected in *Conway v Rimmer*, but it remains true that a party may be aggrieved that the judge has seen material to which he has been denied access.[183] Other practical considerations were put forward by Lord Wilberforce in *Burmah Oil Co v Bank of England*,[184] namely (i) that judges should not lightly undertake to question a responsible minister's assessment of the weight of the public interest in non-disclosure; and (ii) that inspection can be a very time-consuming activity which has to be conducted without the assistance of fully informed argument. Such considerations led Lord Wilberforce to uphold the claim to immunity without inspecting the documents. However, the other members of the House of Lords held that inspection was justified once it was shown that it was likely that the documents would contain material substantially useful to the party seeking discovery. On the facts, this test was satisfied, but after inspection disclosure was refused because it was not found to be 'necessary either for disposing fairly of the cause or matter or for saving costs'.

In *Air Canada v Secretary of State for Trade*[185] it was accepted that the ministerial documents probably did contain material which was relevant to the issues in the case, but without inspection it was impossible to know which side that material would favour. Lord Fraser was of the opinion that a court should not embark upon a private inspection of documents unless persuaded that such an inspection is likely to satisfy it that it ought to take the further step of ordering the documents to be produced publicly. On this basis, Lord Fraser, together with Lords Wilberforce and Edmund-Davies, held that the court should only inspect if the party seeking disclosure has shown 'that the documents are very likely to contain material which would give substantial support to his contention on an issue which arises in the case and that, without them, he might be deprived of the means of . . . proper presentation of his case'.[186] In the words of Lord Wilberforce,[187] there must be 'some concrete ground for belief which takes the case beyond a mere "fishing expedition" '. The judge should only inspect where he has definite grounds for expecting to find material of real importance to the party seeking disclosure; he is not entitled to 'take a peep' on the off-chance of finding something useful, for his function is to see fair play between the parties and he has neither power nor duty to go beyond that to ascertain the truth independently for himself. The reasoning of the majority was based partly on the ordinary principles of discovery and partly on the adversar-

---

[181] [1968] AC 910 at 953.
[182] [1942] AC 624 per Viscount Simon LC at 640–1.
[183] Per Lord Denning MR in *Neilson v Laugharne* [1981] QB 736 at 748–9.
[184] [1980] AC 1090 at 1117.
[185] [1983] 2 AC 394.
[186] Per Lord Edmund-Davies at 435.
[187] At 439.

ial nature of the English trial system. Lords Templeman and Scarman argued that discovery is an exception to the adversarial principle; its function is not only to supply evidence to the other side but also to give some indication of the strength of one's own hand and thus to encourage settlement and save costs. They therefore disputed the need for the party seeking disclosure to show that the material would support his case, and held that the court should inspect documents if they are very likely to be necessary for the just determination of the issues in the case or, in other words, if their disclosure may materially assist *any* of the parties to the proceedings. However, they agreed that the documents should be withheld without inspection because it had not been shown that the documents were likely to contain sufficiently relevant material which was not already available from other sources. Where a prima facie claim to public interest immunity is properly made out, the court is no doubt justified in refusing even to inspect unless a case in favour of disclosure has been made out, in order to prevent litigants from embarking on 'fishing expeditions'. However, it is submitted that the reasoning of Lords Templeman and Scarman adequately achieves this end. Their reasoning appears to have prevailed: ordinarily the modern practice, in a case in which a party satisfies the general threshold test for disclosure but his opponent makes out a prima facie claim to immunity, is for the court to proceed to inspect in order to undertake the balancing exercise.[188] However, it seems that if there is a ministerial certificate demonstrating an actual or potential risk to national security, the court should not exercise its right to inspect.[189]

In order to ensure, as far as possible, that a claim to public interest immunity is not wrongly overridden, Lord Reid in *Conway v Rimmer*[190] said that the party objecting to disclosure should always be able to appeal against the judge's ruling before the documents are produced. The importance of this possibility of appeal, even before the judge inspects the documents, was emphasized in *Burmah Oil Co Ltd v Bank of England*.[191] In *Air Canada v Secretary of State for Trade*[192] Bingham J, the trial judge, was provisionally inclined to order production of the documents but decided to inspect them first. He therefore ordered inspection, but stayed the order pending an appeal.[193]

Partial disclosure

Proper objections to disclosure may sometimes be overcome by allowing names and sensitive or irrelevant material to be covered up. This course has been sanctioned in relation to material protected by public interest immunity[194] as well as material protected on the grounds of confidentiality alone.[195] In *Science Research Council v Nassé* Lord Edmund-Davies seems to have approved Lord Denning's suggestion in the Court of Appeal that disclosure can be limited to the other side's lawyers.[196]

---

[188] See, eg, *Goodridge v Chief Constable of Hampshire Constabulary* [1999] 1 All ER 896, QBD.

[189] See *Balfour v Foreign and Commonwealth Office* [1994] 2 All ER 588, CA, above.

[190] [1968] AC 910 at 953.

[191] [1980] AC 1090 at 1136 per Lord Keith and at 1147 per Lord Scarman.

[192] [1983] 2 AC 394.

[193] The approach to inspection laid down in *Air Canada v Secretary of State for Trade* is inappropriate in criminal proceedings. See generally above at 562, under **The development of the modern law, Criminal cases**. See also per Phillips J in *R v Clowes* [1992] 3 All ER 440 at 455, CCA and per Mann LJ in *R v Governor of Brixton Prison, ex p Osman* [1992] 1 All ER 108, QBD at 117.

[194] See, eg, per Lord Pearce in *Conway v Rimmer* [1968] AC 910 at 988.

[195] *Science Research Council v Nassé* [1980] AC 1028, above.

[196] [1980] AC 1028, HL at 1077, citing [1979] QB 144 at 173.

In *R v Chief Constable of the West Midlands Police, ex p Wiley*[197] Lord Woolf was of the opinion that in general public interest immunity is provided against disclosure of documents or their contents and is not, in the absence of exceptional circumstances, an immunity against the use of knowledge obtained from the documents. If the legal advisers of a party in possession of material which is the subject of immunity from disclosure are aware of the contents of that material, they should consider it their duty to assist the court and the other party to mitigate any disadvantage resulting from the non-disclosure. Thus it may be possible to provide any necessary information without producing the actual document or it may be possible to disclose a part of the document or to disclose on a restricted basis. In many cases cooperation between the legal advisers of the parties should avoid the risk of injustice.

ADDITIONAL READING

Mirfield, 'Regulation of Investigatory Powers Act 2000 (2): Evidential Aspects' [2001] *Crim LR* 91.

[197] [1994] 3 All ER 420 at 447, HL.

Privilege

20

Key Issues

- What is the justification for the rule that no-one should be compelled to answer any question if the answer to it would have a tendency to expose him to a criminal charge ('the privilege against self-incrimination')?

- In what circumstances should the privilege be abrogated by statute?

- What is the justification for legal professional privilege, ie the rules that a client should be able to maintain the confidentiality of (a) communications between him and his lawyer made for the purposes of obtaining and giving legal advice ('legal advice privilege'); and (b) communications between him or his lawyer and third parties, such as potential witnesses, the dominant purpose of which was preparation for contemplated or pending litigation ('litigation privilege')?

- What exceptions should there be to legal professional privilege?

- If material is protected by legal professional privilege, for how long should the protection last?

- If someone other than the client, lawyer, or relevant third party obtains material protected by legal professional privilege, may she be compelled to produce it or give evidence about it?

- What is the justification for the rule that a party to civil proceedings should not be compelled to answer questions about what was said in the course of negotiations held with the other party to the proceedings and designed to settle their dispute ('without prejudice negotiations')?

In the previous chapter, we considered how evidence may be excluded when the public interest in permitting all relevant evidence to be presented at trial is outweighed by some other public interest extrinsic to the trial process, such as the proper functioning of government agencies. The same theme underlies the subject matter of the present chapter which concerns several well-established principles whereby relevant evidence is excluded not because it is unreliable or irrelevant to the facts in issue, but because of extrinsic considerations which are held to outweigh the value that the evidence would have at trial. Three types of privilege fall to be considered: (i) the privilege against self-incrimination; (ii) legal professional privilege (protecting the confidentiality of the lawyer–client relationship); and (iii) 'without prejudice' negotiations (enabling settlement negotiations to be conducted without fear of proposed concessions being used in evidence at trial as admissions). These heads of privilege entitle certain people, whether parties to litigation or witnesses, to refuse to disclose material relating to particular matters, and in some cases to prevent others, such as their lawyers, from doing so. Questions of privilege arise most frequently in connection with oral or documentary evidence to be given at trial, whether criminal or civil, and documents to be produced by a party for inspection at the disclosure stage of civil litigation.[1]

There are important differences between privilege and public interest immunity. First, where a person satisfies the conditions for claiming privilege, he is entitled to refuse to answer the question or disclose the document in issue—there is no question of the judge balancing the particular weight of the claim to privilege against the value of the evidence at trial. Secondly, the heads of privilege are upheld for the benefit of clearly identified people. If those people choose to waive their privilege, or fail to claim it, nobody else can claim it. If a judge improperly rejects a non-party witness's claim to privilege, there can be no appeal for there has been no infringement of either party's rights.[2] If, however, the judge wrongly rejects a party's claim to privilege, for example by requiring disclosure of privileged documents on discovery or by compelling a party who is giving evidence to answer questions as to privileged matters, then that party can appeal since he will have suffered a wrong. Similarly, if a judge improperly accepts a claim to privilege, whether made by a party or non-party witness, then the party who would otherwise have been entitled to call for the documents or tender the evidence will have suffered a wrong on the basis of which he ought to be able to appeal. A third difference from public interest immunity concerns secondary evidence. A successful claim to privilege prevents certain people from being compelled to give evidence of particular matters, but there will be no objection to those matters being proved by other evidence, if available. However, if a claim to public interest immunity succeeds, it will not be possible to prove the excluded facts by any other means.

Privilege also falls to be distinguished from the rules relating to competence and compellability. Privilege only entitles witnesses to refuse to give evidence on particular matters. A witness who is competent but not compellable can choose whether to give evidence at all.[3]

---

[1] Privilege is often relevant at other stages of litigation, eg, in relation to: (i) the special procedures established in *Norwich Pharmacal Co v Customs and Excise Comrs* [1974] AC 133 and ss 33 and 34 of the Supreme Court Act 1981, whereby a non-party or intended party can sometimes be compelled to produce documents for information for use in civil litigation; (ii) the execution of a search order (formerly known as an Anton Piller order), under which the person to whom it is addressed is required to allow an intending claimant to search premises and remove material which may be relevant in subsequent civil litigation; and (iii) requests or orders for further information under PD 18 and CPR r 18.1.

[2] See, eg, in relation to the privilege against self-incrimination, *R v Kinglake* (1870) 22 LT 335.

[3] See Ch 5.

Having chosen to give evidence, such a witness, like a compellable witness, must answer all questions properly put to him (and is liable to be committed for contempt if he refuses) except those in respect of which he is entitled to claim privilege.

The drawing of inferences adverse to a witness or party claiming privilege is not permitted.[4]

The privilege against self-incrimination

The privilege against self-incrimination is deep-rooted in English law and history. It became a part of the common law after the abolition of the Court of Star Chamber,[5] and it is based on a traditional reluctance to compel anyone, on pain of punishment, to give incriminating evidence against himself. Today, the privilege is at a crossroads. Although it is theoretically intact, Parliament and the courts have recognized the unsatisfactory results of the privilege. Parliament has, in prescribed circumstances, abrogated or modified it. The courts, doubtless frustrated by the piecemeal, inconsistent, and somewhat illogical nature of parliamentary reform, have started to substitute a different protection, thereby rendering invocation of the privilege in some civil proceedings superfluous. It is to be hoped that Parliament will give urgent attention to the major problem so powerfully presented by Lord Templeman in *AT & T Istel v Tully*:[6]

> the privilege can only be justified on two grounds, first that it discourages the ill-treatment of a suspect and secondly that it discourages the production of dubious confessions. Neither of these considerations applies to the present appeal. It is difficult to see any reason why in civil proceedings the privilege . . . should be exercisable so as to enable a litigant to refuse relevant and even vital documents which are in his possession or power and which speak for themselves. And it is fanciful to suggest that an order on [the first defendant] to say whether he has received [the second plaintiff's] money and if so what has happened to that money could result in his ill-treatment or in a dubious confession. I regard the privilege . . . exercisable in civil proceedings as an archaic and unjustifiable survival from the past when the court directs the production of relevant documents and requires the defendant to specify his dealings with the plaintiff's property or money.[7]

The classic formulation of this privilege is that of Goddard LJ in *Blunt v Park Lane Hotel*:[8]

> The rule is that no-one is bound to answer any question if the answer thereto would, in the opinion of the judge, have a tendency to expose [him] to any criminal charge, penalty or forfeiture which the judge regards as reasonably likely to be preferred or sued for.

This rule applies in both civil and criminal proceedings, although in civil proceedings a witness can no longer refuse to answer on the ground that to do so would tend to expose him to forfeiture,[9] and in criminal proceedings the position of an accused who elects to testify, is

[4] *Wentworth v Lloyd* (1864) 10 HL Cas 589.
[5] *Holdsworth's History of English Law* vol 9 (London, 1944) 200.
[6] [1992] 3 All ER 523 at 530. Lords Griffiths and Ackner agreed with this view.
[7] For an examination of the historical and theoretical basis of the privilege, see MacCulloch, 'The privilege against self-incrimination in competition investigations: theoretical foundations and practical implications' *Legal Studies*, Vol 26, No 2, June 2006 at 211–22.
[8] [1942] 2 KB 253 at 257, CA.
[9] Civil Evidence Act 1968, s 16(1)(a).

governed by section 1(2) of the Criminal Evidence Act 1898, which provides that: 'A person charged in criminal proceedings who is called as a witness in the proceedings may be asked any question in cross-examination notwithstanding that it would tend to criminate him as to any offence with which he is charged in the proceedings.' Thus section 1(2) of the 1898 Act removes from the accused who testifies the privilege against self-incrimination in respect of the offence or offences charged. In *Jones v DPP*[10] a majority of the House of Lords was of the opinion that section 1(2) permits only such questions as tend directly to criminate the accused as to the offence charged and does not permit questions which tend to do so indirectly, such as questions concerning the misconduct of the accused on other occasions in respect of which evidence is admissible at common law.[11]

The privilege against self-incrimination enables a witness to refuse to answer questions in court and also to refuse to produce documents or things. As to pre-trial proceedings, the privilege may arise only if the claimant seeks to compel disclosure and the production of a document, or to compel an answer to a request for further information in order to assist his case: the privilege does not enable a party to refuse to enter a defence to a civil claim, because there is no *compulsion* to file a defence or to plead anything which provides information to the claimant.[12]

The privilege also applies to search orders,[13] covering not only the parts of the order which require the defendant to produce and verify information and documents, but also the parts requiring him to permit the plaintiff to enter, search, and seize documents,[14] and to disclosure ancillary to a freezing injunction, if production of the documents or information sought would tend to expose the defendant to a prosecution in the United Kingdom.[15] It does not follow, however, that a search order which would expose a defendant to a real risk of criminal prosecution can never be made or executed. Such an order may properly be made if it contains a proviso to the effect that (i) the defendant should be advised of his right to obtain immediate legal advice before execution of the order, including advice that he may be entitled to claim the privilege against self-incrimination; and (ii) the order will have effect only in so far as the defendant does not claim the privilege. If such advice is given in everyday language and the defendant properly understands it but declines to claim the privilege, the order may then be executed.[16]

At common law, there is no exception to the privilege preventing an agent, trustee or other fiduciary from claiming the privilege, as against a principal, in an action brought against him

[10] [1962] AC 635, HL.

[11] Cf *R v Anderson* [1988] 2 All ER 549, in which the Court of Appeal was inclined to think that questioning about the fact that the accused was 'wanted' by the police, which tended to destroy her innocent explanations of prima facie damning circumstances, might have been permissible under s 1(2).

[12] *Versailles Trade Finance Ltd v Clough* [2001] All ER (D) 209, (2001) The Times, 1 Nov, CA.

[13] *Rank Film Distributors Ltd v Video Information Centre* [1982] AC 380, HL. But see now s 72 of the Supreme Court Act 1981, below.

[14] *Tate Access Floors Inc v Boswell* [1990] 3 All ER 303, Ch D.

[15] *Sociedade Nacional de Combustiveis de Angola UEE v Lundqvist* [1990] 3 All ER 283, CA. The privilege is also available in respect of the risk of contempt proceedings either in the action in which the privilege is invoked or in some other action: *Memory Corpn plc v Sidhu* [2000] 1 All ER 434, Ch D. An alleged contemnor cannot be compelled to answer questions at an interim stage the answers to which might expose him to an application to commit for contempt and cannot be compelled to answer a request for further information as regards such an application: *Great Future International v Sealand Housing Corporation* LTL 20/1/2004, Ch D.

[16] *IBM United Kingdom Ltd v Prima Data International Ltd* [1994] 4 All ER 748, Ch D.

by the principal to recover money or property, or an account of such money or property, for which the agent, trustee or fiduciary is accountable.[17]

'Criminal charge, penalty, or forfeiture'

The term 'criminal charge' is self-explanatory, but under section 14(1)(a) of the Civil Evidence Act 1968, if the claim to privilege is made in civil proceedings, 'the right of a person . . . to refuse to answer any question or produce any document or thing if to do so would tend to expose that person to proceedings for an offence . . . shall apply only as regards criminal offences *under the law of any part of the United Kingdom*'.[18] Although there is no *absolute* privilege against self-incrimination under foreign law, the possibility of self-incrimination, or the incrimination of others, under foreign law is a factor which can be taken into account in deciding whether, and on what terms, a disclosure order should be made.[19] However, the scope for restricting disclosure of otherwise clearly relevant facts on this basis is limited and likely to be confined to cases where disclosure might have serious consequences for persons still resident in the foreign state in question.[20] Concerning a 'penalty', section 14(1)(a) provides that if the claim to privilege is made in civil proceedings, the penalty must be provided for by the law of any part of the United Kingdom. Penalties now arise mainly under statutes such as those relating to the Revenue. It does not matter that liability to the penalty may arise without court proceedings, provided that it can ultimately be enforced in English courts. EEC regulations, incorporated into English law by virtue of the European Communities Act 1972, are a potent source of penalties.[21] It seems that proceedings for civil contempt are proceedings for the 'recovery of a penalty' within section 14(1) in respect of which there is a privilege against self-incrimination.[22] Exposure to forfeiture refers to the risk of forfeiting property, a risk against which the courts now have wide powers to grant relief, hence the obsolescence of this part of the rule.

'A tendency to expose'

In *R v Boyes*[23] a witness was handed a pardon in order to overcome his claim that his answers would expose him to criminal liability. He nonetheless refused to answer on the ground that the pardon would not protect him from the admittedly remote possibility of impeachment for his offence, and he asserted that his bona fide claim to the privilege was conclusive of his right not to answer. The court rejected his claim. While acknowledging that, if it appears that the witness is in danger, he should be allowed great latitude in judging for himself the effect of any particular question, the court held:

---

[17] *Bishopsgate Investment Management Ltd (in provisional liquidation) v Maxwell* [1992] 2 All ER 856, CA and *Tate Access Floors Inc v Boswell* [1990] 3 All ER 303, Ch D.

[18] There is no clear authority on the point in relation to criminal proceedings.

[19] *Arab Monetary Fund v Hashim* [1989] 3 All ER 466, Ch D.

[20] *Arab Monetary Fund v Hashim (No 2)* [1990] 1 All ER 673, Ch D.

[21] See, eg, *Rio Tinto Zinc Corpn v Westinghouse Electric Corpn* [1978] AC 547, HL. 'Additional damages' which may be awarded under statutes for breach of copyright are not a penalty: *Rank Film Distributors Ltd v Video Information Centre* [1982] AC 380, CA at 425; *Overseas Programming Co Ltd v Cinematographische Commerz-Anstalt and Iduna Film GmbH* (1984) The Times, 16 May, QBD.

[22] See *Cobra Golf Ltd v Rata* [1997] 2 All ER 150, Ch D and *Bhimji v Chatwani (No 3)* [1992] 4 All ER 912, Ch D, not following *Garvin v Domus Publishing Ltd* [1989] 2 All ER 344, Ch D. Cf, *Crest Homes plc v Marks* [1987] 2 All ER 1074, HL.

[23] (1861) 1 B&S 311, QB.

To entitle a party called as a witness to the privilege of silence, the court must see, from the circumstances of the case and the nature of the evidence which the witness is called to give, that there is reasonable ground to apprehend danger to the witness from his being called to answer . . . The danger to be apprehended must be real and appreciable with reference to the ordinary operation of law in the ordinary course of things; not a danger of an imaginary and unsubstantial character . . . [24]

It is not sufficient to ascertain that the claim was made on legal advice. The duty of the court is non-delegable and therefore it cannot simply adopt the conclusion of a solicitor advising the witness, whose conclusion may or may not be correct.[25] If necessary, the judge may hear the witness's explanation *in camera*. He must make due allowance for the possibility that apparently innocuous questions may, when combined with other material, give rise to damaging inferences.[26] Moreover, it is sufficient to support a claim that the answers sought might lead to a line of inquiry which would or might form a significant step in the chain of evidence required for a prosecution.[27] On the other hand, a claim to privilege will not succeed if the evidence against the witness is already so strong that if proceedings are to be taken at all they will be taken whether or not the witness answers. This is a question of fact for the judge, who should not ignore the possibility that although some evidence is already available to the authorities, additional evidence from the witness may increase the risk of proceedings being taken.[28] The triviality or staleness of the offence may lead the court to treat the likelihood of prosecution as too remote, but it remains to be seen whether protection can be refused on the sole ground that the charge, though likely to be brought, is a trivial one.[29]

Spouses, civil partners, strangers, and companies

In most cases the witness claiming privilege will do so because he fears prosecution himself. If he chooses not to claim the privilege or, in ignorance, fails to claim it—the judge may, but is not obliged to remind him of his rights—no-one else can claim it on his behalf.

A witness in either civil or criminal proceedings cannot claim privilege in respect of questions the answers to which would tend to incriminate strangers.[30] In civil proceedings, under

---

[24] Per Cockburn CJ at 330, approved in *Den Norske Bank ASA v Antonatos* [1998] 3 All ER 74, CA. Cf *Triplex Safety Glass Co Ltd v Lancegaye Safety Glass (1934) Ltd* [1939] 2 KB 395: privilege may be claimed on the ground of exposure to criminal libel proceedings even though such proceedings are rare.

[25] *R (Crown Prosecution Service) v Bolton Magistrates' Court* [2004] 1 WLR 835, DC.

[26] Per Cockburn CJ in *R v Boyes*, ibid at 330; see also *British Steel Corpn v Granada Television Ltd* [1981] AC 1096, HL, especially per Megarry V-C in the Chancery Division (at 1108).

[27] Per Beldam LJ in *Sociedade Nacional de Combustiveis de Angola UEE v Lundqvist* [1990] 3 All ER 283 at 297, CA, citing Lord Wilberforce in *Rank Film Distributors Ltd v Video Information Centre* [1982] AC 380 at 443.

[28] *Rio Tinto Zinc Corpn v Westinghouse Electric Corpn* [1978] AC 547. In *Khan v Khan* [1982] 2 All ER 60, CA a witness in civil proceedings was required to answer questions about his use of the proceeds of a cheque. His conduct 'reeked of dishonesty' and evidence as to his use of the proceeds did not materially increase the risk of prosecution for theft of the cheque.

[29] See per Lord Fraser in *Rank Film Distributors Ltd v Video Information Centre* [1982] AC 380 at 445: the risk of prosecution for trivial offences under s 21 of the Copyright Act 1956 was not enough to establish the privilege, partly because the likelihood of prosecution was too remote, but also because it would be 'unreasonable to allow the possibility of incrimination of such offences to obstruct disclosure of information which would be of much more value to the owners of the infringed copyright than any protection they might obtain from s 21'.

[30] See *Ex p Reynolds* (1882) 20 Ch D 294 (the privilege can be invoked only by someone who does so in good faith for his own protection (or that of his spouse)), cited by Megarry V-C in *British Steel Corpn v Granada Television Ltd* [1981] AC 1096 at 1106, Ch D.

section 14(1)(b) of the 1968 Act, the right of a person to assert the privilege 'shall include a like right to refuse any question or produce any document or thing if to do so would tend to expose the spouse or civil partner of that person to proceedings for any such criminal offence or for the recovery of any such penalty'. However, the privilege remains that of the witness and, if he chooses to answer, the spouse or civil partner cannot complain. In criminal proceedings, however, it seems that a witness cannot claim privilege in respect of questions the answers to which would tend to incriminate his spouse.[31]

Because the privilege is a privilege against *self*-incrimination, office-holders, employees, or agents of a company may claim the privilege themselves, but cannot refuse to answer questions which would tend to incriminate the company or render it liable to a penalty under, for example, an EEC regulation.[32] Equally, the company cannot refuse to answer questions which would tend to incriminate the office-holders.[33]

Statutory provisions affecting the privilege

Pursuant to a variety of statutes and statutory instruments, specified persons in specified circumstances must answer questions for specified purposes notwithstanding that their answers may incriminate them. Some of the provisions abrogate the privilege expressly; others do so impliedly. However, clear language (express or by necessary implication) is required to show that Parliament intended to abrogate such a fundamental principle of the common law.[34] The true effect of any statutory withdrawal of privilege is also a matter of construction, but where a statute revokes the privilege without restricting the use that may be made of the answers, prima facie the answers may be used for any purpose for which they could have been used had the privilege never applied in the first place.[35] Thus if a witness is forced to make an incriminating admission, that admission cannot then be excluded at his own trial as being involuntary.[36] However, use of the answer in subsequent judicial proceedings may amount to a violation of the Article 6 right to a fair hearing, and in any event a criminal court may exclude the admission, in its discretion, if it would be oppressive to admit it.[37]

In *Saunders v UK*,[38] S was convicted of conspiracy, false accounting, and theft. At the trial, evidence was adduced of answers given by S to DTI inspectors appointed under the Companies Act 1985. Under section 434 of the Act, the inspectors could compel a person to answer their questions and the answers obtained could be used in evidence in any subsequent proceedings. The European Court of Human Rights was of the view that although not specifically mentioned in Article 6, the right to silence and the right not to incriminate oneself are 'generally

---

[31] Per Lord Diplock in *Rio Tinto Zinc Corpn v Westinghouse Electric Corpn* [1978] AC 547 at 637 and, but only by inference, *R v Pitt* [1982] 3 All ER 63, CA. Contrast *R v All Saints, Worcester* (1817) 6 M&S 194.

[32] Per Lord Diplock in *Rio Tinto Zinc Corpn v Westinghouse Electric Corpn* [1978] AC 547 at 637–8.

[33] Per Beldam LJ in *Sociedade Nacional de Combustiveis de Angola UEE v Lundqvist* [1990] 3 All ER 283 at 300–1 and per Browne-Wilkinson V-C in *Tate Access Floors v Boswell* [1990] 3 All ER 303 at 314–15.

[34] *R (Malik) v Crown Court at Manchester* [2008] 4 All ER 403, DC at [73], where it was held that para 6, Sch 5 of the Terrorism Act 2000 does not abrogate the privilege

[35] *R v Scott* (1856) Dears&B 47.

[36] Contrariwise if the judge wrongly denies a witness the protection of privilege. Any admission thus compelled will be excluded in the trial of the witness as involuntary: *R v Garbett* (1847) 1 Den 236.

[37] See per French J in *Overseas Programming Co Ltd v Cinematographische Commerz-Anstalt and Iduna Film Gmbh* (1984) The Times, 16 May, QBD and per Ralph Gibson LJ in *Bank of England v Riley* [1992] 1 All ER 769 at 777, CA.

[38] (1997) 23 EHRR 313 at para 68.

recognized international standards which lie at the heart of the notion of a fair procedure under Article 6' and held that use of the statements at S's trial was in breach of his Article 6 right to fair trial.[39] Section 434 was subsequently amended.[40]

The implied rights within Article 6 are not of an absolute character, but can be qualified or restricted, and a statute which does qualify or restrict those rights will be compatible with Article 6 if there is an identifiable social or economic problem that the statute is intended to deal with and the qualification or restriction is proportionate to that problem. *Brown v Stott*,[41] a Scottish case, concerned the introduction of evidence of an admission obtained from the accused under section 172(2)(a) of the Road Traffic Act 1988, under which, where the driver of a vehicle is alleged to be guilty of one of a number of road traffic offences, including driving with excess alcohol and speeding, 'the person keeping the vehicle shall give such information as to the identity of the driver as he may be required to give by or on behalf of a chief officer of police'. Under section 172(3), if he fails to comply with such a requirement he shall be guilty of an offence punishable by a fine, mandatory endorsement, and discretionary disqualification from driving. It was held that evidence of an admission obtained from the accused under section 172(2)(a) did not infringe the right to a fair hearing. Lord Bingham said:

> The jurisprudence of the European Court very clearly establishes that while the overall fairness of a criminal trial cannot be compromised, the constituent rights comprised, whether expressly or implicitly, within Article 6 are not themselves absolute. Limited qualification of these rights is acceptable if reasonably directed by national authorities towards a clear and proper public objective and if representing no greater qualification than the situation calls for.

There was a clear public interest in the enforcement of road traffic legislation and section 172 was not a disproportionate response to the serious social problem of the high incidence of death and injury on the roads caused by the misuse of motor vehicles. The section permitted a single, simple question to be put, the answer to which cannot by itself incriminate the suspect, and the penalty for non-compliance is moderate and non-custodial. Furthermore, all who own or drive motor cars know that by doing so they subject themselves to a regulatory regime which is imposed because the possession and use of cars are recognized to have the potential to cause grave injury. A virtually identical approach to section 172 has since been taken in *O'Halloran and Francis v UK*.[42]

Subsequent attempts to distinguish *Brown v Stott* on the grounds that, under Scottish law, the driver's admission must be corroborated, have failed; and it was applied in *Mawdesley v Chief Constable of the Cheshire Constabulary*,[43] a case of driving in excess of the speed limit. The reasoning of the Privy Council in *Brown v Stott* falls to be compared with that of the European Court of Human Rights in *Heaney and McGuinness v* Ireland[44] H and M were arrested

---

[39] One of the frequently cited decisions of the European Court is *Funke v France* (1993) 60 EHRR 297, but its ratio is far from clear: see the comments of Lord Hoffmann in *R v Hertfordshire County Council, ex p Green Environmental Industries Ltd* [2000] 2 AC 412, HL at 424.

[40] See below.

[41] [2001] 2 WLR 817, PC.

[42] [2007] Crim LR 897, ECHR. The principles and outcome were the same in *Lückhof and Spanner v Austria* (2008) Application Nos 58452/00 and 61920/00, where the penalties for non-compliance were fines and also, in default, imprisonment.

[43] [2004] 1 WLR 1035, QBD.

[44] [2001] Crim LR 481, ECtHR.

on suspicion of involvement in a terrorist bombing. They were required to account for their movements under section 52 of the Offences Against the State Act 1939, which makes it a criminal offence, punishable by six months' imprisonment, for a person detained on suspicion of a defined terrorist offence to fail to account for his movements. They refused to do so and were prosecuted under section 52. They were also charged with membership of the IRA under section 21 of the Act. They were convicted of the charge under section 52, but acquitted of the charge under section 21. The European Court of Human Rights found a violation of Article 6 on the basis that the degree of compulsion created by the threat of a prison sentence under section 52 'with a view to compelling them to provide information relating to charges against them under that Act', in effect destroyed the very essence of the right to silence and the privilege against self-incrimination. As Aikens J observed in *R v Kearns*[45] the Court attached importance to the fact that the purpose of obtaining information under section 52 was to provide evidence for other charges under section 21 of the 1939 Act. *Brown v Stott* also falls to be compared with *R v K*,[46] which concerned the Family Proceedings Rules 1991, whereby parties to ancillary relief proceedings under the Matrimonial Causes Act 1973 are under a duty to give full and frank disclosure of their financial circumstances and, if deliberately untruthful, may face criminal proceedings for perjury. It was held that the rules were intended to abrogate the privilege against self-incrimination because otherwise the purpose of the legislation would be frustrated. It was further held, however, that to use admissions made in such proceedings in subsequent criminal proceedings for cheating the public revenue would violate Article 6: the protection of the public revenue is an important social objective, but the admission of evidence obtained under threat of imprisonment is not a reasonable and proportionate response to that social need.

In *R v Allen (No 2)*,[47] A was convicted of cheating the public revenue of tax by concealing or failing to disclose profits. He had provided a schedule of assets, in compliance with a notice given by the inspector under section 20 of the Taxes Management Act 1970, but had omitted to list his beneficial interest in shares issued by offshore companies. Under section 98(1) of the Act, a person who fails to comply with a section 20 notice is liable to a penalty. The House of Lords held that the section 20 notice could not constitute a violation of the right against self-incrimination, denying the right to a fair trial, because the state, for the purpose of collecting tax, is entitled to require a citizen to inform it of his income and to enforce penalties for failure to do so. A's further application to the European Court of Human Rights failed. It was held that the requirement to declare assets disclosed no issue under Article 6(1), even though there was a penalty for failure to comply. The case was one of making a false declaration of assets, not one of forced self-incrimination in relation to some previously committed offence, nor one of being prosecuted for failing to provide information which might incriminate him in pending or anticipated criminal proceedings.[48]

An important distinction is to be drawn between statements made by the accused under compulsion, which, depending on the circumstances, may involve infringement of the right to silence or the right not to incriminate oneself, and the compulsory production of pre-existing

---

[45] [2003] 1 Cr App R 111, CA at [41].
[46] [2009] EWCA Crim 1640.
[47] [2001] 4 All ER 768, HL.
[48] *Allen v UK* [2003] Crim LR 280. Cf *JB v Switzerland* [2001] Crim LR 748 ECtHR.

documents and materials, which involves no infringement of those rights. According to the majority of the European Court in *Saunders v UK*:[49]

> The right not to incriminate oneself is primarily concerned . . . with respecting the will of an accused person to remain silent. As commonly understood in the legal systems of the Contracting Parties to the Convention and elsewhere, it does not extend to the use in criminal proceedings of material which may be obtained from the accused through compulsory powers but which have an existence independent of the will of the suspect, such as, inter alia, documents acquired pursuant to a warrant, breath, blood and urine samples and bodily tissue for the purposes of DNA testing.[50]

This dictum was applied in *Attorney General's Reference (No 7 of 2000)*[51] where the accused, a bankrupt, completed a preliminary questionnaire and admitted having lost money by gambling. He was then required to produce documents to the Official Receiver under the Insolvency Act 1986, and if he had failed to do so he would have been in contempt of court. He was charged with the offence of materially contributing to or increasing the extent of his insolvency by gambling and the documents which he had produced formed the basis of the prosecution case against him. The Court of Appeal held that use of the documents relating to his gambling would not violate his rights under Article 6. The court adopted the reasoning of Justice La Forest in *Thompson Newspapers Ltd v Director of Investigation & Research*[52] that, whereas a compelled statement is evidence that would not have existed independently of exercise of the power of compulsion, evidence which exists independently of the compelled statement could have been found by other means and its quality does not depend on its past connection with the compelled statement. The principle was also applied in *R v Hundal*,[53] on charges of belonging to a proscribed organization, in relation to items seized following a search under the Terrorism Act 2000.

C plc v P[54] concerned intellectual property proceedings in which indecent images of children were found on a computer which was the subject of a search order. The Court of Appeal held that the offending material was not privileged from disclosure to the police. A majority of the court regarded itself as bound by *Attorney General's Reference (No 7 of 2000)* to reach this conclusion, on the basis that if, in that case, the privilege did not extend to documents which were independent evidence, the same must apply to things which existed independently of a search order. The case was thought to be no different from one in which counterfeit bags of a particular brand, being the subject of a search order, are found to contain drugs or an illegal weapon.[55] However, according to *R (Malik) v Crown Court at Manchester*,[56] until the House of Lords has determined the appeal in *C plc v P*, judges, when exercising discretion in respect of the admissibility of pre-existing documents, should treat the privilege as an important relevant

---

[49] (1997) 23 EHRR 313 at para 69.

[50] However, there are exceptions to the exception, as when the evidence is obtained by forced medical intervention constituting inhuman or degrading treatment involving a high degree of force in defiance of the will of the accused: *Jalloh v Germany* [2007] Crim LR 717, ECHR. See also *Gäfgen v Germany*, Application No 22978/05, 30 June 2008, ECHR, considered in Ch 3.

[51] [2001] 2 Cr App R 286, CA.

[52] (1990) 54 CCC 417 (Supreme Court of Canada).

[53] [2004] 2 Cr App R 307, CA.

[54] [2007] 3 All ER 1034, CA.

[55] See also *R v S* [2009] 1 All ER 716, CA (a key to data in encrypted files).

[56] [2008] 4 All ER 403, DC.

THE PRIVILEGE AGAINST SELF-INCRIMINATION

factor to be taken into account, along with other factors, including the degree of benefit of the material to the investigation, the risk of prosecution, and the gravity of the offence.

A further important distinction has been drawn between the production of information for extra-judicial purposes rather than for use in judicial proceedings. In *R v Kearns*[57] Aikens J, after reviewing the Strasbourg and UK cases, said:

> A law will not be likely to infringe the right to silence or not to incriminate oneself if it demands the production of information for an administrative purpose or in the course of an extra-judicial enquiry. However if the information so produced is or could be used in subsequent judicial proceedings, whether criminal or civil, then the use of the information in such proceedings could breach those rights and so make that trial unfair.

Thus in *Saunders v UK* it was the fact that the information obtained had been used at the subsequent criminal trial that made that trial unfair, not the fact that the information had been obtained in the first place.[58] In *R v Hertfordshire County Council, ex p Green Environmental Industries Ltd*[59] a summons was issued against the company, the local authority having served a notice under section 71 of the Environmental Protection Act 1990 requesting certain information and the company having refused to provide that information. It was held that the section 71 notice did not constitute any form of adjudication and therefore Article 6 was not infringed by its service. In *R v Kearns*, K, a bankrupt was charged with an offence contrary to section 354(3) of the Insolvency Act 1986 of failing without reasonable excuse to account for the loss of part of his property, having been required to do so by the Official Receiver. It was held that section 354 does not breach an accused's right to remain silent or not to incriminate himself and does not contravene the right of a person to have a fair trial under Article 6. First, the demand for information was made in the course of an extra-judicial procedure and not in order to provide evidence to prove a case against K. Secondly, at the time of the demand, there was no other charge against K.[60] Thirdly, there was no possibility that any information obtained could be used in subsequent criminal proceedings. Fourthly, even if section 354 did infringe the 'absolute' right to silence and/or the right not to incriminate oneself, the section 354 regime was a proportionate legislative response to the problem of administering and investigating bankrupt estates.[61]

Typically, statutory provisions do not simply abrogate the privilege against self-incrimination, but also prevent the answers from being used in evidence in any subsequent criminal proceedings in which the person who answered the question is charged with a specified offence. These provisions, individually different, collectively resemble a patchwork quilt to which new additions can always be made. Some important examples are set out below.

Section 98 of the Children Act 1989

Section 98 of the Children Act 1989 provides that in any proceedings in which a court is hearing an application relating to the care, supervision, or protection of a child, no person

---

[57] [2003] 1 Cr App R 111 at [53].

[58] See also *L v UK* [2001] Crim LR 133, ECtHR.

[59] [2000] 2 AC 412, HL.

[60] Cf *Heaney and McGuinness v Ireland* [2001] Crim LR 481, above.

[61] See also *R v Brady* [2004] 3 All ER 520, CA, where it was held that statements obtained on pain of penalty by the Official Receiver under s 235 of the Insolvency Act 1986 could be disclosed to the Inland Revenue for the purpose of investigating possible offences of cheating the public revenue and laying information to obtain search warrants.

shall be excused from giving evidence on any matter or answering any question put to him in the course of his giving evidence on the ground that doing so might incriminate him or his spouse or civil partner of an offence. However, section 98(2) provides that a statement or admission made in such proceedings shall not be admissible in evidence against the person making it or his spouse or civil partner in proceedings for an offence other than perjury.[62] It has been held, in decisions since doubted,[63] that the phrase 'statement or admission made in such proceedings' is to be construed widely to include not only the written and filed statements of the evidence which a party intends to adduce and oral admissions made by a parent to a guardian *ad litem*,[64] but also, at least once the proceedings have begun, oral statements made to social workers charged with carrying out the local authority's duties of investigation.[65] The purpose of section 98 is to protect a witness who is required to give evidence in relation to a child when such evidence would incriminate him or his spouse or civil partner. Thus section 98(2) will not prevent counsel for the accused from putting a 'statement or admission' to his spouse as a previous inconsistent statement in order to challenge her evidence or to attack her credibility.[66]

Section 2 of the Criminal Justice Act 1987

Under section 2 of the Criminal Justice Act 1987, the Director of the Serious Fraud Office may require any person under investigation for a suspected offence involving serious or complex fraud, or any other person, to answer questions, furnish information, and produce documents, but under section 2(8) a statement in response to such a requirement may only be used in evidence against its maker (a) on a prosecution for an offence of knowingly or recklessly making a false or misleading statement (in purported compliance with a requirement under section 2); or (b) on a prosecution for some other offence where in giving evidence he makes a statement inconsistent with it. However, under section 2(8AA), the statement may not be used against its maker by virtue of (b) unless evidence relating to it is adduced or a question relating to it is asked, by him or on his behalf, in the proceedings arising out of the prosecution.

Section 434 of the Companies Act 1985

Under Part XIV of the Companies Act 1985, officers and agents of a company and others possessing relevant information are obliged to answer questions put by Board of Trade inspectors appointed to investigate suspected fraud in the conduct or management of a company. However, under section 434(5A) and (5B) of the Act, in criminal proceedings in which the person who answered such a question is charged with an offence, other than an offence under section 2 or section 5 of the Perjury Act 1911 (false statements made on oath otherwise than in judicial proceedings or made otherwise than on oath), (a) no evidence relating to the answer may be adduced; and (b) no question relating to it may be asked, by or on behalf of the prosecution, unless evidence relating to it is adduced or a question relating to it is asked in the proceedings by or on behalf of the person charged.

---

[62] However, a family court may direct disclosure of such material to the police for the purposes of a criminal investigation: *In re C (a minor) (Care proceedings: disclosure)* [1997] 2 WLR 322, CA.

[63] Per Butler-Sloss LJ and Sir Roger Parker in *Re G (a minor)* [1996] 2 All ER 65, CA.

[64] See *Oxfordshire County Council v P* [1995] 2 All ER 225, Fam Div.

[65] See *Cleveland County Council v F* [1995] 2 All ER 236, Fam Div.

[66] See *Re K (minors)* [1994] 3 All ER 230, Fam Div.

Section 31(1) of the Theft Act 1968

Section 31(1) of the Theft Act 1968 requires questions to be answered and orders to be complied with 'in proceedings for the recovery or administration of any property, for the execution of any trust or for an account of any property or dealings with property' notwithstanding that compliance may expose the witness or his spouse or civil partner to a charge for an offence under the Theft Act. The section goes on to provide that the answers may not be used in proceedings for any such offence.[67] However, neither the revocation of the privilege nor the restriction on the use of the answers applies to any other offences, a limitation which prompted Sir Nicolas Browne-Wilkinson V-C to express the hope that Parliament would urgently extend section 31 so as to remove the privilege in relation to all civil claims relating to property, including claims for damages, but on terms that the statements made in documents disclosed should not be admissible in *any* criminal proceedings.[68]

In cases where there is a claim to privilege in respect of both a Theft Act offence and a non-Theft Act offence, the test, in each case, is whether to answer the question would create or increase the risk of proceedings for that offence. If the test is satisfied in the case of the Theft Act offence, section 31 will apply and prima facie the question must be answered. For the non-Theft Act offence, the test is whether to answer would create or increase the risk of proceedings for that offence, separate and distinct from its connection with the Theft Act offence. If the answer is in the negative, there is no privilege; but if in the affirmative, the privilege will subsist.[69]

Section 13 of the Fraud Act 2006

Section 13 of the Fraud Act 2006, modelled on section 31(1) of the Theft Act 1968, requires questions to be answered and orders to be complied with in 'proceedings relating to property', ie proceedings for the recovery or administration of any property etc, notwithstanding that compliance may result in incrimination of an offence under the 2006 Act or a 'related offence', but prevents the answers from being used in evidence in proceedings for any such offence. 'Related offence' means conspiracy to defraud or 'any other offence involving any other form of fraudulent conduct or purpose'. In *Kensington International Ltd v Republic of Congo*[70] the Court of Appeal was reluctant to construe section 13 narrowly. First, it was held that 'proceedings relating to property' covers *Norwich Pharmacal* proceedings[71] brought to compel disclosure in aid of pending substantive proceedings relating to property, because the proceedings should be viewed as a whole so as to include the substantive proceedings. Second, it was held that 'any other offence involving any other form of fraudulent conduct or purpose' includes offences of offering or giving a bribe notwithstanding that they do not require proof of dishonesty.

Section 72 of the Supreme Court Act 1981

The decision in *Rank Film Distributors Ltd v Video Information Centre*[72] that the privilege against self-incrimination applied to Anton Piller orders, now known as search orders, seriously

---

[67] See also s 9 of the Criminal Damage Act 1971.

[68] *Sociedade Nacional de Combustiveis de Angola UEE v Lundqvist* [1990] 3 All ER 283 at 302–3.

[69] See *Renworth Ltd v Stephansen* [1996] 3 All ER 244 per Morritt LJ at 254, CA; but see also *Khan v Khan* [1982] 2 All ER 60, CA.

[70] [2007] EWCA Civ 1128.

[71] *Norwich Pharmacal Co v Commissioners of Customs & Excise* [1974] AC 133, HL.

[72] [1982] AC 380, HL.

undermined the effectiveness of that remedy, particularly in relation to breach of copyright, which often involves offences of fraud. Accordingly, the decision was rapidly reversed for the purposes of proceedings concerning intellectual property and passing off by section 72 of the Supreme Court Act 1981, the effect of which may be summarized as follows.[73] In proceedings brought to prevent any apprehended infringement of rights pertaining to any intellectual property (ie patent, trade mark, copyright, registered design, technical or commercial information, or other intellectual property)[74] or any apprehended passing off, questions must be answered and orders complied with even though the person complying may thereby expose himself or his spouse or civil partner to proceedings for a related offence or for the recovery of a related penalty. In proceedings for an infringement (or for passing off) which, it is alleged, has already occurred, or proceedings to obtain disclosure of information relating to such an infringement (or passing off), the privilege is withdrawn only in relation to (i) any offence committed by or in the course of the infringement (or passing off); (ii) offences of dishonesty or fraud committed in connection with the infringement (or passing off); and (iii) penalties incurred in connection with the infringement (or passing off). By section 72(3), answers compelled by reason of the withdrawal of privilege cannot be used in proceedings for the offence disclosed or for the recovery of any penalty liability to which was disclosed. Section 72 affects only proceedings for infringement of intellectual property rights and passing off: the decision in *Rank Film Distributors Ltd v Video Information Centre* still applies to the use of search orders for other purposes.

Substituted protection

Re O[75] concerned a disclosure order, requiring the accused to disclose their assets and income, made in aid of a restraint order under section 77 of the Criminal Justice Act 1988, prohibiting them from dealing with any realizable property. The accused faced not only charges under the Theft Act 1968, in respect of which section 31 of the 1968 Act provided protection, but also conspiracy charges, in respect of which section 31 provided no protection. It was held that since the accused could invoke the privilege against self-incrimination, which would frustrate the purpose of the disclosure order, all such orders should be made subject to a condition 'that no disclosure made in compliance with this order shall be used as evidence in the prosecution of an offence alleged to have been committed by the person required to make that disclosure or by any spouse of that person'. The CPS was a party to the proceedings and consented to the order. In *R v Martin and White*[76] it was held that although an affidavit sworn by a person in compliance with such an order cannot become admissible in evidence against him in any subsequent criminal trial, either in the course of the prosecution case or in cross-examination, subject to proper directions from the judge it may be used to demonstrate his inconsistency and thus to impugn his credit.

The decision in *Re O* was approved by the House of Lords in *AT & T Istel Ltd v Tully*.[77] A claim was made for damages and repayment of money obtained by fraud. A major police investigation was launched. The plaintiffs were granted a wide-ranging order for Mareva injunctions and

---

[73] The terms of the section are complex and should be referred to for detail. See also *Universal City Studios v Hubbard* [1984] Ch 225, CA.

[74] Section 72(5).

[75] [1991] 1 All ER 330, CA.

[76] [1998] 2 Cr App R 385, CA.

[77] [1992] 3 All ER 523. See also, applying *Re O*, *Re Thomas* [1992] 4 All ER 814, CA.

disclosure, requiring the defendants to disclose all dealings regarding the money. Paragraph 33 of the order contained a condition identical to that contained in the disclosure order in *Re O*. The order was subsequently varied and the plaintiffs appealed against the variation. Before the appeal, the CPS informed the plaintiffs that it did not seek to intervene in the civil proceedings, that it already had a large amount of potential evidence, and that it would not be prevented by paragraph 33 from using that material or any other material obtained independently of the civil proceedings. The House of Lords restored the original order. Noting that the proceedings were not covered by any of the statutory modifications of the privilege, but were similar to situations in which Parliament had intervened, the House could see no reason why the defendants should blatantly exploit the privilege to deprive the plaintiffs of their civil rights and remedies. The courts were entitled to substitute a different protection in place of the privilege, provided it was adequate. The protection would be adequate if the CPS unequivocally agreed not to make use, directly or indirectly, of the material divulged in compliance with the order. Accordingly, a majority of the House held that, given the terms of para 33 and the clear indication by the CPS that it did not seek to use any of the material to be divulged in compliance with the order, the original order should stand.

On the reasoning of the House, the principle of substituted protection is capable of application in many situations other than those which arose in *Re O* and *AT & T Istel v Tully*. However, those who, in the future, seek to confine the principle, will doubtless rely on the views of Lord Lowry, who emphasized that the decision of the House did not represent a breakthrough in relation to the privilege, being a decision on its own facts.[78]

Legal professional privilege

The common law doctrine of legal professional privilege enables a client to maintain the confidentiality of (i) communications between him and his lawyer made for the purpose of obtaining and giving legal advice, the privilege in this case being known as 'legal advice privilege'; (ii) communications between him or his lawyer and third parties (such as potential witnesses and experts) the dominant purpose of which was preparation for contemplated or pending litigation, the privilege in this case being known as 'litigation privilege'; and (iii) items enclosed with or referred to in such communications and brought into existence for the purpose of obtaining legal advice etc.[79]

Section 10 of the Police and Criminal Evidence Act 1984 (the 1984 Act), which is apparently intended to reflect the common law position,[80] provides that:

(1) Subject to subsection (2) below, in this Act 'items subject to legal privilege' means—
   (a) communications between a professional legal adviser and his client or any person representing his client made in connection with the giving of legal advice to the client;
   (b) communications between a professional legal adviser and his client or any person representing his client or between such an adviser or his client or any such representative

---

[78] [1992] 3 All ER 523 at 544.

[79] For an excellent examination of the topic explicitly aimed more to generate questions than to provide answers, see J Auburn, *Legal Professional Privilege: Law and Theory* (Oxford, 2000).

[80] See the majority view of the House of Lords in *Francis & Francis (a firm) v Central Criminal Court* [1988] 3 All ER 775, below, especially per Lord Goff at 797; and *R v R* [1994] 4 All ER 260, CA, below.

and any other person made in connection with or in contemplation of legal proceedings and for the purposes of such proceedings; and

(c) items enclosed with or referred to in such communications and made—

   (i) in connection with the giving of legal advice; or

   (ii) in connection with or in contemplation of legal proceedings and for the purposes of such proceedings, when they are in the possession of a person who is entitled to possession of them.

(2) Items held with the intention of furthering a criminal purpose are not items subject to legal privilege.

For the purposes of legal professional privilege, 'lawyer' includes, as well as solicitors and counsel, employed legal advisers,[81] and overseas lawyers.[82] It is possible that the privilege may also attach to communications between the police and the Director of Public Prosecutions, if they are seeking legal advice in circumstances analogous to a client approaching his solicitor for advice.[83] The privilege survives the death of a client and vests in his personal representative or, once administration is complete, the person entitled to his estate,[84] and those persons are entitled to either claim or waive the privilege.[85]

A parallel privilege applies to communications between a person and his patent agent,[86] trade mark agent,[87] or licensed conveyancer.[88]

The rationale of the rules of legal professional privilege is that they encourage those who know the facts to state them fully and candidly without fear of compulsory disclosure.[89] In *R v Derby Magistrates' Court, ex p B*[90] Lord Taylor CJ said:

> The principle . . . is that a man must be able to consult his lawyer in confidence, since otherwise he might hold back half the truth. The client must be sure that what he tells his lawyer in confidence will never be revealed without his consent. Legal professional privilege is thus much more than an ordinary rule of evidence. . . . It is a fundamental condition on which the administration of justice as a whole rests . . .

In relation to litigation privilege, it is this confidentiality which enables lawyers to encourage strong cases and discourage weak ones, which is in the interests of the state.[91] However, in the absence of contemplated litigation, it is questionable whether there is any temptation for the client to be less than candid or 'to hold back half the truth',[92] and even if this is a real

---

[81] *Alfred Crompton Amusement Machines Ltd v Customs and Excise Comrs (No 2)* [1974] AC 405; *AM & S Europe Ltd v EC Commission* [1983] QB 878, ECJ per Advocate General Sir Gordon Slynn at 914.

[82] *Re Duncan* [1968] P 306. The term 'proceedings' in this context includes proceedings in other jurisdictions: ibid. However, the fact that the advice given relates predominantly to English law is irrelevant: *IBM Corpn v Phoenix International (Computers) Ltd* [1995] 1 All ER 413, Ch D.

[83] Per Moore-Bick J, obiter, in *Goodridge v Chief Constable of Hampshire Constabulary* [1999] 1 All ER 896, QBD at 903.

[84] *Bullivant v A-G for Victoria* [1901] AC 196, HL.

[85] *R v Malloy* [1997] 2 Cr App R 283, CA.

[86] Copyright, Designs and Patents Act 1988, s 280.

[87] Ibid, s 284.

[88] Administration of Justice Act 1985, s 33. See also the Legal Services Act 2007, s 190.

[89] See *Waugh v British Railways Board* [1980] AC 521 at 531–2, HL per Lord Wilberforce, and also at 535–6 per Lord Simon. As to the court's respect for other confidential relationships, see Ch 19, 577, under **Confidential relationships**.

[90] [1996] AC 487, HL at 507–8.

[91] See per Bingham LJ in *Ventouris v Mountain* [1991] 1 WLR 607 at 611.

[92] See V Alexander, 'The Corporate Attorney–Client Privilege: A Study of the Participants' (1989) *St John's L Rev* 191.

likelihood, it is equally questionable whether it should override the public interest that wherever possible the courts should reach their decisions on the basis of all relevant evidence. As Lord Phillips MR forcefully observed in *Three Rivers District Council v Governor and Company of the Bank of England (No 5)*:[93]

> The justification for litigation privilege is readily understood. Where, however, litigation is not anticipated it is not easy to see why communications with a solicitor should be privileged. Legal advice privilege attaches to matters such as the conveyance of real property or the drawing up of a will. It is not clear why it should. There would seem little reason to fear that, if privilege were not available in such circumstances, communications between solicitor and client would be inhibited.

The protected material

Communications between lawyer and client—legal advice privilege

A client may, and his lawyer must (subject to the client's waiver) refuse to disclose written or oral communications between them made for the purpose of giving and receiving legal advice about any matter, whether or not litigation was contemplated at the time.[94] This applies whether the client or lawyer is a party to the litigation in which the question arises or a mere witness and it applies as much to the production of documents containing such communications as to oral evidence about them. It seems that receipt by the lawyer of a communication from the client is not necessary for the privilege to apply.[95]

The communication must have been confidential and, if not actually made in the course of a relationship of lawyer and client, must at least have been made with a view to the establishment of that relationship.[96] Provided that the communication was made in a professional capacity for the purposes of giving or receiving legal advice, the whole communication will be privileged, including any parts of it in which the solicitor conveyed to the client information which he had received in a professional capacity from a third party: such information cannot be hived off from the rest of what was said so as to become not privileged.[97] However, documents emanating from, or prepared by, independent third parties and then passed to the lawyer for the purposes of advice are not privileged. In *Three Rivers District Council v Governor and Company of the Bank of England*[98] it was held, after a review of nineteenth-century authority, that legal advice privilege only protects direct communications between the client and the lawyer, and evidence of the content of such communications, and that in the case of a corporate client the privilege will only cover communications with those officers or employees expressly designated or nominated to act as 'the client'. Thus the privilege was held not to extend to documents prepared by other employees or ex-employees, even if prepared with the dominant purpose of

---

[93] [2004] 3 All ER 168, CA at [39].

[94] *Greenough v Gaskell* (1833) 1 My&K 98. If litigation does ensue, the standard form of words for claiming the privilege on disclosure is to refer to confidential correspondence etc for the purpose of obtaining legal advice. This is a sufficient description of the documents—the other party is not entitled to a fuller description to satisfy himself that all of the documents are within the scope of the privilege: *Derby & Co Ltd v Weldon (No 7)* [1990] 3 All ER 161, Ch D.

[95] See the obiter suggestion in *Three Rivers District Council v Governor and Company of the Bank of England* [2003] EWCA Civ 474, CA at [21].

[96] *Minter v Priest* [1930] AC 558. However, it seems that a client care letter is not privileged because it merely sets out the terms on which the solicitor is to act for the client: *Dickinson v Rushmer* (2002) 152 NLJ 58.

[97] *Re Sarah C Getty Trust* [1985] QB 956, QBD.

[98] [2003] QB 1556, CA.

obtaining legal advice, prepared at the lawyer's request, or sent to the lawyer. It is submitted that the 'designation' approach is too restrictive, not least because, as one commentator has pointed out, it operates in an unprincipled way to exclude other officers and employees with equivalent or greater authority to act 'as the client', such as, in the case in question, the Governor of the Bank.[99] Equally, however, the 'dominant purpose' test may be too wide and operate to prevent access to relevant facts. The answer may be to adopt the test used in the United States,[100] which limits the corporate client to those who play a substantial role in deciding and directing the corporation's response to the legal advice given.[101]

Legal advice privilege does extend to the instructions given by the client to his solicitor, or by the solicitor to the barrister, and counsel's opinion taken by a solicitor.[102] It does not extend to records of time spent with a client on attendance sheets, time sheets, or fee records, because they are not communications between client and legal adviser, or to records of appointments, because they are not communications made in connection with legal advice.[103] Similarly, such items as a conveyance or other legal document will not necessarily be protected by the privilege, unless made in connection with the giving of legal advice (or in connection with or in contemplation of legal proceedings and for the purposes of such proceedings).[104]

There is generally no protection for communications between opposing parties or their advisers, unless they can be treated as 'without prejudice' settlement negotiations, which are considered below.[105] Thus the privilege does not cover a solicitor's attendance note recording what took place in chambers or in open court, in the course of a hostile litigation, in the presence of the parties on both sides.[106] Similarly, if a solicitor has made an attendance note of a meeting or telephone conversation between the lawyers for each side, although any subsequent communication by the lawyers to their respective clients, informing them about the discussion, advising them, and seeking further instructions, will be privileged, the attendance note itself is not privileged. This remains the case, even if the discussion was 'without prejudice', although that may prevent the note from being given in evidence until the without prejudice ban has been removed.[107]

In *Buttes Gas and Oil Co v Hammer (No 3)*[108] it was held that where a solicitor is instructed by two clients, communications between him and one of the clients will not be privileged against the other client in so far as they concern the subject matter in which they are jointly interested

---

[99] Loughrey, 'Legal advice privilege and the corporate client' (2005) 9 *E&P* 183. As to practical problems relating to pre-litigation risk management to which the approach gives rise, see Passmore, 'Watch what you say', *NLJ* 21 April 2006 at 668.

[100] See *Upjohn Co v United States* 499, US 383, 101 SCt 677 (1981) at 684.

[101] For a good assessment of the implications of adopting the various tests, see Loughrey, ibid.

[102] *Bristol Corpn v Cox* (1884) 26 Ch D 678.

[103] *R v Crown Court at Manchester, ex p Rogers* [1999] 1 WLR 832, DC.

[104] *R (Faisaltex Ltd) v Preston Crown Court* [2009] 1 Cr App R 549, DC at [70], a decision under s 10 of the Police and Criminal Evidence Act 1984.

[105] *Grant v Southwestern and County Properties Ltd* [1975] Ch 185, Ch D: the plaintiff was obliged to produce on discovery a tape-recording of a discussion between the parties even though made for the purposes of instructing his solicitor in connection with contemplated litigation. However, if, after a meeting between opposing parties, one of them makes a record of the meeting for his solicitor, that record will be protected.

[106] *Ainsworth v Wilding* [1900] 2 Ch 315.

[107] *Parry v News Group Newspapers Ltd* [1990] NLJR 1719, CA.

[108] [1981] QB 223, CA (reversed on other grounds, [1982] AC 888, HL), applied in *Guinness Peat Properties Ltd v Fitzroy Robinson Partnership (a firm)* [1987] 2 All ER 716, CA.

but, whether or not the communication is disclosed to the other client, they will be protected as against outsiders. Thus where two parties employ the same solicitor for a conveyancing transaction, communications between either of them and the solicitor, in his joint capacity, must be disclosed in favour of the other. Equally, if one of the parties is then adjudicated bankrupt, the other cannot assert the privilege as against a trustee in bankruptcy, because as the successor in title to the property in question, he should be treated as being in the same position as the bankrupt, and not in the position of a third party.[109] However, the waiver of privilege implied at the outset of a joint retainer ceases to apply in respect of communications made after the emergence of a conflict of interest between the two clients.[110] Similarly, the privilege cannot be claimed by the directors of a company against its shareholders, except in the case of communications made for the purposes of litigation between the company and the shareholders.[111]

'Legal advice', for the purposes of legal advice privilege, does not mean advice given by a lawyer without more, but advice about legal rights and liabilities. However, some communications may enjoy privilege even if they do not specifically seek or convey legal advice. In *Balabel v Air-India*,[112] which concerned a conveyancing transaction, the privilege extended to communications between the appellants and their solicitors such as drafts, working papers, attendance notes, and memoranda. It was held that in most solicitor and client relationships, especially where a transaction involves protracted dealings, there will be a continuum of communications and meetings between the solicitor and client; and where information is passed between them as part of that continuum, the aim being to keep both informed so that legal advice may be sought and given as required, privilege will attach. Similarly, in *Nederlandse Reassurantie Groep Holding NV v Bacon & Woodrow (a firm)*[113] it was held that where a solicitor's advice relates to the commercial wisdom of entering into a transaction in respect of which legal advice is also sought, all communications between the solicitor and the client relating to the transaction will be privileged, even if they do not contain advice on matters of law or construction, provided that they are directly related to the performance by the solicitor of his professional duty as legal adviser.[114] According to *The Sagheera*,[115] the practical emphasis should be on the dominant purpose of the retainer. If it is to obtain and give legal advice, although in theory individual documents may fall outside that purpose, in practice it is most unlikely. If, however, the dominant purpose is some business purpose, the documents will not be privileged, unless exceptionally advice is requested or given, in which case the relevant documents probably are privileged.

The leading authority is *Three Rivers District Council v Governor and Company of the Bank of England (No 6)*.[116] After the collapse of the Bank of Credit and Commerce International (BCCI) in 1991, Lord Justice Bingham was appointed to inquire into its supervision by the Bank of England,

---

[109] *Re Konigsberg (a bankrupt)* [1989] 3 All ER 289, Ch D.

[110] *TSB Bank plc v Robert Irving & Burns (a firm)* [2000] 2 All ER 826, CA.

[111] *Woodhouse & Co (Ltd) v Woodhouse* (1914) 30 TLR 559; *CAS (Nominees) Ltd v Nottingham Forest plc* [2001] 1 All ER 954, Ch D

[112] [1988] Ch 317, CA.

[113] [1995] 1 All ER 976, QBD.

[114] See also *R v Crown Court at Inner London Sessions, ex p Baines and Baines* [1987] 3 All ER 1025, DC: privilege does attach to advice given in conveyancing transactions on factors serving to assist towards a successful completion, including the wisdom or otherwise of proceeding with it, the arranging of a mortgage and so on, but does not attach to the records of the conveyancing transaction itself.

[115] [1997] 1 Lloyd's Rep 160 at 168, QBD.

[116] [2005] 1 AC 610, HL.

which had statutory responsibilities and duties in relation to UK banks. The Bank appointed a Bingham Inquiry Unit (BIU) to deal with all communications between the Bank and the inquiry and solicitors were retained to advise generally on all dealings with the inquiry. One of the main functions of the BIU was to prepare and communicate information and instructions to the Bank's solicitors. The solicitors gave advice as to the preparation and presentation of evidence to the inquiry and as to submissions to be made. After the publication of the inquiry report, depositors and BCCI, by its liquidators, brought proceedings against the Bank and sought the widest possible disclosure from the Bank. The Court of Appeal held that the only documents for which privilege could be claimed were communications between BIU and the solicitors seeking or giving advice as to legal rights and liabilities. The House of Lords allowed the appeal of the Bank. It was held that the policy basis for legal advice privilege was that it was necessary, in a society in which the restraining and controlling framework was built on a belief in the rule of law, that communications between clients and lawyers, whereby the clients were hoping for the assistance of the lawyers' legal skills in the management of the clients' affairs, should be secure against the possibility of any scrutiny from others. Lord Scott accepted as correct the approach of Taylor LJ in *Balabel v Air India*,[117] who had said that for the purpose of attracting the privilege 'legal advice is not confined to telling the client the law; it must include advice as to what should prudently and sensibly be done in the relevant legal context' but that 'to extend privilege without limit to all solicitor and client communications upon matters within the ordinary business of a solicitor and referable to that relationship [would be] too wide'. Lord Scott said that if a solicitor became the client's 'man of business', responsible for advising him on matters such as investment and other business matters, the advice might lack a relevant legal context. The judge would have to ask whether it related to the rights, liabilities, obligations, or remedies of the client under either private or public law, and, if so, whether the communication fell within the policy underlying the justification for the privilege, the criterion being an objective one. It was held that although there may be marginal cases where the answer is not easy, the present case was not marginal. The preparation of the evidence to be submitted, and the submissions to be made, to the inquiry had been for the purpose of enhancing the Bank's prospects of persuading the inquiry that its discharge of its public law obligations was not deserving of criticism and had been reasonable. The presentational advice given for that purpose had been advice 'as to what should prudently and sensibly be done in the relevant legal context', namely, the inquiry and whether the Bank had properly discharged its public law duties, and fell squarely within the policy reasons underlying legal advice privilege.

Communications with third parties—litigation privilege

Litigation privilege is a creature of adversarial proceedings and cannot exist in the context of non-adversarial proceedings.[118] It covers communications between a client, or his lawyer, and third parties—for example, statements from potential witnesses and experts—the dominant purpose of which was preparation for contemplated or pending litigation. The test is whether litigation was reasonably in prospect, which will not be satisfied if there is only a possibility of litigation, even if a distinct possibility, or a general apprehension of future litigation.[119] The privilege, which is a basic or fundamental right, also attaches to the identity and other details

---

[117] [1988] Ch 317 at 330–1.
[118] *Re L* [1997] AC 16, HL.
[119] *USA v Philip Morris Inc* [2004] All ER (D) 448 (Mar), [2004] EWCA Civ 330, CA.

of witnesses intended to be called in adversarial litigation, civil or criminal, and whether or not their identity was the fruit of legal advice.[120] Claims to litigation privilege must set out the purpose for which the documents in question were produced, referring to contemporaneous material where possible. An affidavit in support will be conclusive unless (a) it is clear from the statements of the deponent that he has erroneously represented or misconceived the character of the document; (b) it is contradicted by the evidence of the person who, or the entity which, directed the creation of the document; or (c) there is other evidence before the court that it is incorrect or incomplete on the material points.[121]

The privilege covers documents 'brought into existence', that is created, by a party for the purpose of instructing the lawyer and obtaining his advice in the conduct of the litigation,[122] but not documents obtained by a party or his adviser for the purpose of litigation which did not come into existence for that purpose.[123] A copy or translation of an unprivileged document in the control of a party does not become privileged merely because the copy or translation was made for the purpose of the litigation,[124] but privilege will attach to a copy of an unprivileged document if the copy was made for the purpose of litigation and the original is not and has not at any time been in the control of the party claiming privilege.[125] Privilege will also attach where a solicitor has copied or assembled a selection of third party documents for the purposes of litigation, if its production will betray the trend of the advice he is giving his client,[126] but this principle does not extend to a selection of own client documents, or copies or translations representing the fruits of such a selection, made for the purposes of litigation.[127]

The leading authority is *Waugh v British Railways Board*.[128] The plaintiff's husband, an employee of the defendant, was killed in a railway accident. In proceedings for compensation, the plaintiff sought discovery of routine internal reports prepared by the defendant regarding the accident. The House of Lords held that, in order to attract privilege, the dominant purpose of preparation of the reports must have been that of submission to a legal adviser for use in relation to anticipated or pending litigation. While this was undoubtedly one of the purposes of the reports, it was not the dominant one, another equally important purpose being to inform the Board about the cause of the accident in order that steps could be taken to avoid recurrence. Accordingly, privilege could not be claimed and disclosure of the reports was ordered.

Although application of the dominant purpose test can give rise to difficulty, in many cases of accident investigation it will be possible to conclude that the major purpose was the prevention of recurrence. The courts will not be deterred from reaching such a conclusion, where appropriate, even if those under whose direction the report was prepared depose that its dominant purpose was submission to solicitors in anticipation of litigation and the report itself refers only

[120] *R (Kelly) v Warley Magistrates' Court* [2008] 1 Cr App R 195.
[121] *West London Pipeline & Storage Ltd v Total UK Ltd* [2008] EWHC 1729 (Comm).
[122] Per James LJ in *Anderson v Bank of British Columbia* (1876) 2 Ch D 644 at 656. See also *Southwark and Vauxhall Water Co v Quick* (1878) 3 QBD 315, CA.
[123] *Ventouris v Mountain, The Italia Express* [1991] 1 WLR 607, CA.
[124] *Dubai Bank Ltd v Galadari* [1990] Ch 98, CA (copies) and *Sumitomo Corp v Credit Lyonnais Rouse Ltd* [2002] 1 WLR 479, CA.
[125] *The Palermo* (1883) 9 PD 6, CA and *Watson v Cammell Laird & Co Ltd* [1959] 1 WLR 702, CA.
[126] *Lyell v Kennedy (No 3)* (1884) 27 Ch D 1.
[127] *Sumitomo Corp v Credit Lyonnais Rouse Ltd* [2002] 1 WLR 479, CA.
[128] [1980] AC 521.

to that purpose.[129] In *Neilson v Laugharne*[130] the plaintiff's demand for compensation for alleged police misconduct prompted the police to initiate the statutory complaints procedure. Statements taken for the purpose of that procedure were clearly obtained in anticipation of litigation but it was held that the dominant purpose was that of the complaints procedure. The statements therefore did not attract legal professional privilege in subsequent litigation against the police. In *Re Highgrade Traders Ltd*,[131] by contrast, it was held that the dominant purpose of the preparation of reports procured by an insurance company from specialists in fire investigations, in a case where arson was suspected, was to assess the strength of a claim which, if persisted in, would in all likelihood have resulted in litigation. The insurance company was primarily interested in questions of liability rather than prevention or recurrence. Oliver LJ made it clear that the privilege will attach to a document, whether it was 'brought into existence' before or after a decision was made to instruct a solicitor, provided that litigation was reasonably in prospect and the document was prepared for the sole or dominant purpose of enabling a solicitor to advise whether a claim should be made or resisted.

In *Guinness Peat Properties Ltd v Fitzroy Robinson Partnership (a firm)*[132] it was held that the dominant purpose of a document should be ascertained by an objective view of the evidence as a whole, having regard not only to the intention of its author, but also to the intention of the person or authority under whose direction it was procured. The plaintiffs, building developers, had notified the defendants, engaged by them to act as architects for the construction of a building, of an alleged design fault. The defendants, in order to comply with the condition of their insurance policy, which required immediate notification of claims, thereupon wrote a letter to their insurers enclosing relevant memoranda and expressing their own views on the merits of the claim. In the course of discovery in the action which ensued, the question arose whether the letter was privileged. The defendants conceded that it was not *their* purpose, in writing the letter, to obtain legal advice or assistance. The Court of Appeal held that it could look beyond that intention to the intention of the insurers who had procured its genesis. Their intention, in requiring an immediate written notice of claim, was to enable them to submit it, together with other relevant documentation, to their lawyers for advice on whether the claim should be resisted. The letter was therefore privileged.

In reaching this conclusion, the Court of Appeal distinguished *Jones v Great Central Rly Co*,[133] in which it was held that if a client communicates with a lawyer via a third party who is merely an agent for communication, privilege can be claimed, but that if the third party has to make a preliminary decision on the matter, the privilege is lost. Accordingly, it was held that no privilege attached to information supplied by a dismissed employee to a trade union official for the purpose of enabling the latter to decide whether to refer the claim to the union's lawyers. This case was distinguished in the *Guinness Peat Properties* case on the grounds, inter alia, that the relationship between the trade union and the member was not the equivalent of that between the insurers and the insured where the insurers were, in all but name, the effective defendants to any proceedings. It was further held that since the insurers and the insured had a common interest and a common lawyer, the principle in

---

[129] See *Lask v Gloucester Health Authority* (1985) 2 PN 96, CA.
[130] [1981] QB 736, CA.
[131] [1984] BCLC 151, CA.
[132] [1987] 2 All ER 716, CA.
[133] [1910] AC 4, HL.

Buttes Gas and Oil Co v Hammer (No 3)[134] applied: the letter was privileged in the hands of each of them as against all outsiders.

In *Re Barings plc*[135] Sir Richard Scott V-C doubted the correctness of the decisions in both *Re Highgrade Traders Ltd* and the *Guinness Peat Properties* case on the grounds that disclosure of the documents in those cases would not have impinged upon the inviolability of lawyer/ client communications. In his view, the reason for extending the privilege to documents brought into existence for the dominant purpose of litigation is to prevent the disclosure of documents which will reveal the lawyer's view of his client's case or the advice he has given, and therefore there is no general privilege for such documents independent of the need to keep inviolate communications between client and legal adviser. Thus if the documents do not relate in some fashion to such communications, there is no element of public interest to override the ordinary rights of litigants on discovery. In *Re Barings plc* a report on the conduct of the directors of Barings Bank was prepared on behalf of administrators in compliance with their statutory duty to report to the Department of Trade and Industry, under section 7(3), Company Directors Disqualification Act 1986, where it appears to them that the conduct of directors makes them unfit to be concerned in the management of a company. In subsequent disqualification proceedings, the Secretary of State resisted inspection of the report on the grounds of privilege. The Vice-Chancellor held that the report was not privileged. *Re Highgrade Traders Ltd* and the *Guinness Peat Properties* case were distinguished on the basis that, whereas in those cases the makers of the documents had a choice whether to bring them into existence and it was therefore possible to investigate their purpose in doing so, the maker of a section 7(3) report is obliged by law to make the report, which is not procured by anyone. It was accepted that the statutory purpose underlying section 7(3) was to assist the Secretary of State to decide whether to commence disqualification proceedings, and that Parliament must have expected that the Secretary of State, in reaching his decision, would put the report before his legal advisers for their advice, but it was held that the question of privilege depended not on identifying this parliamentary purpose and expectation, but on whether there was a public interest requiring protection from disclosure sufficient to override the disclosure rights given to litigants. In the absence of any such public interest, it was ruled that the report was not protected from disclosure.

Despite the difficulties of the dominant purpose test, it is usually clear that proofs of evidence from potential witnesses and the written opinions of experts supplied for the purpose of litigation can be kept secret. Under CPR rule 32.4(2), the court will order a party to serve on the other parties any witness statement of the oral evidence which the first party intends to rely on in relation to any issues of fact to be decided at the trial. If a witness statement is not served in respect of an intended witness within the time specified by the court, then the witness may not be called to give oral evidence unless the court gives permission;[136] and if a witness statement is served within the time specified and the witness is called, he may amplify his witness statement only with the permission of the court.[137] Thus, rule 32 does not compel disclosure, but if a party wishes to adduce evidence of fact from a witness at the trial, then he is generally required to disclose all of it in advance.

[134] [1981] QB 223, CA, above.
[135] [1998] 1 All ER 673, Ch D.
[136] Rule 32.10.
[137] Rule 32.5(3)(a).

Once the statement has been disclosed, it is no longer privileged. Thus, it may be relied on, by the other party, in support of an application for specific disclosure of documents referred to in it.[138] Rule 32.5(5) provides that if a party who has served a witness statement does not call the witness to give evidence at trial or put the witness statement in as hearsay evidence, the other party may put the statement in as hearsay evidence. If the party who has served the statement does call the witness, his statement shall stand as his evidence-in-chief unless the court orders otherwise[139] and he may be cross-examined on it whether or not the statement or any part of it is referred to during his evidence-in-chief.[140]

If a party to civil proceedings fails to disclose an expert's report, then he may not use it at the trial or call the expert to give evidence orally unless the court gives permission.[141] As in the case of witness statements, disclosure is not compulsory. A party is therefore free to instruct an expert and, in the event that the expert's report is unhelpful to him, cannot be compelled to disclose it to the other side. Nor will his opponent be able to require the party, his solicitor, or the expert to state in evidence the content of the instructions to the expert or of the report. The costs of the exercise, however, will not be recoverable from the opponent. On the other hand, where a party seeks permission to put in evidence an expert's report, the report must state the substance of all material instructions, whether written or oral, on the basis of which it was written;[142] the instructions shall not be privileged against disclosure;[143] and where the party has disclosed the report, any party may use it as evidence at the trial.[144]

Provision has also been made for the mutual disclosure of expert evidence in criminal cases.[145] The defence, in advance of a trial on indictment, are also entitled to know not only the evidence the prosecution intend to call, most or all of which will have been disclosed by the statements or depositions used by them at the committal proceedings (or served with a notice of transfer), but also, as a general rule, 'unused material', that is statements from persons on whose evidence the prosecution do not intend to rely.[146]

'Items'

Under section 10(1)(c) of the 1984 Act, as we have seen, material subject to legal professional privilege includes items, enclosed with or referred to in communications covered by the above two categories of protected material, which were made in connection with the giving of legal advice etc. An 'item' could include, for example, a model made, or a bodily sample taken, for the purpose of obtaining expert advice. In *R v R*,[147] in which

---

[138] *Black & Decker Inc v Flymo Ltd* [1991] 3 All ER 158, Ch D (citing *Comfort Hotels Ltd v Wembley Stadium Ltd* [1988] 3 All ER 53), a decision under RSC Ord 38, r 2A, the precursor to the current rules.

[139] Rule 32.5(2).

[140] Rule 32.11.

[141] CPR r 35.13.

[142] CPR r 35.10(3).

[143] Rule 35.10(4).

[144] Rule 35.11.

[145] See Ch 18, 552, under **Expert opinion evidence, Restrictions on, and disclosure of, expert evidence in criminal cases.**

[146] The disclosure of unused material, a large topic outside the scope of this work, is governed by the scheme to be found in Part 1 (ss 1–21) of the Criminal Procedure and Investigations Act 1996 (as supplemented by a Code of Practice), under which there is a duty upon an officer investigating an offence to record and retain material and a duty on the prosecution to inform the defence of certain categories of such material which they do not intend to use at trial.

[147] [1994] 4 All ER 260, CA.

a scientist had carried out DNA tests at the request of the defence solicitors on a blood sample provided by the accused, it was held that the prosecution were not entitled either (i) to produce the sample in evidence; or (ii) to adduce the opinion evidence of the scientist based on the sample. Section 10(1)(c) was said to apply to both issues. The word 'made' meant 'brought into existence' for the purpose of obtaining legal advice etc; the sample was an item 'made' for such a purpose; and therefore the accused was entitled to object both to its production and, whether or not it was produced or no longer existed, to opinion evidence based upon it.

The subject matter of privilege: communications not facts

Under the doctrine of legal professional privilege, the client may avoid disclosure of his instructions to his lawyer and of his lawyer's advice to him: the lawyer may still be compelled to give evidence of facts directly perceived by him, even though his perception of them only occurred in the course of an interview with his client. Thus he may be required to admit the fact of having met his client and to give evidence about the physical or mental condition of his client[148] or about his handwriting.[149] Similarly, a solicitor present in court when his client was sentenced may be compelled in a subsequent prosecution to give evidence as to the identity of that person and to produce attendance notes, with anything attracting privilege blacked out.[150] If it is known that the client has shown the solicitor a pre-existing document which becomes relevant in litigation, then subject to the other rules of evidence, it seems in principle that the lawyer should be able to state the contents of the document.[151] These matters must be distinguished from facts conveyed to the lawyer by the client and the contents of documents prepared for the purpose of instructing the lawyer, a distinction which may not always be easy to apply.

Pre-existing documents

Whereas privilege does attach to a document prepared for the purposes of obtaining legal advice, a pre-existing document given into the custody of a solicitor for the purpose of obtaining such advice or sent by a solicitor to a third party in connection with the litigation can, at common law, attract no greater protection in the hands of the solicitor or third party than it had in the hands of the client.[152] Thus in *R v Justice of the Peace for Peterborough, ex p Hicks*,[153] in which the client had sent to his solicitor, for the purposes of gaining legal advice, a forged document, a warrant was ordered to search the solicitor's premises and seize the document. The document was not privileged in the hands of the solicitor because it would have been open to seizure by warrant in the hands of the client.[154] Similarly, in *R v King*[155] the prosecution in a case of conspiracy to defraud were able to subpoena a handwriting expert, instructed by the defence, to

---

[148] *Jones v Godrich* (1845) 5 Moo PCC 16.

[149] *Dwyer v Collins* (1852) 7 Exch 639.

[150] *R (Howe) v South Durham Magistrates' Court* [2004] Crim LR 963, DC.

[151] *Brown v Foster* (1857) 1 H&N 736, although because of its special facts this is not very clear authority for the principle stated. But see also **Pre-existing documents**, below.

[152] But cf *Lyell v Kennedy (No 3)* (1884) 27 Ch D 1.

[153] [1977] 1 WLR 1371, DC.

[154] Dicta of Swanwick J in *Frank Truman Export Ltd v Metropolitan Police Comr* [1977] QB 952, which provide the only authority to the contrary, were doubted in *R v King* [1983] 1 WLR 411, CA.

[155] [1983] 1 WLR 411, CA.

produce documents sent to him by the accused's solicitors as sample handwriting even though the instructions to him, and his report, remained privileged.

Under section 8 of the 1984 Act, warrants of entry and search may be issued if, inter alia, a justice of the peace is satisfied that the material sought does not consist of or include 'items subject to legal privilege' or 'special procedure material'. The phrase 'items subject to legal privilege', as we have seen, is defined in section 10 of the Act. In *R v Guildhall Magistrates' Court, ex p Primlaks Holdings Co*[156] Parker LJ held that section 10(1)(c) does not cover pre-existing documents which were not *made* in connection with the giving of legal advice or in connection with or in contemplation of legal proceedings and for the purposes of such proceedings, but that such documents would constitute 'special procedure material'. Under section 14(2), such material includes material, other than items subject to legal privilege, in the possession of a person who acquired or created it in the course of any trade, business, profession etc and holds it subject to an express or implied undertaking to hold it in confidence.[157] Under section 9, the police may obtain access to 'special procedure material', for the purposes of a criminal investigation, by an application, usually to be made *inter partes*, to a circuit judge. In the *Guildhall Magistrates' Court* case, Parker LJ held that a solicitor's correspondence with his client, and its enclosures, if not privileged, whether by reason of section 10(2) or otherwise, falls squarely within section 14(2) and that if the police are aware that what they seek includes items which are prima facie subject to legal privilege, they should not make an *ex parte* application under section 8, but should proceed under section 9 when the matter can be fully aired before a circuit judge.[158] However, it seems that a solicitor may voluntarily disclose special procedure material to the police because the object of the statutory provisions is to protect from disclosure not the suspect, but the person who has acquired or created the material, and it is for that person to decide whether he wishes to make disclosure, bearing in mind the degree of confidence reposed in him.[159]

Exceptions to the privilege

In *R v Derby Magistrates' Court, ex p B*[160] the appellant was suspected of murder. He admitted responsibility and was charged, but before his trial changed his story and alleged that his stepfather had carried out the murder and that although he, the appellant, was present and took some part, he did so under duress. At his trial, he was acquitted. The stepfather was subsequently charged with the murder and at the committal proceedings the appellant was called as a prosecution witness. Counsel for the defence sought to cross-examine him about the factual instructions he had given to his solicitors prior to his allegation against his stepfather. The appellant declined to waive his privilege. The magistrates issued summonses directing the appellant and his solicitor to produce documentary evidence of the factual instructions, on the basis that the public interest that all relevant and admissible evidence should be made available to the defence outweighed the public interest which protected confidential communications between

---

[156] (1989) 89 Cr App R 215, DC at 225.

[157] A document forged by a solicitor or supplied by him to a fraudulent client is not special procedure material because, from its nature, it could not have been acquired or created in the course of the profession of a solicitor: *R v Leeds Magistrates' Court, ex p Dumbleton* [1993] Crim LR 866, DC.

[158] See also *R v Crown Court at Southampton, ex p J and P* [1993] Crim LR 962, DC.

[159] See *R v Singleton* [1995] 1 Cr App R 431, a decision relating to 'excluded material' within the meaning of s 11 of the 1984 Act.

[160] [1996] AC 487, HL.

a solicitor and a client. An application for judicial review was refused, but the House of Lords allowed the appeal. Lord Taylor CJ, with whose judgment Lords Keith, Mustill, and Lloyd agreed, held that since the client must be sure that what he tells his lawyer in confidence will never be revealed without his consent, there could be no question of a balancing exercise[161]—once any exception to the general rule is allowed, the client's confidence is necessarily lost. The solicitor would have to qualify his assurance and the purpose of the privilege would be undermined. However, Lord Nicholls, who also rejected any question of a balancing exercise, noted that in cases where the client no longer has any interest in maintaining the privilege, the privilege is spent. His Lordship preferred to reserve his final view on the point, but said:[162]

> I would not expect a law, based explicitly on considerations of the public interest, to protect the right of a client when he has no interest in asserting the right and the enforcement of the right would be seriously prejudicial to another in defending a criminal charge or in some other way.

Despite the sweeping pronouncements in the *Derby Magistrates'* case as to the absolute and permanent nature of legal professional privilege, there are exceptions. Statute may override the privilege. For example, in *In re McE*[163] the House of Lords held that the Regulation of Investigatory Powers Act 2000 permits covert surveillance of communications between someone in custody and his lawyer notwithstanding that they are covered by legal professional privilege and despite the statutory right to consult a solicitor privately under section 58 of the Police and Criminal Evidence Act 1984.[164] However, the House was not required to answer the separate question as to what use can be made of information thus obtained. Statute may override the privilege, either expressly or by necessary implication. The latter is not the same as a reasonable implication. In *R (Morgan Grenfell) v Special Commissioner of Income Tax*[165] Lord Hobhouse said:

> A *necessary* implication is one which necessarily follows from the express provisions of the statute construed in their context. It distinguishes between what it would have been sensible or reasonable for Parliament to have included or what Parliament would, if it had thought about it, probably have included and what it is clear that the express language of the statute shows that the statute must have included. A necessary implication is a matter of express language and logic not interpretation.

However, even if a statute does override the privilege, it may still be declared incompatible with the right of privacy under Article 8 of the European Convention on Human Rights, the European Court of Human Rights having said that the privilege is a fundamental human right which can be invaded only in exceptional circumstances.[166]

There are three other specific types of exception. The first, fraud, was referred to by Lord Lloyd in the *Derby Magistrates'* case as 'a well-recognized exception'.[167] The second relates to

---

[161] Overruling, in this respect, *R v Barton* [1973] 1 WLR 115, CC and *R v Ataou* [1988] 2 All ER 321, CA. See also, endorsing Lord Taylor's approach, *R (Morgan Grenfell) v Special Commissioner of Income Tax* [2003] 1 AC 563, HL and *B v Auckland District Law Society* [2003] 2 AC 736, PC.

[162] [1995] 4 All ER 526 at 546.

[163] [2009] 2 Cr App R 1.

[164] See Ch 13.

[165] [2003] 1 AC 563, HL at [45], applied in *B v Auckland District Law Society* [2003] 2 AC 736, PC.

[166] See per Lord Hoffmann, obiter, in *R (Morgan Grenfell) v Special Commissioner of Income Tax* [2003] 1 AC 563 at [7] and [39], citing *Foxley v UK* (2000) 8 BHRC 571 at 581.

[167] [1995] 4 All ER 526 at 543.

reports by third parties prepared on the instructions of the client for the purposes of care proceedings under the Children Act 1989. The third concerns cases in which the instructions given or the advice received are themselves in issue in the litigation.

Fraud

In *R v Cox and Railton*[168] the Court for Crown Cases Reserved held that if a client seeks legal advice intended to facilitate or guide him in the commission of a crime or fraud, the legal adviser being ignorant of the purpose for which the advice is sought, the communication between them is not privileged. The exception also applies if the solicitor *is* a party to the crime or fraud but not, it was held in *Butler v Board of Trade*,[169] if he merely volunteers a warning to the client that his conduct, if persisted in, may result in a prosecution.[170] The exception can only be relied on if there is prima facie evidence of the client's criminal purpose.[171] However, the court may look at the communications themselves, if necessary, to determine whether they came into existence in furtherance of such a purpose.[172]

The exception is not confined to cases in which solicitors advise on or set up criminal or fraudulent transactions yet to be undertaken, but also covers criminal or fraudulent conduct undertaken for the purposes of acquiring evidence in or for litigation, so that where documents have been generated by, or report on, conduct constituting a crime under the Data Protection Act 1984, and they are relevant to the issues in the litigation, they will not be protected from disclosure by legal professional privilege.[173]

There are a number of limitations on the scope of this exception. First, although not limited to crimes, it does not extend to communications concerning all intended legal wrongs. In *Crescent Farm (Sidcup) Sports Ltd v Sterling Offices Ltd*[174] Goff J said:[175]

> It is clear that parties must be at liberty to take advice as to the ambit of their contractual obligations and liabilities in tort and what liability they will incur whether in contract or tort by a proposed course of action without thereby in every case losing professional privilege. I agree that fraud in this connection is not limited to the tort of deceit and includes all forms of fraud and dishonesty such as fraudulent breach of contract, fraudulent conspiracy, trickery and sham contrivances, but I cannot feel that the tort of inducing a breach of contract or the narrow form of conspiracy pleaded in this case comes within that ambit.

Trespass and conversion are also outside the scope of the doctrine.[176] However, privilege will not attach to advice on a scheme, in breach of an employee's confidential duty of fidelity and involving the secret use of the employer's time and money, to take other employees (and the employer's customers) and to make profit from them in a competing business developed

---

[168] (1884) 14 QBD 153, CCR.

[169] [1971] Ch 680.

[170] However, the Board in that case were able to prove a letter since a copy of it had come into their hands and Goff J refused to grant an injunction to prevent such use: see below.

[171] *O'Rourke v Darbishire* [1920] AC 581. But see also *Derby & Co Ltd v Weldon (No 7)* [1990] 3 All ER 161, Ch D: the court will be very slow to deprive a party of the privilege on an interlocutory application and will judge each case on its facts.

[172] *R v Governor of Pentonville Prison, ex p Osman* [1989] 3 All ER 701, QBD at 729–30.

[173] *Dubai Aluminium Co Ltd v Al Alawi* [1999] 1 All ER 703, QBD.

[174] [1972] Ch 553.

[175] [1972] Ch 553 at 565.

[176] Per Rix J in *Dubai Aluminium Co Ltd v Al Alawi* [1999] 1 All ER 703 at 707.

to receive them on leaving the employer's service.[177] Equally, if there is strong prima facie evidence that a transaction has been devised to prejudice the interests of a creditor by putting assets beyond his reach, privilege will not attach to legal advice on how to structure such a transaction.[178]

In *Kuwait Airways Corporation v Iraqi Airways Co*[179] it was confirmed that the fraud exception can apply to litigation privilege, as well as legal advice privilege, but it was held that whereas a prima facie case of fraud may suffice where the issue of fraud is not one of the very issues in the action, where it is such an issue then a very strong prima facie case of fraud is required. In *Chandler v Church*[180] the plaintiffs alleged that the defendant had fraudulently manipulated to his own advantage various share transactions. They sought discovery of communications between him and his solicitors on the basis of prima facie evidence showing that he had obtained their assistance to enable him to mislead the court by putting forward false documents and pretending that certain transactions were genuine. Hoffmann J held that although it does not matter whether the fraud concerns an earlier transaction or the conduct of the proceedings in question, disclosure at an interlocutory stage based on prima facie evidence of fraud in the conduct of the very proceedings in which the discovery is sought carries a far greater risk of injury to the party against whom discovery is sought, should he turn out to have been innocent, than disclosure of advice concerning an earlier transaction. The risk of injustice to the defendant in being required to reveal communications with his lawyers for the purpose of his defence, together with the damage to the public interest which the violation of such confidences would cause, outweighed the risk of injustice to the plaintiffs.[181]

Finally, the exception does not extend to the correspondence between a lawyer and an assignee or victim of a fraudsman. In *Banque Keyser Ullmann SA v Skandia (UK) Insurance Co Ltd*[182] insurance policies, issued to borrowers to cover banks against failure of the borrowers to repay, were assigned to the banks. The loans were not repaid and the banks claimed under the policies. The insurers denied liability on the grounds that the policies had been obtained by the fraud of the borrowers. The contention of the insurers that by reason of the borrowers' fraud no privilege attached to the correspondence passing between the banks and their lawyers was rejected.

Section 10(2) of the 1984 Act, as we have seen, provides that 'items held with the intention of furthering a criminal purpose are not items subject to legal privilege'. In *R v Crown Court at Snaresbrook, ex p DPP*[183] it was held, giving these words their natural meaning, that it is the person holding the items in question whose intention is relevant. This construction was rejected in *Francis & Francis (a firm) v Central Criminal Court*.[184] A majority of the House of Lords, comprising Lords Brandon, Griffiths, and Goff, was of the opinion that section 10(2)

---

[177] *Gamlen Chemical Co (UK) Ltd v Rochem Ltd* [1980] 1 All ER 1049.

[178] *Barclays Bank plc v Eustice* [1995] 4 All ER 511, CA.

[179] [2005] EWCA Civ 286.

[180] [1987] NLJ Rep 451, Ch D.

[181] See also *R v Crown Court at Snaresbrook, ex p DPP* [1988] 1 All ER 315, QBD: where a person has made false statements in an application for legal aid to pursue a civil action, the application, although admissible in a prosecution charging him with knowingly making such a false statement, is privileged in other criminal proceedings even if relevant thereto (see ss 22 and 23 of the Legal Aid Act 1974, re-enacted in ss 38 and 39 of the Legal Aid Act 1988). See per Glidewell LJ at 319. See also per Lord Goff in *Francis & Francis (a firm) v Central Criminal Court* [1988] 3 All ER 775 at 800, HL.

[182] [1986] 1 Lloyd's Rep 336, CA.

[183] [1988] 1 All ER 315, QBD.

[184] [1988] 3 All ER 775, HL.

was intended to reflect the position at common law, and not to restrict the principle of *R v Cox and Railton* to those cases in which the legal adviser has the intention of furthering a criminal purpose; and therefore that the intention referred to in that subsection could be that of the person holding the document or that of any other person.[185] Accordingly, it was held that conveyancing documents innocently held by a solicitor in relation to the purchase of a property by a client, intended by a third party, a relative of the client, to be used to further the criminal purpose of laundering the proceeds of illegal drug trafficking, were not items subject to legal privilege.[186]

In *R v Leeds Magistrates' Court, ex p Dumbleton*[187] a warrant was issued to search for and seize documents held by a solicitor and allegedly forged by him and another. It was held that the documents were not covered by section 10(1), because the phrase 'made in connection with . . . legal proceedings' meant lawfully made and did not extend to forged documents or copies thereof; and in any event the items were held with the intention of furthering a criminal purpose, the word 'held' in section 10(2) relating to the time at which the documents came into the possession of the person holding them.

Proceedings under the Children Act 1989

Care proceedings under the Children Act 1989 are non-adversarial: the court's duty is to investigate and to undertake all necessary steps to arrive at an appropriate result in the paramount interests of the welfare of the child. If a party to such proceedings, on obtaining an unfavourable expert's report, were to be able to suppress it and maintain a case at variance with it, judges would sometimes decide cases affecting children in ignorance of material facts and in a way detrimental to their best interests. For these reasons, in *Oxfordshire County Council v M*[188] it was held that in care proceedings in which the court gives leave to a party to obtain expert reports, it has power to override legal professional privilege and require the report to be filed and served on the other parties.[189] However, the promotion of the welfare of the child does not require that communications between a client and a lawyer should also be disclosed.[190] The same distinction was made in *Re L*,[191] where a majority of the House of Lords rejected a contention that the absolute nature of the privilege attaching to the solicitor–client relationship extends to all other forms of legal professional privilege.

---

[185] As Lord Oliver observed, however, in his powerful dissenting judgment: 'There is not, so far as I am aware, any authority in the common law dealing with the question of whether a criminal intent on the part of a stranger to the relationship of solicitor and client destroys the privilege of the client. If, therefore, the subsection does indeed bear the meaning now sought to be ascribed to it . . . it is breaking new ground and the legislative intent has to be gathered not from some supposed logical extension of the common law rule but from the words which Parliament has chosen to use' (at 793). Cf *Banque Keyser Ullmann SA v Skandia (UK) Insurance Co Ltd* [1986] 1 Lloyd's Rep 336, CA, above, to which none of their Lordships referred.

[186] See also *R (Hallinan) v Middlesex Guildhall Crown Court* [2004] All ER (D) 242 (Nov), where there was evidence of a specific agreement to pervert the course of justice; and *R v Crown Court at Northampton, ex p DPP* (1991) 93 Cr App R 376, DC, where it was the client who had the intention of furthering a criminal purpose. Charged with theft of goods, he had passed an allegedly forged receipt for the goods to his solicitor. It was held that under s 9 of the 1984 Act (see above), the circuit judge should have ordered the solicitor to produce the receipt to the police.

[187] [1993] Crim LR 866, DC.

[188] [1994] 2 All ER 269, CA.

[189] Approving *Re R (a minor)* [1993] 4 All ER 702 and overruling *Barking and Dagenham London Borough Council v O* [1993] 4 All ER 59.

[190] *Oxfordshire County Council v M* [1994] 2 All ER 269 per Steyn LJ at 282, CA.

[191] [1997] 1 AC 16, HL.

The majority approved *Oxfordshire County Council v M*, subject to one qualification: privilege had not been *overridden* in that case because it never arose in the first place, having been excluded by necessary implication from the terms and overall purpose of the 1989 Act. It has also been held that the exception under consideration does not extend to override privilege which has properly arisen and is maintainable in proceedings other than those under the 1989 Act, such as criminal proceedings against the father of the child.[192]

Instructions or advice in issue in litigation

Sometimes the question of what instructions were given to a lawyer or what advice was received may be an issue in the litigation, and this may result in privilege being abrogated. For example, where the court is asked to exercise its power under section 33 of the Limitation Act 1980 to allow an action to be brought out of time, it will be relevant for the court to know what advice the applicant received at various times as to his chances of success.[193] Similarly, the instructions given to a solicitor will have to be disclosed if a question arises whether or not the client authorized him to write letters to his opponent stating that he would accept a certain sum in settlement of his claim.[194]

Duration of the privilege

'As a general rule, one may say once privileged always privileged.'[195] Documents prepared for one set of proceedings continue to be privileged for the purpose of subsequent litigation, even if the litigation originally anticipated never took place;[196] and documents relating to property rights which are privileged in the hands of one person continue to be privileged in the hands of successors-in-title to the property.[197] In order to claim in a subsequent action the privilege which prevailed for the first action, there must be a sufficient connection of subject matter for the privileged material to be relevant to the subsequent action (because if the material is irrelevant the question of disclosure cannot even arise) and the person originally entitled to the privilege or his successor must be a party to the subsequent action; there is no additional requirement that the subject matter of the two actions should be identical or substantially the same or that the parties to the two actions should be the same.[198]

Legal professional privilege is that of the client or his successor in title. Accordingly, a third party from whom a statement was obtained for the dominant purpose of anticipated or pending litigation cannot claim protection in respect of the contents of that statement if he himself becomes a party to wholly independent litigation. *Schneider v Leigh*[199] was an action in libel. The plaintiff was claiming, in other proceedings, damages for personal injuries against a company whose solicitors had obtained a medical report, to which privilege attached, from a doctor whom they intended to call as a witness in those proceedings. The plaintiff regarded the document as defamatory, began the instant action against the doctor

[192] *S County Council v B* [2000] 2 FLR 161.
[193] *Jones v GD Searle & Co Ltd* [1979] 1 WLR 101, CA.
[194] *Conlon v Conlons Ltd* [1952] 2 All ER 462, CA.
[195] Per Lindley MR in *Calcraft v Guest* [1898] 1 QB 759 at 761, CA.
[196] *Pearce v Foster* (1885) 15 QBD 114, CA.
[197] *Minet v Morgan* (1873) 8 Ch App 361; *Crescent Farm (Sidcup) Sports Ltd v Sterling Offices Ltd* [1972] Ch 553, above.
[198] *The Aegis Blaze* [1986] 1 Lloyd's Rep 203, CA.
[199] [1955] 2 QB 195, CA.

and sought disclosure of the full report. It was held that the doctor was not entitled to rely on the company's privilege. The court, however, recognizing that the personal injuries action had yet to be disposed of, ordered that inspection of the report should take effect only on the conclusion of that action.

Where there are likely to be joint proceedings against the client and the third party, it may be that the third party will nonetheless be effectively protected by the client's privilege. In *Lee v South West Thames Regional Health Authority*[200] the health authorities of Hillingdon (H) and South West Thames (SWT) were both involved in the treatment of a patient which went badly wrong. H, for the purpose of getting legal advice about anticipated litigation against themselves, obtained from SWT a report of their involvement. On an application against SWT under section 33(2) of the Supreme Court Act 1981 for pre-action discovery of the report, it was held that although the privilege was that of H and not SWT, it was SWT's right and duty to assert H's privilege until such time as H no longer had an interest in non-disclosure. Since the proceedings against H and SWT would go together, the plaintiff would be unable to use the report against either of them.

Secondary evidence

Legal professional privilege prevents evidence from being given, or documents from being produced, by particular persons: the client, his lawyer, the relevant third parties (where applicable), and any agents for communication, such as secretaries or clerks.[201] If some other person overhears a privileged conversation or obtains a privileged document or a copy of it, he may be compelled to give evidence in that regard or to produce the document or copy. The leading case, *Calcraft v Guest*,[202] involved *copies* of privileged documents, but it is clear that under the principle, the originals, if available, can be produced.[203] The principle operates not only where the communication was disclosed by inadvertence or error on the part of the person otherwise entitled to assert the privilege, but also where the communication was obtained by improper or even unlawful means. However, CPR rule 31.20 provides that in civil cases in which a party inadvertently allows a privileged document to be inspected, the party who has inspected the document may use it or its contents only with the permission of the court.

In *R v Tompkins*[204] an incriminating note from the accused to his counsel was found on the floor of the court and handed to counsel for the prosecution. The Court of Appeal upheld the judge's ruling allowing the prosecution to show the note to the accused and to cross-examine him as to matters referred to in it. It is submitted that the court was correct in holding that the accused could not actually be asked to prove the note, since he was still entitled to assert his privilege in relation to it, but in principle it must have been permissible for the prosecution to tender the note in evidence themselves, subject to the possibly difficult task of proving authorship. In *R v Cottrill*,[205] applying *R v Tompkins*, it was held that a statement made by the accused to his solicitors and sent by them to the prosecution without his knowledge

[200] [1985] 1 WLR 845, CA.

[201] The same restrictions apply to a clinical case manager appointed to assist a severely injured person and involved in the client's litigation by attending conferences with lawyers and experts: *Wright v Sullivan* [2006] 1 WLR 172, CA.

[202] [1898] 1 QB 759, CA.

[203] See per Lord Simon in *Waugh v British Railways Board* [1980] AC 521 at 536; *Rumping v DPP* [1964] AC 814; and *R v Governor of Pentonville Prison, ex p Osman* [1989] 3 All ER 701 at 729–30, QBD.

[204] (1977) 67 Cr App R 181.

[205] [1997] Crim LR 56, CA.

or consent, could be used by the prosecution in cross-examination as a previous inconsistent statement, subject to section 78 of the Police and Criminal Evidence Act 1984.[206]

A litigant who has in his possession copies of documents to which legal professional privilege attaches may use them as secondary evidence in the litigation, but if he has not yet used them in that way, the mere fact that he intends to do so will not prevent a claim against him, by the person in whom the privilege is vested, for delivery up of the copies and for an injunction to restrain him from disclosing or making any use of any information contained in them.[207] In *Lord Ashburton v Pape*[208] Pape, a party to bankruptcy proceedings, obtained by a trick copies of confidential and privileged correspondence between Lord Ashburton and his solicitors. The Court of Appeal granted an injunction preventing Pape from using the copies in the bankruptcy proceedings. The possibility of using privileged material in evidence may thus turn simply on whether the owner can first obtain an injunction to restrain such use. In deciding whether to grant an injunction, the normal rules relating to the grant of equitable remedies apply. Thus delay is a relevant factor, as is the conduct of the party seeking the injunction, including the clean hands principle. Where, as in *ISTIL Group Inc v Zahoor*[209] the privileged documents show that evidence has been forged and that there has been an attempt to mislead the court, the public interest in supporting the privilege will be outweighed by the public interest in the proper administration of justice.

The principle in *Lord Ashburton v Pape* is not confined to cases in which the privileged material is obtained by trickery. In *Guinness Peat Properties Ltd v Fitzroy Robinson Partnership (a firm)*[210] it was held that it may also apply where the privilege is lost by inadvertence. That was a case in which one party to litigation had, on disclosure, mistakenly included in his list of documents to the production of which he did not object, a document for which privilege could properly have been claimed and which should have been included in the list of documents to the production of which he did object. The relevant principles in this situation were summarized by Slade LJ as follows:[211]

1. The court will ordinarily permit the party who made the error to amend his list.[212]

2. Once the other party has inspected the document, the general rule is that it is too late for the first party to correct the mistake by applying for injunctive relief.[213]

3. However, if the other party or his solicitor either (a) has procured inspection of the relevant document by fraud; or (b) on inspection realized that he has been permitted to see the document only by reason of an obvious mistake, the court has power to grant an injunction. Examples include *Goddard v Nationwide Building Society*,[214] in which the plaintiff's solicitors sent the defendant a copy of an attendance note recording

---

[206] See also *R v Willis* [2004] All ER (D) 287 (Dec).

[207] Per May LJ in *Goddard v Nationwide Building Society* [1986] 3 All ER 264 at 270, CA.

[208] [1913] 2 Ch 469, CA.

[209] [2003] 2 All ER 252, Ch D.

[210] [1987] 2 All ER 716, CA.

[211] [1987] 2 All ER 716 at 730–1.

[212] See, eg, *C H Beazer (Commercial and Industrial) Ltd v R M Smith Ltd* (1984) 3 Const LJ 196.

[213] See *Re Briamore Manufacturing Ltd* [1986] 3 All ER 132, Ch D. However, in that case the first party conceded that secondary evidence of the documents would be admissible and the court was not reminded of the decision in *Lord Ashburton v Pape*.

[214] [1986] 3 All ER 264, CA.

conversations with the plaintiff, and the defendant thereupon pleaded the substance of the contents in his defence, and *English and American Insurance Co Ltd v Herbert Smith & Co*,[215] in which a clerk to a barrister instructed by the plaintiff's solicitor mistakenly handed over to the defendant's solicitors a bundle of papers including instructions to counsel, counsel's notes, letters from the solicitor to the plaintiff, and statements of witnesses. In both cases an injunction and an order for delivery up was granted.

4. In such cases, the court should ordinarily grant the injunction unless it can properly be refused on general principles affecting the grant of a discretionary remedy, for example on the grounds of inordinate delay.[216]

In *Webster v James Chapman & Co*[217] Scott J held that the court should balance the interests of the one party in seeking to keep the information confidential against the interests of the other in seeking to make use of it, taking account of not only the privileged nature of the document, but also such matters as how the document was obtained and its relevance to the issues in the action. This approach was rejected in *Derby & Co Ltd v Weldon (No 8)*.[218] The Court of Appeal, without referring to *Webster v James Chapman & Co*, held that where an injunction is sought in aid of legal professional privilege, the court is not required to carry out such a balancing exercise. Dillon LJ said:[219]

> where the privilege is being restored because the inspection was obtained by fraud or by taking advantage of a known mistake, there is to my mind no logic at all in qualifying the restoration of the status quo by reference to the importance of the document. 'You have taken advantage of an obvious mistake to obtain copies of documents; we will order you to return all the ones that are unimportant to you but you can keep the ones that are important' would be a nonsensical attitude for the court to adopt.

In deciding whether disclosure has occurred as a result of an obvious mistake, the party claiming the injunction has the burden of proving, on a balance of probabilities, that the mistake would have been obvious to a reasonable solicitor, rather than to the actual recipient of the disclosed document, although the reaction of the actual recipient can be relevant. A reasonable solicitor, in deciding whether the privilege had been waived, would approach the question without bias towards his client and would take into account such factors as the extent of the claim to privilege in the list of documents, the nature of the document disclosed, the complexity of the discovery, the way it had been carried out, and the surrounding circumstances. Thus in *IBM Corpn v Phoenix International*,[220] from which these principles derive, and in which discovery involving a substantial number of documents had been carried out under a tight timetable and without due care, it was held that a reasonable solicitor would have realized that there was a risk of mistakes being made and would not have concluded, as the recipient had, that a deliberate decision had been made to disclose

---

[215] [1988] FSR 232, Ch D.

[216] If solicitors realize that documents have been mistakenly disclosed to them but, on the instructions of their client read them, an injunction may also be granted to restrain them from acting for the client in the proceedings in question: see *Ablitt v Mills & Reeve* (1995) The Times, 25 Oct, Ch D.

[217] [1989] 3 All ER 939, Ch D.

[218] [1990] 3 All ER 762.

[219] [1990] 3 All ER 762 at 783. See also per Nourse LJ in *Goddard v Nationwide Building Society* [1986] 3 All ER 264 at 272.

[220] [1995] 1 All ER 413, Ch D.

a document containing legal advice. In *Pizzey v Ford Motor Co Ltd*,[221] on the other hand, where discovery was slight and not complex, a reasonable solicitor would have assumed that privilege had been waived deliberately and not in error.

As previously noted, CPR rule 31.20 provides that in civil cases in which a party inadvertently allows a privileged document to be inspected, the party who has inspected the document may use it or its contents only with the permission of the court. The decision should be made in accordance with the principles established in the foregoing cases.[222]

Public policy may also prevent a party from relying upon the principle of *Calcraft v Guest*. In *ITC Film Distributors v Video Exchange Ltd*[223] documents were obtained by a trick in court in the course of civil proceedings. By that stage in the case there were difficulties in the way of granting injunctive relief, but the judge made interesting use of *D v NSPCC*[224] to hold that the public interest that litigants should be able to bring their documents into court without fear that they may be filched by their opponents, required an exception to the rule in *Calcraft v Guest*. The decision, it is submitted, correct in itself, results in an illogical distinction between documents stolen within court and those stolen without.

No less indefensible, it is submitted, is the distinction stemming from *Butler v Board of Trade*,[225] another decision made on grounds of public policy. It was held that the principle of *Lord Ashburton v Pape* cannot be used to prevent the prosecution from tendering relevant evidence in a public prosecution.[226] There is much to be said for allowing the spirit of *Lord Ashburton v Pape* to prevail in criminal as well as civil proceedings.[227]

Waiver

A client may elect to waive the legal professional privilege that he could otherwise assert. Having once waived the privilege, he cannot then reassert it. Thus a litigant who deliberately produces a privileged document for inspection on disclosure or serves notice of a conversation with his solicitor under the notice provisions relating to hearsay in civil cases, cannot at trial claim privilege for that communication.[228] However, if a document has been disclosed for a limited purpose only, privilege will not be waived generally, and the court is precluded from conducting a balancing exercise, because a lawyer must be able to give his client an unqualified assurance not only that what passes between them shall never be revealed without his consent, but that should he consent to disclosure within limits, those limits will be respected.[229] Thus where privileged documents prepared by a claimant for a civil action against a person are handed over to the police in accordance with the claimant's duty to assist in a criminal investigation, charges are preferred against that person and copies of the documents are disclosed to him by the prosecution, this cannot be construed as either an express or implied waiver of the

---

[221] [1994] PIQR P15, CA.

[222] *Al Fayed v Metropolitan Police Commissioner* [2002] EWCA Civ 780.

[223] [1982] Ch 431.

[224] [1978] AC 171. See Ch 19.

[225] [1971] Ch 680.

[226] The same point, in the case of a *private* prosecution, was expressly left open.

[227] Per Nourse LJ in *Goddard v Nationwide Building Society* [1986] 3 WLR 734 at 746, CA; and see *R v Uljee* [1982] 1 NZLR 561, NZCA.

[228] Merely referring to the existence of a document in pleadings or affidavits will not amount to waiver, though quoting from it may do so. See *Tate & Lyle International Ltd v Government Trading Corpn* [1984] LS Gaz R 3341, CA.

[229] *B v Auckland District Law Society* [2003] 2 AC 736, PC.

claimant's privilege in relation to the civil action, because to hold otherwise would be contrary to public policy.[230] Similarly, on the assessment of costs in civil cases, disclosure of privileged material is viewed as a waiver only for the purposes of the assessment: the privilege can be reasserted subsequently.[231]

The principle of waiver is capable of becoming somewhat complicated, particularly in the context of civil litigation, as a result of another principle, namely that a litigant is not entitled to edit his evidence, relying on the favourable parts of a privileged communication but refusing to say anything about the rest. Thus if part of a privileged document is put in evidence at trial, the other side can require the whole document to be disclosed, unless the remaining part concerns such a distinct subject matter as to be capable of severance.[232] The question whether 'cherry picking' is taking place, that is, whether fairness requires the whole document to be adduced so that the court is not misled by seeing only part of it out of context, can only be answered by the judge after he has read the whole of it.[233] The same principles apply at the interim stage of civil proceedings.[234] If cross-examining counsel puts to an opposing witness a statement taken on behalf of his own client, even only a small part of it, he waives his client's privilege in the statement and thereby entitles counsel who called the witness to re-examine him on the whole of the statement. However, the risk of permitting such lengthy re-examination can be avoided either by counsel agreeing that part only of a statement may be put without the whole being opened up for re-examination, or by cross-examining counsel preparing written questions to be handed to the witness either in the witness-box or several days previously.[235] The disclosure of part of a privileged document on disclosure constitutes a waiver of privilege of the entire contents of the document unless, again, the other part deals with a separate subject matter so that the document can be divided into two separate and distinct documents.[236] As to the disclosure of privileged material in interim proceedings, a distinction has to be drawn between a reference to having been given advice to a particular effect, which does not amount to waiver of the right to claim privilege in respect of the advice itself at the subsequent trial, and disclosure of the substance or content of that advice, which does amount to such a waiver.[237]

The principle under discussion, if taken to extremes, could lead to the disclosure of a vast array of otherwise privileged material, including proofs of evidence, memoranda prepared by solicitors, and instructions to counsel.[238] The courts have thus been obliged to find ways of limiting the principle. In *George Doland Ltd v Blackburn, Robson, Coates & Co*[239] a distinction was

[230] *British Coal Corpn v Dennis Rye Ltd (No 2)* [1988] 3 All ER 816, CA.

[231] See *Goldman v Hesper* [1988] 1 WLR 1238, CA. See also para 40.14 of Practice Direction 43–8 and *South Coast Shipping Co Ltd v Havant Borough Council* [2003] 3 All ER 779, Ch D.

[232] *Great Atlantic Insurance Co v Home Insurance Co* [1981] 1 WLR 529, CA. See also *George Doland Ltd v Blackburn, Robson, Coates & Co* [1972] 1 WLR 1338, QBD: if a client seeks to support his credit at trial by reference to what he said to his solicitor on one occasion, he cannot object to being cross-examined as to what he said to his solicitor about the same subject matter on other occasions.

[233] *Derby & Co Ltd v Weldon (No 10)* [1991] 2 All ER 908, Ch D.

[234] *Dunlop Slazenger International Ltd v Joe Bloggs Sports Ltd* [2003] EWCA Civ 901.

[235] *Fairfield-Mabey Ltd v Shell UK Ltd* [1989] 1 All ER 576, QBD.

[236] *Pozzi v Eli Lilly & Co* (1986) The Times, 3 Dec, QBD.

[237] *Derby & Co Ltd v Weldon (No 10)* [1991] 2 All ER 908, Ch D.

[238] Suggested in argument in *General Accident Fire and Life Assurance Co Ltd v Tanter* [1984] 1 WLR 100, though on the facts the judge was able to avoid that result.

[239] [1972] 1 WLR 1338, QBD.

drawn between legal advice and litigation privilege. It was held that oral conversations and documents relating to the subject matter in question were only liable to disclosure insofar as they were covered by the first type of privilege. A different approach, however, was adopted in *General Accident Fire and Life Assurance Co Ltd v Tanter*.[240] In that case privilege had been waived in relation to a conversation which took place at a time when litigation was anticipated and to which the second type of privilege applied. Hobhouse J held that if the party entitled to the privilege puts the conversation in evidence (as opposed to being cross-examined about it) then waiver relates to 'the transaction', that is what was said on the occasion in question, and does not extend to the subject matter of the conversation. Thus although the opposite party is entitled to call for, inspect, and cross-examine on other privileged communications relating to what was actually said in the conversation, he is not entitled to see or use such other privileged communications as may exist relating to the subject matter of the conversation.[241]

Fulham Leisure Holdings Ltd v Nicholson Graham and Jones (a firm)[242] makes clear that the decision-making process may involve a number of different stages. The starting point is to identify the 'transaction' or 'act' in respect of which disclosure was made. That may be identifiable simply from the nature of the disclosure; one is entitled to look at the purpose for which the material was disclosed or the point in the action to which it was said to go. However, the court should determine objectively what the real transaction is. If it is wider than at first thought and only part of the material involved in the transaction has been disclosed, further disclosure will be ordered. Finally, if it is apparent from the disclosure that the transaction is in fact part of 'some bigger picture', then further disclosure will be ordered if necessary to avoid unfairness or misunderstanding of what has previously been disclosed.

The institution of civil proceedings by a client against his solicitor constitutes an implied waiver of privilege. The waiver must go far enough not merely to enable the client to establish his cause of action but to enable the solicitor to establish a defence. Thus it may extend beyond the communications relating to the specific retainer forming the subject matter of the proceedings to communications relating to earlier retainers which are relevant to the issue between the parties.[243]

Without prejudice negotiations

Settlement negotiations

Communications between opposing parties to a civil action, or between their solicitors, do not attract legal professional privilege. In the absence of any other protection, therefore, if one party were to make a concession on the question of liability in the course of settlement negotiations which, in the event, were to fail, the other party would be able to use it against him

---

[240] [1984] 1 WLR 100.

[241] Hobhouse J declined to follow *George Doland Ltd v Blackburn, Robson, Coates & Co* [1972] 1 WLR 1338 insofar as it could be treated as an authority to the contrary. It was also held that the distinction drawn in that case between the two types of privilege was not a criterion applicable in all cases and was not applicable in the instant case. See also *Derby & Co Ltd v Weldon (No 10)* [1991] 2 All ER 908, where Vinelott J, in the case of a single conversation, different parts of which were covered by the different types of privilege, refused to sever the two types of privilege and to say that one was waived but not the other: both had been waived.

[242] [2006] 2 All ER 599, ChD.

[243] *Lillicrap v Nalder & Son (a firm)* [1993] 1 All ER 724, CA. Cf *Nederlandse Reassurantie Groep Holding NV v Bacon & Woodrow (a firm)* [1995] 1 All ER 976, QBD.

at the trial as a damaging admission. In order to remove this risk and thereby encourage the settlement of civil litigation, the rule is that privilege attaches to oral or written statements made 'without prejudice', that is without prejudice to the maker of the statement if the terms he proposes are not accepted.[244] The privilege is the joint privilege of both parties and extends to their solicitors.[245] It can only be waived with the consent of each of the parties.[246] The protection of admissions against interest is the most important practical effect of the rule, but to dissect out admissions and withhold protection from the rest of without prejudice communications would be to create huge practical difficulties and would be contrary to the underlying objective of giving protection to the parties to speak freely about all the issues in the litigation. As Walker LJ observed in *Unilever plc v The Procter & Gamble Co*,[247] 'Parties cannot speak freely at a without prejudice meeting if they must constantly monitor every sentence, with lawyers . . . sitting at their shoulders as minders.'[248] Thus in *Ofulue v Bossert*[249] the House of Lords held that privilege attaches to a statement made in without prejudice negotiations if it is an 'admission' of a matter that the parties do not even dispute and therefore is not in issue. In *Muller v Linsley & Mortimer (a firm)*[250] Hoffmann LJ said that the public policy basis of the privilege is to prevent anything said from being used as an admission, ie for the truth of the facts admitted, rather for some other relevant purpose, for example to show the falsity of the statement or simply to establish the fact that the admission was made.[251] In *Ofulue v Bossert*, however, a majority of the House held that such a distinction was too subtle to apply in practice and would often risk falling foul of the problem identified by Walker LJ (in the passage quoted above).

The basis of the rule is one of public policy, to encourage those in dispute to settle their differences without recourse to, or continuation of, litigation, and in *Barnetson v Framlington Group Ltd*[252] it was held that to give full effect to this policy, a dispute may engage the rule notwithstanding that litigation has not begun. On the question of how proximate negotiations must be to the start of the litigation, the court held that the privilege is not confined to negotiations once litigation has been threatened or shortly before it has begun, because that would be an incentive to the parties to escalate the dispute in order to gain the benefit of the rule. On the other hand, the ambit of the rule should not be extended further than necessary in the circumstances of any particular case to promote the policy underlying it. Auld LJ held that the question is highly case sensitive; that the claim to privilege cannot turn on purely temporal considerations; and that the crucial consideration will be whether, in the course of the negotiations, the parties contemplated or might reasonably have contemplated litigation if they could not agree.

[244] See per Lindley LJ in *Walker v Wilsher* (1889) 23 QBD 335, CA at 337. There is nothing in criminal law akin to 'without prejudice': *R v Hayes* [2005] 1 Cr App R 557, CA, where the prosecution were entitled to cross-examine H on a previous inconsistent statement in a letter sent by his solicitor to the CPS suggesting that he might plead guilty to a lesser offence.

[245] *La Roche v Armstrong* [1922] 1 KB 485.

[246] Inclusion of a without prejudice document in a party's list of documents on disclosure does not amount to waiver: *Galliford Try Construction Ltd v Mott MacDonald* [2008] EWHC 603 (TCC).

[247] [2001] 1 All ER 783, CA at 796.

[248] However, there is nothing to prevent the parties from expressly agreeing that some parts of their discussions are 'without prejudice' and that others are 'on the record', ie unprotected: *R v K* [2009] EWCA Crim 1640 at [49].

[249] [2009] UKHL 16.

[250] [1996] PNLR 74, CA.

[251] See also per Lord Hoffmann in *Bradford & Bingley plc v Rashid* [2006] 1 WLR 2066, HL at 2072.

[252] [2007] 3 All ER 1054, CA.

Without prejudice privilege may be asserted at the trial itself, whether in relation to liability, quantum, or costs,[253] as well as in interim proceedings such as a hearing of a summons for security for costs.[254] The contents of without prejudice correspondence can be disclosed in an application to strike out for want of prosecution, but if it fails, the privilege can be asserted at the trial itself.[255] However where, on an interim application, one party deploys without prejudice material in support of his case on the underlying merits of the claim, the other party is entitled to use other parts of that material at the trial.[256]

If the negotiations succeed and a settlement is concluded, the without prejudice correspondence remains privileged: such correspondence is inadmissible in any subsequent litigation connected with the same subject matter, whether between the same or different parties, and is also protected from subsequent disclosure to other parties to the litigation.[257] Similarly, in a case in which negotiations did not result in a settlement, it was held that it is 'strongly arguable' that the principles governing the admissibility, in subsequent proceedings, of a statement made in without prejudice negotiations to settle earlier proceedings, should be the same as those which would govern its admissibility in the earlier proceedings, and that it is hard to see how the contrary could even be argued where the two sets of proceedings involve the same parties and very closely connected issues.[258] However, if evidence of damaging admissions made in the course of 'without prejudice' communications falls into the hands of the prosecuting authorities, it is admissible in subsequent criminal proceedings against the party who made the admissions, subject to the discretion to exclude under section 78 of the 1984 Act, because the public interest in prosecuting crime is sufficient to outweigh the public interest in the settlement of disputes.[259]

The essential pre-condition for a claim to without prejudice privilege is the existence of a dispute. Thus in *Bradford & Bingley plc v Rashid*[260] the House of Lords held that the without prejudice rule had no application to open communications between a creditor and a debtor which dealt only with whether, when, and to what extent the debtor could meet his admitted liability. For a majority of their Lordships, since the debt was admitted, there was simply no dispute to be compromised.[261] Whether there is a dispute is sometimes a question of some nicety, as in *BNP Paribas v Mezzotero*.[262] While a grievance of M about perceived discrimination was being processed, the employer convened a without prejudice meeting, said to be independent of the grievance, at which M was advised that her job was no longer viable and an offer of a redundancy package was made. In a subsequent tribunal application claiming, inter alia, sex discrimination, it was held that M could rely on what was said at the meeting because there was no dispute at that time. Upholding this ruling, the Employment Appeal Tribunal

---

[253] *Walker v Wilsher* (1889) 23 QBD 335, CA. But see *Calderbank v Calderbank* [1976] Fam 93, below.

[254] *Simaan General Contracting Co v Pilkington Glass Ltd* [1987] 1 All ER 345, CA.

[255] *Family Housing Association (Manchester) Ltd v Michael Hyde & Partners (a firm)* [1993] 2 All ER 567, CA.

[256] *Somatra Ltd v Sinclair Roche and Temperley* [2000] 1 WLR 2453. See also CPR r 31.22.

[257] *Rush & Tompkins Ltd v Greater London Council* [1988] 3 All ER 737, HL. However, the privilege will not prevent inspection of the terms of a settlement if relevant in determining the extent of the liability of a third party against whom one of the parties to the settlement is seeking a contribution: *Gnitrow Ltd v Cape plc* [2000] 1 WLR 2327, CA.

[258] *Ofulue v Bossert* [2009] UKHL 16.

[259] *R v K* [2009] EWCA Crim 1640.

[260] [2006] 1 WLR 2066, HL

[261] Equally, the privilege will not protect correspondence designed to prevent a dispute arising: *Prudential Assurance Co Ltd v Prudential Insurance Co of America* [2002] EWHC 2809, Ch D.

[262] [2004] IRLR 508, EAT.

held that there was no evidence of an employment dispute before the meeting. The grievance related to her continuing employment, not the threat of termination of employment, and therefore could not be treated as evidence of a dispute.

The privilege attaches to any discussions that take place between actual or prospective parties with a view to avoiding litigation, including discussions within conciliation and mediation schemes.[263] The fact that the expression 'without prejudice' is not actually used is 'not without significance',[264] but does not conclude the matter: provided that there is some dispute and an attempt is being made to settle it, the courts should be ready to infer that the attempt was without prejudice.[265] In order to decide whether or not a document was bona fide intended to be a negotiating document, the court has to look at the intention of the author and how the document would be received by a reasonable recipient. If the document is marked 'without prejudice' that is a factor that the court should take into account. It is an indication that the author intended it to be a negotiating document and, in many cases, a recipient would receive it on the understanding that the marking indicated that the author wished to attempt negotiation.[266] However, the heading 'without prejudice' does not conclusively or automatically render privileged a document so marked; if privilege is claimed for such a document but challenged, the court can look at it to determine its nature.[267] The privilege can attach to a document headed 'without prejudice' even if it is an 'opening shot', but the rule is not limited to documents which are offers; privilege attaches to all documents marked 'without prejudice' and forming part of negotiations, whether or not they contain offers, subject only to the recognized exceptions.[268]

There are a number of exceptions.[269] Without prejudice material is admissible if the issue is whether or not the negotiations resulted in an agreed settlement.[270] The rule cannot be used to exclude an act of bankruptcy (such as a letter containing an offer to settle which also states the writer's inability to pay his debts as they fall due).[271] In *Ofulue v Bossert*[272] the House of Lords left open the question whether, and if so to what extent, a statement made in without prejudice negotiations would be admissible if 'in no way connected' with the issues in the case the subject of the negotiations. The privilege cannot be

[263] See *Smiths Group plc v Weiss* [2002] EWHC 582, Ch D. Confidentiality attaches to discussions within such schemes to the same extent that it does to other 'without prejudice' negotiations—there is no broader or more comprehensive 'mediation privilege': see *Brown v Rice* [2007] EWHC 625 (Ch) and *Cattley v Pollard* [2007] 2 All ER 1086.

[264] *Prudential Assurance Co Ltd v Prudential Insurance Co of America* [2002] EWHC 2809, Ch D.

[265] *Chocoladefabriken Lindt & Sprungli AG v Nestlé Co Ltd* [1978] RPC 287 at 288–9. If negotiations begin on a without prejudice basis, they remain so unless the party wishing to change them to an open basis makes this clear to the other party: *Cheddar Valley Engineering Ltd v Chaddlewood Homes Ltd* [1992] 4 All ER 942. However, open letters written after the negotiations and 'without prejudice' correspondence have finished and come to nothing, are not privileged: *Dixons Stores Group Ltd v Thames Television plc* [1993] 1 All ER 349.

[266] *Schering Corpn v Cipla Ltd* (2004) The Times, 10 Nov, Ch D.

[267] *South Shropshire District Council v Amos* [1987] 1 All ER 340.

[268] Ibid, CA at 344.

[269] For a non-exhaustive, but nonetheless extensive, list of the exceptions, see per Robert Walker LJ in *Unilever plc v The Procter & Gamble Co* [2001] 1 All ER 783, CA at 791–3.

[270] *Walker v Wilsher* (1889) 23 QBD 335, CA at 337; *Tomlin v Standard Telephones and Cables Ltd* [1969] 3 All ER 201, CA. It is also admissible on the question whether a mediation resulted in an agreed settlement: *Brown v Rice* [2007] EWHC 625 (Ch).

[271] *Re Daintrey, ex p Holt* [1893] 2 QB 116.

[272] [2009] UKHL 16 at [92].

claimed when an agreement concluded between the parties during the negotiations should be set aside on the grounds of fraud or undue influence.[273] Negligent misrepresentations, however, will not prevent a claim to the privilege.[274] The privilege cannot be claimed if exclusion of the evidence would act as a cloak for perjury, blackmail, or other 'unambiguous impropriety',[275] but this exception should be applied only in the clearest cases of abuse.[276] As to perjury, the exception will apply in the case of a defendant who says that unless the case is withdrawn, he will give perjured evidence and will bribe other witnesses to perjure themselves.[277] However, the test is not whether there is a serious and substantial risk of perjury.[278] The exception will not apply where an admission is alleged to have been made that demonstrates that the pleaded case must be false[279] or where an admission is made that demonstrates that perjury has been committed in the past.[280] As to blackmail, the exception will apply where a claimant says that his claim is bogus and is being brought to 'blackmail' the defendant into a settlement of their real differences.[281] An example of other 'unambiguous impropriety' would be where an employer in dispute with a black employee says during discussions aimed at settlement, 'we do not want you here because you are black': such evidence should not be excluded from consideration by a tribunal hearing a subsequent complaint of race discrimination.[282]

CPR Part 36 codifies the practice at common law whereby a party could make an offer in a letter headed 'without prejudice except as to costs', thereby reserving his right to refer to the letter, should the action proceed to judgment, on the question of costs. Under Part 36, a written offer, called a 'Part 36 offer', may be made with a view to settling the whole or part of a claim. The offer may be made at any time, including before the commencement of the proceedings.[283] If it is an offer by a defendant to pay a sum of money in settlement of a claim, it must be an offer to pay a single sum of money.[284] If the offer is not accepted, normally the court must not be told about it until all questions of liability and quantum have been decided,[285] but if, at that stage, the judgment is no better than the offer, then normally, and unless the court considers it unjust to do so, it will order that the defendant is entitled to the costs that he has incurred since the date of expiry of the 'relevant period',[286] which is usually a period of not less than 21 days specified in the Part 36 offer.[287]

---

[273] *Underwood v Cox* (1912) 4 DLR 66.

[274] *Jefferies Group & Kvaerner International*, 19 January 2007, unreported.

[275] The expression used by Hoffmann LJ in *Forster v Friedland* [1992] CA Transcript 1052.

[276] *Forster v Friedland*, ibid and *Fazil-Alizadeh v Nikbin* (1993) The Times, 19 Mar, CA.

[277] *Greenwood v Fitts* (1961) 29 DLR (2d) 260, BC CA.

[278] *Berry Trade Ltd v Moussavi* [2003] EWCA Civ 715, [2003] All ER (D) 315 (May), CA.

[279] Ibid.

[280] *Savings and Investment Bank Ltd v Fincken* [2004] 1 All ER 1125, CA.

[281] *Hawick Jersey International Ltd v Caplan* (1988) The Times, 11 Mar, QBD.

[282] Per Cox J in *BNP Paribas v Mezzotero* [2004] IRLR 508, EAT. See also per Smith LJ, obiter, in *Brunel University v Vaseghi* [2007] EWCA Civ 482 at [32]; and cf *Brodie v Nicola Ward (t/a First Steps Nursery)* [2008] All ER (D) 115 (Feb), EAT, where, in proceedings for unfair constructive dismissal, the employee was prevented from using a without prejudice letter from the employer's solicitor which, she claimed, was the 'last straw' causing her to resign.

[283] Rule 36.3(2)(a).

[284] Rule 36.4(1). Special provision is made in personal injury claims in respect of future pecuniary loss: see r 36.5.

[285] Rule 36.13(2).

[286] Rule 36.14(1) and (2).

[287] See r 36.2(2)(c) and r 36.3(1)(c).

Matrimonial reconciliation cases

A privilege, similar to that which attaches to 'without prejudice' communications, has been developed to cover communications made in the course of matrimonial conciliation, matrimonial proceedings being in contemplation. In *D v NSPCC*[288] Lord Simon said:

> With increasingly facile divorce and a vast rise in the number of broken marriages, with their concomitant penury and demoralization, it came to be realized, in the words of Buckmill LJ in *Mole v Mole*:[289] 'in matrimonial disputes the state is also an interested party: it is more interested in reconciliation than in divorce'. This was the public interest which led to the application by analogy of the privilege of 'without prejudice' communications to cover communications made in the course of matrimonial conciliation (see *McTaggart v McTaggart*;[290] *Mole v Mole*;[291] *Theodoropoulas v Theodoropoulas*)[292] so indubitably an extension of the law that the textbooks treat it as a separate category of relevant evidence which may be withheld from the court. It cannot be classed, like traditional 'without prejudice' communications, as a 'privilege in aid of litigation . . . '

In *Mole v Mole* it was established that the privilege applies to communications by a spouse not only with an official conciliator such as a probation officer but also to 'other persons such as clergy, doctors or marriage guidance counsellors to whom the parties or one of them go with a view to reconciliation, there being a tacit understanding that the conversations are without prejudice'.[293] In *Theodoropoulas v Theodoropoulas* Sir Jocelyn Simon P, having held that the same rule applied where a private individual is enlisted specifically as a conciliator, said:[294]

> Privilege [also] attaches to communications between the spouses themselves when made with a view to reconciliation. It also extends to excluding the evidence of an independent witness who was fortuitously present when those communications were made and who overheard or read them. I therefore ruled that all the evidence tendered, whether by way of cross-examination of the wife, or in chief from the husband or by calling [a bystander] was inadmissible.[295]

The privilege is that of the spouses and can only be waived by them jointly. The intermediary cannot object to such waiver.

In proceedings under the Children Act 1989, evidence cannot be given of statements made by one or other of the parties in the course of meetings held, or communications made, for the purpose of conciliation. It is important to preserve a cloak over all attempts at settlements of disputes over children. However, an exception exists in the very unusual case where the statement clearly indicates that the maker has in the past or is likely in the future to cause serious harm to the well-being of a child. In these exceptional cases, it is for the trial judge to

---

[288] [1978] AC 171 at 236–7.
[289] [1951] P 21, CA.
[290] [1949] P 94, CA.
[291] [1951] P 21, CA.
[292] [1964] P 311, CA.
[293] [1951] P 21 at 24 per Denning LJ.
[294] [1964] P 311 at 314.
[295] See Law Reform Committee, 16th Report, *Privilege in Civil Proceedings* (1967) (Cmnd 3472) para 36: 'As respects the requirement that matrimonial proceedings must be in contemplation in order that the privilege may attach, it is, we think, a reasonable inference from the fact that a third party has been called in by one or other of the spouses to act as mediator that such proceedings are sufficiently in contemplation to give rise to the privilege, and the courts today readily draw such inference. Where the negotiations take place directly between the spouses it may be more difficult for the court to decide whether such inference should be drawn; we do not, however, see any distinction of principle between the two situations.'

decide, in the exercise of his discretion, whether or not to admit the evidence, and he should do so only if the public interest in protecting the interests of the child outweighs the public interest in preserving the confidentiality of attempted conciliation.[296]

ADDITIONAL READING

Auburn, *Legal Professional Privilege: Law and Theory* (Oxford, 2000).

Loughrey, 'Legal advice privilege and the corporate client' (2005) 9 *E&P* 183.

MacCulloch, 'The privilege against self-incrimination in competition investigations: theoretical foundations and practical implications' *Legal Studies*, Vol 26 No 2, June 2006, 211.

Passmore, 'Watch what you say' (2006) *NLJ* 668.

Vaver, '"Without Prejudice" Communications—Their Admissibility and Effect' [1974] *U Br Col LR* 85.

---

[296] *Re D (minors)* [1993] 2 All ER 693, CA.

Judgments as evidence of the facts upon which they were based[1]

21

Key Issues

● When, and why, should the fact that a person has been convicted of an offence be admissible in evidence for the purpose of proving that he committed that offence (a) in subsequent civil proceedings; and (b) in subsequent criminal proceedings?

---

[1] The word 'judgment' is used here to denote both judgments in civil proceedings and verdicts in criminal proceedings.

It will be useful to begin this chapter by reference to two doctrines, the detailed exposition of which is outside the ambit of this work, namely the doctrines of estoppel by record and estoppel *per rem judicatam*. Under the doctrine of estoppel by record, every judgment is conclusive as against all persons as to the legal state of affairs it effects when that state of affairs is in issue or relevant to an issue in some subsequent proceedings. Thus where a decree of divorce is granted, irretrievable breakdown being established by proof of the respondent's adultery, the decree is conclusive as to the termination of the marriage but not as to the respondent's adultery. Where a judgment is entered against a man for damage caused by his negligence, it is conclusive as to the amount of damages awarded against him but not as to his negligence. Likewise, if a man is convicted or acquitted of theft, the record of the court is conclusive as to the fact that he was convicted or acquitted but not as to the fact that he did or did not commit the theft. Under the doctrine of estoppel *per rem judicatam*, sometimes known as estoppel by record *inter partes*, a judgment is conclusive as to the facts on which it was based but only as against the parties to the legal proceedings in which that judgment was given or their privies. Thus parties and privies but not strangers to the earlier proceedings will be estopped in subsequent proceedings from giving evidence to contradict the facts on which the earlier judgment was based.

The present chapter is concerned with the circumstances in which a judgment is admissible in subsequent proceedings as evidence of the facts on which it was based even though the parties to the subsequent proceedings may be different from those to the earlier proceedings. The problem may be identified by adapting two of the examples already given. If Mr A is granted a decree of divorce from Mrs A, irretrievable breakdown being established by reason of the fact that Mrs A committed adultery with Mr B, can Mrs B, on her petition for divorce, rely on the decree as evidence of the fact that Mr B committed adultery with Mrs A?[2] If D1 is convicted of the theft of certain goods, can the Crown, in a prosecution of D2 for handling those goods, rely upon D1's conviction as evidence that the goods were stolen? Until recently the common law answers to questions of this kind were largely, if not entirely, governed by the decision in *Hollington v Hewthorn & Co Ltd*.[3] That case tipped the balance in favour of the view supported by the bulk of the case law preceding it, that previous judgments are not admissible as evidence of the facts on which they were based.[4]

The action in *Hollington v Hewthorn & Co Ltd* arose out of a collision between two cars. The plaintiff, the owner of one of the cars, brought an action in negligence against the driver of the other car, who had been convicted of careless driving (at the time and place of the accident), and his employer. The Court of Appeal held that the plaintiff was not entitled to admit the conviction of the defendant driver as evidence of his negligence. The decision was based largely on the view that the civil court would know nothing of the evidence before the criminal court (and the arguments that were addressed to it) and that the opinion of the criminal court was irrelevant. The principle of *Hollington v Hewthorn & Co Ltd* was then applied to cases where the subsequent proceedings were criminal. In *R v Spinks*[5] F had stabbed someone with a knife and had been convicted of wounding with intent to do grievous bodily harm. At the trial of Spinks for assisting F by concealing the knife with intent to impede the apprehension

---

[2] See *Sutton v Sutton* [1970] 1 WLR 183, PD.

[3] [1943] KB 587, CA.

[4] But see *Crippen's Estate* [1911] P 108 and *Partington v Partington and Atkinson* [1925] P 34.

[5] [1982] 1 All ER 587. See also *R v Hassan* [1970] 1 QB 423, CA.

or prosecution of 'a person who had committed an arrestable offence', namely F, the Court of Appeal held that the Crown could not rely on F's conviction as evidence that he had committed the arrestable offence of wounding. Since there was no other admissible evidence that F had committed such an offence, Spinks' conviction was quashed.

The rule in *Hollington v Hewthorn & Co Ltd* attracted much criticism. Its effect, in both civil and criminal proceedings, has been largely removed by the Civil Evidence Act 1968 (the 1968 Act) and the Police and Criminal Evidence Act 1984 (the 1984 Act).

Civil proceedings

Narrowly stated, *Hollington v Hewthorn & Co Ltd* had decided that a conviction of a criminal offence is inadmissible in civil proceedings as evidence of the fact that the person convicted committed the offence in question. The Law Reform Committee, observing that the onus of proof in criminal cases is higher than in civil cases, and that the degree of carelessness required to convict of careless driving is, if anything, greater than that required to sustain a civil action for negligence, described the decision as offensive to one's sense of justice.[6] Sections 11–13 of the 1968 Act, giving effect to the Committee's recommendations, overrule the decision insofar as it applies, in civil cases, not only to previous criminal convictions but also to findings of adultery and paternity in previous civil proceedings. After we have examined these statutory provisions, consideration will be given to the extent to which, if at all, the rule in *Hollington v Hewthorn & Co Ltd* continues to apply, in civil proceedings, to previous acquittals and to findings other than those of adultery and paternity in previous civil proceedings.

Previous convictions

Section 11 of the Civil Evidence Act 1968

Section 11 of the 1968 Act not only reverses the rule in *Hollington v Hewthorn & Co Ltd* as narrowly stated, but also creates a persuasive presumption: the person convicted, once his conviction has been proved, shall be taken to have committed the offence in question unless the contrary is proved. Section 11 provides that:

(1) In any civil proceedings the fact that a person has been convicted of an offence by or before any court in the United Kingdom or by a court-martial there or elsewhere shall (subject to subsection (3) below) be admissible in evidence for the purpose of proving, where to do so is relevant to any issue in those proceedings, that he committed that offence, whether he was so convicted upon a plea of guilty or otherwise and whether or not he is a party to the civil proceedings; but no conviction other than a subsisting one shall be admissible in evidence by virtue of this section.

(2) In any civil proceedings in which by virtue of this section a person is proved to have been convicted of an offence by or before any court in the United Kingdom or by a court-martial there or elsewhere—

(a) he shall be taken to have committed that offence unless the contrary is proved; and

(b) without prejudice to the reception of any other admissible evidence for the purpose of identifying the facts on which the conviction was based, the contents of any document which is admissible as evidence of the conviction, and the contents of the information, complaint, indictment or charge-sheet on which the person in question was convicted, shall be admissible in evidence for that purpose.

---

[6] 15th Report (1967) (Cmnd 3391), para 3.

Concerning section 11(1), 'civil proceedings' includes, in addition to civil proceedings in any of the ordinary courts of law, (a) civil proceedings before any other tribunal in relation to which the strict rules of evidence apply; and (b) an arbitration or reference, whether under an enactment or not, but does not include civil proceedings in relation to which the strict rules of evidence do not apply.[7] Subsection (3), to which section 11(1) is subject, provides that nothing in section 11 shall prejudice the operation of, inter alia, section 13, which, as we shall see, relates to proceedings for defamation. A 'conviction' includes one in respect of which an absolute or conditional discharge was imposed.[8] A conviction against which an appeal is pending is 'subsisting' but not one which has been quashed on appeal.[9] The Act has no application to adjudications of guilt in police disciplinary proceedings[10] or to foreign convictions.[11]

There is little dispute that section 11(2)(a) has the effect of reversing the legal burden of proof in respect of the commission of the offence. Thus if A sues B for conduct on the part of B in respect of which B stands convicted, it is for B to prove, on a balance of probabilities, that he did not commit the offence; and therefore it is not sufficient for someone in B's position to establish that the conviction is unsafe, that the judge in the criminal trial, or the Court of Appeal, made an error, or that the prosecution was an abuse of process.[12] There is a divergence of judicial opinion, however, as to what weight should be attached to the conviction in deciding whether the onus resting on B has been discharged. In *Taylor v Taylor*[13] a divorce suit in which the petitioner, in support of her allegation that the husband had committed adultery, tendered evidence of his conviction of incest, Davies LJ thought it probable that the onus of proof of upsetting the conviction was on a balance of probabilities. His Lordship continued, 'but, having said that, it nevertheless is obvious that, when a man has been convicted . . . the verdict of the jury is a matter which is entitled to very great weight . . . '.[14] In *Stupple v Royal Insurance Co Ltd*[15] Stupple had been convicted of robbery from a bank which had been indemnified by the defendant insurance company. Stupple claimed from the defendants certain money which had been found by the police in his possession and which had been paid over to the defendants under the Police (Property) Act 1897. Judgment was given for the defendants. The plaintiff's appeal to the Court of Appeal was dismissed. Buckley LJ said:[16]

---

[7] Section 18(1).

[8] Section 11(5), as amended by the Criminal Justice Act 1991.

[9] See *Re Raphael, Raphael v D'Antin* [1973] 1 WLR 998: rather than finally dispose of civil proceedings in reliance on a conviction subsequently liable to be quashed, the civil proceedings may be adjourned pending the appeal. See also *R v Foster* [1984] 2 All ER 679, CA: the effect of a free pardon is to remove all pains, penalties and punishments ensuing from the conviction but not to eliminate the conviction itself.

[10] *Thorpe v Chief Constable of Greater Manchester Police* [1989] 2 All ER 827, CA.

[11] See *Union Carbide Corpn v Naturin Ltd* [1987] FSR 538, CA. Even if the rule in *Hollington v Hewthorn & Co Ltd* covers foreign convictions, it will not apply where the issues in the criminal and civil proceedings are identical: *Director of the Assets Recovery Agency v Virtosu* [2008] EWHC 149, civil proceedings for a recovery order under s 241 of the Proceeds of Crime Act 2002. See also *Arab Monetary Fund v Hashim (No 2)* [1990] 1 All ER 673, Ch D.

[12] *Raja v Van Hoogstraten* [2005] EWHC 1642, Ch D.

[13] [1970] 1 WLR 1148, CA.

[14] [1970] 1 WLR 1148 at 1152.

[15] [1971] 1 QB 50.

[16] [1971] 1 QB 50 at 76.

In my judgment, proof of conviction under this section gives rise to the statutory presumption laid down in section 11(2)(a), which, like any other presumption, will give way to evidence establishing the contrary on the balance of probability, without itself affording any evidential weight to be taken into account in determining whether that onus has been discharged.

Lord Denning MR, however, took a different view, being of the opinion that although the conviction is not conclusive, it does not merely shift the burden of proof but is a weighty piece of evidence of itself.[17] In *Hunter v Chief Constable of West Midlands*[18] Lord Denning MR went further. In answer to the question how, for the purposes of section 11(2)(a), a convicted man is to prove the contrary, his Lordship expressed the view, obiter:

Only, I suggest, by proving that the conviction was obtained by fraud or collusion, or by adducing fresh evidence. If the fresh evidence is inconclusive, he does not prove his innocence. It must be decisive, it must be conclusive, before he can be declared innocent.

When the case came before the House of Lords, however, Lord Diplock, disapproving this dictum, said:[19]

The burden of proof of 'the contrary' that lies on a defendant under section 11 is the ordinary burden in a civil action, ie proof on a balance of probabilities, although in the face of a conviction after a full hearing that is likely to be an uphill task.

Insofar as it suggests that the party seeking to prove 'the contrary' bears a burden heavier than proof on a balance of probabilities, the approach adopted by Lord Denning MR and Davies LJ, it is submitted, should not be followed. It seems equally untenable that a conviction should *invariably* be regarded as a weighty item of evidence in itself. It is submitted that the weight to be attached to the conviction will depend on the particular circumstances of the case, including, for example, whether the decision was unanimous or by a majority.[20] Clearly, regard may also be had to a transcript of the evidence given in the criminal proceedings, a copy of the judge's summing-up,[21] and any fresh evidence that has subsequently become available to the parties.

Section 11(2)(b) provides for the admissibility of specific types of document for the purpose of identifying the facts on which the conviction was based. Provision is also made for the admissibility of duly certified copies of such documents, which shall be taken to be true copies unless the contrary is shown.[22] A transcript of a judge's summing-up is not admissible under section 11(2)(b) itself, but is admissible, for the purposes referred to in section 11(2)(b), under the Civil Evidence Act 1995.[23]

It would appear that a conviction admitted under section 11 is capable of amounting to corroboration where this is required. In *Mash v Darley*[24] the evidence of the applicant

[17] [1971] 1 QB 50 at 72.

[18] [1981] 3 All ER 727, reported in the Court of Appeal as *McIlkenny v Chief Constable of West Midlands Police Force* [1980] 2 All ER 227 at 237.

[19] [1981] 3 All ER 727 at 735–6.

[20] It has been suggested that assessment of the weight of the conviction would be 'an impossibly difficult task': see *Cross on Evidence* (5th edn, 1979) 458. Cf Zuckerman, (1971) 87 *LQR* 21.

[21] Such evidence is admissible pursuant to the Civil Evidence Act 1995: see Ch 11.

[22] Section 11(4). Corresponding provisions for the admission of copies of such documents under ss 12 and 13 are contained in ss 12(4) and 13(4).

[23] See *Brinks Ltd v Abu-Saleh (No 2)* [1995] 4 All ER 74, Ch D, a decision under the hearsay provisions of the Civil Evidence Act 1968.

[24] [1914] 1 KB 1, DC.

in affiliation proceedings was treated as having been corroborated by evidence of the respondent's conviction of unlawful sexual intercourse with her. Although *Mash v Darley* pre-dates *Hollington v Hewthorn & Co Ltd*, the statutory reversal of the latter may be treated as having revived the former.

Under Practice Direction 16, para 10.1, a claimant who wishes to rely on evidence under section 11 must include in his particulars of claim a statement to that effect and give details of the type of conviction and its date, the court or court-martial which made it, and the issue in the claim to which it relates.

Section 13 of the Civil Evidence Act 1968

Section 13 of the 1968 Act applies to defamation proceedings. In such proceedings, the section, giving effect to the recommendations of the Law Reform Committee, not only reverses the rule in *Hollington v Hewthorn & Co Ltd*, as narrowly stated, but also creates a conclusive presumption: the person convicted, once his conviction has been proved, shall conclusively be taken to have committed the offence in question.[25] The effect of this is twofold: it prevents a convicted person from using the defamation action to reopen the issues determined at the criminal trial[26] and protects from civil liability a person who chooses to state that another is guilty of an offence of which he stands convicted. Accordingly, a defamation action based on the defendant's statement that the plaintiff committed an offence in respect of which he has been convicted will be struck out as an abuse of the process of the court unless the statement also contains some other legally defamatory matter.[27] Section 13 reads as follows:

(1) In an action for libel or slander in which the question whether the plaintiff did or did not commit a criminal offence is relevant to an issue arising in the action, proof that, at the time when the issue falls to be determined, he stands convicted of that offence shall be conclusive evidence that he committed that offence; and his conviction thereof shall be admissible in evidence accordingly.

(2) In any such action as aforesaid in which by virtue of this section the plaintiff is proved to have been convicted of an offence, the contents of any document which is admissible as evidence of the conviction, and the contents of the information, complaint, indictment or charge-sheet on which he was convicted, shall, without prejudice to the reception of any other admissible evidence for the purpose of identifying the facts on which the conviction was based, be admissible in evidence for the purpose of identifying those facts.

(2A) In the case of an action for libel or slander in which there is more than one plaintiff—

    (a) the references in subsection (1) and (2) above to the plaintiff shall be construed as references to any of the plaintiffs, and

    (b) proof that any of the plaintiffs stands convicted of an offence shall be conclusive evidence that he committed that offence so far as that fact is relevant to any issue arising in relation to his cause of action or that of any other plaintiff.

(3) For the purposes of this section a person shall be taken to stand convicted of an offence if but only if there subsists against him a conviction of that offence by or before a court in the United Kingdom or by a court-martial there or elsewhere.[28]

---

[25] 15th Report (1967) (Cmnd 3391), para 26 et seq. Parliament did not accept, however, the Committee's accompanying recommendation that in defamation proceedings evidence of an acquittal should be conclusive evidence of innocence. See *Loughans v Odhams Press* [1963] 1 QB 299, CA, below.

[26] See, eg, *Hinds v Sparks* [1964] Crim LR 717 and *Goody v Odhams Press Ltd* [1967] 1 QB 333.

[27] *Levene v Roxhan* [1970] 1 WLR 1322, CA.

[28] See 636 above, under **Previous convictions**, Section 11 of the Civil Evidence Act 1968.

Previous findings of adultery and paternity

Section 12 of the 1968 Act not only reverses the rule in *Hollington v Hewthorn & Co Ltd* insofar as it applied to previous findings of adultery and paternity, but also creates a persuasive presumption in respect of such findings. Section 12, as amended,[29] provides that:

(1) In any civil proceedings—
   (a) the fact that a person has been found guilty of adultery in any matrimonial proceedings; and
   (b) the fact that a person has been found to be the father of a child in relevant proceedings[30] before any court in England and Wales or Northern Ireland or has been adjudged to be the father of a child in affiliation proceedings before any court in the United Kingdom;
   shall (subject to (3) below) be admissible in evidence for the purpose of proving, where to do so is relevant to any issue in those civil proceedings, that he committed the adultery to which the finding relates or, as the case may be, is (or was) the father of that child, whether or not he offered any defence to the allegation of adultery or paternity and whether or not he is a party to the civil proceedings; but no finding or adjudication other than a subsisting one shall be admissible in evidence by virtue of this section.

(2) In any civil proceedings in which by virtue of this section a person is proved to have been found guilty of adultery as mentioned in subsection (1)(a) above or to have been found or adjudged to be the father of a child as mentioned in subsection (1)(b) above—
   (a) he shall be taken to have committed the adultery to which the finding relates or, as the case may be, to be (or have been) the father of that child, unless the contrary is proved; and
   (b) without prejudice to the reception of any other admissible evidence for the purpose of identifying the facts on which the finding or adjudication was based, the contents of any document which was before the court, or which contains any pronouncement of the court, in the other proceedings in question shall be admissible in evidence for that purpose.

(3) Nothing in this section shall prejudice the operation of any enactment whereby a finding of fact in any matrimonial or affiliation proceedings is for the purposes of any other proceedings made conclusive evidence of any fact.

Modelled as it is on section 11, section 12 of the 1968 Act calls for little comment. 'Matrimonial proceedings' are defined to include, inter alia, any matrimonial cause in the High Court or a county court in England and Wales and any appeal arising out of such cause.[31] Thus a finding of adultery in a magistrates' court would not be admissible under section 12. As in the case of previous convictions under section 11, the legal burden in relation to the finding of adultery or paternity admitted under section 12 is placed upon the party seeking to disprove that finding. The standard of proof required to discharge the burden is proof on a balance of probabilities.[32] A claimant who wishes to rely on evidence under section 12 of a finding or adjudication of adultery or paternity must include in his particulars of claim a statement to that effect and give details of the finding or adjudication and its date, the court which made it, and the issue in the claim to which it relates.[33]

---

[29] By s 29 of the Family Law Reform Act 1987.

[30] 'Relevant proceedings' means proceedings on complaints and applications made pursuant to a wide variety of statutory provisions: see s 12(5), as amended.

[31] Section 12(5).

[32] *Sutton v Sutton* [1970] 1 WLR 183, PD.

[33] PD 16, para 10.1.

Previous acquittals

In *Packer v Clayton*,[34] a case which pre-dates *Hollington v Hewthorn & Co Ltd*, Avory J was of the opinion that in affiliation proceedings, the respondent's acquittal of a sexual offence against the applicant would be admissible to show that the jury were not convinced by the latter's evidence. However, if the principle of *Hollington v Hewthorn & Co Ltd* applies to previous acquittals, they are inadmissible as evidence of innocence in subsequent civil proceedings. This conclusion may be justified on the grounds that an allegation which was not proved beyond reasonable doubt may be susceptible of proof on a balance of probabilities, as it was in *Loughans v Odhams Press*.[35] As a matter of policy, however, it may be argued that a person acquitted of an offence should be granted some measure of immunity from assertions to the contrary. Parliament, it is true, has rejected the proposal that in defamation proceedings evidence of an acquittal should be conclusive evidence of innocence.[36] Whether, at common law, evidence of an acquittal is nonetheless *some*, albeit only prima facie, evidence of innocence, not only in defamation actions but also in civil proceedings generally, is, on the present state of the authorities, unclear.

Other previous findings

Subject to exceptions, the principle of *Hollington v Hewthorn & Co Ltd* would appear to apply in respect of judicial findings in previous *civil* proceedings. In *Secretary of State for Trade and Industry v Bairstow*,[37] the Secretary of State brought proceedings under the Company Directors Disqualification Act 1986, seeking a disqualification order against B. Prior to the proceedings, B had been dismissed by the company of which he had been the managing director, his claim for wrongful dismissal against the company had been dismissed, and his appeal against that decision had failed. The Court of Appeal, in the instant case, held that the principle of *Hollington v Hewthorn & Co Ltd* was not confined to cases in which the earlier decision was that of a court exercising a criminal jurisdiction and accordingly the judge's factual findings in the wrongful dismissal proceedings were inadmissible, in the proceedings under the 1986 Act, as evidence of the facts on which they were based.

The exceptions to which reference has been made are findings of adultery and paternity, which, as we have seen, are now governed by section 12 of the 1968 Act. In the light of the somewhat novel observations of Lord Denning MR in *Hunter v Chief Constable of West Midlands*,[38] a decision on estoppel *per rem judicatam*, there is arguably a third exception. In that case, Lord Denning MR was of the opinion that a party to civil proceedings can only challenge a previous decision *against* himself by showing that it was obtained by fraud or collusion or by adducing fresh evidence which he could not have obtained by reasonable diligence before, to show conclusively that the previous decision was wrong. On this view, if a driver runs down two pedestrians, a finding of negligence against the driver in an action brought by one of the

---

[34] (1932) 97 JP 14, DC.

[35] [1963] 1 QB 299, CA.

[36] See 639 above, under **Previous convictions**, Section 13 of the Civil Evidence Act 1968.

[37] [2003] 3 WLR 841, CA.

[38] [1981] 3 All ER 727, HL, reported in the Court of Appeal as *McIlkenny v Chief Constable of West Midlands Police Force* [1980] 2 All ER 227 at 237–8. Although the views of Lord Denning MR in this respect were to some extent doubted when the case came before the House of Lords, Lord Diplock, giving the judgment of the House, found it unnecessary expressly to consider the topic of issue estoppel: (see at 732–3).

pedestrians could only be challenged in a subsequent action brought against him by the other in the limited way indicated. Applying the principle in *Hollington v Hewthorn & Co Ltd* to the same example, however, the earlier finding of negligence would be inadmissible as evidence of the driver's negligence in the subsequent proceedings.[39]

The principle of *Hollington v Hewthorn & Co Ltd* has been held to apply not only to judicial findings in previous civil proceedings, but also to the previous findings set out in the reports of inspectors under the Companies Act 1967 (see now Part XIV of the Companies Act 1985),[40] to an arbitration award[41] and to the findings of Bingham LJ in an extra-statutory report into the collapse of the Bank of Credit and Commerce International.[42] Similarly, the principle of *Hollington v Hewthorn & Co Ltd* has been held to apply to findings of the Solicitors Disciplinary Tribunal that a solicitor has been dishonest.[43] However, in the earlier case of *Hill v Clifford*,[44] the Court of Appeal held that a finding by the General Medical Council that a dentist had been guilty of professional misconduct was admissible as prima facie evidence of such misconduct in subsequent civil proceedings concerning the dissolution of his partnership, a decision which may be explicable on the basis that the Council was under a statutory duty of inquiry.[45] However, in such a case the court is still entitled to reach its own view of the facts as previously found.[46]

Criminal proceedings

Previous convictions

The application of the principle of *Hollington v Hewthorn & Co Ltd* in criminal cases meant that at the trial of a person charged with handling stolen goods, the previous conviction of the thief was inadmissible as evidence that the goods allegedly received were stolen.[47] Likewise, a woman's convictions for prostitution were inadmissible as evidence of her prostitution at the trial of a man charged with living off her immoral earnings.[48] A final example is *R v Spinks*,[49] where, as we have seen, the conviction of a principal was held to be inadmissible as evidence of his commission of the crime at the trial of the alleged accessory. The Criminal Law Revision Committee thought it was quite wrong, as well as being inconvenient, that in cases of this kind the prosecution should be required to prove again the guilt of the person concerned,[50] and recommended, in respect of convictions of persons other than the accused, a provision in criminal proceedings corresponding to section 11 of the 1968 Act. Section 74 of the 1984 Act not only gives effect to this recommendation but also makes similar provision in relation to the previous convictions

---

[39] In practice, problems of this kind are often avoided by virtue of the procedural provisions relating to joinder of parties and causes of action: see generally CPR Pts 19 and 20.

[40] *Savings and Investment Bank Ltd v Gasco Investments (Netherlands BV)* [1984] 1 WLR 271, Ch D.

[41] *Land Securities plc v Westminster City Council* [1993] 1 WLR 286.

[42] *Three Rivers District Council v Bank of England (No 3)* [2003] 2 AC 1, HL.

[43] *Conlon v Simms* [2007] 3 All ER 802, CA.

[44] [1907] 2 Ch 236. See also *Faulder v Silk* (1811) 3 Camp 126 and *Harvey v R* [1901] AC 601 (inquisitions in lunacy as prima facie evidence of a person's unsoundness of mind).

[45] See per Sir Gorell Barnes P [1907] 2 Ch 236 at 253.

[46] *Clifford v Timms* [1908] AC 12.

[47] *R v Turner* (1832) 1 Mood CC 347 at 349.

[48] *R v Hassan* [1970] 1 QB 423, CA.

[49] [1982] 1 All ER 587, CA.

[50] 11th Report (Cmnd 4991), paras 217 et seq.

of *the accused*: thus without affecting the law governing the admissibility of the accused's past misconduct, it provides that where evidence of the accused's commission of an offence *is* admissible, if the accused is proved to have been convicted of that offence, he shall be taken to have committed it unless the contrary is proved. Before considering the precise terms of section 74, it may first be noted that it is without prejudice to (i) the admissibility in evidence of any conviction which would be admissible apart from the section;[51] and (ii) the operation of any statutory provision whereby a conviction or finding of fact in criminal proceedings is made conclusive evidence of any fact for the purposes of any other criminal proceedings.[52]

Section 74 of the 1984 Act, as amended by the Criminal Justice Act 2003, provides that:

(1) In any proceedings the fact that a person other than the accused has been convicted of an offence by or before any court in the United Kingdom or by a Service court outside the United Kingdom shall be admissible in evidence for the purpose of proving, that that person committed that offence, where evidence of his having done so is admissible, whether or not any other evidence of his having committed that offence is given.

(2) In any proceedings in which by virtue of this section a person other than the accused is proved to have been convicted of an offence by or before any court in the United Kingdom or by a Service court outside the United Kingdom, he shall be taken to have committed that offence unless the contrary is proved.

(3) In any proceedings where evidence is admissible of the fact that the accused has committed an offence, if the accused is proved to have been convicted of the offence—

 (a) by or before any court in the United Kingdom; or

 (b) by a Service court outside the United Kingdom, he shall be taken to have committed that offence unless the contrary is proved.

Section 75(1) of the 1984 Act provides that:

Where evidence that a person has been convicted of an offence is admissible by virtue of s 74 above, then without prejudice to the reception of any other admissible evidence for the purpose of identifying the facts on which the conviction was based—

(a) the contents of any document which is admissible as evidence of the conviction; and

(b) the contents of the information, complaint, indictment or charge-sheet on which the person in question was convicted, shall be admissible in evidence for that purpose.[53]

Concerning the terminology of section 74, 'any proceedings' means any criminal proceedings.[54] A person is 'convicted' for the purposes of the section only if the conviction, which includes a conviction in respect of which a probation order or absolute or conditional discharge was imposed,[55] is 'subsisting'.[56] A subsisting conviction means either a finding of guilt that has not been quashed on appeal or a formal plea of guilt that has not been withdrawn; whether the accused has been sentenced or not is irrelevant.[57] A 'Service court' means a court-martial or a Standing Civilian Court.[58]

---

[51] Section 74(4)(a): eg proof of a witness's conviction pursuant to s 6 of the Criminal Procedure Act 1865. See Ch 7.

[52] Section 74(4)(b). The saving appears to have been included not with any particular statute in mind but because of local and private enactments and the possibility of future public enactments: see Annex 2 (Cmnd 4991) 233.

[53] Provision is also made for the admission of duly certified copies of such documents: s 75(2).

[54] Section 82(1).

[55] Section 75(3).

[56] Section 75(4).

[57] *R v Robertson*; *R v Golder* [1987] 3 All ER 231, CA. See also *R v Foster* [1984] 2 All ER 679, CA, above.

[58] Section 82(1).

Foreign convictions, apart from convictions by Service courts outside the United Kingdom, are clearly not covered by section 74, but may be admissible under the bad character provisions of the Criminal Justice Act 2003[59] and, if admissible, may be proved under section 7 of the Evidence Act 1851.[60] The rule in *Hollington v Hewthorn & Co Ltd* does not apply, in criminal proceedings, to foreign convictions, since it has been treated as a rule 'governing the admissibility of evidence of bad character' and thus abolished by s 99(1) of the Criminal Justice Act 2003.[61]

Section 74(1) and (2): convictions of persons other than the accused[62]

Section 74(1) has an obvious application where proof of the commission of an offence by a person other than the accused is admissible to establish an essential ingredient of the offence with which the accused is charged. Thus where A is seen transferring goods to B and they are jointly charged with handling the goods, A's guilty plea is admissible at B's trial to prove that the goods were stolen.[63]

In *R v Robertson; R v Golder*,[64] a decision under the original version of section 74(1), it was held that evidence of the commission of the offence may be relevant not only to an issue which is an essential ingredient of the offence charged, but also to less fundamental evidential issues arising in the proceedings. It was also held that the subsection is not confined to the proof of convictions of offences in which the accused on trial played no part; and that where the evidence is admitted, the judge should be careful to explain to the jury its effect and limitations.[65] In the case of Robertson, who was charged with conspiracy with two others to commit burglary, evidence that the others had been convicted of a number of burglaries was admissible because it could be inferred from their commission of these offences that there was a conspiracy between them and that was the very conspiracy to which the prosecution sought to prove that Robertson was a party. Golder was convicted of a robbery committed at garage X. Two of his co-accused pleaded guilty to that robbery and also to another committed at garage Y. The evidence against Golder consisted primarily of a confession statement, which he alleged to have been fabricated by the police, in which he referred to both robberies. It was held that evidence of the guilty pleas of the co-accused was admissible: proof of their commission of the offence at garage X was relevant because it showed that there had in fact been a robbery at that garage; and proof of the commission of both offences was relevant because it showed that the contents of the alleged confession were in accordance with the facts as they were known and therefore more likely to be true. *R v Robertson; R v Golder* was applied in *R v Castle*,[66] where C and F were charged with robbery and F pleaded guilty. At an identification parade, the victim said 'yes' in respect of C, 'possibly' in respect of F. Evidence of the guilty plea was admissible because relevant to the issue of the reliability of the identification of C: by confirming the correctness of the 'possible' identification of F, it also tended to confirm the correctness of the positive identification of C.[67]

---

[59] See Ch 17.

[60] *R v Kordasinski* [2007] 1 Cr App R 238, CA. Section 7 is considered in Ch 9.

[61] *R v Kordasinski*, ibid. Section 99(1) is considered in Ch 17.

[62] See generally Roderick Munday, 'Proof of Guilt by Association under Section 74' [1990] *Crim LR* 236.

[63] *R v Pigram* [1995] Crim LR 808, CA.

[64] [1987] 3 All ER 231, CA.

[65] See also per Staughton LJ in *R v Kempster* (1989) 90 Cr App R 14 at 22, CA and *R v Boyson* [1991] Crim LR 274, CA.

[66] [1989] Crim LR 567, CA.

[67] *R v Castle* was followed in *R v Gummerson and Steadman* [1999] Crim LR 680, CA, a case of *voice* identification. See also *R v Buckingham* (1994) 99 Cr App R 303, CA.

In *R v Robertson; R v Golder* it was stressed that section 74 should be used sparingly and not where, although the evidence is technically admissible, its effect is likely to be slight, particularly if there is any danger of contravening section 78 of the 1984 Act.[68] Moreover, a judge, in deciding an application under section 78, should make a ruling, one way or the other, and if he decides to admit the evidence, should give a cogent reason for his decision.[69] In *R v Kempster*[70] it was initially unclear whether the prosecution were relying on the evidence to prove the guilt of the accused or merely to prevent mystification of the jury. Although in the event the jury were encouraged to use the evidence to prove guilt, there was no clear or informed decision by the judge as to any adverse effect it might have had on the fairness of the proceedings. Quashing the convictions, the Court of Appeal highlighted the importance of ascertaining the purpose for which the evidence is adduced before deciding whether it should be excluded under section 78, and held that if the evidence is admitted, the judge should ensure that counsel does not seek to use it for any other purpose. Similarly, in *R v Boyson*[71] the Court of Appeal, *per curiam*, deprecated what it saw as the growing practice of allowing irrelevant, inadmissible, prejudicial, or unfair evidence to be admitted simply on the grounds that it is convenient for the jury to have 'the whole picture'.

Whether a conviction admissible under section 74 should be excluded under section 78 depends on the particular facts. In *R v Mattison*[72] M was charged in one count with gross indecency with D, and D, in another count, was charged with gross indecency with M. D pleaded guilty, M not guilty, his defence being a complete denial. It was held that evidence of the guilty plea was relevant to M's trial but the judge, given M's defence, should have exercised his discretion under section 78 to exclude it.[73] That decision falls to be compared with *R v Turner*.[74] T and L were driving separate cars. L overtook T, hit an oncoming vehicle and killed the passenger in his own car. The prosecution case was that the drivers were racing. L pleaded guilty to causing death by reckless driving. T, tried on the same charge, denied racing. It was held that the guilty plea was relevant, because the prosecution case was that L had been the principal, T the aider and abettor, but that it did not establish that L and T were racing, the essential issue at T's trial. The judge having made it clear that the evidence did not amount to an admission by L that he was racing, there was nothing unfair in admitting it.[75]

The question of exclusion under section 78 is of particular importance in conspiracy and related cases. In *R v O'Connor*[76] B and C were jointly charged in one count with conspiracy to

[68] See also *R v Skinner* [1995] Crim LR 805, CA.

[69] *R v Hillier* (1992) 97 Cr App R 349, CA.

[70] (1989) 90 Cr App R 14, CA.

[71] [1991] Crim LR 274, CA. See also *R v Hall* [1993] Crim LR 527, CA and *R v Mahmood and Manzur* [1997] 1 Cr App R 414, CA.

[72] [1990] Crim LR 117, CA.

[73] Where a co-accused pleads guilty but the prosecution do not seek to rely on s 74, it may be sufficient, depending on the circumstances, for the jury to be told that the guilty plea is not probative against the accused: see *R v Turpin* [1990] Crim LR 514, CA. In a case involving joint enterprise, it is insufficient for the judge to direct the jury that they must be sure that each of the accused was a party to the enterprise—they should be told that it is essential that they put the guilty plea of the co-accused out of their minds: *R v Betterley* [1994] Crim LR 764, CA. However, a warning will not suffice if the jury cannot properly consider the case of the accused in isolation from that of the co-accused, in which case the judge should discharge the jury and order a new trial: *R v Fedrick* [1990] Crim LR 403, CA. See also *R v Marlow* [1997] Crim LR 457, CA.

[74] [1991] Crim LR 57, CA.

[75] See also *R v Bennett* [1988] Crim LR 686, CA and *R v Stewart* [1999] Crim LR 746, CA.

[76] (1986) 85 Cr App R 298, CA.

obtain property by deception. B pleaded guilty, C not guilty. Evidence of the guilty plea was admitted, together with the details in the count against him, as permitted by section 75. It was held that the evidence should have been excluded under section 78 because B's admission that he had conspired with C might have led the jury to infer that C, in turn, must have conspired with B. The same reasoning was applied in *R v Curry*.[77] C was convicted of conspiracy to obtain property by deception. She was charged with two others, W and H. H pleaded guilty. The prosecution case was that W drove the accused to the shops where C, with H's knowledge, used H's credit card to obtain the goods, H's intention being to report the card as stolen so as to avoid liability for payment. Evidence of the guilty plea was admitted to establish the existence of an unlawful agreement to deceive. The conviction was quashed on the basis that the evidence clearly implied as a matter of fact, albeit not law, that C had been a party to the conspiracy. The court said that section 74 should be used sparingly, especially in cases of conspiracy and affray, and should not be used where the evidence, expressly or by necessary inference, imports the complicity of the accused. *R v Lunnon*[78] was distinguished. That case also involved three accused jointly charged with conspiracy, but it was held that evidence of the guilty plea of one of them had been properly admitted to prove the existence of the conspiracy because the judge had separated for the jury two questions, whether there was a conspiracy and who was a party to it, and had made it clear that despite the evidence, they could acquit the accused.[79]

Section 78 may also be invoked successfully on the basis that the prosecution, by relying on section 74, do not have to call the person convicted, thereby depriving the defence of the opportunity to challenge or test him in cross-examination.[80] The argument was rejected in *R v Robertson; R v Golder*[81] on the basis that R's name did not appear on any of the burglary counts to which the co-accused had pleaded guilty, and that even if the co-accused had given evidence in accordance with their pleas, R's counsel would have been unlikely to cross-examine them or, if he had, would have seriously prejudiced R. However, as Staughton LJ observed in *R v Kempster*,[82] although such cross-examination may be unlikely in some cases, or else turn out to be a disaster, one cannot always assume that.

An application under section 78 may succeed where a co-accused has pleaded guilty but the evidence was far from conclusive against him, on the basis that to allow the conviction to be proved might deprive the remaining accused of the opportunity to challenge that evidence.[83] An application may also succeed where, a co-accused having pleaded guilty towards or at the end of the prosecution case, it would be unfair to admit evidence of the plea because, had it been entered and put in evidence earlier, cross-examination might have been conducted differently.[84]

---

[77] [1988] Crim LR 527, CA.

[78] [1988] Crim LR 456, CA.

[79] Cf *R v Chapman* [1991] Crim LR 44, CA where C and seven others were charged with conspiracy to obtain by deception. It was held that a guilty plea by one of the others to two specific counts of obtaining by deception, incidents in which he was involved with C, were relevant and admissible and did not inevitably import the complicity of C. See also *R v Hunt* [1994] Crim LR 747, CA.

[80] This was part of the ratio in *R v O'Connor* (1986) 85 Cr App R 298, CA, above.

[81] Above.

[82] (1989) 90 Cr App R 14 at 22, CA.

[83] *R v Lee* [1996] Crim LR 825, CA.

[84] See *R v Chapman* [1991] Crim LR 44. The evidence may also be excluded under s 78 where it adds little to an already strong case: *R v Warner* (1992) 96 Cr App R 324, CA. See also *R v Humphreys and Tully* [1993] Crim LR 288, CA.

Section 74(2) has the effect of placing the legal burden in relation to the commission of the offence (by a person other than the accused) on the party seeking to disprove it. Where that burden is borne by the accused, the standard of proof required to discharge it is the standard ordinarily required where the legal burden on a particular issue is borne by the accused, namely proof on a balance of probabilities.[85]

Although in most cases section 74(1) has been relied on by the prosecution, in appropriate circumstances it may also be used by an accused to adduce evidence of the convictions of a co-accused which are relevant to an issue in the proceedings.[86]

Section 74(3): convictions of the accused

It is clear from the wording of section 74(3) that its purpose is not to define or enlarge the circumstances in which evidence of the fact that the accused has committed an offence is admissible, but simply to assist, where such evidence is admissible, in proving that fact.[87] The conviction is admissible as evidence of the commission of the offence and the accused shall be taken to have committed the offence unless the contrary is proved. The subsection operates to place on the accused the legal burden of disproving the commission of the offence on a balance of probabilities.

Section 74(3) appears to apply in three types of situation. The first is where the accused denies that he committed some previous offence which the prosecution seek to prove as an element of the offence with which he is charged, for example where he is charged with murder, the victim having died subsequent to his conviction for assault, or where, having convictions recorded against him, he is charged with perjury because in some previous proceeding he testified that he had never committed an offence. The second situation is where the accused's commission of an offence, other than that with which he is charged, is admissible as evidence of his bad character under section 101 of the Criminal Justice Act 2003.[88] The subsection presumably also applies in a third situation in which, a conviction having been proved as part of the prosecution case pursuant to statutory provisions such as section 101 of the Criminal Justice Act 2003, section 27(3)(b) of the Theft Act 1968 or section 1(2) of the Official Secrets Act 1911, the accused denies having committed the offence in question.

It could be argued that section 74(3) also applies where, after a finding of guilt or a guilty plea, a previous conviction is proved in order to guide the court on the question of sentence, but the accused denies having committed the offence in question. However, it is submitted that in such a situation, the question whether the accused committed the offence is irrelevant: it is the *fact* of the previous conviction which is relevant to the determination of an appropriate sentence, and if the accused denies the conviction, it can be proved in the ordinary way under section 73 of the 1984 Act.[89]

Previous acquittals

In the absence of some exceptional feature, evidence of an acquittal is generally inadmissible in a subsequent trial.[90] The reason is that in most cases it is not possible to be certain why the

[85] See *R v Carr-Briant* [1943] KB 607, Ch 4.
[86] See *R v Hendrick* [1992] Crim LR 427, CA where, on the facts, the convictions were irrelevant.
[87] *R v Harris* [2001] Crim LR 227, CA.
[88] See Ch 17.
[89] See Ch 2, 49, under **Convictions and acquittals.**
[90] *Hui Chi-ming v R* [1991] 3 All ER 897, PC.

jury acquitted, but evidence of an acquittal will be admissible where there is a clear inference from the verdict that the jury rejected a witness's evidence because they did not believe him and his credibility is directly in issue in the subsequent trial.[91] Even if admissible, however, evidence of the acquittal is not conclusive evidence of innocence and does not mean that all relevant issues in the trial were resolved in favour of the accused.[92]

ADDITIONAL READING

Munday, 'Proof of Guilt by Association under Section 74' [1990] *Crim LR* 236.

---

[91] *R v Deboussi* [2007] EWCA Crim 684, considered, with the other authorities, in Ch 2, 19, under **Relevance and admissibility.**

[92] *R v Terry* [2005] QB 996, CA, disapproving the dictum of O'Connor LJ in *R v Hay* (1983) 77 Cr App R 70 at 75. See also *R v Colman* [2004] EWCA Crim 3252.

Proof of facts without evidence

22

Key Issues

- When, and why, should facts in issue be presumed in the absence of evidence in rebuttal (rebuttable presumptions of law)?

- When, and why, should a fact be treated as established and not open to any evidence in rebuttal (judicial notice)?

- When, and why, should a party admit a fact in issue so that it ceases to be in issue and therefore evidence of it is neither required nor admissible (formal admissions)?

Facts in issue and relevant facts are treated as established by the courts only in so far as they are proved by evidence. To this general rule there are three exceptions. Certain facts may be presumed in a party's favour in the absence of proof or complete proof and no evidence is required to establish facts that are either judicially noticed or formally admitted.

Presumptions

Definitions and classification

Where a presumption operates, a certain conclusion may or must be drawn by the court in the absence of evidence in rebuttal. The effect of this is to assist a party bearing a burden of proof, the degree of assistance varying from presumption to presumption. In some cases the proof required to establish the fact in question may be less than it otherwise would have been. In other cases no proof may be required at all or the other party may be barred from adducing any evidence in rebuttal. Presumptions are based on considerations of common sense and public policy but not necessarily those of logic. Certain facts or combinations of fact can give rise to inferences which justify legal rules that in such circumstances a conclusion may or must be drawn. For example, if after an operation a swab is found to have been left in a patient's body, it seems reasonable enough to infer, in the absence of explanation by the surgeon, that the accident arose through his negligence.[1] If a surgeon uses proper care, such an accident does not, in the ordinary course of things, occur; negligence may be presumed. However, there is another presumption that a person is dead if he has not been heard of for over seven years. There is, of course, no logic in the choice of 2,556 days' absence for these purposes as opposed to say 2,560 days' absence.[2]

The law of presumptions is as beset with the problems of terminology and classification as the subjects of burden and standard of proof with which it is closely interrelated. A useful starting point is a conventional classification into rebuttable presumptions of law (*praesumptiones iuris sed non de iure*), irrebuttable presumptions of law (*praesumptiones iuris et de iure*), and presumptions of fact (*praesumptiones hominis*). It is the first of these categories which forms the main concern of this chapter, the second comprising rules of substantive law expressed as presumptions, and the third consisting of a number of examples of circumstantial evidence also expressed as presumptions. A further category which falls to be considered, presumptions without basic facts, comprises a number of rules relating to the incidence of the burden of proof. In the ensuing analysis of these four categories reference will be made, by way of example, to the more important of the common law and statutory presumptions, some of which are considered in greater depth later in this chapter. Distributed throughout English law there are numerous common law, equitable and statutory presumptions. This chapter deals with the most important of them, a comprehensive treatment being beyond its scope.[3]

Rebuttable presumptions of law

Where a rebuttable presumption of law applies, on the proof or admission of a fact, referred to as a primary or basic fact, and in the absence of further evidence, another fact, referred to as a presumed

---

[1] See *Mahon v Osborne* [1939] 2 KB 14, CA.

[2] See per Sachs J in *Chard v Chard* [1956] P 259 at 272.

[3] The statutory presumptions arising under ss 11 and 12 of the Civil Evidence Act 1968 and s 74 of the Police and Criminal Evidence Act 1984 are considered in Ch 21 and certain presumptions relating to the due execution of documents are considered in Ch 9.

fact, must be presumed. The party relying on the presumption bears the burden of establishing the basic fact. Once he has adduced sufficient evidence on that fact, his adversary bears the legal burden of disproving the presumed fact or, as the case may be, an evidential burden to adduce some evidence to rebut the presumed fact. The standard of proof to be met by the party seeking to rebut the presumed fact is determined by the substantive law in relation to the presumption in question.[4] For example, there is a rebuttable presumption of law that a child proved or admitted to have been born or conceived during lawful wedlock (the basic facts) is legitimate (the presumed fact). A party seeking to rebut the presumed fact by evidence of, say, the husband's impotence, is, in civil proceedings, required to meet the ordinary civil standard of proof on a balance of probabilities.[5] Other examples to be considered in detail later in this chapter are the presumptions of marriage, death, and, in testamentary cases, sanity, and the maxims *omnia praesumuntur rite esse acta* and *res ipsa loquitur*, the last-mentioned arguably being a presumption of fact.

Where a rebuttable presumption of law places a legal burden on the party against whom it operates, as does, for example, the presumption of legitimacy, it may be referred to as a 'persuasive' or 'compelling' presumption.[6] In such a case, the legal burden of disproving the presumed fact is on the party against whom the presumption operates. Where a rebuttable presumption of law operates to place an evidential burden on that party, as does, for example, the presumption of death, it may be referred to as an 'evidential' presumption.[7] In such a case, the legal burden of proving the presumed fact is borne by the party in whose favour the presumption operates. If he adduces prima facie evidence of the basic facts, an evidential burden is placed on his adversary. The adversary may discharge this burden in the usual way and, if he does so, the effect will be as if the presumption had never come into play at all; the party bearing the legal burden of proof must satisfy the tribunal of fact to the required standard of proof in the usual way. The terminology of 'persuasive' and 'evidential' presumptions is apposite only in civil proceedings. Subject to express or implied statutory exceptions and cases in which the accused raises the defence of insanity, in criminal proceedings the prosecution bears the legal burden of proving all facts essential to their case. It follows from this general rule that where a common law presumption operates in favour of the accused, the prosecution will always bear a *legal* burden (requiring them to disprove the presumed fact beyond reasonable doubt).[8] Likewise, although there are a number of statutory presumptions which operate to place on the accused a legal burden of proof (which may be discharged by the adduction of such evidence as might satisfy the jury on a balance of probabilities),[9] where a common law presumption operates in favour of the prosecution, the accused will never bear more than an *evidential* burden (which may be discharged by the adduction of such evidence as might leave a jury in reasonable doubt).

Irrebuttable presumptions of law
Where an irrebuttable presumption of law, sometimes referred to as a conclusive presumption, applies, on the proof or admission of a basic fact, another fact must be presumed and the party

---

[4] Unfortunately, as we shall see, the authorities are often in conflict as to the amount of evidence required to rebut certain presumptions.

[5] Section 26 of the Family Law Reform Act 1969, below.

[6] See Lord Denning, (1945) 61 *LQR* 380.

[7] See Professor Glanville Williams, *Criminal Law (The General Part)* (2nd edn, London, 1961) 877 et seq.

[8] See *R v Willshire* (1881) 6 QBD 366, below, and *R v Kay* (1887) 16 Cox CC 292, both relating to the presumption of marriage.

[9] For example, s 1(1) of the Prevention of Crime Act 1953. For further examples, see Ch 4.

against whom the presumption operates is barred from adducing any evidence in rebuttal. Such presumptions amount to no more than rules of substantive law expressed, somewhat clumsily, in the language pertaining to presumptions. Indeed, there is no valid reason why the rather cumbersome phrase 'irrebuttable presumption of law' could not be applied to every rule of substantive law. The following examples may be given. Section 50 of the Children and Young Persons Act 1933 provides that: 'It shall be conclusively presumed that no child under the age of ten years can be guilty of an offence.' Under section 76 of the Sexual Offences Act 2003, in certain sexual cases, including cases of rape, if it is proved that the accused did the relevant act (intentional penetration of the vagina, anus, or mouth) and that he intentionally deceived the complainant as to the nature or purpose of the act, or intentionally induced the complainant to consent to it by impersonating a person known personally to the complainant, it is conclusively presumed that the complainant did not consent to the act and that the accused did not believe that the complainant consented to it. This is a somewhat convoluted way of saying that one of the ways in which rape may be committed is by intentional penetration and the intentional deceit or inducing of the kinds described (ie irrespective of whether the complainant consented and what the accused believed in that regard).[10]

Presumptions of fact

Where a presumption of fact applies, on the proof or admission of a basic fact, another fact *may* be presumed in the absence of sufficient evidence to the contrary. Presumptions of fact are sometimes referred to as 'provisional presumptions' to indicate that a party against whom they operate bears a provisional or tactical burden in relation to the presumed fact. Unlike rebuttable presumptions of law, establishment of the basic fact does not have the effect of placing either an evidential or legal burden on that party. Thus presumptions of fact amount to nothing more than examples of circumstantial evidence. Certain facts or combinations of facts can give rise to inferences which the tribunal of fact *may* draw, there being no rule of law that such inferences *must* be drawn in the absence of evidence to the contrary. However, presumptions of fact can vary in strength and on the operation of a strong presumption of fact, if no evidence in rebuttal is adduced, a finding by the tribunal of fact against the existence of the presumed fact could, at any rate in civil proceedings, be reversed on appeal. Examples of circumstantial evidence which have recurred so frequently as to attract the label 'presumption of fact' include the presumptions of intention, guilty knowledge (in cases of possession of recently stolen goods), continuance of life, and seaworthiness.[11]

The presumption of intention.   There is a presumption of fact that a man intends the natural consequences of his acts. In criminal proceedings, this presumption was treated as a presumption of fact[12] until the House of Lords in *DPP v Smith*[13] held that, in certain circumstances, it constituted a presumption of law. This conclusion was statutorily reversed by section 8 of the Criminal Justice Act 1967, the effect of which has been to re-establish the presumption as one of fact.[14] The section provides that:

---

[10] See also s 13(1) of the Civil Evidence Act 1968 (Ch 21); and s 15(2) and (3) of the Road Traffic Offenders Act 1988 and *Millard v DPP* (1990) 91 Cr App R 108, DC.

[11] See also *Re W (a minor)* (1992) The Times, 22 May, CA: there is a presumption of fact that a baby's best interests are served by being with the mother, although with children the situation might be different.

[12] See *R v Steane* [1947] KB 997 and per Lord Sankey in *Woolmington v DPP* [1935] AC 462 at 481.

[13] [1961] AC 290.

[14] See *R v Wallett* [1968] 2 QB 367, CA; *R v Moloney* [1985] 1 All ER 1025, HL.

A court or jury, in determining whether a person has committed an offence—

(a) shall not be bound in law to infer that he intended or foresaw a result of his actions by reason only of its being a natural and probable consequence of those actions; but

(b) shall decide whether he did intend or foresee that result by reference to all the evidence, drawing such inferences from the evidence as appear proper in the circumstances.

In civil proceedings it remains unclear whether the presumption of intention is one of fact or law.[15]

The presumption of guilty knowledge.   Where an accused is found in possession of goods which have been recently stolen, an explanation is called for and if none is forthcoming the jury are entitled, but not compelled, to infer guilty knowledge or belief and to find the accused guilty of handling stolen goods. Where an explanation is given which the jury is convinced is untrue, likewise the jury are entitled to convict. However, if the explanation given leaves the jury in doubt as to whether the accused knew or believed the goods to be stolen, the prosecution has not proved its case and the jury should acquit.[16] This presumption may operate to the same effect in the case of theft.[17]

The presumption of continuance of life.   Where a person is proved to have been alive on a certain date, an inference may be drawn, in the absence of sufficient evidence to the contrary, that he was alive on a subsequent date.[18] The strength of this presumption depends entirely upon the facts of the case in question. In *R v Lumley*,[19] on a woman's trial for bigamy, a question arose as to whether her husband was alive at the date of the second marriage. Lush J said:[20]

> This is purely a question of fact. The existence of a party at an antecedent date may, or may not, afford a reasonable inference that he is living at the subsequent date. If, for example, it was proved that he was in good health on the day preceding the marriage, the inference would be strong, almost irresistible, that he was living on the latter day, and the jury would in all probability find that he was so. If, on the other hand, it were proved that he was then in a dying condition, and nothing further was proved, they would probably decline to draw that inference. Thus, the question is entirely for the jury.

The presumption of seaworthiness.   Where a ship sinks or becomes unable to continue her voyage shortly after putting to sea, an inference may be drawn, in the absence of sufficient evidence

---

[15] See *Kaslefsky v Kaslefsky* [1951] P 38, CA; *Jamieson v Jamieson* [1952] AC 525, HL; *Lang v Lang* [1955] AC 402, PC; *Gollins v Gollins* [1964] AC 644, HL; and *Williams v Williams* [1964] AC 698, HL.

[16] See *R v Schama and Abramovitch* (1914) 11 Cr App R 45; *R v Garth* [1949] 1 All ER 773, CCA; *R v Aves* [1950] 2 All ER 330, CCA; and *R v Hepworth and Fearnley* [1955] 2 QB 600, CCA.

[17] In a case of handling, the prosecution is not obliged to adduce evidence that the goods were handled 'otherwise than in the course of the stealing' (see s 22(1) of the Theft Act 1968): the inference that in the proper case the jury are entitled to draw, namely that an accused was the guilty handler, includes the inference that he was not the thief. However, if the accused is in possession of property so recently after it was stolen that the inevitable inference is that he was the thief, as when he is found within a few hundred yards of the scene of the theft and within minutes after it took place, then if the charge is handling only, the jury should be directed that if they take the view that the accused was the thief, they should acquit him of the handling: *R v Cash* [1985] QB 801, CA, applied in *A-G of Hong Kong v Yip Kai-foon* [1988] 1 All ER 153, PC. See also *Ryan and French v DPP* [1994] Crim LR 457, CA.

[18] See *McDarmaid v A-G* [1950] P 218, *Re Peete, Peete v Crompton* [1952] 2 All ER 599; and *Chard v Chard* [1956] P 259.

[19] (1869) LR 1 CCR 196.

[20] (1869) LR 1 CCR 196 at 198. See also per Denman CJ in *R v Harborne Inhabitants* (1835) 2 Ad&El 540 at 544–5.

to the contrary, that she was unseaworthy on leaving port. In the absence of evidence in rebuttal, the tribunal of fact should be directed that an inference of unseaworthiness at the start of the voyage may be drawn. If, in these circumstances, a tribunal of fact were to find the contrary, it would be such a finding against the reasonable inference to be drawn that it would amount to a verdict against the evidence.[21]

Presumptions without basic facts

All of the presumptions defined in this chapter up to this point may be explained in terms of a basic fact on the proof or admission of which another fact may or must be presumed. Presumptions without basic facts come into operation without the proof or admission of any basic fact; they are merely conclusions which must be drawn in the absence of evidence in rebuttal. In other words, they are rules relating to the incidence of the legal and evidential burdens expressed in the language pertaining to presumptions. The following examples may be given. In criminal proceedings, reference is often made to the presumptions of innocence and sanity. Both are more meaningfully expressed in terms of the incidence of the burden of proof. The presumption of innocence is a convenient abbreviation of the rule that the prosecution bear the legal burden of proving any fact essential to their case.[22] Likewise, the presumption of sanity refers to the rule that the accused bears the legal burden of proving insanity when he raises it as a defence.[23] In *Bratty v A-G for Northern Ireland* two members of the House of Lords referred to 'the presumption of mental capacity'.[24] The reference was to the rule that the evidential burden in relation to the defence of non-insane automatism is borne by the accused.

A final example of a presumption without basic facts is the presumption that mechanical instruments of a kind that are usually in working order, were in working order at the time when they were used. This conclusion will be drawn by the court in the absence of evidence to the contrary, the party seeking to rebut the presumption bearing an evidential burden. The presumption has been applied in the case of speedometers,[25] traffic lights,[26] breath-test machines,[27] and public weighbridges.[28] The presumption, it is submitted, also applies in the case of computers, with the consequence that a party introducing computer-generated evidence need only produce evidence that the computer was working properly at the relevant time if his opponent introduces some evidence to the contrary.

The presumption of marriage

There are three discernible presumptions of marriage: a presumption of formal validity, a presumption of essential validity, and a presumption of marriage arising from cohabitation.

[21] See per Brett LJ in *Pickup v Thames & Mersey Marine Insurance Co Ltd* (1878) 3 QBD 594 at 600, CA. See also *Anderson v Morice* (1875) LR 10 CP 609 and *Ajum Goolam Hossen & Co v Union Marine Insurance Co* [1901] AC 362, PC.
[22] *Woolmington v DPP* [1935] AC 462. The presumption of innocence also applies when an allegation of criminal conduct is made in civil proceedings: see *Williams v East India Co* (1802) 3 East 192. Concerning the standard of proof to be met in these circumstances, see *Hornal v Neuberger Products Ltd* [1957] 1 QB 247, CA, considered in Ch 4.
[23] *M'Naghten's case* (1843) 10 Cl & Fin 200. In testamentary cases, the presumption of sanity is not a presumption without basic facts but a rebuttable presumption of law: see below.
[24] [1963] AC 386 per Viscount Kilmuir LC at 407 and per Lord Denning at 413.
[25] *Nicholas v Penny* [1950] 2 KB 466.
[26] *Tingle Jacobs and Co v Kennedy* [1964] 1 All ER 888n, CA.
[27] *Castle v Cross* [1985] 1 All ER 87, DC.
[28] *Kelly Communications Ltd v DPP* [2003] Crim LR 479 and 875, DC.

Although this threefold classification is accorded scant recognition in the authorities, differences in the basic facts giving rise to each, and in the standard of proof required to rebut each, warrant a discrete analysis.

The presumption of formal validity

The formal validity of a marriage depends upon the *lex loci celebrationis*. A failure to comply with the formal requirements of the local law may make a marriage void. Under English law, a Church of England marriage (otherwise than by special licence) may be void because of irregularities such as failure duly to publish banns or to obtain a common licence. In the case of other marriages under English law, examples include cases of failure to give due notice to the superintendent registrar and cases in which a certificate and, where necessary, a licence have not been duly issued. However, on the proof or admission of the basic facts that a marriage was celebrated between persons who intended to marry, the formal validity of the marriage will be presumed in the absence of sufficient evidence to the contrary. The authorities almost always include among the basic facts the cohabitation of the parties following the ceremony of marriage[29] but the presumption has been held to apply to death-bed marriages.[30] It is submitted that cohabitation is not among the basic facts giving rise to the presumption.

The leading case relating to an English marriage is *Piers v Piers*.[31] A marriage ceremony had been celebrated between two persons who had shown their intention, at the time, to marry. The ceremony was performed in a private house but there was no evidence that the bishop of the diocese had granted the necessary special licence. The House of Lords held that the marriage was formally valid.[32] An example of the application of the presumption to a foreign marriage is *Mahadervan v Mahadervan*.[33] Rejecting as irrational legal chauvinism an argument of counsel for the husband that there was no presumption in favour of a foreign marriage the establishment of which would invalidate a subsequent English one, Sir Jocelyn Simon P applied the presumption and held the foreign marriage to be formally valid.

In civil proceedings, the presumption operates as a persuasive presumption placing a legal burden on the party seeking to rebut formal validity.[34] The standard of proof to be met by that party is high. In *Piers v Piers* Lord Cottenham cited with approval the words of Lord Lyndhurst in *Morris v Davies*:[35] 'The presumption of law is not lightly to be repelled. It is not to be broken in upon or shaken by a mere balance of probabilities. The evidence for the purpose of repelling it must be strong, distinct, satisfactory, and conclusive.'[36] Lord Campbell said:[37] 'a presumption of this sort in favour of marriage can only be negatived by disproving every reasonable possibility.' In *Mahadervan v Mahadervan* Sir Jocelyn Simon P held that the presumption can only be rebutted by evidence which satisfies beyond reasonable doubt that

[29] See, eg, per Barnard J in *Russell v A-G* [1949] P 391 at 394.

[30] See *The Lauderdale Peerage Case* (1885) 10 App Cas 692, HL and *Hill v Hill* [1959] 1 All ER 281.

[31] (1849) 2 HL Cas 331.

[32] See also *De Thoren v A-G* (1876) 1 App Cas 686, HL; *Re Shephard, George v Thyer* [1904] 1 Ch 456; and *Russell v A-G* [1949] P 391.

[33] [1964] P 233. See also *Spivack v Spivack* (1930) 46 TLR 243 and *Hill v Hill* [1959] 1 All ER 281.

[34] In criminal cases where the prosecution bear the legal burden of proving the validity of the marriage, the presumption operates to place an evidential burden on the accused: see *R v Kay* (1887) 16 Cox CC 292.

[35] (1837) 5 Cl&Fin 163 at 265.

[36] The word 'conclusive' hardly seems apposite and its use has been criticized: see Harman LJ in *Re Taylor* [1961] 1 WLR 9, CA.

[37] (1849) 2 HL Cas 331 at 380.

there was no valid marriage.[38] In relation to matrimonial causes more generally, although the authorities remain in conflict, subsequent trends favour the ordinary civil standard[39] and it is likely that in future this lower standard will be applied. When Lord Cottenham in *Piers v Piers* adopted the words of Lord Lyndhurst in *Morris v Davies*, an authority on the presumption of legitimacy, the evidence in rebuttal of that presumption was required to meet a high standard of proof. The presumption of legitimacy is now rebuttable by evidence which satisfies the ordinary civil standard on a balance of probabilities.[40] It is submitted that the standard of proof to be met by the party seeking to rebut the presumption of marriage should also be the ordinary civil standard.

The presumption of essential validity
A marriage may be void on the grounds that the parties lacked the capacity to marry. Under English law, for example, the parties may lack the capacity to marry if they are related within the prohibited degrees or if either of them is under the age of 16 or already married. However, on the proof or admission of the basic fact that a formally valid marriage was celebrated, the essential validity of the marriage will be presumed in the absence of sufficient evidence to the contrary. In the words of Pilcher J in *Tweney v Tweney*,[41] 'The petitioner's marriage to the present respondent being unexceptionable in form and duly consummated remains a good marriage until some evidence is adduced that the marriage was, in fact, a nullity.' Although the matter is far from clear, in civil proceedings the presumption would appear to operate as a persuasive rather than evidential presumption, placing a legal burden on the party seeking to rebut it.[42] However, the standard of proof required to rebut the presumption is lower than that in the case of the presumption of formal validity. In *Gatty and Gatty v A-G*[43] it was held that evidence of a valid prior marriage sufficed. A similar conclusion was reached in *Re Peete, Peete v Crompton*.[44] A woman, W, made an application under the Inheritance (Family Provision) Act 1938 as the widow of Y. W had separated from her first husband X prior to 1916 and in 1919 went through a formally valid ceremony of marriage with Y. The question arose as to the essential validity of the subsequent marriage. The court held that the application failed. Although a presumption of essential validity arose in relation to the subsequent marriage, there was some evidence before the court, namely the existence of the first marriage, that in 1919 W lacked the capacity to marry Y. However, where the prior marriage is of doubtful validity, there is authority that the presumption is not rebutted.[45]

In most of the cases where the presumption of essential validity has fallen to be applied by the courts, one of the parties to a marriage has been married previously. The question has been whether the earlier marriage had terminated by the time of the subsequent ceremony. This issue may in turn require consideration of the presumption of death, the presumption of continuance of life, or even the presumption of essential validity in relation to the earlier

[38] [1964] P 233 at 246.

[39] *Blyth v Blyth* [1966] AC 643 and *Bastable v Bastable and Sanders* [1968] 1 WLR 1684.

[40] See s 26 of the Family Law Reform Act 1969, below.

[41] [1946] P 180 at 182.

[42] Cf *Axon v Axon* (1937) 59 CLR 395, HC of A.

[43] [1951] P 444.

[44] [1952] 2 All ER 599, Ch D.

[45] *Taylor v Taylor* [1967] P 25. Cf *Monckton v Tarr* (1930) 23 BWCC 504, CA.

marriage. Two conflicting presumptions applied to the same facts in *Monckton v Tarr*.[46] A, a woman, married B in 1882. B deserted A in 1887. In 1895, at which time there was no evidence that B was alive, A married C. In 1913, at which time A was still alive, C married a woman D. D made a claim for workmen's compensation as the widow of C. The employers alleged that the 1913 marriage was void because of the 1895 marriage. D replied that the 1895 marriage was void because of the 1882 marriage. D's claim was dismissed by the Court of Appeal. Although a presumption of essential validity arose in relation to the marriage of 1913, the same presumption applied to the marriage of 1895. These two presumptions cancelling each other out, it was for D to prove C's capacity to marry her and this she could only do by showing that B was alive at the date of the 1895 marriage, something which she had failed to do. A different approach was adopted, however, when a similar problem arose in *Taylor v Taylor*.[47] There was some weak evidence that a woman, W, had married X. Subsequently, in 1928, X married another woman Y. Y left him and in 1942, when X was still alive, married Z. Z petitioned for a decree of nullity alleging that his marriage to Y was void because of the 1928 marriage. Y replied that the marriage of 1928 was void because of the earlier marriage between W and X. It might have been expected, on the reasoning employed in *Monckton v Tarr*, that the court would have held that the presumptions in favour of the 1928 and 1942 marriages effectively cancelling each other out, it was for Y to prove her capacity to marry Z and that she had failed to do this, the weak evidence adduced to show the marriage between W and X being insufficient for the purpose. However, Cairns J, expressing a preference for the preservation of existing unions, rather than their avoidance in favour of doubtful earlier and effectively dead ones, held that the marriage of 1942 was valid. The evidence of the earlier marriage of doubtful validity, that is the marriage of 1928, did not suffice to rebut the presumption of essential validity in relation to the marriage of 1942.[48]

The presumption of marriage arising from cohabitation

On the proof or admission of the basic fact that a man and woman have cohabited as if man and wife, it is presumed, in the absence of sufficient evidence to the contrary, that they were living together in consequence of a valid marriage.[49] The authorities suggest that in civil proceedings this presumption operates as a persuasive presumption.[50] Evidence in rebuttal is required to meet a high standard of proof: it must be 'clear and firm'[51] or 'of the most cogent kind'.[52] In *Sastry Velaider Aronegary v Sembecutty Vaigalie*[53] the issue concerned the validity of a marriage ceremony which had taken place between Tamils in Ceylon. The Privy Council, of the opinion that the party in whose favour the presumption operated was under no obligation

---

[46] (1930) 23 BWCC 504, CA.

[47] [1967] P 25.

[48] Cf, in this respect, the available evidence in rebuttal in *Re Peete, Peete v Crompton* [1952] 2 All ER 599, above.

[49] In cases where, pursuant to local law, a valid marriage may come into existence by the consent of the parties without a formal ceremony, such consent is presumed: see *Breadalbane Case, Campbell v Campbell* (1867) LR 1 Sc&Div 182.

[50] In criminal proceedings in which the prosecution rely on this presumption, the authorities suggest that the presumption, by itself, is insufficient to discharge the evidential burden: see *Morris v Miller* (1767) 4 Burr 2057 and *R v Umanski* [1961] VLR 242. Proof or admission of cohabitation supported by the production of a marriage certificate does suffice for these purposes: *R v Birtles* (1911) 6 Cr App R 177.

[51] *Re Taylor* [1961] 1 WLR 9, CA.

[52] *Re Taplin, Watson v Tate* [1937] 3 All ER 105, Ch D. Some of the cases suggest an extremely high standard of proof: see, eg, *Re Shephard, George v Thyer* [1904] 1 Ch 456.

[53] (1881) 6 App Cas 364, PC.

to prove that the ceremony had complied with the requisite customs, held the parties to be validly married. Although in this case evidence was given that a ceremony had taken place, it is clear that the presumption applies in the absence of such evidence.[54]

The presumption of legitimacy

On the proof or admission of the basic fact that a child was born or conceived during lawful wedlock, it is presumed, in the absence of sufficient evidence to the contrary, that the child is legitimate. The presumption may be rebutted by evidence showing that the husband and wife did not have sexual intercourse as a result of which the child was conceived.[55] The evidence in rebuttal may be evidence of: non-access; the husband's impotence;[56] the use of reliable contraceptives; the blood groups of the parties; the results of a DNA test; the minimal nature of the husband's access to the wife; an admission of paternity by another man;[57] the wife's cohabitation with another man for an appropriate period of time before the birth of the child;[58] the results of a DNA test excluding the husband as the father combined with evidence of sexual intercourse with another man who refused to comply with an order for a blood test;[59] or the conduct of the wife and illicit partner to the child.[60] Evidence of adultery by the mother will not rebut the presumption in the absence of evidence that at the time of conception sexual intercourse between the husband and wife did not take place.[61]

Either birth or conception during wedlock suffices to give rise to the presumption. Thus where a child is born to a married woman so soon after the marriage ceremony that pre-marital conception is indicated, the presumption applies.[62] Likewise, the presumption applies where a child is born to a woman so soon after the termination of her marriage that conception during the marriage is indicated.[63] In *Re Overbury, Sheppard v Matthews*[64] the presumption was applied in such circumstances notwithstanding the remarriage of the mother prior to the birth of the child. Six months after her first husband's death a woman had remarried, giving birth to a girl two months later. Harman J held that the child was the legitimate daughter of the first husband, there being insufficient evidence to rebut the presumption. In a case such as this, the presumption could have operated in favour of the child's legitimacy by virtue of her birth during the second marriage. However, in cases where *paternity* is in issue, it is obviously correct to treat the date of conception, and not the date of birth as the determinative factor, so that provided the child can be proved to have been conceived during the first marriage, it

---

[54] *Re Taplin, Watson v Tate* [1937] 3 All ER 105. This remains the case even if the period of cohabitation was short: see *Re Taylor* [1961] 1 WLR 9, CA. Cf *Re Bradshaw, Blandy v Willis* [1938] 4 All ER 143. See also *Breadalbane Case, Campbell v Campbell* (1867) LR 1 Sc&Div 182.

[55] See per Sir James Mansfield CJ in the *Banbury Peerage Case* (1811) 1 Sim&St 153. Under s 48(1) of the Matrimonial Causes Act 1973, the evidence of a husband or wife shall be admissible in any proceedings to prove that marital intercourse did or did not take place between them during any period.

[56] *Legge v Edmonds* (1855) 25 LJ Ch 125.

[57] *R v King's Lynn Magistrates' Court and Walker, ex p Moore* [1988] Fam Law 393, QBD.

[58] *Cope v Cope* (1833) 1 Mood&R 269 and *Re Jenion, Jenion v Wynne* [1952] Ch 454, CA.

[59] *F v Child Support Agency* [1999] 2 FLR 244, QBD.

[60] *Morris v Davies* (1837) 5 Cl&Fin 163 and *Kanapathipillai v Parpathy* [1956] AC 580.

[61] *R v Mansfield Inhabitants* (1841) 1 QB 444 and *Gordon v Gordon* [1903] P 141.

[62] *The Poulett Peerage Case* [1903] AC 395, HL.

[63] See *Maturin v A-G* [1938] 2 All ER 214 (termination by divorce) and *Re Heath, Stacey v Bird* [1945] Ch 417 (termination by death of husband).

[64] [1955] Ch 122, Ch D.

will be held to be the legitimate offspring of the first husband, even if born, say, four or six months after the second marriage. In a case where marriage takes place so soon after termination of an earlier marriage that it is unclear whether conception occurred during the first or second marriage, it is submitted that although a presumption operates in favour of the child's legitimacy by virtue of birth during the second marriage, it should not be determinative of paternity, if that is in issue.

The presumption applies, although it may be more easily rebuttable, where there is a maintenance order in force against the husband (unless it contains a non-cohabitation clause),[65] where proceedings for divorce or nullity have been commenced[66] and even where the husband and wife are living apart, whether or not under a separation agreement.[67] However, the presumption does not apply where a decree of judicial separation or a magistrate's separation order is in force.[68] In such circumstances, it is presumed that the parties did not have sexual intercourse. Accordingly, if the child is born more than nine months after the separation, there is a presumption of illegitimacy rebuttable by evidence of intercourse between the husband and wife.

The authorities suggest that in civil proceedings the presumption of legitimacy operates as a persuasive presumption. At common law, evidence in rebuttal was required to meet a high standard of proof[69] but the matter is now governed by section 26 of the Family Law Reform Act 1969, which provides that:

> Any presumption of law as to the legitimacy or illegitimacy of any person may in any civil proceedings be rebutted by evidence which shows that it is more probable than not that the person is illegitimate or legitimate as the case may be and it shall not be necessary to prove that fact beyond reasonable doubt in order to rebut the presumption.

Thus the party seeking to rebut the presumption bears the legal burden of proving illegitimacy on a balance of probabilities and, in accordance with general principles, will fail if the evidence is such that legitimacy is as probable as illegitimacy.[70] In the words of Lord Reid in *S v S*,[71] which were adopted and applied in *T (HH) v T (E)*:[72]

> That means that the presumption of legitimacy now merely determines the onus of proof. Once evidence has been led it must be used without using the presumption as a make-weight in the scale of legitimacy. So even weak evidence against legitimacy must prevail if there is no other evidence to counterbalance it. The presumption will only come in at that stage in the very rare case of the evidence being so evenly balanced that the court is unable to reach a decision on it.

---

[65] *Bowen v Norman* [1938] 1 KB 689.

[66] *Knowles v Knowles* [1962] P 161, where the presumption was applied on a finding of conception as a result of intercourse between the husband and wife at a time after a decree nisi had been granted but before it had been made absolute. Wrangham J was of the opinion that the presumption involved both a presumption of paternity and a presumption as to the date of conception.

[67] *Ettenfield v Ettenfield* [1940] P 96, CA.

[68] *Hetherington v Hetherington* (1887) 12 PD 112.

[69] See per Lord Lyndhurst in *Morris v Davies* (1837) 5 Cl&Fin 163 at 265, above.

[70] See per Denning J in *Miller v Minister of Pensions* [1947] 2 All ER 372 at 374. However, if the case involves a finding that someone other than the mother's husband is the father of the child, the standard of proof to make the finding of paternity is a heavy one, commensurate with the gravity of the issue and although not as heavy as in criminal proceedings, more than the ordinary civil standard of balance of probabilities: *W v K* (1986) 151 JP 589.

[71] [1972] AC 24 at 41.

[72] [1971] 1 WLR 429.

The presumption of death

Where there is no acceptable affirmative evidence that a person was alive at some time during a continuous period of seven years or more, on the proof or admission of the basic facts (i) that there are persons who would be likely to have heard of him over that period; (ii) that those persons have not heard of him; and (iii) that all due inquiries have been made appropriate to the circumstances, that person will be presumed to have died at some time within that period.[73] One of the difficulties of this presumption stems from the fact that evidence in rebuttal may be indistinguishable from evidence which negatives one of the basic facts. This was the case in *Prudential Assurance Co v Edmonds*,[74] a decision of the House of Lords which suggests that once the party against whom the presumption operates has adduced sufficient evidence for the possibility of the existence of the absent person to be put to the tribunal of fact, the presumption has been rebutted. It would seem that the presumption is of the evidential and not persuasive variety.

The basic facts

In *Chard v Chard*[75] the presumption did not arise because there was no evidence of the first basic fact, that is of persons likely to have heard of the person whose death was in question.[76]

Prudential Assurance Co v Edmonds[77] concerned the second basic fact, that the person whose death is in question has not been heard of. In a claim on a policy of life assurance, it was alleged that the assured, one Robert Nutt, was not dead. Members of the family gave evidence that they had not heard of him for more than seven years but knew that his niece believed that she had seen him in Melbourne, Australia. The niece gave evidence that when she was aged 20, standing in a crowded street in Melbourne, a man passed her whom she recognized as her uncle. She did not speak to him because he was lost in the crowd as she turned to do so but said he resembled her uncle as she remembered him from five years earlier. The House of Lords, being in no doubt that it fell to the tribunal of fact to decide whether or not to accept the niece's evidence, held that if the jury had been satisfied that she was mistaken, the basic facts giving rise to the presumption would have been established.

There is a conflict of authority as to whether the presumption arises without proof or admission of the fact that all due inquiries appropriate to the circumstances have been made.[78] The explanation is probably that the extent of the inquiries to be made depends upon the circumstances of the case in question, and that in some cases the circumstances are not appropriate to the making of any inquiries whatsoever.[79] There is some authority that proof of the third basic fact may render proof of the first unnecessary, presumably on the basis that to adduce evidence that a person has made all due inquiries appropriate to the circumstances is also, in some cases, to adduce evidence of a person who would be likely to have heard of the absent person.[80]

---

[73] See per Sachs J in *Chard v Chard* [1956] P 259 at 272.

[74] (1877) 2 App Cas 487.

[75] [1956] P 259.

[76] Friends and relatives will not be treated as persons likely to have heard of the absent person where it is shown that the latter did not intend the former to hear of him: see, eg, *Watson v England* (1844) 14 Sim 29 and *Re Lidderdale* (1912) 57 Sol Jo 3.

[77] (1877) 2 App Cas 487.

[78] See *Willyams v Scottish Widows' Fund Life Assurance Society* (1888) 4 TLR 489 and *Chipchase v Chipchase* [1939] P 391. Cf *Bradshaw v Bradshaw* [1956] P 274n.

[79] See *Bullock v Bullock* [1960] 2 All ER 307.

[80] *Doe d France v Andrews* (1850) 15 QB 756.

The presumed facts

The presumption of death allows the court to presume the fact of a person's death. However, proof of the mere fact of death may be of little or no assistance to a party seeking to establish that an absent person died unmarried, childless, or without next-of-kin. It is reasonably clear that although these additional issues are not proved by the basic facts giving rise to the presumption of death, but require additional evidence,[81] the amount of such additional evidence may be less than would have been required if the presumption had not applied.[82]

A question giving rise to more complexity is whether the presumption of death operates to establish not only the fact of death but also the date of death. Proof of the mere fact of death is of limited use to a party seeking to establish death before or after a particular date. It seems clear from the authorities that the presumption establishes only the fact of death, additional evidence being required to prove that the death took place at a particular period. In the words of Giffard LJ in *Re Phené's Trusts*:[83] 'the law presumes a person who has not been heard of for seven years to be dead, but in the absence of special circumstances it draws no presumption from the fact as to the particular period at which he died.' However, there are two views as to the date on which the fact of death may be presumed. On one view the fact of death may be presumed at the date of the proceedings (ie a continuous period of absence for seven years or more runs back from the date of the proceedings). A second view is that the fact of death may be presumed at the end of a continuous period of absence for seven years (ie a continuous period of absence for seven years runs forward from the date of the disappearance of the absent person). Whichever view is taken, if a party seeks to establish that death occurred on a particular date prior to the date on which the fact of death is presumed, additional evidence will be required. A party seeking to establish that death occurred on a particular date prior to the date of the action, will only be assisted by the second view. Thus if there is no evidence that X was alive during a continuous period of nine years from 1987 to 1996 and a party seeks to establish that X was dead in 1995, the matter coming before the court in 1996, that party will fail on the first view but succeed on the second.

A case which is consistent with both of the above views is *Re Phené's Trusts*.[84] In *Lal Chand Marwari v Mahant Ramrup Gir*[85] the Privy Council interpreted the decision in that case as an authority for the first view. Other decisions, however, are only consistent with the second. In *Re Westbrook's Trusts*[86] the property of an intestate, who had disappeared, was divided among such of his next-of-kin as were shown to be alive at a date seven years after his disappearance. Those who had died before that date were excluded. On the first view, the fact of the intestate's death would have been presumed, in the absence of any additional evidence that he had died on an earlier date, at the time of the proceedings and the court would have divided the estate among such of his next-of-kin as were living at that date. In *Chipchase v Chipchase*[87] a woman charged her second husband with adultery, desertion, and failure to maintain. Her

[81] See *Re Jackson, Jackson v Ward* [1907] 2 Ch 354.

[82] See *Dunn v Snowden* (1862) 32 LJ Ch 104, *Rawlinson v Miller* (1875) 1 Ch D 52 and *Greaves v Greenwood* (1877) 2 Ex D 289, CA.

[83] (1870) 5 Ch App 139 at 144, CA.

[84] Ibid.

[85] (1925) 42 TLR 159 at 160.

[86] [1873] WN 167, criticized in *Re Rhodes, Rhodes v Rhodes* (1887) 36 Ch D 586. See also *Re Aldersey, Gibson v Hall* [1905] 2 Ch 181.

[87] [1939] P 391.

first marriage was in 1915. In 1928, not having heard of her first husband since 1916, she remarried. The magistrates dismissed the complaint on the basis that she had failed to establish the validity of her second marriage by evidence that the first husband was dead in 1928. The Divisional Court held that the presumption of death applied and remitted the case back to the magistrates for them to consider whether there was any evidence in rebuttal. On the first view, the fact of the first husband's death would have been presumed at the time of the proceedings in 1939 and, in the absence of additional evidence that he died on any earlier date, the decision of the magistrates would have been upheld. It is submitted that the first and stricter view deprives the presumption of death of so much of its value that the laxer second view is to be preferred.

Statutory provisions

There are a number of statutory provisions which fall to be considered in connection with the presumption of death. The most important of these are as follows.

Section 184 of the Law of Property Act 1925. This section provides that:

> In all cases where, after the commencement of this Act, two or more persons have died in circumstances rendering it uncertain which of them survived the other or others, such deaths shall (subject to any order of the court), for all purposes affecting the title to property, be presumed to have occurred in order of seniority, and accordingly the younger shall be deemed to have survived the elder.[88]

In *Hickman v Peacey*,[89] Lord Simon was of the view that the word 'circumstances' in this section is not confined to deaths occurring as a result of a common disaster. It remains unclear, however, whether the statutory phrase 'where . . . persons have died' refers not only to persons whose deaths have been proved, but also to those whose deaths have been presumed.[90]

Section 19 of the Matrimonial Causes Act 1973. Section 19(1) provides that any married person alleging that reasonable grounds exist for supposing that the other party to the marriage is dead may present a petition to the court to have the same presumed and to have the marriage dissolved. Section 19(3) provides that:

> the fact that for a period of seven years or more the other party to the marriage has been continually absent from the petitioner and the petitioner has no reason to believe that the other party has been living within that time shall be evidence that the other party is dead until the contrary is proved.

This statutory presumption is easier to raise than its common law counterpart. Apart from the continual absence, the only basic fact to be established relates to the belief of the petitioner, who must give evidence.[91] In *Thompson v Thompson*[92] the provision was construed by Sachs J to mean that during the period of seven years nothing should have occurred from which the

---

[88] This rule has been modified, for the purposes of disposing of the estate of an intestate, where spouses die in circumstances rendering it uncertain which of them survived the other. The spouse is treated as having predeceased the intestate: see s 46(3) of the Administration of Estates Act 1925 (added by s 1(4) of the Intestates' Estates Act 1952). In cases not relating to the title to property, see *Wing v Angrave* (1860) 8 HL Cas 183.

[89] [1945] AC 304 at 314–15, HL.

[90] See *Re Watkinson* [1952] VLR 123.

[91] *Parkinson v Parkinson* [1939] P 346.

[92] [1957] P 19.

petitioner could have reasonably concluded that his or her spouse was alive. The court left open the question whether the petitioner is required to have made all due inquiries appropriate to the circumstances, but it is submitted that a failure to do so could be relevant to the issue of the reasonableness of the petitioner's belief. The fact that the parties parted under a separation agreement does not prevent the operation of the presumption.[93]

The proviso to section 57 of the Offences Against the Person Act 1861. After defining the offence of bigamy, section 57 continues:

> Provided that nothing in this section contained shall extend . . . to any person marrying a second time whose husband or wife shall have been continually absent from such person for the space of seven years then last past, and shall not have been known by such person to be living within that time . . .

The prosecution, in order to prove bigamy, must show that the first spouse was alive at the date of the second marriage.[94] Where this has been done, the accused may rely upon the proviso, which amounts to a defence, to secure an acquittal.[95] The prosecution bear the legal burden of proving that the first marriage was valid and that the accused went through a second marriage knowing that the first spouse was alive. *R v Edwards*[96] suggests that the accused bears the legal burden of proving that the first spouse was continually absent for seven years[97] and that he or she did not know that the first spouse was living within that time. However, there is also authority that the prosecution bears the legal burden in relation to the accused's knowledge.[98]

Omnia praesumuntur rite esse acta

On the proof or admission of the basic fact that a public or official act has been performed, it is presumed, in the absence of sufficient evidence to the contrary, that the act has been regularly and properly performed. Likewise, persons acting in public capacities are presumed to have been regularly and properly appointed. In civil proceedings, the maxim operates as an evidential presumption and may be rebutted by some evidence of irregularity. The operation of the presumption may be illustrated by the following authorities. In *R v Gordon*[99] proof that a police officer had acted as such was sufficient on a charge of assaulting a police officer in the course of his duty: evidence of due appointment was not required.[100] In *R v Roberts*,[101] on an indictment for perjury committed in the presence of a deputy county court judge, the judge was presumed, in the absence of evidence to the contrary, to have been duly appointed.[102] In

---

[93] *Parkinson v Parkinson* [1939] P 346.

[94] Proof that the first spouse was alive before the second marriage may give rise to an inference that he or she was alive at the date of that marriage: see *R v Lumley* (1869) LR 1 CCR 196.

[95] In Australia, the proviso has been treated as a statutory presumption of death in relation to one party to a marriage on the remarriage of the other: see per Evatt J in *Axon v Axon* (1937) 59 CLR 395 at 413, HC of A and *Re Peatling* [1969] VR 214 (Supreme Court of Victoria).

[96] [1975] QB 27, Ch 4.

[97] See also *R v Jones* (1883) 11 QBD 118 and *R v Bonnor* [1957] VLR 227.

[98] *R v Curgerwen* (1865) LR 1 CCR 1.

[99] (1789) 1 Leach 515.

[100] See also *Doe d Bowley v Barnes* (1846) 8 QB 1037.

[101] (1878) 14 Cox CC 101, CCR.

[102] See also *R v Verelst* (1813) 3 Camp 432. But there is no presumption that a court or tribunal has jurisdiction in relation to any given matter: see *Christopher Brown Ltd v Genossenschaft Oesterreichischer* [1954] 1 QB 8 per Devlin J at 13. See also, in the case of an attorney, *Berryman v Wise* (1791) 4 Term Rep 366.

R v Langton[103] the presumption applied to establish the due incorporation of a company which had acted as such. In *R v Cresswell*,[104] on proof that a marriage had been celebrated in a building some yards from a parish church, in which building several other marriages had also been celebrated, it was presumed that the building was duly consecrated. In *TC Coombs & Co (a firm) v IRC*[105] it was presumed, in the absence of evidence to the contrary, that a tax inspector who had served notice under section 20 of the Taxes Management Act 1970 (requiring stockbrokers to deliver documentary information relevant to the tax liability of one of their former employees) together with a General Commissioner, who had given his consent to the notices, had both acted within the limits of their authority, with honesty and discretion.

The authorities are in conflict as to the applicability of the presumption in criminal proceedings. Although there are cases in which the prosecution has relied on the presumption to establish part of its case,[106] in *Scott v Baker*,[107] on proof that a breathalyser had been issued to the police, the court refused to presume that it had been officially approved by the Secretary of State. It was held that the presumption may not be used to establish an ingredient of a criminal office if the regularity and propriety of the matter in question is disputed at the trial.[108] However, there is also authority that it is insufficient merely to dispute regularity; evidence must be adduced.[109]

The presumption of sanity in testamentary cases

Although in criminal cases the presumption of sanity is a presumption without basic facts, a rule relating to the incidence of the burden of proof expressed in the language pertaining to presumptions, in testamentary cases it operates as a rebuttable presumption of law casting an evidential burden on the party against whom it operates. On the proof or admission of the basic fact that a rational will has been duly executed, it is presumed, in the absence of sufficient evidence to the contrary, that the testator was sane. In *Sutton v Sadler*[110] the heir-at-law of a testator brought an action against the devisee alleging the insanity of the testator. The devisee produced the will, proved its due execution, and called witnesses to prove the competency of the testator. The plaintiff gave evidence of the testator's insanity. The trial judge directed the jury that the heir-at-law was entitled to succeed unless a will was proved but that on the production of a duly executed will he bore the burden of establishing the incompetency of the testator so that if they were left in doubt on the matter, the devisee would succeed. The jury found for the devisee. The Court of Common Pleas held that the jury had been misdirected. The devisee bore the legal burden of proving that he was the devisee under a duly executed will. Proof of the due execution of a rational will gave rise to the presumption of sanity placing an evidential burden on the heir-at-law, the legal burden of proving the competency of the

[103] (1876) 2 QBD 296.
[104] (1876) 1 QBD 446, CCR.
[105] [1991] 3 All ER 623, HL.
[106] See *Gibbins v Skinner* [1951] 2 KB 379, where it was held that on proof that speed limit signs had been placed on a road, the presumption could operate to establish the performance of a local authority's statutory duties pursuant to the Road Traffic Acts; and *Cooper v Rowlands* [1972] Crim LR 53, where a man in police uniform who administered a breath test was presumed to have been duly appointed.
[107] [1969] 1 QB 659, DC, approved by the Court of Appeal in *R v Withecombe* [1969] 1 WLR 84.
[108] See also *Dillon v R* [1982] AC 484, PC.
[109] *Campbell v Wallsend Slipway & Engineering Co Ltd* [1978] ICR 1015, DC at 1025.
[110] (1857) 3 CBNS 87.

testator resting with the devisee. Accordingly, if the heir-at-law had raised sufficient evidence for the issue of insanity to go before the tribunal of fact, they should have been directed to find against the devisee unless satisfied that he had discharged the legal burden by proving on a balance of probabilities that the testator was sane. A new trial was ordered.

Res ipsa loquitur[111]

In the ordinary course of things bags of flour do not fall from warehouse windows,[112] stones are not found in buns,[113] cars do not mount the pavement,[114] and slippery substances are not left on shop floors[115] unless, in each case, those who have the management of the thing in question fail to exercise proper care. The normal rule, that in negligence actions the claimant bears the legal and evidential burden, is capable of causing injustice in cases such as these. Although the claimant is able to prove the accident, he cannot show that it was caused by the defendant's negligence, the true cause of the accident, in most cases, being known only to the defendant. In these circumstances, the claimant may be assisted by the principle of *res ipsa loquitur*. Translating into the terminology of presumptions the statement of the principle given by Sir William Erle CJ in *Scott v London & St Katherine Docks Co*,[116] the presumption may be defined as follows: on the proof or admission of the basic facts that (i) some thing was under the management of the defendant or his servants; and (ii) an accident occurred, being an accident which in the ordinary course of things does not happen if those who have the management use proper care, it may or must be presumed, in the absence of sufficient evidence to the contrary, that the accident was caused by the negligence of the defendant. This definition allows for three possible classifications of the principle, as a presumption of fact, as an evidential presumption, or as a persuasive presumption, for each of which support may be found in the authorities.

Some authorities suggest that the principle is no more than a presumption of fact or provisional presumption, an example of circumstantial evidence: proof of the basic facts gives rise to an inference of negligence which the tribunal of fact may draw in the absence of evidence to the contrary. A party against whom the presumption operates bears the provisional or tactical burden in relation to negligence: if he adduces no evidence, he is not bound to lose but it is a clear risk that he runs and a finding by the tribunal of fact in his favour could be reversed on appeal.[117] Other authorities suggest that it is an evidential presumption: on proof of the basic facts, negligence must be presumed in the absence of evidence to the contrary, and the party against whom the presumption operates bears the evidential burden: he will lose unless he adduces some evidence but where, on all the evidence before the court, the probability of

---

[111] This phrase has been used despite the strictures of the Court of Appeal in *Fryer v Pearson & Anor* (2000) The Times, 4 Apr: 'People should stop using maxims or doctrines dressed up in Latin which are not readily comprehensible to those for whose benefit they are supposed to exist.' The authors applaud the attempt to accommodate the lay client, but rather fear that some doctrines—eg estoppel *per rem judicatam*—will need explanation whatever language they are couched in.

[112] *Byrne v Boadle* (1863) 2 H&C 722.

[113] *Chapronière v Mason* (1905) 21 TLR 633, CA.

[114] *Ellor v Selfridge & Co Ltd* (1930) 46 TLR 236.

[115] *Ward v Tesco Stores Ltd* [1976] 1 WLR 810, CA.

[116] (1865) 3 H&C 596 at 601.

[117] See, eg, per Greer LJ in *Langham v Wellingborough School Governors and Fryer* (1932) 101 LJKB 513 at 518 and per Goddard LJ in *Easson v London & North Eastern Rly Co* [1944] KB 421.

negligence is equal to the probability of its absence, he will succeed, the plaintiff having failed to discharge the legal burden of proving negligence.[118] Finally, there are authorities to suggest that the principle is a persuasive or compelling presumption: negligence must be presumed in the absence of evidence to the contrary, the party against whom the presumption operates bears the legal burden of disproving negligence, and he will lose not only where he adduces no evidence but also where on all the evidence before the court the probability of negligence is equal to the probability of its absence. To succeed, he must disprove negligence on a balance of probabilities. The evidence he adduces must either reveal the true cause of the accident and thereby convince the tribunal of fact that negligence is less probable than its absence or show that he used all reasonable care.[119]

It is submitted that there may be no anomaly in the fact that the courts have adopted such different approaches towards this presumption. Given that the facts calling for the application of the principle vary enormously from case to case so that in some the inference of negligence is slight, in others all but irresistible, efforts aimed at confining the principle to a single category seem ill-founded. At the risk of uncertainty, classification according to the facts of the case in question seems preferable. If the thing speaks for itself, it may do so with degrees of conviction. The hardship caused to the claimant may be remedied by placing the tactical, evidential, or legal burden on the defendant depending on the strength of the basic facts in question.

Conflicting presumptions

Where two presumptions apply to the facts of a case, the court may be required to draw two conclusions, the one conflicting with the other. If the two conflicting presumptions are of equal strength so that each operates to place a legal or, as the case may be, evidential or tactical burden on the party against whom it operates, one obvious and equitable solution is to treat the two presumptions as having cancelled each other out and to proceed, as if no presumption were involved, on the basis of the normal rules relating to the burden and standard of proof. As we have seen, this was the solution adopted in *Monckton v Tarr*,[120] where the same presumption of essential validity applied to two different ceremonies of marriage. However, when a similar conflict of presumptions arose in *Taylor v Taylor*,[121] Cairns J preferred to preserve an existing marriage rather than avoid it in favour of an earlier doubtful one. This approach suggests that the strength of a presumption may be gauged by reference to the comparative likelihood of the two presumed facts, or even to general considerations of public policy, as opposed to the nature of the burden placed on the party against whom it operates. Inherently imprecise, such an approach has the obvious advantage of flexibility compared to any set formula. In cases where the two presumptions are, by reference to the burden placed on the party against whom they operate, of unequal strength, there is a dearth of authority. To say

---

[118] See, eg, *The Kite* [1933] P 154 at 170. See also per Lord Porter in *Woods v Duncan* [1946] AC 401 at 434, HL; per Lord Pearson in *Henderson v Henry E Jenkins & Sons and Evans* [1970] AC 282 at 301, HL; per Lawton LJ in *Ward v Tesco Stores Ltd* [1976] 1 WLR 810 at 814, CA; and *Ng Chun Pui v Lee Chuen Tat* [1988] RTR 298, PC.

[119] See per Lords Simon, Russell, and Simmonds in *Woods v Duncan* [1946] AC 401, HL at 419, 425, and 439 respectively; per Asquith LJ in *Barkway v South Wales Transport Co Ltd* [1948] 2 All ER 460, CA at 471; *Walsh v Holst & Co Ltd* [1958] 1 WLR 800, CA; *Colvilles Ltd v Devine* [1969] 1 WLR 475, HL; and the speeches of Lords Reid and Donovan in *Henderson v Henry E Jenkins & Sons and Evans* [1970] AC 282, HL.

[120] (1930) 23 BWCC 504, CA.

[121] [1965] 1 All ER 872.

that the presumption of greater strength should prevail, is to acknowledge that the conflict is more apparent than real. Where, for example, the confrontation is between a presumption of law and a presumption of fact,[122] the determinative factor is the incidence of the legal burden of proof; whether the presumption of law operates to place a legal or evidential burden on the party against whom it operates, the party bearing the legal burden of proof will lose on the issue in question if he fails to discharge it by adducing sufficient evidence to meet the required standard of proof. *R v Willshire*,[123] often cited as an example of conflicting presumptions, is, it is submitted, properly understood in this sense. The accused was convicted of bigamy, having married D in the lifetime of his former wife C. In fact he had gone through four ceremonies of marriage: with A in 1864; with B in 1868; with C in 1879; and with D in 1880. The prosecution, who bore the legal burden of proving the validity of the ceremony in 1879, relied upon the presumption of essential validity. The accused sought to show that the marriage of 1879 was void. He could prove that A was alive in 1868 by virtue of his earlier conviction of bigamy in that year (he married B in the lifetime of A) and he relied upon the presumption of fact as to the continuance of life to establish that A was still alive in 1879. The trial judge did not leave the question whether A was alive in 1879 to the jury but directed them that the defendant bore the burden of adducing other or further evidence of A's existence in 1879. On appeal, this was held to be a misdirection and the conviction was quashed. Lord Coleridge CJ, in the course of his judgment, referred to a conflict between the presumption of essential validity and the presumption of continuance of life. Although the judgment is consistent with the view that the two presumptions had cancelled each other out, it is equally consistent with the ordinary operation of both, the determinative factor being the incidence of the legal burden.[124] The prosecution bore the legal burden of proving the validity of the ceremony of 1879. Once they had proved the basic facts giving rise to the presumption of essential validity of that ceremony, the defendant bore an evidential burden to adduce some evidence in rebuttal.[125] He had successfully discharged this burden by relying on the presumption of the continuance of life and accordingly the jury should have been directed that they could only convict if the prosecution had satisfied them beyond reasonable doubt that the ceremony of 1879 was valid.[126]

Judicial notice

Judicial notice without inquiry

Certain facts are beyond serious dispute, so notorious or of such common knowledge that they require no proof and are open to no evidence in rebuttal. In criminal and civil proceedings, a court may take judicial notice of such a fact and direct the tribunal of fact to treat it as established notwithstanding the absence of proof by evidence. To require proof of such facts, which in some cases could cause considerable difficulty, would be to waste

---

[122] Or between a persuasive and evidential presumption.

[123] (1881) 6 QBD 366, CCR.

[124] There is considerable variance in the reports of the judgment of Lord Coleridge CJ: see 6 QBD 366 and cf 50 LJMC 57.

[125] The presumption of essential validity operates as a *persuasive* presumption only in civil proceedings: see above.

[126] See also *Re Peatling* [1969] VR 214 (Supreme Court of Victoria): the presumption of validity can prevail over that of continuance by virtue of the greater strength of the former.

both time and money and could result in inconsistency between cases in relation to which common sense demands uniformity. Any attempt at a compilation of the numerous facts of which judicial notice has been taken would be pointless. It will suffice to refer to the following examples: a fortnight is too short a period for human gestation;[127] the duration of the normal period of human gestation is about nine months;[128] the life of a criminal is an unhappy one;[129] the advancement of religion and learning through the nation is one of the purposes for which the University of Oxford was established;[130] cats are ordinarily kept for domestic purposes;[131] the streets of London are crowded and dangerous;[132] a postcard is the sort of document which might be read by anyone;[133] flick-knives[134] and butterfly knives[135] are made for use for causing injury to the person; and reconstructed trials with a striking degree of realism are one of the popular forms of modern television entertainment.[136] A final example of general application is that the court is taken to know the meaning of any ordinary English expression.[137] In all of the above examples, the doctrine of judicial notice was expressly applied, but more often than not judicial notice of a fact is taken without being stated. For example, when evidence is adduced that a burglar was found in possession of skeleton keys, judicial notice is tacitly taken of the fact that skeleton keys are frequently used in the commission of the crime of burglary; the fact is not required to be established by evidence but is taken as established as much as if express judicial notice had been taken of it. Judicial notice of certain facts is expressly required by statute. Most of these provisions require judicial notice to be taken of the fact that a document has been signed or sealed by the person by whom it purports to have been signed or sealed. This applies to any judicial or official document signed by certain judges,[138] and summonses and other documents issuing out of a county court and sealed or stamped with the seal of the court.[139] Judicial notice shall be taken of the European Community Treaties, the Official Journal of the Communities, and decisions of or opinions by the European Court.[140] Statute also requires judicial notice to be taken of Acts of Parliament; evidence is not required to prove either their contents or that they have been duly passed by both Houses of Parliament. Every Act passed after 1850 is a Public Act and to be judicially noticed as such unless the contrary is expressly provided by the Act.[141] At common law, judicial notice is taken of Public Acts passed before 1851, but in

---

[127] *R v Luffe* (1807) 8 East 193.

[128] *Preston-Jones v Preston-Jones* [1951] AC 391, HL. A child born to a woman 360 days after the last occasion on which she had intercourse with her husband, cannot be his child (per Lord Morton).

[129] *Burns v Edman* [1970] 2 QB 541.

[130] *Re Oxford Poor Rate Case* (1857) 8 E&B 184.

[131] *Nye v Niblett* [1918] 1 KB 23.

[132] *Dennis v White* [1916] 2 KB 1.

[133] *Huth v Huth* [1915] 3 KB 32, CA.

[134] *R v Simpson* [1983] 1 WLR 1494, CA.

[135] *DPP v Hynde* [1998] 1 All ER 649, DC.

[136] *R v Yap Chuan Ching* (1976) 63 Cr App R 7, CA. Judicial notice of this fact related to the formulation by the court of the appropriate direction to be given to the jury on the standard of proof in criminal proceedings. Thus the fact judicially noticed was not a fact in issue but was relevant to the question of law which formed the subject of the appeal.

[137] *Chapman v Kirke* [1948] 2 KB 450 at 454.

[138] Section 2 of the Evidence Act 1845.

[139] Section 134(2) of the County Courts Act 1984.

[140] Section 3(2) of the European Communities Act 1972.

[141] Section 3, s 22(1), and Sch 2, para 2 of the Interpretation Act 1978.

the absence of express provision to the contrary, a private Act passed before 1851 must be proved by evidence.[142] Statutory instruments must also be proved,[143] although some have acquired such notoriety that judicial notice may be taken of them.[144]

Foreign law is a question of fact, the proof of which normally calls for an expert witness.[145] Generally speaking, therefore, foreign law cannot be the subject of judicial notice.[146] Exceptions include: (i) the common law of Northern Ireland;[147] (ii) Scots law in civil cases, of which judicial notice may be taken by the House of Lords (on account of its appellate jurisdiction); (iii) the law in relation to maintenance orders in all parts of the United Kingdom;[148] and (iv) in civil but not criminal cases,[149] notorious points of foreign law, for example that roulette is legal in Monte Carlo.[150]

Judicial notice after inquiry

The doctrine of judicial notice also applies to facts which are neither notorious nor of common knowledge. Such facts may be judicially noticed after inquiry. In making inquiries before deciding to take judicial notice, the judge may consult a variety of sources including certificates from ministers and officials, learned treatises, works of reference, and the oral statements of witnesses. Such a procedure resembles but remains distinct from proof by evidence: the judge is not required to make such an inquiry, the rules of evidence do not apply, the results of the inquiry may not be rebutted by evidence to the contrary, and the judge's decision constitutes a precedent in law.[151] Proof by evidence bears none of these characteristics. However, although it is easy to distinguish between the processes of judicial notice after inquiry and proof by evidence, there is clearly a fine line separating non-notorious facts from those requiring proof by evidence in the ordinary way.[152] The matter is of more than theoretical or academic interest. To take judicial notice after inquiry of a non-notorious fact which is indistinguishable from a fact to be proved by evidence in the ordinary way, is improperly to usurp the function of the jury as the tribunal of fact. This may be justified, however, where the issue is such as to require uniformity of decision. In *McQuaker v Goddard*,[153] the plaintiff having been bitten by a camel while feeding it on a visit to a zoo run by the defendant, the question arose whether a camel was a wild or domestic animal for the purposes of the law relating to liability for animals. Books about camels were consulted and expert witnesses gave conflicting evidence on oath

---

[142] Production of a Queen's Printers copy or an HMSO copy suffices for these purposes: s 3 of the Evidence Act 1845 and s 2 of the Documentary Evidence Act 1882: see Ch 9.

[143] See Ch 9.

[144] *R v Jones* (1968) 54 Cr App R 63, CA.

[145] See Ch 2.

[146] *Brenan and Galen's Case* (1847) 10 QB 492 at 498.

[147] *Re Nesbitt* (1844) 14 LJMC 30 at 33.

[148] Section 22(2) of the Maintenance Orders Act 1950.

[149] *R v Ofori (No 2)* (1993) 99 Cr App R 223, CA.

[150] *Saxby v Fulton* [1909] 2 KB 208, CA.

[151] An exception exists in the case of judicially noticed facts lacking constancy, eg the Crown's view on the status of a foreign government. If the matter arises in a subsequent case, a fresh ministerial certificate should be obtained.

[152] In *Duff Development Co v Government of Kelantan* [1924] AC 797 the court acted on information supplied by a Secretary of State. It was said that such information was not in the nature of evidence (per Viscount Finlay at 813). Lord Sumner, however, referred to the information as the best evidence (at 824). See also per Lord Denning in *Baldwin and Francis Ltd v Patents Appeal Tribunal* [1959] AC 663 at 691.

[153] [1940] 1 KB 687, CA.

concerning the behaviour of camels. The trial judge, without resort to the doctrine of judicial notice, held that camels were domestic animals. The Court of Appeal, affirming this decision, held that judicial notice could be taken of the matter. Coulson LJ held that the evidence concerning the behaviour of camels was not evidence in the ordinary sense: 'The reason why the evidence was given was for the assistance of the judge in forming his view as to what the ordinary course of nature in this regard in fact is, a matter of which he is supposed to have complete knowledge.'[154]

Despite the scope for abuse of the doctrine, the authorities show that, in general, the courts are cautious not to take judicial notice of a fact requiring proof by evidence in the normal way.[155] Most of the cases in which judicial notice has been taken after inquiry relate to facts of a political nature. An example is to be found in *Secretary of State for Defence v Guardian Newspapers Ltd*,[156] in which it was held that the classification 'secret' appearing on a document originating in a government office was a matter of public record of which the House of Lords was entitled to take judicial notice: Lord Diplock referred to the Statement on the Recommendations of the Security Commission,[157] presented to Parliament by the Prime Minister in 1982, in which it is stated that 'secret' means that the document contains information and material the unauthorized disclosure of which would cause serious injury to the interests of the nation. In cases of this kind, the source of information, a minister, is treated as indisputably accurate for reasons of public policy, namely the desirability of avoiding conflict between the courts and the executive. Judicial notice after inquiry has also been taken of customs, professional practices, and a variety of readily demonstrable facts including, for example, historical and geographical facts. Such cases can usually be justified on one of two grounds: the fact in question is either readily demonstrable by reference to sources of virtually indisputable authority or comes before the court so frequently that proof in each case is undesirable for reasons of cost, time, and uniformity of decision. Judges also take judicial notice of the common law of England, the source of information, when necessary, being the reports of previous cases, and of the law and custom of Parliament, including parliamentary privilege.[158]

Political facts

Judicial notice has been taken of the relations between the government of the United Kingdom and other states, for example the existence of a state of war, the status of foreign sovereigns or governments, the membership of diplomatic suites, and the extent of territorial sovereignty. In *R v Bottrill, ex p Kuechen-meister*,[159] the Court of Appeal took judicial notice of the fact that the country was still at war with Germany, accepting as conclusive a certificate of the Foreign Secretary to this effect. In *Duff Development Co v Government of Kelantan*[160] the House of Lords took judicial notice of the fact that Kelantan was an independent state and the Sultan its

---

[154] [1940] 1 KB 687 at 700.

[155] See, eg, *Deybel's Case* (1821) 4 B&Ald 243; *Collier v Nokes* (1849) 2 Car&Kir 1012; *Kirby v Hickson* (1850) 14 Jur 625; and *R v Crush* [1978] Crim LR 357. But see also *Mullen v Hackney London Borough Council* [1997] 1 WLR 1103, CA, considered below at 671, under **Personal knowledge**.

[156] [1984] 3 All ER 601 per Lord Diplock at 610, HL.

[157] (Cmnd 8540) (1982).

[158] See *Stockdale v Hansard* (1839) 9 Ad&El 1.

[159] [1947] KB 41.

[160] [1924] AC 797. See also *Mighell v Sultan of Johore* [1894] 1 QB 149, CA; *Carl Zeiss Stiftung v Rayner & Keeler Ltd (No 2)* [1967] 1 AC 853, HL; and *GUR Corpn v Trust Bank of Africa Ltd* [1986] 3 All ER 449, CA.

sovereign ruler, accepting as conclusive information to this effect supplied by the Secretary of State for the Colonies. In *Engelke v Mussmann*[161] the statement of the Foreign Office as to the defendant's membership of the staff of the German ambassador was treated as conclusive. In *The Fagernes*[162] the Court of Appeal, on the instructions of the Home Secretary, accepted that a collision in the Bristol Channel had not occurred within the jurisdiction of the High Court.

Customs and professional practices

Although, as a general rule, judicial notice is not taken of facts proved by evidence in earlier proceedings,[163] there is an exception in the case of general customs. In *Brandao v Barnett*,[164] an action against bankers to recover exchequer bills, the defendants rested their defence upon the general lien of bankers on the securities of their customers. The House of Lords took judicial notice of the custom of bankers' lien; it had been judicially ascertained and established and justice could not be administered if proof by evidence was repeatedly required in each case. After consultation with suitably qualified expert witnesses, judicial notice will also be taken of the professional practices of conveyancers,[165] accountants,[166] and ordnance surveyors. In *Davey v Harrow Corpn*[167] Lord Goddard CJ noted that according to the practice of the ordnance survey, where a boundary hedge is delineated on an ordnance survey map by a line, that line indicates the centre of the existing hedge. The court could take notice of that practice as at least prima facie evidence of what such a line indicated.

Readily demonstrable facts

Certain facts, although not notorious, are readily demonstrable after inquiry. The day of the week that a given date fell on, the longitude and latitude of a given place, and the date and location of a well-known historical event are all readily demonstrable by reference to suitably authoritative almanacs, historical or geographical works, or the oral statements of suitably qualified experts.[168]

Personal knowledge

A question which has given rise to considerable difficulty is the extent to which a judge or juror is entitled to make use of his personal knowledge of facts. For these purposes a useful distinction, albeit not always drawn by the courts, is between personal knowledge used in the evaluation of evidence adduced, a matter quite distinct from the doctrine of judicial notice, and personal knowledge of a fact in issue or relevant to a fact in issue.

The evaluation of evidence

It seems reasonably clear that, in assessing evidence adduced in court, a member of the tribunal of fact is entitled to make use of personal knowledge whether it is of a general or specialized

---

[161] [1928] AC 433, HL.

[162] [1927] P 311.

[163] *Roper v Taylor's Central Garages (Exeter) Ltd* [1951] 2 TLR 284.

[164] (1846) 12 Cl&Fin 787, HL. See also *George v Davies* [1911] 2 KB 445 at 448 and *Re Matthews, ex p Powell* (1875) 1 Ch D 501.

[165] *Re Rosher* (1884) 26 Ch D 801.

[166] *Heather v PE Consulting Group* [1973] Ch 189.

[167] [1958] 1 QB 60 at 69, CA.

[168] See *Read v Bishop of Lincoln* [1892] AC 644, where reference to suitable works was approved on the question whether the practice of mixing communion wine with water was contrary to the law of the church. Cf *Evans v Getting* (1834) 6 C&P 586.

nature. In *Wetherall v Harrison*[169] the issue was whether the defendant had a reasonable excuse for failure to give a blood sample. The defendant gave evidence that he was unable to give a sample because he had had a sort of fit. The prosecution gave evidence that the fit had been simulated. One of the justices, a practising doctor, gave his views on the matter to other members of the bench. The justices also drew on their own wartime experiences of the fear that inoculations can create in certain individuals. An appeal by case stated against the acquittal was dismissed. Concerning the extent to which use could be made of local or personal knowledge, the Divisional Court was of the opinion that judges and arbitrators should be treated separately from justices and jurors. That the latter bring into the court room and make use of their manifold experience was seen as an advantage. Stressing that it would be quite wrong if a justice gave evidence to himself or other members of the bench in contradiction of the evidence adduced, Lord Widgery CJ held that it was not improper for a justice to draw on special knowledge of the circumstances forming the background to a case in considering, weighing up and assessing the evidence adduced.

Personal knowledge of facts in issue or relevant to the issue
It is clear from the above-cited dictum of Lord Widgery CJ that a member of the tribunal of fact may not make use of his personal knowledge of facts in issue if this amounts to giving evidence in contradiction of that adduced. However, if the fact is notorious, it seems that notice of it may be taken.[170] In *R v Jones*[171] it was contended that in order to show that the accused had been given an opportunity to provide a specimen of breath for a breath test, it was necessary to prove that the device in question, the Alcotest R 80, was of a type approved by the Secretary of State. Rejecting this argument, Edmund Davies LJ held that the court (including the jury) was entitled to take judicial notice of the fact that the Alcotest R 80 was of an approved type.[172] In the case of facts which are not notorious, a member of a tribunal of fact may not act on his personal knowledge of the matter in question. Rather than supplement or contradict the evidence in this way, he should be sworn as a witness and give evidence, thereafter playing no further part in the proceedings.[173] In some cases, however, the use of personal knowledge has been approved. In *R v Field (Justices), ex p White*,[174] a case brought under the Sale of Food and Drugs Act 1875, the issue was whether cocoa contained a quantity of foreign ingredients. Despite the absence of evidence to establish the matter, the justices, acting on the knowledge of the subject that some of them had acquired in the navy, found for the accused. Although Wills J observed that, in future, evidence should be heard,[175] the finding was not disturbed. In *Ingram v Percival*[176] the accused was convicted of unlawfully using a net secured by anchors for taking salmon or trout in tidal waters. The only issue being whether the place where the net was fixed was in tidal waters, the justices had acted on their own knowledge. Lord Parker CJ held that justices may and should take into consideration personal knowledge,

---

[169] [1976] QB 773, DC.
[170] This has been referred to as 'jury or magistrate notice'.
[171] [1970] 1 WLR 16, CA.
[172] [1970] 1 WLR 16 at 20.
[173] *R v Antrim Justices* [1895] 2 IR 603.
[174] (1895) 64 LJMC 158.
[175] (1895) 64 LJMC 158 at 159–60.
[176] [1969] 1 QB 548.

particularly when it relates to local matters. In *Paul v DPP*[177] it was held that in a case of 'kerb crawling', justices, for the purpose of deciding whether or not the soliciting was 'such . . . as to be likely to cause nuisance to other persons in the neighbourhood',[178] were entitled to take into account their local knowledge that the area in question was a heavily populated residential area, often frequented by prostitutes, with a constant procession of cars at night.

When a judge takes judicial notice of a notorious fact, he is making use of his general knowledge. The extent to which a judge may make use of his personal knowledge of facts in issue or relevant to the issue is not clear from the authorities. In *Keane v Mount Vernon Colliery Co Ltd*[179] Lord Buckmaster held that 'properly applied, and within reasonable limits' it was permissible to use knowledge of matters within the common knowledge of people in the locality. Similarly, in *Reynolds v Llanelly Associated Tinplate Co Ltd*[180] Lord Greene MR said that whereas it is improper to draw on knowledge of a particular or highly specialized nature, the use of knowledge on matters within the common knowledge of everyone in the district is unobjectionable. These two cases and others cited in support of the same principle were all decided under the Workmen's Compensation Acts, under which the county court judges sat as arbitrators and could take into account, when assessing compensation, their own knowledge of the labour market, conditions of labour, and wages.[181] However, in *Mullen v Hackney London Borough Council*[182] the Court of Appeal has treated the principle as being of general application in any county court case. The judge in that case, in deciding the financial penalty to impose on the council for its failure to carry out an undertaking to the court to repair a council house, took account of the fact that the council had failed to honour previous undertakings to the court in similar cases. On appeal it was held that the judge was entitled to take judicial notice of his own knowledge of the council's conduct in relation to the previous undertakings, since even if not notorious or clearly established, it was clearly susceptible of demonstration by reference to the court records, and there was nothing to suggest that the judge had relied on his local knowledge improperly or beyond reasonable limits. It is submitted that this decision confuses and misapplies the separate principles relating to judicial notice and personal knowledge. As to judicial notice, the facts in question were clearly not notorious or of common knowledge, and bear no resemblance to the kinds of fact of which judicial notice has been held to have been properly taken after inquiry. As to personal knowledge, it appears to have been used, without good reason, without notice and to the unfair disadvantage of the council, as a substitute for evidence.

Formal admissions

It is important to distinguish between formal and informal admissions. An informal admission is a statement of a party adverse to his case and admissible as evidence of the truth of its contents, by way of exception to the rule against hearsay, subject to compliance with the relevant statutory conditions including, in civil cases, the notice procedure.[183] Unlike a formal

[177] (1989) 90 Cr App R 173, DC.
[178] See s 1(1) of the Sexual Offences Act 1985.
[179] [1933] AC 309 at 317.
[180] [1948] 1 All ER 140, CA.
[181] See Christopher Allen, 'Judicial Notice Extended', (1998) *E&P* vol 2(1) 37.
[182] [1997] 1 WLR 1103.
[183] As to criminal cases, see Ch 13. As to civil cases, see Ch 11, 337, under **Evidence formerly admissible at common law**.

admission, it is not conclusive: its maker may adduce evidence at the trial with a view to explaining it away. However, a fact which is formally admitted ceases to be in issue. Evidence of such a fact is neither required nor admissible. Thus a party who makes a formal admission, which is generally conclusive for the purposes of the proceedings, saves his opponent the trouble, time, and expense of proving the fact in question. A party who fails formally to admit facts about which there is no real dispute may be ordered to pay the costs incurred by his adversary in proving them. Legal advisers owe a duty to their clients to consider if any formal admissions can properly be made.

Civil cases

CPR rule 14.1(1), (2), and (5) provides as follows:

(1) A party may admit the truth of the whole or any part of another party's case.
(2) He may do this by giving notice in writing (such as in a statement of case or by letter).[184]
(5) The permission of the court is required to amend or withdraw an admission.[185]

CPR rule 14.1A(1) provides as follows:

(1) A person may, by giving notice in writing, admit the truth of the whole or any part of another party's case before commencement of proceedings (a 'pre-action admission').[186]

In civil proceedings a fact may be formally admitted in a variety of ways. In addition to an express admission in his defence,[187] a fact may be admitted by default, ie by a defendant failing to deal with an allegation,[188] or by either party in response to a notice to admit facts,[189] or in response to a written request, or court order, to give additional information.[190] Prior to the trial, formal admissions may also be made by letter written by a legal adviser acting on behalf of a client.[191] At the trial itself, a party or his legal adviser may admit facts thereby rendering any evidence on the matter inadmissible.[192]

Criminal cases

Under section 10(1) of the Criminal Justice Act 1967, a formal admission may be made of 'any fact of which oral evidence may be given in any criminal proceedings', words which make it clear that the section cannot be used to admit evidence which would otherwise fall to be excluded because, for example, inadmissible opinion or hearsay.[193] The admission, which may be made before or at the proceedings in question by or on behalf of the prosecutor or defendant, is conclusive evidence in those proceedings of the fact admitted. Ordinarily, it

---

[184] Special provision has also been made for the making of admissions where the only remedy which the claimant is seeking is the payment of money: see CPR rr 14.1(3) and 14.4–14.7.

[185] Para 7 of Practice Direction 14 contains a non-exhaustive list of factors to which the court must have regard when considering an application to withdraw a Part 14 admission.

[186] Special provision is made for pre-action admissions made in proceedings falling within the pre-action protocol for personal injuries, for the resolution of clinical disputes, or for disease and illness claims: see r 14.1A(2)–(5).

[187] See CPR r 16.5(1)(c).

[188] See CPR r 16.5(5).

[189] See CPR r 32.18.

[190] See CPR rr 18.1 and 26.5(3), and PD 18.

[191] *Ellis v Allen* [1914] 1 Ch 904.

[192] *Urquhart v Butterfield* (1887) 37 Ch D 357, CA.

[193] See *R v Coulson* [1997] Crim LR 886, CA.

should be put before the jury, unless it contains material which should not be before them.[194] The admission is also treated as conclusive for the purposes of any subsequent criminal proceedings, including an appeal or retrial, relating to the same matter to which the original proceedings related.[195] The admission may, with the leave of the court, be withdrawn.[196] The making of an admission under the section is subject to certain protective restrictions: if made otherwise than in court, it shall be in writing;[197] if made in writing by an individual, it shall purport to be signed by the person making it (in the case of a body corporate the signature being required to be that of a director, manager, secretary, clerk, or other similar officer); if made on behalf of a defendant who is an individual, it shall be made by his counsel or solicitor; and if made at any stage before the trial by such a defendant, it must be approved by his counsel or solicitor (whether at the time it was made or subsequently) before or at the proceedings in question.[198] Where a party introduces in evidence a fact admitted by another party, or parties jointly admit a fact, then unless the court otherwise directs, a written record must be made of the admission.[199]

ADDITIONAL READING

Carter, 'Judicial Notice: Related and Unrelated Matters' in Campbell and Waller (eds), *Well and Truly Tried* (Sydney, 1982).

Zuckerman, *The Principles of Criminal Evidence* (Oxford, 1989), Chs 6 and 8.

---

[194] *R v Pittard* [2006] EWCA Crim 2028.

[195] Section 10(3).

[196] Section 10(4).

[197] Section 10(2)(b). In court, counsel may admit a fact *orally*: *R v Lewis* [1989] Crim LR 61, CA. Cf *Tobi v Nicholas* [1987] Crim LR 774, DC.

[198] Section 10(2)(c)–(e).

[199] Rule 37.6, Criminal Procedure Rules 2005, SI 2005/384.

INDEX

C

B51 074 833 6

KT-494-613

DIN

ROTHERHAM LIBRARY & INFORMATION SERVICE

DINNINGTON

2/11.

16 MAR 2011

18 APR 2011

2 6 APR 2014

6 JUN 2014

2 6 FEB 2015

This book must be returned by the date specified at the time of issue as
the DATE DUE FOR RETURN.
The loan may be extended (personally, by post, telephone or online) for
a further period if the book is not required by another reader, by quoting
the above number / author / title.

Enquiries: 01709 336774

www.rotherham.gov.uk/libraries

NOURISH

NOURISH

DELICIOUS GOODNESS FOR EVERY STAGE OF LIFE

JANE CLARKE

PHOTOGRAPHY BY HOWARD SOOLEY

COLLINS & BROWN

To Maya
& Martin

ROTHERHAM LIBRARY SERVICE	
B514833	
Bertrams	14/02/2011
AN	£20.00
DIN	613.2

First published in the United Kingdom in 2011 by
Collins & Brown
10 Southcombe Street
London W14 0RA

An imprint of Anova Books Company Ltd

Copyright © Collins & Brown 2011
Text copyright © Jane Clarke 2011

All rights reserved. No part of this publication may
be reproduced, stored in a retrieval system, or
transmitted in any form or by any means
electronic, mechanical, photocopying, recording
or otherwise, without the prior written permission
of the copyright owner.

ISBN 978-1-84340-577-1

A CIP catalogue for this book is available from
the British Library.

10 9 8 7 6 5 4 3 2 1

Reproduction by Mission Productions, Hong Kong
Printed and bound by 1010 Printing
International Ltd, China

This book can be ordered direct from the publisher
at www.anovabooks.com

Contents

Introduction

For me one of the driving forces (if not the major one) in setting up my practice over 15 years ago – where today I treat people ranging from young to old, through every stage of their lives – was realising that if we are to be able to nourish our bodies throughout our lifetime, the food has to be delicious. While one can stomach the odd mouthful of healthy gruel, or indeed get a bizarre buzz out of sticking to an abstemious, punishingly boring diet for a week or two, when it comes down to enjoying life, we need to find foods that are easy, inspiring and scrumptious.

This is the job I love: turning life around for people who have lost their way with eating or who have found themselves in a situation where their body is struggling. It's not about being a holier-than-thou puritan food faddist who is everyone's worst nightmare, or being overwhelmed with the intricate details of the number of micrograms of a specific nutrient within each meal – what I hope this book will give you is knowledge of the key foods to focus on throughout every stage of your life. Whether you're feeling great already and just want to do a little fine-tuning to ensure you're eating the right foods, or need help getting over health problems and want to know how you can enjoy eating the most nourishing foods in a practical and easy way, I hope *Nourish* inspires you.

Keeping it simple

While searching for the words to introduce this, my eighth book, I came across two quotes which for me sum up why I've decided to write it – the first being the words of Voltaire.

'Nothing would be more tiresome than eating and drinking if God had not made them a pleasure as well as a necessity.'

Addressing the nutritional needs and appetites of every member of the family, each chapter follows a typical life stage – the prime years of adulthood, pregnancy and new life, feeding growing children, middle age, cooking for teenagers, and the over 60s. As such it will appeal to every woman with responsibilities, whether you are a mother, wife, lover, sister, daughter or friend. I've chosen not to focus on babies and toddlers as this is a specialised area that has been widely covered in much detail, not least in my own books *Yummy!* and *Yummy Baby!* Here I wanted to equip the woman typically at the heart of the family, whose stamina and dedication supports the wellbeing of a raft of others, right through midlife and beyond.

In the past I used to find a lot of enjoyment in spending a significant chunk of my time cooking, and I still do when I can manage to set aside a few hours at a weekend while my daughter Maya is out playing. But it's now more often the case that like most people, I'm juggling different aspects of my life: being a mum to the most gorgeous and smiley but minxy and chatty seven-year-old daughter, being alongside both my darling and my parents, and doing the work I love. My job involves a lot of travelling between the rural idyll where I write and my practices in London and Leicester and I find that balancing the different roles in the different locations requires me to simplify things far more than ever before.

Keeping things simple doesn't worry me; as you can see from books and films such as *Food Inc* and *Fast Food Nation*, there are worrying consequences in moving away from food that's as simply produced and locally sourced as we can get. I'm not a food-mile fanatic – we have to see far beyond food-mile labels and look at the overall environmental effect of both transportation and production in order to try and make an informed decision over whether a particular food is worth eating. I find all the equations so mind-boggling, that it's hard to decipher whether one food is more environmentally friendly to eat than another ◆. So I have decided to pare down my decision-

Read more on:
◆ *Pages 108–109 & 146*

making process and my shopping habits, and working with the amazing Slow Food Movement (www.slowfood.org.uk), I do what I can to support good local food producers. It's easy to use the Internet to buy from passionate suppliers that I read and hear about from friends.

However, I'm not ashamed, and nor do I think anyone else should be, to buy produce from abroad – be this buffalo mozzarella from Puglia, *prosciutto San Daniele*, a slice of Brie or a German pumpernickel bread – for these should and can be part of our lives. I passionately believe we have great ingredients, food producers and chefs in our own countries, but we shouldn't think that we ought not to enjoy being part of a food world.

I also don't shy away from wanting to keep things simple when I'm cooking. People seem obsessed these days with trying to make a complicated meal every evening, especially for children, yet if we look back at the classic teas we grew up with – a lightly fried egg (or flat egg, as Maya calls it) on wholemeal toast or a bowl of pasta with a simple tomato sauce stirred through it – they are completely delicious and provide nourishment for a growing body (and an adult body who doesn't have the energy to make anything more complicated at the end of a long day).

As well as having basic cooking skills, we need to be able to work out the difference between true nutritional fact and the rubbish splashed across the newspaper headlines or in TV programmes. Pseudo-nutritionists' self-made nonsense has left a lot of people confused and feeling as if there's no way they can eat well and healthily in today's society. But nothing could be further from the truth – yes, it's hard with modern pressures to find the time to shop or know what's the best and most nourishing food to buy (not least when food companies are working hard to make their food look super-healthy with labels that aren't easy to decipher), but I hope you will find that you can actually glean all the nourishment you need from simple and delicious foods. For me, online delivery companies, which need not be expensive, are providing an incredibly important link between our farmers and small producers, and us, the consumers. Once you've sourced them and got into the routine of ordering, your goal of eating healthy and scrumptious food can be achieved; so let's keep my second quote, the words of Leonardo da Vinci, in the back of our minds.

'Simplicity is the ultimate sophistication.'

My favourite staples

I think we've lost our way a bit, being scared nowadays at seeing ingredients such as custard, cream, crème fraîche and butter in recipes, but it's perfectly possible to eat well and include these ingredients. In the recipe section (see pages 210–251) you'll find a selection of dishes that frequently appear on our table, and can be varied according to what's in season or what you fancy. All these recipes are good for the whole family, but in certain circumstances particular ones can be especially helpful, so I've given suggestions throughout the book to point you in the right direction.

If you're wondering about the calories, I hope this won't be a constant concern for you – it's not so much about how many calories foods have in them, it's whether these calories exist alongside anything nourishing in other ways. For example, a fig-stuffed Bramley apple with a dollop of Greek-style yoghurt will have more calories than the apple on its own, but as a breakfast, one of these will keep you satisfied until lunchtime. So really it's a question of how useful these calories are; if we look at the choice between, say, cooking with ingredients such as a nut butter as opposed to a low-fat spread, one will taste delicious and the other won't. And there is no difference between a large amount of a low-calorie food and a small delectable slice of something higher in calories – it's about controlling your appetite, savouring your food, cooking with good-quality ingredients and serving the food in a way that makes you feel satisfied in every sense.

I also feel with children that to ban sweet foods from the house is counterproductive and unnecessary; you build up the idea of a forbidden food being far more attractive, so they're likely to binge on it when you're not looking. If you cook some chocolate brownies using a good high-cocoa-bean chocolate, for example, the intensity of the chocolate is such that even the most chocolate-loving child will manage only a small piece. If you get them to enjoy it after a meal rather than on an empty stomach, the absorption of the sugar will be slower, which means it's less likely to send a sugar-sensitive child off in a tizzy. If you're trying to tempt the appetite of someone in their later years, a sliver of chocolate brownie with a drizzle of single cream will be sure to get them off the starting block.

Keeping a food diary

There are many occasions when it's helpful to keep a food diary. Often we don't realise what we're eating or how much of it, until it's written down in front of us. A carefully detailed record can be quite an eye-opener and may point to an obvious and simple solution.

It's also an extremely helpful record to take along if you need to seek medical advice. Try to include as much detail as possible and write down any changes and irregularities along with what you consider to be normal patterns.

DATE & TIME	FOOD & DRINK CONSUMED	QUANTITY	SYMPTOMS
	Give as much detail as you can about ingredients too. If your child is involved, they could collect and stick on the labels of anything they buy, such as confectionery, to make them feel part of the process and help you monitor their snacking away from home.	Use household measures, e.g. teaspoon, slice, small bowl etc.	Are you tired, constipated, nauseous? Do you have tummy aches or headaches? Has a rash appeared? Note down any changes to symptoms, which occur both before and after you've eaten.

Cooking and eating is serious business

I found it especially hard to keep within my allotted word count, particularly in the chapter on looking after teenagers, as there are some big issues to discuss. I think we're heading for huge problems with our next adult generation if we don't get food, cooking and eating in the home back on an even keel. The reason why so many young people struggle with obesity, eating disorders, anxiety over body image and mood swings – be this the usual typical teenage grumpiness and volatility or more serious depression – is that so many homes have become ready-meal reheating places rather than those where we sit together to eat and communicate. Often young girls start playing around with mad depleting diets and develop problems because there hasn't been enough good nourishing food in the house and no one has been able to take the time to teach them how to cook and eat properly. If you can keep some simple foods in the fridge and cupboard so that your teenagers can throw together something quick and nourishing, they'll be far less likely to want to go out for fast food. Yours will be the home their friends will want to come to eat at, and although this can be overwhelming at times, it gives you the opportunity watch what they're eating – you can pick up on eating-related problems, protect their bodies from being overwhelmed by too much fast food junk, and, above all, show love and affection through food and eating together.

When it comes to our later years, nourishing food becomes even more important, not least to meet the specific demands that an ageing body places on us but also to ensure that we are still fuelling our bodies with energy. This could be a body that's very fit and healthy, or one which has aged or is struggling with a health problem such as heart disease, dementia or cancer. As relatives and friends of older people, knowing which foods they can best nourish themselves with, and how to help them do this, provides an essential ingredient in living our lives alongside and caring for each other. So often hospitals and care homes get it wrong, as they seem to put the provision of delicious, nutritious food at the bottom of their list of priorities, so that even if you're healthy in old age, getting the right nourishment is difficult. For some older people, health problems arise for no other reason than the fact that they're not being catered for and looked after properly, which is scandalous and inexcusable. I just wait for the time when someone will sue their hospital or care home for the consequences of malnutrition; I can see the dangers of becoming litigious, but when it comes to a basic human right to be well fed and nourished, it's a cause worth fighting for.

Taking the time to enjoy a nutritious meal should be one of the most rewarding aspects of our later years. One of my favourite restaurants in Paris is *Le Train Bleu*, which is the most beautiful, ornate train restaurant at La Gare de Lyon. Elegant, mature Parisian women sit there in their finery, eating a small herb omelette accompanied by a green salad and a glass of wine. To me, this epitomises how elegant life and eating can be if we know what our bodies need, treasure the ingredients and know how to find and prepare them. Every stage of life can embrace this philosophy, and I look forward to moving on to the next phase knowing that I will still be able to enjoy food, and therefore, life.

Getting to grips with the boring science

I'm generally not a lover of charts and tables as I think we have become far too figure- and measure-focused. I prefer to think of meals like an Italian would – simple, delicious dishes, made up of handfuls of this and a dash of that – rather than obsessively looking at labels like a neurotic shopper. It's far easier as an adult to judge when you need more or less, but when feeding our children or elderly parents, it can sometimes be helpful to have a simple visual place to start. The eat well plate on the next page helps us see what food groups our bodies need. Actually, this is a model that applies to everyone over the age of five and can be gradually introduced for younger children, too as they begin to eat with the rest of the family.

You will see that the two biggest segments are carbohydrates and fibre and fruit and vegetables. Roughly one third of our intake should be from the first carbohydrate group of starches and one third from fruit and vegetables. Of the remaining third, most of it should be from the protein groups of milk and dairy, meat and fish, and non-dairy sources of protein such as tofu. Less than one sixth of our diet should be made up from the fat and sugar group, and of course it is best to eat good fats found in oily fish, nuts and seeds and more natural sugars, be this from fresh or puréed fruit or honey for sweetness. That said, cakes and puddings shouldn't be seen as an evil so long as they're eaten in the right proportions and ideally have some nourishing ingredients in them such as fruit, oats, wholemeal flour, spelt ◆, nuts, nut butters etc. Bear in mind that it isn't necessary to follow the model at every meal, but rather over a day or two.

Read more on:
◆ *Page 182*

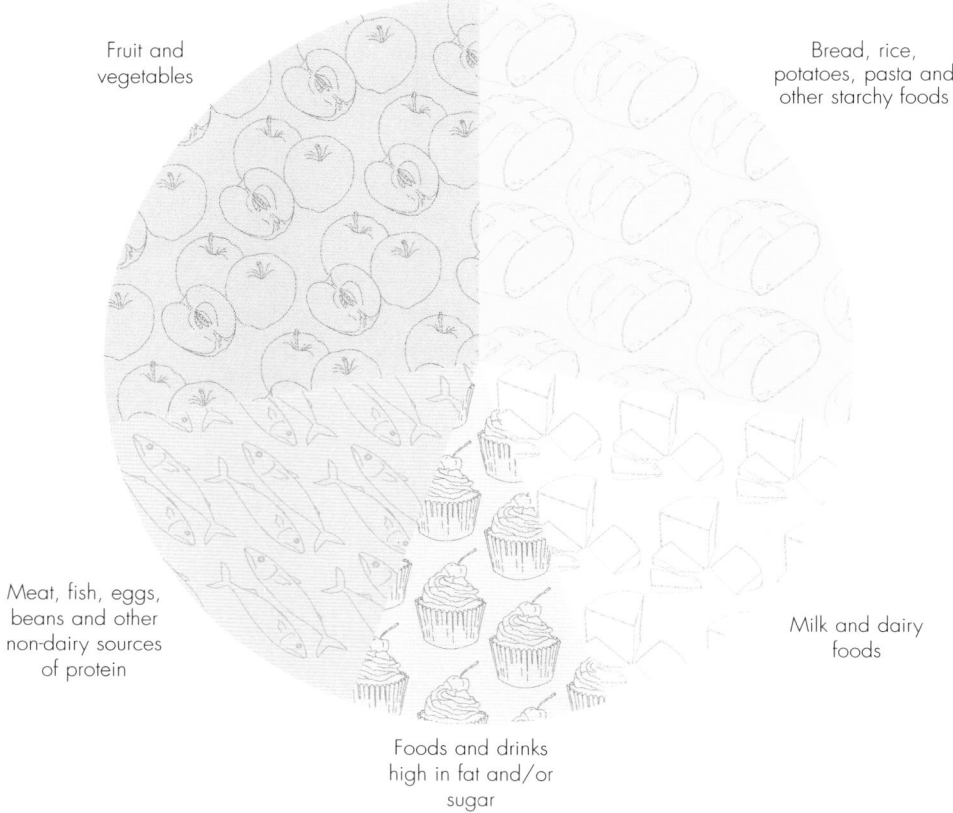

Fruit and vegetables

Bread, rice, potatoes, pasta and other starchy foods

Meat, fish, eggs, beans and other non-dairy sources of protein

Milk and dairy foods

Foods and drinks high in fat and/or sugar

Carbohydrates

Carbohydrates that are grain-based, as opposed to fruits and vegetables, are broken down into complex and simple varieties. These should form a large part of our diet because they are the best source of the energy you need in order to get around and to feel well and energetic. Complex carbs are incredibly rich in nutrients and give you consistent energy throughout the day, reducing the likelihood of you becoming tired and grumpy, which can be the case with simple refined carbohydrate/sugary foods.

The great complex carbs, which have had the least processing, are unsweetened mueslis, porridge oats, wholemeal and wholegrain breads, wholemeal muffins, pitta breads, cornbread, brown rice, millet, spelt, barley and buckwheat noodles. Simple carbohydrates are those that have had most of their fibre removed and may well have been bleached and refined – these are found in the white breads and pastas (and of course the biscuits and cakes) we see in the supermarket. We can usually, and indeed should try to, include some of these simple carbohydrates in our diet, unless as an adult you find that they just don't suit you. We should try not to make them our only source of carbohydrate because most of the goodness has been removed along with the husk of the grain, so we don't find as much of some of the minerals and vitamins that occur naturally in the complex carbohydrates. Most white flour used for bread is fortified with calcium ◆, iron, niacin and other B vitamins, and this can be good especially for children and adults who aren't able to tolerate dairy products or simply don't like them. However, it's much better if you can include some wholemeal and wholewheat carbohydrates in your diet as well.

Just as too much simple carbohydrate means we don't feel satisfied enough after eating (it's the fibre within the husk in complex carbs that makes you feel full), it's not good, especially for children and older people, to eat too many complex high-fibre carbs either. Too much wholegrain can be bulky and upset the gut, which means that you don't get enough energy from your food. As a result, young children (below 13 months) may not grow as well as they should, some people may feel tired all the time, and in extreme situations (though I've only seen this a few times) wholegrain can reduce the absorption of essential minerals such as iron and calcium. A lack of these minerals means children could develop weak bones and iron deficiency anaemia ▲, which though common in older people is thankfully rare in little ones.

Read more on:
◆ Page 20
▲ Pages 70–71

Fibre

Fibre is needed to help keep our digestive system working efficiently and our hearts healthy; it also helps to balance our blood sugar, which affects our energy levels, our ability to concentrate and learn and reduces the chances of us developing conditions such as diabetes and certain cancers. Fibre is found in two main forms in our diets – soluble and insoluble – and we need both.

Soluble fibre is found mainly in fruits, vegetables, pulses and grains such as oats. Insoluble fibre is found in the husks of grains such as wheat and rye, so rye bread and the wholemeal varieties of bagels, muffins, cakes, etc. are rich sources. Insoluble fibre tends to keep the gut moving well and while soluble fibres can help the gut, they're more efficient in maintaining blood sugar levels and the heart through their positive effects on cholesterol and other fats in the blood. To maximise the amount of fibre in your diet, it's best to keep the peel on fruits such as apples and pears and to include some wholegrain products, such as porridge for breakfast or wholemeal bread in sandwiches.

Fruit and vegetables

Fruit and vegetables are also classified as complex carbohydrates and they're great for both children and adults. From the age of five you should be having five portions of fruit and veg a day, so that you get plenty of vitamins, minerals and fibre. Although we recommend five portions of fruit and vegetables a day, I think we'll soon be increasing this to seven, as there are so many benefits to eating a plentiful 'crop' of fruit and vegetables. Every cell in the body will benefit from the nutrients contained in fruits and vegetables.

It's good to vary the fruits and vegetables as much as possible because some are particularly rich in certain minerals and vitamins (spinach in iron and carrots in beta-carotene (vitamin A), for example). Tinned, frozen, cooked and dried fruits and vegetables can be as nutritious as fresh ones; if you bear in mind how practical they are, they can be great ingredients to turn to. If they've been heat-treated, tinned fruits and vegetables contain a little less vitamin C, but most manufacturers compensate for this by adding vitamin C to their products in supplement form. Opt for tinned fruits in natural fruit juice, not sugary syrup. Although wrongly seen as inferior, frozen fruits and vegetables are frozen soon after they have been picked, which means they are just as healthy as fresh (unless you're lucky enough to grow your own or have a generous neighbour, allotment or local market). I find frozen berries a particularly useful standby, and defrost them as and when I need them to use in smoothies, cereals, crumbles and compôtes. Fresh, raw fruits and vegetables usually contain more vitamins and minerals than cooked ones, but they can sometimes play havoc with your digestive system, in which case you may find that cooked fruits suit you better, for example: poached peaches or pears (in a juice such as orange juice, not in wine); baked apples; apricots, plums, greengages; or roasted and puréed vegetables such as roasted butternut squash with shavings of Pecorino cheese or pieces of buffalo mozzarella.

Proteins

Smoked haddock salad, page 225

Proteins are essential for growth, brain development, healthy bones and the production of happy hormones called endorphins. Amino acids are the building blocks of proteins and there are a total of 22 – eight of which (ten for children) are called essential because we can't make them in our body and must therefore get them from our food.

Proteins are divided into two groups: animal and plant. Animal proteins include chicken, seafood, fish, red or white meat from pork, beef, game and lamb, eggs, milk, butter, yoghurt and cheese. They are sometimes referred to as primary proteins, as they contain all eight essential amino acids and are considered to be the most important ones for growth. Plant foods rich in proteins are pulses, legumes, lentils, tofu and other soya products, and you can get some protein from cereal grains such as quinoa and from buckwheat and seaweed. As delicious as these foods are, they are referred to as incomplete proteins because they don't contain all of the essential amino acids, so you'll need to eat a combination of nuts, seeds and grains in order to receive all you need ◆. Children should have some protein along with carbohydrate every day, but adults don't always need the starch found in bread etc.

Read more on:
◆ *Page 98*

Roast mackerel with potatoes & thyme, page 223

Fats

We all, especially children and older people, need fats in our diet. Fats are necessary for brain function, particularly to help children learn, behave and concentrate; they provide some insulation under our skin so we don't lose too much body heat (this is particularly the case with older people); they produce essential hormones to ensure healthy growth and development, especially in children, teenagers and those wanting to become pregnant. Some fat is also needed to ensure good absorption of fat-soluble vitamins such as vitamin D.

The majority of normal-weight people should be eating enough good fat and not just tucking into low-fat foods, which can sometimes be high in sugar, taste inferior and leave you feeling deprived. It's all about knowing which are the better fats for us to eat. The long chain omega-rich fatty foods (see below) are most effective and good for virtually every part of the body. Other fats from dairy produce such as butter, cheese, cream, yoghurt and milk are fine to include in your diet, as in the right amount, they also contribute calcium, magnesium, vitamin A and a little vitamin D.

Omega-3 fatty acids

The most effective omega-3 fats occur naturally in oily fish as eicosapentaenoic acid (EPA) and docosahexaenoic acid (DHA). They also occur naturally in seeds as alpha-linolenic acid (ALA). Good sources include linseed (flaxseed) oil, linseeds, soya bean oil, pumpkin seeds, walnut oil, rapeseed oil and soya beans. They are good for healthy brain function, the heart, joints, and general wellbeing.

The body can convert ALA into EPA and DHA, but not very efficiently. This is why oily fish plays such an important role in a non-vegetarian diet. Oily fish contain EPA and DHA in a ready-made form, which enables the body to use it easily. The main sources of oily fish include salmon, trout, mackerel, herring, sardines, pilchards and kippers, either fresh, frozen, canned or smoked. Unfortunately the exception is tinned tuna, as it doesn't contain the high levels of omega oils found in fresh and frozen tuna but is still a good source of protein.

Vitamins and minerals

The reason I haven't included a specific nutrients chart, with quantities of this and that, is that I want you to feel completely free to find out what works for your own body. Everyone is different and our needs change constantly – one day we may need to stock up on a plentiful supply of energy, while other days we rely on these stores to keep us going. Both of these scenarios are fine, but it's important to know the sort of nutritious food pillars you should try to include each day, bearing in mind that on days when you're not able to nourish your body as well as you'd like, your body will have enough in reserve. There are plenty of websites and books that will give you more detail in milligrams and micrograms, charts and diagrams, but I want *Nourish* to be the place you turn to for inspiration, just as much as knowledge.

Fat-soluble vitamins

Vitamins are classified as fat- or water-soluble. Fat-soluble vitamins are absorbed with fat through the intestine into the circulation and then stored in the liver.

Vitamin A (beta-carotene) is needed for healthy growth, skin, teeth and vision. It protects against infections and is a powerful antioxidant, so helps prevent diseases such as heart disease and cancer. The best sources are cantaloupe melon, pumpkin, squash, carrots, peaches, apricots, red and orange peppers, tomatoes, liver, egg yolk, dairy produce, mackerel and herrings.

Vitamin D is important for the absorption of calcium, building and maintaining strong, healthy bones and teeth. It also helps muscle function and works with vitamins A and C to boost your immune system. Vitamin D is mainly manufactured by the skin when it's exposed to sunlight, but the following foods are also good sources: sardines, herrings, salmon, tuna, dairy produce and eggs.

Vitamin E is an antioxidant needed for healthy skin, a good strong immune system, a healthy heart, and in creams helps reduce scarring. It's found in all vegetable oils, avocados, broccoli, almonds, sunflower seeds, eggs, soya and wholegrains, which include oatmeal, rye and brown rice.

Vitamin K is great for building and maintaining healthy, strong bones and essential for helping blood to clot properly – you may recall that babies are given an injection of vitamin K straight after birth. Vitamin K can be found in bio yoghurt, egg yolks, fish oils, dairy produce and green leafy vegetables.

Water-soluble vitamins

With the exception of vitamin B12, which is stored in the liver, water-soluble vitamins remain in the body for a short time before being excreted by the kidneys – so you need to keep up your intake.

Vitamin B1 is needed for energy production, carbohydrate digestion, heart function and helps children concentrate and their brains generally to function well. It is found in wholegrain foods, such as good cereals and bread, oats, rye, millet, quinoa, legumes, pork and liver.

Vitamin B2 is needed for digestion of carbohydrates, but also fats and proteins, and generally helps our bodies derive enough energy from food. It's also needed for hair, nails and the development of sex organs. The best sources are bio yoghurt, fish, liver, milk, cottage cheese and green leafy vegetables such as spinach.

Vitamin B3 (also known as niacin) is good for the sex hormones and other hormones connected to the digestive system, such as insulin, the hormone that regulates blood sugar levels in the body, and also for thyroxine, serotonin and other mood and brain hormones. Vitamin B3 is generally found in the same foods as vitamins B1 and B2.

Vitamin B5 is needed for conversion of fats and carbohydrates into energy and also for supporting the adrenal glands, which regulate the stress response in the body. It also ensures a strong immune system. We find it in wholegrains, rye, barley, millet, nuts, chicken, egg yolks, liver and green leafy vegetables.

Vitamin B6 is needed for a strong nervous system, for an equally robust immune system and to help repair the body when it gets injured. The main sources include poultry such as chicken and turkey, lean red meat, egg yolks, oily fish, dairy produce, cabbage, leeks and wheat germ.

Read more on:
◆ *Pages 70–71*

Folic acid or folate, if from the natural source (vitamin B9) is perhaps most famous for its role in preventing neural defects during pregnancy, but it's also good for the immune system, energy production and preventing anaemia ◆. It's found in good old dark green leafy vegetables such as kale, spinach, asparagus, broccoli, Brussels sprouts, egg yolks, carrots, apricots, oranges and orange juice, pumpkins and squashes, melons (particularly the cantaloupe variety), wholewheat and rye. You can also get cereals and bread fortified with synthetic folic acid.

Vitamin B12 is needed for growth, digestion and nerves, as well as the production of energy and healthy blood cells. It's found in red meats such as beef, liver and pork, shellfish and other fish, eggs and dairy produce; for vegetarians, you can also find it in seaweed and spirulina.

Vitamin C is needed for a strong immune system, a healthy heart, good skin, preventing diseases like heart disease and cancer in later life, and helping bumps, scratches and cuts to heal properly. The best sources are kiwi fruits, blueberries (in fact, all berries), pomegranates, citrus fruits, potatoes, pumpkins and squashes, sweet peppers, green leafy vegetables, cabbage, broccoli, cauliflower and spinach.

Biotin is needed for hair and nails, skin and energy production. It's found in brewer's yeast, brown rice, nuts, egg yolks and fruit.

Minerals

Calcium is essential for bones, teeth and the heart, and is needed to help our muscles work properly. It's found in dairy produce, small-boned fish such as sardines and anchovies, green leafy vegetables (except spinach, which contains oxalic acid, hindering our ability to absorb calcium), soya products such as soya milk, soya mince and tofu, almonds, sesame seeds (so tahini and hummus are great), sunflower seeds (which I roast and give Maya as a snack with sultanas and raisins) and dried fruits such as apricots. You can also buy calcium-fortified breads, even orange juice, although it's much better to get most of your calcium requirement from natural sources.

As dairy products are such a rich source of calcium, three portions each day should be sufficient to meet an adult's daily need of 700mg of calcium. Try to choose low or reduced fat versions to avoid too much unhealthy saturated fat. A portion includes a glass (200ml) of full-fat, semi-skimmed, 1 per cent or skimmed milk; 250ml calcium-fortified soya milk; 40g hard cheese, such as Cheddar, Brie, feta, mozzarella or Stilton; 125g soft cheese, such as cottage cheese or fromage frais; a small pot (150g) of low-fat plain or fruit yoghurt; fruit smoothie made with 200ml milk or 150g yoghurt.

Iron is important for growth and development and crucial in the production of healthy red blood cells, which carry oxygen around the body. It can be found in liver, lean red meat and egg yolks, as well as foods suitable for vegetarians such as lentils, fortified breakfast cereals, dried apricots and figs, nuts, spinach, kale, seaweed (if you can get your children to eat it!), watercress, broccoli, baked beans, oatmeal, avocados, asparagus, sunflower and sesame seeds and fresh herbs, particularly parsley.

Magnesium helps the body deal with stress, generate enough energy and build strong healthy bones. It also helps the muscle and nervous systems. It's found in citrus fruits, green vegetables such as broccoli, cabbage, nuts and seeds, bread, fish, meat, dairy produce, dried fruits (especially figs and raisins), tomatoes, garlic, carrots, potatoes, aubergines, onions and sweetcorn.

Selenium, which works alongside other antioxidants such as vitamin E, is essential for the immune system and to protect us from skin cancer. It's found in brazil nuts, which can be ground into a delicious mix with seeds to sprinkle on cereals or in porridge, all fresh fruits and vegetables, shellfish, sesame seeds, wheat germ and bran (so healthy cereals are a good source), tomatoes and broccoli.

Zinc is best known for being involved in the immune system, but it's also good for sexual development, regulating moods, the nervous system and brain function. Sources include fish and shellfish, lean red meats, wholegrains, poultry, nuts and seeds, eggs, cauliflower, berries, dairy produce such as yoghurt, oats, rye, wheat germ, brown rice and buckwheat.

Potassium is found abundantly in many foods, and is especially easy to obtain in fruits and vegetables such as chard, mushrooms, and spinach. It can help your muscles and nerves to function properly, lower your risk of high blood pressure and heart problems, ease fatigue, irritability and confusion, and reduce chronic diarrhoea. Older people are more at risk of too much potassium in the body as their kidneys are less able to eliminate any excess.

Sodium is a component of salt, which is naturally present in the majority of foods. Most people eat more salt than is good for their health. It's recommended that adults eat no more than 6g of salt (equivalent to 2.5g of sodium per day). The daily recommendations for children are 2g (1–3 years old), 3g (4–6 years old), 5g (7–10 years old) and 6g (11+ years old). Three-quarters of our salt consumption comes from packaged foods, such as breakfast cereals, soups, sauces and ready meals, so it's easy to inadvertently have too much. Don't mistake sodium levels on labels for the salt content – you need to multiply this by 2.5 to get the salt value ◆.

Read more on:
◆ *Page 46*

Food storage

Something I've found that makes an enormous difference to how fresh and tasty food stays is to look closely at how we wrap and store it. For example, transferring opened tinned foods into sealed plastic containers stops the food being spoilt by contact with the air and metal – once you lose the protective heat-treated seal of the unopened tin, food can spoil very quickly. Often re-sealing technology doesn't live up to expectations, and you're better off taking the food out of the packet and putting it into a plastic container or a good-quality resealable bag. With good wrapping, we not only reduce our risk of food poisoning, but also reduce our food wastage and the contribution that makes to carbon emissions from landfill sites.

If you haven't already found them, try the specially designed food-preserving bags that can make a bag of salad leaves last for days after opening instead of collapsing and drying up. Banana bags, indulgent as they sound, keep bananas fresh as you can store them in the fridge for a couple of weeks (without these special bags bananas go black in the fridge).

Making the most of your fridge

Try not to put too much food into your fridge, as you want the air to circulate properly – this keeps the temperatures at the required levels to keep the food fresh and not spoil. As with cupboards, stock them in rotation so that you use the older yoghurts, etc. before new ones.

Most butchers don't recommend leaving uncooked meat or poultry wrapped in clingfilm or plastic for long, as it goes slimy and can't breathe. Ideally, remove all packaging and wrap it in greaseproof paper, then put it on a plate so that it doesn't drip anywhere. Cold cuts and salamis dry out easily, so wrap them well. Fresh and smoked fish can stay in its sealed bag and is best well wrapped.

Cheese tends to sweat and spoil more easily wrapped in clingfilm – it keeps better in waxed paper, which prevents it from drying out. Oils and butters can go rancid with heat and time (oxidised fats are unstable and aren't good for the heart), so buy enough butter for the week or freeze it in small portions. I'm careful to keep bottles of oil in a cool place away from the cooker, and I keep special extra virgin oils in the fridge (they turn cloudy as they cool, so you need to get them out about an hour before you want to use them). Eggs are often debated over – I don't keep mine in the fridge, but many recommend you do, as this maximises freshness. However, cold eggs tend to crack more easily when you boil them, and if you want to make meringues or mayonnaise you need to get them out of the fridge for a few hours beforehand.

Fruit and vegetables are best left unwashed before they're popped into the fridge, but I tend to wash everything apart from salad and soft berry fruits (best left in their punnets) beforehand, as it means I can just grab something as I fly out of the door. Do check out the stay-fresh-longer bags as they've made a real difference to my food spend and to how much enjoyment Maya gets out of a crisp, fresh-tasting carrot as opposed to a slightly off-peak one. It's always a good idea to wash salad in fresh, cold water and eat it within a day of purchasing. Pure fruit and no-added-sugar jams need to be stored in the fridge, as they don't have the usual high sugar content to act as a preservative.

Be aware of food poisoning

Don't panic if your child picks up a bit of food off your kitchen floor and pops it into their mouth – it's not ideal, but it won't kill them and there are real advantages for their immune systems if you don't keep them in a sterile environment. Children (and adults) need to get into the habit of washing their hands after going to the toilet and before meals, but at the same time, the old saying 'Dirt is good' is true. However, when cooking for young children and older people, you need to be vigilant with food hygiene because they are more at risk of poisoning from wrongly stored or badly cooked food. Food poisoning is more common when budgets are stretched, as it can be tempting to think that best-before dates can be extended a little to help eke out the shop for a few more days. Although with correct storage some extra time can be safe, as with food hygiene, you need to be careful when it comes to children, older people or anyone with a compromised or vulnerable immune system. Best-before dates are there for a reason – to protect us from food poisoning bacteria – so take notice of them even if it means wasting food.

The freezer – my life saver

Bolognese sauce, page 218

Now I'm a mum, I'd be lost without my freezer. Not only does it mean that I can cook meals in advance, but also, from a very practical point of view, it has simplified my shopping routine. I tend to freeze portions of sausages and bread, and also freeze milk (which has to be pasteurised). I also freeze small bags of freshly grated Parmesan, as the taste is far superior to the ready-grated kind. Eggs can be frozen if they're beaten lightly (don't freeze whole), either yolk and white together or separated into yolks and whites for use in sauces or to make meringues. You can freeze egg whites without doing anything to them, but with yolks you need to beat them a little and add a pinch of salt or sugar (remember to label which you've added!). Boiled eggs, mayonnaise, custard, yoghurt (unless it's made into a frozen yoghurt pudding) and single cream don't freeze well, although double cream can be frozen when whipped.

Don't use frozen food for dishes that require re-freezing, as not only can this affect the texture of the dish, but more importantly it may increase the risk of food spoilage or poisoning bugs growing. Freezing doesn't kill all bacteria, which is why you must make sure all food is well wrapped in special freezer bags, plastic containers or extra strong foil, and that it is reheated and defrosted thoroughly. Remember that young children and older people are more likely to get ill with food poisoning, so you need to be extra careful that you reheat to the correct temperatures to completely cook the food. It's fine to then let it cool down a little, but make sure you don't just heat it to a lukewarm temperature you think is right for your little one to eat, as if you do this not all the bugs will have been killed.

Freezing is also a good way to take advantage of good buys in supermarkets, as you can buy more for less money and most importantly not waste any. Picking your own fruit and popping it into the freezer is best of all, as you're getting the most nutritious fruit fresh from the plant. For a family a freezer is a life and sanity saver, and the frozen produce can be great nutritionally as well as in cost value.

Freezing bread

Bread freezes well but goes stale more easily in the fridge, so to make best use of a loaf, divide it as soon as you've brought it and freeze it in manageable quantities – if you're making a packed lunch it works well to freeze a couple of slices in a small bag and take it out of the freezer last thing at night. It also means you can have different breads on different days and not have to waste any. If bread is more than a few days old turn it into croutons or use it for bread and butter pudding or as the base of a soup. It can also be whizzed up to make breadcrumbs (which can also be frozen) to use as a coating for fish fingers or chicken drumsticks, or to go in burgers, falafels, home-made sausages or stuffing.

Freezing fruit

Most fruits freeze well, and this can also be a good way to preserve some vitamin C. Freezing puts a time freeze on the natural reduction in vitamin C, meaning you end up with fruits higher in vitamin C once they come out of the freezer.

Berry fruits are best frozen separately on trays, then packed together in plastic containers. Stone fruits such as plums, damsons and peaches can be frozen with stones in, but I tend to take the stones out and then, like berries, freeze them separately on trays and pack them together once frozen. They're all great for future jam, fruit sauce, chutney and compôte making. With cooked fruits I've got into the habit of filling small freezer bags that I can take out and throw into the microwave for a few minutes if I want a late afternoon snack or in the mornings for Maya to have with porridge (it takes only about five minutes to go from frozen to hot).

Citrus fruits freeze surprisingly well – simply peel and segment oranges (ideally seedless) and freeze as above to make delicious little popsicles for children. This is also a good base for making marmalade if you have a glut of oranges, lemons, limes, grapefruits or other citrus fruit. Finely grated lemon, lime and orange rinds freeze well in ice-cube trays and are great for adding to fruit crumbles, cakes, curries, etc.

Freezing herbs and spices
Herbs and spices can be made economical and practical to grow by freezing them, chopped, in ice-cube trays, to be popped out ready to season sauces, tagines, curries, casseroles, soups, etc. I don't think frozen herbs work as well in raw dishes, as they're slightly mushy when thawed. Alternatively make up a batch of herb-based sauces, such as basil pesto. I find that grated fresh ginger also freezes well and is a great addition to soups, stir-fries and curries.

The natural oiliness of spices means that they can turn rancid easily in a hot light kitchen, leaving the final dish somewhat fusty and unpleasant. So only buy small amounts at a time and ideally store them in small dark jars and in a cool place. Whole spices tend to last longer and give a fresher taste. You can freeze most spices as long as they are well wrapped.

Tandoori chicken, page 221

Check out your cupboards

Like the fridge and freezer, if you look at the way you store dry and tinned foods, the family shop will stretch further and the food will stay fresh, taste good and reduce the likelihood of any little creatures making a nest! The ideal is a cool, dark larder with slate or tiled shelves and racks for vegetables, etc., but this isn't usually the norm. The best choice of cupboard in which to store your food should be as cool as possible, not near an oven, and well ventilated. Even tinned and packet foods will deteriorate and spoil in hot rooms.

Dried goods such as flour can grow moulds – especially the wholewheat versions, which contain more fat because the grains have natural oils in them. Storage jars are ideal for opened dry goods, but remember not to just top them up but use the oldest rice, pasta, etc. first. Tear off the use-by date from the packet and pop it into the jar so that you can keep on top of using food at its best. Cereals can go off and lose their freshness quicker than you think, so keep the waxed inside packets tightly sealed or transfer into storage jars if little hands have loosened their packaging. The same applies to porridge oats – there is a natural oiliness in the whole flakes of oats, so keep them well wrapped. As tempting as BOGOF (buy one get one free) deals are, they often make us buy too much food, so that you end up eating it past its best or throwing it away – unless you're a dab hand with the freezer, in which case making a big batch of pasta sauce with tomatoes bought on offer is ideal.

In Your Prime

Having endured the teenage years and come out the other side relatively unscathed, our bodies now enter the prime age. Generally considered as our 20s, 30s and 40s, we should be looking and feeling our strongest and best. In theory, being an adult brings autonomy but in practice we are hit by all sorts of demands. Finding time to shop for the sorts of nourishing foods you know you should be eating and having the energy to cook alongside the pressures of everyday life, isn't easy for anyone, including me.

But what I'm hoping you'll gather from this book is that there is nothing wrong with the occasional day or meal when there isn't a salad, fruit or wholegrain in sight – for me a classic comfort meal would be delicious sourdough bread, thinly sliced and toasted, along with a board of cheeses and a good tangy pickle – and also that nourishing foods can be quick and easy to prepare as long as you have well-stocked cupboards. This can help you to live healthily and yet still lead a rewarding work and social life – not the easiest of balances to get right.

As to what your body needs now that you've moved into a life stage that doesn't involve as much growth and development as when you were a young child or a teenager, the foundations are in essence the same as for any other stage in life – you need a balance of different nourishing foods to enable you to feel and look your best.

Our body needs fuel

How much food we need largely depends on what sort of day we have ahead of us and how our body is feeling. On average we say that three meals a day with a couple of nutritious snacks in between is a good pattern to work to. However, whenever the work and home environments produce practical and emotional challenges, we can be fooled into thinking that because we feel hungry and may not have time for a proper lunch, it's okay to grab some nibbles or reward a stressful afternoon by dipping into a stash of chocolate biscuits.

Don't forget that the body often craves the distraction of eating – you start to feel hungry when really you want an excuse to take a break or need some classic oral satisfaction – yes, food can be a comfort, but not when it ruins your appetite for a nourishing breakfast, lunch or evening meal. You may feel that working long hours requires you to eat more, especially if you feel hungry, but the reality is that unless you're involved in an extremely active job or working out big-time in the gym, if you answer every hunger pang with a nibble, your weight is quickly going to start piling on.

If it's a break you need, have a drink of something that's not loaded in sugar and fats – it's no surprise, I'm sure, to hear me say that a can of a fizzy, sugary drink can tot up an astronomical sugar hit that shouldn't be ignored. A can of cola can contain as much sugar as a slice of delicious, gooey chocolate cake, although admittedly without the fat (but I'd rather have the chocolate cake!). Don't be misled into thinking that a glass of fruit juice doesn't deliver a sugar hit of its own, because it does, in the form of fructose. Fructose in its original form within a piece of fresh fruit, should be considered as a different thing from when it is drunk as a juice or smoothie. Although juice contains useful vitamins and minerals, the fructose can cause just as much of a sugar high feeling, and therefore a sugar crash, as an artificially flavoured canned drink. It has the same hefty calorie hit, which can really start to add up if you're a big fruit juice drinker. When it comes to your teeth, the stickiness of thicker fruit juices such as smoothies, while delicious, can hang around in the mouth more than a thin juice and corrode teeth. Apart from the sugar content which causes decay, too many fruit drinks can erode enamel and stain teeth.

Watch the energy-rich foods

You may have been one of those teenagers who could eat almost anything they liked – fry-ups, takeaways, snacks of chocolate mid-afternoon – without affecting your weight, but when we reach our mid-20s and go through to our 40s, the chances are that our metabolism will slow down and the effects on our health begin to show. Unless we're careful either with the quantities of fats and sugars we consume or are very active, our weight will go in the wrong direction – up and out. Even if our weight doesn't change, our body shape can – more fat can accumulate around the bits we often have hang-ups about, such as hips, waist, etc., so we start to feel negative about our body. On the inside, excess saturated fat in particular can cause a rise in levels of the bad sort of cholesterol (LDL – see below), which can cause all sorts of health problems. Diets rich in saturated fatty acids are also associated with the development of insulin resistance, which can contribute to developing diabetes ◆, and dyslipidaemia (abnormal blood fat levels) as part of 'Metabolic Syndrome' (a cluster of risk factors for cardiovascular disease).

Read more on:
◆ *Page 157*

HDL and LDL cholesterol

There are two types of cholesterol: high-density lipoprotein (HDL), or 'good', and low-density lipoprotein (LDL), or 'bad'. LDL is the kind of cholesterol that can be deposited in our arteries and cause problems, while HDL is the good kind, which picks up LDL and takes it back to the liver to be broken down. HDL helps to counteract the damaging effects of LDL – so, put perhaps more simply, we should keep our LDL levels down and try to boost HDL. Below 5mmol/l (millimoles per litre) is our preferred total cholesterol level, but to make up this figure the ideal is that LDL cholesterol should be 3.0mmol/l or less and HDL cholesterol should be 1.2mmol/l or more. The TC/HDL ratio (that is, your total cholesterol divided by your HDL cholesterol) should be 4.5 or less. This reflects the fact that for any given total cholesterol level, the more HDL the better. It's the balance between these two types of cholesterol that (along with eliminating other risk factors such as smoking, diabetes and high blood pressure) really protects us against the risk of heart disease and stroke.

This means watching foods rich in saturated fats – butter, cream, cheese, fatty meats and foods containing all of these ingredients – as once inside the body, the liver turns this fat into cholesterol.

Cholesterol-busting tips

- Use skimmed, semi-skimmed or 1 per cent milk (slightly lower than semi-skimmed) and look to the cheeses that are lower in fat or eat less of the full-fat cheeses.

- Choose lean cuts of meat such as steaks, or good-quality, high-meat-content sausages. Another tip is to buy good-quality, low-fat sausage meat, mix it with falafel-type ingredients such as chickpeas, herbs and spices, roll it into balls and cook them like little rissoles. Alternatively make a sausage, tomato and potato pie and serve with ratatouille, caponade or roasted vegetables.

- Cuts of meat such as brisket, oxtail, ham hocks and shoulders and braising steak, are economical to buy. These can usually benefit from longer, slower cooking methods such as casseroling, making hot pots or tagines, and the meat can be made more tender by marinating. It's a good idea to cook these dishes the day before, so you remove the excess fat that forms on the surface when left to cool, but so often the flavours improve with time and through reheating.

- Don't be put off by cheaper cuts of meat that have some fat marbled through them – the cooking process requires some fat for flavour and tenderness, and overly lean meat can be as tough as old boots. Use a good-quality, not over-fatty meat and remove the excess fat after cooking. You can buy fat-removing brushes or use kitchen paper to soak up any excess fat. Using a non-stick frying pan helps, as does using a minimal amount of oil.

Focus on fibre

Fibre is one of our best allies. When we're young, too many fibre-rich foods can fill us up, preventing our body from gleaning enough energy from our diet and absorbing key minerals ◆. When we become adults, the benefits of having a diet rich in fibrous foods are so great, and the downsides are usually so minimal – exceptions arise for people with a sensitive digestion, such as those with IBS ▲ – that we can simply say for the majority of us that the more fibre we can eat the better. But that doesn't mean we can plough our way through a loaf of wholemeal bread, as this will tot up many calories and leave our stomach feeling completely stuffed. What I mean is that if we can look at the foods we eat and see if we can incorporate a higher-fibre version, or add some fibre-rich foods to a meal, this will most likely bring some tangible benefits.

The advantage of boosting the amount of fibre in our diet is that within hours, if not sooner, we will start to feel different. Okay, to

Read more on:
◆ *Pages 18–21*
▲ *Pages 181–182*

Chicken & chickpea burgers, page 220

begin with when we start eating more fibre we might feel a little bloated, but this is normal and due to the fact that we've changed our diet and it takes a while for the gut to adjust and feel great. (By the way, we should always ensure that we drink plenty of water when we boost our fibre, as this helps the fibre to work and prevents constipation – surprisingly, even though fibre is usually good for preventing this, in the short term fibre and no water can bung us up.) Eating fibre-rich foods correctly can help alleviate bloating, constipation and provide other short- and long-term benefits.

You might think the fibre message is one that is well and truly understood, but in fact we're just not eating enough of it. We should be eating 18g a day, yet the average for an adult is only 12g – which, bearing in mind that this is the average, means there are many people falling way below the 18g a day target. This is why so many people have digestive problems, don't feel satiated enough after their meals and are therefore more inclined to overeat and be overweight.

Here's a little science. The term 'fibre' is branded around on products and in marketing messages but it sometimes isn't as well understood as it should be. The connotation of 'fibre' is that it tends to equate with boring and worthy foods, when really it could perhaps benefit from a touch of re-branding so that people would associate it with satisfaction. It's wondrously beneficial in so many ways and at the same time it can be delicious. The word actually describes something we used to call 'roughage', which doesn't sound very pleasant in my book, but in a way this describes it better, as fibre consists of the edible parts of plants that are not broken down and absorbed in our small intestine.

You may have seen the terms 'soluble' and 'insoluble' bandied around, and in essence these are different types of fibre which are named according to the kind of beneficial effect they have in our body. Some (insoluble) are better at helping to get the gut moving as it should, and therefore are the ones to focus on when you're trying to prevent constipation, while others (soluble) are better at helping us to control blood cholesterol and the sugar levels in our blood – which can then have an impact on our energy levels, the temptation to nibble and moods. The reason you should try to incorporate a good mix of soluble and insoluble fibre is in order to glean the benefits right across the board – from reducing bowel problems right the way through to feeling satiated when you've eaten, having healthy blood fat and well-controlled blood sugar levels.

The different types of fibre in the foods we eat behave differently when they meet the bacteria that lives in our large intestine – some fibrous foods are partly fermented, others completely, by these gut bacteria, and this fermentation process, unpleasant as it sounds, is something we want to encourage. This is because the gases

Read more on:
◆ Pages 136–139
▲ Page 20

Chickpea, tomato
& sausage hot pot,
page 212

produced, such as carbon dioxide, methane and hydrogen, and short-chain fatty acids (butyrate, acetate and propionate), are extremely beneficial to our health. For instance, the short-chain fatty acids are absorbed into the cells of the gut wall, where they can be used as fuel, or pass on into the bloodstream, where they can have all sorts of positive effects such as decreasing the risk of developing bowel cancer ◆. This is one of the most common cancers alongside breast and lung cancer, and hundreds of people are diagnosed with the disease every day. Eating a diet rich in fibre is one of the most effective ways to prevent the disease.

Essential iron

Iron is an important nutrient for growth and development ▲ but something that many people (women in particular) tend to lack. One of the reasons for this is that we used to be much bigger red meat eaters than we are these days – maybe it's fears over the relationship between poor-quality, fatty red meat and the development of heart disease and cancer, or the fact that for moral reasons we are preferring to eat more of a fish, white meat or vegetarian diet. I don't eat as much red meat as I used to simply because I prefer to eat more of everything else – I love bean- and lentil-based dishes such as dahl or curry, or a chickpea tabouleh-style salad with roasted vegetables, more than a simple roast – and I admit I'm fussy about where I source my meat, so would rather wait until I can get hold of meat that I have confidence in eating. I also try to make red meat go further – I'd prefer to pay a little more for good-quality, well-sourced brisket of beef and make it stretch to a couple of meals: first making a casserole slow-cooked with root vegetables, then mincing up the cooked meat to make a shepherd's pie, and often making a third meal by using the vegetables and meat as a soup.

Sometimes, however, I crave a good steak, most often on a Friday evening when I'm tired, and this is completely healthy. Most of the studies that link red meat with ill health either don't distinguish whether we're talking about a fatty red meat product such as low-meat-content high-fat sausages, or a lean good-quality steak – and there is a vast difference. It's perfectly possible to be healthy and eat meat if you ensure that it isn't high in fat and that your overall diet is rich enough in other nutritious foods to ensure that your blood fat levels (one of the chief concerns over a diet heavy in fatty red meat) stay within the ideal range. I would say that eating good-quality red meat once or twice a week is about the right frequency.

Read more on:
◆ Page 20
▲ Pages 37–38
● Pages 38–40

Oxtail soup,
page 235

If meat turns your stomach and you need to up your iron intake, there are non-meat sources of iron such as dark green leafy vegetables, eggs, soya, dried fruits like prunes, figs and apricots, fortified breakfast cereals, etc., but the iron is not as well absorbed by the body. You need to ensure that in the same meal you have some food that's rich in vitamin C, as this will help your body absorb the iron ◆. In practical terms this could mean either a fresh fruit salad or bowl of fresh berries after a meal or a glass of freshly squeezed juice. Bear in mind that frozen vegetables can contain more vitamin C than so-called fresh, which can make the practical issues of boosting fresh veg and fruit in the diet easier.

Be careful not to reduce iron absorption

Check that you're not having too much tannin in tea, as this inhibits the absorption of iron – tannins are not to be confused with caffeine, as they're two completely different things, and decaffeinated teas contain just as much tannin as normal tea. One option is to go for herbal teas ▲; alternatively you don't need to refrain from enjoying a proper 'cuppa', but instead of having it with or straight after a meal, leave it a couple of hours so that the tannins within the tea don't interfere with the iron absorption. Tannin levels within a cup of tea increase the longer you leave the leaves seeping, so a lighter-coloured, weaker tea is another way to reduce tannin levels. This brings caffeine levels down as well – although caffeine doesn't have as negative an effect on iron absorption as tannins – but you do need to watch that you don't take in too much caffeine for your general health ●.

Phytates in bran and oxalates in spinach, nuts, chocolate, parsley and rhubarb can reduce the iron effect too, so just make sure you're choosing other green leafy vegetables as well as spinach and that your diet isn't too bran-based.

A warming cup of tea

The average Briton consumes a phenomenal 2.5kg of tea a year, second only to the Irish globally, while ironically in India and China, where some of the finest teas are grown, the annual consumption is more like 500g. There is a lot to be said in favour of tea, not least what a delicious restorative beverage it can be. Drinking tea, whether black, white, green, or something more exotic-sounding like Oolong or rooibos, is now seen as a good way to take in antioxidants and other substances known as bioactives that may

Read more on:
◆ *Pages 201 & 207–209*
▲ *Page 20*

help reduce the incidence not only of heart disease, but also of Alzheimer's and other types of dementia ◆.

Drinking a cup of tea is a great way to top up your fluid intake. Although I'm a huge fan of water and there is a slight diuretic effect in tea, so that we don't glean quite as much water as we would from hot water and lemon, sometimes a cup of tea just hits the spot. It can be an easy and enticing way to take in the benefits of milk, such as calcium ▲, and a little caffeine. It's less potent a caffeine hit than coffee would be, and it may suit you not to have as powerful an energiser – I can drink tea when I'm anxious and it will be calmative, whereas a coffee would tip me into feeling more jittery and anxious.

Herbal teas are not only a great alternative to black, white, green etc., but also have many useful medicinal properties. I don't see the harm in looking to traditional herbal teas, as we could do well to just listen to our ancestors; just ask your doctor or pharmacist if you're taking medication of any sort – most of the ingredients in herbal teas are safe, but herbs are drugs and therefore can be as potent as some medications, particularly when drunk in large quantities. We're quite right to be more careful with children and not to let them drink too much of it, but if they're well, there is nothing wrong with them having a cup of tea. It's warming, soothing, and far better for them than a fizzy drink.

Although research is still in its infancy in terms of real-life tea drinkers (as opposed to a laboratory result), we are able to deduce that the antioxidants found in teas in varying amounts may well be useful in fighting the day-to-day battle of preventing heart disease, and these antioxidants, along with substances we call bioactives, may have a role to play in keeping our brains healthy and our immune systems strong.

Quality is everything

One of the frustrations I have when choosing tea in some supermarkets is that it's very hard to find out much about it, other than assuming that the more you pay for it the finer the quality (though this isn't always the case). For this reason I like to support and source passionate small tea producers, who source the teas themselves and can give you so much information about individual varieties. I particularly like silver tip tea, which is unique in that it is just the leaf buds that are used, unlike all other teas, which are made up of the opened leaves. These mature buds have not yet opened to the sun and therefore have not begun to photosynthesise, making them especially low in caffeine and tannins.

White, green, Oolong and black teas all come from the leaves of *Camellia sinensis*. White and green tea are set apart by the way they are processed. Black teas are processed through fermentation, which results in some of the beneficial nutrients being converted into other compounds. Green tea, however, is steamed to prevent oxidisation and retains more antioxidants, which have been attributed to making it more effective at preventing and fighting various diseases. White tea is the least processed of all teas and therefore contains the highest concentrates of antioxidants. In the Far East, white silver tip tea has long been used as an aphrodisiac and is known for its ability to soothe a hangover. Oolong is a tea that falls between black and green tea and undergoes only a small amount of fermentation during processing. Some laboratory studies have suggested that it is good for enhancing the body's ability to metabolise fats, largely because of its extremely high levels of a particular bioactive called polyphenol, but we're far from being able to say that this would be able to have an impact on global obesity and heart disease. But watch this research!

Water is best fresh and should not be re-boiled, since the oxygen content is diminished, which affects the tea. For black, green and white tea the water should be below boiling point because the amino acids (which produce the tea's flavour) dissolve at lower temperatures than tannin. Tea made with water at 100°C will be more astringent and less sweet. Ideally you should stop the kettle when small bubbles form along the sides of the kettle, just before it reaches a rolling boil. Tea purists say that white tea is best infused when the water is at about 70°C and green and black teas around 85°C. For Oolong tea, on the other hand, hotter temperatures are critical to getting the top notes of flavour and fragrance, so use freshly boiled water.

A few of my favourite herbal teas

Wild rooibos (red bush) is a tea I didn't used to like, but I suspect it was because I'd only tried fusty bags from health food stores. I'm now a fan, as a good rooibos can be lovely. It doesn't belong to the tea family as it's a legume and is therefore 100 per cent caffeine free, which can be useful if caffeine isn't your thing or if you want to avoid stimulating effects.

Lemon verbena (*Aloysia triphylla*) (the French call it *verveine*) is a leafy herb with a wonderfully refreshing lemon flavour. Pop a good pinch in the pot and leave it to stand for three to five minutes. Traditionally lemon verbena is believed to help aid digestion and alleviate stress. Studies aren't conclusive, but I do find it calming when anxiety levels are going up.

Chamomile (*Matricaria recutita*) is a beautiful flower and makes a delicious infusion. Although you can buy chamomile in teabags, I find the tea they make bitter and fusty, far inferior to that made with the dried flowers. Chamomile has long been respected for its ability to soothe sore stomachs and is renowned as a gentle sleep aid.

English peppermint has the tradition of being a good digestive tea, and can be just the thing to sip after a meal, but if you have problems such as stomach ulcers you should watch that the tea isn't made too strong as mint can very occasionally aggravate symptoms. There is a world of difference between mint tea from small sources passionate about their product and the stale mint teabags available from the more usual outlets.

Steaming coffee

As with tea, I tend to be somewhat particular about the type of coffee I enjoy and when I drink it. Some people find that too much coffee can make them jittery and aggravate anxiety. Caffeine is a key component of coffee and the one we nutritionally tend to focus on, although energy drinks and tea contain some caffeine too. Even though studies are somewhat inconclusive and the physiological mechanisms behind the effects of caffeine can be a little complex, my philosophy is that if you're going to have a cup of coffee, make it a good one and cut out downing a coffee for the sake of it. This way you'll be able to enjoy coffee as part of your day, and glean a little caffeine hit which can be useful to get your body going in the morning or to help ease a headache or migraine ◆. When you would usually have had that habitual, unnecessary, lousy-tasting coffee, you can replace it with water, which is by far the most hydrating and beneficial fluid. There is quite a lot of confusing information out there about caffeine sensitivity surrounding bones, heart disease and brain health, so I just want to highlight where the studies have got us to at the moment.

Read more on:
◆ *Pages 43–47*

Bones

While caffeine can have an impact on calcium absorption and bone metabolism, it seems that if we have a consistently good intake of calcium we can still enjoy a little caffeine. Therefore a coffee in our day isn't going to undo all the good work we're trying to achieve with our bones. However, I would say that the majority of people struggle to meet the recommended calcium intake, and if you have bad habits such as not exercising or smoking, you may need to increase the amount of calcium-rich foods you consume. If you're looking for one thing in your life you can do to help with your bones (especially if you've been told that you have low bone density), maybe keeping your coffee intake in check is one of them.

Heart health

When it comes to preventing heart disease, the relationship coffee has with our blood cholesterol levels and other heart disease risk factors is a little confusing, to say the least. Some studies show that in older people drinking coffee can actually offer protective effects against heart disease, while others show that heavy coffee drinkers may find that their risk of developing heart disease will be high. Some people with heart disease or other heart-related problems such as high blood pressure are told to cut out coffee altogether, as it can interfere with their medication. The long and short of it seems to be that if you have a couple of cups a day (the old mantra of moderation in everything springs to mind) then you're not putting your heart at any risk; however, watch what you're adding to the coffee. You could be introducing some saturated fat and calories if you're a cream or full-fat loving latte drinker, and sugar if you like it sweet.

It has also been suggested that drinking decaffeinated coffee could lead to a rise in harmful cholesterol levels, which in turn can increase the risk of heart disease and diabetes ◆. However there are hundreds of studies that do not show increased health risks associated with drinking caffeinated, and particularly decaffeinated, coffee. If you only drink one cup each day, these claims probably have little relevance because your daily coffee dose is relatively low.

Brain health

Studies have shown that being a coffee drinker could in fact help to preserve some of our cognitive function – probably due to its effect on the way chemicals transmit thoughts in our brain. Some studies even show that people who drink coffee have a decreased risk of developing Alzheimer's in later life ▲, but we need far more research to show consistent results before we start thinking that the coffee pot should be permanently by our sides. The other argument is that too much caffeine can adversely affect the way the brain works if you're struggling with mood disorders such as depression. As always, everyone is different, so if you love coffee have a couple a day, ideally in the morning, as although the evidence is mixed as to

Read more on:
◆ Page 157
▲ Page 201

whether caffeine aggravates sleep disorders like insomnia, many people I treat do find that either only drinking coffee in the morning or stopping it altogether helps them sleep better.

Enjoying coffee at its best

If you're going to drink coffee, make it a good-quality one you will truly enjoy. I love espresso with a little milk (the French call it a *noisette*, while the Italians refer to it as a *macchiato*), but I also enjoy a slightly longer coffee made in either a filter or a cafetière. In the latter case if I'm at home I'll grind my own coffee beans. The trick with both filter and cafetière coffee is to drink it freshly made, ideally within the first 15 minutes as this gives you the best flavour. With filter coffee in particular, if you leave it standing on the hot plate it will turn bitter.

Taking it with milk is a personal choice – I prefer a touch of hot milk with an espresso and a little more with a filter or cafetière coffee, because it not only enables me to have a longer drink, but it also provides an opportunity to take in some calcium-rich milk. You can of course use soya or oat milk and other types of non-dairy milk, but they can often curdle if you put them into coffee when it's too hot.

Drinking water

Many research bodies advise us that we should be drinking six to eight glasses of fluid every day, which usually works out at about one to one and a half litres, depending on how large the glasses are. I recommend that two and a half litres a day is the optimum amount of water we should be drinking, and I'm not alone – the World Health Organisation (WHO) recommends that women should drink over two litres of water a day, with men needing closer to three litres. You need even more if you live in a hot climate, have a very active job or work out a lot – a good guide to how much extra you need when you work out is to think about drinking roughly an extra litre per hour of hard exercise. Everyone is different in how much water they can comfortably drink, and when you push your water intake up you may spend a lot of time in the bathroom to begin with. Your body will get used to it, especially if you can stagger your water intake throughout the day – say a glass an hour.

Most nutritionists don't like to say whether we should be drinking water or other fluids such as juices, etc., but it's my experience that the more plain water you drink, the better your energy levels, your skin and digestive system will be; in fact the list of benefits is endless.

It's fine to include the odd glass of fruit juice, tea or coffee but you can treat herbal teas in the same way as plain water. I would always say that the ideal amount of water should be drunk in the form of plain water or herbal teas, and anything else is extra. I realise that drinking two and a half litres of water and then putting tea and coffee on top of that is an awful lot, but it's something to aim for as I see so many people who feel great when they drink a similar amount (as I reach for yet another glass!).

It helps to have water on your desk when working, or a jug of water in a prominent place at home, as it serves as a constant reminder to drink. Try adding fresh mint, lemongrass or thin slices of cucumber, lemon, lime or orange to a jug of cold water, as these can infuse a subtle flavour and look pretty. It helps too to have a nice glass or mug instead of a plastic cup – all these little things make a difference to whether you're inclined to drink the water.

What kind of water?

If you totted up two and a half litres of water a day over a lifetime it would amount to a significant amount of money if you drank only bottled water. And the health benefits of bottled water versus tap water may surprise you – tap water is just as hydrating and healthy, so it's worth putting up with the odd snooty waiter's tut-tuts. The main water suppliers are under a legal obligation to maintain a safe drinking water supply to your house, so if you're concerned that the water that comes out of your tap doesn't taste right or isn't good for you, get in touch with your supplier. Bottled waters can have higher salt levels than many tap waters and don't offer the same fluoride protection. Water fluoridation is the addition of fluoride to our water supply to help prevent tooth decay. The World Health Organisation suggests a level of fluoride from 0.5 to 1.0mg per litre, depending on climate, but bottled water typically has unknown fluoride levels, and some domestic water filters remove some or all fluoride. But bottled waters can be more to your taste and can be more practical. And don't forget sparkling water, which I love to drink sometimes with meals.

If portability is a key concern, think about carrying around a flask or bottle filled with tap water. This is a much more environmentally friendly way to carry water around, without getting through large numbers of bottles, which need to be recycled or create waste. If the taste of the water that comes out of your tap isn't to your liking·you could try a water filter (fitted to your tap or one of the smaller jug-style ones) or simply placing a jug of cold water in the fridge for a couple of hours can improve the flavour too. It's important to replace water filters as frequently as instructed by the manufacturer, to ensure that they continue to filter the water correctly and hygienically. If you have tap water or opened bottled water in the fridge, drink it within 24 hours, especially if you have been drinking it directly from the bottle. There are food poisoning bugs that like to hang around in stagnant water, which may be fine to shrug off when you're fit and healthy, but in the vulnerable, such as the young, old or unwell, could cause health problems. We consider water to be harmless and 99 per cent of the time it is, but we need to be careful, as with food, to store it correctly.

If you're looking for a non-dairy source of calcium, remember that if you live in a hard water area the calcium content of your tap water will be higher than in a soft water area. Bottled waters have to declare their calcium content, so look at their labels to see if there is a water higher in calcium that you like.

Being sensible about alcohol

Those wanting to drink sensibly should drink a maximum of two to three units a day (14 units a week) for women and three to four units a day (21 units a week) for men and avoid binge drinking. Drinking this amount of alcohol affords you all the benefits we often read about, such as reducing risk of heart disease, however it's a good idea to have one or two alcohol-free days during the week and to try to spread your weekly allowance out evenly. Despite several PR messages about beer containing antioxidants, red wine being the healthiest drink for your heart, and so on, let's just knock the implied notion of 'the more you drink the healthier you will be' on the head. There is no real evidence that red wine is better than any other alcohol, and resveratrol, the component concerned, may work well in a test tube but not so well in the body. Sorry to be the bearer of such news, but see it this way – choose the drink you enjoy and drink just a small amount for the pleasure and the health benefits, be this red wine, white wine or beer. Your body will react to alcohol in a unique and different ways, so watch how you drink it: it can disrupt sleep, lower energy and mood levels, and can for some be a strong contributory factor in carrying too much weight.

Alcohol is not only calorific but can also increase appetite, reduce your resolve to eat well and make you crave fatty and salty foods, which can easily be consumed in great quantities if you are in an alcohol haze. Eating salty crisps, nuts, olives, canapés or nibbles with alcoholic drinks makes us thirstier, as the body tries to get us to drink more water to enable it to get rid of the excess salt. We should quench this thirst with water and not another quaff of something alcoholic, as alcohol is also dehydrating. Food is good at helping to slow down the absorption of alcohol, but ideally, we should have something substantial and low in salt – the combination of salt and alcohol can make hangovers far worse.

I don't want to dwell on the negatives too much, but when we have stressful and busy lives it can be far too easy to slip into a habit of drinking too much alcohol. This is especially easy because many people still tend to assume that a glass of wine is just one unit, and it's not – it can be two or three units in the case of some of the enormous glasses that are used nowadays. Pints or half litres of beer can be easier to get a realistic check on how much you're drinking as they're a consistent measurement, but the alcohol content of beers and lagers can vary enormously and you need to bear this in mind when you decide what to drink.

Drinking alcohol on an empty stomach will make its effects more pronounced, as you need food to slow down its absorption into your body. Drinking plenty of water also reduces the effects of the alcohol, so maybe have a couple of glasses of water first and then enjoy wine or beer with your meal, with more water alongside. Be mindful that bubbles increase the speed of alcohol absorption, so champagne and sparkling wine often have the most dramatic alcoholic effects – and mixing drinks increases the chances of being hit with a hangover.

Alcohol and the mind

If you have problems controlling what you eat – whether it's wanting to binge on everything in the fridge or you are desperately trying to get a healthy eating routine going – my experience with treating patients is that alcohol can be a real menace. It can make you eat too much, as you seldom feel full at the right moment, and can dissipate all your good intentions. If you are prone to under-eating, alcohol can meddle with your thought processes and make you feel more anxious, colouring your perception of reality. So consider knocking alcohol on the head while you're trying to get a grip on food and the path of eating the right foods.

Headaches and migraines

At some time or other you're bound to get a headache, but sometimes they become frequent and you may suspect that they are more like migraines, which are typically experienced on one side of the head. Migraine sufferers experience visual auras, extreme pain, sickness and an inability to cope with bright lights and sounds. Physiologically headaches and migraines are very different and although we still don't really know what causes them, doctors believe that they are brought on by chemical changes in the brain's nerve cells. Many factors can trigger a migraine or headache, such as certain foods, tyramine, caffeine, MSG (a flavour enhancer found in many processed products and Chinese food), alcohol, hormonal changes in the menstrual cycle or stress. The first thing is to check with your doctor that the diagnosis is correct, and then it's a simple case of seeing what you can change in your lifestyle to reduce their frequency and ferocity.

The frustrating thing about headaches and migraines is that there are often so many contributing factors. Sometimes you can eat or drink a trigger food and be completely fine while at other times you'll be staying well away from them when a headache or migraine hits you. All we can do is identify and then eliminate as many of the triggers as possible – some being easier to deal with than others. Women in particular may find that they are more affected at particular times of the month, but keeping a food diary ◆ for a few weeks can help you to identify vulnerable times or general trends you can look at improving. This can equally apply to men, and can also be exacerbated when you have other lifestyle factors coming into play, such as greater pressures at work or home, or have to do a lot of travelling.

Read more on:
◆ *Page 11*

Roasted butternut squash & spicy sweetcorn soup, page 234

Tyramine

Tyramine is an amino acid that we naturally have in our body, but is also found in particular foods and drinks that may provoke headaches and migraines. Tyramine is mostly found in offal, mature cheese, peanuts, peanut butter, chocolate, broad beans, cured sausage, sauerkraut and herring (especially pickled). In fact as a broad stroke, anything fermented, pickled or marinated is best avoided.

Caffeine

The causes of headaches and migraines are ill understood and most people react in their own way to caffeine. What we do know is that caffeine in medication or drinking coffee with migraine medication can increase the speed at which the drug is absorbed, and therefore the rate at which your head starts to feel better.

What we also find is that if you dramatically cut down your caffeine intake you're likely to get a withdrawal headache, which sometimes triggers a migraine. I would suggest that if you are having a lot of caffeine-rich drinks and think they might be a contributing factor to your headaches or migraine, see if you can gradually cut them out rather than going cold turkey – try this over a few days and then, once you're down to two or three a day (a pretty good level to be at), you can enjoy a couple of espressos in the morning and a delicious cup of tea in the afternoon. This enables you to enjoy them, hopefully without exacerbating headaches, and if you keep at this level for a couple of weeks you will soon see if you feel any better. Some migraine or headache sufferers feel much better by not having anything caffeinated at all, while sometimes a cup of coffee or tea can prevent the first signs of a headache or migraine from getting worse.

Alcohol

We can be slightly more precise about alcohol. It's my experience not only from treating patients but also from being a migraine sufferer myself, that drinking alcohol on an empty stomach, or when dehydrated, exhausted or stressed, can also saddle you with an alarming headache or migraine. Although some people find that champagne and red wine are the worst offenders, for many others (myself included) white wine is worse. But it all depends on the type of grape and the additives, such as sulphites, which have been added. It's worth keeping a note of what you drink and how it affects you, as it could be a simple case of avoiding specific wines. Avoid mixing your drinks and line your stomach with food before, during and after drinking alcohol.

Unfortunately, alcoholic drinks don't have to declare their contents so you can't always find out what goes into them. (Note that it's worth keeping an eye on the labels of soft drinks too – even cordials such as elderflower – as they may contain sulphites.)

Keeping blood sugars within the comfort zone

Read more on:
◆ Pages 154–155

It does seem that eating regularly and avoiding very sweet, high-GI (glycaemic index) foods can be a key contributing factor in managing or avoiding headaches and migraines. Some endocrinologists dismiss the notion that sugar can cause symptoms in people who don't have a hormonal problem such as diabetes, but this isn't what I see in myself or my patients. I find that the problem is exacerbated by eating very sweet or high-GI foods on an empty stomach. This means biscuits, cakes, sweets and sweet drinks ◆. If you absolutely crave a sweet snack, try pears, dried

Be mindful but not scared of salt

Official guidelines state that adults should eat less than 6g of salt a day (less for children). If you look at this amount on a teaspoon it is shockingly small and if you consider that most of us use a pinch when we're cooking, it can soon add up. Although I use a lot of alternative seasonings in my food – garlic, black pepper, fresh chilli, fresh herbs and spices, lemon juice – sometimes there are still moments when I reach for the salt and needn't feel guilty. But as a general rule, taste before you season and avoid putting salt on the table as this only adds to the temptation to grab some.

We need to strike a balance – the odd dip into some salted crisps, olives or smoked trout or salmon with capers isn't going to harm you, as the body easily steps into action and gets rid of the salt (in urine). I think that to vilify salt and reduce our intake so that food becomes bland can lead to overeating. If food is tasty and well seasoned it's usually easier to stop eating when you feel full. If food is boring it often takes more to hit the 'I'm satiated' bell. So in my mind, it's better to use it judicially, cutting it out gradually so that you learn to live with less.

I am not denying that there are worrying risks in having a diet that is high in salt. It has a profound impact on our heart, largely through aggravating blood pressure and if we reduce our salt intake by around 2.5g a day it could reduce the risk of stroke or heart attack by one quarter. But it's not just our hearts and brains that can suffer – high salt intake has been linked with osteoporosis and cancer, specifically of the stomach – so we do need to do something about it.

Having salty-tasting foods as treats, rather than the norm, is an obvious way to go, but I suspect the real reason that salt is made such an issue in the health headlines is that in some sectors of the processed food industry there are far higher levels of salt than you would imagine (this is where Guideline Daily Amounts can be very useful on the labels of processed foods). Be extra careful if you find yourself heading towards the cheaper, economy lines, as some of them contain nasty surprises. Some supermarkets are able to sell them for less because they fill sausages, meat pies, ready-meals and ready-made sandwiches with cheaper filler ingredients such as flour, starch, etc., but since these are pretty bland in their own right, some manufacturers whack in hefty amounts of salt to make them appetising.

One of the most shocking examples is breakfast cereals. They're traditionally seen as sweet foods, but the high sugar content fools the taste buds into not clocking the fact that there can be a lot of salt in them too. Porridge and natural wholegrains generally have low levels of salt, but there are a lot of others that don't, so be particularly vigilant with processed foods – the labels will help.

Among other things, too much salt can aggravate high blood pressure, bone loss and fluid retention. Because our taste buds can fade in their accuracy, we may think we need more salt to make food appetising, which is a problem. Not only will we eat more processed foods, which will often contain a lot of salt, but if we're shaking the salt cellar over food that has been salted beforehand, we are probably taking in too much.

apricots, plums, grapes, dates or kiwi fruit, as these seem better tolerated, as does eating something sweet after a meal containing protein as the protein helps to slow down the absorption of the sugar, making its less pronounced.

Skipping meals is a common trigger for headaches and migraines, especially breakfast. But this isn't an excuse for constant nibbling – three meals a day plus a couple of snacks should help you to get into a routine of preventing headaches. If you feel a migraine coming on, try to have something bland, for example a couple of rice cakes or a slice of toast and a glass or two of water, as sometimes this can lessen the severity. If nausea is a problem, just try a few mouthfuls and then rest to let the food settle – sometimes a very small amount of food can really help. Relaxing is beneficial too – but this is not to say that exercising won't be a good thing in your life, as it can be a good stress-reliever. As with most things, having regular sleeping times – both going to sleep and waking – can help as a lifestyle measure.

Cellulite

Contrary to popular thinking, physiologically, cellulite isn't any different to any other sort of fat and therefore isn't caused by toxins *per se* – it's just one of those very annoying aspects of being a woman. However, it isn't just a female issue and can be the bane of men's lives too – some adults will spend a fortune on creams, potions, brushes and massages to try to reduce the orange peel-like skin around their thighs. When it comes to food and drink, you should find that eating a nourishing diet, light in calories and high in fruits and vegetables, should pay off. It's also especially helpful if you can incorporate fat burning exercises. As much as I'd love to conjure up a miracle here, there aren't any specific cellulite-banishing foods, despite the claims made for foods such as grapefruit.

Depression

There is growing evidence to show that if we eat a well balanced and nourishing diet we are less likely to develop depression. Scientists believe in some cases it could be conected to an over-heated immune system – recasting depression as an inflammatory condition like heart disease or rheumatoid arthritis. But the symptoms of depression are very varied, as is the degree to which we suffer, and so while not eating well can be a contributing factor, it would be wrong to imply that all depression is caused simply by what we do or don't eat.

Depression is clinically defined in many textbooks and I don't want to dwell on the medical aspects of this illness, but from a nutritional perspective over the years I have often (but not always) seen that by changing the foods we eat we can influence our moods and reduce the other classic symptoms, such as poor sleep, low energy and disturbed appetite. Appetite can go either way – putting us off all foods or eating compulsively to try to make ourselves feel better. Depression can make us crave different foods, which can knock out supplies of other nutrients in the body.

A lot of anti-depressant medication can disrupt the way we eat. Some suppress appetite and if our excess weight is an exacerbating factor in feeling low about ourselves, losing a few pounds and getting in control of what we eat can be a huge factor in helping us to work our way out of a depression. Other anti-depressants can make us crave foods, which if we've been on the underweight end of the weight spectrum can be a useful tool to make us eat something, particularly if we have been suffering from an eating disorder ◆. But more commonly, some anti-depressant medication can both make us crave overly sweet foods and all the starchy stuff to such a great extent that weight gain becomes a problem. This can be a real hurdle for some people, especially women, who I've found can be reluctant to take anti-depressant medication if it's going to make them put on weight.

Read more on:
◆ Pages 170–171
▲ Pages 70–71
● Pages 180–181

Easy apple &
greengage strudel,
page 246

But nine times out of ten, if we can improve the balance of nutrients in our diet, the symptoms improve and in some cases we may be able to stop or reduce taking the medication. In any case check whether you're meant to take drugs on an empty stomach or with meals and discuss with your doctor if your medication is adversely affecting your appetite. Do keep in contact with your doctor or therapist, as it's good to keep them in the loop and to let them know if your weight is changing, as your dose of medication may need to be adjusted. I mention this because sometimes we think that doctors won't be interested in what we eat, but in fact by keeping them informed you can ensure that your medical care is appropriate and working.

It's also important to establish from your doctor's assessment whether there are nutrition-related factors which may well be causing you to feel low, such as iron deficiency anaemia ▲ or coeliac disease ●. Certain drugs taken for other health problems, such as some blood pressure medication and particular contraceptive pills, can have mood-lowering effects too, and your doctor can ensure that you're receiving the right help.

If you just don't feel like eating

Read more on:
◆ Page 19

Pearled spelt with
broad beans,
asparagus & dill,
page 216

Although in times of plenty our bodies lay down stores of many nutrients, which we can draw on when we're not eating so well, if the days of not eating much or well turn into weeks and months, over time our nutrient stores can become depleted. As I've mentioned before, a lack of iron can lead to iron deficiency anaemia, which in itself can cause many of the classic depressive symptoms such as lethargy, low mood and disrupted sleep. Lack of the B vitamins ◆ too can cause depression, as can not eating enough selenium, a mineral that we most commonly find in fruits and vegetables.

The long and the short of it is that if we're off our food and are not eating a diet rich in all the vitamins, minerals and other nutrients our body needs, we can soon start to feel low. Rather frustratingly, appetite can go, which is in fact the opposite of what we really need our bodies to feel – it would be handy if our natural survival instincts kicked in and we started craving the foods that would nourish us and replenish the stores, but often this just doesn't happen. The less we eat the less we feel like eating – and this is particularly common in people who don't have appetising food available to them. Out of sight, out of mind, is a real problem for people who live on their own or are the ones who have traditionally been the cooks. Having to cook for someone else can help, as it stops us slumping into the 'I won't bother putting anything together' phase. So often if you can just get past the first mouthful, your appetite will kick in and you may find you actually enjoy eating.

It helps to stick to three meals a day with a couple of snacks in between, as one of the mistakes that some people with depression make is just snacking on biscuits and other easy-to-grab foods, which takes away the appetite for a proper meal. If you just feel like eating bowls of pasta and mashed potatoes, or having slice after slice of toast, this is fine in the short term – a few days of eating like this isn't going to harm you, and indeed it's much better to be eating something rather than nothing. But in the medium to long term, your body and your brain in particular won't benefit as much. So if you can, try to find something you feel like eating, even if it's putting tomatoes and cucumber into a sandwich or throwing tinned sweetcorn and frozen spinach into an omelette – this way you'll start to build up the spectrum of nutrients we know help your body to perform at its best.

As to how you manage the practical aspects of shopping and cooking, it will depend largely on what works. Sometimes it can help to try the main weekly shop option, so that you stock up on foods and can then simply throw something easy together with little effort. This can work especially well if you're more of a planner – writing

Read more on:
◆ *Pages 252–253*
▲ *Pages 21–25*

out a week's meal plan can help some people shop well and persuade them into eating food they perhaps wouldn't have thought about on the shopping day.

On the other hand, buying food on an almost daily basis can help to cut down on food wastage and, depending on the shops you choose, be just what you need to get your appetite going; for example, seeing the food – a fresh pasta sauce in a deli, for instance – or asking the advice of a passionate procurer or food shop owner, can give you an idea of what's good and how you could cook it. I'd try both ways of organising your shopping and eating, and perhaps also look online for a few inspiring small suppliers who could send you something delicious ◆.

Sometimes it helps to invite a close friend to eat with you, as the added dimension of having to put something together for them can make you feel more inclined to be creative and eat something better than a slice of toast. You could also ask or take up the offer of a friend who's a good cook to bring something round or to stock up your freezer with a few nourishing dishes. It doesn't have to be anything complicated – a few batches of bolognese sauce or ratatouille can be great for times when you just can't muster the enthusiasm to make anything for yourself. Don't forget that many people love being asked to do something practical, and can feel chuffed that you like their cooking enough to ask them – so often those around us feel useless when someone they care about is suffering from depression, and if you can give them the task of cooking something nutritious then this is a win-win situation. If you have the inclination to cook yourself, make more than you can eat in one meal and put some in the freezer or fridge ▲.

If you find your weight spiralling out of control

The first thing to do is to check with your doctor to see if weight gain is a side-effect of any medication you're taking. If it's impossible to change drugs, the likelihood is that the physiological, metabolic changes that have led to your weight gain will have a ceiling in their effect – it's often only at the beginning of taking a new drug. Of course there are instances when you may have been through a particularly anxious or severe depressive spell and you've been eating well but have still lost weight. If the drug you're taking or the therapy that you're receiving enables you to feel happier and less anxious the simple fact that you're feeling better means your body won't be continually burning up food and will start to feel that it can relax. So if you continue to eat the same amount of food your weight will slowly start to creep back on.

I wouldn't recommend for anyone, but particularly when you're suffering from depression, the idea of trying to eat what's commonly referred to in the media as a cleanse or detox or a very low-calorie diet, as your body needs good nourishment when you're depressed, and depriving yourself can leave you feeling depleted in every sense. It can also change the way your body metabolises medication, which could unsettle your regime. This is not to say that things like cutting out the very sweet and fatty stuff and, say, drinking more water and fewer artificial drinks shouldn't be attempted, as I've often seen that patients who take control of what they eat and have a nourishing, healthy diet can get themselves out of a depressive dip. Of course taking charge of your eating also gives you a practical strategy, something you can build into your day-to-day plan, which can be a really positive way to help get you through depression.

It can help to keep a food diary ◆ for a few weeks, to monitor simple things like ensuring that you're eating regularly and drinking enough water as these can be things we lose track of. Alcohol is a depressant as well as an appetite stimulant (and can also be contraindicated with some anti-depressant medication), so see if you can cut down on the amount you drink. Alcohol can also exacerbate many of the symptoms of depression and can cause you to feel out of control if eating disorders or bingeing are a current issue or if you've struggled with them in the past – it can play havoc with your perception of what you have or haven't eaten, and staying away from it can be one big thing that could help ▲.

I hate it when doctors pooh-pooh the notion that changing eating habits is a useless thing to try for people suffering with depression, as my experience shows quite the opposite. In an illness where so much structure can be lost, and the depression can take such an overwhelming hold on day-to-day life, it's helpful to be able to focus on something which is not only practical for the individual but, as I mentioned before, for those around them to be able to feel they're doing something useful. If you can provide the body with good, nourishing meals all sorts of depression-related symptoms can disappear or at least lessen in their severity. In my opinion it's incredibly important for anyone who's suffering from any level of depression to be given the right nutritional support – if you look at the cost of so many aspects of managing depression and other types of mental illness, the costs of eating the right food pale into insignificance, and let's not forget that so much can be communicated and gained on an emotional level from eating delicious nourishing foods. As John Gunther said, 'All happiness depends on a leisurely breakfast', which is reiterated in the Jewish proverb that states, 'Worries go down better with soup.'

Read more on:
◆ Page 11
▲ Pages 42–43

Chicken with winter vegetables, page 222

Nurturing a
New Life

Making the decision to have a child is a momentous one for many women. As Elizabeth Stone once said, 'It is to decide forever to have your heart go walking around outside your body.' Becoming pregnant or deciding to be a mum to a child is an enormous and gorgeous, if overwhelming, concept. It's a time when our body changes, along with our moods, our relationships and how we see the world.

The changes to our body in pregnancy, and the responsibility we have for providing the right nourishment for a new life, can be somewhat daunting. We can begin to feel the need to start looking at food under a microscope, and see meal planning as a military exercise. This is a shame, as other than the foods we need to avoid (because they carry a high risk of food-poisoning bacteria, which in the case of listeria and salmonella can cause untold damage to an unborn child), we simply need to eat nutritious food with just a few tweaks to meet the additional demands of a growing baby. So the aim of this chapter is to take you through what is best to eat to keep you both as strong and healthy as possible, to support a plentiful nourishing supply of breast milk and to get your body back in to shape.

Trying to get pregnant

Getting pregnant can be the easiest thing in the world for some couples while for others it seems an impossibly difficult and upsetting hurdle to overcome. While fertility treatments such as IVF are miracle-makers when all other efforts have failed, there are many cases where looking at lifestyle can be the first stop to help a couple with conception. The strong relationship that exists between exercise, drinking, eating, and how you cope with stress and juggle the demands of everyday life is so powerful that more often than not fertility specialists will recommend that you look into them before you head down the route of assisted fertility treatment. Even if you are already receiving an additional drug or procedure, you should pay attention to how you live, as all the areas covered in this chapter have a role to play. And of course the guidelines apply to every couple trying for a family, whether with treatment or without.

There are definite relationships between conceiving a healthy baby and parents who have enough of the specific nutrients that I discuss throughout this chapter. It's important, however, to keep the role that food plays in perspective as there are many different aspects involved in conceiving a child. If you get all het up and start treating your eating and drinking habits as a military operation, it is only going to make you both pretty miserable, which is hardly conducive to getting pregnant. It's a fine and often difficult line to tread between eating and living well to maximise your chances of conceiving, and allowing yourself a relaxed and fun Friday night.

Read more on:
◆ Page 11

When you're planning and trying to conceive, a good starting point is to look at the real way you eat and drink, not just what you think you do, as there can be a big difference between the two – we all fool ourselves at times! Keep a food diary for a couple of weeks ◆. I know it's cumbersome, but I guess you've probably started thinking about your life in weeks if not days: is it a good day to have sex or not? So a food diary in which you record not just what you eat but also how much shouldn't be too arduous a task. Then you can see what you're doing and work through a few points where you can improve the chances of getting pregnant. And looking at your diet isn't just worth doing if you're a woman – men need to take note, as eating well can improve the quality and quantity of sperm produced, as well as food and drink having an impact on libido for you both. I see many couples in my practice who are desperate to conceive and want to explore how nutritional supplements can improve their chances, but studies show time and time again that your body is best nourished from eating a well-balanced diet.

Non-food changes that increase the chances of conceiving

- **Stop smoking:** Smoking has been linked to both infertility and early menopause in women and to sperm problems in men. It also reduces the success of fertility treatments.

- **Be active:** Keeping active, with at least 30 minutes of cardiovascular moderate-intensity exercise a day (working out at the gym, swimming, cycling, or brisk walking), helps you stay fit and produces endorphins that boost mood. Many patients of mine also find that when they start exercising on a regular basis they feel more positive about their bodies, so that libido increases – there's nothing like feeling more toned and less wobbly for getting you in the mood! Weight is far easier to keep under control with some calorie expenditure. Watch, though, that the exercise doesn't become too intensive and obsessive, as too much can exhaust a pressurised and stressed body and low body fat levels can upset the reproductive hormone cycles ◆.

- **Keep cool:** For men it's particularly important to keep cool – for optimum sperm production the testicles need to be a couple of degrees cooler than the rest of the body. So it's best to avoid tight underwear and jeans, saunas and steaming hot baths.

- **Relax:** Try to reduce stress levels as much as possible. Although stress doesn't cause infertility, being overly worried and stressed can adversely affect menstrual cycles and also lower libido. So try to build in some 'you' time that's relaxed – try not to get overly anxious and controlling over eating and living the right lifestyle, as this is counterproductive.

- **Avoid drugs:** Recreational drugs such as marijuana and cocaine affect sperm counts, as do some prescription drugs – both men and women can have their chances of conception reduced by certain drugs, so discuss this with your doctor if you're taking regular medication. Being exposed to certain paints or pesticides within an industrial workplace may also affect sperm quality.

Body weight and fertility

Read more on:
◆ Page 122

Broad bean &
pistachio hummus,
page 231

The consensus of opinion is that being over or underweight can disrupt your periods and hinder conception, which is why we encourage anyone trying to get pregnant to have a body mass index (BMI) of between 20 and 25 ◆. However, it's more subtle than just what women weigh, as fertility can also be affected by the amount of fat that's carried (as in percentage). This means that even if you're of ideal weight it can be worth looking at your diet and the way you exercise to see if you can reduce your body fat content to within the range of 20–25 (the average body fat content of women is about 28 per cent). You may be surprised when you step on either a scale, which is able to measure the percentage body fat, or get the trainer in your local gym to do some simple measurements to give you an indication of whether they think your body fat level is too high. The likelihood is that if you have a BMI within the ideal range your fat percentage won't be far out, but it's worth looking to see if you can change the way the fat is distributed by exercising well.

But at the other end of the weight and body fat spectrum, being underweight has a profound effect on fertility – your body is at its most fertile when it has a body fat content of around 22 per cent, as the fat is needed to support the manufacture of the necessary hormones to enable you to ovulate and menstruate. If you have a BMI of less than 19, it's worth checking your body fat percentage to see whether you need to increase the amount and variety of the foods you eat. Your body fat percentage isn't usually lower than this unless you're either on the very skinny side, or are suffering from a condition, an eating disorder like anorexia, or a phobia of eating well. But it's also possible to have too low a level of body fat if you're a sports fanatic, and although you have a normal BMI the fact is that you're made up of too much muscle and not enough fat.

Mother nature needs you to have enough fat prior to conception to be able to support a healthy pregnancy, and afterwards – if you decide – to enable you to breastfeed since the milk is largely produced from your fat stores. The desire to be a mum can sometimes be just what you need to get you out of the routine of not eating enough or over-exercising. If you're underweight prior to or while you're pregnant you also have a higher chance of giving birth to a baby with too low a body weight and all the health problems this can bring into play, such as higher rates of heart disease and type 2 diabetes in later life. I don't mean to scare you by this, just give you some extra encouragement should you need it: if you can get your body weight and body fat levels up to a good level to support you both during pregnancy, not only are you going to be giving your baby the best possible start in life but you will also be strong enough once you've given birth to enjoy being a mum.

A word of reassurance, too, that while there are some women who blame being overweight on having children, which can scare the living daylights out of anyone who thinks that being an overweight mum is the last thing you want be, be comforted by the fact that there is no reason why you can't return to having a great body after giving birth if you eat and exercise well. It's the change in eating habits and motivational issues that influence how successful a woman is at getting her body back into shape; the only physiological issue that has any impact great enough to be important is breastfeeding – you can generally lose weight more successfully. So if you're worried that getting pregnant means you will turn into a hippopotamus and not be able to get your body back, this isn't going to happen unless you eat too much during pregnancy and don't do any exercise.

The dad-to-be's diet

Read more on:
◆ *Pages 18–21*

My mum's chicken pie,
page 219

Generally, the dad-to-be's diet should be every bit as balanced, varied and nutritious as that of the mum-to-be. As a future dad it helps to ensure your diet includes zinc, folates and other foods rich in antioxidants, such as vitamin C ◆. All of these help your body to make normal functioning sperm. Great sources of zinc include dark chicken meat and lean red meat, shellfish, milk and dairy foods, bread, baked beans and good cereal products – so if you need an excuse to enjoy a good-quality lean steak this is it! It's tempting to think that supplements could further increase your zinc intake and therefore your chances of conceiving, but studies don't show this – however, if you're not much of a meat lover you could take a supplement containing 15mg of zinc each day.

Vitamin C is best gleaned from a diet rich in fresh fruit and vegetables. Not only does your body absorb vitamin C from fruits and vegetables (frozen vegetables and fruits can be a very practical and rich source of vitamin C too), but the nutrient package within these foods provides other useful fertility-associated nutrients such as folate. People are often astounded by how little vitamin C we actually need in our diet to meet our body's requirement – it's only 60mg a day, which you can easily hit by eating an orange or a small (125ml) glass of orange juice. So as you can see, if you're managing to eat the recommended five portions of fruit and veg in a day – say having a bowl of fresh fruit in the morning and then salads and vegetables as a significant part of your two other meals – it's easy to meet your body's vitamin requirements without a pill in sight. Smoking reduces your body's ability to absorb vitamin C, so try to knock it on the head.

Fertility treatment

Infertility is thought to affect about one in seven couples – most of the women will eventually become pregnant naturally, but waiting can be frustrating and upsetting, while a significant minority will not be successful after years of trying. Often the treatment of infertility involves taking drugs, which can have side effects in varying degrees depending on the treatment you receive and your body's ability to cope – some women find them more upsetting than others and it's impossible to tell how your body will react. The most common reported side-effects for taking drugs orally include abdominal bloating, nausea, breast tenderness, hot flushes and mood changes. At a time when you could really do with feeling at your best, since IVF and other fertility treatments are invasive and stressful enough, the drugs themselves can play havoc with your body. However, these effects can often be improved and managed by looking at the way you eat and drink.

I'm not going to say that food can be a miracle cure, but many women I've treated do seem to find that tweaking the way they eat can take the sting out of the treatment and help them to feel more 'normal' and like the person they want to be. For instance, if you're feeling bloated, it could just be that something as simple as cutting down on the amount of wheat-based foods you eat and including more rice, beans and lentils could help. After all, a large tummy is the last thing you want if there are people around you who know you're trying to get pregnant before you've been successful.

If you're feeling sick a lot, watch that you don't fall into the trap of not eating much. Eat small nourishing meals, maybe juggling the time of day when you have your main meal – often it can suit you better to have this at lunchtime instead of in the evening. If you find that breakfast is a no-no, as you're just feeling too sick to eat anything, don't stress about it. You can make up for it during the rest of the day – maybe have a brunch which is more substantial. Some women also feel that for their body to change and make them feel lousy is unfair, especially when many of the drug side-effects are similar to actually being pregnant. Even if you're trying to relax and not think about getting pregnant every minute of every day, your body may be continually reminding you that you're not. It's a lot to deal with, so if making changes to what and how you eat makes you feel better, it can be a positive and empowering thing to take control of. If you find yourself craving sweet food, try to restrict the high-GI ◆ options as they seldom make you feel great bar the initial buzz – it's much better to choose something nourishingly sweet. Some women find that sniffing a vanilla pod can take away their sweet cravings – strange but it can work!

Read more on:
◆ *Pages 154–155*

Pearled spelt with broad beans, asparagus & dill, page 216

Inspiring vegetables

- Samphire can be bought from fish stalls in markets or from good online grocers. Simply steam it and then marinate in a herby dressing. It's delicious with fish and roasted meats, or a few slices of charcuterie and warm bread.

- Golden and yellow beetroot are wonderful in salads, especially when roasted. Mashed beetroot on toast is delicious too, topped with sliced tomatoes and a dollop of hummus.

- When you're making a salad dressing mix the ingredients over a gentle heat and pour over the salad leaves while still warm. You can either eat it straight away, in which case you will benefit from the aromas of the warmed oil, or alternatively if it's a salad made from vegetables such as beans or roasted vegetables let the vegetables marinate in the dressing for a few hours and then eat them at room temperature. If you like a hint of sweetness in your salad dressing, try using maple syrup. It has a far more complex flavour than sugar, so the dressings have an interesting note.

- Experiment with tapenades and herb and spice blends such as harissa. You can use them to roast vegetables, in which case they can be rubbed in or stirred through like a marinade.

- If you're making a salad as a main meal and fancy a cheese hit but don't want to use much, finely crumble a cheese such as feta or a Wensleydale or Lancashire cheese into it. Alternatively, grate a good Pecorino or Parmesan cheese very finely.

- Be more courageous with chillies – there are so many different varieties with varying strengths of kick. Just a quarter of a teaspoon of freshly chopped chilli can impart a warming kick to a salad dressing, marinade or stir-fry. Using flavours such as chilli or freshly ground pink peppercorns instead of black means that you find yourself using less salt. The more complex flavours you use, the more your taste buds will be stimulated and the more satisfied you'll be after your meal.

- Traditionally, western cuisine has not been the most adventurous in using fresh herbs, and when we do use them we tend to use just one – mint with lamb, sage with pork, tarragon with chicken, etc. Try mixing a few together, as you can get some very good combinations. I particularly like mixing fresh basil, dill and parsley in a salad. Mint goes well with basil too – a tip here is to use a plastic knife or tear the leaves, as metal knives turn them black.

- Add fruit to salads, for example wafer-thin segments of very fresh orange, apple, pear, fig, peach, plum, or something more exotic such as pomegranate. Vegetables which are technically fruits, such as peppers, go well in salads, particularly if they're roasted.

Eating well in pregnancy

The old wives' tale of eating for two has long been discredited, as although our body needs some extra calories each day (and a few extra milligrams of some essential vitamins like folic acid, and minerals such as iron and calcium), there's only one place that eating enough for two will take us – being fed up and looking and feeling like a beached whale. The physiological reality is that, although we need extra calories as our pregnancy progresses, we will become less active as we can't dart around in the same way, so our body just doesn't burn up as many calories. However, it should also be said that many of my pregnant patients do confess to at long last being able to step out of the food jail they've been in – a place of always feeling they should be slim. Finally, they can eat and not feel guilty. And why not? As long as you don't overdo it, enjoy this time of your life.

Pregnancy can be the perfect time to instil some good, nutritious eating habits if you've previously relied on your body's good will to put up with fast living, too much drinking, and bad eating. You may need to wait until after the first trimester, if nausea ◆ is preventing you from being able to stomach anything more than white toast (which, by the way, can be a very nourishing food to eat, try not to worry too much that you're not managing to get through your five-a-day, etc., as the amazing thing about pregnancy is that your baby will take what it needs from your stores. Also, your pregnant body will soon cotton on to the fact that it needs to be extra efficient at absorbing the essential nutrients from smaller amounts of food. The one person who loses out if this continues is you, the mum, as it can leave you deficient in minerals such as iron. Iron deficiency anaemia ▲ is particularly risky during the last trimester of your pregnancy, when the baby draws on your iron stores to support its rapid growth spurts.

If you've not managed to eat well during pregnancy, you can end up feeling depleted after the birth when your body really needs to be feeling strong; be this to support breastfeeding (which we know to be the best possible start for your baby), or to keep up with the constant demands of being a new mum.

Essentially when you're pregnant you should try to eat in the same way as you would normally – a good balance and spectrum of all the foods featured in the eat well plate ●. The calories you require to support your baby's growth and development aren't the same throughout the whole of the pregnancy – most of the extra is needed during the second and third trimesters. Try to hold back and just eat as normal during the early months, and this will help stave off feeling too enormous later on.

Read more on:
◆ Pages 71–73
▲ Pages 70–71
● Page 14

Studies show you only need an extra 200kcals per day during the third trimester, and if you bear in mind that this more or less equates to a sandwich made from a couple of thin slices of wholemeal bread with something like lean ham inside, or a large banana and an apple, you'll see that it isn't very much. If you've been struggling with gaining enough weight, say if you're suffering with sickness, have always been on the light side or continue to lead a very active life, you may need slightly more than this. Really the best way to check whether you're eating the right amount is to keep an eye on your weight – a gain throughout the three trimesters of about 12kg is about right. Of course, there are lots of individual variations in weight gain and 12kg is an average. If you're heavier to start with you may gain less, whereas if your pre-pregnancy weight was on the low side, you may gain more. Some weeks your weight won't change much, but keep in touch with your obstetrician and health team so that they can help monitor your baby's growth and development and see how you're thriving too. If you find you are gaining more than is desirable, try to reduce the frequency of your snacks, take time to sit and savour your food, make sure you're not trying to quench thirst with food, keep a food diary ◆, try eating and exercising at different times and watch that you're not eating too many high-fat, high-sugar foods.

Read more on:
◆ *Page 11*

Beans with tomato, coriander & coconut milk, page 215

Safe eating in pregnancy

One of the most important things to watch out for when you're pregnant is that the foods you eat are safe for the two of you. This means looking at how you choose, prepare and cook produce in order to reduce the risk of exposing your unborn baby to both food-poisoning organisms (such as salmonella and listeria) and toxic food components. You also need to pay attention to the alcohol and caffeine you drink, and also at which nutritional supplements you take, as some just aren't suitable when you're expecting.

This can all sound alarming, but once you've read the fine print of the few things to avoid and how to reduce the risk it's pretty simple. It has astounded me over the years that some pregnant women who have fought tooth and nail to get pregnant ask me which foods to avoid only to then try to persuade me into saying it's okay for them to eat something they shouldn't. They just don't realise that during pregnancy, the bacterial infection that can arise from eating a food which contains listeria, for example, is extremely serious and life-threatening for the baby – it's not just a question of being off-colour for a couple of days. Yes, it's a shame not to have a soft-boiled egg and soldiers, but peace of mind is worth far more.

What a mum eats whilst pregnant (and breastfeeding) is also a factor in whether their child suffers from eczema. Although the studies show mixed results, there is some evidence to suggest that if you eat a diet rich in fruits and vegetables, especially those rich in beta carotene (the orange red and yellow fruits and vegetables) you are less likely to give birth to a child with eczema. Interestingly another recent study showed that if you have a diet rich in vitamin E such as olive oil and avocados ◆ your baby is less likely to suffer from an allergy-type wheeze. Rather than thinking you need to start measuring levels of these specific nutrients, I'd just treat research like this as encouragement to nourish your body as well as you can throughout pregnancy. If you have a particular worry over eczema (perhaps if you have a strong history of atopic eczema and allergies in your family), then it could be worth you taking an omega-3 supplement containing 2g combination of EPA and DHA, which has also been shown to be protective against developing eczema in the first year of life if taken whilst pregnant.

Read more on:
◆ Pages 18, 107 & 110

Listeria

Listeriosis can cause miscarriage, stillbirth, birth defects or severe illness once your baby is born. Foods to avoid are pâté, mould-ripened soft cheese, such as Brie and Camembert, blue-veined cheeses such as Stilton, unpasteurised milk and milk products. Hard cheeses such as Cheddar or other cheeses made from pasteurised milk, such as mozzarella, cottage cheese and processed cheese spreads, are all fine. Hard goat's cheeses are also fine to eat – it's the soft, chèvre-like ones you need to avoid. If you fancy your cheese soft, melt it on toast.

Listeria bacteria are destroyed by heat, and you should always, but particularly when you're pregnant, thoroughly heat food as per the instructions. Don't reheat ready-prepared meals, especially if they contain poultry. The real bane, I think, is having to avoid ready-prepared salads and cold dishes which you won't be reheating before you eat – quiches, flans and cold meat pies. If you buy salad leaves, wash them thoroughly in lots of running cold water and do the same with all fruits and vegetables in order to reduce the risk of contracting listeria.

Salmonella

Salmonella is the most common cause of food-poisoning and in severe cases can cause miscarriage or premature labour. Salmonella poisoning is most likely to come from raw eggs or uncooked poultry, so you need to stick to hard-boiled eggs avoiding raw or partially cooked eggs and all products containing them such as homemade mayonnaise, soufflés and custards. However, you can eat commercially produced mayo, as these almost always use pasteurised egg and don't contain any raw egg ingredients – but check the labels to make sure. It's possible to buy certain classifications of eggs from hens that have been vaccinated against salmonella, but this doesn't mean they are salmonella-free, so you still need to avoid eating them raw etc.

With poultry in particular you need to make sure that it's cooked all the way through – slicing through a chicken breast to check there are no cool spots. A chicken brick is one of the best ways to ensure that the chicken is well cooked but not dried out and rubbery. You need to watch how you handle raw poultry too – washing your hands thoroughly afterwards. And pay attention to how you store raw and cooked foods in your fridge, so that you don't get any cross-contamination from dripping raw chicken ◆.

Read more on:
◆ *Pages 21–23*

Toxoplasmosis

Toxoplasmosis is caused by the organism *Toxoplasma gondii*, which can be found in raw meat, unpasteurised milk and cat faeces. If you contract it when you're pregnant it can, in rare cases, infect your baby via the placenta and lead to severe abnormalities such as blindness and brain damage. To reduce the risk of contracting it you need to avoid eating all raw and undercooked meat – steaks should be well cooked all the way through. Cooking it should be fine, but you need to be extra vigilant in washing your hands and wiping down surfaces. You also need to steer clear of unpasteurised milk and milk products (this is particularly the case with goat's milk). Give the job of cleaning out the cat litter tray to someone else or wear gloves if you have to do it. The same applies if you're gardening – always cover your hands so that they're not coming into contact with the soil. Ideally (although this is often impractical) the cat should go elsewhere for the few months of your pregnancy or be kept out of the kitchen, as they can transmit bacteria just by walking on kitchen surfaces.

Campylobacter

Campylobacter is one of the most common forms of food-poisoning, but if you contract it while pregnant it can cause miscarriage, stillbirth and induce premature labour. The most common sources of infection are poultry, unpasteurised milk and milk products, domestic pets and soil, so if you take the precautions listed above, you will reduce your risk. But you should also be careful with untreated water – both drinking it and coming into direct contact with it – and soil. Gardening gloves need to be on the shopping list from day one.

Peanuts

Twenty years ago peanuts weren't an issue, but it appears that peanut allergy is increasing in both adults and children. An allergic reaction can cause anaphylaxis, which is extremely serious and requires emergency treatment because the symptoms of respiratory obstruction and shock develop so quickly. We don't really know why this happens: some say we're bringing up our children in too clean and sterile an environment, which means that their immune systems don't develop the right level of response; others blame the use of more and more peanuts and peanut oil in our diet – Asian cuisine, which uses peanuts in many of its dishes, is playing a more prominent place in our eclectic tastes for food. Peanut oil is also being used in food and skin preparations, all of which concerns some immunologists enough to wonder if this is to blame.

It can all seem confusing, and we don't have the answers yet, but what we do know is that unless you have a strong history of allergies, such as asthma or eczema, in either of the parents' families, you should continue to eat peanuts while pregnant and breastfeeding as there is no evidence that this will cause your child to develop a peanut allergy. Even if you do have a family history of peanut allergy, there is no clear evidence to say if eating or not eating peanuts during pregnancy will affect the chance of your baby developing a peanut allergy. And in fact there is some evidence to suggest that by not including small amounts of peanuts in your diet, your unborn baby is unable to develop a tolerance to nut proteins, and you could be increasing the risk of the allergy developing. If you look at cultures where nuts are endemic within their cuisine from an early age, you seldom find peanut allergies.

Vitamin A

Although vitamins are vital for our overall health when it comes to being pregnant, you need to watch the amount of vitamin A you consume as high levels can be toxic and cause problems for your baby's growth and development. You not only need to steer well clear of any nutritional supplements containing vitamin A (such as cod liver oil), unless specifically prescribed by your doctor, but you also need to avoid foods that are naturally rich in this vitamin, namely liver and liver products such as pâté and liver sausage. Normal sausages are fine, as they're not full of liver – the liver is where the vitamin A is stored in animals and is therefore potentially toxic to unborn babies.

Drinking the right fluids

Read more on:
◆ Page 72

As well as watching your alcohol intake ◆, it's wise to check that you're not drinking too much tea, coffee and other drinks such as cola, as all of these hit high on the caffeine stakes. Although the evidence isn't conclusive, too much caffeine for women may well lower the chance of conceiving. Caffeine intake during pregnancy should be limited to 200mg a day, which works out roughly (although amounts vary between types of coffee, etc.) at three mugs of instant coffee, six cups of tea or eight cans of cola a day. I know it sounds a lot, but if you had a couple of mugs of coffee, a can of coke and a chocolate bar in one day you'd already be almost up to the limit.

One theory suggests that stimulants affect ovulation by causing changes in hormone levels, which in turn hampers conception. In contrast, caffeine may actually help men's fertility by stimulating sperm motility; although the evidence again isn't conclusive, so I would suggest that you both stick to the rough guide of 200mg a day as a good all-round target. For women it makes particularly good sense, I think, to get into a good caffeine habit while you're trying to conceive, as current recommendations are to keep your intake low once you become pregnant.

Essential fatty acids

As previously mentioned, oily fish are incredibly rich in one of the most beneficial types of fat: omega-3 fatty acid ◆. Although some studies widely reported in the press have suggested that taking an omega oil supplement during pregnancy may offer certain benefits, such as helping to ensure the baby develops a healthy brain and nervous system, some studies suggest that taking a supplement could even improve your baby's intelligence. At the moment the evidence is not conclusive enough to make us think that we need anything more than a couple of 140g portions of an oily fish such as salmon, trout, mackerel, herring, sardines, pilchards, kippers or fresh tuna each week. We can glean all the omega oils we need by eating this way – don't go over the two portions a week, as oily fish tends to store pollutant residues in their flesh, which we don't want to expose any unborn child to. If you've been taking supplements, it's best to stop as the Department of Health advises that pregnant women should avoid fish oil supplements during pregnancy because of their potentially high vitamin A content ▲.

If you're trying to get pregnant you should avoid eating shark, swordfish and marlin, and not eat too much tuna – no more than four medium cans or two fresh tuna steaks a week. This is because the mercury in these fish can potentially harm your unborn child's nervous system. All other fish are great for you, although as with the other oily fish, a couple of 140g portions a week is the desired amount.

Read more on:
◆ *Pages 17–18 & 101*
▲ *Page 64*

Smoked mackerel pâté, page 224

Folates and folic acid

It is now well recognised that folic acid ◆ also known as vitamin B9, is of critical importance both before and after conception in protecting your baby against neural tube defects. This is why we recommend that all women trying to get pregnant take 400mcg of folic acid each day, and continue right up until the end of the first trimester. Even if you fall pregnant unexpectedly, you should start taking the supplement straight away and continue to take it up until the end of the twelfth week. Our body doesn't absorb folic acid as well when it's in its natural folate form as it does when it's synthetic folic acid (this is one of those rarer occasions when the synthetic form outdoes the natural form), but it's good to eat foods rich in folate too as they are generally nourishing foods to include within the scheme of your diet. If you have a family history of neural tube defects you should discuss it with your doctor, who may recommend you take larger doses of folic acid.

Your pregnant body's needs

For some women, eating well while they're pregnant can be the easiest thing while others find foods they previously loved unpalatable and just crave starchy foods. They can therefore get into a bit of a muddle over how to balance what they know they should be eating with what will actually stay down and feel okay. Alternatively some women feel worried that their weight will spiral out of control so much that they'll end up feeling huge and not the person they want to be once they've given birth. Dieting while pregnant is not a good idea because it can compromise your baby's growth and development and also leave you feeling exhausted and depleted.

In this part of the book I want to take you through the key points of how best to balance your nutritional needs with those of your baby – which foods are best to focus on and which ones not to over-indulge in. Bear in mind that when you're pregnant you always need to have 'Is this safe for us to eat?' in the front of your mind ▲.

Read more on:
◆ *Page 19*
▲ *Pages 61–65*

Nutritional supplements

You should avoid nutritional supplements other than folic acid unless an accredited clinical dietician has specifically prescribed them for you. This includes herbal remedies and some essential oils, as their stimulating effects on the body can be strong enough to cause problems – don't fall into the trap of thinking everything labelled natural and herbal is safe to take. Remember that opium, heroin and morphine can all be traced back to the poppy plant; and few would call these natural or safe!

Vitamin D

We've become more aware not only of how important vitamin D is for general health and bone strength ◆ but also of the significant problem in the northern hemisphere with women just not getting enough exposure to the sun's rays to manufacture vitamin D. Asian and Afro-Caribbean women living in cold climates are particularly at risk of having poor levels vitamin D, as dark skin is less efficient at manufacturing vitamin D from the sunlight. If you prevent your skin from being exposed to sunlight by covering up for religious or cultural reasons, your vitamin D levels can also be compromised. Low levels during pregnancy affect the growth and development of your baby, but you can ensure you both get enough vitamin D by taking a 10mcg supplement each day. You may also want to take a supplement while breastfeeding as we don't glean enough vitamin D from our diet to match our increased requirement whilst we're producing large volumes of milk.

Calcium

Although demands for calcium ▲ on the mother are high, during the latter stages of pregnancy your body will adapt through hormonal changes. You absorb more nutrients from your gut as a result of hormones such as oestrogen, lactogen and prolactin being present in your pregnant body, your body retains more of the calcium you absorb too – all this means that you don't need to take in more than the 700mg recommended for all women.

A well-balanced diet will give you all the calcium you need, however, you do need to pay particular attention to how much calcium you're including within your diet if you consume few or no dairy products, are vegan or have a poor vitamin D status (see above). Women who have a diet that is largely vegetarian and packed full of high-fibre foods, such as wholegrain, fruits and vegetables, can also hinder the absorption of calcium (despite the fact that these food are generally considered healthy). So it's this combination of factors which will require you to see whether you need to start including more non-dairy sources of calcium in your diet, the best ones being nuts, fortified soya milk and other soya products such as tofu (in moderation), dark green leafy vegetables and dried fruits. You may also benefit from taking a calcium supplement, although they are not usually very well absorbed.

Read more on:
◆ *Page 18*
▲ *Page 20*

A note about soya

There have been some concerns over the potential hormonal effects of eating a soya-rich diet when pregnant and whether or not it's a good idea to give a soya-based formula milk to a baby. The main concern seems to focus around the compounds known as phytoestrogens in soya and their effect on the development of the testicles. Animal studies have suggested that by mimicking oestrogen, these compounds could prevent the proper development of the reproductive system, causing a variety of problems later in life. But as these studies are based on rats and mice, it's difficult to assess what the result means for humans. Lots of mays and coulds, but I would suggest that if you're pregnant, avoid an overly soya-based diet. And when it comes to soya infant formula, you should only use it under the guidance of your doctor if your little one isn't able to tolerate any other infant formula.

If you're a young mum in your teens, since you're still growing and therefore have an increased need for calcium yourself, you may need to up your consumption of calcium-rich foods to cover what you both need – bear in mind that your baby will take from your calcium supplies first, and if you're not eating enough to meet what they need, as well as to ensure you're holding on to enough for yourself, you could end up with weak bones later in life. Dairy products are some of the best foods to include in your pregnancy diet, as not only do they contain the highest amounts of calcium but our bodies are able to absorb and use the calcium from these foods more easily than from non-dairy sources. If you can't take in dairy, for whatever reason, check out the alternative calcium-rich options mentioned above.

Iron deficiency

Iron is one of the most essential nutrients for the growth and development of your baby and for enabling you to manufacture more red blood cells to support the pregnancy. We stop having periods and therefore don't lose any iron through menstruation, and get better at absorbing and mobilising our iron stores during pregnancy. Therefore it should be possible if you're eating an iron-rich diet when you're pregnant to meet the extra demand your pregnancy places on you. More and more women have low iron stores without knowing it. If you don't like eating much meat, whether you need to take an iron supplement will largely depend on your pre-pregnancy iron stores

Bolognese sauce, page 218

and how iron-rich your diet is throughout the pregnancy. The best way to check this is to keep in touch with your doctor so that they can run regular blood tests. If you find yourself suffering from any of the symptoms of iron deficiency anaemia, such as feeling depressed, overly tired, pale, breathless or losing your hair, your doctor may encourage you to start increasing the iron content of your diet or recommend a supplement. Iron deficiency anaemia can also make you more prone to infections and increase the risk of haemorrhage before or after the birth – when anaemia is severe it can hinder the development and growth of your baby. This shouldn't happen if you're in regular contact with your health team, are eating well and don't have any other underlying health problems that hinder iron absorption, such as coeliac or Crohn's disease. Occasionally in very severe cases you may need iron injections.

Feeling sick

This used to be referred to as morning sickness, which for many women is the time of day when it's at its worst. Some other women find themselves feeling continuously nauseous and off eating, which is a lot harder to manage. You've probably heard, and it's right in some cases, that the nausea is usually at its worst in the first trimester and for women who have undergone fertility treatments. Often you get changes in your senses too, which can put you off eating as your sense of smell can be heightened. Perfumes, smoke and the smells of certain foods can turn your stomach, which can be most frustrating if you're trying to eat a nourishing diet.

When you're feeling sick, try to get someone else to do as much of the food preparation as possible as it's often the cooking of foods that can make you feel queasy before you've even eaten a mouthful. Be aware that you need to be extra careful when reheating foods to ensure that they're well cooked and are not going to pose any food poisoning risk to you ◆. It's a great idea to get a willing friend or relative to stock up your freezer with some meals for moments when you're feeling below par. Another solution is to cook more than enough for a meal when you're not feeling sick, and in this way get ahead, as it takes no more effort to make enough pasta sauce for four meals as it does for one.

There's really no rhyme nor reason to why morning sickness or indeed daily sickness makes you go off or crave certain foods, but one thing which does seem to help is to have a little something before you try to get moving in the morning such as plain biscuits or crackers. Sometimes a more savoury style crispbread can do the trick

Read more on:
◆ Pages 61–64

The line on alcohol

The Government advises that when trying to conceive, women should give up alcohol altogether, while men shouldn't drink more than three to four units a day and should avoid binge drinking to prevent damaging the sperm. Although this is the official line, I think it seems horribly one-sided – perhaps it can be good for you both to take some time off the alcohol or at least cut your intake down. Being teetotal may not be what every couple wants or needs, as there is often anxiety within your relationship when trying to get pregnant. For example, you're both so desperate to succeed that having sex is dominated by thermometers, dates, positions, etc. In this case, a glass or two can lift the mood and make sex far more enjoyable. Make sure you've got some food in your stomach, if you don't want to fall asleep or feel woozy and therefore not in the mood.

The advice over whether or not it's safe to drink any alcohol while pregnant is hugely controversial. No one seems to agree and there doesn't seem to be objective data to give us a real steering on this. Some advise total abstinence, but the consensus seems to be that one to two units a couple of times a week is about the right level – it's always best to check for the latest advice. Bear in mind, though, that while so often we see one glass of wine given as a unit on the alcoholic drinks tables, this refers to a pub measure (125ml) of wine, not the large glasses we tend to serve ourselves at home. One thing researchers do seem to agree on is that you can't store up your unused units and then have a whole bottle in an evening – binge drinking must be avoided at all costs.

Alcohol, like caffeine (and nicotine) passes from your blood into your breast milk. Whilst some research shows that alcohol can disrupt the release of two key hormones – oxytocin and prolactin – responsible for milk production, the odd glass of wine, beer or any alcohol is completely fine for you to drink, whilst breastfeeding. The old wives' tale of alcohol being good for milk production is nonsense. I find that the best way to enjoy alcohol is to feed your little one first, but at times, the odd glass can provide a much-needed respite before you start feeding.

– nibble a couple before you get out of bed. Ginger is also especially good at relieving nausea.

Not eating for a while can bring on nausea waves, so try eating little and often rather than going for just three main meals a day. This said, you need to watch that you don't just become a grazer and make sure you sit down to eat nourishing, well-balanced meals. Starchy foods seem to help stave off nausea more than protein-rich foods, so if you're having, say, a salad with chicken at lunchtime, put some crackers, bread or a small bowl of steamed rice with it and this could well settle your stomach. Many cultures consider rice to be one of the most settling of foods to eat when you're feeling sick. Try some cardamom-infused rice, which is not only delicious, but the slightly perfumed taste can help to settle your gut. Uncooked foods also seem to sit more comfortably and require less effort, but do make sure that you wash fresh fruit and vegetables well.

You may find that your whole body and eating clock goes through some weeks of turmoil. Play around with mealtimes and what you have in each meal too – eating a main meal at lunchtime may suit you better than in the evening. If you have a few days when you just can't stomach much, don't panic. The likelihood is that on other days, even if it's later on in the pregnancy, you will feel like eating something completely different. Remember that your baby will take exactly what they need from you, whether this is from what you've been eating that day or from your stores. A healthy diet will replenish your reserves and keep you in a good shape, so that when you've given birth you're not on your knees having been drained of all goodness.

Food cravings

Some women get the wildest of food cravings, which they feel they have to give in to – I don't have a problem with that as long as you try to build them into a structured and balanced diet. Enjoy the cravings, but don't mistake it for your body trying to tell you that you need more of something – there isn't any scientific proof that this is the case.

If you're craving very sweet, high-GI foods, watch their effect on your weight, as although there isn't any link between eating too much sugar and developing gestational diabetes (see below), it can be that you're gaining weight at a rate at which your body can't cope, specifically your pancreas. Very sweet foods, as is the case with high-fat foods, tend to be instantly gratifying but can leave you feeling pretty empty soon after. Try to incorporate cravings and preferences for specific foods into a well-structured plan rather than hoovering up an enormous tub of ice cream when watching TV, as delicious as it is!

Sometimes it's a craving for salt that hits the spot, in which case make sure that this isn't aggravating your blood pressure. Beware that salty foods can make you feel puffed up, making swollen ankles ten times worse.

Gestational diabetes

Gestational diabetes (GD) occurs in around 2 per cent of pregnancies and it usually crops up in the latter stages (most commonly in the third trimester). Your pancreas starts to struggle with the extra demands of a little person inside you so much so that it just can't maintain your blood sugar levels within the acceptable limits. Most women don't know they have it, as the symptoms of feeling more tired, etc. can be put down to being heavily pregnant, and it's usually not spotted until you have a urine or blood test. Gestational diabetes can usually be easily controlled by watching what, how much and when you eat. Occasionally insulin is needed, which requires a little more fine tuning (in which case you will also be referred to a dietician for specific help). More often than not, by watching that your diet is well-balanced, doesn't contain too many sweet foods like biscuits, cakes, sweet drinks, etc., and not too high in calories, you can keep blood sugar levels in check. Moderate exercise will help to maintain blood sugar levels too.

Constipation

Constipation is common in the latter stages of pregnancy when the baby presses on your internal organs and hormones slow down your bowel's ability to push food through. It can usually be relieved by upping your water intake and eating not only more of the higher-fibre foods such as wholegrain breads, cereals, pulses, nuts, fruits and vegetables ◆, but also specific fruits and juices such as prunes, figs and rhubarb. These can either be soaked, stewed or made into compôtes and will make a delicious start to your day, providing some much needed bowel-moving fibre, especially if served with Greek-style yoghurt and toasted nuts – scrumptious!

Although it's not recommended to drink too much caffeine during pregnancy ▲, a hot cup of coffee or tea can act as a bowel

Read more on:
◆ Pages 30–32
▲ Pages 64–65

Raspberry baskets, page 245

stimulant, which could be just what you need to get things moving again. An alternative is to try hot water and fresh lemon, as there seems to be something about the warmth of the water that can get the body working.

Feeling uptight, stressed and exhausted can make constipation worse, and although it's far easier to write this than to put into practice, try to take your time in the bathroom – maybe have a warm bath, which will help to relax you before you try to go to the toilet. It's so often when you're rushing that constipation arises. Setting the alarm clock half an hour earlier in the morning is one idea, if this gives you time to be alone and peaceful in the bathroom before the madness of the day kicks in. Occasionally severe constipation can cause you to develop piles. If this becomes a real problem and monitoring your eating, drinking and relaxing doesn't seem to help, exercise can often make things easier. Exercise produces hormones that encourage the bowel to get moving as well as being a good stress reliever. It may work better if your hectic routine doesn't lend itself to yoga or relaxation – doing something you enjoy such as swimming could be just the constipation tonic you need. Some mums-to-be find that gentle massage and reflexology helps too.

Iron supplements can sometimes cause constipation, so talk to your doctor about changing to a different one, such as a herbal supplement if you suspect this. Don't take over-the-counter laxatives without consulting the doctor, as you need to ensure the remedy is safe for your baby.

Breastfeeding

There are countless nutritional reasons why breast is best, whether this is for just a few days or until your baby is ready to be weaned. These include: providing everything your baby needs to develop and thrive for the first six months, in the right amounts, at the right temperature and fresh; boosting your baby's immune system while their own is still developing – making them less likely to suffer from illnesses, such as diarrhoea, and vomiting, respiratory, ear and urinary tract infections, allergies, insulin-dependent diabetes, obesity and high blood pressure; it is also much cheaper than bottle-feeding. It is also a great opportunity for you to connect and bond with your baby though skin-to-skin contact. Breastfeeding also helps your womb to contract back to its normal size, and since milk draws on the fat stores laid down during pregnancy, it can help you lose your pregnancy weight. There are other advantages that will benefit your baby in the longer term – research has shown that breastfed babies are able to cope with stress later in life and interestingly, that they are more emotionally resilient if their parents divorce or separate.

However, as with all areas of parenting, you can only try your best, and if breastfeeding isn't possible or for you then this shouldn't mean disaster – there are perfectly good alternatives.

What should I be eating?

It may sound predictable, but a breastfeeding mother should eat a balanced diet with just a couple of tweaks. If you can eat well not only will you produce milk that's nourishing for your baby, but you will be far more likely to feel healthy yourself. Don't forget that your baby takes nutrients from you such as vitamins, minerals, fat, protein and carbohydrate.

Mums can find that they need to eat little and often or can feel ravenously hungry. So you may want to juggle your eating pattern to fit around these changes, such as having a larger breakfast or eating a cooked meal rather than a sandwich in the middle of the day. You need to make sure you eat a balance of things to produce good milk and leave enough nutrients for yourself. I would recommend that you eat an extra 300–400 calories per day for the first three months of breastfeeding and then an extra 400 calories a day, which equates to an extra good small meal, such as a cheese sandwich or a large banana and a couple of shortbread biscuits. Any more than that and you will find that your body holds onto the extra fat that was laid down during pregnancy and you won't be able to shift the weight.

Read more on:
◆ *Page 65*

Damson, pear & walnut muffins, page 250

When it comes to avoiding foods, the good news is that you can now eat those pregnancy no-nos, such as blue cheese. You do need to watch that you stick to just a couple of portions of oily fish each week, as you did during pregnancy ◆. Apart from the fish issue, there really aren't any hard rules, as everyone is different, but sometimes you may notice that your little one reacts badly after you've eaten certain foods. If they have more severe reactions to your milk, such as developing a skin rash or hives, have difficulty breathing, wheezing or congestion, or their stools turn green or mucousy, seek medical help.

I think that breastfeeding mums should drink about two and a half to three litres of water a day. This might sound a huge amount, but if you bear in mind that non-breastfeeding women should drink two and a half litres a day, it's not a lot extra for milk production. Some women feel completely fine, not drinking this much, but I have to say that most end up feeling tired, ratty, headachy and constipated if they don't drink enough.

Feeling low

Being a new mum is exhausting and many women go through a period of 'baby blues' in the first few days after giving birth. There are various physiological and hormonal reasons for feeling down, while others just find that being responsible for a new life is overwhelming. Sadly, the difficulties in the first few weeks and months can lead to depression. You don't need to feel alone in this — ten to 15 per cent of new mothers suffer from post-natal depression, with many more experiencing weeks or months of intermittent feelings of low mood. Some women can even experience depression before giving birth.

I'm by no means saying that eating and food can cure what can be a very distressing and difficult time in a woman's life, but it's my experience as a mum that the types of foods you put inside your body can have an influence on how you feel emotionally, just as much as physically. We arrived home in the depths of winter and when my own mum, who had come with us to India to collect Maya, walked out of the door to go home, I was alone with a tiny, fragile, poorly baby. She was 15 months old but weighed under 4kg and depended on me hugely to pull her through.

Read more on:
◆ *Pages 47–51*

Chicken soup,
page 233

One of the first signs of depression is under or overeating, but by making sure you eat properly and resting as much as you can, the symptoms can become bearable. Sometimes medication is needed to treat the depression ◆, and although it is possible to breastfeed while taking some anti-depressants, some trigger side-effects such as weight gain. Some people get withdrawal symptoms when they stop taking them, which can compound how lousy you feel. In conjunction with your doctor's advice, looking at the types of foods and the way you're eating can enable you to help yourself through this tough time. So if you're feeling low, whether this be for a few days or something deeper and longer-lasting (in which case do seek some professional support), have a look at what you're eating, as food can be a great healer too.

Caring For Children

Much has been written about the nutritional needs of babies and toddlers, but there is a lot of confusing dietary information and you can feel anxious as a parent of a growing child. Weaning and the 'terrible twos' can be problematic, but it's vital that you establish good eating habits early in your child's life. For many parents, the time when their child starts going to school presents practical challenges: mornings become more rushed; school meals may be far from ideal, seldom offering what you'd like your child to eat; packed lunches can be time consuming to make and often come back hardly touched. All these issues are exacerbated by the fact that your child is that bit older, making them more opinionated about what they want and don't want to eat. At this age they're likely to be influenced by what their friends are eating, and perhaps one of the trickiest areas to navigate is how to withstand the pester-power antics from food manufacturers' marketing schemes.

Fortunately, I have a child who loves and appreciates food, likes to take an interest in how food is grown, prepared and shopped for (well, not all the time!). It has been, and continues to be, a glorious stage of my relationship with my seven-year-old daughter, but also a crucial one as good eating habits and an interest in food are instilled at an early age. I've chosen a few particular areas for discussion where I hope I can give reassurance and practical advice on how to move forward into your child's school-age.

Good eating habits

There are times when children won't eat the food you put in front of them ◆, or you're pushed for time and have to grab something or cook something quickly that you know isn't ideal. But don't worry – children are much more resilient than we give them credit for, and ride the waves of coping with the odd not-great-eating day at times when you have to resort to this. Many children see fast and pre-packed food as a treat, so don't stress!

Three meals a day is the optimum eating routine, each containing something from every food group ▲. Even if your child isn't much of a breakfast eater, it's important that they eat something – they've had to tap into their nutrient reserves overnight, so their body needs a fresh supply of nourishment to get them through the morning. If they're off their main meals, don't sit there for hours waiting for them to give in (unless it's a trend) – give them a drink and something like a piece of toast and a banana to tide them over to the next meal.

It's not always easy, but the more you can eat together the better. Your children will see you eating similar foods and they love to copy and share. They will also see that the best way to eat is at a table concentrating on food and enjoying it – this is the perfect age to instil good habits.

Read more on:
◆ *Pages 104–105*
▲ *Page 14*
● *Pages 16–17*

Roasted cherry tomato, basil & mozzarella pizza, page 239

Variety measured in handfuls

Use as wide a variety of foods as possible, to keep children's tastes diverse and also because each food has something unique about it. If you can introduce strong and varied flavours from an early age, there's less chance that you'll have a fussy child later on. If food is too samey and bland they'll develop conservative tastes.

A way to ensure that all the basic nutrient requirements are covered is to try to get into the habit of trying a different type of protein ● with each meal and a couple of different vegetables. There isn't any recommended number of portions of fresh fruit and veg for children *per se*, but I go for five a day (portions are smaller, though), the same amount that adults should be having.

Although variety is good, don't get hung up on having something different at every mealtime. Children can go through phases, and sometimes they will be in a bad mood, so just go for an easy option to avoid tempers getting more frayed; they're not going to start suffering from scurvy or some other vitamin deficiency disease if they don't have any fresh veg for a day – just try to get back into the swing of healthy eating as soon as you can.

Make the most of leftovers

Children don't need food that's freshly cooked from scratch every mealtime. Using yesterday's leftovers – for example bubble and squeak with an egg – can make a perfect tea. The only nutrients that aren't as plentiful in reheated and leftover food are vitamin C and folate. Fibre, proteins, energy, all the other vitamins and minerals are there in just as much abundance as they were in the first place, and if you want to increase the vitamin C level in a meal, for instance, serve it with some frozen or fresh vegetables – or simply have some fresh berries or other delicious fruit afterwards.

Start the day

Mornings can be chaotic, and it can be hard to get your child to sit down and eat breakfast, but the first meal of the day is one of the most, if not the most important of the day. Studies have repeatedly shown that children who eat breakfast have far higher vitamin, mineral and fibre intakes and are better nourished, which helps them to thrive in the classroom and enjoy playtime and sports.

For younger children, the best breakfast should be rich in slow-release energy, which can come from bread, muffins, crackers, cereal, porridge and fruit. The one thing that changes when children are a bit older is that their body is mature enough to cope with wholegrain versions of these carbohydrate-rich foods. When they're younger too much fibre can fill them up too quickly, compromise the absorption of minerals such as calcium and iron and prevent them getting enough energy from their diet ◆. Young children should be eating some of the less fibrous white breads, but from the age of 13 months they can eat the same as the rest of the family and tuck into wholegrain muffins, pitta breads and delicious mueslis and pastas.

Read more on:
◆ *Page 100*

Baked apples,
page 240

Cereals can appear tempting, especially when you see the added vitamin and mineral flags, but they're seldom (especially the ones marketed at children) as healthy as they seem. They're often so full of sugar and salt that I just wouldn't touch the majority of them, apart from the odd treat. (I remember childhood holidays when we were allowed to choose from the selection of small boxes of children's cereals. Having my own little box to open contributed to the fun!) It's best to choose an unsweetened, simple wholewheat, oat- or bran-based cereal and then add fruit to make it sweet enough for your child's palate and for extra goodness.

You can get a large variety of types and quality of porridge oats – I used to hate them, but realised that when I made porridge using organic jumbo oats it had a great texture and natural nuttiness, as opposed to the mushy wallpaper paste a ground inferior oat turns into. Try toasting oat flakes in the oven or under the grill until they're golden brown, and add to porridge for a different taste and texture. If children are struggling with the larger oat flakes, just whiz them in a blender for a few seconds to make them smaller.

If you have the time and your child is up for a more substantial breakfast, there are a lot of benefits to be gleaned from including protein: protein not only gives the body a good hit of amino acids, but also slows down the absorption of the carbohydrate from the wholegrain, so that the energy you experience after eating, say, a boiled egg with your toast should be longer lasting.

There's a lot of nonsense written about eggs, which can make many parents restrict them in their child's diet, largely because they contain what has recently become a scare word – cholesterol. Yes, eggs do contain cholesterol, but the body is able to break it down, and they don't cause the bad sort of cholesterol to increase. In fact eggs are one of the most perfect foods for children (as long as there isn't an allergy issue) – they're versatile, easy to store, last a long time and can be boiled, scrambled, poached or fried within minutes. You could try beating them lightly with a dash of milk and dip slices of bread in to make scrumptious eggy bread – a good way to get reluctant egg-eaters to glean their goodness. Eggy bread is delicious with savoury toppings like sautéed mushrooms, lean ham, crispy pancetta, baked beans, grated cheese, tuna, or any oily fish like mashed sardines. Sardines tinned in tomato sauce are cheap, rich in omega-3 fatty acids and very more-ish when served on eggy bread, as is smoked trout or salmon, either on its own or with some cream cheese, or something vegetarian such as sliced tomatoes, grilled haloumi and cucumber or hummus … Virtually any topping works well with the light and yet satisfying eggy bread. Sweet toppings are delicious too – chopped fruit with a dollop of thick natural yoghurt, nut butter and banana is a Maya favourite.

Packed lunches

The reality is that despite recent school meals campaigns, many of our children's schools are reluctant to change their ways, or, as is the case with Maya's school, don't have a kitchen, making cooked meals out of the question. For whatever reason, thousands of children are either packed off with a lunchbox or given money to buy something on the way to school.

Children need a good lunch – the school day is long and the demands on their energy are great, whether it's a physically active day, or mentally draining. We know how it feels to be ravenously hungry – mood can dip, ability to concentrate goes out of the window – and our children are just as badly off, if not more so, since their early learning years require an enormous resilience in order to accumulate all the necessary life skills. If we put something into our stomachs that doesn't feel comfortable – too much, too salty, too sugary – our gut can start complaining, we get tummy aches, and if the food is too heavy all the body wants to do is sleep. We forget that our stomach is a muscle and needs oxygen to work. If you're running around, the oxygen may either be 'taken away' from the stomach, in which case you experience heavy, stitch-like discomfort, or the body's response to a big a meal is to release sleep-inducing hormones. School days sadly don't accommodate this luxury, so the trick is to put food in your child's lunchbox that is nourishing and sustaining enough to get them through the day but not too heavy to slow them down.

Knowing where to start can be tricky, but as with all meals, the ideal is to include something from each food group ◆, as this replenishes energy stores, provides proteins for muscle strength, as well as vitamins, minerals and fibre. The solution is traditionally a sandwich, and this is what most parents find the easiest to put together. The bread choices we have today give us so many options, from traditional white and wholemeal sliced, to soft, crusty rolls, flat breads and dark rye-type pumpernickels ▲. The more you use your freezer, the more chance you have of making a bread-based lunch slightly more tantalising than the same old bread and filling. But this is not to say that a classic cheese or jam – I tend to use pure fruit spreads, or alternatively choose a jam with the highest fruit and lowest sugar content – sandwich should be frowned upon. You can freeze sandwiches if you wrap them well – just take a frozen pack out in the morning, and by lunchtime it will have thawed and be fresh-tasting. Fillings that do well frozen are charcuterie ham, jam (pure fruit spreads) or egg mayonnaise. Sometimes the sandwich can be a little on the soggy side, but children won't notice this, if you don't point it out – they're usually so ravenous and happy to have something inside their stomachs!

But there is life beyond the sandwich – crispbreads and crisp rolls are another option, as children like the crunchiness, and enjoy dipping crackers into a little pot of hummus or guacamole. I wrap the crispbreads in some foil to keep them dry and therefore crisp when they're opened The only thing you need to watch out for with crackers – which can be plain, wholemeal, seedy or those delicious Scandinavian crisp rolls – is that some of them can be rather salty,

Read more on:
◆ *Page 14*
▲ *Pages 94–95*

Roasted tomato & couscous salad, page 226

Read more on:
◆ *Page 46*

Oxtail soup,
page 235

so check the label. Not only is too much salt bad for anyone's health ◆, but it tends to make children thirsty, which could be a problem at school, depending on whether your child is lucky enough to be allowed access to water during the rest of the day. Crackers can work well with slices of charcuterie ham, roast chicken, cheese, etc., or, if your child isn't bothered by a slightly softer crispbread, can make a sort of sandwich with cream cheese, a soft cheese such as Camembert or a nut butter and sliced cucumber. Or they could be eaten alongside a flask of soup or a casserole from the night before. Dry foods can get stuck in children's teeth (crackers and crisps are the common culprits), so make sure they have a drink or eat some slippery fruit such as a few grapes or a satsuma, to wash them down.

Cold lunches can include pasta or rice salad, or couscous. Maya has recently got into potato salad, which is delicious in the summer when the potatoes are small, new and waxy, but also in winter, when even the older potatoes work well, as does combining them with sweet potato for another nutritious option (since it's a good source of beta-carotene). I make a simple new potato salad with a classic dressing, and use it as an easy way to make a good lunch out of not a lot of anything – a few added pieces of torn salami are delicious, as is something more exotic (there is no reason why children shouldn't like it) – smoked eel.

The great thing about thinking outside the traditional food box is that some foods, since they're not considered trendy, can be inexpensive, as producers know they can't let price be another barrier on top of unfamiliarity. The same can be said for cheaper cuts of meat such as ham hock, oxtail or offal – if your child enjoys eating liver, these make very nourishing casseroles or soups, that can be popped into a child's thermos flask for a hot lunch on a winter's day. They will also tide them over if you tend to find them ravenously hungry when you pick them up from school and you still have a long journey home or homework to finish before tea.

To snack or not to snack

Snacking is very different from nibbling or constant grazing, where your child consumes calories that don't register on the 'I've eaten' radar. A proper snack, which they eat when they can enjoy and concentrate on it, will keep them satiated for longer. The more you can help your child to be comfortable and okay with feeling hungry, the more able they will be to judge how much food they should be eating as they grow older. They are also less likely to struggle with excess weight and will have healthier teeth too.

Knowing when to give your child a snack depends on the situation and on your child — some days they won't be able to last from breakfast to lunch without a snack, while other days you'll be lucky to get just three meals into them, so snacks aren't necessary. It's best not to set yourself hard and fast rules, but have things with you in case it's one of those days when they need to eat more. Avoid getting into the routine of always giving them something between meals, as sometimes they don't need anything and the last thing you want is to fill them up on a snack so that they don't touch their main meals ◆. When they ask for food, check that they're not actually thirsty, as they can sometimes confuse their needs.

Smoothies and juices

Smoothies and juices can be a great way to get children to take in a dose of vitamin C and folate ▲, along with some energising fruit sweetness which, if it's a no-added-sugar smoothie, can be better for them than one of the sugar-laden canned drinks. But, and it's a big but, I think we've become somewhat cajoled into believing that our children can drink an unlimited amount of these drinks. The latest claim from a well-known brand of smoothie, that each smoothie counts as two portions of the recommended five portions or fruits and veg a day, triggers some concerns for me. The notion that just one bottle can count towards two portions means you can become less resolved to get your child to eat more vegetables or pieces of fresh, unadulterated fruit, which have advantages over a smoothie because children have to chew them. This helps with speech development in younger children, which is a good thing.

Some smoothies can even give a child a sugar high, as they can drink quite a lot in a short space of time and there is a lot of fructose (natural fruit sugar) in them, which can aggravate mood and energy levels. The combination of a thick, sticky consistency, acids and sugars, albeit natural, in smoothies can lead to tooth decay.

No-added-sugar fruit squashes can be a useful and tasty addition if you want to make water a little different, but don't set a precedent for always giving your child squash from an early age. If you give them plain water as the norm and fruit squash as a treat, this stops them being so used to a sweet-tasting drinks. Be aware that several squash brands can contain additives and colourings, which in susceptible children can aggravate behaviour moods and energy levels and in extreme cases are linked to increasing the symptoms of attention deficit hyperactivity disorder (ADHD) ●. Cordials such as elderflower or ginger and lemon are very sweet, so again just use a dash every now and then.

Read more on:
◆ Page 86
▲ Page 19
● Pages 116–118

My top snacks

If you can choose a snack with an intense flavour, such as a dried fig, your child will get that wonderful taste acknowledgement, rather in the way a few squares of 75 per cent or other good-quality chocolate will make you feel satiated. Snacks can be substantial, such as a small pot of pasta twirls with a couple of chunks of cheese, or a small filler such as an apple, a few grapes or a rice cake. Stock up on plastic containers of different sizes or save re-usable packaging and small plastic bags, washed well to store ready-to-eat snacks. It's worth buying a cooler bag and a flask that you can use for both keeping tap water cool and soup warm.

Snack ideas

- Fresh fruit or drained tinned fruit in natural juice, e.g. tangerines and chunks of pineapple.

- Dried fruits – ideally those without sulphur dioxide. Watch the ones with yoghurt coating, as they're often high in sugar.

- Raw vegetables, such as carrot, cucumber, celery, fennel, cherry tomatoes, etc. Serve with a little pot of hummus, bean dip, guacamole, tsatziki, or even make a dip from leftover cooked carrots and butternut squash blended with some natural yoghurt – whiz with a hand-held blender to the required consistency and serve with cucumber or celery sticks.

- Chunks of cheese or lean meat.

- Cottage cheese, with small rice cakes or grissini to dip.

- Wholemeal bread with wafer-thin ham, grated or cream cheese or nut butter – think beyond the peanut, as there are delicious hazelnut, Brazil and cashew nut butters too.

- Cooked cold pasta, drizzled with a little olive oil.

- Home-made soup – you can make it more substantial by adding pasta, beans, lentils etc.

Juices vary enormously and some juice connoisseurs say they can taste the difference, but nutritionally there is no difference between a juice made from concentrate, a chilled, freshly-made juice and one in a carton stored on the shelf. I tend to go for blended apple mixes – I also use apple juice to sweeten cakes and biscuits and to soak muesli in overnight. Apple has one of the lowest GI values, which is a measure of how quickly a food gets absorbed and raises the blood sugar level, so it's my preferred juice for Maya too. The combination of fruit acids and fruit sugars can erode tooth enamel, which is why many dentists are encouraging parents to get their children to drink less juice. I'd suggest that a small glass of fresh juice, especially after a meal containing iron-rich foods each day is a good amount to aim for. Another option is to dilute fruit juice concentrate (available from health food shops and online).

Dairy foods

Children of all ages can glean a lot of nourishment from dairy foods such as milk, yoghurt, cream, fromage frais and cheese. These foods provide the body with easily absorbed calcium as well as vitamins A and B12, plus protein and other vitamins and minerals, all of which are key for growth and healthy bodies ◆.

Whether you choose a full-fat or low-fat variety largely depends on how much fat you want your child to consume. The majority of the fat in dairy foods is saturated fat, and an excess of this can cause children (just as much as adults) to produce too much bad cholesterol, which can fur up arteries and increase the risk of heart disease. Cheeses, yoghurts and other types of dairy produce vary in the amount of saturated fat they contain, but it's not the best use of your brain power to go through their individual typical nutritional compositions – it also shouldn't be necessary with children to make a choice of cheese based on its fat or other nutrient content. I would suggest instead getting into some wise cheese-eating habits, as below, so you can enjoy the delicious upsides of cheese and not suffer from too many of the downsides.

Read more on:
◆ Pages 16–21
▲ Pages 110–111

Tandoori chicken,
page 221

Yoghurt

Yoghurt can be tricky – often packed with sugar, colourings and sweeteners – so my advice is to steer clear of the flavoured ones (even those with a misleading picture of fruit on the front). Go for the full-fat natural kind, either runny or the thicker Greek yoghurt, and add your own sweetness. This could be fruit compôte, stewed fruit, honey or nuts (not whole until your child is five), so at least you know what they're eating. Alternatively, you could make your own frozen yoghurt.

Use plain yoghurt in savoury dishes such as dips and soups and make a mayonnaise-style dip by using half natural yoghurt to half mayonnaise to give a lighter taste, or for coating chicken in a spicy masala yoghurt marinade. Better still, choose one containing live probiotic cultures ▲.

Milk

Once children are past the age of two – the recommended age when you can make the switch from full-fat (3.5 per cent fat) milk – one of the best ways to make sure they don't consume too much saturated fat is to change them over to semi-skimmed (about 1.7 per cent fat). They will most likely be getting enough fat and calories from the rest of their diet, and the good news is that these lower-fat milks contain just as much calcium and actually, in the case of 1 per cent and skimmed (0.1–0.3 per cent fat) milk, they do a touch better, containing slightly more calcium than full-fat milk. Taste-wise, semi-skimmed and 1 per cent milks are enjoyable and work well in sauces and other recipes, so it's an easy shift to make in the family's diet. Skimmed milk, in my opinion, is an acquired taste and doesn't work as well in cooking, since it lacks body when it's used in sauces, but it really depends what you're used to – if your child is a guzzler of milk and you're looking for a way to tweak their fat intake, 1 per cent milk may be the way to go.

Read more on:
◆ *Page 130*

Calcium is an essential nutrient for all children to help grow strong bones and reduce the risk of developing osteoporosis when they're older ◆. Many children don't receive the recommended daily intake of 500mg, which equates to 65g Cheddar cheese or 460ml milk.

There is no nutritional difference between ultra heat treated (UHT) milk and fresh milk – you get just as much protein, calcium, etc. So UHT milk can be a good option to use in cooking, especially as that way the slightly different taste isn't so noticeable. UHT milks are cheaper too, and since they're non-chilled products they last a long time – although when opened they need to be refrigerated in the same way as fresh milk.

There are subtle nutritional differences between the different dairy milks, such as goat's, sheep's and the classic cow's milk (sheep's milk is higher in calories than the other two, which are pretty similar). The fats in goat's milk are slightly different, which means that some children may find them easier to digest (they tend not to give them tummy aches), but this difference is so subtle that really the choice between whether you give your child cow's, goat's or sheep's milk should be down to preference. However, it is useful to know that the calcium, phosphorus, sodium, magnesium, zinc, and iron levels are higher in sheep's milk, which could influence your choice of milk. Bear in mind that the alternative dairy milks are more expensive than cow's milk, but essentially they all provide calcium and many other great nutrients such as B vitamins. When it comes to non-dairy milks the story changes, and there are huge differences that need to be considered. A word of warning when searching the Internet for information on non-dairy milks: remember that anyone can write an

Read more on:
◆ Page 102

article and spout all sorts of pseudo-scientific rubbish, usually based around the simple notion that cow's milk is the devil's juice and you're 'poisoning' your children if you give it to them. This is nonsense, and unless your child has a genuine intolerance to cow's milk protein or lactose, or you're bringing them up vegan ◆, I would suggest using cow's milk as your main milk in their diet and using the other milks as variations in cakes, puddings, etc.

Soya milk

Soya milk is widely available in supermarkets and health food shops, and is increasingly being offered in cafés. There are many different varieties: sweetened, unsweetened, organic, fresh, long-life, vanilla-flavoured, mineral-enriched (such as calcium) and vitamin-enriched. Although you can also buy chocolate, strawberry, banana and other fruit-flavoured soya milks, be aware that these can be high in sugar – at least if you make your own you can control the amount of sweetness you add.

Some parents have real concerns about the presence of phytoestrogens in soya milk. These are oestrogen-like substances that occur naturally in many plants, including soya. There is some unease about the possibility that a large intake of phytoestrogens could have an adverse effect on a child's hormonal development, especially because children weigh much less than adults and the effect could therefore be potentially more pronounced. However, while studies on animals have shown that large amounts of phytoestrogens affect the development of reproductive organs and fertility, there is no evidence that there would be similar effects on people. So giving your child soya milk in the way that we typically use cow's milk, say a glass of milk a day, with perhaps a small pot of soya yoghurt and a meal based around soya protein, should be fine.

Too much of any food isn't good for us and it may be that in the future we will find out that too much soya milk isn't a good thing for children. So for this reason, if you're avoiding cow's milk for a health or medical reason, such as lactose intolerance, keep a variety of non-dairy milks in your child's diet – this way you'll be getting a spectrum of nutrients and minimising the potential health risks of too much of any one of them.

Rice and oat milks

Rice and oat milks contain far less protein, fat and calcium than cow's milk (depending on whether it's full-fat or semi-skimmed, of course). You can make up the difference in your child's diet with protein, fat, etc., but as far as calcium is concerned, the calcium even in the fortified versions of these milks isn't as well absorbed by the body as it is from cow's milk. If your child is following a dairy-free diet, seek advice from your doctor or dietician to see if you should be giving a calcium supplement. Rice milk is thinner and sweeter than soya milk and doesn't really work in hot drinks, but it's excellent on its own or with cereal. Delicious milkshakes and smoothies can be made by blending any milk alternative with fruit (either fresh or a dollop of pure fruit spread), good-quality chocolate powder or a non-dairy ice cream, for example one made with soya. Non-dairy milks vary in sweetness, as does fruit, so taste before you add anything sweet such as honey because it may not need much.

Nut and seed milks

Nut milks such as almond milk are available from health food stores, and make delicious smoothies, pancakes and puddings. But check out their nutrient labels, as they seldom provide as many minerals as dairy milks and have high fat and protein levels – though they can be useful if you're trying to boost your child's fat and protein intake and can be an essential part of a vegan or vegetarian diet ◆. Be aware, though, that children can be allergic to all kinds of nuts ▲, not just peanuts, so report any concerns you may have to your doctor immediately.

Read more on:
◆ Pages 98–102
▲ Pages 93–94

You can also make your own nut milks, and I particularly love almond milk. Hemp milk is a new addition to the non-dairy milk selection, which I also love, so check it out!

Tofu

Tofu is made by curdling fresh, hot soya milk, pressing it into a solid block and then cooling it – in much the same way that traditional dairy cheese is made by curdling and solidifying milk. It contains all eight essential amino acids and is a good source of protein. A staple ingredient in Thai and Chinese cookery, it can be cooked in different ways to change its texture from smooth and soft to crisp and crunchy.

Try slicing, marinating and grilling it, or chopping it into smallish pieces and frying it with garlic until golden. Sliced raw tofu can be used instead of mozzarella in the classic Italian salad with tomato and avocado. Silken tofu is a creamy, softer product that works well in puréed or blended dishes such as flans and quiches, and is ideal for making puddings such as mousses. It's better to give children the silken kind rather than the pre-marinated kind as it tends to be less salty, but as long as you're not using salt elsewhere either variety should be fine.

Cheese

- Grate cheese for sandwiches rather than slicing. Grating increases the surface area and makes your taste buds tingle more from a smaller amount of cheese.

- If you're after an intense flavour, use a cheese that has been matured for longer. There are many different varieties – try them in dishes such as cauliflower cheese – blue-veined cheeses are delicious. The advantage of a strong-tasting mature cheese is that you need a smaller amount than you would using a milder one to get the same cheesy flavour. This means you consume less saturated fat, you need less salt when you're flavouring the dish and the piece of cheese will last longer.

- Use a little mustard, either powder or creamed, to bring out the cheese flavour in sauces, soufflés and pies.

- Although chunks of cheese make a nourishing snack, it's a good idea to have something alongside them such as grapes, pieces of apple, crackers or grissini. Not only does this provide some bulk, sustaining your child for longer, but having a couple of different textures and tastes also stimulates the part of the brain that acknowledges satiety.

- If you make your child a cheese sandwich, try to incorporate something rich in fibre such as wholegrain bread, or have an apple with it. If the child also has a drink of water, the fibre in the bread or the apple will swell and stimulate stretch receptors in the stomach that send signals to the appetite centre and make them feel satisfied.

- When slicing cheese, use a cheese slicer, as this gets you out of the habit of cutting unnecessarily thick pieces.

- I'd much rather give Maya a smaller amount of a higher-fat cheese that she'll enjoy than go for a disappointing half-fat or reduced-fat cheese. However, if your child is gaining too much weight, and you have got into the good habits above but are still looking for ways to reduce calories, try some of the reduced-fat varieties available.

- Cut the rind off soft rind cheeses like Brie and Camembert – this reduces the fat content. When you serve these soft cheeses, and also cheeses without rinds, which include sheep's and goat's cheeses, you shouldn't need any butter.

Fats

Read more on:
◆ Pages 17–18
▲ Pages 100–101

Roast mackerel with
potatoes & thyme,
page 223
Cashew nut butter,
page 232

While your child needs some fat to grow and develop, too much of any sort of fat can lead to heart disease ◆. There are many healthier alternatives, so favour the Mediterranean fats as a rule. It isn't good to deep-fry everything, but there's nothing wrong with a drizzle of vinaigrette dressing on a salad, or new potatoes with a small amount of butter. It's all about moderation.

Ideally everyone should have a couple of 140g portions of omega-rich oily fish each week. Girls and women of child-bearing age should stick to two portions (because of concerns over the build-up of toxins in the body, which could harm babies born to them in the future), but boys and everyone else can have up to four portions a week. With recent concerns over the mercury levels in tuna, however, I wouldn't go above a couple of portions of tuna a week for either boys or girls. If you don't like fish, or if you'd like non-fish sources, turn to oils such as hemp and linseed (flaxseed), walnuts and their oil, and seeds such as sunflower and pumpkin. I grind the seeds up to improve absorption and use them in porridge, smoothies, breakfast cereals, crumbles and cakes.

Butter and margarine

Butter and olive- or vegetable-based spreads are good choices. Check the labels to ensure they don't contain hydrogenated fat, as this can lead to trans fats, the unhealthiest sort of fat – although most manufacturers have thankfully removed these from spreads. While too much saturated animal fat isn't the healthiest (it can increase the risk of heart disease), there is nothing wrong with a spread of butter in moderation. One way to keep your salt intake down is to use unsalted butter.

Nut butters
Nut butters provide a delicious, sustaining spread. They are a great source of protein and 'good' mono-unsaturated fats. They also contain fibre and minerals such as zinc. There are so many different ones available, however you can make your own – which I like to do, as you can control what you put in them.

Choosing and using oils

There are so many deliciously healthy oils – rapeseed, hemp, avocado, nut oils – available in supermarkets and they provide a good source of energy ▲. Rapeseed oil, like hemp oil, contains very useful omega-3 fatty acids. Hemp oil varies in its taste and is sometimes a touch strong, so try different brands until you find the one you like best – I favour oils that are lighter on the palate. I love to use avocado or nut oils in dressings and for drizzling over grilled vegetables, sesame seed oil is my chosen oil for stir-fries.

I think it's a shame to use extra virgin and other more boutique oils for simple frying. I tend to use a non-virgin olive oil or a vegetable oil for frying onions, garlic, vegetables, etc. as a base, and then, if the final dish needs a drizzle of something more flavour-enhancing, bring out the bottle of special oil. As well as not wanting the oil to be too hot, you don't want it too cool. Food will soak up oil that's too cool, and therefore the fat and calorie content will be much higher than if the oil is hot enough to make the food sizzle when you pop it into the pan – hot oil quickly seals the food and this stops the fat being soaked up. One test is to drop a piece of bread into the hot oil – if it sizzles and bubbles within a few seconds, the temperature is about right. Bear in mind that nut and other vegetable oils have different burning and smoking points, so try them out to see how they react on your cooker and in your pans. Burnt oils often turn bitter, and oils are more likely to produce trans fats when they get too hot, which aren't good for us – this doesn't usually happen with oils if they're only overheated once, but try not to overheat oils at all. When using oil for deep-frying, use fresh oil if possible, although it's fine to reuse it a few times.

Nuts

Nuts are good to have in your storecupboard. Peanuts are in fact legumes, as in they grow beneath the ground, unlike other proper nuts, such as walnuts and hazelnuts. Whole nuts shouldn't be given to very young children, but once over the age of five, your child should be able to manage them without choking. Ground nuts and nut butters are good to include in your family's diet from an early age (as long as there is no allergy issue).

Crushed nuts can be added to yoghurt to provide a little more nourishment – the crunch factor can be fun too, especially if you make up a bowl of mixed crushed nuts and dried fruits that children can 'tip' or dip their hand into, a far healthier version of the manufactured tippy-style yoghurts that children seem to love.

You can eat nuts straight from the pack, but also try toasting them lightly first to maximise crunch and excite the highly flavoured volatile oils, either in a dry pan or the oven (eight to ten minutes at 180°C/350°F/gas mark 4 will do it; you don't want them black, just

More-ish nutty biscuits, page 247

tinged here and there with golden brown). Throw a few of your toasted nuts over salad leaves dressed with a little nut oil and lemon juice, and toss with crisply sizzled shreds of leftover meat such as roast chicken. Make them into a quick lunch by tossing them with roasted vegetables, crumbled goat's cheese and rocket, or stir into bulgur wheat with lots of chopped mint and cubes of hard goat's cheese or mature Cheddar.

Carbohydrates

Read more on:
◆ *Pages 30–32*
▲ *Page 100*
● *Pages 88–90*

Wholemeal soda bread, page 237

Children need a source of carbohydrate-rich food in each meal. Porridge and wholemeal food all provide a good source of energy as well as fibre ◆. Wholemeal is good news for all the family, although too much fibre is not always a wonder food for young children ▲. To give you an idea, my rule of thumb is, that children over two and a half years old have two-thirds of their bread, pasta, etc. as wholemeal and the remaining third as white. Some children manage to get enough energy and thrive on an entirely wholemeal diet, so it's just a matter of seeing how your little one responds to wholegrain goodness.

Make porridge with semi-skimmed or full-fat milk ● as children need some fat to provide enough energy to grow and to absorb essential vitamins. Try topping porridge with berries (which can be frozen), apple purée, chopped fruit, dried fruits, half a teaspoon of pure fruit spread, a dollop of stewed fruit or a drizzle of honey for a delicious, sweet taste with just a small amount of sugar. The glycaemic index (GI) of honey is slightly lower than granulated sugar, so this breakfast keeps children satiated for longer. Pure fruit spreads and no-added-sugar jams have a more intense fruity taste and don't contain refined sugars, which, I think, is better for everyone.

Bread

There's nothing wrong with white bread (it gives children energy and some extra calcium, iron and B vitamins such as folic acid, since the flour is fortified), but if you can, choose a half and half loaf, which contains slightly more fibre. There are lots of different types of wholemeal bread on the market, from the lighter, fluffy wholemeal bread to the denser, seedy, German-style wholemeal, so try a few until you find one every member of your family enjoys.

If your child isn't gaining as much weight as they should, or if they're unable to finish a meal and have an upset tummy, switch to breads with slightly less fibre – brown, granary or a half and half loaf. Breads like ciabatta and focaccia contain olive oil, are delicious, and are good for them, especially if they have a small appetite – a mouthful contains more calories than wholegrain (because of the oil) and can tempt a little one's jaded palate, although these breads are usually based around white flour, so contain less fibre.

Making bread by hand also means that you can fill it with all sorts of things, from fruit purées, seeds and nuts, to savoury tapenades, and mould it into whatever shape you fancy – you also know exactly what's going into it. You can add almost anything to the bread mixture to make it unique – olives, olive oil, herbs, dried fruits or nuts – or make a brioche-style loaf using milk as a base in which to warm the yeast. Alternatively, for people who can't tolerate dairy produce, use fruit purées or apple juice.

Quinoa

Quinoa (pronounced keen-wah) is an ancient sesame-seed-sized kernel, which we think of and treat as a grain, although technically it's not (it's the seed of the goosefoot plant). Quinoa is a good source of carbohydrate, protein and fibre, and also contains B vitamins and a little polyunsaturated fat. It's gluten-free, so it's useful for children who have problems digesting gluten. You can buy quinoa flour in supermarkets, health food shops and online, to make pancakes, bread and cakes.

The seeds are usually eaten cooked, like rice (although you can sprout them too, see below), but you need to wash them well first, to get rid of any residue that may leave a bitter taste. Cook quinoa for about 15 minutes for a rice-like texture. You can add the uncooked seeds to soups and casseroles (as long as there's plenty of liquid for them to absorb), and you can make them into porridge, just the same as with oats, using water or milk. You can roast the seeds in a non-stick frying pan for a few minutes first if you like, until you get a waft of nuttiness. The toasted seeds will keep in an airtight jar in a cool place for weeks.

To sprout quinoa, soak two tablespoons of seeds in a jar of cold water for two to four hours, then drain and rinse twice a day for two to four days. Sprouts will quickly appear and are delicious in salads or stir-fries.

Vegetarianism

Whether or not you're going to include meat in your child's diet may be your own choice or may come from your child. Life is easier if you can make one meal for the whole family rather than having to come up with both a meat and a veggie option, but try not to make a big issue of it – you could always cook a lamb chop or roast a chicken for the non-vegetarians to have alongside a vegetarian dish.

It's perfectly possible for children to thrive as vegetarians and in fact there are some real plus points, since studies have shown that vegetarian children consume more fresh fruits and vegetables and are therefore less likely to suffer from obesity, bowel cancer and heart disease when they are adults. Nowadays there are many recipes and diverse ingredients available, not just at specialist food retailers and online companies but even in supermarkets.

However, you do need to watch a few areas of your child's diet to ensure that they're getting the key nutrients in plentiful quantities. Some people call their children vegetarian when in fact they eat fish and seafood – technically this isn't what being a vegetarian is about. The majority of vegetarians still include dairy and eggs, which makes things a lot easier as it gives a larger spectrum of foods to choose from (dairy and eggs are excellent sources of protein and key nutrients).

Protein for vegetarians

Legumes: Chickpeas, butter beans, black-eyed beans, kidney beans, borlotti beans, haricot beans (used for baked beans)

Pulses: Lentils, split peas, dried green peas

Soya products: Miso (fermented soya bean paste), tofu (soya bean curd), tempeh (soya meat alternative), tamari (wheat-free soy sauce)

Nuts: Almonds, peanuts, cashew nuts, Brazil nuts, walnuts, hazelnuts, pine nuts, nut milks

Seeds: Sesame seeds, sunflower seeds, pumpkin seeds, linseeds (flaxseeds), quinoa

Protein

Read more on:
◆ Pages 16–17
▲ Page 20
● Pages 19–20

The first essential nutrient to be included in plentiful supplies is protein, which children need to build and replenish a strong digestive, muscular, hormonal and immune system ◆. Animal protein is what we call complete as it contains all the essential amino acids, but unfortunately the same can't be said about vegetable protein, with the exception of soya (and soya products such as tofu) and seaweed. It's simple to get around this by eating a wide variety of plant-based proteins – if you look at the list below you will see there are plenty of delicious foods to choose from.

Vitamins and minerals

If children are eating a varied vegetarian diet containing a plentiful supply of different proteins, cereals, vegetables, fruits and some dairy they should be getting a good balance of essential vitamins and minerals. But calcium, iron and vitamin B12 deserve special mention when you're vegetarian as they can often be lacking.

Calcium is essential for bones and teeth, and is also needed to help muscles work properly ▲. It is much easier to ensure that children take in enough calcium if they eat dairy produce. There is far less calcium in non-dairy foods, so if dairy isn't on the menu every day, discuss the issue of your child taking a calcium supplement to help ensure they're reaching their requirement.

The most easily absorbed sources of iron are liver and lean red meat, but for vegetarians some iron can be found in egg yolks, peaches, apricots, figs, nuts, bananas, green leafy vegetables, seaweed, watercress, avocados, fresh herbs (particularly parsley), pot barley, baked beans in tomato sauce (always a good standby), nuts, oatmeal, lentils, sunflower seeds, fortified breakfast cereals, wholemeal bread and brown rice. Unfortunately, however, unlike meat sources, vegetarian sources of iron need a helping hand from vitamin C to be absorbed. The secret is to eat vitamin C-rich foods in the same meal as the iron-rich ones – this means getting into the habit of serving iron-rich vegetables followed by a portion of fresh or tinned-in-juice fruit. All fruits contain vitamin C but some are richer than others: kiwis, strawberries, blueberries, blackcurrants, papaya, oranges and mangoes.

Vitamin B12 ● is found in almost all foods of animal origin, but vegetarians can also find it in yeast extract, fortified breakfast cereals, seaweed and spirulina. Dietary deficiency of vitamin B12 is rare in younger people and only occurs among strict vegans. B vitamins particularly vitamin B12, are often low in the vegan diet. You can buy fortified cereals, soya drinks, spirulina (a form of algae available in capsule or powder form, which you can stir into smoothies) and low-salt yeast spreads (the full-blown ones are far too high in salt for kids). However, it's not easy to get children to eat enough of these foods to cover their basic requirement, so consider giving them a supplement containing 1.2mcg per day until they're nine years old and then increase this to 1.8mcg per day.

Fibre

Read more on:
◆ Pages 112–113

Butternut squash & red lentil dahl, page 214

In general we all need to eat more fibre – a high-fibre diet is satisfying, since fibre helps keep us satiated, reduces the risk of heart disease and many cancers, and helps to keep our day-to-day gut movements healthy and regular. But with children, especially vegetarian children, you need to ensure they're eating enough but not too much. Too little fibre can cause constipation, which is miserable for children ◆, but on the other hand too much can lead to your child becoming listless, low in energy and (especially common in vegetarian children) anaemic. This is because too much bulk from fibrous foods and too many phytates, which bran and other wholegrain cereals contain, inhibit the absorption of iron.

Vegetarian children are more susceptible to this scenario simply because a vegetarian diet naturally tends to focus on vegetables and fruits. Parents who choose to be vegetarian can be great vegetable cooks and lovers of all food healthy and wholegrain, so before too long, if vegetables and bulky wholegrains are too large a part of a young child's diet, their body can be overloaded with fibre. Note also that too much fibrous food without enough water can in itself cause constipation, so children need to have a good couple of glasses of water with a meal in order to provide enough fluid to enable the fibre to work for rather, than against, keeping the gut regular.

Watch out for your child's weight not increasing as it should, or you might notice that they are more tired and grumpy than usual. Any of these signs could indicate too much fibre in their diet.

Getting the energy levels right

Children, especially vegetarian children, need good healthy sources of energy in their diet, which they usually glean from fats and carbohydrates. There are two main types of fat: those that come from animal foods such as butter, cream, cheese, yoghurt and milk, and those that come from vegetables, seeds, nuts, olives, avocados and oils, such as rapeseed, hemp, sunflower and safflower oils. I like to base much of my diet around vegetarian sources of fat for two reasons: first, cakes, muffins, biscuits, sauces, etc. are delicious when made with nut milks, or oils such as rapeseed or hemp, nut butters, seeds and other energy-rich ingredients. Second, vegetable fats largely (with coconut oil being one notable exception) consist of unsaturated fats such as monounsaturated fats – some of the healthiest types of fat for our hearts ◆.

This isn't to say that animal fats are bad for children – there are great advantages for including dairy foods in a vegetarian diet. They are great energy-giving foods and also provide calcium and vitamin D. You just need to watch that vegetarian children don't have their diet dominated by too much dairy (an easy trap to fall into, since dairy foods can be pretty more-ish and provide an easy and practical option) – a diet too rich in dairy can be higher in calories than even a young, growing child needs, racking up their saturated fat intake, which their cardiovascular system won't appreciate.

Although soya milk and soya products contain plenty of protein, they tend to be very low in fat, so they're good for children's hearts but are not great for boosting energy. Include other vegetable fats too – for example, you could make porridge made with soya milk but then stir in a dollop of nut butter or a teaspoon of ground seeds and nuts.

Omega-3 fatty acids

Omega-3 fatty acids are hard to find if you follow either a vegetarian or a vegan diet. The main dietary source of omega-3 will be from ALA ▲, unfortunately, due to the body's inefficiency at converting ALA to EPA and DHA, it's hard to provide these two vital fatty acids in the amounts the body needs. You'd have to really be tucking into lots of plant sources of ALA, which isn't that practical, so I'd suggest giving your child a vegetarian omega-3 supplement just to cover their needs. This will take the pressure off, and means you can enjoy using seeds, nuts, etc. as part of their general diet without thinking they've got to consume a certain amount in order to meet their omega-3 requirement. It's not easy getting a vegan diet right for your child, so do as much research as you can, and ask your doctor to refer you to a paediatric dietician who can assess and advise you on the overall nutrient levels of your child's diet.

Vegetarian ready-made foods

Read more on:
◆ Page 17
▲ Pages 17–18

We all need a helping hand now and again, so having a stock of ready-made frozen foods such as vegetarian sausages and burgers can be a life-saver when you need to put together a quick and easy meal. But don't assume that the word 'vegetarian' on the label or the lack of meat means they're full of healthy ingredients – you would be shocked to see that fat, sugar, additive and salt levels can be high (in some cases far greater than the non-vegetarian options). So check the labels and try to balance a high value with something nutritious alongside.

The vegan diet

It's a lot easier to follow a vegan diet now that supermarkets, health food shops and online suppliers stock such a wide variety of non-animal dairy produce and ready-made vegan meals. Feeding a vegan child can be a little daunting, as you need to avoid all animal produce, so here are a few of my storecupboard favourites.

- Seed pastes like tahini can be stirred into bean salads and is the basis of hummus (a staple in our house). Tahini can be spread on bread or crackers as a butter substitute, stirred into a bowl of pasta or used to top jacket potatoes.

- My favourite – nut butters such as peanut, cashew, hazelnut and almond. They are yummy on bread and rice cakes and good in vegetable casseroles and bakes. Whole nuts should be avoided until your child is over the age of five.

- Vegetable oils – check out rapeseed, avocado, nut and hemp oil – can not only give a different taste to recipes but also contain different fatty acids, for example walnut oil is rich in omega-3 fatty acids and avocado oil is rich in monounsaturated fats. Too much fat isn't good for any child, but since the vegan diet is generally very bulky, it's important you don't shy away from using oil or something rich in each meal. Vegan children need the calories and energy hit that fats bring, so drizzle oils over vegetables, dip bread in oil at the table, make a sandwich with creamy hummus and roasted vegetables or top warm toast with tahini and sliced peaches. Try to buy speciality breads made with olive oil, such as focaccia, or make your own, as they're higher in fat and more energy-rich than standard breads.

- Avocados are wonderfully creamy and rich in fat – good on jacket potatoes, in salads and sandwiches, even mashed on rice cakes spread with nut butter and sliced banana.

Cooking the slow way

It's all very well and good throwing something to eat together at the end of the day, but one of the ways I juggle being a working mum is to rethink the food preparation routine so that we can walk through the door and know that all we have to do is find a plate. Slow cooking works especially well for me, as I'm an early riser – I can prepare the meal before Maya wakes up and still have time at the end of the day, when we're both tired, to concentrate on getting through homework knowing that tea is taken care of.

If you want to shift your own routine around, either get up earlier, or, if you're more of a night owl, prepare your evening meal the night before. Think about investing in a slow cooker – they're electric and are built with safety sensors so that they can be left for hours to gently cook the food. (You can set them to come on automatically so that the casserole's cooked by the time you get home.) Alternatively, if you're an Aga enthusiast, find the right sort of cooking pot to allow the casserole to simmer away all day in the slow oven.

There are many nutritional advantages to letting foods cook slowly. First, if you give ingredients time to simmer, mix and infuse, the natural flavours will develop and deepen, so you should need less salt at the end (get used to tasting your food just before you serve to prevent adding salt from force of habit). Try using black pepper first to see whether that tweaks the flavours sufficiently and maybe a squeeze of fresh lemon too. Using garlic, and intense herbs like bay and sage, are my favourite ways to provide big flavours without using much salt. Casseroles and tagines work well if you add some wine before cooking, as it enhances the flavours but the alcohol evaporates, so the calorie and alcoholic impact is nil. Remember to use only wines you'd be prepared to drink and don't just bung in any old past-it plonk!

Slow cooking means that vegetables and pulses such as beans and lentils are well cooked making them easy to digest. It also means that less confident cooks can use root vegetables such as celeriac, swede and parsnips, without having to worry about the exact timing – just throw it all in and let the casserole do the work for you. I always love mushy vegetables in sauces, and children with sensitive guts ◆ find them easily digestible. They absorb more antioxidants from a cooked carrot than they would from a raw one, which may upset their gut and pass through before they've had a chance to properly digest and absorb all the goodness from it. One-pots are fantastic for children who don't like the look of vegetables in their crisp state – you can trick them into eating a meaty casserole knowing that there are four or five vegetables in the sauce. You can

Read more on:
◆ *Pages 114–115*

*Chicken, tomato
& sausage hot pot,
page 212*

even liquidise the sauce if they're particularly fussy eaters, add extra stock and blend everything to make a hearty soup. While heat (especially over a long time) destroys a lot of the vitamins B and C, within a casserole you keep all the cooking liquid that the water-soluble vitamins such as vitamin C leach into, so you'll still get some nutrients from the sauce.

Cooking slowly allows you to choose more economical cuts of meat such as knuckles, hocks, oxtail, brisket, and also use pheasant and other game, which need slow cooking to tenderise the flesh. If you're worried about the higher fat content of cheaper cuts, first think about what you're going to serve them with – maybe jacket potatoes, a quick-soak couscous, or a hunk of fresh wholegrain bread. You can reduce the fat content by using the sauce from the casserole instead of butter or oil on these accompaniments: stir it into couscous instead of adding oil, or use bread to mop up the juices instead of spreading it with thick lashings of butter. If you have time to let the casserole cool down, you may like to skim the fat off the top, either with one of the fancy brushes or pipettes you can buy, or just by lifting the fat off if it's gone solid. But remember that, in spite of the huge anti-fat lobby that's so prevalent in our society, we – especially children – need some fat in our diet for flavour and to help our bodies absorb fat-soluble vitamins ◆. No one can convince me that eating a home-cooked casserole containing good fresh ingredients including high-fibre vegetables, beans or lentils is anything other than great for my family's health.

Read more on:
◆ *Pages 18–19*

Fussy eating

Food tantrums can break any parent's resolve. Maybe it would help if we just ditched the notion that mealtimes should be relaxed and without any emotional outbursts, whether from you or your child, and regard anything other than complete meltdown as a positively great mealtime! Joking aside, until you've been a parent and experienced how food and emotions can be so entwined, it's impossible to know how tough it can be to get right. I could write a whole book on how parents need to lead the way with instilling good eating habits, but what may work on one occasion and for one child may not work with the next. What I do know, from helping many parents with fussy eaters, is that the sooner you can instil the idea that you eat what you're given the better. Modern lives where children eat separately from their parents, and the concept of 'meals for one' or 'children's meals', imply that everyone can in theory have something different to eat. What we have created is a nation of very fussy eaters who have been allowed to dictate what they fancy eating. It's hard as a parent when you're shattered and want to avoid conflict at mealtimes, but beware of giving in when toddlers try to manipulate what they eat.

It's ideal if you can either sit and eat the same food with your children, or at least cook one pot of food so that they know this is all that's on offer. Okay, children will have preferences, and there will be foods that they're less keen on, but stick to your guns and reward them for trying even a small mouthful of the food – say with a sticker chart. Although getting into the habit of rewarding them with a chocolate or something sweet they love isn't ideal, don't feel bad if you sometimes resort to this.

Not cooking them something else when they refuse to eat is a really tough thing to do. You may well fear that they'll end up ravenously hungry or wake up in the night, and of course there will be times when you can let the bar down, but it's generally best to stick with the policy that you eat what you're given and don't get anything else. Hungry children will eat eventually, and they'll soon start to change when they know their fussy eating requests don't get much of a reaction. Obviously try to choose something they will enjoy, and see some wins on their sticker chart at the next mealtime if you can, but if they start playing up and saying they no longer like this, then you know it's a behavioural rather than a taste issue. To test whether they truly dislike something or are just being difficult, I'd suggest trying each new food eight or ten times before putting it to one side for a few weeks – at which point try it again and see if the sticker chart motivates them then. Just because they didn't like it before doesn't mean it won't prove a hit in a few weeks' time. The more calm and clear you are that they will only get what's been cooked, the sooner they will respond – but it takes the patience of a saint!

Tired all the time?

Read more on:
◆ Page 11

My mum's chicken pie, page 219

If you've noticed your child is below par and lacks go-getting energy, there may be a simple solution or you may need to do a bit more investigating, such as keeping a food diary ◆ to check that they're getting a varied diet of nourishing foods.

Check they're getting enough exercise, as lack of fresh air and running around can make them feel tired. I find when Maya's over-tired the best thing is a walk or cycle ride as the exercise produces endorphins which lift her mood and increases her metabolism, making her physically tired enough to go to sleep as soon as she hits the pillow. Lack of sleep is an obvious cause, but maybe you could do things differently in the evening to help them nod off – TV last thing before they go to bed could be causing dreams or stopping them getting off to sleep early, while a bath followed by a story and a few drops of lavender oil on the pillow usually works a treat.

Tiredness can be a key symptom of dehydration. Many little ones don't drink enough water – it's especially easy to become dehydrated when the weather's hot or if they're been especially active. They also need more water if they've eaten a salty snack such as a packet of crisps.

Anaemia (the lack of haemoglobin, which carries oxygen in the blood around the body so that our cells can use it to produce energy) causes children to be constantly tired, pale, possibly headachey, with lots of crying. See your doctor who can diagnose anaemia with a blood test. It's usually caused by too little iron in the diet, so focus on boosting their intake of iron-rich foods ◆.

Read more on:
◆ *Page 20*

Too much fibre can prevent children from getting enough energy in their diet. It's hard to give exact guidelines, as some children can glean enough energy when they're eating wholemeal all the time but others may need a break from the wholegrains. Try more white pasta and bread to see if it makes a difference.

Surviving tantrums

While it's perfectly normal for young children to lose it occasionally, there's losing it in a small and containable way, and then there's those dreaded meltdowns which often happen when it's the last thing you need. I've found that what children eat and drink, and when they do it, can have an impact on lessening the severity of the meltdowns.

Make sure they're drinking enough water, as a dehydrated child is far more likely to be a moody one. About one to one and a half litres of water a day is a good target to aim for, but remember, when they're having a meltdown they often get hot and sweaty, so they lose more fluid. If water doesn't interest them, try adding a small amount of apple juice, as this can feel like a real treat and since apple juice has one of the lowest GI values it's less likely to aggravate blood sugar levels – which I find can be a precipitating factor in tantrums.

Try to get children to eat regularly. Sometimes we're caught out and schedules go wrong, and this can be one of the reasons why they're more likely to get out of control – they just haven't had enough food to keep their blood sugar at the best level and this can affect mood. When you know it's going to be a stressful or important day, try to think ahead as much as you can to ensure mealtimes are regular. I find a big breakfast with eggs, grilled sausages and wholemeal toast sets us off on a good footing. If you're already mid-meltdown, cajole them into having something to eat if you suspect that lack of nourishment could be a trigger. Don't fall into the trap of choosing a food that they see as a real treat (otherwise you may find these tantrums happen more frequently) and avoid food with a high GI value such as biscuits, chocolate, cakes and sweets as these can aggravate their moods even more. It's best to offer something like a piece of fresh fruit or banana on a slice of wholemeal bread – even a packet of low-on-the-salt crisps isn't a bad option. A sandwich with a lean protein filling would be good too, as the protein helps to slow down the absorption of the carbohydrate in the bread and therefore enables their blood sugar level to be better controlled.

Eczema

Eczema is an inflammatory skin condition, which causes dry, itchy skin that can drive little ones wild enough to want to scratch and claw away at their bodies. This can make the skin break and bleed and can lead to secondary infections. Genes definitely play a part, but there are also environmental and lifestyle factors, as well as diet, that can have an impact on whether your child suffers from eczema. Eczema is far more common than we'd think and is not only a complex skin condition to treat, but as I've found over the last couple of years with Maya, can be distressing for us both.

There are so many triggers responsible for the skin flaring up and how eczema affects your child will vary greatly. It can range from the odd patch on their elbows and behind their knees to those who can be literally covered from top to toe, and need to have bandages on at night to soothe and protect bleeding limbs and to stop them scratching.

Read more on:
◆ *Page 62*

Children and babies over six months who suffer from eczema can eat the same foods as those recommended for pregnant and breastfeeding mums ◆. However, since most kids aren't that great at eating sardines, mackerel, herrings etc., if your child has eczema, I would also give your child an omega oil supplement containing 2g of EPA and DHA. You can get some easy-to-swallow chewy capsules, but liquid forms are also available or you could crack open the capsules and mix them in with milk and juices if your child finds them unpalatable. You need to be patient, as it can take several weeks for the skin to calm down, and once their skin has improved they need to keep taking the supplement.

If your child can avoid the offending food allergen, their skin will dramatically improve. The most common are: milk (usually cow's milk,

Organic food and farmers' markets

The recent debate over whether or not organic food is healthier for us than non-organic food has highlighted how complex an issue this is. One of the main problems is that it's very hard to compare an organic product with a non-organic one, while there are so many subjective factors such as how easy a food has been to source, how it tastes, how well it cooks, how it makes us feel, and what it has cost. In my opinion, there is little point in overstretching our budget for imported organic food if it doesn't cook well.

To qualify for organic status, farmers must adhere to strict regulations on artificial fertilisers and pesticides – pests and diseases are controlled using wildlife, and some farmers boost the nitrogen content of soils by planting clover. Livestock must be fed organic feed, have access to land for regular exercise (poultry must be free-range) and be kept in appropriate shelter. These conditions naturally reduce the risk of disease so drugs and wormers are only allowed in emergencies, which again many organic food eaters prefer. Lots of people who choose organic produce are sympathetic to this farming ethos.

Reports have shown that organic produce doesn't necessarily contain any more vitamins or minerals than non-organic food. The meat from an organic steak may not contain any more iron than a non-organic steak (so won't necessarily correct low iron levels in your body more effectively), but many people prefer to support smaller organic producers who are passionate about animal welfare. If the fact that the meat is organic makes you feel more comfortable eating it, then this simple fact will in the end benefit your iron status as you'll be eating more.

It angered me to see the report published in 2009 by the Food Standards Agency (FSA). Although this had promised a comprehensive review of scientific evidence, it included comments such as 'There is no evidence of additional health benefits from eating organic food.' I know the non-organic food lobby just loved to interpret this as evidence supporting the organic movement as a waste of time. But people need to look at the fine detail in the report and reach their own conclusions, taking what they did find into consideration: for instance, they found that in organic vegetables there was 53.7 per cent more beta-carotene as well as 38.4 per cent more flavonoids, 12.7 per cent proteins and 11.3 per cent zinc.

There has been a great deal of criticism over the methodology used in the FSA's research, and many people feel they didn't consider evidence from recent studies (although there was some concern over the scientific validity of some of the studies, which reported the nutrient levels of organic foods). However, we need to interpret the results in terms of the differences we value in own our lives.

The organic label, especially when we're talking about imported produce, which won't have the same high standards as ours, doesn't automatically mean that the food is healthy – processed meats and other organic foods can have high levels of saturated fats, salt and sugar. The legislation that surrounds how much of the food needs to contain organic ingredients in order to be able to call itself organic varies from product to product, so I always think it's best to check the labels of organic food in the same way as you would with non-organic produce. Products like organic cola and organic sweets made with just as high levels of refined sugar should be given just as wide a berth as non-organic. It's also worth bearing in mind that some producers haven't yet received their organic certification, but that doesn't mean their produce isn't of a high quality. On the other hand, not all free-range is organic – for example, free range chickens may be fed genetically modified feed. Again, it's always worth checking the label.

As to the argument that organic food tastes better than non-organic, this is a silly thing to say because it depends on each and every food. We all have the right to choose – how I base my decision on whether to buy organic depends on the individual food and supplier, and I like to support some good organic food producers but I don't like to base my decision just on their organic label. For me, quality, price and whether the food has travelled from afar when I could have supported a good local supplier are all accounted for in my decision-making.

I am passionate about the good, clean, fair mission of the slow food movement, but do think that in recent years, the local farmers' market movement has slightly backfired. You get some good small producers selling great-quality foods at good prices but you can also find over-priced poor-quality food being sold in a trendy-looking market, which you would have been far better off buying from a supermarket. It angers me when people (especially those struggling with food budgets) get ripped off by market traders or are made to feel guilty for not feeding their family on locally produced market-bought produce. I shop in a combination of supermarkets, I use the Internet for getting to other smaller suppliers, and if I can, I go to a good farmers' market or support local suppliers for certain ingredients. I especially enjoy educating Maya about where food comes from and for her to see small producers at markets when we have the time.

Read more on:
◆ Page 117

but could be sheep's or goat's), eggs, citrus fruits (usually oranges are the no-no), seeds, nuts (especially peanuts), shellfish, wheat, soya (yes, soya can be a problem too, in which case you might have to use rice, hemp or oat milk) and food additives (particularly the azo dyes and benzoate preservatives ◆). Non-food irritants that can aggravate eczema include: detergents, soap, shampoo, household chemicals, rough clothing, heat, scratching, hard water, house dust and house mites, moulds, pets and wool.

You need to weigh up the benefits – for just the odd patch of eczema behind the knee you might decide that other than trying to make your child's diet well-balanced, with some omega oil supplements thrown in for good measure, it's just not worth trying to get them to exclude foods. But for more serious eczema cases, changing their diet and avoiding the offending foods can be the only way to make life bearable. I would strongly recommend seeking professional advice from a paediatric dietitian if your child has severe eczema and you suspect that a food allergy may be aggravating it.

Probiotics and prebiotics

The word 'probiotic' means 'for life', but we're more used to hearing the term 'friendly bacteria'. We all have these bacteria living in our gut, some more than others, and their main purpose is to maintain a healthy digestive system. It's my view that if we can incorporate probiotics and prebiotics in our children's diets in an enjoyable and delicious way, we're at least nourishing them well for today and at best for a healthy future too. Stress, too much alcohol, too much junk food, IBS, cancer, diabetes and infections that necessitate taking antibiotics can all upset the balance of bacteria. Sometimes a week or so of not eating the foods we know to be nourishing can be enough to destabilise a child's gut flora enough to make them feel out of sorts. And of course if your child is under the weather their gut could do with a helping hand to rebalance the bacteria.

Most probiotics help digestion by breaking down tough fibres, enzymes and other proteins found in food. Probiotic bacteria are the resilient bacteria that can survive the stomach's acids and reach the intestine, where they benefit health-producing nutrients such as vitamin K and ferment organic acids, which are absorbed into the bloodstream for energy. They also play an important role in fending off more harmful disease-causing organisms known as pathogens.

Including live probiotic yoghurt in your child's daily diet is one thing, but it is possible to help your child's gut do much of the work for itself, without or as well as actively boosting the probiotic content of their diet. You can do this by incorporating prebiotic-rich foods, which can be seen as the 'grow-bag' for a healthy gut as they aren't digestible by the body's own enzymes, so they travel through the stomach unaffected. The two main prebiotics can be found in asparagus, bananas, barley, chicory, garlic, Jerusalem artichokes, leeks, milk, onions, tomatoes, wheat and yoghurt. Generally the fresher the vegetable the higher the amount of prebiotics, but we don't yet know how often we need to eat these foods, or how much – one onion may have a lot more prebiotics in it than another onion, for example, and there are no visual or labelling tell-tale signs.

If you have a child who is really struggling with their gut – constipation, diarrhoea or IBS – find either a combined prebiotic and probiotic or a specific prebiotic supplement. Some prebiotics are added to breakfast cereals, juices and yoghurts. Children may initially become a little windy when they start boosting their intake of prebiotic foods or powder, but this soon subsides.

There's no such thing as a miracle food

What's important to realise is that as with all foods, probiotics and prebiotics are not miracle workers. Just because a product (whether it is a tablet, a drink or a food) contains them doesn't mean it is all-round nutritious, as some are high in sugar. Since research has shown that probiotics can help treat diarrhoea (particularly in children) caused by antibiotics and tummy bugs, for me, this justifies trying to make my daughter's diet as rich in probiotics and prebiotics as possible. I have seen some kids who have taken probiotics following an episode of acute diarrhoea or constipation recover very quickly.

There is some research to show that taking probiotic and prebiotic supplements on a daily basis may also prevent food poisoning, improve symptoms of lactose intolerance, reduce susceptibility to skin problems such as eczema, help control IBS, strengthen the immune system and reduce cholesterol levels. I don't think we should all start dashing out and buying supplements because in order to be sure of maintaining a healthy dose of good bacteria in the gut, your child really needs to take probiotics indefinitely, which can be a hassle and expensive. So unless this is something you want to invest in every day, I'd suggest adopting an overall habit of including some probiotic natural yoghurt in their diet most days. Note that if your child is lactose-intolerant you need to check the label, as some supplements contain lactose.

Constipation

It's what every parent dreads – seeing your child in agony on the toilet is upsetting, especially when they're at such a sensitive stage in their lives. The whole issue of not being able to go to the toilet when they and you want them to can be a worry, and the last thing you want is for them to be afraid of going because it's so painful and then perhaps getting so blocked up that when they do go they have accidents or painful diarrhoea.

Sometimes when children are going through a tough time at school – with exams or bullying, for example – the body can exhibit this upset in their gut. They may complain of tummy ache, or have trouble going to or staying off the toilet. This is why when you're treating children for gut symptoms like this it's important to see if you can dig a little deeper as to how happy they are, and whether something needs to be sorted outside their diet (I've seen so many children with tummy problems whose parents have either started them on bizarre exclusion diets or sent them off for expensive, unnecessary and uncomfortable tests when really what's needed is some good old-fashioned listening and good eating). Getting back to proper eating habits should be the first priority, but alongside this you could also enlist the help of a probiotic supplement (and see if you can do more on the prebiotic side of their diet) to rebalance temporary upsets.

Food can be the cause and cure of children's gut problems as much as adults', so the more we can do to help them get over constipation, the better. If, having tried the tips on the following pages, your child still remains constipated, visit your doctor, who may prescribe a mild laxative. Don't abandon my nutritional advice, however, because the more you can help to relieve your child's constipation through food, the less you will rely on laxative drugs. Above all, remember to be relaxed about your child's eating and toilet habits. Uptight children are likely to develop bowel problems, so the more you can do to calm them down (and appear clam yourself), the fewer problems you'll all experience.

Make sure you boost their fluid intake. Dehydration can be one of the most common reasons why children get constipated so get them to drink plenty of plain water ◆. It doesn't matter whether the water is cold or room temperature, although sometimes room temperature water works better with a sore tummy. Plain water is the most hydrating, but if you need to make it a touch more interesting, mix it with a little fruit juice in the proportions of one third juice to at least two thirds water. Chamomile tea is very soothing for a constipated gut, so get them to try some either (safely) hot, or

Read more on:
◆ *Pages 40–42*

Pearled spelt with broad beans, asparagus & dill, page 216

cooled. I like to add a little aloe vera to the water or juice – this natural plant extract can soothe a sore tummy and also loosen the stool to get things moving.

Lack of fibre is right up there with lack of water as a key reason why your child might be struggling to pass a stool. Fibre needs plenty of water to help it swell and stimulate the gut to move, so if you boost the fibre in their diet and not the water, you can make constipation ten times worse. Focus on boosting your child's fibre intake by choosing wholemeal bread, wholegrain cereals, oats, spelt, quinoa etc., plenty of fruits and vegetables (raw or cooked are both fine as fibre levels don't diminish with cooking), lentils, beans, seeds and nuts.

All fruits seem to have a particularly strong laxative effect. The most powerful ones are figs, dates, apricots, papayas, prunes, rhubarb and soft fruits such as plums and greengages, but whatever you can get your child to eat will help. You can buy small pots of prune-based fruit purée to use on cakes, pancakes, toast and ice cream. It's easy to make your own by simmering the dried fruit in a little orange juice until soft. Try not to see it as a medicinal thing – fruit purées are delicious. You could also give your child a small glass of prune juice every day, either on its own or mixed with freshly squeezed orange juice.

Check your child is not eating too much fast food. A diet too heavy in fast-fried ready-made food and not enough fresh vegetables and good home cooking is more likely to bung children up. This can explain why holidays can be a nightmare for their gut – their routine can be disrupted, especially if they're having to travel on planes for a long time and not only don't get much of an opportunity to roam around and get their gut muscles working but have to eat strange food at strange times. It's a hassle, but the more I travel with Maya, the more convinced I am that the answer is for me pack food for us to eat on the plane that we will both enjoy, and that we know will make us feel good at the end of the flight rather than the pre-packaged aeroplane food that is served.

Some children are allergic to, or intolerant of, wheat or dairy produce. If you suspect that your child has tummy troubles after eating a specific type of food, keep a food diary ◆ for a couple of weeks, making a record of when they go to the loo and any other symptoms such as headaches. Having analysed the food diary, if you think you can see a pattern, give your child less of the suspect food, and if this strategy has positive results, ask your doctor to refer you to a paediatric dietician for advice on how best to balance your child's diet. It may be something more serious such as coeliac disease ▲ so don't delay in speaking to your doctor if the symptoms don't improve.

Read more on:
◆ *Page 11*
▲ *Pages 180–181*

Pan-roasted Padrón peppers, page 231

Excess wind

Sometimes specific foods can trigger children to be more windy, as can too much spicy or fatty food. Keeping a note of what they eat and how their gut is can give you some pointers, but for use immediately if they've got it now, try some weak fennel tea. You can make your own or use a tea bag. Sometimes resting up, a warm bath or hot water bottle can help, but at other times getting them running around can get air moving in the right direction too.

A word of caution before you start taking specific foods out of your child's diet. I more often see good results with children when we look at a few simple things: Is your child sitting up straight when eating? Slouching makes it uncomfortable to swallow food and they end up swallowing a lot of air at the same time; try to get them to slow down with their eating – hard, I know, but fast eating means they generally put too much food in their mouth and then struggle to swallow it and end up overloading their tummy; try to discourage talking while they're eating, as this helps the digestive system work more efficiently and is less likely to lead to a windy, painful gut; make sure they're sticking to regular mealtimes and not eating too many snacks; look at the section on probiotics ◆, as sometimes wind is caused and aggravated by too many bad bacteria – especially if they've just finished a course of antibiotics or have had a cold; if you're tempted to start cutting out specific food groups since you suspect an intolerance, discuss it with your doctor, who can refer you to a dietitian for help; fennel tea is made with just a teaspoon of fennel seeds – simply infuse in boiling water for a couple of minutes, strain, and allow to cool to the right temperature.

Read more on:
◆ *Pages 110–111*

Upset stomach

If sickness and diarrhoea lasts for more than 12 hours or if you're worried, call your doctor. If your child is being sick and passing loose or watery stools, keep them off food – much as they may cry out for something to eat, the last thing they need is anything inside more inside them, as it'll only come up or pass through again and cause stress to their gut when it's not in great shape. Try to get them to take regular sips of something liquid, as it's important to keep them as well hydrated as possible.

Tummy soothers

If your child has a tummy ache caused by a tummy bug or anxiety, first, I'd reach for ginger. You could try crystalline ginger, which you can buy in health food stores, to chew on, but this can be covered in sugar, so it's better to make fresh ginger tea. Grate some fresh ginger root, place in a small saucepan and cover with boiling water. Simmer for about eight to ten minutes then strain it and add some honey, or a little fresh lemon. If you pop it into their favourite mug to sip, the ginger can dissipate the tummy ache and nausea.

Alternatively try peppermint, which has a strong antispasmodic effect and can take away tummy ache as well as wind: pop a few fresh mint leaves into a teapot and cover with boiling water. Again you can add some honey.

Finally Peter Rabbit's favourite, chamomile tea. You can either use a tea bag and let it infuse for three to five minutes, or use the dried flowers, which I like and which you can get from good health food shops. The dried flowers make a sweeter, honey-like tea – use just a pinch of the dried flowers and infuse in the boiling water for three to five minutes. Chamomile is also great for calming children down if they've come back from a party wired, or if they're over-tired and bouncing off the walls.

Honey

You may be a little curious as to why I said I didn't recommend crystalline ginger coated with sugar for kids, but on the other hand suggest adding honey to their tea. The reason for this is that although honey can be just as calorific as sugar, and when eaten on its own it can stick to teeth and cause tooth decay, when it's added to tea it loses its stickiness, so it shouldn't be as damaging for children's teeth. Honey also contains a few B vitamins, and when it's diluted in tea, your child won't get the same sugar hit as when chewing a sweet. If they have a sore throat caused by a virus, a teaspoon of room temperature honey, on its own, is the way to help them get over it.

Warning! Children under one year old shouldn't be given honey, as it may cause infant botulism.

Attention Deficit Hyperactivity Disorder

It's pretty likely that there will be one or two children in your child's year group (boys are four times as likely to have the condition than girls) that, rightly or wrongly, have this label attached to them. If the classic symptoms of Attention Deficit Hyperactivity Disorder (ADHD) – insomnia, lack of concentration, moodiness and frequent destructive outbursts – sound familiar, then the first step is to talk to your doctor who can refer you to a paediatric team for expert assessment and advice. Although you may recognise traits and behaviour patterns which suggest to you that your child has ADHD, don't slip into the mistake of self-diagnosing, or equally accept a doctor's first diagnosis and drug prescription without having your child properly assessed by a specialist. It's far too easy to put the wrong label on a child, which will only result in incorrect treatment when perhaps psychological or nutritional therapy could be more effective.

It has to be said that some of the studies into the relationship that food plays in altering mood and behaviour throw up mixed results, but from my experience and those of many colleagues working in this area, changing the diet of children with ADHD can make a noticeable difference. Since the side-effects of dietary and behavioural change (apart from being hard work and needing lots of determination) are minimal, I urge all parents of children with ADHD or other behavioural issues to look at some key aspects of their diet. The first area to focus on is the general overall healthiness of the diet: small, frequent, healthy meals, lots of water, fresh fruits and vegetables and a high intake of essential fatty acids. It is also essential to strip out the baddies – too many of the high-GI foods and additives. With careful fine tuning of the diet, I have turned children with huge behavioural issues around, and the results can be literally life-changing.

Replacing high GI foods with wholegrains

Read more on:
◆ Pages 154–155

Smoked mackerel
pâté, page 224

Despite the fact that many parents swear that sugary foods turn their little ones wild, there is little scientific evidence to prove that they have a bad effect on behaviour. But my feeling is that since foods that are highly processed, overly sweet or have a high glycaemic index (GI) have little to offer nutritionally, it is worth trying a lower GI diet ◆. This may just help to reduce some of the symptoms, but will also benefit their health in so many other ways, such as making them less likely to be overweight and suffer from tooth decay. High-GI foods don't just include the obviously sweet foods like biscuits and cakes. In fact, as you will read throughout this book and see from many of the pudding and cake recipes, if you use wholegrain ingredients and use fruits as a base, you can make something scrumptious which shouldn't have as negative effect on their blood sugar levels as a refined, processed biscuit. It's also worth looking at starchy foods — white rice, white bread and boiled potatoes — to see if changing to wholegrain versions brings about any benefits as although the GI value in wholegrain versions of these food is still high, they offer a lot of other nutritional benefits and don't tend to have the same negative effects. I often warn my patients that changing their child's diet might make them more moody or lethargic to begin with, but this is just the stage of being weaned off the rapidly absorbed sugars. Within a few days they should start to find a more consistent energy level and hopefully you'll see some other positive mood and behavioural effects too.

Additives

Manufacturers put some additives in our foods to stop them going off and to give good texture, but when it comes to children and additives, I try to keep well away from tartrazine (E102), quinoline yellow (E104), sunset yellow (E110), carmoisine (E122), ponceau 4R (E124), allura red (E129) and sodium benzoate (E211). Both studies and my own experience have shown that kids who eat a diet free of these additives (in addition to looking at other areas of their diet and lifestyle) are much healthier, more evenly behaved and can concentrate better.

The salicylate issue

On rare occasions, children with ADHD have reacted to a group of naturally occurring chemicals known as salicylates. In such cases they should be referred to a paediatric dietitian. If you suspect a problem, you may want to try removing the salicylate-rich foods — apples, oranges, nectarines, tangerines, grapes, cherries, cranberries, peaches, apricots, plums, prunes, raisins, almonds, tomatoes, cucumbers, peppers — from your child's diet just for a few weeks to see if behaviour improves. It's a huge list of healthy foods, but if you notice your child craving and eating a lot of any item on the list, just try reducing the quantity to a more balanced amount into their overall diet. (I have to say that tomatoes are the only thing on the list that I've really experienced as a trigger.)

The goodies

Finally, but very importantly, one of the most exciting areas of research into the relationship between foods and behaviour focuses on getting children to eat more of the oily fish that are rich in omega-3 fatty acids ◆. The reason why oily fish come to the rescue is that they contain beneficial fatty acids, which positively influence the signals that are sent back and forth between the brain and parts of the body. EPA in particular has been shown in many studies to have the power to stabilise mood swings and generally improve mood, behaviour, concentration and learning abilities of children with ADHD. Vegetarian non-fish sources of omega-3 fatty acids aren't the long chain beneficial omega-3 fatty acids that have been shown to be most useful, so if your child is following a vegetarian diet, I would discuss giving them an omega-3 supplement with your doctor.

Sometimes kids with ADHD can have food intolerances, and avoiding these foods (most typically wheat or milk) can improve their behaviour. Ask to be referred to a paediatric dietitian for some professional support. I would stress how useful it is to keep a detailed diary of what your child eats ▲ for a good couple of weeks, as this can give you and any professionals from whom you seek advice a real idea of which foods could be aggravating the child's behaviour. Try to keep the diary as secret as you can, apart from asking them what they've eaten at friends' homes or at school, as they can quickly cotton on and start playing up which muddies the waters!

If this sounds daunting, remember that children with a short attention span will feel positively stimulated, interested and therefore better able to concentrate and behave well if they see their parents preparing different foods and then sitting down to eat as a family – this is just one example of how eating and behaviour modification are intertwined. If there is no way that your child will eat fruit or vegetables, give them a daily multivitamin and mineral supplement (one which lists the dietary reference values for the nutrients and is free of bad additives and E numbers) to ensure that their body receives some nutrients. It's particularly worth looking at zinc and iron supplements as low ferritin (iron store) levels have been associated with higher hyperactivity symptoms in children. This should make them feel better so that in turn their eating habits and behaviour improve.

Read more on:
◆ Pages 17–18 & 101
▲ Page 11

Wholemeal soda bread, page 237

The Middle Years

'What's happening to my body?' is a common thought as we hit our 50s and 60s. We may look in the mirror and see lines appearing, weight piling on and our body shape changing, all of which affects our confidence at a time when most of us need every ounce we can get. Typically both women and men find their middle starts expanding, and yet the bits we wish would preserve their voluptuousness, be this our breasts or bums, seem to lose their peachiness. These changes combined with not having as much get up and go as we used to, and often a lower libido and all that entails, means that the onset of middle age can cause considerable anxiety.

But enough of the doom and gloom – there are so many gorgeous, inspirational, men and women such as Richard Gere, George Clooney, Judi Dench and Isabella Rossellini, who I think are even more attractive now that they have grey hair and 'expression lines', as my darling calls them. In many ways, entering middle age can feel like you are being given a new lease of life. As our grown-up children move away and we prepare for retirement, we still have the energy and enthusiasm for life that keep us vibrant and beautiful. It can be incredible to see a patient turn from someone who feels that all the above changes are inevitable into a person who feels healthier and happier in every respect. I aim to guide you towards the foods that are spot on for your body now that it's entered the middle-aged stage.

Putting on weight

As we age, our body's energy requirement decreases, although there are times – if there are underlying health problems such as recovering from an operation – when the body needs extra. Many people mistakenly think that they are eating and exercising as they have always done, so can start to fill out. You may have seen headlines recently suggesting that according to some studies we should be restricting our calorie intake even more tightly in order to maintain an ideal body weight and body fat measurement. Although we do need to monitor our calorie intake I feel that (a) restricting it even further is not realistic, and therefore even the most determined would feel they were failing and (b) we shouldn't be wavering from the aim of enjoying nourishing, delicious foods. We face plenty of challenges in our work and family lives, and we certainly don't need to add food to our list of worries – food can give the greatest of pleasures at times when lots of things seem like hard work, and we need to retrain our bodies so that we follow healthy eating patterns.

Apple or pear and BMI

The body mass index (BMI) is used to determine whether a person is under or overweight. Although BMI gives us some idea of the health risks associated with being a certain weight for your height, it doesn't take into account a person's body fat content and is not as accurate if you're an athlete, pregnant or breastfeeding, very young or very old. Waist circumference and waist to hip ratios are now believed to be much more reliable measures of future health risk as it's the fat around our middle that poses most danger.

Most of us store body fat in one of two distinct ways – around our hips and thighs, or around our middle. Those who store fat around the middle are often known as having an 'apple shape' or 'beer belly', while those who store fat around the hips and thighs are known as having a 'pear shape'. The shape of your body is directly linked to your risk of poor health. Too much fat around the body increases our risk of developing heart disease, diabetes, stroke, breast and colon cancers, osteoarthritis and emotional problems such as low self-esteem and depression. Over the past few years, scientific research has demonstrated that being an apple shape puts a person's health at greater risk than being a pear.

Effect of hormones

Read more on:
◆ *Page 11*

*Quick Caesar salad,
page 227*

Many of the changes that occur in our bodies in mid-life happen because our hormone balance begins to alter. The hormonal shifts that occur – for example, women's oestrogen levels and men's testosterone levels start to decrease – can mean that men lose muscle bulk, and may start putting on fat around the middle, while women may start noticing a spare tyre forming, or those dreaded bat wings under the arms. Muscle bulk, muscle strength and our skin's elasticity all change, which means we can pile on weight and start changing physically in ways we would prefer not to. Some body changes can be tackled by exercise alone, but mostly it's a combination of a good diet and exercise that gives us the greatest chance of success.

Exercise

Put simply, body fat gets deposited when we take in too many calories and don't burn up enough in our everyday life. We lead such sedentary lives now – I notice that even though I live in the countryside and spend a huge amount of time outside, gardening, walking and cycling Maya to school, there can be days when I find I've sat glued to the computer all day with only my hands doing any activity. We can be shocked at how little exercise and activity we do – in the same way as keeping a food diary ◆, try keeping an activity diary for a couple of weeks and I bet you'll find that your diet is far too high in energy for the amount you expend.

Exercise specialists usually recommend a combination of muscle development and aerobic fat-burning exercise, such as running, swimming, cycling and brisk walking, as not only do toning and muscle development exercises such as lifting light weights, yoga and pilates improve posture and body shape, but our metabolic rate can rise as our muscle mass increases. If we combine this with cardiovascular exercises, which are good fat-burners, slowly but surely our metabolic rate will climb and our body shape will start to head in the direction we want it to. People often worry about their weight, but in fact more health risks are linked to how much body fat we're carrying than what the scales say – this is certainly the case with heart disease, diabetes and certain cancers, specifically breast cancer. Okay, joints don't like having to work extra hard and energy levels might be lower if we're having to hoik a heavier body around, but if our weight is largely muscle and we're keeping our body fat levels within the ideal range it's highly likely our body's not going to run into half the health problems it would do if it was carrying too much fat.

Watch what you eat and drink

The easiest way to reduce our body fat level is to take a careful look at the concentrated sources of calories. The obvious one is fat, but it's not that simple – and indeed we need some good fats in our diet at this stage in life, to protect our bones, heart, etc. We need to look at the amount of refined sweet foods we're eating, and at our portion sizes of all foods – even if we're talking about a full-of-fibre wholemeal bread sandwich, if we eat too much of a good thing then our weight and our body fat will just stay too high.

The most calorie-dense foods are those rich in fat and sugar. On the sugar side, women going through hormonal changes may find they get raging sugar cravings that can get them into all sorts of trouble, as they're often pretty addictive and only satisfying for a few moments. We know how at different times in our menstrual cycle our body can crave sugar or chocolate, and the menopausal oestrogen shifts can sometimes bring these all back again even more strongly. You'll be particularly prone to sweet cravings if you're struggling with the emotional changes encountered at this stage of your life. In short I'd try avoiding all sweet foods other than fresh fruits. Go cold turkey on them all – you may well be shouting and looking at the biscuit and chocolate shelves like a crazed person for a few days, but if you keep walking, chanting a mantra or doing whatever helps to distract you, within 48 to 72 hours you'll be past the danger zone and won't need half as much will-power to resist. Alternatively, some people find sniffing a vanilla pod or essence good for breaking the sweet craving.

With our decreasing metabolic rate we sometimes don't need the same amount of food. Just step back and have a look – keep a food and emotions diary for couple of weeks and see if you're perhaps eating more than you need, not really through greed but because of the simple fact that you have always eaten this much. It could be that if you serve yourself less and eat it slowly, you could cut down your food intake enough to ensure your weight and body fat levels stay in check.

Not only is alcohol incredibly high in calories but it increases our appetite, takes away our will-power to eat well, and has a tendency to make us pile on fat around the middle – the beer belly shape. Plus the health risks of drinking too much ◆, are serious and, particularly with women, underestimated and taken far too lightly. I'm not trying to come across as a killjoy, but it can be astonishing how cutting right down on the amount we drink, can have a very positive effect. It can help with decreasing body fat levels, increasing energy, improving sleep (helpful in combating hot flushes, anxiety, snoring or sleep apnoea), boosting our self-esteem and making us feel far younger in body and mind. I don't buy the excuse that there is so

Read more on:
◆ *Pages 42–43*

much social pressure in and out of the workplace to drink like a fish – there's too much known about the health risks of drinking too much, and work ethos has altered so that boozy lunches can easily be got around if there's a will to change.

Worrying weight loss

So often we associate hitting middle age with gaining too much weight, but this isn't always the case. Stress, depression, anxiety and unhappiness over the way our body is changing, along with the complexities of life around us (be this children leaving home, or parents becoming ill or dying), or being faced with a diagnosis ourselves, can all make the way we eat move in the opposite direction.

Weight loss without any obvious reason should always be checked with your doctor even if you're not feeling unwell in any other way. If you are suffering from depression, although it may seem a bonus to shift a few pounds at first, losing too much weight and not eating properly is only going to make it harder to come out the other side. Eating can be the last thing on your mind, and some drugs prescribed for depression can put you off your food, but try not to slip into poor eating habits ◆.

If your weight is dropping too low and your appetite is off, often it's a case of forcing yourself to eat a little. Take up any invitations from friends and family to join them at mealtimes, and if they offer to stock up your fridge say yes! Not eating enough and low blood sugar levels will make you feel weak and reduce your appetite further, so it could be that small meals, almost snacks, will suit you better. But make sure they're nourishing – much better to have a slice of wholemeal bread with good-quality peanut butter and a small banana than a packet of biscuits.

Read more on:
◆ Pages 47–51

Menopause

Many of us dread the word 'menopause', but I actually prefer it to the term 'change', which can make women feel that they shouldn't talk about the fact that their body is entering a new phase in their life. The menopause affects women in completely different ways, but the most common symptoms include hot flushes, sweating, insomnia, anxiety, impairment of memory and fatigue. Long-term consequences can include a decline in libido, osteoporosis, heart disease, even dementia, all linked to reduced oestrogen levels. The reason we now

Menopause | 125

even hear people refer to the time leading up to the menopause as the peri-menopause is, I think, thankfully a result of women feeling more comfortable to discuss such a sensitive time in their lives.

The usual age to start going through the menopause is when we hit our late 40s or early 50s and it seems to have a more profound effect on women's bodies and the way they feel than men. Some women can sail through with only the odd hot flush, but others have a pretty miserable time: weight seems to pile on, emotions are all over the place and their body can start to look and feel old and tired. The physiological reason why the body starts changing in such a way is largely down to a drop in oestrogen production – but as with most hormones, once one of them starts to alter it can have a knock-on effect on other hormones. Some menopausal symptoms such as lack of libido and vaginal dryness can be exacerbated by low testosterone levels, so sometimes testosterone therapy can be given alongside the more common oestrogen and progesterone therapies. Indeed, having adequate testosterone helps us to maintain strong healthy bones and good levels of HDL cholesterol ◆. Women usually produce enough testosterone from their adrenal glands to ensure that these health benefits are covered, but it could be worth discussing with your gynaecologist whether a little testosterone top-up could ease menopausal misery. With the male menopause, testosterone therapy may help too.

Female menopause

Two very important health issues come into the spotlight during these menopausal years. First, lower oestrogen levels can reduce our bone density by as much as two or three per cent during the five or so years after the menopause. This may not sound much in percentage terms, but it can be significant enough to put bones at a far greater risk of fracture as a result of developing osteoporosis ▲.

Second, it is the female hormones that provide a level of protection against heart disease and storage of fat around the waist. As women approach the menopause, their oestrogen level drops dramatically, so this protective effect disappears and puts the body at a similar risk to men. Women who are a pear shape may also find that their body changes into more of an apple, and weight starts to gather around the middle, increasing the risk of developing type 2 diabetes ●. Although it can appear to be less serious than type 1, studies are in fact now finding that this type of diabetes can cause blindness and kidney, heart and circulation problems when blood sugar levels aren't controlled. Since type 2 usually remains undiagnosed for longer, the likelihood is that the higher blood sugar

Read more on:
◆ Page 29
▲ Page 130
● Page 157

Beans with tomato, coriander & coconut milk, page 215

levels will have a considerable amount of time to cause damage. Insulin-dependent type 1 diabetics tend to be regularly monitored by doctors and dietitians, and the issue of having to inject themselves tends to make sufferers take their health more on board, whereas type 2 diabetics can be a little more laissez-faire, leading to all sorts of problems. The good news is that we can make a dramatic difference to our likelihood of developing any of these conditions simply by watching the way we eat, treat our bodies and lead our lives.

Many women associate menopause and diet with soya and phytoestrogens – nature's oestrogen mimickers. There seems to be an absence of menopausal symptoms, in countries where diets are naturally rich in phytoestrogens, such as the Far East and Japan. This doesn't mean that one is responsible for the other or that Westerners metabolise and benefit from the phytoestrogenic foods in the same way. Genetics and environmental factors play a huge part in how our bodies react to specific foods, so as yet we can't say whether a diet rich in phytoestrogenic foods is beneficial to women going through the menopause or not. But it could be worth a try if you're really struggling, and indeed there are some positives about including some of these foods even if they don't have much of a positive effect on the symptoms you're trying to relieve: they're usually high in fibre and protein, low in saturated fats, and some women prefer the taste of soya milk to cow's milk. If you are vegetarian or vegan, soya-based foods like soya milk, soya yogurt, tofu, miso and tempeh can be an invaluable part of your daily routine. The sort of level some women seem to find beneficial is if they drink a couple of large glasses of soya milk each day. You might want to think about one of the calcium-enriched soya milks, because they can also be useful for helping to abate some of the bone effects of the menopause.

If soya isn't your thing, other sources of phytoestrogens include pulses (lentils, chickpeas, beans, etc.), beansprouts, peanuts, linseeds (flaxseeds) and yams (sweet potatoes). We don't know how much you need to eat to glean any benefits, which is frustrating and you also need to bear in mind that too many legumes such as lentils and beans may make you feel bloated. Fortunately this is usually just in the short term, as your body will adapt to these wondrous high-fibre foods so it's worth persevering. Research is far more definite about showing that when you're going through the menopause there is a lot to be said for focusing your diet around a variety of fruits and vegetables (I would try to have about eight portions a day, if you can). You should also aim to eat up to four 140g portions of omega-3-rich foods a week ◆, as these can help ease some of the hormone-induced symptoms such as hot flushes, breast tenderness and mood swings. Some women find cutting out caffeine helps the symptoms – studies don't back this up, but I'd still give it a try.

Read more on:
◆ Pages 17–18 & 101

Chicken & chickpea burgers, page 220

As you will have read at the beginning of this chapter, one of the most significant issues to watch when you enter this time in your life is not overdoing the calories, as not only is weight gain far more likely but your metabolism also changes. It's important when you're looking at beneficial foods such as oily fish that you cook them lightly and incorporate them into a light and healthy nourishing diet; piles of smoked salmon on a bagel smothered in cream cheese isn't going to help ease any hot flush – it'll just find its way right down to your midriff and stay there! If you can lose some pounds by eating little and lightly, the likelihood is that many menopausal symptoms will become less noticeable.

Male menopause

Although the way we eat and the amount of exercise we do can have a significant impact on how our bodies look and feel during middle age, hormonal changes that occur in a man's body can also be a major player. It's only been in the last few years that we've started talking about men's hormones, which may in part be down to the fact that there is now a male HRT, which doctors are becoming more familiar with. Men don't tend to suffer in silence or accept that low energy levels, a changing body shape, poor libido and sexual ability should be something just to put up with – and quite right too.

Hormone replacement therapy (HRT) is one option to consider if you have low testosterone levels, but first I just want to point you back to the beginning of this chapter to have a look through the nutritional watch points. Some of the symptoms you experience as a man when you hit middle age may not be down to a hormonal imbalance – it could be the way you're eating drinking and living. Getting fatter, feeling sluggish, low in mood, etc. need not be inevitable – I see many patients in their mid-50s or 60s who at first are resigned to the fact that it's middle age, yet within a few weeks they can turn the situation around.

Men can be brilliantly focused on getting their body into shape once they make the decision to do so – it's often a company medical showing up high LDL cholesterol or a friend being diagnosed with a heart problem or cancer, which can be the kick up the backside. Traditionally women still do a lot of the food shopping, cooking and organising, which can of course make it easier if they get on board with the lifestyle and food changes. It doesn't take long to experience the benefits – even a few days of eating well and exercising can get you off the starting block to feeling younger and fitter, which when you're talking about libido, sexual function and energy levels can have a big impact.

Supplements and herbal remedies

Supplements and herbal remedies that are rich in phytoestrogens are marketed at combating menopausal symptoms. However, there is limited evidence as to whether a diet rich in phytoestrogens helps relieve symptoms such as hot flushes, so I'd urge you to discuss taking any herbs or supplements with your doctor or clinical dietitian. Some herbal remedies have been found to contain high levels of toxic metals and even steroids, and they can interfere with other medication, so it's not something to be dabbled with.

Some women swear by herbal remedies such as black cohosh, dong quai and ginseng for helping them through this rocky hormonal time, but others find they make no difference, which can be disappointing, especially when you're trying to stay away from the conventional hormonal replacement therapies.

Bone health

Bones continue to grow in density (with a good and continuous supply of calcium and vitamin D) until our late teens and early 20s. This is a particularly crucial stage in our bone health, so we should make a point of encouraging healthy eating and living at a time when many young people think that they can throw caution to the wind and not worry about it. If we build strong bones while we're young we reduce the risk of our bones becoming fragile when we're older. The effects of what we eat on our skeleton are powerful and wide-ranging. It's absolutely critical that we look at how we can optimise our bone health much earlier on in our lives in order to reduce the rate and impact of bone diseases such as osteoporosis. We tend to think of bones as being inanimate and something we can't really influence, but in fact our skeleton is very much a living part of us: bone cells are busy throughout our lives manufacturing new bone, and this process, although most evident in childhood and the teenage years, continues to be vitally important throughout the rest of our lives.

Often we only start to think about our bones when we enter middle-age and doctors start suggesting bone scans or instigating discussions as to whether taking hormonal replacement therapy (HRT) is for you — bone protection is one of the benefits offered by HRT. Even if you don't have a high risk of osteoporosis, since this disease is largely preventable and at least the impact and severity of it can be reduced by eating and living well, this can be a good time to check up on how you're nourishing your bones.

Osteoporosis

Osteoporosis (also known as brittle bone disease) is a disease of the bone which is characterised by a low bone mass and deterioration in the structure of the bone which ultimately causes the bones to become fragile and more likely to fracture. Not only can osteoporosis cause a great deal of pain and discomfort, especially when fractures happen, but also the costs of looking after people who suffer osteoporotic fractures (most commonly the hips, wrists and spine) are enormous. Yet it is largely preventable — how we eat, live and exercise has an enormous impact on how healthy our bones are. Therefore, by looking at nutritional factors that influence how dense and how fragile our bones are, this gives us a real way forward in trying to reduce the risk of suffering from osteoporosis.

We need to pay particular attention to our bone health after the age of 50 because, particularly in women when we reach the menopause, our bone density rapidly decreases — we lose an average of about 2–3 per cent over the next five to ten years, the loss being at its greatest in the early post-menopausal years ◆. There is a strong genetic link that can place us more at risk of developing osteoporosis, while smokers, people who aren't physically active (couch potatoes as they're so often referred to), people who have a lower than ideal body weight or eating disorder, people with bowel and digestive or kidney problems, or have to take regular medication such as corticosteroids or anti-convulsants are also more at risk than others.

Calcium for healthy bones

Dairy produce has always been highlighted as the best source of calcium, but some people can't take it, either because they have a lactose intolerance or are allergic to cow's milk protein, while others just don't like eating dairy foods. Luckily, there are a few other sources to tuck into, which lately we've found to be pretty good at providing the body with easily-absorbed calcium ▲.

One frequent dilemma women can struggle with is balancing the need to eat enough calcium-rich foods to keep up their bone density without having too much high-saturated dairy food, which can

Read more on:
◆ *Pages 125–128*
▲ *Page 20*

Roast mackerel with potatoes & thyme, page 223

Read more on:
◆ Page 29
▲ Page 20
● Pages 20–21

Cauliflower cheese,
page 217

increase levels of LDL cholesterol ◆. Lower-fat dairy foods can be helpful as they not only contain less saturated fat and therefore don't increase your production of LDL cholesterol but in fact, low-fat milks contain slightly more calcium than the full-fat versions.

I'm generally not a lover of low-fat products, as I think the taste falls down and some heavily-processed low-fat foods can be filled with sugar to make up for the missing taste bud-satisfying fat. To get the right balance, choose a dairy food that tastes good, such as a natural yoghurt or fromage frais. The fat content of yoghurt seems to vary a lot – from the runny no-fat variety, which I find disappointing, to the Greek-style yoghurts which can be up to 12 per cent fat. Although they're higher in fat I tend to go for the latter, as they're more satisfying, so you don't feel the need to eat so much. The best solution would be to find something in the middle that you enjoy.

Cheeses that are lower in fat include Gouda, Emmental, Parmesan, fromage frais, fresh feta, ricotta and cottage cheese. The fat content of goat's and sheep's milks varies, but it's harder to source lower-fat versions of these less popular dairy milks. The non-dairy sources of calcium ▲ are all good things to include in your diet, but I don't think their contribution is good enough to meet your calcium requirement at this stage in your life, especially if you have low bone density or have been diagnosed with osteoporosis.

Vitamins and minerals

Our bones need magnesium ● and although, I'm not fond of counting our food in milligrams of this or micrograms of that, the recommended daily intake for magnesium is 270mg for women and 300mg for men, which equates to 66g of Brazil nuts or 100g of pine nuts. This is an awful lot to incorporate into your diet, so it may be where a combined calcium, magnesium and vitamin D supplement could work for someone who has low bone density, other strong risk factors, or for anyone who doesn't eat much dairy.

Vitamins K and D are also essential for bone health. If you're over 65 and can't absorb enough vitamin D from the sun, you need to take 10mcg. If you suspect that your vitamin D status may be low or you have low bone density, discuss the issue of taking a supplement before you reach this age with your doctor.

Caring for our bones

We all need some fat in our diet to support the absorption of essential vitamins and some minerals, but we also need to have

Read more on:
◆ Pages 17–18
▲ Page 46

enough fat on our bodies to ensure that the hormonal environment is conducive to helping to protect our bones. A small amount of fat on your body helps to cushion the effect of a fall, making a fracture less likely, but too much fat hinders the way we can move. Falling when we're overweight can place an enormous load on our bones and therefore increase the risk of a fracture, and we can be less successful at manoeuvring our body into a safer falling position. It helps to ensure that your body weight is within the ideal range and that the type of fat you choose is as healthy as possible ◆. Although studies don't yet tell us why, it's thought that the fatty acids within oily fish and the vegetable-based oils help to support good bone health.

It's another place where the studies don't give us strong evidence either way, but we do know that high salt intakes have been associated with an increase in the amount of calcium we lose in our urine. If we bear in mind that too much salt also has a negative effect on our heart health, I think it's a good opportunity to see how you can keep your intake down ▲.

Bones don't like too much alcohol. Chronic alcohol abuse tends to damage the cells that manufacture new bone and also interfere with the way our livers behave, which can have a profound impact on the metabolism of key nutrients such as calcium and vitamin D.

Finally, too much caffeine isn't good either, as it can interfere with the amount of calcium we absorb, so enjoy a small amount of good-quality caffeine-rich food or change to something caffeine-free. Some people I see with diagnosed low bone density or osteoporosis, or who really want to maximise the amount of calcium their body can absorb, prefer to give up caffeine altogether. But equally, studies don't show that a couple of caffeine drinks a day will do any harm to your bones.

Weight bearing exercise

Smoking and being inactive can severely harm your bones, and it's particularly important on the exercise side to include some load-bearing exercise – brisk walking, jogging, running, aerobics, boxing – something in which your body is placing a downward load on your bones. Yoga and Pilates can help you to move more easily and protect yourself from falling badly so do have a role to play in reducing the risk of fracture. However, when it comes to their efficacy at stimulating the bone cells to manufacture new healthy bone, they are not as efficient as load-bearing exercise. I would suggest a combination of different types of exercise, some load-bearing and some to increase your flexibility.

Tahini

Tahini is a thick paste made out of sesame seeds that's commonly used to make Middle Eastern dishes such as hummus, babaganoush (roasted aubergine dip) and halvah (a very sweet dessert). I prefer to go for the Greek or Lebanese brands rather than those in health food shops and supermarkets, which use unhulled sesame seeds and tend to be overpowering and heavy. It conveniently keeps for weeks in the fridge if sealed, but will go rancid if left opened in a warm cupboard. It's a source of calcium, but also of some protein, B vitamins, iron and essential fatty acids. However, it's laden with sesame oil, which, although mainly the healthier type of unsaturated fat, is hefty in calories, so don't overdo it.

I like to make it into a sauce by taking 150ml of tahini paste along with the same amount of water, 80ml lemon juice, two peeled cloves of garlic and a pinch of salt, and mixing them all together in a blender until smooth and creamy. Then I add about 25g of finely chopped flat-leafed parsley and mix well. I use this sauce on vegetables or as a sort of pesto-style dressing for salads or on cooked roast meats like chicken.

Water and waterworks

Ideally, you should continue to drink a couple of litres of water every day. However, you may find that as your bladder, kidneys and pelvic floor muscles (for men the prostate gland) age, your ability to do anything other than visit every public convenience in the country is compromised! Women can strengthen their pelvic floor muscles by doing regular exercises, which should help you to cope with drinking a lot of water. Night-time waking and needing to go to the bathroom can be troublesome even if you don't drink that much, so you may well find that if you suddenly up your water intake in the hope of having all the health benefits of being well hydrated, going to the toilet all the time becomes a real pain. I would suggest that you take a few weeks to increase your water intake gradually – concentrating the increase during the day, as opposed to downing a lot with your evening meal. This gives the kidneys time to acclimatise to the increase in water intake, so that eventually you should be able to drink close to the ideal two and a half litres a day without too much disruption to sleep ◆.

Read more on:
◆ *Pages 40–42*

Reducing our health risks

Avoiding the diseases we dread, such as cancer, heart disease, dementia and diabetes, can sometimes seem an overwhelming and impossible task. However, there are specific nutrients and foods that are particularly good for helping us do this if other aspects of our lifestyle, and health or strong genetic factors, make us vulnerable. But the pillar principles – eating at least five portions of fruits and vegetables a day and small amounts of good fats etc. – are essential before we begin to look at other areas of our diet.

Healthy brain

Read more on:
◆ *Pages 201 & 207–209*
▲ *Page 46*

The reason I wanted to mention dementia in this chapter is simply because so many aspects of it – the diagnosis, treatment and day-to-day living with the disease – should be addressed as early as possible. Some of the drug treatments can have quite profound effects on slowing down the disease, and when it comes to nutrition, as with so many scenarios in our lives, the better nourished we are, the less likely it is that other complications will arise and the healthier, stronger and happier we'll feel. I cover it in much more detail in the last chapter ◆ but I think we can do a huge amount in our 50s and 60s to prepare our bodies for old age. Having a healthy body not only reduces the risk of developing certain diseases, but the symptoms are more manageable and we recover more quickly.

Watch your salt intake

Ensure that the amount of salt you eat is reasonable ▲, as the risk of both high blood pressure and other heart-related problems increases with age. Too much salt can cause high blood pressure, and also aggravates bone loss and fluid retention, which some women find is a side-effect of taking HRT. Our feet can swell more than they used to when we were younger, which can be a sign of heart or other health problems, so if it's persistent check in with your doctor.

Bother with bowels

You may find that as your hormone levels alter your bowel habits also start to change – typically you may have been as regular as clockwork until you hit this middle-aged zone. The majority of bowel problems can be sorted by tweaking your diet, but it's worth finding out about constipation and irritable bowel syndrome (IBS) ◆.

Bowel cancer affects thousands of people and claims many lives every year, yet is completely curable if caught early and treated quickly. If you're at all worried by your change in bowel habit or have bleeding, abdominal pain or have lost a lot of weight and feel exhausted, see your doctor – the words 'bowel' and 'cancer' aren't often talked about, and it can lead to some people going around with symptoms which should be investigated but aren't. Don't just think it's IBS and something you have to put up with.

Preventing cancer

Developing cancer continues to be one of the most common worries we harbour about our health, and the anxiety increases as we get older – not just because cancer risk increases with age, but because it's pretty likely that even if we don't suffer from cancer ourselves, we know someone who has it now or has had it in the past. In fact it's estimated that more than one in three of us will develop some form of cancer at some point in our lives, so its impact continues to be significant.

The incidence of the different cancers varies hugely, but the four most common cancers (breast, lung, bowel and prostate) make up over half of all cases. A lot is talked about breast cancer, and it continues to be one of the most common types, but I also want to highlight the enormous number of people who are diagnosed with bowel cancer every day, with men and women being fairly equally affected. However, despite numerous campaigns and headlines being placed across the news broadsheets, we still seem to have an inordinate problem in talking about bowels. When a woman finds a lump in her breast she is highly likely to get straight on to seeing her doctor, but the problem with bowel cancer is that we often don't feel a lump. Since our gut is so often changeable, from times when we're completely fine to when constipation causes us grief or food seems to go straight through us, to go and talk to a doctor about our bowels just doesn't come easily to many of us. Often, therefore, the disease goes undiagnosed for a long time, and I fear that more and more people will go on without noticing the symptoms ▲ or addressing the problem. So it's up to us to become more familiar with our bodies and to be persistent with seeking the right specialist care if we have any worries over our bowels.

A massive two-thirds of bowel cancer cases could be prevented by eating, drinking and living well, but this is not to say that if you are

Read more on:
◆ *Pages 181–182*
▲ *Pages 139*

Fruity beetroot cake, page 251

diagnosed with bowel cancer or any other type you should think it's all down to the way you've been living your life. Cancer is a complex disease, and there are many, many factors that influence whether or not you get it. Smoking should perhaps be put in a box of its own, since we all know that being a smoker takes your risk of developing cancer right up. To throw a figure around, smoking 20 cigarettes a day increases your risk of developing lung cancer by a massive 2,000–4,000 per cent, but our genes, where we live and the type of work environment we're exposed to, also play a large part.

We do know that by eating a certain way we can significantly reduce our risk of some types of cancer. The strongest links between cancer risk and what we put into our mouths is with bowel cancer, but it also applies to other parts of our digestive system, from the mouth, throat and stomach to the most common type of cancer, breast cancer.

The 'cancer-preventing' storecupboard

Surprise, surprise, fruits and vegetables are at the top of the list! As with all areas of science, studies differ in how effective certain foods are in preventing cancer. We do know, however, that eating healthily – and particularly fruit and vegetables – help to reduce the risk of certain cancers, including those of the mouth, throat, stomach and lung. We don't know exactly why, but they house a plentiful supply of nutrients and what we call bioactive substances (these are in a way 'super nutrients' found in plants which have a very positive effect on our health). It's the combination of all these nutrients that gives these foods specific antioxidant properties, which help reduce the impact of free radicals and cigarette smoke, which can trigger abnormal behaviour within cells and lead to cancer developing.

Fibre seems to be a key component in reducing the risk of certain cancers, particularly bowel cancer, because of its stool-bulking effect. Producing an easy-to-pass stool decreases the amount of time that waste products and toxins, which can cause some cell changes, spend in the bowel. Fibre also undergoes useful fermentation (brought about by the presence of bacteria) in the bowel, and in doing so produces what we call short-chain fatty acids, including one type called butyrate. This may all begin to sound a little complicated, but the long and the short of it is that fermentation protects the cells from changing in the wrong way – so fibre on all fronts should be something we treasure in our diet ◆. So we should be eating a plentiful supply of fruits and vegetables – this is where the five-a-day mantra comes from ▲, as we know this is the sort of level we should be getting through.

Read more on:
◆ *Pages 30–32*
▲ *Page 16*

Detecting bowel cancer

If you notice any of the following changes and they last longer than four to six weeks you should report them to your doctor. These symptoms are unlikely to be caused by cancer, but it's better to play safe.

- Bleeding from the bottom without any obvious reason.
- A persistent change in bowel habit to looser or more frequent bowel motions.
- Tummy pain, especially if severe.
- A lump in your tummy.

You will see many adverts for vitamins and minerals which imply that they hold the answer to staving off diseases such as cancer. I can understand that it may appear easier and more scientific to take a pill, but not only do we know that the body finds it easier to absorb some nutrients when they're eaten as part of a normal diet, but research shows an increased risk of some cancers in people taking specific antioxidant supplements in large doses. This is not to say that taking a general standard multivitamin or mineral is going to harm you, but neither is it going to benefit you as much as eating a diet rich in fruits and vegetables.

Does meat cause cancer?

The two words 'cancer' and 'meat' seem to have appeared together in many health headlines, but it's a bit more of a complex relationship than it can initially appear. While studies have suggested that a high consumption of red or processed meat – bacon, ham – is linked with an increase in the risk of colorectal (or bowel) cancer, the evidence is a lot stronger for a link between a diet heavy in processed meats than if we ate some really good-quality lean steak a couple of times a week. There is a huge difference between a diet of processed poor-quality meat (whoever wants to eat that stuff anyway?) and the quality kind, but good-quality lean red meat seems to have been thrown into the same pot as the poor-quality, fatty stuff. The reality of being able to eat good-quality meat alongside a diet rich in fruits, vegetables and wholegrains is shown in studies to be completely fine, and indeed lean red meat provides us with some easily absorbed iron and omega-3 fatty acids. Okay, we can get these omegas from oily fish, but there is a lot to be said for including some good-quality lean meat in your diet if you would like to.

There is a wide spectrum of processed meats, from the kind that is not so great for us to eat, to the kind that is not so bad for us as long as we don't eat too much of it. Overall, studies suggest that eating about 50g of processed meat a day (around two slices of ham or a slice of bacon) may increase the risk of bowel cancer by around 20 per cent, but they don't really distinguish whether they're talking about a piece of cheap salami or a slice of well-reared pancetta. So it leaves us a little in the dark – although for me this just makes a stronger case for choosing our meat well and eating a smaller amount of good quality. To put the role some meats can play into perspective, studies suggest that by smoking 20 cigarettes a day our lung cancer risk is 100–200 times greater than the effect of eating more than the recommended amount of processed meat!

In studies too (I don't want this chapter to be too study-heavy, but for me it shows how complex a subject area the whole relationship between cancer and what we eat is), we use the term 'red meat' to include pork, lamb, beef and processed meat. Scientists advise us to limit our consumption of processed meat and to keep our consumption of red meat to 500g a week or less, which gives us real scope for enjoying some delicious meat-based meals. Bear in mind that a bolognese sauce made with 500g of lean, good-quality beef mince should serve six hungry adults.

Salt and cancer

Read more on:
◆ Page 46

Health campaigns highlight the relationship between eating too much salt and ill-health, such as aggravating blood pressure and the loss of calcium from our bones, and attention is also drawn to the role it can play in increasing our risk of developing cancer. As you'll read in numerous sections of this book ◆, I am not an anti-salt queen – for me there is little point in having food which is bland, and sometimes we just need a pinch of salt to bring out great flavours.

When it comes to salt's relationship with cancer, studies are in their infancy, but we've found that the stomach can be more likely to fall prey to cancer if you have a high-salt diet. Smoked foods can be some of the worst culprits – this includes, unfortunately, delicacies such as smoked fish – herring, mackerel and salmon – and rashers of bacon and ham, so watch your consumption of these. There isn't any need to avoid them completely, just be mindful that you should try not to have too much, and should serve them with something fresh like a big, leafy salad packed with lots of raw vegetables.

Give your body a dose of wholegrain goodness as well – I think healthy, nutritious eating is all about knowing that if you have something, say, salty, fatty or sugary, you partner it with a food that is right up there in its almost-holiness. So a few slices of smoked salmon on warm wholegrain bread, served with a big watercress, raw spinach and tomato salad, is far better for you than if you have the same smoked salmon with white bread, a poor quality margarine, and a bag of crisps. This is why I think it's not always altogether helpful to look at labels on processed foods and feel that you have to go for the lower salt version, as sometimes it's bland. I'd rather have a smaller amount of a higher-salt food and make sure that the rest of my diet evens it out.

Cancer and weight

Not so talked about is the relationship that exists between carrying too much weight and cancer, but it's there, and significantly so when we look at specific cancers such as oesophagal, bowel, pancreatic, endometrial (the lining of the womb), kidney, gallbladder and breast (in post-menopausal women). To put a context on the risk, men are a staggering 50 per cent more likely to develop bowel cancer if their weight rises and puts them into the obese zone, while the figure for women is 25 per cent.

As to how much exercise we need to do, while the recommendation is for at least half an hour five times a week, I sometimes think this sort of statement makes us feel as if it's not worth doing any less than this, which just isn't the case. Something is always better than nothing, even if it's cycling to work, or getting off the bus a few stops early and walking. It can be shocking to realise how inactive a life we lead as we try to cram everything in, so think of exercise as a good thing in order to see if you can just make your everyday life less sedate and your cancer risk factor will go down.

The drink factor

I think we've been placing a little too much belief in the powers of the antioxidants which exist within the bottle – both the supplement tablets on the health food shelf and the alcohol we drink. Seldom a week passes without a headline discussing the beneficial antioxidant properties of beer or red wine, the oldest antioxidant shouter. We now know that it's only in the laboratory setting that red wine's antioxidants offer us any real benefits, and I suspect that the other types of alcoholic antioxidants won't fare any better.

Not only is it not good to see alcohol as a cancer preventer, but studies find a convincing relationship between drinking too much alcohol and the development of mouth, throat, oesophagus, liver and bowel cancers. Alcohol is a key factor in increasing the risk of breast cancer in women, and unfortunately we seem to be seeing some pretty worrying drinking habits. Headlines and news items highlight binge drinking teenagers getting into all sorts of trouble, but I'm far more concerned about women in their middle age, as this is a far more private style of drinking, one that seems to have become part of our society. Women can buy wine very easily and cheaply, and it can be so easy to get into the habit of opening a bottle in the early evening or to share a bottle or two when eating out. The strains that life places us under when we hit middle age – elderly parents, children leaving home, a pressurised workplace – can cause the drinking habits of many a woman at this stage in her life to place her at risk of a lot of health issues, and cancer is right up there with them. I say this because I don't think we shout loudly enough about the dangers of drinking, especially for women, and yet ironically some women set their minds at looking to super-nutrients in health food shops but don't think about their alcohol intake ◆.

Read more on:
◆ Pages 42–43

Milk and cancer

There has been a lot of confusing information in the newspapers recently about dairy products and cancer, and in my opinion it's a case of watching and waiting for more clear research to come to light. Recent research shows that a higher intake of calcium (found in dairy products) can protect against bowel cancer, but some early research also suggests that there could be a link between dairy intake and the risk of developing prostate and ovarian cancers. For breast cancer the evidence is conflicting. A link between breast cancer and dairy products has been suggested, possibly because of the saturated fats they contain, or contaminants that could be present, but there is no clear evidence to support this. Another theory is that dairy products might help protect against breast cancer, but again, this needs to be backed up by firm evidence.

A large study called European Prospective Investigation of Cancer (EPIC) is currently looking at the relationship between diet, lifestyle and cancer. It will produce reports on diet and lifestyle and a variety of cancers over the next ten to 20 years, starting with bowel cancer and breast cancer. For the time being I believe that we should continue to include some dairy foods in our diet, as they're such a good supplier of calcium. If we incorporate all the other key food groups like fruits, vegetables and wholegrains, we'll get a good

Read more on:
◆ Page 14
▲ Page 129

spectrum of nutrients which should balance each other out – remember, the healthiest diet is one that includes variety right across the food groups ◆.

Soya and other phytoestrogens

Phytoestrogens are chemicals found in plant foods (phyto means 'plant'). They have a similar structure to the female sex hormone oestrogen and have been found to influence the effects of the menopause ▲. There are different types of phytoestrogens – some are found in soya bean products (isoflavones), whereas others are found in the fibre of wholegrains, fruit, vegetables and flax seed (lignans).

The main type of phytoestrogens in the western diet are lignans – so we're talking about foods like wholemeal bread, fruits and vegetables as opposed to soya bean products, which most of us don't eat that much of. However, these soya isoflavone types of foods seem to be the ones that are attracting the most research, as in certain parts of the world the diet is very heavily soya-based and the results of rates and types of cancers require some in-depth exploration. Whether soya is good or bad seems to be one of the hottest-contested and debated topics surrounding cancer, so I feel it requires a bit of space here.

A joint study was reported in July 2002 by Cancer Research UK, the National Cancer Institute of the USA and the National University of Singapore, which found that women with a soya-rich diet had breast tissue that was less dense than that of women with a low-soya diet. Higher density breast tissue has been linked to a higher risk of breast cancer, so this is the first study to directly link eating soya with an effect on breast tissue. Asian women, who eat the highest amount of soya foods, were found to have a lower risk of breast cancer. However, it's not clear whether genetic make-up (which influences the way that the body metabolises food) and environmental factors interact with the soya and therefore produce different effects in the body. What we can say is that in other parts of the world, most women do not eat enough soya to reduce their risk of breast cancer.

How to deal with cancer

Food has the power to nourish, so understanding what your body needs can be a key way to enhance the effects of conventional cancer treatment. Focusing on your diet if you have been diagnosed with cancer can be therapeutic in so many ways. It can not only provide key nutrients that can help your body fight the cell changes that cancer triggers, but also being able to take control of something yourself can have a positive effect on how you feel. The challenges you face when you're diagnosed with cancer vary considerably, from having to undergo surgery to enduring chemical or radioactive therapies, and it would be hard to cover them all in this chapter. But I want to take you through a few key ideas I've developed during the time I've been treating people with cancer, in the hope that they inspire you to see food, nutrition and nourishment as something positive and empowering on which to draw.

Some oncologists and cancer care surgeons and physicians don't consider diet to have any positive role to play in cancer treatment, which saddens me, because it's such as shame that some doctors put people off from exploring how food can be a great healer in its holistic sense. Although it's unlikely that eating a specific food will cause any significant change, in its truest medical sense, what you eat can not only support your immune system but can help a great deal with many of the unpleasant side-effects of the treatment, from a sore mouth to feeling sick, puffy, bloated and exhausted. Understanding everything there is to know about food and nutrients can help to relieve suffering and make the difficult relationship between cancer, eating and illness just a little easier. Doctors have hit out at pseudo-nutritionists who tell patients they can fight cancer without the need for medical intervention, and despite us having some supportive findings that the way we eat can have a positive effect on our immune systems, pseudo-nutritionists shouldn't lay claim to this. Of course there are instances when people have turned their back on conventional medicine and eaten their way to recovery by following diets that are bizarre and pure as they see it. We can't explain why these things happen, but turning their back on conventional treatment can be a worrying scenario for many cancer care surgeons and physicians, who would much prefer their patients to see nutritional intervention as a complementary therapy rather than an alternative. And this is exactly where I stand.

Some doctors are also concerned when patients start to blame their cancer on a food they've eaten, or worry when their appetites change. Because the patients have heard from somewhere that white bread and pasta is bad when you have cancer, they can start worrying unnecessarily if they can't stomach wholegrains or any raw fruit or vegetables. Just as we know that nutrition has a positive role to play in helping to get our bodies in the right space to fight cancer, we also know that worry and angst don't do much to help. It doesn't matter if you have some days when you just fancy or can only stomach plain pasta or rice, or can just about manage to eat a biscuit – no food is going to harm you. As to the mad notion that's bandied

Tandoori chicken, page 221

about saying that sugar feeds cancer cells, so you should avoid all forms of sugar (fruit included), this is utter nonsense! All cells need sugar for energy – it's a simple biochemical reaction that supports life in every cell – so to say that you should stop all sources and provision of sugar to your cells, be these cancer or non-cancerous, is as crazy as saying that because all cells require oxygen we should stop breathing to prevent abnormal cell activity. So, let's move on to how best to eat when you're undergoing chemo and biological therapies (including vaccines and monoclonal antibodies), hormone therapies and other cancer drugs.

It has to be said that not all cancer treatments cause side-effects such as sickness and heart burn; how you feel could be down to the cancer itself, or to other drugs you're taking, such as painkillers or antibiotics. It's also important not to assume that sickness is definitely going to happen, or that if it does you should suffer in silence. Managing side-effects of drugs and symptoms is a key part of your oncology team's role, so don't be afraid to keep asking for their advice. After saying all this, feeling sick, even if you're not actually sick, is a pretty common side-effect of many cancer treatments (and of course anxiety can put us off our food too), so the more you can do to try to reduce your anxiety levels the more you may find that the intensity of the nausea waves lessens.

A note on cancer treatment

If you are undergoing treatment for cancer, there may be times when your immune system is particularly challenged – the cancer itself can also reduce your ability to fight what you would normally be able to ward off. So you need to be particularly careful about food hygiene, and also about avoiding the foods that carry a higher risk, such as raw eggs, and unpasteurised dairy products like milk and cheese.

Depending on how compromised your immune system is (your medical team can keep you up to date on your blood results), you may just need to eat cooked fruits and vegetables rather than raw, for the time being. The heat and the time the food is cooked for helps to reduce the bacterial content of food, so it's ideal to just eat freshly prepared cooked foods: a soup made from chicken broth, with some strips of soft chicken breast and noodles can have so much more nourishment in it and be tolerated far better than a chicken nugget cooked by a fast-food outlet. An oaty fruit crumble can give your body some much-needed fibre antioxidants, such as beta-carotene, if you make it with plums and blackberries, while a bowl of fruit compote with some thick Greek-style yoghurt can be refreshing, delicious and full of safe-to-eat goodness.

The case against meat

The production of meat, especially beef, has a profound effect on global warming, not only because it requires astronomical volumes of water to produce but also because gases given off by cattle significantly contribute towards the greenhouse effect. It is always a good idea to consider the meat source and production process, although in reality, this should apply to everything we eat, not just meat.

Globalisation plays a huge role in the meat debate. Supermarkets search far and wide for cheap suppliers, often ignoring the increase in food transportation-related pollution. For example, living in Britain you would ideally choose British over New Zealand lamb and British over Danish bacon, but you may also consider whether or not the produce is organic – it's up to you to decide where your priorities lie. Foreign produce is not to be rejected *per se* – it is sometimes the only option, but try to weigh up the distance it has travelled over your necessity or desire to buy it. The best option is to buy local produce as often as possible, and that really does mean local, as much of the national goods supplied are sent to various different distribution centres all over the country. Don't forget that you're also more likely to receive fresher food if you buy it from local sources.

Since 1950, worldwide production of meat has increased fivefold, yet this is unsustainable – water and soil resources are being polluted and rapidly depleted. Meat is often intensively reared to cut costs, paying no attention to animal welfare. Apart from the question of animal rights, intensively-reared livestock is often kept in unhygienic and unnatural habitats, leaving livestock in a poor condition and reducing the quality of the meat. Crops used for animal feed are routinely grown using huge amounts of fertilisers and pesticides, and the animals themselves are often fed antibiotics to prevent diseases. These can enter the food chain and cause all sorts of problems in humans. In the last few decades, there have been several serious health scares involving meat. Bovine spongiform encephalopathy (BSE), E. coli and salmonella all pose threats to us, particularly to the young and the elderly. Regulations have been put in place to avoid contaminated meat, but the risk cannot be completely removed. If we take action to avoid meat produced in these ways, farmers, supermarkets and governments will be forced to change their policies.

But it's not all bad. Meat is an important part of our economy and an invaluable source of protein. Beef, in particular, is a great source of iron and omega-3 fatty acids. When I look at the ethical and health issues surrounding meat, two or three organic meat meals a week, with a good selection of nutritious vegetables, beans, lentils, wholegrains and fruit, feels about right. Let's not forget that although a good vegetarian diet with lots of beans, lentils, wholegrain, etc. is of course fantastically healthy, a diet full of processed foods such as fried vegetarian sausages, too much dairy and oily pastries, isn't. In fact, a vegetarian diet can be far higher in saturated fats, calories and sugars, and far lower in fibre, etc. than a meat-based diet.

Eating soya when you've been diagnosed with cancer

Although studies still don't give us any clear guidance on eating soya-rich foods if you have been diagnosed with an oestrogen-dependent type of breast cancer, I would suggest staying away from soya as much as possible. A little isn't going to cause anything disastrous, I just mean that you shouldn't choose the soya-rich options on menus, or think about becoming vegan at this stage in your life. Sadly I think the possible downsides of creating an environment that could potentially encourage the growth of these tumour cells far outweighs any potential benefits you may glean from soya. If you're vegetarian this presents a practical hurdle, as so many vegetarian foods are soya-based, so try to focus on lentils, beans, nuts, seeds and grains like spelt and quinoa as good sources of protein, which are all delicious when cooked well.

Nausea

Read more on:
◆ *Pages 71 & 73*
▲ *Pages 61–64*

When experienced as a side-effect of cancer treatments, feeling sick is completely different, but I suggest that you begin by reading about morning sickness during pregnancy ◆, as so many of the tips I give there can help if you feel queasy. Because your immune system is being strained by the cancer and by the potent chemicals being put inside you, it's also very apt to look at the food hygiene issues I mention in the pregnancy section ▲, as the last thing you need is to develop a food-poisoning infection that will make you feel worse and interfere with your treatment. Intake of oily fish should be limited in pregnancy and for women of child bearing age, but this doesn't apply here, so if you fancy some smoked trout or salmon or a little smoked mackerel pâté you can have up to four 140g portions in a week.

I would suggest that you think twice before you start downing the so-called 'supplement drinks' that are on sale in pharmacies for anyone who is experiencing poor appetite or nausea. These high-calorie, high-protein, high-fat drinks can have their role in a minority of situations, when nothing else suits or is available, but they're pretty sickly and can fill you up so that you're not able to eat a nourishing meal later on. If you could have a soup made with a good stock, with some thick Greek yoghurt added to it, served in a beautiful little bowl, this would

Read more on:
◆ Page 11
▲ Page 90

Cauliflower cheese,
page 217

feel far more normal and something all the family can share instead of sipping on a nutri-drink. I feel that we need to gain confidence in real food and how this can be tweaked to fit our cancer treatment.

You may find that nausea comes in waves and certain times of the day are less problematic for eating, so try to keep an open mind and capitalise on those times of the day when you don't feel so sick. We get set in our routines, but you may find that you need to have your evening meal earlier on or that you have five smaller meals instead of your usual three. If you keep a food and symptom diary ◆ as you're going along, this can help you work out how the spectrum of the different foods and nutrients is working out over a 24-hour period.

Remember, though, that your body can do with good supplies of as many of the key nutrient groups as possible, so if you can manage some fruits and vegetables and a few sources of protein as well as what appeals most – toast, pasta, etc. – then this is a real plus. You could find that cooked vegetables suit you more than raw ones, as they aggravate acid levels, but as long as you keep cooking time to a minimum you will still glean some useful vitamins such as vitamin C. In the case of beta-carotene, be reassured that the body is more easily able to absorb it from a cooked carrot than from a raw one – so don't worry that you're not getting much nourishment if all you fancy is cooked fruit and vegetables. Something simple such as a jacket potato stuffed with a little butter, salt and freshly ground black pepper may soothe and appeal.

If you don't feel like chomping your way through a steak or a piece of chicken, think about incorporating protein in something more appealing, such as a small portion of shepherd's pie, which contains all sorts of vegetables as well. Experiment with the topping, which could include cauliflower or carrots as well as the traditional potato. If you're feeling lousy and don't fancy a plate or bowl of anything, then a big mug of clear, consommé-style soup could be both comforting and nourishing.

You could also incorporate egg or nut milks ▲ into pancakes as they provide a little unobtrusive protein. If you can also manage it, a sliver of lean ham or smoked fish, or some pure fruit spread or sliced banana and a little butter on top can be especially nourishing and delicious. We so often just need ideas to get us out of the rut which chemotherapy and being labelled as ill tends to throw us into.

Sore mouth and swallowing difficulties

As with sickness, a sore mouth or an unpleasant taste are pretty common side-effects. One of the reasons why the mouth and the gut tend to be hit hard when we undergo many of the cancer treatments is that the drugs hit the cells, which rapidly divide, and this includes our gut (the skin and the hair being two other targets for a similar reason). As with sickness, discuss it with your doctor to see if your drugs can be tweaked, but if you find that your mouth is sore this can affect the type of foods you feel like eating. Sometimes a mouth can be more sore when it's dry, so drink plenty to keep it moist.

If hard or dry food is a no-go, try dishes like risotto, loosened with plenty of stock or something very saucy like cannelloni or lasagne made with plenty of rich tomato and meat sauce. Soup and noodle dishes can work too and if you use a good base stock and perhaps throw in some soft poached chicken or small prawns, you can have all the key nutrient groups in a delicious, comforting, easy-to-swallow meal.

You may find that softer breads work better, and are even easier without the crusts on. They are easiest to swallow when fresh with plenty of moist fillings inside, such as egg mayonnaise (made with ready-made mayo), cream cheese and very thinly sliced and peeled cucumber. Poached fish such as trout with mayonnaise or a little cream cheese are good too. Salt beef can be very soft, and if you add some thinly sliced tomatoes and a little mild mustard it can make a delicious sandwich.

Try to make soups as nourishing as possible by adding ingredients such as Greek yoghurt, crème fraîche or cream at the end, as this boosts the calorie content, while croutons can add interest if the soup feels too liquidy. One thing doctors worry about when we're undergoing cancer therapies is losing too much weight, as this can alter our blood work and disrupt our body's reaction to the invasive drugs and therapies. Try to keep this in mind and think about what you can add to dishes – olive oil, butter, cream and finely grated Pecorino or Parmesan cheese to puréed and mashed vegetables, for example, or a thick creamy custard made with full-fat milk to stewed fruit, served with a soft melt-in-your-mouth fine buttery biscuit. If porridge is your thing in the morning, make it with full-fat milk and add some cream and brown sugar or honey before serving. Putting a good layer of butter or nut butter on toast could make it easier and more enjoyable to eat, as well as higher in fat and therefore a more intense calorie hit.

Casseroles and tagines tend to produce soft textures and can be a good option if you add some little dumplings or serve them with gnocchi. Cooking meat for a long time, for example a slow-roasted shoulder of lamb, can render the meat ready to melt in the mouth ◆. With fish, the way you cook it can make a big difference, as can the size of the fish – bear in mind that the amount of time and effort you have to put into preparing foods can take the edge off your hunger, so you don't really want to be picking your way through small-boned, fresh sardines, especially if missing a bone could mean you catch what is already a sore mouth or throat. I'd go for larger,

Read more on:
◆ Pages 103–104

Pearled spelt, goat's cheese & chard risotto, page 213

fleshier fish, where the bones are easier to remove, and if you bake or poach them in stock, the flesh can be delicious. An obvious choice would be to make a fish pie, as the creamy sauce and soft, fluffy, buttery mashed potato often hits the spot. They can be made in small ramekins, enough for one or two to share so that one cooking effort can be turned into a few meals that you can freeze and use later, when you're not feeling up to cooking.

Sorbets, ice creams and frozen yoghurts need not be seen as treats but more of a necessity! The coolness can be soothing, but sometimes you may need to let them melt slightly, as anything extremely cold can cause more irritation. Sorbets can be more refreshing, but they're usually lower in calories than ice creams and frozen yoghurts (which, by the way, can be even higher in fat than ice creams). Small pots of sorbet, ready-made ice cream desserts and cold yoghurt or *mousse au chocolat* are worth keeping in your fridge, as they sure beat hospital food! Bear in mind that home-made ice cream sometimes contains raw egg, which can cause salmonella poisoning if your immune system is compromised, so watch out. Do take up offers of having food cooked for you, and let friends and relatives stock up your fridge and freezer, as it's one less thing for you to do. It can also be good for those around us to feel they're doing something helpful, healing and comforting.

Healthy heart

Read more on:
◆ *Page 122*
▲ *Page 157*

Chicken & chickpea burgers, page 220

You probably don't need me to spell out how widespread and costly heart disease is – its effects on our day-to-day lives and our society are enormous. One of the most heartening (excuse the pun) headlines should be that we can in theory have a big role to play in reducing the incidence of cardiovascular disease, as most of the risk factors bar genetics are in our control. We often read about how smoking, high blood levels of the wrong kind of cholesterol and being inactive or overweight – particularly if we're storing fat around the middle ◆ – all increase our risk of developing heart disease, but so does having the less-talked-about type 2 diabetes ▲. There are other risk factors coming to light through research, including high levels of an amino acid called homocysteine, low birth weight, the presence of inflammatory markers and other immune system factors. It's early days for some of the researches to give us clear guidelines, but not for others: we do know that keeping our weight within the ideal range, not smoking, keeping active with a healthy blood pressure, and keeping our blood fats in check, will all make an enormous difference to the risk we place on our hearts and circulation.

Read more on:
◆ *Page 29*

Chicken soup,
page 233

I'm going to focus in this section on how, by eating certain foods, you can get your heart and blood vessels in good shape. The cholesterol story is pretty well documented – too much LDL cholesterol is bad and too little HDL cholesterol isn't the best either ◆. If you're unlucky enough to have already been diagnosed with heart disease, getting your diet in order is even more important. Not only can you help to prevent any further furring up of your arteries, but there is also some evidence to suggest that you could in fact help to reduce any damage that's already been done – so it's never too late to look at eating and living healthily.

Getting the balance right

It's important to look at your diet and the way you're living, even if your doctor puts you on cholesterol-lowering drugs, as reducing your risk of heart disease isn't just about tackling one aspect. In eating and living well you help to reduce the likelihood of any cholesterol depositing in your blood vessels, as well as the chances of experiencing other risk factors such as high blood pressure. If you eat well you're far more likely to feel well and lose any excess weight you put on. I think men especially sometimes think all that matters is their cholesterol level, and for some taking a statin pill seems to be the way to fix the problem. It's more complex than that, but I hope this section inspires you to believe that eating for a healthy heart is easy and delicious, especially since the arrival on our supermarket shelves of great oils such as avocado, rapeseed and hempseed.

It's a good idea to try to get the ratio of the bad and the good sorts of cholesterol right because by eating well we can ensure a good balance: we want a high HDL and a low LDL level. Diet is incredibly important and shouldn't be a hardship or difficult to follow, as we now have such a vast array of produce at our fingertips, either in the supermarket, or if we use the Internet to source small suppliers. What we need to concentrate on is the Mediterranean diet (see below) as this will correct the balance of good and bad cholesterol and provide very useful antioxidants, which help reduce the likelihood of LDL hardening the arteries.

Concentrating on the Mediterranean diet

The Mediterranean diet – from Italy, Spain, France etc. – is what we typically call a diet based around lots (five-plus portions) of fresh fruits and vegetables every day. It incorporates a wonderful variety of colours and types, so we glean a good spectrum of vitamins and beneficial substances our hearts love. It's fine to have favourites and to go through phases when we buy a large amount of something because it's economical, or in season, but it's best not to get into a rut and have too much of any one type of fruit or vegetable all the time. Every fruit and vegetable has something in its favour: some have more vitamin C, others are higher in beta-carotene, another antioxidant, while others are better in the fibre stakes.

It's easy to get into the habit of always buying the same things, so if you're a little stuck in your ways get a few cookbooks out, or tap into websites and food magazines to target a few different fruits and vegetables. I get around the issue of not having too much of one particular fruit or vegetable by using my freezer a lot, not only to buy frozen vegetables like peas, broad beans and spinach, but also to freeze the vegetables I've grown when they're at their best. I make soups, vegetable sauces, casseroles, trays of roasted vegetables, as well as blanching crops like French and runner beans so that they're there in the freezer when I need them at some other time of the year. If you get into this habit you'll also have the advantage of knowing that you've picked your vegetables at their best and frozen them quickly (vitamin C and other vitamin and mineral levels don't diminish much in the freezer, so when you come to eat them they'll still be nutritious). This can also be a way to get the best out of the supermarket 'buy one get one free' offers: even making a large batch of tomato sauce and freezing it in usable quantities can be very economical in both money and time.

You're better off with vegetable rather than animal fats, which need to be kept to a minimum. Olive oil is the classic Mediterranean choice, but try rapeseed, hempseed, and avocado and nut oils, such as walnut oil, in dressings. They contain omega-3 fatty acids, which help to reduce your risk of heart disease even further. Unless you're underweight, use vegetable oil sparingly, in non-stick pans, and drizzle it, perhaps even using a sprayer to minimise the amount. There are as many calories in vegetable oil as there are in butter and it can lead to weight gain, which, especially round your waist, can lead to high blood pressure and heart disease ◆, the last thing you need.

You could consider one of the butter-like spreads rich in plant stanols or sterols, which can reduce cholesterol levels, but I have to say I don't like the taste much. You need around 2g of either stanols or sterols each day (the amount you'd get if you spread one of these margarines on four slices of bread) in order to lower cholesterol by about ten per cent over time. They need to be consumed regularly, but they aren't the only way to lower your risk of heart disease. Some people walk away from their doctor or supermarket thinking as long as they use spreads, drinks or yoghurts containing sterols their hearts will be fine. I don't recommend my patients use them, as I think it's far better to look at being more creative with the food you're eating to achieve your healthy heart goal; but, this said, if you're looking for a few products to help improve your blood cholesterol balance, these are an option.

Read more on:
◆ Page 29

Green olive & parsley focaccia, page 238

Although meat is lambasted as not being desirable on the menu if you have a high level of LDL cholesterol ◆, a piece of lean meat is completely fine. Not only can it be pretty low in calories while being extremely satisfying, but lean meat also contains some monounsaturated fats, including the beneficial long-chain omega-3 fatty acids, and minerals such as iron and zinc. The poorer-quality fatty cuts need to be avoided, as they can deal you a very hefty dose of LDL-producing saturated fat – as also do the creamy sauces sometimes served alongside the meat. I think a good pattern to get into if you like lean red meat is to have it twice a week.

The rest of the time I'd focus more on oily fish – again a couple of times a week. They're a very good source of omega-3 fatty acids, which, although they don't have much of a direct impact on either LDL or HDL levels, have benefits that reduce your overall risk of heart disease. As with meat, you need to be clever with the way you eat them – making a smoked mackerel pâté with butter isn't the ideal way, as the saturated fat in the butter increases LDL, and the salt, which aggravates blood pressure, far outweigh the benefits of the oily fish.

For the rest of your week, go for meals based around chicken (well cooked and not too buttery), white fish, game, and lentils and beans for veggie days. Choose wholegrains such as porridge (which our hearts love, as oats are wonderfully rich in a special type of soluble fibre) and wholemeal bread.

Fatty liver

The image these two words conjure up is not pretty, and it can be worrying when you're told that your liver is too fatty, but the good news is that you can turn the situation around easily by eating and drinking well. Having a fatty liver is most likely down to having too much of a lesser-known type of fat in your blood, called triglyceride – although some people with high triglyceride levels also have too much LDL cholesterol, which requires a little refining of what you eat. High triglyceride levels can also be associated with carrying too much weight – luckily the type and style of eating you need to adopt when you have a fatty liver is compatible with losing weight, so you can hopefully get some good results on more than one level. Of course if you can bring down your weight, specifically the amount of body fat you're carrying, this helps to reduce your overall risk of developing hardened arteries and heart disease, as well as giving you all the other benefits of being lower in body fat. Sometimes a diagnosis of a fatty liver is just the impetus you need to make some good changes in how, what and when you eat.

Triglyceride levels

The first stage in reversing a fatty liver is to reduce your triglyceride levels, which in turn will help your liver to shed some of its fatty deposits. This process tends to take weeks, if not months, so we're looking at a change of lifestyle here, not a quick fix. Triglyceride is a type of blood fat that's aggravated not only by saturated animal fats – butter, cream cheese, fatty meats, lard, dripping, etc. – but also by vegetable fats, which is where the treatment for someone with a fatty liver differs from that for someone with a raised bad cholesterol level.

Our liver doesn't distinguish animal fat from vegetable fat, so if you need to reduce your triglyceride levels, make sure your total fat intake is lowered (setting oily fish aside for the moment, as the long-chain omega-3 fatty acids can be beneficial). This means keeping your intake of vegetable fats, oils, avocados, nuts, nut butters, nut oils, etc. down as well, though you don't need to avoid them completely, as food often needs a little oiliness to give it good flavours. A vinaigrette dressing on a salad or a drizzle of olive oil over a dish of pasta is completely fine, but there is no point in going along with the Mediterranean diet, which can be heavy on the olive oil, or spreading your toast with thick layers of peanut butter, thinking you're doing your liver a favour, as you're not. A little drizzle or a thin scraping are the descriptions to think of here, not lashings.

The reason I set oily fish apart from other animal fats is that they contain the good long-chain omega-3 fatty acids, which can help reduce blood triglyceride levels and therefore help your liver. Once they're past the childbearing age, women can eat up to four 140g portions a week ◆ – but don't worry if you're not much of an oily fish fan, as just a couple of portions will give you sufficient omega oils to improve your blood-fat levels.

Read more on:
◆ *Pages 17–18 & 101*

Cashew nut butter, page 232

GI values

In addition to watching your fat intake, you need to watch the sweet stuff, as triglyceride levels are aggravated by high-GI foods. I can hear the sighs, but simply put, this means staying away from sugar, glucose, honey, sweet foods like biscuits, cakes, chocolate, fruit juices and ice creams. It also unfortunately means not overdoing the sweeter fruits and fruit juices, because although they contain some additional benefits such as antioxidants and fibre, too much high-GI fruit isn't good either. This means you need to steer clear of bananas, melons, raisins, grapes, dates, mangoes and pineapples. Instead, focus on citrus fruits such as oranges, clementines, satsumas and grapefruit, stone fruits such as apricots, plums and greengages, plus apples, pears, rhubarb and berries – they may not be exotic, but they're scrumptious. The trick for dealing with the fact that these fruits are slightly more tart is to cook them well – for instance, cooking rhubarb with an apple, a vanilla pod and some orange zest or star anise imparts lovely flavours that occupy your taste buds so that the tartness isn't so apparent. Roasting or chargrilling fruits also changes how tart they taste. On the vegetable front there are just a few to watch – baked and mashed potatoes, cooked carrots, squash and swede as they have a higher GI value too. All the others are good to include, so you should think bowls of steamed greens, ratatouille, big veggie soups and stuffed vegetables.

With fruit juices you have to be especially careful not to think that more is good, as unfortunately when fruit is changed into a juice some of the fibre is lost. You don't need to avoid juice, but you should have perhaps just a small glass every other day instead of the more common daily habit many seem to have got into since the arrival of ready-made smoothies. One way to make the drink last longer is to dilute it with a little water, or, if you're very thirsty, quench your thirst with water first.

Other good foods to eat are beans (borlotti, cannellini, kidney, black-eyed, haricot, etc.), lentils (ranging from the black or dark green Puy lentils to red and yellow and wholewheat pasta. And of course you can get spelt and other grain pastas, which, although they generally don't contain as much fibre as the whole durum wheat pasta, do have more fibre in than the white, so they're a good middle-ground to try. All these higher-fibred grains, beans and lentils are fantastic for helping to get a good triglyceride level.

When it comes to bread, since wholemeal bread very surprisingly has roughly the same high-GI value as white bread (wholegrain rye bread such as pumpernickel has one of the lowest GI values of the breads), I would suggest that you don't just choose bread according to its GI value – breads are generally best in their wholegrain form, be this the fluffy wholemeals or the darker, seedier, malty German-style wholegrains – as they provide fibre, B vitamins and other nutritional benefits. When it comes to your liver just watch that you don't eat too much of them. I think the superfood and positive nutritional labelling culture has led to a mentality that more is always better – but more cereal with added fibre or more wholegrain bread can lead to being overweight as well as having too fatty a liver. Less (that's good nutritional quality) is what I would call more here.

Seeing the results

If you make these sorts of changes to your diet as well as looking at how and what you're generally eating, you will most likely find that any excess weight will come off gradually and easily. If you reach your ideal weight and body-fat level you need to ensure that you don't keep losing it, as this isn't healthy either and can leave you depleted – so just check that you tuck into good-sized portions of nourishing foods and eat enough.

If you were of an ideal body weight and fat level (which is rare but not unheard of) when you were told you had a fatty liver, have a go at incorporating as many of these changes as possible, making sure you don't reduce your portion size. You could find that if you cut right down on fats and sugars you may find that your weight drops too low or you find yourself exhausted and ratty because your body is just not receiving enough of the good stuff, which includes calories. As I mentioned, this should be a lifestyle change, not something where you sort it out and then go back to your old ways, as the likelihood is that your liver will complain again in the future.

The only thing you may think it's a good idea to be pretty black and white about avoiding is alcohol. Since alcohol unfortunately aggravates a fatty liver, your doctor may want you to avoid it altogether for a while. Although people are generally told that a couple of glasses of red wine is a good health-protecting mantra, it appears now that we shouldn't put red wine up on a pedestal. You should treat it like any other alcoholic drink and either have it in moderation or consider avoiding all alcohol until your triglyceride levels return to normal and your doctor gives the all-clear.

Liver cleansing

If you want to consider complementary remedies, carrot and pomegranate juices are said to be good for the liver. Pomegranate juice provides some antioxidants and may also help reduce bad LDL cholesterol levels, while carrot juice has been used as a liver cleanser for centuries. If you like either of these, try having a small glass a few times a week – be aware, though, that pomegranate juice can be rather sweet, so is best diluted, and too much carrot juice can turn your skin orange! Others swear by taking milk thistle – the usual dose is up to 300mg three times a day.

Diabetes

Diabetes is a life-long condition that, if not managed well, can lead to kidney damage, blindness and a higher risk of developing heart disease and stroke. Diabetics have too much glucose in their blood (which comes from digesting carbohydrate and is also produced by the liver) because their pancreas either: doesn't produce any insulin; doesn't produce enough insulin to help glucose enter the body's cells; or the insulin that it does produce doesn't work properly (known as insulin resistance).

Type 2 diabetes is the most common form and usually occurs when you hit middle age or in your older years. However, South Asian and black people are at greater risk and it can appear when they're much younger, although it is rather alarmingly also becoming more common in children and teenagers of all ethnicities. It does not usually require insulin for treatment (unlike type 1 diabetes), instead, patients must eat healthily and take drugs to help their system handle sugars more efficiently.

If you're diagnosed with type 2 diabetes, it's important to get to grips with your eating habits, as they can have a profound effect on how your body copes and how you feel. You don't need to resort to eating diabetic products (which can be unpleasant and expensive) as your eating style should be no more complicated, and just as delicious, as everyone else who follows a well balanced and nourishing diet. This can include some delicious cakes and biscuits, as long as you eat them in moderation (as everyone should) and make them as nutritious as possible by basing them on wholegrain ingredients such as wholemeal flour and fruits. This way you'll not only be enjoying some scrumptious cakes, but also taking in valuable fibre, vitamins and minerals, which, in combination, help your body stay and feel well.

If you're carrying too much body fat, then losing this healthily and steadily can have a very positive effect on your blood sugar levels. It's also particularly important to build a good exercise routine into your schedule as this will not only help you to lose weight, but will help the body maintain good blood sugar levels. Since having diabetes also increases the likelihood of developing heart disease, it's good to ensure you are eating the right types of fats as this will also help to reduce your risk.

Teenage Needs

This is a key age for experimentation, which as a parent, you can use to your advantage. As teenagers' interests begin to change you can introduce them to new foods and win their taste buds over to things they wouldn't previously touch (when they are hungry they'll eat anything). Often it is at this age that we start to become interested in cooking and begin to learn to cook for ourselves. This brings about a new understanding of food, which yields many positives as long as teenagers are taught the importance of a healthy diet and good-quality food.

This is a time when you are going to need your parenting skills more than ever. Teenagers may appear physically grown up – more than capable of looking after themselves in many ways – but actually they still require a lot of attention, time, support and of course love. You may have to find diplomatic ways of conveying all these things – they are not little children any more – but it is your job and not theirs to keep the lines of communication open. Nine times out of ten they may push you away, but the one time they don't it is absolutely vital you are there. It's a challenging time all round, but if you approach it with a positive outlook, the great thing is that you can instil healthy habits that will sustain your child throughout their life. When all lines of communication are down, sometimes being able to sit and eat together can be just what you need to open the channels up again – though this is not the time to harp on about the vegetables not being eaten. Let it go and relax – something in their stomach, even if it's a takeaway, even better if shared with you, even in silence, can be just what you need to draw a line in the sand.

Parenting teenagers

Pause for a moment and think about what being a teenager was like in your day: a melting-pot of hormones, emotions and body changes that played havoc with your confidence, mood and sense of wellbeing. Few people ever describe their adolescence as 'the best years of my life', and frankly it's no wonder. You may find the slamming doors, uncommunicative grunts and baffling language hard to deal with, but do have some sympathy. Teenagers today have it worse than we did in so many ways: more exams, which equals more stress; and more exposure to unrealistic 'perfect' body shapes, while fast food and excessive alcoholic intake play a huge part in teenage social life. Excess can lead to them gaining far too much weight and all the associated health and psychological problems. Let's not forget, too, that teenagers are inheriting a world which at times feels unsafe, confusing and pessimistic no matter how old you are – all in all, it's no wonder the teenage years are often not the easiest to work through.

A time for sensitivity

You probably don't need me to say this, as you'll know how sensitive you need to be around your teenager, but this is not the time for jokes about chunky thighs or spots – such comments are not only unkind, but positively destructive. The number of teenagers and older adults among my patients who can recite a remark by a parent as something that tipped them over the edge into an eating disorder is horrifyingly significant. There's a fine line to tread when knowing what to say about their body if they're either end of an ideal body weight. Of course it's your role as a parent to help them if they're gaining too much weight, but equally it's not good to focus on it, as that can cause their confidence to be dashed, leading them to either eat secretly, or lose all the excess weight and more, swinging right down into anorexic behaviour.

Some parents, especially mums, can be so fearful of their child becoming anorexic that they never talk about weight or eating issues – they think that if it's not discussed, their teenager won't think about it. But I don't think this helps – being able to talk with your child about any sensitivities they have and coming up with practical help to get them through it can be invaluable. The likelihood is that they will all be talking about it at school and see some of their friends sadly having big issues with disordered eating – be this anorexia, bulimia or being overweight. At least if you keep the lines of communication open you have a chance to put their minds at ease and to instil some common-sense, simple, what's-good-to-eat knowledge. Celeb-style magazines often spout utter nonsense about what celebrities supposedly eat and don't eat, and they also come up with copious amounts of pseudo-nutritional facts which can prey on your child's mind and get passed around their peer groups. If you're able to dismiss these by getting them to read this book and eat nourishing foods with you, you have a good chance of getting them through the teenage years unscathed by the mad disordered eating-world they're surrounded by.

This is not the time to start banging on about how you wish you were two stone lighter. Deal with that yourself quietly and without fuss. You also need to be aware that concerns over eating and body image aren't exclusive to females – society exerts many pressures on young men too. Gone are the days when a stocky man with a bit of a paunch was seen as a solid bet – models and fashion all provide a very different example of how young men feel they should look. Many want to be perfect, all muscley and six-pack-ridden, so be sensitive. It's a good idea to write down in a private notebook issues you don't want to pass on to your child, and keep referring to it.

The right foods

Read more on:
◆ Page 14

The adolescent years are physically dominated by the production of the sex hormones such as oestrogen, progesterone and testosterone, which bring about all sorts of physical and emotional changes. Little girls go from a child shape to the more curvaceous womanly shape that is defined by an increase in body fat levels, whereas boys start increasing their muscle mass and filling out – all of which requires teenagers to eat enough nourishing foods to enable the body to mature correctly. On a practical level, this doesn't mean you need to change the balance of the types of foods teenagers eat very much ◆. Boys don't need to start tucking into whole chickens or downing protein shakes, and neither do girls need to start increasing their fat intake – so long as they eat well, the body should take care of the changes. Really, you should think in terms of the teenage body just needing more of the types of nourishing foods they ate as children.

There are a couple of watch points for girls: if they're dieting or not eating much, and are restricting their fat and protein intake in particular, their menstrual cycle could be disrupted, which has the potential to affect their fertility and bone health in the future. Menstrual bleeding means that each month girls lose some iron, which you should try to replace by eating an iron-rich diet ◆. Iron also provides a key role in cell replication, so it's essential for teenagers, both boys and girls, to eat enough to meet their growth needs. Sometimes, though not always, the body craves what it needs – in the case of red meat, you could find your teenager craving a lean steak, and this can be the case particularly with girls at different times of the month. Mind you, boys can eat large amounts of red meat too, and although they need to have enough to provide iron, it's important that the meat they eat is lean and good quality so that their intake of trans fats and saturated fat isn't too high.

Rapid growth, coupled with a fast lifestyle and poor dietary choices, can result in iron-deficiency anaemia, which can make you look and feel tired or breathless, experience poor concentration and affect mental and physical development in children and teenagers. Teenage girls are particularly at risk because their iron stores are depleted each month following their period, as are infants over the age of six months, menstruating or pregnant women, vegetarians and vegans, and people with conditions that affect absorption of food, e.g. IBS ◆.

Read more on:
◆ *Pages 181–182*

Weight problems

The teenagers I see as patients are often struggling with their weight – eating either too little or too much. Comfort-eating often signifies that their emotions are in turmoil, so if you can find a way to make sure they eat regularly, you can save them a great deal of unhappiness, both now and later on. You need to explain to them that what they do has a real impact on how their bodies will be in the future – a badly nourished body during the teenage years carries a greater risk of developing problems, such as osteoporosis and infertility. This can be a pretty compelling reason to help some girls click out of the notion of extreme underweight being seen as attractive. If you starve yourself during your teenage years, it may also have a pretty devastating effect on your metabolism as when you do begin eating normally again, the weight can pile on. I see many 40-something women who look back with huge regret at not being kinder to themselves when they were younger.

The best way to encourage teenagers to have a comfortable relationship with food is to eat with them as much as possible and teach them simple cooking skills. Don't nag, though, as the last thing food should become is a battleground. The aim is to try to get enough good food into their systems so they won't have the urge to binge. The secret lies in always having delicious and nutritious food available that takes only minutes to prepare.

Girls in particular often develop a phobia about sweet food, which they perceive as being fattening. You need to help them build up their confidence, introducing sweet dishes that are wholesome and healthy, such as carrot cake or date and walnut cake. It is important they learn that eating something sweet does not equate with their weight spiralling out of control.

Be sensitive to the fact that your daughter in particular may not want to eat stodgy dishes. I think it's completely counterproductive to try to get teenagers to eat food that you know makes them feel uncomfortable. If you insist on it you're going to have a battle on your hands – either then or, worse case scenario, if they eat it and then disappear off to the bathroom.

Dieting

Read more on:
◆ *Pages 170–171*

Tomato & herb salad, page 227

Mothers in particular can worry that by explaining the calorific value of food to ours daughters, in a bid to help them prevent piling on the weight in later years, we are wilfully inflicting potential eating disorders upon them ◆. What absolute nonsense! We have a far greater problem in our westernised society with obesity than with anorexia or bulimia, and if you enable your child to know how to be able to select healthy foods, this is ideal – what food contains and how much or little they need to eat are among the most important life skills you can teach them.

If your child is unhappy about gaining extra weight, don't tell them they look fine – take their concerns seriously. Plenty of teenagers put on so-called puppy fat and it is the fat, not the losing of it, that can lead to a negative body image. In addition, being overweight can lead to children being horribly bullied. When that happens, they can suffer all kinds of psychological problems, from low self-esteem to feeling suicidal. So if they come to you asking for help, make sure you provide it, rather than leave them struggling on their own. However, it is also important to encourage them to have a realistic expectation of what their body can look like – what was your own body shape like at this age? Help them achieve a look that gives them confidence, but which is also as healthy as possible.

Sensible, controlled dieting can be an excellent opportunity for you and your child to talk about food and introduce good habits for the future. Show them that it is possible to control weight through delicious, nutritious dishes, rather than extreme behaviour. Help them by not keeping items such as crisps and biscuits at the front of the cupboard although there may be members of the household who don't have a problem with their weight, so you don't want to make them completely off the radar. Try to replace the space they filled with snacks such as dried fruit, unsalted nuts, crispbreads, etc. It also helps to have a fridge full of light foods such as raw vegetables, soup, stewed fruits and natural yoghurt that they can have if they've come home ravenous and need something small.

As an eating pattern, place the emphasis on plenty of vegetables and salads, with moderate amounts of protein, such as chicken and fish. Don't ban any food – just encourage moderation. Bread, pasta, potatoes and rice can all be enjoyed if eaten in sensible quantities. Even chocolate is fine if you buy good quality, 70 or 85 per cent, which is virtually impossible to eat in huge quantities even though it's delicious. Stay positive about food and don't chastise children if they fall off the wagon. It is a fine line to tread, but if you can instil a basic love and appreciation of food, rather than allowing it to become the enemy, you will have more chance of them developing bodies they are happy and comfortable with for the rest of their lives.

Taking time over meals

In an ideal world we would eat with our children every evening, but life is not that perfect. Eat with them when you can – at least once or twice a week – or the second-best scenario is to sit with them and talk while they eat. Food is a social activity and one we usually enjoy more when there are other people around. Eating on our own is quite lonely, which is why so many people sit in front of the television, but try to discourage this at least some of the time – food is something that needs concentration in order to fully appreciate it. Teenagers who eat while they're watching TV, wandering around or on the phone are far more likely to become overweight and have problems with digestion. The gut needs to be still to deal with food, so try to encourage them to sit down, even for a snack – it takes nothing more medicinal than this.

Read more on:
◆ Page 14

Teenagers often rush their food, so again encourage them to eat slowly, as this will help the body recognise when it is satisfied. As with all stages in life, their meals should include a good balance of foods from the key groups ◆. If a meal is too light it will leave them complaining of being hungry later on – you may think a simple salad is all you need at lunchtime, but their rapidly maturing bodies need something more substantial. Equally, something that is very sweet, fatty and low in fibre and protein – typically fast-food junk – will satiate them only for a short time. People get addicted to fast food and want to eat more and more of it because of the lack of satisfaction as well as the high fat and salt content.

Ten tips for helping your teenager lose weight

- Hydration plays a big part, so get them to drink at least two and a half litres of water throughout the day – weak squash (no added sugar) also helps.

- Encourage them to only eat at mealtimes – if they need a snack they should sit and eat it slowly, concentrating on what they're eating.

- Keep to three meals a day plus fruit snacks between meal. Insist on them eating breakfast, even if it's just a banana and yoghurt or a smoothie (home-made, ideally). This will improve their moods and energy and make them less inclined to snack mid-morning.

- Cook nourishing meals for the whole family to share; don't isolate your teenager and make them feel different because they're on a diet that no one else is happy to eat.

- Don't keep crisps, biscuits, chocolates or fizzy drinks in the house. Suggest that once a week they can enjoy a treat outside the home, say a cake at a coffee shop.

- Make sure the fridge and cupboards are stocked with plenty of simple nourishing foods, so that hunger doesn't lead to snacking on something junky.

- Teach them five quick dishes they can make for themselves – even a toasted sandwich made with wholemeal bread is a good made-in-a-minute option.

- Choose activities that expend energy. Sports are an obvious option, but don't forget boxing, martial arts and dancing, as these are fun and good for burning calories. It's amazing how short walks and less time in the car, can help and exercise gets your body to manufacture mood-enhancing endorphins.

- Try not to eat in fast-food restaurants. There's nothing wrong with a simple *pizza Margarita* and a salad with the dressing on the side (so you can control how much you add), but watch Caesar and blue cheese dressings, de luxe salads with croutons or bacon bits, etc., as they're all high in fat and sometimes sugar, and you've probably read that many fast-food salads contain far higher calorie values than a simple burger made with good-quality lean red meat, especially without cheese.

- If you feel it will help, set some targets and non-food rewards – losing about a kilo (two pounds) a week is roughly what to expect, although we're all different. It may be that simply noticing clothes getting looser week by week rather than actually weighing seems the better strategy.

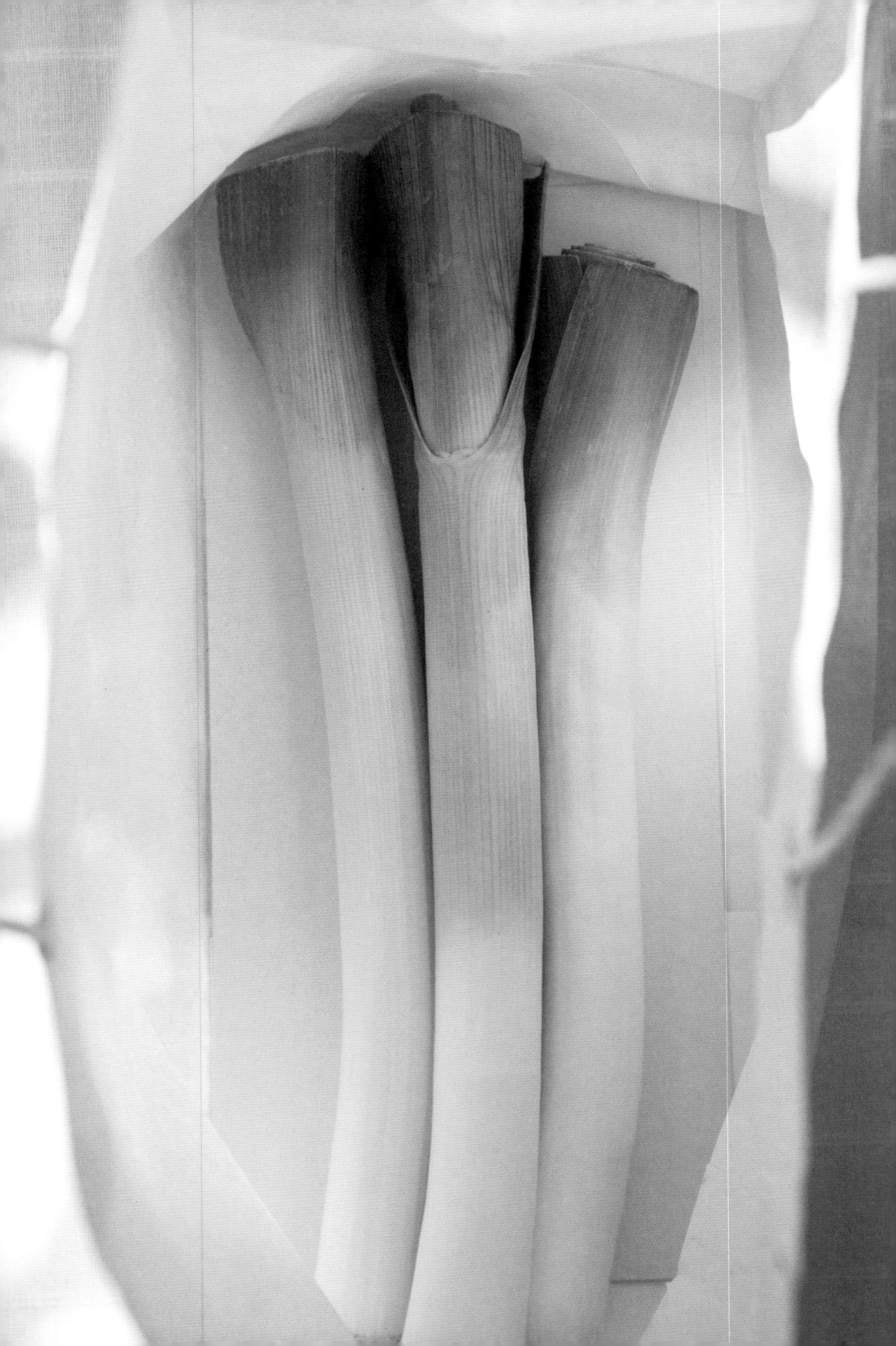

What's in the cupboard?

In reality, a lot of the time your teenager will want to 'graze' or grab a quick snack before bolting out the door again and will rarely sit down for a proper meal. The trick as a parent is to ensure that there is good food available when we want it, however, the last thing we need is for our house to be seen as a juice and salad bar with nothing but boring health food fodder around. This will only lead to teenagers staying well clear and eating out all the time, as they crave something more substantial – and this may be junk and processed foods, which you'd rather they avoid. With sensitive girls, in particular, you don't want to give the impression that they should only be eating salads and low-fat yoghurts, but on the other hand it's not a good idea to stock cupboards with copious amounts of crisps, sweet drinks and chocolate bars. You need to provide a good selection – some treats like good-quality chocolate and unsalted nuts and dried fruits, but also plenty of foods that provide stomach-filling goodness as a snack or a more substantial meal put together in no more than ten minutes.

When it comes to main meals, make sure you have a few good staples such as pasta (ideally wholemeal, but white is still good), which teenagers can boil and stir a dollop of pesto or tomato sauce into – show them how to make a quick snack so that they have the confidence to do so. Another good storecupboard staple is good jumbo porridge oats that they can grab in the morning with a chopped banana, a handful of frozen berries or a dollop of apple sauce. I've got into the habit of soaking the oats in milk overnight in the fridge, which makes not only a good porridge but also a base for adding seeds, nuts and dried fruits (you can soak the oats in apple juice if you prefer, and stir in a dollop of creamy yoghurt along with the nuts and fruits). Keep a stock of fish fingers in the freezer, plus individual packs of wholemeal bread rolls and pitta breads that can quickly be made up into a fish 'burger'. Eggs are another essential standby – fried, boiled, poached or in an omelette, they make easy, nutritious dishes that cost little time or money.

It's good to get teenagers into the habit of eating properly, but if all this feels like too much effort and they're flying out the door, then whip them up a smoothie with fruit and oatmeal that can be devoured in less than two minutes.

It's also worth remembering that teenagers often travel as a group. If you want to monitor whether your own son or daughter is eating a nutritious diet, the clever thing to do is make sure yours is the house known for always having food available. As well as keeping the cupboard well stocked, keep dishes in the freezer that will satisfy the hungry hordes. There are many simple things – a simple tomato, meat or vegetable sauce – that they can dip into or that you could turn into something such as a sausage bake, lasagne, cottage pie, or a batch of meatballs; then all they need to do is microwave it and serve with a warmed pitta bread, dollop of relish and a few salad leaves for a meal in minutes. It's also good to have a few lighter dishes for the girls, such as chicken casseroles and vegetable stews. Don't forget to have some sweet things around – carrot cake, date and walnut muffins, fruit crumbles, sorbets, etc. – as the more you encourage teenagers to eat at home, the less chance there is of them eating in fast-food outlets or skipping meals altogether.

Teach them to cook!

Teach your children to cook from as early an age as possible. You'll be surprised how interested many teenagers are in cooking (thanks to the many TV food programmes and inspirational celebrity chefs) and it may become something they excel at. Even if they're not keen on learning much, anyone can be taught how to boil pasta, bake potatoes, whip up scrambled eggs or heat up baked beans. If you know they love a particular dish of yours, teach them to cook it. Let them see that preparing food is fun, enjoyable and much more than a chore. I think the most useful piece of kitchen equipment to have with a teenager around is a hand-held blender to rustle up quick soups and smoothies. Remember that as they learn to cook they will probably ruin every frying pan you own and leave the kitchen in a terrible mess.

When teenagers exhibit worrying eating patterns, I think cooking has a role to play in enabling them to build up a healthier relationship with food. If they're worried about their weight, they can so often think sauces are packed with calories, or that you put lots of fat in dishes when really there isn't much at all. Magazines come out with such nonsense about food that it can be a nightmare for someone sensitive. If teenagers cook (shopping is also a good thing to get them to do) they can take control of food in a more constructive way – once they're involved in the food preparation they can put together something lighter that they're happy with but the rest of the family can still join in with eating. This helps take the spotlight off their sensitivities and keeps the lines of communication open. If you serve something rich and overwhelmingly stodgy, you will only exacerbate their fear and they will most likely refuse to eat with you, resulting in all sorts of chaos and unhappiness in the home. But if they are involved in cooking the food themselves, it takes the pressure off you – so let them cook and let them feel proud of doing something helpful and pleasing.

Tandoori chicken, page 221

Eating disorders

I know I'm going to challenge the traditional views of how to treat what we can loosely term disordered eating. Let me just say here that I'm not talking about the very underweight, anorexic teenagers who need specialist help, I'm talking about the far larger group of teenagers who struggle with eating and body weight. The traditional way of treating teenagers with eating disorders is to force them to eat regular high-calorie meals in order to get them to put on weight. Simply put – and I'm not saying all clinics are like this but the majority of them seem to be – if you don't eat the food and put on weight you don't earn rewards such as seeing relatives, getting your own music, etc. It's my experience that this therapy doesn't work, as all that happens is that they are forced to eat, gain weight, and then, as is highly likely, struggle so much with what they're meant to eat and how their body is feeling that they will get into a mess again and lose far too much weight as a result.

Although everyone is different, and a key element in helping your child with an eating problem is to get good psychological help if you feel it's gone beyond what I call worried eating, I think it's far better to allow them to eat lighter foods. They might not have as much, say, carbohydrate (which many don't seem to like to eat in large amounts), but I think it's much more important for them to eat regular meals containing nourishing ingredients, such as roast chicken with a salad that has a few beans or lentils thrown into it. If you offer light meals your teenager will feel comfortable about eating and you can add bulk to it for other family members by serving extra pasta or bread in a separate bowl. If you are going out for a meal, choose a place where your child can order sushi or salad rather than everything-with-chips.

Being aware about what they are eating does not necessarily equate to an eating disorder. The teenage years are tough emotionally and physically, and if your child is sensitive and conscious about food they need to know they can talk to you about issues and not either get their head bitten off or be forced to eat what you think they should be eating. The more laid-back you are, the sooner they're likely to click out of controlling their weight and join in with the rest of the family. Experimentation is a normal part of the teenage years, and food is often a part of that. If you respect this and offer healthy nutritious meals in moderate portions, there's no reason why it should escalate into anything serious.

People with eating disorders are usually not comfortable around any food at all. Having a preference for the low-fat variety simply indicates a quite normal teenage preoccupation with how their body looks. The warning signs are: that they don't want to eat with you; that they say they've had a meal, but you never see them eating one; that they blatantly skip meals; that they won't even eat something you know they love; that it seems that they say are not hungry all the time; that their weight has changed significantly in either direction over a couple of months; that they have rituals around how they eat; that they are particularly body-sensitive; that they over-exercise; and that they start to cut themselves off from the rest of the family. In addition, they may start to wear dark-coloured clothes that appear to shroud them, which can be a sign that they are feeling ashamed of their body.

If your teenager fits any part of this description, do not panic. Do not immediately march them down to the doctor or arrange for them to be admitted to a specialist centre as you could be adding fuel to the fire. If you can keep your child eating with you, no matter how small an amount they consume, you have a chance to pull the situation back from the brink. Do not offer high-calorie, high-fat dishes in a bid to 'build them up' – they are more likely to be tempted by a food they perceive as non-fattening. Don't stand over them insisting they eat or turn food into a battle of wills between you and them and don't let them see how anxious you are. If you are co-parenting, it is important that the two of you work together on a cohesive course of action, agreeing to discuss it only in private. If you do show

support and a great deal of common sense, it is possible that you will be able to gently wean your teenager off the food-phobic path. Only when you have exhausted all possibility of recovering the situation yourself – and if their weight is clearly plummeting – should you seek professional help for anorexia.

Bulimia (classically bingeing on food and then purging through self-induced vomiting) can be a much harder problem to spot. Look out for a very slim body with a face that looks puffy and bloated – the latter can be brought about through fluid retention caused by repeatedly making oneself sick. Bulimics may not have the outward signs to trigger concern, but inside they are doing a lot of damage to their bodies. This can result in ulceration, indigestion and even breathing difficulties from stomach acids leaking into the oesophagus – serious hardcore bulimia can result in electrolyte imbalances that can be extremely serious. If your child asks for help and it's not happening that often, you may want to see if you can sort it out as a family. Help them to break the routine by first listing the foods they do feel comfortable about eating, no matter how few this is. As previously mentioned, it is important to help them eat regular, light meals and end the dangerous cycle to which bulimia can lead.

(Note: boys are just as capable of developing a serious eating disorder as girls.)

Teenage moods

We all remember these, don't we? The slamming doors, the you-don't-understand-me mantra, the sudden onset of tears … Well, I'm not promising miracles, but you will be delighted to know that there are plenty of practical ways that you can help to deal with those adolescent mood swings.

Depression and anger

Read more on:
◆ Pages 180–181

Maya's chocolate brownies, page 244

By this, I don't mean actual clinical depression, but the sudden lows teenagers encounter, almost as though they're plummeting through the floor. Sudden anger is often a sign of depression, which manifests itself in teenagers prone to tantrums.

The first thing you should check, with girls in particular, is whether they are iron-deficient, as depression can be one of the first signs of anaemia. Coeliac disease ◆ is an intolerance to gluten and can be a lesser-known culprit, as it diminishes the gut's ability to absorb iron and other key nutrients. Both anaemia and coeliac disease can affect sleep, which in turn can lead to depression.

You should also consider their refined sugar intake, as it is my experience that too much can cause an instant high followed by a dreaded crash, which plays havoc with teenage moods. It's worth checking to see if teenagers are eating or drinking lots of sweet stuff and be aware that it seems to have its most powerful effect when they consume it on an empty stomach. Having said this, the highest GI foods, which raise blood sugar levels, are in fact, not that sweet-tasting – white rice, white bread, bran flakes etc. – so you may be better off encouraging them to eat the wholegrain varieties.

Is your teenagers' caffeine consumption too high? Are they having too many high-energy, high-sugar drinks and not enough water? Being dehydrated can itself be a mood dampener – often we feel low and moody but within minutes of drinking a glass of water the mood can lift. Are they actually eating enough? Remember how crotchety they were as small children when they were hungry? Well, there is no difference now they are twice the size – and in fact those growing bodies require more food than ever. The hormonal changes that are going on can also change their appetite, which explains why girls can have the munchies at certain points in their menstrual cycle and boys can have an enormous appetite when their increase in testosterone production calls them to start bulking up. Skipping breakfast, smoking and too little exercise can also be important factors in affecting moods.

Broken heart

The melancholic pain of a broken heart is different from depression. Love is a powerful force, no matter how old you are, so don't make light of the pain your child is suffering. This is not the time to say there are 'plenty more fish in the sea.' Teenagers can feel absolutely invalided by the hurt they are going through so you should also heed any warning signs of negative body image – the idea that 'he wouldn't have dumped me if my thighs weren't so enormous.' Broken hearts can lead to a severe loss of confidence, which, in rare cases can spiral into an eating disorder ◆.

Going off food is often a sign of heartbreak, as the very thought of eating can make the broken-hearted feel nauseous. It is important to get some food into their system, as the nausea will only get worse on an empty stomach and their bodies will quickly become depleted of vital nutrients. Even if it is only a soup or a smoothie, it will do them the world of good. Girls in particular often crave sweetness when they are unhappy. Rather than see them munching sadly through sweets and chocolate bars, introduce some delicious home-made treats, such as chocolate mousse or comforting chocolate brownies. Give them plenty of love and sympathy, but don't overtly criticise the lost boyfriend or girlfriend – they may be back together in a week or two!

Anxiety

Teenagers today have good reason to be anxious: they are stressed out with too many exams, are bombarded with 'ideal' bodies through the media and are faced with an increasingly uncertain world. It is your responsibility to help them through their worries and fears. Much of this centres on the same advice given for depression (see above): plenty of water, not too much caffeine, regular nourishing meals, moderate alcohol and nicotine intake and some light exercise. Good sleep is also a huge factor ▲.

A high-fibre breakfast such as porridge, muesli, fruit, yoghurt or wholemeal toast followed by a protein-rich food such as eggs, beans or smoked salmon is a good option if they've got a big exam session ahead. Surprisingly, couscous made with nuts and dried fruits can be good too – I think it's the combination of easy eating and the sweetness of the dried fruits, without liquid, that makes it a good stomach-settler. If they are too nervous or feel too sick to eat, try to get them to eat just a couple of pieces of fresh fruit – bananas have a particularly good stomach-settling effect. A piece of fruit or a fruit smoothie – ready- or home-made – is another good stopgap.

Read more on:
◆ Pages 170–171
▲ Page 177

Spicy fish casserole,
224

Read more on:
◆ Pages 37–38
▲ Pages 154–155
● Page 11

Too much caffeine can exacerbate anxiety, so although a warming cup can be good to wake them up, watch that they don't have too much. Try to keep them off energy-stimulating drinks, as they can make them feel wired and unable to concentrate on the task in hand. If you find you have a very nervous teenager and think that a cup of something soothing and calming is what's needed, try giving them a herbal tea – the ones that traditionally have been used to calm include chamomile, catnip, bergamot and lemon balm. More potent sedative teas include skullcap, blue vervain, valerian and hops, which you could try in the evening to help them wind down ◆.

Make sure they are drinking enough water and encourage them to hold off on sweet or fizzy drinks, chocolate, sweets, biscuits and other sugary snacks – fresh fruit, dried fruit, unsalted nuts, smoothies, yoghurts and soup are far more beneficial. At night, starchy foods such as wholegrain rice, pasta, potatoes and bread can make them feel more relaxed and prone to a better night's sleep.

Panic attacks are bad news no matter how old you are, but can be absolutely terrifying for teenagers. The adrenaline rush causes a racing heart, sweating and anxiety and is often followed by feeling completely shattered. The first thing to ban is caffeine, although interestingly, research shows that people who drink a lot caffeine become tolerant to it, so it is less likely to make them more anxious. It's the teenagers (and adults) who are particularly sensitive to it, or suddenly increase their caffeine intake, who may notice a difference. Alcohol and certain illegal drugs such as cannabis can also feed anxiety, so try to discourage your teenager from wild nights out.

Look at how generally well balanced their diet is. If you eat regular, nutritious meals you are far less likely to suffer from anxiety than someone overdoing the fast-food, high-GI type ▲. Try instead to go for medium- to low-GI foods, which include most fruits (except bananas and dried fruits), raw vegetables, pasta (white or wholemeal), porridge, rye bread and rice (brown or white).

Teenage bodies

Some teenagers (especially boys) can be extremely skinny, so you are lulled into thinking that they're not eating enough or are avoiding junk food when in fact, this is often not entirely true. They are very good at filling their bodies with unhealthy food without anyone realising or any weight gain. They can still do themselves some damage, so as a parent, you need to watch what they're eating. Perhaps you could occasionally ask them to keep a food diary ● or do it as a family so that you don't alienate them or put them under any pressure.

Menstruation

When girls start menstruating their bodies can go through all sorts of physical and emotional changes as a result of the alterations in sexual hormones such as oestrogen, progesterone and testosterone. Mood swings can rock from one extreme to the other and teenage girls can suffer from very bad menstrual cramps, become bloated and uncomfortable, and develop spots. Forget all the nonsense sold to us in tampon adverts, that imply that you should carry on as normal through your period. The fact is that any young woman should be allowed to feel under the weather, because periods can be debilitating. Nature is a powerful force; one theory as to why women feel so exhausted before their period is that it is the last time in the month you have the potential to get pregnant. By slowing you down, nature makes it more likely a man will catch you and mate with you! Many young women need some extra TLC at this time, so keep a diary of your daughter's menstrual cycle and be prepared to be extra nurturing if she is unfortunate enough to suffer with bad period pains, bloating and moodiness.

Pain and bloating are enough to make any young woman feel negative about her body, particularly when they are so out of her own control. IBS symptoms ♦ are common during menstruation, because the gut becomes sensitive to changes in oestrogen and progesterone levels. For some girls, menstrual discomfort and mood swings can lead to a scenario where they try to stop being women by starving themselves, a dangerous move that can lead them to developing an eating disorder ▲. If you talk to your daughter about how she is feeling and show concern and sympathy, she is less likely to become fearful about what she is going through.

Happily, there are also practical steps you can take to help her through it. Perhaps one of the most significant nutritional challenges is the fact that starting menstrual bleeding is the first time girls are confronted by a regular loss of iron. You need to up her iron levels, both immediately before menstruation and during it. She may not be keen on the idea of eating liver – the traditional old wives' cure – but she can also take in iron through lean steak, eggs, dried apricots and green-leaf vegetables, such as kale, dark Savoy cabbage, rocket and spinach. Try to keep her off strong tea and coffee, especially when eating iron-rich food, as they diminish iron absorption.

Bloating is another down side of menstruation and one that figure-conscious teenagers can find particularly upsetting. Some foods, such as cauliflower, Jerusalem artichokes and onions produce a lot of wind ●, so may be better left off the menu. Cooked vegetables are also generally kinder to the gut than raw ones. Fluid retention can also be aggravated by too much salt and not enough

Read more on:
♦ Pages 181–182
▲ Pages 170–171
● Page 114

potassium, so prepare dishes based around herbs and lemon juice, rather than salt and pickles.

Water is essential (fluid retention is not caused by water), and a diuretic tea such as dandelion may help. Smoothies are also easy to digest, and again, ones that are potassium-enriched are ideal, such as banana and orange or grapefruit and raspberry.

Boys' bodies

Read more on:
◆ Page 47

While girls are coping with periods, boys are having a similarly confusing time with an overload of testosterone. Testosterone isn't just a male-only hormone – women produce it too – and the same applies to the female hormones such as oestrogen, which boys also manufacture. Boys often overproduce oestrogen during puberty, which can give them slightly larger breasts and even cellulite ◆, which usually disappears. The hormonal cocktail that surges into action during puberty causes boys' bodies to undergo similarly rapid changes in shape, albeit less rounded and more about building muscle than women. The hormonal shifts can also change their skin, making it more prone to spots, oiliness, and of course smelliness. And need I mention the moods and the changes in energy levels? One minute they're perfectly happy to be out clubbing all night and the next they won't move from their bed all day!

We often talk about how some girls are preoccupied with their body shape and the way their body is changing into that of a woman, but we shouldn't forget that this time of change can be equally challenging and upsetting for boys. Boys often worry about not growing up as fast as their peers (or growing too fast) and height and bulk start to become very important. Some boys feel shy about developing facial hair and a deeper voice, while for others developing a six-pack can become a preoccupation – we only need look at advertising campaigns and men's magazines to see that there is huge social pressure for boys and men to have the perfect body.

Boys can get confused with what to eat – so you need to step in here. They often think they need to start drinking protein shakes and eating whole chickens in order to bulk up, but this isn't the case – it's the combination of good regular exercise, both aerobic and non-aerobic. Running, swimming, cycling and longer-lasting lower endurance exercise alongside muscle development and weight training will increase chances of having the flat-board stomach and chest that many aspire to! Note – a gym workout does not mean a huge increase in calorie intake. You may feel ravenous afterwards but you'll not be doing your body any favours if you double the amount of food you eat.

Sleep

At any age, sleep is important. Unfortunately, teenagers often slip into bad sleep patterns, going to bed too late and then feeling exhausted during the day. Iron deficiency can also cause poor sleep, so it can be something that girls suffer from during menstruation. Lack of sleep can also lead to terrible mood swings and poor performance at school. Caffeine is very often a culprit in exaggerating all of this, so watch teenagers' consumption of high-energy drinks, tea, coffee and chocolate. If they want a sweet 'fix', try to provide it with fresh fruit or home-baked flapjacks, which are packed full of oats, carrot cake made with wholemeal flour etc. These are far more gentle on the body and less likely to unsettle blood sugar levels, which can be disruptive to sleep patterns.

Try to introduce comforting soporific foods, such as bananas, wholegrain rice or pasta, in the evening, which fill the stomach and are also very relaxing. Starchy, warm dishes are the perfect inducement for sleep but avoid dishes with lots of spices in them, because some people find them to be quite energising and may irritate the gut, which can also disrupt sleep. You only need to sniff some chilli powder to see what effect it has on your heart rate and how powerful it can be!

Milky drinks have a fantastic lulling effect, but remember that milk contains a natural sugar called lactose, which is slowly released so you don't necessarily need to add anything else to it. Chocolate, which contains a caffeine-like substance called theobromine, can be a stimulant, but if that is what appeals, make your own by melting a couple of squares of 70 per cent cocoa chocolate into the milk, as this is good quality with very little sugar in it. Plain milk with a touch of honey is sweet and comforting, particularly for people who don't like the natural sweetness of milk. Most hot chocolates are fine – whatever your teenagers fancy, serve it in a nice big mug and let them really savour the experience. Look out for night-time milk – literally milk taken from cows that are milked at night – as this contains a higher amount of the sleep-inducing chemical, melatonin.

Hair

The appearance of our hair is crucial to our self-esteem, so hair loss can be upsetting, particularly for teenagers. If hair is thinning, take your teenager to the doctor to check for anaemia or low ferritin levels (the body's store of iron). Are they eating enough? If protein levels are low, hair will be affected. A low-fat diet will also have an impact because the follicles need sufficient oils – if for no other reason, this can be a good motivator for getting your son or daughter to be less strict with themselves. There are other complaints that can affect hair, ranging from digestive ones, such as Crohn's disease, to skin conditions such as eczema. The contraceptive pill can also have an impact and lacklustre hair can be a sign of psychological problems, such as bullying at school, so always heed such warning signs.

If your child wants to eat well to achieve a healthy mane of hair, the secret lies in plenty of iron-rich foods, such as good-quality red meat, game or offal. One or two good-quality red meat meals each week should be enough to keep iron levels healthy. If this is a teenage turn-off, encourage them to eat plenty of green, leafy vegetables, such as spinach, dark green Savoy cabbage, curly kale, broccoli and asparagus. Egg yolks, pulses (including baked beans) and fortified cereals are also beneficial, but try to choose a healthy, low-sugar, low-fat version if possible. Proteins have the double benefit of meeting the hair follicles' high requirement for amino acids.

Read more on:
◆ Pages 98–102

Many children decide to become vegetarian ◆ in their teenage years, so you need to make sure that they eat a balanced diet. An extreme vegetarian or poor diet can also cause hair loss later in life. If your child is a strict vegetarian or vegan, you may need to seek professional help, because it can be hard to increase ferritin stores to a sufficient level without the help of supplements. Iron supplements are notorious for their negative effect on the gut so you need to make sure you consult a doctor or nutritionist. In order to assist the body to absorb iron, you need to increase the intake of foods rich in vitamin C: berries, mangoes, kiwis, oranges, citron pressé and smoothies. Serve an iron-rich meal with a small glass of orange juice or offer fruit for dessert. Don't allow coffee, tea or cocoa drinks during or after such a meal, because the polypherols block the body's absorption of iron. Also watch out for green teas, because although their polypherols are generally seen as a good thing, they can also block iron absorption, so it's best to drink them between rather than with meals.

Skin

Spotty skin is the cause of much teenage angst, so it might be that your child can be persuaded to eat more healthily on the grounds of vanity if nothing else. It is a myth that chocolate causes spots and that dairy products block the pores. What the skin does need is plenty of hydration and enough replenishing nutrients, such as zinc, vitamin C and iron. Antioxidants and omega-3 fatty acids are also essential, and can be taken through a good combination of vegetables, juices and oily fish. Oily fish are also a rich supplier of protein, essential for growth and development, which are after all occurring at a breakneck speed at this age.

If your teenager is vegetarian or vegan, I'd suggest they take a vegetarian omega-3 supplement to cover their needs. This will take the pressure off, and means they can just enjoy eating seeds and nuts as part of their general diet without thinking they've got to consume a certain amount in order to meet their omega-3 requirement. You also need to make sure that your teenager's diet is high in fresh fruits and vegetables, that they drink plenty of water and generally eat a well-balanced diet ◆.

Read more on:
◆ Page 14

Cashew nut butter,
page 232

Food intolerances – facts and myths

The incessant bombardment of nonsense food stories in the press means that many teenagers convince themselves they are intolerant to something. I see many people in my practice who think that their symptoms, such as bloating, wind, an uncomfortable gut or skin conditions, are down to intolerance of a food such as wheat, when in fact the problem within their body comes purely and simply from their lifestyle: not enough good, regular meals, eating the wrong things, too little sleep, too much alcohol or nicotine. So instead of rushing to exclude foods, one of the best things you can do is teach teenagers about the impact of food on their gut.

This is particularly important if their diet isn't that well balanced in the first place – if they're fussy eaters, the last thing you need is for them to be even more limited in their food choice. This can cause all sorts of spin-off problems, such as being worried about food and the way their body looks, as well as leading to physical problems such as lack of energy and depression. For girls, restricted eating can prevent their body from maturing, so try to get them to eat a well-balanced diet for a few weeks and see if the symptoms disappear. If they don't, then you can of course explore whether specific foods need to be targeted.

Candida

As deeply uncomfortable as the symptoms can be, there is a lot of nonsense around about the effects of too much *Candida albicans* in the system, and teenagers may start to believe that they should be following an anti-candida diet. It is true that sometimes, if you have had to take a lot of antibiotics, you can end up with an overgrowth of candida (which can cause thrush). However, the idea that certain foods will do the same is irrational: all food is eventually broken down into glucose, which is the only fuel we can use in our bodies. The idea of cutting out sugar, yeast, mushrooms and alcohol in order to kill candida bacteria is really pseudo-science.

Sometimes symptoms such as headaches, bloating and tiredness do in fact improve on an anti-candida diet, but that is simply because this diet is healthier than usual – cutting out sugars, fast food and alcohol never did anyone any harm. If your teenager wants to follow such a diet, take it as an opportunity to explore some healthy eating together and to talk about what the body really needs in order to stay healthy. Try to dissuade them from following any diet that involves fasting or excluding certain food groups; as they need a balanced diet for general health, and there is a danger they will build up a bad relationship with food and end up more moody and depressed than when they started. They can also become low on valuable nutrients, which can affect the look of their skin and hair. When it comes to the problems caused by too many antibiotics, introducing probiotics and prebiotics ◆ can help reinstate the bacterial balance within the colon, which can help ease problems such as wind and bloating. You can offer these either as a supplement or in something tasty such as Greek-style yoghurt.

Read more on:
◆ *Pages 110–111*

Lemon polenta cake, page 249

Coeliac disease

Coeliac disease affects one in 100 people and is caused by a reaction to various proteins found in wheat, rye, barley and oats, including gluten. These proteins damage the part of the small intestine that enables the body to absorb food properly. The disease runs in families and particularly affects people from the Punjab region of India, Pakistan, the Middle East and North Africa. It is also common among people with type 1 (insulin-dependent) diabetes, autoimmune thyroid disease, osteoporosis, ulcerative colitis and epilepsy.

Diarrhoea and malnutrition are the most common symptoms of coeliac disease. Children may fail to gain weight and grow properly, while adults may find they lose weight. Malabsorption of essential proteins can also leave people feeling tired and weak, because of anaemia caused by iron or folate deficiency. Other possible problems include mouth ulcers, vomiting, abdominal pain, itchy rashes on the elbows and knees, infertility, osteoporosis and bowel cancer. Some people who are intolerant to wheat may have

Read more on:
◆ *Page 130*

Wild rice salad,
page 228

undiagnosed coeliac disease so it is important to consult a doctor. Although there is no cure, it can be controlled by carefully following a gluten-free diet and it is important to understand which foods are gluten-free and which contain wheat, barley and rye. Many can be successfully substituted and recipe books and gluten-free foods are readily available. A diet rich in calcium and vitamin D and regular weight-bearing exercise are also essential to help prevent osteoporosis from developing ◆.

Irritable Bowel Syndrome (IBS)

This is an umbrella term for a number of symptoms, the most common being: bloating, gripes, constipation, diarrhoea, wind, nausea or a bad taste in the mouth. Although any serious symptom should be checked with a doctor, more often than not these sorts of digestive symptoms are signs that an aspect of their lifestyle needs to be tweaked and this is not necessarily just based around what they eat. It's good to see if there are emotional reasons for their gut being upset before rushing them to see a gastroenterologist or embracing some sort of food exclusion diet at home – it might be an indication that your teenager is having a tough time at school or college, for example, as emotional upset can sometimes manifest itself physically in this way. Sometimes teenagers just won't articulate why they're struggling with something, as life can feel pretty complicated, and this affects the way their body deals with food – anxiety and stress can increase acid secretion in the stomach, which can change the way that food is dealt with. It can make us more tense and less able to go to the toilet, so we can get into a troublesome cycle of constipation or the opposite, having to rush to the toilet when we're worried. Of course, being preoccupied with woes can make us skip meals, eat things on the run, crave foods that aren't the best to eat – so all in all it's not surprising that IBS can start at this age. (Menstruation can also trigger IBS-type symptoms.)

A good place to start with nutrition is to explain to your teenager that the food they eat has a very real effect. If they go to the pub and then for a Chinese takeaway at midnight, they will suffer the consequences the next day. Of course you can't expect them to always eat healthily, but do try to help them understand the link between the foods they eat and how they feel. The gut is a muscle and it needs oxygen in order to work. If we eat and then dash off somewhere, the oxygen will be pumped to our legs, not the gut – and the gut may start to complain. Try to get teenagers to cut down on alcohol and nicotine, drink enough water and eat small, well-balanced, nourishing meals three times a day.

Read more on:
◆ *Pages 110–111*
▲ *Page 11*
● *Pages 94–95*

Pearled spelt, goat's cheese & chard risotto, page 213

In addition to eating well, you could increase the level of prebiotics and probiotics in their diet – this means looking into natural or Greek-style yoghurt, as this is a natural probiotic if it contains live cultures, which survive passage through the GI tract. Eating live probiotic natural yoghurt helps them to build up good levels of bacteria, which can alleviate some symptoms of IBS ◆. Prunes (and figs) are natural laxatives, delicious with probiotic yoghurt as a good quick breakfast or with something like a no-added-sugar muesli-type better-for-you breakfast cereal. The combination of natural yoghurt, fruit and high-fibre cereal can often provide a good remedy for painful constipation.

If bloating is a problem, encourage teenagers to keep a food and symptom diary ▲, recording everything they eat and drink for a week. From this you will be able to see if they're eating a healthy diet or whether a simple thing like eating more fruit and a high-fibre cereal or wholemeal bread instead of white, could suit them better ●. You may like to see if they prefer a diet that's not heavily wheat-based – which can so easily be the case when they're huge cereal fans, have a sandwich lunch and then eat pasta in the evening. Maybe a tweak or two, changing to, say, rice or rice noodles or even a spelt or other cereal-grained pasta, might just address the imbalance. We so often get stuck in a routine, but if we can think outside the box and be a touch more adventurous with what we eat, IBS can become a thing of the past.

A note on spelt

Spelt is a distant cousin of wheat and has a lot of its versatility making delicious bread, pasta, cereals, etc. However, some people find (for reasons largely unknown, as research studies are still in their infancy) that spelt seems to suit their digestive system better than wheat. The structure of the protein in the spelt is different – gluten being more brittle and differently absorbed by the gut – and if you look at well-sourced and well-produced brands (which are usually organic and don't come into contact with contaminants), you may find that your body prefers spelt-based products. Spelt comes in the form of pearled spelt, which you can make into a risotto, as flour for all sorts of delicious bread, pastries and biscuits, and also as pasta. You can also buy pastas, biscuits and other traditional products made with buckwheat, oats and rice, so check these out too.

Glandular fever

Glandular fever, which is caused by the Epstein-Barr virus, can be a horribly debilitating illness common to this age group. Affecting people in numerous ways, from aching joints and depression to exhaustion, it can develop into ME and chronic fatigue syndrome. It is important, therefore, to support the immune system with a healthy nourishing diet rich in antioxidants found mainly in fruits and vegetables. Zinc and selenium also benefit the immune system, so encourage teenagers to eat foods such as unsalted nuts, red meat, chicken, shellfish, pulses and wholegrains.

Although it's tempting for teenagers to just grab something when they're feeling lousy, it's best if they avoid the pattern of grabbing a quick fix of energy, and then slipping back into sleep or inactivity. Not only does the crash that follows undermine the body's ability to get stronger, but if this is all you eat then you run the risk of becoming depleted in essential vitamins, minerals and other key recovery nutrients such as proteins and complex carbs. Structure can also be useful when it comes to activity, as research has shown that if you include a daily programme of exercise and activity, as opposed to just lying around with little to distinguish your days from nights, the recovery time from illnesses such as Epstein-Barr virus and ME shortens.

If they are suffering from a very sore strep throat (which often coincides with the Epstein-Barr virus), you should look to dishes that will slip down with relative ease, such as fruit sorbets, soups, soufflés and risottos.

Coughs and colds

Colds and sniffles are much less serious adolescent complaints, but can affect the moods and behaviour of your teenager. Dairy products are not responsible, as many believe, for causing blocked sinuses – and to deplete the body of calcium at this age is a mistake. The answer is to strengthen the body's immune system through nourishing soups and the like. Honey and lemon is a classic and effective remedy for cold symptoms as it has powerful soothing and healing effects. I usually have some when I'm feeling under the weather or going down with a cold (or indeed want to try to stop myself catching one of Maya's). Whatever the illness, hydration is very important: aim to drink two to two and a half litres of water a day, staggered sensibly, with just the occasional cup of tea or coffee.

Spicy fish casserole, page 224

Looking After the Older Generation

As we enter our late 60s and early 70s, our bodies, along with the way we eat and the lifestyle we lead, tend to change significantly. There can be huge differences between a 70-year-old who's sprightly and continues to lead a very active life, and someone who due to physical or mental health problems needs a lot of care. For the vast majority, reaching this stage of life brings new nutrition- and food-related challenges.

Eating well or feeding someone nourishing food can be such a pleasure, and something we can hopefully have some control over. However, this can be more difficult in hospitals and care institutions as they don't seem to be able to get it right at all, in my opinion. Why shouldn't this stage in our lives incorporate eating delicious food we know is good for us?

As I've dotted around the various ages through this book I've found myself with even more difficulties in making generalisations, but I've identified some concerns that are good starting and discussion points. I hope they will inspire you to look at other sections of the book to see how you can tackle and work your way around them.

Look after yourself

Some of the challenges that arise as we reach old age are because old habits die hard. The temptation is to think that we can eat whatever we want and continue a similar lifestyle – after all, that's what we've always done. However, both our body's ability to deal with the food we eat and all other aspects of our lifestyle begin to change and our diets need to reflect that. We are also more at risk of developing certain diseases such as heart disease and stroke. But help is at hand, as we have far more sophisticated health screening and diagnostic tests now, so that we can look at things such as cholesterol levels and see whether our blood vessels are furring up, which is information that wasn't available in the past. We also know so much more about how making changes to our diet can have a really positive effect on our health before problems begin to appear and it feels like it's too late to do anything about it.

Although I don't want to imply that life should be focused entirely around food, it's especially important when you reach this stage of your life not to let things go when considering what you eat. You need to maintain interest in your body, as the difference between looking and feeling well, and being healthy on the inside can be strongly influenced by the foods you eat. You may find that frequent health niggles that start to appear at this age, such as constipation, poor energy levels, heart disease and diabetes can be made far more manageable by eating the right foods and caring for yourself. If you're looking after someone in this age group, food will enable you to give them so much pleasure and can be a great healer.

Sadly it's far too easy to fall through the cracks of the modern-day health system, and illnesses that need treating can be misdiagnosed or missed altogether. Even if you are lucky enough to be under the care of a good doctor or nurse, get back in touch with them if you find that your appetite starts going off, you're losing weight or notice any other changes in your eating habits. It's always best to catch weight loss early than to get into real difficulties when your appetite has gone and other symptoms arise as a result of not eating enough. Some drugs adversely affect appetite, so keep in regular contact with your doctor and discuss changing to an alternative if you think it could be more appropriate.

We often take weight loss and lack of appetite far too lightly, and many institutions don't prioritise eating nourishing meals. We should do far more to turn the situation around, rather than prescribing supplement drinks as if they're the answer to everything. Life should be more about eating nourishing, scrumptious food, and even more so when we're older.

Vegetables

Read more on:
◆ Pages 112–113
▲ Pages 32–33

Cauliflower cheese,
page 217

Vegetables are one of the most important groups of foods to focus on throughout our lives, but particularly as we get older, as they offer so many nutritional benefits, not least fibre. Lack of fibre leads to constipation ◆ and can mean that we don't get enough or any satisfaction from the meals we eat. This can lead to us eating too much of the higher-calorie fatty and sugary foods, which ultimately ups the risk of gaining too much weight with further consequences. Our body is at a stage when it could do without being put under too much weight as we carry the excess load.

One of the problems, looking at the practices in institutions and hospitals and at some older people's cooking habits, is that the vegetables that they eat are generally over cooked and not at all delicious or nutritious. If we overcook vegetables we lose most, if not all, of the vitamin C, and although there will still be some fibre our levels of essential vitamins can be too low. Lack of vitamin C means our immune system won't be receiving as much help as it could do with, and can compromise our ability to heal leaving us vulnerable to infections. Lack of vitamin C also reduces our body's ability to absorb iron, which we need a plentiful supply of throughout our lives. If we don't eat much red meat, we need to give our body a helping hand in absorbing iron from other iron-rich foods such as eggs, green leafy vegetables, lentils and beans ▲.

There is a case for using the freezer well when it comes to practical ways to boost our vegetable intake, as frozen vegetables – spinach, broad beans, peas, etc. – preserve their nutrient content and can be a good source of vitamin C, especially if cooked lightly, and are also fantastic for fibre. We can stock up the freezer and just use what we need rather than leave unused ones to rot in the vegetable rack. Tinned vegetables can often be disappointing, rather mushy and bland, but improved canning technology over the last few years that there are a few good exceptions: tinned sweetcorn, garden peas and asparagus spears tend to be fine, as can spinach and artichoke hearts. An omelette with peas and finely chopped prosciutto or streaky bacon can make a quick scrumptious meal, and throwing peas or sweetcorn into a ready-made pasta sauce stirred into pasta, along with pesto, or soup can be another easy way to up vegetable intake.

You can also buy pretty good soup nowadays, both tinned ones and fresh in pouches and cartons, with a good vegetable content (and often lower in terms of salt and sugar than the chilled soups). And of course it's a good idea to stock the freezer with individual portions of vegetable pasta sauces, soups, ratatouille, tagines and vegetable casseroles, if you're looking after someone. You don't lose

Read more on:
◆ *Pages 30–32*
▲ *Page 100*

any of the fibre or vitamins and minerals by blending a soup either, so if swallowing is an issue, a blended soup can be a great source of vegetables.

Vegetable juices are a fantastic way to glean vitamin C, folate and fibre. Make them fresh at home, using a juicer, or buy ready-made juices such as beetroot and apple or apple and rhubarb.

Keeping things moving

Not being active tends to slow down the way the lower part of your gut works and you may suffer from constipation, in which case you could find that you need to increase your fibre ◆ and water intake; doing gentle exercise such as yoga, walking or swimming can help to get things moving. Some medication can also have a constipating effect, so discuss this with your doctor – it could be that changing your drugs (codeine, for example, can be dire at bunging you up) could help ease things too. The most common constipation remedy to be handed out is lactulose, which can have its place, but it can also aggravate the bloated feeling – it's very sweet, and I think it's much better to see if you can get your gut moving by tweaking your diet.

Make sure that your diet includes lots of fibre-rich foods such as wholegrain bread, brown rice, quinoa, spelt, oats and cereals, plus fruits, vegetables, beans and lentils ▲, but you also need to keep your fluid intake up by drinking plenty of water. There are a couple of herbal teas renowned for getting the gut moving – those made from tamarind, dandelion or yellow dock, and infusions made by steeping fresh root ginger or four to five senna pods in 150ml of hot water (alternatively, you could try senna tablets from health food shops and pharmacies).

Being active helps the gut to move – even walking or yoga or swimming, something not too stressful on the heart or any other part of your body, can help to kick-start the gut into working better. Exercise can also help to reduce stress and anxiety levels, which can be contributing factors to constipation.

If you still have a problem with constipation, your doctor may prescribe a laxative, but don't be surprised if you find yourself feeling more bloated – this can be an uncomfortable side-effect and is the last thing your sore, constipated gut needs. If your constipation isn't too bad, or if you prefer to see if you can tackle it without taking laxatives, it could be worth trying to boost your intake of the naturally laxative-effecting fruits such as prunes, figs and apples. Sometimes just a few glasses of prune juice (which I suggest making up from prune juice concentrate), wholemeal toast spread with prune spread, or some stewed apple and rhubarb, can get the problem sorted quickly.

Drinking enough water

As we get older our ability to recognise when we need to be drinking more water or fluid decreases, and many people find that the less they drink the less they want to drink. Some care homes and hospitals don't want their elderly patients to drink much because of the practical issues of continence that this can trigger. I find this atrocious, as lack of fluid can cause all sorts of health problems: not least, it can make you feel shattered, fed up, constipated and can affect your concentration. Some care homes have their heating on quite high, and while residents may not be sweating, they can still lose a lot of water this way. Whatever the reason, we need to keep our fluid intake around two and a half litres a day.

As you know, I'm a huge fan of water – it's the most hydrating of fluids, meaning that you will glean the maximum hydrating properties from drinking it. If cordial makes the water more appetising, a glass or two a day can be a good way to up your water intake ◆. Tea and coffee have a mild diuretic effect (you lose a little bit of the water you've taken in as it stimulates your kidneys to get rid of it), but there is nothing wrong with a few cups of tea or coffee a day contributing towards this amount either. There is a lot of good to be gleaned from drinking tea ▲, but you should watch that you're not too generous with the sugar. The only liquid which has a dramatic diuretic effect is alcohol, so this shouldn't be seen as part of your two and a half litres a day target. If you don't have any contraindications for drinking alcohol, such as pancreatitis or being on certain medication, a few units a week can be pleasurable. And a little glass of something before a meal can be a good aperitif – especially useful if your appetite is off.

Read more on:
◆ *Pages 40–42*
▲ *Pages 33–38*

Rhubarb

Rhubarb is high in fibre, vitamin C, folate and beta-carotene, and is especially yummy when cooked with the juice of an orange or a little apple juice. Although spring tends to be the time when the majority of rhubarb hits the shops, and the more greenish-tinged rhubarb I grow pops up from May through to October. You can find force-grown rhubarb in the depths of winter but it tends to be more pink in colour and less tannic in taste, and therefore has a more delicate hit which may suit your palate better. Rhubarb can easily be cooked or blanched and frozen.

Butter

Many of us are big butter fans, but we shouldn't see it as being the only and the best source of fat, or use it in large quantities. Fats of all sorts contain a lot of calories, and when we were younger and more active, our body was probably able to justify a buttery slice of toast or portion of vegetables. As we get older, however, we tend to become more sedentary and our metabolic rates lower (unless we're very unwell), so if we're not careful too much butter can increase our weight and also our levels of LDL cholesterol, which can ultimately lead to heart disease.

I don't want to say that butter should be banned altogether, but if you've been told by your doctor that your LDL cholesterol level is too high ◆ cutting down on butter can be one way to help bring it back down to a safe level. We do all need some fat in our diet to help us absorb fat-soluble vitamins and stop us from losing body fat, which is a good insulator and cushioning under our skin, so replace saturated fats with some other vegetable-based mono- or polyunsaturated fats. Try olive, rapeseed or avocado oil, or perhaps choose an olive oil based spread for your sandwiches, even if you are adamant that toast doesn't taste the same without butter. Every step you can take to ensure that you're not eating too much saturated fat is welcome.

Sugar

While a delicious sable biscuit or melt-in-your-mouth ginger nut with a cup of tea or a small portion of apple crumble with custard or a *crème caramel* after a meal can be part of our day, if we were to keep a record of how much sweet stuff we consume the amount might be higher than we'd expect. As part of our culture, we consider giving people gifts of sweet foods, such as a box of chocolates or truffles, to be one of the best ways to show we care about them. However, if we're not careful and we eat too much, we can hit problems when our refined sugar intake goes too high – for one thing, we increase the risk of tooth decay. Preserving our teeth and gum health is incredibly important, and sweet drinks, biscuits, etc., combined with poor oral hygiene, can conspire against us maintaining a healthy set of teeth and gums. If we have a small appetite, drinking too much sweet tea and nibbling on too many biscuits can make it far less likely that we'll be able to eat a nourishing meal later.

Read more on:
◆ *Page 29*
▲ *Page 157*

Too much sweet food can pile on the weight too, which increases our risk of developing diabetes ▲ and heart disease, and

Read more on:
◆ Pages 194–199

Poached rhubarb &
blueberries, page 240

can aggravate joint problems such as arthritis ◆. If we're carrying too much weight, getting around and exercising is far more difficult, so all in all it's a good idea to see if we can watch the amount of sweet foods and drinks we consume. There are so many delicious ways to enjoy sweet foods but at the same time reduce to the effects of having too much. The best scenario is if we can get our sweet hit from fresh fruits, perhaps a delicious orange or a slice of apple cake made with wholemeal flour, and in that way introduce some other health benefits such as fibre. If you can stick to three meals a day, with, say, a piece of fresh fruit as a between-meal snack, this is a good way to ensure that your body receives a good balance of the essential nutrients.

If you're having problems with your teeth that are affecting your ability to eat fresh fruits with tough skin, one solution is to peel or cook them. I cook Bramley apples in a large pot with frozen raspberries and poach peaches, nectarines and plums, then either freeze them in smaller portions or keep them in the fridge to dip into as a base for puddings or simply warmed up with a dollop of yoghurt. The only thing you need to bear in mind is that you won't receive as high a vitamin C hit from fruit when it's cooked, but it still provides a good source of fibre and other nutrients such as potassium and some folate. Do discuss any dental problems you're having with your dentist, as it may be that something can be done to make eating fruit easier and you don't need to suffer in silence.

Avoid getting low in vital nutrients

As we get older our body tends to become less efficient at absorbing or manufacturing nutrients; for instance, the skin isn't as good as it used to be at manufacturing vitamin D, so if we're not spending much time in the sun our vitamin D level can be worryingly low. This is why we are encouraged to take a 10mcg vitamin D supplement. But research also shows that older people can lack enough iron, calcium, B vitamins such as folate, and zinc – a lesser-known mineral which we need for a strong immune system and to maintain a healthy appetite.

Mass-produced food is notorious for being devoid of much nutrition, and is often not that appetising when it arrives. If you're a relative or friend of someone who's having to rely on institutionalised food, you could try to improve their nutritional status. It may be that as well as a vitamin D supplement, a more general vitamin and mineral supplement could help make up a few of the essentials, but discuss this with a doctor to ensure that it doesn't interfere with any medication they're taking.

Avoid grazing

Just as large meals can put you off eating well, so can being a constant nibbler, as the nibbles usually end up being high in fat, salt and sugar and lower your appetite for nourishing meals. While constant nibbling on biscuits, nuts, sweets, etc. can do this, so can sipping on the supplement drinks often prescribed by doctors when appetites are poor.

Reduce the risk of food poisoning

Read more on:
◆ *Pages 61–64*

When we're young and fighting fit it can be easy to get through a bout of food-poisoning, but when we're older it can be far more serious and in some cases, life threatening. We need to avoid foods we know carry a greater risk, such as runny eggs, soft cheeses, especially if they're unpasteurised, and pâtés ◆. We also need to be particularly careful with keeping foods well wrapped, fresh and stored well. This is where a freezer and a microwave can be useful, as they can reduce the length of time that food is sitting around and potentially growing food-poisoning bugs. As long as food is defrosted and cooked well, it can be a very practical answer. Flasks are great for soup, risotto, pasta, casseroles, vegetable curry, dahl, ratatouille and one of Maya's favourite school lunches, cauliflower cheese, if you need to cook something in the morning or early afternoon and you want it to be warm enough to eat later on.

Arthritis

The majority of people with arthritis, whether it's rheumatoid, osteoarthritis or gout, wonder if their diet might be either the cause or the cure of their joint problems. It's a big area of interest, not least because there are lots of supplements that promise to be the best thing for our joints, either in preventing arthritis or, if we already have it, in making a difference to the way it affects us. Cod liver oil and glucosamine are two of the most popular supplements, with green-lipped mussels and turmeric being more recent headline grabbers. As well as this, it has already been suggested that if we avoid acid-producing foods such as oranges and red meat, or have a daily dose of apple cider vinegar, our joints will love us.

Yet some doctors completely dismiss the notion that a diet or supplement will make any difference, and some can make you feel as though there isn't anything we can do to help ourselves other than lose weight. This is a shame, because I've found that we can make a significant difference to our symptoms and our overall health. We also need to bear in mind that when we go through a particularly rough time with arthritis, especially rheumatoid arthritis, we can lose a lot of weight quickly and all of a sudden look and feel much older.

Osteoarthritis and rheumatoid arthritis

Studies show, and indeed it seems to be widely considered, that diet can have a bigger impact on rheumatoid arthritis than the more common type – osteoarthritis. However, I'm going to deal with the latter first, because we are more likely to suffer from it in old age.

Osteoarthritis (OA) is a degenerative condition that develops when the cartilage around our joints, especially weight-bearing joints such as the knees and hips, wears away and new bone tissue grows beneath. This prevents the joints from moving as smoothly as they should, causes painful inflammation and over time, the joints may become distorted, causing further discomfort as muscles become strained and nerves get trapped. The main risk factors for developing OA are getting older, having a genetic predisposition to it, trauma or injury to a joint, and sometimes repetitive activity (which is the case with professional sports people) can make the joints become arthritic. Carrying too much weight is a strong risk factor, especially for developing OA in the knee – the joint which seems to suffer most from excess weight strain.

Of course a big problem resulting from osteoarthritis is that because the pain discourages movement, we don't feel like exercising even more, so unless we change our diet the weight can start piling on. This puts an even greater strain on the joints, particularly the knees, and up goes the inflammation and the pain. Interestingly, the link which exists between being overweight and having OA of the knee can be easily understood, as the less weight the knee has to support the less strain put on the joint, but the link that studies have found with being overweight and suffering from OA is far more complex than simply being mechanical. It's thought that being overweight and carrying too much body fat has an effect on blood fats and on hormones such as oestrogen which may explain the link which exists between OA and a greater risk of developing heart disease.

Whatever the subtleties physiologically, if you're carrying too much weight the first and most important thing to do is to try to bring your weight down sensibly: a couple of pounds (1kg) a week is a good rate. You need to do this healthily, as the last thing you need is to go on any sort of crash nutrient-depleted diet that will leave you feeling weak and ill. Sometimes doctors can be too forceful in their 'go away and lose weight' tactics, and you can feel bullied into going on a crash diet, but this isn't the answer – it's possible to sustainably lose weight by eating well without exacerbating any of your other symptoms. I think that one of the reasons why some people give up trying to lose weight is because they go on a diet that's so strict that it leaves them feeling weak and even more awful than they did before. It's interesting that if you're not overweight in the first place you have a lower risk of developing OA, but even if you have already been diagnosed, any shift in weight, however small, should help to make some of your symptoms better.

When it comes to the specifics as to what your diet should look like now that you have osteoarthritis, the main parameters should be the same as for anyone else your age. The more intricate links that have been found between specific foods and symptoms of arthritis seem to be connected with rheumatoid arthritis (a complex inflammatory condition that affects both young and older people). However, some people with osteoarthritis do seem to find that certain foods upset them or ease their discomfort, so although the evidence for the following areas of nutritional strategies is far stronger with rheumatoid arthritis, you may find something that could help you, whichever type of arthritis you have.

The overall diet can be best summarised by Mediterranean food – fruits, vegetables, oily fish being a few of the things to enjoy ◆. Most arthritis sufferers say that they can't eat too many oranges, tomatoes or other acid-producing foods as they make their joints feel worse. Interestingly, there is no hard scientific evidence to support cutting out any specific food, but rather than dismiss it completely I think it's worth keeping a food and symptom diary for a fortnight or so ▲. At the end of that time you can see if there is any relationship between what you eat and drink and how your joints and the rest of you feels.

My theory is that as long as you eat an overall healthy diet, you may just find that taking down the amount of specific foods or indeed leaving something out helps. If you feel better eating white instead of red meat, for example, this is fine, but my big word of caution here is that your diet should be healthy overall and full of nourishing foods. You need to watch out if you're cutting out fresh fruits, as these can be one of your richest source of vitamin C, if not the richest. Vitamin C is an essential vitamin for helping our body repair cuts and pressure sores and recover from illnesses – so it's important on every front to keep your fruit and vegetables up to the five-a-day target.

We don't understand exactly why, but diet rich in the long-chain omega-3 fatty acids found in oily fish ● stimulates the body to

Read more on:
◆ Pages 151–153
▲ Pages 11
● Pages 17–18 & 101

Roast mackerel with potatoes & thyme, page 223

produce substances that can sometimes dampen the inflammatory response and alleviate arthritic pain. Although it has to be said that the evidence for long-chain omega-3 fatty acids being helpful is largely shown with rheumatoid arthritis, sometimes people with osteoarthritis experience some relief too. Since there is evidence to show that vitamin D (in which oily fish are wonderfully high) is also important in helping to relieve and slow down the progression of osteoarthritis, I recommend that it's good to ensure oily fish are a big part of your diet. Another option for increasing your long-chain omega-3 fatty acid intake would be to take a fish oil supplement, as this may help to reduce inflammation – you need one containing a total of 500–750mg of the fish oils EPA and DHA. Cod liver oil, although one of the most widely used supplements taken by OA sufferers, hasn't been shown to fare well, and even though some people swear by avocado and soy bean, again the studies don't give us much evidence for the benefits in taking them.

Getting back to your diet and the types of fat you eat, I'd strongly recommend that you choose monounsaturated fats as your main source of fat, as these are largely regarded as being neutral when it comes to inflammation (unlike the omega-6-rich oils – sunflower, safflower and corn oils – which are best kept down in your diet). Rheumatoid arthritis can increase your risk of heart disease, so choosing a diet based around a small amount of monounsaturated fat will also help you protect your heart.

Another common supplement is glucosamine (an amino acid sugar), but again there confusion here as the industrial studies show them to be advantageous while independent ones don't. But some people swear by glucosamine, and some studies have shown that if taken regularly over several years it can be effective in increasing the rate at which cartilage is able to repair itself. The usual dose is 1–2g per day. You may well see some glucosamine supplements that contain chondroitin (another component of cartilage), and although studies have cast doubt on whether these supplements, whether taken individually, or combined, actually show convincing results, my view is that if you find they do provide some relief, since there isn't any harm in taking them and there is little traditional medicine-wise which offers miracles, then I wouldn't stop taking them.

Gruesome gout

Unlike most forms of arthritis, gout tends not to last very long. It's an extremely painful inflammation that usually only affects one site – most often the joint at the base of the big toe, which some people describe as being so excruciatingly painful that it's as if someone has rammed a red hot poker into it. It seems to be more common in middle-aged or older men, and especially among those who love rich food although I'm seeing more and more women with hot, swollen, painful toes. There is, however, also a strong genetic link.

The inflammation of gout is caused by the release of crystals of monosodium urate monohydrate, which usually comes from the natural product of metabolism, uric acid. Sometimes this is caused by a build up of unwanted uric acid in the body, but a diet which is rich in purines (see below) can also increase levels of uric acid and trigger gout. There is a saying that 'the associates of gout are the associates of plenty', but more specifically, as well as not too much of the rich stuff, you should look to watching the amount of purine-rich food you eat. Keeping away from these as a general rule can reduce the likelihood that a gout attack will painfully spring itself upon you – it could also stop the first signs of gout (if you're in tune enough with your body to notice when perhaps the joint is feeling different, or indeed if your doctor has advised you that your uric acid level has come back high in a blood test) and prevent an attack from occurring.

The foods richest in purines and therefore best avoided or kept to a minimum include game, offal and meat extracts such as stock cubes, pâtés, sausages, meat pies and yeast extract (Marmite). Those red meat lovers among you may well be relieved to know that lean cuts of red beef, lamb and pork, as well as poultry, are slightly lower in purines, so are fine for you to eat in moderation. It's game and offal that can get you into the most trouble.

When we talk about oily fish, it's usually in a positive way, i.e. these are good for the joints, since they're rich in the long-chain omega-3 fatty acids. But unfortunately if you either have a genetic predisposition to gout or find that your diet is otherwise high in purines you also need to be very mindful that mackerel, sardines and herrings are purine-rich. Sadly anchovies, sprats, whitebait, and shellfish such as crab and prawns, are also high in purines, so I would suggest that if gout is on your radar you either look to taking an omega-3 supplement or stick to salmon and fresh tuna (which have lower levels of purines). More generally on the fish front, white and oily fish (salmon and fresh tuna, mentioned above) are great to eat, but too much smoked food such as smoked salmon, pickled herrings and rollmops isn't good for gout.

You could also look to include some of the vegetarian sources of omega-3 fatty acids, including hemp, walnut and linseed (flaxseed) oils – use these oils in salad dressings or as alternatives for frying or drizzling over vegetables. You could also sprinkle linseeds and walnuts (also good for your heart and blood pressure) on wholegrain cereals such as unsweetened muesli and porridge. However, unfortunately the types of omega-3 fatty acid you find in foods other

Read more on:
◆ Pages 17–18 & 101

Butternut squash & red
lentil dahl, page 214

than oily fish aren't of the long-chain variety, so I'd see using some of these oils and nuts as an added bonus, not as your main omega-3 fatty acid source ◆. Be aware that too much oil of any sort will up your calorie intake, which may not be a good thing.

Finally, as if I haven't been enough of a killjoy already, and although they're usually seen as great nutritious foods, you may find that if you're particularly predisposed to gout, steering clear of dried fruits, peas, asparagus, cauliflower, spinach, lentils, mushrooms and mycoprotein (Quorn) could be just what your body needs to get its uric acid levels down. Wholegrain bread and cereals are good generally, but you need to avoid wheatgerm (generally bought as a single cereal in health food stores) and bran. Watch out for the deluxe mueslis, as they can be packed with dried fruits, which may just aggravate your gout.

Alcohol has been firmly associated with gout and historically, we can trace a link back to port and Madeira being the worst gout-triggering drinks. This was probably because they used to sweeten these alcoholic tipples with lead shot, chronic low-grade lead poisoning being a risk factor for gout. But nowadays, when port and Madeira are less commonly quaffed, we know that alcohol of any sort doesn't help gout, and indeed beer drinkers can be some of the hardest hit. You'll probably be warned off all alcohol if you're mid-attack, but afterwards drinking plenty of water alongside your alcohol can help to flush it out of your system and make it less of a menace. It's good to drink two and a half litres of water a day anyway, as this helps to lower the salt levels in your blood, which helps blood pressure and general health too.

Eye conditions

Most of us value our sight more than any other sense, and would fight tooth and nail to preserve it. The most common age-related eye conditions include cataracts, glaucoma and diabetic retinopathy, but one of the perhaps lesser-known conditions is age-related macular degeneration (AMD). This is a disease that gradually destroys sharp, central vision and ultimately leads to our eye or eyes struggling with fine sight details. In some cases AMD advances so slowly that we hardly notice any change in vision, but for others the disease progresses faster and may lead to a loss of vision in both eyes.

Research into what we can do to reduce the risk of AMD isn't conclusive, but there is some interesting research, which suggests that our diets can have an impact. Smoking is a major risk factor for both AMD and cataracts, and if you have the early stages of AMD your doctor will probably encourage you to quit, as you can slow down the disease quite profoundly by doing so. When we look beyond giving up smoking, it does seem that an antioxidant-rich diet with a good variety of fruit and vegetables is once more where we should focus our attention, as it's thought that the physical changes which occur in the eye are largely down to free radical damage. And as with most areas of our body, the eye doesn't just need you to be tucking into vegetables and fruits. There is some evidence to suggest that oily fish ◆ can also reduce your risk of developing AMD.

Antioxidant nutrients found in fruit and vegetables hold some power when it comes to protecting our eyes from AMD; they like to scavenge and react with free radicals to prevent them from damaging us. Admittedly research has tended to be shown in a laboratory setting, so we don't know yet how this will translate if we eat a diet rich in these specific nutrients; but since they have been shown more widely to be great for us, let's follow this line of thought.

The key eye-benefiting antioxidant nutrients are vitamin C and the carotenoids lutein and zeaxanthin. Vitamin C is much talked about, but the highest hitters with the stranger-sounding carotenoids are spinach, kale, broccoli and red and orange peppers. Zeaxanthin is found in greatest quantities in mangoes, oranges, red and orange peppers, nectarines, papayas, squashes and honeydew melons. The good news for lutein and zeaxanthin is that unlike vitamin C, which is very sensitive to heat and time, the carotenoids are more robust and don't tend to deteriorate as rapidly with cooking. Our body's ability to absorb and use these carotenoids also improves with cooking, so small ravioli stuffed with ricotta and spinach or a thick Tuscan-style bean soup with peppers and curly kale would be a couple of delicious options to try – if the spinach was raw or just steamed you'd glean some useful vitamin C too.

However, rather than feeling as if you have to eat something rich in lutein or zeaxanthin every day, I would instead suggest that you ensure you have them as part of your five-a-day mantra and try to have a good spectrum of colours to maximise your chances of gleaning a range of antioxidants. One of my main reasons for suggesting that we shouldn't focus on eating only these specific fruits and vegetables is that to see the benefits we should be having a diet containing about 6mg of lutein daily – and this would amount to eating about 200g of spinach every day, which is an awful lot. Lutein and zeaxanthin supplement tablets can be bought in health food shops, but I wouldn't recommend taking them unless recommended by a doctor or dietitian. It's very easy to take supplements that are unnecessary so you're much better off ensuring that your diet is rich in a good spectrum of vegetables and fruits, including those rich in lutein and zeaxanthin.

Read more on:
◆ Pages 17–18 & 101

Smoked mackerel pâté, page 224

Dementia

As we get older we fear a deterioration in the way our brain functions perhaps even more than cancer or any other disease. Much of this fear surrounds dementia, for the simple reason that it is very ill understood and until you've had someone close to you develop this disease, nothing prepares you for the immense challenges it presents. Also, unlike cancer and heart disease, where there are public awareness campaigns the issue of dementia is still seen as something to be hidden, and admitting that there is any presence of brain disease is something very few are happy to do. Research into dementia is slow because people are far more likely to support cancer research than contribute to an Alzheimer's charity. Dementia is progressive, which means that the symptoms will gradually get worse, but how fast it progresses will largely depend on the individual and on how early on they can access support and treatments.

It can be a very difficult issue to bring up and discuss within families, so many people would prefer to try to ignore the problems; to broach the idea of someone dear to you having problems with their brain is often met with denial and aggression. It is all in all a very upsetting problem, but one that can have a big impact on our quality of life.

It's hard to cover all the elements of how food and dementia influence each other, but I have a real 'bee in my bonnet' about the fact that the concern for dementia sufferers' nutritional wellbeing doesn't feature high enough on the list of priorities in care homes, hospitals or if someone is living alone. It absolutely should be at the top of the list, because it can have such a profound effect on the disease and the lives of all concerned. Care homes can charge a significant fee so there is no excuse for poor-quality food, even on the tightest budgets. I think it's atrocious how many dementia sufferers and those who are generally old and frail have their food plonked in front of them with no one to help them eat it. Someone should be there to sit and take the stalks off grapes, peel a clementine, cajole without pestering someone who has a poor appetite, help them to eat and ensure that if they don't manage to eat much during that meal this is noted and monitored.

Dementia is seldom the same for everyone, but we usually experience memory loss, a change in moods, anxiety, depression and aggression. It can be a very disempowering condition, and is often frightening as we don't understand what's happening to us. Part of the problem, too, is that dementia can really start to affect our ability to communicate, which can lead to isolation and our needs won't always be met. As you might expect, our ability to carry out even the most basic of everyday tasks gradually disappears and we become more and more reliant on others.

Diverticular disease

Chicken & chickpea burgers, page 220

As we get older our gut changes in all sorts of ways, even when our diet apparently stays the same. We have some ideas as to why this happens although it's usually a combination of things – being less active, certain drugs and our gut 'holding' upset and tension inside. This can be a sensitive subject, as we may look all right on the outside, but tension, grief or upset of any sort can make bowel movements difficult. Sometimes the less we're able to go to the toilet the more uptight we get, making our gut even more unpredictable. All in all, the more we can do to try to reduce the anxiety surrounding our bowel habits, by doing gentle exercises, eating nourishing good-for-the-gut foods, drinking plenty of water, and trying to reduce stress and boost happy endorphin levels, the sooner our gut will settle down. Do check out one of my favourite anti-anxiety machines, the Pzizz machine, as this meditation device can make a real difference to the way the gut behaves.

Being constipated is one of the things that can increase the risk of developing diverticular disease, which is thought to be present in at least half of the population over 65. Diverticular disease happens when the walls of the intestine weaken, forming pockets or sacs (diverticula). Many people never know they have diverticula in their intestine because they have no symptoms, and luckily only 25 per cent of sufferers are struck down with symptoms of severe abdominal pain, intermittent diarrhoea and constipation.

Diverticula often develop because our diet is relatively deficient in fibre-rich foods, which help to prevent constipation – it's the straining involved in passing a stool that weakens the intestinal walls, causing diverticula to form. So preventing constipation is important to ensure that diverticula don't develop in the first place.

Sometimes diverticula can become infected and cause rectal bleeding, pain and fever; if untreated this can prove to be serious, as the infection can become widespread and cause all sorts of complications. If you're diagnosed with an infection, the advice completely changes – the last thing you need is roughage, as it's too much for a sore, infected intestine to deal with. You need a low-fibre diet, which means switching from high-fibre foods to white rice, pasta, white fish such as grilled Dover sole, seabass and some fresh prawns, chicken, a few cooked (not raw) fruits and vegetables. For the immediate future, stay away from vegetables and fruits with seeds such as tomatoes, courgettes, marrows, grapes (this is simply because sometimes seeds get trapped in the diverticula, aggravating the infection), and wind-inducing vegetables like Brussels sprouts, cabbages, beans and lentils.

Read more on:
◆ *Pages 110–111*

Vegetable soup with lime & herbs, page 232

Once the infection has been treated successfully (which most likely will need antibiotics, as a gut infection is a serious medical condition), look to see if you can improve your gut bacterial flora. First take a combined prebiotic and probiotic supplement ◆, to help ensure that the bacterial balance in your gut returns to normal after the course of antibiotics. Then, once your infection has cleared up, start gently building up your fibre intake, so that your gut returns to a good non-constipated state. But gently does it.

Recovering from surgery

We are at our most vulnerable when we've undergone an operation, because the operation puts our body under a lot of strain – the physical trauma of being cut into and the hormonal responses to being operated on can use up a lot of stores, such as fat, muscle, vitamins and minerals. Even with the best hygiene standards in the operating theatre, any operation introduces bacteria and viruses into our body that can challenge our immune system. Furthermore, if we're undergoing surgery it's possible that we've not been feeling at our best for a while, may not have been eating well and may have other health problems that will hinder our recovery. It's unusual that we go into the operating theatre feeling 100 per cent. And indeed, after the operation it's highly likely that we'll have a few days when our body is unable to tolerate much, if any, food, as the anaesthetic often affects the bowel.

Even for people who are in theory able to cope with a nourishing meal, hospitals and care homes can be atrocious at providing appetising, nutritious foods and ensuring that patients eat enough of it to enable their bodies to recover. So often it is down to us, the relatives, to take the issue of eating for recovery into our own hands. Being able to look after someone we care about in this way can be incredibly valuable, as we so often feel helpless.

I want to take you through the foods and nutrients needed to recover that are often contrary to those that patients and relatives think they need. It's not all about fruits and vegetables rich in the skin- and body-repairing nutrients such as vitamin C. Of course vitamin C is a valuable nutrient but when our body is recovering from surgery or any situation that has depleted our energy stores, we need more than anything to eat plenty of calories. Our body needs a plentiful supply of calories to repair skin and muscle, build new bone, fight other infections, and prevent any further loss of the padding we have underneath our skin. But often there is another challenge, that of not having much of an appetite, so we need to focus on small amounts of nourishing, calorie-rich foods. This is not the moment for nibbling on a few grapes thinking they're a good source of vitamin C – your body needs fat, carbohydrate and protein. In particular, being ill or having an operation often depletes your protein reserves, and although this is putting somewhat complex physiological processes into very simple terms, each meal you eat should include a protein-rich food as well as a good source of starchy carbohydrate with some good fat alongside it.

Fine-tuning the fibre

When recovering from an operation, you may find that high-fibre, carbohydrate-rich foods fill you up too quickly. A good alternative is a white bread sandwich with a protein-rich filling such as ham (wafer-thin honey roast ham, proscuitto etc.), fish such as smoked trout or mackerel, eggs (ensuring they're hard-boiled to prevent salmonella poisoning), chicken or cheese. You may find a big steak off-putting, but a small portion of shepherd's pie, made with beef or lamb mince in a rich gravy and topped with a crunchy layer of buttery mashed potato, could hit the spot.

However, a common side-effect of surgery or being bedridden for a while is constipation, and if you start eating white bread and pasta instead of the wholemeal variety you may not get enough fibre to kick-start and encourage the bowel to get moving. One way round this would be to eat fruit and vegetable options such as compote of fruits, poached fruit with custard or panacotta, juices, soups or porridge with honey and berries on top. In order to ensure that the meal isn't full of too much fibre and not enough calories, the solution would be to add something high in fat or sugar to up its energy content: stirring cream into soups; adding honey or brown sugar to porridge; using thick Greek-style yoghurt and full cream milk on cereals.

Small, nutritionally powerful and delicious

Recovering from any illness, especially if you've had an operation or have pressure sores, requires a plentiful supply of vitamin C and other skin- and tissue-healing nutrients such as zinc (see below). Stir thick yoghurt into a home-made smoothie, serve cream with strawberries, bake peaches with dark muscovado-style sugar or maple syrup, or have a vegetable or fruit juice in between meals. Make sure it's not too close to a mealtime, as liquid fills you up so quickly that to have a juice as a starter or a soup could just scupper the chance of being able to eat anything more substantial. Whereas

I don't usually like *nouvelle cuisine*, preferring to cook big pots of something hearty in the middle of the table that everyone dips into, this is an instance where a little espresso cup of a creamy leek and potato soup mid-meal could just be what's needed – small and delicately presented, it will often be just what you fancy too.

Bolognese sauce, page 218

Lack of zinc can exacerbate any poor appetite – the less zinc-rich foods we eat, the less inclined we are to want to eat; it's a vicious cycle we would do good to break. Zinc-rich foods include lean red meat, nuts, seeds, shellfish such as oysters and prawns, crumbly cheese such as Cheshire, Lancashire and Parmesan, and wholegrains, but while I'm not usually a fan of unnecessary vitamin and mineral supplements it may be a good idea, especially if you're off your food, to take a 200–220mg zinc sulphate supplement two or three times a day (discuss it with your doctor to ensure that this complements any other drugs, as sometimes they can interfere). This may not only bring back the appetite but also helps with wound healing, etc.

Low iron levels can be common after an operation (when you will have lost some blood), and also if you've not been eating well for a while. Check your iron level, which is linked to your haemoglobin level, as low haemoglobin levels not only hinder healing but can also make us exhausted and have low moods. Even if our haemoglobin level is normal our ferritin (iron store) levels can be low, which can lead to hair loss and poor wound healing, so you may also like to check this out with your doctor. As with zinc, if your appetite is off it may be that an iron supplement providing something like 200mg of ferrous sulphate may be useful, although some people don't tolerate this well. It can cause constipation or diarrhoea, in which case discuss with your doctor whether one of the more gentle iron supplements might be suitable alongside focusing on this aspect of your diet.

Vitamin D is vital for wound healing, and since our ability to synthesise this vitamin in our skin decreases with age and can be particularly poor if you're spending a lot of time indoors recuperating, it's even more important to take a 10mcg supplement each day.

Drinking enough

It can be tempting to think that taking lots of mineral and vitamin supplements will get you better more quickly, but this isn't the case – there is nothing better, nothing more nourishing in its truest and most complete sense, than eating and drinking well. You need to keep up your fluid intake and usually I would suggest keeping the majority of the fluid as water, as there is nothing more hydrating. When you're trying to increase your calorie, protein, fat and other nutrient intakes it can be good to include milky drinks, which provide protein, fat, calories, calcium, zinc – the full-fat versions are the most nutrient-dense and you can add honey to them. It may surprise you to hear that I'm also a fan of cordials, squashes and juices, as they provide some glucose, which can be a good source of energy. Or indeed, a cup of tea can be milky sweet and makes the perfect boost with a biscuit ◆ while soups make a nourishing drink too.

Read more on:
◆ Pages 33–38

Tooth decay

We become far more susceptible to tooth decay as we get older, and of course losing our teeth and having to rely on dentures, is not as valuable as having your own set of healthy teeth. One of the biggest problems for older people who have been unwell for a while is that their dentures can become less well-fitting, as the gums can retract and become sore if the body is run down – all of this can put you off your food, and here starts another destructive vicious cycle.

Some medications, like antibiotics and laxatives, can be very high in sugar, while others can exacerbate a more common ageing scenario: the decrease in the amount of saliva we produce. All these factors have a negative impact on our teeth, so the more we can do to prevent tooth decay when we're older the better. I bring up this subject now because I've mentioned above that sweet drinks can be a good way, as can biscuits, etc., to boost your calorie intake when you're recovering from an illness or operation, but too much sweet stuff, even if it's just a seemingly harmless cup of sweet tea, can ultimately cause tooth decay. So just watch that you're not having too much and on a too frequent a basis – five sweet hits during a day is about the right sort of level, as this gives the mouth enough time in between to recover and rebalance its acidity levels (which go up when you've eaten something sweet). This highlights a real problem with relying on some of the very thick and sweet supplement drinks – using a straw can help reduce the impact on the teeth.

It can also give us an added impetus to think of savoury alternatives to sweet treats, especially if you think you're treating by giving them another slice of cake when perhaps a sandwich or a slice of toast with some cheese on top would actually be far more nourishing snack and better for their teeth.

Good oral hygiene and using a fluoride-rich toothpaste can help too – most pastes contain fluoride, it's true, but you can get some especially high-fluoride ones for older people who are most at risk of tooth decay (wait 30 minutes after eating before you brush too).

Dementia care

The foods we eat can have a very significant influence our lives, and not only on our physical health. The level to which we're well nourished can have an impact on our moods, and when it comes to reducing the risk or the progression of dementia, although research is still in its infancy, there are a few very important relationships between nutrients and brain health that are worth exploring.

The first of these surrounds the overall levels of nourishment and the likelihood of developing dementia. We do know that having a nourishing, well-rounded diet gives our brain the best chance of not succumbing to the disease, because strong relationships exist between eating well and reducing the likelihood of suffering from a stroke, for instance; but over and above eating a well-balanced diet, full of wholegrain, fruits and vegetables, there is some new research that suggests that the omega-3 fatty acids ◆ in particular can play a significant role in reducing some of the risk. Also, when dementia is diagnosed, it looks as if eating a diet rich in omega-3 fatty acids could help to slow down the progression of the disease. It's all well and good saying that we should therefore be eating a couple of portions of oily fish a week, but the other far greater challenge we face with dementia is that as the disease progresses, our ability and desire to eat deteriorates. Which is really why we need to focus on what we can do to meet these practical challenges head on.

Read more on:
◆ *Pages 17–18 & 101*

My mum's chicken pie, page 219

There are some very practical issues that dementia presents, not least the fact that memory loss and confusion mean that some people may forget to eat; from one meal to another, time of day and the importance of eating can be lost and when dementia hits hard, even the presence of food on a plate in front of you doesn't necessarily mean you'll know it's there to be eaten. Our ability to judge temperature can disappear too, so if food is served too hot it can burn our lips or throat, and physical skills like keeping our mouths closed while food is inside, to help us chew and swallow, can become difficult.

We may not be able or be safe enough to cook or prepare food on our own, while depression, low energy and constipation can all make eating difficult. Unlike when we have food battles with our young children, when we're dealing with an adult, particularly our parents, who is strong and possesses the language to lash out, much as we try not to let words and actions wound us, they do – we're all human and have our limits. It sounds so basic, and I don't mean it to be patronising, but there are a few things to try to keep in the forefront of your mind, or to write down and stick on the wall as visual mantras.

Try to keep calm

A calm, regular routine is reassuring for someone with dementia – even being ten minutes out in a routine, or sitting at a different table, or with friends they don't usually eat with, can upset them. The requirement to always stick to the same routine can be isolating for you, the carer, as your whole day is dictated by something that used to be flexible and sociable. One way around this is to feed them in the same way, at the same time, and then for you yourself to eat with friends afterwards. You will then be more able to enjoy a nourishing meal, which is obviously very important. If we don't manage to feed ourselves properly when we're having such demands placed on us we're not going to be any use to anyone.

Try to keep things simple

While we try to juggle so many tasks when caring for someone, it can be tempting to try to hurry, which only increases the likelihood of upset and for very little food to get eaten. Because concentration needs to be maximised to enable the person we're caring for to eat and focus on swallowing or getting the food from fork to mouth, etc., it helps not to have the radio or the TV on as a rule. This said, I do have some patients who find that listening to meditative music can help take some of the aggression out of the situation if the meal's heading that way. It can certainly help us to step back for a minute and find the strength we need to go back with a calm attitude.

If you're finding that the person you're looking after is frustrated by not being able to eat when the sole focus is on eating, you might find that sitting in front of the TV with a plate of something easy to nibble, such as sandwiches or crisps, or soft fruits such as bananas, could just mean that these get eaten while they're being distracted by the programme. One thing to remember is that if they're very upset or agitated, or if they're drowsy and not very responsive, feeding can cause choking – so try to leave a bit of time before you try, and seek advice and help if you're having problems with these aspects.

As the dementia progresses it's highly likely that appetite and ability to eat will change – this can sometimes be sudden, though it's more common for it to fall off more subtly – so you will probably have to become flexible in your routine. Don't feel that changes in appetite or ability to eat are always down to the disease itself – sometimes medication can put them off their food and interfere with hunger messages in the brain. We also shouldn't forget the simple fact that sometimes they can't remember if they've eaten, so they may say they want more food when physically they don't need it.

Chicken with winter vegetables, page 222

I think we tend to assume that as dementia progresses the biggest challenges are weight loss, and getting them to eat enough of the right foods, but before taking you through some ideas as to how to best get around this, I want to point out that sometimes gaining too much weight becomes an issue – people with dementia can forget that they've eaten, and have difficulties knowing when to stop, as they lose the ability to register and respond to the fullness feeling. If they become overweight it not only creates physical challenges of helping them walk, etc., but poses a health risk too. So much as an occasional treat is good, keeping to the basic structure of an overall nourishing diet is best.

What to do about poor appetite

Our appetite and desire to eat anything is influenced by many factors. For instance, if we are constipated the body can take away our appetite if the gut isn't able to get rid of what it doesn't need. But many other physical problems can have an influence too, such as a sore mouth, badly fitted dentures, or just the sheer effort involved in eating for those who suffer from dementia. When our mood is low or we're angry, eating can be the last thing we feel like doing. Some of us don't like to eat on our own, which can be a real issue if we live alone or away from family.

What we do know about a poor appetite is that the less we eat, often the less we fancy eating. Malnutrition can kick in, and all sorts of problems start occurring – pressure sores, poor wound healing, depression, etc. – which would never have arisen had the person been well nourished. So if you suspect that your relative or friend in a care home isn't getting the right types of foods or that they're not getting any help with eating, make a nuisance of yourself and either try to persuade someone to sit with them while they're eating, or ask if you can bring in some food. Ensuring someone is well nourished reduces the likelihood of other medical problems arising that will require more acute and often expensive care.

If you're looking after someone at home and their appetite is off, I suggest you first try tempting their appetite. Although your individual situation will mean that some things work better than others, it will give you some ideas about how to make food as nourishing as possible, in small and practically workable ways. If you're struggling with the physical aspect of cutlery, plates, etc., seek advice and support from organisations that work with the elderly and their carers, or your doctor and district health care teams, as there are some fantastic adaptations of these home basics that can make feeding and eating far easier. Don't suffer in silence – the help is out there.

Roast mackerel with potatoes & thyme, page 223

Recipes

If I'd had room I would like to have included more recipes, but the ones I've given here are some my favourite staples, which you can use as a starting point. You can give them a twist – try varying the base of a soup or the topping on a pizza, for example. By changing the texture, or adding something like a dollop or two of Greek-style yoghurt and some toasted wholemeal croutons, you can make a soup you are enjoying with your young family equally appropriate for an elderly parent, spouse or friend.

I've included some recipes that use ready-made ingredients you can keep in the freezer, for times when you need to rustle up a quick but nutritious meal. While there are weekend moments that lend themselves to making your own puff pastry, you can also now buy really great ready-made pastries that don't contain the hydrogenated fats we've worried about in the past. Rolled out and filled with fruits, they make a delicious contribution towards your five-a-day target.

Chickpea, tomato & sausage hot pot

SERVES 4

2 tbsp olive oil
2 large onions, roughly chopped
4 cloves garlic, thinly sliced
1 leek, finely chopped
400g (14oz) good quality, lean sausages (I like to use a variety)
1 tbsp dried chilli flakes
175ml (6fl oz) dry sherry, or white or red wine
8 ripe tomatoes, roughly chopped
200g (7oz) canned chickpeas, drained and rinsed
1 bay leaf
1 small bunch of fresh parsley, roughly chopped

Warm the olive oil in a deep, heavy-based pan or flameproof casserole. Add the onions and cook over a medium heat for a few minutes. Add the garlic and leek, and cook with the onions until they turn a pale golden colour.

Cut each sausage into four and add them to the pot with the dried chilli flakes. Pour in the sherry or wine, bring to the boil and add the tomatoes, chickpeas and bay leaf. Bring to the boil, then turn down to a simmer and leave to cook, half-covered, for 45 minutes.

Stir from time to time and, if necessary, add a little water to make a thick, rich tomato sauce. Just before serving, stir in the parsley.

Other herbs work well, such as chopped coriander or torn basil.

This is also delicious served with little dumplings or mashed potato, or it can be blended to make a scrumptious soup.

Pearled spelt, goat's cheese & chard risotto

SERVES 4

250g (9oz) pearled spelt
½ tbsp olive or rapeseed oil
2 medium shallots or 1 small onion, finely chopped
1 litre (1¾ pints) hot vegetable stock
2 handfuls of chard or spinach leaves
50g (2oz) soft goat's cheese
freshly grated Parmesan or Pecorino cheese
salt and ground black pepper

Soak the spelt in cold water for 10 minutes. Heat the oil in a large pan and cook the shallots until soft but not brown. Drain the spelt, add it to the shallots and pour in one-third of the stock. Bring to the boil then turn the heat down to a simmer and gradually add the remaining stock a ladleful at a time, stirring constantly.

When the spelt is cooked but not mushy (as you still want it to have a slight bite to it), tear the chard leaves, stir them in and leave them to soften for 1–2 minutes. Add the cheese and season to taste.

This risotto can be made with Arborio rice instead of spelt and all kinds of other ingredients, such as mushrooms, peas or broad beans, which can be thrown in from frozen at the chard stage, as they only take a couple of minutes to cook.

Butternut squash &
red lentil dahl

SERVES 3–4

   1 medium squash, unpeeled and halved
   300g (11oz) red lentils, rinsed
   1 tsp ground cumin
   ½ tsp ground turmeric
   1 cinnamon stick
   2cm (¾ in) piece of fresh root ginger, peeled and grated
   1 litre (1¾ pints) hot water
   rice, chapattis or naan bread, to serve

FOR THE TARKA

   1 tbsp olive oil
   2 red onions, thinly sliced
   2 garlic cloves, thinly sliced
   1 red large chilli, cut into thin strips

Preheat the oven to 190°C (170°C fan oven) mark 5. Place the squash on a baking sheet and bake for 30–40 minutes until it turns golden and soft. Allow to cool slightly and then discard the seeds, scoop out the flesh and set aside.

Meanwhile, put the lentils, cumin, turmeric, cinnamon, ginger and hot water into a pan. Bring to the boil, then simmer over a low heat, stirring occasionally, for 30 minutes or until very soft.

Remove the cinnamon stick from the lentils and discard. Add the squash, stirring to break up any lumps.

To make the tarka, heat the olive oil in a frying pan, add the onions and cook on a very low heat until golden and caramelised. Add the garlic and chilli to the tarka and cook over a low heat for 10 minutes. Serve the dahl in bowls with a spoonful of the tarka to garnish.

Beans with tomato, coriander & coconut milk

SERVES 4–6

400g (14oz) dried haricot beans or chickpeas, soaked overnight
1 tbsp olive oil
2 medium onions, thinly sliced
3 garlic cloves, finely chopped
seeds from 8 green cardamoms
2 tsp coriander seeds
1 tsp yellow mustard seeds
1 tsp cumin seeds
2 tsp ground turmeric
salt and ground black pepper
3 small hot chillies, deseeded and finely chopped
2 x 400g (14oz) cans chopped plum tomatoes
400ml (14fl oz) water
a pinch of sugar
250ml (9fl oz) coconut milk
a large handful of fresh coriander leaves
juice of 2 limes or lemons

Rinse the beans and cook in fresh water for 1 hour or until tender. Heat the oil in a large, deep pan, add the onions and cook over a medium heat until softened and slightly golden. Add the garlic and cook for 2–3 minutes.

Crush the cardamom, coriander and mustard seeds using a pestle and mortar or heavy rolling pin, then stir them into the onions. Add the cumin seeds, ground turmeric and salt and pepper, and cook for 5 minutes.

Add the chillies, tomatoes, water, sugar and cooked beans. Simmer over a low heat for 35–40 minutes. Stir the coconut milk into the sauce, simmer for 5 minutes, then add the coriander leaves and the lime juice.

Alternatively, you can use 3 × 400g (14oz) cans beans or chickpeas, drained and rinsed.

Pearled spelt with broad beans, asparagus & dill

SERVES 4

125g (4oz) fresh spinach, washed
50g (2oz) broad beans, blanched for 1 minute
50g (2oz) peas, thawed if frozen, blanched for 1 minute
8 asparagus spears, blanched for 2 minutes
225g (8oz) pearled spelt, cooked for 20 minutes
a handful of fresh dill, torn into small fronds
4 tbsp extra virgin olive oil
juice of 1 lime or lemon
1 tsp finely chopped chilli (optional)
salt and ground black pepper

Put the spinach in a dry pan over a low heat and cook in the water that clings to the leaves after washing for 3 minutes or until wilted. Remove quickly and drain in a colander.

Put the broad beans in a bowl and mix with the peas, asparagus, pearled spelt and spinach. Add the dill and dress with olive oil, lime juice and chilli, if using. Season and toss together lightly with your fingers. Serve quickly while the flavours are fresh.

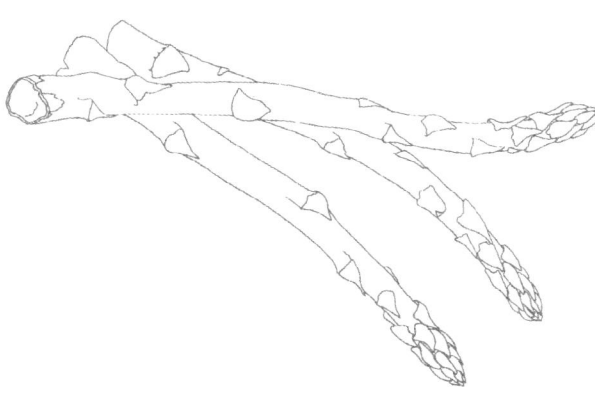

Cauliflower cheese

SERVES 4

- 25g (1oz) butter, plus extra for greasing
- 1 large white cauliflower and 1 large green cauliflower, trimmed and broken into florets
- 25g (1oz) plain flour
- 600ml (1 pint) milk
- 100g (3½ oz) mature Cheddar cheese, grated
- 1 tbsp Dijon mustard, or 1 tsp made-up English mustard
- a pinch of grated nutmeg
- ground black pepper
- 25g (1oz) fresh wholemeal breadcrumbs
- 50g (2oz) freshly grated Parmesan cheese

Preheat the oven to 200°C (180°C fan oven) mark 6. Lightly grease an ovenproof dish that is large enough to hold the cauliflower in one layer. Steam or boil the cauliflower for 5–6 minutes until just tender, then drain and set aside.

Melt the butter in a pan over a low heat. Add the flour and stir for 1 minute, without browning. Remove from the heat and gradually beat in the milk. Return the pan to the heat and simmer gently, stirring frequently, for 10 minutes or until the sauce is thickened and creamy.

Remove the pan from the heat and stir in 75g (3oz) Cheddar cheese and the mustard. Season with nutmeg and pepper. Put the cauliflower in the greased dish and pour over the sauce.

Mix together the breadcrumbs, Parmesan and the remaining Cheddar cheese, and sprinkle evenly over the cauliflower and sauce. Bake for 25–30 minutes until browned and bubbling. Serve immediately.

If using non-dairy milk, butter and cheese, you might want to add other vegetables, such as sautéed mushrooms and herbs, to the sauce to give it some extra flavour.

Bolognese sauce

SERVES 8

3 tbsp olive oil
50g (2oz) smoked streaky bacon, diced
1 onion, finely diced
2 celery sticks, finely chopped
2 carrots, finely chopped
2 garlic cloves, finely chopped
1 tsp fresh thyme leaves
1 bay leaf
1 tsp dried oregano
400g (14oz) can chopped tomatoes
1 tbsp tomato purée
1 tsp anchovy essence or anchovy sauce
1 tbsp Worcestershire sauce
900g (2lb) good quality lean minced beef
125g (4oz) fresh chicken livers, finely chopped (optional)
750ml (1¼ pints) dry red wine or water
1 litre (1¾ pints) hot chicken, beef or lamb stock
salt and ground black pepper

Heat 1 tbsp oil in a large, heavy-based pan and fry the bacon until crispy. Add the onion, celery, carrots, garlic, thyme, bay leaf and oregano, and cook over a medium heat until the vegetables have softened. Stir in the tomatoes, tomato purée, anchovy essence and Worcestershire sauce.

In a separate frying pan, heat 1 tbsp of oil and fry the minced beef in small batches until browned. Drain off any fat and add to the tomato mixture. Add another 1 tbsp oil to the pan and fry the chicken livers, if using, until brown and crusty, then add to the tomato and mince mixture. Deglaze the frying pan with 2–3 tbsp red wine, scraping any sediment from the bottom. Pour the remaining wine and the stock into the tomato and meat mixture. Bring to the boil, reduce the heat and simmer, stirring occasionally, for 2 hours, adding a little water if it gets too dry. Season to taste.

My mum's chicken pie

SERVES 3–4

butter, for greasing
2 medium onions, roughly chopped
1 garlic clove, peeled
500g (1lb 2oz) cooked chicken meat, breast and legs
juice of 1 lemon
a few leaves of fresh sage or a few sprigs of parsley
ground black pepper
375g (13oz) shortcrust pastry, thawed if frozen
1 egg, beaten

Preheat the oven to 200°C (180°C fan oven) gas 6. Grease a 25.5cm (10in) pie dish. Put the onions, garlic, chicken, lemon juice, fresh herbs and pepper into a food processor or mincer and mince until you have a mixture that resembles chunky sausage meat.

Roll out half the pastry and line the pie dish. Put in the chicken mixture and spread it level. Roll out the remaining pastry and put it on top. Squeeze the edges together. Cut a couple of slits in the middle of the pie to allow steam to escape while it's cooking. Brush the pie with the egg, and bake for 50 minutes–1 hour until the pastry is golden brown.

If you make your own pastry you could use half white and half wholemeal flour.

Chicken & chickpea burgers

SERVES 4

450g (1lb) roasted chicken
200g (7oz) canned chickpeas, drained and rinsed
1 small onion, roughly chopped
1 garlic clove, roughly chopped
2 tsp finely chopped fresh sage
175g (6oz) wholemeal breadcrumbs
1 egg, beaten
salt and ground black pepper

Put the chicken, chickpeas, onion and garlic in a food processor or mincer and mince to combine. Alternatively, chop finely and mash together with a fork, or put the ingredients in a clean plastic bag, tie the end, then put on a hard surface and hit with a rolling pin until mashed together.

Put the mixture in a bowl, add the sage, 50g (2oz) of the breadcrumbs and enough of the egg to bind the mince without it becoming too sloppy. Season to taste.

Spread the remaining breadcrumbs on a large baking sheet and, taking a handful of mixture at a time, form a ball, then roll in the breadcrumbs until completely coated. Grill until the coating turns golden brown. Serve immediately.

Try replacing the chickpeas with broad beans or canned beans such as haricot, butter or borlotti. The burgers can also be made with other roasted meats such as ham, roast pork or beef.

Tandoori chicken

SERVES 4

1.25kg (2 lb 12oz) chicken pieces, legs and/or breasts, skinned
3 tbsp lemon juice
450ml (¾ pint) Greek yogurt
1 onion, coarsely chopped
1 garlic clove, chopped
2.5cm (1in) piece fresh root ginger, peeled and chopped
1–2 hot green chillies, roughly sliced
2 tsp garam masala
coarse sea salt
lime or lemon wedges, to serve

Cut each chicken leg into two pieces and each breast into four. Make two
deep slits crossways on the meaty parts, making sure that they don't start at
an edge and that they are deep enough to reach the bone. Spread the
chicken pieces out on two large platters. Sprinkle one side with a pinch of
salt and half the lemon juice, and rub in. Turn the pieces over and repeat
on the second side. Set aside for 20 minutes.

Put the yogurt, onion, garlic, ginger, chillies and garam masala in a
blender or food processor and whiz until smooth. Place in a bowl with the
chicken. Rub the marinade into the slits in the meat, then cover and chill for
1–2 hours, or overnight if possible.

When you're ready to cook, preheat the oven to 240°C (220°C fan oven)
mark 9 and set a shelf in the top third of the oven where it is hottest. Put the
chicken in a single layer on a large, shallow baking tray and bake for
20–25 minutes until cooked through. Lift the chicken pieces out of their
juices and serve with lime or lemon wedges.

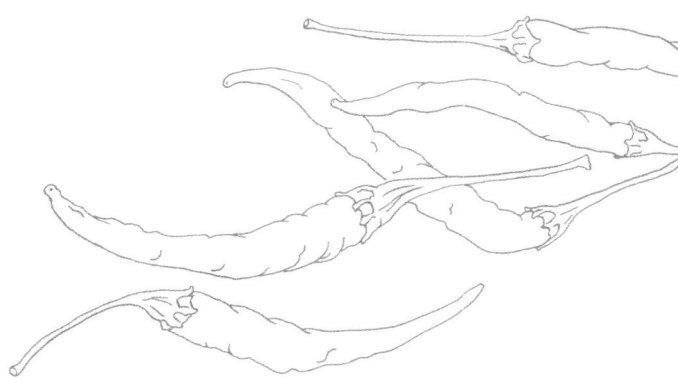

Chicken with winter vegetables

SERVES 4

1 medium-sized chicken, giblets removed
large bunch of flat-leafed parsley
4 bunches of thyme
3 bay leaves
1 small head each of fennel and celeriac, finely chopped
1 leek, roughly chopped
4 carrots, chopped into large pieces
75cl bottle dry white wine
450g (1lb) small waxy potatoes, peeled
salt and ground black pepper
Dijon mustard, to serve

Preheat the oven to 200°C (180°C fan oven) mark 6. Put the chicken in a large, heavy casserole. Remove the leaves from the parsley and set them aside. Put the parsley stalks, thyme, bay leaves, fennel, celeriac, leek and carrots into the casserole. Pour in the wine, season and cover with a lid. Cook in the oven for 2½ hours.

Remove and discard the parsley stalks and thyme stems. Transfer the chicken to a serving platter and cover it with clingfilm. Put the potatoes in a pan of lightly salted cold water, bring to the boil and simmer until cooked. Finely chop the reserved parsley leaves and add them to the cooked vegetables, check the seasoning and stir well.

Serve the thick parsley and vegetable soup as a first course, then serve the chicken and potatoes with the mustard.

Roast mackerel with potatoes & thyme

SERVES 2

  300g (11oz) small new potatoes, cut into 2cm (¾ in) slices
  3 tbsp olive oil
  4 tbsp fresh thyme leaves
  salt and ground black pepper
  1 tbsp sherry vinegar
  2 large or 3–4 small mackerel fillets, cleaned and deboned
  watercress and tomato salad, to serve

Preheat the oven to 180°C (160°C fan oven) mark 4. Put the potatoes into a shallow dish, drizzle with 1 tbsp oil and sprinkle with 3 tbsp thyme leaves, salt and lots of pepper. Coat the potatoes well, then bake in the oven for 40 minutes or until golden and tender when pricked with a fork.

Mix the remaining oil, the sherry vinegar and the remaining thyme with salt and pepper in a small bowl. Put the mackerel skin-side up on top of the potatoes and spoon over the herby dressing. Put it back into the oven and cook for 15–20 minutes until the mackerel is cooked and slightly crispy. Serve with a watercress and tomato salad.

This recipe works equally well for any oily fish, such as herrings and sardines, although the cooking time will change depending on the size of the fish.

Spicy fish casserole

SERVES 4

400g (14oz) new potatoes, scrubbed and cut into thick slices
3 tomatoes, peeled and quartered
3 garlic cloves, chopped
2.5cm (1in) piece of fresh green or red chilli, finely chopped,
½ tsp paprika
½ tsp ground cumin
juice of 1 lemon
500g (1lb 2oz) white fish fillets, skinned
25g (1oz) fresh flat-leafed parsley, chopped
2 fresh mint sprigs, leaves chopped
4 large handfuls of spinach
ground black pepper

Put the potatoes, tomatoes, garlic, chilli, paprika and cumin into a large pan and add 1 litre (1¾ pints) water and half the lemon juice. Simmer for 25 minutes or until the potatoes are tender.

Add the fish fillets and cook for another 10 minutes, then gently break up the fish into smaller pieces and add the herbs and the spinach. Cook for a further 1 minute, then stir. Season with pepper and add the remaining lemon juice.

The flavours of this dish will develop if you cover it well and chill it, then eat the following day.

Smoked mackerel pâté

SERVES 4 AS A STARTER

200g (7oz) smoked mackerel fillets (without pepper), skins removed
200g (7oz) Ricotta cheese
a squeeze of fresh lemon juice
2 tbsp Greek yogurt
ground black pepper

Add all the ingredients to a food processor or blender, season with ground black pepper and whiz together until smooth.

Spread the pâté on toast or flatbreads or use in sandwiches. For sandwich rolls, spread over fresh, soft, good-quality white or wholemeal bread, crusts removed, then roll up. Cut across the roll into slices.

Smoked haddock salad

SERVES 4–6

200g (7oz) spelt or other grain, such as quinoa or wild rice, rinsed
2 naturally smoked haddock fillets
3 black peppercorns
½ onion
1 each dill and parsley sprig
½ cucumber, chopped into small pieces

FOR THE YOGURT AND HERB DRESSING

4 tbsp Greek yogurt
2 tbsp finely chopped fresh parsley
2 tbsp finely chopped fresh dill
1 tbsp finely chopped fresh chives
½ tsp finely chopped preserved lemon or a dash of lemon juice
salt and ground black pepper

Put the spelt into a large pan of cold water and bring to the boil. Cover and simmer for 20 minutes or until cooked but not mushy. Immediately drain and rinse under cold water to prevent it from cooking further.

Put the haddock into a deep frying pan and add the peppercorns, onion and sprigs of herbs. Add cold water to just cover. Gently poach the haddock by cooking just below simmering point for 5 minutes. Remove from the pan and allow to cool.

To make the dressing, mix together the yogurt, herbs and preserved lemon. Add black pepper to taste and very little salt if needed (the haddock is already salty).

In a large bowl flake the haddock, removing any bones, and add the cucumber and spelt. Add the dressing to the haddock mixture and adjust the seasoning if necessary. Serve cold.

Roasted tomato & couscous salad

SERVES 6–8

16 large ripe plum or round tomatoes
2 tbsp muscovado or soft brown sugar
4 tbsp olive oil, plus extra for drizzling
2 tbsp balsamic vinegar
coarse sea salt and black pepper
2 onions, thinly sliced
250g (9oz) brown rice, mograbiah, pearled spelt or quinoa
400ml (14fl oz) chicken or vegetable stock
a pinch of saffron threads
250g (9oz) couscous
1 tbsp chopped fresh tarragon
1 tbsp nigella seeds
1 tsp finely chopped sun-dried tomatoes
100g (3½ oz) of labneh or thick yogurt
a handful of stoned olives green, sliced

Preheat the oven to 150°C (130°C fan oven) mark 2. Cut the tomatoes into quarters lengthways, or slice them in half if using round tomatoes, and put on a baking tray, skin-side down. Sprinkle with sugar, 2 tbsp olive oil, the balsamic vinegar and salt and pepper. Roast in the oven for 2 hours or until the tomatoes have lost most of their moisture.

Put the remaining olive oil in a large pan and sauté the onions over a high heat for 10–12 minutes, stirring occasionally, until a dark golden colour. Put the rice into a large pan of slightly salted boiling water and simmer for 15 minutes or until tender but not mushy. Drain and rinse under cold water.

Boil the stock in a pan. Add the saffron and a little salt. Put the couscous in a large bowl and pour over the boiling stock. Cover and leave for 10 minutes. Fluff up with a fork. Add the rice, tomatoes and juices, onions and oils, tarragon, half the nigella seeds and the sun-dried tomatoes. Adjust the seasoning. Serve at room temperature with a dollop of labneh and a drizzle of oil, the remaining nigella seeds and the sliced olives.

Tomato & herb salad

SERVES 4

a handful each of basil, mint (spearmint – *Mentha spicata* – is best for salad if you can find it), curly-leafed parsley and chives
3 handfuls each of Italian rocket and ruby chard
4–6 ripe baby tomatoes, quartered
1 ripe avocado, peeled and sliced
extra virgin olive oil, for drizzling
leaves from 1 thyme sprig

Tear the basil, finely chop the mint, parsley and chives, and put into a salad bowl. Throw in the rocket and chard leaves, the tomatoes and the avocado. Drizzle with enough olive oil to lightly coat the leaves, scatter with the thyme leaves and mix well.

Quick Caesar salad

SERVES 2

1 slice wholemeal, white or granary bread, cubed
1 tbsp mayonnaise
1 tbsp Greek yogurt
2 garlic cloves, crushed
4 tbsp freshly grated Parmesan cheese
6 anchovy fillets, chopped
2 hard-boiled eggs, chopped
4 large handfuls of chopped cos lettuce
ground black pepper

Preheat the oven to 230°C (210°C fan oven) mark 8. Put the bread on to a baking sheet and bake, turning twice, for 10 minutes or until golden brown all over. Allow to cool while you make the salad.

Put the mayonnaise and yogurt into a small bowl and mix in enough water to make a pourable consistency. Add the garlic, Parmesan cheese and plenty of pepper. Put the remaining ingredients into a large salad bowl, drizzle with the creamy dressing and top with the croutons.

Serve with lean roast meats such as chicken, ham, roast beef or cold salmon, tuna, roasted cod or sea bass. It's also delicious with a simple tomato salad or some steamed asparagus or green beans.

Bought croutons can be used if you prefer.

Wild rice salad

SERVES 4

250g (9oz) wild rice
65g (2½ oz) shelled pistachio nuts
150g (5oz) soft, dried unsulphured apricots, soaked in hot water for
    5 minutes
leaves from 1 small bunch of fresh mint
1 small bunch of rocket
3 spring onions, roughly chopped
zest and juice of 1 lemon
2 tbsp olive oil
1 large garlic clove, crushed
sea salt and ground black pepper

Put the rice in a large pan and cover with water, bring to the boil then reduce the heat and cook for 30–40 minutes, or until *al dente*. Drain and rinse under cold water. While the rice is cooking, toast the pistachio nuts in a dry pan over a medium heat for 8–10 minutes, then coarsely chop. Drain the apricots and chop them coarsely. In a bowl, mix the rice, pistachio nuts and apricots. Add the remaining ingredients, toss well and season with salt and pepper to taste.

Salsa verde

SERVES 6–8

350g (12oz) fresh flat-leafed parsley
25g (1oz) fresh basil leaves (optional)
50g (2oz) canned anchovies
3 tbsp capers
2 garlic cloves, crushed
1 tbsp finely chopped shallots or onions
4 tbsp breadcrumbs
3–4 tbsp white wine vinegar or lemon juice
about 125ml (4fl oz) olive oil

Put all the ingredients, except the olive oil, into a blender or food processor and whiz until smooth. Slowly trickle the olive oil into the mixture and gently stir to make a smooth, green sauce. If the sauce is too thick, dilute it with a little more olive oil. Serve with raw or cooked vegetables, pasta or jacket potatoes, or spread it lightly over wholegrain bread or toast.

Carrot & spring vegetable salad

SERVES 4

100g (3½ oz) baby carrots
200g (7oz) green beans
100g (3½ oz) shelled fresh broad beans
100g (3½ oz) shelled fresh peas
150g (5oz) mangetouts
100g (3½ oz) baby asparagus
100g (3½ oz) each rocket and watercress, divided into sprigs
a few fresh chives, roughly chopped
a few fresh basil leaves, torn
olive oil, to drizzle
a squeeze of lemon juice

FOR THE MAYONNAISE

2 egg yolks, at room temperature
1 tsp Dijon mustard
2 tbsp fresh lemon juice
ground black pepper
a pinch of salt
250ml (9fl oz) olive oil

To make the mayonnaise put the egg yolks into a food processor or blender with the mustard, lemon juice, a pinch of salt and some ground black pepper. Whiz until pale and frothy, then very slowly add the oil in just a thin drizzle, whizzing slowly as you drizzle, until the mayonnaise becomes thick and glossy. Adjust the seasoning to taste and put to one side.

Steam the carrots for 6–8 minutes, then the beans, peas, mangetouts and asparagus for 3 minutes or until *al dente*. Once they're cooked, drain and rinse briefly with cold water to stop them cooking. Mix them in a bowl with the rocket and watercress. Toss in the fresh herbs, add a very light drizzle of olive oil and a squeeze of lemon juice. Serve with the mayonnaise to dip into.

Roasted aubergines with tahini

SERVES 3–4 AS A SIDE DISH, 2–3 AS A MAIN COURSE
2 medium aubergines, each cut into four lengthways
100ml (3½ fl oz) olive oil
seeds from 4 cardamom pods, ground (optional)
25g (1oz) pine nuts, toasted

FOR THE DRESSING
2 tbsp Greek yogurt
1 tbsp tahini
½ tsp very finely chopped preserved lemon, or lemon or lime juice
   to taste
1 tbsp olive oil
1 tsp thyme leaves
sea salt and ground black pepper

Preheat the oven to 200°C (180°C fan oven) mark 6. Cut each piece of aubergine into three short, fat lengths. Put in a roasting tin and drizzle with the olive oil. Shake the roasting tin to ensure the aubergines are coated. Season with salt, lots of ground black pepper and the cardamom, if using. Roast for about 40–45 minutes until the aubergines are soft and toasted.

To make the dressing, mix the yogurt, tahini, preserved lemon, if using, and olive oil in a blender or use a fork or a small whisk. Season to taste with salt and black pepper and then add most of the thyme leaves. If you haven't added the preserved lemon, add a dash of lemon or lime juice and stir.

In a bowl, gently mix the aubergines into the dressing while they are still warm. Leave for 20 minutes and then serve scattered with the toasted pine nuts and the remaining thyme leaves.

Broad bean & pistachio hummus

SERVES 4

1kg (2¼ lb) frozen broad beans
2 tbsp shelled pistachio nuts
leaves from 2 fresh basil sprigs
2 tbsp extra virgin olive oil, plus a little extra if necessary
juice of half a lemon
ground black pepper

Steam the broad beans for 2 minutes until they're cooked but not mushy. Rinse and cool thoroughly under cold water and remove the skins by squeezing the bean at one end – the bright green centre should just pop out.

Toast the pistachio nuts in a dry pan for 2 minutes over a gentle heat, being careful not to let them burn. Put them into a food processor or blender and blend to a fine nut powder. Add the beans and the basil, oil and lemon juice, and whiz to a mash. You can add a little extra oil or lemon juice, if you like, depending on how smooth and tart you want the hummus to be. Season with pepper.

Serve as a sandwich filling, or on jacket potatoes or pasta. Or make a delicious salad with romaine lettuce leaves, new crisp baby carrots and sliced raw vegetables, which you can dunk into the hummus.

Pan-roasted Padrón peppers

SERVES 4

200g (7oz) small, sweet Spanish (Padrón) peppers
olive oil, for shallow frying
sea salt

Rinse the peppers and dry them. Warm a shallow pool of olive oil in a frying pan then cook the peppers over a gentle heat until they have softened. (Alternatively, roast them at 180°C (160°C fan oven) mark 4, in a baking dish with a little oil.) They will puff up and the skin will blister slightly. Drain on kitchen paper and salt generously. Serve torn and added to salads or other dishes for a peppery hit.

You can buy Padrón peppers from some supermarkets or specialist delis.

Cashew nut butter

MAKES ONE 200G (7OZ) JAR

200g (7oz) cashew nuts, unroasted and unsalted
3 tbsp extra virgin groundnut or rapeseed oil
1 tsp clear honey
½ tsp sea salt

Put the nuts into a food processor and pulse until quite fine. Add 1–2 tbsp
oil and process, adding more oil if needed, until you have a creamy paste.
Add the honey and salt. Store in the fridge in an airtight container and use
within a week.

*You can also use almonds, peanuts or hazelnuts. Stir in a few chopped
nuts at the end if you'd prefer a chunky butter.*

Vegetable soup with lime & herbs

SERVES 4

2 garlic cloves
2 litres (3½ pints) vegetable stock
4 lemon grass stalks, bashed
5cm (2in) fresh root ginger, peeled and thinly sliced
8 lime leaves, crushed or whole
the juice of 2 limes
2 large flat mushrooms, cut into thick slices
2 handfuls of frozen peas
2 handfuls of frozen broad beans
2 small hot chillies, deseeded and thinly sliced
a pinch of golden caster sugar
20 mint leaves
a large handful of coriander leaves

Smash the garlic to a pulp and simmer it with the stock, the lemon grass,
ginger and the lime leaves for 7 minutes. Add the lime juice, mushrooms,
peas, broad beans and chillies. After 2 minutes remove the lemon grass
and lime leaves, and season with a pinch of sugar. Add the mint and
coriander leaves.

Chicken soup

SERVES 4

5cm (2in) piece of fresh root ginger, peeled
1 chicken, about 1.4kg (3lb)
2 celery sticks
1 medium onion
2 ripe tomatoes
2 whole star anise
6 black peppercorns
1 lime
20 mint leaves, roughly chopped
a handful of flat-leafed parsley or coriander, roughly chopped
salt

Bash the ginger with a weight to crush slightly. Put the chicken into a large pan and add the celery, onion, tomatoes, ginger, 1 star anise and the peppercorns. Pour over enough water to cover. Bring to the boil briefly, then turn down the heat, cover and simmer for 1 hour.

Remove the chicken from the pan and set aside to rest. Measure out 1.4 litres (2½ pints) stock and pour into a clean pan. Add the remaining star anise, the lime juice to taste and a pinch of salt. Bring to the boil and leave to simmer for 7–10 minutes. Slice the chicken breasts thinly, then put several pieces in each bowl. Spoon over the hot stock and scatter with the mint and parsley.

Roasted butternut squash & spicy sweetcorn soup

SERVES 4

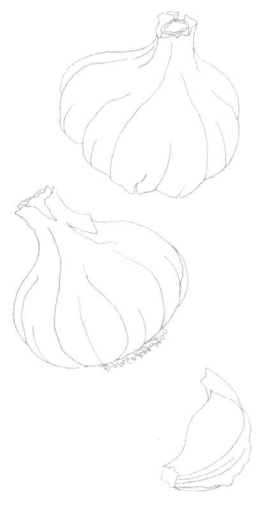

- 750g (1lb 10oz) butternut squash, or any squash or pumpkin, cut into 2cm (¾ in) pieces
- olive oil, for drizzling
- 1 tsp ground cumin
- 1 tsp ground coriander
- seeds from 6 cardamom pods
- 25g (1oz) butter
- 1 onion, finely chopped
- 2 garlic cloves, finely chopped
- 1 tsp turmeric
- 1 tsp ground ginger
- 2 celery sticks, finely chopped
- 1 leek, finely chopped
- 500g (1lb 2oz) sweetcorn, rinsed and drained if canned, thawed if frozen
- 275ml (10fl oz) semi-skimmed milk
- 750ml (1¼ pints) vegetable or chicken stock
- ground black pepper
- a handful of wholemeal croutons and a swirl of natural yogurt, to serve (optional)

Preheat the oven to 180°C (160°C fan oven) mark 4. Put the squash on a baking tray, drizzle with olive oil and roast for 25 minutes or until golden.

Meanwhile dry-roast the cumin, coriander and cardamom seeds in a small frying pan for 2–3 minutes until they change colour and start to jump in the pan. Crush them finely, using a pestle and mortar.

Melt the butter in a large pan, then add the onion and garlic, and cook for 5 minutes or until soft. Add the ground seeds with the turmeric, ginger, celery and leek, and stir well. Cook for a further 3 minutes, then add the squash and sweetcorn. Season with black pepper. Stir well, then cover and cook over a low heat for 10 minutes. Add the milk and stock, replace the lid, bring to the boil and simmer gently for 20 minutes.

Take the soup off the heat. Whiz in a food processor or blender, leaving a little texture – it doesn't need to be absolutely smooth. Serve with wholemeal bread croutons and, if you like, add a swirl of yogurt.

Oxtail soup

SERVES 4–6

1.25kg (2lb 12oz) oxtail, jointed and excess fat removed
4 tbsp plain flour
about 2 tbsp olive oil
1 large carrot, roughly chopped
1 turnip, roughly chopped
1 celery stick, roughly chopped
1 large onion, roughly chopped
1 bay leaf
a few thyme sprigs
1 tsp black peppercorns
2 tsp tomato purée
300ml (½ pint) red wine or stock
1.1 litres (2 pints) beef stock
2 tbsp butter, softened
a handful of flat-leafed parsley, chopped
salt and ground black pepper

In a shallow bowl, mix 2 tbsp of the flour with salt and pepper. Heat half the oil in a large, heavy-based pan until hot. Coat the oxtail pieces with the seasoned flour, shaking off any excess, and fry for 2 minutes on each side or until evenly browned, then remove from the pan.

Add the remaining oil to the pan with the vegetables, herbs and peppercorns. Cook for 4–5 minutes until the vegetables begin to soften. Stir in the tomato purée and the remaining seasoned flour, adding a little more oil if necessary. Stir frequently for another 1–2 minutes.

Pour in the red wine and scrape the base of the pan with a wooden spoon. Boil for a few minutes. Return the oxtail to the pan and pour in the stock to cover. Bring to a simmer and skim off any scum that rises to the surface. Partially cover the pan and cook gently for 3 hours or until the oxtail is very tender and comes off the bone easily. With a pair of kitchen tongs, carefully move the oxtail pieces to a large bowl and leave to cool slightly.

Strain the cooking stock through a fine sieve into a clean pan, pushing down on the vegetables with the back of a ladle to extract as much liquid as possible. Pull the meat from the oxtail and shred into small pieces. To thicken the stock, mix the remaining 2 tbsp of flour with the butter, then whisk into the simmering stock, a little at a time. Simmer for 5 minutes. Taste and adjust the seasoning, then add the shredded meat to the pan to warm through. Sprinkle with lots of chopped parsley before serving.

Breadsticks

MAKES 16

35g (1¼ oz) fresh yeast
175ml (6fl oz) warm water
400g (14oz) strong white, wholemeal, Granary or spelt flour, or a
    combination
1 tsp salt
1 tbsp olive oil
1 tbsp fresh thyme leaves or 1 tsp dried oregano
3 tsp caraway or fennel seeds
25g (1oz) butter, melted, plus extra for greasing
semolina, for dusting

Dissolve the yeast in the water, then combine it with the flour, salt and olive oil in a large bowl and mix together to make a smooth elastic dough. Knead for about 10 minutes to knock out some of the air and to develop the dough. Cover and leave to rest in a warm place for about 1 hour.

Divide the dough into two. Add the thyme leaves or dried oregano to one half and the caraway or fennel seeds to the other. Knead both balls of dough again. Roll each out into a rectangle measuring 23 x 16cm (9 x 6¼ in) and cut each rectangle into eight lengths. Put the dough pieces on to a greased baking sheet, cover and leave for 10 minutes in a warm place to rise.

Meanwhile, preheat the oven to 220°C (200°C fan oven) mark 7. Brush the breadsticks with melted butter, dust with semolina and bake in the oven for 10–15 minutes until tinged golden. Transfer to a cooling rack and eat warm.

Wholemeal soda bread

MAKES A 800G (1LB 12OZ) LOAF

25g (1oz) melted butter, plus extra for greasing
400g (14oz) wholemeal flour, plus extra for dusting
1½ tbsp caster sugar
2 tsp bicarbonate of soda
½ tsp salt
225ml (8fl oz) buttermilk
225ml (8fl oz) water

Preheat the oven to 220°C (200°C fan oven) mark 7. Grease a 20.5cm (8in) square cake tin and dust with flour. Measure the flour into a large bowl, then add the butter and rub it between your fingertips until evenly dispersed. Add the sugar, bicarbonate of soda and salt, and toss this through.

In a large jug, measure the buttermilk and thin down with the water. Stir this liquid through the dry ingredients quickly and evenly, then scrape the dough into the tin and smooth it down. Place an oiled piece of foil over the top of the tin, squeeze tightly in at the corners so that it stays in place and bake for 20 minutes. Remove the foil.

Reduce the heat to 200°C (180°C fan oven) mark 6 and bake for a further 10–15 minutes until brown on top. Remove from the oven and leave to cool in the tin for 5 minutes. Take out of the tin and cool on a wire rack.

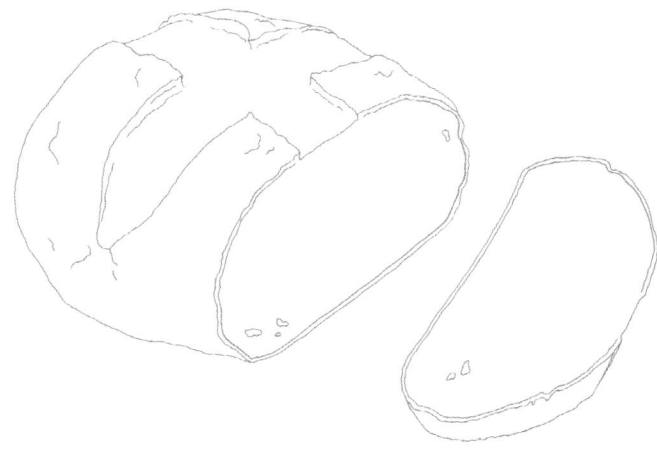

Green olive & parsley focaccia

MAKES 1 LOAF

450g (1lb) strong bread flour, plus extra for dusting
1½ tsp salt
2 tsp fast-acting yeast (or a 7g packet)
400ml (14fl oz) luke-warm water
semolina, for dusting
a large handful of green olives, pitted and roughly chopped
3 tbsp olive oil, plus extra for greasing
1 garlic clove, finely chopped
small bunch of flat-leafed parsley, chopped
leaves from 4 thyme sprigs
coarse sea salt

Put the flour, salt and yeast into a large bowl, mix well then pour in the water and mix to make a sticky dough. Flour the work surface generously, then turn out the dough and knead lightly for 5 minutes or until it no longer sticks to the surface. You may need to add a little more flour if the dough becomes too sticky, but it should be a little more moist than a loaf dough. Put the dough into a lightly floured bowl and cover with a tea towel or clingfilm. Put in a warm place to rise for 1 hour or until doubled in size.

Grease a 30.5cm (12in) diameter baking tin with a little oil. Dust with a thin layer of semolina. Knock back the dough on a floured surface for 2–3 minutes and then spread it in the baking tin. Leave to rise for 30 minutes. Preheat the oven to 220°C (200°C fan oven) mark 7.

Mix the olives with 1 tbsp oil. Stir the garlic, parsley and thyme leaves into the olives. With a floured finger, push several holes deep into the dough, then spread the olive and herb mixture over the top. Scatter with sea salt.

Bake for 25–30 minutes until pale golden, crisp on top and springy within. Drizzle with the remaining olive oil, then allow to settle. While still warm, free the bread from the pan with a palette knife, then cut or tear into pieces.

Roasted cherry tomato, basil & mozzarella pizza

SERVES 4

1 quantity focaccia dough (see Green olive & parsley focaccia)
oil for greasing and drizzling
6 canned anchovy fillets, well rinsed
16 ripe cherry tomatoes, halved
6 green or black pitted olives
125g (4oz) small mozzarella balls or torn mozzarella
a few basil leaves, torn
Parmesan cheese shavings

Make up the focaccia dough as explained in step 1 of Green olive & parsley focaccia (page 238). Roll out the dough and divide into four pieces. Roll each piece into a circle and put onto greased baking sheets. Leave to rise for 30 minutes.

Dry the anchovy fillets on kitchen paper. Preheat the oven to 220°C (200°C fan oven) mark 7.

Gently push down the centre of the pizza base to leave about a 2.5cm (1in) rim around the edge. Scatter the cherry tomatoes over the pizza and add the anchovy fillets, olives and mozzarella on top. Finish by scattering over the basil, then drizzle with a little olive oil. Bake for 20 minutes or until the cheese has melted and the base is crisp and golden. Serve with a few shavings of freshly grated Parmesan cheese.

You can adapt the topping by adding a tomato sauce, canned fish, such as sardines, or slices of salami or prosciutto, smoked salmon, lean ham or roast chicken. Alternatively, add steamed asparagus spears, canned artichoke hearts or sliced mushrooms.

Baked apples

SERVES 4

- 50g (2oz) sultanas
- 50g (2oz) dried unsulphured apricots, finely chopped
- 25g (1oz) currants
- 25g (1oz) dried figs, stalks removed and finely chopped
- 1 tbsp pure fruit apple and pear spread
- 2 tbsp fresh orange juice
- 2 tbsp dried coconut shavings (optional)
- 4 cooking apples
- custard, natural yogurt or ice cream, to serve

Preheat the oven to 180°C (160°C fan oven) mark 4. Make the filling by putting all the ingredients, except the apples, in a bowl. Mix together, then leave for 20 minutes to allow the flavours to blend.

Core the apples, then cut them in half crossways. Put on a baking sheet, skin-side down. Stuff the mixture into the middle of the apples. The filling will also spread over the top.

Cover with foil and bake on the middle shelf of the oven for 25–30 minutes, until the apple is soft. Serve with custard, natural yogurt or ice cream.

The apples are also delicious cold and make a tasty breakfast dish.

Poached rhubarb & blueberries

SERVES 4

- 250g (9oz) rhubarb
- 200g (7oz) blueberries
- 2 tbsp water
- about 2 tsp maple syrup or clear honey

Preheat the oven to 170°C (150°C fan oven) mark 3. Cut the rhubarb into short lengths and put into an ovenproof dish with the blueberries. Add the water and drizzle the maple syrup over. Stir gently and bake for 1 hour or until the fruit is soft, then taste to see if you need any more maple syrup or honey (this will depend on the sweetness of the fruit and your personal taste). Serve warm or thoroughly chilled.

Poached peaches & nectarines

SERVES 8

4 firm peaches
4 firm nectarines
75g (3oz) pure fruit spread, such as orange or grapefruit, or jam
with no added sugar
4 thinly pared strips of orange rind
½ tsp rose-water (optional)
rose petals (optional)
custard or yogurt, to serve

Choose a pan large enough to fit all the fruit tightly in a single layer. Pour 600ml (1 pint) cold water into the pan and add the fruit spread and orange rind. Gently heat until the spread has dissolved, then bring to the boil.

Carefully put the peaches and nectarines into the pan using a slotted spoon. Cover and cook for 8 minutes, turning the fruit over if it is not completely submerged in the liquid. Reduce the heat, cover and simmer gently for a further 5 minutes or until the fruit is tender.

Remove the pan from the heat and cool the fruit in the syrup for 15 minutes. Using a slotted spoon, remove the fruit and transfer to a serving dish. Set aside.

Bring the liquid in the pan to the boil and boil until it has reduced by half. Allow to cool slightly, then add the rose-water, if using, and pour over the fruit. Cool completely before serving with custard or yogurt and with rose petals, if you like.

The fruits are also good sliced over muesli, porridge or yogurt for breakfast, and can even be mashed and spread on toast.

Brown bread & hazelnut frozen yogurt

SERVES **4**

65g (2½ oz) soft, fresh wholemeal breadcrumbs
65g (2½ oz) light muscovado sugar
65g (2½ oz) golden caster sugar
100g (3½ oz) skinned hazelnuts
100ml (3½ fl oz) double cream
400ml (14fl oz) Greek yogurt

Put the breadcrumbs in a bowl and add the sugars. Whiz the hazelnuts in a food processor or nut mill until they are like coarse gravel, or chop them finely by hand. Thoroughly mix the nuts into the breadcrumbs and sugar, then spread out in a shallow layer over a baking tray. Put under a hot grill and grill until the sugar, nuts and crumbs are deep golden – be careful, as the sugar can burn very easily. Leave to cool then break up into small pieces.

Mix the cream and yogurt together in a bowl. Add the sugared crumbs and stir well.

Using an ice cream maker: pour into the ice cream maker and churn until frozen, then transfer to a freezerproof container and freeze until needed.

To make by hand: put the mixture into a freezerproof container and freeze for 1–2 hours until it starts to form crystals around the edges. Stir well, using a fork, to break up the crystals, and freeze again. Repeat twice more, then leave to freeze until needed.

Before serving, take the yogurt out of the freezer and allow it to soften a little.

A little cream gives a frozen yogurt a good texture, but if you want to reduce the fat content use 500ml (18fl oz) yogurt and omit the cream.

Frozen raspberry & blackberry yogurt

SERVES 4

100g (3½ oz) raspberries
50g (2oz) blackberries
1 tbsp apple concentrate
400ml (14fl oz) Greek yogurt
3 tbsp double cream
1 tsp vanilla extract

Using an ice cream maker: whiz the berries with the apple concentrate in a blender to make a purée, then pour into the ice cream maker, with the yogurt, cream and vanilla extract. Churn until frozen, then transfer to a freezerproof container and freeze until needed.

To make by hand: mix the yogurt with the cream and vanilla extract. Put in a freezerproof container and freeze for 30 minutes.

Meanwhile, whiz the berries with the apple concentrate in a blender to make a purée. Take the yogurt mixture out of the freezer and stir well with a fork to break up the forming ice crystals. Mix in the fruit purée. Freeze for another 1–2 hours until it starts to form crystals around the edges. Stir with a fork, freeze for 2 hours and stir once more, then leave to freeze until needed.

Before serving, take the yogurt out of the freezer and allow it to soften a little.

Maya's chocolate brownies

MAKES 8–10

    300g (11oz) golden caster sugar
    250g (9oz) unsalted butter
    250g (9oz) plain chocolate with 70% cocoa solids
    4 large eggs
    65g (2½ oz) plain wholemeal flour
    65g (2½ oz) good-quality cocoa powder
    ½ tsp baking powder
    a pinch of salt

Preheat the oven to 180°C (160°C fan oven) mark 4. Line a 23cm (9in) square baking tin with baking parchment. Put the sugar and butter into a large bowl and beat, using an electric whisk, until the mixture turns soft, white and fluffy. Break the chocolate into pieces and set 50g (2oz) to one side. Put the remainder into another large bowl set over a pan of gently simmering water. Leave until the chocolate has melted – do not let the water touch the base of the bowl or boil over. Meanwhile, chop the reserved chocolate into very small pieces. Take the melted chocolate off the heat and add the chocolate chunks.

Break the eggs into a small bowl and beat them lightly with a fork. Sift together the flour, cocoa powder, baking powder and salt. Add the beaten eggs, little by little, to the chocolate mixture, mixing well between additions, and continue until you have added all the egg and you have a mixture similar to chocolate custard. Using a metal spoon, gently fold in the flour and cocoa.

Spoon the brownie mixture into the prepared tin, smooth over the top and bake for 30 minutes. The top will rise slightly and the cake will appear slightly softer in the middle than around the edges. Pierce the middle of the cake with a skewer; it should come out sticky, but the mixture shouldn't be uncooked. If necessary, put the cake back into the oven for another 3–5 minutes. Leave to cool in the tin then turn out and cut into squares. (Alternatively, serve them hot from the oven with ice cream, yogurt or crème fraîche.)

Raspberry baskets

SERVES 4

450g (1lb) raspberries
1 tbsp elderflower cordial
6 sheets of filo pastry, thawed if frozen
25g (1oz) butter, melted, plus extra for greasing
50ml (2fl oz) whipping cream
50ml (2fl oz) Greek yogurt
icing sugar, for dusting

Preheat the oven to 200°C (180°C fan oven) mark 6. Put the raspberries in a bowl and drizzle with the elderflower cordial. Lightly mix and leave to infuse while you make the baskets. Cut the filo pastry sheets in half to form 12 squares. Put four small upturned ramekin dishes on to a large, greased baking sheet and brush them with a little of the melted butter.

Brush 3 squares of the filo pastry with melted butter. Place 1 sheet, butter-side up, over a ramekin, pressing it down the sides. Add the other 2 sheets at different angles to form a basket. Repeat with the remaining ramekins, pastry squares and butter to make three more baskets. Bake for 8 minutes or until they turn golden. Leave the baskets to cool slightly before carefully removing them from the ramekins.

Whip the cream until thick and stir in the yogurt. Divide between the baskets. Top with the raspberries, and drizzle with the raspberry juice from the bowl. Lightly dust with a little icing sugar just before serving.

Use Greek yogurt and omit the cream, if you want to keep the fat and calorie content down.

Use any other berry if you prefer, or add a spoonful of stewed fruit.

Easy apple & greengage strudel

SERVES 4–6

75g (3oz) butter, plus extra for greasing
1kg (2¼ lb) cooking or tart eating apples, peeled, cored and finely sliced
250g (9oz) greengages or plums, halved and stones removed
2 tbsp sultanas
1 tbsp slivered, toasted almonds
finely grated zest and juice of ½ lemon
2 tbsp clear honey
1 tsp ground cinnamon
2 tbsp wholemeal breadcrumbs
flour, for dusting
1 packet, about 350g (12oz) filo pastry, thawed if frozen
icing sugar, for dusting

Preheat the oven to 200°C (180°C fan oven) mark 6. Butter a large baking sheet. Put the apples, greengages, sultanas and almonds into a bowl and add the lemon zest and juice, honey and cinnamon. Mix until the apple slices are completely coated with honey.

Melt 25g (1oz) butter in a pan and fry the breadcrumbs until crisp. Set aside. Melt the remaining butter. Lay out a clean tea towel, dust lightly with flour and cover with a layer of filo to form a rectangle about 40.5 × 60cm (16 × 24in) – join two sheets by overlapping them slightly if necessary. Brush with butter, cover with another layer of filo and sprinkle with breadcrumbs. Spread the filling along a long edge, leaving a margin at each end. Tuck the ends over the filling. Pick up the two corners of the cloth nearest to the filling and roll the strudel away from you, allowing it to curl over itself.

Put the strudel on the baking sheet. Brush with a little more butter and sprinkle with a few drops of water. Bake for 40 minutes or until crisp and golden brown and the apple filling is soft – test by inserting a skewer. Dust with icing sugar and serve warm, with custard, yogurt or cream.

More-ish nutty biscuits

MAKES ABOUT 12

- 100g (3½ oz) butter, at room temperature
- 50g (2oz) light muscovado sugar
- 50g (2oz) golden caster sugar
- 100g (3½ oz) cashew or peanut butter
- 25g (1oz) salted, roasted cashew nuts, roughly chopped
- 25g (1oz) unsalted peanuts, roughly chopped
- 100g (3½ oz) plain wholemeal flour
- ½ tsp bicarbonate of soda
- ½ tsp baking powder

Preheat the oven to 190°C (170°C fan oven) mark 5. Line a baking sheet with baking parchment. Beat the butter and sugars together using a food processor or electric whisk until the mixture becomes pale and smooth. Mix the nut butter into the butter and sugar mixture with most of the nuts, holding back a handful or two.

Sift the flour, bicarbonate of soda and baking powder over the mixture, and stir gently to form a soft dough. Spoon heaped tablespoonfuls of the dough on to the lined baking sheet. Flatten each mound slightly.

Scatter over the remaining nuts and bake for 12–14 minutes until the biscuits are pale golden and dry on top – they should be slightly moist inside. Cool slightly on the baking sheet, then transfer to a cooling rack to cool completely.

Although best eaten fresh, these biscuits will keep for 2–3 days in an airtight tin.

You can use any combination of chopped nuts and nut butters. If you're watching your salt intake, you can use unsalted nuts and butters. The salted nuts contrast well with the sweetness here – I don't think we should be afraid of using a little salt in home cooking.

Blackberry & apple crumble cake

SERVES 8

150g (5oz) butter, softened, plus extra for greasing
150g (5oz) caster sugar
3 large eggs
75g (3oz) plain white flour
1½ tsp baking powder
100g (3½ oz) ground almonds
1 cooking apple, cored, quartered and thinly sliced
150g (5oz) frozen blackberries

FOR THE TOPPING

100g (3½ oz) cold butter, straight from the fridge
50g (2oz) plain white flour
50g (2oz) plain wholemeal flour
100g (3½ oz) demerara sugar
2 tbsp whole rolled oats
icing sugar, for dusting

Preheat the oven to 180°C (160°C fan oven) mark 4. Grease and line a 20.5cm (8in) loose-based springform cake tin, 6.5cm (2½ in) deep, with baking parchment. Beat the butter and sugar together until the mixture becomes pale, smooth and fluffy. Lightly beat the eggs, then add them gradually to the butter and sugar mixture, beating briefly after each addition. If the mixture starts to curdle, stir in 1 tbsp flour. Sieve the flour and baking powder over the mixture and fold in using a metal spoon. Fold in the almonds.

Spoon the mixture into the cake tin and smooth the top. Arrange the apple slices on top of the cake, pressing them down slightly. Scatter over the blackberries.

To make the topping, rub the butter into the flours, then stir in the sugar and oats. Sprinkle the crumble over the top of the cake. Bake for 1 hour, then insert a skewer into the centre. It will be wet from the fruit but with no cake mixture. Leave to cool, then dust with icing sugar.

Lemon polenta cake

SERVES 8

3 large eggs, separated
100g (3½ oz) golden caster sugar
zest and juice of 1 lemon
50g (2oz) fine polenta
25g (1oz) ground almonds

FOR THE FILLING (OPTIONAL)

125g (4oz) mascarpone cheese
2 tsp orange juice
½ tsp orange zest
1 tbsp natural yogurt
½ tbsp maple syrup

Preheat the oven to 180°C (160°C fan oven) mark 4. Grease and line a 20.5cm (8in) cake tin then lightly butter the base. Using a food processor or electric whisk, beat the egg yolks and the sugar at high speed until they turn pale, thick and creamy. Gradually add the lemon juice to the creamed mixture, beating until it starts to thicken.

Mix the lemon zest, polenta and ground almonds together and stir them into the egg and sugar mixture. In a clean bowl beat the egg whites until almost stiff. Fold the egg yolk mixture into the whites using a metal spoon. Transfer the mixture to the lined cake tin and bake for 30 minutes or until the centre is cooked and the top is lightly browned. Insert a skewer into the centre – it should come out clean. Using a palette knife, turn the cake out on to a cake rack and leave to cool.

Cut the cake in half horizontally if you want to fill it. Put the bottom half on a cake plate. To make the filling, beat the mascarpone in a bowl. Add the orange juice, zest, yogurt and maple syrup, and beat until smooth. Spread over the cake and replace the top half, or spread half the filling over and use the other half to top the cake.

Damson, pear & walnut muffins

MAKES 12 LARGE MUFFINS

- 25g (1oz) vegetable oil, such as rapeseed or groundnut oil, plus extra for greasing
- 150g (5oz) unsweetened breakfast flakes (such as buckwheat and rice cereal flakes, or oats and a bran-type flake)
- 150g (5oz) plain white flour
- 100g (3½ oz) plain wholemeal flour
- 125g (4oz) golden caster sugar
- 1 tsp ground allspice
- 25g (1oz) walnuts, chopped
- 1 tsp baking powder
- a pinch of salt
- 150g (5oz) natural yogurt
- 50ml (2fl oz) milk
- 2 large eggs
- 1 large firm pear (or 2 small pears)
- 200g (7oz) damsons (fresh or frozen), stones removed and cut into eighths

Preheat the oven to 200°C (180°C fan oven) mark 6. Grease a 12-cup muffin tray. Combine the cereal flakes and dry ingredients in a large bowl. Gently combine the yogurt, milk, oil and eggs in a second bowl, using a fork.

Grate the pear and squeeze out and discard any excess liquid. Add the pear and damson slices to the dry ingredients. Pour the oil mixture into the fruit and dry ingredients and combine gently, but thoroughly, with a metal spoon. Do not overmix – use big scooping movements to mix well without beating.

Divide the mixture equally among the muffin cases. Bake for 20 minutes, then reduce the oven temperature to 180°C (160°C fan oven) mark 4 and bake for a further 10 minutes until firm and lightly golden.

Fruity beetroot cake

SERVES 8–10

    150g (5oz) white self-raising flour
    75g (3oz) wholemeal self-raising flour
    ½ tsp bicarbonate of soda
    1 tsp baking powder
    ½ tsp ground cinnamon
    175ml (6fl oz) rapeseed or sunflower oil
    225g (8oz) light muscovado sugar
    3 eggs, separated
    150g (5oz) raw beetroot, coarsely grated
    juice of ½ lemon
    75g (3oz) sultanas
    75g (3oz) mixed seeds, such as pumpkin sunflower, hemp or
        linseeds (flaxseeds)

Preheat the oven to 180°C (160°C fan oven) mark 4. Lightly butter a 20.5 x 9 x 7cm (8 x 3½ x 3in) loaf tin and line the base with baking parchment.

Sift together the flours, bicarbonate of soda, baking powder and cinnamon into a large bowl, then tip the bran left in the sieve into the bowl (if you want to keep it).

In another bowl, beat the oil and sugar using a food processor or electric whisk until well combined. Gradually beat the egg yolks into the oil mixture.

Fold the beetroot into the mixture, then add the lemon juice, sultanas and seeds. Fold the flours and raising agents into the mixture while beating slowly.

In a clean bowl, whisk the egg whites until light and almost stiff. Fold gently into the mixture using a large metal spoon. Pour the mixture into the cake tin and bake for 50–55 minutes until risen and firm, covering the top with a piece of foil after 30 minutes. Insert a skewer into the centre – the cake should be moist inside but not sticky. Leave to cool in the tin for 20 minutes, then remove from the tin and cool completely on a cooling rack.

My favourite suppliers

BRINDISA and **GARCIA & SONS** are London-based suppliers of Spanish delicacies such as pimientos del Padrón and amazing olives and charcuterie.
www.brindisa.com
www.garciacafe.co.uk

LA FROMAGERIE was founded in London by my dear friend Patricia Michelson, who sells not only wonderful cheeses, but also delicious charcuterie, chocolates and amazing German rye breads.
www.lafromagerie.co.uk

THE RARE TEA COMPANY is a boutique tea company. They source and sell gorgeous teas from black to silver tip and green – and their herbal teas such as lemon verbena are also delicious. You can order online from anywhere in the world.
www.rareteacompany.com

MONMOUTH COFFEE COMPANY has shops in London selling not only an extensive range of delicious coffees (sold ground or as beans, so that you can grind them yourself) but also very good decaffeinated coffee that has had the caffeine removed by steam, so there are no chemicals involved.
www.monmouthcoffee.co.uk

NATOORA sells amazing fresh produce, from mozzarella di bufala to olive oils, salad leaves and big bunches of fresh herbs with the roots still on that you don't find in the supermarkets. Their products are available to order online for delivery throughout the UK.
www.natoora.co.uk

LE PAIN QUOTIDIEN is famous all over the world for delicious sourdough and other breads and nut butters, among other delicacies.
www.lepainquotidien.com

THE SPICE SHOP is a wonderful shop just by London's Portobello Road market, which sells spices and rose/orange blossom. You can also order online from anywhere in Europe.
www.thespiceshop.co.uk

LAKELAND is brilliant for kitchen gadgets and I'm particularly a fan of their food storage bags. They have shops throughout the UK and you can also order online.
www.lakeland.co.uk

SHARPHAM PARK is run by my dear friends Roger and Monty Saul, who sell spelt and all things deliciously spelty (cereals, biscuits, pastas, etc.). Available throughout the UK.
www.sharphampark.com

GOOD OIL products are available in supermarkets and sell hemp oil and hemp products such as salad dressings. You can also buy online direct from the UK, US, Germany and France.
www.goodwebsite.co.uk

GOODNESS DIRECT is the home organic foods, vitamins and herbal remedies, fresh foods, cruelty free toiletries and foods for those with special dietary needs. Order online for delivery throughout Europe.
www.goodnessdirect.co.uk

THE WATERMILL stock their own organic stoneground flours, dried fruit, nuts, seeds, pasta, herbs, spices, beans and peas, chocolate, coffee, teas, herb teas and more. They deliver to the UK from their shop in Cumbria.
www.organicmill.co.uk

Acknowledgements

A large number of people have generously shared their time, knowledge and support with me in writing this book. My family continue to be amazing and I am also lucky enough to have a set of very treasured friends, who have pulled me out of writers block dips, listened to my screams as recipes have flopped and inspired me to keep going until the final page was delivered. In particular I'd like to thank Cat Vinton, Vanessa Fairfax, Martin, Lesja Liber, Jo Milloy, Diana Houghton, Katingo Giannoulis, Justine Conant, Amanda and Diana Preston, Caroline Peppercorn, Navin Poddar, Matt Utber, Marcella Ocaranza and Dawn Harlow. I couldn't enjoy my writing and my work without such a supportive group of colleagues who in their own way point me in the right direction, in particular my agent along with Susan Hutter, Sara Stanner, Paul Chiape, John Evans and my treasured editor Annie Lee. And when it came to turning my manuscript into a beautiful book, I want to thank Katie Cowan, Caroline King, Howard Sooley, Jane McIntosh, Jilly Sitford and Martin Topping at Ome Design, Sarah Rock, Tim Hart and his team at Hambleton Hall for the lovely location and Juilian Carter for his help at Hambleton Bakery.

Picture Credits
All photography by Howard Sooley except author photograph page 6 and inside cover by Cat Vinton (www.catvphotography.co.uk). Illustrations by Jilly Sitford at Ome Design (www.omedesign.co.uk.)

Index